THE OATH OF

From this day forth, I re... freemate. No man shall bind me *di catenas* and I will dwell in no man's household as a *barragana*.

I swear that I am prepared to defend myself by force if I am attacked by force, and that I shall turn to no man for protection.

From this day forth I swear I will give myself to no man save in my own time and season and at my own free will, at my own desire; I will never earn my bread as the object of any man's lust.

From this day forth I swear I shall never again be known by the name of any man, be the father, guardian, lover or husband, but simply and solely as the daughter of my mother.

From this day forth I swear I will bear no child to any man save for my own pleasure and at my own time and choice; I will bear no child to any man for house or heritage, clan or inheritance, pride or posterity; I swear that I alone will determine rearing and fosterage of any child I bear, without regard to any man's place, position or pride.

From this day forth I renounce allegiance to any family, clan, household, warden or liege lord, and take oath that I owe allegiance only to the laws of the land as a free citizen must; to the kingdom, the crown and the Gods.

I shall appeal to no man as of right, for protection, support or succor: but shall owe allegiance only to my oath-mother, to my sisters in the Guild and to my employer for the season of my employment.

And I further swear that the members of the Guild of Free Amazons shall be to me, each and every one, as my mother, my sister or my daughter, born of one blood with me, and that no woman sealed by oath to the Guild shall appeal to me in vain.

From this moment, I swear to obey all the laws of the Guild of Free Amazons and any lawful command of my oath-mother, the Guild members or my elected leader for the season of my employment. And if I betray any secret of the Guild, or prove false to my oath, then I shall submit myself to the Guild-mothers for such discipline as they shall choose; and if I fail, then may every woman's hand turn against me, let them slay me like an animal and consign my body unburied to corruption and my soul to the mercy of the Goddess.

A Reader's Guide to the Novels of Darkover

THE FOUNDING

A "lost ship" of Terran origin, in the pre-empire colonizing days, lands on a planet with a dim red star, later to be called Darkover.

DARKOVER LANDFALL

THE AGES OF CHAOS

1,000 years after the original landfall settlement, society has returned to the feudal level. The Darkovans, their Terran technology renounced or forgotten, have turned instead to free-wheeling, out-of-control matrix technology, psi powers and terrible psi weapons. The populace lives under the domination of the Towers and a tyrannical breeding program to staff the Towers with unnaturally powerful, inbred gifts of *laran*.

STORMQUEEN!
HAWKMISTRESS!

THE HUNDRED KINGDOMS

An age of war and strife retaining many of the decimating and disastrous effects of the Ages of Chaos. The lands which are later to become the Seven Domains are divided by continuous border conflicts into a multitude of small, belligerent kingdoms, named for convenience "The Hundred Kingdoms." The close of this era is heralded by the adoption of the Compact, instituted by Varzil the Good. A landmark and turning point in the history of Darkover, the Compact bans all distance weapons, making it a matter of honor that one who seeks to kill must himself face equal risk of death.

TWO TO CONQUER
THE HEIRS OF HAMMERFELL
THE FALL OF NESKAYA

THE RENUNCIATES

During the Ages of Chaos and the time of the Hundred Kingdoms, there were two orders of women who set themselves apart from the patriarchal nature of Darkovan feudal society: the priestesses of Avarra, and the warriors of the Sisterhood of the Sword. Eventually these two independent groups merged to form the powerful and legally chartered Order of Renunciates or Free Amazons, a guild of women bound only by oath as a sisterhood of mutual responsibility. Their primary allegiance is to each other rather than to family, clan, caste or any man save a temporary employer. Alone among Darkovan women, they are exempt from the usual legal restrictions and protections. Their reason for existence is to provide the women of Darkover an alternative to their socially restrictive lives.

THE SHATTERED CHAIN
THENDARA HOUSE
CITY OF SORCERY

AGAINST THE TERRANS
—THE FIRST AGE (Recontact)

After the Hastur Wars, the Hundred Kingdoms are consolidated into the Seven Domains, and ruled by a hereditary aristocracy of seven families, called the *Comyn*, allegedly descended from the legendary Hastur, Lord of Light. It is during this era that the Terran Empire, really a form of confederacy, rediscovers Darkover, which they know as the fourth planet of the Cottman star system. The fact that Darkover is a lost colony of the Empire is not easily or readily acknowledged by Darkovans and their *Comyn* overlords.

REDISCOVERY (*with Mercedes Lackey*)
THE SPELL SWORD
THE FORBIDDEN TOWER
STAR OF DANGER
THE WINDS OF DARKOVER

AGAINST THE TERRANS
—THE SECOND AGE (After the Comyn)

With the initial shock of recontact beginning to wear off, and the Terran spaceport a permanent establishment on the outskirts of the city of Thendara, the younger and less traditional elements of Darkovan society begin the first real exchange of knowledge with the Terrans—learning Terran science and technology and teaching Darkovan matrix technology in turn. Eventually Regis Hastur, the young *Comyn* lord most active in these exchanges, becomes Regent in a provisional government allied to the Terrans. Darkover is once again reunited with its founding Empire.

THE BLOODY SUN
THE HERITAGE OF HASTUR
THE PLANET SAVERS
SHARRA'S EXILE
THE WORLD WRECKERS
EXILE'S SONG
THE SHADOW MATRIX
TRAITOR'S SUN

THE DARKOVER ANTHOLOGIES

These volumes of stories edited by Marion Zimmer Bradley strive to "fill in the blanks" of Darkovan history, and elaborate on the eras, tales and characters which have captured readers' imaginations.

THE KEEPER'S PRICE
SWORD OF CHAOS
FREE AMAZONS OF DARKOVER
THE OTHER SIDE OF THE MIRROR
RED SUN OF DARKOVER
FOUR MOONS OF DARKOVER
DOMAINS OF DARKOVER
RENUNCIATES OF DARKOVER
LERONI OF DARKOVER
TOWERS OF DARKOVER
MARION ZIMMER BRADLEY'S DARKOVER
SNOWS OF DARKOVER

THE SAGA OF THE RENUNCIATES

THE SHATTERED CHAIN
THENDARA HOUSE
CITY OF SORCERY

Marion Zimmer Bradley

DAW BOOKS, INC.
DONALD A. WOLLHEIM, FOUNDER
375 Hudson Street, New York, NY 10014
ELIZABETH R. WOLLHEIM
SHEILA E. GILBERT
PUBLISHERS
http://www.dawbooks.com

First Paperback Printing, August 2002
1 2 3 4 5 6 7 8 9

DAW TRADEMARK REGISTERED
U.S. PAT. OFF. AND FOREIGN COUNTRIES
—MARCA REGISTRADA.
HECHO EN U.S.A.
PRINTED IN THE U.S.A.

The Shattered Chain

For Tracy
In return for telling me the joke about the spaceman, the
leronis, and the three Dry-Towners.

City of Sorcery

To Donald A. Wollheim
This, as all my books

THE SHATTERED CHAIN

PART I
ROHANA ARDAIS,
Comynara

PART II
MAGDA LORNE,
Terran Agent

PART III
JAELLE n'ha MELORA,
Free Amazon

Twelve years elapse between
the first part and the second.

PART I

ROHANA ARDAIS,

Comynara

Chapter 1

Night was lowering across the Dry Towns, hesitating as if, at this season, the great red sun were reluctant to set. Liriel and Kyrrdis, pale in the lingering daylight, swung low over the walls of Shainsa.

Inside the gates, at the outskirts of the great wind-swept marketplace, a little band of travelers was making camp, unsaddling their mounts and off-loading their pack animals.

There were no more than seven or eight of them, and all were garbed in the hooded cloaks and the heavy tunics and riding-breeches of the mountain country, the faraway land of the Seven Domains. It was hot in the desert lands of Shainsa, at this hour when the sun still burned with some force, but the travelers still wore their hooded cloaks; and though every one of them was armed with knife and dagger, not one of the travelers carried a sword.

This was enough to alert the crowd of Dry-Town loafers, hanging around to watch the strangers pitch camp, to what they were. When one, sweating under the weight of laden saddle-bags, slung back hood and cloak to reveal a small shapely head, with dark hair close-cropped as no man—or woman—of Domains or Dry Towns ever wore it, the hecklers began to collect. So little goes on, ordinarily, in Dry-Town streets, that the watchers behaved as if the arrival of the strangers were a free show arranged for their benefit, and they all felt free to comment on the performance.

"Hey, there, come have a look at this! Free Amazons, they are, from the Domains!"

"Shameless bitches, that's what they are, runnin' around like that with no man to own to 'em! I'd run the lot out of Shainsa before they corrupt our decent wives and daughters!"

"What's the matter, Hayat, you can't keep hold of your own wives? Mine, now, they wouldn't run loose for all the gold of the Domains. . . . If I tried to cut 'em loose they'd come back cryin', they know when they're well off. . . ."

The Amazons heard the remarks, but they had been warned and were prepared for this; they went quietly about the business of making camp, as if their observers were invisible and unspeaking. Emboldened by this, the Dry-Town men came closer, and the jokes flew, free and ribald; and now some of them were addressed directly to the women.

"Got everything, haven't you, girls—swords, knives, horses, everything except what it takes!"

One of the women flushed and turned, opening her lips as if to reply; the leader of the group, a tall, slender, swift-moving woman, turned to her and said something, urgently, in a low voice; the woman lowered her eyes and turned back to the tent-pegs she was driving into the coarse sand.

One of the Dry-Town idlers, witnessing the little exchange, approached the leader, muttering suggestively: "Got your girls all right under your thumb, haven't you, then? Why not leave 'em alone and come along with me? I could teach you things you never dreamed about—"

The woman turned, pushing back her hood to reveal, beneath graying close-cropped hair, the gaunt, pleasant face of a woman in middle years. She said in a light, clearly audible voice, "I learned everything you could possibly teach me long before you were housebroken, animal. And as for dreams, I have nightmares like everybody else, but thanks be to the Gods, I've always waked up so far."

The bystanders guffawed. "One in the eye for you, Merach!" Now that they had turned their jokes on one another instead of on the women, the little band of Free Amazons went quickly about the business of setting camp: a booth, evidently for buying or selling, a couple of sleeping tents and a shelter to guard their mountain-bred horses against the fierce and unaccustomed sun of the Dry Towns.

One of the onlookers came forward; the women tensed against further insult, but he only asked politely enough: "May one inquire your business here, *vahi domnis?*" His accent was thick, and the woman addressed looked blank; but the leader understood, and answered for her: "We have come to sell leather goods from the Domains; saddles, harness and leather clothing. We will be here for trading at daylight tomorrow; you are all invited to come and do business with us."

A man in the crowd yelled, "They's only one thing I'd ever buy from women!"

"Buy it, hell! Make *them* pay for it!"

"Hey, lady, you going to sell them britches you're wearing so you can dress like a woman?"

The Free Amazon ignored the jeers. The man who had come to question her said, "Can we direct you to any entertainment in the city this night? Or"—he hesitated, looked appraisingly at her, and added—"entertain you ourselves?"

She said with a faint smile, "No, thank you very much," and turned away. One of the younger women said in a low-indignant voice, "I had no idea it was going to be like this! And you *thanked* him, Kindra! I'd have kicked his dirty teeth down his throat!"

Kindra smiled and patted the other's arm soothingly. "Why, hard words break no bones, Devra. He made an offer with such politeness as was in him, and I answered him the same. Next to these"—she swept the crowd of loafers with an ironic gray glance—"he was the soul of courtesy."

"Kindra, are we really going to trade with these *gre'zuin?*"

Kindra frowned faintly at the obscenity. "Why, yes, of course. We must have some reason for staying here, and Jalak may not return for days. If we have no apparent business here, we will be prime objects for suspicion. Not trade? What are you wearing for a head, today? *Think,* child!"

She moved on to a woman who was piling saddlebags within the shelter, asking in an undertone, "No sign yet of Nira?"

"None so far." The woman addressed glanced uneasily around, as if fearful of being overheard. She spoke pure *casta,* the language of the aristocrats from Thendara and the plains of Valeron. "No doubt she'll seek us out after nightfall. She would have small liking for running the gauntlet of these folk; and for anyone dressed as a man to enter our camp openly and unchallenged—"

"True," Kindra said, looking at their watchers. "And she is no stranger to the Dry Towns. Yet I cannot help being a little fearful. It goes against the grain to send any of my women in man's dress, yet it was her only safety here."

"In man's dress . . ." The woman repeated the words as if she felt she must have misunderstood the other's language. "Why, do you not all wear man's dress, Kindra?"

Kindra said, "Here you betray only your ignorance of our customs, Lady Rohana; I beg you to keep your voice low when we might be overheard. Do you truly believe I wear man's dress?" She sounded affronted, and the Lady Rohana said quickly, "I meant no offense, believe me, Kindra. But your dress is certainly not that of a woman—not, at least, a woman of the Domains."

Deference and annoyance mingled in the Free Amazon's voice as she said, "I have no leisure now to explain to you all the customs and rules of our Guild, Lady Rohana. For now, it is enough—" She broke off at another outbreak of guffaws from the bystanders; Devra and another of the Free Amazons were leading their saddle-horses toward the common well at the center of the marketplace. One of them paid the watering fee in the copper rings that passed as currency anywhere east of Carthon, while the other led the animals to the trough. As she returned to help Devra with the watering, one of the idlers in the crowd laid hands on her waist, pulling her roughly against him.

"Hey, pretty, why don't you leave these bitches and come along with me? I've got plenty to show you, and I'll bet you never—*eeyah!*" His words broke off in a howl of rage and pain;

the woman had whipped a dagger from its sheath, slashing swiftly upward, laying open his filthy and tattered clothing to expose bare, unhealthy flesh, a line of red creeping upward along the quarter-inch-deep slash from lower belly to collarbone. He stumbled back, staggering, falling into the dust; the woman gave him a contemptuous kick with one sandaled foot, saying in a low-fierce voice, "Take yourself off, *bre'sui!* Or next time I'll spill your guts, and your *cuyones* with 'em! Now get the hell out of here, you filthy bastards, or you won't be fit for anything but selling for he-whores in the Ardcarran bordellos!"

The man's friends dragged him away, still moaning more with shock than pain. Kindra strode toward the woman, who was wiping her knife. She raised her eyes, grinning with innocent pride at how well she had defended herself. Kindra slapped the knife out of her hand.

"Damn you, Gwennis! Now you've made us all conspicuous! Your pride in knife-play could cost us our mission! When I asked for volunteers on this trip, I wanted *women,* not spoiled children!"

Gwennis' eyes filled with tears. She was no more than a girl, fifteen or sixteen. She said, her voice shaking, "I am sorry, Kindra. What should I have done? Should I have let the filthy *gre'zu* paw me?"

"Do you really think you were in danger, here in daylight and before so many? You could have freed yourself without bloodshed and made him look ridiculous, without ever drawing your knife. Your skills were taught you to guard against real danger of rape or wounding, Gwennis, not to protect your pride. It is only men who must play games of *kihar,* my daughter; it is beneath the dignity of a Free Amazon." She picked up the knife where it had fallen in the dust, wiping the remnant of blood from the blade. "If I return it to you, can you keep it where it belongs until it is needed?"

Gwennis lowered her head and muttered, "I swear it."

Kindra handed it to her, saying gently, "It will be needed soon enough, *breda.*" She laid an arm around the girl's shoulders for an instant, adding, "I know it is difficult, Gwennis. But remember that our mission is more important than these stupid annoyances."

She left the women to finish the watering, noticing with a grim smile that the crowd of idle watchers had evaporated as if by magic. *Gwennis deserved every harsh word I gave her. But I am still glad she rid us of those creatures!*

The sun sank behind the low hills, and the small moons began to climb the sky. The square was deserted for a while, then some of the Dry-Town women, wrapped in their cumbersome skirts and veils, began to drift into the marketplace to buy water from the common well, moving, each of them, with the small metallic clash of chains. By Dry-Town custom, each woman's hands were fettered with a metal bracelet on each wrist; the bracelets were connected with a long chain, passed through a metal loop on her belt, so that if the woman moved either hand, the other was drawn up tight against the loop at her waist.

The Free Amazon camp was filled with a smell of cooking from their small fires; some of the Dry-Town women came close and stared at the strange women with curiosity and contempt: their cropped hair, their rough mannish garb, their unbound hands, breeches and low sandals. The Amazons, conscious of their stares, returned the gaze with equal curiosity, not unmingled with pity. The woman called Rohana finally could bear no more; leaving her almost-untouched plate, she got to her feet and went into the tent she shared with Kindra. After a moment the Amazon leader followed her inside, saying in surprise, "But you have eaten nothing, my Lady. May I serve you, then?"

"I am not hungry," said Rohana, stifled. She put back her hood, revealing, in the dim light, hair of the flame-red color that marked her a member of the telepath caste of the *Comyn*: the caste that had ruled the Seven Domains from time unknown and unknowable. It had been cropped short, indeed, but nothing could conceal its color, and Kindra frowned as the *Comyn* woman went on:

"The sight of those women has destroyed my appetite; I feel

too sick to swallow. How can you endure to watch it, Kindra, you who make so much of freedom for women?"

Kindra said with a slight shrug. "I feel no very great sympathy for them. Any single one of them could be free if she chose. If they wish to suffer chains rather than lose the attentions of their men, or be different from their mothers and sisters, I shall not waste my pity on them, far less lose sleep or appetite. They endure their captivity as you of the Domains, Lady, endure yours; and truth to tell, I see no very great difference between you. They are, perhaps, more honest, for they admit to their chains and make no pretense of freedom; while yours are invisible—but they are as great a weight upon you."

Rohana's pale face flushed with anger. She said, "Then I wonder you ever agreed to this mission! Was it only to earn your pay?"

"There was that, of course," Kindra said, unruffled. "I am a mercenary soldier; within reason, I go where I am hired to go, and do what I am best paid to do. But there is more," she added in a gentler tone. "The Lady Melora, your kinswoman, did not connive at her own captivity, nor choose her form of servitude. As I understand what you told me, Jalak of Shainsa—may his manhood wither!—fell upon her escort, slew her guards, and carried her away by force; wishing, for revenge or sheer lust of cruelty, to keep a *leronis* of the *Comyn* enslaved and captive as his wife—or his concubine, I am not certain."

"In the Dry Towns there seems no great difference," said the Lady Rohana bitterly, and Kindra nodded. "I see no very great difference anywhere, *vai domna,* but I do not expect you to agree with me. Be that as it may, Lady Melora was carried away into a slavery she had not chosen, and her surviving kinsmen could not, or did not, choose to avenge her."

"There were those who tried," Rohana said, her voice shaking. Her face was almost invisible in the darkened tent, but there were tears in her toughened voice. "They vanished without trace, until the third; he was my father's youngest son, my half-brother; and had been Melora's foster-brother, reared as her playmate."

"*That* tale I have heard; Jalak sent back the ring he wore still on his fingers," Kindra said, "and boasted he would do so, and more, to any other who came to avenge her. But that was ten years ago, Lady, and if I were in the Lady Melora's slippers, I would not have lived to endanger any more of my kinfolk. If she has dwelled for twelve years in Jalak's household, surely she cannot be in any great need, by now, of rescue. By this time, one would imagine she must be resigned to her fate."

Rohana's pale face stained with color. "So in truth we believed," she said. "Cassilda pity me, I, too, reproached her in thought, wishing her dead rather than living on in Jalak's house as a shame to us all."

"Yet you are here now," Kindra said, and although it was not a question, Lady Rohana answered. "You know what I am: *leronis,* Tower-trained; a telepath. Melora and I dwelt together, as young girls, in the Dalereuth Tower. Neither of us chose to remain lifelong, but before I left the Tower to marry, our minds were joined; we learned to reach one another's thoughts. Then came her tragedy. In the years between, I had indeed all but forgotten; learned to think of Melora as dead, or at least gone far beyond my reach, far, far beyond my touch or my thoughts. Then—it was not more than forty days ago—Melora came to me across the distances; came to me in thought, as we had learned to do when we were little maidens in the Tower at Dalereuth. . . ."

Her voice was distant, strange; Kindra knew that the red-haired woman was no longer speaking to her, but to a memory; a commitment. "I hardly knew her," Rohana said, "she had changed so greatly. Resigned to her place as Jalak's consort and captive? No; simply unwilling to cause"—Rohana's voice faltered—"more death and torment; I learned then that my brother, her foster-brother, had been tortured to death before her eyes, as a warning lest she seek rescue. . . ."

Kindra grimaced with horror and revulsion. Rohana went on, steadying her voice with a fearful effort. "Melora told me that at last, after so many years, she bore a son to Jalak; that she would die before giving him an heir of *Comyn* blood. She did not ask rescue for herself, even then. I think—I think she wants to die. But she will not leave her other child in Jalak's hands."

"Another child?"

"A daughter," Rohana said quietly, "born a few months after she was taken. Twelve years old. Old enough"—her voice shook—"old enough to be chained." She sobbed, turning her face away. "For herself she asked nothing. Only she begged me to get her daughter away; away out of Jalak's hands. Only so— only so she could die in peace."

Kindra's face was grim. *Before I bore a daughter to live in the Dry Towns, captive, chained,* she thought, *I would lay hands on myself and the life within me, or strangle the babe as she came forth from my womb! But the women of the Domains are soft, cowards all!* None of this showed in her voice, however, as she laid a hand on Rohana's shoulder, saying quietly, "I thank you for telling me this, Lady. I did not understand. So our mission is not so much to rescue your kinswoman—"

"As to free her daughter; that is what she asked. Although— if Melora can be freed . . ."

"Well, my band and I are pledged to do all we can," Kindra said, "and I think any of us would risk our lives to save a young girl from living chained. But for now, Lady, you will soon need all your strength, and there is neither courage nor wisdom in an empty belly; it is not fitting that I should lay commands on a *Comynara,* but will you not join my women now and finish your meal?"

Rohana's smile wavered a little. *Why, beyond her harsh words, she's kind!* She said aloud, "Before I joined you, *mestra,* I pledged myself to conduct myself in all ways as one of your band, and so I am bound to obey you."

She went out of the tent, and Kindra, standing in the doorway, watched her take a place by the fire, and accept a plateful of the stewed meat and beans.

Kindra did not follow at once, but stood thinking of what lay ahead. If it came to Jalak's ears that anyone of the Domains was in his city, he might be already on guard. Or would he so despise the Free Amazons that he would not trouble to guard against them? She should have insisted that the Lady Rohana dye her hair. If any spy of Jalak's should see a redheaded *Comyn* woman . . . *I never thought she would be willing to cut it.*

Maybe courage is relative; for her, maybe it took as much courage to cut her hair as for me to draw knife on a foeman. . . .

It is worth risk, to take a young maiden from Jalak's hands, from chains to freedom.

. . . Or such freedom as any woman can have in the Domains.

Kindra raised her hand, in an automatic gesture, to her cropped, graying hair. She had not been born into the Guild of Free Amazons; she had come to it through a choice so painful that the memory still had power to make her lips tighten and her eyes grow grim and faraway. She looked at Rohana, sitting in the ring of Amazons around the fire, eating, listening to the women talk. *I was once very like her: soft, submissive to the only life I knew. I chose to free myself. Rohana chose otherwise. I do not pity her, either.*

But Melora was given no choice. Nor her daughter.

She thought, dispassionately, that it was probably too late for Melora. There could not, after ten years in the Dry Towns, be much left for her. But there was evidently enough left, of what she had been, to spur her to an enormous effort to get freedom for her daughter. Kindra knew only a little of the telepathic powers of the *Comyn*; but she knew that for Melora to reach Lady Rohana, over such distance, after so long a separation, must have taken enormous and agonizing effort. For the first time, Kindra felt a moment of genuine sympathy for Melora. She had accepted captivity for herself rather than allow any more of her kinsmen to risk death by torture. But she would risk anything, to give her daughter a choice; so that her daughter would not live and die knowing nothing but the chained world, the slave world, of the Dry-Town women.

Lady Rohana did well to come to me. After so many years, no doubt, her Comyn kin wished Melora dead, wished to forget she dwelt in slavery, a reproach to them.

But that is why the Free Amazons exist, in the final analysis. So that every woman may, at least, know there is a choice for them . . . that if they accept the restrictions laid upon women, on Darkover, they may do so from choice and not because they cannot imagine anything else. . . .

Kindra was about to leave her tent, to return to the fireside and have her own meal, when she heard a small, strange sound: the whistle of a rain-bird; such a bird as never cried here, in the Dry Towns. Quickly she turned, nervously alert, seeing the small, slight form that wriggled under the back flap of the tent. It was very dark, but she knew who it must be. She said in a whisper, "Nira?"

"Unless you think some rain-bird has gone mad and flown here to die," said Nira, rising to her feet.

Kindra said, "Here, get out of those clothes; another woman around our fire will never be noticed, but in men's clothes you would collect another crowd here. We had quite enough of that while we were off-loading."

"I heard," Nira said wryly, slipping out of her boots, unbuckling the shortsword she wore—contrary to Domain law—and concealing it in the clutter of the tent. Kindra flung the younger woman a shirt and loose Amazon trousers, saw that she was very faintly silhouetted by firelight, and turned the tiny lamp lower still until they were in darkness. Nira was folding up her disguise; as she stepped into her clothes, Kindra came and asked in a whisper, "Was there any trouble? What news, child?"

"No trouble; I passed for any trader's lad from the mountains, any apprentice; they thought me a beardless boy with his voice still unbroken. For news I have only gossip of the marketplace, and some from the servants at Jalak's door. The Voice of Jalak, who keeps his Great House when the Lord is away, has received a message that Jalak, and his wives and concubines and all his household, will return before noon tomorrow; and one of the slave-girls told me that they would have returned tonight, except that his Lady is heavy with child, and could not ride so far this day. Jalak has sent word for the midwives to be in readiness at any time after his return, and his servants are making bets about whether this will be the son he wants . . . it seems he has begotten nothing but girls, whether by wife, concubine or slave-girl, and that he has promised that the first of his women to bear him a son shall have rubies from Ardcarran and pearls brought from the sea-towns at Temora. Some old midwife says that she can tell by the way Lady Melora carries her child, low and broad, that it is a son; and Jalak will do nothing to endanger her while he has this hope. . . ."

Kindra's face twisted in distaste. She said: "So Jalak is camped in the desert? How far away?"

Nira shrugged. "No more than a few miles, I gathered. Maybe we should have arranged to attack his tents. . . ."

Kindra shook her head. "Madness. Have you forgotten? The Dry-Towners are paranoid; they live by feud and combat. On the road, take my word, Jalak will be guarded so that three cadres of City Guardsmen could not come at him. In his own house he may be a little more relaxed. In any case, we cannot stand against open attack. A quick strike, a guard or two killed, and ride like hell; that's the only kind of chance we have."

"True." Nira had dressed in her own clothes again; they were about to leave the tent when Nira laid her hand on Kindra's arm, detaining her. "Why must we have the Lady Rohana with us? She rides but poorly; she will be no use at all in a fight—she hardly knows which end to take hold of a knife—and if she is recognized we are all dead women. Why did you not demand that she wait for us at Carthon? Or is she like those men who hire a watchdog and do their own barking?"

"I thought so myself at first," Kindra said, "but the Lady Melora must be warned, and ready to leave with us at a moment's notice; the slightest delay could ruin us all. The Lady Rohana can reach her mind, without warning Jalak, or rousing his suspicions as even the most cautious message could do." Kindra grinned wryly in the darkness of the tent. "Besides, which of you wants the task of caring for a pregnant woman on the journey back? None of us have much taste for it—nor any skill should she need nursing. Or do you want to try?"

Nira laughed ruefully. "Avarra and Evanda forbid it! I stand reproved!" she said, and went to join the other women around the fire. After a moment Kindra went to join them, taking the plateful of food they had saved her (it was cold by now, but she ate without noticing), listening to the women talking softly as they cleared away the dishes, set a watch. Mentally, she checked them over.

She had handpicked this group from volunteers, and with all of them except the young girl Gwennis, she had worked before. Nira, who could pass as a man when she must, learned to use a sword. *Against Dry-Towners we may need it.* By the Charter of the Guild of Free Amazons, it was not lawful for any Amazon to bear a sword. *Too threatening to the men of the Domains for women to play with their precious toys!* Yet that law was not always honored; Kindra felt no guilt that she had allowed Nira to teach the others what she could of handling a sword. Then there was Leeanne, who had been neutered at fourteen and looked like a slim boy: breastless, hard-bodied and spare. Another who had known the neutering operation—which was illegal, but still turned up sometimes as a *fait accompli*—was Camilla, born of a good family in the Kilghard Hills; she did not use her family name Lindir, for they had long disowned and disinherited her. Camilla was nearing middle age, and like Kindra, had spent most of her life as a mercenary fighter; she was scarred with multiple knife-scars. Also Kindra had chosen Lori, who had been born in the Hellers and fought with two knives, mountain style; and Rafaella, Kindra's own kinswoman. Not all the Free Amazons were fighters, of course, but for this mission Kindra had chosen, mostly, the best fighting women she knew. Then there was Devra, who was not a great fighter, but skilled beyond anyone Kindra had ever known at reading the trackless lands of mountain or desert, so that Kindra had chosen her, warning her to keep out of any close-quarters fighting. And Fat Rima, who was altogether feminine in appearance and manner, and so heavy she could ride only the biggest horses; but Kindra knew she was skilled at making and managing a campsite, and their comfort was valuable, too, on a trip like this; and like all Amazons, Rima was completely able to defend herself. *And she has other skills that may be needed before we reach Thendara!*

Kindra reflected. Then there was the girl Gwennis, and Lady Rohana.

Anyone who knew the Free Amazons, Kindra thought, could tell at once that the Lady was not one of them: her walk, her speech, her riding. But there was no one here, the Goddess be praised, who knew that much about them!

They had finished putting away the supper gear; Kindra surrendered her empty bowl, to be scrubbed with sand by Fat Rima. Rafaella brought out her small *rryl* and laid it across her knees, striking a preliminary chord or two. "Kindra, will you sing for us?"

"Not tonight, Rafi," she said, smiling to soften the refusal. "I have plans to make; I'll listen to the rest of you."

Devra began a song, and Kindra sat with her head in her hands, her mind not on the music. She knew she could trust every one of these women with her life. Lady Rohana was an unknown, but she had more reasons than the others to work at Kindra's command. The others had all volunteered; partly, at least, because like every Free Amazon from Dalereuth to the Hellers, they hated the Dry-Towners with a deadly hatred. The Domains themselves had made an uneasy peace with the Dry Towns, and kept it; there was no love lost between Domains and Dry Towns, but there was a bitter memory of the long wars they had fought, without any conclusive victory on either side. The Domains might accept the present state of truce out of political expediency; and their women with them. *The Domains live under men's laws. They accept the enslavement of the Dry-Town women because it pleases them to think how benevolent, by contrast, they are to their own women. They say all men must choose their own lifestyles.*

But no woman who had ever cut her hair and sworn the Oath of a Free Amazon would ever accept that compromise!

Kindra had early freed herself from a life that now seemed to her as enslaved, as weighted with invisible chains, as that of any Dry-Town woman who walked in her ornamental bracelets and fetters of possession; she felt that any woman who truly chose, and would pay the price, could do as much. *Yes, even the women of the Dry Towns.* Yet, for all her lack of sympathy for any woman who bowed her head to a man's yoke, she felt a surge of hatred and loathing for the men who perpetuated this kind of slavery.

Should I tell them my plans now? She raised her hand and listened. Lady Rohana, who had a sweet, small, untrained voice, and Gwennis, who had a very light, true soprano, were singing a riddle-song from the Domains. Kindra decided not to disturb them. *Let them have a night's undisturbed sleep first.* "Set good watch around the camp," she said. "Some of these Dry-Towners may have ideas about how Free Amazons might like to spend their nights, and I doubt we'd care for their notions."

Chapter 2

At high noon the marketplace of Shainsa lay sweltering under a direct sun, beating down on the dry stone, the sun-bleached stone walls of houses and buildings that turned blind faces to the light.

In spite of the insults and jeers that the loafers of the streets had flung at the Free Amazons, their booth, a light woven-wicker affair intended for transport on horseback, had been doing a flourishing business all morning; the mountain-tanned leather commanded a good price in the Dry Towns, where few animals could by husbanded and leather and textiles were scarce. Their stock was vanishing, in fact, so quickly that Kindra was beginning to fret; if any happenstance delayed Jalak's return, and their wares for sale were exhausted, their lingering in the town might cause some suspicion. *Must I lay the groundwork for an accident to one of the pack animals?* she wondered. Then there was a stir in the marketplace, an almost visible murmuring of rumor, and idlers, passersby and children began to drift toward the great gates. *Jalak,* she thought. *It must be Jalak returning, nothing else could create so great a stir.*

Leaving the booth in the hands of Devra and Fat Rima, she moved idly with the crowd toward the gates, Rohana at her side. She muttered, in a tone that could not be heard six inches away, "Now, if ever, you must get a message through to your kinswoman. Tell her to be alert to move at a moment's notice; we may have only a few minutes to strike and we must take it when the occasion offers. It will not be until after nightfall;

thereafter, she must be ready. Also, find out precisely where she sleeps, and if she is guarded and by how many; and where her daughter sleeps, alone or with other royal daughters."

Rohana leaned against the Free Amazon's arm, feeling suddenly sick and faint with the enormous responsibility. Now it was suddenly all on her shoulders. Someone jostled them; Kindra glared, steadied Rohana on her feet and the jostler flung a jeering phrase at them that made the *Comyn* woman blush with indignation, more for Kindra's sake then her own. She knew the Free Amazons were often accused of being lovers of women; she supposed some of them were. Yet all Kindra's kindness to her had been entirely impersonal, almost motherly, and Rohana felt a surge of anger that Kindra should suffer such insult on her behalf. *How absurd to be thinking of that now! As if I—or Kindra—could possibly care what some Dry-Town nothing thought of either of us!*

There was a blare of horns, a strange, hoarse fanfare. First came a dozen of his guards, in trappings so alien to Rohana as to make little impression on her except the general one of rude splendor: sashes and baldrics, elaborately gilded tunics, high headdresses. Then *cralmacs,* furred and tailed humanoids with great gold-colored eyes, wearing only their own fur and elaborate jeweled sashes, riding on the great shambling *oudhraki* of the far deserts: a legion of them, it seemed. More guards, less elaborately and ceremonially dressed this time, but armed with the long, straight swords and daggers of the Dry-Towners. Rohana thought, *Just as well that Kindra's band did not try to strike him encamped by night.* And then came Jalak himself.

Rohana had to turn away before she had more than a sight of his thin, hawk-keen face, sun-bleached under thick pale hair, fierce bristling mustachios; there were times when it seemed to her that so immense a force of hatred *must* somehow communicate itself to its object, that he could not fail to be aware of her thoughts. Rohana, a telepath since girlhood, lived with that as reality; but Jalak seemed impervious, riding amid his guards with a set, impassive face, looking neither to left nor right.

Near him rode—she supposed—a couple of his favorites,

slaves or concubines; a slim girl with lint-white hair, chains jeweled, her body muffled in a scant fur smock, but her long legs bare to the fierce sun; she leaned toward Jalak and murmured and cooed to him as they passed. On Jalak's other side a thin, elegant boy, a pretty minion: too curled, too jeweled and perfumed to be anything else. ·

Behind Jalak and his favorites rode an assembly of women, and among them, outstanding for her flame-red hair (now, streaked faintly with gray), rode Melora. Rohana felt faint. She had been prepared for this; Melora had come to her in thought. But seeing her like this, in the flesh, changed beyond recognition (*And yet, Cassilda pity us, I would have known her anywhere, anywhere . . .*), Rohana felt that her pain and pity would overwhelm her and she would sink down, fainting.

Kindra's hand closed painfully on Rohana's arm, the nails digging into the flesh; Rohana recalled herself. This was her part in the rescue, the thing only she could do. Deliberately, she reached out and made contact with her kinswoman's mind.

—*Melora!*

She felt the shock, the start and flutter. She was suddenly afraid lest Melora should see her, make some sign of recognition.

—*Betray nothing; do not look for me or try to see me, darling, but I am near you, among the Free Amazons.*

—*Rohana! Rohana, is it you?*

But Rohana, from her place in the crowd, saw—and felt a sudden, fierce pride in her kinswoman—that Melora rode on without making any visible sign; her eyes fixed, apparently, on nothing; slightly slumped in her saddle; the taut, thin, careworn face beneath the graying red hair showing nothing but weariness and pain. Suddenly Rohana was struck with fear and compunction. She thought, *She is so heavy, so near her time, the child weighs on her so. How can we possibly get her away in safety?* She sent the concerned question.

—*Can you ride, Melora, can you travel, so far in pregnancy?*

The answer was almost listless. —*It is easy to tell you do not know the Dry Towns; I would be expected to ride even closer to my time than this.* Then the answering thoughts were fierce with hate.—*I can do what I must! To be free I would ride through hell itself!*

Painstakingly, then, but by bit, Rohana relayed Kindra's message; received Melora's answer, even while the caravan passed on, passed by the marketplace. At the rear came a few more guards, who indifferently tossed small coins, copper rings, wrapped fruits and sweetmeats into the crowd, watching with dead eyes, as the beggars scrambled for them. Kindra and Rohana, not staying to watch the painful spectacle, turned back toward their booth. Once safely inside it, Rohana relayed the information she had received.

"Jalak sleeps in a room at the north side of the building, with his favorites of the moment, and Melora; not that he has any interest, at the moment, in sharing her bed, so she told me; but at the moment she is his most prized possession, bearing his son, and he will not let her out of his sight. There are no guards within the room, but there are two guards, and two *cralmacs* armed with knives, in the antechamber. Until this last pregnancy, Jaelle—that is her daughter—slept in her mother's room; now she has been moved to a room in the suite set apart for the other royal daughters. She complained that the noise the little ones made kept her from sleeping; Jalak is indulgent with girl-children if they are pretty ones, and allotted her a room to her own use, with a nurse there. It is at the far end of the royal children's suite, and looks out on an inner courtyard filled with blackfruit trees."

She anticipated Kindra's next question, saying, "I have the plan of the building so clear in my mind that I could draw it for you from memory."

Kindra laughed and said, "Truly, Lady, you would make a Free Amazon someday! Perhaps it is our loss that you did not choose our way, after all." She went to the women still in the booth, saying in an undertone, "Sell what you can; but what cannot be sold by nightfall, be prepared to abandon. Do not strike the booth; if we leave it standing they will expect us to be here come morning. Be sure the horses we used as pack animals are ready to be saddled for Melora and her daughter. . . ."

That afternoon seemed endless to Rohana. The worst of it lay in that she must behave exactly as usual—or at least as near to usual as was possible for her, here in the Dry Towns, far from her accustomed ways of occupying herself. She tried not to fidget visibly, knowing it would only disturb the Amazons, who seemed quite calm, selling their wares, tending their animals, idling around the camp, And yet, as the afternoon wore on, it seemed to her that she could see small signs that they were not, after all, quite so indifferent as they seemed to the coming battle. Camilla sat cross-legged at the back of the booth, sharpening her great knife to a razor edge, whistling an odd, tuneless little melody that, after a time, began to set Rohana's teeth on edge. Kindra sat drawing patterns again and again in the sand and quickly rubbing them out again with the toe of her boot. Rohana wondered how Melora was passing the time, but resisted the temptation to follow her in thought. If Melora could take some rest before sunset, let her do so, by all means!

How will she travel? She looks not more than three days from her time—if so much!

Slowly, slowly, the great red sun declined toward the hills. It seemed to Rohana that no day in her lifetime had worn away so wearily, with every hour stretching into lifetimes. *Not even the day my second son was born, when I seemed to lie for hours stretched on a rack of pain tearing me asunder . . . even then, something could be* done. *Now I can only wait . . . and wait . . . and wait. . . .*

Kindra said quietly, as she passed, "This day must seem longer still for your kinswoman, Lady," and Rohana tried to smile. That, at least, was true.

"Pray to your Goddess that the Lady Melora does not go into labor this day," Kindra said. "That would be the end of hope. We might still rescue her daughter, but if the Great House was ablaze with lights, midwives running here and there to attend to her . . . even that would be made more difficult than we could manage."

Rohana drew a deep breath of apprehension. *And she is so near to her time. . . .*

She tried to form, in her heart, a prayer to the Blessed Cassilda, Mother of the Seven Domains; but her prayer seemed to hang on the dead air, waiting, like everything else. . . .

And yet, as all things mortal must, even the day wore to an end. The Dry-Town women, veiled and chained, came to buy water at the well, and again they lingered, fascinated even through their scorn, to watch the Amazons moving about, tending their horses, cooking their meal. Rohana offered what help she could; it was easier if her hands were busy. She watched the Dry-Town women come and go in the marketplace, thinking of Melora, her hands weighted by the jeweled chains, her body weighted with Jalak's hated child. *She had been so light and quick, as a girl, so frolicsome and laughing. . . .*

They finished their meal, and Kindra signaled to Rafaella to take her harp, strike a few chords. She said in an undertone, "Come in close, and listen; act as if you were only listening to the music."

Rohana asked in a low voice, "Can you play 'The Ballad of Hastur and Cassilda'?"

"I think so, Lady."

"I will sing it. It is very long, and my voice," she added, with a self-deprecating smile, "is not so strong that anyone passing by would think it odd if you kept very quiet to listen to me—but not so soft that Kindra cannot talk more softly still, and be heard."

Kindra nodded, pleased at Rohana's quick comprehension of her plan. Rafaella played a short introduction, and Rohanna began, hearing her own voice wavering:

"The stars were mirrored on the shore,
    Dark was the dim enchanted moor;
    Silent were field and tree and stone. . . ."

The other women clustered in close, as if to listen to the ancient ballad; Rohana heard her own voice falter, fought to steady it. She must somehow collect herself to remember all the seemingly endless verses, string it out while Kindra gave soft, detailed instructions to every one of the Amazons. *Get hold of yourself,* she ordered and commanded herself: *This is something you can do, while they do the real work . . . the dangerous work, the fighting. . . .*

Yet they are women. I learned to think fighting was for men; I could never carry a knife, strike, see blood flow, perhaps suffer wounding, die. . . .

Sing, damn you, Rohana! Stop thinking, sing.

"He lay thrown up along the shore,
The sands were jeweled evermore,
And to the shore Cassilda came
And called him by a mortal name. . . ."

Struggling to remember the next lines, she heard Kindra, in a low, tense voice, detailing the information she had been given, pointing to the pattern she had scratched in the sand by firelight.

"Jalak sleeps here, with his favorites and Melora; there are no guards in the room, but just outside . . ."

"Cassilda wept and paled and fled,
Camilla knelt and raised his head,
He left his high immortal fire
For mortal man's entranced desire;
White bread and wine and cherries red . . .

"—No, damn it, I skipped a verse," she said, breaking off in vexation, then realized it did not matter; no one was listening anyway.

"Brought by her doves through morning bright,
Camilla came, and bowed her head;
He ate and drank by mortal light;
And as his brilliance paled away
Into a dimmer earthly day
Cassilda left her shining loom:

> A starflower in his hand she laid;
> Then on him fell a mortal doom. . . ."

"Are the windows accessible by ladders?" asked Gwennis, and Kindra snapped, "They might be, if we *had* ladders. Next question, but no more stupid ones, please! We have time to kill, but not *that* much time!"

> "Into the heart of Alar fell
> A splinter from the Darkest Hell,
> And madness raging on him came,
> He cried again on Zandru's name,
> And at the darkened forge he made
> A darkly shining magic blade;
> An evil spell upon it cast. . . ."

"Devra and Rima, you will stay here, and the moment we come in sight, get moving! Be sure that the guards at the gate make no outcry. . . ." Kindra looked meaningfully at Rima.

The fat woman laid a hand on her knife, with a grim nod. Kindra said, "Camilla, you ride lighter than any of us; you will carry the child on your saddle. Lady Rohana—*no, go on singing!* You must be ready to ride close to Melora, to be alert for anything she needs; we shall all be busy enough evading pursuit and dealing with anyone who might come after us."

Rohana felt a shudder take her, seize her body and shake it like a rabbithorn in the grip of a wolf. Her voice faltered; she tried to cover it with a cough, and doggedly went on, knowing she was garbling the words horribly:

> "He could not see the—something—plan
> That gave a God to mortal wife,
> That earthly love with a mortal man—
> Should bring to man a—something—life,
> Camilla fell without a cry—"

Damn, damn, I've skipped two whole verses again. . . .

> "And Hastur, shielded by her heart,
>   Knew he could die as mortals die. . . ."

"Lori, you handle the *cralmacs;* I understand you know how they fight. Those long blades . . . anything else? Leeanne?"

"Remember that sometimes the Dry-Towners poison their swords. Don't neglect even a scratch. I've got some ointment that is supposed to neutralize their worst poisons. . . ."

> "Then Hastur son of Light had known,
>   (For so had ruled the Shining Sire
>   When first he left the Realm of Fire)
>   Once more his star must burn alone . . .
>   For on the earth he might not reign
>   If he should cause one mortal pain,
>   Or in that hour he must return
>   To the far realms that were his own. . . ."

"We'll never be readier than now," Kindra said softly. "Finish the damn song, Rafaella, and get your dagger."

Gratefully Rohana began the last verse:

> "And ever more the cloud waves break
>   Along the fringes of the lake,
>   And tears and songs still whisper there
>   Upon the still and misty air. . . ."

It was an unnerving experience, knowing they were all listening now, but impatient of every note, eager for her to finish. *Damn it, no more eager than I!*

> "They built a city in the wild,
>   Fit for his rule, the kingly child,
>   And singing of Camilla's doom
>   They wrought for her an opal tomb."

She skipped the little postlude and rose impatiently, letting Rafaella put her harp away. Earlier in the afternoon she had packed the few possessions she had brought on this journey into a small bundle. Inside the tent the Amazons moved quickly and efficiently by the light of a single shaded candle, stowing food and necessary belongings in their saddlebags. Rohana watched, keeping out of their way, Devra and Fat Rima moved away toward the city gates, and Rohana felt another shudder take her; their business was to assure that those gates would be unguarded when they came back this way in a hurry, fleeing. . . .

Don't be squeamish! The guards there are Dry-Towners; they've probably deserved death a dozen times over. . . .

But they have no quarrel with any of us! There must be some good men among them, who have done nothing more than live as their forefathers have lived for centuries. . . .

Angry at herself, Rohana stifled the thought. *I hired Kindra's band to get Melora and her child away. Did I really believe it could be done without bloodshed? You cannot take hawks without climbing cliffs!*

Kindra beckoned the red-haired woman to her side. She said in an undertone, "I had thought to leave you here with these; but we shall need you, in case your kinswoman must have help—or reassurance. Come with us, Lady, but look to yourself if there is fighting; none of us will have time or thought to protect you, and Jalak's men may think you one of us and attack. Have you any kind of weapon?"

"I have this," Rohana said, showing the small dagger she carried, like all *Comyn* women, for personal protection. Kindra looked at it, trying to conceal her scorn. "It would be small service in a fight, I fear. But if we fail—I do not think we will fail, but nothing in this world is absolutely certain but death and next winter's snow—if we fail, at least it will keep you from falling alive into Jalak's hands. Are you prepared for that, *vai domna?*"

Rohana nodded, hoping the Amazon could not see that she was trembling. And again it flickered fleetingly through her mind, as had happened more than once during the twenty days she had been in their company, that perhaps Kindra had some small spark of psi power, that she followed Rohana's thoughts a little more than might happen by chance, for the Amazon's hard-boned hand descended briefly on her shoulder; only for a moment, a light touch, and hesitant, lest the noblewoman angrily refuse her sympathy. "My Lady, do you think none of us is afraid? We have not learned not to fear; only to go on in the face of fear, as women are seldom taught to do on our world." She turned away, her voice brusque again in the darkness. "Come along, Nira: to the front, you know the way step by step, we know it only from my Lady's drawings and maps."

Thrust to the rear of the small group of women, Rohana followed, hearing her pounding heart, so strongly it seemed to her that the thumping must almost be audible in the dusty, deserted streets. They moved like ghosts, or shadows, keeping in the lee of buildings, stealing along on noiseless feet. Rohana wondered where they had learned to move so silently, found she was afraid to speculate. For a panic-stricken moment she wished she had never begun this, that she were safe at home in Castle Ardais, on the borders of the Hellers. She wondered how her children fared without her, how the cousin who had managed her estates after her husband's death a few years ago was dealing with the business, what was happening far away in the mountain country. *This was never any place for me. Why did I ever come here? War, revenge, rescue, these are matters for men!*

And the men were content to let Melora pine away and die, captive! She hardened her resolve and stole along at the rear of the little column, trying to pick up her feet and put them down as silently as the Amazons, not to stumble against a chance stone.

The city was a labyrinth. And yet it was not very long before the women in front of her stopped, drew close together in a knot, seeing across an open, wind-swept square the loom of the Great House where Jalak of Shainsa ruled. The house was a great squared building of pale bleached stone, glimmering faintly by the light of a single small gibbous moon: a blind windowless barrack, a fortress, the two doors guarded by tall guards in Jalak's barbarous livery. Silently the Amazons turned, slipping through the shadows and along the side of the building. Rohana had heard Kindra's plan, and it seemed to her a good one. Every outside door into a Dry-Town house was guarded; against direct attack at the doors a couple of guards could hold it indefinitely. But if they could somehow get through the small side gateway into the courtyard, make their way through the garden—hopefully deserted, at this hour—and get into the house through the unguarded *inside* doorways, they might get into Jalak's chamber.

She had heard Kindra say, through her singing, "Our best hope is that there has been peace in the Dry Towns for many moons. The guards may be bored, not as alert as usual."

She could see the guard at the side gate now. *Evanda be praised, no more than one.* He lounged against the wall; Rohana could not see his face, but she was a telepath, and even unsought, his thoughts were clear enough: boredom, dullness, the sense that he would welcome anything, even armed attack, to relieve the monotony of this watch.

"Gwennis." Kindra murmured. "Your move."

(When this plan had been put forward, Gwennis had protested, sullenly. "Does it have to be me?" and Kindra had said, "You're the prettiest.") Now there was no protest, the band's discipline held. As Gwennis deliberately scuffed a stone loose against the wall, Rohana felt the Amazon leader thinking, *This is the worst moment of risk. . . .*

The guard straightened, alert to the noise.

He's alert, we can't take him unawares; so we have to get him away from the gate, get him out into the center of the square, Kindra thought.

Gwennis had swiftly divested herself of knife and dagger, torn her tunic slightly down the front. She sauntered out into the moonlit square, and the guard was instantly alert, then relaxed, seeing a woman alone.

We are taking advantage of him, yes. Of the centuries-old Dry-Town contempt for women as helpless, harmless chattels. Victims, Kindra reflected bitterly.

The guard did not hesitate more than half a minute before stepping away from his post at the door, moving purposefully toward the young girl. "Hey, pretty thing—are you lonely? One of the Amazons, huh? Have you got tired of them and come looking for some better company?"

Gwennis did not raise her eyes. Rohana had heard the argument about that, too. ("I won't seduce him to his death. If he minds his own business he is safe. I won't use a feminine trick.") But the guard had already left his post, and Gwennis' silent indifference to him had provoked his curiosity; he came swiftly toward her, saying, "Ha—caught you without that knife you wear all the time, huh? Now you'll see what it's like really to be a woman. Who knows, you might even like it better. Here, come here and let me show you a thing or two. . . ." He reached for the girl, roughly pulled her against him, spun her around, one hand covering her mouth to stifle a cry . . . his words broke off in a strangled gasp. Lori's long knife, thrown with deadly accuracy, went straight into his throat. A moment later Lori herself bent over him, delivering a swift, fatal death-stroke to the great vein below his ear. Kindra and Camilla dragged him into the shadow of the wall, out of sight of any chance passerby; Gwennis scrambled up, fastidiously wiping her mouth as if she could wipe away the guard's rude touch. Kindra rummaged at the dead man's belt, found his keys and began to try them one by one in the heavy lock. *Locked on the outside, not within. Less against invaders than against the escape of one of his women. . . .*

The lock was stiff; it seemed to Rohana, quaking in the quiet street, that it creaked loudly enough to alarm the whole town, but after a moment it gave and the door swung noiselessly inward. The band of Amazons crowded inside, shrinking against the inner wall, pushing the door closed.

They stood in a quiet and deserted garden. Here in the Drylands little grew unless it was planted, except thornbush; but Jalak, tyrant of Shainsa, had spared no expense to create an oasis for himself and his pampered women and favorites. A multitude of fountains splashed, tall trees towered overhead, flowers grew in lush profusion, with a sweet, damp, rank smell. On silent feet, guided by the sketch Rohana had made after the rapport with Melora, the women threaded their way along the bricked pathway, and paused in the shadow of a grove of blackfruit trees.

"Leeanne," Kindra whispered.

As the slender, sexless figure moved away toward, Rohana knew, the chamber where Melora's twelve-year-old daughter slept with her nurse, Rohana found herself wondering incongruously how a neutered Amazon thought of herself. *Not as a woman, surely. A man? Some indefinable third thing?* She dismissed the thought impatiently. *What nonsense to be thinking about now!*

They moved toward the unguarded garden door; a moment later they were actually inside. Rohana, moving now from memory of her rapport with Melora, began to move directly toward the guarded room where Jalak slept.

Was Melora awake, alert for them, expecting them? All this afternoon she had resisted the temptation to reach out for telepathic contact with her cousin, but now she yielded; reached for rapport, more easily as the long-neglected skill came back.

—*Melora, Melora!* And suddenly, in a half-forgotten sensation of blending and merging, she *was* Melora, she . . .

. . . She lay silent, facing the wall, every muscle tense and alert, willing herself to relax, be patient, wait. . . . In her body the heavy child kicked sharply, and she thought, with weary patience, *You are so strong and lusty, little son, and, Avarra pity me, I have not even the heart to wish you more like to die. It is not your fault but your ill fortune that you are Jalak's son. . . .*

Will it truly be tonight? And the guards . . . how, how? The memory that had been with her, night and day, for ten years now of her foster-brother Valentine, broken, writhing, his fingers cut from his living body, covered in blood, after atrocities too many and too dreadful to think about. . . . *Oh, Evanda and Avarra, Aldones, Lord of Light, not Rohana, too. . . .*

No! I must not remember that now! I must be strong. . . .

Painstakingly, muscle by muscle, she forced herself to relax. Jalak slept now, deeply: the first, sated sleep of the night.

Beyond him she saw, by the dim moonlight from the courtyard window, the pale forms of the two favorites who shared his bed. They, too, slept; Danette—pale, nude, her long scattered hair enfolding her; Garris snoring a little, lying on his back, folded against Jalak's long body. At first this had infuriated and humiliated her to silent tears and passionate rebellion; after ten years she was only wearily relieved that *she* need no longer share his bed. During these months while she carried his son, Jalak, proud, and as near to kindness as he ever came, had yielded good-naturedly to her plea and allowed her to have a bed of her own, that she might sleep in peace and rest well. For years now she had been freed at night, like other Dry-Town women, from the chains she wore by day; only while she was still a rebellious prisoner had she been forced to wear them night and day. More than once, in that first faraway year, she had flown at his throat . . . ceasing only when she knew her furious resistance excited, amused, stimulated him. . . .

Poor Danette, how she hates me, how she gloated when she took my place in Jalak's bed, never guessing how willingly I would have resigned it years ago—and she hates my child worse than she hates me, she knows she is barren. If only I were. . . . I wish Garris no ill. His parents sold him in the brothels of Ardcarran when he was no older than Jaelle . . . he loves Jalak no more than I . . . perhaps less. Cruelly as the Dry-Towners treat their women, there are at least laws and customs to protect women to some degree, and not even such laws protect such as Garris. Poor little wretch . . . he still cries. . . . How slowly this night seems to pass. . . .

She stiffened, every nerve in her body alert. *What sound was that?* The next moment the door came crashing inward and it seemed all at once that the room was full of . . . *of women?* Jalak woke with a bellow, snatching up his sword where it lay ready, night and day, to his hand; he yelled for the guards . . . a yell that went unanswered. Already on his feet, he yelled again, naked, leaping at the first who came against him; they crowded him against the wall, and Rohana, seeing through her own eyes now—although she shared Melora's thought, *Where are the guards?*—saw the Amazons force him against the wall, saw him disappear behind what looked like a wall of women, slashing, darting in with their knives; saw the long ripping cut with which Kindra darted in, slashed, the tendons at the back of his knee. He fell, howling, struggling. Danette, wide-eyed, kneeling upright on the bed, shrieked.

"Garris! Garris! Get his sword! They're only *women. . . .*"

"Silence that bitch," said Kindra, and Camilla's rough hands muffled Danette's shrieks with a pillow. Garris sat upright, looking down at the writhing, howling Jalak with an unholy joy. . . . Rohana caught up a furred cloak from the foot of the bed, wrapped it over Melora's scanty nightgown. "Come—quickly!"

Guided between her kinswoman and the Amazon leader, Melora stumbled into the hall; her foot slipped in the blood of the guards who had been killed there. *Are they all dead? All?* Even Jalak's howls had stopped. *Dead, or unconscious from loss of blood?*

She saw through the still-open door that Garris had caught up Jalak's sword; Nira whirled, her own sword at the ready, but Garris rushed past them, not even looking at her, disappearing down the hallway, with—evidently—no thought in mind but his own escape.

Rohana hurried Melora along, out into the silent garden. It was so silent that it took her breath away; fountains splashed, trees rustled undisturbed in the wind, no sound or light to show that somewhere inside there in the Great House, eight or ten of Jalak's fighting men and perhaps Jalak himself lay dead.

None but Jalak himself had had opportunity to strike a single return stroke; but that single slash had gone to Nira's thigh and she limped, leaning heavily on Camilla's arm. Lori came and bent beside her, roughly wadding the wound with her kerchief, wrapping it hastily with the belt of her tunic. Leeanne came out of the darkness, carrying in her arms a small form in a long nightgown, barefoot. She set the little girl on her feet, and in the dim light Rohana caught a glimpse of a small, surprised, sleepy face.

"Mother—?"

"It's all right, my darling, they are my kinswomen and our friends," Melora said in a singing voice; she stumbled, and Kindra put a hand under her elbow.

"Can you walk, Lady? If not, we can carry you somehow—"

"I can walk." But Melora stumbled again and put out her hand to clutch at Rohana's arm, thinking, *For the first time in a dozen years I am outside that wall with unbound hands— walk? I could run, I could fly.* Hurrying along between them, stumbling, she lost track of where her steps were taking her. *Anywhere. Anywhere away from here. Like Garris. . . . Poor little creature, I hope they do not hunt him down for Jalak's murder. . . .*

She felt the knives of pain in her side and back, felt the weight of her unborn child dragging at her, not caring. *Free, I am free. I could die now, happy. But I must not die and delay them. . . .*

The deserted marketplace was a silent wilderness of empty stalls, deserted booths. Rima and Devra came out of the dark, near where the horses waited. "The gates are clear," Rima said, with a suggestive gesture—a finger drawn across her throat.

"Come, then. Leave everything but your own saddlebags and food for travel," Kindra said, leading Melora to a horse with a lady's saddle. "Before you mount, *domna,* get into these clothes; they may not fit well, but they will be better for riding than that nightgown."

Melora felt Rohana slip her gown over her head, under cover of the darkness; help her into the long, loose trousers, tie them around her waist; slip a fur-lined tunic over her head. The faint smell in their folds made her want to weep with recognition and thankfulness: the spices and incense used to sweeten the air in every home in the Domains. She caught back a sob, letting Rohana help her to her saddle, slip suede boots—far too big—on her feet.

She looked around anxiously for Jaelle; saw that one of the Amazons had wrapped her in a cloak and lifted her to a saddle behind her, where she sat alert, amazed, her long straight hair streaming down her back, too excited and astonished even to ask questions.

Kindra took the reins of Melora's horse, saying, "Sit your horse as best you can, Lady; I will guide her." Melora clung to the saddle-horn (unfamiliar, after so many years, to ride astride again!) and watched, tensed against the pain of moving, as Kindra moved to the front of the little column of riders. She said in a low, tense voice, "Now ride like hell, all of you. We may have as many as five hours before the sun comes up and somebody finds Jalak in his blood; but we won't have more than that no matter how lucky we are, and from this day on for the next three dozen years, no Free Amazon's hide will be worth a *sekal* anywhere in the Dry Towns. Let's *go!*"

And they were off. Melora, clinging to her saddle, bracing herself as best she might against the jolting of her horse's gait (though she realized that Kindra had indeed provided a horse with an easy gait, the best available for a pregnant woman), looked back for an instant at the black loom of the walls of Shainsa.

It's over, she thought, *the nightmare is over. Thirteen years of it. Jalak lies crippled for life, hamstrung, perhaps dying.*

I hope he does not die. Worse, oh, worse for him to live and know that a pack of women has done this to him!

I am avenged, and Valentine! And Jaelle will live free!

They rode into the night, unpursued.

Chapter 3

To the end of her life, the Lady Rohana Ardais never forgot that mad ride, fleeing from the walls of Shainsa; alert at any moment for some small sound behind them that would mean Jalak—or his dead body—had been found, and the hunt for them was up.

For the first hour it was very dark, and she rode blindly after the sound of hooves from the other horses, with only dim shadows ahead. Then Kyrrdis rose, a brilliant half-circle above the horizon, so bright that Rohana knew it was not more than an hour or two ahead of the sun; and by its blue-green light she could make out the forms of the other horses and their riders.

They were traveling more slowly now. Even the swift horses from the plains of Valeron could not keep up the pace of those first hours. She wondered how Leeanne had found their road in the darkness; the Amazon's reputation as a tracker was evidently well-deserved. She could see Jaelle, a huddled, dark small form, collapsed in sleep against Camilla, clinging drowsily to the saddle. What did the child think of all this?

She was reared in the Dry Towns. Perhaps, to her, all this is quite normal: murder, midnight raids, the stealing of women. What if her loyalty is to Jalak? After all, he is her father.

None of us has any idea what Jaelle is like. . . . We have thought only of Melora's wishes. . . .

Melora is a telepath. She must know her child's heart. . . .

In the final hour before dawn they stopped to breathe the horses; Leeanne went to the top of a nearby hill to spy out any sign of pursuit. Rima came and put some bread and dried meat into Rohana's hand, poured wine into the cup at her saddle-horn.

"Eat and drink while you can, Lady. There won't be much time for breakfast if we are being pursued. There are a few hiding holes between here and Carthon, and Kindra knows all of 'em, but mostly our safety lies in a good long start. So you eat now."

Rohana chewed a mouthful obediently, although her mouth was dry, and the stuff tasted like stale parchment. She thrust it into a pocket of the unfamiliar Amazon trousers; maybe later she could manage to swallow it. She sipped at the wine, but it was too sour to drink, almost; she rinsed her mouth and spat it out again.

She led her horse slowly for several steps, hearing its deep, panting breaths slowly quiet to normal; rubbed its head absently, leaning against the warm, sweating body. She thought, not for the first time since she had undertaken this long journey, how fortunate it was that she was hardened to long riding, hunting with hawks in her distant mountain home. *If I were the kind of woman who did little more than sit over her embroidery-frames, I would be half dead of saddle-sores.* This made her think of Melora again (*How weary she must be!*) and she made her way through the Amazon crew: dismounting, slumped to rest, eating, talking in low tones. She noted that Jaelle had been lifted down and was sleeping heavily, curled up on someone's cloak, and covered with another. *At least they seem to be looking after her well. I do not suppose any of them know much about children.*

She looked around for Melora, seeing that Kindra was helping her kinswoman out of the high saddle; but before she could approach them, Nira, the crude bandage loose around her thigh, intercepted her. "Can you dress this wound by moonlight, *domna?* It hinders my riding more than I thought, or I would wait for the light."

Rohana felt a moment's impatience; then, remembering that Nira's wound had been incurred in their service, felt ashamed of herself. "I'll try. Come here, away from the shadows, where the light is brightest." She rummaged in her saddlebag for the few items of women's gear she had brought, found a clean, unworn shift and tore it into strips. Like everything else it was gritty with the sand of the Dry Towns, but clean.

She had to cut the bandage, and then the trouser leg, away with a knife; it was stuck to the wound with clotted blood. Nira swore under her breath, but did not flinch as Rohana washed the ugly cut with the sour wine—*At least the stuff is good for something,* she thought—and bandaged it tightly, pressing the hard pad of bandage against the wound. "It should be stitched; but I cannot do that by moonlight. If it begins to bleed again, I will do what I can when it is light."

Nira thanked her. "Now, if that bastard Jalak doesn't poison his weapons—one hears such things of Dry-Town men—"

"He does not," Melora said quietly beside them, and Rohana rose, folding what remained of the torn shift, to see her cousin standing there. Her face was dim in the moonlight, but even so it looked swollen and unhealthy. "Jalak would think that a coward's way; it would mean he did not believe his blows were strong enough to kill, and he would lose *kihar*—lose prestige, you would say, be shamed before his peers, if he stooped to a poisoned blade."

Nira got up awkwardly, grimacing as she put weight on her wounded leg. Her boot crunched on sand as she drew it on. She said wryly, "That is a comforting thought, Lady, but is it fact, or is it a sentiment seemly for a loving wife?"

"It is true, on the honor of my House," said Melora quietly, but her voice trembled, "and only my own Gods know how little I was a loving wife to Jalak, or anything else but a pawn to his filthy pride."

"I meant no offense," Nira said, "but I make no apology either, Lady. You dwelt in his house a full thirteen years, and you did not die. I would not have lived to shame my kinsmen so, even though my father is no great *Comyn* lord but a small-farmer in the Kilghard Hills."

"You have shed blood in my service, *mestra;* could I take offense, unless my pride were as great and evil as Jalak's own? As for my own life—can you see in the darkness?" She thrust out her wrists, took Nira's fingers in her own and guided them. Rohana, watching, touching, saw and felt the rough calluses from the metal bracelets on the chains; and above them on each darkly tanned wrist, a long, ragged, seamed scar. "I will bear them to my death," she said. "And after that, I was chained day and night—chained so tight I could not feed myself and had to be fed by the women and carried to the bath and to the latrines." Her voice shook with anger and remembered humiliation. "By the time I had healed, my child had quickened in me, and I would not kill the unborn with my own death." She looked at the dark form of her daughter, huddled and lost in sleep, saying, "How did you get her away? Jalak had given her into the charge of his fiercest woman-guard. . . ."

Leeanne had come back from the hilltop in time to hear this last; she said: "There is no sign of pursuit so far; not even a sand-rat seems to be stirring between here and Shainsa. As for your daughter's nurse, Lady, she sleeps past any waking; I do not like to kill women, but she came at me with a dagger. I was sorry to kill her before the child's eyes, but I had little choice."

"I will not weep for that one," said Melora with a grimace. "Indeed I think there will be small weeping for her, even in Jalak's house. She was my chief jailer before Jaelle was born, and I hated her worse than Jalak's own self. He was cruel because it was his nature and he had been reared to be so; but she was cruel because she found pleasure in the pain of others. I trust Zandru will delight in her company in hell; to be sure he will be the only one who has ever found such pleasure. Had I ever been trusted with a weapon again, even at table, I would have sunk it into her throat before turning it on myself." She turned to Rohana; for the first time there was a moment to exchange a quick, awkward embrace. "*Breda* . . . I am still not sure this is no dream, that I will not waken in Jalak's bed."

With the touch of Melora's swollen hands in hers, Melora's wet face pressed against her own, the rapport wakened again; Melora's mind lay open to her, and more: sharp physical discomfort, pain. Rohana thought, panicked. *Can she ride? Will she go into labor here and now, in the desert, far from help, delaying us . . . ?*

Gently, Melora loosed Rohana's hands and the contact lessened. "It is easy to see you know little of the Dry Towns. May you never have cause to know more! I would have been expected to ride, even nearer to my time than this. Don't worry about me, *breda*." Her voice broke in a sob. "Oh, it is so good, just to speak to you in our own tongue. . . ."

Rohana was desperately uneasy about her; she was not highly skilled in midwifery, but as mistress of Ardais she had seen many births; she knew Melora needed rest and care. But the Amazons, at Kindra's signal, were already mounting again, and indeed there seemed no choice.

Kindra came to inspect, briefly, Nira's bandaged wound. "So far there is no sign of pursuit, but with dawn someone will certainly find Jalak—or his corpse. And I would greatly prefer not to fight Jalak's men, or end my days chained in a Shainsa brothel."

Even in the dim light Melora's smile was perceptible. "It may be there will be no pursuit; most likely Jalak's heirs have found him dead and are already squabbling over his property and his wives, and the tenancy of the Great House. The last thing they would want would be to recapture a son of his with a valid claim!"

"Aldones grant it be so," said Kindra, "yet some kinsman of Jalak might seek *kihar* by avenging him—or some rival might want to make very sure any son with a valid claim did not survive him."

Melora gave Rohana's hands a convulsive squeeze, but her voice was calm. "I can ride as far as I must." Her eyes went to her sleeping daughter. "Can I have her with me on my own saddle?"

"Lady, you are heavy; your horse should not carry such a doubled weight," Kindra said. "Those of us who ride lightest will take turns to carry her, so that she can sleep a little longer. Can she ride? We have a spare horse for her, if she can sit alone on a saddle."

"She could ride almost as soon as she could walk, *mestra.*"

"That will do for when she wakes, then; for now, she can sleep," said Kindra, and lifted Jaelle, still sleeping, to her own saddle; she clambered up beside her, while Rohana assisted her cousin to mount. She was fearfully clumsy, and seemed unsteady in the saddle, but Rohana said nothing. There was nothing to say; Kindra was right and they both knew it. She gathered up her own reins, took the reins of Melora's horse to lead it onward across the desert.

Melora was gazing wistfully toward the sunrise. "At this hour, I always long for—oh, I don't know—some snow, or rain, anything but the eternal sand and hot dry wind."

Rohana said softly, "If the Gods will, *breda,* within a tenday you will be back again in our hills and see the snow at every sunrise." Melora smiled, but shook her head. "I can ride now, and guide my own horse, if you think it better."

"Let me lead it, for now at least," Rohana said, and Melora nodded and leaned back in her saddle, bracing herself as best she could against the motion of the beast.

The sun rose, and Rohana saw, as the miles went by under the feet of their horses, that the character of the land had changed. Flat, barren sand-desert had given way to low, rolling hills as far as the eye could see, and a low scruffy ground-cover of thorn-trees and gray feathery spicebush. At first the smell was pleasant, but after a few hours of riding through it, Rohana felt that if she ever again ate spicebread at Midwinter Festival it would choke her. Her throat was dry; she almost regretted the wine she had not been able to drink. Hour by hour Melora seemed more unsteady in her saddle, but she made no word of complaint. Indeed, she did not speak at all, riding head down, her face stony-gray with effort and patience.

As the sun climbed the light grew fiercer, and the heat. Some of the Amazons drew loose folds of their shifts or tunics over their heads; Rohana did likewise, finding the heat preferable to the direct glare. She was beginning to wonder how long Melora could continue to ride—and she herself was weary and saddle-worn almost to the point of dropping from her saddle—when

Leeanne, riding ahead, turned back, held up her hand and called to Kindra, who rode quickly ahead to join her, while the others came to a gradual halt.

After a moment Kindra came riding back. "In the next ravine there is a water hole; and some rocks for shelter from the sun. We can lie there during the heat of the day." As they followed her along the path Leeanne indicated, Kindra dropped back to ride beside Rohana and Melora.

"How is it with you, Lady?"

Melora's attempt at a smile only stretched her mouth a little. "As well as I can hope for, *mestra*. But I don't deny I shall be glad to rest a little."

"So shall we all. I wish I could spare you this. But—" She sounded apologetic, and Melora gestured her to silence. She said, "I know perfectly well that you and yours have put your heads in jeopardy for me, and more. God forbid I should complain about whatever you must do for your safety and ours."

Something about the words made Rohana's breath catch in her throat. Melora had sounded, for a moment, almost precisely her old self: gracious, gentle, with the winning courtesy she had shown to her peers and inferiors alike. *She spoke as she would have spoken when we were girls together in Dalereuth. Merciful Evanda, is there really any hope that one day she will be herself again, live out her life happy and free?*

The water hole was a dull, glimmering sheet of water, less than twenty feet across; it looked pallid and unhealthy, but Kindra said the water was good. Behind it a cluster of blackish-red, forbidding rocks, casting purple shadows on the sand, turning the omnipresent fluff of spicebush to a lavender shadow on the barren space. Even the shadow of the rocks made Rohana think more of snakes and scorpions than cool, inviting rest, but it was better than the burning glare of the Dryland sun at midday.

Rohana helped Melora to dismount, steadying her uneven steps. She guided her to a seat in the shadow of the rocks and went to lead her horse to the water, but Kindra stopped her. "Care for your kinswoman, Lady," she said, taking the bridles of their horses, and, lowering her voice, "How does she, really?"

Rohana shook her head. "So far, she is managing. There is really no more I can say." She knew perfectly well that anyone skilled in such matters would say that Melora should not ride at all. But Kindra knew that, too, and there was simply nothing to be done.

She said, "Are there any signs of pursuit?"

"So far, none," said Leeanne, and Jaelle, who had slid down from her horse, came up to them, and stopped, shyly, at a little distance. She said, "How do you know we are not pursued, *mestra?*" She spoke the language of the mountain country with a faint accent, but understandably; and Kindra smiled at the child.

"I hear no sound of hooves with my ear to the ground; and there is no cloud of sand rising where men ride, within the distance my eyes can see."

"Why, you are as good as Jalak's best trackers, then," said the little girl in wonder. "I did not know that women could be trackers."

"Living in Shainsa, little lady, there is much you do not know about women."

Jaelle said eagerly, "Will you tell me, then?"

"Perhaps when I have time; just for now, do you know enough about horses to know that these must be watered and cooled?"

"Oh, I am sorry—am I delaying you? Can I help, then?"

Kindra handed the small girl the reins of the horse Melora had ridden. "Walk him slowly back and forth, then, till his breathing quiets and the sweat is almost dry around his saddle. Then lead him to the water and let him drink what he will. Can you do that, do you think?"

"Oh, yes," said Jaelle, and walked off, holding the horse's reins. Kindra followed with Rohana's horse, and Rohana stood, looking after Jaelle. She seemed tall for her age, lightly built, with delicate bones, her hair flaming red, hanging halfway down her narrow back; she wore the nightgown in which she had been wakened—fine-spun Dry-Towns linex, smoothly loomed and embroidered—although one of the Amazons had put a short jacket, much too big for her, around her shoulders. Her feet were bare, but she walked on the hot sand without apparent discomfort. Rohana could not see that the child resembled Melora, except for her flaming hair; but there was no discernible resemblance to Jalak, either.

She returned to Melora, who had stretched out her clumsy body on her riding cape, and closed her eyes. Rohana looked at her with disquiet, then composed her face hurriedly as Melora opened her eyes. "Where is Jaelle?"

"She is helping Kindra to water the horses," Rohana said. "Believe me, she's quite safe and well, and seems not overwearied by the ride." Rohana lowered herself to the shade beside her cousin. "I wish I had even a little of her energy."

Melora stretched out her thin fingers, clasping Rohana's hand in hers as if hungry for the reassurance of the touch. "I can see how you have wearied yourself for me, too, cousin. . . . How came you into the company of these—these women? *You* have not deserted husband and children as they do . . . ?" The question was evident without words, and Rohana smiled in reassurance. "No, love. My marriage—as I knew it would be—is well enough: Gabriel and I are as happy as any other couple."

"Then how—"

"It is a long story," Rohana said, "and not easy in the telling. It seemed to me that everyone had forgotten you; I had all but forgotten myself, thinking you dead or—or resigned to your life." She added, half defensively, "It had been so long."

"Yes, a lifetime," said Melora with a sigh.

"When you came to me, at first I thought it a dream. I made the journey to Thendara and spoke to some of the Council; but they said they could do nothing, the time was not right for war with the Dry Towns, and they would send no others to die. I had all but resigned myself to thinking that nothing could be done, when by chance—or who knows, by the work of some Goddess—a little band of Free Amazons met with me on the road. They were hunters and traders, and had a mercenary soldier or two to protect them; and in talk with them, I learned that while their band did not venture into the Dry Towns, they knew of one who would. So I went to the Guild-house and spoke with Kindra; and she agreed to attempt the rescue. And so—"

"So here you are," said Melora, almost with wonder, "and here I am. It was true. I had resigned myself, and when I knew I bore Jalak's child again, and that child a son—I was ready to die." Her eyes went to her daughter; Jaelle had finished walking the horse, and was standing beside him as he drank from the water hole. "She is past twelve; at thirteen she would have been chained. I think if you had not come I would have killed her, somehow, and then myself. . . ."

Rohana saw the deep shudder that ran through her cousin's body. She put out her hand quickly to clasp Melora's. "It is past, love. All past. Now you can begin to forget."

Forget? While I bear Jalak's son? Melora did not speak the words aloud, but Rohana heard them anyway. She said very gently, "Well, for now you can rest, and you are free, and safe for the moment. Try to sleep, dearest."

"Sleep." Melora's smile was wry. "I cannot remember when I really slept last. And it seems a pity to sleep now, when I am with you again, and safe . . . and I am happy. . . . Tell me all the news of our kinfolk, Rohana. Does Marius Elhalyn still rule in Thendara? What of our people, our friends—tell me everything," she said yearningly, and Rohana had not the heart to silence her.

"That is a long story and would take many days and hours in the telling. *Dom* Marius died the year after you were taken; Aran Elhalyn keeps the throne warm from year to year, and as usual the Lord of Hastur is the true ruler; not old Istvan, he is senile, but Lorill Hastur, who was his heir. You recall that Lorill and his sister Leonie were with us at the Dalereuth Tower, when we were girls; I thought perhaps Lorill would move against Jalak for your sake—"

Melora sighed. She said, "Even I knew better than that; the Hasturs must think of more important things then the dues of kin, or how are they better than the Dry-Towners with all their feuds and little wars? There is peace otherwise?"

"Peace, yes . . . Lorill has brought the Terrans from Aldaran to Thendara; they are building a spaceport there, and he has defended his move before the Council; some of them fought it all the way, but Lorill prevailed, as the Hasturs usually do."

"The Terrans," said Melora, slowly. "Yes, I had heard; men like us from another world, come on great ships from the stars. Jalak told such tales only to laugh at them; in the Dry Towns they do not know that the stars are suns like ours, lighting worlds not unlike our own, and Jalak loved to scoff at such tales and say these so-called off-worlders must be clever rogues indeed to fool the Seven Domains, but that no sensible man from the Drylands would be caught so. . . ." She shut her eyes, and Rohana thought, for a moment, that she slept; and was grateful. Knowing that she, too, should try to rest, she closed her eyes, but a shadow fell across her face, and she opened them to see Jaelle standing there, looking down at them. She said in a whisper, "It is you who are my—our kinswoman, Lady Rohana?"

Rohana sat up and held out her arms; Jaelle gave her a quick, shy embrace. "How does my mother, kinswoman? Is she asleep?"

"Asleep; and very weary," said Rohana, rising quickly to her feet. She drew the child away so the sound of their voices would not disturb Melora.

"I will not waken her, but I wanted to see—" and her voice trembled. Rohana looked down at the small serious face, the wide green eyes.

Comyn, she thought; *she does not look like Melora, but her* Comyn *blood is unmistakable. It would have been wrong, entirely wrong, to leave her in Jalak's hands; not only inhuman but wrong!*

Jaella said, almost in a whisper, "She should not ride now; the baby will be born so soon. . . ."

"I know that, dear. But we are not safe here, except for a little rest. When we reach Carthon, we will be back in Domain country; and out of Jalak's reach forever," Rohana said quietly.

"But—what will it do to her? The riding, the weariness—" Jaelle began hesitantly, then dropped her eyes and looked away. Rohana thought, *Has she* laran? Even in the telepath caste of the

Comyn, the Gift did not begin to show itself much before adolescence; a trained *leronis* could make educated guesses about a child Jaelle's age, but it had been so long since Rohana had used her telepath training that she could not even guess about Jaelle. *Now, when I need to know, the Gift deserts me. . . . Why must women have to choose between the use of* laran *and all the other things of a woman's life?*

She looked down at Melora, wiped out in exhausted sleep, and thought of the time when they had been young girls together, in the Tower at Dalereuth, learning the use of the matrix jewels that transformed energies; working as psi monitors, in the relay nets that kept communications alive in the vast spaces of Darkover, learning the technology of the Seven Domains.

There had been three of them, all the same age: Rohana, and Melora, and Leonie Hastur, sister to that Lorill Hastur who ruled now behind the throne at Thendara. Rohana's family had insisted that she marry, and she had left her work in the Tower—not without regrets—and gone to marry the heir to the Ardais Domain, to supervise the great estate there, to bear sons and a daughter to that clan. Leonie had been selected Keeper; a telepath of surpassing skill, she was now in charge of the Tower at Arilinn, controlling all the working telepaths on Darkover. But Leonie had paid the Keeper's price; she had been forced to renounce love and marriage, living in seclusion as a virgin all her life. . . .

Melora had been given no choice. Jalak's armed men had seized her and carried her away to imprisonment and chains . . . rape and slavery and long suffering.

Rohana's weariness was giving her strange thoughts. *Did Jalak really change her life so much? Do any of us have choice, really? At our clan's demand, to share a stranger's bed and rule his house and bear his children . . . or to live isolated from life, in loneliness and seclusion, controlling tremendous forces, but with no power to reach out our hand to any other human being, alone, virgin, worshiped but pitied. . . .*

Jaelle's small hand touched hers lightly, and the little girl said, "Kinswoman . . . you are so white. . . ."

Rohana quickly returned to reality. She said matter-of-factly, "I have eaten nothing. And in a little while I must wake your mother and see that she eats something, too." She went with Jaelle to where the Amazons were sharing out food and drink; this time she diluted the wine with water from the well and found it sour but drinkable. Kindra went to look at the sleeping Melora and came back, saying, "She needs rest more than food, Lady; she can eat when she wakes," and looked at Jaelle, saying, "You will be sunburned and saddle-sore if you try to ride in that nightgown, *chiya*. Gwennis, Leeanne, Devra, you are smallest, can you find the little one some clothes?"

Rohana was surprised and warmed to see how immediate the response was; all but the tallest of the women went at once to their saddlebags, searching, sharing out what they had: an undervest here, a tunic there, a pair of trousers (Leeanne's, and even these had to be rolled up almost to the knees). Camilla, whose feet were slender, brought out a paid of suede ankle boots, saying, "They will be too big, but laced tightly, they will protect her while she is riding and keep her feet from the sand and thornbushes." They were embroidered and dyed, evidently her own holiday gear, and Rohana was more surprised than ever; a neuter, she would have thought, could hardly have maternal feelings.

Jaelle let Rohana undress her and clothe her in the strange garments, looking around hesitantly toward her mother but forbearing to disturb her. She did say shakily, as Rohana belted in the bulky long trousers, and began to lace up the pretty, dyed-leather boots, "I have always been told it is not seemly for a woman to wear breeches, and—and, I am *almost* old enough to be called a woman."

"Better breeched than bare, Jaelle," Rohana said, adding more gently, "I know how you feel. Before I came on this journey, I believed nothing could force me to wear breeches and boots, but necessity is stronger than custom; and, as for seemliness—well, you cannot ride in that tattered nightgown with your bare haunches in the wind."

Camilla came and checked the fit of the boots. "If they are

too loose and make blisters, child, tell me and I will find an extra pair of thick stockings. How do women manage to ride in the Dry Towns, little lady?"

"The saddle is made like this"— Jaelle demonstrated—"so that a woman can sit sidewise and her skirts are not disordered."

"And will slip and fall if her horse stumbles," said Gwennis, "while I can ride as fast and far as any man, and I have never had a fall. But in the Domains, little one, you can wear those clumsy riding-skirts your kinswoman prefers to wear."

"Clumsy they may look," Rohana retorted, "yet I ride well enough in them that I can hunt with hawks in the mountains; in a bad season, when the men cannot spare time for the hunt, the little children or sick people have never had to go without birds or small game for their table, riding-skirts or no; I ride as well in them as in these." *And I wish I were wearing them now,* she thought, but knew the Amazons would have had small sympathy for that.

Gwennis ran her hand along Jaelle's long tangled hair. "It is a pity it should snarl so."

Jaelle's eyes filled with tears; she looked up at Rohana's cropped head and said, "Do you have to cut it?"

Rohana said firmly, "No indeed. But let me comb and braid it tight, so it will not tangle while you ride." She made Jaelle sit down and began to comb the waist-length, fire-red hair. She felt again a pang at the thought of her own hair, which had been her pride, her one claim to beauty. *Gabriel will be angry when he sees my hair, hacked short like an Amazon's.* She thought defensively, as if answering her husband, *I had no choice, it was for Melora's sake.* But Jaelle's should not be sacrificed.

Kindra came and looked at Jaelle, dressed in the too-large odds and ends of Amazon garb, but she made no comment. She drew Rohana aside for a moment and said, "Do not tell the child, and do not disturb your kinswoman, but there is a small cloud of dust at the horizon. It probably has nothing to do with us—it is not in the direction of Shainsa, from which pursuit would come; but I must warn my women, and you, Lady, should be wary."

"Should we be ready to ride again?"

Kindra shook her head. "No. In the heat of the day we dare not; we would die of heat prostration as painfully as on a Dry-Towner's sword. We will hide ourselves among the rocks and hope that this dust has nothing to do with us, or with Jalak and his men; sleep if you can, Lady, but stay near to Melora and the little one, and caution her, if she wakes, to stay hidden in the shadow of the rocks." She signaled to Devra and Rima, saying, "I shall set you two on watch; Leeanne and I have been leading and tracking all the night, and Nira has lost enough blood that she needs rest. But call me at once if that dust seems to turn in our direction. Lady, go now and try to sleep. And you too, *domnina*," she added to Jaelle.

"May I bring my bread and finish it before I sleep?" Jaelle asked, and Kindra said, "Of course," as she went away to rest. Gwennis, reaching into her pocket, smiled at Jaelle and said, "Are you hungry, *chiya?* Here is a sweet for you; suck it before you sleep, and it will keep your mouth from getting too dry in this heat."

Jaelle accepted the candy with a small, shy inclination of her head. She looked around at the Amazons with curiosity—though Rohana could see that she was trying hard to repress it and, in politeness, ask nothing. At last she said to Gwennis, "Some of you look—almost like men. Why is that?"

Gwennis glanced at Rohana; then said, "Yes; Leeanne and Camilla. They have been neutered; their bodies are not actually those of women. There are some women who feel that woman-hood itself is too great a burden to be borne, and choose this way, even though the laws forbid it."

"But you are not like that," Jaelle said, and Gwennis smiled.

"No, *chiya*. It is troublesome to be a woman, from time to time—I imagine you are old enough to know so much—but all in all, I think I would rather be a woman than not, even if it were easy or simple to find anyone, in these days, who will risk the laws against that sort of mutilation. All in all I find it more plea-sure than trouble."

Rohana, too, had been curious about this; like all women reared in the protective, pampered world of the Domains, she had always thought—when she had thought about the Amazons at all, which was seldom—that they were mannish women, or plain girls such as would burden their families to find any sort of husband. But, except for the two neutered women, and the mountain tomboy with the two knives, none of them were anything like that. Kindra was gentle and almost motherly, as was Fat Rima; and the others seemed none too different, clothing and cropped hair apart, from her own waiting-women. As for Gwennis, she seemed almost like a little girl herself, not much older than Jaelle, or Rohana's own daughter.

Jaelle smiled at Gwennis and said, "You would be beautiful if you let your hair grow long."

It was Rohana's own thought. Gwennis said with a kindly smile. "Why, perhaps so, little sister, but why should I want to be beautiful? I am not a dancer, or an actress, or a lyric performer, that I should need so much beauty!"

"But if you were beautiful, you could make a good marriage," Jaelle said, "and you would not need to be a soldier or a hunter to earn a living."

"But, little one," said Gwennis, laughing, "I do not want to make a marriage, not even a good one."

"Oh?" Jaelle pondered this for a moment; it was easy to see that this was a new idea to her. "Why not?"

"For many reasons. Among others," she said deliberately, "lest I should find that my husband sought to keep me in chains."

Rohana felt it like a blow; Jaelle put her hand to her mouth and bit at the knuckle. Her face went white, then a desperate, agonized crimson. She made a small strangled sound, turned away and ran to her mother's side, flinging herself down on the blanket beside her and burying her head in her arms.

Gwennis looked almost as dismayed as the child. She said, "My Lady, I am sorry, I should not have said that."

Silently, Rohana shook her head. She said at last, "She had to know."

Suddenly Jaelle has realized what this is all about. Before this it has been an adventure, safe because her mother is here; but she has not truly understood. And now—now she knows.

And a shock like this, to a girl just on the threshold of wom- *anhood . . . a girl with extraordinary telepath potential . . .* Rohana was not sure just how she knew this, but she was sure of it. *What will it do to her?* Slowly, Rohana went and laid herself down in the shade beside Melora and Jaelle. Melora slept heavily. Jaelle's face was buried in the blanket, her thin shoulders trembling violently. Rohana reached out to draw her close, comfort her, as she would have done with one of her own children; but Jaelle resisted her stiffly, and after a moment Rohana let her be. *I am almost a stranger to her,* she thought in despair. *I can do nothing for her. Not yet.*

Chapter 4

The days and nights had passed, and Rohana had given up expecting pursuit or capture. If there had been pursuit at all, it had taken the wrong direction or been left hopelessly behind. Or else Melora was right, and Jalak's heirs, finding him dead or wholly disabled, were busily dividing up his remaining wives and his property.

Gradually the character of the land had changed: the first days had seen dry, burning, gritty sand, broken only by scruffy thornbushes and feathery spicebush; now there were endless, trackless leagues of low, rolling dunes, covered by grayish Dryland bracken, with now and again a sharp black outcrop of rock. *As if,* Rohana thought, recalling the old tale, *when Zandru made the Drylands, even the very rocks rebelled and broke through their cover, thrusting up in rebellion . . . the very bones of the world refusing to be covered in these barren leagues of desert and sand. . . .*

It was nearing twilight; the fierceness of the sun was tempered by the lengthening angle of the shadow. All that day they had seen no living thing, and Kindra had cautioned them to drink sparingly from their waterskins. "Should anything delay us," she had warned, with a sharp glance at Melora, "we might not reach the next water hole this night . . . and we cannot carry too much in reserve."

Melora rode just ahead of her, head down, braced stiffly in her saddle. She had not spoken since they left the site of their noonday rest, and when Rohana would have felt her forehead for fever, she had turned away, refusing the touch, refusing even to meet Rohana's searching eyes. Rohana was desperately worried about her. This trip was far too long, far too arduous for any pregnant woman. Melora had not complained; Rohana had the chilling sense that she had ceased to care. She seemed to have expended all the effort of which she was capable in making the original contact with Rohana that had resulted in her rescue; that accomplished, it seemed to Rohana that Melora no longer cared. She had not even asked any further questions about her home, about their kin, about what lay ahead when they should leave the Dryland country and return to the Domains.

The sun descended, a great blood-colored orb, blurred at the horizon with the first clouds Rohana had seen since they crossed the river at Carthon. Kindra, riding ahead, stopped to let Rohana come up with her, and pointed to the purpled sunset. She said, "Those clouds hang over Carthon; and beyond Carthon we are in the Domains again. Even if Jalak came so far, he would have to come with an army. Safety lies there. How does the Lady Melora?"

"Not well, I fear," Rohana said soberly, and Kindra nodded.

"For her sake I shall be glad when we cross the river and we can travel at a pace more fitting her condition. It goes against me, to force the pace this way, but there is no safety for any of us in this country."

"I know," Rohana said, "and I am sure Melora understands. She knows, better than any of us, the dangers for women of the Domains, here in the Dry Towns."

Kindra said, "Well, we will make camp yonder"—she pointed to one of the great black tumuli of rock, upthrust like jagged teeth against the low horizon—"and there, if the Goddess is good to us, we will cook some hot food, and perhaps even wash the dust from our faces."

"Do you know every water hole in this territory, Kindra?"

The woman shook her head. "I have never traveled here before, but I can see the *kyorebni* circling as they do only over water. And tomorrow before midday perhaps we will ford the river, and be safe in Carthon." She grimaced. "I am hungry for hot roast meat and good hot soup instead of this unending porridge and dried meat and fruit, and some fresh-baked bread instead of hardtack."

"Me too," Rohana said, "and I shall stand surety for the best meal we can buy in the best cookshop in Carthon, believe me, once we cross the river!"

Kindra looked back and said slowly, "Pray to your Goddess, Lady, that *domna* Melora is able to enjoy that meal. Ride back to her, Lady Rohana, and reassure her that we will make camp just a little farther on. She seems almost ready to fall from her saddle." Her face, in the gathering darkness, was deeply troubled.

Rohana did as she was bidden, sighing. It seemed that never in her life had she known such prolonged and incessant fatigue. The thought of sleeping in a bed under a roof, eating hot, fresh-cooked food, bathing in a hot tub of scented water, comforts she had taken so much for granted that she never even thought about them, made her whole body ache with an almost sensuous longing.

She supposed the Amazons would think such longings soft and weak. Well, she would show then that she could endure hard living if she must; she was *Comynara* and she would be strong as any man of her caste. But she wished there were a few comforts for Melora.

Melora was riding next to Fat Rima; as Rohana neared them the big Amazon lowered her voice and said, "Look to your kinswoman, Lady. No, she has not complained, but I earned my bread for a time as a midwife in the Lake Country, and she has a look to her that I do not like."

It's good to know there is a midwife among us, at least. Rohana drew her horse even with Melora's; Melora raised her head, slowly and wearily, and her look shocked Rohana. Her face was swollen, with a dull pallor; even her tight lips were colorless. She tried to smile at Rohana, but could not quite manage it. Her face contracted in a sudden spasm of pain, and Rohana knew at once what her kinswoman had been trying to conceal.

"*Breda,* you are in labor!"

Melora grimaced. "For some hours, I fear," she said apologetically. "I had hoped we could reach a campsite near to water. I am very thirsty, Rohana," she added, in the first hint of complaint Rohana had heard from her lips.

She leaned over and took Melora's hands in her own. She said, "We are very near to water, love; can you ride just a little way farther, just a few hundred steps more? See?" She pointed through the falling dusk. "One or two of them are already dismounting; see there? Listen; I can hear Jaelle laughing."

Melora said softly, "She is like a little animal let out of a cage. I am so glad that they are so good to her. Poor little rabbit, I have had so little strength to spare for her, on this journey. . . ."

"I am sure she understands," Rohana said softly.

"I hope she does not," Melora said, and in the twilight her face twisted. They were near to the place where the others were dismounting; again Rohana heard Jaelle's light merry laugh. In the days of the journey she had quickly become a favorite with all the Amazons; laughing, chattering, full of endless questions about the world and the life before her. They had competed with one another for the privilege of carrying her on their saddles when she grew weary, saved her such tidbits and choice morsels as they could scrounge from their sparse meals, told her stories and sang songs to while away the tedium of the trip, even fashioned her small toys and playthings from odds and ends.

If nothing else, we have freed Jaelle, and she is a daughter of whom any of the Domains could be proud. Jalak's blood may be a handicap when the time comes for her to make a good marriage, but that can be overcome. She has laran, *I am sure; I will have her tested when we come to Thendara. . . .*

She slid from her horse, relinquished it to Rima, who came to lead it away, and tenderly helped Melora from her saddle. Melora's knees buckled and Rohana had to support her cousin's weight in her arms; she held her upright, but suddenly frightened, called to Kindra. After a moment the Amazon leader came from the shadows, took in the situation with one appraising glance. "So your time has come, *domna?* Well, only two things in this world are sure, birth and next winter's snow, and both come when they will and not when it is convenient. Thanks to the Goddess, we are near to water. A pity we had to abandon the tent; no child should be born with only the sky for a roof."

"Better under the free sky than in Jalak's Great House," Melora said fiercely, and Kindra held her hand for a moment. "Can you walk just a little, Lady? We will prepare a place for you to rest."

"I can do what I must," Melora said, but she leaned very heavily on her kinswoman, and Rohana felt an all-encompassing dread. Here, in the black night, in the desert, with no skilled hands to help . . . *Rima had been a midwife, perhaps; but the Free Amazons renounced womanhood. . . .*

"I had hoped that I could hold out till we reached Carthon," Melora said, and Rohana realized that her kinswoman was sharing her sense of unease and dread. Rohana must somehow manage to be strong and confident.

She said, "Look. They are making a fire, we will have light, and some hot food, and there is water near," as she guided Melora's steps toward the kindled blaze. "And we are in luck; one of these women was once a midwife!"

She was dismayed, now that she could see Melora by firelight: hands and ankles swollen, eyes red and feverish. *She should have told us hours ago; we should have stopped . . . but then the child would have been born without water near. . . .*

Melora sank down gratefully on the pile of blankets that the Amazons had arranged for her. For a moment she buried her face in her hands; Rohana could hear her breathing, loud and hoarse like an animal. Then she raised her head and said plaintively, "I am thirsty, Rohana—will you bring me a drink?"

"Of course." Rohana began to rise, but Melora clutched at her hands. "No, no stay with me. Did I tell you why I suddenly knew I must escape, get Jaelle away, or kill her myself before this child was born?"

"No, dear, you didn't tell me—"

"When I found her—playing with Jalak's other little daughters—they had all of them, even Jaelle, tied ribbons about their hands, playing at being grown up, and in chains—"

Rohana felt herself shudder, deep down in the bones. She said quickly, "Dear, let me go. I will fetch you a drink; do you think you could eat a little?" She left Melora lying on the pile of blankets and went to the darkness near the water hole, kneeling to rinse the cup, trembling, glad to hide her face in the darkness.

After a little she managed to control herself and come back. Kindra said from the fire, "Tell her we will have some hot food soon, and something to drink; it may strengthen her for what lies ahead. And I think we can manage torchlight later, if we need it."

Rohana somehow managed to thank her. She came back and knelt beside Melora, who was lying with her eyes closed; Rohana held the cup to her lips, and Melora gulped it thirstily. Rohana said, "We shall have some hot food for you soon; try to rest." She went on talking, saying anything that crossed her mind, trying to sound encouraging; after a few minutes, Melora put out a hand to stop the flow of chatter.

"*Breda*—" She used the *casta* word for "sister"; in the intimate inflection it also meant "darling." "Don't lie to me. In memory of what we both were, once, don't try to pretend, as if I were still an outsider; what is going to happen?"

Rohana looked at the sick woman, heart-wrung. *So after all she is still* Comyn, *still telepath; she can read me so easily.* "What can I say to you, Melora? You know as well as I that no woman so far in pregnancy should travel so far or so fast. But other women have survived worse than this, and lived to frighten their granddaughters with the tales of what they endured. And I'll be with you."

Melora clasped her hand. "Better you than the evil crone who brought Jaelle into the world," she said, clinging to her cousin's fingers. "She would not even free my hands. . . ." She ran her fingertips, as with a long-habitual gesture, along the jagged scars at her wrists. "Jalak swore if I bore a son he would give me whatever I asked, save my freedom; I had it in my mind to ask for her head."

Rohana shuddered, was grateful when Fat Rima approached

them; she said, "Here is our midwife; she will do what she can for you, *breda*."

Melora looked up at her; she felt—Rohana sensed it—skeptical and more than a little frightened. But she said (again, poignantly, Rohana was reminded of the lighthearted and gracious girl Melora had once been), "I thank you, *mestra;* I did not know any of the Free Amazons would choose such a womanly trade."

"Why, Lady, we earn our bread at any honest work," Rima said. "Did you truly think we are all soldiers and hunters? The Guild-house in the city of Arilinn, where I was trained, has a speciality of training midwives; and we compare everything that is known about the problems of birth from Temora to the Hellers, so we are the best of midwives; even on the great estates, sometimes, women will send for us. Now, my Lady, let me see how far this thing has gone, and how long you must expect to wait here." She knelt, feeling all about Melora's body with gentle, expert hands. "Well, it is a strong child, and a big one, too."

She broke off as Jaelle came running toward them. The child's face was drawn and white in the firelight. "Mother—oh, Mother—" she said and burst into tears.

Rima said firmly, "Come, my child, that will not help Mother. You are almost a woman now yourself; you must not behave like a baby and trouble us."

Melora dragged herself upright, letting herself lean heavily on Rohana. "Come here, Jaelle. No, let her come to me, I know she will be good."

Struggling to fight back her sobs, Jaelle came and knelt beside her mother; Melora seized her in a fierce embrace and said, not to any of them, "It was worth it all. You are free, you are free!" She kissed the small wet face hungrily, again and again; then laid her hand under Jaelle's small quivering chin and looked at her a long time in the wavering firelight before saying, "You must go now, my darling, and stay with the other women. You cannot help me now, and you must leave me to those who can. Go, my dearest love, and try to sleep a little."

Crying, Jaelle let Gwennis lead her away into the darkness beyond the campfire. Rohana heard the child sobbing softly for a long time; then she was quiet and Rohana hoped she had cried herself to sleep. The night wore on slowly. Rohana stayed with Melora, holding her hands, now and then sponging her sweaty face with cold water. Melora was still and patient, doing what she was told, trying to rest between the spasms; now and then she talked a little, and after a time Rohana, with a shudder, knew Melora had lost track of where she was and what was happening. She talked to her own mother, years dead; once she started up with a shriek, crying out curses in the Dry-Town language; again and again she sobbed and entreated them not to chain her again, or cried out, over and over, "My hands! My hands!" and her fingers went again and again to the long ragged scars at her wrists. Rohana listened, murmured to her soothingly, tried now and again to break through the delirious muttering. . . . *If Melora knew she was here and free, here with me. . . .* She tried, with all her telepathic skill, to reach her cousin's mind, but all she could feel was horror and long dread.

Blessed Cassilda, mother of the Domains . . . Evanda, Goddess of light, Goddess of birth . . . merciful Avarra . . . what she must have endured, what horror she must have known. . . .

None of the other women slept, although Kindra had ordered them all to bed; Rohana could sense, like a tangible vibration in the air, their awareness, their concern. *At times like this it is a curse, to read the thoughts of others. . . .*

Once, when Melora slept for a moment, in exhaustion, Rima met Rohana's eyes over the struggling body and shook her head briefly. Rohana closed her own eyes for a moment. *Not yet! Don't give up hope yet!*

Rima said, pityingly, "She has no strength left, I think, to be free of the child. We can only wait."

Rohana suddenly knew if she stayed there another moment she would break into hysterical screams and sobs, herself. She said thickly, "I will be back in a moment," and rose, plunging away, around the campfire, toward the crude latrine the Amazons dug at their camps. She leaned against the harsh rock-face, covering her face, struggling not to vomit or scream. After a moment, controlling herself a little, she went to the fire, where a pot had been left with the hot drink of fermented grain, which the Amazons used in place of bark-tea or *jaco,* just simmering. She dipped herself out a cup and sipped it, fighting for self-control. Kindra, tall and almost invisible in the darkness, stopped and laid a hand on her shoulder.

"Bad, my Lady?"

"Very bad." Rohana felt for a moment that the hot bitter brew would choke her. "She is not—not a woman who could ever have borne children easily; and here, without skilled help, after so much suffering—after this hard journey—without care or comfort . . ."

Kindra's sigh seemed to come from the very depths of her being. "I am sorry, truly sorry. It is cruel that she should suffer so much for freedom, and never live to enjoy it, after so much courage. It must add greatly to her suffering, to know that even if her child is born alive, there will be none to suckle him or care for him."

A resentment she had not known she felt, against these women who had chosen to spare themselves the pains of womanhood, surged up in Rohana, out of control. She had forcibly to restrain herself from flinging the scalding contents of her cup at the older woman. She said bitterly, "You! What would *you* know of that fear for a child?"

"Why, as much as you, Lady," said Kendra. "I bore four children before I had turned twenty. I was given in marriage very young, and my first child died before I could bring him forth; the midwives said I should not try to bear another, but my husband was eager for an heir. My second and third children were daughters both and he cursed me. I came very near to death with my fourth child—he was three days in the bearing—and this time, instead of curses, when he saw our son, he showered me with gifts and jewels. And then I knew a woman's lot in our world was wholly accursed; I was of no value; the daughters I bore him at risk of my life were of no value; I was nothing but an instrument to give him sons. And so when I could walk again, I left my children sleeping, one night, and cut my hair, and made my way alone to the Guild of Free Amazons, and there my life began."

Rohana stared at her in horror. She could think of nothing to say. Finally she stammered, "But—but all men are not like that, Kindra."

"No?" Kindra said. "I rejoice you have not found them so, Lady, but that is luck and good fortune, and no more." She glanced at the reddening sky, and said, "Hush," listening to the sounds that had changed, in the last few minutes, from long, patient sighs to harsh, gasping breaths and hoarse short grunts of effort. She said quickly, "Go to her, Lady. It cannot be long now."

There was enough light in the sky now so that Rohana, coming to kneel beside Melora, could see her kinswoman's face, strained and swollen as she fought, panting, for breath.

"Rohana—Rohana—promise me—"

Rima said, imperatively, "Don't talk, dear; pay attention now. Take a good deep breath, and hold it. Come now, dear, that's right, another nice long breath. Now, bear down—come on, hold on tight, just push—"

Rohana let Melora take her hands, cling to them with agonized strength as the inexorable process of birth seized her body, wrenching her into spasms. Rima said, in the singsong that Rohana supposed was common to all midwives, "Come on, now, sweet, that's a good girl, another nice big push, hard now. That's right, *that's* a good girl, come on now, just a little bit more—"

Rohana felt Melora's nails dig into her hand; the contact wrung her with agony. Wide open to her cousin, she felt the tearing pain wrenching at her own body, gasped with the weight of it. *Too much, too much . . . worse than when Kyril was born. . . .* She felt the smothered scream Melora was fighting back, thought in dismay, *Gabriel stayed with me; now I know how he felt . . . I know now he felt all I was enduring. I never knew . . . too much, too much. . . .*

She felt the pain ebb away, felt Melora relax for a moment. Rima said authoritatively, "Come on, now, breathe deep, get ready for the next one; a few more good ones like that and it'll be all over." But Melora ignored her, clutching at Rohana's hands. She gasped, "Rohana, promise—promise—if I die— care for my children. My baby, take my baby—"

She gasped, and arched her body again under the fierce, wrenching pain. Rohana could not speak; she reached for contact with Melora again, directly to her mind.

—I swear it, darling, by the Blessed Cassilda and by the Lord of Light. . . . They shall be as my own children, may the Gods seize me if I make any difference between them and the children born of my own body. . . .

Melora whispered, "Thank you—I knew—" She collapsed again. "Over her head, dark with sweat, Rima looked up, and Rohana met Kindra's eyes. Kindra said quietly, "I had better fetch Jaelle now."

Rohana looked up indignantly; looked at the swollen, unconscious body, the spreading bloodstains, feeling the wrenching agony seize Melora again, and herself flinched before the terrifying assault on body and mind. She said in violent indignation, "How can you? Is this any place for a little girl . . . ?"

Kindra said gently, but inexorably, "It is her right, Lady. Would you wish to sleep through your mother's death-bed? Or are you still lying to yourself, Lady Rohana?" She did not wait for Rohana's answer. Rohana, kneeling, letting Melora grip her hands with that anguished death-grip, heedless of Melora's nails digging into her and drawing blood, was seized again by that moment of terror she had known at the climax of her own child-beds. . . . *Breaking, tearing, splitting, coming apart . . . dying. . . .* Rohana struggled to keep herself a little apart from Melora's terror, to give her kinswoman some strength, something to cling to outside her own agony and fear. She held Melora, murmuring endearments, whispering, "We're with you, love, we're right here, we're going to take good care of you . . ." but she did not know what she was saying.

For the first time and last time Melora shrieked aloud, a long, terrible cry of anguish and dread; and then, just as the sun was rising, into the terrible silence there was another sound: a strange sharp, shrill sound, the uplifted howling of a newborn child.

"Praise to Evanda," said Rima, holding up the naked, bloody child, feet first. "Listen to how strong he is! I didn't have to slap *this* one into life—"

Melora whispered, almost inaudibly, "Give him to me," and reached out for him, her face changing. *The never-failing miracle,* Rohana thought. Always, no matter how hard and terrible the birth, there was this moment of joy, when the face changed, alight and glowing. *Melora looks so happy, so happy; how can she?* Rohana wondered, not remembering her own happiness. Rima wrapped the baby in a fold of clean towel she had laid ready, and placed him on Melora's flaccid belly. She said matter-of-factly. "He will do well enough."

"Jalak's son," Melora whispered, and the joyous smile slipped away, "What will become of him, poor little wretch?"

Rima said sharply, "My Lady—"

Melora reached out her hands. She said, "Jaelle—Jaelle, come here and kiss me—oh, Jaelle—"

Rima reached out in consternation; blood came forth in a great gush, and Melora sighed and fell back, her face white and lifeless. And there was no sound in the sunrise except the crying of Melora's motherless children.

"Will you truly have Jalak's son to foster, Lady Rohana?" Kindra asked.

The sun was high in the camp. Jaelle had cried herself to exhaustion and was lying on the sand between them, limp, like some bedraggled little animal. Rohana was half sitting, half lying against a pile of saddlebags. She had wrapped the naked child and thrust him inside her tunic against her breasts, where he squirmed and nuzzled, already lively and seeking the nourishment he did not know would be denied him. Rohana patted the warm bundle tenderly. She said, "What else can I do, Kindra? I swore to Melora that her children should be to me as my own in all things."

Kindra said fiercely, "He is a male of Jalak's blood; do not your kinsmen and your foster-brother's blood cry out for revenge, that you should cherish him? Is there not blood-feud and a life between you and Jalak's son, my Lady?" She bared her knife, handed it to Rohana, hilt first. She said, "He cost Melora her life, so she came never to her hard-won freedom; and he is Jalak's son. Avenge your kinsmen, Lady."

Chilled, sick with horror, Rohana knew that Kindra spoke no more than simple truth. The men of the Ardais and Aillard Domains would have echoed her words: Jalak's son must pay for Jalak's crimes.

She felt the child move against her body, warm and strong. *Melora's child; and I took him up from her dead body.* She looked at Jaelle, who was curled tight beside them, her eyes shut in rejection. *She is Jalak's child, too. Must she pay?*

Kindra said earnestly, "Rohana, he will die, whatever you do now. There is no nurse for him, no food, no proper care. Don't wring your heart for him; let him lie here beside his mother."

Slowly, Rohana shook her head. She handed back the knife, meeting the Amazon's eyes. She said, "Blood-feud and revenge are for men, Kindra. I am glad to be a woman, and bound by no such cruel law. Let this child's life, not his death, pay for my foster-brother's death; Ardais lost a son in Valentine, so this boy shall be called Valentine." She laid her hands, as if in ritual, on the small squirming body, "And he shall be foster-son to Ardais, in place of the one who died at Jalak's hands."

Kindra put the knife away, raised her face with a grim smile. She said, "Well, spoken, my Lady. An Amazon would say so, indeed; but I had not thought you were so free to discard the laws of your clan and caste."

Rohana said violently, "I hope I will always feel free to ignore any law so cruel! It may be that he will die, as you say; but not at my hands, and not if I can save him!"

Kindra nodded. "So be it," she said. "I will speak to Rima; she has fostered motherless babes before this. Our women sometimes die in bearing, too, and Rima is skilled in all the secrets of the Arilinn Guild-house." She rose, saying, "There is another child of Melora's who needs your care; look to her, Lady.

She went off to join the other Amazons, who were burying

Melora in the hill behind the water hole. Rohana turned to Jaelle and began to stroke her hair gently.

"Jaelle," she coaxed, "don't cry any more, darling. I know nothing can heal your grief, but you must not make yourself ill with crying. I swore that I would be a mother to you, always. Come, darling, look at me," she pleaded. "Don't you want to see your little brother? He needs someone to love and comfort him, too." She added, "*You* had your mother for twelve years, Jaelle; this poor little mite lost his mother before she had ever looked into his face. He has none but his sister; will you not come and help me to comfort him?"

Jaelle pulled away with a shudder of violent revulsion, her sobs rising again to a frenzy, and Rohana, in despair, let her go. Jaelle had not spoken since Melora's death; Rohana feared that in those last moments of Melora's life, spent in terror and dread, in the fear of death, the child's mind had been roughly opened to the terrifying telepathic rapport, her latent Gift wakened in that dreadful instant of shock and agony.

No one could have blamed Melora for reaching out, with her last conscious thought, in the only way for which she still had strength—for one last, desperate attempt to touch her beloved child. But what had it done to Jaelle?

As if he sensed Rohana's desperate unease, the baby began to stir and fret and whimper inside her tunic again. She stroked him, thinking of the long leagues that still lay between them and Carthon, where she might at least find a wet-nurse for the child. For him it was a simple matter of survival; handled, fed, carefully cared for, he would survive. But what of Jaelle? She would not die, but what had that shock done to her? Only time would tell.

Perhaps the Amazons can do more for her than I. I am, in her mind, still part of that moment of terror and death. But perhaps they can comfort Jaelle and help her.

She must leave it to them, at least until Jaelle was calm and recovered her senses. After that—Rohana looked longingly at Jaelle's soft tangled hair, but dared not touch her—after that, only time would tell.

Chapter 5

Twelve days later, Rohana looked down from the top of the pass that led away into the valley of Thendara.

"Jaelle," she called, turning back, "come here and see the city of your forefathers!"

Obediently the young girl rode forward, looking at the ancient city that lay in the valley below them. "This is the city of the *Comyn*? I have never seen so big a city; Shainsa is not half so large." She looked down with fascination and, it seemed, with dread, at the wide flung buildings, the *Comyn* Castle beyond. "Tell me, kinswoman, is it true that the *Comyn* are descended from the Gods? My—I have heard it said, and I have heard—I have heard it denied. What is the truth?"

How deftly she avoids either her father's name or her mother's! In twelve days she has spoken of neither of them. Rohana said, "I can tell you only what I have heard myself. The story goes that Hastur, son of Aldones, Lord of Light, came to our world at Hali; and that he wooed and won Cassilda, daughter of Robardin, mother of the Domains; and thus all those of the blood of Hastur are kin to the Gods. If it be true, or only a beautiful fable, I know no more than you; but this much is true beyond question. All those of the blood of the Hasturs, all the kin of the Seven Domains, have the *laran* powers, the psi gifts that set them apart from all other men born on this world."

"Are all of the *Comyn* of Hastur blood, then?"

"In the beginning, yes; although in the great days of the Towers they were separated into the seven families we now call the

Domains. All are of the blood of Hastur and Cassilda. But it is sure that none of us are Gods or anything like it, my child."

Would that we were. I should know better what to do with you, little one. Rohana sighed, touching the warm sleeping weight where Melora's baby slept, tucked inside her tunic for warmth; it was cold at these heights, even in summer. Jaelle was no longer openly hostile to Rohana, but she had not turned to her for comfort, either. Nor had she been willing to touch her little brother, or so much as look at him.

Every one of the Amazons—even the two neutered women, Leeanne and Camilla—had shared the burden of the newborn child in those first dreadful days, before they reached Carthon and found a wet-nurse for him. They had all spared sugar and meal to make gruel for him, and, knowing that Rohana was exhausted and burdened with grief, had taken turns to carry him and try to soothe his fitful crying. Only Jaelle had steadfastly ignored her brother; had refused, even when urged repeatedly by Kindra, whom she adored, to hold him in her arms or even look at him.

As if her thoughts had reached him, the baby Valentine began to stir and fret, and Rohana beckoned to the wet-nurse from Carthon; she rode forward, took the child from Rohana, and opening her dress, lazily put the child to her breast. She was, Rohana thought, a singularly stupid woman—*I would not let her rear a pet dog, let alone a child*—but he throve on her milk, and for now that was all that mattered.

Should any woman alive be allowed to live so ignorant that she is no better than a dairy-animal? The Free Amazons openly despised her, and with the pride seen in the invincibly stupid, the wet-nurse treated them with contempt. Rohana—sharing their contempt for the woman, but needing her services—tried to mediate an uneasy peace.

Rohana stretched her back (the sling in which she carried the baby during the day gave her cramps in the shoulders) and tried to think ahead. She had pledged Melora that she would rear the children as her own. Her husband would not object; he had said often that he would welcome more children, regretted that

Rohana had borne only three. But now reaction had set in, after Rohana's first elation at saving Melora's son alive. *What have I taken upon myself? My eldest is already almost grown; my daughter is already five, and since two of our children are sons, Gabriel agreed I need have no more. And now when I thought I was done with it, again I have all the worry and trouble of rearing a very little one! No doubt Gabriel will begin to talk, again, of having another so he will not be brought up alone.*

Am I only an instrument to give him sons? she thought, and was horrified at herself. Quickly she turned her thoughts elsewhere: *What place can we make in the Domains for the son of a Dry-Towner? And Jaelle, so cold and withdrawn, will she ever accept me?*

It was too much to expect, that she could find comfort in the child. I am a mother myself, that was the greatest comfort to me, that something remained of Melora . . . but Jaelle is a child. She sees only that poor little Val robbed her of their mother. . . .

Kindra drew her horse close to Rohana's. She said, "Lady, is that where the Terrans are building their spaceport? What do they want here, these men from another world?"

"I do not know." Rohana gazed at the great dirt-colored slash beyond the city of Thendara, where, it seemed, several miles of the valley had been ripped open by their enormous machines and smoothed to an eerie, unnatural flatness. Part of the area had been paved, and buildings were sprouting in strange, unlikely shapes. "I have heard that our world is at a crossroad of their travel roads among the stars; they seem to have trade caravans between the many worlds as we have between the towns in the Lake Country. I don't know what their trade may be, no one has bothered to tell me, though I think Gabriel knows." She fancied a look of contempt from Kindra. *Why should I be content with ignorance? Oh, damn these Amazons, they are making me question everything: myself, Gabriel, my very life!*

It made her voice edgy. "These people, they call themselves the Terran Empire, came first to Caer Donn, near Aldaran, and began a spaceport—a small one, they could not build so wide in the mountains there—and dealt with the accursed Aldarans.

Hastur offered them a place here to build their spaceport where the climate would be more to their liking—I have heard that to them our world seems cold—and so we can keep watch over their doings; but of course we have nothing to do with them."

"Why not?" asked Kindra. "I should think that a race which can travel from star to star as readily as I can ride from here to Nevarsin would have a great deal to teach us."

Rohana said stiffly, "I do not know; Hastur has willed it so."

"How fortunate are the men of the Domains, that they have the son of Hastur to teach them," said Kindra, her gray eyebrows lifting. "A stupid woman like myself would have felt that a race which can make trade caravans among the stars might outreach even a Hastur in wisdom."

Rohana was annoyed by the sarcasm, but she felt too deeply indebted to Kindra to take her to task for it. "I have heard it explained thus: Hastur feels there is much in their way of life that might be more of a threat than we can know at once. They have, for a beginning, leased the spaceport here for five hundred years, so that we will have plenty of time to choose what we can learn from them."

"I see," said Kindra, and was silent, thinking it over, studying the enormous slash on the horizon, where strange machines crawled and unknown shapes grew against the horizon.

Rohana, too, was silent. As they rode this last mile, it seemed that she was, in a curious way, changing worlds. For near to forty days she had lived in a world as alien to her as the world of the Terrans below; then she had grown used to it, and now she must again change worlds, make ready to reenter her own.

At first the world in which the Amazons lived had seemed hard and comfortless, strange and lonely. Then she had realized that most of the strangeness was not the physical lack of comfort at all. It was quite different. It was easy to get used to long hours of riding, to unfamiliar and ugly clothes, to bathing as one could in stream or river, to sleeping in tents or under the sky.

But it was not nearly so easy to give up the familiar support of known protections, known ways of thinking. Until she came on this journey, she had never quite realized how much all her decisions, even small personal ones, had been left to her father and brothers, or, since she married, to her husband. Even such small things as *Shall I wear a blue gown or a green? Shall I order fish or fowl for the table tonight?* had been dictated less by her own tastes and preferences than Gabriel's wishes. She had not realized, until Jaelle and the newborn Val were hers for fostering, how much even what she had said to the children or done for them had been based, openly or not, on how well Gabriel would think of her for her dealings with them.

A strange, painful, almost traitorous thought kept returning: *Now that I know how to make my own decisions, will I ever be content again to let Gabriel decide for me?"*

Or, if I do go back, is it only because it is so much easier to do exactly what is expected of a woman of my caste?

They had ridden through the great city gates of Thendara now, and people came out to stare at the sight of a *Comyn* lady in the company of an Amazon band. Inside the city Kindra dismissed most of the Free Amazons to the Guild-house in Thendara. Accompanied only by Kindra, Jaelle, and the wet-nurse with the baby, Rohana rode on to the *Comyn* Castle.

In the suite that had belonged to the Ardais clan for uncountable years, Rohana summoned the skeleton staff of servants who remained there all year round—most of the Ardais retainers returned home to Castle Ardais, with their masters, when Council season was over—and ordered that comfortable quarters be found for the wet-nurse and the baby; that Kindra be treated as an honored guest; and that Jaelle, whom she introduced as her foster-daughter without going into details, be made comfortable in a room near her own, and provided with suitable clothing.

Then she dispatched a message to the Princess Consort announcing her return, and summoned her own personal maid, bracing herself for the inevitable: the woman's shocked reaction to her hacked-off hair, her completely unsuitable clothes, the state of her hands and complexion, roughened with riding and outdoor living.

It will be worse than this, when I return to Ardais. Why should I need to be always beautiful? I am not a dancer, or a

*lyric performer. And I have long ago made my good marriage.
But there are those who would think Melora's rescue too dearly
bought at the cost of my hair and my complexion!*

Just the same, even while she chafed at the woman's cluck-
ings and scoldings for getting herself in such a state, it was good
to lie again at full length in a hot bath, scented with balsam;
good to soothe her roughened and chapped skin with creams and
healing lotions, to be dressed again in soft feminine garments.

When she was ready, word had come that the Lady Jerana
would receive them; and that the Lord Lorill Hastur wished to
receive the Free Amazon leader as well. When Rohana relayed
this royal command—for though veiled in exquisite courtesy,
that was what it was—Kindra smiled wryly.

"No doubt he wishes to be certain I have not committed the
Domains to war with the Dry Towns."

"Nonsense," said Rohana irritably. "He is Melora's kinsman
too; I am sure he wants to thank you!"

"Well, Lady, whatever it is, it is for me to obey the Lord Hastur," said Kindra, "so we shall see."

When Jaelle was brought to them, Rohana drew breath in
amazement at the child's surprising beauty. The grime of travel,
and her ill-assorted cast-off garments, had obscured it before.
She was tall for her age, her skin very pale, dusted with a few
faint amber freckles; her hair had been washed and hung below
her waist, the color of new copper. She had been prettily dressed
in a delicate green gown, just the color of her eyes. Truly, Rohana thought, a daughter of whom any *Comyn* household could
be proud. But would they see it? Or would they see only that she
was Jalak's daughter?

The Lady Jerana, Princess Consort of Aran Elhalyn (she had
been born an Aillard and was Rohana's cousin), a languid, fair-
haired, spoiled-looking woman, greeted Rohana with the embrace due a kinswoman, kissed Jaella coldly and spoke
graciously to Kindra.

Why shouldn't she be gracious? It's all she has to do in life,
Kindra thought.

"So this is our dear Melora's child," said Jerana, looking the girl up and down. "A pity she is Jalak's daughter as well; it will be hard to arrange a marriage for her that suits her station. Has she *laran?*"

"I do not know. I have not had her tested." Rohana's voice was cold. "I have had other things to think about."

Lorill Hastur said, "Such brilliantly red hair often indicates an extraordinary degree of psi power; if she were so gifted, she could be sent to a Tower, and the question of marriage need not arise."

Rohana thought that in any case it was too soon to worry about the marriage of an orphan only twelve years old, who had not yet recovered from multiple shocks; but she did not say so. She suspected Lorill picked up the thought anyway. He was a slightly built, serious-looking man about Rohana's own age; like many of the Hasturs, his flaming hair had already begun to turn white. He frowned in Jaelle's direction, and said tactlessly, "I suppose there is no doubt she *is* Jalak's child? Now if Melora had been already pregnant when she was captured, or if we could put it about that this was the case—"

Jaelle was biting her lip; Rohana feared she would cry. She said coldly that, unfortunately or not, there was no doubt about the girl's parentage.

"I assume Jalak is dead?"

Kindra said that they did not know for certain. "But there was no pursuit, Lord Hastur, and when we reached Carthon, there were already rumors of change in the Great House at Shainsa."

"Of course you know what troubles me," Lorill Hastur said. "Your rash act—I am speaking to you, Rohana; I know the Free Amazon only did what you employed her to do—your rash act could have plunged us into war with the Dry Towns."

Kindra's eyes met Rohana's in a brief, vindicated grin. She might as well have said, aloud, "I told you so."

"Lorill, you are Melora's kinsman, too! Should I have left her to die in slavery, and her child in Jalak's hands?"

The man looked deeply troubled. "How can I say that? I loved Melora; I cannot express my grief that she did not live to enjoy her freedom. As a man, and her kinsman, what else can I say? But the peace of the Domains is in my hands. I cannot go to war to right one person's wrongs, or I am no better than the Dry-Towners with their endless tyrannies of blood-feud and revenge. I must try to do what is best for everyone within these Domains, Rohana; *Comyn* and commoner alike. What of our farmers and peaceful citizens who live along the borders of the Drylands? Must they live in fear of revenge and reprisal by the Dry-Towners? And if the truces we have worked so hard to make are broken, that is all they can hope for."

Suddenly Rohana felt sorry for him. He was speaking only the truth. His personal feelings could not be allowed to conflict with his duty as Councillor. He was Melora's nearest living kinsman; the duty he had shirked, for whatever good reason, had been done instead by women. That could not be easy for a Hastur to swallow.

"Kinsman, that is of little moment now. What does matter is the guardianship of Melora's children."

"Children?" Jerana asked. "Has she others?"

"The son she died in bearing, Lady." Rohana glanced uneasily at Jaelle. Jerana should have had tact enough to send the child away before discussing her future before her; but it was not for Rohana to suggest it.

Jerana said, "Oh, they can be fostered somewhere. If Melora had lived, I suppose we'd have had to do something for them, but we can't be expected to take any kind of responsibility for the children of some Dry-Town tyrant. Put them out to fosterage somewhere and forget about them."

Even Lorill flinched at the brutal tactlessness of that. Rohana said firmly, "I pledged Melora before she died that I would rear her children as my own." *Melora knew our kinfolk better than I, it seems.*

Jerana shrugged. "Oh, well, I imagine you know best. If Gabriel does not object, I'll leave it to you." Rohana realized that Jerana was glad she could dispose of it so perfunctorily.

Lorill Hastur turned to Kindra and said, "Was it you who accomplished the rescue, *mestra?*"

"My women and I, Lord Hastur."

"We are deeply in your debt," Lorill Hastur said, and Rohana realized he was trying to soften Jerana's indifference. "You did what my kinsmen and I failed to do. What reward will you ask of me, *mestra?*"

Kindra said with dignity, "My lord, the Lady Rohana has paid my women generously; you owe me nothing more."

"Still, there is a life between us," Lorill said.

"No, for I failed. My appointed task was to restore the Lady Melora to her kin," said the Free Amazon.

Rohana shook her head. "You did not fail, Kindra; Melora died free, and she died happy. But it is for me, not you, Lorill, to offer her what extra reward she will ask."

Kindra looked up at them both, and moved to Jaelle's side. "Then, since you both offer a gift," she said, "I ask this: give me Jaelle to foster."

Lorill Hastur said, in shock, "Impossible. A child of *Comyn* blood cannot be reared among Free Amazons!"

Rohana, too, had felt a moment's shock at this request—such a presumption! But Lorill's words angered her as much as Jerana's rudeness had done. "Fine words, Lorill. But you were willing to sit uncaring in Thendara, and let her be reared in chains by Jalak." She beckoned Jaelle to her, and said, "Jaelle, before your mother died, I swore to her that I would rear you as my own daughter, born of my body. I know she meant I should keep you in my house, bring you up as my own child. But you are twelve years old; and if my own daughter, at twelve years old, came to me and said, 'Mother, I do not want to live with you, I want to be fostered by such and such a one,' then—if her choice of foster-mother were such a one as I could trust—then I would consider carefully her wishes in the matter. You have heard Kindra ask for you, and"—she looked with angry defiance over Jaelle's head, at Lorill Hastur—"it is *mine* to decide. But will you not come with me to Ardais, and be *my* daughter?" she pleaded. "I loved your mother, and I will be a mother to you as well. You will have my daughter and her friends for playmates and sisters, and you will be brought up as your mother and I were reared, as a *Comynara,* as is fitting for our caste."

Jaelle, darling, you are all I have of Melora. . . .

The hard little face was unyielding, strangely set. "And when I am grown, kinswoman?"

"Then, birth or no, Jaelle, I will arrange for you a marriage as good as for my own daughter—" and then she knew, suddenly, that she had lost. Jaelle's face went cold.

She said, "I only want to live where I will never be in subjection to any man. If Kindra will have me to foster—" She went and laid her hand in the Free Amazon's, and said, "I do ask it, kinswoman."

Rohana thought, almost in despair, *It is too late to treat her as a little child. She has known so much that would age her before her time.*

Still, she was a *Comyn* daughter, and might have *laran.* She said gravely, "Kindra, she must not be neutered. Promise me that."

Kindra's face held outrage. "I see you have understood all too little of the Amazons, Lady. We do not neuter women."

"I saw the two of your band—Leeanne and Camilla—"

"We do not neuter our women," Kindra repeated implacably. "Now and again, a woman will be so maddened with hate for her own womanhood that she will persuade or bribe some healer to break the law for her sake; often they come to us afterward, and we cannot cast them out; there is usually nowhere else they can go, poor souls. But women who come to us first, instead, usually learn self-respect, not self-hate. I do not think—if she is fostered among us—that she will come to such hatred." She put her arms lightly around the child's shoulders, turned to Jaelle and spoke directly to her, but not as if she spoke to a child at all; she spoke as if to an equal, and Rohana felt a strange emotion that after a moment, incredulously, she identified as *envy.*

"You know, Jaelle, you cannot, by the laws of our Guild, be accepted yet as an Amazon; even our own daughters must wait until they are legally old enough to be counted as women, to marry, or to choose. When you are fifteen, you will be permitted to make that choice; until then, you will be only my fosterling."

Lady Jerana said querulously, "I think this whole business is outrageous; can't you stop it, Lorill?"

Rohana thought, with anger she did not know she possessed, that it had been outrageous enough to discuss the girl before her face as if she were deaf, dumb, blind and feeble of wit. Lorill Hastur seemed to echo her indignation as he said, "It is Rohana's right to choose where Jaelle should be fostered, Jerana; she first consulted you, and you chose not to exercise your privilege of decision. Now I will defend Rohana's right to choose."

Oh, good for you, Lorill! She looked at him gratefully, thinking that being Chief Councillor couldn't be the most pleasant of jobs. Jerana's pretty, vapid face was spiteful.

"Well, Rohana, at least you need not worry about finding someone to marry Jalak's daughter; I have always heard that the Free Amazons are eager to find pretty young girls whom they can convert to their unnatural way of life, turning them against marriage and motherhood, making them haters of men and lovers of women. It was clever of you to let Jaelle among them. . . ."

White with anger, Rohana felt that she would like to slap Jerana's sneering mouth, silence the filthy implication of those words. Then, as she saw Kindra smiling, she knew her sojourn with the Amazons had changed one thing forever.

She would return to her old life, and the world of women. For the rest of her days she would tune her decisions to the invisible winds of Gabriel's whims, perhaps. But one thing would never be the same; and it was a difference that changed the world.

Rohana knew, now, that she was living that life *by choice;* not because her mind was too narrowly bounded to imagine any other life, but because, having known another life and weighed it, she had decided that what was good in her world—her deep affection for Gabriel, her love for her children, the responsibility of the estate of Ardais that demanded the hand of its lady—outweighed what was difficult, or hard for her to accept.

And so nothing that any woman like Jerana might say could ever hurt her or make her angry again. Jerana was simply a stupid, narrow, unimaginative and spiteful woman; she had never had any opportunity to be otherwise. Kindra was worth a hundred like Jerana. *I am free. She could never be,* Rohana thought.

She said, almost gently, "I am sorry you feel that way about it, Jerana, but this seems to me a happy choice for Jaelle; you did not choose to foster her yourself, and since you do not love her, it is just as well. I would be selfish indeed to keep Jaelle tied to the ribbons of my sash, just to comfort me in my bereavement."

"You will give her to that—that Free Amazon, that shame and scandal to womanhood?"

Rohana said serenely, "I know her, Jerana, and you do not." She held out her arms to Jaelle and said, "I told you that if my own daughter made such a choice, I would listen to her. Be it as you wish, then." She folded Jaelle in her arms, and for the first time the little girl hugged her, hard, kissing her on the cheek, her eyes shining. Rohana said, "I give you to Kindra to foster, Jaelle. I bid you be a dutiful daughter to her; and do not forget me."

Then, letting Jaelle go, she stretched her hands to the Free Amazon. The older woman's calloused, sunburned hands met her own; the level gray eyes looked straight into hers. She said quietly, "Lady, may the Goddess deal with me as I with Jaelle."

Rohana's mind lay open to the touch. Again, and for the last time, she felt the Amazon's immense kindness, steadiness; she knew she would trust Kindra with her life—or with this other life so precious to her. She was surprised to feel that her eyes were filling with tears.

She thought, *I almost wish I were coming with you, too. . . .*

Kindra said softly, aloud, "So do I, Rohana." There was no formal "My Lady" now; they had gone too deep for that. Rohana could not speak, even to say good-bye; she laid Jaelle's hand in Kindra's and turned away.

The last thing Rohana heard, as they left the audience chamber, Jaelle skipping along at Kindra's side, was the little girl asking eagerly, "Foster-mother, will you cut my hair?"

PART II

MAGDA LORNE,

Terran Agent

Twelve years elapse between the
first part and the second.

Chapter 6

If there was a noisier job anywhere in the Galaxy than building a spaceport, Magda Lorne hoped she'd never have to listen to it.

And a *long* job. This one, it seemed, had been building most
of Magda's life. She had been born at Caer Donn, the Terran
Empire's first foothold on Darkover; had been eight years old
when the HQ had been moved here to Thendara; and the spaceport had been under construction ever since.

Even the violence of the autumnal storm had only dulled, not
silenced, the roar of the building machines, although the mountains behind the city had disappeared into a blur of white snow,
and even the old town beyond the HQ was all but invisible.
Magda went through the heavy storm doors into the unmarried
women's quarters and simultaneously slammed out storm and
noise. Inside it was soundproofed. The lights here were yellow
Earth-normal. At least this building was finished, she thought,
and *quiet*. All during her brief marriage to Peter, they had lived
in Married Personnel Quarters; unfinished and the soundproof-
ing still not complete. And she wondered, sometimes, just how
much the perpetual tension of the noise had contributed to the
breakup of that marriage. She shrugged the thought off, opening
the door of her room. *It would never have worked, no matter
what the conditions. I don't think I was ever in love with Peter,
and I'm perfectly sure he was never in love with me. We'd just
been together too much,* her thoughts ran on the familiar track,
and not quite enough, not quite enough to get it out of our

systems. When that wore off, we realized there wasn't anything else to hold us together.

Recalling her marriage to Peter, her thoughts continued along an annoying, smooth and familiar groove. *Where is he? He's never been away so long before. I hope nothing's happened to him.*

She sternly admonished herself not to worry. Like herself, Peter Haldane was a graduate in Alien Anthropology from the Empire University; like herself he had been brought up since childhood on Cottman IV, which the natives called Darkover; and like herself, when they returned to the planet that both was and was not their home world, they had gone directly into Empire Intelligence work. The Empire might call the work they did *Intelligence* and think of it as elaborate spying, but to Magda, and Peter, and the others like them—not many, here on Darkover—it was the best training for an alien anthropologist: to mingle with the people of their world, to get to know them in a way anthropologists not reared here never could. Peter was evidently on a lengthy assignment somewhere. But this time he had been gone so *long!*

And there were the *dreams. . . .*

Magda knew she should report the dreams. In the course of her Alien Psychology credentials, she had been tested for psi potential; and had tested very high. Just the same, she was reluctant to make an official report of her recurrent dreams—all of which, without exception, warned her that Peter Haldane was in trouble—as if to do so might give them some reality. *Dreams are just dreams, that's all. . . .*

Nevertheless, when she finished shedding her heavy outer layer of clothing, she went to the communicator button.

"Personnel? Lorne here. Is that you, Bethany? I don't suppose Haldane has reported back, or sent word, has he, in the last twenty-eight?"

"Not a word, Magda," the woman in the coordinator's office replied. "I knew it; you're still carrying around a yen for Peter, aren't you? You've been on the button every twenty-eight, asking for news."

"Yen be damned," Magda said irritably. "In case you've forgotten, I've known Peter since I was five years old; we grew up together, and I worry." *And that,* she thought, cutting the connection, *is why I don't report the dreams. I'm sick and tired of every bored woman here speculating, out loud, how long it will be before Peter and I get together again! Is it going to get so bad that one of us has to put in for a transfer and leave Darkover? Damn it, I grew up here, this is my home, too!*

I wonder if Peter feels that way too? We never talked about it. We never talked much about anything, outside of bed. That was half our trouble. . . .

She still felt irritable as she took off the Darkovan outfit she wore for her work outside the HQ gates. She wore the ordinary dress of a woman of Thendara: a long, full skirt of heavy cloth, woven in a tartan pattern, a high-necked and long-sleeved tunic, embroidered at the neck, and ankle-high sandals of thin leather. Her hair was long and dark, coiled low on her neck and fastened with the butterfly-shaped clasp that every woman wore in the Domains. Magda's was made of silver, a noblewoman would have worn copper, a poor woman's clasp would have been carved of wood or even leather; but no chaste woman exposed her bare neck in public.

She hung the Darkovan clothes away, first rubbing their folds with an aromatic mixture of spices; it was as important to smell right as to look right, in the Old Town. She showered and got into Terran clothes, thin crimson tights and a tunic with the Empire emblem on the sleeve. They felt chilly, and she thought it made no sense to wear thin synthetics here and heat the buildings to a temperature that made them practical. It just made the Terrans unfit for the climate.

It's like the yellow Earth-normal lights everywhere in the HQ; it just keeps everyone from adapting to the red sun. I know, it's Empire policy everywhere; and when spaceport personnel are likely to be transferred all across the Galaxy at a few days' notice, of course maintaining a stable set of standard conditions makes sense.

But it's hard on those of us who really live here. . . ."

She was trying to decide whether to have food sent to her room, or to go to the HQ cafeteria and eat in company, when the communicator summoned her again.

"Lorne here," she said, in no pleasant temper. "I'm off duty, you know."

"I know—Montray here. Madga, you're an expert on the Darkovan languages, aren't you? Isn't there a special inflection for speaking to the nobility, and a feminine mode of address?"

"Both. Do you want a capsule lecture, or a library reference? My father compiled the standard text, and I'm working on a revision."

"Neither; I want you to translate," the coordinator said, "You're our only resident female expert; and I'm mortally afraid of offending the lady by some improper form of speech. I've heard about the various gender taboos, but I don't know half enough about them, and that's a fact."

"The lady?" Magda's curiosity was piqued; noblewomen were rarely seen even on the streets of Thendara.

"A lady of the *Comyn*."

"Good God," Magda said. She had rarely set eyes on a single member of this royal and aloof caste; even the men of the *Comyn*, if they felt the need to speak with one of the representatives of the Empire—which didn't happen often—did not hesitate to summon them into Thendara instead. "One of the women of the *Comyn* has summoned you?"

"Summoned, nothing! The lady's in my office right now," said Montray, and Magda blinked.

She said, "I'll be there in three minutes." Her normal duties did not include working as a translator, but she could understand why Montray was unwilling to use the regular staff.

This was completely unprecedented; a woman of the Comyn, *in Montray's office. . . .*

Magda put on her outdoor clothing. She had removed her butterfly-clasp; she started to coil up her long hair on top of her head. The Darkovans certainly knew that Terrans went, in Darkovan clothing, into the Old Town, just as the Terrans knew that a considerable number of the Darkovans who worked at construction jobs on the spaceport were paid to pass along information about the off-worlders to the Darkovan authorities. But neither side took official notice of it. It was important for Magda to look like any other Terran translator. But her bare neck prickled at the exposure.

I ought to act as if I didn't even know about the proper degree of exposure for a Darkovan woman. But she felt bare and immodest; she took the braid down and let it hang loose down her back.

The noise had shut down now to a nighttime roar; her feet, in thin shoes, slid on the slippery, sleeted sidewalks. She was glad to get into the Temporary HQ building, where Temporary Coordinator Russ Montray—Darkover wasn't important enough in the Empire, yet, to be assigned a proper Legate for liaison with the native residents—met her in the outer office.

"It's good of you to do this for me, Magda. It won't hurt to let them know we have some people who can speak the language the way it really ought to be spoken." He was a plump, balding man in his forties, with a habitual worried look; even in his centrally heated office, with the thermostat turned up to the maximum, he always looked, and was, cold. "I took the lady into my inner office," he said, and held the door for her.

He said, in his poor and stumbling *cahuenga* (the lingua franca of the Trade City), "Lady Ardais, I present to you my assistant, Magdalen Lorne, who will speak with you more easily than I can do." He added to Madga, "Tell her we are honored at her visit, and ask what we can do for her. She must want something, or she'd have sent for us instead of coming here herself."

Magda gave him a warning look; she guessed, from the flash of intelligence in the lady's eyes, that she understood Terran Standard—or that she was one of the occasional telepaths rumored to be found on Darkover. She began, *"Domna,* you lend us grace. How may we best serve you?"

The woman looked up, meeting Magda's eyes; Magda, who had spent her life on Darkover and knew the nuances, thought, *This woman is from the mountains; the women of the lowlands are more timid with strangers.* As custom demanded for all of the *Comyn*, she had brought a bodyguard—a tall, uniformed man in the green and black of the City Guard—and a lady companion, but she paid no attention to either of them. She said quietly, "I am Rohana Ardais; my husband is Gabriel-Dyan, Warden of Ardais. You speak our language well, my child; may I ask where you learned it?"

"I spent my childhood at Caer Donn, Lady, where the citizens mingled more with the Terrans than is the custom here; all my playmates were Darkovan children."

"Ah, that explains why you speak with the accent of the Hellers," Rohana said. Magda, studying her with the eyes of a trained observer, saw a small, slightly built woman, not nearly as tall as Magda herself. It was hard to tell her age, for there were no telltale lines in her face, but she was not young; the heavy auburn hair, coiled low on her neck and confined with an expensive butterfly-clasp of copper set with green gems, was liberally streaked with gray. She was well and warmly clad in a heavy dress of thick green wool, woven and dyed and elaborately embroidered. She bore herself with great poise, but her hands, clasped in her lap, moved nervously on one another.

"I have come here, against the will of my kinfolk, to ask a service of you Terrans. Perhaps it is foolish, a forlorn hope—" She hesitated, and Magda told her that it would be an honor to serve the Lady Ardais.

Rohaha said quietly. "It is my son; he has disappeared. We feared foul play. Then a workman who is employed here in your port on one of your great buildings—surely it is no secret that many of these are paid by us to tell us what we wish to know about your people—one of these workmen, who knows my son slightly, reported to us that he had seen my son here, at work. This was some months ago; but it seemed to us, at last, that any rumor was worth investigating. . . ."

Startled, Madga relayed Rohana's words to the coordinator. "It is true that we employ many Darkovans. But—your son, Lady? Most of those we employ are put to work as common laborers, running machines, doing carpentry and building—"

"Our son is young, and eager for adventure, like all men his

age," Rohana said. "To him, no doubt it would seem a great adventure, to mingle with men from another world. He would not
hesitate to work as a layer of bricks or a pavement-maker, for the
sake of that. And as I say, he was seen and recognized here." She
handed Montray a small packet wrapped in silk; he unwrapped
it, slowly, glancing at Magda as she translated Rohana's words.

"I have brought a likeness of my son; perhaps you could ask
those of your men who are responsible for the work crews of our
people, when he was last employed here."

Inside the silk was a copper locket; Montray opened the clasp
to reveal a miniature painting. His eyebrows rose as he looked
at it.

"Take a look at this, Magda."

He handed it to her, and she looked on an elaborately painted
likeness of Peter Haldane.

"I can see by your faces that you both recognize my son,"
Lady Rohana said. Magda's first thought was, *This is impossible, insane!* Then sanity came to her rescue. *A chance resemblance, no more. A fantastic coincidence.*

Montray was on the communicator. "Get me a personnel
solido and photos of Peter Haldane, Bethany. Magda"—he
turned back to her—"you can explain."

Magda tried. She could see faint beads of perspiration along
the lady's hairline; whether from nervousness or from the heat
of Montray's office—or both—she could not tell.

"Chance resemblance? Impossible, my child. He was recognized by the color of his hair, and that color is borne by none but
Comyn, or those of *Comyn* blood."

"It is not rare among Terrans, my Lady," Magda said. (She
had known this; Peter had made jokes of it. "On the Darkovan
side they think I must be some nobleman's bastard!") "It carries
among us no claim to nobility, but means only that one's parents
had red hair, and a certain racial makeup." She broke off as
Bethany came in, took the small solido and personnel printout
that bore a color photo of Peter Haldane. She handed them to
Lady Rohana without comment.

Rohana studied them a moment, then looked up, her face

gone white. "I cannot understand this. Are you very sure he is not one of ours, in some disguise that has misled you?"

"Very sure, my Lady; I have known Peter Haldane since childhood."

"How can this be? One of your Terrans, so like to one of us . . ." Her voice wavered. "I can see that anyone might be deceived, if this man wore Darkovan dress. And your man is missing, too?" Not until hours afterward did Magda realize that she had not told Rohana this. "Strange. Well, I see I must search elsewhere for news of my son."

When she had taken leave of Montray, formally, she turned to Magda, lightly touching her hand. She looked at her, a long and searching look. "Somehow I think I have not heard the end of this matter," she said. "I thank you for your courtesy. A day may come when I can help you, my girl; until then, I wish you well."

Magda was almost too surprised to speak; she managed a formal word of thanks, but Rohana kindly waved her away, summoned her companion and the sweating Guardsman and departed.

Left alone with Magda, Montray exploded, "Well, what do you think of that!"

"I think the poor woman is worried to death about her son."

"Almost as worried as you are about Haldane, huh?"

"A lot more. Peter is a grown man, and entirely on his own. Why should I—"

"Damned if I know *why* you should, but you are," Montray said. "And I gather her son is a grown man, too. But on a damn feudal world like this where fighting duels is the most popular indoor sport, I gather there's real cause for concern if the man of the house doesn't come home."

"Feudal is hardly the proper description—"

"OK, OK, Magda, you're up on all the little nuances and fine points; I'm not, I don't want to be. All I want is away from this damn place; you can have my job any time I can get a transfer out—or you could, except that on a world like this a woman wouldn't be allowed to take it. I should think you'd want out, too. The point is: I understood most of what the lady was saying to you. It looks like you've made a useful contact. It's not easy for a woman to do anything much on this world, but if you have an in with someone on the top levels, in the *Comyn*—"

Magda found she did not want to explore this point just now. She reminded Montray, rather tartly, that she had come here in off-duty time; he told her to put in a voucher for the extra pay, and let her go.

Yet, back in her own quarters, removing her heavy clothing, she thought about what he had said. Rohana had spoken formally at first, and when she had called Magda "my child" she had spoken in the inflection normally used to a servant or an inferior—or someone like a translator. But at the end she had called her "my girl," in the intimate mode she would have used to a young woman of her own caste. Was it only random kindness?

Outside, the snow had turned to heavy sleet; Magda went to the window, drawing aside the curtains to look out through the doubled, soundproof glass into the silent raging of the storm.

You're out there somewhere, Peter, she thought. *What are you up to? If there's really any such thing as ESP, I ought to be able to reach you somehow. Damn it, Peter come home, I'm worried, damn you.*

She thought, *How Peter would laugh at me. He's somewhere, following some obscure lead he's found.* Magda knew she was a good Intelligence officer; knew Peter was considered a gifted one. A woman could not do too much in the Intelligence line on a planet like Darkover, where strong codes and taboos regulated female behavior; Magda knew that elsewhere, on a less strongly patriarchal planet, where men and women were equals, she could have had more scope for her talents. *Yet Darkover is my home. . . .*

One of the messier moments, during the tense weeks before the showdown that had ended their brief marriage, had been Peter's accusation that she was jealous, jealous because he was allowed to accomplish more than she was on a world like Darkover. And of course, it was true. . . .

Oh, Peter, come home. I'm worried. Feeling foolish, yet taking it seriously, Magda strained in concentration—as she had done at the New-Rhine-Rakakowski Institute on Terra, making her significantly better-than-chance scores on her ESP cards—to try to send a message, if such a thing were possible. *Peter, Peter, we are all worrying. At least let us know you are safe.*

But there was no sense of contact, and at last, drained and weary, feeling it had been an idiotic endeavor, Magda gave up and went to bed.

That night she dreamed of Peter Haldane, but he was laughing at her.

Chapter 7

The season drew on, and the cold thickened. Magda, who had been born in the mountains, did not mind the cold; at least, not when she could wear suitable clothing for it. But most of the Terrans burrowed indoors like animals in their winter holes, venturing out only when they must; and the crews of the starships that touched down here confined their stay to the minimum, seldom venturing out even into the port and never going into the Old Town.

Even Magda, careless of official disapproval, wore her Darkovan dress more and more around the HQ, suffering the inconvenience of long skirts and heavy petticoats for their warmth. One afternoon when she came in from a day spent in the Old Town, it was snowing so heavily that the idea of changing into the thin Terran synthetics seemed insane; she went directly to Personnel, and the station where her observations were recorded. Montray's pretty assistant, heavily sweatered, looked at her with envy. "I don't blame you for going native. I'm almost tempted to transfer to your section so I can dress for the climate! I don't know how you manage to get around in those things— but they do look warm!"

Magda grinned at her. "Usual question."

"Usual answer, I'm afraid," Bethany said soberly. "No word from Peter. This morning the boss took him off the active-duty list; he's officially reported PMOD—provisionally missing on duty. Pay suspended subject to official contact, and so forth."

Madga flinched. The mechanism was in motion for having him declared *Missing, presumed dead.*

Bethany said, trying to comfort her. "Nothing's final yet. Maybe he found a friendly place to stay and just settled in for the winter. He couldn't travel in this, even if he was all right."

Magda's smile only stretched her mouth. "It's not nearly winter yet. The time when travel becomes impossible and all business shuts down for the spring-thaw is almost four months away. The passes aren't even closed into the Hellers."

"You're joking!" Bethany looked into the raging storm and shivered. "But you should know, you've been out in it. Summers, I think you have a peach of a job—nothing to do but mix with the crowds in the city and listen to gossip. But in weather like this—I'm surprised they didn't name this planet *Winter.*"

"They couldn't; there's already one called that. Read the records someday. Speaking of records, I'd better get mine set up.

"Is that really all you do—listen to gossip?"

"That, and a lot more. I take note of the fashions being worn by women, make linguistic notes on new expressions and changes in the local argot . . . languages change all the time, you know that."

"Do they really?"

"Do you use the slang expressions now that you did when you were seven years old? It doesn't matter if an agent uses some outdated expressions; people do pick up little tags of speech from their parents, and everybody tends to use expressions that were common in their own teens, when peer relationships were being established. The one thing no undercover agent on the Darkovan side can do is speak as if he'd learned the language from a book; so I work all the time keeping us all up to date. Montray gets away with it because he's meeting people as a Terran, and it's a compliment for him to go halfway by speaking their language at all; speaking it too well would be a subtle form of one-upmanship that would rouse all kinds of psychological resistances in the Darkovans he meets. They're *supposed* to be able to speak better than he does. But the agents who work on the Darkovan side can't make mistakes even in slang. And everybody has to keep up with common usage."

Bethany looked puzzled. Magda elucidated: "Well, look. For instance, there's a word which means, literally, 'entertainer,' or 'singing woman.' It's in the standard texts. But if you called a ballad-singer, or one of the soprano soloists with one of the orchestras in Thendara, by that word, her father or brother would call you out in a duel—call a man out; a woman using such a term would simply be regarded as very vulgar and ill bred."

"An *entertainer?*" Bethany repeated the word in amazement. "Why? It sounds inoffensive enough."

"Because for decades that particular word has been a polite euphemism—the kind of word you can use in front of a lady— for 'prostitute.' No respectable woman on Darkover would soil her mouth with the word *grezalis*—that's vernacular for 'whore'—and no man but a boor would use it in front of her. The respectable concert soprano is a 'lyric performer,' and don't forget it if you go to a concert in Thendara!"

Bethany shivered. "I had no idea a translator's work was so complicated."

"It's true; you have to take extra pains to avoid giving offense. One of my main jobs is to check through official speeches to make sure our translators and speech-writers avoid words with accidentally offensive connotations. For instance: you know how our standard official speeches—not just on Darkover—are full of expressions of friendship and brotherhood? Well, the commonest expression for 'friend and brother' in the *casta* language—that's the official language in Thendara—is red-flagged as an absolutely taboo term for official speeches here."

"Why, for heaven's sake?"

"Because the commonest expression meaning 'friend and brother,' if you don't get the inflection just right, can get you in an *incredible* amount of trouble. In the impersonal inflection it expresses the purest sentiments of fraternal charity and humanitarian concern, and is perfectly suitable for official and diplomatic use. Just the same it's red-flagged, because a lot of our officials simply cannot *pronounce* the language well enough, and even if they *mean* to use the impersonal inflection, they're likely to *sound* like the wrong one. And if you use that word— the same word—in the personal inflection, it means 'brother' in the sense of family intimacy and closeness, and is too familiar; while if you happen to use it in the intimate inflection, you're defining the person addressed as a homosexual—and your lover. Do you see now why it's an absolutely forbidden term in official language?"

"Good God! I certainly do." Bethany giggled. "No wonder Montray has his own private linguist to write his speeches!" The women exchanged a conspiratorial chuckle; Montray's ineptitude in the Darkovan language was a standing joke in the HQ. "And so that's why you go over all his speeches personally? You know everything about Darkover, don't you, Magda?"

Ruefully, Magda shook her head. "No, certainly not. No Terran can." *And if any Terran could, no Terran woman could.* The thought was as bitter as ever. But she put it aside.

"It would have been different, if the Terran HQ had stayed at Caer Donn. There, the Terrans and Darkovans met more or less as equals, and we could mingle with them *as* Terrans. There was no need for undercover agents. But here we have to work undercover; the *Comyn* have completely refused to cooperate. They leased us land for the spaceport, let us hire workmen for construction jobs and allowed us to build the Trade City, but beyond that—oh, hell, Beth, didn't you get all that in Basic Orientation?"

"Yes, I did; Class B Closed, very limited trade, spaceport personnel restricted to the Trade City. No fraternization."

"So, you see? No other Terran children will get the kind of chance that Peter, and Cargill, and I did—to grow up playing with Darkovan children, learn the language from the ground up. That's why there are so few of us who can actually pass, on the Darkovan side, *as* Darkovan—and I'm the only woman."

Bethany asked, "Then why didn't they keep the HQ at— where was it—Caer Donn? If they were so much friendlier there?"

"Partly the climate," Magda said. "If you think this is cold, you should see what winter's like in the Hellers. Everything comes to a dead stop, from midwinter-night to the spring-thaw. The climate of Thendara is pleasant—well, moderate anyway—by contrast. Then there was the problem of roads and transport. There's just not enough *room* at Caer Donn for the kind of spaceport the Empire wanted, not without leveling a major mountain or two, and the Ecological Council on Terra wouldn't have given permission for that even if the locals hadn't objected. Then there's the question of trade and influence. The Aldarans back at Caer Donn rule over miles and miles of mountains, forests, valleys, little villages, isolated castles and a few thousand people. In the Domains there are five good-sized cities and a dozen little ones, and Thendara alone has almost fifty thousand people. So there really was no choice at all, for the Empire. But it means Empire agents, anthropologists and linguists, have to work undercover, and we're still working out the parameters. There are literally thousands of things we don't know yet about this culture. And the *Comyn*'s policy of not helping us at all is a terrific blockade; they don't *forbid* people to work with us, but the people here just *don't* do anything the *Comyn* disapprove of. And that means that those few of us who can pass as Darkovan can practically name our own terms; because even keeping up with the language is a difficult and complicated undercover job. Of course I can't do *all* the things, here, that a male agent would do. One of a male agent's prime tasks, in linguistics, is to keep up with the dirty jokes; and of course I don't hear them."

"Why would anyone need to know dirty jokes? Is this for the Folklore Reference section?"

"Well, that too. But mostly to avoid accidentally offensive—or unintentionally funny—references. You grew up on Terra; would you say, in a serious and formal context, that somebody or other was *always in the middle?*"

"Not unless I wanted my audience to crack up and start snickering and leering. I see what you mean; you have to red-flag the punchline of the current dirty jokes or any specially notorious old ones. But you don't hear the dirty jokes—"

"No; I have my own specialty. I mentioned that some expressions aren't used by women—or in front of them, among the polite. There are also special expressions used mostly *by* women. Darkover isn't one of those cultures that has a special women's language—there are some of *them,* Sirius Nine for instance, and *there's* a real translator's nightmare! But no culture is ever completely free of 'women's talk.' Not even Terra. For instance, I came across a footnote in my language history text saying that women in one of the major prespace cultures used to refer to their menstruation as 'the curse.'"

"Did they really? Why?"

"God knows; I'm a linguist, not a psychologist," Magda told her. "Listen, Beth—this is fun, but it isn't getting my work done."

Magda bent over her keyboard and began to type her day's notes into the computer terminal for analysis, programming and storage by the computer experts who would later code them.

A joke is making the rounds in Thendara, she typed. *Heard on three occasions in the last five days. Details vary, but basically concerns two (three, five) Terrans who were on an outdoor escalator on the port, which malfunctioned, stranding the Terrans for several hours (three days in one version) between the first and second level pending repairs. Implications: Terrans are so addicted to mechanical transport that walking down a half flight of unmoving stairs is physically or psychologically impossible. The implications of this: Darkovan concept of Terrans as physically weak, incapable of effort. Secondary implication: envy of Terran access to machinery, the ease of Terran lifestyles? The growing frequency of jokes about Terrans, most of which appear to concern our life-style with special reference to its physical ease, would imply . . .*

"Magda," Bethany interrupted, "I just got a flash from Montray; do I tell him you're here?"

Magda nodded. "I'm still officially on duty."

Bethany spoke into the communicator, listened a moment and said, "Go on in."

Inside, Montray frowned irritably at Magda's Darkovan

clothes. "A messenger just brought word from the *Comyn* Castle," he said. "One of the Big Names over there—one Lorill Hastur—has just sent for me, and included a request that you—you personally—be brought along to translate. I imagine your friend, the Ardais lady, has been talking about your special skill with the language. So I have a problem." He frowned. "I know perfectly well that it's not according to protocol, and probably improper, too, to take along a woman as official translator on the Darkovan side. On the other hand, I understand one simply *doesn't* ignore a request from the *Comyn*. Who are the Hasturs, anyway?"

Magda wondered how Montray could live on Darkover, even in the Terran HQ, for as much as a year, and still not know precisely who the Hasturs were, and why. "The Hasturs are the most prominent of the *Comyn* families," she said. "Lorill Hastur is the real power behind the throne. The prince, Aran Elhalyn, is popularly referred to as 'keeping the throne warm with his royal backside, which is the most useful part of him.' Most of the Hasturs for the last two hundred years have been statesmen; they used to sit on the throne as well, but they found it interfered with the serious business of government, so they gave up their ceremonial functions to the Elhalyns. This Lorill is the Chief Councillor—roughly equivalent to a prime minister, with a supreme court judge's power thrown in."

"I see. I suppose it's important not to offend him, then." Montray scowled at Magda. "You can't go as an official Terran translator in *that* outfit, Lorne!"

Magda said, "I'm sure it will offend them far less than what I'd normally wear around here. You do know, don't you, that a Terran woman's ordinary dress would be considered, on the Darkovan side, indecent even for a prostitute?"

"No, I didn't know that," Montray said. "I suppose I'd better take your advice, then; you're supposed to be the expert on women's customs."

But as they went through the great gates, past the black-leathered Spaceforce man on duty, Montray scowled. "See what you've let me in for? He probably thinks I've picked myself up a Darkovan girlfriend."

Magda shook her head, reminding him that the Spaceforce guards knew her, and were accustomed to seeing her in Darkovan clothing; she never went into the Old Town without it. But, too late, it occurred to her that she had, perhaps, let Montray in for trouble on the Darkovan side. Terrans were not precisely popular in the Old Town, and the sight of a Terran escorting a respectable Darkovan female could indeed cause some trouble, if some Darkovan hothead wanted to take advantage of it.

This is idiotic. I know fifteen times as much about Darkover as Montray ever will; yet by strict protocol I'm not even qualified to be an official translator, far less for any position more advanced than that; just because I'm a woman, and Darkover is a world where women don't hold such positions.

So by accident of birth, I'm permanently disqualified from the work I know best, while an idiot like Montray needs a specially qualified linguist to write his speeches, and two more to hold his hand in case he gets lost or has to ask his way a hundred meters outside the gates! I should have Montray's job. He isn't even qualified for mine!

Montray was shivering; Magda had no sympathy for him. Montray knew what the climate was like; he had authority to dress for it, or modify the official uniform in some more suitable way, but he didn't even have the imagination for that.

I ought to get right off this damn world. There are plenty of planets where I could do the kind of work I'm best fitted for.

But Darkover is the one I know best. And here, I'm only fit for a woman's job!

And I can only do even that because I'm a Terran. Darkovan women don't even do my kind of work!

At the gates of the *Comyn* Castle, a man in the green-and-black uniform of the City Guard asked their business. He used the derogatory mode, and Magda bristled.

Montray would not have noticed, but Magda told him stiffly that they had been personally summoned by Lord Lorill Hastur. The Guard went away, returning almost immediately; this time he spoke in the respectful mode, saying that the Lord Hastur had given orders for them to be conducted at once into his presence.

The hallways of the *Comyn* Castle were drafty, cold and all but deserted. Magda knew that at this season of the year, most of the *Comyn* had withdrawn to their own estates throughout the Domains; they gathered here only in Council Season, near midsummer. The Hastur Domain was far away on the borders of the Hellers; she supposed Lord Hastur had stayed here only because events in the capital city required his presence. She carefully studied the corridors, the hangings and ornaments, wanting to make the most of an opportunity which, for her, might never come again; no woman could hold an official post on Darkover, and she would probably never again enter the *Comyn* Castle.

At last they were led into a small audience chamber where Lorill Hastur awaited them: a slight, serious man, with dark red hair winged with white at the temples. He greeted them with courteous phrases, which Magda translated automatically. She had seen that the only other person in the room was Lady Rohana Ardais.

Magda would have said, if asked, that she did not believe in precognition and was skeptical about ESP. Yet the moment she saw the slender, copper-haired woman, in a dress of violet-blue, seated quietly on a cushioned bench, she *knew.*
This has to do with Peter. . . ."

"My kinswoman has made the long journey from Ardais purposely to speak with you," Lorill Hastur said. "Will you explain, Rohana?"

"I came to you from a sense of obligation," Rohana said, "because you were kind to me when I came to you in deep trouble about my son." She spoke to Montray, apparently, but it was obvious that the words were meant for Magda.

"My husband and I have just received a message from Rumal di Scarp."

Magda could not quite control a shudder as she translated. "Sain Scarp is the most notorious bandit stronghold in the Hellers," she explained to Montray. (As a child, that word had been used to frighten her little friends into good behavior: "The men from Sain Scarp will get you!")

Lady Rohana continued: "Rumal hates the men of Adrais with a deadly hatred; my husband's father hanged half a dozen of his men from the walls of Castle Ardais. So now Rumal has sent us a message: that he holds our son Kyril prisoner in the *forst* of Sain Scarp; and he has named a ransom which we must pay before Midwinter, or Kyril will be sent back to us"—Rohana shivered slightly—"in pieces."

Montray said, "Lady, my deepest sympathies. But the Terran Empire cannot entangle itself in private feuds—"

Rohana's eyes blazed. She did not wait for Magda to translate. "I see you still have not understood. When, after I spoke with you, I returned to Castle Ardais, I found my son safe and well at home; he had delayed because of frostbitten feet, and came when he was able to travel. When we received the word from Sain Scarp, he was in the room with us, and he thought it a tremendous joke."

Magda turned pale, knowing what Rohana's next words would be. "I knew, then, having seen the portrait you showed me, just who is being held in Sain Scarp. Your friend," she said to Magda. "Is he your lover?" She had used the polite term, for which the nearest Terran equivalent was "promised husband"; the derogatory mode would have implied "paramour."

Magda forced her words through dread. A whole childhood spent hearing tales of bandits in the Hellers made her throat tight. "He was my"—she searched for the precise Darkovan equivalent for "husband," for there were at least three forms of Darkovan marriage—"my freemate. We have separated, but we were childhood friends and I am deeply concerned for his safety."

Montray, who had followed all this with difficulty, was scowling. "Are you certain? It is rare for any of my men to go so far into the Hellers. Could it not be some other kinsman with a resemblance to your son, Lady?"

"Rumal sent this with his message," Rohana said, and held out a man's neck-ornament on a fine copper chain. "I know it is not my son's; it was made in Dalereuth, and such work is not sold in the Hellers, nor worn much.

Montray turned it uneasily in his hands. It was a carved medallion of some blue-green semiprecious stone, encircled in finely worked copper filigree. "You know Haldane better than I do, Madga. Do you recognize it?"

"I gave it to him." Her mouth was dry. It had been shortly before their short-lived marriage; the one and only time they had traveled together to the plains of Dalereuth. She had bought it for herself, but Peter had admired it so extravagantly that Magda, who after all could not wear a man's ornament, had made him a present of it, in return for—She raised her shaking hands to the nape of her neck, touching the silver butterfly-clasp she always wore.

He took off the one I had worn, and pinned this one there . . . as only a lover would dare to do . . . and I let him. . . .

"That's pretty conclusive," Montray said. "Damn him, he knew better than to try to get into the Hellers alone. What chance is there that this bandit—di Scarp—will turn him loose, if he finds out he's got the wrong man?"

"None," Hastur said. "The mountain bandits remember all too well those first few years at Caer Donn, when Aldaran deceived the Terrans into believing it was permitted to use your weapons against them. I hope, for his own sake, that your young man does not reveal his identity."

Montray said, "Doesn't that just prove that we were right to help the Aldarans, and that you were wrong to stop us? They are still ravaging your people worse than ever, and your Darkovan Compact makes it impossible to attack them effectively. You should have let us finish wiping them out!"

"I must respectfully refuse to debate the ethics of Compact with you," Hastur said; "it has kept Darkover free of major wars for hundreds of years, and is not open to debate. We still remember our Ages of Chaos."

"That's all very well," Montray said, "but doesn't it mean anything to you that an innocent bystander may be murdered in a quarrel that is none of his, and that you are condoning their actions by making it impossible for our people to rescue him?"

"It means a great deal," said Hastur, and his eyes glowed with sudden anger. "I might remind you that he is hardly an innocent bystander, having walked into this situation of his own free will. We did not require him—for that matter, we did not even give him leave—to travel in the Hellers. He went of his free choice and for your purposes, or his own—not ours. But we did not forbid him to go, either; and it is really none of our affair if he suffers the same fate that our own men risk whenever they go there. I might remind you, also, that there was no compulsion upon us ever to tell you of his fate. Nor do we refuse you leave to rescue him, if you can do it as secretly as he went there."

Montray shook his head. "In the Hellers, with winter coming on? Impossible. I'm afraid you're right; he knew the risks he was taking, he knew what would happen if he got caught. I'm afraid he'll have to take whatever he brought on himself."

Magda said in horror, "You're not going to—to abandon him, just write him off?"

Montray sighed heavily. "I don't like it either, Magda. But what else can we do? He knew the risks; you all do."

Magda felt her spine prickle, as if the small hairs on her body were all standing on end. Yes, that was the rule of the Intelligence service. *The first law and the last is secrecy. Get into trouble, and there's no way to pull you out again.*

"We can ransom him," Magda flared. "I'll stand surety for the ransom myself, if you begrudge it!"

"Magda, it's not that. We'd gladly pay to get him loose, but—"

"Impossible," Lorill Hastur said, "Rumal di Scarp would never negotiate with the Terrans; the moment he knew his prisoner was a Terran he would take pleasure in killing him out of hand—by means I would prefer not to describe before women's ears. Your man's only hope is to conceal his origin." He turned to Magda and said, courteously not looking at her (a gesture which spoke a great deal about the quality of Magda's Darkovan dress and manners), "Not knowing otherwise, I would have taken you for a woman of the Hellers. Does your friend speak the language, and know our customs, as well as you?"

"Better," Magda said truthfully. Her mind was racing. *We must think of something! We must!* "Lady Rohana, they evidently still believe he is your son. Can *you* negotiate with them for his ransom?"

"It was my first thought. I would gladly do this to save a life. But my husband has forbidden me, once and for all, to go near Sain Scarp on any such mission. It was only with difficulty that I won his consent to come and tell you this much."

"Magda, it's no use. The only hope would be for Peter to escape on his own," Montray said. "If *we* go, and try to ransom him, as a Terran, we are only hastening his death-sentence."

She said fiercely, "If I were a man, I would go myself and negotiate for his ransom! There is no man alive in the Hellers who would know me for a Terran! If I could use the lady's name, and negotiate as if for a kinsman . . ." She turned, appealing directly to Rohana.

"Help me think of a way!"

I know she can do it, if she will. She is a law to herself, this lady of the Comyn, *she will do what she thinks right and no one will forbid her. . . .*

Rohana said to Hastur, "I told you this girl had spirit and strength. I will not disobey Gabriel—it is not worth the argument—but I will help her, if I can." She turned to Magda, and said, "You would be willing to go yourself into the Hellers? With winter coming on? Many men might shrink from such a journey, my girl." Again she spoke as if to a younger woman of her own caste. Magda set her chin, and said, "Lady, I was born near Caer Donn; I am not afraid of the mountains, nor of their worst weather."

Montray said harshly, "Don't be a damned fool, Magda! You're supposed to be the expert on women's customs on Darkover; but even *I* know that no woman can travel alone and unprotected! You may have guts enough—or damnfoolishness enough—but it's impossible for you to travel alone, here on this planet. You tell her, my Lady," he appealed to Rohana. "It would be impossible! Damn it, I admire her spirit, too, but there are things women just can't do here!"

"You are right," Rohana said. "Our customs make it impossible for a woman. An ordinary woman, that is. But there is one way, and only one, in which a woman can travel alone without danger and scandal. The Free Amazons alone do not accept the customs that bind other women."

Magda said, "I don't know much about the Free Amazons. I've heard the name." She looked straight into Rohana's eyes, and said. "If you think I can do it . . ."

"Once before, I employed a Free Amazon on a mission no man would undertake. It was a scandal, at the time." She looked at Lorill with a mischievous small smile, as if, Magda thought, she were evoking a shared memory. "So it will evoke no great scandal—or if it does, no more scandal then I can bear—when it is known that I have sent a Free Amazon to Sain Scarp to negotiate in my place for my son's release. And if Rumal di Scarp should chance to hear it rumored that my son Kyril is safe at Ardais then he will only think that he has captured instead some kinsman or fosterling of our house, whom we are redeeming out of kindness or a bad conscience; and he will sneer at us for being so gullible, but he will take the ransom anyway and be glad to get it.

"I think I know enough of the Free Amazons to make it possible for you to pass as one, unchallenged. But there may be dangers by the way, child; can you defend yourself?"

Madga said, "Everyone in Intelligence—man and woman alike—is trained in unarmed combat and knife fighting."

Rohana nodded. "I had heard about this," she said, and Magda wished she knew *how* this information had come to Darkovan ears. *Probably the same way we learn things about them!*

"Go back, now," Rohana said. "Arrange for the journey, and for the ransom, and come to me at dawn tomorrow morning. I will see that you have the proper clothing and necessities, and that you know how to carry yourself as a Free Amazon."

Montray burst out, "Are you really going to do this hare-brained thing, Magda? Free Amazons! Aren't they lady soldiers?"

Rohana laughed. "It is easy to see you know nothing about them," she said. "Indeed, it is comforting to think there is something you Terrans have not managed to discover about us!" Madga had to grin ruefully at that. "Yes, many of them are mercenary soldiers; others are trackers, hunters, horsebreakers, blacksmiths, midwives, dairy-women, confectioners, bakers, ballad-singers and cheese-sellers! They work at any honest trade; for one to serve as a messenger and negotiate in a family feud is completely respectable, as such things go."

"I don't give a damn whether it's respectable or not," Magda told Montray, and Rohana smiled approvingly.

"Good," she said. "Then it is settled." She gave Magda her hand, with a kindly smile. "It is a pity, but you will have to cut that lovely hair," she said.

Chapter 8

Magda woke in the gray dawn, hearing the thin patter of sleet on the roof of the travel-shelter. It was her seventh night on the road, and until now the weather had been fine.

She had till Midwinter Night. With anything like reasonable weather, she had ample time. But could anyone expect reasonable weather in the Hellers, at this season?

From the far end of the shelter she could hear the soft stamping and the rustling breaths of her saddlehorse and the pack animal, an antlered beast from the Kilghard Hills, better suited to the mountain weather than any horse. She wondered what time it was; it was still too dark to see.

It did not occur to her to regret—or even to think about—her chronometer. Like all Terrans allowed to work undercover on any planet anywhere in the Empire, she had undergone a long and intense conditioning, designed to make it virtually impossible for her to act in any way not consonant with her assigned character; and there was no item, in all her luggage and gear, of off-world manufacture. This was a habit of years; everyone in Intelligence learned the almost hypnotic mechanisms which meant that the moment she left the Trade City, Magdalen Lorne of Linguistics was gone, left wholly behind her; even her name was gone, packed away in a very small corner of her unconscious mind. *Magdalen* had no precise Darkovan equivalent; when she was a small girl in the mountains near Caer Donn, her Darkovan playmates had called her *Margali*.

She turned over restlessly in her sleeping bag, raising nervous fingers to her shorn head. It felt cold, strange, immodest.

Lady Rohana, in the long briefing session that had preceded her departure, had been sympathetic about that, too.

"I traveled once, in disguise, with a band of Free Amazons," she said, "and I had to cut my hair; I can still remember the shock I felt. I remember that I cried, and how they laughed at me. It was worse for me, probably, than for you: you are accountable to no one, but I knew how angry my husband would be when he knew."

Magda had asked, "And was he angry?" and Rohana smiled, a reminiscent smile. "Terribly. It was already done, so there was nothing he could do about it; but I felt his anger for almost a year, till it had grown to what he called a respectable length."

Magda heard the sleet beginning to abate and crawled out of her sleeping bag. Shivering in the fireless hut, she dressed quickly in the clothing Lady Rohana had provided: loose trousers, a long-sleeved and high-necked undertunic of embroidered linen, a fur-lined overtunic and riding-cloak. She had even measured Magda's foot and sent a servant to buy boots in the marketplace. Magda laced the high boots and led her animals outside, feeding them from the stacked fodder in the nearby shed and slipping the prescribed amount of coins into the padlocked box there. She led them one by one to the watering trough, breaking the ice there with the small hammer on her saddle. While they munched and drank, she went inside, quickly made a small fire and boiled some water, stirring it into the precooked, powdered mixture of grains and nuts that made a kind of instant porridge. Mixed with a few shreds of dried fruit, it was edible when you were used to it.

The ransom was safely hidden in her saddlebags, converted into the copper bars that were the standard Darkovan currency. In Terran exchange it was no more than a couple of months' salary for a good agent; they probably wouldn't even bother to take it out of Peter's "hazard" pay.

Why am I doing this? Peter's a grown man, able to take his own risks. I'm not his guardian. I'm not even his wife any more.

I don't love him that much, not any more, not now. So why? But she had no answer, and it nagged at the back of her mind as she set off down the trail. She stopped at the indicator post near the travel-shelter, locating the next three shelters along this trail. One was at a reasonable distance for a large caravan with heavily laden pack animals; a second was located at a good day's ride for a party traveling at an easy pace but without much gear; the third was about at the limit of a long day's hard ride for a solitary traveler. *Maybe I can sleep there tonight.* . . . She turned from the post and started along the trail, feeling a faint unease she could not identify; then it came to her.

I'm out of character, reading the travel-post. Most Darkovan women can't read. . . . Literacy even among men on Darkover was by no means universal, though most men could spell out a placard or scrawl their own names; among women it was extremely rare, and her small Darkovan playmates at Caer Donn had been astonished and slightly shocked—and a little envious—when they discovered that Margali could read, that her own father had taught her. *Out of character. Damn it, this whole trip is out of character.*

Magda clucked to her horse, and started along the trail. Rohana had warned her: "I traveled with the Free Amazons, but not as one of them; I do not deceive myself that I know all of their ways and customs. If I were you, I would avoid any meeting with real Amazon groups; but most of the folk in the hills where you will travel know *nothing at all* about them. So no one will question your disguise, if you are careful."

And in seven days she had not been challenged, though once she had had to share the travel-shelter with two men, traders from the far hills. By law and custom, these shelters, put up centuries ago, and kept inspected and stocked even in wartime by the border patrols, were sacred places of neutrality, and must be shared by all comers; anything else would have condemned other travelers to die of cold and exposure. By law, even blood-feuds were suspended in the shelters, as Magda had heard was the custom during forest fires. The men had glanced briefly at

Magda's short hair and Amazon clothing, spoken a few formally courteous words, and ignored her entirely after that.

But since then she had met no one; the advanced season had sent most travelers home to their own firesides. The clouds had thinned and gone, and the great red sun of Darkover, which some poet in the Terran Zone had christened The Bloody Sun, was rising between the peaks, flooding the high snowfields with flaming crimson and gold. As she rode up into the pass, it seemed that a sea of flame bathed the high snowcaps, a brilliance of solitude that exhilarated and excited her.

But the sunrise subsided, and there was nothing but the lonely silence of the trail. Silence; and too much time to think, to ask herself again and again: *Why am I doing this? Am I still in love with the bastard?*

Pride, maybe, that a man who shared my bed—however briefly—should be abandoned and left to die, with no one to help him?

Or maybe, when we were growing up in Caer Donn, just the few of us among all the Darkovan children, we absorbed their codes, their ethics. Loyalty, kinship's dues. To the Empire, Peter is only an employee, expendable. To me, to any Darkovan, that's an outrageous notion, an obscenity.

She crossed the path before the sun was more than an hour high in the sky, her ears aching with the altitude, and began to descend into the next valley. At noon she stopped at a little mountain village and indulged herself by buying a mug of hot soup and a few fried cakes at a food-stall. Some curious children gathered around, and Magda guessed, from their eagerness, that they saw very few outsiders; she gave them some sweets from her saddlebags, and lingered, resting her animals before the climb to the next pass, enjoying her first taste of fresh food since she had left Thendara.

They were all curious as kittens; they asked where she had come from, and when she told them "Thendara," they stared as if she had said "From world's end." She supposed that to these children, never out of their own hills, Thendara *was* the world's end. But when they asked her business, she smiled and said it was a secret of her patroness. Lady Rohana had given her permission to use her name. "I will give you my safe-conduct, too, under my seal. In the foothills there are many who owe service to Gabriel and to me." She had also cautioned her against any but the most casual contact with genuine Amazons, but had advised her that if she met any by chance, she would be asked for her Guild-house, and for the name of the woman who had received her Oath. "In this case, you may say Kindra n'ha Mhari; she is dead these three years"—and a fleeting sadness had touched Rohana's eyes—"but she was my dear friend, and I do not think she would grudge this use of her name. But if the Gods are kind you will get to Sain Scarp, and, hopefully, back again, without using it."

She had finished eating, and was watering her animals at the village trough when she saw a pair of men riding into the square. By the cut of their cloaks she knew they were from the far Hellers; they were bearded, and wore wicked-looking knives in their belts. They looked at Magda and, she fancied, at her laden saddlebags, with a regard that made her uneasy. She cut short the watering, clambered hastily into her saddle, and took the trail out of town. She hoped they would stop there for a good, long rest, and she would not see them again.

For a long time the trail led upward between heavily wooded slopes. The ice and snow were melting in the noon sun and the trail was slushy underfoot; Madga let her horse find its own pace, and when the road grew steepest, dismounted to lead it. She paused at a bend in the trail, where the trees thinned at a giddy height, looking down at the narrow line of road far below. There she saw, with consternation, what looked like the same two men she had seen in the village. Were they following her?

Don't be paranoid. This is the only road northwest into the Hellers; am I the only one who could have legitimate business along it? She stepped to the edge, careful not to slip on the muddy, slushy cliff, and looked down at the men riding the trail. Could she even be sure they were the same two men? Yes, for one man had been riding a roan horse; they were not common at any latitude, and to see two in the mountains in the same day's ride was entirely unlikely. As if to dispel her last doubt, one looked up, apparently saw Magda silhouetted along the edge, and leaned over to speak urgently to his companion; they drew at their horses' reins, edging in toward the cliff where they would not be visible from above.

Magda felt panic grip and drag at her, a physical sensation like a cramp along her leg muscles. She hurried back to her horse, ordering herself sternly to be calm. *I'm armed. I've been combat-trained since I was sixteen, and first knew I was going into Intelligence.* On any other world, she knew she would have been expected to take this kind of chance routinely, man or woman. Here she'd been sheltered by Darkovan custom.

If it came to a fight—she laid her hand on her knife for a moment, trying to reassure herself—it would be better to make a stand in the pass. She could defend herself better there than on the downslopes. But need it come to a fight? Terran agents were trained to avoid confrontations when possible. And she would have bet that even Free Amazons didn't go around looking for trouble.

Suddenly she knew that she could not, *could not* force herself to make a stand here and face them. She commanded herself to stay here and think it through, but even while she tried to form her thoughts clearly she was guiding her horse away down the slope, down the trail, hurrying and urging it more, she knew, than a good rider would ever do (there was a mountain proverb of her childhood, "On a steep road let your horse set the pace"), yet she knew she was almost racing downhill, hearing small stones slip and slide beneath the horse's hooves.

It was not long before she realized she could not go on like this; if one of her animals should fall and break a leg she would be afoot and stranded. She drew the horse to a stop, patting its heaving sides in apology. *What's wrong with me, why did I run away like that?* Behind her, the road to the pass lay bare and unoccupied. *Maybe they weren't following me at all. . . .* But she felt the vague unease, the "hunch" she had learned, in years of successful agent work, always to trust; and it said, loud and clear: *run, hide, disappear, get lost.* The woman who had trained her, far away on another world, had said: "Every good under-cover agent is a little psychic. Or they don't survive long in the service."

Now what? She couldn't outrun them, burdened as she was with luggage and pack animal. Sooner or later they would come up with her, and then it would come to a fight.

She looked at the ground, covered with melting snow and mud, an amorphous trampled brownish mess. *Lucky. In new snow they'd see my tracks . . . and see where I left the trail, which would be worse. . . .* But in the running, muddy water and slush all tracks vanished as fast as they were made. She turned aside from the road, leading the animals through a small gap in the trees; turned back to obliterate, with a quick hand, the marks in the snow where she had crossed the edge; led them some distance from the road and tethered them in a thick grove of ever-greens, where they could not be seen.

Then she slipped back, found a concealed vantage point where she could conceal herself between trees and underbrush, and gnawed nervously on some dried fruit as she waited to see the success of her trick.

It was nearly an hour before the riders she had seen came down the slopes, hurrying their mounts as much as they could in the mushy trail underfoot. But neither of them even glanced in Magda's direction as they hurried past. When they were out of sight, she crawled shakily from her hiding place. She noted peripherally that her knees were weak and trembling, and that the palms of her hands were clammy and wet.

What's the matter with me? I'm not behaving like a trained agent—or even like a Free Amazon! I'm behaving like a—like a bunny rabbit!

And why am I panicking now, anyway? I did the sensible thing. Any of our agents, man or women, on any world, in that situation, would have done just what I did. Kept out of trouble. . . .

Yet she knew, no matter how she tried to rationalize it, that her flight had not been a considered thing, based on her standing orders to avoid a fight where possible. It had been, quite simply, a rout. *I panicked. That's the long and short of it. I panicked, and I ran.*

I behaved like . . . like. . . . Realization flashed over her. *Not like a Terran agent. Not like a Free Amazon. Like an ordinary, conventional Darkovan girl.*

The kind I've taught myself to be, in Thendara. The kind I was brought up to be, in Caer Donn. . . .

The short winter day was drawing to a close, and she thought, *I'll camp here tonight, in the woods; I'll let them get a good, long start. By tomorrow they'll have gone through two or three of those little villages, and with luck they'll think I just found a place to stay in a village, and give up.*

Or, possibly, they were respectable traders on their own lawful business and in a hurry to get home to their wives and children, she considered.

She put up her small tent. It was a compromise, the maximum possible protection in bad weather combined with the minimum possible in weight and size; a combination of an undersized tent and an oversized sleeping bag. It was the standard Darkovan traveler's model. She knew already that no sane person ever spent a night outdoors if he could possibly help it, which was why the roads were lined with the travel-shelters and huts and why they were sacred places of neutrality.

But she spent that night in the open anyway. By good fortune the weather kept fine, even the predawn snowfall unusually light; but Magda knew, as she emerged shivering, this was a bad sign. Clouds scudded thick and black, away north, and a high wind had already begun to toss the tips of the evergreens, promising a severe storm on the way.

In the lonely silence of the trail she went over and over her failure. However she rationalized it, it *was* a failure; she had panicked.

I've taught myself always to behave that way, whenever I step on the Darkovan side. It was the standard Intelligence conditioning: build yourself a *persona,* a character for whatever planet you're working on, and never step out of it, even for an instant, until you're safely back inside the Terran Zone.

But the personality I built for myself in Thendara won't work here. Because of the particular society on Darkover, and the way women live. It was different for the men. But I was the only woman; and I never realized how far I had come from ordinary agent's training. . . ."

She tried to think it through, to analyze just what basic changes she would have to make in her basic Darkovan *persona* for this assignment, but the attempt made her so overwhelmingly anxious that she had to give up the effort. *The trouble is, I've been trained never to think of Terra outside the Zone.* Now she was trying to bring a process as automatic as breathing under voluntary control; and it wasn't working.

I can't be a Free Amazon. I don't know enough about them. Even Lady Rohana said she didn't know enough about them. So I can be only my basic Darkovan persona, pretending to be a Free Amazon. Lady Rohana seemed to think it would be effective enough to fool people who didn't have much to do with Free Amazons; but I'd just better hope I don't meet any real ones!

This caused another of those weird small repercussions which, for years, she had thought of as "hunches" and learned to trust. Oddly, this one iced her blood; she had physically to pull her cloak tighter about her shoulders against the sudden runnel of cold down her spine. *It would be just my luck, to meet a couple!*

Peter always said I had a talent for bluffing. Better get used to thinking of him by his Darkovan name.

She had a sudden moment of blank terror when the name refused to come to her mind, when she wholly blanked on it. It lasted only a few seconds, and the panic ebbed away as the name came back to her. *Piedro. That's in the Hellers. In the lowlands they'd call him Pier . . . why did I blank on it like that?*

It was an hour past noon when she passed one of the shelter huts; it was empty, and she hesitated, tempted to stay there overnight. But she had already lost half a day, and always, at the back of her mind, was the thought of the Midwinter deadline. She must not only be at Sain Scarp by Midwinter, but she must leave some leeway for return to Thendara before the winter storms closed the passes. *I can't see us camping on Rumal di Scarp's doorstep all winter.*

Nor did she particularly want to spend the winter cooped up anywhere, alone with Peter. *Once I used to daydream about something that would isolate us, so we had time only to be alone together. . . . Even now, it might be . . . pleasurable. . . .* Exasperated, Magda told herself to snap out of it. She wondered, half annoyed, if Bethany had been right all along; *was* she still half in love with Peter? *I should have taken another lover right away, after we separated. God knows I had enough chances. I wonder why I didn't.*

She checked the notice board, and discovered that there was another shelter just about half a day's ride distant. As she turned her back on the shelter she felt again the curious, almost physical prickling of the "hunch," but told herself fiercely not to be superstitious. *I'm afraid to go on, so I find reasons, and call it ESP!*

The trail steepened and grew rough underfoot; by midafternoon the thickening clouds lay so deep on the mountain that Magda was riding through a thick white blanket of fog. The dim gray world was full of echoes; she could hear her horse's hooves sounding dimly, behind and before her, like invisible, ghostly companions. The valley was gone, and the lower slopes; she rode high and alone on a narrow trail above the known world. She had never been afraid of heights, but now she began to be afraid of the narrowness of the dim trail, of the white nothingness that hemmed her in on every side and might hide anything—or worse, nothing. Her mind kept returning to the cliffs and crags below, where an animal, putting a foot down wrong, might step off the trail, go plunging down the mountainside to be dashed to death on the invisible rocks far below. . . .

As the darkness deepened, the fog dissolved into fine rain and then into a thick, fast-falling snow, wiping out trail and landmarks. The snow froze as it fell, and the slush underfoot crunched and crackled under her horse's hooves; then the wind began to howl through the trees and, where they thinned, to roar across the trail, driving icy needles of sleet into her face and eyes. She pulled up her cloak's collar and wrapped a fold of her scarf over her nose and chin, but the cold made her nose run, and the water froze on her nose and mouth and turned the scarf to a block of ice. Snow clung to her eyelashes and froze there, making it impossible to see. Her horse began to slip on the icy trail, and Magda dismounted to lead it and the faltering pack animal, glad of the knee-high boots she was wearing; a woman's soft low sandals or ankle-high, tied moccasins would have been soaked in a moment.

I should have stayed in that last shelter. That was what the hunch was all about. Confound it, I ought to listen to myself!

Her feet were freezing, and she was seriously beginning to wonder if her cheeks and nose were frostbitten. Normally cold did not bother her, but she was chilled now to the bone; her thick fur-lined tunic and cloak might have been dancing silks.

She sternly told herself not to be frightened. The woman who had trained her in Intelligence work had told her that human stock was the hardiest known in the Empire. Man's home planet, Terra, had contained extremes of temperature, and, before civilization, ethnic types had developed who could, and did, live in unheated houses made of ice blocks, or on burning deserts sufficient to blister the skin. She could survive outdoors, even in this storm.

But frostbite could delay me, beyond the Midwinter deadline.

The light of her saddle-lantern glinted on one of the small arrow-shaped signs of a travel-shelter. Her antlered pack beast threw back its head and whickered. Magda turned off the trail and trudged down the narrow path, leading toward the dark building she could just see. The road crunched with rutted and frozen sleet, much trampled. As she came through the trees, she saw the loom of two buildings; it was one of the large shelters, with a separate building for animals. Then she swore softly to herself. Through the crack of the door a faint light was visible: the shelter was occupied.

Oh, damn. I should go on. Why take chances? But the next shelter might be another half-day's ride away; and she was soaked, chilled and freezing. Her cheeks felt numb beneath her hand, and her eyes smarted. *Just to get out of the wind for a minute or two. . . .*

While she delayed, her horse and pack animal had made up their own minds; they tugged at the reins, plunging ahead of her inside the dark barn. There was a good, dusty smell of fodder and hay. It seemed warm and pleasant. She set her saddle-lantern in a safe place, and set about unsaddling the horse, off-loading her pack beast. *I wouldn't have the heart to take them out in this storm again.* Several horses and pack animals were already chomping on fodder and grain; Magda fed her animals, then sat down by the light of the saddle-lantern and pulled off her boot. She drew a sharp breath of dismay as she saw the whitish patches along the reddened flesh under the wet stocking. *I need fire,* she thought, *and something hot to get the circulation going.* She had lived on Darkover much of her life, and knew the danger signs. There could be no question, now, of camping outdoors.

She would simply have to rely on the traditional neutrality of the travel-shelters, and on the disguise she wore. After all it had excited no comment or question from the traders she had met that other night.

She gathered up her saddlebags and started into the main building. Almost automatically she drew up her cloak collar to cover her bare neck; then, self-consciously, put it down where it belonged. Her Amazon's dress and short hair were the best protection in this situation; ordinary female dress and manners would make what she was doing unthinkable.

She pushed the door open and stepped into the light of several lanterns. There were *two* parties of travelers in the long stone-floored room, one at each end, around the fireplaces. As she saw the men near the door, her hear sank; she almost wished she had taken her chances in the woods. They were a party of big rough-looking men, wearing strangely cut cloaks, and Magda fancied there was something more than impersonal curiosity in their eyes as they turned to look at the newcomer.

The laws of the road meant it was for Magda to speak first.

She spoke the formal, almost ritual words, hearing her voice, light and almost little-girlish in the huge echoing room:

"As a late-comer I crave leave from those who have come before to share shelter."

One of the men, huge and burly, with a fierce-looking reddish-gold moustaches, spoke the formal greeting, "Be welcome; enter this neutral place in peace, and go in peace." His eyes rested on her with a look that made her skin crawl. It wasn't just that the man was unshaven, and his clothes far from clean; that could be bad weather and traveler's luck. It was something in his eyes. But the laws of the travel-shelter should protect her. She clutched her saddlebags and edged past. Both fireplaces had been preempted, but she could build a small fire near the stone shelving along the center wall, She need not even struggle with tinder; she could borrow a light. (But not, she resolved, from the big man with the moustaches!)

At the far end, five or six figures were gathered; they turned when Magda spoke, and one of them, a tall, thin figure, lean to gauntness, came toward her.

"Be welcome, sister," the figure said, and Magda heard the voice in astonishment. A woman's voice, low-pitched and almost husky, but undeniably a female voice. "Come and share our fire."

Zandru's hells, thought Magda, involuntarily calling on a Darkovan God in her dismay, *what now?*

They're Free Amazons.

Real ones!

The tall gaunt woman did not wait for Magda's acquiescence; she said, "I am Camilla n'ha Kyria, and we are traveling on a mission to Nevarsin. Come, lay your things here." She relieved Magda of her saddlebags, led her to the fire. "You are half frozen, child! You had better get out of those soaked things, if you have dry ones to put on; if not, one of us can lend you something, till your own garments have felt the fire." She pointed to where the women had strung cords and hung spare blankets over them for privacy; by the light of the lantern they had hung there, Magda saw the stranger, Camilla, clearly. She was tall and emaciated, her face deeply lined with age—and what looked like knife scars—and her hair all gray. She had taken off outer cloak and tunic, wearing only the embroidered linen undertunic of a Thendara woman; beneath it her body was so spare and flat that Magda knew her for what she was: an *emmasca,* a woman subjected in adolescence to the illegal neutering operation.

Magda went behind the curtaining blankets, and got out of her wet clothing, slipping into spare trousers and tunic. She was glad of the privacy of the blankets, less because of the rough-looking men at the far end—they could hardly have seen her in the dim shelter—than because of the other women. Had Lady Rohana been right about every detail of her clothing and gear?

A slight woman, with hair the exact color of new-minted copper bars, put her head around the blankets. She said, I am Jaelle n'ha Melora, elected leader to this band. Are your feet frozen?" She bent down to look carefully at Magda's feet and toes.

"No, I don't think so," Magda said, and Jaelle touched one foot with careful fingers. "No, you were lucky. I was going to say Camilla has some medicine for frostbite, if you need it, but I think even your cheeks are all right; you got out of the wind just in time. Put your stockings on, then, and come to the fire."

Magda gathered up her wet clothes and hung them on the poles the women had rigged there for drying their own garments. On a small grille over a bed of coals, some small birds were roasting, and they had slung a hook and kettle, in which some kind of hot steaming soup was cooking. It smelled so good that Magda's mouth watered.

Jaelle said, "May we know your name and Guild-house, sister?"

Magda gave her alias, and said she was from the Guild-house at Temora; she had purposely chosen the farthest city she knew, hoping that the distance would cover any small differences in dress and manners.

"What a night for travel! I do not think there will be so much as a bush-jumper stirring in these hills between here and Nevarsin," Jaelle said. "Have you journeyed all the way from

Temora? Surely your clothes are of Thendara make; that leather-work and embroidery is found mostly in the Venza hills."

There was nothing to do but brazen it out. Magda said, "They are indeed; such warm clothing cannot be bought on the seacoast—it is like trying to buy fish in the Dry Towns. My patroness was generous in providing me with clothing for my journey, and well she might be, sending me into the Hellers at this season!"

"Will you share our meal?"

Prudence dictated having as little to do with the strange women as possible. Yet they seemed to take it so much for granted that it might cause comment and arouse suspicion. Besides, the food smelled too good, after days of powdered porridge, to refuse. She made the usual polite reply: "Gladly, if I may be allowed to contribute my share."

Jaelle gave the expected answer, "It is not necessary, but will be welcome," and Magda went to her saddlebags for some confectionery with which she had provided herself for just such an occasion. The woman who was cooking accepted the sweets with a little cry of pleasure. "These, too, are made in the Thendara valley. I have not tasted this sort for years, and I am afraid we shall all be shamefully greedy! Except for Jaelle, who hates sweets like a true Dry-Towner!"

"Shut your silly face," said Jaelle, turning harshly on the cook, and the older woman bridled and looked sullen. Magda could see now that all the women were older than Jaelle, though most of them seemed young, except for Camilla. *So young; and their elected leader. She is younger than I, I am sure! And beautiful. I don't think I have ever seen any woman so beautiful!* Jaelle, like the rest, wore the shapeless Amazon clothing: loose trousers, tunic; but this did not conceal the slender, feminine body, the delicate poise of the flame-colored head on her shoulders, the features delicate and pale, and so regular that they would have been almost ordinary, except for the eyes, which were very large and framed in thick dark lashes.

"You have met Camilla," Jaelle said. "That is Sherna"—she pointed to the woman who was cooking their meal—"and that is

Rayna, and that is Gwennis. And in a few minutes, we will have something to eat. Oh, and there are two latrine closets in this shelter; we have taken this one"—she pointed—"for our own use, so that you need not go down among the men to . . ." She spoke, with complete insouciance, a word Magda had never heard a Darkovan woman speak; she had seen it only in textbooks, for no man would have used it before her.

I'd better not talk much. Among themselves, at least, they don't use the euphemisms thought polite for women!

She noticed, too, that a roughly printed sign hung on the outside of the latrine the women had preempted, warning the men away. The trained anthropologists made another assumption at the back of her mind: *They expect me to know how to read. And some of them, at least, can write.* That, too, was a faint shock.

"Here, come and eat." Sherna ladled hot soup into Magda's own cup; divided one of the roast birds with a knife and handed her a share. Like the others, Magda sat on her unrolled blankets to eat. She told herself not to be nervous; she had eaten in Darkovan company often enough before this.

The Amazon Jaelle had pointed out as Gwennis—Magda thought she must be about thirty, a slender pretty woman in a blue linen undertunic—asked, "May we know the nature of your mission, Margali, if it is not secret?"

Magda had begun to suspect that among strange bands of Amazons this kind of polite interrogation was customary. In any case, after accepting the invitation to share their fire and meal, she could not retreat into churlish silence. *I was a damn fool. I should have camped in the woods.* But outside the walls of the shelter she could still hear the howling of the storm, giving her the lie.

"It is not secret, no; but it is a family matter of my patroness."

Rayna, a tall, slender woman with hair so curly that it frizzled all about her head like a small halo in the firelight, said, "And no doubt you will be proud to name her for us?"

Lady Rohana foresaw this. Bless her; I'd never have dared to name her without her permission. "It is my privilege to serve the Lady Rohana Ardais on a mission to Sain Scarp."

Camilla, who was sitting next to Jaelle on her rolled-out blankets, pursed her lips and glanced quickly at the rough-looking men, now sitting around their fire and talking loudly as they gobbled food from a big kettle.

Magda thought, *Can those men be bandits? Is it possible they are from Sain Scarp?* The thought set her to prickling with her "hunch" again; she did not hear Jaelle speaking to her and had to ask her to repeat what she had said.

"I said: the Lady Rohana, is she still so very lame from that fall she took from her horse? Poor old woman, and so soon after losing her husband, too; what a tragedy!"

After an incredulous moment, Magda realized what was happening. Nothing to do but brazen it out boldly. She set down her plate with a good display of offended pride.

"You have had later news than mine, or you are testing me, *sister*." She spoke the customary address with heavy irony. "When last I saw the Lady Rohana she was hearty and strong, and to call her old would have been grave insult; I do not think she is twenty years older than I. As for her husband"—she rummaged quickly in her mind for his name—"I have not been privileged to meet *Dom* Gabriel, but she spoke of him as alive and well. Or is there another Lady Rohana in the Ardais Domain whom I have not been privileged to know and serve?"

Jaelle's lovely face looked troubled now, and contrite. She said, "You must not be angry with me, Margali; the Lady Rohana is my kinswoman, and the only one of my kin who has been kind to the family disgrace. As you can guess, her honor is dear to me, and I would not hear her name bandied about without her leave. I beg you, give me pardon."

Magda said stiffly, "You had better see the safe-conduct I carry."

"Oh, please"—Jaelle looked very young now—"don't trouble yourself. Sherna, pour her some wine. Drink with us, Margali. Don't be angry!"

Magda accepted the wine, sweat breaking out on her palms; she wiped them furtively on her tunic. *Just my luck. But I managed that one. What else are they going to throw at me?* She sipped the wine, nibbling at some sweets and the nuts Rayna was passing around; they had been pickled in something tart and highly spiced, and she noticed that Jaelle, who had refused Magda's confectionery, ate the spiced nuts with relish.

She's young. But I'd better not underestimate her!

A burst of noise from the men around the other fire interrupted her, and she twisted around to look at them. They were drinking hard, passing a bottle from hand to hand and laughing uproariously; loud enough to drown out the howling of the storm outside. She strained her ears to listen, thinking, *If they are from Sain Scarp, they might know something of Piedro. . . .*

Camilla's hand came down on her wrist like a vise; Magda almost cried out with the pain of it. "*For shame,*" said the old Amazon, in a voice that cut like a knife. "Is this how Temora House teaches her daughters to behave, shameless girl, staring at drunken men like some harlot of the streets? Turn your back on them, you ill-mannered brat!"

Magda pulled her hand free of the wiry old fingers. Her eyes filled with tears of outrage and humiliation. She said in a whisper, "I was only wondering if they are bandits. . . ."

"Whatever they are, they are nothing to us." The old woman spoke with firm finality. Magda rubbed her wrist, wondering if there would be a bruise.

I'm doing everything wrong. I'd better keep my mouth shut, and go to bed so soon as I can. She lay back on her unrolled blankets, pretending sleep. The drunken laughing and singing of the bandits went on. Around the women's fire there was a little more soft-voiced conversation, some quiet laughing and joking—they were teasing Sherna about something that had happened at midsummer-feast. Magda understood none of it. The women waterproofed their low suede ankle-boots, tidied saddlebags, cleaned and put away eating utensils and began to ready themselves for bed.

Someone said, "I wish Rafi were here with her harp; we could have a song, better than that noise!" She flicked a quick, oblique glance over her shoulder at the drunken crew at the far end, but, Magda noted, did not turn to look. Amazon etiquette?

Camilla said, "Rafi was with me when we punished those two women in Thendara city. You are new-come to us, Rayna, Sherna, you have not heard? You, Margali, you came here from Thendara; has the tale made the rounds yet in the marketplace?"

"What tale?" Magda did not dare to pretend sleep too deep to answer.

"You have not heard, either? Well, it came to our ears that in the Golden Cage—you know of the Golden Cage?" she asked, waiting, and Magda nodded. The Golden Cage was a notorious brothel not too far from the Terran Zone; she knew that it was patronized by spacemen and Empire tourists sometimes.

"It came to us that there were two *entertainers*"—she spoke the polite term with irony—"who had cut their hair short and were nightly presenting an exhibition of a particularly indecent sort—I am am sure that every one of you can imagine the details—which the old freak running the place announced as 'Love Secrets of the Free Amazons.' So Rafaella and I—"

"Dear aunt," said Jaelle, yawning, "I have known since my fourteenth year, and so have we all, that there are lovers of women in this world, and that there are pretended lovers of women, and that some men have nothing better to do with their manhood than indulge in naughty fantasies about them. Do you think we are so bored that you must entertain us with dirty stories, Camilla dear?"

"Then you haven't heard how we punished those bitches for pretending to be Amazons, and bringing scandal and disgrace to our name? Can you guess, Margali?"

Magda said "No," not trusting herself to say any more. *This is being told for my benefit. Somehow I've given myself away. That old* emmasca *has eyes like a gimlet.*

Camilla said, savoring the words, her eyes lingering on Magda, "Why, Rafi and I went there by night when their leering audience had gone, we dragged those shameless wenches out into the main square, we stripped them naked and shaved their heads bald as an egg, and their private parts, too, and smeared them in pitch, and rolled them in wood shavings."

"I should have been there," said Jaelle, her eyes glistening with savage relish. "I would have put a torch to them and watched them sizzle!"

"Oh, well, we left them there in that state to be found by the guard; somehow I do not think, after being so shamed, that they will pretend to be Amazons for their filthy charades. What do you think, Margali?"

Magda tried to make her voice steady, but there was a lump in her throat, an she knew what caused it: stark fear. She said, "Probably not; but I have always heard that a *grezalis* follows her trade because she is too stupid to learn any other, so it may have been a lesson wasted."

"You were too hard on them," said Sherna. "It is the foul old pervert who runs the place that I would have treated so. He staged that filthy show; it was not the women's fault."

"On the contrary, I think you were too easy on them," Jaelle said. "Shaming such women is useless; if they were not dead to shame, they would never have been in such a place."

"All women are not made harlots of their free will," Sherna argued; "they must earn their bread somehow!"

Camilla's voice was harsh, rasping like a file. "There is always an alternative," she said, in a voice that effectively shut off comment.

Magda, watching the grim old face, wondered again, *What kind of awful experience could make a woman hate herself so much that even neutering seems preferable to retaining any trace of female function?* The neutering operation had been illegal on Darkover for centuries; not even the strictest enforcement of the laws had managed to stamp it out.

Jaelle yawned again, asking Rayna, who was the tallest, to put out the lantern. Another woman banked the fire so it would keep a few coals through the night. Magda pillowed her head on her saddlebags as she saw the others doing, laid the knife from her boots beside her head.

Now that the danger seemed over, and the acute fear of discovery had subsided, she found herself elated. She had learned more about Free Amazons in one evening than twelve years on the Darkovan side had taught all the agents. She knew that because before leaving her post she had read through everything actually known about them, including folklore, rumors and dirty jokes, and it all fitted on a printout she could hold in one palm. *If I carry this off, I'll have something to brag about for the rest of my life; that I could spend the night with them and get away undetected.*

One after another, the Amazons dropped off to sleep. Old Camilla snored very softly. Sherna and Gwennis, who lay side by side, talked for a few minutes in whispers, then slept. Magda, in spite of the long day's hard riding, was too tired and tense to sleep. The noise around the other fire did not subside, but grew louder; Magda wondered if it was deliberate, a way of expressing hostility the men dared not show. There was loud talk, drunken singing, some of the songs of such a bawdy nature Magda knew they would never have been sung directly before any woman with the slightest pretense to respectability.

For a time she listened, then grew bored and irritable. Were there no laws of polite use for the shelters, to determine how late one party might continue to carouse when sharing a shelter with another group of travelers? Damn them, were they going to keep up that racket all night? It was surprising the Amazons put up with it, but then, their code evidently forbade them to take notice of the band of men.

The songs came to an end; there was a brief lull, a minor fight broke out and was settled, and in another lull Magda heard one of the men say loudly ". . . held at Sain Scarp . . ."

Magda went tense, straining herself to hear even one more word, but the loud drunken talk started up again. *They do know something about Peter! If I could only hear!*

Blurred by the conversation she seemed to hear the word *Ardais*—she was never sure—and her resolve stiffened. She *must* hear! The Amazons were all sleeping now. She would slip very quietly along the dark wall. . . . She had partially undressed; she sat up and drew on trousers and undertunic in the dark; slid quietly from her blankets and went barefoot along the wall, clinging to the shadows. She could see Jaelle sleeping on her stomach like a child, her face on her bent arm. Magda tiptoed toward the far end of the room, holding her breath; was rewarded by hearing one of the men say ". . . Ardais cub . . ." and ". . . send him back at Midwinter . . ."

"And what answer did the lady . . ."

"You think he tells me all that? All I can . . ." It was drowned out in a burst of drunken laughter, than one of the men stiffened.

"What's that?"

"Mouse or rat, probably. Pass me the jug, you—"

Magda froze, but the first speaker got up, suddenly strode straight toward where Magda huddled in the shadow; she turned to slip away, missed her footing and fell full length. Above her she heard a great shout of laughter. The next minute hard hands came down on her and she was picked up bodily and carried into the center of the circle of men.

The man holding her set her on her feet, guffawing loudly.

"Some mouse or rat, Jerral!"

Magda saw that her captor was the big burly mustachioed man whose eyes had frightened her when she first came into the shelter. He bent toward her, taking her chin in his ham-sized hand.

"Tired of sleeping alone, *chiya?*" He used the word for "little girl," which in family intimacy is affectionate; elsewhere, contemptuous. "Which one of us you got the hots for, hey? Bet it's me; saw you looking at me before."

Magda was wildly trying to get her breath, to *think*. She *would* not, she *could* not struggle and plead with these men!

"Yeah, we've all heard about the Free Amazons," said a big black-bearded man, digging Magda's captor in the ribs with a wicked leer. "Let's wake up the rest of the girls and get them to join the party! What about it, little rabbit, did you come to ask if there was a drink for you here?"

Oh, God, what have I done? I've been responsible for breaking the shelter-truce, if I've involved the other women in this, made these men think. . . . Furtively she felt for her knife; realized, in horror, that she had left it lying by her saddlebag.

"What's wrong, *chiya?* Not a word to say? Well, we'll loosen up your tongue, soon enough," said the big man who had grabbed her, and she felt his fetid, drunken breath hot on her face, the evil, bristling mustachios brush her cheek. He jerked her undertunic down around her shoulders. "Hey, a pretty one, too. Stop shoving, Rannar, you'll have your turn soon enough—I caught this one. You want a girl, go wake up one for yourself!" He ran his hands down her bared body. Magda jerked away, caught him by the arm, tried to wrench him in a judo throw; he sidestepped, with a leering shout. "Hey, pretty, I know a trick worth two of that! So you're a fighter, too? We can *really* have some fun with this one," he said, leering. Magda's arms felt numb.

What's the matter with me? She felt him take her shoulder, twisting it cruelly; she could not keep back a cry of pain.

"Now let's not have any more nonsense, precious. Just be a good little girl and we won't hurt you, no, we won't hurt you at all," he muttered, running his hot hands down across her breasts. She backhanded him, hard, across the mouth; rearing back in drunken rage, he struck her a blow that flung her, half stunned, to the floor. "Damn it, you bitch, none of that! Hold her, Rannar—"

She fought and struggled, gasping, silent, afraid if she opened her mouth that some word of Terran Standard would escape her. The men clustered around, shouting encouragement to the men who held her. Magda had been trained in unarmed combat since her sixteenth year; she tried to catch her breath, to find the strength to strike effectively, but she found herself held too hard.

Why can't I defend myself? How did I get this far? Suddenly, as a drowning man's whole life is said to flash before his eyes, Magda knew the answer. *I've psyched myself, for years, into behaving like a normal Darkovan girl. And they're too timid to fight—they expect men to protect them. I'm conditioned to that, and it canceled out my Terran agent's training. . . .*

She hardly knew it when she started to scream. . . .

Chapter 9

Suddenly a light flared in Magda's eyes; a torch came down, blinding the man who held her. He reared back, yelling. Then there were half a dozen knives, it seemed, bared and leveled at Magda's captors.

"Let her go," said a low, level voice; Magda saw Jaelle's face above the torch. The man who held her backed away; Magda pushed the other man aside, pulled herself free and scrambled to her feet, clutching her torn tunic around her. The mustachioed man yelled something obscene, rushed forward, grabbing up his sword; there was a blur of blades, a clash, a howl, and the man fell, clutching at a slash across his thighs. Magda saw blood on Jaelle's knife. One of the women helped Magda to gather her torn clothing around her, while the men clustered together, muttering.

"Look out," Gwennis said sharply; the women fell back, braced, knives like a wall in front of them. Magda, thrust unregarded to one side, watched the slow, grim advance of the bandits, the unflinching barricade of the women's knives. Everything seemed sharply focused as she stood there waiting for the clash: the rough, menacing faces of the men, the equally unyielding faces of the women; the torchlight, the dark shadowed beams, even the patterns of the stone-flagged floor, seemed etched forever on her memory. Later she never knew how long that taut, sharply focused *waiting* lasted—it felt like hours, days—for the inevitable rush, clash of swords, tension drawn tighter, tighter. She felt like shrieking, *Oh, don't, don't, I didn't mean* . . . and physically raised her hands to cover her mouth so that she would *not* cry out.

Then one of the men swore roughly, dropped the point of his sword. "The hell with all this. Not worth it. Put your knives down, girls. Truce?"

None of the women moved, but the bandit leader—the big, black-bearded man who had held Magda down—gestured to his men, and one by one they lowered their swords. When the last one was down, the women slowly relaxed, letting the points of their knives drop toward the stone floor.

Jaelle said, "You have broken shelter-truce by laying hands on one of ours. If I reported this at a patrol station you could all be outlawed, with any hand free to kill you for three years." The strange beauty of her face in the torchlight, copper hair haloed around her pale features, made a strange contrast to her hard words. The leader said drunkenly, "You wouldn't do that, would you, *mestra?* We weren't hurting her none."

"We could all see how much pleasure she took in your advances," Jaelle said dryly.

The mustachioed man said thickly, "Ah, hell, she came to *us;* how'd we know she wasn't looking for a bit of fun?" The wound across his thighs still oozed blood, but Magda could see now that it was no more than half an inch deep: painful perhaps, and humiliating, but not disabling or dangerous. Jaelle wasn't even trying to kill him.

Jaelle swung around to Magda; her eyes glinted like green fire by torchlight, and Magda felt sick with shame and dread. *I am responsible for all this.*

"Did you come to them of your free will? Were you looking, as he says, for a bit of fun?"

Magda whispered, "No. No, I didn't." She could hardly hear herself speak.

"Then"—the Amazon leader's voice was a whiplash that cut—"what were you doing that they could think so?"

Magda opened her mouth to say, "I wanted to hear what they were talking about," but stopped before a single word could get out. Camilla had warned her: spying on men was not proper behavior for an Amazon. She could not disgrace these women, who had protected her without any obligation to do so, by bringing shame or contempt on them. They had welcomed her to their meal and fireside; dressed as an Amazon, she had violated one of their strictest codes of behavior. Now she knew she must lie, quickly and well, a lie that would not involve the Amazons in her misbehavior. She said shakily, "I—I had a cramp, and I turned the wrong way in the darkness, looking for the privy. When I saw I was wrong I tried to get away before they saw me, and I slipped and fell."

"You see?" said Jaelle to the men. Her eyes flicked Magda's face like the blow of a whip.

She knows I'm lying, of course. But she knows why. It was all the amend she could make.

Jaelle said, "You have broken shelter-truce, for which the penalty is three years' outlawry. And you have attempted to rape a woman here, for which *our* penalty is castration. Think yourselves lucky that your man did not succeed. And now gather up all that is yours, and be gone. By law we need not share shelter with outlaws and rapists."

Blackbeard said, and the drunken dismay in his voice was actually comical, "In this storm, *mestra?*"

"You should have listened to the voice of the storm before you broke shelter-truce," Jaelle said, and her face was like stone. "Outside, like the dirty animals you are! And if one of you sets foot over the threshold while we are still here, I swear, I will cut out his *cuyones* and roast them over the fire there!" She gestured with her knife. "Out! No more talk now! Out!"

Fumbling, drunken, muttering obscenely, they gathered up their belongings; grumbling and angry, but before the gleam of the women's knives, their massed, indomitable *waiting,* they went. When the door had closed behind the last of them, Jaelle said, "Rayna, Gwennis, go and be sure they do not disturb our horses and gear." She handed the torch to Sherna, and came slowly toward Magda. "You. Are you hurt?" Did they do anything worse than tear your clothes and maul you?"

"No." Magda's teeth were chattering with shock and

reaction. *I've been false to everything. To the Amazons, by behaving immodestly before men. To the mission I came on, by not finding out what I risked so much to know.* She felt sick, shamed, exhausted with the violence of her emotions.

Jaelle put an arm around Magda, supporting her. The action was not kind, but contemptuous. She said, "Give her some wine before she finishes this by falling in a faint at our feet!"

She shoved Magda down on a bench; Camilla held a cup to her lips. Magda pushed it away. "I don't want—"

"Drink it, damn you!" Camilla forced the cup against her mouth; Magda gulped, choked, swallowed again. Camilla said viciously, "You! I warned you, you bitch! Who let you out of the Guild-house in this state, with no notion of how to behave? If they had not all been as drunk as monks at Midwinter Feast, it would have come to a fight, and we could all have been raped, or killed. You deserve to be beaten and sent back to the Guild-house!"

Sherna had built up the fire again; the women came in from the barn, and Rayna said, "They have gone; good riddance. I hope they freeze in the storm."

Jaelle was standing with her back to the fire, looking formidable. Camilla shoved Magda toward her.

"Jaelle, you are our chosen leader; it is for you to deal with her. If you say so, I will beat her bloody for you; it would be a pleasure!"

Jaelle said at last: "Let her go, Camilla; if I decide she should be beaten, I can do it myself. Well," she said to Magda, "What have you to say for yourself?"

It's not over yet. I've got to go on bluffing. She said, with a spurt of defiance. "You are not *my* chosen leader. Do I owe *you* an explanation of my conduct?"

Jaelle said angrily, "You could have involved us all in your stupidity—or your wantonness, whatever it was! What is one of our first basic rules? Never get yourself *into* anything you can't get yourself out of again! No one forces a woman into danger; but having taken a risk, you should be able to meet it. Now you have reinforced one of the old dirty stories about us, that we fight only in wolf packs and never meet our enemies fairly! Yes, damn you, I think you owe me an explanation; not me alone—all of us."

That was fair enough. She said at last, truthfully, "I heard a part of what they were saying; and it seemed to me that it bore on the business that brought me into these hills, I felt I had to hear it."

Jaelle considered that for a moment, frowning. Magda noticed, incongruously, something she had not seen until that very moment; Jaelle, standing there so secure and confident, was wearing nothing but her underwear. They all were. And somewhere at the back of her mind, the trained anthropologist, never off duty, was making notes: *So that's what Free Amazons wear for underwear.*

Old Camilla's voice was sharp. "Don't listen to a word she says, Jaelle. Men's boots, with a knife in them? And who let her out of the Guild-house in this shape, to disgrace us all? Any girl from the Guild-house, even a girl of fifteen, would know how to defend herself against rape, even unweaponed. There is something wrong here!"

"Yes, very wrong," said Jaelle. "Someone has behaved irresponsibly, allowing her to go about alone before she knew how to behave. You shame whoever took your Oath," she said to Magda. "Who was she? Name her to us; she is responsible for your conduct!"

God help me, now I'm in for it! Well, the woman is dead, so Rohana told me, and it won't involve any living person in trouble. She said, "I took the Oath at the hands of Kindra n'ha Mhari."

"You lie!" Jaelle raised her arm and struck Magda a blow that made her head ring. She slapped her again and again across the face. "You lie, you bitch," she said, trembling. "Kindra n'ha Mhari was my foster-mother; I dwelt with her seven years before her death, and every one of her oath-daughters is known to me by face and name! How dare you slander a dead woman? You lie, lie, *lie!*"

Magda's head was pounding with the pain of the blows. What now? *What now?*

Old Camilla thrust her face at Magda; she was white and shaking. She said, "If you were a man, I would call challenge upon you. Kindra n'ha Mhari took me in when I was alone and desperate; I have been a member of her band for thirty years, and I loved her as a twin sister! I don't know who or what you are, that you think you can misuse her name, but you will not do so again! Rayna, Gwennis, get her saddlebags; we will see if there is something in them to give us a clue to this filthy bitch of an impostor!"

Rayna got down and started to go through Magda's belongings by torchlight. Finally she pulled out the safe-conduct, handed it to Jaelle.

"It bears the Lady Rohana's name and seal. A forgery, no doubt, but you had better see it, Jaelle."

Jaelle turned it curiously in her hands, held it closer to the fire to see better. "Light the lantern, Rayna; we need light for whatever is going to happen," she said. "I cannot read in this murk." When the lantern was lighted she stood examining it for some time and finally said, "It is not a forgery; I know my kinswoman's handwriting too well for that. And the seal is genuine." She read aloud: ". . . Call upon all those who owe loyalty to the Domain of Ardais to give such aid as is in their power . . ."

"Stolen," said Camilla, her mouth lifting in a sneer.

"No, for it bears her name and a good description." She went to Magda and handed her the safe-conduct. "Did my kinswoman truly give this to you?"

"She did."

"No one can force Rohana to do anything she does not want to do," Jaelle said, "and I have never known her to lend her name to any wickedness. Are you truly on a mission in her name?"

Magda nodded. Jaelle said, "But you are not an Amazon, are you? How came you to try to pass yourself off as one, Margali— if that is truly your name?"

"It is the name I bore as a child." Magda blinked, for a

moment afraid she would cry. But she spoke without faltering. "My mission is an honorable one, and it was the Lady Rohana who suggested to me that I dress and bear myself as an Amazon." She raised her head, still stinging with Jaelle's blows. "I have disgraced no one! If I had avoided your camp, no harm would have been done; but in this storm I did not want to sleep out of doors."

"No," said Jaelle. "You narrowly escaped frostbite as it was. So you thought you could get through the night without betraying yourself—"

"And then it seemed to me that those men knew something of importance to my mission. Something so important that nothing else seemed to matter."

"What prompted you to wear men's boots? Was it only ignorance?"

"Lady Rohana provided the boots," said Magda, "but I knew no better."

Camilla laughed suddenly. "I told the Lady Rohana that her ignorance of our customs would make trouble sometime; but it came many years later than I thought it would! Well, she meant well; I suppose if you had met no real Amazons you might have passed, indeed, as one of us."

Jaelle said curiously, "But, were you not afraid to travel in the Hellers, alone, and with winter coming on?"

A few hours ago Magda would have said, "No, I was not afraid." Now, having tasted fear, she was more honest with herself. "I was afraid, yes. But it seemed to me that my mission was more important than fear."

For the first time Jaelle's eyes were a little kinder. "So you felt the dress of an Amazon would protect you? Well, the disguise even deceived us, for a little while, and it seems to me that in general you tried to conduct yourself in such a way as to bring no disgrace upon our dress and name. It is not your fault you failed. But what put it into your head to come alone on such a mission, my girl? Was there no man to whom you could turn, no relative, no father, no warden, overlord or guardian? What is the mission on which you must travel alone?"

Having no better idea, Magda told the truth; or as much of it as she dared. "A near kinsman"—*(A husband is related, damn it, related by marriage at least . . .)*—"is held at Sain Scarp for ransom; if he is not ransomed by Midwinter, he will be tortured and killed."

"And no man in your family or household would help you? But I do not understand this," Jaelle said. "If you had the right to appeal to the Lady Rohana, you would have had an equal right to appeal to her husband or to her sons for their aid."

Magda said steadily, "I have no right to appeal to the Lady Rohana. She aided me out of kindness and charity, because I had none other to help me."

"Ah, that is like her," said Jaelle. "No lame dog of the mountains ever came limping in vain to her doorstep." She sighed and yawned, covering her mouth with a small hand, so graceful it was hard to believe she had wounded a man, had beaten Magda with those same small hands. "Well, I am not your guardian, and your affairs are none of my business; normally I would feel bound to help anyone under the shelter of my kinswoman's patronage. But there is a more serious point at issue here. It seems to me, truly, that you have shown a spirit almost worthy of a true Amazon, venturing alone into the Hellers in the decline of the year, instead of calling upon some man for protection. You were stupid, yes, and you were unlucky; but if stupidity were a crime, half the human race would be outlawed at every crossroad, and—how says the proverb? *If ill luck were cheese, dairy-women would go wanting work.* Just the same"—she frowned—"no one may be allowed to impersonate a Free Amazon. Camilla has told us how one such impersonation was punished!"

Magda shuddered, but forced herself to say boldly, "You have said it yourself: I did nothing to disgrace you. And I know that Lady Rohana was allowed to travel with your band, dressed as one of you."

"True. But the law requires that before this is allowed, the woman must have the permission of the elected leader, and the consent of every one of the women who is to travel in their company."

"Then give me such permission," Magda challenged, and Jaelle broke into an unexpected smile.

"I almost wish the laws of our Guild permitted it," she said half aloud. "A thousand pities Rohana did not know how inflexible is that law. Had she sent for me, and asked that leave, *before* you had shown yourself in Amazon's dress, I almost believe—" She sighed, and said, "Well, the law does *not* allow me to give you that permission once you have invaded the privacy of my women in disguise: unknowing, perhaps, in ignorance of your crime, but invaded nonetheless. There was a day—and if we are not vigilant it could come again on Darkover—when we were invaded constantly by enemies, spies, seeking to learn something of our ways and weaknesses, or to carry tales about us, hoping to slander us to our disadvantage. The penalty for a man who invades us in disguise is death or mutilation, as we may choose and as circumstances dictate. For a woman the penalty never changes. Before you depart from us, the lie must become truth: You must take the Oath of the Free Amazons, here and now."

Magda's first reaction was, *Oh, is that all?* Jaelle saw the relief in her face, and her voice hardened. "Don't dare to take it lightly," she said, "for if you swear it, and later betray it, any Free Amazon on Darkover may kill you where you stand; you are a dead woman the moment you put your nose out your own window!"

It flashed across Magda's mind: *An oath under duress is not valid.* That was the Terran Magda; in the next moment the Darkovan girl Margali, who had grown up at Caer Donn, absorbing the way of life, the codes, the beliefs of her Darkovan playmates almost more deeply than those of her parents, thought, *An oath I cannot betray; how can I do this?*

The conflict was terrible; she felt as if she were being wrenched apart. *I have come and gone between two worlds with impunity; now I must pay the price, and I do not know if I can!* She put her hands over her face, in a futile attempt to conceal her emotions. *If I refuse, will they kill me here and now?*

"Will you take the Oath?"

Magda said, "What choice have I?"

"None, I fear. I owe it to my women, and to every woman of the Guild, that none shall invade us and carry our secrets outside. If you will not swear, we will simply have to carry you, as prisoner, back to the nearest Guild-house, and there keep you until you are willing to be sworn, or until Midwinter Night when all our Guild meet in reunion and our judges can hear your story and decide what is to be done with you. It may be that no penalty will be exacted, that you will be sworn to secrecy about what you have seen and you will be allowed to depart."

"To that much I will swear willingly," said Magda, and meant it.

"But I am not empowered to take *that* oath from you. That can be given only by a judge, and at Midwinter Night, and only after hearing everything that bears upon the case; if, for instance, you had several young children and there were none else to assume their care or you had already sworn a Keeper's oath to a Tower. If you prefer, then, we can take you now to Neskaya Guild-house—it is only a tenday ride from here—and leave you to be judged at Midwinter."

And by that time Peter would be dead by torture!

I guess I'll have to take their damned Oath. It will give me time to decide what to do. . . .

Probably all it entailed—she remembered the few Darkovan oaths whose content and form she had heard—was a pledge not to harm any Free Amazon, and not to betray any of their secrets. *And I don't know any of them, so that's safe enough to promise! I can do that much honorably.*

But if there is more? She felt a kind of despair. "I will take the Oath," she said, fighting to keep her voice steady.

Jaelle nodded. "I thought you would," she said. "Come, let us get it over with, then; we are all weary, and you more than any, I should imagine. Come here to the fire and stand among us."

Magda obeyed. Jaelle was standing directly before the fire, her back to the flames; Magda noticed again how very young she looked. How old could she be? Twenty-two, twenty-three . . . hardly more than that! The women made a circle around them. Camilla came to Jaelle and said in an undertone, "You are young for this; do you want me to take her Oath?"

Jaelle patted the lined old cheek. "Dear aunt, you are always ready to spare me or shield me, but if I am old enough to be elected leader of a band, surely I am old enough to punish intruders, or to take an Oath."

She said to Magda, "Bare your breasts before us."

Startled, confused, Magda fumbled with the laces of her torn tunic. Part of her, at this moment, the trained agent who never stopped taking mental notes for later use, was excited—the graduate anthropologist participating in an unusual and secret tribal custom; but the rest of her was just a frightened girl, ashamed as any girl reared in Caer Donn would have been ashamed, to stand with her body bared before strangers. She fumbled with the laces; Sherna came and pulled the tunic down so that she stood before them bare to the waist, shivering. She clenched her fists at her sides, resisting the impulse to cover herself with her hands, as one by one the women came and solemnly inspected her bare breasts.

This must have been an ancient way of making sure they were not invaded by men in disguise. I'll bet there was a time when the candidate—or the intruder—had to strip herself bare, head to foot. She bit her lip hard to keep from breaking into nervous laughter—or tears. *I feel like a horse in the market!*

When every one of the women had looked her over, Jaelle said, "Have we all verified that this is in truth a woman, and not a man come in disguise to mock us? If there are any doubts we shall have this one stripped naked; any of you has the right to demand it." Magda was no longer able to be elated at this verification of her guess; she stood shivering, her eyes cast down. But no one demanded it, and Jaelle nodded.

"So be it; we accept you as a woman. Now, you have cut your hair and come among us of your free will; so I call upon you to repeat the Oath given in the days of Varzil the Good, to the Guild of Free Amazons, in accordance with the Charter kept at Nevarsin. In the presence of these witnesses, repeat after me:

From this day forth I renounce the right to marry save as a free-mate. No man shall bind me *di catenas* and I will dwell in no man's household as a *barragana*."

Stumbling over the words, Jaelle prompting her at intervals, Magda repeated the words. "No man shall bind me . . ." *Nothing,* she thought, *is less likely than that I should ever want—or any Terran-born woman should be allowed—to marry* di cate-nas, *by the old religious ritual. And a* barragana *is simply a kept woman, a concubine.*

"I swear that I am prepared to defend myself by force if I am attacked by force, and that I shall turn to no man for protection."

Magda repeated the words; again, feeling that she was actu-ally disintegrating. *Two of me—the Terran Magda, the Darko-van Margali—and they're breaking apart! Who am I? Who will I be after this?*

". . . Turn to no . . . no man for protection. . . ."

I've been taught to defend myself since I was sixteen years old. On any other world I would have been doing it all along. Here I was sheltered, and when I finally had to try, I couldn't. Without Jaelle's band I'd have been beaten up and probably gang-raped. I might have survived it—people do—but it would have been a hell of a thing to live with!

"From this day forth I swear I shall never again be known by the name of any man, be he father, guardian, lover or husband, but simply and solely as—" Jaelle broke off. "What was your mother's name?"

Magda rummaged wildly in her mind for the Darkovan equivalent of "Elizabeth." *What's wrong with me? I heard it often enough: I'm disintegrating!* She said, after a perceptible pause, "Ysabet."

". . . As Margali *nikhya mic* Ysabet," said Jaelle, speaking the words in full without the common abbreviation, and Magda repeated them, biting her lip, fighting for self-control. Nothing so far in the oath had troubled or frightened her, but this did. Known only as Margali n'ha Ysabet. *Oh, Dad, do I have to give up your name, too? I didn't mind giving up Peter's, when we separated. But you, Dad, do I have to renounce you, too?* The face of David Lorne, graying, gentle, scholarly, seemed to swim in her mind, to shake his head at her in reproach. *Oh, God, Peter, are you worth this?* Margali n'ha Ysabet . . . Magdalen, daughter of Elizabeth. No more than that?

"From this day forth I swear I will give myself to no man save in my own time and season and of my own free will, at my own desire; I will never earn my bread as the object of any man's lust."

Well, no woman in her right mind would object to swearing an oath not to become a prostitute. Then she suddenly felt troubled. If a woman had no occupation of her own, that could also mean—a wife?

"From this day forth I swear I will bear no child to any man save for my own pleasure and at my own time and choice; I will bear no child to any man for house or heritage, clan or inheritance, pride or posterity; I swear that I alone will determine rearing and fosterage of any child I bear, without regard to any man's place, position or pride. . . ."

The Terran Magda thought, *Well, that makes sense.* But the girl reared in Caer Donn discovered that she was choking as she spoke the words. *Peter wanted a child. I didn't, then, but I was ashamed of not wanting it; I was almost as disappointed as he, to find I was not pregnant. I wanted so to please him. I knew I'd failed him—and now I can never . . . never make it up to him. . . .* She heard herself, to her own shame and horror, sob aloud. *He wanted that so much, and I failed him in that, I failed him in everything. . . .*

Jaelle waited for her sobs to quiet, repeating inexorably, " . . . Any man's place, position or pride. . . ."

Magda repeated the words, but found that she was crying as she spoke them. She ordered and commanded herself to be calm. *What's happening to me? Why am I coming apart like this?*

"From this day forth I renounce allegiance to any family, clan, household, warden or liege lord, and take oath that I owe allegiance only to the laws of the land as a free citizen must; to the kingdom, the crown and the Gods."

Magda repeated the words mechanically. She was almost too exhausted by emotion to hear them or understand their sense.

"I shall appeal to no man as of right, for protection, support or succor: but shall owe allegiance only to my oath-mother, to my sisters in the Guild and to my employer for the season of my employment."

And what of my loyalty to the Empire? Magda repeated the words, forcing them past the lump in her throat.

"And I further swear that the members of the Guild of Free Amazons shall be to me, each and every one, as my mother, my sister or my daughter, born of one blood with me, and that no woman sealed by oath to the Guild shall appeal to me in vain. . . ."

Magda discovered that her throat was thick again with unshed tears. She thought, *My mother is long dead. I never had a sister, and I shall never have a daughter. Yet I swear. . . .*

Jaelle reached out her hands, clasped Magda's cold hands in her own. She said quietly, "Margali n'ha Ysabet, I accept you before the Goddess as oath-daughter; henceforward you shall be as daughter and sister to me and to every one of us in the Guild. Here in the presence of these witnesses, I declare that you are from this moment sealed by Oath to the Guild of Free Amazons, subject only to our laws, and I give you freedom of the Guild: and in token I exchange with you this greeting." She drew Magda close and solemnly kissed her on the mouth. "Kneel," she said softly, "and repeat: From this moment, I swear to obey all the laws of the Guild of Free Amazons and any lawful command of my oath-mother, the Guild members or my elected leader for the season of my employment. And if I betray any secret of the Guild, or prove false to my oath, then I shall submit myself to the Guild-mothers for such discipline as they shall choose; and if I fail, then may every woman's hand turn against me, let them slay me like an animal and consign my body unburied to corruption and my soul to the mercy of the Goddess."

Too late to retreat. Numb, desperate, Magda heard herself stumble through the words that condemned her to betray someone. *Whatever I do now, I am forsworn. What shall I do, what shall I do?*

Jaelle raised her to her feet, hugged her close. "Don't cry, my sister," she said softly, using the word in the intimate mode. "I know, it is a great and solemn step to take, and few of us have taken it without tears."

Camilla wrapped her in her tunic. "Poor little thing, you are chilled to the bone! Jaelle, how could you let her go through that long oath, standing there almost naked? When we had once seen her, you might have stopped to let her cover herself!" She wrapped a blanket over the tunic, drew her to the fire.

Jaelle laughed in apology and said, "Forgive me, Margali; I had never accepted an Oath before, I was nervous, afraid I should forget some of the words—"

"Drink this, it will stop your shivering." Gwennis handed her the cup they had given her before, which she had not finished. She heard her teeth chattering against the rim of the cup; she sipped slowly, trying to get control of herself. They all crowded around her, hugging her, comforting her. Rayna murmured, "Don't feel bad, we all cry, you didn't cry nearly as much as I did!"

Jaelle said, "Now you must forgive us for being so rough with you before; now we are all your sisters. From tonight, every Amazon is your sister, but those who witnessed your oath are your family, and special, always." She looked affectionately around the circle, saying, "Are you not? Camilla cut my hair for me, nine years ago."

Gwennis said, in an undertone like a private joke, "How dare you chide her for crying, Jaelle? *You* didn't cry, I remember!"

"But I was fostered among you," Jaelle said. "Now we will finish this bottle of wine in our sister's honor, then we must all sleep. Tomorrow we must think how best to send her to the Guild-house, but for tonight we will celebrate."

They are all so kind to me now. I don't deserve it. Magda, calm now and exhausted, asked Gwennis, "Where am I to be taken?"

"To Neskaya Guild-house, or perhaps to Thendara, which is

our own house," said Gwennis. "Every new-made Amazon must spend half a year in the Guild-house, learning our ways and un-learning the vicious old ways you have been taught since girlhood—all the things you were taught about seemly behavior for a woman. Your childhood put chains on you; there you will be taught to free yourself, to be what you best can be."

Oh, God! I took this oath to escape being sent to the Guild-house, to gain time! Am I forsworn for nothing, then?

Each of them had something to say to her. Sherna, who was a plump and pretty girl, came and knelt beside her. "I came to the Amazons two years ago, when I fully realized that I had no share in my father's estate; all my brothers shared, but not I; for me there was nothing ahead but marriage to some man who could help my brothers to manage my father's lands. They re-fused two men I liked because, they said, they would not dwell under one roof with them; and would have forced me on a friend of theirs. So when I knew I had no right to refuse, but could be made to marry at their wish and not mine, I cut my hair and came to the Guild-house. Do you know what I feared most?" She grinned, such a droll grin that Magda had to smile. "I feared they would tell me I could never lie with a man again! But, I thought, better that than marry to please my brothers. . . ."

Jaelle sat beside her. "It is customary for oath-mother and daughter to exchange gifts. I have no gift for you, Margali; I had not foreseen this. I must think of something."

They're so kind to me. So overwhelmingly kind. They act as if I were their long-lost sister. The Oath means so much. . . .

Magda said, "My mission—I had told you it was life and death. . . ."

Jaelle said, "We will discuss that in the morning. It may be that you owe no loyalty to any man, even to a kinsman. But for now we must all sleep."

The women finished their wine and went to their sleeping rolls again. Rayna put out the lantern. It was very quiet, except for the diminishing, faraway howl of the storm. Camilla, who lay next to Magda, reached out her hand in the darkness and pat-ted her gently on the cheek.

"You were not the first to shiver through the Oath," she said. "When my Oath was taken, I—you know I am *emmasca*—I had nothing like to a woman's form, and so three of the witnesses refused to believe I was not a man and I had to be stripped. Kindra was so distressed by that, that she, too, forgot to have me covered afterward. I was so humiliated, I wept for hours; but it was half a lifetime ago, and now I can laugh about it. Someday you will laugh, too, sister. Sleep well."

"You, too—sister," Magda said with difficulty. It was the first time in her life that she had ever spoken the word in the intimate mode.

One by one the women dropped away into sleep, Magda was almost too weary to think straight. *I can't go to a Guild-house and let Peter die by torture! An oath under duress is not valid . . . my first loyalty is to the Empire.*

She was very weary; sleep began, against her will, to steal over her. Bits and pieces of the Oath seemed to echo in her mind. *Bear no child except at my own will . . . did I want Peter's child, then? If not, why did I cry that way? Or did I only* want *to* want *it . . . because I had failed him so?*

She thought, at the very edge of sleep, that she would rather like to go to a Guild-house, if it were not for her mission. *I could be as strong and effective here, as an Amazon, as on any planet where women are free.*

Whatever I do, I am forsworn. I can betray my Oath to my sisters—or betray my first allegiance to the Empire. All my life, never knowing it, I have been two women: one Terran, one Darkovan. And now I am torn. I must betray someone, or Peter dies by torture.

Is Peter worth the sacrifice of my integrity? Can I give up that, too? With a life at stake?

Sleep took her suddenly, and she plummeted into it like bottomless darkness.

She dreamed of Peter Haldane; he was lying in the dark, on stone; cold and alone and frightened. And it seemed to her that as he had done only once or twice in the brief term of their love, he held out his hands to her, laid his head against her breast: off guard, vulnerable, no longer concerned to keep up the mask of strength, of masculine infallibility. She kissed him and soothed him in her dream, and he whispered to her, "You are the only one I can trust, Mag. I trust you. Everybody else is out to cut my throat, but you don't compete. I'm not afraid of you, Mag, you're the only one I'm not afraid of." And she wanted to cry but knew she could not, that it was for her now to be strong enough for both of them. . . . In the dream she wiped away his tears and comforted him, saying, "Darkover is not an easy world for men, either." But when she woke she was alone, in her lonely and solitary bed.

Chapter 10

Magda woke late; it was full daylight in the shelter, and the Amazons had built up the fire and were cooking breakfast. She closed her eyes, pretending sleep, knowing that she could delay the decision no longer.

I took the Oath to gain time. I do not want to break it. I have learned—and learned too late—that I am almost more Darkovan than Terran, and an oath is sacred. But that does not matter now. I cannot let Peter die, alone and by torture. I am an agent of Terra, and Peter is my colleague.

Once she had formulated that clearly, all the emotional reasons on the other side surged up inside her; but she forced them down with a great effort, her face set in rigid calm. *I have made my decision. I will not even think about any other possibility.*

Even if it's a wrong decision?

Stop that! No more wavering!

She set about wondering how she could carry it out. They were planning to send her to the Guild-house at Neskaya, which was a good long way from here. But it was in a different direction from Nevarsin, which was their immediate mission. Surely they would not alter their route to take her to Neskaya; one or, at the most, two would be detailed for that. She would pretend submission until they were off guard and trusted her—*How skillful I am at betrayal!*—then slip away and take the fastest route back to Thendara. *They will be looking for me at Sain Scarp, and if I go directly there, having betrayed my Oath to them, they will have a legal right to kill me on sight, and Peter will die, under torture. Once in Thendara—what then?*

All I can do is tell Montray I've failed, that—literally—he sent a woman to do a man's job, and on his world, a woman couldn't handle it. He will have to send someone else. There will still be time, just barely.

And what's ahead for me, on this world, after that?

Nothing. . . .

Magda accepted the fact that this meant exile from her own world, which was Darkover. She could never again take up her old work in Thendara; once she stepped into the Darkovan zone, any Free Amazon was legally entitled to kill her on sight. She would have to put in for a transfer, go somewhere else.

To a planet where a woman can have something genuine to do. She thought, bleakly, that at least her coup with the Free Amazons—*I've quadrupled all existing knowledge about them*—would bring her an offer worthy of her capabilities.

The thought of leaving Darkover brought sharp, tearing pain, almost a physical agony. But there was no other way. She knew she could no longer endure the ordinary life of a woman on this world, nor the limited work that a woman could do here for the Empire.

If I could live here as a Free Amazon . . . but the price of keeping her Oath was Peter's death by torture.

He is Darkovan, too. Would he accept his life, knowing I had bought it by oath-breaking and the sacrifice of integrity? The thought was too painful to endure. Magda forced herself to get up, to break off the endless, useless self-questioning.

Jaelle, already dressed, was standing by the fire, making up a hot drink from roasted grain; Magda had tasted it a few times in Caer Donn. She dipped up a cup for Magda, and said, "I made them let you sleep; you must have been wearied to death. The others are out with the horses, making ready to go. This morning you and I take the road for the Guild-house, where your name will be written on the rolls of the Charter."

Magda said, in a last desperate attempt to get through to her,

"I have told you my mission is life and death; my kinsman will die by torture if I do not ransom him at Midwinter."

Jaelle looked sympathetic. But she said, "By Oath, sister, you renounced loyalty to any man, and to any household, family or clan. Your loyalties are to us now."

Magda clenched her fists in utter despair. Jaelle said gently, "When we reach the Guild-house, you may lay your case before the Guild-mothers; it may be that when they have heard all, they will decide that your claim does not violate the oath, and send someone in your place to ransom him. There would be time for that. But I am not empowered to make that decision."

Magda turned abruptly away. *So be it,* she thought grimly; *on your own head, Jaelle, even if I have to kill you.*

The other women came from the barn, laughing, chattering, talking of the ride ahead. Jaelle said, "The rest of you may ride when you will, but you must choose another leader; Margali and I must ride for Neskaya."

"Oh, Jaelle," Gwennis protested, "you took this mission because your brother is there, and you have not seen him in years! Appoint one of us to take her to Neskaya for you! I will gladly change with you."

Jaelle laughed, shaking her head. "Why, I just reproved Margali, reminding her that out first loyalty is to Guild, not kindred! As for my brother, a boy of twelve has little need for a visit from a grown sister; I can see him at Ardais in Midsummer, and anyway, no doubt *Dom* Gabriel has taught him enough about the family disgrace that I am sure he would rather be spared my visit!"

Magda asked, "Is your brother a monk, then?"

"Oh, no! But he has been sent there, like many *Comyn* sons, to learn to read and write and to hear something of our history. He is Rohana's fosterling; I have seen him but once since he was three years old."

Pretending interest, she asked the nature of the mission.

"At Nevarsin, the monks keep the record of much knowledge lost elsewhere since the Ages of Chaos. They will not teach women, and we are not even allowed to stay in the guest-house, but we have leave to use their library. Our best scribes, a little at a time, are transcribing their books on anatomy and surgery, as well as those on birth and the diseases of women—books you would think they would turn over to us entirely, since the monks can make no use of them. We are allowed to have only two scribes there at a time; Rayna and Sherna are going there to change with two women who have been there for half a year, and Gwennis to keep house for them in the village, while Camilla will escort the others home."

Magda toyed with a bowl of the powdered porridge. She was curious, but asked no more questions. It went against the grain to pretend friendliness with a woman she might have to kill.

Soon after, the other women rode away, leaving Magda and Jaelle alone. While they were saddling their horses, Jaelle discovered that hers had a loose shoe.

"I wish I had discovered it before Gwennis left," she said. "She is no blacksmith, but I have seen her make emergency repairs. Well, we must stop in the nearest village. Just look at that!" She handed the shoe to Magda, who stood weighing it in her hand as Jaelle bent to examine the horse's hoof.

I could stun her with it and get away now. . . .

But she waited too long; Jaelle turned back and held out her hand for the shoe, dropping it into her saddlebag.

It was a bright morning, almost cloudless, with a brisk cold wind blowing. Jaelle sniffed the wind, started to throw a leg into her saddle—and at that moment Magda heard a savage yell and two men rushed them from the woods, knives drawn. In split-second shock, Magda recognized two of the bandits from last night: the black-bearded bandit leader, and the big man with the mustachios whom Jaelle had wounded. Magda heard herself shout a warning; Jaelle whirled, half out of her saddle. Then she was fighting, backed up against her horse, the two men almost hiding her from Magda's sight. Magda thought, *Run! Get away now, they're saving you the trouble of killing her—*

But already she had her own knife out, was running toward them. Blackbeard whirled and Magda felt his knife graze her arm, a pain like fire, as she plunged her own knife deep into his chest; felt it turn on bone and slip. He slithered, with a groan, to the ground. Jaelle was still fighting with the other man; she saw that Jaelle was bleeding from a long slash on the cheek. Then she heard Jaelle scream with agony as the bandit's knife drove down toward her breast; she fell to the ground and at that instant Magda felt her knife sink into the man's back.

He fell with a harsh sound, air escaping from lungs already no longer breathing. Slowly, feeling sick, she pulled out the knife.

I haven't fought anyone since combat training, ten years ago. Now I've killed one and wounded another. She looked at Jaelle, unconscious on the ground, almost under the body of the man Magda had killed. *Is she dead?* The thought did not bring relief, but a wrenching agony. *She fought for me, last night. And I would have betrayed her. . . .*

Jaelle stirred, and Magda knew that Jaelle's life still stood between her and her mission. She was still holding the bloody knife with which she had killed the bandit. She saw Jaelle's eyes move to the knife; she lay still, looking up at Magda without a word. Magda suddenly knew that she could not kill anyone in cold blood; above all she could not kill this woman who lay bleeding and helpless in the snow at her feet.

What good is Peter's life if I buy it with another death? I will save him honorably if I can; not otherwise.

She knelt beside Jaelle. Her face was covered with blood; more blood was soaking through her shoulder. She lifted the sticky clothes clinging to the wound.

The bandit's knife had gone under the collarbone and sliced down toward the armpit; a bad wound, painful and dangerous but not, Magda thought, necessarily fatal. She got out her knife again and cleaned the blade, saw that one of Jaelle's eyes was open—the other was clotted shut—and that she was watching the knife. Magda said irritably, "I've got to cut these clothes off so I can stop the bleeding." She slit Jaelle's tunic and eased it gently away from the skin; Jaelle gasped with the pain but did not cry out. She only said, wetting her lips, "Did you—kill them both?"

"One is surely dead. I don't know about the other, but he isn't in any shape to harm us," Magda said.

Jaelle said, her breath coming loud, "Bandages . . . in my saddlebags. . . ."

Magda got up, edging between the dead bandit and Jaelle's horse, which, smelling the blood, shifted its feet uneasily. She led the horse away and took down the saddlebags, hunting in them; she found two or three rolls, and what looked like a small, primitive first-aid kit. *That cut probably needs stitches, but I can't do it.* She made a pressure bandage, strapped it around Jaelle's shoulder, turned her attention to the long, hideous gash along Jaelle's face; it had laid her cheek open to the bone. Jaelle said, in a hoarse, frightened voice, "Can't see out of . . . this eye. . . ."

Magda went to the well behind the shelter, dipped up the icy water, came back and sponged the dreadful gash. The eyelashes parted; a little more sponging showed that the eye had only been stuck shut with blood from a small nick in the eyelid. Magda pushed the eyelids open; Jaelle gasped with relief.

"Can you walk? You can't lie out here in the snow." Magda knelt, slipped an arm around the woman, managed to hoist her to her feet; Jaelle tried to walk, but collapsed against Magda. Magda managed, somehow, to get her inside the shelter and lay her on one of the stone benches. She started to build a fire, put some water to boil, thinking that some bark-tea, or some of the Amazon grain-brew, would do them both good. And if Jaelle was in shock—and she looked like it—she had better be kept warm. Not knowing how Jaelle had stowed her own blankets, Magda got out her own and wrapped Jaelle up in them; shoved one of the stone slabs into the fire, thinking she could heat it, wrap it in something and put it at the hurt woman's feet. When the water boiled she poured it on the bark for tea, and went out to put the animals away—they wouldn't be going anywhere right away. The second bandit was definitely dead. She had to drag him out of the way to get the horses and her pack beast into the stable again.

When she came into the shelter Jaelle was conscious. She whispered, "I thought you had gone."

Remotely, like something someone else might have thought, it occurred to Magda: she could have escaped. After doing her best for Jaelle, she could have left her here to recover, and felt no particular guilt. Now it was something she could never have done. *I swore to treat every Amazon as my own mother, sister or daughter. . . .*

She fumbled for words, saying, "We are oath-bound—sister."

Jaelle put out her hand, a groping gesture that made Magda's heart ache, remembering how quick and skillful those hands had been. She whispered, "I told you—oath-mother and oath-daughter exchange gifts. I did not ask for such a gift as this."

Magda felt embarrassed. "You'd better not talk anymore. Are you cold?" She got another blanket, put the hot stone at Jaelle's feet, propped her up to sip a little of the boiling tea. Jaelle touched her sleeve. "Tend your own wound."

Magda had forgotten it. "It's only a scratch."

"Just the same. Some mountain bandits . . . poison their blades," Jaelle said with difficulty. "Do as I say."

By the time Magda had finished Jaelle was asleep or unconscious again. And asleep or unconscious she remained all that day. Magda made herself some soup from dried meat, late in the day, and tried to rouse Jaelle to eat, but Jaelle only moaned and muttered and pulled away from her hands; Magda knew that she was feverish. Once she woke and asked quite clearly for a drink of water, but when Magda brought it she was stuporous again and would not swallow.

Are there injuries I did not see? Or were the wounds poisoned after all? Magda found that she was fighting terror and dread. *I don't want her to die! I don't!*

By nightfall Jaelle's skin was blistering hot, and Magda could not rouse her even for a moment. Jaelle muttered and flung herself around; once she began with her free hand to tear at the bandage on her face. Magda pulled her hand away, but a few minutes later Jaelle was clawing at the bandage again.

Magda, thinking that if she got the bandage loose she might hurt herself, make the scar worse, took a roll of the bandage and tied Jaelle's hands at her sides. She was not prepared to hear Jaelle begin to scream: wild screams of panic and terror.

"Oh, no, no, no, no . . . don't chain my hands, don't— Mother, mother . . . don't let them . . . oh, don't . . . oh, no, no!" and the thin tearing screams again. Magda had never heard such terror. She could not bear it. Quickly she cut the bandage, lifted Jaelle's hands one after another to show that they were free. Somehow that penetrated Jaelle's delirium; she stopped shrieking and lay back quietly. About an hour later she began restlessly to tear at the bandage on her face again, but Magda had no notion of repeating whatever had terrified her so; instead she took the unconscious woman's hands firmly between her own and held them tight. She said quietly and firmly, "You must not do that; lie still, you will hurt yourself. I will not tie your hands, but you must be still." She repeated this over and over, several times, with variations.

Jaelle opened her eyes, but Magda knew she did not see her. She muttered, "Kindra," and later, "Mother," but let her hands rest in Magda's without struggling. Once she said, to no one present, "It hurt. But I didn't cry."

Most of that night Magda sat beside Jaelle, listening to her delirious mutterings, holding her hands tight whenever she tried to tear at the bandages or, as she started to do later, to climb out of bed, under some agitated impression—Magda gathered from her raving—that she was needed somewhere else, at once. Magda had nothing to give her for the fever; there were some medicines in Jaelle's saddlebags, but Magda did not know how to use them or what they were. She sponged her several times with the icy water from the well, and tried to make her drink, but Jaelle pulled away and would not swallow. Toward morning she sank into quiet; Magda did not know whether she was asleep or had lapsed into a coma and was dying. In either case there was nothing she could do. She lay down at the unconscious woman's side and closed her eyes for a moment's rest; suddenly the shelter was full of gray light and Jaelle was lying with her eyes open, looking at her.

"How do you feel, Jaelle?"

"Like hell," Jaelle said. "Is there some water, or tea, or something? My mouth has not been this dry since I left Shainsa."

Magda brought her a drink; Jaelle gulped it thirstily and asked for more. "Did you stay by me all night?"

"Until you fell asleep; I was afraid you would tear off your bandages. You tried."

"Was I delirious?" When Magda nodded, Jaelle said with a wry grin, "That explains it; I dreamed I was back in the Dry Towns, and Jalak—well, it was frightful nonsense, but I have rarely been so glad to wake up." She put a tentative hand to the bandages.

"You will have a dreadful scar, I am afraid."

"There are some women in the Guild-house who think their scars a good advertisement for their skill," said Jaelle, "but, then, I am not a fighter."

Magda had to smile at that. "I should say you were quite a fighter."

"I mean, not a professional fighter. I do not normally hire myself out as soldier or bodyguard," Jaelle said, and shifted her body uncomfortably. "I don't remember much after you cut off my tunic."

"I'll tell you more after I dress your wound," Magda said. Jaelle had run so high a fever that Magda feared to find infection; but there was at least no renewed bleeding, though the edges of the wound looked ugly. Poisoned? Jaelle said, "I have some *karalla* powder in my saddlebags; it will keep the wound from closing too soon with rot beneath." At her directions Magda sprinkled the wound with the gray stuff before rebandaging it, Jaelle was exhausted and pale, but coherent; she ate some of the dried-meat soup, with Magda's help, and drank more water.

"You killed both of them? That does surprise me!"

"It surprised me, too," Magda confessed.

Jaelle uneasily fingered the bandage on her face. "I am not

one of those who make a fetish of displaying their scars, but I may have to pretend that I am. Better scarred than buried—or blind! Camilla told me, once, that there were some men who found knife-scars on a woman irresistible." She sank back wearily against the rolled saddlebag under her head. "It was a fool's wound, really. Gwennis, or even old Camilla, could have driven them both away without taking a scratch."

She closed her eyes and slept again. She was somnolent, or sleeping, most of that day, but the fever did not return. Magda had little to do, after the animals had been tended. She thought about burying the dead bandits, but that was a task entirely beyond her strength. She stayed near Jaelle, in case the wounded girl should need anything. The sight of the bandage on Jaelle's face troubled her deeply. *She was so beautiful! In the Terran Zone they could repair that ugly slash as good as new; here, I suppose, she will bear that terrible scar until she dies!*

It occurred to her again that now, with Jaelle well on the way toward recovery, she could make her escape, leave her to recover at leisure, and not even have the other woman's death on her conscience. But by now the thought was very remote.

On the next day Jaelle was able to get up and walk about a little, moving her arm cautiously; swearing at the pain, but moving it, nevertheless. "I don't want the muscles to freeze and the arm to lose its strength," she said irritably, when Magda urged her not to risk tearing it open again. "I know what I am doing." Now that she was no longer somnolent with shock and exhaustion, she was in a good deal of pain, and it made her irritable and restless. Late in the afternoon Magda woke from a brief doze to find Jaelle staring at her as if trying to remember something. *Does she remember thinking I was going to kill her?* She remembered, with some shock, the moment when she had stood over Jaelle, not yet sure herself what she intended. Jaelle had been as still as a wounded animal awaiting the hunter's death-stroke. . . .

Jaelle said quietly, at last, "I did not expect you to stay with me, Margali; I knew you took our Oath unwillingly. It is customary for oath-mother and daughter to exchange gifts; you have given me my life, I know."

"Don't!" Magda could not bear to start thinking again about her indecision. She got up and went out of the shelter, looking at the lowering gray sky, heavy with unfallen snow. Midwinter was only a few days distant; and on that day Peter Haldane would meet a dreadful death, suffering the penalty of Rumal di Scarp's blood-feud with the Ardais clan. Magda leaned against the outside wall of the shelter and gave herself up to helpless, desperate weeping.

After a long time she felt a soft touch on her arm; Jaelle stood there, looking very pale and troubled.

"Is he so dear to you—the kinsman of your mission?"

Exhausted, struggling for self-control, Magda could only shake her head and say, "It is not only that."

"Then tell me what it is, my sister." Jaelle took Magda's hand. She said, "Don't stand here in the cold."

More because she remembered that Jaelle herself must not be kept in the cold with her unhealed wound, Magda let herself be led inside. Jaelle stumbled, fell heavily against her; Magda caught her, eased her down on one of the stone benches.

"Now tell me, sister."

Magda shook her head, exhausted, "I told you all."

"But this time," Jaelle said, "the truth, will you not? I do not understand you, Margali. You were lying when you took the Oath; you were not lying. You were telling the truth; you were not telling the truth. Even your name—it is your name; you have another name. Tell me."

Magda's defenses were down. "How did you know?"

Jaelle said, "I was born daughter to the *Comyn*; I have some *laran*." Magda did not know the word as Jaelle used it; it usually meant a gift or talent. "I have not had the training to use it properly. Lady Rohana—she is my mother's kinswoman—wished me sent to a Tower to be trained in its use; I would have none of that crew. So my gift is erratic; I cannot use it when I would, and when I would not, it thrusts itself on me, undesired. It was so when you took the Oath; I could feel, within myself, that you were torn two ways, and in such fear . . . there was no need for such terror as *that*. And now I can read your thoughts, but only a little, Margali—if that is your name. You are oath-bound, but so am I; as you are sworn, so am I oath-bound to you, never to hurt or betray you. Tell me, my sister!"

Magda said wearily, "I was born in Caer Donn. My true name—the name my parents gave me—is Magdalen Lorne, but the Darkovan children with whom I played could not say that name; they called me *Margali,* and that is my name as much as the other."

"The—the *Darkovan* children?" Jaelle whispered, and her eyes were wide, almost with fear. "What are you, then?"

"I am . . . I am . . ." Magda struggled, the words sticking in her throat. This was basic. *You never tell any outsider who you are. Never.*

Jaelle is not an outsider. She is my sworn sister. Suddenly all conflict was gone. The lump in Magda's throat dissolved, and it seemed that she drew the first free breath she had drawn since she first entered this shelter several nights ago. She said, and her voice did not falter, "My mother and father were Terrans, subjects of the Empire; I am Darkovan, born in Caer Donn, but I am an Intelligence agent and linguistics expert for the Empire, and I work from Thendara."

Slowly, Jaelle nodded. "So that is it," she said at last. "I have heard something of the Terrans. One of ours in Thendara Guild-house—an *emmasca* who can pass herself off as a man: they all can, but many of them will not—hired herself out with the workmen among those building the spaceport, and she told us something of your people. But I did not know the Terrans were human, except in form."

Magda smiled at that way of putting it. She said, "The records of the Empire say that Darkovan and Terran are one stock from the far past."

"Does Lady Rohana know you are *Terranan?*"

"Yes; she saw me first there."

"This explains why you had to appeal to her," said Jaelle; she was just thinking out loud. "Your kinsman, is he Terran, too?"

"Yes; but taken prisoner by Rumal di Scarp because of a chance likeness to Lady Rohana's son."

"He is like Kyril? That will not endear him to me," Jaelle said. "I love Rohana well; Kyril is another matter entirely. But that does not matter now. You love this man so very much? Is he your lover, then?"

Magda said slowly. "No; although for a time we were"—she hesitated, used the Darkovan word—"freemates. But it is more than that. We were children together, and he has no one else. To my superiors in Thendara, he is—expendable; so I took this duty upon myself to save him from death and torture."

Jaelle bit her lip, frowning, idly fingering the bandage on her cheek. She said, "I must think. Perhaps—you are in the employ of your service, under bond for a legitimate service? A Free Amazon is bound by law to fulfill any work she hires herself of her free will to do, and it could be legally said you must complete this pledge and honor your conditions of employment." Again, she was thinking out loud. "You say you do not love him. How *do* you feel about him, then?"

"I don't know." Magda searched her mind; surprised herself by saying, "Protective."

Jaelle looked at Magda with that intense, frowning stare which made Magda wonder if the girl was really reading her thoughts. She said, "Yes; I think no man has ever meant more to you than that, not yet. You have, I think, the true spirit of an Amazon, and if you had been born among us, I think you would have come to us in the end. This must have been what Rohana saw in you."

She was silent for some time, thinking; suddenly she laughed.

"There is only one man living whom I love less than Rumal di Scarp," she said. "I would love to cheat Rumal of his prey! And you are oath-bound to obey all lawful commands of your employer. And there is a life between us; and it is required of me that I give my oath-daughter a gift. I will come with you, Margali, to Sain Scarp!"

Magda said, again with that sense of conflicting loyalties,

"Jaelle, I can never thank you for this, but first you should know: it will cause much trouble for you in Thendara. Lorill Hastur has forbidden anyone in the Domains to take part in this affair."

"You do not listen very well," Jaelle said. "I do my own thinking, not the blind will of Hastur. Like all people, I must obey the laws of the land, but the whims of Hastur are not yet the laws of Thendara, and Lorill Hastur has no right to forbid any Free Amazon, under the Charter, to accept any lawful work. Lorill Hastur is my kinsman—though the only time he saw and spoke with me he seemed not very eager to accept the relationship—but he is not the keeper of my conscience! The Free Amazons owe no allegiance to any liege lord, even if he calls himself the son of Hastur. And it seems to me that if the Terrans could give you, a woman, and born in Caer Donn, the strength and spirit to venture alone into the Hellers, and the—" She hesitated, looking away. "And at the same time, the integrity to honor an oath, even under such conditions of strain, then it seems to me that these *Terranan* might have something to teach even a Hastur, and that the Free Amazons should be their friends and allies. So I will give you leave, and I will help you, to rescue your friend."

Magda said hastily, "It must not be known that Peter is a Terran!"

"No, indeed! Rumal would take delight in hanging him from his castle wall that same day!" She held out her hands to Magda and said, "I think I can ride tomorrow; we will ride, then, for Sain Scarp."

Chapter 11

Before leaving the shelter, next morning, Jaelle insisted on stripping the bodies of the dead bandits; an unpleasant task, as they had frozen hard in the bitter cold. They dragged them away from the path. "The *kyorebni* and the scavenger wolves will do the rest," Jaelle said cheerfully. "We could never have buried them with the ground frozen hard, so they can do our work for us."

The day was overcast and grim as they set forth, and Magda was anxious about Jaelle; exposure to cold, with an unhealed wound, could be dangerous. Yet once the pass of Scaravel was closed, no amount of haste could bring them to Sain Scarp before Midwinter Night.

They made good time for the first three days; but on the fourth day it began to snow in earnest, and Jaelle looked troubled as they began to ride upward along the road to the pass.

"If we get through before dark, there is nothing to fear; Sain Scarp is a two-day ride beyond it, and there is nothing else so high as Scaravel. But if we are delayed today, or if we have to pass Scaravel in the darkness . . ." She was silent, frowning, obviously worried.

Near midday they came to a little village on the mountainside, where they bought some hot soup at a food-stall, and bargained for fodder for their animals. They were about to ride on when the lashings on Magda's pack animal suddenly gave way, and the pack slipped; the beast snorted and neighed, frightened by the bumping of the heavy pack hanging under its belly.

Magda slid down and ran to free it from the swaying bumping burden, but the frightened animal kicked and reared, and it was half an hour before, even with Jaelle's help, Magda could quiet the creature enough to get the remaining strap unbuckled and the pack off. Then they had to find a harness-maker who could mend the strap or make a new one; and when Jaelle came back after talking at length with the harness-maker (his dialect was so thick Magda could not understand him), she looked grave.

"Lady Rohana, with her escort, crossed Scaravel three days ago, on her way to Ardais," she said, "and the pass was open then; since then, no traveler has climbed toward the pass. We may find it blocked already; if not, this storm will surely close it till spring-thaw. Come what may, we must cross Scaravel tonight, or we cannot reach Sain Scarp in time. Let us find some more of that woman's good bean soup before we take the road; we'll get little warm food tonight."

Less than half a mile out of the village, Magda looked back down the trail and saw that the thickening snow had already blotted out the lights behind them. Jaelle wrapped a fold of her scarf across her bandaged cheek; her voice sounded muffled through it. "If these folk were not all living in the very shadow of Sain Scarp—and probably in their pay, or at least in fear of them—I think I would have left the horses here and tried the pass on foot. But I would not put such a strain on their honesty. There is a saying in the hills: 'Don't trust your bone to another man's dog.' "

It was less than an hour before they had to light their saddle-lanterns; the small lamps, fueled with resin, cast dim light for a few feet in every direction, but beyond that the light scattered into fog against the curtain of the falling snow. The trail was beaten deep between rocks, and Magda was glad, for the snow blotted out landmarks, and they might stray from the trail and never find it again. But when she said this to Jaelle, the other woman laughed through the muffling of the scarf.

"Just keep going up until there's no farther you can go! My-self, I'm glad of the snow; so near to Sain Scarp, Scaravel is no pass to travel alone in good weather. I have no doubt that is how your friend was taken! But on a night like this, even a bandit would be home by his own fireside!"

Higher and higher they rode, and Magda began to feel the dull, internal ache in ears and sinuses, born of the high altitude, which no amount of yawning or pressing her fingertips against her ears could completely dispel. The cold was bitter, and they began to feel the wind of the heights, which set the thick snow streaming almost sidewise against their faces and heaped it under their feet till they sank knee-deep in drifts and they had to dismount and lead their protesting horses. They moved slowly against the wind, each woman isolated in her own cocoon of darkness and silence. To Magda the world had shrunk to a circle less than ten feet wide, containing herself, the front half of her horse, the tail of Jaelle's saddle-horse just ahead and the soft crunching of the antlered pack beast that plodded along on his broad hooves after her lantern. Outside this narrow circle was nothing; only darkness and a wind that screeched like all the demons of Zandru's legendary ninth hell. Up, and again up, with the protest of knee muscles with every step, and her breath short. She wrapped her thick scarf heavily over her chin, and felt the wind freezing it, from the moisture of her breath, to an ice-mask.

She felt herself bump into something hard and soft at once, recoiled from the intrusion of something else into her private co-coon, and discovered it was Jaelle, who had turned her horse somewhat so it stood sidewise of the trail to block it. She put her head close to Magda's and shouted, "Let's stop for some food; it seems hours since we ate, and higher up it's dangerous to stop!"

They formed the animals into a triangle, nose to tail, and stood at the center of this crude windbreak, chewing on some dried-meat bars and fruit, which were the first things Magda could find at the top of the saddlebags. The world had shrunk so small that Magda found herself staring at the small pattern of blue birds knitted into the back of Jaelle's woolen mittens, and wondering if Jaelle had knitted them herself.

Then above them, sweeping down from the heights and even drowning out the shrieking wind, came a shrill, eerie cry; a long, paralyzing howl that made Magda's ears ring and almost physically paralyzed her. She gasped with the sound, then knew what it must be, even before Jaelle said: "Banshee. I was afraid of that; let's just hope the wind distorts its sense of direction. And remember it would rather have the horses than us, so keep in their shelter."

Magda had heard about—but never actually *heard*—the shattering, paralyzing scream of the great flightless carnivores who lived above the snowline and were attracted by the warmth and movement of their prey. Again the ghastly screech came, and it seemed to her that the meat-bar she was chewing had turned to leather in her mouth.

Jaelle was trying to make herself heard above the howl of the wind again. "What, Jaelle?"

"This is where we have to decide. I'm not an expert on Scaravel, but I *have* been over it in daylight, and I gather you haven't. Above here the trail narrows, so we can't turn around, and there's not even a level spot to spend the night. Beyond here, we're committed, because there's no stopping till we're on the other side. But it seems to be open now. It's a risk either way, but it's *your* risk, and your neck. Try it in the dark, or wait here? It's not a particularly good trail even by daylight."

Magda thought of the narrowing trail, the terrible carnivores of the heights, her own aching legs and wind-burned face. And Jaelle, beside her, was not really well enough to travel. *It's not Jaelle's mission at all. If I lead her to her death . . .*

"What would you advise?" Magda asked.

"I wouldn't advise; I'd try not to get into such a spot. But being in it, I'd probably go on. Just the same, I didn't want you to go at it thinking it's easy or safe, because it's not. This is your last chance to lose your nerve."

And this was the last chance. If they did not make it across Scaravel tonight, and it proved to be blocked by daylight after the night's snow . . . She said, "But what about you, Jaelle? You're still not strong—"

"There's almost as much risk to turn around here and go

down," Jaelle said, "and if we stay here, we might freeze. I can make it if you can."

Magda was not so sure; but having come so far, she was unwilling to retreat or give up. She swallowed the last of the dried meat, and said, "All right, then, we'll try. Want me to break trail? You've been doing it this far."

"From here on we don't break trail; we let the horses do it," said Jaelle, "and we stay between them, in case any banshee is prowling around looking for a midnight lunch!"

The trail was really steep now, but between the two saddle-horses, crowded together on the narrow path, the howling of the wind reached them less fiercely. The snow crunched hard underfoot, and they clung to the saddles on the horses to keep their footing. The trail twisted and turned between great rocks that gave some slight shelter from the wind, but now and then Magda caught, between the horses' legs or over their backs, a faraway and eerie glimpse of great chasms and cliffs, of dizzy gulfs of space dropping away from the trail; and, hastily turning her eyes back into the enclosing world—the horses on either side, Jaelle pressed close against her elbow—she was glad of the darkness that concealed the giddy heights to either side. They struggled along side by side, so close that Magda could hear the other woman's labored breathing; again and again, from the heights above them, they could hear that eerie, demoralizing banshee cry. The horses stirred and stamped; Magda's horse tossed its head, and she hauled on the bridle, trying to calm and quiet the frightened animal.

"Won't the saddle-lanterns attract the banshees, too?"

"No, they're blind," Jaelle said. "They sense warmth and movement, that's all. I remember—"

Magda never heard what she remembered. In the next moment there was another high, chilling banshee scream—this one almost on top of them—and a screech from the pack animal behind them, and Magda's horse reared, struggling, at the very edge of the cliff. The pack beast went down, screaming, plunging, kicking in the snow, and over its struggling body Magda caught a blurred glimpse of a huge, naked, buzzardlike head, an enormous ungainly body, the beak plunging into the pack animal's soft underbelly and rearing up, dripping gore. Magda pulled out her knife, backing away, waiting for the moment to strike. The naked head whipped around in her direction, weaving, darting, and Jaelle caught her wrist and dragged her back.

She said in a harsh whisper, "Let it eat! It's too late to save the animal, and if it's full it won't turn on us!"

Magda knew that made sense, but the screaming of the dying beast, the terrified screams of the other horses and the foul stench of the great predator turned her sick. She covered her face with her hands as the wicked talons struck down, scraping, raking, and the evil beak plunged down, again and again, as the banshee gorged his fill. Jaelle pulled Magda down behind the horses, and the women lay there concealed, trying not to hear or to see as the creature ate with little growling clucks and snarls.

God, those talons! One blow from them almost ripped the animal in half! Magda thought.

It seemed a long time before the banshee jerked up its huge head, darting it from side to side without interest, then plunged back once for a final tidbit and lumbered heavily away. The talons left great sloppy prints of blood and filth on the snow. Magda, struggling to control her sickness, got up slowly. The antlered pack beast lay almost still, and—this was the ultimate horror—whining thinly, still alive. Magda could not stand it. She bent swiftly, drew her knife across its throat, and with one final twitch, it lay still. Behind the horses Jaelle was lying in the snow, retching weakly, helplessly.

Magda went to her. "Come on! Help me get the pack off that thing, and onto our horses! And then let's get the hell away from here before all that thing's brothers and sisters come around looking for another helping!"

Jaelle came, wiping her face on her sleeve. Her face looked grotesque, red and blotched. "Oh, that was horrible—horrible—"

"It was. But it could have been a lot more horrible if it had grabbed one of us instead," Magda said, and bent over the dead animal to cut the straps that held the pack to the half-eaten carcass. *The same strap we so carefully had replaced in the vil-*

lage! With Jaelle's help she managed to haul it off the dead animal, though their hands were slimy with blood and entrails before they finished. Magda hoisted it to the back of her horse.
"We can divide up the load tomorrow," she said. "Right now
we'd better get moving."

Numbed by fatigue and horror, the women stumbled upward,
higher and higher; and suddenly, rounding a curve in the deep-
beaten trail, they were not climbing anymore. They stood in the
top of the pass of Scaravel, and there was no way to go but
down. Magda was too weary even to feel relieved. Jaelle was
stumbling with fatigue and weariness, and Magda wished it
were safe for her to ride. Certainly she could not go on much
longer.

The going was easier now, although the horses had a tendency to slip and stumble; before long Magda felt the lessening
ache in her ears that told they were losing altitude. She recalled
hearing that banshees nested only above the timberline; when
they reached the first clump of gnarled trees, thick wind-tangled
evergreens, she could feel the tension running out of her like
water. She stumbled along for another hundred feet or so, found
a thick grove of trees where the horses would be a little protected from wind and the still-falling snow. Jaelle was dazed, out
on her feet; she stood blinking, unaware what was going on.
Alone, Magda tied the horses and blanketed them, managed to
get up one of the tiny tents, got Jaelle out of her snow-caked riding-cloak and boots and shoved her into her blankets. She fell
into her own without stopping to take off anything but boots.
The tent was much too small for two—Magda had thought it
was too small for one—but claustrophobia was better than taking the time to get up the other one; besides, they needed the
warmth. She thought, as she fell asleep, *I'd bring the horses in
if I could get them in.* Even the faraway wail of another banshee—or the one who had attacked them?—could not keep her
awake.

The weather cleared in the night, and they looked on a dazzling white world, with evergreens bent almost double under
their weight of snow. When Magda dressed Jaelle's wounds,

they looked dull-white and macerated; they had been frozen, and this would make the scarring worse, but there was nothing to be done about it. She used some of the water she had boiled for porridge to try to clean them, but there was not much she could do. Jaelle ate listlessly, but she did eat, and Magda was glad; that glazed, numb look of exhaustion had frightened her. When she had done, she pointed to a low peak in the next range.

"Sain Scarp," Jaelle said. "If the weather holds we will be there tomorrow." Magda's eyes were sharp, but try as she might, she could see nothing but trees.

Jaelle laughed. "I doubt Rumal di Scarp will entertain us, so we may not have much of a Midwinter Feast this year! But no doubt your kinsman would rather eat porridge on the open road than feast with Rumal! And if the weather holds fine, we might reach Ardais by Midwinter; you cannot see it from here, though if you have good eyes you can see it from the very top of Scaravel. But I am not going back up to look now!"

Now that they were actually within sight of their goal, Magda found herself wondering about Peter again. How would he feel, to be rescued at a woman's hands? An hour later, as they rode down the trail through the melting snow, Jaelle voiced the same question.

"Your kinsman, will it damage his pride too much, to accept rescue at a woman's doing? Or don't the *Terranan* have that kind of pride?"

"Not usually. On other worlds men and women usually share the risks equally," Magda said. *But Peter was reared on Darkover, like me. And I found my Darkovan training too strong even for the Empire. Will it damage him, destroy him, as it might a Darkovan man?*

And suddenly Magda understood something about herself that she had never realized before.

Brought up as I was, at Caer Donn, only a Darkovan could have attracted me; they say the way you react to the opposite sex is conditioned before you're seven years old. None of the Terran men I knew seemed right, none of them had the right sort of emotional—or sexual—wavelengths for me. The sexual cues were all wrong. So Peter was literally the only man I knew to whom I reacted as to a male at all.

And when I was ripe for a love affair, he was the only man I knew; literally the only one. It wasn't that I cared more for him than others; it was that there were no others.

She realized that this might very well be the most important insight of her life, and resolved that she must somehow manage to hold on to it, even after she met Peter again.

Sain Scarp was an enormous fortress, isolated beyond a long rock causeway. The next day at noon the two women rode across the causeway, and Magda, at least, had the sense of eyes watching them from the tower at the far end. At the end of the causeway a big, rough-looking man stopped them, demanding their business.

Now. This is the culmination of it all; everything else that has happened—even the Amazon oath, dividing my life in two—was all for this. Strangely, Magda had almost forgotten that. She said, "I am the Free Amazon Margali n'ha Ysabet"—(how strange that sounded)—"come on a mission from the Lady Rohana Ardais. There is a prisoner and a ransom to be paid. Carry this word to Rumal di Scarp." They waited, shivering in the bright cold air, until the bandit chieftain came.

Afterward she could never remember what Rumal di Scarp looked like, except that he seemed a small man to carry such weight of rumor and horror tales: a small, wiry, hawk-faced man with fierce eyes. Behind Rumal, his hands bound, Magda saw a slender, familiar figure. *Peter!* He was thin and pale, dressed in shabby and torn mountain garments; a narrow fringe of coppery-red beard shadowed his face, but Magda knew him.

Rumal di Scarp came slowly toward them. "Well, *mestra,* I hear there is a ransom to pay. Who are you?"

Silently, Magda held out her safe-conduct; Rumal took it, handed it to the huge bandit at his side, who overshadowed him physically as much as the little man seemed to dwarf his giant companion in every other way. The man read it aloud to Rumal. "Lady Rohana Ardais . . . empowered to deal in a family matter . . ."

Rumal took the safe-conduct, crumpled it contemptuously and tossed it back to Magda. He said, laughing, "Gallant are the men of Ardais, that they send women to pay ransom for their menfolk! Why should I deal with you?"

Jaelle said, "Because I am the Lady Rohana's kinswoman, and if you do not honor your word I will spread it far and wide, from the Hellers to Dalereuth, that Rumal di Scarp does not honor his bargains. And then you may sit here in Sain Scarp and make soup from the bones of your captives for all the good they will be to you, since no one will ever again pay a single coin in ransom!"

Rumal made a gesture of contempt, signaled for Peter to be brought forward. "Well, there he is, heir to Ardais, whole and well, sound in wind and limb as a horse in spring market. And so, my ladies"—he used the intimate inflection, which made it sound even more contemptuous—"let us see the color of that ransom, then."

Magda knew her hands were trembling as she counted out the copper bars. Rumal shrugged, signaled to his giant henchman to wrap the ransom money in a cloth and take it away. "You have your kinsman. Take him away, then."

Jaelle looked at him defiantly, and said, "His horse and gear?"

"Oh, that," said Rumal. "That I kept to cover the cost of feeding him between snowfall and Midwinter Night, lest the ransom grow too great for one horse to carry." He said ironically to Peter, "Farewell, my Lord; fortunate is that man so loved by his kinsmen that they entrust him to a woman's ransoming. See that you repay these ladies well for their courtesy, my Lord, since no doubt it was only their pleas that persuaded the menfolk of your clan to ransom you at all. And now—" He made a deep, graceful bow, whose very courtly grace sent a shudder of horror through Magda, much worse than if he were ugly or deformed. "Farewell, *Dom*; a safe journey and a fortunate homecoming."

Peter made him a deep, equally ironic bow. "My thanks for your hospitality, *Messire* di Scarp. May I sleep the night in each of Zandru's hells in turn before I taste of it again."

"A churlish speech," Rumal drawled, "but the color of money is not brightened by courteous words—nor dimmed by boorish ones." He turned on his heel and walked away, not looking back.

Peter reached out and seized Magda's hands in a hard grip. His own were shaking. "It *is* you," he said. "I dreamed—I dreamed—" His voice caught, and for a moment she thought he was about to weep, but he managed to control it, clutching her fingers painfully hard in his own.

She said, and her heart was wrung with pity, "You are so thin and pale! Have they been starving you?"

"No, no, though the fare was not what I could have hoped for in the Hellers," he said, still clinging to her hands.

Jaelle broke in: "There is a horse for you at the end of the causeway; we traded for it in the last village. I thought Rumal would keep yours, as he did. I hope it suits you."

"*Mestra,* I would ride a rabbit, or walk from here to Thendara in my bare feet, it is so good to be beyond these walls," he said. "Come, let us get out of bow-shot. . . . How came this to be? I had utterly lost hope that you would ever know where I was, or how, even, I had died."

Jaelle was studying him curiously as they came to where they had left the horses. "I cannot believe it! This is not a joke? You are not my cousin Kyril? Are you truly—*Terranan?*"

"I am," Peter said, and glanced curiously at Magda. "Who—and what—?"

"She is my friend and sister, Peter," Magda said quietly, "and she knows who we are, so there is no need for pretense."

Peter bent over her slender hand. He said, "How can I speak my thanks, *mestra?* Midwinter Night is too near for me to pretend I was not afraid."

Jaelle looked back, saw that Rumal and his men had turned to watch them from the end of the causeway. She said, with a hesitant laugh, "Now, indeed, I believe you are not my cousin Kyril. I think he would rather be hanged in fragments from Rumal's walls than confess himself afraid!" She added, after a moment, "No doubt they are watching and wondering why you do not greet me as a kinswoman."

From anyone else Magda thought that would have sounded almost unbearably flirtatious; Jaelle only sounded embarrassed. Peter said, "That will be my pleasure, then—kinswoman." He bent forward and made as if to give her a brotherly embrace and kiss on the cheek. Jaelle colored and lowered her eyes; suddenly, gently, Peter took Jaelle's slender hand up in his again, bent and laid a light kiss on her wrist.

Magda, watching, thought unexpectedly, *I'm free of him. Before, I would have been unendurably jealous—to see that look in his eyes, turned on any other woman. I nearly went mad when he danced with Bethany at a New Year's party last year. Now I do not care.* Her love, her guilt, her concern, had been a part of her so long that she felt cold, flat and empty. Now she looked at him with sympathy, with concern for his thinness and pallor. . . . *As if he were my brother, my child. But not a lover. Not now.*

Jaelle started to move away, then suddenly reached out and caught Peter's hand. She said, "I cannot believe it. You are so like to my cousin Kyril, and yet . . . let me see your hands! How many fingers have you?"

"Normal number," said Peter, "four and a thumb—oh, my God!" He was looking down at Jaelle's slender hand, lying in his own. "You have six fingers on each hand," he said numbly.

"Yes. The Ardais and the Aillard blood—those who bear it have the extra finger," Jaelle said. "Is it wholly unknown among Terrans? Rohana is Aillard by birth, and her husband an Ardais; and all of her children have the Aillard hands." She began to laugh hysterically. "If Rumal had—had bothered to count your fingers—" she got out between spasms, "you would now be hanging—in pieces—from his castle wall."

She could not seem to stop laughing; Magda came and tried to calm her, and at last, really frightened, reluctant but afraid that it was the only way to stop her, took her shoulders and shook her hard. Jaelle began to cry as hysterically as she had laughed. "You'd be dead," she got out between sobs, "you'd be dead—"

She has ridden too far; she is still not strong. Magda said to

Peter, "Can you take her on your saddle? We must get away from here before nightfall," and watched as Peter tenderly lifted Jaelle on his horse, got on and supported the drooping girl, his arm holding her upright against him. Magda mounted her own horse, and took the reins of Jaelle's, leading it after them. And already—she realized a long time afterward—she knew then what was going to happen.

PART III

JAELLE n'ha MELORA,

Free Amazon

Chapter 12

The ceiling was painted blue, with a border and a design of little stars in gilt. At first Jaelle could not imagine where she was. Then she remembered that she had slept in this room during her one extended visit to Castle Ardais, in her sixteenth year.

"Before you renounce your heritage as *Comynara*," Kindra had warned her, speaking more seriously than she had ever before spoken to her foster-daughter, "you must first know what it is that you are renouncing." So to Ardais Jaelle had gone, protesting, to remain a full half-year. She had not been happy there; she had felt, she told Rohana once rebelliously, like a fish in a tree.

But I am not fifteen years old anymore! Why am I here? She shifted her weight, and at the sharp stab of pain in her wounded shoulder, remembered. Where were her Terran companions? They had come late at night, she remembered, and she had told the servants at the gate to bear word to the Lady Rohana that her kinswoman had come to spend Midwinter Night, bringing two friends. She remembered Rohana, graciously welcoming them all, and her dismay when she saw Jaelle's bandaged face. The rest was blurred.

Jaelle was lying in a big bed, wearing a long-sleeved nightgown, trimmed with lace at the neck and wrists. She supposed it belonged to Rohana, or to her daughter; she herself possessed no such garments, and it was too fine for a servant. One of the sleeves had been slit to accommodate the folds of bandage at her shoulder; her face, too, had been bandaged freshly. She looked around the room and saw a second bed near the window, and the Terran woman asleep in it, but at that moment Magda turned over and looked at her.

"You look better," she said. "When you were carried up here the night before last, I thought you were dying." Magda got out of bed and came to Jaelle's side. She, too, was wearing one of the lace-trimmed gowns, though she was so tall it came only midway down her calves. Her dark short hair had been washed and was curling around her cheeks.

Jaelle said, "I really don't remember anything after we got here; did you carry me here, or—" She hesitated, not remembering his Darkovan name, unwilling to use the Terran one where they might be overheard.

"No; *Dom* Gabriel himself did you that honor."

Jaelle smiled wryly. "Poor *Dom* Gabriel! How my kinswoman's husband dislikes me! Or, at least, dislikes having a Free Amazon in the family!"

"He seemed genuinely anxious about you," Magda protested, and Jaelle laughed a little. "Oh, anything belonging to Rohana he will treat kindly—pet dogs, Free Amazons, even Terrans, I suppose." She felt the smile stab ferocious pain through her bandaged face. "Does he know?"

"Rohana told him only that we were friends of yours," Magda replied. "She warned me afterward that the house was full of Midwinter guests, and we must be careful. Of course, when *Dom* Kyril met Peter, he was tremendously curious. He asked who Peter was, and Peter told him his usual tale—that he was born in Caer Donn, that he did not know his father's name. *Dom* Kyril said after that, 'Having seen you, I think I could put a name to your father's clan, at least.' And, like you, he looked at once at his hands."

Jaelle lay back, astonished at herself. *So weary, after sitting up only a few minutes?* Her shoulder throbbed as if it were afire. "Where is—where is he?"

"Alseep in the next room," Magda said, pointing to the connecting door. "Lady Rohana apologized that she could give us only these rooms; I told her that in any case you should not be left alone at night. You slept all of yesterday; you did not wake even when *Domna* Alida came to dress your wounds."

"So I have lost a day," Jaelle said. Now she remembered, fuzzily, how they had come here. Rumal di Scarp would be expecting them to head at once for Ardais; would find it suspicious if they turned in any other direction. In any case, Scaravel was blocked behind them by the snow. Magda had felt that since Lady Rohana had arranged this mission, she had a right to know of its success.

Jaelle remembered, too, how Peter had ridden at her side, had helped her whenever they stopped to rest the horses. Much of that time, she had been in a daze of pain and weariness, but she remembered how when they stopped, he had coaxed her to eat, and how, when she could no longer sit in her saddle without falling, he had taken her again before him on his saddle and held her against him. All else was blurred, but she could remember, with a sharp tactile memory, the feel of his arms around her. She had been ashamed of her weakness and secretly a little glad of it, for it let her lean against him, rest her head on his shoulder through the swaying dizziness of pain and fever. . . .

She thought, with a sharp sting of guilt, *Appeal to no man for protection* . . . and closed her eyes, feeling tears of weakness sliding down her cheeks. She felt Magda's gentle hand on her wrist. "I will let Lady Rohana know you are awake," she said.

Rohana came before long, small and queenly in a fur-trimmed gown; she bent and kissed Jaelle on the cheek not covered with the bandage. "How are you feeling, my child? And how came you by this dreadful wound? Margali has told me very little, only that you fought for her."

"I suppose she did not tell you that she saved my life," Jaelle said, "nor that she is oath-bound to the Guild, and my sister."

Rohana asked very seriously, "Is this allowed, my child, that a *Terranan* should be accepted by Oath into the Guild?"

"The Guild-mothers must give the final decision on that," Jaelle said, "but the Guild Charter excludes no woman; it is the Oath, not the parentage, which makes an Amazon under the

Charter. And my sister chose to honor her Oath; to stay and fight for me, and to care for me afterward, when she could easily have abandoned me to die."

Rohana said gently, "Then she is kinswoman here, too, my darling." Relieved, Jaelle slipped back into exhausted sleep—or stupor—again, and over her head Rohana's eyes met the Terran woman's. "Someday you must tell me how this came about."

"I am not sure myself," Magda said with a troubled smile, "but I will honor my Oath, whatever comes."

"For her sake? Only for friendship?"

"No. Not entirely. Perhaps—" Magda hesitated, searching for words. "Perhaps because I have two worlds to serve, and I think I can best honor both loyalties this way."

"And your husband? What will he say to this?"

"He is not my husband in law; we parted more than a year ago. Certainly he is not the keeper of my conscience."

"I thought—" Rohana stopped. Like all telepaths, she had a horror of seeming to intrude in any personal matter. But it had seemed to her, when she met Magda in the Trade City, that the Terran woman was wholly committed to her former lover; and she had had misgivings when she saw Magda in Amazon garb. It had seemed to her that in spite of the spirit and strength she had admired, Magda was all too feminine for the part she must play. It had seemed to her that Magda was much like herself, committed to taking a man's part for a woman's reasons.

She felt completely at a loss; and that was a new sensation for Rohana. It also roused questions she thought she had settled, completely and without any doubts, years ago. She was glad to put her self-questioning aside when Magda asked, "Is it right for Jaelle to sleep so much? Is she worse than I feared?"

"I do not know: Alida says that neither wound is healing as it should. She will know more today."

"It is my fault," Magda said, looking down at Jaelle with dread. Asleep or unconscious again? "She exhausted herself trying to help us."

Rohana's hands closed very lightly over hers. Magda did not yet know enough of the telepath caste to know how very rare a gesture it was, or what trust it indicated. "My dear child, don't blame yourself. Since Kindra died, there has been no one, no one at all who could make Jaelle do anything she did not want to do, or prevent her from doing her own will; so whatever she did was freely done." She looked down at Jaelle with a detached, sad tenderness. She said, and Magda felt that Rohana was not really speaking to her at all, "In many ways she is dearer to me than my own daughter. Yet I have known for many years that I must let her take her own way."

She turned to go. "*Domna* Alida will see her this morning; she is Tower-trained, and has great skill in such matters." She went away.

Shortly after, Peter came through the connecting door. "How is Jaelle?" he asked, in a low, troubled voice.

Magda repeated what Rohana had said, and he shook his head, dismayed. "I hate to think she would put herself in such danger for us," he said. "But listen to me, Magda; we have to leave here, as soon as we can. You know we can't stay here for Midwinter, as Lady Rohana expects, when there might be someone here who recognizes us!"

"Rohana won't tell."

"Perhaps not. But among the household there are two or three men from Caer Donn who may recognize me . . . remember me from the days when Terrans and mountain men could mingle freely. If they do . . ."

Magda was sympathetic, but for the moment another concern seemed more important. She said, "I cannot go without Jaelle's leave; perhaps I cannot go at all. Certainly I would not go while she is ill and needs me." She flung at him, in sudden rage, "Does an oath mean nothing to you?"

"Not one wrested from you by force," Peter said, "and in any case you had no right to give it. I know you were forced into it, but still—"

It was her own reasoning, and it made her angrier than ever, as he went on, persuasively, "I know you have always had a great love for pretending yourself Darkovan, and a pride in your skill at it. But there is a time to forget all that. Your first loyalty is to the Empire—do I have to remind you of that?"

He had taken her hands in his; she wrenched them away. "Then say I *chose!* I feel I can serve best this way, but if it comes to choice . . . !" She was trembling all over. He said, trying to conciliate, "I didn't realize you felt like that; you know I would never interfere in a matter of conscience, Mag. But why does this girl mean so much to you? It's not like you to have this kind of—this kind of emotional attitude over another woman. It's not quite—" He hesitated, unwilling to say it, and Magda, guessing what he refused to say, was angry again.

"Think anything you damn please! If you believe that, you'll believe anything!"

"Mag, I didn't say I believed—"

"You're a fool, Peter," she said in disgust. "Do you really believe no woman could be loyal to another woman out of common humanity and integrity? Jaelle saved my life; and do I have to remind you that if she had not risked hers to cross Scaravel Pass with an unhealed wound, you would still be counting the days to Midwinter Night in Rumal's dungeons? And you want me to leave her, not even knowing if she will live or die, or be scarred for life?"

"Do *you* need to remain? I thought these people were her closest kinfolk!"

"Yes," Magda said, "but by Oath she has had to renounce all her kinfolk; as her oath-daughter I am the closest kin she has beneath this roof." She said this with absolute certainly, knowing that, in spite of Rohana's deep affection for Jaelle, she would have said the same thing. Rohana had taken it for granted that Magda had a duty, and a right, to stay with Jaelle and care for her; more than Rohana's own right. Camilla had said, jesting, that Rohana was still ignorant about the ways of Free Amazons. But she had her finger on the very pulse of what they meant to one another; more, Magda knew, than she herself did.

Peter's anger had been short-lived, as always. He said, "Probably you know best, Mag; you usually do. And Midwinter Feast is the time for hospitality; probably a couple of extra guests will never be noticed." He walked to Jaelle's side, and stood looking down at her.

"How beautiful she is," he said softly, "or how beautiful she would be, without that terrible scar! How could a woman like that renounce love and marriage?"

Jaelle opened her unbandaged eye; her vision was blurry and unfocused. She said, "It is not love we renounce . . . only marriage . . . bondage. . . ." she stretched out her hand, and Peter knelt beside the bed, taking her hand in his. Her eyes fell shut again, but she kept hold of him.

He was still kneeling there when the door opened again and Lady Rohana came in, with *Dom* Gabriel's sister, who had been described to Magda as a *leronis*. The title translated, usually, as "sorceress" or "wise-woman"; Magda suspected it meant, in this case, "healer." Her name was Alida. She was a small, slight woman with flaming red hair, younger by some years than Rohana, and with a kind of indefinable arrogance which made Magda, for some reason, think of Lorill Hastur.

Lady Alida inclined her head in the faintest of courteous greetings to Magda. She ignored Peter. She pulled back Jaelle's blankets and began to unfasten the cutaway nightgown; then looked, in unmistakable command, at Peter. He had been brought up in the mountains near Caer Donn and understood perfectly well; actually it was even somewhat scandalous that he should have been in the room when Magda was not fully dressed. He let go Jaelle's hand, but she quickly clasped it again, opening her eyes.

She said; "I want him to stay!" She sounded like a child, and Magda wondered if she were delirious again.

Lady Alida shrugged. "Stay, then, if she wants you. But take her other hand, and keep out of my way." Peter obeyed, and Alida, with some minor help from Rohana, got the bandages undone to examine the ugly wounds. Even Magda could see that they were not healing properly, but were swollen and festered. The clean slash on the face had spread and reddened, the nick in the eyelid so swollen that Jaelle's eye was shut.

"This is a poisoned wound! How came she by it?"

Briefly, Magda recounted their fight with the bandits. Lady Alida made a fastidious grimace. "That is no work for women!"

Jaelle flushed with anger. She said pettishly, "I do not need to be told you do not approve of my way of life, kinswoman, but courtesy should prevent you from insulting my sister and guest before me!"

Rohana said in haste, "Alida meant no offense—did you, kinswoman?"

Alida paid no attention to either of them. "What has happened to *your* wound, *mestra?*"

After a moment Magda realized that she was being addressed, and pushed up the long sleeve of the nightgown she was wearing. "It is healing."

"But not as it should," Alida said, her light, cold fingers gently touching the red seam, still puckered and inflamed. "A cut like this should long be closed and sealed, with not even an itch remaining. This still gives you some pain, I can tell—does it not?"

"Yes, a little," Magda said. She had so little experience with such cuts that she had thought it natural. She saw Peter looking up, in surprise and consternation, at her bare arm and the red seam there, and she pushed her sleeve down to cover it.

Alida said, "Jaelle must have been wounded first, and got most of the poison."

Rohana sounded anxious. "Can you help it, Alida?"

"Oh certainly. I learned to treat such wounds at Neskaya Tower; it is nothing much. You were Tower-trained in Dalereuth as a girl; can you monitor for me?"

Rohana nodded. "Certainly."

But Rohana watched, faintly troubled, as Alida uncovered her matrix jewel. She knew she should send the two Terrans away. This, she knew, was one reason why Lorill Hastur had interdicted any serious contact between Terran and Darkovan; he was unwilling they should learn anything about the ancient matrix sciences. Yet, if she should make a point of dismissing Magda and Peter from the room now, she must explain why.

She had told no one here that they were Terrans, but she was sure Gabriel guessed. When he had seen Peter's almost unbelievable likeness to their son Kyril, and heard that he was the prisoner from Sain Scarp, he must have known; but he did not really want to know, Rohana realized, that she had gone against his wishes again. *Because then I would have to tell him, in so many words, that he is not the keeper of my conscience; and even now I do not think Gabriel wants to know that in a way he cannot pretend to ignore.*

And the woman, Magda, was Jaelle's oath-sister and had a right to remain. As for the man—she saw Jaelle clinging to his hand, saw the tenderness in his eyes, and knew what neither of them knew themselves, as yet.

"Put that away, Lady Alida. I will have none of your sorcery," Jaelle said weakly.

"I must, child. There is poison in the wound and it is spreading to your eye; it can damage your sight. If I do not treat it now . . ."

"I do not care," said Jaelle in great agitation. "I will not allow—"

Rohana said sternly, "Stop it, Jaelle. You are behaving like a frightened child who will not have a cut bandaged! I had not believed you so cowardly!"

Alida's voice was kinder. "I know you were afraid of me when you were a child, Jaelle, but I hoped you had outgrown your fear."

"I am not afraid," Jaelle said, shaking with anger, "but I will not have you meddling with my mind! Once is enough for a lifetime!"

Suddenly Rohanna recalled what Jaelle was talking about. On that single extended visit to Ardais, which she had demanded before allowing Jaelle to take the Amazon's Oath, she had insisted that Jaelle be tested for *laran;* Melora's child, and with the flame-colored hair that marked the telepath strain, would surely have one of the *Comyn* gifts. Jaelle had been frightened and helplessly reluctant, but on this point Rohana would not be moved. Alida had done the testing, and Jaelle had come away white as a corpse and looking deathly ill. It was the only time since her mother's death that Rohana had ever seen Jaelle in tears. When Rohana had sent her away, a little calmed and comforted, Alida had said:

"Yes, she has *laran;* I think she is a powerful telepath, but for some reason she is blocking it. I could break her defenses, of course; but whether I could ever put them together again afterward—that is another matter. And since you have allowed her to be fostered among the Amazons, I think she would find life intolerable in a Tower. Let her take her own way."

Rohana had left it at that. She had complied with the law that every child of *Comyn* blood—legitimate or illegitimate; and in law Jaelle was illegitimate—must be tested. More was not necessary. She was sure it was the shock of rapport with her dying mother that had forced Jaelle to barricade her own *laran,* but she had not tried to find out.

But was Jaelle's fear still so acute? *Domna* Alida only said, unoffended, when Jaelle swore at her, "You are ill, Jaelle. You do not know what you are saying. Shall I really put you to the indignity of having your hands tied?"

Magda almost cried out: "No, you mustn't!"

"Jaelle," Rohana persuaded, "you are not one of those Amazons who makes a great thing of swaggering and comparing scars."

Alida said coolly, "If she wishes to end her days looking like a battle-scarred veteran of the campaigns at Corresanti, that is her affair; I am only concerned about her eyesight!"

Peter was still holding Jaelle's hand in his. He raised his free hand to Jaelle's cheek, caressed the smooth skin below the red slash. He said, as if there were no one in the room but himself and Jaelle, "You are so beautiful. It would be so dreadful to let that beauty be spoiled."

Jaelle moved her other hand, clumsily, toward his; and Magda knew—they all knew—that she would not protest further.

That wasn't fair, Magda thought. *Jaelle is too vulnerable. Peter should not have done it. . . .*

Lady Alida moved her hand, and Magda could see the blue

stone in it—a jewel? A brilliant flash, a twisting, sickening *glare* . . . Magda turned her eyes away, unable to endure the sight. The *leronis* said quietly, "You were too busy cursing me to let me explain, Jaelle, but I need not touch your mind for this. I am going to be doing some very delicate cell-reconstruction work, so you must lie as quietly as possible, and try to make your mind as blank as you can, so that your thoughts will not interfere. You can sleep if you wish; it will be all the better if you do. I do not think you will feel any pain, but if you do you must tell me at once, so that your pain will not blur what I am doing."

Magda listened, in amazed curiosity. Hypnosis? All that about making her mind a blank . . . ?

"Rohana, you must monitor," Alida instructed. "And you must warn me if I come too close to the nerves, or to the small muscles near the corner of the eye," Alida warned, and again the blue jewel flashed in her hand. Magda felt a little, twisting ripple deep in her body, almost a sickness. Alida looked up, her face now remote and masklike, looking at Magda without really seeing her.

"Do not look directly at the matrix, *mestra;* many people cannot endure the sight."

Magda turned her eyes away, but found them drawn back. *Fakery, nonsense; but what are they going to do to Jaelle?*

Rohana approached Jaelle, bending over her; ignoring Peter, who still knelt on the far side of the bed, holding Jaelle's hands. Jaelle's eyes had fallen shut again. Rohana ran her fingertips along Jaelle's face, not quite touching her; down across the bared shoulder and the swollen, horribly festered wound there. It seemed to Magda that a line of light followed Rohana's fingertips, began to glow along Jaelle's skin . . . *As if I could see the bones through the skin. . . .*

Rohana said,—*No, not the bones, the nerve currents that lie among them. . . .* But Rohana had *not* spoken, not raised her head; she was bending intently over Jaelle.

Alida was holding the jewel stone before her eyes with one hand, her face set in an almost inhuman calm. Now Magda could see, around the two wounds, a dull pulsing, a kind of glow around the inflamed flesh.

Alida said, "Now," and Rohana began to move her fingertips along the wound in the collarbone and shoulder. She did not touch Jaelle, but as the small lines of light followed her fingers, the swollen flesh seemed to move and ripple, dull colors swirling inside it; to heave, tremble and change color, from angry inflamed red to thick festering purple and then, almost, to a dull black, the lights in the flesh dimming, pulsing. Magda caught her breath; was this some ghastly hypnotic illusion? Blood oozed from the wound.

"Careful," Rohana said tonelessly.

The rippling surface of the open wound slowly paled, turned purple again, and as the lights around it brightened, turned red, then a smooth, healthy pink. . . .

Rohana shifted her hands, drawing her fingertips above the repulsive open gash across Jaelle's face. Alida brought the blue jewel stone close, and Magda, seeing it without sickness this time, found herself caught up in what was happening. She saw with a curious double vision those nerve currents under the skin, the slashed and broken and infected layers of skin and muscle and escaped, oozing blood, the seeped poison around the eye . . . she *felt,* with an inner itch and tension inside her mind, what Alida was doing: lowering her consciousness farther and farther, *into* the cells, exerting the tiniest pressures (*How! How?*) on each cell, so that she actually *felt* the blood and poison as pressures against the light-lines of the nerves, sensed the tiny, delicate membranes, the pressures against them. . . .

"Careful," Rohana said again, a low soft neutral sound, but to Magda, deep inside Alida's awareness, it was like a shriek of warning; and with infinite caution, Alida eased the carefully intricate pressures, moved her touch away from a small ruptured blood vessel, felt and almost *saw* the tiny tensions of fluids so near the eyeball, the glowing inner mechanism of the eyeball and tear ducts, so near, dangerously near. *Ease up just there.* . . . Something in the back of Magda's mind said, *Psychokinesis:* the power of the mind to exert delicate cellular changes. Her consciousness seemed wholly sunk inside that light, bending pressure. She looked at Jaelle from a great distance. *As if I were up somewhere near the ceiling and looking down.* . . . Giddy shifts of perspective.

Magda thought, somewhere back in her mind, *I can do that, too,* and found her attention focused on the healing slash in her own arm, sensed the inner pressures, somehow *wrenched* them into consciousness, feeling a faint sting of violent pain, somehow *outside* herself, which vanished without trace. . . .

She shook her head as if to clear it. She was standing firmly on her own feet, and Alida had covered the blue stone. She blinked as if dizzy, and looked down at Jaelle in amazement and shock. There was now no hideous, festering slash crisscrossing Jaelle's cheek; only a narrow, bright red seam, still jagged and raw, from which one drop of clean blood oozed. The nick in the eyelid was gone, and the closed eye, beneath its fringe of lashes, was no longer swollen.

Alida drew a long sigh of weariness. Mechanically Magda pushed up her sleeve, staring in puzzlement at where the bandit had gashed her arm with his poisoned blade. There was no puckered red line there now; only a firm white scar, which looked long healed. *Did I dream it?*

Alida thrust the wrapped stone inside the front of her dress. She looked at Magda, with a questioning frown, but did not speak to her. "Jaelle?"

Rohana touched Jaelle's forehead lightly. "She is asleep, I think."

"Good; while she sleeps the healing will be finished," Alida said, and gestured to Peter. "Leave her."

He tried gently to withdraw his hand, but the fingers were locked around it. He settled himself into a comfortable position on the floor and said, "I'll stay."

Magda tiptoed to Jaelle's side and drew the nightgown up over the girl's bare shoulder and breast, covered her with a blanket, then followed Rohana and Alida out of the room. Alida stumbled, almost fell against the door; Rohana caught and steadied her on her feet. She said, "Go and rest, Alida. And I thank you for Jaelle's sake."

Magda's mind was whirling. It was *not* illusion! That terrible, festering wound, like a great open, oozing sore . . . and now, as she covered Jaelle with her nightgown, it had not even needed a bandage, but was clean and almost healed. There was also her own arm; it looked like a scar a year old. And somehow, with the aid of the blue jewel, this had all been done through the powers of the mind. *Psi power. I never believed in it, not really. But I saw it. . . .*

Rohana saw Magda trembling, reached out and gently steadied her as she had done with Alida. She said, "Rest, my girl, that is strenuous work. Why did you not tell us you had *laran?*"

And Magda could only stammer, confused and dismayed, "I don't even know what the word *means!*"

Chapter 13

On the eve of Midwinter Day, the long-delayed blizzard swept down from the Hellers, a thick white wilderness of snow and howling wind that effectively damped the preparations for the festival. The house-party guests had already arrived, but Lady Rohana told her guests, with some disappointment, that the usual festivities would have to be suspended. Normally, everyone who lived within a day's ride would have visited Castle Ardais at some time during the day to share in the merrymaking there.

Magda expressed polite regrets for the spoiling of the holiday, but was herself secretly relieved not to have to face more strangers. She had no personal fear. *Dom* Gabriel would not make trouble for his wife's guests, whoever they were; and the strong tradition of hospitality in the Hellers made it unlikely that they would meet with any personal unpleasantness. But it might well mean that other Terrans, after this, would be more carefully watched and restricted in their travel.

Lady Rohana had holiday gifts for them both: long riding-capes trimmed with fur. She also tactfully offered them garments more suitable for the festival, pointing out that they had only traveling clothes with them, and those much the worse for wear. Magda accepted with relief, Jaelle with a wry laugh. She said when Rohana had gone away, "My kinsman is cowardly, to make Rohana do his errands! Margali, you are a translator by trade; see if you can interpret this as I do! I may not have the words quite right, but the music is very clear, and the tune is something like this: 'I refuse to have two Amazons in trousers at my banquet-table!' "

Magda politely refrained from comment on her host, but she felt Jaelle was probably right. Jaelle was up and around now, though until today confined to her room, but she was recovering so swiftly that Magda still doubted the evidence of her own eyes. But there it was before her: the healed scar on Jaelle's collarbone, the red line—perceptible, and a little startling, but no longer disfiguring—across her cheek.

It makes Terran medical science look primitive! Magda thought.

But if it was psi force, what was the function of the blue jewel? Was it only a focus? Magda knew she would never rest till she knew the answer to these questions. The key seemed to be the strange word *laran,* which was colloquially translated as an art, skill, gift or talent; she surmised that a *leronis* was one who used *laran,* and that the meanings of "wise-woman" or "sorceress" were ancillary. Jaelle verified this guess, adding that *laran* meant an inborn gift for psi power, and that while she herself had a little of it, she had not wanted to be trained in its use. When Magda repeated Rohana's remark—that she herself seemed to have *laran*—Jaelle shut up and could not be persuaded to say another word.

In midafternoon the promised festival dresses arrived, brought by one of Rohana's women. Magda's was a rust-colored gown with narrow sable fur trim, and trailing sleeves lined with golden silk; it was one of the prettiest dresses she had ever seen, and fitted her well enough. She felt a twinge of regret as she put it on and brushed her dark smooth hair, thinking of the silver butterfly-clasp that she would never wear again.

Jaelle said, "Among Terran women, is close-cropped hair thought a disgrace?"

"Oh, no. Most women in Empire service wear their hair little longer than men; but I have lived on Darkover most of my life, and kept mine long to be able to mingle unnoticed with women here, so I am accustomed to long hair," Magda said. "I had half expected to be told that Amazons were not allowed to wear women's dress! Is this simply a courtesy to *Dom* Gabriel, then, Jaelle?"

Jaelle laughed merrily. She had put on the delicate green gown Rohana had sent her. She said that it had been made for her cousin, Rohana's seventeen-year-old daughter, whose name was Elorie but who was usually called Lori. With a little pinning at the waist, it fitted Jaelle beautifully. As she brushed her own hair into a burnished coppery helmet and fastened it with a pair of gold bar-clasps from her saddlebags, she said, "Oh, no! Do you think we wear trousers compulsively, like men, you silly girl? We wear them when we have to ride, or work like men, but in the Guild-house, or when working indoors, we wear whatever seems comfortable to us. We are not *required* to wear anything in particular; we simply refuse to accept the social rule that *forbids* women to wear any comfortable garment for reasons of modesty or custom. The only thing we *may* not wear—by our Charter—is a sword." Again, she laughed. "Kindra chided me, now and then, that I spent so much of what I earned on finery; I probably have as many pretty gowns as Rohana, or more, because I need not account to anyone for what use I make of my money!"

Magda felt a little relieved; she was not fond of fine clothes, in particular, but she would have felt strange to think of spending the rest of her life in rough and unattractive work clothes!

Jaelle said delightedly, when they were ready to go down, "I had no idea you were so pretty! When I first saw you, you looked like a half-frozen rabbit, and after that I have not been able to notice!"

Magda herself had been aware of Jaelle's astonishing beauty, even in rough Amazon dress; in the green gown, she was breathtaking. She saw her own opinion confirmed when Peter joined them in the hallway, outside their connecting rooms; he looked at Jaelle in delighted amazement. She smiled at him shyly, and lowered her eyes; Magda knew Jaelle was embarrassed at recalling how she had clung to him when she was weak and ill. Jaelle did not offer him her hand as she had done readily during her illness; strangely, the very omission seemed to create a greater closeness than the frank gesture. *She reacted to him as a child reacts then. Now she is very aware that he is a man and she a woman,* Magda thought.

Peter said softly, "I am very happy to see you recovered, Jaelle," and with something of her own constraint, turned to Magda, and offered her his arm. She took it, mostly because she sensed his embarrassment and tension and it was an old habit, to cover his indecision.

"Have you noticed how like our own celebrations this is? The halls decorated with greenery, the great fire, the exchanged gifts—even the smell of the spicebread!"

She knew he was only saying the first thing that came into his head, to cover embarrassment; it roused an old emotion, a mixture of tenderness and exasperation, so familiar that she felt an old, inner trembling.

"You are lovely, Magda. But I miss your lovely long hair—" He put up his hand to touch the bare nape of her neck: a gesture of intimacy, permitted only to lovers. Magda felt embarrassed. She said in a low voice, "Don't, Piedro." She used his Darkovan name deliberately, to remind him of where they were. Yet she knew it had had exactly the reverse effect; it had recreated the old intimacy.

He said, "Margali," speaking her Darkovan name like a special caress. She saw Jaelle's eyes on them and dropped his hand as if it burned her, so that they went into the Great Hall side by side, but not together.

The kindled Midwinter Fire burned on the great hearth, and *Dom* Gabriel, Lord of Ardais, stood before it, a tall, soldierly man, with graying russet hair, dressed in green and scarlet. When Jaelle stepped toward him with a formal bow, he clasped her, briefly, in a kinsman's embrace, pressing his lips to her cheek.

"I rejoice that you are well enough to join us, Jaelle. A pleasant year to you, and all happiness."

"I thank you for your hospitality, for myself and my friends, Uncle," Jaelle said, and stepped along, to be warmly hugged by Rohana and to exchange greetings with her cousins. Magda and

Peter stood before the Ardais lord; he bowed over her hand, raising his eyes to hers with a puzzled, kindly smile. Madga thought
of what Jaelle had said: "Anything belonging to Rohana he will
treat kindly—pet dogs, Free Amazons, even Terrans . . . !" It
seemed to her for a moment that Jaelle had been hard on him;
from the very touch of his hand she sensed he was a decent man
and a kind one, if a little narrowed by the prejudices of his caste,
and without much imagination. Anyway, if Rohana loved and
obeyed him, he must have more virtues than Jaelle could see in
him.

"Welcome, *mestra,* as my kinswoman's friend; a pleasant
holiday to you, and a fortunate year."

Magda, recalling the New Year's greeting of her Caer Donn
childhood, said, "My year will be brightened by the memory of
your hospitality; may the fires of your hearth never grow cold,
Lord Ardais," and saw the puzzlement grow in his eyes. As she
moved on to exchange formal greetings with Rohana and her
grown children, she thought, *He obviously knows we are Terrans. Is he surprised that we can manage ordinary politeness?*
She wondered if the Ardais lord really thought that a race which
could create a Galactic empire were all ignorant boors without
any sense of good manners. . . .

Lady Alida, at one of the long tables, raised her eyes, looked
directly at Magda and beckoned; Magda could think of no polite
way to ignore the invitation. The *Comyn* lady wore a festival
gown of pale blue; her red-gold hair was coiled low on her neck.
She gestured to Magda to sit next to her, and Magda felt the little prickles of "hunch" touching her again. Alida was a *Comyn*
lady, a *leronis,* and gifted with psi power. A mere trace of this,
in Jaelle, had given Magda away. How could she manage not to
betray herself?

For a time, everyone's attention was on the small delicacies
of the table: a clear soup with golden slices of some delicious
mushroom floating in it; small, hot savory tidbits of different
kinds; spicebread in all sorts of ornamental shapes, gilded and
decorated. But as these were taken away, and the servants—in
their holiday garments, and joining in the feast they helped to

serve—brought the main courses, Alida turned to Magda and said, "While your sworn sister was ill and needed your care, I would not call you from her side, *mestra.* But now she is well," and she looked at Jaelle, laughing between Peter and her cousin and obviously teasing them about their resemblance. "I wanted a word with you. Have you never been tested for *laran,* Margali?"

"No. Never."

"But surely you were aware of your inborn talent, were you not?"

"No," Magda said again, and a faint frown furrowed the lady's high pale forehead.

"But surely . . . as you know, it wakes normally at adolescence; had you no hint of this gift? Or were you committed so early to the life of a Free Amazon that you did not ask for this testing?"

That would have been a good escape, but the lie was too easily discovered; it was a matter of record that she had only recently been made a Free Amazon. She fell back on the literal truth. "Until the other day, my Lady, I had no idea that I had the faintest trace of *laran.* It came as a great surprise to me."

"Well, when Midwinter Festival is over, we must have you properly tested," Alida said, as if the matter were settled. How, Magda wondered, would she get out of *this?* With definite relief, she remembered something else. She never would have believed herself capable of putting this forth with positive pleasure. "After Midwinter, Lady, my duties commit me to the Guild-house."

Lady Alida brushed that aside. "Something will be arranged. An untrained telepath is a danger to herself and everyone around her, and that would apply to all your sisters of the Guild-house." She said no more, politely calling her guest's attention to the musicians who had come to entertain them, and would play later for the dancing.

But enough had been said to ruin Magda's appetite. What was she going to do now?

When the meal ended, the older guests gathered around the

midwinter-fire for gossip and reminiscence (Magda knew these house parties, held when the weather brought all outdoor work to a standstill, were reunions of friends who often did not meet from year to year) while the younger people descended into the lower hall for dancing. Magda had learned to dance as a child—a girl could not reach her eighth year in Caer Donn without learning to dance, and to dance well—and knew most of these dances.

Although she took part with pleasure when Jaelle and Lori drew her into a ring-dance with a dozen other girls, she did not know what the rules of Amazon etiquette were for dancing with men after the group dances gave way to dancing in couples. But after a time, seeing Jaelle laughing and flirting and dancing with all comers, she grew less hesitant. She accepted the invitations, enjoying it on two levels: the Terran agent making mental notes (But would she ever really be that again?), and, to her own surprise, the young girl she had been in Caer Donn, mingling for the first time with young men. It was, literally, the first time since childhood when she had felt herself actually in the company of her own kind.

Magda had never realized until this moment quite how much her curious, between-worlds childhood had robbed her of the ability to mingle with people her own age. Childhood in Caer Donn had prepared her, emotionally and socially, for adolescence and maturity in the same world; instead, before adolescence, she had been torn away and isolated in the Terran Zone with children whose background was only that of the Empire; and at sixteen she had been sent off-world for training. She had felt isolated and completely at a loss with girls or boys her own age in the Empire. Later, when she could mingle with Darkovans in the course of her work, there were many inhibitions against allowing any purely personal contacts; and in any case Darkovan women met men only in their homes and under the proper sponsorship of their families.

But now, as Rohana's guest, she could join in freely. *If I had been exposed to a little of this when I was twenty I would never have married Peter.* The thought troubled her for some reason, and she was glad to turn to a young man of *Dom* Gabriel's household who came up to her, asking for a dance. After a time he said, "Is your name—Margali?"

"Yes, that is what they call me."

"I thought so! You had another name, but none of us could pronounce it, so we called you by that one. You are *Toroku* Lorne's daughter, are you not?" The title was the equivalent of "learned man" or "professor," and had been given her father by the local children. "I knew you when we were children; you used to have dancing lessons with my sisters, Tara and Renata. I am Darrill, son of Darnak."

Now she remembered Darrill, and his sisters. She had once spent Midwinter Night with Renata when she was quite small; she had played with them, visited in their home, and brought them to her own home in the HQ. Darrill had been an older boy, out of their orbit.

He said, "I thought all of you Terrans had gone to Thendara and would not return to the Hellers. What are you doing here?"

"I am Lady Rohana's Midwinter guest—or rather, the guest of her kinswoman Jaelle."

Darrill demanded, "Do they know who you really are? I am *Dom* Gabriel's sworn man, and if you are here under false pretenses, Lord Ardais should know!"

Magda said, trying to control her inner trembling, "My true name and my purposes are known to Lady Rohana; you may ask her if you wish. And I suppose, since she knows, that *Dom* Gabriel knows as well."

He said with a faint grin, "I suppose so; but if the lady knows, it does not really matter whether *Dom* Gabriel knows or not, since it is well known from here to the Kadarin that the lady rules the estate, with *Dom* Gabriel's assistance when he feels so inclined."

She asked after his sisters; he told her the names of their husbands, and how they fared. She wondered if it was really safe to spend time with anyone who knew who and what she really was. But it might be worse to make a point of avoiding him; that would be suspicious conduct indeed. His fear that she was a spy once overcome, he seemed to accept it as quite normal that she be here.

It ought to be normal! Darkovans and Terrans should have a chance to be together, then they will not have a chance to build barriers of ignorance and distrust! Lorill Hastur is wrong, wrong, wrong!

When he had left her—it seemed, with reluctance—she found herself standing next to Jaelle, who had paused, breathless, after a fast, romping dance.

"I think Camilla was right," she said, laughing. "There are men who find scars irresistible on a woman! I have never been so popular!"

"I had half expected to find that Amazons were not allowed to take any notice of men—after Camilla warned me so sternly not even to look at them!" Magda could laugh about this memory now.

"Oh, this is only when there is work to be done, or the men are such as might consider a glance some sort of—of invitation," and Jaelle. "There have been times when I worked with men and they took no more notice of me than of another workman. We learn not to cause trouble—you will learn it, in the Guild-house—so that an Amazon can travel alone in a band of a dozen men, and will be accepted as one of them. But I also know how to behave when I want them to accept me as a woman—at Midwinter Festival, for instance! Or Midsummer, when the dances—in Thendara, for instance—go on all night, and extend into the gardens! And you know the old proverb: 'What is done under the four moons need not be remembered when they have set. . . .' Although for my part I have never had any taste for waiting forty days after, to see if I would bear a child in the spring—" She broke off, saying gently, "I am sorry—it is like talking with Rohana; I forget sometimes that she has been trained to the politenesses of women's speech. I did not mean to shock you, sister!"

Magda had not, of course, been shocked at the words; but she realized that she did not know Jaelle at all, in this madcap mood. And she herself had been brought up to observe the fairly straitlaced sexual taboos of the mountain women. This had been confusing to her during her off-world training and had tended to throw her, more and more, into the company of Peter; he respected them, to some degree shared them.

Jaelle said, "In any case, no one cares much what happens at such festivals; even *Dom* Gabriel will turn a blind eye to whatever happens in the galleries and dark corners, or when the fires burn low. . . . Usually the old people go off to bed early and leave the young people to do as they please." She leaned close to Magda, and whispered, her eyes glowing with mischief, "There is a saying that you never master a language completely till you have learned to make love in it! I saw Darrill looking at you—I am sure he would be happy to teach you."

Magda felt her cheeks flaming, and Jaelle gave her a gentle pat on the shoulder. "I should not tease you, sister. Someday you will know how to take our jests, too. Here is Piedro, come to dance with you at last!"

Instead he took Magda lightly by the elbow, and said, "I want to talk to you for a minute." He guided her toward the refreshment table, dipped himself up some wine from the great cut-crystal bowl there. He said in an undertone, "What did Darrill say to you?"

"Only that he recognized me," she said, "and asked if *Dom* Gabriel knew who I was."

"He asked me the same," said Peter. "I told him that since Lady Rohana knew who I was, I was quite sure *Dom* Gabriel knew it also." He hesitated, about to fill her glass.

"No, I've had enough. I'm feeling a little dizzy," and she nibbled on a bit of cake instead.

Peter said, almost jealously, "I saw you dancing with Darrill. You certainly seem to be enjoying yourself!"

"I am. Aren't you? I've never had a chance to do this kind of thing before! And I've missed it!"

"It never occurred to me you would want to," Peter said. "I have gone to the Midsummer Festivals in Thendara these last three years; if I had thought of it I could have taken you. But"— he hesitated—"at the public festivals—not the ones in private houses like this, where everything is very decorous—but the public dances, where all comers mingle, the party sometimes gets a little wild. Dancing till dawn, pairing off in the gardens and all that; I didn't think you'd want to come.

Magda suddenly felt a violent resentment; he felt it was suitable to go himself, even if the party got a little . . . *wild.* Yet he had decided, without consulting her, that that kind of entertainment was not suitable for *her!* She said dryly, "You might have let me decide it for myself."

He raised his hand to touch the nape of her neck again; a suggestive touch, arousing memories she had tried to forget. He whispered, "I was jealous, darling."

She felt a sudden, almost completely irrational anger. How dared he make that decision for her? Had he felt free, then, to take a casual sweetheart for himself at these festivals—a privilege he felt himself justified in denying to her, as if he were her father or guardian?

He was still bending close to her, fondling her neck; she could feel his warm breath. He was a little drunk; not much. Like herself, he had been taught to take great care with alcohol or other mind-altering drugs, and he knew and watched his own limits carefully. He was a good agent, she thought, a gifted agent, and felt the old fondness surge through her, so that she did not move away when he put his arm around her and drew her into the shadow of the draperies at one side. He bent his head, murmured to her.

She tensed in his arms and said sharply, "Speak *casta;* have you forgotten where we are?"

He brought his lips down on hers and kissed her. "It's good to be alive!" he said violently. "It's Midwinter Night—and I *knew* I was going to die. I *knew* there was no hope of rescue. Oh, Magda, Magda, Magda . . ." His voice faded out. He kissed her, hard enough to hurt. "And I'm alive, and you're here, and we're together again."

At first she did not protest, thinking it was a mere surge of gratitude, awareness of life instead of death; but his embrace grew quickly more demanding, more personal.

"Do you have any idea how much I want you, *need* you, how damnably I've missed you?"

Gently she tried to put a little space between herself and his demanding caresses, but he whispered against her throat, "You feel it, too, I know you do! You want me as much as I want you, or you'd never have come so far for me."

Against her will she felt herself responding; but a cold rational voice was saying in the back of her mind: *Now that you are free of him, do you truly want to start the whole miserable thing over again?* The excitement of the festival, a few drinks, the general atmosphere of license and the straitlaced rules relaxed for once, the fact that he'd been alone a long time and wanted a woman—that's what it was and that's all it was. She wouldn't be fooled into thinking it was more than that. Gently, but inexorably, she removed his hands from her.

"I'm sorry, Peter."

"Mag, Mag, I need you so. Don't you know we belong together?"

"I'm sorry, truly I am," she said with a sigh. "Until a little while ago, I thought so, too. But now I just don't feel guilty about you anymore. Now I'm just sorry I can't give you what you want."

"Is there someone else? That Darrill—"

"No, no. Nothing like that. Don't be foolish, Peter. I haven't seen him since I was nine years old!"

There had never been anyone else. Until now she would have sworn there never could be.

"Mag, you know there can never be anyone else, not for either of us, not on this world."

That, she thought, was partly true; they had shared the Darkovan childhood, the isolation from their peers, which had kept them from finding satisfactory mates elsewhere; drawn together by the knowledge that they were the only ones available for one another. Now she resented this; and resented, even more, how much he took it for granted.

"No, Peter. Whatever you're asking—no."

"I want you," he said, as if in pain. "I want you for always. I want to marry you again. And I want you now. Magda, Magda, come with me now! Our rooms are together, it's as if it had been intended—"

She said quietly, "You know I am not free to marry. Now."

"Oh, that! This Amazon game you are playing—"

"It's not a game." The very softness with which she spoke accentuated the finality of the words.

His voice was bitter. "Have you cut off your womanhood with your hair?"

"No," she said. "I don't think so. But I don't think womanhood means I have to go to bed with you just because you're lonely"—she had begun to use a ruder word—"and want a woman."

He touched her softly, intensely, and she hated her own arousal. He said, in triumph, "You want me, too. You know you do!"

"If I do," she said, suddenly angry, "that is *my* affair and not yours, unless *I* choose to make it so! Oh, God, Peter, why can't you understand? Do you want me just to be *kind* to you?"

He said, trying to hold her, "I'd settle for that," but she wrenched herself free.

"But I won't, and that's final! Peter, let me go. Jaelle is watching us!"

She moved away; only a few inches, but with such finality she might as well have been on one of the moons. Seeing the angry flush of offended pride lying along his cheekbones, she felt almost regretful; but nothing kinder would ever have made him believe her. He swallowed hard, and turned away; she watched him go toward Jaelle, saw the girl hold out her hand, with none of the shyness now she had shown earlier this evening. Peter took the slender fingers in his own, and although Magda could not hear what they said, she saw them move away together.

She watched them circle the dance floor, with a certain sadness. She was really free of Peter now. And suddenly, with her new dimension of awareness, she knew what she had done.

She had seen it, as they left Sain Scarp. Perhaps it was only chemistry, perhaps it was something more; but it had been immediate and unmistakable. Jaelle's weakness and collapse had misdirected Peter's response into protective kindness, self-effacing chivalry.

But it had been there, all the time, behind the kindness and the gentle, impersonal protectiveness. She had seen it again, when Jaelle had clung to Peter in her delirium. And now, feeling almost humiliated, she knew why Peter had come to her tonight; and it was not because he found her irresistible.

Peter was, first of all, a Terran agent; and he knew the rules. And one of them, a major one, was this: never, never—*never*—get seriously and deeply involved with any native woman on any planet where you're assigned. Casual liaisons were condoned, if not approved (every spaceport in the Empire had a red-light district), but anything more serious was forbidden.

And whatever it was between Peter and Jaelle, it was very real, and it was serious. Peter had been trying, a desperate last-ditch attempt, to protect himself against this involvement which could be so disastrous to the rules under which he lived. Magda was safe, Magda was one of his own. And yet . . . not quite.

He's like me; his sexuality somehow got to be Darkovan, just as mine did. He doesn't react to other women. But I'm near enough so that somehow he can be content with me. As I was with him. For a while.

If Magda had come with him, tonight, he could have resisted his own powerful, and dangerous, desire for Jaelle. But Magda had driven him away, with a blow to his masculine pride; and Peter had gone straight to Jaelle to heal that wound.

Now, with sudden dread, Magda found herself worrying about them both. Peter could risk his career for Jaelle. And Jaelle—what would she risk? She was no girl of the spaceport bars, but a woman of the *Comyn*, and, if Magda was any judge, deeply in love.

Irritably, Magda tried to dismiss the whole matter from her mind. It was definitely not her affair. Jaelle was no child; she was only a year or two younger than Magda herself, and, judging by the way she had been talking earlier, quite sophisticated enough to take care of herself. As for endangering Peter's career, Jaelle was not free to marry.

But even while she stood and watched a group of men dancing with torches, an ancient sword-dance, she wondered where in the lowering shadows Peter and Jaelle had gone. . . .

Somehow, the savor had gone from the evening. At midnight or thereabouts, *Dom* Gabriel, Rohana and Lady Alida, with most of the older people, said good night and withdrew, hospitably bidding their younger guests to remain and enjoy themselves as late as they chose.

Darrill sought Magda out again, and urged her to accompany him into one of the long galleries where, he said, there were some very fine ancient murals. From the way he touched her, and spoke, Magda was perfectly sure that he had no more interest in the murals than she did herself. She made some tactful excuse, and when he had gone away, she wondered why she had not taken up the challenge. Peter and Jaelle had long since disappeared and not returned; she wondered what gallery *they* were exploring. From what Jaelle had said, Magda knew it was not regarded as particularly reprehensible to share a good deal of casual kissing—or more, if she wished—on Midwinter Night.

Sooner or later, now that I'm free of Peter, I must find out how I react to other men. . . .

Then, angry with herself, she thought, *Damn it, before I complicate my life with another man, I want to know more about myself! I want to know what I am to myself, not always have to see myself through a man's eyes!*

A strange man came and asked her to dance again; she pleaded extreme fatigue, left the Great Hall and went up to the room she shared with Jaelle. Jaelle had not returned. Magda took off her beautiful gown, readied herself for bed and lay down. She expected to lie awake, worrying about Peter and Jaelle; instead she fell at once into a heavy sleep.

Hours later, she woke to see Jaelle standing in the doorway, barefoot, her face flushed, her short hair tousled. Her eyes were very bright. She came across the room and sat on Magda's bed.

Magda said lightly, "I didn't expect you back until later."

Magda could smell the girl's sweet heavy breath, and knew she had been drinking; was not sober now.

Jaelle said, "Oh, don't be angry with me, sister. I didn't want this to happen, I know how you feel."

"Angry?" Magda sat up and put her arms around Jaelle. "Darling"—the word she used was *breda*—"what right have I to be angry? Do you think—" Abruptly, it dawned on her just what Jaelle *did* think. "Do you think I'm *jealous?*"

Jaelle said with a nervous giggle, "This kind of thing is easier at Midsummer when there are gardens. We have spent most of the night in the long galleries." Her teeth were chattering, whether with cold or nervous excitement Magda could not tell. "I—I should have gone with him as he asked me." She looked at the connecting door into Peter's room. "But—but I wanted to be sure, I don't like deciding things in a hurry and," she added after a moment, looking at Magda in appeal, "I did not want to—to tread on the hem of your garment."

Incongruously Magda realized that she was still making mental notes about the curious idiom. She hugged the trembling girl tight, and said, "Jaelle, anything between Peter Haldane and me was a long, long time ago." As she said it, she knew that it was really true. "Do you love him, *breda?*"

"I don't know," Jaelle said. "I'm not sure. I've never felt like this before."

Magda found herself wondering if Jaelle were a virgin. From her flippant jokes, and sophisticated comments, she had not thought so; but could an experienced woman be so uncertain? As if Jaelle had picked up the thought directly from her mind— and by now Magda was almost ready to believe that—Jaelle said in a low voice, looking down, "It's foolish, isn't it? I've come near to it many times. Before I took the Oath, when Kindra saw that I liked to—to laugh with men and to flirt with them, she told me that before I bound myself, I should take a lover, test myself that way; she said that it might someday seem hard to me that I was bound by law never to marry. But somehow there was never anyone I could—could trust that much."

She added defensively, "So it never came to more than

laughter or foolishness. Nor did I ever leave any man wounded by my teasing, or heart-scalded. But now"—she looked and sounded forlorn—"I have no more laughter. I think I am more afraid now, when I—when I love him, when I want him, than when I was a girl and the very thought of giving myself to any man seemed frightening, an open door to bondage and slavery. . . . I don't know myself anymore!" Her voice was shaking and she was very close to tears. "I don't know what I want! Oh, Margali, Margali—sister, what shall I do?"

Magda felt wrung, helpless. *What can I say to her?* She could understand that to Jaelle, brought up as she had been among women close-bound to one another by oath, it seemed completely natural to turn to another woman for comfort or counsel. *I am bound to treat every woman as my mother, sister, daughter . . . but I've always lived by such different laws . . . God help me, I don't know what to say to her!* If one of her own friends in the Terran Zone—Bethany, for instance—had come to her with such a question, Magda could have turned it off with a casual or even a crude joke. But she could not do that to Jaelle.

What would Rohana have said to her? Finally, in a voice shaking as much as Jaelle's, she said, "Darling, I can't advise you. I don't know if anyone could. You must do what you feel is right." Then, to her own surprise, she found herself whispering the words of the Oath of the Free Amazons: "I swear I will give myself to no man save in my own time and season and of my own free will. . . ."

There was a moment of silence, then Jaelle whispered as if to herself, "In my own time and season," and smiled, tightening her arms around Magda; and Magda knew that somehow, by instinct, she had hit on precisely the right thing to say. She felt Jaelle's lips against her cheek for a moment; then, without a word, Jaelle pressed her hand, and went, on noiseless feet, to the connecting door, which closed a moment later behind her. She did not return.

Chapter 14

Day after day the snow fell, pouring from gray skies as if it had forgotten how to stop. Then, ten days after Midwinter, Magda was awakened by Jaelle, sitting on her bed.

"Wake up, sister, the sun is shining!"

Magda ran to the window. The sky was filled with thick, low, puffy clouds through which erratic sunshine spilled; in the courtyard below, pathways were being cleared by bundled men with long shovels; and horses, their breath streaming in the cold, were being brought around for departing guests.

Magda dressed hastily in her traveling garments, not at all sorry to resume them. Every day their stay was prolonged meant another chance of revealing who they were.

Jaelle began slowly to dress. Since Midwinter, she had spent her nights at Peter's side, although she had been careful not to be found there in the morning by *Dom* Gabriel's servants. When Magda teased her gently about what seemed like hypocrisy, she had said, "I do not care a *sekal's* worth what *Dom* Gabriel thinks of me; he is not my guardian and I owe no man any account of my acts. I care still less what his servants think of me. The servants know, of course; they always know such things. But if no one of them sees me there, then there will be no one whose business it is to inform *Dom* Gabriel. And although he probably knows, too—he is not a fool, and he has seen us looking at one another—if his servants told him in so many words, he would feel compelled to ask Rohana to reprimand me for putting the women of the *Comyn* to shame by sharing a commoner's bed.

And for his peace of mind Rohana would feel she had to come and scold me, even though she and I agreed together when I was fifteen that she was not my guardian and no longer the keeper of my conscience. And she would try not to offend me because she knows that I am a grown woman and by law the mistress of my own acts, and I would try not to be rude to her because I love her. And when we had all forced ourselves to say all these things, I would still go on sleeping with Peter whenever I chose; so it seems to me wiser not to start all that in motion."

That reasoning seemed complicated to Magda, but she had to admit that it probably saved trouble for all of them. It was even possible that *Dom* Gabriel, if it were brought directly to his notice, might feel compelled to call Peter personally to account. By the Amazon Oath, Jaelle had declared her independence of his guardianship, but Magda had heard from Jaelle that some men still refused to recognize the Amazon Charter.

Peter joined them in the hallway; he took Jaelle's hand in his as they went down the corridor, and Magda, watching, thought that the trip back to Thendara, with just the three of them, was likely to be awkward in more ways than one. She did not grudge Jaelle a single moment of her happiness—and that they were happy, no one who saw them together could possibly doubt— but it *was* going to be awkward, and she, Magda, would bear most of the awkwardness!

The immediate family of Ardais, with a bare handful of the house-party guests and estate officials, usually had their meals in a small breakfast room away from the Great Hall. As they came in they heard a burst of laughter. *Dom* Kyril was telling a funny story, which was one of the commonest Midwinter pastimes, at this season when all outdoor work came to a dead stop.

". . . And everybody had to carry around a little torch to thaw out what he said before he could be heard; and this man made quite a bit of money by gathering up all the frozen speeches in a barrow, and carting them around to their owners. Only he wasn't quite as careful as he should have been, to make sure that they were delivered to the right owners, and when the spring-thaw came, and all the words thawed out again, there was a tremendous amount of trouble. The mule-driver thawed out what he had yelled at his team, and found he had the words of an old lady talking to her pet birds; and the young mother scolding her little children got the mule-driver's, and the children cried half the day; and the young wife telling her husband she was to bear his first son, got what the Free Amazon said to the man who—" He broke off and turned a full red as Jaelle giggled. "My apologies, cousin!"

Jaelle said dryly, "Kinsman, I heard all the jokes there are about Free Amazons, before I had turned fifteen; and most of them I heard in the Guild-house from my sisters. I would share them with you, but most of them would shock your delicate male sensibilities." It was the turn of the others to laugh. "Finish your story, kinsman; this is one I have not heard."

Kyril tried to take up where he had left off. "The aristocratic lady entertaining her guests was delivered the chatter of the men from the lowest tavern in the village, while the Keeper instructing her youngest novice found herself hearing what the Dry-Towner bellowed at his minion. . . ."

"Enough," *Dom* Gabriel said, with a glance at Lady Alida. "It seems to me this is a tale for the barracks, son, not for your mother's breakfast table." He glanced up to greet the newcomers, his eyebrows raising in question as he saw the women in Amazon clothing.

Jaelle said, "Uncle, with your leave, we will ride for Thendara today; it is a long journey at this season, and my sister has duties in the Guild-house."

"Impossible," Lord Gabriel said. "This is only the snow-break, my girl; tomorrow at this hour it will be snowing harder than ever. This storm will last another ten days at the least; only the guests who live within a few hours' ride are departing today. You would be well advised to remain until the spring-thaw, at least."

"You are more than kind, Lord Ardais," said Peter, "but we could not so long trespass on hospitality."

"You couldn't possibly travel more than a day's ride before the snow blocked you again," *Dom* Gabriel said. "It seems to me nonsense, to spend the rest of the blizzard in a tent or travel-shelter when you could stay here in comfort."

Magda and Peter knew he was right. And indeed, the weather in the Hellers at this season was proverbial; from Midwinter to spring-thaw, only the mad or the desperate ventured more than an hour's ride from their own firesides.

Toward afternoon the day darkened again, and the next morning the windows were a flurry of white snow, with the wind howling around the towers of Ardais like a banshee hard on the heels of its prey. And at breakfast *Dom* Gabriel said triumphantly, "You see? You had better stay till spring-thaw, all of you!"

Afterward, Lady Alida drew Magda aside and said, "We should arrange for your testing, *mestra,* today; it should not be much longer delayed."

Magda was seized by such panic that she felt it must be perceptible to the *leronis.* As soon as she could get away she went in search of Lady Rohana, and found her in her private sitting room, working on the accounts of the estate. At first this might have surprised Magda; now she knew that every thread in the running of Ardais was spun through Lady Rohana's slender six-fingered hands.

"Forgive me for disturbing you, my Lady; may I speak to you alone for a moment?"

Rohana motioned her inside and dismissed the lady companion without whom, it seemed, she could not move half a dozen steps. "Certainly; this can wait till spring-thaw, if need be. What troubles you, child?"

Magda felt an overwhelming sense of presumption; she had come to a *Comyn* lady to complain about one of the lady's own caste! She said hesitantly, "The Lady Alida is determined to have me tested for *laran,* and I am afraid that if she explores my mind that way it may cause trouble for all of us."

Rohana looked grave. *This is my fault; I should have sent the Terrans away.* She said, "We were both surprised to find you in the rapport when we were working in the matrix. Have you been trained in these powers among your own people?"

Magda shook her head. "Among us, there are not too many who even believe that such powers exist, Lady. Those who believe in them, or claim to be able to use them, are thought ignorant, superstitious, credulous."

"I had heard that." Rohana knew that had been one of Lorill Hastur's reasons for the ban on too much mingling with the Terrans. *They do not believe in these powers; once convinced, they would be greedy to know all about them, and exploit them.*

Rohana said, "Belief or not, you seem to have this kind of *laran,* child. How came you by it?"

"I do not know, Lady. All my life I have been able to use hunches, but I believed it was simply that I had a talent for adding up things which were subliminal—just a little below the conscious levels of perception. And there have been times when my dreams were not—not nonsense, but told me things I did not consciously know; so I have learned to take heed of them."

Rohana leaned her chin thoughtfully on her hands. This meant they must reevaluate most of what they had learned about the Terrans. "Lorill is committed to a belief that Terrans and Darkovans are different races of beings, and that the Terrans are inferior; and he uses their lack of *laran* as proof."

Magda said, "My Lady, I am not supposed to tell this outside the Terran Zone, either; but the Lord Hastur is mistaken. This is not a belief, but a fact that can be proved; Terran and Darkovan are one race. It is known to us beyond question that Darkover was settled by Terrans long ago, by one of what we call the Lost Ships. In an age before the faster-than-light ships that we have now, there were ships that were sent out from Terra—it was not an Empire then—and some of them were lost and never heard of again. There is evidence from your languages that it was settled by a ship whose very name I could give you, and the names of those aboard. It is most likely that this knowledge was lost to you centuries ago, Lady—probably to keep the survivors from pining too much for their lost homeland—but your people are truly Terrans."

"Then psi gifts—you have them, too?"

"It is rumored that once they were more common than now;

now they are very rare, and there was a time in our history when people used to pretend them, or feign them with clever devices and machinery, so they fell into disrepute and their use was considered charlatanry. But there seems evidence that once they were known."

Rohana nodded. "There was a time in the history of the *Comyn*," she said, "when we did selective breeding to fix these gifts in our racial heritage; it was a time of great tyranny, and not a time we are very proud to remember. It led to its own downfall, and we of the *Comyn* are still suffering the aftermath; not only in the distrust the common people have for us, but in that our fertility was lowered by inbreeding; and the gifts are linked to some dangerous recessive traits. But they are powerful, and when misused can be very dangerous. Which brings me to you, child. Normally, psi gifts waken in adolescence; when they waken later there are sometimes dangerous upsets and upheavals. Have you felt any strange sensations, any unexplained sickness without physical cause, any sense of being outside of your body and unable to get back, any wild emotional upheavals?"

"No, nothing like that," Magda said. Then she remembered the moment of altered perspective during the healing, but that had passed off quickly and of itself.

Rohana asked her a number of searching questions about her dreams and "hunches," and finally said, when Magda felt wrung out by the questioning, "It seems to me that your talents are slight, and that you have compensated for them very well. You could, if you wished, probably learn the use of *laran* with ease, and it would be interesting to see what use a Terran could make of this training. I would like to have the teaching of you; but it seems it would make more trouble than it is worth. You are committed elsewhere; and I have already gone against Lorill's will as much as seems wise. Yet," she added, almost wistfully, "if you demand this training, I could not refuse it to anyone with *laran;* and by law, birth and parentage cannot be used to refuse it to you."

Magda said firmly, "I think I have quite enough trouble without that!"

Rohana touched her wrist very lightly, that feather-touch Magda was beginning to guess was peculiar to telepaths among their own. "So be it, dear child. But it you ever have trouble with *laran,* you must promise to come to me."

She sat looking intently at Magda for a moment. "If Lorill is wrong—if it can be proved that what he believes about your people is wrong—I do not need to tell you what it will mean for both your world and mine."

To Magda, with her heightened sensitivity, the force of what she had always called "hunch" raising her perceptions, it seemed at this moment that she caught the very image in Rohana's mind: a great barricaded door, slowly swinging open between two locked-away worlds, two peoples; opening to give a bright and sunlit view. Magda thought, *We should be one people, not two . . . I would do anything for that. . . .*

Rohana said, slowly, more as if she were thinking aloud than speaking, and yet Magda knew she was meant to share the woman's thoughts, "Does it not seem to you, Margali, that there is a design of some sort in this? That of all the Terrans on our world, it should be your friend, who could be so easily mistaken for my son, who should be taken by Rumal di Scarp? I myself, in a quick look, can still be deceived, and must look at their fingers and hands to be certain, until one of them speaks. Does it not seem fantastic to you that of all the Amazons of Darkover, you should fall into Jaelle's hands, and that the two of you should be so tested that you have become sworn friends as well?"

Magda felt uneasy. She said, "Coincidence, Lady."

"One coincidence, perhaps. Two, maybe. But so many, like beads strung on a necklace? No, this is more than coincidence, my friend; or if it is coincidence, then coincidence itself is only another word for a design intended by whatever force it is that shapes the fates of man." She smiled, and seemed to come back to the practical world, saying, "Now I must ask something of you, child. Will you take care in what you say to your friends, and to your superiors in the Terran Zone, at least until I have had a chance to speak with Lorill?"

"Indeed I will," Magda said, smiling a little at the thought of Montray's face if she should ever try to tell him about the matrix operation that had healed Jaelle's wound within a few minutes, or that Lady Rohana had said that she herself had *laran*. If this was ever to be brought up between Darkovan and Terran, she was quite willing it should be someone other than herself who should do it—and she hoped there would be a more receptive audience than Russell Montray!

Rohana rose, and said, "Go now, Margali. I must think this over and decide what to do."

Magda hesitated just a moment. "But what shall I tell Lady Alida?"

"Don't worry about her. I will tell her that I have tested you myself," Rohana said, and her smile was droll. "Don't you realize that is what I have been doing?"

The blizzard lasted for another ten days—almost exactly as *Dom* Gabriel had predicted—and when the weather finally cleared, the roads and passes lay blocked with drifts so deep that the three guests at Ardais were readily persuaded to remain for a few more days. Yet Magda had begun to brace herself, mentally, for their departure, and for whatever lay ahead. She could not return to her old life inside the Terran Zone, venturing outside it only in disguise; she knew the disguise had become her truest self. But what she could do instead—that she did not know either.

She found herself thinking again and again of what Rohana had said about a design in the chain of coincidences that had brought them together; even in the peculiar pattern that had drawn Peter and Jaelle together as lovers. If the Empire was to remain on Darkover indefinitely, sooner or later there would be—as on all planets inhabited by different groups of humans—entanglements, romances, liaisons, and eventually marriages, even children who belonged to both worlds. And someone had to be the first.

Of course, one day Darkover would be an Empire planet. It

was inevitable. The Empire did not conquer; but once the contacted planet saw the pattern of the Tenan Empire, and what it could mean to be part of it, the rulers always asked to be affiliated. When that time came, Terran and Darkovan would all be Empire citizens, and such affairs and romances would concern no one but the two people involved, and perhaps their families. But now it could cause only complications.

Magda hoped their departure would not be too long delayed. Jaelle and Peter were beginning to be a little less careful, and Magda wondered what the end would be. Again and again, seeing them together, she felt the small, indefinable pricklings of "hunch"—or precognition. *Sooner or later, this meant danger. . . .* Yet how could she speak to Jaelle, warn her, without the younger girl thinking that she was jealous, or grudged her the happiness she had found with her lover? Still less was it possible to remonstrate with Peter. So she only watched them with growing disquiet and anxiety.

In anticipation of their imminent departure she began to sort and put together her possessions; Jaelle found her occupied by this, and suggested that most of their traveling clothes were in need of repair, and that they might profitably spend the day in putting them in order. Magda was surprised to find that Jaelle was an expert needlewoman; somehow this had seemed too feminine an art for an Amazon. Magda herself, accustomed to the readily replaceable, cheap synthetics of the Terran Zone, had never mastered the art; had, in fact, been taught to scorn it as being a pointless way of passing time for women who had no useful work to do.

When she said this to Jaelle, the younger woman laughed. "And so it is, much of the time! Last night in the hall, when Rohana invited us to join her women at the tapestry they were making for the hall chair cushions, I thought I should go mad! I love to embroider," she added, "but how Rohana can endure it, I cannot imagine! I myself should go mad, to sit there night after night, surrounded by those fools of sewing-women . . . stitch, stitch, stitch, gossip, gossip, gossip! Rohana runs the whole estate of Ardais, and does it better than *Dom* Gabriel could do, and she sits in Council and gives advice to Hastur, yet there she sits among those foolish girls, and chatters with them as if she had never had a thought in her head more serious than whether to embroider the next cushion with a rainfish or a star-flower! As if it mattered to anyone's backside what was embroidered on a cushion, as long as it was well stuffed!" But even as she spoke, she was setting small neat stitches in the torn fingers of her glove.

Magda, watching her, thought that it made good sense to learn an art of this kind, on a world like Darkover, where warm and durable clothing was a necessity of life. She said ruefully, looking at the mess she had made of the torn tunic, "I am even less skillful with a needle than a sword!"

Jaelle laughed. "My skill with a dagger is incidental," she said. "I told you I was no fighter, but for my first year or two among the Amazons I used to work at Kindra's side. She was my foster-mother and had been a mercenary soldier. And when there was peace in the Domains, she hired herself out as a body-guard to escort travelers through the Kilghard Hills and the Hellers, and protect them against bandits, catmen and what-have-you. For a few years I worked with her; but I did not really like it, and gradually I discovered my real skill."

"What is that, Jaelle?" Magda remembered Rohana saying that the Amazons worked at any honest trade; but she was curious to know which of them Jaelle had made her own.

"I am a travel-organizer," Jaelle said. "People who intend to travel in the hills come and consult me. I can tell them precisely how many pack animals they will need for supplies for any number of men, for the length of their trip, and where to hire or buy them, and where to hire drivers for them, and precisely how much equipment they must buy—or I can buy it for them, on commission. Then I can advise them about how much of the different kinds of food they must buy to keep the men healthy, and provide them with guides and bodyguards, tell them what roads to take, how long the journey will last at the specific season of the year, what passes might be closed or what rivers in flood, and anything else they might wish to know. It is not a business to make anyone rich, but I make a good living at it. Some people only wish for an hour or two of advice, and I give it to them for a fee; others put all the preparations for the trip in my hands, and I do everything from buying pack saddles to choosing meals and equipment they can use at midwinter in the high passes."

"Tell me," Magda said hesitantly. "From what I have seen of Thendara—are there many men willing to turn such responsibility over to a woman?"

"More than you might think," Jaelle said. "Rafaella, who started this business, told me that in the first year or two, her business was almost limited to providing escort service for ladies whose kinsmen had no leisure to escort them and would not trust them to strange men. Amazon bodyguards for women were much in demand because they knew the ladies would arrive unraped! But as it became known that the caravans we organized could take quicker routes, and arrive without running out of fodder, or having to live on porridge-powder for the last four or five days, the ladies themselves began to insist that we be allowed to make plans for their husbands' business journeyings, and so it has grown to a point where we have as much business as we can do."

"It still seems a strange business for a woman—here," Magda said. "I have grown used to thinking that a woman's life on Darkover was always so limited. Oh, *damn* this thing!" She broke off, sucking the finger she had pricked with an incautious stitch.

Jaelle laughed, saying, "Don't bother; give it to one of Rohana's sewing-women. They will be glad to have something to do, and it will give them pleasure to think there is something, *anything* they can do better than a Free Amazon."

Jaelle, Magda thought, was a puzzle; she was devoted to her sisters in the Guild of Free Amazons—and yet she could be so contemptuous of other women! She said, "Do you really think all women would be happier as Amazons, Jaelle?"

Jaelle put her mended glove back with its mate and began to sort out some small things at the bottom of her saddlebag. She said, not looking up, "No, I don't. I used to think so, when I was younger. And I do truly look forward to a day on our world when all women will have the freedoms that we—the Guild—have seized and declared for ourselves; when they will have them by law, and not by revolt and renunciation. But I know now that there are many women who could not be happy living my kind of life." She sat in the windowseat, her legs folded up under her chin, her short hair tousled; she looked like an adolescent girl. She had a bit of ribbon in her hand and was absentmindedly twisting it about her wrists as she spoke. "Rohana's women. They think of nothing but marriage; they are shocked and troubled at the idea of any other life than they live. It seems dreadful to them, to think of hiring themselves out, as men do, at any work for which they have the strength and skills, instead of serving for a time as waiting-women in one of the Great Houses, and then going home, as Lanilla is doing at winter's end, to a marriage arranged by their families. I asked her what her husband was like and she said she did not know, and asked me, 'Does it matter?' It was enough for her that she would have a home of her own, and a husband. Did you ever want to marry, Margali?"

Magda reminded her softly, "I *was* married."

"But only for a time—"

"I did not know when I married that it was only for a time," Magda said, with a twinge of the old pain. They had made so many plans for permanence!

"Tell me; if you had had a child, would you have stayed with him? Do you think it can be a bond between you?"

"My mother found it so," Magda said slowly. "She followed my father to four different worlds; then we came here, and I was born, and she always seemed content."

"Content only to make a home for him? Is that your way, in the Empire?"

"She was a musician," Magda said. "She played on several instruments, and she wrote many songs. She translated many of the mountain songs into the Empire's standard language; and she wrote music for some poems written in *casta*. But my father was always the center of her life; after he died, she seemed to lose all joy in living, and seldom touched her music again; and she did not live very long."

"Rohana married *Dom* Gabriel when she had seen him only twice," Jaelle said reflectively. "To me that seemed frightful, to be given to a man I barely knew, to lie with him, to bear his children. It seemed no better than slavery or rape made lawful! But when I said as much to Rohana, she laughed at me, and said that any man and woman, with health and goodwill, can live together in kindness and make a good life for one another. She said she thought herself lucky that he was decent and kindly and eager to please her; not a drunkard or a gambler or a lover of men, as so many of the Ardais are. To me, that seemed like a man, who has received a cudgeling, rejoicing that he had not been horse-whipped as well. . . ." She was still absently twisting the ribbon around her wrists, looping and uncoiling it. "And now he is truly the center of her life. I cannot understand it, though I find I like him better as I grow older. But there are times, too, when it seems to me that Rohana has as much freedom as any of us, that she does as she wishes and has given up little. . . ."

She drew the loop of ribbon into a tight coil around her wrists, began to coil the loose end around her other arm. She said, "Margali, did you want a child at all? Why did you not have one? You are not barren, are you, *breda?*"

"I did not want a child at once," Magda said. "We were traveling together; I did not want anything to separate us." It had been a bitter quarrel; she looked away from Jaelle, unwilling even now to relive that painful moment.

Jaelle reached out to touch her hand lightly, saying, "I did not mean to pry."

Magda shook her head. "Afterward, when we agreed to part, I was glad I had no child, to remind me always. . . ." *But would we have separated, then?* The touch of Jaelle's hand suddenly heightened the awareness, the contact, and she found herself thinking, *Is she pregnant? Does she think she is, does she want to be?* But all she sensed from the touch of Jaelle's fingertips was . . . loneliness, fear. *I thought Jaelle was so happy.*

Magda knew that from this touch she could use her awakened ESP—what Rohana had called *laran*—to find out if Jaelle were pregnant. The thought suddenly frightened her. She did not want to pry that way, to use this new skill to intrude. She let go of Jaelle's hand as if the narrow fingers had burned her, and found her hand caught in the ribbon Jaelle had been winding and unwinding about her wrists. Caught of guard, she demanded, "What in the world are you *doing* with that thing?"

Jaelle stared down at it, in sudden shock. She wrenched it loose, and flung the ribbon across the room, with a look of horror and loathing. As if, Magda thought, she had found a poisonous snake coiling about her wrists!

"Jaelle! What's wrong, sister?" The affectionate term came readily to her tongue now; but Jaelle's moment of vulnerability had vanished again behind a barricade of flippancy.

She said, "Old habits! A puppy you don't housebreak almost before his eyes are open will still be wetting the floor when he's an old dog. I've had this habit since I was a little girl; Kindra told me that it was just a nervous habit, and that I'd outgrow it. But I haven't, see?"

Magda knew there was more to it than that, but she knew she could not ask questions; knew it with that indefinable inner knowledge she was beginning to trust. Instead she asked something she knew to be safer.

"Jaelle, are you pregnant?"

Jaelle's green eyes met hers, just a flash, and then looked away. She said, and sounded almost desolate, "I don't know. It's too soon to tell." Quickly she jumped off the windowseat, barricading herself again. "Come on, let's find one of those silly women of Rohana's and ask her if she can mend your outfit, and make her happy by thinking she is superior to a Free Amazon!"

Watching the girl as she bundled Magda's torn traveling clothes together, Magda thought, *She's so young and vulnerable! If Peter breaks her heart, I think I'll want to kill him!*

What was going to happen to Jaelle? For that matter—if this involvement was serious and lasting, as Magda was beginning to guess—what would happen to Peter? Could he really sacrifice his career for a woman? And for one who was not, by Oath, even free to marry?

It was easy to talk about the inevitability of liaisons, love affairs, even marriages between members of separate peoples on Empire worlds. Magda had thought of them as inevitable statistics, before this. But it was different—completely different—when you knew the people involved, and guessed what they meant in purely human and personal terms. No statistics could give you even a clue to that.

Is this my fault, too? By refusing Peter, did I bring this on both of them?

Chapter 15

The winter drew on; the snow lay deep over Ardais. To Jaelle this was a precious interlude, a time separated from anything else in her life, before or after. For the first time since her thirteenth year, she lived surrounded by ordinary women; she wore women's clothes, shared in the life of the household, and spent her days with women who did not live by the terms of renunciation and freedom of the Amazon Oath.

She had tasted this life—but briefly, and unwillingly—when she was fifteen. Rohana had insisted that she must know the life she was to renounce, before she made that renunciation irrevocable.

But I was too young, I could not see it clearly.

And now it is too late. All the smiths in Zandru's forges can't mend a broken egg, or put a hatched chick back into the shell. I can never, never be one of them, not now.

I do not think I want to be. But I am not sure, not now. . . .

And there was the Terran, her lover. . . .

Like any young woman in the grip of her first serious love affair, it seemed to her that he filled her whole sky. The Guildhouse and the life there seemed very far away. She knew this was only an interlude, that it must end, but she tried to live entirely in the present, neither remembering the past nor thinking ahead to the future, but simply savoring each moment as it passed.

But there were times when she woke in the night, held close in her lover's arms, and realized that she no longer knew what she was doing, or who she was, or what lay ahead for either of them. None of the thousand uncertainties could be answered in words, or even asked; so she would turn to him in desperation, holding herself close to him, demanding the one thing she could be sure about, the one certainty they shared. She had ceased to be cautious. She no longer cared to conceal what was between them. She knew that sooner or later this would precipitate a crisis, but in some indefinable way she felt that even this would be a relief from the terrible uncertainty.

And then, one night, when she woke, she heard around the towers the soft dripping of rain and running of melting snow, and knew that the spring-thaw had begun. Now reality would close again over their enchanted isolation; and whether anything would remain, she could not even guess. She dared not even weep, for fear of waking him. She knew he would have only one comfort to offer, and now even that was no comfort at all, before the knowledge of the inevitable.

When I took the Amazon Oath, I believed I had made it impossible for any man to enslave me. Yet here I lie, bound in chains of my own making! What can I do? Oh, merciful Goddess, what shall I do?

By the time the sun rose, red and dripping behind the fogbank, she had fought her way to calm, and was able to discuss their impending departure serenely. "I must cut my hair; it has grown too long here."

Peter came and passed his hand through the silky strands, long enough now to touch her shoulder blades. "Must you? It is so lovely."

"Nothing in the Oath binds me to it," she admitted. "It is custom, no more; to show, when we work with men, that we do not seek to entice them with feminine wiles."

He put his arms around her, and held her close. "Must we part, then, my precious? I know you are pledged not to marry, but—is there no way, no way at all that you can remain with me? I cannot bear to let you go. Do you truly want to leave me so soon?"

She said, through the pounding of her heart, "I can remain with you for a time as freemate, if you wish."

"Jaelle, beloved, do you have to ask if I wish it?" He held her so tightly that he hurt her, but she almost welcomed the pain.

She thought sadly, *Have I come to this?*

"Don't cut your hair," he begged, caressing the locks at the nape of her neck, and she smiled and sighed.

"I will not."

He did not know, and Jaelle would not tell him, that Free Amazons who elected to remain for a time as freemate to a lover did not cut their hair; by custom, close-cropped hair was a sign among them of commitment to solitude.

She was dressed and ready before him. Since they made a point of coming downstairs separately, she started down to the small breakfast room. The sun, flooding in brilliantly through the stone-arched windows, would at any other time have given her pleasure, after so many dark days. Now it only meant the end of an interlude that could never come again. She might remain with Peter, but never again in such complete isolation, mutual self-absorption; the outside world would intrude, with other work, other commitments, and she grieved for the end of their brief honeymoon.

A hand on her wrist detained her; at a quick glance she thought that Peter had hurried after her, and smiled, but the smile slid off as she realized that the hand had six fingers, and simultaneously, she recognized the voice of her cousin Kyril. *So alike, so different. . . .*

"Alone, *chiya?* Have you quarreled with your commoner lover? I should make a reasonable substitute to console you, should I not? Or did you turn to him because you so much regretted refusing me, when we were younger?"

She picked his hand off her arm as she would have removed a crawling insect. She said, "Cousin, we will all be leaving here very soon. For Rohana's sake, let us try to remain friends, for this short time. I am sorry for all our quarrels when we were not much more than children; don't torment me by bringing them up now that we are grown."

Kyril pulled her against him, in a mockery of a kinsman's embrace, and laid his cheek roughly against hers. "Nothing is farther from my mind than quarreling with you now, Jaelle."

Shocked and angry, she removed herself from his arms. She said, almost in entreaty, "This is not worthy of you, Kyril. I am your kinswoman and your mother's guest. Don't force me to be rude to you!"

"And is *your* behavior so worthy?" he demanded, "when you put our whole family to shame with this bastard from nowhere?"

Jaelle struggled to keep her composure. "If he is truly a bastard of Ardais," she said, "then the shame is in the misbehavior of his parents, and no fault to him. You were born *Comyn*, and legitimate, through no virtue in yourself. And as for *my* behavior—for the last time, Kyril, I owe *you* no account of my actions, nor any man living!"

He gripped her by the arms, his fingers digging cruelly into the soft flesh there. Through the touch her untrained *laran* gift—which she could never control but which, in deep emotion, thrust itself on her involuntarily—made her aware of his frustration and anger, and desire. He wanted her, crudely, sexually, and in a kind of intense, man-to-woman hostility that she had never known since—incredulously, she identified it as what she had sometimes sensed, without understanding, between her father and his women. It turned her physically sick; she thrust him away without trying to conceal her disgust. Her voice was shaking.

"Kyril, I do not want to hurt you under your mother's roof, where I am a guest. But you have known since we were fifteen years old that no Free Amazon trained in self-defense can be—can be raped. Don't put your hands on me again, Kyril, or—or I will have to prove it to you again, as I did then."

She realized, in shame and self-disgust, that she was probably crying.

When we were both fifteen years old, Kyril probably meant no real harm; it was a game he was playing, a game of adolescent pride: a little kissing and fondling, just to prove himself a man and my master. But I would not play that game with him then, and I wounded his pride more than he could endure. And I made him an enemy, and he is still my enemy.

"You bastard bitch," he flung at her, and his face was very ugly; the more terrifying because it seemed such a cruel caricature of the face of her lover. "By what right do you play the whore with this stranger, and then turn away from my touch like any chaste lady? By what right do you refuse me what you so freely give him?"

"You *dare* talk of rights?" Her tears gave way to flaming anger. "Rights? I *choose* my lovers, Kyril—and by what right, then, do you complain that I have not chosen you? I would not have you when you were an arrogant boy of fifteen bullying your mother's fosterling, and I will not have you now when you have grown into"—she caught back the crude obscenity on her tongue—"into her unworthy son!" She turned her back on him, hurrying toward the breakfast room, knowing that he would never dare make this kind of scene before *Dom* Gabriel. She was not overly fond of Rohana's husband, but she knew him for an upright man who would tolerate no offenses toward a woman and a guest at his own table.

But Kyril followed close on her heels, gripping her from behind, his fingers digging into the bruises he had made so painfully that Jaelle cried out. "How dare you talk of my mother and your respect for her? It has not kept you from behaving like a harlot under her roof! Does my father know how you have shamed our kin by flaunting yourself in this stranger's bed? If he does not, my girl, then I promise you he shall know at once, and then your precious lover shall account to the Lord Ardais himself for how he has dealt with his kinswoman!"

"I am not his ward; I am a Free Amazon, and by law I am mistress of my own actions," she said, and again, with that frightening *larun* awareness, sensed that he took pleasure—an active, *sexual* pleasure—in the pain of his hands bruising her arms, in her uncontrollable sobs. She fought hard to get herself under control again. She would not, she *would not* feed that sick thing in him that found pleasure in her suffering. She said, breathing hard, but her voice calm and steady, "What has Piedro done to you, Kyril, that you want to hurt him this way? Why are you doing this? I had thought you his friend!"

"This has nothing to do with Piedro," said Kyril, and he was breathing hard, too. "He is a man; but you damnable Amazon bitches, thinking yourself free of all the rules for women, thinking that you can pretend yourself chaste ladies and demand that we treat you like chaste ladies, and then playing the whore when it suits you, flaunting your lovers—Zandru whip me with scorpions, but I will teach you that you cannot treat men that way!"

She turned her back on him, wrenching herself free of his hands, and went swiftly into the breakfast room. She was shaking so violently that she had to steady herself for a moment against the doorframe. Her heart was pounding, and the bruises on her upper arms, where he had gripped her, ached and throbbed. Magda was already in her place; Jaelle went and slipped into a seat beside her, nervously smoothing her hair. Magda, instantly aware that something was wrong with her friend, reached out her hand below the table, taking Jaelle's hand in her own.

"Jaelle, what's wrong?" she whispered. "You've been crying. . . ."

Jaelle clung to her friend's hand, but she could not control her voice enough to answer. *Do all men hate us that way? Can it really be true that all men hate us so much?*

Kyril had come into the room behind her; he said, "Father—" with a defiant stare at Jaelle.

"Later, my son," said Rohana. "Your father is very much occupied."

And indeed *Dom* Gabriel looked angry and upset, staring furiously at the factor who managed his estate. "No, damn it, man, I'll not have it!"

"Lord Ardais, a thief is a thief, whether he steals copper coins or *sarm*-nuts!"

"Avarra's mercy, man," *Dom* Gabriel said irritably. "Are you seriously trying to tell me that I should hang a hungry man who steals a few bushels of nuts to feed his sons so they can grow up to be my loyal servants?"

"If they steal nuts in one season, *Dom* Gabriel, they will steal the trees themselves in another!"

"Then mark the trees you have ready for felling, and let it be known that any man who touches a marked tree will get a good cudgeling; and turn a blind eye when they help themselves to the downwood. If they cart it away to burn at their hearth-fires, it won't be there to feed forest fire another year! That last burn cost us half a year's profit in resins! But no more hangings, hear me? Or you'll find yourself hanging there beside them!"

The man grumbled, "You might as well paint up a placard at the edge of your forests, Lord Ardais: *Open to every thief in the Hellers, come and help yourselves!*"

"Don't be a fool, Geremy," the Ardais lord said. "No man can own a forest! My fathers have managed the lumber for centuries, and because they were clever at manufacturing resin and paint, and trading with the Dry Towns for sulfur to make bookpaper, we have grown rich from the forests we did not plant! But I grew rich with the aid of the men who live there, and they have a right to feed themselves with the fruit of the trees, and warm their poor homes with the wood from the trees! The Gods hate a greedy man; and when I grow so greedy that I think I own the trees themselves, and the fruits of the trees, and even the men who live among the trees, then it is only a matter of time before these men take the law into their own hands and teach me the lawful measure of a man's ambition!"

"Yes. But, my Lord—"

Jaelle looked at *Dom* Gabriel and shivered slightly; his face was dark with wrath, and she could see that his hands were trembling. It reminded her, faintly but frighteningly, of what she had seen in Kyril. He shouted at the factor, "Not another word, damn it! If you want to work for a bandit, and grow rich, go ask Rumal di Scarp if he needs a *coridom!*"

"Well said, Gabriel," Rohana said softly, reaching over to touch his sleeve. "But calm yourself. No one is arguing with you; we are all, I think, in agreement on that." She stared at the factor. "Are you not, Geremy?"

"Yes, my Lady, certainly!" the man almost stammered.

Jaelle thought, *Why does Rohana always try so hard to placate him? If he shouted like that at my table, I would give him shout for shout—yes, and blow for blow, too!*

Magda saw Peter slide into his seat—he had come in while *Dom* Gabriel was talking—and as he met her eyes, she knew what he was thinking. It was an opportunity given few Terrans, to sit at table with one of the *Comyn* lords and hear him expound his decisions. She knew Peter was making mental notes for a report in Thendara; so in her own way was she. But would she ever deliver it?

The factor had moved to the question of how to mark trees for felling when the thaw had progressed a little further, and the scarcity of ax-heads and saws in recent years.

Gabriel turned to Peter. "You have lived in Thendara; what do you know of the *Terranan?*"

Peter froze, saw Lady Rohana raise watchful eyes to her husband, but the question was obviously innocent, so he answered, "As much as any man in the street knows."

"Can you verify a rumor for me? When they were here in the Hellers, back near Aldaran, I heard that they traded in metal from off-world; that the off-world metals were stronger than our native alloys, and would take a more durable edge. Is this true, or is it like the tales of men with wings for hands, and pots for breathing on their heads?"

"I have never seen any men with wings for hands, nor yet with pots for heads," Peter said truthfully, "but I lived as a child in Caer Donn, and I have seen the off-world metal. It is good solid stuff, and can be traded in bars for forging, and as finished tools, and the tools are probably better than what your smiths can make."

"Rohana, you sit in Council," said the Ardais lord querulously. "Maybe you can tell me why that donkey Lorill has prohibited such trade?"

Rohana said soothingly that she was certain that the ban on trade was only a temporary thing, that the Hastur lord only wished the Council to examine the consequences of their world becoming dependent on resources not native to this planet.

Kyril interrupted. "May I speak now? I have a serious complaint to make, about a breach of hospitality—and decency! This man from nowhere, this nobody, has abused our hospitality—"

Rohana's voice was sharp. "Kyril, I will not have your father worried with such trifles! If you have anything to say, then you may—"

"I was not speaking to you, Mother," said Kyril, staring angrily at her. "Let my father speak for himself; I am weary of hearing you reduce him to a nonentity in his own household! Father, do you rule this household, or does my mother?"

Dom Gabriel turned toward them, and his face was red with an anger that made Jaelle tremble. "I will hear what you have to say," he said. "But I will not tolerate insolence to your mother, my son!"

Kyril said, thrusting out his chin, "My mother, too, has failed in her duty, since she has shown herself powerless—or unwilling—to keep order and decency beneath this roof! Or are you unaware that Jaelle has been seduced by this nobody who calls himself Piedro, and that she has shared his bed from Midwinter Night?"

Jaelle tensed, clenching her fists with mingled rage and distress. She felt Magda's hand close gently over hers, and sensed the mingling of fright and dread in her friend, as *Dom* Gabriel's flushed face, red with rage, turned toward Jaelle. His eyes were squinted close, his mouth contorted.

He shouted, "Is this true? Jaelle, what have you to say for yourself, my girl?"

She opened her mouth angrily. "Uncle, I am not your ward—" she began, and Rohana said in a low voice, almost agonized, "Jaelle, *please*—"

The desperate dread in Rohana's voice somehow got through to Jaelle; she said, more gently than she had intended, "All I can say to you is that I am very sorry to give you offense, sir. I would not willingly have done it." She bit her lip and looked down at the plate in front of her, her hands shaking as she buttered her bread, struggling not to say any more. Rohana's quick, grateful look was reward enough, but it could not calm *Dom* Gabriel now.

He bellowed, "Is this true? Have you made a scandal here in my house, with your love affairs?"

She swallowed hard and raised her eyes to meet his. She said clearly, "There will be no scandal, Uncle, unless you make it!"

Gabriel swung on Rohana, rising from his seat, turning angrily between Jaelle and Rohana. "What of this, my Lady? Did you know of this and say nothing? Did you permit your shameless ward to play the whore while she is under your care? What have you to say to this, Lady? Answer me! Answer me, Rohana," he bellowed.

Rohana had turned dead white. She said in a low voice, "Gabriel, Jaelle is not a child. She has taken the oath of the Free Amazons, and in law neither you nor I have any responsibility for anything she may do, under this roof or any other. I beg of you to calm yourself, to sit down and finish your breakfast."

"Don't you quote that filthy law to me," the man shouted incoherently, and his face was so dark and congested with fury that Magda wondered if he were about to suffer a stroke. "Jaelle is a woman of the *Comyn*! I forbade you to allow her to join these female scandals, and now do you see what you have done? A woman of our clan, seduced and betrayed—" He actually raised his arm as if to strike Rohana.

Jaelle, in horror, rose to her feet. "Uncle! Rohana is not to blame for anything I may have done! If you are going to shout and carry on like a madman, at least shout at me!" she said angrily. "I am a grown woman, and competent in law to manage my own affairs."

"Law, law, don't you talk to me about the law," Gabriel shouted, beside himself. "No woman alive is fit to manage her own affairs, and it doesn't matter what you—law—" He struggled to speak, as if his rage had swollen his throat completely shut, got out a few words of gibberish, then clenched his fists, swayed and came crashing down on the table, shattering crockery and chinaware, overturning a copper pot filled with some scalding hot drink that flooded the table, drenching the cloth. He struck his head hard, seemed to jerk violently on the rebound, and fell heavily to the floor, where he lay with his body arching backward, his heels drumming the floor in repeated, convulsive spasms.

Kyril, motionless with shock, suddenly leaned half across the table, running to lift him, but Rohana was already there, cradling the unconscious man's head against her knee.

"Let him lie till it is over," she said in a low, angry voice. "You have done enough for one morning. Go and call his man to help him to bed. Are you content, Kyril? Do you know now why I begged you not to provoke or trouble him? Do you honestly think"—she raised gray eyes, literally blazing with anger, to her son's—"that anything—*anything* goes on under this roof which I do not know, or permit?"

Jaelle felt a lump in her throat, obstructing speech. She had seen epileptic seizures before, but she had never before seen *Dom* Gabriel in the grip of one. Now, looking at Rohana, kneeling and holding her husband's head, she realized exactly why Rohana spent so much of her life—foolishly, slavishly, she had often thought—in keeping *Dom* Gabriel quiet and content, in averting his rage and calming his anger. Rohana's burden was far heavier than she thought.

Could I myself do so much for any man, however I loved him? And Rohana was given to him by her family, hardly knowing his name. Yet all these years she has managed it so that few outside the household even know his disability! She must have seen the warning signs, and tried to avoid any trouble. . . .

"Mother, I am sorry," Kyril begged. "I truly thought he should know of this."

Rohana swept him with a look of utter contempt. "Did you truly, my son? You cannot bear to think of any woman who does not obey you as if you were a God! And now you thought you had her at your mercy! How petty you are, Kyril! So to salve your wounded pride, and to revenge yourself against Jaelle, you have goaded your father into a fit; and he will be ill for days." She brushed aside his excuses without listening. "Go and call his body-servant, and help carry him to his bed, and no more talk. You have insulted our guests, and I will not forgive you soon for this!"

He went, glowering, and Jaelle came to Rohana's side. "Rohana, I am sorry—I did not realize—"

Rohana sighed and smiled at her. "Certainly not, child; you thought you were dealing with a rational man. You spoke more gently than I would have expected, and you said nothing that was not true. And I know that Kyril provoked you."

Her eyes rested for a moment on Jaelle's arms as if she could see the painful bruises there, and Jaelle thought, *Does she truly read my mind?*

When Kyril had helped to carry the unconscious man away, Rohana rose to her feet. She looked weary and worn.

"I know that you three"—her glance took in Peter and Magda, too—"were planning to leave today. Can you delay one more day? Today I must remain and make certain Gabriel is recovering as he should; tomorrow I can be ready to ride to Thendara with you."

"To come with us? Why?" Jaelle asked.

Rohana looked at Magda and said, "Because I have made a very important discovery; I must talk at once with Lorill Hastur. He is under a misconception which, if it is not corrected at once, can have the gravest consequences for both our worlds. So, if you will have my company on the road to Thendara, tomorrow morning I will be ready to ride with you."

Chapter 16

It was raining when they reached the travel-shelter at sunset, and as the party began to dismount, Rohana said, "I had hoped to reach Thendara today, but I have no great liking for riding half the night. It will be tomorrow for certain."

"I shall be glad to get there," Magda said, but then she began to wonder. Just what awaited her in Thendara? Even this one night's respite was welcome.

As she was unsaddling her horse, Darrill, son of Darnak, came up behind her, lifting the heavy saddle from her hands. She smiled and relinquished it, and stood beside him as he began giving their horses fodder. He waited until most of Rohana's guardsmen had withdrawn—Lady Rohana, as wife of the Lord of Ardais, could not travel without a considerable escort—then asked in a low voice, "Will you be glad to get back to your own world, Margali?"

She said, troubled, "I am not sure it is my world anymore, Darrill. I am sworn to the Free Amazons."

"But surely . . . Piedro told me that was but a disguise, a way of allowing you to travel in safety."

"Piedro does not know anything about it," Magda said, with unexpected sharpness.

"I don't think I understand."

"I am not sure that I understand it myself," she said. "It is true that I took the Oath as a means to an end; not really aware of what it meant. But later I chose, of my free will, to honor it, and I will do so, whatever happens."

Slowly, he nodded. "I can understand that. But what will the Terrans say?"

That, she thought, *is the question. Will I spend the rest of my life as a fugitive from the Empire's justice?* "I will try to get a leave of absence to honor my obligation to the Guild-house," she said. "And after that I think I could work more effectively for the Empire. It would allow me to do many things that an ordinary woman could not do here, otherwise."

He said, very low, "Margali, when I first met with you on Midwinter Night, I was very impressed with your courage and spirit. It seemed to me that no woman of our people could have so much, and I thought it must be only that you were a stranger, a Terran. Now there are times when it seems to me that you are even more like a woman of our own people. You are not like anyone I have ever known before." He raised his eyes, and looked directly into hers, and for a moment Magda thought he would kiss her. Then he swallowed hard, recalled himself, and turned a little away. He said, "Forgive me; I must finish with the horses."

As he went about his work, Magda found herself thinking, *If I am not careful, he will be falling in love with me. And that is a complication I cannot allow now. I must be very careful.* The thought made her a little regretful. *I discovered at Midwinter that I must find new ways of relating to my world; but before I complicate my life with another man, I must find out more about myself!*

It might be flattering to have young Darrill in love with her; but it would be a cruel thing to test her new awareness of men by capturing his interest and perhaps his heart, when she was not free, could not make any permanent or serious commitment to anyone. Jaelle had defended her flirting on the grounds that she had never left any man wounded or heart-scalded by her teasing. *I must be very careful to avoid that, too,* Magda thought.

Inside the travel-shelter, which was one of the largest, the guardsmen, and Peter among them, had made their fire at one end; Rohana with her ladies, and Magda and Jaelle, at the other. As usual, Rohana sent word that Peter should come and join them at their meal. When they had finished, she looked at Peter and Jaelle, close together, their hands linked in the shadows, and said to Magda, "In common humanity, I think we should leave them alone for a few minutes." She raised her voice slightly. "Come, my ladies, I think the time has come to visit the guardsmen at the other fire and see if they are content with their rations and their comfort."

Rohana's maid, a fat and sentimental old woman, looked back with an encouraging smile at Jaelle, as they went toward the other fire, and Jaelle felt herself blushing. Then she forgot the woman, as Peter drew her into his arms for a long, passionate kiss. She sank gratefully into his arms, blessing Rohana for even this moment or two alone with her lover; it would not be more than a few minutes, but while it lasted she could reassure herself. . . .

Finally he loosed her. "I am dizzy with wanting you! At least it will not be long; we reach Thendara tomorrow. Do you still love me, Jaelle?"

She looked up, laughing, into his face. "Can you doubt it?"

"But you avoid me."

"Avoid you? Of course not, love," she said, with a little flicker of laughter. "You certainly do not think I could lie with you in the presence of a half dozen guardsmen and all of Rohana's maids!"

He looked away, uneasy at her directness. "That is not what I meant," he protested, "but we could be together more often on the road; you could ride at my side, spend more time in my company! All during this trip you have treated me like someone you might have met at a public dancing-class, not like your lover!" He used the word in the inflection that made its nearest meaning "promised husband," and she smiled, pressing his hand.

"You are my beloved," she said in a whisper, "and soon we shall be together as much as you wish. But I am an Amazon, Piedro. I have not told you much about our laws and customs, but one of the things we are taught is that there is only one way in which women can travel among men without causing trouble and dissension. And that is by behaving as human beings; not as sexual creatures, women whose major business in life is to attract men to protect and care for them."

"Oh, come, surely Lady Rohana and her companions—"

"Rohana is the wife of their lord, a sacred trust they must safeguard with their lives. And her ladies are covered by her—her special charisma. But I am an Amazon and I have renounced my protected status as *Comynara*. And I am working among them; I organized this journey. So I must not come among them as a woman who is—is free to be desired. Can't you understand?" she begged. "If I spend much time with you, show myself as your lover"—she, too, used the word in the inflection meaning "promised wife," and he pressed her hand—"then I show myself to them as a woman. And they begin to think of me as a woman, and before long they begin to compete in small ways for my favor and attention, and to show themselves before me as men, and soon there is dissension among them all, and ill feeling. So I must be just another worker, one of themselves. They must feel at ease with me, not temper their speech to a woman's ears, or feel compelled to give me their lightest work."

She did not shade her words with the faintest reproof, but Peter recalled that a few days ago she had frowned at him for helping her, unasked, with a heavy load.

He said, "Are you trying to tell me that there is no work which is beyond your strength?"

"No, no indeed!"

"I should think not," said Peter indignantly, looking at the slender girl. "And what do you do, proud Amazon, when you find something beyond your strength?"

She smiled and said, "Precisely what you do among men, when you find something too heavy to lift, or a task needing four hands to accomplish it. You are not a tremendously strong man, I imagine; when a task demands more strength than you have in your arms, I suppose you simply say to one of the other men, 'Come here and help he lift this before I strain my guts!' Well, that is exactly what I do. If I have made it obvious that I do not shirk any work within my strength, then they will help me as they would help another man with a task too heavy for him, and not with any thought of a woman who must be sheltered!"

"I hope you do not always intend to treat me that way!" he said, and she laughed and raised her hand to touch his cheek lovingly.

"When we are alone, beloved, I shall be so fragile and demanding that you will sometimes think I am Lady Rohana herelf, who is not by law permitted to move as much as a day's ride without her maid and her lady companion and half a dozen guards! But you must not expect me to be anything other than I am, my love." She stood on tiptoe, pulled his head down and kissed him quickly. "Enough for now. Rohana and her women are coming back, and tomorrow we will be in Thendara."

"And tomorrow night . . ." Peter said, smiling at her, and for a moment she held herself against him, not at all unwilling to let him know she shared his eagerness. Then, sighing, they moved apart as Rohana with her ladies returned to their fire.

They rode down into Thendara a little after noon. Rohana said as thcy came through the gates, "What will you do now? Jaelle, you must go to the Guild-house, I know, with Margali."

Magda felt a small clutch of fear. *It's here. There's no more delaying. Oh, God, I'm frightened!*

Certainly, within my lifetime, Darkover will be a part of the Empire, and it will make no difference. The usual time from first contact to affiliation is about fifty years, and that's almost half over. But will that come too late to do me any good? Must I be exiled from one world to the other?

She thought this, not knowing that Darkover was to prove unique in the history of the Empire, and that not only her own lifetime but many lifetimes would pass before Darkover and the Empire were reconciled. Just the same, the curious little flash of prccognition iced her blood again, and she pulled her fur-trimmed riding-cloak—Rohana's midwinter gift—about her shoulders.

"This is idiotic!" Peter said, looking back to make certain they were out of earshot of Rohana's women and the guardsmen. "You can't possibly do that, Magda. Somehow or other, we've got to get you out of that nonsense of spending half a year in the Guild-house. I'm sure you'd find it interesting, but we can't possibly afford to lose our only resident female expert. Come back with me now to the HQ, and let the people there think of some way to get you out of it."

Magda said, in exasperation, "Peter, you don't understand. I am oath-bound, and I will honor my Oath. I will try, after, to make it right with the Empire authorities; but the obligation must be met nevertheless!"

"Oh, that," he said in contempt. "You know as well as I do that an oath taken under duress is not valid!"

Jaelle looked at him in shock and dismay; and Magda, with that new, devastating sensitivity to thoughts, knew that Peter had just shocked Jaelle to speechlessness. *An oath is sacred. What kind of man could ignore it?* And if he had no awareness of what the Oath meant to Magda, how could he possibly know what it meant to Jaelle?

Can he ever know, Jaelle thought with desolation, *that it is the very mainspring of my being?* It was only a moment, then her love began to make excuses for him; soon, soon he would understand. She smiled gaily at Peter and said to Magda, "We shall have to teach him better than that, will we not, sister?"

Rohana interrupted, sensing the strain: "The best way is for you, all three of you, to be my guests at *Comyn* Castle tonight. There is room in the Ardais suite for a dozen or more; and you, Piedro, can send word to your Terran supervisor that tomorrow we will all meet with Lorill Hastur. Both of them will be eager to know how this affair has ended."

They agreed to that compromise, and an hour later were all settled in comfortable quarters in the Ardais suite. Magda was tired from the long journey, and lay down for a nap, but she knew that sleep was simply another way of avoiding, for a time, the unendurable conflicts. Tomorrow, at whatever cost, they must be faced.

Peter stood for a few moments at the door of the room the women shared. He said, hurt, "Jaelle, you are avoiding me again!"

"No, my love. In a day or two we shall declare ourselves as freemates, before witnesses," she promised, standing on tiptoe to kiss him with a passion that swept away his doubts. "But just now I am Rohana's guest in _Comyn_ Castle and for her good name I must abide, under this roof, by her laws and rules of conduct rather than my own. But I love you. Never doubt it, promise me, Piedro, promise."

"I promise," he assured her, then, in surprise, bent to wipe the tears from her eyes. "My love, my darling, why are you crying?"

"I—I don't know," she stammered, and although he knew she was evading him, there was nothing he could say. "Even though I am a Free Amazon, Piedro, you must sometimes just let me be a woman, and not always reasonable. . . ."

When he had gone away, and Magda had fallen into an exhausted sleep, Jaelle wandered, restlessly, around the Ardais suite. At this time of year it was deserted; Rohana and her guests seemed to rattle around the empty rooms and corridors like a few pods on a tree stripped by a storm. At last Rohana sought her out.

"Come and sit with me for a little while, Jaelle. It may be a long time before we can spend time together like this; at Council season I have little leisure to enjoy your company, and it may be many years before you can pay me another visit at Ardais."

They sat before the fire that had been kindled in Rohana's room. For a time they said little, but at last Jaelle got out of her chair and came and sat on the hearth-rug beside her kinswoman. She laid her head for a moment on Rohana's knee; hesitantly, Rohana stroked the soft hair. As a girl Jaelle had never permitted caresses and Rohana had quickly learned not to offer them, but for once she seemed to invite them.

At last Jaelle said, "I did not tell you this, but you probably have guessed. Piedro has asked me to remain in Thendara as his freemate; and I have consented."

Rohana looked down at Jaelle with a distant sadness. _She loves him so much; and I know I cannot really understand._ Rohana herself had been given in marriage very young, had obediently married the man chosen by her family, without question, and had never been touched by this kind of passion. At last she asked, with a hesitant tenderness, "Have you ever regretted your Oath, Jaelle?"

"Never before this, never for a moment," Jaelle said. Then, forcing the words out, "Just the same, I think you were right, years ago, when you said I was too young for such a choice."

That struck to Rohana's heart, almost with physical pain. *Merciful Goddess, I gave her freedom, the freedom that had been denied to me. Was I so wrong?* For a moment time slipped out of focus, past and present blending together, and it seemed to Rohana that it was again the last day of Jaelle's long visit to Castle Ardais, in her sixteenth year. Rohana had known Jaelle was not happy there: she detested Kyril and had no great liking for Rohana's younger son and daughter; she thought Gabriel a petty tyrant; she had chafed at the need to wear skirts even for riding; and on the last day of her visit she had come to Rohana like this and told her, defiantly, that she would take the Amazon Oath on the very day she was legally free to do so.

Rohana had foreseen this, but had still been dismayed by the actuality. She felt Jaelle had as yet no idea what she was renouncing.

She had said: "Be very sure, Jaelle; very sure. This is no game, it is your whole life. Don't throw it away like this!" And then she had begged: "Jaelle, will you give me three years, more time, as you gave Kindra, to prove to you that my life is no less happy than hers?"

She knew Jaelle was remembering, too (Or did the girl's awakening *laran* share her thoughts?), when Jaelle said softly, "Three years seemed a lifetime then; longer than I could bear to wait. And—forgive me, Rohana—you wanted to prove your life was happy; and yet I knew *you* were not happy. So it seemed— hypocrisy."

Rohana bowed her head. No; she had not been happy then, but she thought she had concealed it more carefully from Jaelle. She had felt harried then, trapped by the life she led, after her brief taste of freedom. She had been much beset with her adolescent children, and with the three-year-old Valentine, who was at the most active and troublesome age. And at that time she had been pregnant again with a fourth child she did not want; that had been the price she paid for Gabriel's final forgiveness. And though she had not wanted the child, Rohana was too much a woman to bear a child for most of a year and see it die without anguish. So when it had been stillborn, she had grieved as bitterly as if she had longed for it. But she had carried the child, that year, in anger and desperate rebellion, feeling that perhaps she had paid too high a price for Gabriel's goodwill and peace in her home. Now, before Jaelle grown to womanhood, she bowed her head and said, almost inaudibly, "You were right; I was not happy then. Now I feel more guilty than ever that because of my unhappiness you rushed to take the Amazon Oath."

Janelle laid her cheek against Rohana's hand. "Don't blame yourself; I don't think it would have made any difference. Even Kindra said I was stubborn and headstrong; she, too, urged me to delay a little. Perhaps"—she smiled fleetingly—"I am my father's daughter, too, though I do not like to think so."

Never before this day had Jaelle spoken her father's name in Rohana's hearing. She had some idea of what it had cost Jaelle to say this. She was silent, asking after a long time, "Then you will stay with your Terran lover?"

"I—I think so."

But she is not sure. "Is it fair to any man, Jaelle, to give him so little of yourself as a freemate gives?"

"Rohana, I give him what he wants of me! The Terrans do not make their women slaves to their will!"

"Just the same—don't be angry, Jaelle—it seems to me that a freemate gives little more than a prostitute." She used the coarse word *grezalis,* knowing that on her decorous lips it would shock Jaelle into listening. "It seems to me that it is no marriage unless you commit yourself to a man for all times: good and bad, in happiness or misery. You know that when I was wed, Gabriel was nothing to me but a burden I had to bear, because I had been born *Comyn*, and the laws of my caste required me to marry within my clan and bear him children with *laran*."

"And you can call *me* whore? When you were sold like a

slave for your family's pride of position, and I choose to give myself freely to the man I love and desire?"

Rohana put out a hand to stop her. "Jaelle, Jaelle darling, I did not call you a whore, or anything like it! I said: this was how my marriage seemed at the beginning, a grave burden I must bear for my family's sake. Yet now Gabriel is the very center of the world we have built together. A freemate says to her lover, because of this storm of desire, I will remain with you while it suits my pleasure; but if we lose our happiness I will leave you, sacrificing the happiness we have had and the good times that may come in the future, all because of the unhappiness of a year or two. There is no obligation to remain together and work to turn the evil times into good again."

"How can you do that? Do you not live with constant regret for the years of unhappiness you had to share, with no possibility of escape?"

"Not really," Rohana said. "It has taken us a long time to outlive unhappiness, but we have forged a bond that will last till death. And beyond," she added, smiling, "if there is anything beyond."

"You say this bravely," said Jaelle, "but I think . . . oh, Rohana, I do not want to make you angry."

"The truth could not make me angry, Jaelle. Only remember, darling, that it is *your* truth, and not necessarily *my* truth."

"Then I think," said Jaelle, "that because it is too late for regrets, you tell yourself you have never had them. I think you simply would not give up your power and position as wife to the lord of the Domain of Ardais."

"Perhaps," said Rohana, unoffended, "a marriage is spun of many small threads. Gabriel is only a part of my life, but not a part I would willingly renounce now. I did not love him when we were wed, but it would rend my heart into a thousand fragments to be parted from him now."

Jaelle, remembering Rohana's face as she knelt beside the unconscious man, knew dimly that this was true; but it seemed to her that this was only slavery to an ideal, and nothing like the overwhelming passion that had caught her up, almost unwillingly, into Peter's life. She said, trembling, "That is not what I call love!"

"No, I suppose not, dear," said Rohana, taking the small cold hands in hers, "but it is real, and it has lasted."

"Then you think love—love as I know it—means nothing? It seems to me you think marriage can be made by any two, however they feel about one another, as if'—for the first time in a dozen years, Jaelle spoke her mother's name—"as if Melora and Jalak . . . as if my mother, even in rape and captivity, could have built lasting happiness."

"Even that, under some circumstances, darling. But I went consenting to my marriage, with my family's support and blessing; Melora was torn by force from all her kin. But even then; had Jalak and Melora chosen one another, had she run away with him of her own will, or even, afterward, had he loved and cherished her for herself, and not as a pawn to his evil pride, and a memento to his hatred of her folk of the Domains—even then, perhaps, she could have found some peace; not happiness, perhaps, but content."

"Even in chains?"

"Even so, my darling. Had Melora loved Jalak, and willed to please him, she would have known that the chains were a game he played for his pride before all men, and she would have worn them to play the game with him, willingly. . . . Jaelle, if your Amazons made up an army and marched to free the women of the Dry Towns from their chains, no doubt there are some who would hail you as their saviors; but there are others, I am sure, who would bid you turn around and march home again, and not meddle in their affairs. Would you not wear chains to please your lover, Jaelle?"

She said, "He would never ask," but dropped her eyes, remembering her play with the ribbon; the fantasy game she had played as a little girl in the Dry Towns. She said, angry at the memory, "Had you no pity for my mother?"

"Only the Gods know how much," Rohana said. "I risked the anger of Hastur, and came near to destroying what happiness I had found with Gabriel, to bring her away before she bore Jalak a son; and to set you free, because she said she would kill you rather than have you chained in Jalak's Great House. Do you not remember that?" Her eyes flamed with the beginning of anger.

Jaelle took her hand, and after a moment kissed it. Rohana said quietly, "Jaelle, many women wear their chains as I wear the *catenas*." She thrust out her arm, showing her the ceremonial marriage-bracelet, whose twin was locked on Gabriel's arm. "A token of something that would be locked upon my heart forever, even if I refused, as you will refuse, to wear the outward symbol."

Jaelle said softly, "The Amazon Oath binds me not to marry *di catenas*. I never thought I would want to," and her head went down on Rohana's knees, the slender shoulders shaking with the violence of her sobs. "I don't, Rohana! I don't!"

Rohana thought, *Then why are you crying so?* But she did not say so, sensing, through the feel of the girl's head against her knees, the very real heartbreak. She only stroked Jaelle's soft hair, tenderly. At last she asked, "Are you pregnant, darling?"

"No—no. He has spared me that."

"And do you really want to be spared, my precious?"

Jaelle couldn't answer; she was unable to speak. At last Rohana asked, very gently, "Will you stay with him in sorrow as in joy, Jaelle?"

Jaelle raised her flushed face. "I feel now that I would," she said in anguish, "but how can I be sure? How can I know he will love me in the evil times that come to everyone? How can I even know what I will be then? And yet—it seems that it is worth even this. Did you never love anyone, Rohana? Did you never want to give up everything—everything, your pledged way of life, your honor, *everything* because you could not—could not part from—" She put her head down on Rohana's knees, and cried desperately again.

Rohana's heart ached for her, and for a long-healed wound that Jaelle's words had torn. *Yes, there was a time when I would have given up everything: my children, the life I had made for myself, Gabriel—yet the price seemed all too heavy to pay.* At last she said, faltering, "There is nothing in this world that is not bought for a price. Even Kindra; she never regretted her oath, but she grieved to the day of her death for the children she had abandoned. It seems to me that is the one flaw in the Amazon Oath; you women who take it guard yourselves from the risks all women take willingly. Perhaps it is only that every woman must choose what risks she will bear."

Jaelle listened, and the words fell heavy on her heart. *I came too young to the Amazon Oath; most women make these renunciations in grief, knowing that they are real privations. To me it seemed only that I renounced slavery and embraced freedom. I did not weep when I took the Oath. I could never truly understand why so many women made the Oath only with tears. . . .*

"You love, Piedro. Will you stay with him?"

"I—I must, I cannot leave him now."

"Will you bear his children, darling?"

"If he—if he wants them."

"But your Oath binds you to bear them only if you want them," Rohana said. "You must choose, and perhaps it is that which I feel so wrong; that you women claim the right to choose."

"I will never believe that," Jaelle flared at her. "A woman not free to choose is truly a slave."

"But even the freedom to choose does not always guarantee happiness," Rohana said, capturing the cold hands again and caressing them. "I have heard old Amazons lamenting their childlessness, when it was too late to change their minds. And I—" She swallowed hard, for she had never said this to any living being; not to Gabriel, not to Melora, not to Kindra, who for so long had shared her innermost thoughts. "I did not want children, Jaelle. Every time I knew myself pregnant, I wept and raged. You weep because you are not to bear a child, but I cried more when I knew I was. Once I flung a silver bowl at Gabriel's head, and I hit him, too, and I shrieked at him that I wished I had killed him and he could never do this to me again. I hated being pregnant, I hated having little children around to trouble me, I feared childbirth worse, I think, than you feared the sword that gave you this." With light fingers she traced the still-crimson scar across Jaelle's smooth cheek. "Had I been free to choose, I would never have borne a child. And yet now that the children are grown, and I see that they are a part of Gabriel and myself which will survive when we are gone—now, when it would have been too late to change my mind, I find I am glad that the laws of my caste forced me to bear them, and after all these years, I have forgotten—or forgiven—all the unhappiness."

Jaelle said hoarsely, not wanting to show how much this had moved her, "I think, again, that you know it is too late for regrets; so you tell yourself that you have none."

"I did not say that I had no regrets, Jaelle," said Rohana, very low, "only that everything in this world has its price, even such serenity as I have found after so many years of suffering."

"You truly believe that you have paid a price? I thought you told me now that you had everything a woman could desire!"

Rohana lowered her eyes. She swallowed hard, and for a moment she remembered a day, years ago, when she had looked into Kindra's gray eyes and known the price she would pay. She could not face Jaelle; she did not want to cry. She said, "Everything but freedom, Jaelle. I think that would have been too dearly bought. But I am not sure." Her voice broke. "Nothing in this world is sure but death and next winter's snow. Maybe I do not want to be sure. The price I have paid is my freedom. You have your freedom; you are oath-bound to take it even now when you no longer want it. But at what price, Jaelle?"

Chapter 17

Magda woke at twilight, to see Jaelle sitting on the foot of her bed. She looked pale, as if she had been crying; but she was calm.

"Sister," she said, "I know that you took our Oath unwillingly; in a sense it was forced from you. Normally that would not matter; but you are a Terran, and you took it without the knowledge of what it truly implied. Do you want to petition for release from your Oath, Margali? If you do, I will speak for you before the Guild-mothers."

Magda knew that this would solve some of her deep inner conflicts; more, it would free her from the fear of Terran retribution, not directed toward herself alone, but toward those who had aided her to desert her original loyalties. She considered it for a moment, but then she was seized by revulsion. Go back to her life in the Terran Zone, and the narrow, sterile world she had lived there, circumscribed by the little work of importance that a woman could do? She realized now that even through her tears and terror when she had taken the Oath, it had still seemed a major decision in her life; and more, a genuine decision. *Here is a way I can follow. This is what I want, whatever the price I must pay.*

I was not forced to abandon Peter to death. Jaelle saved me from paying this price. But sooner or later I knew there would be a day of reckoning; and now I will meet it, whatever it may be.

She used the formal Amazon phrase. "Oath-mother," she

said, "I told you: I chose of my free will to honor my Oath, and I will keep it, until death take me or the world end."

"Even if it makes trouble for you with your own people, Margali?"

She said what she had said to Darrill on the journey: "I am not so sure they are my own people any more." Her voice was not quite steady. "I have renounced allegiance to—*to family, clan, warden or liege lord.*"

Jaelle took her hands; suddenly she leaned forward and kissed her, as she had done when she accepted her Oath. She said, "Allegiance for allegiance, my sister. We are sworn. But I think you must face the fact—we must face it together—that it may make grave trouble for you."

"I know that," said Magda, and could not keep from trembling a little. "If it had not been for Lady Rohana, I think Peter would have insisted on taking me to the Terran Headquarters, even if he had to do so by force, and under arrest."

"A beautiful reward for your loyalty to him," Jaelle said angrily. "But for you, he would be dead in Sain Scarp this moment!"

Magda felt compelled to defend Peter's point of view. "He is a Terran agent," she said. "To him, I think, loyalty to the Empire transcends any loyalty to persons."

"That is not right," Jaelle said, troubled.

Magda thought, *It's not a point of view any Darkovan can understand; so in many ways Peter is worse off than I. He is Darkovan in so many ways, he can never live at peace within the Empire; but he will never be free to renounce those very things which would prevent him from being wholly at home in Darkover . . . and he will always be torn, an exile. . . .*

"Jaelle," she said, "you told me once that the Free Amazons were allowed to accept any lawful work. If the Terran authorities would give me a leave of absence to honor my obligation to the Guild-house for their training, then when I had completed it, would I be allowed to continue the work I have been doing for the Terrans?"

"Do you mean that you would spy on us?"

"No, of course not," Magda said; the very idea was repellent. "But to build a bridge between our worlds; to help my people better understand all the small ways of your society, your language, your laws and customs—even if I did nothing more than my old work, to keep our translators from unwittingly offending against your customs; and I think I could do more, much, much more."

"That would not violate your Oath," Jaelle said. "By our Charter you may accept any lawful work anywhere. That means that as a sworn Amazon you may work for the Terrans—" She broke off, as if she had seen a blazing light, and said almost in a whisper, "And so can I."

"How would that be arranged, Jaelle?"

"However you wish," Jaelle said. "By our Charter's laws, you must pay a portion of your earnings to the Guild. We renounce family and home, but this means that we have the protection of home and family always. Whenever you are sick, pregnant, unable to work or in a strange city, you can always turn to the Guild-house or to any Amazon there, and find a home where you can be cared for. Your tithes go to maintain the Guild-houses, and you have always sisters and friends there, and you have a lawful right to them. You need never live within a Guild-house unless you choose, although if you choose to live there you are expected to help with the maintenance of the house, to take your turn at housekeeping or gardening or whatever needs to be done. But it is our true home, where we come as others come to their family homes, wherever else we may go."

Magda had known no family life since her father's death; she and Peter had never seriously tried to make a home together. The thought of having a true home, a Darkovan home, to which she could go not as a stranger or a guest, but as of right, gave her a sense of warmth she had not known for years.

Jaelle said, "We can go there in old age when we are past work, or have our children fostered there."

"You bear children, then?"

"If we wish," Jaelle said, and the memory of Rohana's words brought a fleeting sadness to her face. "Did you think we took

Keeper's vows? Our daughters can be fostered in the Guild-house till they are grown, when they can choose for themselves whether to join the Guild or to marry. Our sons are usually given to their fathers to rear, after they are weaned, but if your child's father is unwilling, or you think him unfit to raise your child, or if you do not know who fathered your child—then you can arrange to have him fostered as you wish; though no boy over five years old may live in the Guild-house." She was thinking out loud; suddenly she came back to the present. "Well, you will learn all that during your Guild-house training, sister."

Was it possible that she could share her two worlds? It seemed almost too good to be true. Magda said, hesitating, "You know that Lorill Hastur has forbidden contact between the Terran Zone and his people. It is easy to defy him in the Hellers, Jaelle; but here in Thendara?"

"Yes, that is one of the gravest difficulties," Jaelle said, "but Rohana is pledged to speak to Lorill. Her heart dwells in two worlds, too, and I think it is larger than either of them. And I think it is time that the people of Darkover, not the *Comyn* lords alone, knew something of the Terrans, and what they can do for our world. You heard Gabriel speak about Lorill's ban on trade. Hastur's will is not the voice of God, even to the *Comyn*! Let us find out what some of the others think. Will you come with me now to the Guild-house, sister, and see what we can do to settle this, before we meet tomorrow with Lord Hastur—and with your Terrans? Then we will know where we stand."

Magda hesitated. Then, knowing this was the moment of choice, she nodded.

"Yes, I will."

The next morning, the Lady Rohana sat beside Lorill Hastur in the small Council chamber, awaiting the arrival of the Terran coordinator. Peter Haldane sat across from them, looking both apprehensive and angry. Rohana could not read his thoughts, but she did not have to. This morning, Magda and Jaelle had vanished, and she was certain they had taken refuge in Thendara Guild-house. But they had left a message saying they would appear before Hastur at the Council, and it was not Rohana's duty to explain further when they had not.

Hastur leaned over and asked her in an undertone, "This was the man taken by Sain Scarp? Is he truly identical to Kyril? The resemblance is extraordinary; are we dealing here with Cherillys' Law?"

Rohana laughed. "I have not remembered Cherillys' Law since I was a psi monitor in Dalereuth Tower with you and Melora and Leonie," she said, "But no, it is not that; the Terran has only five fingers on either hand."

"Still, a remarkable likeness, and it goes to bear out what you said about a single race; although it seems fantastic to believe that our people could have come from another star, or that we would ever have permitted ourselves to forget such an heritage. And you told me that the woman has *laran*. May I ask how you found that out? I gave orders that no Terran was to witness a matrix operation."

"Jaelle was dying," Rohana said, "and her sworn sister had a right to remain with her. I can only imagine—" She frowned, trying to think it out. "Alida has the Ardais Gift; she is a catalyst telepath, and contact with her may have awakened latent *laran* in this woman. But if it had not been there, Alida could not have roused it. The man—Haldane—was there, too, and he showed no sign of being aware of what was going on. But whatever the reason, this woman has *laran*, and it means we must revise some of our preconceived notions about Terrans." She said "our" preconceived notions, but she really meant "your"; Hastur knew it and scowled.

He said, "Here is the Terran official, and his interpreter."

Rohana had met Montray before, and had not been impressed; she wondered if she had picked up some shred of Magda's contempt for the man. This time he was accompanied by a young man who spoke *casta* as well as either Peter or Magda, which was as well as any native-born Darkovan. He introduced himself as Wade Montray, the coordinator's son, and politely made himself known to each of them, while his father went toward Peter, glowering.

"So there you are, Haldane! Do you have any idea how much trouble you've caused? And where is Miss Lorne? She should be here! In fact, both of you should have reported back to the HQ last night for orders!"

Peter said rather stiffly, "I have not been informed that any charges have been filed against us. It did not seem proper to give offense to the Lady Rohana when she invited us to remain as her guests. I am certain that Magda will be here at the proper time." He turned toward the door, with an audible sigh of relief. "In fact, she is here. And the young woman with her was instrumental in saving my life, Montray, so you be polite to her, damn it!"

"Nice-looking girl," Montray commented, and Peter stiffened up again. "Montray, you've been on Darkover how long— ten years? If you haven't learned yet that it's not proper to make comments about a woman's looks, I suggest you put in for transfer as fast as you can, or never stick your head out of the Terran Zone!"

Magda had come into the room with Jaelle and three strange women, and was quietly seating herself with them on the fourth side of the room. Hastur said sternly, "Jaelle, what is this? I gave you no authority to invite any outsiders to this conference!"

"I did not ask for it, my Lord." Jaelle spoke respectfully, but with none of the fear most outsiders displayed before a *Comyn* lord. "Lord Hastur, it seemed to me that our Guild is very deeply concerned in these matters that are under discussion this morning, and I therefore asked these representatives to come and state our position before you, and before the Terrans."

Montray demanded, "What did she say?" and his son began quietly repeating Jaelle's words, as Jaelle went on.

"My Lord, my Lady and respected off-worlders," she added, turning to the Terrans. "I wish to present to you *Mestra* Millea n'ha Camilla, Guild-mother of Thendara House." Millea was a tall and bulky woman, conventionally dressed, and as feminine as Rohana herself, "*Mestra* Lauria n' Andrea, the head of the Independent Council of Craftswomen, and *Domna* Fiona n'ha Gorsali, Judge of the City Court of Arbitration."

Rohana thought, admiringly, *Oh, Jaelle, you are far more clever than I ever believed!* The women seating themselves in a dignified row across the room were no ordinary Amazons; they were three of the most powerful women in the city of Thendara. The Council of Craftswomen had successfully fought for the right to be recognized among the city's business; *Domna* Fiona was the first woman ever to be appointed a judge in the history of Thendara. Hastur could not dismiss them as unimportant.

Jaelle said, "Will you grant us the right to hear your deliberations, nobles?"

Hastur looked a trifle annoyed, but nothing could ruffle his long discipline in diplomacy. He rose and bowed politely to the three women. "I will not welcome you to this Council, for you came uninvited," he said, "but this is no secret conclave to work tyrannies; no concerned citizen may be denied the right to hear, and in turn, be heard."

Montray said, his son translating, "We welcome the chance to be heard by any citizens of Thendara. Be welcome, ladies."

Hastur addressed himself to Montray. He said, "When you were last before us, we granted permission for your employee, Magdalen Lorne"—Magda, seated among the Amazons, noticed that he did not hesitate or stumble even slightly over her Terran name—"to venture into the hills and negotiate for the rescue of your employee, the man Haldane, held captive at Sain Scarp. As I now understand the matter, the Lorne woman encountered a band of Free Amazons under the command of Jaelle n'ha Melora, and was required, according to their custom and the laws of their Charter, to swear an oath of allegiance to their Guild. Is this an accurate account of the affair?"

The Guild-mother Millea said, "According to the reports we have had from our sisters, this is true."

Hastur said, "I do not quite understand the difficulty. It seems to me that this is a matter for private agreement among the parties concerned, or at least for the courts of arbitration."

Montray listened with an angry frown; he said something, and his son shook his head, refusing to translate it.

Hastur turned to Magda and said, "Miss Lorne, did you have

these women brought here that you might petition, in the presence of all concerned, to be released from your Oath?"

Magda's voice was low, but very clear. She said, "No, my Lord Hastur. I am willing to abide by the Oath I swore, and to honor it till death. But I am not certain that the Terran authorities will allow me to do so. They may possibly hold that my Oath is not valid, or that because of prior loyalties I had no right to swear it."

Montray said something again, and the young translator said, just audibly, "I told you so."

Rohana, watching, realized that Magda had done an exceptionally clever thing. In private, the Terran ambassador might state that he did not believe in the validity of a Darkovan oath. But if he said so, in the presence of Hastur and three Guild-mothers from Thendara, he destroyed the credibility of every Terran on Darkover for decades to come. And if he didn't know it, and judging by his expression he hadn't, he was finding it out in no uncertain terms, both from the young and expert translator, and from Peter Haldane! From the look of frustration on his face, Rohana could tell, even without need for a scrap of *laran*, that he was consigning all of them, especially Magda, to whatever his Terran equivalent was for the coldest of Zandru's hells!

Domna Fiona said, "The noble guest from Terra appears to find some difficulty in accepting the decision; may we hear it, with Lord Hastur's permission?"

Montray said, waiting for his son to translate, "The difficulty is this: Miss Lorne is extremely valuable to us. She is the only woman qualified to act as an expert on the Darkovan languages, and to advise us on women's customs and the laws governing social usage on Darkover. It seems to us that we cannot, for the moment, spare her to any other work, valuable as it may be, and highly as we may respect those who would welcome her among them."

Rohana knew perfectly well that the polite phrases had been added by the translator, and suspected that Montray's original had been more emphatic and much less courteous. She did not understand enough of the Terran language to be sure.

"If that is the only difficulty, it can easily be settled," *Domna* Fiona said. From the voice, and something about the narrow body in the judicial robes, Rohana suspected the woman was an *emmasca;* but the robes were too bulky to be sure. "If your problem is a lack of adequate experts on women's customs and the languages, then I think we can offer assistance. Sister," and she turned to Jaelle, who stood up nervously.

Her eyes met Peter's briefly across the room. Jaelle said, "Say to the Terran official that if it is agreeable to your people, I will offer myself to take my sister's place in working for you. I speak both *casta* and *cahuenga* fluently, and I can read and write in these and in the language of the Dry Towns; and I think I can help you to fill in what gaps there are in your knowledge of the customs of Thendara. And I think there are others of my sisters who would be willing to do the same, to the limits of your needs. We have been told"—again, briefly, she met Peter's eyes—"that you Terrans have had trouble in finding workers for anything but simple manual labor, and that you have sought for them without success."

Montray said, "That would indeed be welcome." He bowed politely to Jaelle. "But we had heard it was the will of Hastur that the people of Thendara should not give us this kind of assistance."

The Amazon Lauria, head of the Council of Craftswomen, said quietly, "The Lord Hastur speaks for the *Comyn*, and for their sworn followers and those who owe allegiance in the Domains. But the will, or the whim, of Hastur is not yet the law of this land. With all respect, Lord Hastur"—and she made a deep bow to the *Comyn* lord—"we do not accept the right of *Comyn* to lay commands upon the free women of Thendara as to what lawful work they may accept, or what their relations shall be with the men of the Empire from the stars . . . or with their women. By the will of Hastur, the only women who have been permitted to know the men of the Empire are the women in the bars and brothels near the spaceport. We do not believe this will give a true picture of our world to the men of the *Terranan*. So we have come here today to offer you our lawful services in fields more suitable for meaningful communication between our two worlds: as mapmakers, guides, translators or any suitable work at which the Terrans wish to employ Darkovan workers and experts. And in return, knowing that you of the Empire may have much to teach us, we ask that a group of our young women be placed as apprentices among your medical services and other scientific branches of your knowledge to allow us to learn from you. Is that agreeable to you, *messire* of Terra?"

Of course it was agreeable, thought Magda, watching Montray's face; it was what they had hoped for from the beginning, what they had so obdurately been denied on Darkover. She had never realized—and blamed herself for her own insensitivity—that the women of Darkover would resent being judged, by the Terrans, only by the women their men met in the bars and brothels. She herself, with her knowledge of such respectable women as she could meet in the markets and public places of Thendara, had gone a little deeper—but not much.

It wasn't, of course, total cooperation. There weren't that many Free Amazons, and they were rarely in positions of such power as *Domna* Fiona. (It was also the first she had heard of the Courts of Arbitration. *What a lot I have to learn,* she thought, *and what fun I'm going to have learning it!*)

And afterward she would work again for the Terrans, and be one of the first to come and go between the two worlds, helping them to find a way to one another. Two worlds: and she would belong to both! She looked across at Lady Rohana, and the lady smiled. Again Magda had the image of a great door swinging wide, both ways, an opened door between locked-away worlds. . . .

Jaelle was watching Lorill Hastur. He seemed not very pleased, but he capitulated with such good grace as he could. *The fact is, the Free Amazons just aren't important enough—or so Hastur thinks—that he can, with dignity, take any notice of what we do. But where we go, others will follow, for their own reasons.* She caught Peter's eyes across the room, and smiled; and it seemed that her heart stopped at his returning smile.

I have found an honorable way we can be together in his world!

Montray was answering Hastur's gracious words with a little speech about friendship and brotherhood, carefully using all the wrong inflections while his son Wade carefully straightened them out and made them into the proper ones.

How will Montray get along without me to write his speeches? Magda realized, lightheartedly, that she didn't give a damn. She had more interesting things to do.

When it had all been settled, and Hastur and Lady Rohana and Montray—his son at his elbow to keep him from any too offensive mistakes—were exchanging amenities, Peter and Jaelle and Magda met for a moment in the doorway of the Council chamber. Peter knew the custom of the Domains too well to touch Jaelle in public, but his quick glance at her was like an embrace. But he spoke to Magda, with raillery:

"So you've had your own way, Mag, and made us all look like fools—doing what no man could manage to do! Have you really such contempt for us all, then?"

"Contempt? Not really," Magda said, but she could not help flicking a quick look at Montray, which Peter caught. "But he, at least, hasn't done so well with Darkover so far."

Peter said, "Everyone knew you were doing the real work of the coordinator's office, Magda. It's just the way the breaks run, that you couldn't have the title, too. Maybe someday you can have the job."

She smiled without bitterness and said, "No, thanks. Why don't you try for it, Peter?" She felt the strange little prickles of the hunch running up and down her spine as she spoke. "You'll make a good coordinator—or the first Legate, someday. I have something better to do."

"You've already done miracles," he said, clasping her hands warmly, and she shook her head.

"It wasn't I. It was Jaelle—and the Guild-mothers."

He said under his breath to Jaelle, "You are wonderful! I never believed you could do it!"

Jaelle said quietly, "I think you do not believe that women

can do many things, Piedro, in spite of what Margali has done for us both. But perhaps you will learn, someday. I believed, for a time, that women among your people were more free than mine. Now I know that there is really not so much difference between Terra and Darkover. My foster-mother told me, once, that it was better to wear chains than to believe you are free, and weight yourself with invisible chains." Then she smiled at him, a luminous smile. "But there is always hope, and I am committed to a day when we are part of the Empire from the stars, and when we are not all strangers and aliens, but all people are— are—" She hesitated, stumbled for a word, and Peter said, "Where all men are brothers?"

She smiled, caught Magda's eyes and said, "And sisters."

He said, "Well, politics can wait; you and I have other things to think of today! Magda, will you come with us when we declare ourselves before witnesses?"

"I cannot," she said, glancing at the Guild-mothers. "I am not really supposed to leave the Guild-house for half a year after I am sworn." Suddenly she held out her hands.

"Oh, Peter, wish me luck! Don't hold it against me!"

He gave her a brief, almost brotherly hug. "I do, Mag," he said, kissing her on the cheek. "Looks like you'll need luck with those old battle-axes! But it's what you want, so be happy, love."

She said, "Jaelle—" and impetuously Jaelle flung her arms around Magda, holding her tight. Magda whispered. "You be happy, too."

"I'll come and see you," Jaelle promised. "Thendara House is my home, too."

Peter said, "But you must promise not to turn her against me, Magda! Must I cope with all those mothers-in-law?"

Jaelle said, laughing, "No one could turn me against you. But you must learn someday not to speak so of my mothers and sisters!"

She's grown up, Magda thought. *I've always thought of her as a young girl. But she isn't. She's a woman. And she isn't infatuated anymore. She knows him for what he is. And she loves him anyway.*

He would never understand that there could be loyalties—certainly not loyalties between women—that could go deeper than love. But he would do his best for the world they all loved, and his best would be very good indeed. And for that, if nothing else, Magda knew she would always love him a little.

The Guild-mother Millea turned and beckoned to Magda to join them. Magda kissed Jaelle again, and said, "Be good to each other." Then, slowly, but without looking back, she went across the room to join the three women.

Jaelle, standing and watching her go, seemed to catch from her mind the image of a great, opening door, swinging wide on a sunlit world and a brilliantly lighted future.

THENDARA HOUSE

ACKNOWLEDGMENT

Shortly after I completed the novel *The Shattered Chain*, I began writing, for my own amusement, the story of Magda in the Amazon Guild House. At that time Jacqueline Lichtenberg and I were corresponding regularly and frequently, and she suggested that I should also write the story of Jaelle among the Terrans. I said I didn't feel qualified just then to do so, but that *she* could, if she wished. So, for the fun of it, we wrote about half a dozen chapters each, passing them back and forth between us and discussing them, with an eye to eventual professional collaboration. However, we were both busy with other projects, far from Darkover, and Jacqueline's career was taking off in a far different direction. Also, it turned out, we had quite different ideas about where the story was going, and before long we discovered that we were pulling in opposite directions, and, with suitable expressions of regret and mutual esteem, abandoned this particular collaboration; she went back to her own "Sime" and "Molt Brother" seria—if that is the plural of series—and I to write other Darkover and non-Darkover novels, feeling that the botched collaboration was not redeemable, and tossing it into my bottom file drawer with other projects on what I believed would be permanent "hold."

Years later, taking up this collaboration, although I have rewritten almost everything Jacqueline did on it—for our writing styles and themes are very different—I note that my concept of the character of Jaelle has nevertheless been broadened and strengthened by her input on the chapters in which she had the first touch. Although this is not a collaboration, I am still greatly indebted to Jacqueline for allowing me to see a character of my own through her eyes. As she has graciously acknowledged my part in what I consider her best book, *Unto Zeor, Forever*, so I must acknowledge her part in this book of mine.

MARION ZIMMER BRADLEY

PART I
CONFLICTING OATHS

PART II
SUNDERING

PART III
OUTGROWTH

PART I:

CONFLICTING OATHS

Chapter 1

Magdalen Lorne

Light feathers of snow were falling overhead; but toward the east there was a break in the clouds where the dull reddish light of Cottman IV—the sun of Darkover, called the Bloody Sun by the Terran Empire—could be seen dimly through cloud, like a great bloodshot eye.

Magdalen Lorne shivered a little as she walked slowly up the approach to the Terran HQ. She was in Darkovan dress, so she had to show her indent cards to the Spaceforce people at the gates; but one of them knew her by sight.

"It's all right, Miss Lorne. You'll have to go over to the new building, though."

"They finally finished the new quarters for Intelligence?"

The uniformed man nodded.

"That's right. And the new Chief came in from Alpha Centaurus the other day—have you met her yet?"

This was news to Magda. Darkover was a Closed Planet, Class B, which meant Terrans were—officially, at least—restricted to certain Treaty Zones and Trade Cities. There was no official Intelligence Service, except for a small office in Records and Communications, working directly out of the Coordinator's office.

It's about time they opened a branch of Intelligence here. They could do with a Department of Alien Anthropology, too. Then Magda wondered what it would mean to her own somewhat irregular status. She had been born on Darkover, in Caer Donn, where the Terrans had built their first spaceport before shifting to the new Empire Headquarters here in Thendara. She had been reared among Darkovans, before the new policy of standardization of spaceport buildings to Empire-normal yellow lights—a policy making little or no provision for the red sun of Darkover and the fierce cold of the climate. This, of course, made sense for Empire personnel stationed on ordinary Empire planets, who seldom stayed in one post more than a year or so and did not need to acclimatize themselves; but conditions on Darkover were, to say the least, unusual for an Empire planet.

Magda's parents had been linguists who had spent much of their lives in Caer Donn; she had grown up more Darkovan than Terran, one of only three or four people who spoke the language like a native and were capable of doing undercover research into customs and language. She had never been away from Darkover except for three years of schooling in the Empire's Intelligence School on Alpha Colony; then she had accepted a position in Communications as a matter of course. But what had been, to her superiors, only convenient disguise, fitting her for research and undercover work on the planet of her birth, had become to Magda her deepest self.

And it is to that Darkovan self, Margali, not Magda, that I must now be true. And not just Margali, but Margali n'ha Ysabet, Renunciate of the Comhi-Letzii, *what the Terrans would call Free Amazon. That is what I am now and must be henceforth*, men dia pre'zhiuro. . . . Magda whispered to herself the first words of the Renunciate's Oath, and shivered. It would not be easy. But as she had sworn, so would she do. To a Terran, an oath given under duress was not binding. *Darkovan, the Oath binds me without question, the very thought of escaping it dishonorable*.

She wrenched her thoughts from that endless loop in her mind. *A new section for Intelligence*, he had said, *and a new Chief*. Probably, Magda thought with a resigned shrug, someone who knew considerably less about the job than she did herself. She, and her ex-husband, Peter Haldane, had both been born here, were naturally bilingual, knew and accepted the customs as their own. But that was not the way the Empire did things.

The new Intelligence Office was in a tall skyscraper, still shining with newness, high above the Port. By the Terra-normal yellow lights, too bright for Magda's eyes, she saw a woman standing; a woman she knew, or had once known, very well.

Cholayna Ares was taller than Magda, brown-skinned, with white hair—Magda had never known whether it was prematurely grayed or whether it had always been naturally silver-white, for her face was, and had always been, unusually young. She smiled and reached out in a welcoming gesture, and Magda took her old teacher's hand.

"It's hard to imagine you'd give up the Training School," Magda said. "Certainly not to come here—"

"Oh, I didn't exactly give it up." Cholayna Ares laughed. "There was the usual sort of bureaucratic hassle—each group tried to get me on their side, and I said a plague on both their houses, and put in for transfer. So I wound up—here. Not a popular post, so no competition for getting it. I remembered that you came from here, and you liked it. Not many people have a chance of building the Intelligence Service up out of nothing on a Class B planet. And with you and Peter Haldane—didn't I hear once that you'd married him?"

"The marriage broke up last year," Magda said. "The usual sort of thing." She warded her former teacher's look of curious sympathy away with a hard shrug. "The only problem it created was that they didn't send us out in the field together any more."

"If there was no Intelligence Service here, what were you doing in the field?"

"We worked out of Communications," Magda said. "Language research; at one time they had me recording jokes and idioms from the marketplace, just a way of keeping up with language and current slang, so people who *did* have to go into the field wouldn't make stupid mistakes."

"And so, my first day on the job, you come up to greet me and make me feel welcome?" Cholayna asked. "Sit down—tell me all about this place. It's kind of you, Magda. I always knew you'd make a good career in Intelligence."

Magda lowered her eyes. "That wasn't the idea—I hadn't been told you were here." She decided the only way to get it said was to say it. "I came here to resign."

Cholayna's dark eyes showed the dismay she felt.

"Magda! You and I both know what the Service is like! Certainly they should have offered you this job, but I always thought we were friends, and that you'd be willing to stay on for a while, at least!"

Magda had never thought of that. But of course it was the impression Cholayna would get. She wished the new Head had been a complete stranger, or at least someone she disliked, not a woman she had always liked and respected.

"Oh, no, Cholayna! I give you my word, it has nothing to do with you! I didn't even know you were here, I was in the field till last night—" She found she was stammering in her eagerness to convince Cholayna of the truth. Cholayna frowned and gestured her to sit down.

"I think you'd better tell me all about it, Magda."

Uneasily, Magda sat down. "You weren't at the Council this morning. You didn't know. While I was in the field—I took the Oath of a Renunciate." At the bewildered look on her colleague's face she elaborated. "In the files they're called Free Amazons; they don't like the name. I am bound to spend half a year in the Guild-house in Thendara for training, and after that—after that, I'm not sure what I intend to do, but I don't think it will be Intelligence.

"But what a wonderful opportunity. Magda," Cholayna said. "I wouldn't think of accepting your resignation! I'll put you on inactive status, if you like, for the half year, but think of the thesis you can get out of this! Your work is already regarded as the standard of excellence, you know—I did hear that much from the Coordinator," she added. "You probably know more about Darkovan customs than anyone working here. I also heard that the Medic division has agreed to train a group of Free Amazons—" she saw Magda's slight wince and amended—"What was it you called them—Renunciates? Sounds like an order of nuns, what do they renounce? Sounds like a strange place for you."

Magda smiled at the comparison. "I could quote the Oath for you. Mostly what they—we—renounce are the protections for women in the society, in exchange for certain freedoms." Even to her, it sounded like a woefully inadequate explanation, but how could she explain? "But I'm not doing this to write a thesis, you know, or to provide more information for Terran Intelligence. That's why I came to turn in my resignation."

"And that's why I'll refuse to accept it," said Cholayna.

"Do you think I am going to spy on my friends in the Guild-house? Never!"

"I'm sorry you see it that way, Magda. I don't. The more we know about the different groups on any planet, the easier it is for us—and the easier it is for the planet we're on, because there's less chance of misunderstandings and trouble between the Empire and the locals—"

"Yes, yes, I learned all that in the Intelligence School," Magda said impatiently. "Standard party line, isn't it?"

"I wouldn't put it that way." There was something like carefully controlled anger in the older woman's voice.

"But I would, and I'm beginning to see how it can be misused," Magda said, and now she too was angry. "If you won't accept my resignation, Cholayna, I'll have to leave without it. Darkover is my home. And if the price of becoming a Renunciate is to give up my Empire citizenship, why, then—"

"Wait just a minute, Magda—please?" Cholayna held up her hand to interrupt the angry torrent of words. "And sit down again, won't you?" Magda realized that she had started to her feet; slowly she sank down again in the chair. Cholayna went to the console on the office wall and dialled herself a cup of coffee; brought another to Magda, balancing the hot cups in her palm, and sank down to a chair beside her.

"Magda, forget for a minute that I'm your superior officer won't you? I always thought we were friends. I didn't expect you'd walk away without any explanation at all."

I thought we were friends, too, Magda thought, sipping at the coffee. *But I know now I have never had any woman friends at all; I didn't know what friendship was. I was always trying so hard to be one of the boys that I never paid any attention to what other women did, or didn't do. Until I met Jaelle, and knew what it was to have a friend I'd fight for and die for if I must. Cholayna isn't my friend either, she's my superior and she's using friendship to make me do what she wants. Maybe she thinks that is being my friend, it's a Terran way of thinking. I'm just not one of them anymore. If I ever was.*

"Why don't you tell me the whole thing, Magda?" The kindly look in Cholayna's eyes confused Magda again. *Maybe she really thinks of herself as my friend.*

She began at the beginning, telling Cholayna how Peter Haldane, her friend and partner, and for a time her husband, had been kidnapped by bandits who had mistaken him for Kyril Ardais, son of the Lady Rohana Ardais. Fearing to travel alone as a woman, Magda had been persuaded by Lady Rohana to disguise herself as a Free Amazon. When she had later encountered a band of genuine Renunciates, led by Jaelle n'ha Melora, the deception had been discovered.

"The penalty for a man who invaded them in women's clothes would have been death or castration," Magda explained. "For a woman, the penalty is only that the lie must become truth; a woman may not enjoy the freedoms of the Oath without first renouncing the safety and protection of the laws specially protecting women."

"An oath taken under duress—" Cholayna began but Magda shook her head.

"No. I was given free choice. They offered to escort me to a Guild-house where one of the Elders would decide the special circumstances—whether I could simply be sworn to secrecy and released." She sighed, wearily wondering if it had been worth it. "That would have lost too much time; Peter was to be executed at Midwinter if not ransomed. I chose, quite freely, to take the Oath; but I took it with a lot of—of mental reservation. I felt just as you do now. Only between then and now I—I changed my mind."

She knew that sounded ridiculously inadequate. She went on, telling only a little of the cruel conflict in her mind, when she had intended to escape, leave her Oath, even if she must kill Jaelle, or leave her to be slaughtered by bandits; and how she had found herself fighting at the woman's side, saving her life. . . .

Cholayna listened to the story in silence, rising once to refill the coffee cups. Finally she said, "I can understand, to some extent, why you feel obligated."

"It's not only that," Magda said. "The Oath has become very real to me. I feel myself a Renunciate at heart—I think I would always have been one, had I known such a choice existed. Now—" How could she explain it? She drained the cold coffee from the cup and concluded helplessly, "It is something I *must* do."

Cholayna nodded. "I can see that. I don't know if there is a precedent. I've heard of men going over the wall, going native, on some of the Empire planets. I don't think I've ever heard of a woman doing that, though."

"I'm not exactly *going over the wall*," Magda pointed out. "If I were, would I be here in your office, formally turning in my resignation?"

"Which I do not intend to accept," Cholayna said. "No, listen to me—I listened to you, didn't I? There's no precedent for this; I don't think there's any way to give up Empire citizenship for a sworn-in civil servant, and you made that choice when you accepted three years' training in the Intelligence School—"

"I've done enough work to repay the Empire—"

Cholayna silenced her with a gesture. "Nobody questions that, Magda. I am perfectly willing to put you on inactive status, if you must have your six months—half year—how long is the Darkovan year anyhow? But something has come up which ties in very well with what you have told me."

She turned to her desk and took up a file of printouts.

"As it happens, I have a transcript of that Council here," she said, and Magda glanced at the printouts—the Council where Lord Hastur had been forced to accept the validity of a Terran's Oath and where the Guild-mothers had arranged that the Terrans should engage the services of the Renunciate Jaelle n'ha Melora to work in Magda's place in the Terran Headquarters, prior to the employment of a dozen Free Amazons. "—Oh, very well,

Renunciates," Cholayna amended quickly, "to be trained in medical technology by our Medic Department, and possibly in other sciences and skills. With Jaelle working among us, and you in the Guild-house, it seems to me that during this half year you will be especially qualified to determine personnel practices for Darkovan employees in the Empire, especially among women. We are prepared to put you on detached duty. Living among Darkovan women, you can find out which women could handle the culture shock of living among Terrans, as well as letting us know how we ought to treat them for the best communication between Terrans and Darkovans. You are the only person who is qualified to do this, actually living in a Guild-house."

Finally Magda said, "If you already know all this, Cholayna, why did you have me tell it to you?"

"I only knew what you had said," Cholayna replied, "and what the Guild-mothers had said about you. I did not know how you felt about it. Because the student was the right kind of girl when I knew her, doesn't mean the woman who had become a trained Agent was the kind we could trust."

Somehow the words softened Magda's anger, as Cholayna went on. "Can't you see? This is for the good of your Renunciates, as well as for the Empire—to cushion them against the worst of culture shock when they come here? Even, if necessary, to know which Terrans we can trust to deal fairly with them? You know, and I knew before I had been here a tenday, that Russ Montray is no more fit to be Legate, when they get a Legation here, than I am to pilot a starship! He doesn't like the planet, and he doesn't understand the people worth a damn. And I can tell, from the way you speak, that you do."

Is she trying to flatter me, to get me to do what she wants? Or does she mean it? Magda knew, of course, that Montray was considerably less fit than she was herself. Yet on a planet like Darkover, with its strictured traditional roles for men and women, Magda knew she could never be a Legate, or hold any comparable post, because the Darkovans would never accept a woman in such a position. Cholayna herself could hold her post in Intelligence only because she would never come into direct contact with Darkovans, but only with her field Agents.

"Magda, I can tell from the way you're looking at me, that something about this bothers you—"

"I do not want to seem to spy on my sisters in the Guild-house—"

"I never thought of asking that," Cholayna replied, "only that you create, for us, a set of rules for Terrans who must come into close contact with Darkovan women in general, particularly with Renunciates in the service or employ of the Empire. This will benefit us, certainly—but I would think it would benefit your—your Guild-sisters even more."

There seemed no way to refuse that. She would indeed be doing just the kind of service for Darkover, and the Guild-house, which the Guild-mothers had said, at that Council, that they would welcome. She remembered what the Guild-mother Lauria had said:

"We have come here today to offer you our lawful services in fields more suitable for meaningful communication between our two worlds. As mapmakers, guides, translators, or any work for which the Terrans wish to employ Darkover. And in return, knowing that you of the Empire may have much to teach us, we ask that a group of our young women be placed as apprentices among your medical services, and other scientific branches of your knowledge to allow us to hear from you . . ."

And this had been a real breakthrough. Before this day, the men of the Empire had been able to judge the culture of Darkover only by the women they met in the Spaceport bars and the marketplace. When she had heard Mother Lauria say this, she had realized that she would be one of the first to come and go, building bridges between her new world and her old one. She bent her head in capitulation. She was still an Intelligence Agent, no matter how she might resent it.

"As for your resignation—forget it. That isn't the kind of thing you could do without a lot more thought than you've given it. Leave the doors open. Both ways." Cholayna reached out and patted Magda's hand, an unexpected gesture, and somehow it softened Magda's hostility.

"We need to know how we should treat these Renunciates when they are employed by the Terrans. What are their criteria for good behavior? What would offend or upset them? And while you are in the Guild-house, we may ask you to make the final choice of which women we can accept, which women are qualified for Medic apprentices, women with open minds, flexible toward changing customs—"

Magda said patiently, "Do you really believe that most of them are unenlightened savages, Cholayna? May I remind you that for all its Closed B status, Darkover has a very complex and sophisticated culture—"

"With a pre-space, pre-industrial technological level," Cholayna said dryly. "I'm not doubting they have great poets and a fine musical tradition, or whatever else it takes to make you Communications people call a culture sophisticated. The Malgamins of Beta Hydri have a highly sophisticated culture too, but they embody ritual cannibalism and human sacrifice. If we are going to give these people our own highly sophisticated technology, we must have some notion of what they're going to do with it. I suppose you are familiar with Malthusian theories, and what happens to a culture when you start—for instance— saving the lives of children, in a culture where population control cannot proceed, for religious or other reasons, at an equal level? Remember the rabbits in Australia, or don't they teach that classic example of Anthropology 1-A any more?"

She had only the vaguest memory of the classic example, but knew what the theory involved. The expansion of population, taking the brakes off predators or increasing survival at birth, created exponential expansion and resultant chaos. Terrans had been widely criticized for denying medical knowledge to native populations for just that reason. Magda knew of the policy, and the hard necessities behind it.

"I think, when you've had time to go over it in your mind, you'll know why you have to cooperate with us, even for the sake of your own sisters in your—" she hesitated and groped for the word, "Guild-house." She stood up and her voice was crisp.

"Good luck, Magda. While you're on detached duty you'll

get two rises in pay, you know." The gesture put Magda back in the service, and she wondered dimly if she ought to salute.

And I didn't manage to do what I came to do, I didn't resign. I needed, so desperately, to be one thing or the other, not torn between them like this. The real me, the truest me, is Darkovan. Yet too much Terran to be true Darkovan . . .

She had never really belonged anywhere. Perhaps, in the Guild-house, she would find out where she belonged—but only if the Terrans would let her alone.

She went out of the Intelligence office, briefly debated going to her old quarters to retrieve a few cherished possessions. No. They would be of no use to her in the Guild-house, and would only proclaim her Terran. She hesitated again, thinking of Peter and Jaelle, who would be married this morning as freemates— the only marriage lawful for a Renunciate. Jaelle would want her at the wedding; and Peter, too, in token that she bore him no grudge because he now loved and desired Jaelle.

I do not want Peter. I am not jealous of Jaelle. As she told Cholayna Ares, the marriage had been broken before she had ever known Jaelle. And yet somehow she felt she could not endure their newlywed happiness.

She hurried toward the gate and went through, taking off her Terran HQ identity badge and dropping it into a trash can as she went.

Now she had burnt her bridges; she could not return without special arrangement, for she would not be admitted as an employee. On a Closed Status planet, there was no free access between Terran and Darkovan territory. What she had done had committed her, irrevocably, to the Guild-house and to Darkover.

She hurried through the streets until she saw the walled building, windowless and blind to the street, with the small sign on the door:

THENDARA HOUSE
GUILD OF RENUNCIATES.

She rang the small, concealed doorbell, and somewhere, a long way inside, she heard the sound of a bell.

Chapter 2

Jaelle n'ha Melora

Jaelle was dreaming. . . .
She was riding, under a strange ominous sky, like spilt
blood on the sands of the Drylands. . . . Strange faces sur-
rounded her, women unchained, unbound, the kind of women
her father had mocked, yet her mother had once been one of
them . . . her hands were chained, but with ribbon links which
broke asunder, so that she did not know where to go, and some-
where her mother was screaming, and pain crashed through her
mind . . .

No. It was a noise, a blaring, somehow *metallic* noise, and
there was a glaring yellow light cutting through her eyelids.
Then she was aware that Peter was nuzzling her shoulder as he
leaned over her to cut off the blaring sound. Now she remembered; it was a signal, a rising bell like the ones she had heard
on her one visit to the guest-house at Nevarsin monastery. But a
sound so harsh and mechanical could not be compared with the
mellow, tempered monastery chime. Her head ached, and she remembered the party last night in the Terran HQ Recreation area,
meeting a few of Peter's friends. She had drunk more of the unaccustomed strong drinks than she intended, hoping she would
be able to relax her shyness before all the strangers. Now the
whole evening was only a blur of names she could not pronounce and faces not attached to names.

"Better hurry, sweetheart," Peter urged, "don't want to be late your first day on a new job, and I can't afford to—one bad black mark against me already."

Peter had left the shower running. Her back ached from the strange bed; she wasn't sure whether it had been too hard or too soft, but it hadn't felt right. She told herself that was ridiculous. She had slept in all kinds of strange places, and certainly a good, icy shower would wake her up and make her feel refreshed. To her surprise the water was warm, lulling rather than bracing, and she could not remember how to adjust it for cold. Anyhow, she was awake, and went to dress.

From somewhere Peter had produced an HQ uniform for her, and she struggled into it, the long shaped tights that made her feel uncomfortably as if her legs were bare, the ridiculously low and thin shoes, the short black tunic piped with blue. His own tunic was like it, only piped with red. He had told her what the different colors meant, but she had forgotten. The tunic was so tight she could not pull it over her head, and it took her some time to figure why they had put the long fastener in the back where she had trouble reaching it, instead of in the front where it would have been sensible. Why would anyone want a dress that tight, anyhow? Cut looser, and with the press-together seam in the front, it would have been an admirable dress for a woman if she was breast-feeding a child, but this way it seemed a waste of materials—cut a few inches looser, it would have slipped over her head without needing the fastening at all. It felt rough against her skin, since no under-tunic was provided, but at least it had warm knitted neck-folds and tight sleeves. She was frowning at herself in the mirror when he came up behind her, already dressed, and took her shoulders, looking at her in the mirror and then hugging her hard.

"You look marvelous in uniform," he said, "Once they see you, every man in the HQ will be envying me."

Jaelle cringed; this was exactly what she had been taught to avoid. The dress was cut immodestly close to the curve of her breast and her narrow waist. She felt troubled, but when he turned her around and held her close, she buried her face against him, and in his arms, all the tension seemed to flow out of her. She sighed and murmured, "I wish you didn't have to go—"

"Mmmmmm, I do too," he murmured, caressing her, burying his lips in her bare neck—then, abruptly, raised his eyes and stared at the chronometer on the wall.

"Ouch! Look at the time! I told you I didn't dare be late back, this first day," he said, and made for the door. She felt icy cold, in spite of the hot shower, as he mumbled, "Sorry, love, I'm late, but you can find the way down alone, can't you? I'll see you tonight." The door closed, and Jaelle stood alone. Still roused from his touch and his kiss, she realized that he had not even waited for the answer to his own question. She wasn't at all sure she could get down to the office where she had been told to report this morning, in the bewildering labyrinth of the HQ.

She stared blindly at the chronometer, trying to translate Terran time into the familiar hours of the day. It was, as nearly as she could reckon, not yet three hours after sunrise. She remembered a flippant comment of Magda's:

I don't think you'll like it much in the Terran Zone, the other woman had said. *Sometimes they even make love by the clock.*

But she, too, had duties this morning. She could not stand here, staring uneasily at her image in the mirror. Nor could she imagine going among strange men, Terrans, in this immodestly tight dress. Not even a prostitute would go out in such attire! With shaking hands, she unfastened it and got into her ordinary clothes. The uniform was not warm enough, either, for the late-spring weather outside; inside the buildings, heated to almost suffocating warmth, the uniform might be sufficient, but she had to go outdoors—she stared at the little map of the HQ Peter had left her, trying to puzzle out the confusing markings.

She found her way, shivering in the morning drizzle, to the main building and showed the pass Peter had given her. The Security man said, "Mrs. Haldane? You should have gone through the underground tunnel, in this weather," and she looked around, seeing, indeed, no one on the elaborate walks and ramps.

She managed to puzzle out the signs—Peter had given her a crash course in reading the most common signs, and she had been taught a little Standard, which was not really so very different from *casta*—she had been told once that they had descended from a common language group before Darkover was settled, that *casta* was similar to the most common Terran language. She felt reluctant to ask directions from any of the men and women moving around in the rabbit-warren buildings; they all seemed to look alike, in tights, tunics of varying colors and trim, low, thin sandals. She rode up and down a time or two in the elevator until she figured out how it worked. It was not complicated, once you could understand why anyone would *bother*. Did the Terrans suffer from a racial paralysis of the legs, or something, that they could not walk up and down stairs? She supposed it made sense when there were twenty or thirty floors to a building, but why build it so high? They had been given enough room in the spaceport HQ to build rationally!

There was nothing wrong with Peter's legs, at least, she thought smiling; perhaps Terrans were just trained to be lazy.

Outside the section Peter had marked on the map—it was marked, too, with one of those signs that spelled, she knew, the Terran word for COMMUNICATIONS—she presented herself before a man stationed there. She said, "My name is Jaelle n'ha Melora," and proffered her pass.

"Just go over there and present it to the screening device," he said indifferently. She slid the pass through the slot, and the glass screen began to blink with a strange beeping sound.

"What's the matter?" he asked.

She stared helplessly at the blinking, beeping screen. "I don't know—" she began, "they slid my pass back out at me—" and she picked it up, bewildered, from the slot.

He glanced at it and at the screen. He frowned and said "You're out of uniform, and the scanners don't recognize you from the picture—see? And the name you said doesn't match the name on the pass, Miss." She puzzled this out to an honorific, roughly equivalent to *damisela*. Should she correct him? He pointed patiently to the name on the pass and said "You have to repeat the name in the form it's on the pass. See? *Haldane, Mrs. Peter.* Try saying it like that."

She started to protest that her name was Jaelle, that it was forbidden by Oath to a Renunciate to take a man's name, but quickly stopped herself. It was none of his business and how could she explain it to a Terran anyhow? Meekly she repeated "Haldane, Mrs. Peter," before the screen, and the door slid back and let her in. She remembered that some of Peter's friends last night—not the best friends—had called her Mrs. Haldane and she had had to correct them. But was that was Magda's name too, then?

She went into a huge light room with the omnipresent yellow glare. Along the wall were strange machines she did not recognize. A young woman rose from behind a narrow table to greet her.

"I'm Bethany Kane," she said. "You must be Jaelle." Her *cahuenga*, the Trade City language, was barely intelligible, so that Jaelle hardly recognized her own name. Bethany led her to a table with glass panels and strange equipment. "Leave your things here and we'll go up and get started; I'm supposed to take you up to Basic and Medic."

Jaelle could tell that it was a memorized speech—she had obviously brought no "things" to leave, and the young woman seemed to want to say more, but couldn't. On an impulse Jaelle replied in *casta*, "Magda mentioned her friend Bethany to me; you are she?"

Bethany said with a relieved smile "I didn't know you spoke the city language, Jaelle—is that how you pronounce it, Zhay-el-leh?"

Bethany was a slight woman, with medium brown hair, brown eyes—*like an animal's eyes*, Jaelle thought—and she looked pretty and rounded in the Terran uniform which seemed so immodestly cut. How could the woman display herself like that, in an office composed of men and women together? Perhaps, if only women were nearby, it would not seem so—so—
—Jaelle fumbled for the concept; so deliberately enticing. Yet these women worked with men on easy terms and no one seemed to notice. She filed that away for later thought as they passed the uniformed men at a succession of doors and Bethany,

taking her scribbled pass, got them through various tunnels and elevators through what seemed to Jaelle like miles and miles of corridor. Her sandalled feet, accustomed to stoutly laced boots, were aching by the time they reached their goal. She put aside her theory that Terrans were lazy; with this much racing about, perhaps they needed their elevators and escalators.

The next hours were the most confusing of her life. There was a place with lights flashing and glaring into her eyes, and a moment later a small, laminated card slid out of a slot, with a picture Jaelle, for a moment, did not recognize as herself; a small serious-looking red-haired woman with slightly frightened eyes. Bethany saw her grimace at the picture and chuckled.

"Oh, we all look like that in ID pictures. As if we were being lined up and photographed for a prison sentence; something about the lights and the pose. You should see mine!" But, though Jaelle expected her to offer it, she did not, and she supposed it must be some form of figurative speech, social noise. Then an elderly gentleman, round and good-natured, who spoke excellent Darkovan, questioned her at length about her place of birth ("Shainsa? Where exactly is that?" and finally managed to get her to sketch a rough map of the road between the Dry Towns and Thendara) her age, the date of her birth, and asked her to pronounce her name again and again while he scribbled it down in precise markings which, he said, might help others to pronounce it very accurately; Jaelle wondered why he could not simply tell them, or use one of the omnipresent voice recorders—at one point she had been startled to hear her own voice coming from one of them. But she had known there would be many unfamiliar things. At one point he called her "Mrs. Haldane," and when she corrected him, smiled gently and said, "The custom of the country, my dear girl." He used the phrase, which in Darkovan could have become an offensive intimacy, in such a fatherly fashion that Jaelle was warmed instead of offended. "Remember, young woman, you're among Terran barbarians now and you have to allow us our tribal customs. It makes record-keeping simpler that way. You're sharing quarters with Haldane, aren't you? Well, there you are."

"Yes, but I am a Renunciate, and it is not the custom to bear the husband's name—"

"As I say, it's our custom," said the man. "Do you have any proverb which says, When in Rome, do as the Romans do?"

"Who were the Romans?"

"God knows; I don't. Some old territorial people, I imagine. One could translate; when living among barbarians, follow their customs as well as you can."

Jaelle thought it over, felt her face crinkling in a smile. "Yes; we say, When in Temora, eat fish."

"Temora, as I recall, being a seacoast town," he mused. Then he began tapping on the odd keyboard with remarkably nimble fingers—she hoped they wouldn't ask her to use any machine demanding that much dexterity—and silent lights streamed across a glass plate before him. There was a beep, and he raised his eyes at the series of letter-lights on the glass.

"I forgot. Get her prints, will you, Beth?"

"Finger or eye, or both?"

"Both, I think."

Bethany led Jaelle to another machine and guided her hand against a curious flat glass plate; it flared lights, and Bethany guided her face against another with a place for her chin to rest. She jerked back, startled, as lights hurt her eyes, and Beth said soothingly "No, hold your head still and keep your eyes open; we're taking retina prints for positive identification. Fingerprints can sometimes be faked, but eyeprints never."

It took two more tries before she could conquer the involuntary response, twitching back and her eyes squeezing shut. Finally they clipped a laminated card to her tunic, with her picture in one corner and the odd squiggles which were, they told her, coded prints. Bethany said, "You really have to wear the uniform, you know. Twice already today you tripped the monitors with an intruder-alert—they're programmed to ignore anyone wearing uniform, because of the codes inside the tunic patch." She guided Jaelle's fingers to examine a roughness as of metal between the thickness of her uniform neck's cloth; Jaelle thought it had been torn and repaired, but it was evidently intended that way.

"Fortunately, the man on the main gate saw your pass and warned us that you were out of uniform today. But wear it tomorrow, won't you, like a good girl? Makes everything so much simpler."

Simpler; to have everyone looking just alike, like so many painted toy soldiers from a box!

"I know you're working under Lorne," the man went on, "but she got away with it because, working in the Boss's office as much as she did, she could pull rank." Lorne, of course, was the name Magda used in the HQ, she knew, but none of the rest of it was intelligible except that for some strange reason, perhaps a superstitious ritual, she must wear the uniform to keep from touching off alarms within the building. It probably wasn't worth arguing about.

"It's all right for today, your first day," the man added, "but tomorrow, show up in uniform, all right? And wear the badge at all times. It identifies your department and your face."

Jaelle asked, "Why should I have to wear my face, when I am already wearing my face?"

"So that we can see that your badge matches your face, and no unauthorized person gets into Security areas," the man said, and Jaelle, who was already confused, decided it was not worthwhile to go on asking why should anyone want to go where they had no business? It wasn't as if there was anything interesting in here to see.

"Take her on up to Medic, Beth, we're finished with her," said the man. "Good luck, Mrs. Haldane—Jaelle, I mean. Where are they going to put her, Beth? They can't put her in the Boss's office. He tends to make—" the man hesitated, "rude remarks. About certain people's—backgrounds."

Jaelle wondered if the man thought she was deaf, or feeble-minded; she had met Montray, and no one with a scrap of telepathic ability could possibly be in doubt that he disliked Darkover and all the Darkovans. But it was polite of the man to try and spare her feelings; the first politeness she had encountered from Terrans, who were often friendly, but seldom polite. Not, anyhow, as she understood it; they seemed to have different standards of courtesy. Only after they were in the hallway did she realize that while she had answered a great many questions about herself, no one had bothered to introduce him to her and she still did not know his name.

"Next stop, Medic," remarked Bethany, and Jaelle, who knew the Terran word by now, after the long debates about allowing Renunciates to become Medical technicians, protested, "But I'm not sick!"

"Just routine," said Bethany, an answer Jaelle had heard so often that day that she recognized it, though she did not yet know what it meant, as a ritual answer which was supposed to cut off discussion. Well, she had been told it was rude to inquire about the religious rituals of others, and Terrans must have some really strange ones.

They went up farther, this time, than ever before, and Jaelle, catching a random glance out a window, shivered involuntarily; they must be as high as they had been in the Pass of Scaravel, and she clung, feeling dizzy, to a handrail. Was this some form of testing her courage? Well, a woman who had faced blizzards in the Hellers and banshees in the mountain passes would not quail at mere height. Anyhow, Bethany seemed unconcerned.

There was a different kind of uniform on this floor, and since she was to participate in whatever curious ritual was being done this time, she did not complain when they took away her woolen and leather Amazon outfit and dressed her in a white tunic made of paper. The workers here all had the same sign on their tunics, an upright staff with what looked like two snakes coiled around it, and she wondered if work emblems replaced clan or family blazonings here. She waited on benches for peculiar processes, was touched or prodded with strange machines, and they pricked her finger with needles. She shrank back at this, and Bethany explained, "They wish to look at your blood under a—" she used a strange word, and at Jaelle's blank look, elaborated, "A special glass to see the cells in your blood—to see if it is healthy blood." They stuck a glass plate in her mouth, and draped her from breasts to knees with a metal-treated heavy cloth, then left her alone with the machine, which made a curious humming noise, at which she startled and jumped. The young technician, a girl about Jaelle's own age with curly fair hair, swore angrily, and again Bethany explained hastily that they were only taking a picture of her teeth to see if they had holes or damaged roots.

"They could ask me," Jaelle said crossly, but when they tried it again, she held her breath and stayed as still as she could. The technician looked at the plate with pictured teeth and said to Bethany that she had never seen anything like it.

"She says your teeth are perfect," Bethany translated, and Jaelle said, with a sense of injury, that she could have told them that in the first place.

Then there was a room filled with machines, and the technician in charge of them, a man who spoke somewhat better Darkovan than anyone except the man who had questioned her so long in the photographing place, said, "Go in behind those curtains, and take off all your clothes. Right down to the skin. Then come out that end, and walk directly down that line, along the painted white stripe. Understand?"

She looked at him in horror; a good third of the technicians manning the machines were, in fact, male.

"I can't," Jaelle said, clutching in panic at Bethany's arm. "Do you really mean I am to walk through all those machines, completely naked?"

"The machines won't hurt you," Bethany said. "They're the new computerized scanners; no X-rays, nothing harmful or mutagenic. I'll go first and show you, see?" She stuck her head out and said something in Terran to the technicians, and translated to Jaelle; "I told them I'd walk through first and show you that they wouldn't hurt you." She was stripping off her clothes, and Jaelle watched her, making mental notes—*So that's how you manage the back fastenings? Do the tights really tear as easily as that, that she is so careful not to get her fingernails into them?*

"Program the metal-detector for the fillings in my teeth, Roy.

Last time it beeped at me and they kept walking me back and forth half the morning."

"Fillings, teeth, all right," said the man, making some adjustment to the machine. "That's nothing, we had Lucy from Comm up here the other day and we forgot to get records and didn't program it to ignore her IUD. And of course anyone with a pin in a hip or something really fouls it! Go on through, Beth." And as Bethany walked, stark naked, down the row of machines, Jaelle realized that they ignored her absolutely, as if she were male or fully clothed. But when Bethany came back and would have pushed her from the cubicle, she hung back still.

"I tell you, the machines won't hurt you; it's nothing but light."

"—But—they're men—"

"They're Medics," Bethany said. "You're nothing to them but a set of bones and organs; they'd be more thrilled by a Colles fracture than if you had the most wonderful set of tits in the universe. Go on—you're keeping them waiting!"

Jaelle didn't understand quite all of this, but she supposed Bethany was trying to tell her that the men—Medics?—were like monks or healer-priests, interested in nothing but their work. Bracing herself, she stepped out of the cubicle, but to her relief, no one raised an eye, whether male or female, but stayed bent over the machines. One of the women asked in faulty Darkovan, "Wear you any metal? Teeth, fittings, anything?"

Jaelle spread empty hands. "Where would I have it put?" she demanded, and the woman smiled. "Right. Walk so—that side— turn. Stop there. Raise one arm. The other." Jaelle felt like a tamed chervine doing tricks. "Now turn again—lower arm—see? Machine no hurt—"

When she was dressing again, she asked Bethany, "What did those machines *do*?"

"Pictures of your insides, I told you. Tells them you're healthy."

"And as I told *you*, I could have told them that already," said Jaelle. Except for one or two wounds in battle—during her first years as an Amazon, she had fought as a mercenary at Kindra's side—and a broken wrist when she had fallen from a horse at sixteen, she had always been perfectly healthy.

Then they took her and put her into a contoured lounge and pasted gooey flat plates to her head, and pushed her down in the chair. She must have fallen asleep, and when she woke up she had a splitting headache, not unlike the headache she had had when Lady Alida had forced her, at fifteen, to look into a matrix jewel.

"She's very resistant," said one man, as she woke up, and another man answered, "That's normal for the indigenous population. Not used to technological environment. Beth said she spooked at the fluoroscopy machines. Hey—pipe down, she's awake already. Can you understand us, Miss?"

"Yes, perfectly—oh, I see. A language-teaching machine." That was nothing; the *Comyn* could have done that with a matrix and a well-trained telepath.

"Head ache?" Without waiting for her answer, the Medic handed her a small paper cup with a spoonful or so of pale green liquid in the bottom. "Drink this."

She did. He took the cup from her, crushed it in his hand and tossed it into a waste collector. She watched in amazement as it turned into pale slime and flowed out the drain, One moment it had been a cup; then, the next instant, without transition, it was a bit of pale slimy stuff, deliberately discarded and destroyed. Yet it was not old, or outworn, the new crisp feel of it was still in her hand, the *reality* of it. She could still feel it, but the thing itself was gone. *Why?* A few minutes later, changing back into her own clothes, Bethany told her to throw her paper tunic into the same kind of collector. It confused her still, to see the things dissolve and flow down the drain and exist no longer. The man who had worked the language machine—she heard him call it a D-Alpha corticator, which left her no wiser than before—handed her a neat packet of disks.

"Here are your language lessons in Standard for the rest of the week," he said. "Tell your husband to show you how to use the sleep-learner, and you can go ahead on your own."

Another machine! This man had not been introduced to her

either, but she was accustomed to rudeness by now, and was not surprised when Bethany told her to hurry or they would be late to lunch. She had been hurrying all morning, but Terrans were always in a hurry, driven by the chronometer faces she saw everywhere, and she supposed there were some good reasons to serve meals on time; it was rude to keep the cooks waiting. There were no cooks visible, only machines, and it confused her to have to press buttons to get food, but she did what Bethany did. The food was all unfamiliar anyhow, thick porridges and hot drinks and bland textured messes. Sticking a fork in one peculiarly colored red mess, she asked what it was, and Bethany shrugged.

"Ration for the day; some kind of synthetic carbo-protein, I imagine. Whatever it is, it's supposed to be good for you." She ate up her portion with appetite, though, and so Jaelle tried to choke some of it down.

"The food in the Main Cafeteria is better than this," Bethany said, "this is just a quick place to eat and run. I know this was a boring morning, but it's always like this on a new job."

Boring? Jaelle thought of the last job she had undertaken; with her partner Rafaella, organizing a trade caravan to Dalereuth. They had spent the first day talking to their employer, finding out what men he had and how many animals, inspecting pack-beasts and making up their loads, visiting harness-makers to have proper packs made up. While Rafi had gone off to organize the hiring of extra animals, Jaelle had questioned the men about their food preferences and gone to purchase supplies and arrange their delivery. Monotonous, perhaps, and hard work, but certainly not boring!

The food was too strange to eat much; she could not have gotten it down at all had she not been ravenous after her breakfastless morning. The textures were too smooth, the tastes too sweet or too salty, with one fiery bitterness that made her splutter. At least Bethany was trying to be friendly.

Searching her mind, she realized she was still angry about the moment when she had walked naked between the rows of machines. None of the men had been offensive, they had not noticed that she was female. But they should have noticed. Noticed; not looked at her offensively, but noticed that she *was* in fact female and would have feelings about displaying herself before strange men. Possibly they should have had the machines entirely staffed by women, just to indicate that they understood her natural feelings. She hated the idea that they considered her just a nothing, another machine that happened to be living and breathing, a machine no one would have noticed except that it was not wearing the proper uniform! *A lot of bones and organs*, Bethany had said. She felt depersonalized, as if by treating her like a machine they had made her into one.

"Don't try to eat that stuff if you don't like it," Bethany said, noticing her struggle with the food. "Sooner or later, you'll find out which things you like and which ones you don't, and you can get native food—oh, I'm sorry, I mean naturally cooked food, things more like what you're accustomed to eating—in quarters. Some people prefer synthetics, that's all—the Alphans, for instance, have religious objections to eating anything that's ever been alive or growing, so we have to provide complete synthetic diets for them, and it's cheaper and easier to package them for the staff up here. They're not so bad when you're used to them," she rattled on, while Jaelle blinked, thinking of a world where everybody ate this kind of thing, not for convenience or cheapness but because they had religious scruples about eating anything which had once contained life. She supposed it showed, after all, a very elevated ethical sense. Anyway, there was nothing she could do about it.

By now she was numb to shocks and flung her half-emptied plate into the ubiquitous disposal bins, watching it flow away into slime and swirl away down the drain. Small loss, she thought. Upstairs again, in one of the large windowless offices, she felt the unease of incipient claustrophobia—it was unsettling to be not sure whether she was on the fourth floor or the twenty-fourth. She told herself that she could not expect to have everything familiar, among Terrans, and that at least it was a new kind of experience. But the strange sounds and background machine noises scraped away at her nerves. Bethany located a desk for her.

"This is Lorne's place; even when she's here she doesn't use it much, she worked mostly in Montray's office upstairs, but when I heard you were coming in, I had it cleaned out and set up for you. You wouldn't want to work under Montray, he's a—" She used an idiom Jaelle did not understand, comparing him with some unfamiliar animal, but the disapproving tone conveyed her meaning perfectly well. She remembered what she had heard in the Medic office, too . . . Montray, then, was the one who could not be trusted to treat Darkovans with ordinary courtesy. How, she wondered, had this man come to be in a position of authority if his character faults were so extreme that even his own staff felt free to comment on them? She resolved to ask Peter; she literally did not know how to frame the question for Bethany's ears without implying all kinds of insulting things about Terrans in general.

Bethany was explaining, in rapid-fire, how to use the voice-scriber, the throat-mike, the clearing key for erasure, the way in which the words would print on the screen before her. "You don't have to speak out loud, just subvocalize," She struck a key, and said, "Here, like this—watch."

On the screen, printed in luminous pale letters, the words appeared: HERE, LIKE THIS—WATCH. Jaelle swallowed as she slowly spelled them out.

"Wouldn't it be simpler if I just told this to the person who needs to know this?"

Bethany shrugged. "I suppose it could be done that way, but we need it for records—then the next Director of Operations, and the one beyond him, will be able to get it in your own words, years from now."

"Why should anyone be interested, say, fifty years from now, when we are no longer here and Rumal di Scarp is dead?"

"Well, it goes into the record," said Bethany, sorely puzzled herself. *That word again.* "Even by next week, your memory will have distorted what happened. . . . you really should have been debriefed, as Magda should have been, right after it happened, though I understand why it wasn't possible—you all spent the winter snowed in at Ardais, didn't you? But we have to get all this into the record, as clearly as we can. Then other Heads of Departments, or even people on other Empire planets, will have access to the information, even a hundred years from now. It all goes into the permanent record."

But that, Jaelle thought, was impossible; for anyone to report anything with that kind of permanent, frozen, once-for-all objectivity. She said, choosing her words to try and convey her distress, "But the truth I tell now about what happened at Sain Scarp is not the truth I would have told then. And what I tell now will not be the truth fifty years from now. I will have to recall all of it, fifty years from now, to see what the truth is then, because the only truth then will be what we remember—and not just me, but what Margali—Magda remembers, and what Peter remembers, and even what Lady Rohana and Rumal di Scarp himself remembers."

Bethany shook her head, clearly not understanding what Jaelle was trying to convey. "I'm afraid that's too complicated for me. Just tell everything you can remember, and we'll worry about that kind of ultimate truth some other time—all right?"

"But whom am I reporting *to*?"

"Does it matter? Tell it just the way you'd tell it to anyone who asked you what happened out there; put in every little detail you can think of—someone else will be editing the text and if there's anything really irrelevant, she'll cut it out."

"But how do I know what to say if I don't know who I'm saying it to?" Jaelle asked, confused again. "I mean, if you asked me to tell you, I'd tell it one way, and if, say, the *Comyn* Council asked, I'd tell it another way—"

Bethany sighed, and Jaelle could feel her frustration. She said, "I guess my *casta* isn't as good as I thought. It sounded as if you were saying you'd tell two different stories to us and to your own people. That's not what you mean, is it?" At Jaelle's vigorous headshake, she nodded and said, "I didn't think so; you look fairly honest to me, and Magda said nice things about you; I couldn't imagine you being that two-faced. I'll tell you what;

just tell the story into the scriber, as if you were telling it to one of your Guild people, Elders—what's the word—?"

"Guild-mothers?"

"I guess that's it. Tell it as if you were telling one of your Guild-mothers, why don't you?"

She clipped the throat-mike, with its black snakelike attachment, to the neckband of Jaelle's tunic. "That's another good reason for wearing uniform; the standard uniform for your sector has a pocket in the neckband for a scriber-microphone and you can just tuck it in instead of messing around with clips." She demonstrated on her own uniform tunic. Jaelle flinched a little at the thought of being hooked up to any machine, but she supposed she would get used to it. It wasn't dangerous and she was not the barbarian they seemed to think her. It was up to her not to panic like a fish in a tree!

"Now just talk into it softly, or even subvocalize; I won't stand over you, it would only make you nervous, but I'll be right over here at my desk if you need me for anything," she said, and went away. Jaelle sat still, trying to decide what to do first. She said half aloud, "I'm still not sure I know how to handle this thing—" and heard the small humming and rattling sound; luminous letters swam on the screen and she saw in the slightly unfamiliar letters of Standard, her words in Casta "I'm still not sure I know. . . ."

Chagrined, she pressed the clearing key and saw the letters disappear into flashes of light, as her paper cup and dinnerplate had vanished into nothingness. *Is anything permanent here?* she wondered; yet Bethany had been speaking of making her report accessible for all time. It was a sobering thought.

She said slowly, "I don't know where to start . . ." and as the machine hummed again, she saw the words appear in light on the screen. But this time it did not trouble her. How many times, she wondered, had she started out a report to Kindra, or to one of the Guild-mothers, of some mission accomplished or failed, with those very words? As if she had been sitting in the great gathering room in Thendara Guild-house, with the Guild-mothers and her sisters waiting to be told of what she had done, she began in a composed, formal way:

"On a certain night about ten days before Midwinter, I was traveling north to Nevarsin Monastery. With me were a band of the *Comhii-Letzii*, with myself, Jaelle n'ha Melora, as elected leader, Gwennis n'ha Liriel, Sherna n'ha Lia, and Rayna n'ha Devra on their way to take the places of three of our sisters who had been living in Nevarsin to copy records there, and Camilla n'ha Kyria, my oath-sister, as escort and guard. Because of a severe oncoming storm, we camped in a travel-shelter situated half a day's journey north of Andalune Pass. We found the place already tenanted by a band of strange men, about twelve in number; but invoking the traditional neutrality of the travel-shelters, we greeted them politely and made our camp at the opposite end of the building. Shortly after dark, a woman traveling alone, and in the ordinary dress of a Renunciate, entered the building; she identified herself as from Temora Guild-house and was welcomed to our fire. This woman I learned later to be Magdalen Lorne—" She struggled with Magda's Terran name and was quite sure that what appeared on the screen was not what Magda's name looked like in Terran letters. She had once seen it written. She must have mispronounced it so grossly that the machine could not compensate and was reduced to a phonetic transcription of what she had actually *said*. She hit the clearing key and, biting her lip, called Bethany to ask the proper spelling.

To her great relief Bethany showed no exasperation, no sense that she had asked anything terribly stupid; she matter-of-factly spelled it for her and went back to her own desk, and Jaelle went on.

"We did not know her to be Terran or an Agent of Intelligence. We simply made her welcome among us and shared food as was traditional when Renunciates meet on the trail. While we were all sleeping there was a disturbance—"

She went on, the words flowing smoothly now, telling how Magda had been attacked by one of the bandits, breaking the travel-shelter's law of neutrality; when the men had been evicted from the shelter, Magda, under questioning, had been exposed as an intruder, and as the law provided, had been required to take the Oath. The next day Jaelle had turned over her leadership of the group to Camilla n'ha Kyria, in order to escort her new oath-daughter to Neskaya Guild House; when the others had gone, she and Magda had been attacked by two of the returning bandits and had fought them, in an encounter where Jaelle had been severely wounded. Magda, wounded herself, had saved Jaelle's life; and although she could then have ridden away on her mission, had stayed to tend Jaelle's severe and life-threatening wound. Later, Jaelle had discovered Magda's true identity, and had gone with her to complete the ransom of Peter Haldane from Rumal di Scarp.

She went on from there, briefly sketching in the encounter with a banshee-bird in the Pass of Scaravel, the ransom exchange, and the subsequent trip—what she could remember of it, since her memory of that time was blurred by the fever in her wound, and she remembered little of the journey except that Peter had taken her on his saddle when she could no longer ride alone.

She said little about their stay in Castle Ardais, except that they had been treated with kindly courtesy by Lady Rohana and welcomed by *Dom* Gabriel with due and gracious hospitality, even though he did not approve of Renunciates. She mentioned very briefly that Rohana was her kinswoman, and had been her guardian in childhood; even more briefly, that she and Peter Haldane had agreed to marry, upon their return to Thendara, and had done so. If they wanted to know anything more than that, they would have to ask her. How did she know what they wanted to know, and what business of theirs was it, anyhow? She was willing to report the part she had played in Peter's ransom—she supposed he would be reporting that from his own perspective—but while she would have gladly told her Guildmothers how she had come to know Peter well, how she had clung to him during her illness, the growing closeness between them, and how she had first shared his bed after the Midwinter Festival, she was not going to report all that to a faceless machine, for Terrans who did not know either of them.

Inside the windowless room she lost track of time, and only when she looked up and discovered that others were closing up their desks and stations did she realize that her stomach was reminding her fiercely of her sketchy and inedible lunch.

When she stepped from the building into the spaceport HQ plaza, it was past sunset, and fine drizzling rain was falling. In the central cafeteria, which was at least spacious and well-windowed, she felt less claustrophobic than in the shut-in office with its clutter of desks; but everyone looked so alike in uniform that she did not see Peter until he actually touched her on the shoulder.

"Jaelle! What are you doing out of uniform?" But before she could explain, he went on, "I heard that somebody had tripped the monitors all over the station, but I never dreamed it was you!"

She was astonished at the anger in his voice; she started to explain, but he was not listening.

"Let's get on line for dinner—there's always a crowd about this time."

The food looked and smelled better than the synthetics which were all that had been provided in the other building at lunch; some of it was almost familiar, roasted meats and local grains and vegetables. She was relieved to see that Peter's choices and her own were almost identical. Well, of course; he too had been brought up near Caer Donn and was used to Darkovan food. In every way that really mattered to her he was Darkovan, though his protective coloration was so good, here among the other Terrans. It was a disquieting thought; which one was the real Peter?

He explained, too, why she had had to thrust her identity badge into the slot before releasing the food. "We're entitled to a certain number of meals as an employee; extras are deducted from our pay. Let's find a quiet corner, shall we?"

There were no really quiet corners in the cafeteria, not as she understood the word, but they did find a table for two, and sat down together. Around them were laughing, talking workers, mostly in uniform or the white smocks with the emblem of Medic Services. There was a crew of what looked like road workers, still brushing snow from the heavy parkas they wore over their uniforms. It was not, she thought, so different from supper in the Guild-house. She felt, for a moment, fiercely homesick. She thought of Magda, eating her first meal there. Then she looked across at Peter and smiled. No, she was here with Peter and it was where she wanted to be.

But he still looked angry. "Damn it, you've got to wear uniform while you're in the building, Jaelle."

She said stiffly, carefully, "It was explained to me that it creates a problem with the—the machinery. I will—try."

"What's the problem, Jaelle?"

She wondered if she could really make him understand. "It is—is immodest. It makes me look—too much woman."

Was he being deliberately obtuse? He smiled enticingly at her and said, "That's the good part of it, isn't it? Why don't you want to look like a woman?"

"That's not what I meant—" she began, crossly, then broke off. "Why does it matter to you, Piedro? It is my problem, and I must deal with it in my own way. If you wish, I will explain that it has nothing to do with you—that you asked me to, and I refused."

"You can't do that," he said, harried. "I'm working under Montray now, and I'm in enough trouble with him without having him think—" he stopped, but to Jaelle, surprisingly, it was as if he had spoken aloud what was in his mind; *think I can't manage my wife.*

That did make her angry. She said, between clenched teeth, "Why should you think that it reflects on you?"

"Damn it, woman," he burst out. "You're wearing my name! Everything you do reflects on me, whether you mean it to, or not! You're certainly intelligent enough to understand that!"

She stared at him in consternation, knowing that she would never understand. She wanted to get up and walk out of the cafeteria; she wanted to scream at him. She only stared at him, her hands shaking. But before she could move, a voice said behind her, "Peter? I was looking for you. And this must be Jaelle."

A tall, brown-skinned woman, with hair silvered white,

picked up a chair and set it down at their table. "May I join you? I was talking to Magda this morning."

Peter's face changed so rapidly that Jaelle began to doubt the evidence of her senses. "Cholayna? I heard on the grapevine that you were here. Jaelle, this was the Head of Intelligence School when Mag and I trained there; Cholayna Ares."

The woman had a tray of the synthetics Jaelle had refused at lunch, but she ignored the meat and steaming vegetables on their trays. "May I join you? Or am I breaking in on a private discussion?"

"Please do," Jaelle said. There was nothing she wanted less than to be alone with Peter in this mood. Cholayna put her tray on the table and slid into a seat.

"It's nice to see someone dressed properly for this climate. I understand Magda tried to set an example by wearing clothes that fit the weather here, but those half-headed half-brains in the department couldn't think of anything except their wretched machines. Who's running this show, anyway? Old Russell Montray? She made a small sound of scorn. "I wish someone in Head Center would show some intelligence and transfer him back to a space station; he might manage that and do it quite well. He's not really stupid, you know, he simply has no patience with strange planets and alien customs. I thought the essence of being Coordinator on a Closed Planet was to understand the people and the native culture, so that when they got around to setting up a Legate they would know what kind of person to choose. But Montray seems to have made so many mistakes already that it will take a century or more to smooth out the troubles he has caused. I Who sent him here? And whatever could they have been thinking?"

"Political pull, I expect," Peter said, "the wrong kind; not where he wanted the job and somebody with clout fixed it for him, but the kind where somebody wanted to get rid of him, pulled strings, and kicked him upstairs—and he wound up here. They may have thought it was isolated enough that he couldn't make much trouble. Typical bureaucratic thinking—let him go make trouble somewhere else."

"Particularly stupid," Cholayna confirmed with a nod. "This planet may not have a great deal of trade potential, but because of its location, it's an important transit point; in twenty or so years, this will be one of the major intersecting spaceports anywhere in the Galaxy. If this fellow Montray has already created trouble with the locals, as it seems, it could take centuries to repair the damage. I've made a start, I hope, by putting Magda on detached duty, to try and analyze how we ought to be treating Darkovans, in contrast to how we *are* treating them. I will want information from you too on that, Jaelle. As for you, Peter, you know you really ought to be working out of my office, not Montray's; I hope he isn't going to make it a status point to keep you there."

Peter muttered something Jaelle knew to be a polite noncommittal social noise, but once again her erratic *laran* carried his thoughts as if he had spoken them aloud.

Not fair, dammit, I spent five years setting things up so that when Darkover got an Intelligence Service I'd be at its head, and now some damned woman walks in and takes over. Bad enough playing second fiddle to Magda. . . .

She lost the contact then, but she had heard enough to make her look at Peter in dread and dismay. She liked Cholayna, and thought she would like working with her, in spite of the strange color of the woman's skin and her unreadable dark eyes; but if Peter felt this way, what should she do?

Chapter 3

Magda

As the doors of Thendara Guild-house swung shut behind her, Magda thought, with a strange, desperate intuition, *I must never look back. Whatever I was before this, I must leave it forever behind me, and look only ahead. . . .*

Around her a great hall arose, panelled in dark woods and hung with curtains which gave an effect of space and air and light. A snub-nosed young girl had opened the door for her, directed her across the hall and said "The Guild-mother Lauria is waiting for you." She looked curiously at Magda, but only shoved her through another door, where the Guild-mother, Lauria n'ha Andrea, head of the Independent Guild of Craftswomen in Thendara, and one of the most powerful women in the city, waited for her. Lauria was a tall, sturdy woman, her gray hair shorn close about her head, one ear bearing an earring with a carved ensign and a crimson stone. She rose and extended her hand to Magda.

"Welcome, my child. You have been told, I know, that this will be your only home for half a year; until two moons past midsummer Day. During this time you will be instructed in our ways, and while you have the freedom of house and garden, you may not step outside the wall nor into the street, except on Midsummer Festival when all rules are suspended, or under the direct orders of your oath-mother or one of the Guild-mothers."

She smiled at Magda and said, "You have shown us that you are willing to honor your oath, even though you took it unwilling; you will promise me to keep this rule, will you not? You are a woman grown, and not a child."

"I will obey," said Magda, but it seemed a bleak prospect, half a year, through the long, bitter Darkovan winter, oath-bound not to step outside. Well, she had wanted this, why should she complain at getting what she wanted?

"Mind you," Mother Lauria said, "this is within reason. Should the house take fire, or some other catastrophe occur, which all Gods forbid, use your own soundest judgment; you are not pledged to lunatic obedience! You are bound to the house only so that you will not be confused by daily meetings with women who live in ways you must learn not to imitate. Do you understand?"

"I think so." They used to call it *deprogramming;* women on Darkover are brainwashed by the social roles expected of them, till it is a miracle that any of them are free enough to rebel and join the Renunciates. She remembered hearing Jaelle say once, *Every Renunciate has her own story and every story is a tragedy.* In such a traditional society as Darkover, only the desperately rebelling would dare break away.

I have rebelled against my home world and my adopted world too . . . but she cut off that thought as self-pity and turned to the older woman, who beckoned her into a chair.

"I suppose you are hungry and weary? But you do not want to face everyone just now in the dining room for the noon meal, do you? I thought not . . ." and she touched a little bell. The snub-nosed girl who had let Magda inside, appeared in the door.

"Bring something from the dining room, for me and for our new sister," she said, and as the little girl went out—she could not, Magda thought, be more than thirteen—Mother Lauria gestured to a chair beside the fireplace—no fire was burning, at this time of year. "Sit down and let us talk awhile; there are decisions to be made."

At the far end of the office was a great wooden door with copper panels; the door was hacked about as if with an axe, and partially burnt. Magda stared at the battered relic, and Mother Lauria followed her eyes.

"It has been here for more than a hundred years," she said. "The wife of a wealthy merchant in Thendara ran away to us, because her husband had ill-used her in ways too gross to repeat, and had finally required her to sleep in the attic and to wait on her husband and his new concubine in her own bed. The woman took Oath with us; but her husband hired an army of mercenaries and we were forced to fight; he swore he would raze this house over our heads. Rima—this was her name—offered to return to him; she said she would not be the cause of our deaths. But we were not fighting for her alone, but for the right to live without male sufferance. We fought three days—you can see the marks of the battle."

Magda shivered; the slashed, burnt door looked as if, at one point, an axe had chopped halfway through it.

"And you stood against them?"

"If we had not, neither you nor I should be here," said Lauria. "All Gods grant that one day we shall all enjoy our freedom as of right, without keeping it at sword's point; but until that day we are prepared to defend our rights with the sword. Now, tell me a little more about yourself. I have heard the story from Jaelle, of course. Your name is—" she stumbled over it. "Makta-lin Lor-ran?" She made a wry face. "Will it suit you if you use Jaelle's name for you, Margali?"

"That *is* my name," Magda said. "The name my father and mother gave me; I was born in Caer Dunn. I was never called Magda except in the Terran Zone."

"Margali, then. And I see you speak the language of the Hellers, and are fluent in *casta*; can you speak *cahuenga* as well?"

"I can," Magda replied in that language, "though my accent is not good."

"Your accent is no worse than any other newcomer to the City. Jaelle has told me you can read and write; is this in Standard only, or in *casta*?"

"I can read and write *casta*," she said. "For my father was an expert in languages, and he wrote the—" she hesitated, groping for a Darkovan way to explain a dictionary. "A compilation of your language for strangers and foreigners. And my mother was a musician, and made many transcriptions of folk songs and music of the Hellers."

Mother Lauria pushed a pen and a scrap of paper toward her. "Let me see you copy this," she said, and Magda looked at the scroll and began to copy the top line; she recognized the scroll as a poem her mother had set to music. She was not used to Darkovan pens, which were not as smooth as the ones she used for her own work. When she finished, Mother Lauria took the paper in her hand.

"A clumsy hand and girlish," she said severely, "but at least you are not illiterate; many women when they come to us can only spell out their names. You have not the making of a scribe, but I have seen worse."

Magda flushed at this harsh judgment; she felt bruised and offended; she had never been accused of clumsiness in her entire life.

"Let us see what we can do with you, then. You are no scribe. Can you sew? Embroider?"

"No, not even a little," said Magda, remembering her attempt to botch together her trail clothes at Ardais.

"Can you cook?"

"Only for the trail, when traveling."

"Can you weave, or do dyeing?"

"Not even a little."

"Do you know anything of plants and gardening?"

"Even less, I fear."

"Can you ride?"

"Oh, yes, certainly," Magda said, glad to arrive at something which she *could* do.

"Can you saddle your own horse, care for his tack, look after his feed and care? Good; I am afraid we will have to put you to work in the stables," said Mother Lauria. "Do you mind?"

"No, of course not," Magda said. But she had to confess ignorance again when the woman asked if she knew anything of farriery, of metalworking and forging, of veterinary medicine, dairying, cheesemaking, animal husbandry or bootmaking, and she had to answer no to all of these things. Mother Lauria looked a little more approving when Magda said that she had been trained in both armed and unarmed combat; but she said thoughtfully "You have a good deal to learn," and Magda guessed that Mother Lauria was as relieved as she was herself when the fair-haired, snub-nosed girl reappeared with trays and jugs.

"Ah, here is our dinner. Set it down here, Doria."

The girl uncovered the tray; a bowl of some kind of baked grain with a sauce of vegetables, mugs of something which tasted like buttermilk, and some sliced fruit, preserved in honey or syrup. She gestured to Magda to help herself, and ate in silence for some time. Finally, as she folded her napkin, she asked, "How old are you?"

Magda assumed she meant Darkovan reckoning, and told her age; only later did she realize that Mother Lauria had been testing to see if she could reckon the difference between the relatively short Terran year and the much longer Darkovan.

"You have been married, Margali? Have you a child?"

Magda shook her head silently. That had been one of the main causes of tension between them, that she had not given Peter the son he wished for.

"Has that marriage been formally dissolved, as I gather you Terrans can do by mutual consent?"

Magda was surprised that Mother Lauria knew this much. "It has. Terran marriage is not quite like freemate marriage, but it is nearer to that than to the Darkovan *catenas*. We agreed to separate more than a year ago."

"That is fortunate; if you had a child under the age of fifteen, you would be required to make arrangements for its care. We do not allow women to take refuge here if they have obligations outside which have not been met. I assume you have not an aged parent who is dependent on you?"

"No; my mother and father have been dead for many years."

"Have you another lover now?"

Silently Magda shook her head.

"Will it be a great hardship to you, to live without a lover? I suppose, since you and your husband have been separated for some time, you have grown accustomed to sleeping alone; but will it be very difficult for you? Or are you perhaps a lover of women?" She used the very polite term, and Magda was not offended—she supposed that any society composed only of women must attract a certain percentage of those who would rather die or renounce everything than marry. She found this line of questioning uncomfortably personal, but she had promised herself that she would answer everything as honestly as she could. "I do not think I shall find it unendurably painful," and only after she had spoken did she realize how sarcastic it sounded. Mother Lauria smiled and said, "I hope not; but especially during your housebound time, this can be a problem, as anyone but a child would know. Let me think—it is hard to remember what to ask you. Have you been taught methods to prevent the conception of an unwanted child?"

Magda was really shocked now; of course such teaching was routine at puberty for any Terran, male or female, but she had been brought up in Caer Donn and absorbed the Darkovan attitude which considered such things proper only for prostitutes. She said "Yes," but wondered what the older woman must think of her, confessing to such knowledge!

Mother Lauria nodded calmly. "Good. We have the women in the Towers to thank for that; women who work in the matrixes must not risk interrupting their term by an undesired pregnancy, yet it is not possible to require that they remain celibate, sometimes for many years. There is an ancient bond between the women of Neskaya Tower and the Guild of Renunciates, which goes back to the history of the Guild; we were formed, as you may know, in the days of Varzil the Good, from two separate houses of women; the Priestesses of Avarra, who were an order of healer-priestesses trained in *laran*, and the Sisterhood of the Sword, who were, during the time of the Hundred Kingdoms and the Hastur Wars, a guild of woman soldiers and mercenaries. Some day you shall read this history, of course. The Priestesses of Avarra taught us many things which could be done by any women, including those who had no *laran*, though of course it is easier for those who do. Among the Renunciates, it is criminal to bear a child who is not wanted by mother and father, and for whom no happy home is waiting, so we require this instruction for all our women." She took pity on Magda's embarrassment and said, "Oh, my dear, I am sure you feel foolish, but I must deal with blushes, outraged modesty and outright refusal from women who swear they would rather forswear men entirely. But it is our law; every woman, even those who have never lain down with a man and never intend to do so, must know these things. They need never use them, but they may not remain ignorant. Twice in a tenday, at our house meetings, one of our midwives talks to the younger women. Are you strong and healthy? Can you do a good day's work without tiring?"

"I've never done a great deal of manual work," Magda said, relieved at the change of subject, "but when I was traveling I could spend all day in the saddle when I must."

"Good; many women who live indoors, doing only women's work, grow sickly for lack of exercise, and we have not so much sunshine here that we can afford to be without it. You may laugh to see grown women playing games and skipping rope like children, but it is not only little girls who need to run about and exercise. I hope you are not too modest to swim when the weather permits?"

"No, I like to swim," Magda said, but wondered when, on frozen Darkover, the weather permitted!

"Are your monthly cycles regular? Do they give you much trouble?"

"Only when I was living offworld," Magda said; she had found them troublesome in the Empire Training School, adjusting to different gravity and light and circadian rhythms; she had been in and out of the Medic office all the time, while she was on the Alpha color, and had been given hormone shots and various kinds of treatment. Back on Darkover, she had reverted to her usual good health. She explained that, and added, "Before I was sent on this mission—the one to Ardais—I was given treatment by Terran medics to suppress ovulation and menstruation; it is fairly routine for women in the field. At Ardais Jaelle asked me about this—she thought I was pregnant."

"That treatment is something we would find priceless," said Mother Lauria. "I hope your Terrans will help us learn it; when women must work alongside men, or travel for a long time in bad weather, it would be a great convenience. Some women have been desperate enough to consider the neutering operation, which is very dangerous. We do have a few drugs which destroy fertility for a period of half a year or more, but they are too strong and dangerous: I do not recommend that any woman use them. But women who have a great deal of trouble with their cycles, or women who have no talent for celibacy and great ease in getting pregnant—well, we elders cannot forbid them that choice. Now there is a very important decision to be made, and you must make it, Margali."

Magda looked at her empty plate. "I will do what I can."

"You saw the little girl who brought in your dinner? Her name is Doria, and she is fifteen; she will take the Oath at Midsummer. She has lived among us since she was born, but the law forbids us to instruct girls below legal age in our ways. So that you, and she, will be in training together. You are not of our world, Margali. Yes, I know you were born here, but your people are so different from ours that some things may be strange and hard to endure. I know so little of the Terrans that I cannot even guess what those things may be, but Jaelle came here at twelve from the Dry-Towns and she had many difficulties; and a few years ago we had a woman here from the rain forests far beyond the Hellers. She had courage toward us, and good will, but she was really ill with the shock of finding so many things new and strange. And most of these were little things which we all accepted as ordinary to life; we had never guessed how hard she would find it. We do not want you to suffer in that way, so there are two courses we can take, Margali."

The old woman looked sharply at Magda.

"We can tell all of your sisters here that you are Terran born, and all of us can be alert to help you in small things and make allowances for you. But like all choices, this one would have its price; there would be a barrier between you and your sisters from the beginning, and they might never wholly accept you as one of us. The alternative is to tell them only that you were born in Caer Donn, and let you struggle as best you can with the strangenesses. What do you want to do, Margali?"

I never realized what a snob I was, Magda thought. She had not expected them to understand culture shock, and here Mother Lauria was explaining it to her as if she were not very intelligent. "I will do what you command, my lady."

She had used the very formal *casta* word, *domna*, and Mother Lauria looked displeased.

"First of all, I am not *my lady*," she said. "We do not free ourselves from the tyranny of titles imposed by men only to set up another tyranny among ourselves. Call me Lauria, or Mother if you think I deserve it and you wish to. Give me such respect as you would have given your own mother after you were grown out of her command. And I cannot command you in this; it is you who must live by your decision. I cannot even counsel you properly; I know too little of your people and their ways. I am sure that some day, all of us will have to know you are Terran; do you think you can overcome that strangeness? You need not carry that handicap unless you choose; but they might make more allowances for you . . ."

Magda felt doubtful. Jaelle had known she was Terran, and it had certainly helped ease them through some difficulties. Yet, though she and Jaelle had come to love each other, there had been strangeness between them. She said hesitantly, "I will—I will defer to your advice, Lauria, but I think—at first—I would rather be one of you. I suppose all women have strange things to face when they come here."

Lauria nodded. "I think you have chosen rightly," she said. "It might have been easier the other way; but this very ease might have left unresolved some strangenesses you would never settle. And I suppose you do truly want to be one of us—that you are not merely studying us for your Terran records." She smiled as she said it, but Magda detected a faint lift, almost of question in her voice, as if even Mother Lauria doubted her sincerity. Well, she would simply have to prove herself.

Mother Lauria looked at an ancient clock, the kind with hands and some internal mechanism with a swinging pendulum. She rose to her feet.

"I have an appointment in the city," she said, and Magda remembered that this woman was the President of the Independent Council of Craftswomen. "Since you have no close friend in the house now, I have told the dormitory keepers to give you a room by yourself; later, if you make a friend and wish to share a room with her, there will be time enough to change." Magda was grateful for that; until this moment it had not occurred to her that she might have been thrust into a room filled with two or three other women, all of whom had known one another most of their lives.

Mother Lauria touched the little bell. "You are not afraid to sleep alone, are you? No, I suppose not, but there are women who come to us who have never been alone in their lives, nurses and nannies when they are small, maids and lady-companions when they are older; we have had women go into a screaming panic when they find themselves alone in the dark." She touched Magda's hair lightly and said, "I will see you tonight at dinner. Courage, Margali; live one day at a time, and remember nothing is ever as bad or as good as you think it will be. Now Doria will show you over the house."

Magda wondered, as Mother Lauria went away, *Do. I really look that frightened?*

A few minutes later the young girl Doria came back.

"Mother says I am to show you around. Let's pick up the trays and dishes first and take them out to the kitchen."

The kitchen was deserted, except for a small dark-haired woman, drowsing as she waited for two huge bowlfuls of bread dough to rise. She raised her eyes sleepily as Doria introduced Magda to her.

"Margali, this is Irmelin—she is our housekeeper this half-year; we take turns helping her in the kitchen, but there are enough of us living here that no one needs to do kitchen duty more than once in a tenday. Irmelin, this is our new sister, Margali n'ha—what was it, Margali?"

"Ysabet," Magda said.

"I saw you last night," Irmelin said. "You came in with Jaelle—are you her lover?"

Mother Lauria had asked her this too. Reminding herself not to be angry—she was in another world now—she shook her head. "No—her oath-daughter, no more."

"Really?" Irmelin asked, obviously skeptical, but she only looked at the bread dough. "It won't have risen enough to knead for another hour—shall I help you show her around the house?"

"Mother Lauria told me to do it—you can stay in the kitchen and keep warm," Doria laughed. "We all know that is why you volunteered to keep house this term, so you could sit by the fire like a cat." Irmelin only chuckled, and Doria added, "Do you need anything from the greenhouse for supper, fresh vegetables, anything? Margali has no duties yet, she can help me fetch it."

"You might ask if there are any melons ripe," Irmelin said. "I think we are all tired of stewed fruit and want something fresh." Irmelin yawned and looked drowsily at the bread dough again, and Doria went out, fanning herself vigorously with her apron, pulling Magda after her.

"Phew, I hate the kitchen on baking days, it's too hot to breathe! But Irmelin makes good bread—it's surprising how many women can't make bread that's fit to eat. Remind me to tell you sometime about the time when Jaelle took her turn as housekeeper, and Gwennis and Rafaella threatened to dump her out naked in the next blizzard if she didn't get someone else to make the bread—" Doria chattered on, still fanning herself. It was certainly not too hot in the drafty corridor between kitchen and the long dining room where she had sat last night, a stranger, hiding in Jaelle's shadow. And now it was her home for half a year, at least. There were long tables which would, Magda supposed, seat forty or fifty women, piled at one end, stacks of plates and bowls, covered with towels, awaiting the evening. Behind the dining hall was a greenhouse—the inevitable feature of most homes in Thendara—with solar collectors, and a woman wearing a huge overall wrap, kneeling in the dirt and patting soil around the roots of some plant Magda did not recognize. She was a big woman, with curly, almost frizzy straw-colored hair, her fingers grubby with soil.

"Rezi, this is Margali n'ha Ysabet, Jaelle's oath-daughter. Irmelin asked me if there was any fresh fruit for tonight."

"Not tonight or tomorrow," said Rezi, "but perhaps after that; I have a few berries for Byrna—"

"Why should Byrna have them when there are not enough for us all?" demanded Doria, and Rezi chuckled. Her accent was coarse and country; she looked like one of the peasant women Magda had seen in the Kilghard hills, working in field or byre.

"Marisela ordered it; when you're pregnant you'll get the first berries too," Rezi said, laughing.

Doria giggled and said, "I'll make do with stewed fruit!"

They went on through the greenhouse, into the stable where half a dozen horses were kept with several empty stalls; a barn behind, clean and whitewashed with a pleasant smell of hay, held about half a dozen milk animals, and a small dairy where, Doria informed her, they made all their own butter and cheese. Shining wooden molds, well-scrubbed, hung on the wall, but again, the place was deserted. A winter garden, with scattered straw banking some buried root vegetables, looked bleak and chilly. Magda was shivering; Doria said, surprised, "Are you cold?" She herself had not even bothered to pull her shawl about her shoulders. "I thought you were from Caer Donn; it doesn't seem cold at all, not to me. But we can go inside," she agreed, and led the way through a huge room which she called the armory—there were weapons hanging on the walls—but which looked to Magda more like a gymnasium, with mats on the floors and a sign reading, in very evenly printed *casta: Leave your shoes neatly at the side; someone could fall over them.* There was a small changing room at the side, with towels and odd garments hanging on hooks, which reminded Magda of the Recreation Building in Unmarried Women's Headquarters. Behind it was a larger room filled, to Magda's amazement, with steam, and hidden in the steam, a pool of apparently hot water.

She had heard that there were many private houses in Thendara located over hot springs, but this was the first time she had seen it. Another sign read *Please be courteous to other women; wash your feet before entering pool.*

"This was built only four or five years ago," said Doria. "One of our rich patrons had it built in the house; before that, we had only the tubs on the dormitory floors! It's very good after unarmed-combat lessons, to soak out the bruises! Rafi and Camilla are wonderful teachers, but they are rough on anyone they suspect of slacking! I've had lessons since I was eight years old, but Rafi is my foster-mother, and she doesn't like to teach me. Come, let's go upstairs," she added, and they went along another corridor to the stairs. "Here is the nursery at the top of the landing—there is no one in it now except Felicia's little boy, and he will leave us in another moon; no male child over five may live in the Guild-house. But Bryna will have a baby in another month," she said, opening the door to the room, where a small boy was playing with some toy horses on a rug before the fire, and a young woman, sewing on something, sat in an armchair.

"How are you today, Byrna? This is Margali n'ha Ysabet, she is new—"

"I saw her last night at supper," Byrna said, while Magda wondered if every woman in the house had noticed her. She rose restlessly, pacing the room. "I'm tired of dragging around like this, but Marisela said it would be at least another tenday, perhaps a whole moon. Where is Jaelle? I had hardly a minute to speak with her last night!"

Magda realized again how popular her friend must be. "She is working in the Terran Trade City."

Byrna made a face. "Among the *Terranan*? I thought that was against the Guild-house laws!" The tone of her voice made Magda realize how wise she had been to conceal her identity. She knew in general terms of the prejudice against Terrans but had never encountered it at close range before. Byrna asked, "What is your House, sister?" and Magda replied, "This one, I suppose—I am here for half a year training—"

"Well, I hope you will be happy here," Byrna said. "I'll try to help make you welcome when this is over—" she patted her bulging belly.

Doria jeered. "Maybe *next* Midsummer you'll sleep alone!"

"Damn right," said Byrna, and Magda mentally filed that away with what Mother Lauria had told her about contraceptives. "Where is she going to sleep, Doria? In your room?"

Doria giggled. "There are five of us in there already. Mother Lauria said she's to have Sherna's room while Sherna's in Nevarsin." She led Magda along the hallway, pushing open the door of a room with half a dozen beds. She said "We got permission this year for all of us to share—Mother Millea said we could all room together if we promised to be quiet so others could have their sleep. We have a lot of fun. Here are the baths—" she pushed a door, showing a room with tubs and sinks, "and here is where you put your laundry, and here is the sewing room, if anything needs mending and you can't do it yourself. And this is Sherna's room—yours now; she and Gwennis shared it for two years, then Gwennis moved in with her friend—" She gave the word the inflection which made it also mean *lover*. Well, that must be commonplace enough, Irmelin had asked it about her, casually, and gone on to make a comment about the bread dough!

Doria pointed to a bundle on the bed. "Mother Lauria arranged with the sewing room to find you some spare clothes—nightgowns, undertunics, and a set of work clothes if you have to work in the garden or stable. I think most of them were Byrna's—she is so pregnant now that she can't wear any of her clothes, but by the time she has her baby and needs them back, you'll have made your own."

Well, thought Magda, looking at the clothes on the bed, they were sparing no pains to make her feel welcome; they had even included a comb and hairbrush, and some extra wool socks, as well as a warm fleecy thing she presumed was a bathrobe; it was fur-lined and looked luxurious. The room was simply furnished with a narrow bed, a small carved-wood chest, and a low bench with a bootjack.

Doria stood watching her. "You know that you and I are to

take training together? But you are so much older than I—how did you come to the Amazons?"

Magda told as much of the truth as she could. She said "A kinsman of mine was held to ransom by the bandit Rumal di Scarp; there was no one but I to ransom him, so I went alone, and wore Amazon dress to protect myself on the road; when I met with Jaelle's band on the road I was discovered and forced to take the Oath."

Doria's eyes widened. "But I heard—was that *you*? It is like a romance! But I heard that Jaelle's oath-daughter had been sent to Neskaya! Camilla told us, when she came back after escorting Sherna and Rayna and Gwenns to Nevarsin, and bringing Maruca and Viviana home—that must be why Irmelin thought you were Jaelle's lover, that you had come here on purpose to be with Jaelle! But Jaelle is working now in the Terran Zone, isn't she?"

Magda decided she had answered enough questions. "How did you come to the Amazons so young, Doria?"

"I was fostered here," Doria answered. "Rafaella's sister is my mother—you know Rafaella, don't you? Jaelle's partner—"

"I have not yet met her; but Jaelle has told me about her."

"Rafaella is a kinswoman of Jaelle's foster-mother Kindra. Rafi bore three children, but they were all boys. The third time, she and her sister were pregnant at the same time—and the father of Rafi's child was my father, you see? So when Rafi had another boy, my mother wanted a son, so they traded the children for fosterage; Rafaella's baby was brought up as my mother's son and my father's—which of course he *is*—and Rafaella took me, when I was not three days old, and nursed me and everything, here in the Guild-house. I am really Doria n'ha Graciela, but I call myself Doria n'ha Rafaella, because Rafi is the only mother I ever really knew."

Magda was furiously making mental notes. She knew that sisters frequently shared a lover or even a husband, and that fosterage was common, but this arrangement still seemed bizarre to her.

"But I am standing here chattering instead of telling you

what you ought to know. Some years we each look after our own rooms, but this year in House Meeting we chose to have two women from our corridor sweep the floors every day and mop them every tenday. You must keep your boots and sandals in your chest, it is hard on the sweepers to have to sweep around and over them, so anything lying on the floor, they will pick up and throw in a big barrel in the hall and you will have to hunt for them. Do you play the harp or the rryl or the lute? Too bad; Rafi has been wishing for another musician in the house. Byrna sings well, but now she is short of breath all the time—I thought when I grew up to have no ear for music that Rafi would disown me! She has—" Doria broke off as a bell in the lower part of the house began to ring.

"Oh, merciful Goddess!"

"What is that, Doria? Not the dinner-bell already?"

"No" whispered Doria, "That bell is rung only when some woman comes to take refuge with us; sometimes it does not ring twice in a year, and now we have two newcomers in one day? Come, we must go down at once!"

She pulled Magda hastily toward the stairs and they ran down together. Magda, hurrying behind her, felt a curious little prickle which she had come to know as premonition; *this is something very important to me. . . .* but dismissed it, as anxiety born of Doria's excitement, and the stress of so many new things happening to her. Irmelin stood in the hallway, with Mother Lauria, and between them a frail-looking woman, bundled in heavy shawls and cumbered with heavy skirts. She stood swaying, clutching at the railing as if she were about to faint.

Mother Lauria looked about the women gathering quickly in the hall; many of the women Magda had seen last night at dinner, but she did not know their names. Then she turned to the fainting newcomer. "What do you ask here?" Somehow, Magda felt, the words had the force of ritual. "Have you come to seek refuge?"

The woman whispered faintly "Yes."

"Do you ask only shelter, my sister? Or is your will to take the Oath of a Renunciate?"

"The Oath—" the woman whispered. She swayed, and Mother Lauria gestured to her to sit down.

"You are ill; you need answer no questions at present, my sister." She looked around at the women in the hallway, and her glance singled out Magda and Doria where they stood at the foot of the stairs.

"You two are new-come among us; you three will be together in training, should this woman take Oath, so I choose you as her oath-sisters, and—" She looked around, evidently searching for someone. At last she beckoned.

"Camilla n'ha Kyria," she said, and Magda saw, with a curious sense of inevitability, the tall, thin *emmasca* who had witnessed her Oath to Jaelle. "Camilla, you three take her away, cut her hair, make her ready to take the Oath if she is able."

Camilla came and put her arm around the strange woman, supporting the frail, swaying body. "Come with me, sister," she said, "Here, lean on me—" she spoke in the impersonal inflection, but her voice was kind. She suddenly saw Magda, and her face lighted. "Margali! Oath-sister, is it you? I thought you had gone to Neskaya! You must tell me all about it," she said, "but later; for now we must help this woman. Here—" she gestured, "put your arm under hers; she cannot walk—"

Magda put her arm around the apparently fainting woman, but the woman flinched and cried out, in a weak voice, drawing away from the touch. Camilla led her into a little room near Mother Lauria's office, and lowered her into a soft chair.

"Have you been ill-used?" she asked, and took away the shawl, then cried out in dismay.

The woman's dress—expensively cut, of richly dyed woolen cloth trimmed in fur—was cut to ribbons, and the blood had soaked through, turning the cloth to clotted black through which crimson still oozed.

Camilla whispered, "Avarra protect us! Who has done this to you?" But she did not wait for an answer. "Doria, run to the kitchen, bring wine and hot water and fresh towels! Then see if Marisela is in the house, or if she has gone out into the city to deliver a child somewhere. Margali, come here, help me get these things off her!"

Magda came, helping Camilla get off the cut and slashed tunic, gown, underlinen; they were all finely cut and embroidered with copper threads; she wore an expensive copper-filigree butterfly clasp in her fair hair. Magda stood by, helping and holding things, as Camilla bared the woman to the waist, sponged the dreadful cuts; what could possibly have inflicted them? The woman endured their ministrations without crying out, though they must have been hurting terribly; when they had done, Camilla put a light shift on her, tying the drawstrings loosely around her neck, and covered her with a warm robe. Doria came back, troubled, reporting that Marisela was not in the house.

"Then find Mother Millea," Camilla ordered, "and Domna Fiona. She is a judge in the City Court, and we must make a sworn statement about this woman's condition, so that we may legally give her shelter. She is not strong enough to take the Oath; we must put her to bed; and have her nursed—"

The woman struggled upright. "No," she whispered, "I want to take the Oath—to be here by right, not by charity—"

Magda whispered, more to herself than to anyone else, "But what has happened to her! What could have inflicted such wounds—"

Camilla's face was like stone. "She has been beaten like an animal," the *emmasca* said. "I have scars much like those. Child—" she bent over the woman lying in the chair, "I know what it is to be ill-used. Margali—you will find scissors in the drawer of the table." And as Magda put them into her hand, Camilla asked, "What is your name?"

"Keitha—" the word was only a whisper.

"Keitha, the laws require that you must show your intent by cutting a single lock of your hair; if you have the strength to do this, I will do the rest for you."

"Give me—the scissors." She sounded resolute, but her fingers hardly had strength to grasp them. She struggled to get them into her hands. She grabbed a lock of her hair, which had been arranged in two braids, and fumbled to cut it; struggled hard with the scissors, but had not the strength to cut through the braid. She gestured, whispering "Please—"

At the gesture Camilla unraveled the braid, and Keitha snipped fiercely, chopping off two ragged handfuls of hair. "There!" she said wildly, tears starting from her eyes. "Now— let me take the Oath—"

Camilla held a cup of wine to her lips. "As soon as you are strong enough, sister."

"No! *Now* . . ." Keitha insisted; then her hands released the scissors, which slithered softly to the floor, and she fell back, un- conscious, into Camilla's arms.

Mother Lauria said quietly, "Take her upstairs," and Magda, following Camilla's soft command, helped Camilla to carry the unconscious woman up the stairway and into an empty room.

Chapter 4

The waterhole lay dark, oozing black mud and darker shadows; but behind the rocks, the crimson sun was rising. She was old enough to know what was happening on the other side of the fire, she was twelve years old, and in Shainsa a girl of twelve was nearly old enough to be chained, old enough to be near at hand in the birthing rooms. But these women with unchained hands, these Amazons, they had sent her away as if she was only a child herself. Beyond the fire, in the growing sunrise, she could hear her mother's voice, feel the pain thrusting through her own body like knives, see the carrion birds circling lower and lower as the sun rose; and now the sunlight was like the blood poured out on the sands, like the stabbing feel of knives and her mother's anguish, pouring through her body and her mind . . .

Jaelle! Jaelle, it was worth it all, you are free, you are free. . . . but her hands were chained, and she was struggling, screaming, crying out. . . .

"Hush, love, hush . . ." and Peter was patiently untangling her flailing hands from the bedclothes, cradling her in his arms. "It's only a nightmare, it's all right—"

Only another nightmare. Another. God above, she's been having them every night. I don't know what to do for her.

Jaelle squirmed away from him, not quite sure why, only knowing that she did not want to be too close just now. She sought his face, frowning, troubled, for the hostility she could not find in his gentle voice.

"Kyril—" she muttered. "No. For a moment I thought you— you were my cousin Kyril—"

He laughed softly. "That would give anybody nightmares, I guess. Here, count my fingers. Only five." He pressed his hand against hers and she smiled faintly at the old joke between them. He was so like her cousin, Kyril Ardais, save for the six-fingered hands Kyril had inherited from his mother, Lady Rohana.

Kyril's hands, fumbling about her all that summer, until she had finally, sobbing with wrath and humiliation, had to use on him the Amazon training which made a trained Renunciate almost impossible to dominate. A Renunciate, they used to say, can be killed, but never raped.

For Rohana's sake she had not wanted to hurt him. . . .

"Honey, are you all right?" Peter asked. "Should I go and get a Medic? You've been having these nightmares every night . . . how long is it now? Ten days, eleven?"

She tried to focus on his words. They seemed to have some strange echo that ached in the palms of her hands, reverberated in her sinuses. The edges of the room seemed to be outlined with fuzzy lights, swelling up and shrinking and swelling again to loom over her. Her eyes hurt, and she jumped up with a wavering surge of nausea, dashing for the bath. The retching spasms shattered the last remnants of dream; she could not remember now what she had been dreaming, except for a curious taste and smell of blood in her mouth. She swallowed the flat, sickly water from the shower, trying in vain to rinse it away, and Peter, troubled, went to the refreshment console and dialed her some kind of cool drink. He held it to her lips.

"I *am* going to take you to a Medic tomorrow, love," he said, watching her finish the drink, which bubbled and stung her lips; when she put it away he shook his head.

"Finish it, it will settle your stomach. Better?" He examined the headset on the pillow; somehow she had torn it loose in the dream. "There must be something wrong with the language program they gave you, or the D-alpha is out of synch—that can mess up your balance centers," he mused, holding it. "Or maybe it just stirred up something in your subconscious. Take it up to

Medic tomorrow, and ask them to adjust it on the EEG file they have for you." He might, she thought distantly, just as well have been speaking in some language from another Galaxy; she didn't know what he was talking about and didn't care. He held the earpiece to his temple, shrugged. "It sounds all right to me, but I'm no expert. Come on back to bed, sweetheart."

"Oh, no," she said, without thinking, "I'm not sleeping under that damned thing again!"

"But, love, it's just a machine," he said, "even if it is out of adjustment, it won't really hurt you. Baby, don't be unreasonable," he added, his arm around her shoulders. "You're not some ignorant native, from out in—oh, the Dry Towns—to get all shaky, just at a piece of machinery, are you?" He pulled her down on the pillow. "None of us could get along without the sleep-learner tapes."

They lay down again, but Jaelle only dozed fitfully, trying to hear the soft words of the sleep-learner consciously, so that she would not sink again into the morass of nightmare. They had become constant; maybe there was something wrong with the machine? But the nightmares, she remembered, had started before she had brought home the tapes for the machine Piedro called a D-alpha corticator. She would have liked to blame it all on the machine, but she was afraid that was not possible.

Some time before the alarm was due to ring, he woke sleepily, moved it so it would not interrupt them, and began softly caressing her. Still more than half asleep, she yielded herself to this comfort which had become so central to her life and being; she let herself rise with him, as if flying above the world, soaring without gravity or bonds; held tightly in his arms, she shared the delight he knew in possessing her, binding her close with his passion. She had never been closer to him; she reached out blindly to be closer still, closer, seeking that last unknown which would actually merge them into one another's mind and flesh. . . .

My flesh. My woman. My son, immortality. . . . *mine, mine, mine.* . . .

It was not words. It was not feeling alone. It lay deeper than that, further into the base of the mind, at the very depths and foundation of the masculine self. Jaelle did not have the education to speak in the language of the Towers, about the layers of conscious and unconscious mind, masculine and feminine polarity; she could only sense it directly, deep in nerves long denied such awareness. She only knew that what was happening was making things come alive in her body and mind that were not sexual at all, and were quite at variance with what was going on. And some isolated, uncommitted fragment of herself rebelled, in words from the Amazon Oath:

I will give myself only in my own time and season. . . . I will never earn my bread as the object of any man's lust . . . I swear I will bear no child to any man for house or heritage, clan or inheritance, pride or posterity. . . .

Or pride. . . . or pride. . . . or pride. . . .

And at the very moment when she was ready to rip herself from his arms, tear herself away from what had once been the greatest delight in the world, something within her body, deep in a part not subject to conscious will, told her, *no, not now, nothing will happen . . .*

She did not move or draw away from him; she simply lay quietly, not responding, yet too well bred to rouse a man and leave him unsatisfied. But whatever had been binding them together had withdrawn; he was still holding her, caressing her, but slowly, the desire in him ebbed as her own had done, and he lay looking at her, baffled and dismayed. She felt herself hurting inside at the trouble in his eyes.

"Oh, Piedro, I'm sorry!" she cried, at the very moment he released her, murmuring "Jaelle, I'm sorry—"

She drew a long breath, burying her head in his bare shoulder. "It wasn't your fault. I guess it's just not—not the right time."

"And you were already feeling rotten, with all the nightmares," he said, generously ready to make for her the excuses she could not offer for herself; she knew it, and pain stabbed at her again. He got up, and went to fetch a couple of self-heating containers. "Look what I got for us; I know a fellow on the kitchen staff. Coffee; just what you need at this hour." He pulled the tab for hers, and handed it to her, steaming. It was hot, anyhow, and the taste didn't seem to matter. As she sipped it, he nuzzled her neck.

"You're so beautiful. I love your hair when it's this long. Don't ever cut it again, all right?"

She smiled and patted his cheek, still rough where he had not yet shaved. "How would you feel if I asked you to wear a beard?"

"Oh, come *on*," he said, appalled, "You wouldn't do that, would you?"

She laughed softly. "I only meant I wouldn't ask it, love, it's your face. And it's *my* hair."

"Oh, hell!" He rolled away from her, looking stubborn. "Don't I have any rights, woman?"

"Rights? In *my* hair?" It touched the same raw nerve that the moment of deep seeing into his pride had touched; she set her lips and pushed the coffee away. She looked deliberately at the clock face and asked "Do you want to shower first?"

He rolled out and headed toward the bath, while she sat holding her head, trying to focus her eyes on the coffee containers and the wisps of steam that still leaked from them.

The room seemed to be pulsing, getting smaller and larger, higher now, then pressing down on her head. *Something*, she thought, *is wrong with me.* Peter, coming from the shower, saw her bending over, holding her head, fighting the compelling sickness to which she refused to give way.

"Honey, are you all right?" And then, with a smile of concerned pleasure, "Jaelle, you don't suppose—are you pregnant?"

No. It was like a message from deep within her body. She snapped "Of course not," and went to dress. But he hovered near, saying "You can't be sure—hadn't you better check with the Medic anyhow?" and she thought, *how am I so sure?*

I refuse to be sick today, I simply won't give in to it.

She said, "I have a report to finish," and got out of bed. As she forced herself to move, the dizziness receded, and the world became solid again. She was accustomed, by now, to the Terran uniform, the long tights which were astonishingly warm for such thin material, the close-cut tunic. Peter, smelling of soap and the fresh uniform cloth, came to hug her, murmur something reassuring, and dash off.

He wasn't like this at Ardais, she thought fuzzily, and put that away in her mind to think about when it would be less disturbing.

She had long finished the reporting of her trip to Ardais and was working now in Magda's old office in Communications, doing work she considered pointless, upgrading a standard dictionary—that was what Bethany called it—of Darkovan idioms. At least she wasn't working with the damnable sleep-learner-tapes, though she imagined that the work would be transferred eventually to such a tape.

I wonder if the sleep-learner—what did Peter call it, D-alpha corticator—is what's giving me these nightmares? Even he suggested that was a possibility! I'm never going to use it again— I'll sleep on the floor if I have to!

But she worked on conscientiously, upgrading outdated idioms and slang popular in her own childhood, recalling commonplace terms and vulgar language more common than the extremely polite ones. Well, this dictionary had been compiled— she remembered—by Magda's father, years ago in Caer Donn. No one would have used vulgar idiom in front of a learned scholar who was, moreover, an alien. But there were phrases she knew that she would blush to include on a language program to be used before men; furthermore, she was a little doubtful if these particular idioms were ever used among women, except in the Guild-houses.

The fact is, she thought, and wondered why it depressed her, *I do not really know how ordinary women talk, except for Lady Rohana. I went so young to the Guild-house as Kindra's fosterling!*

Well, she would do what she could, as well as she could, and that was all they could rationally expect of her. She was not fully aware that she was stiff with resentment at the unaccustomed uniform, the collar-tab which held the throat-microphone so that she was, for all practical purposes, wired into their machines, the tights which made her legs feel naked. Nakedness would not have bothered her at all, inside the Guild-house with her sisters, but in an office where men came through now and again—though, admittedly, not very often—she felt exposed, and tried to pretend that her desk and consoles could conceal her from them. Once a man walked past her desk—not anyone she knew, an anonymous technician who had come to do something mysterious at Bethany's terminal, pulling out wires and odd-looking slats and peculiar things.

So that's Haldane's Darkovan squaw. Lucky man. What legs. . . .

She looked up and gave the man a blistering glare before she realized that he had said nothing aloud. Her face burning, she lowered her eyes and pretended that he wasn't there at all. All her life she had been plagued with this intermittent *laran* that came and went with no control, forcing itself into her consciousness when she had no wish or will to know what was in another's mind, and often as not, failing her when it would have been priceless. An unwelcome thought intruded on her now, but it was one of her own:

Was I truly reading Peter's mind this morning, is that how he sees me?

No. I was sick, hallucinating. I promised him I'd see the Medic. I'd better go now and arrange it. When the technician had gone, she asked Bethany:

"How do I arrange to see someone in Medic?"

"Just go up there, on your meal break, or after work," Bethany told her. "Someone will make time to see you. What's the matter? Sick?"

"I'm not sure," Jaelle said, "Maybe it's the—the corticator; Peter said it could give me nightmares like that."

Bethany nodded without interest. "If it's not adjusted properly it can do that. Don't bother Medic with it; take the unit up to Psych and they'll adjust it. But if the headaches or nightmares keep up, you probably ought to see a Medic. Or if you're pregnant or something like that."

"Oh, no," said Jaelle promptly, then wondered, *how did she know, why was she so sure?* Maybe she had better check out the Medic after all. She would go on her meal break—she wasn't hungry and the kind of food she could get at the cafeteria at lunchtime wasn't the kind she would regret missing.

But shortly before the time when they left their desks for the meal, there was a curious beeping noise from her desk console. She stared, wondering if she had broken something, if she would have to summon back that technician who had looked at her so offensively.

"Bethany—"

"Answer your page call, Jaelle—" she saw that Jaelle did not understand, and said, "My fault, I forgot to show you. Push that button there—that round white thing that's blinking."

Wondering why they called it a button—it would certainly be hard to sew it on a coat or tunic—Jaelle gingerly touched the pulsing light.

"Mrs. Haldane?" The voice was unfamiliar and quite formal. "Cholayna Ares, Intelligence. Could you come up to my office? Perhaps you would be willing to have lunch with me; I would like to talk with you."

Jaelle already knew enough about Terran speech patterns to know that the words, framed as a polite request, were actually a command, and that there was no question of refusal. She was in Magda's place; the woman she had met last night in Peter's company was Magda's superior officer—at least that was one way of describing it—and therefore Jaelle's as well. She said, trying to tailor her words to Terran forms of politeness, "I should be pleased; I'll be there at once."

"Thank you," said Cholayna's voice, and the light blinked off.

Bethany raised her eyebrows.

"Wonder what *she* wants? I'd surely like to know how she wangled this post out of Head Center! Intelligence, for heaven's sake, when she couldn't go into the field anywhere on this planet! Of course, all she has to do is sit in her office and boss everybody around like a spider in the middle of her web, but an Intelligence officer ought to be able to blend into the scenery, and she'll never be able to do that here! Of course, Head Center may have forgotten what a freak this planet is, and I'll bet anything Cholayna didn't know when she put in for transfer here—"

"I don't think I quite understand," Jaelle said, wondering if she ought to be offended, "Why is this planet such a freak?"

"It's one of the half-dozen or so Empire planets which were settled entirely by a homogeneous group, colonists from one ethnic area," Bethany said. "And though there may have been a few blacks, orientals or what have you on the original ship's crew, genetic drift and interbreeding lost those traits a thousand years before the Empire rediscovered you. A planet with 100 percent white population is rarer than a hen hatched out with teeth!"

Jaelle thought about that for a moment. Yes, she had noticed Cholayna's bark-brown skin and bright brown eyes, but she had simply believed that perhaps the woman had nonhuman blood; there were tales in the mountain of crossbreeds with trailmen or even catmen now and then, though the *kyrri* and *cralmacs* did not, of course, interbreed with humans. "But in the Ages of Chaos," she added, explaining this, "humans were often artificially interbred with *cralmacs*; I simply thought she was only part human, that's all."

"Don't let Cholayna hear you say that," Bethany said, with a shocked grimace. "In the Empire, calling someone half-human is the dirtiest—not the second dirtiest—thing you can say to them, believe me."

Jaelle started to express her shock—what disgusting prejudice! —but then she remembered that among ignorant peoples, even here, there were certain prejudices against nonhumans, and there was no accounting for custom and taboo. *Don't try to buy fish in the Dry Towns.* She held her peace, wondering why, with the vaunted Empire medical technology, they had not discovered or rediscovered this technique and why they did not make use of it.

She said "I had better go up to the Intelligence Office. No, thank you, I can find the way myself."

Cholayna made Jaelle comfortable in a soft chair, and ordered up lunch for her from the console, which seemed to have more choices than the lunch cafeteria.

"I haven't had much chance to talk to anyone Darkovan," she said frankly, "and I know that on this planet I won't be able to do field work; so I have to depend on my field agents. I'm here to organize an Intelligence department, not to work in it. I'll have to depend on you, and on anyone else here who knows the planet and grew up in the field. I didn't want to lose Magda Lorne, but I wasn't given the choice. I want to feel I can rely on you, Mrs. Haldane, as I would have relied on Magda. I hope we can be friends."

Jaelle put a fork into her food before replying. She had never known a woman who was neither the property of some man, nor yet a Renunciate. At last she said, "If you want to be my friend, you can start by not calling me *Mrs. Haldane.* Peter and I are not married *di catenas* and the Renunciate's Oath forbids that I shall wear any man's name—though I can't seem to make Records understand that."

"I'll try and have it fixed," Cholayna said, and Jaelle could see the woman's lively brown eyes absorbing the information. "What should I call you, then?"

"I am Jaelle n'ha Melora. Should we truly come to be friends, my sisters in the Guild-house call me *Shaya.*"

"Jaelle, then, for the moment," said Cholayna, and Jaelle noted with appreciation that she did not hurry to use the intimate name. "I was Magda's friend as well as her teacher, I think. And there is a good deal you can do for us here; I am sure you know that we have agreed to train a group of young women in Medic; perhaps you can make it easier for them among us. You are the first, you know."

Jaelle smiled. "But I am not, of course. Two of my Guild sisters worked on the spaceport when you were building it."

Cholayna said, surprised, "Our employment rolls show no sign of Darkovan women employed—"

Jaelle laughed. "They were both *emmasca*—neutered; you probably thought them men, and of course they would have taken men's names. They wished to see what your people were like, who had come from beyond the stars," Jaelle said. She forbore to add that what they had told, in the Guild-house, had been the subject of many jokes, some vulgar.

Cholayna laughed softly. "I should have known that while we were studying you, you would be studying us in return. I will not ask you what you thought of us. Neither of us knows the other well enough for that, not yet."

Jaelle was pleasantly surprised. This was truly the first Empire subject she had met who did not jump to unjustified conclusions about Darkovan culture. Perhaps Cholayna was the first truly educated Terran she had met, except for Magda, who was more Darkovan than Terran.

"Are you sure you have had enough to eat? More coffee? You are sure?" Cholayna asked, and at Jaelle's refusal, shoved the dishes into the disposal unit, and took up a cassette from her desk. Jaelle recognized her own writing on the label; it was the report she had made up about Peter's ransom and their winter at Ardais. One with Peter's familiar label was beside it.

"I see from this," she said, "that you were born in the Dry Towns, and lived there until you were almost twelve years old."

Jaelle wondered suddenly if the lunch she had eaten had contained something poisonous to her; her stomach heaved, reminding her that she had intended to go and see the Medic. She said curtly, "I left Shainsa when I was twelve and have never returned. I know very little of the Dry Towns: I have even forgotten the dialect of Shainsa and speak it like any stranger."

Cholayna looked at her silently for a long moment. Then she said, "Twelve years is long enough. At twelve, a child is formed—socially, sexually, the personality is fully created and cannot really be changed thereafter. You are far more a product of the Dry Towns than you are, for instance, a product of the Renunciate's Guild-house."

Jaelle caught her breath, not knowing whether the flooding emotion was rage, dismay or simple disbelief. She found herself actually on her feet, every muscle tensed.

"How dare you?" she almost spat the words at Cholayna, "You have no right to say that!"

Cholayna blinked, but did not give ground before the flood of fury. "Jaelle, my dear, I wasn't speaking of you personally, of course; I was simply restating one of the best established facts of human psychology; if you took it as a personal attack, I am sorry. Whether we like it or not, it's a fact; the earliest impressions made on our minds are the lasting ones. Why should it trouble you so much to think that you might be basically a product of Dry-Town culture? Remember, I know very little about it, and there is very little about it in the HQ files; I must rely on you to tell me. What did I say to make you so angry?"

Jaelle drew a long breath and discovered that her jaw was aching behind her clenched teeth. At last she said "I—I did not mean to attack you personally, either. I—" and she had to stop again and swallow and unclench her teeth; if she had been wearing a dagger, she realized, she would have drawn it, and perhaps, before she thought, used it, too. *Why did I explode like that?* The rage slowly drained from her, leaving bewilderment behind.

"You must be mistaken, in this case at least. If I were a product of the Dry Towns, I should be a—a chattel, as women are there; chained, some man's property; a woman unchained is a scandal—she must bear the mark of some man's ownership. I swore the Renunciate's Oath as soon as I was old enough, and I have—have forgotten—everything I have done since I left the Dry Towns has been a way of—"

She stopped, her voice trailing into silence, completing in her mind, *a way of proving to myself that I would never wear chains for any man. . . . Kindra said once to me that most women, and most men too, believe themselves free and weight themselves with invisible chains . . .*

Cholayna brushed her hand absently over her silver-white hair. "If everything you have done since you left the Dry Towns has been a way of proving that you were not one of them, then, whether you live by their precepts or no, they have formed everything you have done. If they had left no influence on you, you would have chosen your way without thinking whether it was their way or the reverse—wouldn't you?"

Jaelle muttered "I suppose so." She was still carefully breathing, forcing herself to relax, to unclench her fists.

Cholayna added, casually, "I know little of the Renunciates, either. You spoke of the Oath, and so did Magda, but I know nothing of it. Is it a secret, or can you tell me what a Renunciate, a Free Amazon. swears?"

Jaelle said tiredly, "The Oath is not secret. I will gladly tell you." She began "From this day henceforth I swear—"

"Wait—" Cholayna lifted a hand. "May I turn on a recording device for the records?"

There was that word again! But what was the point in arguing? It was, perhaps, the only way to make the Guild-house comprehensible to an outsider. She said, "Certainly," and waited.

"From this day I renounce the right to marry save as a freemate; no man shall bind me *di catenas* and I will dwell in no man's house as a *barragana*," she began, and steadily recited the Oath from beginning to end. How could Cholayna believe that she, if she were truly, as the woman said, a product formed by the Dry-Town culture, without hope of change in personality or sexuality or will, could have freely chosen the Oath? Ridiculous, on the face of it!

Cholayna listened quietly, nodding once or twice at some provision or other.

"This is, of course, not strange to me," she said, "for in the Empire, and particularly on the Alpha planet where I grew up, it was taken for granted that women had these rights and responsibilities; although we also admit," she said with a faint smile, "that the father of a child also has rights and responsibilities in determining care and upbringing. Some day, if you wish, I should like to discuss this with you at length. Also, I can see why it was that the Free Amazons—forgive me, the Renunciates— were the first Darkovan women to seek to learn from the Terrans. I have two things to ask of you. The first is that you should visit Magda in the Guild-house and talk with her about choosing suitable women as candidates for Medic training—or whatever else seems suitable."

"That will be my pleasure," Jaelle said formally, but her mind ran counterpoint, *If she thinks I will help to persuade our women to act as Intelligence spies, she may think again.*

"Jaelle, what was your work among the—the Renunciates? What sort of work do they do?"

"Any honest work," Jaelle said, "Among us there are bakers, cheese-makers, midwives—oh, yes, we train midwives especially in the Guild-house in Arilinn—herb sellers, confectioners, mercenary soldiers—" Abruptly she stopped, realizing where this line of questioning was leading.

"No, we are not all soldiers, Cholayna, nor mercenaries, nor sword-women; if I had to gain my porridge with the sword, I should have starved long ago. The outsiders think always of the more *visible* Free Amazons, the ones who hire out as soldiers and mercenaries. There was a time, long ago, when there was a Sisterhood of the Sword—in the Ages of Chaos—it was dissolved when the Guild, the Comhi-Letzii, were formed. The Sisterhood were mercenaries and soldiers, then. You asked what I did? I am a travel-organizer; we provide escort for ladies traveling alone, at least that was how it started, because we could chaperone as well as guide and protect. Later, men also came to us, so that we could tell them how many pack-beasts to hire, what food to buy for them, and how much they would need for the journey—we also act as guides through the worst country and the mountain passes." She smiled a little, forgetting her anger. "They say now that an Amazon guide will go where no man in the Hellers will dare to set his foot."

"That would be invaluable to us," Cholayna said quietly. "Mapping and Exploring can always use guides and personnel who can tell them how to outfit themselves for the weather and the terrain. Lives have been lost for lack of that knowledge. If the Renunciates will consent to work for us, we will be truly grateful." She paused a moment. "I wish, too, that you would consent to talk with one of our agents about what you remember of the Dry Towns, however simple. I am not asking that you should spy upon your own people," she added shrewdly, "only that you should help to prevent misunderstandings—to tell us what your people think *our* people should know about your world, forms of courtesy, ways to avoid giving offense by ignorance—"

"Yes, of course," said Jaelle. She could not remember now why she felt so angry at the very thought of talking about the Dry Towns. She was an employee of the Empire, so employed with the consent of her Guild-mothers, and as such she should obey every lawful command of her employer.

"For instance, we have an Agent—his name is Raymon Kadarin—who is willing to go into the Dry Towns and send back some information from there. I want you to meet him, to see if you think he could go into the Dry Towns without being immediately spotted as a spy. What we know of the Domains—" she broke off as a light began to blink on her desk with repetitive insistence.

"I told those fellows not to disturb us," Cholayna said, frowning slightly, "Just let me get rid of them, Jaelle, and we'll go on. Yes?" she snapped, pressing the blinking stud.

"The Chief's on a rampage," said the disembodied voice. "He's looking all over for that Darkovan—you know, Haldane's girl? Finally Beth said she was in your office, and he made a scene. Can you send her down here double-quick and calm him down?"

Jaelle felt herself clench tight with wrath. She was not *Haldane's girl*, she was not a *girl* at all, she was a woman and an Empire employee in her own right, and if they wanted her, they could have the courtesy to ask for her properly by name! She started to blurt out some of this, then saw Cholayna was frowning, and sensed that the woman was almost equally angry.

"Jaelle n'ha Melora is in my office, and I have not yet finished my conference," said Cholayna coldly. "If Montray wishes to speak with her, he may request her to come to his office when I have finished."

Jaelle had met the Coordinator at the Council and had not liked him. She knew that Magda, too, had small respect for the man who had been her immediate superior; that he knew far less of Darkover than Magda herself, or any of half a dozen agents who worked under him. Peter, too, had said something like that; *Granted, the man's a career diplomat, not an Intelligence Agent, but he ought to know something about the world where he's stationed!*

Cholayna pushed the button and it went dark. "That will hold him for a little while, but I can't guarantee that he won't send for you right away. I've done my best." She smiled at Jaelle, in a sudden, conspiratorial way, and Jaelle realized she liked this woman, she had one friend here, at least.

"Now, how would you like to record what you know of the Dry Towns?" Cholayna asked. "You can put it into a tape for Records, or you can talk directly to the Agent . . ."

I'd rather not do either, Jaelle thought. She hated talking on tape, but she had not learned to relate to the men she found here in the Headquarters. The thought of talking to a strange Terran Agent, to any Terran man without at least the tacit protection of Peter's presence, frightened her. Yet the words of the Amazon Oath tormented her, *I shall appeal to no man as of right, for protection. . . .* what, she thought distractedly, has *happened* to me, since I have come to live here as Piedro's freemate?

Cholayna was still expectantly looking at her and Jaelle realized that she had not answered. She stammered, "I'd—I'd like to think about it a little, before I make up my mind."

What I really want, she thought, is to talk mostly to the women. I feel safe and comfortable with Cholayna, even with Bethany. I feel secure relating to Darkovan men, even those who detest everything the Free Amazons stand for, because I know how to disarm their suspicions, to work among them as one of themselves. She did not think she could learn to do that with Terran men, and she didn't really want to try.

And then she felt ashamed of herself. She was a grown woman, a Renunciate, she should not expect to hide behind Cholayna or even behind Piedro. She said almost aggressively,

"I'll talk to the Agent," and stared at the floor, uncomfortably conscious that Cholayna was looking at her with sympathy.

I'm a big girl now, I don't need to be protected or mothered . . . she told herself, wishing she could feel the truth of that.

The light on Cholayna's desk blinked again, and she said to it, irritably stabbing with one polished nail at the button, "What now?"

"Mr. Montray to see you," answered the voice, and Cholayna raised her eyebrow.

"The mountain cannot fly to the birds, therefore each of the birds must fly to the mountain," she said wryly. "That is an old proverb on my planet, Jaelle. I'm afraid I'll have to let him in. You can go, if you'd rather."

Jaelle shook her head. "I shall have to meet him sometime," she said, bracing herself for the graying, disapproving Montray. The man who entered, however, was a stranger, at least twenty years younger than the man Jaelle remembered.

"You were expecting my father?" he asked at Cholayna's look of surprise. "I'm Wade Montray, and Father sent me up to look the girl over and see what use we could make of her—" He broke off, looked around at Jaelle and grinned apologetically.

"I did not know you were still here; I don't mean to be rude. I believe I saw you at the Council, but we weren't formally introduced."

Now she remembered; he, at least, spoke the language flawlessly and had interrupted some of his father's more tactless and unsuitable comments. "Yes, I remember seeing you, Mr. Montray—"

"Wade," he said, "but I know that isn't easy to say in your language. I'm usually called Monty, miss—" again he broke off. "I am sorry; I don't know the polite address for a Renunciate—"

"I am Jaelle n'ha Melora. If you do not feel ready to use my name, you may say *mestra*. But if we are to work together and I am to call you Monty, I should be Jaelle."

He nodded, repeating the name carefully. "May I take her down to the Old Man's office, Cholayna? Or do you still need her up here? If you do, I'll try and smooth it over a little." He hesitated and said, "Look, he really doesn't mean any harm. It's just—well, he's been running everything, Intelligence, and Communications, Linguistics, all that stuff out of his office, and all of a sudden he doesn't know where his authority leaves off and yours begins, so he's feeling a little raw around the edges."

Cholayna nodded. She looked a little grim. "I can see that it would be hard for him. Technically of course I am not responsible to any planetary Coordinator, but only to Head Center. I'll try not to—to step on his feet, unless he gets in the way too much—I mean, in the way of Empire Intelligence. Jaelle, please feel free to call on me for help any time. And ask Peter to come in and see me sometime tomorrow, will you?" Cholayna turned her attention back to the lights blinking on her console, and Jaelle turned to the door with young Montray. *Monty*, she reminded herself, to distinguish him from his father.

"Your command of the language is excellent," she said, as they went down the hall. "How—"

He grinned at her disarmingly.

"How do I speak the language so well when Father still needs an interpreter? I came here before I was ten years old, and I've always been good at languages. The old man kept expecting, every year, that he'd be shipped out next year to a place he liked better, and so he never bothered with the language. I was shipped offworld for a proper Empire education when I was fourteen, but I liked it here and couldn't wait to come back. Sorry, I didn't mean to bore you with my personal problems. We can take this elevator."

The sickening drop was less frightening now; her legs were almost steady under her as they stepped out. In Montray's office, the plump, balding official was seated near a window looking out over the spaceport.

"I asked you to come down here, Mrs. Haldane," he said, in *casta* so poor and stumbling that Jaelle decided it would not be the least use to correct him about her name, "because I have a special assignment for you. My colleague here, Alessandro Li." A tall man, standing beside his desk, turned and bowed to Jaelle.

"He has been sent here as a Special Representative of the

Senate at Head Center, with diplomatic status, to investigate whether Cottman Four shall retain its Closed World status or be reclassified, and to make recommendations about a Legation here. Sandro, this is the first Native Darkovan woman in Intelligence; she is married to Peter Haldane—"

"I know Haldane's background in Intelligence," the man interrupted. "Alien anthropology specialist; excellent field operative." His *casta* was better than Montray's, though not perfect. He turned and bowed slightly to Jaelle. "It is a pleasure to meet you, *domna*."

Jaelle forbore, for a moment, to correct him. Alessandro Li was a tall man, hatchet-jawed, with steel-gray eyes under protruding eyebrows, the whole face shadowed by bushy dark hair and made—to Jaelle's eyes—ridiculous by a foppishly trimmed moustache.

"Do you think you can fit him to travel incognito in the Hellers and the Kilghard Hills, *mestra*?" Montray asked.

The first thought that came to her mind was an absurd, *not with that moustache*, but she bit it back; after all, the man was new to her world and even from traveling between mountains and Domains she knew that the small things, dress and culture patterns and body language, varied so enormously that their significance could not be taken for granted. She saw, however, a gleam of amusement in Monty's eye and knew that his first thought had been the same as hers. So she studied Alessandro Li for a moment without speaking. At last she said, "He could pass in the Hellers, up around MacAran country; some of them are dark and—and bony, like that. He would have to wear his hair longer, and either shave clean or wear a fuller beard. And he would have to be properly dressed, of course. And there is no way that he could pass until he has more training in the language."

"I wouldn't know about that," said the elder Montray with unexpected humility. "Languages aren't my strong point; that's why I miss Magda; she was my best interpreter. Wasted, of course, as an interpreter; she was the best undercover agent we had. But you think he could, eventually, pass?"

Alessandro Li was trying to meet her eyes; Jaelle colored and dropped her own. There was no way he could know—yet—that this was rude in their society, but Monty spoke up.

"To start with, Sandro," he said, "you don't try to make eye contact with a strange woman, not here in the Domains, unless you think she's a prostitute trying to pick you up. If Jaelle's husband were here, he could call challenge on you for looking at her like that. Call it your first lesson in cross-cultural courtesy here on Darkover."

"Oh, right," the man said promptly, and dropped his eyes. "No offense meant, miss—excuse me—*mestra*, is that right?"

"None taken," she said just as promptly, "but this is the kind of thing I mean. Piedro could help him more than I, of course. And it wouldn't be easy. It would be simpler to prepare—" she gestured toward Monty, who laughed and said, "I'd like to work in the field, of course. But as for sending Sandro out in the field—well, it seems to me that it would make more sense to let the actual fieldwork be done by our trained operatives, the ones who can go out and never be spotted as Terran because in everything that counts they *are* Darkovan; Haldane, Lorne—Cargill, Kadarin, even myself. Then we could report to Sandro and he could make his final decision from that."

Russell Montray leaned his chin on his hands and thought about that for a moment. Finally he said, "There's only one problem with that. Haldane, Lorne, Kadarin—the ones who can really pass in the field—they *are* Darkovan, for all intents and purposes. Yes, they've taken a Service oath, and I'm not questioning their loyalty, but it's natural that they'd think in terms of what's best for Darkover, not necessarily what's best for *us*. No offense meant, Jaelle—" he mispronounced her name, but at least he wasn't calling her *Mrs. Haldane* and she could tell that he meant to be friendly—"but Haldane married Darkovan—and now Magda has pledged to spend half a year in that Free Amazon women's commune or whatever it is. And we don't want the decisions made by someone who's gone native on us; the investigation must be supervised by an objective observer, not prejudiced in favor of the Darkovan view of everything. Do you understand?"

Jaelle stared out the huge window that overlooked the spaceport. One of the Big Ships was there, a ground crew crawling over it, servicing the spaceborne monster which had come here, not because it cared to come to Cottman IV, Darkover, but simply because Darkover was a convenient way station on the way to somewhere else. The quick retort on her tongue, that Sandro Li would be equally prejudiced in favor of the Empire's view, would not mean anything to Russell Montray.

From this height, the service crew around the ship looked tiny as so many scorpion-ants. No wonder this was why the elder Montray thought of the Darkovan view as something distant, irrelevant. He did not know Darkovans personally, he did not wish to know them, they were something other than human, forever set apart. What was it Bethany had said? The filthiest insult, in Empire language, was to call someone half-human.

"I am going to assign you to Sandro Li, to work with him, to be personally responsible for him," he said. "It's your job to work with him on languages, to get him ready for fieldwork, and I'll hold you responsible if anything happens to him."

He had used the words, *personally responsible*, which would have made it a matter of honor and pride to defend him to the death. For a moment Jaelle's hand, automatically, sought for a knife that was not hanging at her belt; the gesture, arrested, made her feel foolish. She said in a low voice, "On my honor by my Oath, I will hold myself responsible for him."

But Monty had seen the gesture. He said, "We're not asking you to be his bodyguard, Jaelle. You weren't hired as a knife fighter. What my father means is—you're to accompany him if he goes off base, make certain he doesn't get into any avoidable trouble, avoid any incidents; train him to get along in the Trade City without getting himself into trouble. Understand?"

She nodded. "First of all," she said, "you must have a Darkovan name. Alessandro is near enough to a name used in the Kilghard Hills, but no one would call a man *Sandro*; it is too much like that of *Zandru*. Zandru is Lord of Choices, good or evil, and of the Nine Hells."

"Equivalent of the devil," Monty put in, and Alessandro Li raised his bushy eyebrows. "What would a child named Alessandro be called, then?"

"Probably—Aleki," Jaelle hazarded, and he pronounced it after her, stumbling. "Ah—lee—kye, is that right?"

She nodded. "And he should—" she hesitated, but these *Terranan* would not know the difference, and why should she hesitate? "Monty, get him to a barber; a Darkovan-trained one. And get rid of that moustache, first thing. Piedro can help to find him proper clothes."

Alessandro Li—*Aleki*, she reminded herself—gently touched the maligned moustache; a little regretfully, she thought. "So begins my transformation into a Darkovan," he said, at last, with a shrug. "All in the day's work, I suppose. Where do I find a barber, Monty?"

The transformation was remarkable; Jaelle had not thought it could make so much difference. His face was transformed entirely by the absence of the moustache which had been its strongest feature, and the barber had trimmed the eyebrows, too, giving the whole countenance an entirely different look. Jaelle was curious about the barber who could effect this kind of change—what did he think? Had she supervised a change which would enable this man to spy on her people?

Who are my people? And why? I have never belonged in the Domains, any more than I belonged, as a child, in the Dry Towns. I have never belonged anywhere except among my sisters in the Guild-house, and now I have forsworn that . . . and she broke off, shocked at herself. She had not forsworn anything. It was her right to take a freemate, as she chose, and to accept any lawful employment. She was building a bridge between two worlds, as her friend and sister Magda was doing, as her beloved Piedro was trying to do. Why must the interests of Terran and Darkovan conflict? Could they not be working at what was best for both?

Aleki was looking at her, awaiting her approval. He had been dressed in the fur-and-leather clothing which any sensible man, traveling in the Venza mountains near Thendara, would wear, and the Terran sandals had been replaced by thick boots.

"No one would think you Terran," she said, and then, confronted with an apparently Darkovan man, was conscious of the immodestly revealing Terran uniform. That was the difference; he took it for granted, a Darkovan would not. To cover her confusion she said quickly, "You don't smell right; Piedro—Peter would be able to advise you about that better than I."

"Haldane? I am eager to meet him," Aleki said. "I know of his work; wasn't he the first Terran to travel to the seacoast, Temora and Dalereuth? Or was that Magda?"

"They were married at that time," Jaelle said, "I believe they share the work and the credit. And if you wish to meet Piedro, nothing is easier; will you join us at dinner?"

"A pleasure; would you object if Monty joined us too?"

"Not at all." Actually, Jaelle was relieved; Monty's presence made the whole affair simply the business of Intelligence.

Peter was waiting for them inside the entrance to the main cafeteria; he recognized Monty at once, and the two men shook hands. Monty introduced Alessandro Li, repeating also the Darkovan name *Aleki* which he had been given.

"A pleasure, Haldane. I know your work. I had hoped to meet Magda as well," Aleki said.

"Well, that could be arranged; she is still in Thendara," Peter said. "Are men allowed to visit the Guild-house, Jaelle?"

"Of course; though they are not allowed to go beyond the Strangers Room," Jaelle said, and she could see Aleki filing away this information in his mind.

"I'll find us a table where we can talk," Aleki said, moving away, as Peter and Monty went with Jaelle toward the food console dispensers.

Behind them someone said, low but clearly audible, "That's Haldane's girl; he picked her up in Thendara. She's gorgeous, at least now he's got her in civilized clothes. Back in the mountains, I hear, they still wear animal skins. What legs!

Lucky man—I've heard all kinds of stories about Darkovan
marriage—"

"I heard a girl and all her sisters share the man," said another
voice, "Reckon this one has any sisters? Or maybe Haldane's
into—"

At the first syllable Peter had stiffened, going silent, and
now, as the words trailed off into obscene speculation, he
whirled, grabbing the man by his shirt front.

"Watch your filthy tongue, you bastard," he growled. But
Jaelle, adrenalin spurting inside her brain, pushed Peter angrily
away.

"This is *my* fight!" She gave Peter another hard shove, so that
he reeled and half fell into Monty's arms, then, her hands stiff-
ening into weapons, caught the man across the throat; he fell as
if he had been struck with a hammer. A deftly aimed kick
stretched the first speaker, moaning and clutching himself, on
the floor. Jaelle, her mouth trembling, and her breath coming in
little catching half-sobs, turned back to Peter.

Then black-uniformed Spaceforce guards were there, dragging them apart; Jaelle tightened, but the man only pushed her
away, almost respectfully, with his arm; Peter put his arm
around her, but she straightened, resentfully. The words of the
Oath. . . . *defend myself by force if I am attacked . . . turn to no
man as of right for protection* were beating in her pulse like little hammers inside her head.

The Spaceforce man said mildly, "Disturbing the peace in a
public place; shall I give each of you a citation? Can't you go
work out in the gymnasium? The cafeteria isn't the spot for martial arts."

Peter snarled, "The filthy bastards were running off at the
mouth about my wife!"

"Hard words break no bones," said the Spaceforce man.
"Anyhow, it looks as if the lady can take care of herself." His
eyes rested a moment on Jaelle, and she could almost *hear* his
thoughts, but all he said was "I don't know what Darkovan customs are, ma'am, and I don't want to know, but our customs
here include, no brawling in public places. You're a stranger, so

I won't cite you this time, but no more fighting in here, all right? Haldane, you ought to teach your lady to behave herself in public." He turned away; his partner picked up the man Jaelle had slammed to the ground, who was shaking his head and ruefully fingering his throat. The other was still moaning; he grabbed the offered arm of the Spaceforce man and said, "Can you help me up to Medic?" He groaned again, staggering as he walked. The first man, with the bruised throat, gulped again and came toward Jaelle; she tensed, but he only husked, "Serves me right; me and my big mouth. I got to hand it to you, lady, you fight like a man," and went to his own table.

Aleki beckoned to them from a table for four in the corner. Peter nodded and went toward the food line. Jaelle was shaking, now that the crisis was over. She chose the first foods she came to, at random, and went back to the table, but when she put a forkful into her mouth she could not swallow.

"I have heard that the Renunciates were fighting women," Aleki said quietly. "Are you trained with a sword as well?"

She said, and knew her voice was small and shaking, "I can handle a knife. I—" her throat closed; she touched the healed scar on her cheek. She was still pulsing with fury.

Animal skins! When one of the prized trade items was the luxurious marl-fur from the Hellers, when the supple tanned and dyed leathers from the Kilghard Hills brought almost their weight in copper!

Monty said, "I have seen fighting like that in the Intelligence School; women as well as men are trained to defend themselves. But I had not expected to find it on Darkover—"

"No, most women are trained only to turn to the nearest male for protection!" Jaelle heard the note of contempt in her voice only after she had spoken, and saw the hurt reflected in Peter's face. He said, sliding into his seat, "They were insulting me, not you, Jaelle. Didn't it ever occur to you that I was the one being insulted?"

"On *my* behalf," she said stiffly.

"All that happened was, you made it worse," he said, setting his chin in the sulky line she dreaded. "Did you hear those men—*teach your lady to behave in public?* That's what you've got to do, Jaelle—learn how to behave in public! I don't care what you do or say when we're alone, but in public it reflects on me if you behave as if you were just out of some wild village in the Hellers!"

"Reflects on *you*—" she broke off. He sounded, it occurred to her, rather as *Dom* Gabriel had sounded when he spoke of the Free Amazons; as if it insulted the men of her family that a woman should learn to defend herself, rather than relying on her menfolk.

He was brought up as a Darkovan, she thought. *I thought, as a Terran, he would understand; Terran women are more independent* . . . and with a queer little sickening lurch inside her, Jaelle thought of what Cholayna had said that day; that the personality was formed by the age of twelve and could not be much changed thereafter.

Had she been so swift to fight—when, actually, it *was* Peter being insulted—because she could not bear the thought that perhaps, within herself, there was a woman of the Dry Towns who wished to be chained, as symbol that she was lawfully the property of some man? Had she lashed out with her fists to silence that voice, not the casual obscenities of the two men? Was Peter, inside himself, a man of the Hellers who felt his wife should turn to him in all ways for protection and care? Could either of them ever escape the doom of their upbringing?

Of course we can, she told herself angrily. Otherwise no woman could ever become a Renunciate; and the Renunciates are all women who have renounced their birthright and overcome the chains put on them in childhood by their upbringing. I too shall overcome. . . .

Several of Peter's friends, who had seen the controversy, made a point of coming over to say something friendly. Evidently the men who had made the rude remarks were not generally liked, and though not many people had heard what remarks started the fight, they disapproved on principle of that kind of rudeness. They lingered on in the cafeteria, drinking and eating and talking, until it took on some of the characteristics of an impromptu party, and finally the kitchen staff had to turn them all out.

But outside, Jaelle turned away invitations to come up to various rooms in quarters and continue the partying. She felt exhausted. She had intended to see the Medic that day, but she had not done so. Peter was still silent and sullen, and she dreaded the reproach that would come into his eyes when they were alone. Had she truly wounded his pride so much?

And should it matter to her—as an Amazon—if she had?

She turned to him as soon as they were alone. "I am sorry—" she said, but he was already speaking. "Jaelle, I didn't mean to be so—" and as they heard each other, they laughed and fell into one another's arms.

"You're wonderful," he whispered. "I love you so much! I know how hard this is for you—" and again, reassured, she felt that she was sheltering in his love, that it was a rock to cling to in this strange and alien place.

But that night, after they had made love till they were exhausted, and she had fallen asleep in his arms, she roused up shrieking from a dream in which her half-forgotten father, Jalak of the Great House in Shainsa, came with chains for her hands, saying she was far past the age where she should have been wearing them, and when she begged Peter to help her, he stood back and held her while the bracelets were slipped lovingly over her wrists.

Chapter 5

Magda sat at supper in the dining hall of Thendara Guild-house, looking back over her fourth full day as a Renunciate. The first day they had asked her to stay with Keitha, who was feverish and ill from the aftermath of the beating she had received; the next day she had been set to help Irmelin in the kitchen. She had been incredibly clumsy about sweeping, and peeling vegetables for supper, but Irmelin had merely made a few grumpy remarks about fine ladies who didn't ever get their hands dirty. She had been gentle and good-natured about showing her how to wield the ungainly mops and brooms, and to slice vegetables without cutting herself. She found herself helplessly resenting the waiting on table, and dishwashing afterward; why had no one ever invented the simplest labor-saving devices to save women from these dehumanizing tasks?

Today had been worse; she had been sent to work in the stables. She did not mind feeding, watering or even exercising the horses, for in the big paddock the sun was bright overhead and the air fresh and clear, but the heavy barn-shovels were worse than kitchen mops, and the smell of manure was sickening. This, she told herself angrily, is why they had an Industrial Revolution on Terra; somebody got sick and tired of shoveling horse manure!

Her partner in this work was called Rafaella; she remembered that Rafaella was Jaelle's partner in their travel-counseling business, and had hoped to find her friendly, but Rafaella had had little to say to her. At the end of the day Magda was exhausted; she had never done manual work before, and she was glad to wash off the dirt and grime; but even though she washed her hair, she fancied that the stable smell still clung to it. The smell of the soap was harsh after the perfumed cosmetics of the Terran Zone. She lingered in the hot pool, trying to soak away fatigue, until Doria and another group of very young girls came in, and there was a lot of noisy and cheerful horseplay, running around naked and climbing in and out of the tubs and playfully squabbling over the soap. The noise they made finally drove her out of the pool room entirely, and only later did she admit to herself that she was jealous of the fun they were all having together.

Now, hungry after her day in the barn, she still found the food hard to get down; it was some kind of meat, or more likely, entrails, stewed with coarse-ground meal, and flavored with a highly spiced sauce; the bread was dark, coarse and unleavened, and there was some stewed fruit in honey which might have been tolerable if it had been chilled, but which was served warm. She was accustomed to Darkovan foods, and liked most of them, but by unlucky chance, the foods tonight were all new to her and distasteful; she nibbled at buttered bread, pushed the stew around on her plate, and longed, angrily and hopelessly, for a good cup of coffee. She had been trained, in Intelligence, to eat any kind of alien food without protest or visible distaste, and usually she managed it, but tonight she felt exhausted and let down. Could she really endure a half year here, among these strange women and in these uncomfortable conditions?

She sat in her place next to Doria; across the table was the elderly *emmasca*, Camilla, who had witnessed her oath, and beyond her was the new woman, Keitha. Today she looked better, with some color in her cheeks, and her bright hair, roughly hacked off for the oath-taking, had been neatly trimmed around her neck. She was wearing Amazon clothing which looked shabby and much-worn; probably from the same castoff-box as Magda's own. She still seemed shy and lost and ate little.

Camilla's gaunt face was kind with concern.

"But you are eating nothing, Margali—don't you like the tripe stew?"

"Oh, is that what it is?" Magda took another forkful and wished she hadn't. "It's very good," she lied, "but I'm not very hungry tonight." She took another piece of bread and buttered it. At least she *could* eat the bread, and with the warm stewed fruit on it, it wasn't too bad.

Mother Lauria rapped with a glass for silence. "Training Session tonight," she said. "It is compulsory for all new sisters and for everyone who has been oath-bound for less than three years, and everyone, of course, is welcome. The Sisterhood is meeting in the music room tonight, so Training Session will be in the armory."

There was a loud and audible groan. "Everybody remember to bring your extra shawls," somebody grumbled, "It's freezing down there!"

"We'll put the mats down for you to sit on," Rafaella said. "And a little cold won't hurt you! It keeps you alert so you won't go to sleep, as you might otherwise after a heavy supper!"

Magda whispered to Doria as they left the dining room, "What is the Sisterhood?"

"It's a secret society," Doria whispered back, "It links the Guild-houses together, that's all I really know about it, and most of the women who belong to it are healers or midwives; Marisela belongs. They're sworn to secrecy about it and they never tell."

Camilla came and linked her arm through Magda's as they went downstairs toward the armory. "I thought Jaelle was taking you to Neskaya. Why are you here? I heard that Jaelle was back for a night or two, but I had no chance to speak to her; I saw the scar on her cheek, though. What happened?"

"She and I were attacked by bandits," Magda said. "We spent the winter at Ardais; she was too ill to travel. Then we came here to Thendara—"

"Well, it is not surprising, that she should want her oath-daughter in her own house," said Camilla. She drew Magda after her into the armory, where women were dragging the mats into a close circle. Camilla tossed Magda a blanket.

"You are cold, I can see, even with your shawl; wrap up in this," she said.

Mother Lauria said, "My sisters, all of you have seen the new ones among us; it is many years since we have had as many as three to be trained together. You all know Doria; Rafaella has done what each of us hopes to do some day, brought a grown daughter or fosterling to take the Oath from her hands. Now it is time for you to know Margali n'ha Ysabet, who took the Oath at the hands of Jaelle n'ha Melora last winter, and Keitha n'ha Casilda, who took oath from Camilla n'ha Kyria here in this house four days ago. Camilla, you are oath-mother to one of these and oath-sister to the other; will you lead us in the first round tonight?"

"With pleasure," said Camilla, "Doria, you have not yet taken Oath, though you have lived among us all your life. Why do you want to take the Renunciate's Oath?"

Doria smiled and said confidently, "Because I was brought up among you; it is my home, and will please my foster mother."

Rafaella said quickly, "That is not a good reason. Doria, did I ever ask or require of you, as a condition of my love, that you should become an Amazon?"

Doria blinked, confused, but she said, "No, but I knew you wished—"

"But what was *your* reason?" asked Camilla, "Yours, not Rafi's."

"Because—well, really, because—I have lived here all my life, and I wanted to be really one of you—not just a fosterling here—but a real Amazon—"

Irmelin asked, "Were you afraid that if you did not take the Oath you would have nowhere to go?"

"That's not fair," Doria said shakily, but Irmelin insisted. "Tell me. If we refused to take your Oath, what would you do?"

"But you aren't going to do that, are you?" Doria protested, "I've lived here all my life, I've just *expected* to take the Oath when I was fifteen—" She looked shocked and afraid.

"Just tell us," Irmelin said, "If we refuse you the Oath, where will you go? What will you do?"

"I suppose—I don't know—back to my birth-mother, I suppose, if she will have me—I don't know, I don't know, I don't *know*," Doria cried, and burst into tears. Camilla shrugged, and turned to Keitha.

"You. Why did you come here, Keitha?"

"Because my husband beat and ill-treated me, and I could bear no more—and I had heard a woman could take refuge here—"

"How long had you been married?" Magda recognized the speaker as the heavily pregnant Byrna.

"Seven years."

"And had your husband beaten you before this?"

"Y—yes," Keitha said shakily.

Byrna made a wry face. "If you had endured his beatings before this, why did you suddenly choose to endure no more? Why did you not try to arrange your life in such a way that you need not endure his beatings and abuse, rather than running away?"

"I—I tried—"

"And so, when your feminine wiles could not soften his heart, you ran away because you had failed as a wife?" asked a woman whose name Magda did not know, "Do you think we are a refuge for any woman who cannot manage her husband?"

Keitha lifted blazing gray eyes and said, "You *did* take me in! Why did you not ask me all of this *before* I took Oath then?"

There was an odd little murmur around the circle, and Magda recognized it, with surprise, as approval. Camilla nodded as if Keitha had scored a point, and asked her, "What form of marriage did you have? Freemate, or *catenas*?"

"We were married *di catenas*," Keitha confessed. Magda remembered; this was the most formal kind of marriage, where the *catenas* or marriage-bracelets were locked on the arms of both parties, and the marriage was difficult to dissolve in law.

"Then you were oath-bound," said Camilla. "What do you think of the proverb which says that one who is false to her first oath will be false to her second?"

Keitha stared rebelliously at Camilla. Her eyes were reddened and a tear was trickling from the corner of one eye, but she said clearly, "I think it nonsense; for your proverb I offer you another; an oath broken by one does not thereafter bind the other. My husband vowed when we were bound by the *catenas* that he would care for me and cherish me; but I had nothing from him but abuse and vile language and of late, beatings till I feared for my life. He had violated his oath many times; at last I chose to consider that, in breaking it, he had released me from observing it." She swallowed hard and wiped her eyes with the back of her hand, but she stared defiantly at the women, and Camilla, at last, nodded.

"So be it. Margali, tell us why you wished to become an Amazon?"

Magda was suddenly grateful that she had been the third one interrogated; she realized that the point of the procedure was to put the questioned one on the defensive, and force her to justify herself. She said clearly, "I did not, at first, wish to become an Amazon; I was forced to take the Oath since I had been found wearing Amazon—Renunciate garb and impersonating one of you."

"And what were you doing running around in Amazon garments?" asked Rafaella.

Magda said, "I knew that no man would molest a Free Amazon; I did not want to create a scandal or expose myself to insult while traveling alone."

"Tell us," said Rafaella, "Did you feel it right to take advantage, unearned, of an immunity which other women had won at the point of their knives, and earned by years of renunciation?"

The hostility in her voice made Magda cringe, but she kept her own words steady.

"I knew too little of your ways to consider whether it was right or wrong. Lady Rohana made the suggestion—that I travel as a Free Amazon—but I myself will take responsibility for what happened."

"And why did you later abide your Oath?" asked a woman Magda did not know. "Since you have taken it under what were really false pretenses, why did you not petition the Guild-mothers to have it set aside?"

Magda glanced at Mother Lauria, impassive, wrapped in heavy shawl and cloak, across the circle. Surely she would say something? But she did not meet Magda's eyes. Magda drew a breath, trying to form her words in such a way that they would convey her meaning without revealing what she had sworn never to reveal while she was in the Guild-house. She could not explain that she felt this the best way to serve her two worlds, building a bridge between Terran and Darkovan; and that somehow she must free herself from the fetters of custom which prevented women from doing anything very important on Darkover. Finally she said, "I felt it wrong to break an oath I had sworn. And since I had no commitment elsewhere—"

That was not really true. She had sworn the Service Oath. Yet in this way she could better serve as a Terran agent, and serve, too, the world she had chosen as her own.

"Commitment!" One of the women pounced on that at once. "Do you think we are simply a place for idle women who have nothing else to do? Why do you think you have anything to give us, in return for the protection of the Guild-house and your sisters?"

"I am not sure," Magda said, struggling to keep her calm, "but maybe you can help me to find out what I have to give."

Camilla said, "That is a good answer," but her words were almost drowned out by Rafaella's hostile voice:

"Don't you think we have anything better to do than to teach ignorant women what they want out of life?"

Magda felt anger stirring in her, and was glad. If she was angry enough, perhaps she would not cry. "No, I don't," she said sharply, "If you did, you would be doing it, not sitting here trying to make us angry!"

There was an outburst of laughter all around the circle, and small sounds of approval. I was right, Magda thought, that *is* what they are trying to do; probably because Darkovan women are taught to be so submissive. They want us to *think*, question our own motives, defend them. The one thing they do not want us to do is to sit here meekly and accept what we are told.

Mother Lauria said "Keitha brought jewels and tried to make

a gift of them to the House. Do you know why they were refused, Keitha?"

"No, I don't," said the fair-haired woman. She moved restlessly where she sat; Magda wondered if her back was still raw
with the dreadful wounds of her beating. "I could understand
why you refused, if they had been my husband's gifts to me. But
they were a part of my dower property from my own mother;
why am I not free to give them to you? Should I give them to
my husband? And I have—" suddenly her voice wobbled,
though she tried to hold it steady, "I have—now—no daughter
to whom I might give them."

Mother Lauria said, "First, because no woman can buy a
place here. I am sure you had no thought of it; but if we accepted
gifts, there might some day be a difference made between the
few women who can pay, and the many who can bring nothing.
Early in our history, we asked women to bring a dowry if they
were able; and we were accused of luring rich women to us, for
the sake of their dowries. Also, none of us is perfect; if we allowed such gifts we might be lured into accepting some woman
not fit for the life, out of greed for her riches. So it is our first
rule; no woman may bring anything to us when she enters here
except the clothing she stands in, the skill of her hands, and the
furnishing of her brain and mind." She smiled and added, "That,
and a more precious gift; her unknown self, that part of herself
which she has never learned to use . . ."

She went on, but Magda did not hear; suddenly it was as if a
voice had whispered in her mind:

*Sisters, join hands and let us stand together before the
Goddess. . . .*

Before Magda's eyes a vision suddenly appeared, as clearly
as if the circle of women seated on the armory mats had vanished; it bore the form of a woman, but taller than womankind;
clothed in the gray and starry robes of the night, gems sparkling
in her dark hair, and her face seemed to look upon Magda with
divine compassion and tenderness. *My daughters, what do you
seek . . . ?*

In confusion, Magda wondered, is this some new test they

have arranged for us? But across the circle she could still hear Mother Lauria saying to Byrna, "You may be excused if you are weary, child," and Byrna, shifting her weight uncomfortably, replying, "No, please—this is the only chance I get to be with all of you!"

Magda could still see, faintly, the shimmering form—but was it inside her mind, a vision, or was it real, standing before her in the circle? She blinked and it was gone. Had it ever been there? Magda wondered if she were going mad. Next, she thought grimly, *I shall be hearing voices telling me I am to be the new women's Messiah!*

Rafaella had evidently been asked to lead the next round of questioning, and Magda shrank inside. Rafaella had been consistently unfriendly. She had heard only half or less of the question;

". . . teach you to be women, and independent, rather than mere chattels of men?"

Keitha answered hesitantly "Maybe,—as cadets are taught in the Castle Guard, to use weapons, bear arms, protect ourselves? That is the way in which boys are taught to be men—"

She braced herself for instant refutation, looking scared, but Rafaella only said mildly "But we want you to be women, Keitha, not men; why should we train you as boys are trained?"

"Because—because men are more self-sufficient, and women are meek because they have not been taught these things—"

"No," said Rafaella, "Although all Amazons must learn to defend themselves if they are attacked, there are women among us who have never held a knife in their hands; Marisela, for instance. Doria, what do you think?"

Doria suggested "Maybe—to learn a trade and get our own living, so we need not depend on any man to feed and clothe us?"

"You need not be an Amazon for that," said a woman Magda had heard called Constanza. "I sell cheese in the market, when we make more than we can eat, and there I see many women who earn their own living; they work as maids or servants, or they do washing, or work at leather-crafts. Some do so because they have shiftless or drunken husbands, and they must support their little children alone; and I know a woman who works as a maker of wooden dishes because her husband lost a leg riding mountain trails. Yet she defers to him in everything, as he sits in his wheeled chair at the back of their stall. That alone is not the answer."

Rafaella asked, "Margali, what do you think?"

Magda hesitated; she was sure nothing she would say could be the right answer, that this part of Training Session was only to make the newcomers unsure, to dispel their early and ignorant prejudices. She looked around the circle of women, as if she might find an answer written in one of the faces. Two of the women, she saw, were seated under a single blanket wrapped round them both, their hands enlaced, and as she looked, one of the women turned to the other and they exchanged a long kiss. She had never seen public lovemaking between women before, and it startled her.

Rafaella was still awaiting her answer. Magda said uncertainly, "I don't know. Perhaps you will tell us."

"We are not asking what you *know*, but what you *think*—if you know how to think," Rafaella said waspishly.

Thus urged, she tried to put some of her inarticulate thoughts into words.

"Perhaps—by getting us out of women's clothing, stop using the women's language—because these affect the way we think, the words we use, the way we walk and talk and dress—" she fumbled, "because we have been taught to behave in certain ways and you will teach us different—better—ways of behaving—"

And then she was unsure, remembering Jaelle's love of finery, and the way in which, talking to *Dom* Gabriel or to Lady Rohana, Jaelle's language had been as proper as the Lady's own.

"You are all right in a way," said Camilla, "and you are all wrong. Yes, you will all learn to protect yourselves, by force if you cannot do so by reason or persuasion; but this in itself will not make you the equals of men. Even now, a day is coming here in Thendara when every little matter need not be put to the sword, but will be decided more rationally. For now, we accept the world as men have made it because there is no other world available, but our goal is not to make women as aggressive as men, but to survive—merely to survive—until a saner day comes. Yes, you will all learn a way to earn a living, but being independent of a husband is not enough to free you of dependence; even a rich woman who marries a poor man, so that they live upon her bounty, considers herself, by custom, bound to serve and obey her husband. Yes, you will learn to wear women's clothes by choice and not from necessity, and to speak as you wish, not to keep your words and your minds in bonds for fear of being thought unmannerly or unwomanly. But none of these is the most important thing. Mother Lauria, will you tell them the most important thing they will learn?"

Mother Lauria leaned forward a little, to emphasize what she was saying.

"Nothing you will learn is of the slightest importance, save for this: you will learn to change the way you think about yourselves, and about other women.

The difference is in the way you think about yourselves. . . . Magda thought soberly that the Guild-mother was right. Magda herself had grown up to take it for granted that she would earn her own living, had gone to the Empire Intelligence school on Alpha, had been taught to defend herself in both armed and unarmed combat. And in the Terran Zone she had had no special restrictions of dress or language.

Yet I am as much a slave to custom and convention as any village girl in the Kilghard Hills. . . . Was it Lady Rohana who had spoken, once, about women who think themselves free and weight themselves with invisible chains?

Men too suffer in chains of custom and convention; perhaps the woman who most needs freedom is the hidden woman within every man. . . . Magda did not know where the thought had come from; it was not her own, it was as if someone had spoken it clearly within the room, and yet no one was speaking except Mother Lauria; but Magda lost track of what the Guild-mother was saying. She blinked, expecting to see again the form of the woman in gray and silver, the evening sky, divine compassion in her eyes . . . but no, there was no trace of it; her eyes opened on grayness in which strange faces moved, men and women, and before her in the gray waste a tall white tower gleamed . . .

Quickly a voice—a man's or woman's, Magda could not tell—said, "There is an intruder; someone has strayed here, perhaps in a dream! Lock your barriers!"

And suddenly the grayness was gone, and Camilla snapped, "Margali, have you gone to sleep here among us? I asked you a question!"

Magda blinked in disorientation, wondering if she was going mad. She said "I am sorry; my mind was—was wandering." *It was indeed,* she thought, *but wandering where?* "I am afraid I did not hear what you asked me, oath-sister."

"What, do you think, is the most important difference between men and women?"

Magda did not know whether Keitha or Doria had answered this question; she had no idea how long her mind had been drifting in the gray wasteland. The faces she had seen there, the image of the woman who must, she realized, be a thought, form of the Goddess Avarra, were still half-lingering in her mind. She said, trying to gather her scattered thoughts, "I think it is only a woman's body that makes the difference." This was the enlightened Terran answer, and Magda was quite sure that it was the right one; that the only difference was the limited physical one. "Women are subject to pregnancy and menstruation, they are somewhat smaller and slighter as a general rule, they do not suffer so much from cold, their—" she stopped; it was doubtful if they would understand what she meant if she said their center of gravity was lower. "Their bodies are different, and that is the main difference."

"Rubbish," Camilla said harshly. She made a gesture indicating her spare, sexless body, arms muscled like a man's, an *emmasca,* a woman who had been subjected to the neutering operation. "What am I then, a banshee?"

Before the angry look in the older woman's eyes, Magda said

meekly, "I don't know; I thought—I had been told—that a neuter, an *emmasca*, was made so because she refused to think of herself as a woman."

Camilla reached for Magda's hand and gave it a little squeeze. Her voice was still stern, admonishing, but she gave Magda a secret smile as she said, "Why, that is true; I began by refusing to accept myself as a woman. Womanhood had been made so hideous to me, so hateful, that I was willing to accept mutilation rather than see myself as a female. Some day, perhaps, you will know why. But that is not important now. What is important is that here, in the Guild-house, I learned to think of myself as a woman, and to be proud of it—to rejoice in my womanhood, even though—even though there is, in this *emmasca* body of mine, very little that is female."

She was still holding Magda's hand. Self-consciously, the younger woman drew it away. Camilla turned to Doria and asked "What do you think is the difference between men and women?"

Doria said defiantly, very determined not to be caught out again. "I say there is no difference at all!"

This answer provoked a perfect storm of jeers and laughter, with a few obscene remarks, about the politest of which was "When did you father your first child, Doria?"

"You just said the physical difference wasn't important," protested Doria, "Camilla cut Margali to pieces for saying the difference was a physical one, and if the physical one makes no difference—"

"I never said—nor did Camilla say—that the difference was not important," said Mother Lauria, "and it would take someone far more stupid than you, to believe that there is no difference. The difference is there, and not insignificant. Keitha, have you any idea?"

Keitha said slowly, "Maybe the difference is in the way they think. The way they—and we—are taught to think. Men think of women as property, and women think—" she frowned, and said as if discovering something. "I don't know what women think. I don't even know what I think."

Mother Lauria smiled. She said, "You have come very close to it. Perhaps the most important difference between men and women is in the way society thinks about them; the different things that are expected of them. But there is no really right answer, Keitha. You, and Margali and Doria too, you have all said a part of the truth." Stiffly she rose to her feet. "I think it is enough for tonight. And I heard the bell in the hall telling us that the Sisterhood have finished. I told the girls in the kitchen to bring us some cakes and something to drink. But let us go into the music room for that—it *is* getting a little chilly in here."

A little chilly—that struck Magda as a masterpiece of understatement; her own fingers were blue with cold, and she felt that the cold of the stone floor seeped up through her legs and buttocks, even through the thick mat. Hugging the blanket round her, she rose and went after the others.

She was hungry after the supper she had not been able to eat; the cakes were short and crisp, decorated with nuts and dried fruit, and she ate several of them hungrily, and drank a huge mug of the hot spiced cider they had brought for those women who did not drink wine. Her mind was still full of the discussion; a form, she knew, of simple therapy, forcing people to think, to protest, to break up old habits of thought. But she hoped all the sessions would not be like this. She felt intensely uncomfortable, her mind still picking over the questions and the many answers that had been given. Why had she chosen to be an Amazon? What is the difference between men and women? She was still testing and re-formulating answers, things she might have said, and that, she supposed, was the reason for the discussion. She heard one of the women say to another "It's an intelligent group," and the listener reply skeptically, "I'm not so sure of that."

"Oh, they'll learn," the first replied, "We did."

Doria's eyes were still red when Magda joined her. "I certainly made a fool of myself, didn't I?"

"Oh, that's what they intended you to feel," Magda said lightly. "Cheer up, you didn't sound any sillier than I did."

"But I grew up here, I *should* have known better," said Doria, threatening to dissolve into tears again. One of the younger girls—Magda recognized her as one of Doria's roommates—came and wound her arms around Doria, saying comforting things to her, and led her away. Magda raised her eyes and found Keitha looking at her with a faint ironic smile.

"Trial by fire," Keitha murmured, "Do you think we survived, fellow victim?"

Magda laughed. "Considering that their whole objective was to put us on the defensive, I think so," she said. "It's likely to get worse before it gets better."

"Are all the sessions like that, I wonder?" Keitha asked aloud, and a woman who had not been present at the session—she had been introduced to Magda as Marisela, the house midwife and healer—came up and smiled at them both. She said "No, of course not; the next session I will conduct, at which time I will instruct you all in the female mysteries, supposing that some of you may have had mothers who were too shy to speak of such things to their daughters."

"At least I will not be so completely ignorant at that," Keitha said, "I have delivered children on my husband's estates, and I was thought to have some skill as a midwife."

"Oh indeed?" said Marisela, interested. She was a pretty woman, dressed, not in the Amazon boots and breeches, but in ordinary women's clothes, a tartan skirt and shawl, over a full-sleeved tunic and bodice. "Then there will be no question of teaching you a trade; perhaps they will send you to Arilinn Guild-house when your half-year is finished, to learn the midwife's art and some of the special skills which the women in the Towers have taught us. If you have even a trace of *laran*, it will be very welcome. What about you, Margali? Have you any of the skills of a healer or midwife?"

"None," confessed Magda. "I can bind a wound on the trail, or bandage a cut or scratch, but nothing more." But as Marisela drew Keitha away, and the two sat down to talk together, Magda thought of the word she had used. *Laran*, the Darkovan term embracing telepathy, clairvoyance, and all the psychic arts.

Rohana had tested her, during the winter she spent at Ardais, and told her that she herself had some trace of it.

Was that how she had come to see the curious visions she had seen? Had she been, unwittingly, spying on the meeting of the Sisterhood, with the *laran* she did not really understand and did not know how to control? It seemed, for a moment, that around Marisela's slender shoulders she could almost see the gray mantle of Avarra. . . . she wrenched her thoughts back to the music room and began inspecting some of the instruments. Some were familiar; her mother, who had spent her life studying Darkovan folk music, had played several of them. She recognized some *rryls*, both a small hand-held one and another tall one played standing before it; they were something like harps. Other instruments she would have classified as lutes, dulcimers and guitars, though there were no reed or brass instruments visible. There were a few others so alien she could not even imagine how they would be played.

"Do you play an instrument, Margali?" Rafaella asked, almost in a friendly way.

"I am sorry; I did not inherit even a little of my mother's gift for music," she said. "I love to listen, but I have no talent."

The couple who had been embracing under the blanket in the armory were snuggled together in a corner now, the taller girl leaning on her friend's shoulder, the other's hand just barely touching her breast. Magda turned her eyes away, feeling uncomfortable. In public, like this? Well, it was, after all, their home, and they were young, not more than sixteen or so. Caresses as simple as this, exchanged in public by young people—if they had been boy and girl, instead of two young girls—would not have turned an eyebrow in the Terran Zone. Suddenly, with intense loneliness, she wished she were there.

She wondered if Jaelle were wishing the same thing. *Everything that seems so strange to me here,* she thought, *is dear and familiar to her.* She wondered if Jaelle felt equally alienated from everything she knew.

"Are you feeling homesick, Margali?" asked Camilla, behind her, and put her arm around Margali's waist.

"A little, maybe," Magda said.

"Don't be angry with me for speaking to you so roughly, oath-sister; it is part of the training, to make you think." She followed Magda's eyes to the girls embracing in the corner.

"Thank the Goddess for that! Janetta has been moping so since Gwennis left, I was beginning to be afraid she would throw herself out the window! At least, now, she seems to be comforted."

Magda did not know what to say. Fortunately, before she had to answer, Doria grabbed her elbow.

"Come and help me take the cups back to the kitchen, Margali, and put away the cakes that are left over. Irmelin is sulking because we did not eat them all up—do you want another one?"

Magda laughed and took another of the crisp little cookies. She helped Doria and Keitha gather up plates and cups, brush crumbs from the table and throw them into the fireplace. Rafaella was running her hands over the surface of the large *rryl* and Byrna called out "Sing for us, Rafi! We haven't had music for a long time!"

"Not tonight," Rafaella said. "I am too hoarse, after eating all those cakes! Another time; and besides, it is late, and I have to work tomorrow!" She covered the harp and went out of the room. Doria and Magda took the rest of the cups to the kitchen, and turned up the stairs. Just ahead of them, she saw Janetta and her friend, still clinging to one another, so mutually absorbed that they stumbled on the stairs and had to steady each other. Byrna behind Magda, sighed, watching them go off, arms still round one another, toward their room.

"Heigh-ho; there are two who will not sleep alone tonight," she said as the door closed behind them, "I almost envy them." Another deep sigh as she clasped her hands over the weight of her child. "What a she-donkey I am—what would I do with a lover now if I had one? I am so tired of this—"

With a clumsy impulse to comfort, Magda hugged her. "But you're not really alone, you have your baby—"

"I'm just so *tired*, I want it to be *over*," said Byrna, and her voice caught in a sob, "I can't *stand* dragging around like this any longer—"

"There, there, don't cry—it won't be long now," Magda said, patting her shoulder gently. She led the sobbing woman to her own room, helped her off with her shoes—for Byrna was now so clumsy in the waist that she could not reach her feet—helped her into her nightgown and tucked her into bed. She kissed her on the forehead, but did not know what to say. Finally she said, "It can't be good for your baby, to cry like this. Think of how good you'll feel when it is all over," and as she looked up, she saw Marisela on the doorstep.

"How are you feeling, Byrna? No signs yet?" she asked, and Magda, feeling superfluous, went away. Some of the women were still clustered in the hall; they exchanged goodnights, and went toward their own rooms, but Camilla lingered a moment.

"Are you lonely, oath-sister?" she asked gently, in an undertone. "Would you come tonight and share my bed?"

Magda was stiff with astonishment; for a moment she did not believe what she was hearing. It took an effort not to pull away from Camilla's hand. She reminded herself that she was in a strange place and it was for her to adapt to *their* customs, not the other way round, Camilla had certainly meant no offense. She tried to turn it off lightly by a laugh.

"No, thank you, I think not." *I've had some weird proposals, but this* . . . Camilla's touch was not unpleasant, but Magda wished she could free herself from it without distressing the other woman or sounding unfriendly.

Camilla murmured "No? But I have not yet been welcomed back among you, oath-sister—" Her fingertips were just lightly touching Magda, but Magda was very aware of the touch and it embarrassed her. She was aware that some of the women still in the hallway were looking at them; but she was anxious to keep from offending Camilla, who had done nothing offensive by her own codes. She tried gently to free herself from the other's touch and murmured very softly "I am not a lover of women, Camilla. But I thank you and I am glad to be your friend."

The other woman laughed, unoffended. "Is that all?" she

said, and, smiling, released Magda. "I thought you might be lonely, that is all; and we are oath-bound, and there is no other close to you in this house, with Jaelle away from us." She leaned forward and kissed Magda gently. "We are all lonely and unhappy when first we come here, however glad we are not to be where we were before. It will pass, *breda*." She used the intimate inflection, which could make the word mean *darling* or *beloved*, and that embarrassed Magda more than the kiss. "Good night; sleep well, my dear."

Alone in her own bed, she thought about the evening. She knew intellectually that the raising of unanswered, and unanswerable questions, the deliberate arousing of emotions never fully faced, was taking its toll. She could not sleep, but lay awake, restlessly going over and over the questions and the many answers in her mind. Doria's tears, the two young girls embracing, Byrna's outburst, Camilla's kiss on her lips—all spun together in fatigued, almost feverish images. What was she doing here among all these women? She was a free woman, a Terran, a trained Agent, she need not wrestle with all these questions so important to the women enslaved by Darkover's barbarian society.

Invisible chains. . . . it was as if a voice had whispered it in her mind. Where was Jaelle now? Lying in Peter's arms, in the Terran Zone. Mother Lauria had asked if she would find it too difficult to live without a lover. No, *that* was not what she wanted . . .

And then, abruptly, the image of the Goddess Avarra drifted before her eyes again, her compassionate face, her hands outstretched as if to touch Magda's. Through all the unanswered questions and the turmoil in her heart, Magda suddenly felt a great peace and contentment washing outward through her mind.

She slept, still pondering; what is the difference between man and woman? What makes a *Comhi-Letzis?* She slept, and in her dream she knew the answer, but when she woke she had forgotten it again.

Chapter 6

"Yes, certainly, you could pass within the Dry Towns as a native," Jaelle said, studying the face of the tall, thin man before her, his beaked nose, high forehead, the shock of silver-gilt hair above it, "Fair hair is not common in the Domains, but most Dry-Towners are light-haired and pale-skinned. Your main problem would be the—the interlocking of customs and family relationships. You would have to have a very good story to cover what you were doing; it would be safer to pose as a man of the Domains, a trader."

The man Kadarin nodded thoughtfully. He spoke the language, she thought, flawlessly. She could not guess his origin. "Perhaps you should travel with me, and keep me informed about customs—?"

She shook her head. Never, she thought, never. "I would have to wear chains and pretend to be your property," she said, "and the Amazon Oath forbids it. Surely there must be men among your Empire Intelligence—" she only heard the sarcastic tone in her voice after she had spoken, "or even women who are capable of that."

"I'll manage," he said, "but I wish you could tell me more. Cholayna Ares said you had actually lived there till you were twelve—"

"Behind the walls of the Great House of Shainsa," she reminded him, "guarded night and day by women-guards; I went beyond the walls only twice at a festival. And all I knew has been wrung out of me anyhow, by your damned D-alpha corti-cator or whatever you call it!"

Under light hypnosis, she had dredged up memories she had not even known she had. Playing with Jalak's other daughters, twining ribbons about their arms, pretending they were old enough to be chained like women. The sight of a would-be in-truder into the women's quarters, his back flayed to ribbons, staked over a nest of scorpion-ants, and the sound of his screams; she could not have been more than three years old when her nurse had inadvertently let her see that, and until the session with the corticator she had wholly forgotten. Jalak, list-lessly petting his favorites in the Great Hall at dinner. Her mother, in golden chains, holding her on her lap. Being punished for trying, with one of the boy-children of the house, to steal a glimpse out through the walls. . . .

She shoved them all away, slamming her mind shut; that was over, over, except in nightmares!

And her mother's death on the sand of the desert, her life bleeding away . . .

"I can tell you no more," she said curtly, "Dress yourself as a trader new to the Dry-Towns, speak softly and challenge no man's *kihar*, and you will come safe away. A foreigner may do in ignorance what one of their own would be killed for attempting."

Kadarin shrugged. "It seems I have no choice," he said, "I thank you, *domna*. And in return for all my questions, may I ask you one thing more, a personal question?"

"Certainly you may ask," she said, "but I cannot promise you an answer."

"What is a lady of the *Comyn*, with all the marks of that caste, doing among the Renunciates?"

The word *Comyn* dropped into the silence of the room, quiet and inoffensive, was, for Jaelle, weighted heavily with painful memory. She said, "I am not *Comyn*," and left it at that.

"*Nedestro*, then, of some great house?" he probed, but she shut her lips and shook her head. Not for worlds would she have told him that her mother had been Melora Aillard, bearing all the *laran* of that house, Tower-trained; kidnapped into the Dry Towns, married to Jalak of Shainsa . . . rescued by Free Amazons, only to die bearing Jalak's son, in the lonely deserts outside of Carthon. Yet before his steel-gray eyes she wondered if perhaps he had enough *laran* to read it in her mind.

Laran! The *Terranan* had something worse than *laran*, with their damned corticator which could stir up all the forgotten nightmares in the brain! She was told they had a strong psychic probe, too, but she had refused to submit to that. If she would not have a properly trained *leronis* meddling with her mind, when they would have sent her to a Tower, why should she submit to the crudely mechanical machines of these *Terranan*? She was relieved to see the man Kadarin rise and take leave of her with a courtly bow. Where had he come from, she wondered, what was his race of origin? He was not like anyone she had ever seen before.

She put the thought aside; she was to spend the rest of the morning working with Alessandro—Aleki, she reminded herself of his Darkovan name—preparing him by speaking of the background of the Domains, and elementary forms of courteous address among them.

They had been working for several days, in one of the smaller offices in the new Intelligence department, sometimes with the presence of the younger Montray—Monty—and sometimes alone together. Jaelle did not object to this; Aleki's manner was completely impersonal; he never seemed to regard her as a woman, but simply as a colleague. Jaelle, nervous and suspicious at first, now felt almost friendly toward him.

Aleki's first business had been to read through everything about Darkovan society which had been gathered by agents working in the field. Much of it was signed by Magda Lorne or by Peter Haldane, a fact which made it especially interesting to Jaelle; how much they had discovered about her world! Today she found him running through the account she herself had made of her trip into the Hellers, and comparing it with Magda's account and Peter's. As she came in he pushed it all aside and greeted her.

"But I do have some questions to ask you," he said. "Before we begin, are you thirsty? May I get you something? It may be a long session—I have a lot to say. Coffee? Fruit juice?"

She accepted the fruit juice, and took a seat at the table across from him. He fussed with the console, fetching some sort of hot drink for himself, and brought it, steaming, to the table.

"All three reports I have here, as well as some of the others," he said, "speak of wintering in Castle Ardais—am I saying it right?"

"Are-dayze," she corrected him gently, and he repeated it.

"How is it that you, a Free Amazon—and I understand they are not very highly regarded in the society—were accepted as a guest at Castle Ardais, with Haldane and Lorne, and no questions asked? Is hospitality so open in the mountains as it is on the rest of Darkover?"

This man is very intelligent; I must not underestimate him. "Lord Ardais would indeed shelter anyone homeless in his Domain," she said, "but I was welcomed as kinfolk there; Lady Rohana is—is a kinswoman of my mother."

"And you are related, then, to *Comyn* . . . for I understand the Ardais are of the *Comyn*? I do not entirely understand how it is that the *Comyn* rule all the Domains," he said. She could almost feel his curiosity, a palpable presence, and cursed the unwanted *laran* which thrust itself upon her, not controlled or desired.

"Nowhere in these Records," Aleki said, "is there any indication of how the society of Darkover took on such a feudal cast, or why the hierarchy called *Comyn* rose to power. Of course, what we know of Darkovan history is far from complete—"

"Most of us know little more," Jaelle said carefully. "What records we do have of the origin of Darkovan society are lost in what we call the Ages of Chaos. At that time—" she hesitated, knowing she should not speak—it was the will of the Hasturs that no Darkovan should speak to the *Terranan*—of the heyday of the Towers and of the old matrix technology which had all but destroyed their world.

"About the earliest time of which we have much history," she said, "is about five hundred, seven hundred years ago, when all these lands—" she touched the map he had copied, lying on the desk, "were divided up into a hundred or more little kingdoms."

"It seems a small country to be divided up into a hundred kingdoms," Aleki commented, and she nodded.

"You must understand, many of the kingdoms were very small; they used to say that a lesser king could stand on a hilltop and look out over his whole kingdom, unless a resin-tree had grown up that season to hide a half of it," she told him. "There is a children's game called 'king of the mountain'—is it played on your world?—where one child scrambles to the top of a hill and the others try to push him off, and whoever succeeds is king—until someone else pushes him off in his turn. It seems some of the smaller kingdoms were much like that. I know the names of only a few of them—Carcosa, Asturias, Hammerfell. About the time of the signing of the Compact—surely you know the Compact?" she broke off to ask him.

"Isn't that the law in the Domains that no weapon may be used which does not bring the user within arm's reach of death?"

"That's right," she said, "It reduced wars to the minimum; and, as I said, about the time of the signing of Compact, there was a series of wars called the Hastur Wars, and slowly, one by one, the Hasturs conquered all these lands; then they broke them up again into what we call the Seven Domains, each ruled over by one of the Great Houses of the Hastur-kin; the *Comyn*. The Domain of Hastur rules over the Hastur lands to the east, the Domain of Elhalyn over Hali and the western hills, the Altons rule over Armida and Mariposa, and so forth and so on. . . ."

"I can see the Domains outlined on the map," said Aleki. "What I want to know is how they came to power, and why the common people should obey them so unquestioningly. If you are a kinswoman of Lady Rohana, as you say, then you are evidently akin to *Comyn* and must know something of their history and power."

"I know no more than anyone knows," Jaelle evaded, "and through all this land there are very few who have not some trace of *Comyn* blood. Even I, and I am, as you pointed out, no more than a simple Renunciate."

She had begun to feel that this was some sort of testing, like a Training Session before she had taken the Oath. Again, all her hidden conflicts and loyalties were being brought out and explored. He persisted:

"I still do not understand why the common people should so unquestioningly do the will of the Hasturs."

"Do you people in the Empire not obey your governors and rulers?"

"But our rulers are chosen from among ourselves," he answered. "Though we still call ourselves 'Empire,' we are an Empire without an Emperor, and structured like a Confederation—do you know these terms? We offered Darkover full membership, with autonomous government and representation in our Senate by members chosen by themselves. Almost all planets which we occupy are more than happy to be members of a star-spanning Empire, rather than remaining isolated barbarians bound to their own solitary worlds. Yet Darkover has not joined the Empire, and we do not know why; we do not know whether it is truly the will of the Darkovan people or only the will of the Hasturs and of the *Comyn*."

For the first time she sensed that he was being wholly honest, and that he was puzzled. After a moment she asked him quietly, "Was Darkover given a choice? Or did you simply come here, establish yourselves, and *then* offer us membership in your Empire?"

"Darkover—Cottman Four—*is* an Empire colony," Alessandro Li said quietly. "You were colonized from Terra, many years ago. When we came here, we knew that; you had lost your history—perhaps within those Ages of Chaos of which you speak. The *Comyn* have chosen not to make this fact known to your people, so that you people may reclaim your heritage. Normally, local planets are pleased to have the resources of a star-spanning civilization."

It was a temptation to repeat the arguments she had heard, against the Empire and against the *Terranan*, but how could she speak for *Comyn*? And if she did, Aleki might badger her for more detail than she felt able to give. She realized that this long explanation had been given in order to draw her out, to get her to speak unguardedly, and she withdrew carefully from the offered gambit.

"I personally see no reason for making Darkover just another of the worlds of the Empire," she said. "But I am not privy to the mind of Hastur. The Hasturs have probably gone into the matter much further than I, and I for one am content to let them judge these matters."

"Wouldn't you prefer to have a voice in the decision yourself?" he asked her curiously, "rather than mindlessly obeying the will of a ruling caste?"

"I do not *mindlessly obey* the will of any man, be he Hastur, husband or God," she flashed back at him. "But the *Comyn* have studied this subject and I have not had the opportunity to know all sides of the matter as they have. Piedro has explained your system of representative democracy to me, and it seems only a way for the decisions to be placed in the hands of those unfit to make them. Would you rather listen to the voices of a thousand—or a million—fools, or to the voice of a single wise man well trained in these matters?"

"I do not automatically assume that a thousand, or a million, of the common people must be fools, or that one who speaks for the ruling class must be wise," he retorted swiftly. "And if the thousand, or the million, are fools, is it not the business of the wise to instruct them, rather than letting them remain ignorant?"

"You are making an assumption I do not accept," replied Jaelle, "which is that instructing a fool will make him a wise man. There is a proverb which says—a donkey may be schooled for a hundred years, and only learn to bray louder."

"But you are not a donkey. Why do you assume that your fellow commoners are not competent to learn as well as you?"

"I am not ignorant," she said, "but I cannot see as far as the *Comyn*. I have no *laran*, and even if I learned as much as I am capable of learning, I cannot read the minds and hearts of men, nor see past and future as they can do. It is this which gives them the strength to rule, and the wisdom which persuades the head-blind to accept their wisdom."

"*Laran*," he said quickly, "what is *laran*?" And Jaelle realized a moment too late that he had led her into this debate, just for this reason—that she might speak, unguarded. She cursed the pride that had led her to enjoy sharpening her wits on this *Terranan*.

"*Laran?*" she repeated blandly, as if she hardly remembered what she had said. But he had, of course, one of those forever-be-damned *records*, the words she spoke had been recorded on to one of their wretched devices and he could listen over and over to what she had said, analyze it, know what she had betrayed.

"*Laran*. I know what the word means, of course—psychic power, which most Terrans consider superstition. And your people believe that the Hasturs have it?"

She hesitated just a moment too late before answering; she should have said quickly that yes, the common people superstitiously believed in the powers of the *Comyn*. But now it was Alessandro Li who backed away, courteously.

"I think we have done enough for one day, Jaelle. We would not want to be late for the Coordiantor's reception tonight."

"Certainly not, since you're the Guest of Honor," she answered, and at his startled look cursed herself again; worse and worse; she remembered that she had not been told this, that Piedro had not known.

"How did you know that? Are you psychic yourself?" he asked. She said, "Oh, no, when there is an—an important guest such as yourself, it doesn't take *laran* to guess that the Coordiantor will honor him at a reception." She stood up quickly. "I'm afraid my mind was wandering a bit."

"I hope I have not tired you; I'm afraid I am a very demanding taskmaster," he said in apology, "but we'll break this up for today; you can go and make yourself beautiful for the reception. I am looking forward to knowing your husband better. I know his work in records, of course, he must be quite an exceptional man, to have attracted so competent a wife."

She ordered herself not to blush at the compliment, resisting the impulse to tug at the immodestly short skirt. Years of Guild-house training should have made her immune to this kind of thing. She stood up, remembering the sharp teaching of the Guild-mothers, *your body language says more than your words, if you behave like a woman and a victim, you will be treated as one; try to stand and move like a man when you are working among men.* She said in her most businesslike manner "I am sure Piedro will be honored," and strode away.

She should warn Piedro; this man was sharp, he could put together small hints in an uncanny way. He might lead Piedro to talk too much. How could she blame her husband, when she had done the same thing? But she had made the mistake of underestimating Li; Piedro at least would be forewarned.

How much does Piedro know? Goddess! I wish I could talk to Magda! she thought.

At one of the high windows overlooking the spaceport, she paused, casting an eye at the great, declining, bloodshot eye of the sun. Perhaps she had time to go through the streets of Thendara to the Guild-house, talk with her oath-daughter. . . . but no. There was this accursed reception to get through, and Piedro had warned her this morning that all the invited personnel were expected to be at their finest; he had suggested that she visit the personal-services department and have her hair done.

She shrugged and decided to do exactly that. She had been curious about it anyhow; it was a ritual which all of the women here at HQ seemed to undergo at frequent intervals, and she knew that Peter would be pleased if she went to considerable lengths to make herself beautiful for him. And in the last few days she had been working so hard in Aleki's office that she had seen Peter only when he was asleep, or nearly so.

The personal-services area was on the cafeteria floor, painted in a rosy pink color which made Jaelle, raised under a red sun, feel comfortable and soothed. She had begun to think of this time among the Terrans as an adventure, something to relate with pride to the young Renunciate novices when she was old and housebound.

She punched her ID card into the first machine, and a sign flashed: TAKE A SEAT AND RELAX, YOU WILL BE ATTENDED SOON.

She read the afterimage of the words—sign reading was an exercise in reading swiftly. To Jaelle it was gone before she could focus her eyes. She took one of the gently contoured pink chairs, and waited, thinking over the last days. Time! Alessandro Li was fiendishly aware of time, even more than average Terrans, who were all clockbound to an incredible degree. She had heard gossip among the women in Communications; Bethany said that under normal circumstances, an official on his level would have done nothing, not even requisitioning an office to work in, until after the official reception; but he had begun work immediately, and had kept her with him most of these days. She felt wrung dry, as if he had actually pressed her and squeezed out all the juices of her knowledge; and this was only a beginning. There was so much tension in the awakening memories—for she had told him, and Kadarin, things she did not know that she knew or remembered—that even when she returned to their apartment she would lie awake, aching, her mind racing, too tired to sleep, hardly closing her eyes until it was time to get up. Time! Time! She lived at the mercy of a clock face, time to work, time to eat, time to make love, time, always time!

At home, she had been able to call an attendant whenever she needed something she could not do for herself; even in the Guild-house, where none was servant to another, women did for each other these sisterly services. It was never hard to find some sister who would help you to lace your dress, curl your hair or cut it, lend cosmetics or clothing. Here everything was done by machines, it seemed. At length another sign flashed, YOU MAY GO IN NOW, and she took her courage in her hands and went into the pink room; and stopped cold in the doorway.

Rack that tilted every which way, chairs that tilted and turned to the tables, clamps to hold the head, straps to hold the victim in place. . . . the darkness reeled around her for a moment and she had literally to hold to the door. For a moment she was a child again, back in the insane years before her real life had begun, a child who had secretly crept to the door of a hidden room to steal a glance, not knowing it was her father's torture chamber. . . .

Mother! Mother! For a moment she wanted to run, shrieking, as she had done then, to hide her head in her mother's lap—

Then, abruptly, it was just another room, a Terran room filled with machinery, that did with metal fingers what flesh and blood could have done better. She could even make out, now, robot machines for cutting hair, for curling it, for smoothing cosmetics . . . perfumed sprays. The room smelled and looked calm and soothing, but Jaelle could not force herself to step inside; finally she managed to free her feet, which seemed, as they had seemed then, rooted to the ground. She fled down the corridor, through the cafeteria, out the heavy doors and across the hard paving, forgetting to use the underground tunnel, never seeing the Terran eyes that turned to watch her fleeing form, stare at her. She threw herself, gasping, on her bed and buried her face in the pillows, glad beyond belief that Piedro was not there to demand explanation of her curious behavior. Had she disgraced him again? She no longer knew or cared.

It seemed only moments later—had she slept for a few minutes, an hour?—when the door chimed softly. A visitor at this hour? Or had Piedro forgotten his key-card again? Keys and locked doors, for her, belonged to matrix laboratories, dungeons—torture chambers!

Braced to welcome Peter, she was amazed to find Bethany Kane standing in her door.

"Jaelle, honey—are you all right? I saw you running across the court as if the devil was after you! Listen, is that bigwig from the Senate bothering you? He has no right to do that! I dropped in, but his secretary said you'd gone down to get your hair done—can I come in? People are sleeping on this corridor and I don't want to wake them up." She came in, as Jaelle gestured, then suddenly took in Jaelle's disheveled appearance.

"What's the matter? Not going to the reception? I was going down to have my hair done, too, I thought we could go together—"

Bethany went and stood before Jaelle's dressing-table, running her fingers through her own hair. "I'm a mess, and Montray will expect everyone on the staff to look their best. Do you have some extra curlers? Or are you going down to the beauty shop—?"

She was looking expectantly at Jaelle, and Jaelle said woodenly, "I did go down. But I—I decided not to go in."

"Honey, was somebody down there nasty to you? If they were, you ought to put them on report. They're there to wait on people, and if anybody made a single nasty remark—"

"Oh, no." Jaelle smiled faintly. "I didn't see any people down there at all—I thought it was all done by machines!"

Bethany chuckled. "Well, most of it is, but there *are* people there to make sure the machines do what they're expected to do," she said. "You've let your hair grow lately, haven't you? What are you going to do with it tonight?"

Jaelle shrugged. "It's not long enough to braid; what is there to do with it?"

Bethany surveyed her with consternation. "You're not going like *that*, are you? Honey, Peter would *die!* Here, sit down, let me see what I can do. Why, you've never even used the cosmetic console in the dressing room, have you? Show me what dress you're going to wear, and I'll figure out something."

Bethany managed, in the next twenty minutes, to show her several features of the bath and dressing table that she had not known existed. She was creamed, curled, elaborately made up, her hair elegantly fluffed into reddish-gold curls. For a little while it felt as if Bethany was indeed one of her Guild-sisters, and she was readying herself for Festival in the streets of Thendara at Midsummer. It was certainly easier than the strange, terrifying room full of machinery would have been, and at last she surveyed herself in the mirror with a certain pleasure; the new Jaelle who looked out at her would hardly have been recognized by the Guild-sisters. Bethany's deft fingers had arranged her hair into a soft halo, deftly accented her high cheekbones and the green glint of her eyes, softened her freckles to a gilt blur, and done something to her eyes so that they looked deep-set and mysterious.

"You look marvelous," Bethany said. "You're going to be the hit of the reception! I didn't realize you were a beauty, Jaelle!"

Somehow she felt disloyal to the Guild-house. Dressing and preening herself like this, for a group of *Terranan?* Well, she rationalized, it was part of the job, to look her best—even Bethany had said so. Impulsively she hugged her.

"Thank you, Beth," she said, and Bethany yipped, "Look at the time! I've got to get down and change my own dress, or I'll be late! Anyhow, Peter will be coming in pretty soon—"

Bethany had hardly gone when he came in, breathless.

"Sweetheart, you look wonderful—you've done something to your hair, haven't you? I came to pick up my dress outfit— I'll have to dress over there. Do you know what they've had me doing, the last three days?"

"No, I don't," she said, "You've hardly seen me, you haven't told me anything."

"Don't nag, love, I'm in a real hurry. They've had me crawling around in the dust of the old Records section, trying to clear space for a new model corticator programmer. The place is filled up with old file boxes and *books,* for God's sake, I didn't know we still had any, and look at the dust!" He held out filthy hands. "I haven't seen the light of day this week! I should be getting hazard pay, all the germs in there—anyhow, Montray wants me in his office in ten minutes." He flung the suit over his arm. "Where are my dress shoes?"

"In the closet, I suppose." She was pleased that Peter had noticed the pains she had taken with her appearance, but he had so quickly taken it for granted.

"Well, for heaven's sake, *get* them for me, will you? I'm late, and I've got to do something about this damned beard—" he vanished into the bath, and Jaelle, fuming, went to pull out his shoes. She had performed many jobs in her life, but that of valet was new, and she didn't see why she had to perform as his body-servant; if he needed that kind of personal servant, why didn't he hire one for himself? Inside the bath Peter bellowed out a gutter curse and something metal crashed against the wall. He stormed out, raging.

"Jaelle! I hear so much about how great you are down in the office, keeping the desks stocked and doing all the little chores

Mag used to do, and now I find you've let me run out of depila-
tory! Hellfire, girl, do you think I can go to the Coordiantor's reception looking like a spaceport tramp?" He rubbed his beard.
"Now somehow I've got to make time to hit the barbershop!
Here, give me those!" He grabbed the shoes she was holding.
"Don't be late to the reception, hear me?" And he was gone,
without a word, without a kiss, without really looking at her at
all.

Jaelle sank down, shaking, the ache inside her so enormous
and empty that she could hardly breathe. Somehow, the slam of
the door behind him had broken something in her, a self she had
created here, the reflection of herself in Piedro's eyes. As it
broke, she felt her teeth clench, the soft beauty Bethany had
painted on her face suddenly vanishing into the cold, tough-
minded Amazon Kindra had trained.

She was tempted not to go to the reception at all. But it was
part of her job. . . . *obey any lawful command of my employer* . . . and Magda would have turned herself out stunningly
because, if Magda had been doing the work she was doing,
Magda would have seen herself as the appointed assistant of the
Guest of Honor and known she must do him credit.

The cafeteria level had been rearranged into a gala banquet-
ing hall, already filling with brilliant uniforms, costumes from a
dozen different worlds. There was a bar at one end, dispensing
drinks which looked delicious, brightly colored and cool. Wait-
ers were carrying trays of little tidbits, and the cafeteria tables
had been moved, combined into formal patterns, draped with
linen and adorned with flowers. Real flowers. Well, thanks to
Lady Rohana, she knew how to behave at a formal banquet. A
man she knew slightly from Communications offered her a
drink from the bar and she accepted it, saying a few formal
words of small talk without hearing herself. She looked around
for Peter, but he had not yet appeared. She thought of him in the
clutches of the curious beauty-shop machines, having his hair
and beard attended to, and cringed.

"Jaelle?" It was Wade Montray, bowing to her. "You look
very beautiful tonight." She accepted the compliment as the so-

cial noise it was, hardly personal at all. "Sandro Li is looking for you. See—over there by the head table, next to the Coordiantor."

She made her way through the crowd toward him, brushing aside greetings. Crowds had never bothered her before this, and certainly this was not as crowded as Midsummer in Thendara, but for some reason she felt strange, taut, and it seemed to her that too many people were looking at her, *there's that Darkovan girl, the one Haldane married, some sort of Darkovan nobility, no I heard she was a Free Amazon, a soldier, a fighter, look at the knife scar on her cheek. . . .*

Aleki bowed to her. He was wearing some sort of formal clothing strange to her, dark-red, with gold lace and decorations on his breast; she supposed it was suggestive of his Imperial rank. He was very unlike the informally dressed man she knew from the office.

"I told you to make yourself beautiful for tonight, but I did not realize that you would dazzle us all," he said, smiling at her, and for a moment it seemed that he was ready to seize her, to grasp at her . . . no; he was smiling courteously, he had not touched her, why was she so intensely, painfully aware that he desired her, that he had not touched a woman for a long time and that he wanted her? The Amazon in Jaelle cringed, but he had said nothing, his manner was perfectly correct, why was she so open to him just now? She felt as if the room were full of a ringing silence.

His voice seemed to reverberate from very far away. For an instant it seemed that the few sips she had had of her drink were nauseating her and that she would disgrace herself by vomiting here before the whole assembly. She grabbed at vanishing self-control and said as calmly as she could, "I didn't hear you, sir. It's a little noisy in here."

He looked around cheerfully. "We *are* a noisy crowd tonight, aren't we? I asked if you could hunt up Peter Haldane for me."

She had had no chance to warn Peter against this man, who was so alert to find out what she had no wish to let him know about Darkover. Her eyes searched the crowd for Peter's familiar shape, and she braced herself to cross the crowded room through the onslaught of mental voices.

How do the Comyn *who have full* laran, *like Lady Rohana, ever manage to appear anywhere in a crowd?* For the first time in her life, she wished she had had some of the training given routinely to the telepaths of the *Comyn*, to control her *laran.* . . . but then, it had never seemed to her that she had enough *laran* to be worth training! She moved through the crowd, carefully keeping her face blank, she would not stare about her in panic like a mushroom-farmer in the big city for his first Festival!

She knew Peter would be wearing gray, the steel-gray which was so becoming to his red hair and gray-green eyes. She looked through the crowd and finally saw a red head. She made her way to his side and touched his arm.

"Alessandro Li wishes to speak with you," she said formally.

"Let's not keep him waiting, then," he said, and took her arm. She pulled upright, bracing herself.

"I can walk by myself," she said stiffly.

"Honey, are you still mad at me? Let's not fight, not here at a party!"

She drew a long breath. She said, "Piedro, listen to me, please. Li is very curious about the *Comyn*; he's determined to find out what lies behind it. For three days he has been after me with his questions; don't underestimate him. I did. And I don't know what he wants, but I am not sure it is good for Darkover. I may have told him too much already; be careful what you say to him."

Peter grimaced. He said "I can't afford to play games with an Imperial bigwig. I've got to cooperate. Montray—the Coordinator, not Monty, Monty's a decent sort—old Montray just threatened me—he wants to send me offworld."

"Peter!" Suddenly she forgot her quarrel with him, at the shocking thought that she might somehow lose him. "What? Why?"

"They've located a planet something like Darkover—feudal setup, low technology, all that—and he says with my experience here, I'd be a good one to send there. Personally, I think he's afraid I'll have his job if I stay here; I know twice as much, ten times as much, about Darkover as he does and he's afraid somebody will find it out. And if I can convince Sandro Li that I'm really needed here to unravel this mystery—do you see?" He swung around and caught her wrist. "Jaelle, I'm fighting for my life, as much as you were when you and Mag met the banshee on the trail. Won't you back me up? I want to stay on Darkover—with you. Help me, don't fight me, beloved!"

People slid by, on either side of them. In this crowd, so filled with voices she did not really hear, voices that penetrated her mind brutally, she could not think clearly. She swallowed hard and said "Come along; just—just be careful what you say, or even what you hint, or he'll get it out of me."

Li greeted Peter with great cordiality, indicating, as people began to move toward the banquet tables, that Peter and Jaelle were to be seated near him at the head table.

She was aware, at least partly from the subliminal chatter of telepathic sound, that the Terrans here in Thendara Spaceport regarded Li much as the common people of Thendara would have regarded the Heir to Hastur; here to judge them, in authority over them. Peter was talking to Li with all the charm of which he was capable, emphasizing to the Imperial investigator that he knew more about Darkover than any other man working here. She could tell that Aleki was impressed. She also realized what neither Montray nor Peter had bothered to tell her; that on Li's report depended, not only the future status of Darkover in the Empire, but the future of the Terran installation. He had the power to withdraw the Empire entirely, except for a few officials to tend the spaceport; or to increase the HQ staff until it was a full colony administration; he could open the world to trade, or close it completely.

The fate of Darkover in relation to the Empire is in this man's hands. Even the Hasturs have little to say about it. This is too much of a responsibility for me! It is too great a responsibility for anyone!

At one point in the dinner, when the main course had been finished and they were lingering over sweets and tiny, delicious glasses of variously-scented and colored cordials, Aleki said, "In your work I have found frequent mention of Miss Lorne's work. Why is she not on the station? Is she on leave offworld? I found her name on the *inactive* roster."

Cholayna Ares, tall and elegant in low-cut draperies of fire-red which accented her smooth dark skin and frost-white hair, leaned across to them and said, "She is on detached duty in Thendara, Sandro; she is in the Renunciate Guild-house."

"I am extremely eager to meet her," Li said. "Do you suppose that I could request her to come in for an interview?"

"I doubt it," Jaelle said, "she is serving her housebound time among the Amazons; she is not allowed to leave the House for that period—"

"But that is barbarous!" Li said. "To imprison an Empire citizen—"

"Hardly imprisonment," Jaelle said calmly, "since it is voluntary."

Peter leaned forward. He had, Jaelle suspected, drunk a little too much. He said "I can tell you anything Magda could tell you, Sandro. Most of the places she went, she managed to go while she was under my protection. You don't realize yet how many doors are closed, here, to any woman. Magda's a fine agent; If she'd been born a man, she'd be the Legate by now! But here on Darkover, no woman could be accepted that way. And now she's gone over the wall, gone native. I can fill in most of Magda's reports for you."

"Can you really?" Li's face was sharp, and intent.

"I can and I will." Peter reached for another drink.

"I'll take you up on that," Sandro Li said, and turned to listen to the speaker at the head of the table.

An hour later, Jaelle faced Peter across the small room they shared. She knew he had drunk too much; his face was flushed, his speech incoherent, but he was not so drunk he could disclaim responsibility for what he had done.

"Peter, don't you realize? That man is out to destroy

Darkover—the Darkover we know—to turn it into another Terran colony! And you're helping him!"

"I think you're exaggerating. In any case, what does it matter? He's only here to investigate how well the HQ is doing its job on Darkover. I owe him cooperation; so do you and so does Magda. If it weren't for men like him, there would be *no* Empire."

"Would that be such a misfortune?"

He took her shoulders and turned her toward him. She permitted it, not sure why she didn't kick him away.

"There's no reason Darkover can't accept what's good about the Empire while keeping what's good in its own way of life. It's not wrong to hate ignorance and poverty. Look, *chiya,* I was born on Darkover, it's my home too, I love it—I want to stay here, be part of it." He bent to kiss her, burying his face in her scented hair. "I was fighting—I *am* fighting—for the right to stay here, as any man would fight for his land, his home, his wife. I do it with words instead of a sword, that's all. But I *am* Darkovan. You heard what Cholayna said when she heard about our wedding?"

She had heard; somehow it had nested in her heart, almost with pain. Cholayna had said; *with your red hair and Peter's, what beautiful children you will have.*

"I want a son," he whispered, "as much as any man of the Hellers would want a son. A son to live here on Darkover, our world. . . . Jaelle, Jaelle . . ."

He picked her up and carried her to the bed. She allowed it, even enjoyed his touch; he laid her down, whisked away the filmy green of her dress, flinging it unheeded to the floor. As he drew her into his arms once again he was wholly open to her She could feel it in him, like an eternal and unhealed wound, Magda's refusal to give him the child he desired. His body possessed hers but it was she who possessed his mind, he was at her mercy . . .

. . . *and suddenly she knew him as Magda had known him, he really believed that he could treat her as valet, comrade-in-arms, personal servant, breeding-animal, and somehow repay*

it all just with the ardor of his lovemaking. . . . the rage that
boiled up in her then cut off thought; she twisted aside, a knee,
a shoulder, both arms stabbing up, and he rolled helplessly
aside, shocked and vulnerable. She sprang up, crouching into a
defensive posture, and he lay stunned, staring at her in absolute
disbelief.

"Sweetheart—what's wrong?"

"Next time, *ask* me if I feel like making love!" The confusion
and outrage on his face felt good to her. "Next time I might even
agree to bear you a child. But ask. Don't—don't take!" She felt
she could not endure to look at him. He thought he had only to
caress her and she was enslaved to his will!

He was sitting on the bed, drunk and miserable. "Jaelle, what
did I do wrong? Tell me!"

She did not know. What did happen to love? Now she only
wanted to hurt him, to lash out at him, to jeer at his vulnerability! She said, low and hard-faced, "Don't ever—*ever*—take me
for granted, *Terranan!*" and slammed the door of the bath behind her, turning on the water full force. She stood under the
shower and cried, cried till she felt empty and helpless as she
had left Peter there. When she came out of the shower he was
asleep, a bottle empty on the floor beside him; he reeked of the
cheap Darkovan wine from the port. She threw the bottle down
the disposal chute, pulled her cloak from the closet and fell
asleep on the floor by the bed.

She woke late, and he was gone; she had not even heard him
leave. And she was glad.

Chapter 7

Someone was calling Magda's name, in her sleep, from very far away.

"Margali—Margali!"

It was dark in the room; outside it was snowing hard. Camilla, wrapped in a thick furred gown, was standing by her side. Magda sat up and asked, "What is it? I'm not on kitchen duty, Camilla." There was no particular hour to get up; but for the convenience of women who worked in the city, an early hot breakfast was served, and the women on kitchen duty were roused early to cook and serve it. Anyone sleeping through this breakfast had to rummage in the pantry for cold bread, or go hungry until dinner.

"I'm sorry to wake you at this hour, *breda*, but Byrna is in labor and should not be left alone; will you come and sit with her for a time?"

Magda got out of bed, huddling her thick nightgown round her, her feet cringing at the touch of the stone floor. "Where is the midwife?"

"It always happens this way—babies come in clusters! Marisela has slept in the house these last ten days, but tonight of all nights she was called out to the other end of the city. But it is Byrna's first child, and there is no great hurry. You will have time to wash your face and dress."

Magda went down the hall to the community bath and splashed her face with cold water; she flinched at its cold bite, knowing that if she stayed here a hundred years she would never, never get used to this. It had never seemed to occur to anyone that anyone would want a warm bath in the morning, so in the morning there was no hot water—it was as simple as that. Magda supposed that when you were doing hard manual work it made sense to wash off the day's grime in the evening—she still remembered her tenday in the stables, and how welcome a hot bath had been then. But it was one of those cultural differences that really hurt.

"What time is it?" she asked Camilla, as they went down the corridor.

"Just after midnight. We have taken her upstairs, so she can make as much noise as she likes, and not fear waking anyone who needs sleep. Rafaella is upstairs with her now, but Rafi is pledged to leave at sunrise and she must have a little sleep."

In the fourth-floor room, a fire had been lighted, and Byrna was walking back and forth in front of the fire, wrapped in thick shawls over her chemise. She turned and said "Thank you for coming to stay with me, Margali—I'm sorry to get you up like this—"

"It's all right," said Madga, taking her hands awkwardly. "How are you feeling?"

"It doesn't hurt as much as I thought it would, not yet," Byrna said, "It's like a bad case of cramps, and it sort of comes and goes; between times I feel fine."

"And it won't even hurt that much, if you remember what Marisela told you, and breathe into it," Rafaella said, coming to put her arm around Byrna's waist. "I've had four, and I know." She gave Byrna a hug, and went to the door with Magda. She said, "Do you know how to handle this early stage?"

Magda shook her head. Rafaella always made her feel stupid and incompetent. "I've never been with a woman in labor before."

Rafaella raised her eyebrows. "At your age? Where, in Avarra's name, were you brought up? Well, all you can do at this stage is to keep her cheerful, remind her to relax if she starts to tense up. The most she can do, at this stage, is not to interfere with what's going on inside. Let her drink as much water as she wants, or tea—" she added, indicating a kettle boiling over the fireplace on its long arm, "and if she feels faint, put a spoonful of honey in it. Don't worry if she vomits, some women do. The important thing is just to be with her, reassure her."

Magda faltered. "What if the—the baby comes before the midwife gets here?"

Rafaella stared at her in puzzlement. "Well, so what? If it comes all by itself, that's the best thing that could happen. They do sometimes come like that, no pain, no fuss. If it does, just wrap it in anything handy—don't cut the cord—just lay it on top of her and go and yell for somebody who knows what to do; any of the Guild-mothers would know." She added impatiently, "There's nothing to handling a baby that comes by itself; it's when they *don't* that you need help! Camilla will be in and out; if Byrna starts wanting to push, tell Camilla to go and get somebody in a hurry, but I don't think that will happen for hours yet. And for heaven's sake, calm down, you'll frighten Byrna if you're this nervous! If there were anybody else, I'd never leave her to you, of all people! But how was I to know anyone your age would be so ignorant?" Rafaella went and hugged Byrna again, said, "Have a nice little Amazon for the house, won't you?" and went away with Camilla, leaving Magda alone with Byrna. They looked at each other rather helplessly; then Byrna said "Oh—it's starting again," and grabbed Magda around the waist, leaning heavily on her, breathing hard and panting softly. When it was over she drew a long, gasping breath and said "*That* one really hurt!"

"Well," said Magda, "maybe that means it won't be as long as you think."

"I want to rest for a while." Byrna dropped down on the mattress which had been laid on the floor, covered with clean, but ragged sheets, She sighed restlessly.

"My oath-mother promised to be here for the birth, but I have heard there are floods in the Kilghard Hills, and she could not travel." She blinked tears from her eyes. "I'm so lonely here, with no oath-sisters in the House—everyone's been so kind to me, but it's not like having my oath-sisters here."

Those who witness your oath are your family. . . . Magda remembered the swift growth of her own bond with Jaelle, and
that Camilla had treated her with unusual friendliness. "Byrna,
we are all your sisters, bound by the Oath—every one of us
here."

"I know. I know." But Byrna blinked tears away and her
hands clenched into fists. She closed her eyes, shifted her weight
again and seemed to fall asleep for a moment. Magda rose and
mended the fire, tiptoed back and sat beside the apparently
sleeping Byrna.

After a long time Byrna stirred and twisted restlessly. "Even
when I'm breathing the way Marisela told me, it hurts, it hurts
so much, and Marisela promised it wouldn't . . ."

Magda tried to remember random things she had read. "Just
breathe quietly; try to feel as if you were floating," she said, and
Byrna was quiet again, resting. After a time she hoisted herself
up wearily and began to walk, leaning on Magda. "They said it
would go faster if I could stay on my feet."

Later, Camilla came back, carrying a cradle in her arms.
"How are you feeling, Byrna? Look, here is a cradle for your little one; I found it in the storeroom, and an embroidered blanket;
I made this one myself, fifteen years ago, for Rafaella's last
baby. Doria slept under it. And now she is nearly an Amazon
herself!"

"It looks like new," Byrna said, caressing the woolly fabric,
and Camilla laughed. "No baby uses it for very long. How do
you feel?"

"Awful," Byrna said, "and it seems to be taking a long time."

Camilla felt about her body. "You're coming along well
enough. It may not be as long as we think. Try to walk some
more, if you can."

She disappeared again, and the time seemed to stretch out.
Byrna walked and Magda held her upright, holding her when the
contractions seized her; later she lay down to rest, or slept a little, moaning. After three or four hours, gray light began to steal
through the window.

"Look," Magda said, "it's morning. The sun will be up

soon." Byrna did not answer, and Magda thought she had dozed again, but then she heard the woman whimper softly. "What's the matter? Is it very bad? Lie back and relax, Byrna—"

"Lie back, Byrna, don't make a fuss, Byrna, relax, Byrna," the woman mimicked savagely, sitting up on the bed. "Don't I know it all?" "You don't really give a damn," Byrna flung at her, and started to cry, "There's nobody here who cares, and I'm so miserable—" She sobbed, curling herself up, holding herself, and Magda was dismayed. She felt she was breaking all the rules—surely nothing like this would ever have been allowed in Medic HQ in the Terran Zone—but she sat down on the edge of the mattress beside Byrna, laying a tentative hand on the shaking shoulders. "That's not true, Byrna. I'm really sorry your oath-mother isn't with you, but I'll try to help you all I can, really I will. And it will be over sooner than you think."

Byrna flung her arms around Magda and burst into agonized, passionate crying. Magda patted her, helplessly.

"Is it so bad? Don't cry, they say the worse it is, the sooner it is to being over." It was one of the few things she could remember from the midwives' lecture a few days ago. "If you feel so bad now, then this is the worst, you'll feel better soon when you start to bear down, But please, lie down again—try to relax—"

"It isn't the pain," Byrna said distractedly, "I could stand that, it isn't that—" she clung to Magda, moaning. Magda held her, letting Byrna clutch at her hands with bone-crushing force. She could *feel* the deep, racking shudders that passed through Byrna, and it reminded her of that moment under the matrix, when Lady Alida had gone deep into the cell-structure of the wound on Jaelle's face and Magda had found herself sharing it. *Laran. Must I feel everything she feels?*

But the paroxysm passed and Magda wondered if she had merely imagined it. She persuaded Byrna to lie back on the pillows, sponged the sweat from her face, and persuaded her to sip a little tea with honey. Tears were still rolling down Byrna's face, and to distract her Magda asked, "Do you want a boy or a girl?"

"A girl, of course—I was there when Felicia had to give up her son, since no male may live in a Renunciate house after he is five. She said he would soon be a stranger to her, yet she did not want to leave the House and her sisters, and hire a nurse to keep him when she was at work, and face all the dangers of a woman living alone in the City—I think if I bear a son I will give him up at once, before it tears my heart to let him go. Felicia wanted a son, she said she did not want to be troubled with fifteen years tied down to rearing a girl, but now that Rael is gone she is moping like a chervine that has lost her calf. I will not be that foolish, I will give him up at once."

"Who is your child's father, Byrna? Or would you rather not tell—"

"His name is Errol, and he is a cousin of mine. His wife has no son, and she said she would welcome a child of his to foster—" and then Byrna began to cry harder than ever. Magda, alarmed, asked, "*Breda*, what is it?"

Byrna wept "I can't stand it, I can't stand it—"

"The pains? Sister, shall I go and call Camilla, or one of the Guild-mothers? Keitha has had children, too, she might know—"

"No, no, not the pain—" she sobbed till her whole body shook. "Only—only—I am oath-breaker, forsworn—"

"Byrna, don't—this is no time—"

"It's true, true! That is why I wanted my oath-mother here, to confess to her, to have her forgiveness—" Her body convulsed again and Magda was sure she was making it worse with her violent crying.

"The Oath—" she wrenched out, twisting and writhing, "I am sworn . . . *bear no child save in my own time and season*. . . . I have been taught, I know there are ways of preventing the conception of a child I did not want—but it was Midsummer, and I—I wanted to please Errol, so I lay with him even though I was *raiva*, ripe for conception, and not—not protected—but I was lonely, and he wanted me—we have been lovers for many years; at one time we had spoken of marriage, but I was—at that time I wanted to be independent, to do only my own will, so I chose the Guild-house, and went away to Dalereuth, and then, when I came back to Thendara, I found that he was married, and unhappy. And it seemed—oh, I hardly know how to tell you, so *right* somehow, with the music, and the dancing, and a—a starlit night with all the moons above us, and yet—I knew it was wrong, to risk this, to risk it—and so I am forsworn, forsworn—"

Magda was confused, not aware of the particular ethical point involved. She remembered how, at Midwinter Festival at Ardais, she had come near to surrendering herself to Peter, just because the old habit of love for him was so strong, and he had wanted her so much. But she could have done so, thanks to Terran medicine, without this kind of risk. *She* had been properly protected against conception . . . and she remembered what Mother Lauria had said on her first day in the house, that this training would be beyond price to the Renunciates. It was a sin that they did not have proper contraceptives, so that women need not take this kind of risk, bear unwanted children . . . and suffer this kind of guilt.

She held Byrna till her sobbing quieted a little, and said gently, "It is too late for regrets of that kind, *breda*. Done is done. Now you must just think of your baby." What a foolish thing to say, she thought, as she mouthed the phrases; what else had Byrna been thinking about for all these months?

Obediently Byrna lay down; and then a look of surprise came over her face. She began to gasp deeply, to breathe in a new way, gulping in deep breaths and letting them out in a harsh, straining groan. Magda admonished her to relax, but Byrna seemed not to hear, gasping out between the heavy groans "Something's happening—it doesn't hurt as much now—"

Oh, God, Magda thought, she's beginning to bear down, I've got to go and call somebody who knows what to do—

Byrna gasped "I need to—to *hold* something—" and grabbed at Magda's hands, straining, hauling, her face reddening with the effort. Magda tried to brace herself against panic.

"O-o-h," Byrna groaned, but curiously it was not a sound of

pain; only of tremendous effort; Magda could almost feel it in her own body and it was a curiously satisfying sensation—what the hell was happening to her? More to the point, what was happening to Byrna?

Byrna clutched her hands and let out a long howling cry, more a grunt than a scream. "It's coming," she yelled, "I can *feel* it, it's coming, it's coming *now*—" She gulped air again and gave herself over to the groaning, straining effort. Magda tried to wrest her hands away.

"Let me go and call somebody, Byrna—"

"No, no, don't leave me—" Byrna grunted the words out and went into a long shriek; Magda could not free herself. Maybe someone would hear Byrna yelling, but she could not get free without hurting her, maybe she should run and call somebody— but Byrna was tugging at her hands, crying out, that hard yell ending in gasping grunts.

Oh, Camilla, why don't you come back—!

The door burst open and Keitha was in the room. She said briskly, "I heard her, and I've delivered enough babies to know what that kind of yell means. Here, let me—" she drew the shawl and chemise back. "Get behind her, Margali, hold her up—yes, like that, hold her up, that's right." Magda obeyed, numbly, not knowing what was going on; Byrna was sitting half-upright, her legs spread, Magda behind her, gripping her around the waist. Byrna arched her body, strained, howling aloud, as Keitha braced her knees upright. She said swiftly, "No time to call anybody, no time to wait—I can manage."

Byrna gasped and yelled again, her body arching with effort. She was babbling, but Magda could not understand the words. Keitha knelt before her, and out of the corner of her eye Magda saw something red, slick, wet, streaked with blood. Byrna's harsh gasps and cries were blood-curdling; Keitha murmured something reassuring, and then Magda saw the wet, wriggling body of the child as Keitha lifted it, gently, tilted it head downward. There was a faint mewing wail, then the newborn baby began to scream indignation at leaving his warm nest. His.

Magda could see the tiny folded genitals against the little body. Byrna relaxed against Magda, held out her arms.

"Let me hold him," she whispered. "Oh, Keitha, give him to me."

"He's beautiful," Keitha said, smiling, and laid the naked child on Byrna's belly. He wriggled toward the breast, and Byrna guided him gently; Magda suddenly wanted to cry, she wasn't sure why.

I didn't want a child, she thought, any more than Byrna did. Yet she's so happy with it now. He's so beautiful, she thought, looking blissfully at the baby against Byrna's body, and I could have had Peter's child, and I would have been as happy as that— she felt her breath catch in a sob.

"Margali," said Keitha, "Go and call Mother Millea. I would go myself, but I can manage the afterbirth, if I must, and you can't."

But Magda had not reached the door before Camilla came in, and beside her, heavily wrapped in outdoor cloak and hood, was Marisela, who looked at them and laughed as she took off her mantle.

"So you have cheated me out of a birth-gift, Keitha? Well, I have been up all night delivering twins; both born backward and I thought the mother would bleed to death. But they are both alive, and so is their mother, and they were both sons, so the father—" she made a wry face, "forced a double fee on me. So I am glad the hard part is already over." She went quickly and washed her hands in the basin near the fire, then came and said, "Let me see. Well, you managed that nicely, Keitha; she is not torn, even though it came so fast? Well, he is not very big. Here, little man," she said, taking up the baby and handling him in her expert fingers, turning him over, checking the cord, the stumpy little toes and fingers, putting a finger in his mouth to see if he sucked at it, swiftly inspecting nose, ears, the back of his pudgy neck, "Well, what a fine little fellow you are, every finger and toe where it should be." She laid him down again at Byrna's breast. "How do you feel, Byrna?"

"Tired," the woman said blissfully, "and sleepy. And hungry. Isn't he *beautiful*, Marisela?"

"He is indeed," said Marisela. She was a small, competent-looking woman, her hair cropped in Amazon fashion, but she wore women's clothing. She said, "I will send one of your friends down to get you some hot milk with honey; you are not bleeding much, but I will put something in it anyway, and then you will sleep for a while. And when you wake up, you shall have as big a breakfast as you want to eat." She looked at Magda and said, "You are the new one, aren't you? I forget your name—"

"Margali n'ha Ysabet," Magda said.

"I am sorry; I spend so much of my time out of the house I sometimes do not remember you all. I remembered you, though, Keitha," she said, touching Keitha's cropped golden head, "Did I not deliver your daughter? She must be a big girl by now."

Keitha's face crumpled. She said, shaking, "She—she died just before Midwinter, of the fever—"

"Ah, Goddess, I am sorry!" Marisela exclaimed.

"I—I begged my husband to send for you, who know so much of healing, but he would not—would not let a Renunciate under his roof—"

"Ah, I am sorry, but I might have been as helpless as they," said Marisela gently, "I am skilled, but against some fevers there is no help. But now you are here, and some day, Keitha, we must talk. For the moment, I am grateful to you for doing so well with Byrna's baby. I must finish this," she added, holding her dripping hands well away from her, exactly as Magda had seen Medics do in the Terran HQ, and bent over Byrna to check the afterbirth. "Camilla, will you wrap up Byrna's little man?"

Magda watched Camilla's long, callused fingers, tender on the child; Camilla held the baby, crooning, for a moment against her meager breast. How can a neuter, a woman who has no female hormones—and besides that, she must be fifty at least—appear so motherly? How, in any case, did a neuter, an *emmasca*, think of herself, of children? Magda could not even

guess. She had always believed that this kind of motherly feeling was a matter of hormones, no more than that.

"Margali," Marisela said, "Go down to the kitchen, and heat
some milk; put honey in it, and bring it up here for Byrna, to
have with her medicine, before she sleeps."

Magda went downstairs, feeling weary; now she must stir up
the banked fire and heat some milk! To her aching relief, however, Irmelin was already there, quietly moving around the huge
stove. Rafaella was there too, dressed for riding, eating a bowl
of hot porridge at the table.

"So Byrna's had her baby? And now Marisela wants some
hot milk and honey for her," Irmelin said, kindly. "You sit down
there by Rafi and have some tea; I made myself some when I
came down, it's poured out there. So Byrna's had her baby—
what was it? Boy or girl?"

"A boy," Magda said, drinking the hot tea gratefully as
Irmelin put the milk to heat.

Rafaella swore, slamming her fist on the table. "Hellfire!
Poor brat, and she'll have to give him up—Zandru's hells, how
well I remember that! There ought to be a better—hellfire!" She
slammed out, leaving her porridge-bowl knocked over, spilling
milk and runny porridge over the table. Magda stared after her,
wondering what was the matter.

Irmelin watched her, sighing, but she came and mopped up
the milk without speaking. She said curtly, "Drink your tea,
Margali, and take this up to Byrna," and her eyes were distant,
her lips set. Magda sipped at the sweet milky tea, longing almost
passionately for a strong cup of black coffee. Her head was
aching, and she felt exhausted. She took the milk upstairs.

The baby, wrapped in blanket and kimono, was lying in
Byrna's arms; Byrna had been washed, her hair combed and
braided, and she was lying with her eyes closed and peaceful.

"Let me put him in the cradle while you drink your milk,
breda," Camilla said, holding the cup to her lips, but Byrna
clung to the baby. "No, I want to keep him, please, please—"

Marisela told them to go and get some breakfast, saying she

would stay with Byrna for a few hours, to make sure she did not begin bleeding, and Camilla sighed as they went down the stairs.

"Poor little thing," she said, "I hope Ferrika will come here in time to comfort her before she yields up her child—I am troubled about her." She put her arm around Magda, and said, "You are weary, too—had you never delivered a child before?"

"Never," said Magda. "Had you?"

"Oh, yes—I could have managed, had Keitha not been there. Rafaella's second son was born like that, and long before she looked for it; she had not counted her time properly and did not know she was within forty days of labor." She began to laugh. "We were riding together near Neskaya Guild-house: we had been on fire-watch. She barely had time to get her breeches off; the child was born into my hands as I bent to see if she was truly in labor. We wrapped it in my tunic and she rode home beside me!" The tall *emmasca* chuckled. "I have heard that Dry-Town women ride till the very day they are delivered, but this equalled anything I had ever heard!"

The smell of breakfast cooking rose up the stairs, but Camilla did not turn toward the diningroom; instead she pulled the house-door open. The street was empty and dark, snow still falling heavily, though the light was stronger. Magda felt lost in the world of thick snowflakes, lost, very alien in this strange world. She felt that if by chance she should look in a mirror she would not recognize herself. Camilla heard her sigh, and tightened her arm around Magda's shoulder.

"You are weary of being housebound, I can imagine; but dark and dismal as the days are now, it would be worse to be shut up inside in the full summer. The time will pass before you know it. Look, there is blood on your tunic, and on your wrist," she added, picking up Magda's hand. "We have an old saying in the hills where I was brought up; if blood is spilt on you before breakfast, you will shed blood before nightfall. Are your courses due?"

For a moment Magda did not quite understand the phrase, which Camilla had spoken in the *cahuenga* vernacular; Camilla repeated the question in *casta* and Magda shook her head.

"Oh, no, not nearly." The snowflakes, whirling up from the street, felt cold on her cheeks. Camilla looked at her, troubled.

"But you have been here more than forty days and you have not had them—*breda*, are you pregnant?"

Damn it, was everybody watching her so closely as that? She said in exasperation "Damnation, no!"

"But how can you possibly be sure—" Camilla's face changed. "Margali! Have you taken a fertility-destroyer?"

Again, for a moment, Magda did not understand; when she did she thought that was probably the nearest equivalent to the Terran medical treatment which had suppressed menstruation and female function. She nodded; it saved argument.

"Don't you know those drugs can *kill* you, child? Why do you girls do it?" Camilla broke off and sighed. "I of all people have no right to lecture you, being what I am . . . and beyond that danger forever. It has been so long, so long since I can even remember what it was like to be driven by those hungers and needs. But at times—when I think of Byrna's face when she looked at her child—I wonder." The deep sigh seemed to rack her whole body; but her lips were pressed tight together, and she stared impassively at the falling snow. Magda had wondered before; what could drive a woman to the illegal and often fatal neutering operation on Darkover; it would not have been simple even for Terran medicine, yet she had seen more than one *emmasca* in her travels. She did not speak her question aloud, but at her side Camilla stiffened and looked away from her, staring into the whirling snowflakes, and Magda wondered if the woman could really read her mind.

Camilla said at last, "Only my oath-mother, Kindra, knows all; it is something of which I do not often speak, as you may imagine, but you are my sister and should know the truth. I—" she stopped again for a moment, and Magda protested, "I did not ask—you do not need to tell me anything, Camilla—"

She does read my mind! How? Magda remembered, with a curious sting of apprehension, how at Ardais she had stood by as Lady Rohana and the *leronis* Alida worked with the matrix to heal Jaelle's wound, and how she had found herself within the matrix, working with *laran*.

Camilla said, "Once I—bore another name, and my family was not unknown in the Kilghard Hills. My mother said," she added, her voice flat and detached, "that there was Hastur blood in my veins; which means probably that I was Festival-born, and not the daughter of my father. I was destined for a great marriage, or for the Tower, a *leronis*. My father's freehold was attacked one day by bandits; they slew many of my father's sworn men, and me they carried away, with some of his cattle, to be a plaything for them. You can imagine, I suppose, how they used me," she said, still in that flat, detached voice. "I was not yet fourteen years old, and mercifully I have forgotten much."

"Oh, Camilla!" Magda's arms tightened around the older woman's spare body.

"I was ransomed, and rescued, at last," Camilla went on, rigid in Magda's arms, "My family was concerned, I think, mostly that I was spoilt for a grand marriage. And a *leronis* must be—" she paused, considering and turning over words, almost visibly, "untouched. I was not yet old enough even to know that I was with child by one of the—animals who had stolen me. I remember no more; my mind was darkened. I am told I laid hands on my life." Her eyes were distant, looking inward on horror; at last she gave herself a little shake and her voice was alive again.

"It mattered no further to my family what became of me. I was healed, but I knew I could never again endure the touch of any man without—horror. The Lady of Arilinn it was, Leonie Hastur, sanctioned it, that I should be made *emmasca*; and so it was done. For many years I lived among men, as a man, and refused to admit even to myself that I was a woman. But at last I came to the Guild-house; and there I found, again, that womanhood was—was possible for me." She smiled down at Magda. "It was half a lifetime ago; sometimes for years together I remember nothing of that old life, or who I was then. We should go and sleep; only when I am weary do I talk such morbid rubbish."

Magda was still speechless, horror-stricken, not only by
Camilla's story, but by the frozen calm with which she told it.
Camilla smiled again at her and said "My oath-mother Kindra
said once to me that every woman who comes to the Guild-
house has her own story and every story is a tragedy, one which
would hardly be believed if it was played in a theatre by actors!
When I saw Keitha's scars—I too was once beaten like an animal, and bear scars like hers on my body; so the story is fresh in
my mind, and raw again."

Magda protested, "Surely that is not true of all Renunciates,
though? They cannot be all tragedies! Surely some women simply come here because they like the life, or choose it for themselves—Jaelle, she told me, grew up in the Guild-house,
foster-daughter to Kindra—"

"Ask Jaelle, sometime, about her mother's death," said
Camilla. "She was born in Shainsa; but it is her story, not mine,
and I have no right to tell it."

Magda laughed uneasily. "My story is no tragedy," she said,
trying to speak lightly. "It is more like a comedy—or a farce!"

"Ah, sister," Camilla said, "that is the true horror of all our
stories, that some men, hearing them, would think them almost
funny." But there was no mirth in her voice. "You should go to
breakfast. I will give no lesson in swordplay today." She held
out her arms and gave the younger woman a quick, warm hug.
"Go and sleep, *chiya*."

Magda would have rather stayed; she did not want to be
alone. But she went obediently up to her room and to bed. An
hour or two later she found herself awake, and unable to sleep
again; she went to the kitchen and found herself some cold food;
afterward, at loose ends—for the Guild-mothers had excused
her from any duties today—she went into the library and read,
for a time, the history of the Free Amazons. It crossed her mind
that she should make careful notes, to file all this in the Terran
records one day, but she did not want to think about that just yet.
Later in the day Mother Lauria found her and asked her to take
hall duty, the lightest of the assigned tasks inside the house. This
meant only that she should go to the greenhouse and find flow-

ers and leaves there for the decorations, which were beginning to fade, and afterward, stay in the hall and let anybody in or out, or answer the door if anyone came to the House on business.

Magda was learning simple stitches, but she still disliked sewing; she brought down a cord belt she was braiding, and sat working at the intricate knots.

Two or three times she got up to let someone in, and once brought a message to Marisela, which she gave at the door of the room where Byrna was sleeping, the baby tucked in beside her. She was half asleep, in the gray light of the hallway, when suddenly there was a loud and shocking banging on the door.

Magda jumped up and pulled the heavy door open. A huge burly man, expensively dressed, stood on the doorstep: he glowered at Magda and said, using the derogatory mode, "I wish to see the woman who is in charge of this place." But the inflection he used made it obvious that his meaning was, "Get me the bitch who is in charge of this rotten dump."

Magda noticed that there were two men behind him, as large as himself, both heavily armed with sword and dagger. She said, in a polite mode which was a reproof to him, "I will ask if one of the Guild-mothers is free to speak with you, *messire*. May I state your business?"

"Damn right," growled the man, "Tell the old bitch I've come for my wife and I want her right now and no arguments."

Magda shut the door in his face and went quickly to the Guild-mother's sanctuary.

"How white you are!" Mother Lauria exclaimed. "What's wrong, child?"

Magda explained. She said "I think it must be Keitha's husband," meanwhile glancing at the huge, copper-sheathed door commemorating the battle which had claimed their right to a woman who had, like Keitha, taken refuge here generations ago.

Mother Lauria followed her eyes.

"Let us hope it does not come to that, my child. But run down quickly to the armory, and tell Rafaella—no, Rafi is away with a caravan to the north. Tell Camilla to arm herself quickly, and come. I wish Jaelle were here, but there is no time to send for her. You arm yourself, too, Margali; Jaelle told me that you fought with bandits when she was wounded near Sain Scarp."

Magda, her heart pounding, ran down to the armory and quickly armed herself with the long knife the Amazons did not call a sword—though Magda could not see the difference. Camilla, arming herself, looked grim.

"Nothing like this has happened for ten years and more—that we should have to defend the house by force of arms as if we were still in the Ages of Chaos!" She looked doubtfully at Magda. "And you are all but untried—"

Magda was all too aware of this. Her heart pounded as they hurried along the stairs, side by side. Mother Lauria was waiting for them in the hall. There was a furious banging on the door, and Mother Lauria opened it again.

The man on the doorstep began to bluster. "Are you the woman in charge of this place?"

Mother Lauria said quietly "I have been chosen by my sisters to speak in their name. May I ask to whom I have the honor of speaking?" She spoke with the extreme courtesy of a noblewoman addressing the crudest peasant.

The man snarled, "I am Shann MacShann, and I want my wife, not a lot of talk. You filthy bitches lured her away from me, and I want her sent out to me this minute!"

"No woman is allowed to come to us except of her free will," said Mother Lauria, "If your wife came here it was because she wished to renounce her marriage for cause. No woman within these walls is wife to you."

"Don't you chop logic with me, you—" The man spat out a gutter insult. "You bring my wife out here to me, or I'll come in there and take her!"

Magda's hand tightened on her knife, but the Guild-mother's voice was calm. "By the rules of this place, no man may ever pass our walls except by special invitation; and I am afraid I really have nothing more to say to you, sir. If the woman who was once your wife wishes to speak with you, she may send you a message and settle any business left unsettled between you, but until she wishes to do so—"

"Look, that wife of mine, she gets mad at me sometimes, once she ran away to her mother and stayed almost forty days, but she come cryin' back to me again. How do I know you're not holding her there and she wanting to come back?"

"Just why would we do a thing like that?" asked Mother Lauria mildly.

"You think I don't know what goes on in places like this?"

"Yes," said Mother Lauria, "I think you do not know at all."

"Keitha, she's too much a woman to get along without a man!" Shann blustered, "You send her out here right now!"

"I'm really afraid, you know," said the Guild-mother with great composure, "that you are going to have to accept my word: Keitha n'ha Casilda has expressed no desire to return to you. If you wish to hear this from her own lips, we allow visitors on the night of High Moon, and you are welcome to come, un-weaponed, alone or with members of your immediate family, and speak to her either alone or in our presence, as she herself wishes. But at this hour and on this day no man may enter here unless he has business here, and you, sir, assuredly have none. I ask you now to take yourself and your men away from here, and not to create a commotion on our doorstep."

"I tell you, I'm coming in and get my wife," Shann shouted, whipped out his sword and started up the steps. Camilla and Magda, long knives drawn, quickly stepped forward and blocked the way.

"You think I'm not a match for a pair of girls?" He whipped the sword down, but Camilla, moving swiftly as a striking snake, caught his blade with hers and struck it from his hand. He missed his footing on the stairs and stumbled, almost falling. He shouted to his men "Come on! Let's get in there!"

Magda braced herself for another attack. The white light of the snow in the street, the two huge men slowly advancing, Camilla at her shoulder, the knife-scars on her face white and drawn. For Magda the scant few seconds it took for the men to mount the first step seemed to last an eternity.

Then the men were on them and Magda felt herself thrusting, twisting the steel; the man's sword clanged, whipped sideways, slashed quickly back, and Magda felt a line of fire slice along her leg.

It didn't hurt, not yet, but while she blocked the next stroke—skills learned in Intelligence training, years ago, were coming back rapidly—what she mostly felt was shock.

You get this kind of training, it's routine, but you don't expect to have to use it, not really. You find you can do it, her thoughts raced, *but you don't believe it, not while you're doing it, not even while you're bleeding.* Her mind lagged behind but her body was fighting, driving the men back, down the steps. One slipped in the snow and Magda felt the sword go in under his breastbone before she fully knew it, felt the body sliding back off the blade, pulled by its own dead weight. She brought her knife up to guard against the next man; did not realize that Shann had gone down, bleeding, under Camilla's sword; that Camilla had said, to the third man, "Had enough?"

Magda did not hear: she was going after the third man in a flurry of sword-strokes, forcing him back and down the steps. Her blood sounded loud in her own ears and there was a blurry haze, blood-colored, before her eyes. A voice inside her seemed to be screaming, *Kill them, kill them all!* All of her rage against the Darkovan men who had kept her from the work and the world she wanted, her terror of the bandits who had disarmed her and shown her her own weakness—it was almost a sensual frenzy, letting the sword move almost without volition, until she heard someone shouting her name. By now the sound meant nothing. She saw the man before her slip, stumble to his knees. Then another sword struck hers down; she whirled to face her attacker and in the moment before she struck, she saw Camilla's face; it made her pause, just a moment, and her sword went flying with a violence that knocked her hand numb.

"No, Margali! No! He surrendered, didn't you see him raise his sword in surrender?" Camilla's hand bit into her wrist, a cruel grip that paralyzed her fingers.

Magda came to her senses, shaking; she looked, in consternation, at the man she had killed, and Shann next to him, groaning in his blood at the foot of the stairs. The third man had backed off and was staring in dismay at a wound in his forearm, from which fresh blood welled up.

Camilla said furiously "You have disgraced your knife!" She pushed Magda down, hard, on the steps, and went down the stairs to the wounded man.

"I most humbly beg your pardon, sir. She is new to fighting, and untried; she did not see your gesture of surrender."

The wounded man said, "I thought you women were going to kill us all, surrender or no! And this is no quarrel of mine, *mestra!*"

Camilla said, "I have honorably sold the service of my blade for thirty years, comrade. My companion is young. Believe me, we will so deal with her that she will not so disgrace her blade again. But are you not Shann's sworn man?"

The mercenary spat. "Sworn man to that one? Zandru's hells, no! I'm a paid sword, no more. It's no business of mine to lose my life for the likes of him!"

"Let me see your wound," Canilla said, "You shall have indemnity, believe me. We have no quarrel with you."

"And I have no quarrel with you, and no blood-feud, *mestra*. Between ourselves, I'd say that if his wife left him he'd given her cause four times over, but my sword is for hire, so I fought while he fought. But he is no kin or sworn comrade." Awkwardly, with his unwounded hand, he thrust the sword back into its sheath, and pointed to Shann. "I'll go find his housefolk and his paxmen to haul him home; he's nothing to me, but when I fight at a man's side, I don't leave him to bleed to death in the street." He looked regretfully at the man Magda had killed. "Now *he* was a pal of mine; we've been hiring out our swords together for twelve years come Midsummer."

Camilla said gravely, "Who grudges his blood to a blade had better earn his living behind the plow."

The man sighed, made the *cristoforo* sign of prayer. "Aye, he's laid his burdens now on the Bearer of the World's Wrongs. Peace to him, *mestra.*" He looked at his wounded arm. "But it goes hard to have blood shed after surrender!"

Mother Lauria came down the steps. "You shall have whatever indemnity a judge names as fair. Camilla, take him to the Stranger's Room and bind up his wound."

Camilla turned angry eyes on Magda. She said, with savage contempt, "Get inside, you, before you disgrace us further!"

Puzzled, feeling betrayed, Magda managed to stumble inside. The wound in her thigh, which she had hardly felt at the time, began to throb as if it had been burned with fire.

She had fought for the House. She had done her best—had the man truly surrendered before she struck him?

In the mountains I disgraced myself because I was afraid to fight, then when I fight I disgrace the Guild-house. . . . She felt sobs choking her, and braced herself against them; if she let herself cry now she would break into hysterical crying and never be able to stop. . . .

"Breda—" said a soft, troubled voice, and Keitha's pale, tear-stained face looked into hers. "Oh, how cruel she is! You fought for us, you are hurt too—and she cares more for that soldier's wound than yours! And you have shed your blood for us! Come, let me, at least, look after your hurt—"

Magda let herself lean heavily on Keitha as they went up the stairs. Keitha went on, indignant, "I saw it all—how can Camilla be so unjust? So the man had surrendered—what of that? I wish you had killed them all—"

Magda's leg had begun to hurt so badly that she felt dizzy. Blood was dripping on the floor. Keitha drew her inside the bathroom on their floor, pushed her down on a little wooden bathing stool and gently pulled off the slashed breeches. The cut was deep, blood still welling up slowly from the bottom. Magda clung to the stool, suddenly afraid of falling, while Keitha sponged the wound with icy water. While she was working on it, Mother Lauria came slowly up the stairs and stepped inside.

She looked coldly at the two women. "How badly are you hurt, Margali?"

Magda set her teeth. "I don't know enough about wounds to know how bad it is. It hurts."

Lauria came and examined the slash herself. "It is a clean

wound and it will heal; but painful. Did you get it from a sur-rendered man fighting for his life?"

Magda said clearly, "I did not; it was the first man, the one I killed, and I was fighting myself for my life, since I suppose he would not have stopped at killing me."

"Well, that's something," Mother Lauria said.

"How can you blame her so!" Keitha cried. "She fought to defend us, she is hurt and bleeding, yet you let Camilla bully her and call her harsh names, then you come and bully her further, before her wound is even bandaged—"

The Guild-mother's face was stern. "To kill a surrendered man is *murder*," she said. "If Camilla had not struck down her sword, she could have killed a defenseless man and brought blood-feud on us. As it is, we are fortunate that he was only a hired mercenary; had he been one of MacShann's sworn men, they would be bound to avenge him! Thendara House would have had to answer challenge after challenge, and it could have destroyed us! Fortunately, his wound is not disabling, and Camilla has been a hired mercenary herself and knows their codes of honor. She is dressing his wound in the Stranger's Room, and she hopes he will accept a cash indemnity for the wound so shamefully given."

Magda lowered her head, accepting the guilt. Yes, she had lost control, she was to blame. She remembered Cholayna Ares, in Intelligence School, warning them. *Never lose control, never lose your temper; never kill unless you wish to kill.* To keep her fear at bay, she had clung to her anger, and it had disgraced her. She sat trembling, feeling that Mother Lauria's anger was a tan-gible thing, a sort of red glow around the woman. And then she wondered if she were going mad.

Lauria turned on Keitha in angry scorn.

"And you, you have not even inquired whether he who was your husband is alive or dead! Are we to be assassins for your grudge?"

Keitha said furiously, "I care nothing, truly, whether he lives or dies! Am I to return good for evil like a *cristoforo*? I have re-nounced him forever!"

"Not true," said Mother Lauria. "If you had truly renounced him, you would not fear to know whether he lived or died, and could tend, like Camilla, the wounds of a fallen foe without hatred."

"She had not suffered at his hands—" Keitha began.

"What do you know of what Camilla has suffered at the hands of men?" Mother Lauria demanded, and Magda remembered what Camilla had told her . . . had it been only this morning? It seemed so very long ago. Mother Lauria sighed.

"Well, Margali's wound still bleeds; fortunately, Marisela is still in the house, though I hate to wake her like this when she was up all night. Margali, do you realize what you have done?"

Magda was still fighting the urge to hysterical crying.

"I didn't know—I did not see that he had surrendered—"

"When you take sword in hand it is your business to know," said Mother Lauria grimly. "There is no excuse in this world, or the next, for striking down a surrendered man. Name your oathmother!"

It had the force of a ritual demand; Mother Lauria knew perfectly well what the answer was.

"Jaelle n'ha Melora."

"You have disgraced her too," Mother Lauria said, "and when you are well again, she shall deal with you!" She went away, and Magda sat sobbing on the bench. Her leg hurt fiercely, but in her distress she hardly felt it.

"Well, what have we here?" asked Marisela cheerfully, as she came in, and Magda looked up, frightened; would Marisela too think it her duty to scold and browbeat her? She deserved it, whatever they might say or not say. And they would hold Jaelle responsible, and that was the worst!

But Marisela only knelt to examine the cut with gentle, experienced hands. "Nasty, but it will heal; the muscle is not much damaged. I will have to stitch this. Can you help me get her to her room, Keitha? It will be easier to do it there, and afterward, I fear, she will not be in much shape for walking, poor little rabbit." She stroked Magda's cheek and added, "This is a miserable thing to happen when you first take sword in our defense. Help her to her room, Keitha, while I fetch my things."

It was a nightmare of pain and effort, but somehow Keitha got her to her room and into her bed. Magda felt a twinge of fear through the pain, when Marisela came in—in the Terran Zone, she knew, a cut this deep would be sewn under anesthetic! Marisela sponged it with some icy stuff that numbed it slightly, then quickly and skillfully put in several stitches; Magda was by now so unstrung that she could not be brave, but disgraced herself again, she felt, by sobbing like a child. Keitha hugged and comforted her, and Marisela held some kind of fiery cordial to her lips; it made her head swim. Afterward Marisela kissed her on the forehead, said, "I'm sorry I had to hurt you so, *breda,*" and went away. Keitha sat beside her, holding her hand.

"I don't care what they say! To me it is no disgrace! They should not bully you that way!"

But now it was over, and the hysteria subsiding, Magda knew what Camilla meant. She had disgraced her steel.

I can't do anything right, she thought. I was a failure in the Terran Zone, a failure as a wife—I couldn't even give Peter the son he wanted—now I have failed here too, disgraced Jaelle, disgraced Camilla who taught me—I have failed here too, she thought.

Keitha held her, whispering, "Don't cry, Margali." She turned Magda's head between her hands and kissed her; and to Magda's dismay and horror, she felt no impulse to push the kiss away; instead her awareness was strange, intense, frighteningly sexual; she felt herself returning it, pulling Keitha closer, even though, in that sudden overwhelming awareness, she knew Keitha had not meant it that way, had meant only to comfort her as she would have kissed her own child, that Keitha would have been horrified if she had had any idea how Margali had interpreted her gesture. She could feel Keitha's compassion and kindness as a warm flood of soft colors wrapping her, just as she had felt Mother Lauria's rage, a red halo surrounding her and lashing out to strike . . .

What was in that stuff Marisela gave me, anyhow? I am

drunk, drugged, I am going mad . . . was this why she had failed with Peter, was it this Camilla had read in her the other night, was this what she really wished for when her defenses were down? Had Peter been right, when he accused her of being half in love with Jaelle herself, and jealous of him?

But she was too exhausted to be afraid. She let herself float, remembering the moment at Ardais when she had been inside the matrix. The bed was floating, it was like being far out in space, swirls of light tracing themselves round and round *inside* her eyes, faster and faster. For a moment she was back there at Ardais, with Lady Rohana looking up at her, troubled, and saying, *If you have trouble with* laran *you must promise to tell me at once.* But how could she, Magda wondered, when Rohana was *there* and she was *here?* It seemed that Keitha was calling to her from very far away, but she thought, Keitha is my friend, I do not want to upset or frighten her as I was frightened of Camilla that night, so she hid herself and did not answer. And then there was another face in the darkness, a beautiful woman's face, pale, surrounded in a cloud of pale reddish-golden hair, and all blue as if she saw it through the color of a pale blue fire, and at the last, yet another face; round, calm, practical, a woman's face under close-cropped greying hair, an Amazon, saying quietly, *We must do something for her, she belongs to us and she does not know it yet.*

A Terranan?

She is neither the first nor the last to claim a heritage in an unknown world.

And then the world went away and did not return.

Part II:

Sundering

Chapter 1

It was snowing. The world outside the high HQ tower, beyond the windows of Cholayna Ares's office, was lost in a flurry of white, and Jaelle, looking out into it, wished she were outside in the snow, not in here, in the yellow light, where no hint of natural weather ever penetrated.

Peter saw her look out wistfully into the storm, and pressed her hand. Since the night of Alessandro Li's reception, he had been gentle, apologetic, tender with her; she could not hold on to her anger, and in the past weeks he had tried, again, to be the man she had loved at once in Sain Scarp, had clung to at Ardais. He had tried, conscientiously tried, in spite of his Terran upbringing, to remember her independence, never to take her for granted. She had begun to hope again; perhaps, perhaps, even if they had lost what first drew them together, they could grow into something stronger and better than before. *That first intense sexual glow, I should have understood, I could never expect that to last forever, but now that I am no longer a delayed adolescent in the grip of her first infatuation, perhaps Piedro and I can find something more mature, more genuine. It was not all his fault, either. I have been selfish and childish.*

He said gently, "I'd like to be out there, too, walking in the snow," and for a moment, so great was their attunement, she wondered if perhaps he too had rudimentary *laran*; many, perhaps most, Terrans did. As they grew closer, perhaps it would develop and she could have with him the kind of understanding she craved.

Cholayna smiled at them both and said with a glimmer of irony, "If you two lovebirds can spare me a moment—" and Peter let go of Jaelle's hand and she saw the self-conscious color creeping up his face. Cholayna said, "Oh, don't apologize. I wish I could give you both a year's leave so you could go off for a proper honeymoon, but conditions really don't allow it. By now, Magda should have had plenty of time to decide if there are any women in the Thendara Guild-house who would be suitable for Medic technicians, and perhaps others we could use here in different employment. What's the possibility that she could come here to talk about it, Jaelle?"

"Absolutely zero," Jaelle replied promptly. "I told you; she is in her housebound half-year for training, and during that time she cannot leave the house except at the direct command of a Guild-mother."

Cholayna frowned a little and said, "I understood you were her superior; can't you send for her and order it?"

"I suppose I could," Jaelle said slowly, "but I would not do that to her. It would set her apart from the others and she could never recover, if she is really to be one of them."

"I think you're being overconscientious," Peter said. "The decision to use Free Amazons—excuse me, Renunciates—in Terran employment is an important one for both our worlds and it should be implemented as soon as humanly possible, before we lose the momentum of that decision."

"Just the same, we don't want to disturb Magda's cover," said Cholayna, "If she has gone among them as one of them we don't want to single her out in any way. Jaelle, could you go there and talk privately to her?"

Jaelle was suddenly overcome with a flood of homesickness. To visit the Guild-house, to be one with her sisters again! "I'd be glad to do that, and I can talk to Mother Lauria about it, too."

"The only thing wrong with that," Peter said wryly, "is that I can't come with you, can I?"

"Not to the Guild-house, I'm afraid," she said, but smiled, thinking that one day before long they would surely walk in the snow together, through the city she loved. He loved it too, he had spent years living as a Darkovan in her world. Why had she begun to think of him as a Terran and alien? Somehow she must help him, as well as herself, to recapture the Darkovan Piedro she had loved.

"I want to talk a little about the kind of woman we need here," said Cholayna. "Above all, they must be flexible, capable of learning new ways of thinking, doing, capable of adjusting to alien conditions. In fact—" she smiled at Jaelle and it was like a warm touch of the woman's hand, "like you, Jaelle; capable of surviving culture shock."

"Ah," Peter said, "but there aren't any more like Jaelle. When they made her, they broke the mold."

"I don't think I'm as unique as all that," she said, smiling, but already her mind was running over the women she knew in the Guild-house. There might be others she did not know as well, suited to training among the Terrans. Rafaella would never make a Medic technician, but she might be useful as a mountain guide, would certainly be valuable to the Terrans for her knowledge of travel in the hills and the Hellers. Marisela—Jaelle frowned for a moment, thinking of the midwife's skill and the adaptability which allowed her to work in the city with women who despised the ordinary Free Amazon. Marisela, certainly, would benefit by this kind of training, but could they spare her in the Guild-house? She shrugged it off, deciding that she would talk it over with Mother Lauria, and raised her eyes to meet Cholayna's smile.

"Where were you?" she asked, smiling, and Jaelle laughed and apologized. "Thinking over the women in the Guild-house."

Cholayna laughed and dismissed her. "Well, go and talk it over with your Guild-mothers. Some day, perhaps—would it be possible for me to visit a Guild-house?"

"I don't know why not," Jaelle said, responding again to the woman's spontaneous friendliness. "I think Mother Lauria would like you very much. I wish you could have known my oath-mother, Kindra." They were, she decided as she went down to her quarters, very much alike in many ways. Although Cholayna had grown up in a world where no one had made it difficult for her to learn and grow, and she had come to her strength, not by revolt and renunciation, as an Amazon must do, but simply by choosing this work. . . .

And then Jaelle was shocked at herself. Was she criticizing her own world, in favor of the *Terranan*? Had a few tendays here corrupted her so much?

Corrupted? Is it corruption, then, to love Peter or to appreciate his world? She slammed the door of her quarters and tore off her uniform with shaking hands. It was, indeed, time to revisit her home!

She got into her embroidered linen undertunic, heavy drawers and the thick woollen breeches and overtunic; sat down to lace her boots. Swearing, she ran her hand through her thick hair. Time, and more than time, to have it cut. No, damnation, why should she? She was living as Peter's freemate—*which the terms of her Oath permitted her to do*, she reminded herself severely. Yet the thought persisted; what would Rafaella say, or Camilla, when she appeared in the Guild-house with long hair instead of the distinctive Renunciate cut which proclaimed her independence of any man? Oh, damn them all! She fingered a pair of scissors, looked reflectively in the mirror, remembering Peter's hands caressing her hair. She actually set the scissors to her neckline, then swore again, angrily, and flung them down. It was her own hair and her own life, and if she wished to please her beloved freemate that too was her privilege. Yet the sting of guilt remained.

If it was snowing outside, she should have creams to protect her face against the wind and chill. She rummaged in the drawer, appreciating the soft perfumed Terran cosmetics; the perfume was a little stronger, the texture somewhat smoother, than those she could have bought in the market or the ones that some of the women made in the Guild-house when funds were short for a time. As she was smoothing the stuff on her face, she encountered the small calculating device of beads which she used to keep track of her women's cycles by the movement of the moons; the beads colored like the four moons, violet, peacock-blue, pale green and white. She slid down a violet bead, for she had noted that Liriel's disc was full, and stopped, staring at the beads. She should have pulled down a red bead for bleeding, at least a tenday ago. She had been so disrupted by the dreadful fight with Peter, and the distress accompanying it, and after it, her exacting work with Cholayna and Aleki, that she had simply pulled down the beads mechanically every day without noticing.

Was it simply the disruption of the cycles which, she had been warned, might come with living by artificial yellow light? Or was it possible that she might have become pregnant, that Peter, in the ecstatic reunion which had followed their quarrel, had managed to make her pregnant?

She could not help a deep-based flicker of pleasure at the thought, immediately followed by doubt and dread. Did she really want this? Did she want to be at the mercy of some small parasite within her body, sickness, distortion, the appalling ordeal of birth which had killed her own mother? For a second her mind flickered the terror of a nightmare. . . . *red spilling into the parched sand of a waterhole, sunrise and blood* . . . and a sharp stab of pain in her hands told her that without knowing it she had clenched her fist so tightly that her nails dug into the palm. Nonsense, what was she thinking, this mixture of old nightmares?

Peter will be so pleased when I tell him! For a moment she anticipated the delight that would spread over his face, the tenderness and pride that would light his eyes.

Pride. The words of the Oath reverberated in her mind, *Bear a child only in my own time and season; bear no child for any man's heritage or position.* . . . Oh, nonsense, she told herself. Peter was not *Comyn,* even though he looked so much like Kyril, he had none of the particular pride in heritage which was so much a part of *Comyn* life. The sneaking thought remained, *Rohana too will be pleased, that I have chosen to bear a child for the Aillard Domain,* and she slammed that thought shut, too. Not for Aillard. Not for Peter. For myself, because we love each other and this is the surest confirmation of our love! *For myself, damn it*!

But she slammed the drawer shut on the beads, almost with guilt, when she heard Peter's step.

"Jaelle? Love, I thought you were going to the Guild-house—"

"I am just going," she said, and tried not to look guiltily at the drawer. *If he were telepathic like Kyril, he would know without being told, without even seeing the beads.* She had once explained the device to him, but he had never paid much attention to it, though he admitted he had seen them for sale in the market and wondered if they were a kind of abacus. He had shown her how an abacus worked, telling her it was the most ancient Terran variety of calculator.

"Surely you won't go in this blizzard, Jaelle—"

"You've been in the Terran Zone too long, if you call this little flurry of snow a blizzard," she said gaily. She wanted to get out into the bracing cold of the weather, not skulk here in the debilitating artificial heat of the HQ buildings.

"Let me go with you," he said, pulling on his outdoor boots and jacket. She hesitated.

"Love, in Amazon clothing I should not walk through the streets of the city with you this way, and it will expose you, too, to comment and gossip—" and at his blank look she elaborated, "You are still in uniform."

"Oh. That. I can change," he offered, but she shook her head.

"I would rather not. Do you really mind, Peter? I'd rather be alone now. If I come to the Guild-house in the company of a Terran—or of any man—there will be talk which will make my mission harder."

He sighed. "As you wish," he said, pulling her close and kissing her. The kiss lingered suggestively.

"Wouldn't you rather stay here where it's nice and warm?"

The thought was tempting. Had she fallen into the Terran way of making love by the clock, with no room for emotional spontaneity? But, firmly, she disengaged herself from his arms.

"I'm working, darling. I really do have to go. As you're fond of reminding me about Montray, Cholayna's my boss."

He let her go almost too promptly. "You'll be back before dark?"

"I might spend the night in the Guild-house," she said. "It's not the sort of thing I can do in an hour or so." She laughed at his crestfallen look.

"Piedro, love, it's not the end of the world, to sleep apart for a single night!"

"I suppose not," he grumbled, "but I'll miss you."

She softened. "I'll miss you too," she whispered into his neck, hugging him close again, "but there are going to be times when you're out in the field, and I'll have to stay alone. We might as well get used to it now."

But the hurt look in his eyes followed her down the stairs, out into the chill of the base, past the Spaceforce guards which separated the HQ from the Trade City. Feeling the welcome cold of snow on her cheeks, she still wished she had softened their parting with her good news.

But there would be time enough for that.

It would be better, Magda thought, if someone would call her names. Anything would be better than this endless, reproachful silence, this careful courtesy.

"Are you quite ready, Margali?" Rafaella asked. "Will you work with Doria and Byrna? I think they need more practice in falling."

Magda nodded. The big room called the armory was filled with the white light of the snow outside, for the windowshades had been rolled back to let in maximum light. Mats were unrolled on the floor, and a dozen women were doing beginning exercises in stretching and bending, in preparation for the lesson in unarmed combat which Rafaella was about to give.

Magda remembered her third day in the house, when she had had her first lesson under Rafaella. After several days of struggling with unfamiliar tasks, baking bread, trying to learn to milk dairy animals, struggling with heavy barn brooms and shovels, it had been a great relief to come upon something she could actually do. She had been thoroughly trained in unarmed combat skills in the Intelligence School on Alpha, and she was eager to show Rafaella that she was not a complete idiot.

She had been prepared—then—to like Rafaella, knowing

the slight, dark woman was Jaelle's partner in their travel-counseling business. Also, on her first evening in the House she had heard Rafaella singing to the harp. Magda's own mother had been a notable musician, the first Terran to transcribe many of the Darkovan folk ballads, and to make the historical connections between Darkovan and Terran music. Magda was no musician herself—she had a good sense of pitch, but no singing voice— but she admired the talent in others. She had been ready not only to like, but to admire Rafaella.

But Rafaella had been, from the first, persistently unfriendly, and when, in that first lesson, it became apparent that Rafaella expected her to be completely stupid, as clumsy as the house-bred Keitha, Magda had summoned all her knowledge of Terran *judo* and Alphan *vaidokan*. When she had twice thrown Rafaella on her back, the older woman had stopped the lesson and frowned at her.

"Where in Zandru's hells did you learn all that?"

Too late Magda realized what she had done. She had learned it on a planet half a Galaxy away, from a Terran-Arcturian woman who had trained both her and Peter in self-defense; but she was in honor bound to Mother Lauria not to say so.

"I learned it—when I was a very young woman," she said. "A long way from here."

"Yes, I remember, you were born in the Hellers near Caer Donn," said Rafaella. "But did your father permit such learning?"

"He was dead by that time," said Magda truthfully, "and there was no other who had a right to object to it."

Rafaella looked at her skeptically. "I cannot imagine any man but a husband teaching such things to a woman," she said, and Magda said, again truthfully, "My freemate had no objections."

Quite without intending it, Magda remembered a time early in their marriage—before the growing competitiveness that had destroyed it—when she and Peter had worked together in un-armed combat techniques. Rafaella scowled at her.

"Well," she said, "it is certain that I can teach you nothing more; rather, you have much to teach us all. I hope you will help me, and the rest of us as well, to learn some of those holds. I suppose it is a technique known in the mountains." And so Magda had become a second teacher of the lessons in unarmed combat. It was not as easy as she thought it would be; she had learned the techniques to use them, not to teach them, and she had spent considerable time working alone, trying to figure out how she did things. But it had given her some much needed self-esteem, and she had even, a little, managed to disarm Rafaella's unfriendliness. Until the day when she had fought for the house and disgraced them. Camilla had managed to disarm the man's anger, and they had escaped blood-feud at their door, but they had had to pay a heavy cash indemnity which the house could ill afford. Magda had been kept in bed almost a tenday after the wound, and had just been allowed up.

"Are you able to work this way?" Rafaella asked. "You do not want to break the wound open and start the bleeding again."

"Marisela said I should exercise it carefully," she said, "or it would grow stiff."

Rafaella shrugged and turned her back. "You know best," she said, and went to the corner where she was trying to induce Keitha—without much success—to relax and fall perfectly limp on one of the mats.

Byrna, wearing an old pair of trousers too large for her, wrapped twice about her waist, touched Magda's shoulder. She said "Don't be upset; Rafi is like that. She's cross because she's been teaching unarmed combat here in the House for the last twelve years, and now you come here, a newcomer, and you are better at it than she is. She's jealous, can't you tell?"

Magda was not sure, but she said firmly, "Shall we get started?" and began to do the ballet-like stretching exercises which preceded a workout. Her leg hurt, and she stopped, rolled up her trousers and looked at it. It was firmly scabbed over; she knew the pain was only the stretching of muscles gone soft while she had been in bed.

"Me too," said Byrna, groaning, "Marisela warned me to exercise all the time I was pregnant, and I was too lazy, and now every muscle shrieks at me!" She winced as her arm jostled her full breasts. "And I will have to go upstairs in half an hour and feed the little one! But I suppose I should get a little exercise, so I will get back into condition somehow."

"Come over here and work with me, Byrna," said Rafaella, "I have had the experience of working out while I was nursing a hungry suckling, and I can show you how to recover your muscles quickly. And you, Margali," she added formally, "will you do me the favor of working with Keitha for a time?"

Magda thought; of course; *as soon as I begin talking with someone who is really friendly to me*—for since the night when Byrna's child was born, she had grown to know and like the other woman very much—*Rafaella calls her away, and I am alone again.* Keitha obediently came to her, moving stiffly, and Magda said, "Try to make your whole body soft and limp, Keitha. Until you stop being afraid of hurting yourself, you will always be tense, and then you *will* hurt yourself." Keitha, she thought uncharitably, was as stiff as a barn broom; when Magda urged her to fall over, she stiffened and went down, putting out an arm to try to break her fall.

"No, no," Magda urged. "Try to *roll* as you fall. Limp—like this," she said, demonstrating, falling relaxed and unhurt on the mat, and Keitha, though she tried bravely to imitate Magda, could not repress a cry of pain.

"Ow!" She rubbed her bruised shoulders and hip. Magda was tempted to lose patience with her, but she said only "Watch how Doria does it." She looked up as some of the other women approached, asking, "Do you want to work with us?"

The other women said, with perfect politeness, "No, thank you," and went to the far end of the room, pointedly ignoring them.

Keitha is friendly, and Byrna, and Doria. For the others, I don't exist, Magda thought, and shrugged, turning back to Doria. The one thing she had not wanted was to get into direct competition with Rafaella; but somehow she had managed that too.

"Keitha, I won't let you hurt yourself," she said, trying to encourage the woman to relax. "Look, like this—" and again she let herself go limp, landing easily. After two or three more tries, Keitha, though still stiff, had lost some of the terrified rigidity which had made every fall a painful ordeal. Well a lifetime of decorous, ladylike movement was not easy to overcome.

Byrna and Doria started practicing holds together; Doria tripped and fell clumsily, and as she picked herself up, Magda, watching, realized something which she had not noticed, even in herself, until she noticed it in Doria.

"It is not so much a matter of *movement* as of *breath*," she said. "Try and visualize the center of your body *here*, and try to breathe from it." She pointed at the center of her abdomen. "This point here, your center of gravity, really doesn't move; your body moves around it. That is why methods of self-defense designed for men are not really so suitable for women; a woman's center of gravity is lower, because of a man's bony structure."

"But some women are built almost like men," Doria protested, "Rafi—she's so tall and thin—" and she looked at her foster-mother, who stopped work and listened. Magda felt self-conscious as she said, "It is not so much a matter of male or female as a matter of different bone structure; everyone must learn precisely where her own—or his own, for a man—where the particular balance point is for the body, and learn to move around it. Part of it can be done through what we call centering, in the—" she stopped and gulped; she had been about to use the Old Terran word *dojo*, still used in the Alpha Colony for a martial arts school—"in the place where I studied," she hastily amended. "You can learn this *centering* through breathing and meditation, and through physical practice, learning to move your body around this absolute physical point, wherever it is. I am taller and heavier than you are; it would be different for me than for you, and different yet for Rafaella, or Camilla—she looked around the room to see if the old *emmasca* was there. She was, but she was busy at refining the grip on a knife hilt, and seemingly paying no attention to the lesson. Rafaella, however, had stopped working with her group and had moved closer to listen, and Magda felt, again, the self-consciousness as she finished, hunting for the right words—it was not easy to find equivalents for the Terran style of martial arts and translate them into

Darkovan; she had to use the language of Darkovan dancing, for there was no other. "It is a kind of balance; you find a place where your center is motionless and your body moves *around* it, balancing on that spot."

"She is right," Camilla said, raising her head. "This I had to learn for myself, when I studied swordplay among men; it may be one reason I am better with a sword than many men. They did not notice, thinking me a man, and it is true that I am very tall and thin, but my center is still lower than a man's of my height; I had to learn to compensate for that, and the constant practice to match myself against men gave me more skill than many of them." She came and touched Doria's shoulder. "You are very thin, and your hips still very narrow—I do not think you are quite full grown yet; your balance will change as you grow, but once you have learned how to find your center, you will know how to recognize the changes."

Some of the women were moving and balancing curiously, trying to test for themselves whether what Magda said was true. Keitha said scornfully, "It sounds like that old mystical theory—that the center of a woman's body is in her womb!"

Rafaella chuckled. "Nothing mystical about it. That's exactly where it is." Keitha made a gesture of revulsion, and Rafaella added, "Ask Byrna if her balance did not change when she was pregnant?"

"Indeed it did," Byrna said, "and I still have not recovered my old balance, having carried the child so long!"

Rafaella said directly to Keitha, "Why do you think a child is carried just *there*? Because it is exactly where the body is balanced and can best take the weight of a child." She looked Keitha over with an experienced eye. "I should imagine you would carry very low—am I right?"

Keitha said sullenly, "Yes. What of it?"

"That is your trouble in movement," Rafaella said. "You are trying to brace your body from the small of your back, as a man does and you should bring your weight forward—try to stand like this," she added, readjusting Keitha with a careful hand. She looked at Magda with momentary camaraderie. "You are so tall I would judge that you carry very high, don't you?"

"I don't know," Magda said, "I have never been pregnant."

"No? Well, when you are, I am sure you will notice the change in balance," Rafaella said. "Keitha, if you bring your weight forward—look how Margali stands—you will balance more easily." She moved away, and Magda said, "Doria, will you try with me? I want to show them—"

Doria turned to her, taking the braced stance for practice, and Rafaella reached out and moved her roughly into position.

"Not that way, stupid thing," she said. "How dull you are, Doria!"

Magda drew a deep breath, and said, carefully, "Rafaella, I think Doria would do better if you were not constantly standing over her and correcting her. She is doing well enough."

"She is *my* daughter," Rafaella flared, "and it is not enough for her to do *well enough!* That is all very well for outsiders—" she looked scornfully at Keitha, "who have never been taught to believe in themselves and have to learn here what every girl should learn before she is ten years old! But Doria was brought up among us, and there is no excuse for her to be so stupid and clumsy!"

Doria was struggling with tears again, and Magda bit her lip; Rafaella was so anxious for the girl to excel that she kept Doria constantly on the edge of hysteria. "Rafaella, forgive me, but it was you who asked me to teach Doria, and I believe it is for me to say when she is doing well or not—"

"It is for you to say *nothing!*" Rafaella snapped. "You ignorant hill-woman, it is not even sure that they will let you stay among us, after what you have done!"

Magda fought twin impulses; to turn on her heel and walk out of the armory, to slap Rafaella harder than she had ever hit anything in her life. She felt again the terrifying surge of fury which had overcome her when she had fought for the house; she knew with her last grip on sanity that if she struck Rafaella now, with the skills she had learned in Alpha's Intelligence School, she would kill the woman with her bare hands. Shaking, her hands gripped into fists, she walked a little away from them.

Camilla said peacefully, "Rafaella, at Doria's age a girl can learn better from a stranger than from her mother—"

Rafaella put her arm around Doria and murmured, "Darling, I only want to be proud of you here in our own Guild-house, that is all. It is only for your own good—" and Doria burst into tears and clung to Rafaella.

At that moment the door opened and Mother Lauria looked in to the armory. Her eyes widened at the scene—Doria sobbing in Rafaella's arms, Magda with her back to them all, the rest staring—but she said only, "Is Margali here? You have a visitor in the Stranger's Room; I am sorry to call you from your lesson—"

"Oh, *she* has nothing to learn from any of *us*," Rafaella said, but Mother Lauria ignored the sarcasm.

She beckoned Magda to the door. "There is a Terran, a man, who has come and asked for you by the name you are known by here."

Magda's throat tightened; who could it be but Peter? And why would he come? Had something happened to Jaelle? "What is his name? What does he want?"

Lauria said disdainfully "I cannot remember his barbarian name. You need not meet him unless you wish; I can have the girls send him away."

"No, I had better go and see what he wants. Thank you, Mother." Magda was grateful that the Guild-mother had come herself to give this message; it was not usual for her to put herself out this way for anyone, rather than sending a message.

"Please yourself," Mother Lauria said, and went away. Magda was suddenly conscious of her hot, flushed face, her sweat-soaked tunic, her hair straggling in damp wisps about her face. She went into the room behind the armory, washed her face in cold water, stripped off the sweaty tunic and put on the fresh one she had learned to keep there for after a lesson. She laced her overtunic and was combing her hair neatly back when Rafaella came in.

She said scornfully, "Are you readying yourself to meet a lover?"

"No," said Magda struggling for composure against the rage that kept threatening to get out of hand again, "but I have a guest in the Stranger's Room and I do not want him to think that a Free Amazon must be a filthy slattern from a dung-heap, either!"

"Why are you so concerned with what a man would think of you? Is it so important to you that men must notice your beauty, your desirability?" Rafaella asked with a curl of her lip, and Magda held herself by force from answering, walking past Rafaella in silence. Some day, she thought, some day I will slap that look off her face, it would be worth whatever they did to me for it! She went down the hall to the little room at the front of the house that they called the Stranger's Room. She was still shaking with anger, ready to fling defiance in Peter's face—how dared he break in upon her here?

But seated on one of the narrow chairs, she saw a complete stranger. She had seen him somewhere before, but he was certainly no one she knew well; and she fancied he looked with surprise and disdain at her tunic and breeches, her cropped hair. She said curtly, "May I ask your business here?"

"My name is Wade Montray," he said, "And you are Magdalen Lorne—Margali, as they call you here?" He spoke Darkovan, she noticed, and very good Darkovan at that. Language tapes, the ones she and Peter had made, no doubt. He tiptoed quietly to the door, and looked into the hall. "Nobody listening, and I doubt if they have the technology to bug a room, but you can't be too careful."

Magda said frigidly, "I doubt if anyone here would trouble to intrude on a private conversation, being sufficiently busy with their own affairs. If we have to talk, by all means talk freely." Yes, she had met this man, he was the Coordinator's son, like herself, brought up on Darkover. She felt immense distaste for the suspicion in his voice; had she really once been a part of the vast paranoia of the Intelligence Service?

"I wanted to be careful not to blow your cover here, Miss

Lorne. Jaelle Haldane will be down here in a few days to talk with you, so Cholayna says, and I really ought to leave it to her. But she has her job and I have mine. I have to travel into the Hellers this winter, and I understand you were there last season. Your report's full of intriguing gaps, and I need to know more about what you know of that ruling caste—*Comyn*, is it? And you spent the winter at Castle Ardais as the Lady Rohana's guest; there's a lot you could tell us."

"There is nothing to tell, really, except what I put in my report," Magda said cautiously. "I do not suppose you are interested in the menu for Midwinter Festival feast, the names of the men with whom I danced at the Festival Ball, or the depth of snow on the day after Festival."

"Look, I'm interested in everything—absolutely everything," said Wade Montray. "Your previous reports have been very full; I'm curious to know why you filed such a sketchy one about this mission!"

"I went on leave," Magda evaded, "and I did file a report with Cholayna Ares; check with her."

"I understand, but under the circumstances, I'd appreciate it if you'd come down to the HQ and file a fuller report," said Montray. "Haldane does good work, but I don't think he has quite the grasp of the situation that you do."

He was trying to butter her up now; she recognized it with distaste. The Training Sessions had made her very aware of the techniques which men used to get on the favorable side of a woman, and she was angry at the familiar condescension. "I remind you I am on leave, and that this is my first leave of absence in six years; you have no right to interrupt it."

"Oh, I'll see that you get extra pay for breaking into your vacation time," Montray said, and Magda was resentful suddenly at the Terran idea that her wishes could be set aside by an offer of extra pay! Were all the Terrans as mercenary as that?

"I am sorry, I would rather not. What would you do if I had gone offplanet, as I would have had every right to do? Why should you assume I am required to be accessible?"

"Oh, come on," he said, and she noted that his smile was singularly sweet, "It couldn't hurt you that much to come down on a free afternoon and fill in the gaps for me, could it? For that matter, we could get you a special bonus if you would keep a log while you're here and file a full report on whatever happens in the Guild-house, we don't have a lot of data on the Free Amazons—excuse me, Renunciates, I did remember that—and if we're going to be employing them for Medic and Tech training, we need all the help we can get."

"I absolutely refuse," she said angrily, and he changed his tack.

"Have it your own way," he said. "I didn't mean to upset you. You're certainly entitled to spend your leave in peace and quiet, if you want to."

Peace and quiet! That's the last thing I would find here, especially now! Against her will she smiled at the thought, not knowing that the smile transformed her face and made a mockery of her annoyance. Seeing it, he was encouraged.

"Look, Miss Lorne, off the record—all right? I don't want to break into your leave, but why not come out of here, where we can talk without worrying about who might overhear us; we can have a quiet drink somewhere in the Trade City, and you can fill me in on what I need to know. I have a scriber with me; I can just put it into Records, or if you like, I'll keep it off the record, for my ears only. No trouble, no fuss, and then I'll leave you in peace. How about it?

Unexpectedly, she was tempted. To go away from here, out of the perpetual atmosphere of distrust and hostility, to slip back into her familiar Terran self; even the thought of a drink, or of some Terran coffee, was intolerably tempting. She sighed, regretfully.

"I'm really sorry, I wish I could," she said, smiling, "but it's quite impossible, Mr. Montray." She had slipped into speaking Terran Standard, and suddenly realized it.

"Mr. Montray is my father," he said, grinning, "I'm Monty. And why is it so impossible?"

"In the first place, even if I could go, it wouldn't do for a Renunciate to be seen sitting around in a bar with a Terran in uniform." Quite against her will, she realized that she was smiling; her eyes twinkled with amusement. "And I couldn't go; I'm pledged to remain here in the house until Midsummer, and I can't leave without permission of the Guild-mothers."

"And you put up with it? A free citizen of Terra? Imprisoned?"

"No, no," she said. "It's part of the training system, that's all. And you yourself said you didn't want to blow my cover. If I, a probationary Renunciate, went off with a Terran—well, you can imagine what they would say."

Damn what they say; but I gave my word, and I'll keep it or die trying.

He took it philosophically, and rose. "If you can't, you can't; but I warn you, I'll come back at Midsummer," he said, "and I'll get that report somehow." He held out his hand; suddenly homesick for a familiar gesture, Magda took it. She watched him go, thinking with some regret that he was a familiar voice from a world she had renounced—and now, paradoxically, found that she missed.

She returned to the armory, but the lesson had ended; a few of the women were soaking in the hot tub, but Rafaella was among them, and Magda, though her hurt leg was aching and she would have enjoyed the heat of the tub, decided against joining them. She decided to take advantage of the privilege still allowed her, and go up and lie down. For the first time she was beginning to doubt her ability to endure for the half year of housebound training.

She liked the women here, most of the time. She even liked Rafaella, or would if the woman would let her, and she liked Camilla and Doria and Keitha, very much. But it was the little things, the cold baths, the food, the stupid insistence on manual work, and now the constant friction, since that fight when she had lost her temper. She couldn't really understand how they felt about it; the man had, after all, been attacking the House. Even if she had killed him, he would have deserved it.

Could anyone, ever, completely renounce their world? Had she been a fool to try? Should she simply give it up, tell Mother

Lauria it was too much for her, petition to have her Oath, her forced Oath, set aside after all? Maybe she would not have to make that decision; maybe, when they came to review the dreadful thing she had supposedly done, they would expel her from the Guild-house and that would relieve her of the choice.

And how would I face Jaelle, then?

There was no regular noon-meal served in the Guild-house; anyone who was hungry at mid-day went down to the kitchen to find cold bread or meat, and after a time Magda, who was used still to the Terran mealtimes, and liked a light snack at noon, went down to the kitchen. She poured out a mug of the bark-tea which always simmered in the kettle over the banked fire—it wasn't coffee, but it was hot and the kitchen was cold, and her hands curved around the hot mug with comfort—and sliced bread from a cut loaf, spreading it with butter and soft cheese from a crock. It was too much trouble to slice the cold meat in the cool-room, and it was too cold in there anyhow. She sat nibbling, wondering where Irmelin was. The bread for supper was rising at one end of the table in a huge bowl, puffing up under a clean towel. She was brushing up the crumbs and rinsing her mug—one of the strictest rules, that anyone coming to the kitchen for food must leave it as clean as they found it—when Irmelin stuck her head in the door.

"Oh, Margali? You weren't in your room. I hoped you would be here," she said. "Will you take hall duty? Byrna is nursing the baby."

Magda shrugged. "Certainly," she said, and started for the hall, but Irmelin held her back, the chubby woman's face alive with curiosity.

"Are you not Jaelle n'ha Melora's Oath-daughter?"

"Yes, I am," Magda said, and Irmelin nodded. "I thought so; she is here to see Mother Lauria, and they have been closeted in her office for hours—" Her eyes widened, and she added, "I suppose Mother Lauria sent for her to discuss what they're going to do about you! I hope they let you stay, Margali! I think

Camilla was too hard on you—we can't all know the honor code of mercenary soldiers, and I don't know why we should!"

With her very kindness she had managed, again, to destroy Magda's peace of mind. Was it so serious that they would send for Jaelle from the Terran Zone? But Irmelin added fussily, "Go, now, sit in the hall to let people in, I have to knead down the bread and get it into the pans for tonight's dinner, and if Shaya will be here I want to make some spicebread."

Magda sat in the hall, listlessly plaiting the belt, and remembering against her will the last time she had worked on it. When the doorbell rang again she was braced for trouble, and when she found a man, in the green and black uniform of a Guardsman, on the doorstep, she set her chin aggressively.

"What do you want?"

"Is Byrna within?"

"You can see her in the Stranger's Room, if you wish," Magda said.

"Oh, I am glad she is up again," the young man said.

"May I tell her who is asking for her?"

"My name is Errol," he said, "and I am the father of her son." He was a very large, very young man, his cheeks still downy with the first shadow of beard. "My sister has just had a baby and she has offered to nurse this one with her own, so I came to take him away."

So soon. He is only a tenday old. Oh, poor Byrna. Her distressed look must have reached the very young man, for he said uncertainly "Well, she *told* me she didn't want to keep him, so I thought the sooner I took him off her hands, the better it would be for her."

"I will go and tell her." She showed the young man into the Stranger's Room, and hesitated, wondering what to do now; but the doorbell rang again and fortunately, Marisela stood on the steps.

"What shall I do, Marisela? The father of Byrna's baby is in there—" she pointed, "and wants to take him away—"

Marisela sighed; but she only said, "Better now than later. I will tell her, Margali; go back to the hall, child."

Magda obeyed; and after a considerable time she saw Errol coming from the Stranger's Room, carrying a thickly wrapped bundle in his arms, with the clumsiness of a man not accustomed to handling babies. Marisela, at his side, was talking attentively to him, and she left Marisela to let him out; it struck her that probably, at this moment, Byrna was in need of some sympathetic company. If anyone came to the door, they could just knock until Irmelin, in the kitchen, heard them and could leave her bread-rolls long enough to let them in!

She found Byrna in her room, flung across her bed, crying bitterly. Magda didn't speak; she only sat down beside Byrna and took her hand. Byrna raised her tear-blurred face, and flung herself, sobbing, into Magda's arms. Magda hugged her, not trying to talk. She had had half a dozen things ready to say; but none of them seemed worth the trouble.

They shouldn't have let him take the baby. It's too soon. Everything we know tells us that at this stage, Byrna needs her baby as much as he needs her! It's cruel, it's not right . . . and through the woman's trembling in her arms, it seemed that somehow she could *feel* the vast pain and despair. She said nothing, just held Byrna and let her cry herself into exhaustion, then laid her gently down on her pillow.

"He's too little," Byrna sobbed, "he needs me, he really needs me—but I promised, I didn't know when I promised how much it would hurt—"

There was nothing Magda could say; she was relieved when the door opened and Marisela came in, Felicia at her side. "I hoped someone would come to stay with her. Merciful Avarra, how I wish Ferrika had come back!" She bent over Byrna, said gently, "I have something to make you sleep, *breda*."

Byrna could not speak. Her eyes were swollen nearly shut with crying, her face blotched and crimson. Mariscla held her head as she sipped the cup at her lips, laid her down. "You will sleep after a little."

Felicia knelt at Byrna's side, took her hands and said, "Sister, I know. I really do, remember?"

Byrna said, her voice hoarse and ghastly, "But you had your

little boy for five years, five whole years, and mine is still so little, only a baby—"

"And it was that much harder for me," Felicia said gently. Her big gray eyes filled with tears as she said, "You did right, Byrna, and I only wish I had had the courage to do the same, to give him up at once to the woman he will call mother. I kept him here for my own comfort, and then when he was five years old, he had to go among strangers, where everything is different and they will expect him already to know how to be what they call a little man—" she swallowed hard. "I took him to my brother's house—he cried so, and I had to tear his hands away and leave him, and they had to hold him, and I could hear him all the way down the street, screaming 'Mother, Mother—' " Her voice held endless pain. "It is so much better—to let him go now, when all he will know is love and kindness and a warm breast—and if his foster mother has nursed him herself she will love him so much more and be gentler with him."

"Yes, yes, but I want him, I want him—" Byrna sobbed, and clung to Felicia; Felicia was crying now, too, and Marisela drew Magda gently out of the room.

"Felicia can help her now more than anyone else."

Magda said, "I should think she would make it worse—isn't it cruel for them both?"

Marisela put her arm round Magda and said gently, "No, *chiya*, it is what they both need; grief unspoken turns to poison. Byrna must mourn for her child, even though it is like death. And she can help Felicia, too; Felicia has not been able to cry for her son, and now they can weep together and be eased by knowing the other truly understands. Otherwise they will both sicken with the first sickness that comes near them, and Byrna, at least, could die. Give the Goddess her due, child, even when her due is grief. You have never borne a child, or you would know." She kissed Magda's cheek and said gently, "Some day you too will be able to weep and be healed of your grief."

Magda watched Marisela go down the stairs, staring after her in amazement. She supposed Marisela was right—she had come to respect the woman, she knew as much as most Medics, in her own way, and she supposed she had a good grip of the psychology of the matter; everyone knew that stress could cause psychosomatic illness, though she was surprised that Marisela would think of it. But certainly Marisela was wrong about *her*, she had no particular sorrows, she had nothing to cry about! Anger, yes, enough to burst with it. Especially lately. Resentment. But grief? She had nothing to cry about, she had not cried more than three times in her adult life. Oh, yes, she had cried when she had been hurt and Marisela had stitched up her leg without anesthetic, but that was different. The idea that she might have some unknown and hidden grief for which she should be healed, struck her as the most fantastic thing she had ever heard.

There was the sound of a mellow chime; the bell warning women who had come in from working in the city that dinner would be served in an hour and that they should finish bathing, and changing their garments. Magda went upstairs, still frowning. She passed Byrna's closed door, hoping that the woman was sleeping.

I was sad, but not enough to cry about it, when I realized that Peter had not managed to make me pregnant; and then, when we separated, I was glad not to be burdened with a child. And especially now—what would I do here with a child? I could now be in Byrna's predicament. The idea is ridiculous. Marisela could use some sensible Terran training, both in medicine and psychology.

As she stripped off her clothes to change for dinner, she sighed at the thought of confronting Rafaella again at the meal, or meeting the unspoken resentment of the others. But there was nothing she could do about it, and she would not hide in her room and let them know that it bothered her. She was a Terran; and even more than that, she was a Renunciate, and she would somehow manage enough strength to get through this time.

Chapter 2

Inside Mother Lauria's office the women heard the chime, and Mother Lauria sighed. "I must go, Jaelle; it has been good to have this talk with you. You will spend the night in the House, won't you? It does not matter which women you and I think are qualified, I cannot require of any woman that she leave her sisters and take employment among the Terrans. She herself must wish to go."

"But we cannot let any woman go who wishes," Jaelle insisted, "They must be the right ones—we do not wish them to fail and the Terrans think us silly women, think the women of Darkover are all fools and children who hide behind the safety of home. And they should not be lovers of women, for that is a thing the Terrans despise. I would like to consult with Magda about it—"

"The very last one. She is new to us—"

"She has been among you three moons; as long as I have been among the Terrans."

"But the women in the House do not know she is Terran; they would wonder why I consulted with a newcomer, instead of a veteran who has been among us for years. I might as well ask Doria!"

"You could do worse; children's eyes see clearly," Jaelle said. "I am sure Doria knows our faults and weaknesses as well as I do myself. But before we make any decisions I would like to speak privately, at least, with Magda. I can see that you would not want to call her out from the rest and consult with her—"

Jaelle felt troubled; she had not known Magda had chosen to be anonymous here. But Mother Lauria had risen, firmly, and the interview was over.

Jaelle went and washed her hands in the downstairs scullery. Her home, she realized, and for the first time since she was eleven, she had no designated place here! She went into the dining hall, and after a moment, there was a cry of "Jaelle!" and she was caught enthusiastically in Rafaella's arms.

Jaelle returned the hug and laughed gaily at her partner's surprise.

"You didn't expect to see me, did you? How is the business?"

"As well as can be expected, when you have been away so long," Rafaella returned, half teasing, but with a note of real resentment. "To work among the *Terranan*! How could you?"

"I am not the first, and shall not be the last," Jaelle said quietly. "You will hear about that in House Meeting. And you have left the House to live with a freemate, more than once, have you not?"

"But with a *Terranan*!" Rafaella's vivacious face grimaced in fastidious distaste. "I would as soon couple with a *cralmac*!"

Jaelle laughed. "I have never lain down with a *cralmac*," she said, "and know nothing about their bed manners, though in the mountains I once knew a woman who said she slept every night between her two female *cralmacs* for warmth, so they cannot be as disgusting as all that! But, seriously, Rafi, the Terrans are men like other men, no more different from us than hillmen from lowlanders; differing from us only in language and customs, no more. They are far more like to us than the *chieri*, and there is the blood of the Ancient Folk in all the Hastur kin. I had not thought to hear you, of all people, repeating superstitious nonsense about the Terrans, as if they had horns and tails!"

Perhaps, she thought, it is no miracle that Magda chose to be anonymous here, if this nonsense about the Terrans is common to the women here! I thought the sisters of my own Guild-house had better sense! But she let it pass—she had no wish to quarrel with her friend and partner.

"But tell me about the work and how it goes, Rafi. You could take someone else into partnership for a time, you know, while I am away, or even permanently—there is enough work for three, most years. And how is my baby, Doria?"

"Your *baby* is in her housebound time, and will take the Oath at Midsummer," Rafaella returned dryly. "If she can manage to be admitted—she is at the very worst stage in growing up— every time I say a word to her, she bursts into tears! I am really ashamed of her. The business? Well, I have had to turn down two caravans, but we are doing well enough. There is a new maker of saddles—"

"Can you find somewhere else to talk?" asked a tall, slender woman, hair gleaming faint gold, a long apron pinned over her trousers. Rafaella took her friend's shoulder and shoved her along so that the woman could set plates and bowls along the long table. "Our sister Keitha, she came to us at the same time as your oath-daughter Margali," Rafaella said, and turned to introduce Jaelle. Women were streaming into the hall now, singly and in little groups, standing about and talking, finding seats, amid clattering dishes. There was a good smell of hot bread fresh from the oven, and Jaelle sniffed, appreciatively.

"Real food! I'm starved!"

"What's the matter, don't the Terrans feed you? You've certainly gained weight," Rafaella said, raising her eyebrows. "Or is there another reason for that, Shaya?"

Jaelle smiled at the pet name, given her in this house when she was younger than Doria, but drew a little away from Rafi; she didn't want to talk about that yet.

And yet if I had a child, I could keep it and raise it myself with Peter's help, I would not need to face the fact that it might be a son whom I must give up when he was five years old. I have always felt that Amazons should not have children; there are enough unwanted girls whom we can take into our homes and our hearts, as Kindra took me.

But I was not unwanted. Mother—mother loved me, I think, though I cannot remember her at all. Sometimes, in the dreams I have been having under those damned machines, I think I remember her a little. And Rohana would gladly have fostered me. Yet I chose to come here . . .

Magda, coming into the dining hall, felt a sudden wave of dismay and distress, and stopped hesitantly on the threshold. What was happening to her? She was having peculiar small hallucinations all the time now. Was she losing her mind? She looked around the room, saw Rafaella by the fireplace, talking to a woman, but not an Amazon, for the woman's hair was long and coppery-red, curling at the tips. Then the woman laughed and turned her head toward the door, and Magda froze; Jaelle!

She was sure she had not made a sound, but Jaelle turned as if Magda had called her name, her face filled with delighted surprise.

"What is it, Jaelle, what's happened, why are you here?" Were they, in fact, discussing her crime? She had been told that the matter must be taken up with her oath-mother. But Jaelle said gaily, "I am not housebound, *breda*; I would have come before, but this was my first chance—I have been very busy, as you can imagine."

Magda searched her friend's eyes; there was more in them than a casual visit. The whites of the eyes seemed bloodshot, but she knew how rarely Jaelle cried. *Perhaps*—a nagging, intrusive thought, *Peter doesn't let her get much sleep.* She dropped the thought as if it had burned her. *You'd think I was jealous!*

"Mother Lauria and I have been discussing the women who can be chosen to learn Terran medicine, but I want to talk with you about that. Not here, though." The chiming of the supper bell interrupted them; Mother Lauria came in and took her seat, and Jaelle sniffed with delight.

"I am so tired of food that comes out of machines! Real bread, fresh baked—and tripe stew, if I'm not mistaken. Wonderful! Here, let's sit here," Jaelle said, seizing her hand, responding to Camilla's beckoning hand, bending to give Camilla a quick hug and kiss. "Well, Aunt, you look hearty and well, did Nevarsin's climate agree with you? Come sit by me, Margali, let's eat and you tell me everything they've been doing to you around here!"

Magda laughed. "That would take more than an evening!"

"*Breda*—" Jaelle said, startled, as if actually seeing her for the first time. "*Chiya*, what have they been doing to you here? You *have* lost weight," she scolded, "The housebound season is hellish for everyone, I know, but you mustn't let it affect you this way!" Then Jaelle took Magda in a close embrace, long and hard and deliberate.

Magda could not see the tears Jaelle hid against her shoulder, though she sensed that Jaelle was clinging to her as if for comfort. But she also saw Janetta's knowing smirk, and sensed that all eyes were on them. She pulled back a little.

"Don't, Jaelle!" She could not conceal her unease; the room seemed suddenly full of a ringing silence, as if all the noises of dishes and silverware were echoing in a vast, vaulted chamber from many miles away.

Jaelle withdrew, frowning. She asked, almost formally, "Have I wronged you somehow, oath-daughter?"

"Oh, no," Magda said, shocked; lowering her voice, she murmured, "It's only—I didn't want—I mean, everyone in the Guild-house already believes I am your lover . . ." her voice trailed off. She was half expecting Jaelle to reply sensibly, "What does that matter?"

However, Jaelle only murmured, "I see," and sat down as if nothing had happened. But her look sent a chill through Magda; it was the same look Jaelle had given her that first night, when Jaelle had rescued her from the bandits bent on rape; icy, detached, verging on contempt. The next moment, though, it was gone and Magda was wondering if she had imagined it, as Camilla and young Doria were hugging and kissing Jaelle and trading around so they could all sit together around the corner of the table.

Jaelle said over Doria's head, "This is my baby, Margali; she was no more than three when I came here as a fosterling, and she has always been my pet and plaything—and now look at her, all grown up and ready for the Oath! I'm so proud of you, *chiya!*"

Doria glanced at Magda with a tiny shared grin, and Magda thought, *she hasn't seen us shaking all over at Training Sessions or she wouldn't be so proud of us! Thank heaven there won't be one tonight; I couldn't stand it, in front of Jaelle!* Or, she wondered, was there? Tripe stew usually appeared on the nights of Training Sessions or the almost equally frightening House Meetings. She had never lost her distaste for tripe stew; as the dish passed, she shook her head, passing it to Jaelle. Jaelle stared.

"Really? It's my favorite and I'm starved for it! Well, the less there is for you, the more for the rest of us!" She helped herself liberally. "Sisters, you'll never appreciate the food here until you have to try to eat what the Terrans call food!" She was exaggerating, almost a burlesque.

"You can have my share, and welcome," Magda said, trying to hide her bitterness. Here was Jaelle, home, feasting and laughing and enjoying herself as if she'd been locked in solitary confinement on bread and water. While in the Terran Zone Jaelle had fifteen choices at every meal, and didn't even have to help cook them, music from several different planets, all the books ever written, rounds of parties and visiting among Base personnel—as Peter's wife she would be required to attend most of the official functions—sports, swimming (and in an indoor, properly heated pool at that), and all kinds of games and recreation. *And here I am, struggling with stable brooms, and in disgrace at that . . . and fed on tripe stew, dammit!*

Magda found a bowl of something which tasted faintly like baked yams or pumpkin—and helped herself. Then someone passed her the leftover dish, filled with some mixture of grain baked with cheese and reheated in milk. "I saved this *just for you*, Margali." Magda gritted her teeth, knowing that this was intended as a subtle insult; most of the women considered the stuff barely fit to eat even when it was served fresh, but it made its appearance on the table, because it was cheap, all too often since the House had been let in for the enormous cash indemnity by the man Magda had wounded. She told herself not to be hypersensitive—everyone knew how much she disliked the tripe stew—and helped herself without comment. But just last night, the girl who had "saved" it for her had made, just too loud, a comment about how their food budget had suffered, and why.

She was buttering herself a piece of bread when Jaelle said quietly, "You don't have to eat that *reish*, Margali!"

The word she had used meant literally, stable-sweepings; horseshit. Magda took a spoonful.

"Never mind, I like it, really, better than the tripe stew."

"You couldn't! Listen, *breda*, you're my oath-daughter, you don't have to take that kind of treatment from anybody! Not in my own house!" Now it seemed that, from the light touch of Jaelle's hand on her wrist, the woman's own rage flowed into Magda, she was filled with fury, *how dared they treat her that way!* A grain of sanity insisted in Magda that it was all very silly, she really liked the grain-and-cheese dish as well as anything else they served here, but through her own sanity she felt Jaelle's fury, a slight to her oath-daughter was a slight to Jaelle as well. Jaelle took the dish in her hand, and stood over the woman who had handed it to Magda.

"That's very generous of you, Cloris, but knowing how much you like it, we couldn't possibly deprive you of it!" Jaelle said, eyes flashing, and dumped the whole soggy mess on Cloris's plate. Magda knew—and Cloris did, too—that she had come very close to dumping it on Cloris's cropped curls. "A present— from *my oath-daughter*!" She put enough emphasis on the words that Cloris bent her head, color rising in her round cheeks, and put a fork into the mess, choking down a mouthful. Jaelle stood over her, triumphant, for a moment, then came back to her seat, where Magda was pretending to eat the baked-pumpkin stuff, and picked up her own fork.

Slowly, the tension in the room dissolved. Camilla and Doria were asking a hundred questions about the Terran Zone; they spoke a rapid-fire *cahuenga* that Magda could hardly follow, but she did sense Jaelle's anger melting away as she talked on, and after a time it was the old Jaelle, merrily regaling her friends with larger-than-life adventures in faraway places; all the little foibles of the Terrans grew and seemed hysterical.

Magda felt a stab of resentment. Jaelle wasn't telling them

anything she couldn't have told them, yet she was honor bound, oath-bound, to say nothing about it. She had made the wrong decision. If they had known she was Terran, they might have accepted her differences and blamed her less, they would have excused her blunder in the sword-fight as unfamiliarity with custom, not dishonorable negligence. She had been so proud of her own ability to pass as a Darkovan; Peter had warned her once that it would destroy her! Magda blinked back tears of self-pity, and pushed the food around listlessly on her plate. Jaelle had forgotten her, and the only two people in the house who really liked her, Doria and Camilla, were so wrapped up in Jaelle that neither of them had a word to say to her. The hall, which was large and drafty, seemed colder than ever; there was a cold draft blowing on the back of her neck where her hair used to be, she'd probably have a cold tomorrow, and these people didn't have a decent antiviral drug in the house!

She rose quietly and slipped toward the door. No one would know or care that she was gone. But as she paused on the threshold, Mother Lauria rose in her place.

"Before you all go off to your evening tasks or to rest," she said, "Jaelle will be leaving at first light tomorrow; so there will be a few minutes in the music room, if you wish to greet her, before House meeting. Remember, the meeting is obligatory for everyone tonight." Her eyes locked for a moment with Magda's, and Magda felt the old tightness in her throat.

House Meetings were somewhat less disturbing than the Training Sessions, whose very purpose, of course, was to upset and humiliate the probationers, breaking old patterns—to teach us, Keitha had said once, to be women, not girls or ladies. Keitha usually came away from them in tears, but Magda had not yet been reduced to tears, though she usually lay awake for hours afterward turning over all the things she knew she should have said, or suffered racking nightmares. The meetings, by contrast, were usually routine affairs—the last one had taken up two hours complaining that the women who cleaned the third floor did not keep the baths stocked with towels or menstrual supplies! But Magda knew that in this meeting, her Oath was to be called into question. Rafaella had all but told her so this afternoon in the armory. She knew she would never be able to face the psychological assault troops, and remembered Marisela's words, with dismay. Are they never going to be satisfied until they can get me to break down and cry in front of them all, was that what they were waiting for? Magda shoved the curtain aside and fled, running up the wide stairway, taking the steps three at a time; half sobbing, she stumbled, slid down a couple of steps, scrambled up, and gained the upper hallway, locking herself into the second-story bath by the simple expedient of blocking the door with a stool. She felt nausea rising, the very walls seemed to bulge outward around her, blurring before her aching eyes.

Jaelle found her there, sitting on the floor, clutching a towel over her eyes, swaying back and forth, unable even to cry. "*Chiya*," said Jaelle, kneeling on the floor beside her, "What is it? What have we done?"

Magda let the towel drop and for a moment it seemed that Jaelle's words, her very presence, held the bulging walls in place, forced the words into solidity. *Of course, she is* Comyn, *a catalyst telepath, an Aillord*, she thought, and irritably wondered what the words meant and where they had come from. She was battling the impulse to throw herself into Jaelle's arms, cling there and cry herself senseless, to enfold the other woman within herself, cling to her strength. . . . then inside her, a spark of defiance flared. Jaelle had the strength to face the Terran Zone's culture shock, to make jokes about it at supper, then come up and offer solace to Magda because she couldn't! She could not display weakness—not before Jaelle, of all people. She bit her lip, tasting blood in her mouth as she fought for control.

Jaelle, seeing the unfocused eyes, the beads of sweat filming Magda's brow under the clinging curls, thought quite logically that Magda was simply afraid; she knew her Oath would be challenged tonight, and, knowing what the Oath had cost Magda, she ached for her friend. But Jaelle had been a soldier before anything else. Kindra and Camilla had schooled her to hard stoicism, reinforcing the rigid strength of a desert-born woman, and the last months had been, for her, the hardest fight of her life! And Magda was not facing the machines and dehumanizing life of the Terran Zone, she was here surrounded by the love and concern of all the Guild-house sisters!

She said, with a sting of harshness meant to be as bracing as the first touch of cold water in the morning, "Margali n'ha Ysabet, listen to me!" Magda's Amazon name rang out like the clash of a sword. "Are you a woman, or a whimpering girl? Would you disgrace your oath-mother in our own House?"

Magda's rising pride grabbed that and held on to it, *I can do anything she can do, anything any Darkovan woman can do!* It gave her the strength to pull herself to her feet, and say through set teeth, "Jaelle n'ha Melora. I will not disgrace you!"

Jaelle knew, with the knowledge which she could never control, but which, from time to time, thrust itself on her undesired, that the spiteful tone was armor against total nervous disintegration; all the same, the cold tone hurt. She said icily, "Downstairs in the music room, before the clock strikes again," turned her back and added, with chilly detachment, "You had better wash your face first." She turned and went, fighting the awareness that what she really wanted to do was put Magda into a hot bath, rub her back until the tension went out of her, then tuck her up comfortably in bed and comfort her, as she would have done for Doria when the child had gotten into one of the inevitable fights that faced an Amazon fosterling in the Thendara streets from the street girls—and boys.

But Margali is a woman; my oath-daughter, but she is not a child, I must not treat her like one!

Left alone, Magda had an insane impulse to change into Terran uniform and confront them on that basis, fling their damned Oath into their faces and storm out before they could throw her out. *If I had a uniform in the building, I might,* she thought, then was glad she had not, knowing she would regret it all her life. Magda was Darkovan enough to guard the integrity of her given oath with her very life; yet a traitorous part of her self persisted, as she washed her swollen mouth, in knowing that she might be going back in the morning to the Terran Zone with Jaelle—or

without her. Either way, it would not be her fault, she would not
have given up. All the tension, which had been building to impossible heights since the sword fight, would be over. Painful as
the breaking would be, it could not help but be better.

In the music room, Jaelle and several others were clustered
around Rafaella, begging her to sing.

"Rafi, I have had no music since I went to the Terran Zone;
nobody plays there, nobody sings, the music comes out of little
metal screens, and is only sound to mask the sound of machines,
not real music at all. . . . sing something, Rafi, sing 'The Ballad
of Hastur and Cassilda. . . .' "

"We should be here all night, and Mother Lauria has called
us for House Meeting," Rafaella protested, but she took up the
small *rryl* which looked to Magda like a cross between a guitar
and a zither, and began softly tightening the pegs, bending her
ear close as she tuned the instrument. Then she sat down, holding it across her lap, and began to sing softly, a ballad Magda
had heard in Caer Donn as a child. Her mother had told her it
was immeasurably old, perhaps even of Terran origin.

> When the day wears away,
> Sad I wander by the water,
> Where a man, born of sun,
> Wooed the *chieri* daughter;
> Ah, but there is something wanting,
> Ah, but I am weary,
> Come, my fair and bonny love,
> Come from the hills to cheer me . . .

And a curious, haunting refrain in a language Magda did not
know; she would like to ask Rafaella where she had learned
the song, what was the language of the ancient refrain, to
check it against the Terran language banks. . . . but she held
aloof. Surely Jaelle had confided in her best friend how she
had found Magda in the bathroom having hysterics, they were
all waiting for her, the last to arrive . . . yet the old song recalled her childhood, her mother, who had always worn Dark-

ovan clothes for warmth in the frigid hills of the Hellers,
wrapped in a tartan shawl; the very sound of the *rryl* was like
the one her mother had played, and Magda had tried for a time
to learn the chords;

> Why should I sit and sigh,
> All alone and weary. . . .

The soft arpeggios of the accompaniment died; Mother Lauria came up behind Magda and laid a warm, dry hand on her
shoulder. Magda turned, and the old woman said softly,
"Courage, Margali." But the kindness in her voice was blurred
in Magda's ears. Magda only thought, does she think I am
going to disgrace them all by breaking down? Damn her anyhow! Mother Lauria read the defiance in her face, and sighed,
but she only propelled Magda into the center of the group,
where the women were finding seats, on chairs and benches and
on the floor on cushions.

Rafaella put the *rryl* carefully into its case and sat down
cross-legged beside Jaelle, as silence fell on them all. Mother
Lauria said, "Shall we begin? I will take the meeting myself,
tonight."

They brought an armchair for the Guild-mother and placed it
at the center, and Magda felt a renewed stab of misgiving. Usually the Guild-mothers or elders presiding over the meeting sat
on the floor, informally, like everyone else. Normally there were
House Meetings only every forty days, and the trainees were not
allowed to speak at all in them; they were gripe sessions, or serious discussions of House finances, policies, visiting hours and
work assignments.

Magda wondered if she was building up nightmares out of
nothing. After all, the woman was old and had a lame knee; she
was the oldest of the Guild-mothers and her knee would not let
her sit on the floor for a long meeting!

Lauria opened soberly, "The House has been alive with talk
and gossip for more than a tenday. That is not the way to handle
troubles, with talk and secret slander! Tonight we must talk of

violence, and other things; but first let us have this trouble in our House spoken openly, not whispered in corners like naughty children talking smut! Rafaella, you have had the most to say, let us hear your grudge openly!"

"Margali," said Rafaella, turning to look at her, and Magda felt all the eyes of the women turning to follow, "She has disgraced us; she has brought a heavy indemnity upon us, she has dishonored her steel, and she does not even seem to realize the gravity of what she had done."

"That's not true," Magda cried out. "What makes you think I don't realize it? But what would you have me do? Weep night and day?"

Mother Lauria said, "Margali—" but Jaelle had already silenced Magda with a hand on her shoulder. "Hush, *chiya*. Let us handle this."

A girl called Dika—Magda did not know her full name— said, "See, even now she has not learned manners! And it's common knowledge that her Oath was irregular, taken on the trail! She should have been questioned in a Guild-house before she was ever allowed to come among us!"

"And she sits there brazen, not caring," Janetta said, and Magda suddenly realized—distantly, intellectually—what they meant. It was a cultural reaction she was lacking. Yes, she spoke the language, had learned it as a child—but she had been separated from the Darkovans who were native to her at an early age, she did not have the right body language, the right subtle signals to show her very real remorse and guilt; they were expecting a reaction she did not know how to give, and that was why they were so hostile all the time. All, that was, except Mother Lauria, who knew she could not be expected to react quite as she should, and knew why. She understood her guilt, in their framework, but she didn't know how to show them that she knew it!

This has always been my curse; too much Terran to be Darkovan, too much Darkovan ever to be happy in the Terran Zone . . . I came to the Amazons to find my own freedom to be what I really am, but I don't know what that is, and how can I find it if I do not know what it is I must find here?

Mother Lauria said, "There has been too much gossip and too little truth about the irregularity of Margali's oath. Jaelle, she took the Oath at your hands, and Camilla, you witnessed it; let us hear the truth from your lips, before us all."

Magda listened while they told the story, mentioning that she had been traveling under safe-conduct from Lady Rohana Ardais; there were small murmurs all round the room at this, for Lady Rohana was a much-loved and respected patron of the Thendara Guild-house. Camilla told how they had administered the Oath under threat, as the Amazon Charter required, and why. Mother Lauria heard her out in silence, then asked formally, "Tell us, Margali, did you take the Oath unwillingly?"

Mother Lauria knew that perfectly well; she had been at the Council where it had been discussed in full. She gulped down her misgivings, and said, hearing her voice thin and childish under the high ceiling, "At first—yes. It was something I had to do, before I could be free to keep my pledge to my kinsman. I was afraid I would have to make promises I could not, in conscience, keep." Should she tell them, here, that she was Terran and that by Terran law an oath under duress was invalid? No; there was enough trouble here between Terran and Darkovan without her adding to that old quarrel. "But as Jaelle said the Oath to me, I—I seemed to find the words of the Oath engraved somewhere upon my heart—believe me, the Oath is now at the very center of my being . . ." Her throat tightened and for a moment she felt again that she could cry.

Jaelle's hand was on Magda's shoulder, reassuring. "Have I not told this company how Margali fought for me, when she could have held her hand, and my death would have freed her from all obligation? She abandoned the mission which meant so much to her because she would not leave me wounded, to freeze or die alone. She brought me across the Pass of Scaravel, under attack by banshees, and later brought the three of us to Castle Ardais under little more than the strength of her own will." Jaelle fingered the narrow red scar on her cheek and said vehemently, "No woman here has an oath-daughter more faithful under trial!"

"But," said Rafaella, "Camilla has told us how she first failed to defend herself against a gang of drunken bandits. And did she not kill that one who wounded you in a fever of bloodlust and revenge, rather than disciplined self-defense? I submit that she is unstable and unfit to bear steel, and that she has proved it again in this house, not a tenday past."

Jaelle said angrily, "Rafi, who among us comes to this house fit to bear a blade? Why do we have training sessions, if not to teach us what we do not know? Would you send Keitha, or Doria, to defend this house at blade's point?"

"Doria would never have struck a defenseless man who had surrendered his weapon," Rafaella began angrily, but Mother Lauria motioned her to quiet.

"What Doria would have done is not at issue. But you have raised a fair question; if Margali has learned nothing among us in her time here—"

"But," said Magda, pulling away from Jaelle's restraining hands, "I have learned—truly! I know what I did was wrong—"

"Margali," said Mother Lauria, "you will be silent until you are spoken to."

Magda sank back, biting her lip, and Mother Lauria continued, "Margali's Oath has been formally called into question; and therefore three of you, other than her oath-mother, must speak for her; and they must be from those who have been oath-bound for at least five years."

Magda felt curious calm settling over her. At least, this was the end. She had done her best; but mentally she was already returning the borrowed clothing to the sewing room, gathering her few possessions, and walking out into the ice-glazed streets of Thendara, wholly alone for the first time in her life. *I have done ine best I can. But Cholayna will have her triumph; she refused to accept my resignation. Did she know I would fail?*

But Camilla said angrily, "If you are going to call Margali's Oath into question, question mine too! I was angry, yes, furious enough to beat her senseless, but what she did was my fault, and not her own; I put her beside me to defend the House, because I knew she was a skilled fighter—and I thought, in the haste of the moment, that this was enough. I had forgotten that her skill with a knife outstripped her training; I forgot that, facing men for the first time in many moons, she might well go berserk with all the repressed rage we have been systematically raking up inside her mind in the Training Sessions."

She turned to Rafaella and said seriously, "Few of us come here with any knowledge of fighting; we learn it here, only AFTER we have learned to discipline our emotions. If I had had to face men in the middle of my own training here—I who had lived among men as a mercenary soldier—I would have killed them all, I think. I don't know where Margali came by her skill at fighting, but she has much to teach us as well as to learn from us—you yourself have seen that, Rafi, this very day you had her helping you to teach unarmed combat! She has many skills, though she is not yet fit to use them anywhere outside our training hall. I forgot how she had come to us and how she had behaved outside; it is my business to know such things, and when I had gotten over being angry with her, I realized it was my fault and not hers, and I will take full personal responsibility—" she used the formal phrase—"for the mistake which exposed her weakness."

She came and stood beside Magda; then dropped down behind her on the floor, and Magda saw the stern pride in her face. At that moment, any resentment she had ever felt against the old *emmasca* for her harshness, her threatened beatings, dissolved, never to return. The word "personal responsibility" was the one used in the most serious matters of honor, and Camilla had engaged hers in this matter.

She is my oath-sister, and she takes that sisterhood seriously—more seriously than I do myself! Magda said spontaneously, "Camilla, no! My hand struck the blow of disgrace! I should have known better, I take responsibility for it—"

"You will be silent, Margali," Mother Lauria said harshly, "I will not say this again. One more word without leave, and I will send you from the room to await the decision elsewhere! One has spoken. Two more are required."

Marisela said in her sweet reedy voice, "I will speak for

Margali. Have you not heard from this how much Margali has learned? She does not shirk responsibility, even when another has offered to assume it for her—even if she spoke out of turn, her intentions were good. Margali cannot be held to blame that she failed a test which should never have been laid on her. Yet we have, all of us, silently been holding her to blame for a tenday and more—and which of us could withstand so much disapproval from her sisters for so long, in the midst, of her housebound time and thrust, evening after evening, into the Training Sessions and all their weight of distress—and still come down among us, composed and quiet, and ready to shoulder all blame?"

She looked earnestly round the circle. "Sisters, we have all been where Margali is now—feeling like fumbling children, all our old certainties lost, and with nothing yet to put in their place. Look at her—she sits there not knowing whether we will throw her into the street to fend for herself, or make her way alone back wherever she came from—yet this is the woman who, laboring under all we have laid on her in these last days, still found it in her heart to go, unasked, to comfort Byrna. None of us here—not one, not even those of us who have borne children and had to give them up—could find a moment for our sister, because she is from another House. I speak for Margali, sisters; this woman is truly one of us and I, for one, do not challenge her Oath."

There was a long silence. At last Mother Lauria said in that curiously ritual way, "Two have spoken, but a third is wanted."

And the silence was prolonged; until Magda felt her legs gather under her to take her from the room as sentence was pronounced. Whether or not they threw her out, she would not stay under this roof to Midsummer if all of them felt her dishonored.

Rafaella stirred, and Magda braced herself to listen to Rafaella's gloating, her accusations. Instead Rafaeilla said, slowly, "In simple justice—I must speak for her myself."

For a moment Magda did not understand the words, as if the words had been in the alien language of the song Rafaella had sung.

"She fought to defend us; not wisely, perhaps, but without hesitation; she took up the blade knowing she could have died here on our doorstep, and who will fight for an oath she does not, in fact, believe and honor? She fought, perhaps, with hatred when she should have fought with discipline, but I do not think she is incapable of learning discipline, in time. More than this, I know that Byrna would have spoken for Margali if she were able to be here—I call Marisela to witness for that. Margali has given generously to all of us, including my daughter, in training hall—in a time when she needs all her strength for her own learning. Not many of us could have done this during our own training time—I know I could not."

"Nor I," said Camilla roughly.

"It is usually not required of us. We have required of Margali more than most of us have to give; perhaps instead of blaming her because she has not done perfectly, we should give her credit that she has not done worse under such heavy demands. And more than this, She has made me see something to which I have been blind—" Rafaella stared at the floor, her slender musician's hands twisting restlessly. She said at last, "She has made me see that I have been unfair to Doria, as well as to her. I am not Kindra; *she* managed to foster Jaelle in this house and still put her through her housebound time here without favoritism—and without demanding more of her than Jaelle could give. Margali has made me see that I cannot do this with Doria. I think Doria should be sent to another Guild-house for her housebound training and for her Oath." Magda saw her swallow hard, and she dashed her hand across her eyes, but then she raised her head and stared tearlessly at Mother Lauria. "I speak for Margali, and I ask, when you have considered this, that you send Doria away. I am not fit to train her; I am too eager that she should—should honor my pride, rather than her own good."

Mother Lauria looked up at Magda. She said quietly, "Three have spoken. Margali's Oath shall stand. As for Doria—I have thought of this myself, Rafaella, but I had hoped it could be avoided. She is a child of this house—"

"I don't want to go away," Doria cried. "This is my home, and Rafi is my mother—"

"But I am not," Rafaella said harshly, "You were born to my sister; so I thought I could be—impersonal with you. But I cannot; I—in my pride, I have asked too much of you. You know that an Amazon who has a birth-daughter in her own House must send her elsewhere for her training—"

Mother Lauria held up her hand. "One thing at a time! Doria, you know you must be silent here unless asked to speak! Rafi, we will talk of this later; for the moment, we have not done with Margali. Three have spoken for her, and by the laws of the Renunciatēs, her Oath must stand. But we cannot have the House torn with dissension. I will have no more gossip and silent slander; if there is anything to be said against Margali, say it here and now, and thereafter be silent, or say it before her face."

Mother Millea said, "I have no objection to allowing Margali to stay among us. I do not dislike her. But the truth is, she did bring indemnity and disgrace upon us, and I do not think she fully understands all the laws of our Charter. If Jaelle were living here, it would be Jaelle's responsibility to instruct her oath-daughter in these things. Since she is not, we might consider extending the housebound time, so that she may complete her training—"

Oh, no, Magda thought, *I couldn't take it. . . .*

Mother Lauria said, "There is precedent for that, too; the housebound period may be extended another half year if a woman has not sufficiently learned our ways to be trusted in the outside world. Still, I am reluctant to do this with a woman Margali's age. If she were a girl of fifteen, I would certainly demand it, but surely there is a better way than this."

Camilla said, "It is pure chance that it was Jaelle and not I who took her Oath; we were both present. I will volunteer to instruct her myself, as Jaelle might do."

"And I," said Marisela, and Mother Lauria nodded. She said "If any of you has an unspoken grudge against Margali, speak it now, or be silent hereafter for all time."

Magda, glancing hesitantly around the circle, seemed to hear

...da wondered if she only fancied the pain in the woman's

And behind her it seemed that Jaelle had spoken aloud, then
...gda realized with dismay that somehow she was reading
...le's thoughts, that no one except herself could hear; *Camilla
...s no less foster mother to me than Kindra—perhaps more,
...ce she had no child and knew she would have none. I love
...milla, but it is so different from the way I love Piedro. I love
...m . . . sometimes . . . at other times I cannot imagine why I
...ver even liked him. Never, never could I turn against one of my
...isters that way. . . .*

And Magda was thinking, in a desperate attempt to distance
the subject by intellectualizing it, they talked a lot about the differences between men and women, but none of their answers
ever satisfied her. She could get pregnant and Peter could not,
that was the only difference she could see in the world of the
Terrans, they did not share the most dangerous of vulnerabili-
ties. And then somehow she felt as if her whole sense of values
had done a flipflop, he had been dependent on her, and now on
Jaelle, to give him the son he so desperately desired . . . before,
she had always seen herself as taking all the risks, but now Jaelle
could bear him a son, if she would, *if she would*. . . . now he was
at Jaelle's mercy as he had been at hers; she saw it almost with
a flash of pity. Poor Peter. And then, in a flash, *was Jaelle pregnant?* Then the sudden linkage broke and slammed shut and
Magda was alone in her mind again, confused, not knowing
which were her thoughts and which came from elsewhere. She
had missed some of what Camilla was saying.

"I have gone to some lengths to prove myself the equal, or
more, of any man, but I am past that now; I can admit my own
womanhood and I need not prove it to you. Why does it distress
you to think of me as a woman, Keitha?"

Keitha cried out, "I cannot understand you! You are free of
the burden none of us can endure, and yet you choose to be
woman, you *insist* upon it . . . does not even neutering free
you?"

Camilla's face was very serious now. "It is not the freedom

unspoken fragments of thought. Marisela said quietly, "I can tell
that your grudges are too petty to speak, in the light of this—is
it true? I think Margali is an extraordinary woman, and one day
we will all be proud to claim her as one of us."

Janetta, one of the younger women who had not been allowed to speak for Margali—and Magda had not expected it, for
Janetta was the lover of Cloris, who had created the crisis over
the leftover dish at supper—said thoughtfully, "I think some of
us have forgotten what it was like to go through training. Rafi is
right; I couldn't have done it, but it wasn't asked of me. But I
think maybe we expected too much of her, because she was
Jaelle's oath-daughter."

The third of the Guild-mothers, who had sat silent through
the entire proceeding—Magda remembered hearing that she
was a judge in the Court of Arbitration, and wondered if that
was why she had taken no part in the affair—said in her rusty
old voice, "I think there is a lesson for all of us in the way we
have been behaving; none of us is more than flesh and blood,
and we must not ask more of a sister than we would be willing
to endure for ourselves. That is true of Rafaella and Doria as
well as Margali."

Rafaella had been leaning against Jaelle's shoulder; she
turned around and held out her hand to Magda. She said,
"Janetta is right; I had forgotten, and I was angry with you this
afternoon because you made me see what I was doing to Doria.
I—I don't want to lose her. But for her own good, I see now that
I must leave her training to others. Will you forgive me?"

Magda took the hand Rafaella gave her, feeling embarrassed.
"I ought to have put it more tactfully. I was rude—"

"We were both rude," said Rafaella, smiling. "Ask Camilla
sometime what I am capable of—" she raised her face, laughing,
to the old *emmasca*. "When we were both in training together,
we drew our knives on one another! We could both have been
sent away for that!"

"What did they do to you?" Magda asked, and Camilla
chuckled, pressing Rafaella's shoulder.

"Handcuffed us together for ten days. For the first days we

did nothing but fight and scream at each other—then we discovered we could do nothing without the other's help, and so we became friends. They do not do that any more, not in this House—"

"But then, we have not had any two trainees draw knives on one another since then," Mother Lauria said, smiling as she overheard them. "But we have not yet learned all we can from this affair. It is still painful to speak of it; but we must speak of it *because* it is painful. Keitha, your Oath has not been called into question, you are not here on trial, but tell us, Keitha, why, after Margali had wounded the surrendered swordsman, you were heard to declare that we should have killed them all?"

Magda had to admire the old woman's skill as a psychologist. She felt the pressure lifted from her shoulders, yet she did not feel Keitha was being attacked in her stead; only challenged, as usual during Training Sessions.

Keitha took time to frame a reply, knowing it would be torn to shreds before the words were well out of her mouth. Finally she said, "He had no right to follow me here—he would have killed some of you, killed Camilla certainly, dragged me back unwilling, raped me—by the Goddess," she burst out, and Magda could see that she was trembling, "I wished then that I had Margali's skill with a blade, so that I could have killed him myself and not put my oath-sisters to the trouble!"

"But," Camilla said gently, "the men with him were only hired swords, and they followed the code of the sword; when he was himself felled, they surrendered at once. What is your quarrel with them, oath-daughter?"

"A man who hires out his sword to such an immoral purpose—does he not then forfeit protection? If not of men's laws, at least of ours?"

Rezi said angrily, "I think Keitha is right! Those men who fought alongside her husband agreed to what he was doing, they would have served their own wives the same—how do they deserve to be treated better than he?"

Camilla's soft voice—so feminine, Magda suddenly realized, in spite of her lean angular body and abrupt manners—came

quietly out of the dimness in the shadow of the r
men see that we women cannot abide by civiliz
havior, they will turn all the more quickly agains

"Civilized rules! *Their* rules!" Janetta sounde
Mother Lauria ignored her.

"Keitha, was it those men you hated? Or was it
wished to see punished in them?"

"It is Shann I hate," she said in a low voice, "I v
him dead before me—I wake from dreams of killin
there no one here who has ever hated a man?"

"I think there is no one here who has not," said Rafa
Mother Lauria went on as if she had not heard. "Hate c
shackle stronger than love. While you hate, you are still
to him."

Camilla said quietly, "Hate can lead you, if you cannot
the one your hate, to turn upon yourself. I sacrificed my
womanhood so that no man could ever desire me again. It v
hate cost me this."

Magda remembered the grim story Camilla had told, an
wondered how the old woman's voice could sound so calm. Keitha flared, "And is that such a price? You don't know what you
have been spared!"

Camilla's voice was hard. "And you don't know what you
are talking about, oath-daughter."

"Is that not why you became a mercenary? To kill men in revenge for the choice they cost you?" Keitha asked.

Jaelle said into the silence, "I have known Camilla since my
twelfth year; never have I known her to kill any man needless,
or for revenge."

"I fight often at the sides of men," Camilla said, "and I have
learned to call them comrades and companions. I hate no man
living; I have learned to blame no man for the evil done by another. I have fought, yes, and killed, but I can admire, and respect, and even, yes, sometimes, love where love is due."

"But, you," Keitha said, "*you* are not a woman anymore."
Camilla shrugged slightly. "You think not?" she said, and

you think it, oath-daughter," she said, holding out her hand to Keitha, but Keitha ignored it.

"It is easy for you to be sentimental about womanhood," Keitha cried, tears running angrily down her face, "You have nothing more to lose, you are free from the desire of men and from their cruelty, you can be a man among men or a woman among women as you choose, and have it all your own way—"

"Does it seem so to you, child?" Camilla took Keitha's hand gently in hers, but the younger woman wrenched it away in angry revulsion. Camilla's face twisted a little, as if in pain.

"Can I really be a woman among women? You are not the first who has refused to accept me as one of you, though it does not often happen in my own House. Perhaps men are a little kinder; they accept me as a comrade even when they know I have nothing to offer them as a woman, they defend my back and offer their lives for mine by the code of the sword. My sisters here could do no more. Yet I am all too aware that I am not one of them."

Keitha, savage in aroused hatred, said viciously, "Yet you sit here and dare to boast of your comradeship with our tormentors and oppressors!"

"I was not boasting," Camilla said quietly, "but it is true that I have come to know men as few women have the chance to know them. I no longer want to kill them all for the vileness of a few."

"But doesn't everyone here have a tale to tell, of men worth nothing but our hate? I am filled with it—I will never be free of it—I want to kill them, to go on killing them, but I would be more merciful than they, I could kill them cleanly with the knife where they kill and torture, enslaving the body and the soul—I will never be free of it until I have struck down a man and seen him die—"

"Is that why you came here, Keitha?" asked Marisela gently, "to learn to kill men?"

Mother Lauria said "A man? And any man will do?"

"Are they not all the same in their treatment of women?" Keitha demanded.

Mother Lauria looked round the circle. "Here sits one," she said, and her eyes came to rest on Jaelle, "who has said the same thing so many times that their sound is a permanent echo within this room; yet she has taken a freemate and dwells with him outside the Guild-house. Jaelle, can you talk to Keitha about men, and whether they are all the same?"

Magda could feel Jaelle's agitation, like a living presence, though Jaelle was silent and did not move. Finally she said "I do not know what to say, Mother, I would prefer not to speak yet—"

"Is that because you need it, perhaps, more than the rest of us? You know the rules; none of us may spare ourselves, nor ask our sisters to speak of what we will not share—"

But Jaelle looked steadily down at the rug, and Mother Lauria shrugged. "Doria?"

The girl giggled nervously. She said, "I have never known any man well enough to love him—or hate him either. What can I say?" She turned to Jaelle and said, "You were the last woman I would ever expect to take a freemate! You had said so often that you wanted nothing of men—"

Mother Lauria looked at Jaelle so long and intently that the younger woman said, "Don't—I will speak." But then she was silent for a long time, so long that Magda actually turned to look at her, to see if she was still physically present there. At last she said, "Men—are all the same—just as, in a way, women are all the same. Each man is different, yet they all have something in common which makes them different from women, I don't know what it is—"

There was a round of giggles and laughs all round the circle, and the tension slackened a little, but Jaelle said, distracted, "I don't think that was what I meant. I have lain with only this one man. I like it—I suppose he is not much different from Keitha's husband—better mannered, perhaps; they have laws in the Terran Zone, no man may lay violent hands on his wife, no more freely than on any other citizen. But I would have to ask some woman who has had many lovers whether they are all the same in this way—"

Rafaella said with a faint laugh, "It is a common illusion of young women that men are all different from one another," but then she said into the laughter from the rest, "No, seriously; no man is like another, but they are not so different, either."

"In the Terran Zone, a woman is not her freemate's property, not in law," Jaelle said, "but there is something in a man which seems to drive him to *possess* . . . I never knew this existed before." She shook her head, and her hair, the color of a new-minted copper coin, cascaded around her shoulders and her face, gleaming in the firelight. "In intimacy—the mind—it is raw—I don't know—" she said half aloud, running her fingers through her hair, shaking it into place with a gesture of pride and defiance.

And suddenly it seemed Jaelle was at one end of the room and all her sisters were at the far end; Magda knew it had never been there before between Jaelle and her sisters, but it was there, a gulf wider than the abysses between the stars; she thought, *I could get up now and proclaim myself a Terran and I would be less alien than Jaelle at this moment.* Jaelle was far away, alien, alone, with nothing save her pride and her flaming hair and the word, *Comyn,* which echoed softly in Magda's mind, echoed from all over the room. *Comyn.* The very word was like a solid wall which separated Jaelle from the only family she had ever known.

They had known of her blood, of course, knew that Lady Rohana was her close kinswoman; but never in all these years had Jaelle spoken any word or given any hint that she cared for her *Comyn* blood; her red hair seemed no more than an accident of birth. Now it was in the room with them, and Magda, looking at the faces which were suddenly those of strangers—and she knew that she saw them through Jaelle's eyes—sensed fear; a wary fear reserved for gods, not men; for *Comyn,* aliens, outsiders, rulers. . . .

For this moment, Jaelle was an outsider, not a cherished sister, and they all knew it. Trying to break that frightening silence, Magda turned and took Jaelle's hand in her own. She said, "I think it is a game they like to play with us; possession. They like to think they own us; they know they do not and it makes them insecure. Women do not—do not suffer so much from separation as men do. Perhaps we should not blame them so much for trying to pretend they own us. It is their nature. They have nothing else."

"Their nature!" Felicia spoke from the shadows, her eyes still swollen, her voice husky. "Are we not to blame them for possessiveness, when I have seen my son torn from me, sobbing, screaming my name—" she turned on Lauria, in shaking anger. "Their nature! Does their nature demand that they shall have command of the world, of their women and their sons, that they and they alone have a right to immortality through their children? What kind of world have they built, where a woman must give up her sons, to be taught to fight and kill as a sign of manliness, never to weep, never to show fear, to instill into his nature the need to *possess*. . . . to possess his women and his children, to make him into the kind of man from which I fled— is it not in my nature, too, to desire my sons? And I am denied this here among you—" She put her face in her hands and began to cry again, heartbrokenly.

Janetta flared, "Would you have your sons grow up among us, then, to turn on us and try to possess us when they are grown?"

Rafaella snarled, "There should be a better way than to return them to that very world, to be made into the kind of men we hate! Perhaps, if they were reared among us they would be different—"

"They would still grow to be *men*," Janetta cried, "and they do not belong here in the Guild-house!"

Mother Lauria raised her hands, trying to impose silence, but the clamor grew. Magda was thinking, almost in despair, not knowing whether the thoughts were hers or another's, *We give up our sons because that is all men want of us. Perhaps what they are trying to do here is hopeless and unnatural. . . .*

Jaelle said into a sudden silence, "I have thought—sometimes—I would like to have a child. I have—have thought some of you foolish for allowing yourselves to become pregnant." She folded her hands in her lap to keep from wringing them. "But how do you know? The Oath says—we must bear children only in our own time and season. But how do you—how do you *know* whether it is your own wish, or—or only a wish to please *him*?"

"If you had borne two or three children," Keitha said with great bitterness, "you would know."

"Would you?" Rafaella asked, and Magda felt the confusion and dismay, Rafaella had borne sons and given them up, and she was torn apart with Felicia's misery . . . *how do I know all this?*

Cloris said, "Do we not spend all our time here learning to know our own minds and our own wishes from what men expect of us?"

"No," Jaelle said. "There's no way for ordinary minds to know, they can teach that only in the Towers—oh, there's no talking to you, you don't even have *laran*, how can you know?" And suddenly Magda realized again that Jaelle had not said this aloud, that she had flung no more at Cloris than a strangled "No—" and stopped, shaking. Marisela leaned over and took Jaelle's hand, a firm clasp that silenced the red-haired woman. Magda too was held silent, hardly hearing what Mother Lauria was saying:

"You have given us another important thing to consider; how do we know when we do our own will, or the will of another whose approval is important to us?" She went on talking, but Magda was no longer listening, and heard only snatches of the rest of the House Meeting. One of the women said ". . . if we all chose never to bear children, and if all women were as we were, then should we be as extinct as the *chieri*, the desire of a woman to bear is as inborn as the desire of a man to engender," and Janetta said in protest, "That is not a true desire from within us, it is a desire we have been told we must have! I have never known a man, I never shall; I do not feel it is right that a Renunciate should renounce men and their world and their property, and continue to lie with men, to love them, to bear them children for whom we must take these wretched compromises! If we have given up men's rule, cannot we give up the power over men which comes from lying with them?"

Marisela asked gently, "Would you have us all lovers of women, Janetta, as some men say we are?"

"And why not? At least I will never bear a child to be snatched away into the world I have renounced and made into the kind of man I hate!"

"Yet I would not want to live in a house without children," someone said. "Life would be worse without such as Doria, and Jaelle who was fostered among us—and the House is empty—" Magda could feel Felicia's awful grief for her child, and Marisela's memory of Byrna's baby. . . .

Mother Lauria said gently, "The wish for children is after all a natural desire, and cannot be dismissed as something born of man's pride alone. That can be destroyed quickly enough by ill treatment, sometimes even in men it can be destroyed. There are men with no desire for women, and I think that sad, too. This is part of what we share with men, too; the wish for children, our immortality, companions for our old age, or even, like our little Doria, little ones to cherish and care for and watch them growing to womanhood among us—"

"And for that selfish desire," Janetta argued, "you would bear a child into a world which enslaves women and corrupts men to go on enslaving them?"

Magda found a curious picture floating in her mind; a woman, beautiful, queenly . . . chained, hung about with heavy chains that hindered her, weighed her down . . . the image shattered; was she hallucinating again?

". . . but you had a choice, Felicia; you could have kept your son, by living outside the House, or even with your son's father."

"It seemed I could not bear either choice," Felicia said, shaking, "I could not bear to leave my sisters. Yet no woman can teach a man to live as a man. A man who could live by our code would be an effeminate, never at ease anywhere—I would not condemn my son to such a fate."

"Yet if we despise the way men live," said Mother Lauria, "Is it right to allow them to bring up our sons to be more of that kind of men?"

Keitha said, "I would prefer a man to be effeminate rather than to be masculine at the cost of all decency and consideration."

Mother Lauria said quietly, "Some day, perhaps, there may be another answer for us. But the world will go as it will, not as you or I will have it. May the Goddess grant that some changes come in our lifetime; yet we, who are changing the world, will always suffer for it. I do not think your suffering is wasted—nor Keitha's, nor Camilla's, nor Byrna's—every one of us is suffering to show the men of the Domains that perhaps we would rather suffer than live by their rules. And yet if men and women are to live forever barricaded from another, how then shall the human race go on?"

Marisela said slyly, "Perhaps as they say the Terrans do it— with machines," and the room broke up into an uproar of laughter; even Mother Lauria laughed. Only Magda did not laugh; she was not intending to tell Mother Lauria about the worlds where that was actually the normal procedure. The women began unwinding stiffened legs, rubbing cold hands over the fire: they clustered in small groups, talking softly, while some of the others went to the kitchen, bringing back a huge kettle of hot cider and plates of cakes and sweets. Magda dipped up a cup of the hot, spicy drink and stood by the fire, separated from the others. Camilla, Rafaella and Jaelle were clustered near the fire; the moment of alienation Magda had seen, when Jaelle seemed suddenly apart from all of them, was gone as if it had never been. Magda wondered if she had imagined it. Mother Lauria came, leading Doria by the hand, and gestured Rafaella away, and Jaelle, looking up, signalled Magda to join them. She took up a plate of the crisp little fried cakes which always made their appearance on these nights, and went over to Jaelle.

"Where is Camilla?"

"She went to speak with Keitha," Jaelle said. "That is a bad situation, Margali; Camilla is her oath-mother, there should not be so much hostility between them."

"I cannot imagine what has caused it," said Mother Lauria, joining them, with Rafaella and Doria at her side. "I thought you would like to know, we have settled it that Doria shall go to Neskaya for her training—"

Fine, Magda thought, *one more friend gone!* Doria hugged Magda shyly.

"I'll miss you, Margali, and Keitha,—I don't want to go away," she said tearfully. "This is my home, but—but—"

"But everyone leaves her home for training, and you may not be different," Jaelle said, "Remember, Kindra made me spend half a year with Lady Rohana at Ardais, so that I might know for certain what the life was, that I was renouncing—so that no one could say I had renounced it without a clear idea of the choice I was making. At least you, Doria, are going to another Guildhouse. I know many of the women in Neskaya—you will find many friends there, and they are all your sisters, after all."

Behind her, Magda heard Rafaella ask, "But what can Keitha possibly have against Camilla? Surely not just that she is an *emmasca*, neutered—she could not possibly be as cruel or bigoted as that, could she?"

"I do not think it is only that," said Jaelle. "Camilla is a lover of women; she has been kind and affectionate with Keitha, and possibly Keitha has misunderstood her affection—"

Magda's face burned, though rationally she knew the words were not directed at her, neither woman knew anything about the moment when she had kissed Keitha, in her delirium after being wounded—how could they? And she was sure Camilla had not told either of them of the encounter where she herself had rebuffed Camilla.

"Keitha is a *cristoforo*," said Rafaella, "and they are as bad as the Terrans on that subject. But Camilla is not the type to press her wishes where she is rebuffed, even gently. Certainly Keitha does not think of Camilla as a danger to her, does she? Margali, you know her as well as anyone here, what does she think?"

"I don't know what Keitha thinks," Magda said, "I don't even know what I think myself. But if Keitha cannot see that Camilla is a good and honorable woman, then it is certainly her loss."

"But there cannot be hostility between a woman and her oath-mother," said Rafaella, "it is un-natural and wrong. Something must be done about it!" She hovered with her hand over the plate of sweet cakes, then shook her head, laughing. "I have eaten too many already, I am as greedy as if I were four months pregnant! Jaelle, are you spending the night in the house? You surely can't go back through the streets of Thendara at this hour, can you? And listen," she added, pausing, and they could hear the violence of sleet against the windows, the wind that hurled itself incessantly around the corners of the houses in the street.

"I like hearing it," said Jaelle, though Magda shivered. "In the Terran Zone, we are so insulated from the weather, we never know whether it is snowing or the sun is shining—"

"If you are staying, would you like to sleep in my room? They moved Marisela out because she had to come in and out so often, a midwife's sleep is like a farmer's at calving season! And Devra is still in Nevarsin, so there is plenty of room there—"

"Yes, and perhaps we can have a few minutes to talk about the business," Jaelle said. "I think you may need to take a partner, after all, for the next year or two—"

"Jaelle! Are you pregnant, then? I would like to meet that freemate of yours, if he could change your mind about something like that," Rafaella said, teasing, but Jaelle shook her head. She said, "It's too soon to be sure, Rafi. Believe me, you would be the first one I would confide in, but of course there is always the possibility. In any case I will be with the Terrans for at least a year, I have given my word. There is also—"

"There is also the matter of which women to send to learn their medical techniques," Mother Lauria said, "and I will try to consult you about that, Rafaella, before we make the final decisions. Perhaps when she finishes her housebound time in Neskaya, Doria might like to go; I was thinking of sending her to Arilinn, for midwife's training. She has clever hands and she is good with animals, she might be good at that too. But not tonight," she added, looking around the room, where only a few small groups of women remained, the others having scattered. Three or four were settled down in a corner by the hearth, drinking wine, as if they had decided to make a night of it; two others were absorbed in some kind of card game; Irmelin with two of her helpers was gathering up the used plates and mugs. Mother Lauria said, "I had hoped to bring this up in the meeting, but it went otherwise and I did not want to keep you all too late. Margali, will you and your Oath-mother come for a moment to my office before you go upstairs?"

Magda had to admire the deft way Mother Lauria had singled the two of them out—*you and your oath-mother*—as if it had only to do with Magda's challenged oath. Rafaella gave Jaelle a goodnight kiss. "You had better sleep with Margali tonight; you and I always spend half the night talking, and I am sleepy." She punctuated the words with an enormous yawn. "We can talk business at breakfast. But don't stay away so long next time, love—the Terrans can't be keeping you as busy as all that, can they?"

Jaelle hugged her goodnight. "Sometime I'll tell you all about Terran clocks!"

In Mother Lauria's office, the Guild-mother said, "You have had a chance to see us and to remember our strengths, Jaelle—have you any suggestions?"

Jaelle's smile wavered. Magda thought she looked very tired. She said, "Only negative ones; I do not think Janetta would suit the Terrans—or the other way around."

Mother Lauria nodded. "It is a pity," she said. "Since Janni is clever and learns quickly, I am sure the Terrans would find her excellent at their—*technology*." She used the Terran word; there was no equivalent one in *casta*. "I think Keitha, too, would be valuable, and such learning valuable to her; Marisela is already taking her along on maternity calls—Keitha is a skillful midwife already, and with Terran training too, she could take Marisela's place here when Mari is away on Sisterhood business."

"I have never understood the Sisterhood," complained Jaelle.

The old Guild-mother smiled faintly. "Nor do I; nor does anyone who is not sworn to them, Shaya. But they go far, far back into the history of the Renunciates; some say they were the original Renunciates. Be that as it may—I do not think Keitha is yet able enough to control herself around strange men." She sighed. "We should be thinking which of our best women we wish to send for the Terran training, not only which ones are able to survive among them! It is one of the strengths of our training, that it makes us hard and inflexible, and yet that is a weakness too . . . no society which is not open to new things can grow and change as we need to do. Kindra used to say that we should learn from everything which came into our lives."

Magda said hesitantly, "Perhaps we should simply describe what the Terrans want in House Meeting, and ask which women would like to volunteer—and perhaps let one of the Terran women come here so that the—the Guild Sisters can see that Terran women are not so different." Cholayna Ares, she thought, she would understand the Amazons and the Guild-house, and the Renunciates would respect her strength and integrity. Yet Cholayna's brown skin might arouse their xenophobia. She told herself she was being silly; certainly these women could learn to respect a woman of a different ethnic group!

"That might be arranged. I myself would like to meet with some of these Terran women, Margali. Among other things—" her smile was kind. "I think it might help me understand you better. Sooner or later there must be meetings of this kind."

Jaelle said "Perhaps—perhaps you could come and visit the HQ, Mother? And perhaps—" she made the suggestion hesitantly—"invite some of them to dinner in the Guild-house and let them speak in House meeting about what they offer, and what they ask?"

Magda was glad the suggestion had come from Jaelle instead of herself; though she smiled at the thought of a regular Empire Recruiting agent here in the Guild-house. Well, why not? There were women here capable of profiting by Terran education; she could, for instance, see Rafaella as a starship captain!

"I will think about it, and that is all can say at the moment," Mother Lauria said, "though I would gladly visit there. And now I must send you both to bed."

Dismissed, Jaelle looked at her hesitantly. "You don't mind, do you? She took it for granted that as your oath-mother I would prefer to stay in your room—"

"All right by me," Magda said, remembering the many nights she and Jaelle had spent together on the trail. Alone in their room, Magda asked, "And Peter, is he well?"

"Oh, yes, very well." Jaelle had lapsed into a brooding silence, which Magda was reluctant to disturb. She found Jaelle a nightgown; it was far too long, and Jaelle looked like a child dressed in her mother's clothes. She sat on the edge of the bed, saying, "This reminds me of when I first came here. There were no children in the house, and Kindra could find nothing to fit me; I learned to sew by cutting everything down to my own size!"

"How old were you when you first came here, Jaelle?"

"Oh, eleven, thirteen—something like that, I don't remember much."

"Where were you born?" she asked.

Jaelle frowned and said curtly, "Shainsa. Or so I'm told; I remember little about it. Your Terrans have already been after me to allow them to hypnotize me with one of their machines and tell them every little thing I remember. But I don't want to remember—that's why I forgot it in the first place."

"I don't even know where Shainsa is. Isn't it one of the Dry Towns?"

"Yes. In the desert beyond Carthon," said Jaelle, clipping off her words in distaste. "I didn't have time to bathe before supper; I think I'll try and find a free tub."

She went off to the common bath, and Magda, chilly even in the long warm nightgown, crawled into bed under the extra blankets she had managed to cadge. Her feet felt like ice; she tucked them alternately behind her knees, wondering why no one on Darkover had ever invented a hot-water bottle. *Maybe I could be a public benefactor and re-invent the warming pan,* she thought fuzzily, wondered why Jaelle was taking so long—had she fallen asleep in the tub? She did not wake when Jaelle came back in the dark, crawling over her to the wall side of the bed, to lie there fighting sleep until the familiar night sounds of the

House, and the familiar scent of the mattress stuffed with sweet-grass lulled her into the deepest sleep she had known since she went to the Terran Zone.

Magda dreamed. She was downstairs in the training hall—or was it the great ballroom at Ardais where she had danced, at Midwinter? Lady Rohana was there too, but with her hair cut short like an Amazon's; and Peter was there as well, but they had to cross the pass of Scaravel before the snows began, and he kept trying to urge her to leave the ballroom with him. But now Peter belonged to Jaelle and had no right to try to persuade her this way. Finally she went out with him on to the balcony, but the balcony had become the causeway leading to the bandit stronghold of Sain Scarp, and Rumal di Scarp was there, so she drew her knife and defended the steps of the house against him, her blade moving as if by its own volition, defending Peter from his attack, and she went on, and on, disregarding his surrendering gesture, even though she knew that she would disgrace herself as an Amazon; but she didn't stop, she went on slashing and striking until he lay dead at her feet in a pool of blood. The blowing snow in the pass turned to a stinging sandstorm, and beneath the shadow of a great rock she saw the pool of blood, crimsoning the desert in the light of the rising sun, and she was screaming, screaming—

With a rush and a gasp, she woke, realizing that she was kneeling bolt upright in the bed, the covers flung on the floor, and it was Jaelle who was screaming . ... no, she was no longer sure there had been any screams at all, except in the dream whose fragments were even now fading to the shocking memory of blood on desert sand. The room was filled with pale light from the snow outside, reflecting the small green moon.

"Damn dream," said Jaelle, gasping. "I'm sorry, *chiya*. I've been having nightmares—want me to sleep on the floor?"

Magda shook her head. "I was having a nightmare too—it's my fault as much as yours. I always have nightmares after the Training Sessions."

"You too? I used to lie awake after session for hours because I was so afraid of the nightmares I got. What was yours?"

Magda groped at vanishing fragments of nightmare. "Sain Scarp. Fighting someone. A pool of blood—I'm not sure," she said though, with eidetic terror, she could see Peter's face at the center of the pool of blood.

"I was dreaming about—I think it was my mother," said Jaelle, off guard for a moment. "Awake I can't even remember her face—I was so young when she died. But I have nightmares about her. I know she died in the desert, but that's all I've ever been able to remember." Yet Magda could see the nightmare in her mind. Clear, the blood spreading on the sand, frozen horror that would not let her move. Deliberately, to break the paralysis, she leaned over and tugged the blankets.

"Aren't you too hot with all these?" Jaelle asked.

"Hot? God, no, I'm freezing," Magda said, crawling gratefully under the blankets again. She wished for hot coffee or something like it. "Lady Rohana was there too, only she was dressed like an Amazon, or there were Amazons there too, I don't remember . . . somebody was bleeding to death—no, it's gone. What's the matter, Jaelle?

"Nothing, only I'm cold after all," Jaelle said, her teeth chattering. "It's so hot in Quarters, I've gotten used to it. Here, let's try and keep each other warm." She pulled Magda close, and the other woman's body warmth was like an anchor, welcome, somehow solidifying the wavering edges of the light.

"Peter never had any patience with dreams," Magda said, finding the image floating in her mind without knowing why, "He always said no one was interested in them but Psych and Medic—if I just had to talk about my dreams, I ought to go down and find a psych-tech who would at least have a professional interest in them. Does he do that to you?"

Jaelle shook her head. "I didn't know the machines could give you nightmares, until he told me."

"But a properly adjusted corticator shouldn't bother you so much," Magda said, concerned. "You should make sure they have it properly adjusted to your alpha rhythms, of course. Who are you working with?"

"I can't remember all their names. There are so many—"

"You ought to have an office to yourself, at least," Magda said. "I spent years getting out of that madhouse down in the Co-ordinator's office; you mean, after all the time I put in getting out of that mob scene, you let them put you back there? Jaelle, as a special resident expert in languages, you deserve a private office—you have to fight for your privileges, especially being a woman, or they'll walk all over you!"

Jaelle drew a deep breath of relief; so her loathing of the crowded office with the jammed, claustrophobic desks was not simply a sign of personal failure, as Peter often seemed to think; Magda hated it too.

"You're a special expert, not a routine clerk," Magda re-minded her. "Insist on what's due you. They'll expect it and re-spect you for it." She thumped her pillow into a more comfortable position. "One thing I really miss here is a clock with a luminous dial, I never know what *time* it is!"

And that was one of the things Jaelle appreciated most; being free of the tyranny of the continual emphasis on time. She sup-posed it was one of the cultural differences that went deepest. She only said "I don't think I'd ever miss it," and snuggled under the quilt. Magda buried her face in the pillow, and Jaelle moved into the warmth of her body.

After a time they began to dream again. They were in some kind of tower, at the very top of a tower, and she and Magda were standing at opposite ends of a circle; somehow Magda seemed to look out from her own eyes and from Jaelle's too, holding up, in their arms, a glittering rainbow-colored arch, like a glittering geodesic dome . . . the word *geodesic* came into Jaelle's head, alien, but she was not really curious about what it meant nor did she wonder from what odd experience Magda had become aware of its meaning. The dome was transparent but very strong, it would protect those below who were working— it was very important work but what they were doing neither of them could quite see, though Marisela seemed to be down there working, and there was a pleasant-looking man in his forties, wearing the green and gold of the Ridenow Domain, who looked up at Jaelle and suddenly met her eyes, and for a long minute they looked at one another, so that Jaelle knew that if she ever met this man in real life she would recognize him at once. He said softly, *Are you here out of time, or astray in a dream,* chiya? and she had no answer for him. And there was another Amazon there, her face round and snub-nosed—Jaelle had seen her somewhere but could not remember her name. Something was growing under their hands, and Magda felt very proud of what they were doing. Someone said in her hearing, *Every one of us here has had to outgrow at least one life*, and Magda heard someone repeating a fragment of poetry—she knew it was very old:

> He who lives more lives than one,
> More deaths than one must die . . .

and she said fretfully, "It's bad enough to have to die once, isn't it?"

"Oh, there's nothing to dying," Marisela said, "I've done it a few hundred times. You'll get used to it."

Magda seemed to be talking to a tall man with fair hair whose face Jaelle could not see. He reminded her a little of Alessandro Li but he wasn't, and he picked up Magda bodily and carried her across a sudden, blazing strip of fire . . . Jaelle felt the fire sear Magda's feet, and tried to run to her, but the dome was slipping through her fingers. And then she was in Peter's arms, and he was holding her down, only it was not Peter, it was her cousin Kyril Ardais, and she heard herself say fretfully that she should have counted his fingers before going to bed with him. Only somehow it was not Kyril either, it was one of the bandits who had attacked them, and Magda was in Peter's arms . . . no, Magda knew it was not rape, she knew she had gone willingly into Peter's arms only now when she had left him she knew that in a very real sense he had been using her all that time, dominating her because he knew she was his superior in their shared work, and now Jaelle was going to have his child, but they were alone, trying to climb down the cliffside of a mountain, ice-steps hewed into the side of the mountain, and she was looking for Lady Rohana, because Jaelle was pregnant by one of the bandits and she was going to die in childbirth unless she could bring Lady Rohana to her in time. She was dying, she was bleeding to death on the sands of the desert, there was a blizzard with sand that cut like blowing snow in their faces, and Jaelle was lying on the sand bleeding, and yet as she twisted and screamed in childbirth, it was somehow Magda's child she was trying to bear, the child Magda should have borne Peter but she had left Jaelle to it. . . .

And they woke again in each other's arms, clutching each other tightly, the heavy blankets and quilts kicked off them. Magda pulled away, reaching for the blanket, but Jaelle held her.

"Oh, the Gods be thanked, I am here safe, here with you, *breda,*" she said, gasping, holding Magda tight, "I was so frightened, so frightened—" and she pulled Magda down close to her. "What were you dreaming this time?" And she held Magda tightly and kissed her.

Magda felt the kiss and for a moment it blended into the magical way in which she had shared Jaelle's thoughts in the dream. Then, shocked and shaking, she pulled away. What had this place done to her? She felt weak and drained and the early snow-reflected light at the window sent knives through her head. Jaelle looked up at her and the laughter died in concern. "It's all right, Margali," she said in a whisper. "There's nothing to be afraid of, you're here with me, *bredhya.*" She tried to pull Magda down again into the comfort of her arms. But Magda pulled free, stumbling, her dressing robe dragging on the floor behind her. The floor felt unsteady, bulging and rippling under her feet, and when she got into the bath and splashed her face with icy water it seemed to burn her skin without clearing her vision or cooling her fever.

Irmelin was there under the icy shower; the very sight made Magda shiver. She looked surprised to see Magda.

"Awake so early? You are not on kitchen duty, are you? Or helping Rezi with the milking?" She moved aside, and said, "I'm finished here," and picked up her towel. She stopped a moment, concerned, watching Magda clinging to the basin. "Are you ill, Margali?"

Magda thought, Yes, something is wrong with me, but she only shook her head.

"There is blood on your nightgown," said the plump, smiling woman. "If you take out the stain now with cold water, you will be doing a kindness to the women who are working in the laundry this moon."

"Blood?" Magda was still in a stupor of horror from the dream; she started to say, *but I'm not even pregnant.* She caught herself—how foolish! She bent to look; it was true. The heavy nightgown was spotted with blood.

Well, that explained part of the dream, anyhow; explicitly sexual dreams had always heralded the onset of her menstruation. The treatment she had been given in the Terran Zone, to suppress the cycles of ovulation, must have worn off. She had not been expecting it. Peter had always laughed at the sexual dreams she had at that time, saying that if she had been equally passionate earlier in her cycle, he might have been able to make her pregnant—she cut the thought off, angry at herself for remembering. She went to the cupboard where supplies were kept, and Irmelin, watching her, said, "You really do look unwell, Margali. If I were you I would ask Marisela for some of the herb medicines she keeps for such things, and then go back to bed and try to sleep."

She did not want to disturb Marisela's rest, but it was a temptation; to go back to bed, to huddle there and complain of sickness, to put it all aside. And the thing which made her feel sickest was that she wanted nothing more than to go back to Jaelle, let the woman comfort her, find the same kind of rapport she had had with Keitha after the fight, when Marisela's drug had worn down her defenses, and this time follow it as far as it would lead. But she could not face Jaelle, she could not face anyone with this thing, whatever it was; she was helpless, unprotected . . . she felt entangled, enmeshed in conflicting loyalties like spiderwebs. Her hands shook as she washed out her nightgown.

I am jealous of Jaelle. Not because she has Peter, but because Peter has her, now . . . he accused me of this once and I would not believe it.

She went back to the room, hurrying into her clothes, Jaelle sat up and watched her, troubled.

"Oath-daughter," she said. "What have I done? What are you worrying about? Did you think—" and she stopped, not able to follow Magda's troubled thoughts; the erratic *laran* she could never command had deserted her again, and she did not know what Magda was worrying about, she only knew the other woman was desperately troubled, and could not imagine why. Why would Magda not accept her comfort? Magda put on her shoes and clattered down the stairs, running; when Jaelle followed, some time later, Magda was neither at breakfast in the dining room, nor anywhere else in the house, and when she asked if anyone had seen her, Rafaella said, puzzled, that Margali had volunteered to help with the milking in the barn.

And suddenly Jaelle was angry: *If she would rather do hard work in the barn than face me and have this out together, so be it.* She sat down by Rafaella and dipped up a dish of porridge, flooding it with milk and shaking her head when Rafi passed her the honey jar.

"Very well," she said. "Let's talk about the business, for I should be back at the Headquarters by the third hour after sunrise."

Chapter 3

Jaelle was sure, now, that she was pregnant, though there was as yet no trace of the early-morning sickness. And that brought back a memory from the Guild-house, years ago. It had been before Kindra died. Marisela had said, in one of the first midwives' lectures Jaelle had been allowed to attend after her body had matured, that morning sickness was at least in part because the body and mind were in disagreement; one or the other, mind or body, rejecting the child when the other wished for it. And she would not have been surprised if this sickness had come in her confusion.

She had not yet told Peter. Part of her confused mind wondered if she was being spiteful. He wanted a son so very much. Did she take malicious pleasure in denying him the knowledge that would mean so much to him? No, she was sure it was not that.

In my heart what I want is for him to know without being told. To read it in my heart and mind as even Kyril, much as I despise him, would know. And this made her guilty again, that she so much wanted—no, *needed*—Peter to be what he was not. Yet she had rejected, with so much determination, her *Comyn* heritage. Rejected it again and again, the first time when, as a child, she had asked for fostering in the Amazon house rather than remaining with Rohana; Rohana had loved her mother and would have gladly fostered Melora's daughter. She had rejected it again, when at fifteen she had chosen to take the Oath rather than to honor the training of a *Comyn* daughter, to be trained in *laran* in a Tower, and then to marry a *Comyn* son as they decreed. They had not wanted her to renounce her heritage. She stood too near the head of the Aillard Domain—Jaelle was not sure how near; she had not wanted to know.

The Oath was specific; bear no child for any man's house or heritage, clan or inheritance, pride or posterity. As she had asked in the Guild-house: how did she know whether she wanted a child for herself, or because Peter so much wanted it? And what of a woman's heritage? Did she not wish to bear a daughter for the Guild-house, or for her mother's inheritance?

And why should she think so much about it now? Since she was already pregnant, there was not very much she could do about it. She had deliberately neglected the contraceptive precautions that the Terran Medics had carefully explained to her. A child had chosen her, even if she had not really chosen the child.

Yet, when she walked that morning into Cholayna's office, it struck her that she would very much like to confide in Cholayna.

Yet—confide in a stranger, when she had not even told the father of her child? Was this only the habit of turning to another woman for comfort or validation? She remembered that she had sought reassurance, almost permission, of Magda, before she shared Peter's bed, and had rationalized it by telling herself that she wished to be sure her friend would not feel jealous, because Peter had once been Magda's husband.

But Cholayna was her employer, not her friend or oath-sister!

"Jaelle," Cholayna said, "I am to talk this morning with one of the Renunciates, a—Guild-mother?" She hesitated, stumbling a little, on the title. "Her name is Lauria n'ha Andrea—did I pronounce that right? And I want you present as interpreter."

"It will be my pleasure," Jaelle said formally, thinking that Mother Lauria had lost no time. "But you speak the language so well I do not think you truly need an interpreter."

Cholayna said with her quick smile, "I may pronounce the words properly, but I need someone to be sure I use all of them properly. Do you know what I mean by *semantics?* Not the meaning of the words, but the meaning of the meanings and the way different people use the same words to mean different things."

Jaelle repeated that she would be honored, and Cholayna started to speak into her communicator. "Ask the Darkovan lady—" and stopped herself. "No, wait. Jaelle, would you be kind enough to escort her into my office yourself? She is known to you."

Jaelle went to obey, thinking that Cholayna had an intuitive grasp of the right gesture, the personal touch, which would make her invaluable in dealing with Darkovans. Russell Montray did not have that intuitive sense. Yet Peter would have had it, or Magda, and she thought Monty would know, or be capable of learning it. And it was her personal responsibility to be sure that Alessandro Li learned it.

Mother Lauria was in the waiting room, her hands composedly clasped in her lap, her clear blue eyes moving around the room, studying every detail.

"What a pleasant place to work, Jaelle, though I suppose the yellow lights must be a little difficult to tolerate at first." As they went into the inner office, she asked, "Is it proper courtesy to bow to your employer, as we would do to one of our own, or to clasp her hand, as Camilla has told me the Terrans do in greeting?"

Jaelle smiled, for Cholayna had asked her the same sort of question. "For the moment, a bow will do," she said. "She is well trained in our courtesy and knows that we do not offer our hand unless it is a sincere offer of friendship."

But as the two women bowed to one another, Jaelle suspected that beyond the courtesy there was, at once, a sincere liking for one another, tempered with mutual respect, as Cholayna welcomed Mother Lauria, urging her to a comfortable seat, offering her refreshment. "Can I offer you fruit juice or coffee?"

"I would like to try your Terran coffee; I have smelled it in the Trade City," said Mother Lauria, and as Cholayna dialled her a cup from the refreshment console, sniffed the cup appreciatively. "Thank you. An interesting mechanism; I would like to know how this arrived here. I still remember, when I was told that messages came over wires, looking up to watch for the papers to come swinging along the wire. It was not till much later that I realized that what traveled over the wire were electrical pulses. And yet the idea was logical to me at that time, though I know better now." She took a sip of the coffee, and Cholayna briefly explained the refreshment console, that the essence of the drink was kept in stock there and immediately mixed and reconstituted with hot or cold water as the computerized combination required.

Mother Lauria nodded, understanding. "And the yellow lights, they are normal for your home star?"

"For the majority of the suns in the Empire," Cholayna qualified. "It is rare for a sun to have as much red and orange light as the sun of your world, and many of the people who work here will not be here long enough to make it worth the trouble of adapting to a different light pattern. But if it is more comfortable for you, I can adjust the lights here to what you would consider normal." She touched a control, and the lights dimmed to a familiar reddish color. At Jaelle's look of surprise, she smiled.

"It's new; I had it done just the other day. It could have been installed all over the HQ if anyone had had the imagination to think of it. It occurred to me that if we are to have Darkovan women working in Medic, some compromise will have to be made between what is comfortable for natives to this planet, and career employees accustomed to a brighter sun. I, for instance, come from one of the more brilliant worlds, and I can hardly see in this light, so I must have a work area tasklighted for my own eyes. But this is restful when I am not reading." She added, "I imagine that your eyesight is comparatively much better. On the contrary, I suppose you have less tolerance to ultraviolet—if you had sun reflecting off snow, for instance; you would need to be much more careful to guard against snowblindness."

"I have heard women who travel in the Hellers say that this is a problem for them," Mother Lauria confirmed, "and I am sure you know that one of the major items of Terran trade here is sunglasses."

"While I can tolerate desert sunlight on my own world

without any kind of eye protection," Cholayna said, smiling, "and people from dimmer suns must safeguard themselves very carefully against sunburn or retinal burns; Magda told me that in her first week on Alpha she was nearly blinded. I have noticed that the normal lights in here are difficult for Jaelle to tolerate."

"I did not think you had noticed," Jaelle confessed. "I have tried not to show discomfort."

"But that is foolish," Cholayna said. "Your eyesight is valuable to us. There is no reason your quarters should not be wired for red light—Peter too was brought up on Darkover and would appreciate it, I am certain. It is only necessary to speak to the technicians. My own skin tones, too, are an adaptation by my people to a more brilliant sun," she added.

"That, I should think, would be one of the difficulties our people would have should they take to traveling in space."

"You are quite right," Cholayna confirmed, "and if your women work among our medical technicians, we must make some kind of accommodation, for our lights, which are even brighter in Medic than up here, may make them uncomfortable or even damage their eyes. For instance," she added to Jaelle, "I have noticed that whenever you have been in Medic, even though you have not complained, you seem to develop headaches."

It had not occurred to Jaelle before, but now she did realize it; that at least a part of her intense reluctance to go down to the Medic floors was an unconscious distaste for the more brilliant lights down there!

"This is one of the reasons I came here," Mother Lauria confessed, "I wished to see for myself the conditions under which our women, when they come to you for teaching, will be expected to work."

"It would not be difficult at all to arrange a tour of the Medical facility for you," Cholayna said. "I can ask one of the Medic aides to show you around the hospital, or it can be arranged for a day when the new trainees can come with you. We have a standard orientation program in the Empire for planetary natives being given training. There are so few Darkovan employees now that it has not yet been done, and I am afraid that Jaelle, and a few of our others, have simply had to handle the cultural changes as best they can. But of course once we begin to have a number of them, such a program will have to be implemented at once—" She stopped, glanced at Mother Lauria and then at Jaelle.

Jaelle said promptly, "I do not quite understand 'orientation program' myself, Cholayna, and I am sure Mother Lauria does not."

Cholayna explained, and Mother Lauria instantly comprehended.

"It is like Training Session for newcomers to the Renunciates; even though they have not changed worlds, it is so different a life that they must be taught how to adapt," she said. "I think it would be best, then, Cholayna—" Jaelle noticed that Mother Lauria used the Empire woman's given name easily, which she herself had not yet learned to do—"if you came to visit us in the Guild-house and spoke to our young women. Then you could arrange the tour and orientation procedures. And it might be possible to arrange a similar program," she added after a moment, "for Terran, or Empire, women who, like Magda, are to be sent into the hills and back country of our world, so that they will know how to behave, and—" her eyes twinkled—"not run the risks Margali, Miss Lor-ran, had to undergo."

Cholayna chuckled too. "That had occurred to me, of course. We would be very grateful to you, Lauria. It is not even a question of spying, but all of our women who work in such things as Mapping and Exploring occasionally have to take refuge, because of bad weather or something of the sort, in the outlands, and it is better if they know how to behave and do not outrage local opinions of how a lady should comport herself."

When Mother Lauria rose to go, they had arranged that in a tenday Cholayna should come to dine at the House, that Jaelle would accompany her, and that afterward she should talk with Marisela and the other women who had had some basic training in medical techniques. Later she would address the whole Guild-house in House Meeting, and discuss the women to be given training. As Jaelle conducted her outside, Mother Lauria said, "I like her, Jaelle. I had expected a woman from another world to be more alien."

"I feared you would think her strange, and perhaps feel reserve or dislike, because she is so very alien," Jaelle said, and Mother Lauria shrugged.

"The colors of her skin and hair? I have traveled in the Dry Towns, child; I know their coloring and the bleaching of their hair are an adaptation to the desert; it is not strange to me that a woman from a brighter sun should have a different skin color. Beneath that skin she is a woman like ourselves. A roan horse and a black can travel equally far in a day's journey, and I am not fool enough to judge her by the way the skin of her foremothers has adapted to protect her against the sun of her childhood. I was impressed, too, by the practicality of her clothing, for an active woman who must work among men."

Jaelle looked down self-consciously at her close-fitting Terran uniform. "That is strange, I still feel this clothing is not modest."

"But you were born and reared in the Dry Towns," Mother Lauria said, smiling, "and all your childhood you knew that a woman's garb was to make it easier for a man to see and admire her body. Beneath the Amazon, you are still a woman of the desert, Jaelle, as we are all the daughters of our childhood. I was born in the Kilghard Hills, I knew that a woman's clothing was to keep her from the free movement of a man's work. I admire your employer's uniform, and what you are wearing, because they so admirably allow free movement, without false modesty. I am rebelling against one kind of restriction in women's clothing, and you against one that is quite other."

Jaelle bit her lip and was silent. This was so much like what Cholayna had once said to her that she was beginning to wonder if it was really true.

"I thought I had forgotten everything from the Dry Towns." Lauria shook her head.

"Never. Not in your lifetime. You were almost a grown woman when you left there. You can choose not to remember, as no doubt you have done; but not to remember should be choice, not failure."

To return to the outdoors, they had to pass through the hallway outside the Communications office, the "madhouse" as Magda had called it. As they passed, Bethany came out and almost stumbled into Jaelle.

"Oh, Jaelle! I was coming up to Intelligence to look for you—you're needed in Montray's office, the Coordinator, that is. Something about a Mapping and Exploring plane down in the Kilghard Hills, and field people in to talk to the M & E people up here; Piedro's there too, and they want you right away."

"I will go as soon as I have escorted Mother Lauria to the gates," Jaelle said in *casta*, which she knew Bethany spoke well, and introduced the woman to Margali. Mother Lauria greeted her kindly and added, "I wished to add; we would welcome some of your associates when you come to visit the Guild-house. It is not right that women should be separated by language and customs. That is the kind of difference that matters more to men."

Jaelle thanked her, but really she couldn't see Bethany in a Guild-house, even as a visitor. She called over her shoulder to Bethany "Talk to Cholayna on the intercom; tell her I'll go right down to the Coordinator's Office."

"Right," Bethany replied, and Jaelle, frowning, went down the escalators with Mother Lauria. The old woman, frowning, said, "I can well see that ordinary women in ordinary skirts would be endangered on a device like this! Truly, your uniforms are more sensible. But, Shaya, my dear, if you are wanted you must go at once to your work; I am neither so old nor so crippled that I cannot find my way out, even from this labyrinth!"

Jaelle gave the old woman an affectionate hug for goodbye. "It is only that I am reluctant to say goodbye to you—I miss all of you more than I thought I would," she confessed.

"Then the remedy is simple, you must come back to us more often," Mother Lauria said. Jaelle stood at the foot of the stairs, watching the small, sturdy, determined woman walk away through the uniformed people on the base. She was so much herself, Jaelle thought, and here everyone seemed all alike, as if they had put on the same face with their uniforms. Yet, as she stood watching Mother Laura, she felt, suddenly, a little dizzy at the realization. . . .

Every one of the Terrans here on this base, space workers around the Big Ships out there, technicians down in Medic or up in Mapping or Communications, the port workers who looked like thronging ants from the view station high above the port where Peter had taken her one day to watch one of the ships taking off, the men and women who repaired machines or kept track of traffic on computer monitor screens, the Spaceforce men who guarded the port gates or kept order in the big buildings, even those who supervised laundry or cleaning machines or cleaned tables in the cafeteria—every one of these many people, more here on this small base than in the city of Thendara, every one of them was like Mother Lauria, a separate person with feelings and different ideas of his or her own, and perhaps if she knew and understood them as well as she knew Peter or Mother Lauria or Cholayna, she would understand that person and like or dislike him or her for what he was, not just as a "Terranan." But of course, why have I never thought of this before? She stood without moving on the escalator until a uniformed Spaceforce woman in black leathers, hurrying down the escalator, pushed her gently aside as she ran.

Jaelle looked after her. She thought, *she is a fighting woman, she would appreciate knowing about us, the Amazons, how do I seek her out and make friends with her? What kind of training would make a woman choose that life among the Terrans?* She watched the leather-clad woman out of sight, and suddenly she knew that this woman was someone she would like, wished that she could follow her on her work. . . . and at that moment it seemed that she heard an enormous babble of voices, disjointed fragments of thought, here, there, from the woman in leather, from the guard standing quiet at the gates. Even though she could not see him it seemed that she looked through his eyes as he let Mother Lauria out of the gates, and at the same time she heard Piedro demanding to know where she was, she should hurry . . . he was up in the Coordinator's office, pacing, and for the first time she saw Piedro through Russ Montray's eyes, envy for the younger man's freedom of movement, he had the work he wanted on the planet he wanted, and I am stuck here on this frozen lump of a world hanging over a desk . . . what the Coordinator wanted, she suddenly knew, was shining in her mind then, a glowing world of water and rainbows shining, and little shimmering gliders skimming over the water, and he saw his own son choosing a world where dressing like an animal in fur was real, and she looked down through strange eyes into the glare of a welding arc on some unimaginable part from the inside of one of the spaceships, and worked the arc with skilled fingers, knowing that the part was a Joffrey coil and that metal fatigue would cause it to part in some strange stress . . . all this flared and blazed through her mind in a single instant, too much for any one to tolerate at once, and the stress from high in a Tower above the port where a woman's hand hesitated over a communications device, bring the ship down now, or wait, no, half a second more, and someone scalding himself with a kettle of boiling soup up in the kitchen . . .

Then it all overloaded and Jaelle slid to the surface of the stair, collapsed and fell down half a dozen steps, jarring, unconscious, to the ground. Dimly she heard voices, concerned questions, someone pulling at her identification badge to see who she was, for the first time she understood through the eyes of the technician what the badges were for, and she saw someone hurrying down from Medic, and the immediate jangle of thoughts here, has she broken that wrist? She landed pretty hard . . .

No! No! It's too much!—Jaelle tried to scream but her voice was only a whimper, her hands went up to cover her ears but it was not sound and there was no way to shut it out. Then she overloaded and as she slid down into welcome unconsciousness she wondered what a fetal position was and why it should surprise them.

Piedro's face wavered above her as she opened her eyes. A Medic pulled him away. "Just a minute. Mrs. Haldane, do you know where you are?"

She blinked and decided she did. "Medic—Section Eight, right?" Too late she realized that he had called her Mrs. Haldane and she had decided not to answer to that name.

"Do you remember what happened?"

She took a tiny mental peek at it, and decided she did not want to talk about it—*blazing stars, the battering of ten thousand thoughts, a Medic stitching up a torn eyelid, arclight flare, murder in an angry mind*—she slammed the doors of her mind on panic and confusion. "I think I must have fainted. I forgot to eat breakfast this morning."

"That would explain it." the Medic said, "Nothing much wrong, Haldane, if she wants to go back to work it's all right—if she feels like it. If not, I'll write her a half-day clearance."

"God, I was scared," Peter said, squeezing her hand, "when Spaceforce called that they'd found you unconscious on the stairway—you shouldn't go around skipping meals, love."

"I was late," she evaded, and inside, irritation flared, *it doesn't matter to him except that it made him late for that meeting with the Coordinator! He didn't even think about what every Darkovan man would be eager to know about his wife.* And then she was confused, when he had made it clear that he cared about having a child she was angry and now when he seemed not to care she was angry again! She leaned on his shoulder, for a moment, but at the touch it came flooding back again and she straightened and drew away. He misinterpreted the gesture.

"Still feeling faint, love? We'd better stop by the cafeteria and feed you." She demurred—they were already late in the Coordinator's office—but he insisted on taking her down to the dining building and getting her a quick meal. She didn't want it, but thought, it serves me right for lying, and forced the stuff down, hoping it wouldn't come right up again. He had gone to great pains to fetch her things, from the limited lunch selection of synthetics, that he had seen her eat, and she was touched, but again she found herself carefully evading his fingertips, and after a moment she realized why.

Do I really think that if I touch him he will be able to read my mind? Where did I get that idea?

Or is it that I do not want to know for certain that he cannot?

Still, it seemed his instinct had been right. The food seemed somehow to block the enormous overload of sensation and reduce it to manageable proportions. Had she been under less tension, she might have enjoyed the visit to the Coordinator's office, high above the port with a vast view reaching from the Venza Mountains high above the city, and the *Comyn* Castle, at one edge of the sky, and at the other, a vast expanse stretching halfway to the plains of Valeron, dim and blue at the edge of an indistinguishable horizon. The Coordinator was there, with his son and Cholayna Ares and many people Jaelle did not know, admiring the view.

Alessandro Li was speaking of it as they came in: "Grand view you have up here, Russ!"

The Coordinator turned his back on it, shrugging. "Not my type of scenery and the sun's the wrong color," he said. "Can't see worth a dawn." *I should imagine the natives would go blind.* It was a moment before Jaelle realized that he had not said that aloud. Damn it, if she was going to be hearing both what people would say and what they did *not* say, it was going to be an uneasy conference! It also occurred to her that he had been here quite long enough for his eyes to be as well adapted to the light as Magda's or Piedro's except that he had so carefully insulated himself from that light. She tried, as she found she could, to draw within herself and avoid the contact, and the effort turned her pale.

"We might as well get down to business," Montray said, "Some of our field men came in last night with a report of a downed plane out in the Kilghard Hills. I think they've finally found Mattingly and Carr."

"Remember, I'm new here," Li said, "Who are Mattingly and Carr?" It was Wade Montray, Monty, who answered.

"Mapping and Exploring," he said. "About three, four years ago. Plane went down in the Kilghard Hills somewhere in a freak storm, and although we sent our airsearch people, we never saw a sign of it; we imagined it must have been buried in the snow somewhere in the wild country. Now some of our field people have spotted it—"

"I can show you exactly where," said one of the men, and unrolled a huge sheet of paper with markings on it which Jaelle did not understand, but his words told her it was intended for a map, a sort of aerial picture of the Kilghard Hills—or, rather, a symbolic representation of the Hills as they might look from high above. He pointed. "We have to get back the downed plane before the locals start salvage work—"

"Why would they do a thing like that?" someone asked.

It was Peter who answered.

"This is a metal-poor planet," he said, "the metal of the hull would make anyone who found it rich. Not that we'd normally begrudge the salvage. But the plane's instrumentation—we don't want them knowing what kind of surveillance we've been running on them."

Li asked "They have no aircraft at all?"

"None to speak of. They do use gliders in the mountains, mostly as a recreational item, though I heard once that they were used for messages and fast relay in firefighting. As I said, we don't want them to know how closely we've been studying their countryside outside the Trade Zone—treaty restricts where we can and can't go, though they aren't stupid and they must know we have some field people out. But I think we ought to hear whatever it was they said," Peter added, and the man from Mapping and Exploring nodded. "Bring the people in."

Cholayna said, "This is the sort of thing I am beginning to hope we can do openly with the new Darkovan employees. If their surveying techniques are primitive, they might find it useful, and good for trade relations as well."

"You'd think so," the Coordinator grumbled, "but they don't seem to have invented it in all the years they've been here. If ever there was an example of a planet regressing to the primitive—"

"I'm not so sure," Cholayna dissented, but Alessandro Li said quietly, "Let's hear the report first. We can argue about cultural acceptance later."

The men who came in were apparently ordinary Darkovans, but they spoke flawless Terran, and Jaelle, curious about who they might be, without any attempt to reach for the information, found the awareness she needed. They were all the sons of Terran spaceport personnel from the old days at Caer Donn, mostly by Darkovan women of the lowest class from the spaceport bars and wineshops; they had been given Terran education, then sent back into fieldwork from Intelligence. Cholayna was thinking that this was all wrong, but that nothing could be done as long as the families of Darkovan women were adamant in rejecting the children of such mixtures. With irritation Jaelle switched off the knowledge and tried to follow what was going on.

The men had snapshots, too, which were passed around, and when they came to Jaelle she said, "I know this area. I have traveled near it—" and pointed to the peculiar configuration of one of the hills, like a falcon's beak. "It is not too far from Armida— the Great House of Alton," she added at a curious look from Cholayna. "Rafaella and I have escorted caravans past there."

"Do you know the people at—what was it, Armida?" asked Li, and she shook her head ruefully.

"No indeed! I saw the old *Dom* Esteban, before he was lamed, once in the City, and once when I was a young girl I rode to Arilinn City and saw Lady Callista, who was Keeper there, riding out with a hawk. But know them? No indeed. They are the highest of *Comyn* nobility, folk of the Hastur-kind—" She chuckled. "To them, a Renunciate would be among the lowest of the low!"

"Yet you do have relatives among them," Piedro said, "Lady Rohana at Ardais was hospitable to all of us for your sake, Jaelle."

Li's eyes were sharp on her, but Jaelle only said, "Oh, Rohana is a rare soul—she has no prejudice against Free Amazons and other low forms of life! Besides, my mother was her first cousin and I think they had been lovers when they were young girls in the Tower. Some of them are my kinfolk, but I assure you," she added, laughing, "none of them would be proud to claim the relationship!"

"However that may be," Russ Montray said dryly, "You do believe that you could find the place where this picture was taken, Mrs. Haldane?"

She took the rough aerial photograph and studied it.

"Unless a blizzard should cover it again," she said, "which is not at all unlikely. But it is a difficult place to get into. I cannot imagine how a plane could have fallen so far. But then I do not understand how your planes stay up, so perhaps it is not surprising that I do not understand it when they do not. But we do not have to worry about finding it," she added, "They will bring it to us."

Russ Montray jerked his head toward her, in sharp disapproval. "What was that you said?" he demanded, and Jaelle felt again that fuzzy consternation, she had spoken out of a certainty that even now was ebbing away like the tides.

Montray said, his lips pressed together tightly in scorn, "I don't know where you got your information, Mrs. Haldane, but the facts are, shortly after we received this news from our men in the field, we had a message from the—" he frowned, fumbled; Monty filled in for him quickly.

"From one of the aides of the Regent, Lord Hastur, in the City. They also have located our plane and they have offered to retrieve the bodies of the men in return for a share of the salvage in the metal."

Jaelle pressed her hand against her head. This was absurd, she never got headaches! Well, she had never been pregnant before either; she supposed it was natural enough.

The Coordinator said, "I think we should tell them, hands off! It's our ship and our metal and what the hell do these Darkovans think they are anyhow? Just another Terran colony like any other—"

"I venture to remind you," Peter said softly, "of the Bentigne Agreement, that a Lost Colony which established its own culture is not subject to automatic attachment by parent stock in the absence of cultural continuity. And in the case of Darkover there is less cultural continuity than in any other planet I studied in the Intelligence School."

Monty said, "It seems a fair enough arrangement. Mounting a full-scale salvage operation into the Kilghard Hills would be expensive—even if we could get permission to do it, which isn't by any means certain—"

"It's our plane," his father insisted. "We certainty have a right to recover it, and we don't want the natives mucking around with the machinery—they'd probably be dumb enough to melt it down for the metal!"

"The operation would belong to Intelligence," Cholayna said quietly, "though certainly the Coordinator's office has some interest in the matter. What's the problem, Russ? Didn't you bother to get permission for the Mapping and Exploring flights, and are you afraid you'll have to answer for illegal surveillance outside the Trade Zone?"

Typical Montray trick, Jaelle found herself picking up the thought, and realized her arm was linked with Peter's and she was once again reading his thoughts. Certainly Russell Montray was incompetent, if even his own subordinates felt this way about him! *Possibly the whole history of the Empire on Darkover has been bungled because some damned bureaucrat wanted to get rid of Russ Montray and pushed him out here.* It was hard to believe that a civilization spanning the stars could have made a mistake as petty as this—wouldn't a stellar empire make mistakes only on the grand scale?

"Whatever the case may be," Montray said, frowning, "we have been summoned to speak with the Regent, and you, Mrs. Haldane, are familiar with their protocol; you are our choice for interpreter. Can you be ready to go in an hour?" His chilly eyes rested on her, but it was over her head that he spoke to Cholayna Ares. "I'm trusting you to find the leak in Intelligence Services; Mrs. Haldane shouldn't have found out about it before I saw fit to release it. You ought to check your people, Ares."

"I'll let you go in a few minutes to be ready for the trip into the City," Cholayna said. "I wish I could go with you; perhaps some day I'll have a chance." Jaelle heard; *some day when this planet isn't quite so xenophobic; visiting the Guild-house will be a good start.* "But before you go, Jaelle, just how *did* you hear about the envoy from the Hasturs? I know I didn't leak it to you—couldn't, I didn't know it myself. You're on good terms with Sandro—Aleki, I mean. I won't let it get back to him, but was he talking when he shouldn't?"

Jaelle shook her head. "Peter didn't know either," she said. "That's the truth, Cholayna, I don't know where I picked it up. Somewhere—someone in that room knew and I must have read it in his mind and thought it was something everybody knew. I don't know how I did it. . . ."

Cholayna laid a light hand on her arm. "I believe you, Jaelle. I've heard something about the ESP that's common on this planet. The earliest reports spoke of it, then everything closed down. I've suspected before this that you were psychic. Don't worry about Montray. I'll smooth him down." Jaelle read in the woman's mind an uncomplimentary epithet she did not understand. "Go and get ready for the trip, and be sure to dress warmly; it's a beautiful day, but my own ESP, such as it is, tells me there's a storm coming up."

But she did not even glance toward the window, and Jaelle was sure she was not speaking of bad weather.

Jaelle was ready, even eager, for the trip into the City, but Peter spoilt her enthusiasm at once; he was furious when he saw she was wearing Darkovan clothing.

"What are you trying to do to me, dammit?"

She realized now she would never understand him. "What has it to do with you? We are going over to my side of the wall this time! And you should know how our people—" she said *our* people deliberately, trying to remind him, "react to Terran uniform; not even a prostitute would dress this way in Thendara. Why, Magda was intelligent enough to know that—" she stopped herself before she said something unforgivable.

He scowled at her and said, "You are going as an employee of the Empire and of the HQ—" but he stopped there, jerked his head forward and said, sullenly, "Let's go."

At least he knew he could no longer make arbitrary demands

of her which she would obey without protest, simply out of a desire to please him. And she had yielded so far, she wore uniform around the HQ, understanding that in a sense it made her invisible, not singled out everywhere as *that Darkovan woman Haldane married*. But she would not wear it in her own city.

Outdoors the weather was so mild and pleasant that she felt even Peter must toss off his sullen mood; one of those wonderful days in early spring when, although snow is still only a cloud-flicker away, the soft air seemed to hold all the beauty of summer. It was a delight to walk the cobbled streets of the City, away from the sounds of machinery and the bland characterless music that was supposed to mask the sound and never did. Peter himself, and Li, and Monty, and even the Coordinator, whose intolerance of cold weather was a joke all over the HQ, had come out wearing light summer uniform. She slipped her arm through Peter's, unable to endure a barrier between them on this lovely day.

"Piedro! Would it really please you to have me dress as if I were a shameless woman? I know it is custom in the HQ, but would you really display me in this way before all the strangers in the street? Even if Cholayna visits the Guild-house, I shall supply her with proper clothing!"

He stopped then, and thought it over for a minute. Then he said quietly, "It's not fair to you, and I know it. I shouldn't blame you. But especially right now, while Li is here examining the status of the colony—they're saying I wrecked my career; I could have been the first Legate here. I don't see why it should make any difference, especially as you are adapting so well to life in the HQ, and there's really no question of conflict of interests. But I felt it might be better, just now, not to—not to ram it down their throats, that I'd married across the wall."

He stopped, and Jaelle felt as if he had slapped her. But it was nothing she had done. He had married her knowing who and what she was, and what it might do to his career. Now if he was having second thoughts, she should not blame herself for them. She had never guessed at this kind of ambition which would be willing to build on a lie! She stared straight ahead, blinking back tears she would not shed. All her pleasure in the beauty of the day had gone. Now, in the afternoon sky, there was as yet no trace of the late-afternoon fog preceding nightly sleet or rain. Jaelle's life often depended, traveling in the hills, on her ability to judge weather conditions for a whole caravan, and she felt a little uneasy prickle down her spine.

There's a storm coming. Maybe Cholayna did mean weather after all.

The Terran escort left them at the formal outer gates of the *Comyn* Castle, where a very young cadet, unshaven fuzz downy on his cheek, very stiff in his shiny new uniform, informed them self-consciously that the Lord Hastur had sent an honor guard to escort the guests. Peter replied politely, in flawless *casta*, but Jaelle wondered if he knew what was perfectly clear to her, that the guard was not to do them honor but to keep these clumsy intruders out of places where they were not wanted.

They were guided into a room Jaelle had never seen before, but she guessed at once that it was the Regent's presence chamber. She had never thought they would be allowed to see Prince Aran, not even to pay their respects; had supposed they would be fobbed off with some minor functionary, but it seemed that the Hastur would deal with them himself. So it was serious. Prince Aran Elhalyn, like all the princes of the *Comyn*, held purely ceremonial and ornamental functions; the real power of the Council lay in the hands of the Hasturs.

Guarded by two more of the youthful cadets in green and black uniform, some unidentifiable metal fragments were laid out on a polished table. The Terrans began to drift over to examine them, when one of the young cadets cleared his throat hesitantly, and Jaelle tugged urgently at Peter's arm. He spoke in an undertone to Coordinator Montray, who turned as, between two more of the Guards, a slender, pale-haired man, not much over thirty, came into the room. He wore elegant blue and silver, the colors of the Hasturs, and his manner was quiet and unassuming; yet Jaelle could see how much in awe of him all the Guardsmen were.

He said, "I am Danvan Hastur, and my father, the Regent, has been unexpectedly called away on family business; he sent me to make you welcome; please forgive him, it is not intended to slight you that I am sent in his place." He bowed to the strangers, and Peter translated this for the Terrans.

The Coordinator said, "Haldane, say whatever is suitable about the honor he does us, and tell him as diplomatically as you can that the sooner we get down to business, the sooner he can get back to family matters or whatever they are."

Jaelle stood listening quietly while Peter translated in his perfect *casta*; the young Hastur listened with a bland smile, but Jaelle, nevertheless, had the feeling that he understood what Montray had really meant.

When the formalities had been concluded, Hastur gestured them toward the table. "These are the bits of the fallen aircraft which contain identifying numbers or letters, which of course our people could not read. Everything else, I am assured, is only bare metal, and you must realize that these people, although they are very poor, are very honest; in returning these materials, they are renouncing what would to them be a fortune. It would be generous of you to reward them in some way."

Montray said, "In our culture people don't expect rewards for common honesty—no, don't translate that," he added with a wry face. "Their sense of duty is probably different from ours. If I live here a thousand years, and it seems I'm going to, I'll never understand a world where honesty isn't taken for granted as duty, and rewards kept for something unusual."

Aleki said cynically, "Oh, come, Montray, you can't be that naive. Matter of relativity. Suppose somebody left a hill of diamonds lying around and told you to guard this heap of worthless rocks? That's the whole history of Terran civilization— taking valuable things that the natives never thought were valuable, and trading them for worthless junk. How do you think we got the plutonium on Alpha?"

"It *was* worthless to them, with their current level of civilization—or lack of it," argued Montray, "but we can talk ethics some other time, if you don't mind. Right now, tell him we appreciate the courtesy, and make a note to send the farmers or whoever found this stuff, some kind of reward."

Jaelle, remembering a conversation at Ardais, volunteered quietly, "A few good metal tools—spades, hammers, axes—would be the most welcome reward possible."

"Thank you, Jaelle. Make a note of that, Monty," Aleki said, "and Haldane, start getting the data on those fragments before they're moved."

Peter went with Jaelle to read off the numbers and record them on his pocket scriber.

"Flight recorder, tapes intact," Peter said. "We can find out why the plane crashed, though I suppose, in the Kilghard Hills, bad weather and crosswinds are as far as we have to look." He sorted through the neatly packaged fragments. "Only three ident disks? Mattingly. Reiber. Stanforth. There is a Carr listed in the records. His disk must still be out there in the wreck. How many bodies did they find?"

Jaelle translated the question, and Danvan Hastur shook his head. "I fear I have no idea. You must question the men, who said they are willing to guide you to the wreckage. But they told me that they buried the bodies decently. The plane was, you understand, at the very bottom of a nearly inaccessible ravine; they felt that transporting the men out would have been unnecessary labor, since nothing could now be done for them."

Jaelle paused with a piece of metal in her hand, a picture suddenly clear in her mind, *a plane crashed on a high ledge, perched there precariously for moments, then when a single figure made its way outside, the sudden precipitous crash into the irrecoverable depths* . . . she clutched at the edge of the table, dizzied, wondering at the vertigo which had suddenly overcome her.

"One of the men survived the crash?" she blurted. "What happened to him?"

Hastur's pale eyes met hers and Jaelle realized she had spoken in her own language. "How did you know there was a survivor, *mestra?* Have you *laran?*"

She blundered, "I held this—and I saw him, plunging out of the plane, on to the ledge, when it fell—"

Peter turned to look at her, startled, and she realized she had drawn all eyes to herself. Hastur ignored the other Terrans. "It is true there was a survivor of the crash; he is living at Armida. I have a message from the Lord Damon, Regent of Armida for the Lord Valdir, who is still legally a child, that the man Carr is in his employ. He was asked if he wished to send a message to his kin, and declined, saying he had no living relatives and the Terrans had no doubt presumed him dead for many years."

"That can't be allowed," said Coordinator Montray when this was translated to him, "he must return and regularize his status."

Monty said under his breath to his father, "No, sir, that was what that business was all about last year. Private contracts between Terran citizens and Darkovan employers are legitimate, if we want to be able to hold contracted Darkovans to their terms of employment." He asked Lord Hastur, "Tell me only this, sir, who is the patron of the man Carr?"

"The Lord Damon Ridenow himself," said Hastur, and Monty's eyebrows went up. "That settles *that*, Father. The rule says that if a Darkovan of substance makes himself personally responsible for the Terran employee, it's legal, and there's nothing we can do about it. Lord Domenic out at Aldaran asked for a dozen Terran experts in aircraft design—he wants to try and get helicopters or some form of VTOL aircraft working out there. Lorill Hastur has half a dozen hydroponics experts working with solar technology out on the Plains of Arilinn. If Lord Armida wants to keep this Carr working for him, all we can do is put it into records that he's alive and well somewhere in the Domains, and leave it at that."

They ended the session by bundling up the logged thirty pounds or so of assorted debris to be returned to the HQ for study. Lord Hastur stated, "I am willing to mount a salvage operation, complete with guides to take you there, when weather permits. But I think we must meet soon and discuss the rules under which your overflights for Mapping and Exploring are permitted."

The Coordinator said, "With respect, sir, we do not accept your jurisdiction over our flights. You are making no use of your airspace whatever and there is no traffic problem. We intend to continue all necessary mapping flights, and, while we are grateful for your cooperation, it should be abundantly clear that we ask this cooperation as a favor, we do not admit that we are required to do so. Our position is unchanged; Darkover is an Empire colony and while we will not interfere with the self-determination of your people, we do not admit that these overflights come under your jurisdiction to protest."

Hastur's face went pale with anger. "About that, sir, you must speak with my father, with Prince Aran and with the *Comyn* Council; you are invited to appear before us at Midsummer, if you wish, and present your case. And now, I fear, duty calls me elsewhere. May I offer you help in having these things transported to the Terran Zone? And it would be welcome if you would speak with the people who brought these things and make arrangements to sell them the metal for adequate compensation or to have it transported." He arose and departed, followed by his escort, and the Terrans were left alone.

"Cool customer," said Aleki, "I'd give a lot to know why everybody is so damned deferential to these *Comyn*—Jaelle," he added, "aren't you related to some of them?"

"Only distantly," she lied, eager to get away from them and suddenly unwilling to remain there any longer.

"What about that damned metal? It's no good to us, but we don't want to disturb the local economy by leaving it out there to start what amounts to a gold rush, either. We've got the important part here—" Li gestured to the identification disks, flight recording box, the fragments which identified the particular aircraft. "Should we waive the rest of it out there? Haldane, Monty, you know local conditions; what do you recommend?"

Peter said, "The Regent of Alton has the reputation for being a reasonable and honorable man. Granted, I've never met him personally, but he has that reputation. I suggest we send someone to discuss it with him; after all, it's on his land."

"Good idea," the Coordinator said, "and at the same time we

can find out about this man Carr. What the hell, if he wants to take some job over the wall, nobody's stopping him, and after all, he didn't come in to collect his severance pay!" He laughed uproariously, and Jaelle could not help but see the grimaces of the other Terrans behind his back. Did anyone take this man seriously?

"But we've got to make sure," the Coordinator went on, "that they're not holding this man Carr out there to squeeze out everything they want to know about the Terrans. Brainwash him. We might wind up having to send someone out to rescue him!"

Peter said in his dryest tone, "Somehow I cannot imagine the Regent of Alton would be guilty of anything so dishonorable."

"Look here, whose side are you on anyhow?" demanded Montray. "You always take all these native bastards right at face value and if they're as simple as all that, how come they're not doing what all the other natives on uncivilized planets do when the Empire lands on their world—coming up and begging for a piece of the action? Something's going on out there that we don't know about and I've got a gut feeling that those bastards you call *Comyn* have something to do with it!"

Monty said, and his tone would have frozen liquid hydrogen, "However that may be, sir, I suggest you keep your voice down. We are, after all, in *their* territory and if there is anyone here who speaks even a little Terran Standard, you have just insulted their highest nobility. We can discuss what Haldane is to do when we are safely behind the walls of the HQ again."

Jaelle said in a tone almost as stiff as Monty's, "If you question your safety, I venture to remind you that the word of a Hastur is proverbial, and Lord Danvan has assured us of our safety. Nevertheless, I suggest that we should be gone from here before we give him cause to regret his courtesy!"

"Let's load up that stuff, then," Li commanded. "We can give it to Spaceforce when we get down to the gates; until then, Monty, Haldane, you're able-bodied, can you divide it up between you? Careful with that recorder box, I'll take that," he added, and tucked it into a uniform pocket. "I'll turn it over to

Flight Operations personally, though I don't suppose it will tell us anything except bad weather. All right, let's get going."

One of the cadets remaining cleared his throat self-consciously and said to Jaelle, "*Mestra*, will you kindly inform the *Terranan* captain, or officer—I don't know his proper designation, acquit me of deliberate failure in courtesy—that the Lord Hastur has required us to give any assistance desired in transporting your property through the gates and to the City. They need not burden themselves like animals; we are here to assist them."

Jaelle relayed the information; the Coordinator said, "I'll bet they'd like to get their hands on it, wouldn't they?" but quickly, before that could sink in, Peter said, "Thank you, friends," to the cadets in the most courteous inflection, then added, "Monty, let him take it, Li, hand him the flight box; it will come to no harm, and when someone of Lord Danvan's rank offers a courtesy it should be accepted gracefully."

"Who the hell do you think you are, Haldane?" growled the Coordinator, but Aleki said under his breath, "He's the resident expert on protocol, sir, he has the right to override you on matters of this kind; dammit, don't make an issue of it!"

Russell Montray sullenly gave up the recorder box to the leader of the cadets, and they went out toward the gates.

As they passed through the corridor outside the Presence Chamber, Peter said in a low voice, "Against the wall, everybody. Someone's coming through and by their look I would say they were high placed in the *Comyn*. Let them pass and for God's sake act respectful!"

Jaelle could almost hear the Coordinator's snarl that they were Terrans and they didn't bow down to feudal lords from any damned pre-space culture, but he did not speak aloud and they moved against the wall in varying attitudes of courtesy, grudged or real. The man in the lead was somewhat like the young Hastur-lord who had spoken with them, though his hair was gray through the silvery blond, and the others were crowded behind him. Then there was a cry of recognition.

"Jaelle! My dear child!" And in a moment Jaelle was in Lady Rohana's arms.

Lady Rohana Ardais seemed to have shrunk; she was smaller, more frail. There was more gray in her dark-red hair than Jaelle remembered.

"My dear, I looked for you in the Guild-house, but I did not find you there, and the Guild-mother was not there to tell me where you could be found! Blessed be Avarra who guided me to this meeting, child!"

Lorill Hastur took Jaelle briefly into a kinsman's embrace. She was surprised by that, as if it had happened to someone else. Surely he could see that she was a Renunciate, that she had among other things renounced what status she might ever have had in *Comyn*.

"I remember as a child," he said, and touched the feathery edges of her short hair, "It is almost all I remember about you; how lovely your hair was, and what a pity that the Renunciates should sacrifice it."

She dropped him a confused curtsy and for the first time in her life the dress of a Renunciate seemed awkward.

"But who are all these people, my child, and how is it that you come among them?"

Danvan Hastur, behind his father, said quietly, "They are the Terran embassies who have come to speak about the downed aircraft on Armida lands, sir."

Jaelle pushed Peter forward and said shyly, "This man, Lord Hastur, is my freemate. He was born in Caer Donn and has lived among Darkovans most of his life."

"Rohana spoke of him," said Lorill Hastur, "and I remember that he was among those who helped to formulate the concept of making *medical technology* available to our people through the employment of Renunciates in the Trade City." He nodded courteously to Peter. "Rohana, if you would like to speak with your foster-daughter, I can spare you for a time from our counsels," and passed on.

"Do stay and talk with me," Rohana said, clinging to Jaelle's arm, "There are so many things we have to say."

Jaelle looked hesitatingly at Peter. He said, "It's very kind of you, Lady Rohana, but my duties—"

"Stay if you want to," Montray said, but as the great door swung open before them, wind lashed through the room, and he shrank back. Jaelle realized that she should have expected this—why had she not been sensitive to the very unseasonable weather? This was the sudden late-spring blizzard that could sweep across from the pass unseen until it struck full force, blanketing the city in white-out within minutes and without warning. Once Jaelle had been caught out in it at Midsummer Festival itself. "Zandru's Kiss," she said aloud, then explained to Montray, hesitating. "I fear we must seek hospitality here—we cannot go out in this. My Lord Hastur—"

He turned back to her and nodded. He said to one of the waiting cadets, "Conduct the Terran dignitaries to guest quarters, if you will," and Monty thanked him with flawless courtesy. Russell Montray had the good sense to keep quiet.

"And you, Jaelle, and your freemate," Rohana said, "you will of course be my guests tonight." She smiled gaily. "I did not know that the weather would be so favorable for my wishes!"

But as the Terrans were conducted away to guest suites, Peter watched uneasily; and when he and Jaelle were together in the luxurious guest rooms in the Ardais part of *Comyn* Castle, he said restlessly, "I don't feel right about this, Jaelle. I don't think Montray knows enough of Darkovan protocol, and I should be there with him."

"Monty will get along all right," said Jaelle, "and I've been working every day with Aleki; if he doesn't know enough to keep the old man out of trouble, he's not as good as I think he is."

"That's the point," Peter almost snarled. "You really don't understand all this, do you? You never have. I need to be there, Jaelle—not tucked away somewhere in the lap of luxury while somebody else reaps the reward. I want old Montray's job, it's just as simple as that, and if I'm not there, this newcomer, this Sandro Li, is going to step in and take over by being on the spot, and where am I? Out in the cold, good for a field agent, but never considered for top administration!"

Jaelle was, for a moment, speechless with shock. The idea that anyone would actually scheme for one of the tiresome administrative jobs, the kind of thing forced upon the *Comyn* by birth and the inescapable inherited requirements of nobility, struck her with such shock that for a moment Peter seemed a stranger to her.

"Then of course you must go at once," she said when she could speak at all. "We cannot let you be passed over in your *ambition.*" She used the stinging derogatory inflection as one would speak of a toady office-seeker, sniffing around for bribes and preferment, but he seemed not to understand that she had insulted him, and Jaelle stood wondering why she had ever been able to endure his presence at all. He was not the man she had loved at Ardais, he was not anyone. He was a dirty little manipulating office-seeker, caring only for preferment and his work. Why had she never seen it before?

"I knew you'd understand. After all, it's to your benefit to, if I make good at this job," Peter said, smiling—*of course, he is content now that he has his own way*—and dropped a quick kiss on her forehead before she could bend to escape it. She stood silent in the middle of the big room, not even taking off her outer garments, tears stinging her eyes. She had made so many excuses not to see him for what he was. And now she was trapped, she was bearing his child.

Melora—my mother—must have felt like this in the Dry Towns. She must always have believed that somewhere there was rescue, and that her kindred would ransom her. And then she knew I was to be born and that no matter what should happen, rescue or no, the world would never be the same.

I am bound for my term of employment, and when Peter knows about the child he will never let me go.

. . . bear children only in my own time and season, at my own will and never for any man's place or pride, clan or heritage. . . . the words of the Oath rang in her mind, and she knew she was forsworn. She had known it in the Amazon Guild-house that

night when they spoke of children, and now there was no escaping the knowledge; she had been blind to it then, but now it was clear to her. . . .

The servant at the doorway had stood unmoving, but now she came and gently took Jaelle's cloak from her, laying it aside, and asked in a soft deferential way if she could bring the lady any refreshment. Jaelle had spent so many years, first in the Guildhouse where no woman was servant to another, and then among the Terrans where service was not personal at all, that she felt awkward as the woman took her cloak. She murmured thanks and declined refreshment, wanting only to be alone, to come to terms with the new and unwelcome knowledge thrust on her.

But the woman persisted: "If you are sufficiently refreshed, the Lady Rohana wishes you to attend her in her private sitting-room."

That was the last thing Jaelle wanted. But she had come to *Comyn* Castle of her free will and now she was, like any other woman of the Domains, subject to *Comyn*. Rohana was her kinswoman; more, she was a patron and benefactor of the Guildhouse and there was absolutely no way to refuse her polite request. She could have stalled, said she was too tired for speech, delayed by asking for food or drink which Rohana would have been bound by hospitality to give her. But why did she not want to talk with Rohana, who had never showed her anything but the greatest kindness?

In the little sitting-room, which was the identical twin of the room at Ardais where Rohana went over her estate accounts with her steward, and saw *Dom* Gabriel's clients and petitioners, Rohana was waiting for her.

"Come here, my dear child," she said, and from habit Jaelle started to take her place on the little footstool at Rohana's knee; then realized what she was doing and withdrew, taking an upright chair across the room from her kinswoman. Rohana saw what she was doing, and sighed.

"I sought you at the Guild-house," she said, "but the Elder in charge could tell me only that you were working among the Terrans, and I did not know how to look for you there. I came to Thendara at least partly for your sake, Jaelle, on *Comyn* business—"

Jaelle heard her own voice sounding as harsh as a stranger's.

"I have no business with the *Comyn*. I renounced all that when I took oath, Rohana."

Rohana held up her hand. She said, as if Jaelle were a disruptive adolescent still fourteen years old, "You have not heard what I came to say. You are interrupting me, *chiya*." The reproof was given gently, but it was a reproof, and Jaelle colored, remembering that by her own choice, she was not Rohana's equal in the *Comyn*, but a subject and a citizen and very much Rohana's inferior. She murmured a ritual formula.

"Your pardon, Lady."

"Oh, Jaelle—" Rohana began, then composed herself again.

"I do not suppose, behind the walls of the Terran spaceport, that you have heard. *Dom* Gabriel is dead, Jaelle."

Now Jaelle, saw what she had not seen, the dark dress of mourning, the swollen eyes, still red-rimmed with weeping. *She mourns him, though she was given to him unwilling, and he used her ill for most of his wretched life.* She had not loved the dead man; yet she remembered jesting with Magda at Midwinter Festival.

Oh, anything belonging to Rohana he will treat with courtesy . . . puppies, poor relations, even Free Amazons. He had never been knowingly unkind to her. "Oh, Rohana, I am truly sorry!"

"It is better so," Rohana said calmly, "he had been ill for many moons; he would have hated to be disabled or helpless. A tenday ago he fell in a fit, and none of the medicines we had could restore him; he had thirty seizures between midnight and dawn, and Lady Alida said that if he woke again he would probably never know me again, nor the children, nor who he was nor where. I was, in a dreadful way, relieved when his heart failed." She closed her eyes for a moment and Jaelle saw her swallow, but she said calmly, "The Dark Lady indeed showed mercy."

This was so true that Jaelle had nothing to say except, "I am truly sorry for your grief, Rohana. He was always kind to me in his own way." Then she recalled that Rohana's oldest son was five-and-twenty; while Gabriel lived, Rohana had been Regent for her ailing husband, but now she was subject to her own son, who would succeed his father. "And now Kyril is Lord of Ardais."

"He feels himself quite ready to be Lord of the Domain," said Rohana. "I wish this had come when he was older—or else when he was much younger and still willing to be ruled by me."

Jaelle could honestly mourn for *Dom* Gabriel, at least a little; but she had never had anything but dislike and contempt for her cousin Kyril and Rohana knew it. "I rejoice I am not born an Ardais and therefore at his command."

"As do I," Rohana said wryly. "His first act as Warden was to arrange a marriage between his sister Lori and Valdir, Lord Armida. Valdir is not yet fifteen, nor Lori either, but that did not stop Kyril; he wanted that Alton alliance. He has never forgiven me that I did not interfere a few years ago, when Lady Callista of Arilinn left the Arilinn Tower, to get her for his wife. I had hoped Lori would marry your brother Valentine, Jaelle—my daughter to marry back into the Domain of my birth. But of course your father and Valentine's was a Dry-Town man, and so Kyril has already forbidden the marriage—he is now Valentine's guardian."

Jaelle had seen her brother Valentine fewer than a dozen times in her life; he had been born when her mother died and she had not wanted to remember. *Dom* Gabriel would never have been unkind to a child, but Kyril had detested his young cousins; Jaelle had escaped to the Guild-house, but for Valentine there had been no escape till his tenth year, when he was sent to Nevarsin monastery.

"Valentine and Valdir are *bredin*; when Valdir marries, Valentine will go with him as his paxman, and no doubt Valdir will find him a good marriage somewhere," Rohana said. "You need not fear for him."

"I hardly know him," said Jaelle, "but I am glad he will be out of reach of Kyril's malice. But Lori, how does she feel about making a marriage with a kinsman she hardly knows?"

"Oh, she thinks him charming," said Rohana, "All the Altons are brilliant, and I think Valdir likely to be one of the best of them. You do know that the last Heir, young Domenic, was killed in Thendara, in a swordplay-accident, a few years ago, and the Domain is under a Regent, Lord Damon Ridenow, who married Domenic's sister Ellemir. But Valdir will be fifteen this summer, and assume his place as Warden of the Domain—"

"I know," Jaelle said, and felt a curious prickle in her mind which dismayed and annoyed her. Why had the affairs of the Altons been brought to her mind just now? The downed plane on Alton lands. Peter, saying that the Regent of Alton was an honorable man. Somehow it made her think of the curious dream she had shared with Magda; there had been someone in Ridenow colors, green and gold . . . what had the affairs of the *Comyn* to do with her?

Rohana sat up straight and Jaelle could see that she was angry. Had Rohana read her mind? She did not know that she was virtually broadcasting her annoyance and displeasure, and that Rohana, whose *laran* was fully trained and under control, was as annoyed by her undisciplined mind as Jaelle would have been angered by one of the young girls making a noisy disturbance in the Guild-house when the House was supposed to be quiet.

"I am sorry the affairs of the *Comyn* are so tiresome to you," she said dryly, "but you must bear with me while I rehearse them to you, since you are, after all, deeply involved in them—"

"When I took the Oath of the Renunciates—"

"When you were permitted to take that Oath because of my intercession," Rohana reminded her coldly, "You were allowed to take the Oath, and renounce your place in the succession of the Aillard Domain through your mother, Melora, only because I certified to them—not quite truthfully, I now fear, though I did not know it then—that you had no usable or accessible *laran*. But though you can renounce your own heritage, you cannot renounce it for your unborn daughter."

"I have no daughter, born or unborn—" Jaelle began, but Rohana met her eyes.

"You still lie to yourself, Jaelle? Or will you have the insolence to lie to me, and deny that you are carrying a daughter by
your Terran lover?"

Jaelle opened her mouth; and closed it again, knowing that
she had nothing to say. She had known, and barricaded her mind
from the knowledge. Rohana went on, quietly.

"When I was born, there were many daughters in the Aillard
succession. That was more years ago than I like to remember,
and time has not been kind to our Domain. My mother, Lady
Liane, married a man who took her name and rank, rather than
she taking his." The Aillard, alone among the *Comyn*, traced descent through the female line, mother to eldest daughter. "My
mother had two younger sisters; her youngest was your mother's
mother, Jaelle. Melora and I were cousins and *bredini*; we were
fostered together in Dalereuth Tower. I left there to marry
Gabriel; Melora was kidnapped by Dry-Town bandits and bore
Jalak of Shainsa two children. You and your brother Valentine."

Jaelle said, her mouth suddenly dry, "Why do you tell me
what I have always known?"

"Because my eldest sister, Sabrina, had no daughters, but
only sons. My sister Marelie married into the Elhalyn Domain
and for better or for worse, her sons and daughters belong to that
Domain and are not Aillards. I wished Gabriel to renounce his
father-right in Lori, but he would not, and in later years he was
too ill for me to persuade him; so that Lori was reared, not for
the Heirship of a Domain, but for marriage. But you have not
married, Jaelle; you are still an Aillard; in fact, you have taken
vows which mean that any daughter you bear is *yours*, not your
husband's. Your daughter, Jaelle, will be Heir to Aillard,
whether you like it or not. And she will inherit the powers of the
Domain."

"No! I will not allow it—"

"You cannot stop it," Rohana said, "Such is the law. We have
been watching you since Melora died. Obviously, Sabrina was
not pleased to see Melora replace her—"

"Especially since the father of Melora's child was a Dry-
Town bandit," Jaelle said dryly.

"Nevertheless, Sabrina is now past childbearing; so she cannot bear a daughter. Melora had an older sister—"

"Did *she* have children for the Domain?"

"We thought that she would do so," said Rohana, "She bore a *nedestro* daughter to Lorill Hastur; festival-gotten, so we had her married off for convenience to a small-holder. That girl would now be—God help us, how the years pass!—she would be past forty. I saw her once when she was young; she was very beautiful, and she was destined for a Tower."

"Why can she not be Heir to the Domain? Or are the Hasturs jealous of their daughters?"

Rohana shook her head. "Before she was fifteen, she was stolen by bandits; she was ransomed, but she ran away again—perhaps she had a lover among them—and we never heard anything else of her. Though Leonie of Arilinn told us not to look for her—either she was dead or something had happened to her which meant she could never return to her people. I am sure she is dead now. So the succession passes to you, Jaelle, for better or for worse; and if not to you, to your daughter. This is why I brought you here; to tell you this."

Jaelle realized that, without knowing it, she had crossed her hands over her belly, as if to protect the child within, the child she had never thought of except as a tie to bind her to marriage and to Peter. But this was worse than child to a Terran, if she must bear a child to *Comyn*, to be servant and master alike. *Comyn*. She *would* not. She was sworn to bear no child for place or position, house or heritage—

"And as Regent for your unborn child, who is Heir to Aillard, you must take a seat on the council," Rohana said, "although Lady Sabrina is still Regent by name. Unless you wish to make Sabrina your daughter's Guardian," she added icily. "Then you may continue to pursue your own wishes as a Renunciate and neglect your duty. But you must give birth to your daughter and place her properly in the hands of *Comyn*, to be brought up as her birthright dictates."

"She is half Terran," said Jaelle rebelliously.

"You still do not understand, do you, Jaelle?" Rohana said.

"This is not the first time that the female line of the Aillard has died out; but it must not do so again. We have been unfortunate now for three generations. Your duty to the *Comyn*—"

"Don't talk to me about my duty to the *Comyn*," Jaelle said, stifled. "In all the years of my life what have they ever done for me?"

"I do not ask for you," Rohana said coldly. "You renounced that life before you were old enough to know what it means. Life demands of everyone that they make promises before they are old enough to abide by them; *honor* is abiding by these pledges even when it becomes difficult."

Jaelle had been thinking something like this . . . *had she forsworn her Oath to the Renunciates when it became difficult? . . .* and she lowered her eyes. Rohana said again, more gently, "You made your own choice. But you cannot make that choice for your daughter. I know enough of the Renunciates to know that even a Guild-mother cannot make that choice for her daughter, even if the girl was born under the Guild-House roof. Your daughter must be reared knowing her duty to *Comyn*, that she is Heir to Aillard, and you must know what it is that is demanded of her. I ask you, Jaelle, to take a seat in Council this summer, when Kyril is installed as Warden of Ardais and when your daughter is chosen for Aillard."

"What is the alternative?" asked Jaelle.

"I hope you will not force us to think of alternatives, Jaelle. Only if the child dies, or you die in childbirth, would that be a viable option."

I am not a slave and I do not want my daughter enslaved. I want to live for myself, not for that arrogant caste which rejected my mother and abandoned her to slavery, then rejected me because I was my father's daughter as well as my mother's. She said aloud, "The *Comyn* would have none of me because of my Dry-Town blood. Now you say they will overlook it in my daughter, and her Terran blood as well?"

"At that time," said Rohana quietly, "they had a choice. There were other heirs to Aillard. Since that time there have been deaths. Death gives a woman no choice, either, and she is a harder task-mistress than the *Comyn*. Necessity does not consult convenience, Jaelle."

And the dead women, Jaelle thought, had been Rohana's kinswomen.

Blood, spreading on sand, dark shadows of the waterhole, pain splitting her forehead... somehow she managed to force the picture out of consciousness again. Rohana watched her narrowly but said nothing, and Jaelle was grateful. Somehow she feared that Rohana must look right into her mind, see her dawning *laran*, reach out to take her from her refuge among the Renunciates ... *no refuge. I have abandoned them too. Where does duty send me? Duty to whom? To* Comyn, *to the Terrans my employers, to Peter my freemate, to my sisters in the Guild-house? There is no escape from conflicting oaths ... no more than from birth or death....*

She said, "Kindra used to tell me, nothing is inevitable but death and next winter's snow. There must be another answer even for this."

"Ah, Jaelle," said Rohana, gently, leaning forward to stroke the younger woman's soft hair, "Life is not as simple as that. I do not demand any choice from you now. I did not ask you here to bully you. Go away and think about it, darling. Ask Peter what he thinks—she is his daughter too, and whatever the Renunciates may think about it, he has some rights over his child. You need not decide now. Even when the child is born, I only ask that you should not close too many doors too soon. Leave her a choice, too. Your mother risked, and lost her life, so that you might have a choice, so that you would not grow up in chains. That, I suppose, made me soft with you, so that I did not insist on bringing you up strictly by the laws of a *Comyn* daughter; Melora was given no choice, I was given no choice...."

Jaelle looked sharply at Rohana, but then realized that Rohana had not spoken of herself, she had said aloud only, *Melora was given no choice.* She repeated it now, "Melora was given no choice, and she had died to give you choice, so I would not force anything upon you. You have had many years of freedom; is it not time, now, to do something for someone besides yourself?"

Maybe she is right, maybe she is right . . . maybe I owe something to those who came before me, those who will come after me . . . Rafaella tried to choose for Doria, and it is not working, Doria has had to be sent away . . .

She bowed her head and said "I will think about it. But surely you did not travel this long road from Ardais only to argue with me about the destiny of my daughter . . ."

Rohana seized on this so eagerly that Jaelle knew Rohana, too, must have been troubled by their quarrel. "Not only for that, of course," she said, "but to bury Gabriel, and to hear Kyril installed as Warden for the Domain. . . . There will be a special session of Council called; the Hasturs are already traveling here from Carcosa, and Prince Aran with his wife and daughter. Word has been sent through the Domains—but I do not suppose all this is of the slightest interest to you, child. Go and rest; you will need your sleep. I will ask them to send you some supper, something light, and you can rest well and in the morning go home, or stay here and talk with me again, just as you choose. I will send you more precise details about when the Council is to meet, and you really should try to be present for your daughter, and to meet the other members of the Domain—you do know, child, that you have family members other than myself and Kyril. You should know them!"

"I am no more eager to know them than they have been to know me all these long years since Mother died," Jaelle said, but she said it gently; she realized she was just as unwilling to hurt Rohana's feelings as ever.

The guest suite where she had been taken was quiet and empty, and Jaelle ate some of the soup and roast bird which Rohana had sent to her. She supposed that Peter was dining with the Terran group in the faraway guest suite where they had been sent, and almost wished she were with them. But she was not sufficiently familiar with *Comyn* Castle to try and find her way there. She drowsed on a soft chair, hardly aware of how comforting it felt to be among familiar things. No, not familiar, she had never known luxurious surroundings like this. Since she was old enough to remember she had known only the tidy, comfortable, but completely non-luxurious surroundings of the Guild-house. Luxuries like these might have been hers all the time if she had chosen to remain with *Comyn* rather than honoring her Renunciate Oath, and why was she thinking of that now? After a time she fell asleep, to be wakened by Peter coming in very late.

"I'm sorry I woke you, love," he said. "I would have come back sooner, I wouldn't have wanted to leave you alone here, but I knew you were with Lady Rohana and she'd look after you. I felt obligated to take care of them."

"Of course you had to," she said warmly. It was one of the things she loved about him, his sense of duty. *Did that mean she had none of her own?* She shied away from this question.

"Have you had dinner? Rohana sent me in all kinds of lovely food, and I could hardly eat any of it," she said, "There's all kinds of cakes and cold fowl and wine there on the side table—"

"I ate something with the others," he said. "They don't appreciate good food, except Monty. Sandro Li—what is it you call him, Aleki?—wouldn't touch any of it, he said he didn't trust natural foods, they weren't as safe and couldn't be as nourishing as the kind scientifically computed for vitamin and mineral content. Makes me want to be out in the field again." He took up a leg of fowl in one hand and a slice of some kind of nut pastry in the other and came toward her, gnawing hungrily on the bone. "I come to stay in a place like this, I realize how—how alien the Terran Zone really is. Poor girl, you've been at your wits' end there, haven't you? Maybe in a few weeks when this Carr business is all settled, we can get away for a few weeks, make a trip into the back country, the mountains—Daleruth maybe, I have always loved the seacoast and you haven't been there at all, have you? Leave everything behind us and just make the trip down through the mountains by road—just the two of us, get back to each other again. Hey, hey—" he came and bent over her, dropping the roast meat in a clumsy haste to take her in his arms, "You're crying, Jaelle—I've been a beast, haven't I, getting all tied up in worrying about business and promotion and all that nonsense and never remembering what's really important! It takes something like this to remind me that there are other things in life. I'm sorry I was so nasty to you earlier. It would serve me right if you hated me after all that, but I don't know what I would do without you, Jaelle, I love you so much. . . . I need you—"

She buried her face into his neck, sobbing. Why had they grown so far apart? And he did not even know any of this, did not know about *Dom* Gabriel's death, or the demands Rohana had made, or their child—

"Listen, Peter," she said earnestly, reaching up to pull his face against hers, "you do know that Rohana is my kinswoman, and she had so many things to tell me, so much I cannot decide it all alone." In a rush, she told him everything, but as she had hoped, he paid little heed to what Rohana had said about her child being Heir to the Aillard Domain.

"The important thing," he said, holding her close, "the one that's important, that's our baby, Jaelle. We've had a lot of trouble, but now it's all going to be worthwhile, now we have someone other than ourselves to think about." He kissed her so tenderly she wondered why she had ever doubted him.

"That comes first, Jaelle. Just you, and me—and the baby."

Chapter 4

Magda was beginning to feel restless, almost claustrophobic; the women were friendlier, even Rafaella, but she was so tired of being indoors; sometimes she would step into the garden just to breathe the air of freedom. Even, she thought wryly, if the air of freedom smells a little too much of the stables!

She was still wearing castoffs from the box of outworn clothing, but tradition demanded that she must make herself a full set of clothing before the end of her housebound half year. She understood, after a fashion, why this was so—women of the upper classes, coming to the Renunciates, were accustomed to wearing clothing made only by the labor of servants and others, and it was necessary that they should know the cost of their labor. Keitha, on the other hand, enjoyed a chance to sit and sew and was now covering the neck and sleeves of her new undertunic, with daintily embroidered butterflies. Magda envied the ease with which she did it.

"Oh, this is restful for me," Keitha said. "At any moment Marisela may summon me out to attend a confinement, so I will rest and embroider while I can—"

"It is not restful for me," Magda said, biting her lip as she stabbed her finger again with the needle. "I would rather muck out barns than sew a single seam!"

"That is obvious from your work," said Keitha, examining the stitches with a critical eye. "What was your mother thinking of!"

"She was a musician," Magda said, "and I do not think she could sew any better than I can; she was always busy with her lute, or with her translations." Elizabeth Lorne had played nine instruments, and had collected over three hundred mountain folk-songs of Darkover. Magda, who had little musical talent, had not been close to her mother, though in these last months she had been more and more aware of how like her mother she was, absorbed in her work, craving something to do for herself. She wondered, now when it was too late to know, what her mother's marriage had really been like. She had surely not let herself be consumed in David Lorne's career among the Terrans but had always done her own work. . . .

"My mother said I must never ask a servant to do anything for me that I could not do for myself," Keitha said. "Otherwise a lady is slave to her own servants. Now I am grateful for it, though I do not like to work with horses. But Marisela says I must learn to attend to my own horses and saddle and tack, because a midwife is required to go by law to any woman within a day's journey who has need of her, and farther if she can. And Marisela says I may not always have serving men or women to look after my animals for me."

Magda smiled a little; *Marisela says* had become the most important words in Keitha's vocabulary. Magda had begun to suspect that one of the main points of Amazon training was to regress women to their adolescence, so that they could grow up again in a way that would not make them subservient to fathers, brothers, the men who ruled most Darkovan households. If it took them back to the stage of having crushes on other women, well, that was not a crime either, though it was surprising to see it in Keitha, who had been brought up as a *cristoforo* and had made some unkind remarks about lovers of women in the Guild-house.

She pricked her finger again with the needle, swore as she tried to tie off a short end of thread. Camilla was not the only woman who had made such an offer to Magda, but she had always smiled and refused in such a way, she hoped, as not to give offense. It had been harder to refuse Camilla, who had been her friend when she so desperately needed friends.

But I am not a lesbian. I have no interest in other women . . . and that brought her mind back to that unsettling episode with Jaelle. Well, that had been a dream, a shared nightmare, it had no real significance. But as she struggled with her thread, trying to poke the end through the eye of the needle, she remembered the night it had been brought up in Training Session. . . .

. . . Cloris and Janetta had claimed that any Renunciate who had love affairs with men was a traitor to her Renunciate Oath. "It is men who oppress us and try to enslave us, like Keitha's husband who beat her and tried to bring her back by hired mercenary soldiers. . . . how can a free woman love men who live like that and would drag us back to them?"

"But all men are not like that," Rafaelle had insisted, "The fathers of my sons are not like that, they are content to leave me free. They might like it better if I would dwell with them and keep their house, but they allow my right to do as I will."

And Keitha had cried out, at white heat, "We leave our husbands and come here for refuge, thinking ourselves safe from pursuit, and then we find we are not safe from our sisters either! Here in this house, no later than yesterday, one of my sisters made—made an unlawful request of me—"

Mother Millea said in her gentle, neutral voice, "I suppose you mean by that, Keitha, that someone asked you to go to bed with her. Who styled that request unlawful? Or did she not leave you free to refuse if you would?"

"I call it unlawful," Keitha cried, and Rezi said, laughing, "You called it something worse than that, didn't you? I confess that I am the vicious criminal involved, and she fled from me as if she thought I would rape her then and there, without even the courtesy to look me in the face and tell me, no thank you!"

Keitha was red as fire, tears dripping down her face. "I would not have named you," she said angrily, "but you boast of it?"

"I will not let you make me ashamed of it," Rezi said. "Among men, if two young boys swear to be friends all their lives and allow no woman to come between them, even if they marry and have children later, none denies their right to place their friendship first among all things! *Donas amizu!*" she said scornfully. "All the writers of songs have nothing but honor for a man who places his *bredu* higher than wife and children, but if two women so pledge one another, it is taken for granted that when the girl grows to womanhood, her oath means only . . . *I will be loyal to you until my duty to my husband and my children comes first!* My love and loyalty are all to my sisters, and I will not waste love on a man, who can never return it!"

Magda thought, confused, *but all men are not like that, Rafaella is right,* and lost track of what was being said. Now she thought, *I wonder if Keitha is intellectually honest enough to recognize what is happening between her and Marisela; or if Marisela will ever make her aware of it?*

Janetta put her head in at the door and said, "Margali, Keitha, Mother Lauria wants you both down in the hall."

Magda gratefully bundled her sewing into an untidy ball and thrust it into the wooden cubbyhole bearing her name. Keitha stopped to fold her work more neatly, but Magda heard her steps behind her on the stairs and they ran down side by side.

Camilla was there, dressed for riding, and Rafaella and Felicia, with a little group of women Magda did not know; but on their sleeves they bore the red slashmark of Neskaya Guildhouse.

"Margali, Keitha, are you weary of being housebound? Are you willing to put yourself in some danger? There is fire in the Kilghard Hills, on Alton lands; the Guild women are not required by law to go, but we are permitted to share this obligation, when all able-bodied men are required to go. There is no law which says you *must* go," she repeated carefully, "but you may go if you will."

"I will go," Magda said, and Keitha added more timidly, "I would be glad to go, but I do not know what use I should be."

"Leave that to us," said one of the strange women, "if you cannot fight the fire, you can help around the camp, but we can use every willing pair of hands."

Mother Lauria looked at them one after the other, then said,

"Good; I will send you, then." Magda realized that they had in effect been ordered to go; the housebound time required that they remain indoors unless specifically ordered to go by a Guild-mother.

"You must learn to bear yourself properly among men, and to work with them as one of themselves, not with a woman's special privilege. You are in the charge of Camilla and Rafaella; you are to obey them implicitly, and to speak to no one, and especially to no man, without their permission. Is that understood? Good; go and dress yourselves for riding, and wear your warmest clothes and cloaks, and strongest boots. Fetch clean linen for four days, and be down here before the clock strikes again."

As she made ready to ride, and rolled her clean underlinen in the small canvas bag Rafaella had given her, Magda was shaking with excitement. She was a little frightened, too; but, she reminded herself, she was stronger than many men required by law to meet this obligation. *And I am a Renunciate.*

As they saddled their horses, Rafaella said quietly to Keitha and Magda, "Some of the men with whom we will travel will try to lure you into conversation; or they will make rude and suggestive remarks. Whatever they say to you, you may not reply to them, not a single word; pretend if you wish that you are deaf and dumb. If they lay hands upon you, you may defend yourself, but you must accustom yourself to the fact that they resent us, and learn to live with it, since there's no helping it."

The detachment of men waiting at the City gates was an ill-assorted crew. At their head were three dozen young Guardsmen in uniform, commanded by a smart young officer not yet out of his teens.

"Valentine Aillard, *para servirte, mestra*," he said, giving Rafaella a cool and courteous nod. "Your women are welcome; we can use every pair of hands. Have you rations and tools?"

"They are on our pack-animals there," Rafaella said, and gestured to the women to fall into line. The polite young officer had evidently made it clear to his Guardsmen how they were to behave, for, though the Guardsmen looked at them with some

curiosity, there were no overt signs of resentment. It was otherwise with the other men, traveling to the fire-lines with the
Guardsmen but all too obviously not under military discipline.
There were soft whistles, coos intended to attract attention, and
leers; and as they took their place in the line, a murmured obscene phrase or two. Magda ignored them; Keitha was as red as
a bellflower. She drew her hood over her head, and Magda
thought she was crying under its shelter. The women from
Neskaya House, all of whom were in their forties or older, rode
by the men without a glance their way, while Camilla—Magda
remembered that at one time she had been a mercenary soldier—rode ahead with the Guardsmen, chatting casually with
them.

Keitha whispered, "Why is she allowed to speak with them
when we are not?"

"Probably because they do not yet trust us to know how to
behave," Magda whispered back. "Do you *want* to talk with
them?"

"No," Keitha whispered vehemently. "But it seems to me
strange that she will talk and be friendly with the same men who
are treating us so badly."

That had occurred to Magda too, but she supposed Camilla,
who had been a Renunciate for many years, had managed somehow to make the distinction between men who accepted her as
one of themselves and those who treated her as a woman to be
cajoled. In any case Camilla was a law to herself.

All afternoon they rode, and well into the night; finally the
officer at the head of the column called a halt and they camped
in a meadow; the Amazons cooked over their own fire, and later
laid their blankets in a circle. Rafaella said, "Keitha, you will
sleep with me, and Margali, you with Camilla. Whenever we are
among men this way, we always sleep two and two; just to make
it abundantly clear to any men that we are not seeking company.
And if anyone does get the wrong idea, you can protect one
another."

Magda could see the sense in this, although she was sure that
the men around the other fire, if they did not get the idea that the

women wanted their company, were sure to get another idea which might be almost equally mistaken. She reminded herself sternly that it was none of their business what the men thought. Still, it made her self-conscious when she spread her blankets with Camilla's.

Rafaella asked one of the women from Neskaya, "Where is my daughter? I had hoped to see Doria with you."

"I told her she could come if she wished," the woman said, "and she was as eager to get out of the house as any of us; but it was the first day of her cycles, and hard work and hard riding at such a time are no pleasure; I could see she was really feeling ill, so I did not try to persuade her to go."

Rafaella said angrily, "I do not like to think of my daughter shirking! I have ridden and worked hard when I was seven moons pregnant, and she let that stop her?"

The other woman shrugged. She said, "There is no law to say that all women must react alike to their bodies; because you do not mind hard work, would you force it on her? I am sure, if the fire was near and we really needed every available hand, she would have been right beside us—she does not strike me as lazy or slothful. There were enough of us who were willing and even eager to come. Don't worry over her, Rafi; she is out of your hands now. If she really shows any sign of slacking—and so far I have seen no sign of it—let the Neskaya Guild-mothers deal with her."

Rafaella sighed and said, "I suppose you are right," and was silent. After a time the other woman said gently, "I think perhaps the children of Renunciates have a harder time than those who come to us from the outside world. We expect so much more of them, don't we?" and Magda saw the strange woman stroke Rafaella's hair gently. "I have a daughter who chose to leave the Guild and marry. She is happy, she has two children, and her husband treats her as well as even I could wish, but I still feel I failed with her. At least your daughter has taken Oath, my sister, and is no man's servant or slave."

Camilla murmured into Magda's ear, "And if I had said that to Rafaella, she would have slapped me. I am glad that someone

else thought to do so." She stood up and called the women
around the fire. "Before we sleep," she said, "Annelys will give
you some instructions in firefighting." Annelys was the woman
from Neskaya Guild-house; she gathered the women around
their fire and gave them some rudimentary instructions about the
theory of firefighting, what to do under various conditions, elementary safety precautions; although she emphasized that most
of them would be put to doing ordinary manual work on the fire-
line and would not need to know what was going on, but only
obey instructions precisely. Around the other fire, Magda could
hear one of the young officers telling the men almost the same
things; his voice was mostly a sound with no words distinguishable but now and then a chance silence or a gust of wind their
way would bring them a few words.

"If it were only the Guardsmen," Camilla murmured—she
was sitting between Magda and Rafaella—"we would all work
together and camp together too. But some of these men are
riffraff and we do not trust them. After a time you will learn
which men can be trusted and which cannot. Always err on the
side of caution. You should know that."

Annelys heard her and said, "I am not so sure that any men
can be trusted completely. They are not when I am in charge of
any work details of Renunciates, believe me, Camilla."

Camilla shrugged. "Maybe I am more trusting than you. Or
perhaps it is only that I have nothing more to lose, and any man
who lays a hand on me will draw back a bleeding stump—and
knows it perfectly well!"

Annelys yawned. "Well, today was a long hard day, and tomorrow will be longer and harder still. Let us sleep, my sisters,"
she said, and bent to cover the fire. Magda was tired and sore
from riding, and the ground was hard beneath the thin blankets,
but even as she told herself that she could not possibly sleep
under such conditions, she drifted off. She woke once in the
night, seeing the campfire like a sullen red eye, still smoldering;
Camilla had moved close to her, and Magda put her arms around
the woman, glad of the warmth, for she was cold. Camilla murmured something drowsy, shifted her weight in her sleep, and

Magda snuggled close; Camilla kissed her lightly and Magda felt her drift off into deep sleep again.

But Magda felt troubled. As she had done all too often in the last few weeks, she found herself examining her thoughts closely.

Jaelle. Exactly what had happened between them? They had wakened in one another's arms, out of a shared dream, the *laran* she had not known she possessed . . . and Jaelle had pulled her down and kissed her, not the casual light kiss she could have taken for granted, the offhand sleepy kiss Camilla had just given her, but a real kiss, the kiss of lovers, with an intensely sensual awareness which frightened Magda. Like many women whose experience has been entirely conventional, she found it hard even to imagine that she could respond to such a thing. Jaelle had not been angry . . . but Magda had run away. Now, close to Camilla, she tried again to test her own feelings. Camilla, too, had once asked this of her, and Magda had refused her but she no longer knew why.

Is this what I want, then? Is this why my marriage failed, because at heart I am a lover of women . . . ? She felt troubled, alien to herself. Finally, telling herself firmly that hard work awaited her tomorrow, she managed to drift off into uneasy dreams.

Before noon the next day they began to smell and hear the fire, a roaring, a dull acridness in the air, lurid red against the sky. Along the hillside a row of grimy forms, men and boys, stretched out with hoes and rakes, scraping a firebreak in the soil; when they reached the camp, they found others felling trees within the firebreak.

Magda and Felicia were put to scraping firebreak-lines with the men; Keitha, they judged, was not strong enough to work on the lines, so they sent her to the fire-camp where women were cooking and hauling water. Camilla was sent to the tree-felling party with Annelys and some of the others.

Magda could not, where she was working, even see the fire, but she could hear it; the grubby hoe in her hands scraped blisters, even through her gloves, and her back began to ache before she had been at the work for an hour, but she kept on. After an hour or so, some men brought a pail of water along, and she straightened and drank in her turn. The man beside her on the line looked at her for the first time, her smudged face and filthy hands, the rough riding clothes, and said, "Zandru's hells, it's a girl! What are you doing here, *mestra?*"

"The same thing you are doing, man—fighting a fire," Magda said before she remembered that she had been ordered not to speak to any man, good or bad, and lowered her head, draining the cup and returning it to the old man who was carrying the water bucket. The old man said, "What is a nice girl like you doing out here among all the men, girlie? Shouldn't you be back at the camp, where my wife and daughters are?" But Magda shoved the cup into his hand and picked up her hoe, bending to grub away at the line, and after a time the man, grumbling, moved on to offer his cup to the next man.

No one had bothered to explain to Magda what they were doing, but Annelys's explanation had told her a little, and she supposed that the idea was to scrape away everything burnable beyond a certain distance, so the line was barren of anything which could support the fire. At dusk they were relieved by another party, Magda was almost too weary to stand; her hands were blistered and her back felt as if it would never stop hurting. Down in the camp there was a place to wash hands and face, and the women passed them big bowls of bean soup which had been simmering all day over the cookfires within the ring. Magda wished there was a place to bathe, but they were all in the same predicament, grubby and sweating and smelling of smoke. Magda started off toward the latrine, but one of the Amazons from another Guild-house grabbed her and reminded her that they always went two by two, for protection, and though Magda felt self-conscious about going to the rough latrines before the other woman, when she saw the faces of some of the men outside she was glad.

Barbarian. Among the Terrans I could work among the men and no one would touch me unless I invited it! Yet a thousand years of different customs set them apart. The ordinary women, protected by their long skirts and the caps on their braided hair, walked where they wished alone, and no one would dare to touch them because they were known to be the property of some man who would avenge any rudeness offered to his possessions. The Free Amazons belonged only to themselves and therefore they were any man's for the taking. . . . *Barbarian*, Magda thought again. But the Terrans had their own faults. . . .

When the Amazons had spread their bedrolls, again two by two, at their own end of the camp, Keitha who had joined them, whispered, "The women were worse than the men. They stared at me as if I were something with a thousand legs which they had found in their porridge bowl, and one of them asked why I was not home caring for my children. And when I told them—"

"Never mind," said Rafaella gently. "We have all heard it. We have had time to get used to it, that is all, and you will too. Remember to be proud of what you are and what you have done; if they do not understand, that is their worry and not yours. We have all done well for the Domains today; go to sleep, love, and don't let anyone make you think less of yourself for doing what you think right." Magda was surprised at the kindness in Rafi's voice; in general she had little patience with Keitha's timidity.

Camilla murmured, "It's true, though, the men are not nearly so bad as the women. Once the men get it through their heads that we work to the limits of our strength and want no special privileges, they accept us. The women never do. They feel that by working beside men, we endanger their privileged status; how can they convince their husbands that they are fragile and delicate when we are there to give them the lie? Keitha thought she was going to easier work than ours because she is not strong—"

"Do you accuse me of shirking?" Keitha blazed.

"Never, oath-daughter; your work is suited to your strength as ours to what *we* can; but it is just as well you should have encountered this. I would a thousand times rather work amid the hostility of men, than of women. Your trial is far more severe than ours. No woman thinks me a danger when I work beside her husband—" she added grimly, and Magda, looking at the scarred and haggard old *emmasca*, knew Camilla's scars burned as deep inwardly as outwardly, "but you are young and pretty, you could have a man, a husband, a lover whenever you chose. They will forgive me for renouncing what they think I could never get even if I wished it. But they will never forgive you, and you may as well know it now as later."

The next morning was damp and dripping. "Let us pray that it will smother the fire," Camilla said grimly as she drew on her boots. "Margali, child, let me see your hands." She drew a harsh breath as she examined the blisters. "Here; put on some of this cream, it will harden the skin a little," she said, and made Magda smear her hands with it before she drew on her gloves. They stood in line with the men for breakfast, bowls of thick grainy porridge, cooked with onions and other herbs. There were buckets of beer and pails of a hot grain drink. There were more comments from the men, but Magda kept her eyes down and pretended not to hear. Camilla, on the other hand, laughed and jeered with the men; many of them knew and evidently respected her. She told Magda that she had served alongside them in the last border war.

As she took up her place beside Felicia on the fire-lines, a man called softly, "Hey, pretty things, what are you doing with that old battle-ax? What did they do, get hold of you before you knew what you were missing? Come over here with us and we'll show you a good time—"

Magda ignored the comments, staring straight ahead. She had a hoe which was too short for her, and stopped to trade hoes with Felicia, who was not as tall as she was. While they were settling into place again, a man ran down the slope.

He was small and slender, with dark-red hair, wearing a cloak of orange and green. "The fire's jumped the break up that way," he shouted, "Don't go up there! Get back and move the men, move up the carts, we've got to bring the camp back down—"

There was a stir in the ranks of men. "It's Lord Damon," they heard someone say, and the men hastened to do as they were told. Magda was set to piling up food supplies and blankets on a wagon, and as she handed them up to Felicia, she could see the man they had called Lord Damon, talking in low worried tones with the line bosses, drawing maps on the ground with a long stick. Someone handed him a mug of beer; he took a sip or two, rinsed his mouth and spat on the ground, coughing, then drained the cup and asked for another. His clothes, though fine, were filthy and rumpled as if he had slept in them on the ground like the others. His voice was hoarse with fatigue and smoke.

"Stop gawking," Camilla told her harshly, "Go over to that other wagon and lead the horses away; carefully, now, don't let them bolt!"

Magda started down the slope, her hand on the bridle of the near horse. The animals, smelling of fire, snorted and reared in the harness, balking and neighing, and finally Magda unknotted her sash to tie over her mount's eyes; but the animal smelled the smoke in the cloth and reared, shying away. Magda called to Keitha to bring her apron and tied it around the animal's head. Now it came peacefully as Magda urged it along with soft words.

Lord Damon came down a little way toward them. "A good thought," he said. "Stay to the right of the dry watercourse there, as you lead them down, and set up camp there—" he pointed, "in the shade of that grove of featherpod trees where the men have been felling them. Make a firebreak around the camp, at least three spans wide. Go with them—" he pointed out half a dozen women who followed the wagon down, and after a time, another wagon lumbered along. The blindfolded horses came quietly to Magda's touch on the rein, as she urged them along step by step.

"So there, good fellow, come along, that's right—"

At the indicated spot the women began off-loading the wagons, piling bowls and kettles and blankets into the arms of waiting helpers. Magda worked hard, pulling down loads of blankets.

"Here," she said, piling a final armload into a woman's

hands, "these are ours, from the Guild-house; could I trouble you to set them down over there?"

The woman glared at her and let the blankets drop deliberately from her arms into dead leaves and brambles. "Take them yourself," she said. "I am no servant to you filthy *lemvirizi*—"

Magda gasped at the foulness of the word. "Sister, what have we done to deserve this? We are here helping your people to fight the fire—"

The woman glared at her, twisting her face. "The Gods send forest fire to punish us for our sins, because we tolerate such as you among us; a sign that the very ground itself cries out against such filth as you. I am no sister to any of your kind!" She turned her back on Magda and strode away, and Magda, shaking all over, bent to pick up the fallen blankets. Tears stung her eyes; she tripped over a loose stick on the ground and almost let them fall again.

"Let me help you, sister," said a soft voice, and Magda looked up at a strange woman; her hair was cropped like an Amazon's, and she wore a Renunciate's earring, but she wore ordinary women's dress, skirt and tunic. She took a part of Magda's load, but Magda stood silent, staring. She knew the woman, she had seen her, heard her voice somewhere . . .

"Are you one of us, Sister?"

"I am Ferrika n'ha Fiona," said the woman. "Pay no heed to these ignorant women, we will teach them better some day. I am midwife at Armida," she added, over her shoulder, as she dumped the load of blankets where Magda had asked and bent to straighten them, but someone called out, "Where is the healer-woman? They are bringing three men down with burns!" and Ferrika said swiftly, "I will speak with you later," and hurried away, her tartan skirts trailing in the dust. Breeches, Magda thought, really made much more sense out here, if the woman was a Renunciate why didn't she dress like one?

Later she was sent to clear away brambles, a hard dirty job that snagged her clothing and tore her gauntlets. A new firebreak was being built and it seemed so far from the fire that Magda asked in dismay, "Do they really think it will come down here?"

In answer the woman pointed. "Look."

Magda drew a breath as she saw that the fire had topped a hill to the right of them and was burning across where their camp had been last night, little tongues of flame racing down across bramble and underbrush. Here and there a resin-tree would take fire and shoot up like a flaming torch, sparks flying hundreds of feet in the air.

"Everybody to the lines down there," a man shouted. "Women, too, all of you, from the camp! If there aren't enough shovels, grub it up with hoes, rakes, bare hands if you have to, we're working against time!"

Magda worked where they sent her, back bent, trying not to look up or listen to the fire. The smoke hurt her throat and the dust from the firebreak made it hard to breathe; Magda pulled her tunic up over her mouth and tried to breathe through it as some of the men did, wishing for a moment that she had a woman's kerchief. Some of the villager women were working beside her in the lines, their skirts tucked up to their knees, but still caught on dead branches and tore on briars; and Magda thought that her own Amazon breeches were more modest as well as more comfortable, and wondered why she was thinking then about that? They were hauling at brush and brambles now so that the men could get at the trees to fell them, and around her she heard fragments of snatched, breathless conversation— felling these trees was a sacrifice of good timberland but anything was better than letting the countryside burn! A man touched her on the shoulder—the noise made it difficult to hear connected words—and beckoned her to one end of a two-man saw; she was quite sure he had no idea she was a woman, for she did not see any of the other Amazons doing such work, but she went without comment.

As the young boys carrying water came down the line, she saw the man she had seen this morning, the one they had called Lord Damon, riding along the bare patch. She supposed he was in charge of the whole operation, a kind of engineer.

"No good," he said vehemently to someone Magda could not see. "They've got to pull out up there and let it burn; it's gone anyhow, and the best we can do is put all our men down here on this side. That way we can hold the line and keep it from burning over toward Syrtis—there are five villages down there, man!" He looked down to where the workers were straightening their backs for a moment, drinking as the buckets were passed; he saw Magda and gestured to her.

"You led the horses this morning, didn't you, lad? Good thinking. I need someone with his wits about him to carry a message to the men on the other side of that ridge up there. Give your end of the saw to that man there—" he pointed—"and come here."

She remembered that she had been ordered not to speak to any man; but that could hardly apply to listening to orders given by the man who was bossing the job! He was hardly looking at her; his eyes were troubled, surveying the distant roar and swirl of smoke and fire.

"Go up along that ridge there, and you'll come to a gang of men working under a big man, fair as a Dry-Towner; ask for *Dom* Ann'dra if you can't find him. Tell him he must pull out all the men along that ridge and let it burn out, it's hopeless. Tell him I need all the men he has down here on the east side, to keep it from burning over toward Syrtis. Have you got that?"

Magda repeated the message, pitching her voice as low as she could. "And who shall I say sent the message, *vai dom?*"

He looked straight at her for the first time. "Oh, you're not one of my men, are you? You're one of the group they sent out from Thendara, right? Tell him Lord Damon sent word. Run along, now."

Magda went off as quickly as she could through the heavy tangled underbrush. As she climbed the slope she could see the fire on the other hill they had left that morning, burning down relentlessly toward the new firebreak; where they had breakfasted was all afire now, but there was a long stretch of clean firebreak between the workers and the fire. The stench was horrible, with overtones of roasting meat, and Magda thought of the animals trapped in the fire. As she caught sight of the gang of men, she saw, with them, a gaunt, familiar figure in gray tunic and heavy trousers; Camilla. Magda recognized her only by the low Amazon boots; Camilla had tied a sweat-rag over her face, for the dust and heat were terrible. She was the only worker on the line who had not stripped to the waist.

Magda would have spoken to her, but her message was too imperative; she went along the line, looking for a tall fair-haired man. But the smoke was thicker here, rising from the other slope, so she could hardly see; she asked a man hastily "Where is *Dom* Ann'dra? A message from Lord Damon—"

The man coughed and pointed through a thick haze of smoke, and Magda plunged into it; behind her someone shouted but she could not distinguish the words. Now she saw, indistinctly, a tall man in a board-brimmed hat, fair-skinned and well over six feet tall.

"*Dom* Ann'dra?" she called, and the man turned. "I gave orders no one should follow here—"

"A message from Lord Damon," she said quickly, coming up to him, coughed for a moment, then quickly repeated her message. Her eyes were streaming with the smoke. The tall man, Ann'dra, swore angrily.

"He's right, of course, but I'd hoped we could save the pastures up here; horses will go hungry this summer! All right, go down as fast as you can, and tell him I'll have everyone down there in half an hour, got that?"

Magda nodded, coughing too hard to speak; his face, blackened with smoke, took on a look of concern.

"You should get out of the smoke as fast as you can, lad. Come this way—" he motioned her along, back toward the workers, taking the hat from his head and waving it in great sweeps.

"Pull back, men, pull back, Lord Damon needs us below— Raimon, Edric, all of you, grab the tools and get down—" he shouted, abruptly his voice took on a new sound of warning.

"Hi! Look out there, drop everything and *run*—break-through over there!" Magda stared in horror as a wall of flame leaped from nowhere and came roaring up the little gully she had crossed on her way up here. The thick, choking smoke was suddenly sweeping all around her, and when she started to run she was overwhelmed by coughing, stumbled and fell. Then she was picked up in strong arms and carried to clearer air; *Dom* Ann'dra set her down after a minute and stared at her.

"God almighty," he said but he had spoken in Terran! While Magda stared at him he shook his head and said in the mountain tongue, "Sorry—I mean, we've got to make a run for it; have you something you can tie over your face?" Magda ripped at her undertunic; it was no time to think about modesty! The smoke was so thick no one could see anyhow.

"Good," he said tersely, and took her hand. "Don't be scared, I won't let go of you, but you've got to trust me; you might get a bit scorched, but better that than roasted for the devil's supper! Hang on, now!" Holding hands, they ran directly toward what looked like the center of the fire. Magda felt a blast of heat, smelled her hair singing and searing pain in the soles of her feet; she heard herself screaming, but she ran on, her hand held tight in the big man's grip. Then they were through the flame and out of the smoke, coughing and choking and gasping. Her eyes were streaming; suddenly the world went dark and she slid to the ground.

"Ferrika!" she heard *Dom* Ann'dra bellowing, "Is the healer-woman in the lines? Well, get *somebody* up here, and make it fast! We've got to get this youngster down fast, he risked his life to get through—" and Magda felt herself lifted up; he scooped her up, arms beneath shoulders and knees, as if she had been a child. Then he drew a quick breath, staring down at her in consternation and said in a whisper, "Good God, it's a girl!"

She said in a shaky whisper "Don't—I am all right—put me down—"

He shook his head. Only then did she realize that he was still speaking Terran. "Put you down, *hell,* your boots are burned half off your feet. And who are you?"

"I am a Free Amazon from Thendara—"

"Yeah," he said in an undertone, staring skeptically, "that's what you say. Now who in the hell *are* you? Intelligence?" His eyes flared at her like steel filings in flame, out of the blackened, grimed mess that was his face. "Whoever you are, you've got guts enough for three, girl. Those boots aren't going to be good for much."

Ferrika, the Renunciate Magda had seen briefly in camp, came hurrying toward him; at her side was Camilla.

"Vai dom, the Amazon from Thendara says the messenger is one of hers and she will take her to her sister—" She stopped and cried out with compassion as she saw Magda's burnt boots, the raw blistering of her flesh that showed through. "Sister, let me take you where we can care for those feet—"

Ann'dra nodded. "Look after her; I've got to get these men down to Lord Damon, and you people get off the ridge as fast as you can. I need to find out what Damon needs, and do it right away!"

Ferrika and Camilla made a chair of their arms to carry Magda. Now she could feel terrible pain in the soles of her feet, but she followed *Dom* Ann'dra with her eyes.

Intelligence, huh? And he had spoken Terran, too. Yet Damon seemed to know and accept him as one of them. What was going on here? She was coughing and choking, her eyes were streaming and her chest hurt; she realized that Ferrika and Camilla had set her down on a blanket. Rafaella appeared from somewhere with a stoneware mug of cold water, holding it to Magda's mouth. Camilla said, "I saw the fire sweep around you, Margali, and I thought you had been killed. . . ."

Rafaella's voice was tart. "I notice she managed to fall where there was a handsome man to carry her to safety."

"Let her alone, Rafi, can't you see she's hurt?" Camilla snapped, "Should she have stayed there to burn? I am not sure I would have had the courage to run through the fire like that, even if the Hastur Lord himself, let alone *Dom* Ann'dra, held my hand!"

"Who is *Dom* Ann'dra?" Magda asked, coughing.

"Brother-in-law to the Regent; he married the Lady Ellemir's twin sister," Ferrika said, and glanced up at the burning ridge, scowling. "What are the *leroni* about, up there? I heard—" and she broke off abruptly. "Sister, let us dress those

feet of yours. And you, Camilla," she added sharply, "no more
work on the lines for you. There is *livani* tea in the kettle, it is
good against the smoke; get yourself a cup quickly, and bring
some here for your sister—" She looked into Magda's eyes,
puzzled. "I do not know your name," she said, "but surely I
have seen you before—"

"You helped me with our blankets this morning," Magda
began, but Ferrika shook her head.

"No, before that," she said, and abruptly Magda knew where
she had seen the snubbed nose, the freckled, round face and
green eyes, before this. The night of her first Training Session,
when her mind had drifted to the Sisterhood . . . and she knew
that Ferrika recognized her, too, and was staring at her in puzzlement. She said something in a strange language, but Magda
only shook her head, not understanding. Ferrika looked more
perplexed than before, but she only said, "Drink this, it will clear
your throat."

Magda sipped at the hot, sour drink; she made a wry face at
the taste, but it did soothe her smoke-rasped throat and somehow it made her nose stop streaming. Camilla, too, was sipping
the stuff; she wiped her smoke-blackened forehead with her torn
sleeve.

"Let me see those feet. Are you hurt anywhere else?"

Camilla knelt anxiously beside them. Magda's forehead was
singed a little, her eyebrows burnt and some of her hair singed,
but the burn was not serious. Camilla held her hand while Ferrika gently cut away the ruined boots, scowling.

"These soft-leather things—you can see why they are not
suitable for work on the lines!" Ferrika scolded. They had burnt
through quickly, and the last remnants had to be picked away
from the burned flesh with tweezers; Magda flinched, but did
not cry out.

"A bad burn," Ferrika said, "You will do no walking for a day
or two. It may be deeper than it looks." But to Magda's surprise,
she did not touch the burn, only held her hand over the flesh,
two or three inches away, first one foot, then the other. When she
sighed and straightened, she looked relieved. Magda thought of

Lady Rohana, concentrated and serious but not touching Jaelle's dreadful wound. *Laran*?

"Not as bad as I thought," Ferrika said, "but not superficial either; skin, but no serious burning into the muscle. With proper boots you would not have been hurt at all. I must bandage them, and she must be carried; she must not walk on those feet at all."

Tears were streaming down Magda's face. She thought it must be the aftermath of the smoke. "I came to help and I am a burden—"

"You are honorably wounded," Camilla said gruffly. "We will care for you."

Ferrika was rummaging in her case of medicines. It looked very like the one Marisela carried. "Bathe her face with this lotion, Camilla, while I dress her feet. But she must not walk on the bandages, either, and we must find her a pair of boots from some old man in the campsite, who can go barefoot without trouble."

"I had forgotten," Magda said with a sharp catch of breath, "I had a message for the Lord Damon—"

"Give it to one of the women, then," said Ferrika, "for you are not going anywhere on those feet."

Magda repeated the message to Rafaella, who nodded and hurried away. She lay back, closing her eyes and trying to ignore the pain as Ferrika smeared her feet with some sharp-smelling herb salve, and wound them in thick loose bandages. Camilla gently sponged her face with the cooling lotion.

"Poor child, when I saw the smoke close round you I was sure you were dead—I thought I had lost you, Margali—" she repeated hoarsely, holding Magda close against her. Magda realized, shocked, that the older woman was almost crying. Camilla rarely showed emotion. But Ferrika straightened up and said, "I must get back to the lines; others need my skill," and Camilla rose.

"I too must get back to the lines—"

"You stay here," Ferrika commanded, and Camilla looked angrily at her.

"What do you think me?"

"I think you too old for this work; you should never have come out," said Ferrika. "You will be more use in the camp among the women."

"I would rather work among the cows!" Camilla said scornfully, and went before Ferrika could say anything more. Ferrika sighed, looking after the elderly *emmasca* as she strode away.

"I should have known better; always Camilla must be stronger than anyone, man or woman! Stay here and rest, Margali," she commanded, and went. Magda lay back on the blanket; her feet hurt less than they had, but the pain was still enough to make her tremble. After a time it subsided to a dull ache; she lay on the blankets, alone except for a woman who was tending the fires at the back, and an old man who lay on one of the blankets, covered up warmly and breathing raucously; when the woman came to look at her Magda cringed, remembering the scorn and contempt one of the women had shown, but the strange woman only said, "You must call out to me if you need anything; more tea?" Magda felt fiercely thirsty and sipped another cup of the hot sour herb drink.

"I heard that someone had been burned, but I thought it was one of the messenger boys," she said. She moved her head indicating the old man on the blanket. "Gaffer Kanzel was overcome by the smoke this morning, but he'll do well enough with rest; what's his son thinking of, to let the old man come? I must go and tend to the supper—you're one of the Renunciates from Thendara, no?"

Magda nodded and the woman said, "I have a sister in Neskaya Guild-house; I'll trade work, one of your sisters is at the next fire, so she can come and be close to you." She went off and after a minute Keitha came up to her.

"I heard someone had been burned, but I did not know it was you," Keitha said, bending over her. "That was a nice woman who sent me here; she says she has a sister who is one of us. And I heard there are Renunciates among the healer-women who are helping here, too—"

"One of them bandaged my feet."

"I have a fire to tend, and stew to keep from burning,"

Keitha said, "but I will come and bring you drinks—she said you must drink as much as you possibly can. Do your feet pain you much, Margali?"

"I'll live," Magda said, "but they hurt, yes. But go and do your work, don't worry about me."

Reluctantly, Keitha went back to the fire, and Magda lay on her blanket, trying to get into a comfortable position on the hard ground. After a time she fell into an uneasy drowse, waking when the sky was crimson with sunset. Keitha came to give her more of the hot herb-tea and a plate of stew, but Magda could hardly swallow, though Camilla came and skillfully propped her up, and would have fed her with a spoon if Magda had let her.

"No, no, I am not hungry. I can't swallow," she said. "I am only thirsty, very thirsty—"

"That is good; you must drink as much as you can, even if you cannot eat," said Ferrika, standing over them, and they looked up to see the slight, dark aristocrat who had been called Lord Damon.

"*Mestra*," he said to Magda, "I am sorry for your injuries; I sent you into danger, not even knowing you were a woman."

She said, "I am a Renunciate," proudly, at the same moment that Ferrika protested, "You know better than that!"

She spoke without the slightest hint of deference and Lord Damon grinned at her. He looked tired and disheveled; he was chewing on a strip of smoked meat, half-heartedly, as if he were too tired to sit down and eat properly. His face was still grimed with smoke, but Magda noted that his hands were scrubbed clean, as he set the meat aside and said, "Let me look at your wounds, *mestra*, I too have something of the healer's arts."

And after a whole day fighting fire on the lines he still must go around the camp and see who is wounded . . . well, what would you expect of Damon? For a moment Magda thought someone had spoken the words aloud, but she realized that she had heard them as she was beginning to hear unspoken thoughts. She saw Lord Damon's face contract slightly as he unwrapped the bandages, and knew, without being told, that he felt, physically, the pain he caused her for a moment. *Perhaps he is too tired to shut it out.* Then it was gone, and he said quietly, "Painful, I am sure, but not really dangerous. But be careful not to let the bandages get wet or dirty; otherwise the burns will become infected; do you understand that this is important? You must not try to be brave and walk on them, you must let your sisters carry you everywhere; and drink as much as you can, even if it means you must let them carry you to the latrines every hour or two; the burns create poisons in your body and you must rid yourself of them." His manner was as courteous and impersonal as a Terran Medic's, and Magda was astonished.

He straightened to go. "Carry my compliments to the Guild-mothers in Thendara and tell them that again I have cause to be grateful to the Sisterhood."

Rafaella bowed deeply. "You honor us, *vai dom.*"

"It is you who honor us," Damon said, and touched Ferrika lightly on the shoulder. "I will leave you with your sisters for the moment; you know how to get in touch with me if you need me," he said and walked away. Ferrika went to look at one of the women who had scalded her hand on a stew kettle, and from across the circle of the camp Magda heard her ordering others who had inhaled smoke to drink more of the tea which was kept boiling on great kettles over the cookfires.

"He doesn't treat her like a servant," Keitha said, and there was the faintest hint of criticism in her voice. One of the strange women said, "Maybe she isn't."

"You do not know Ferrika," said Camilla coldly, "if you are hinting that she is his concubine. She is a Renunciate."

"Maybe," Magda said, "she's just his friend." The others gave her skeptical looks, but what Magda had sensed between the *Comyn* aristocrat—what were the *Comyn* anyhow?—and the Renunciate was an easy acceptance, a kind of equality she had not yet seen given by any man to a woman on Darkover.

Someone called from another fire "*Mestra'in*, we have heard that there is a minstrel among you; will it please you to come and play and sing for us? We have worked hard for our music!"

Rafaella rummaged in the packs they had slung across their horses. Magda had not known that she had brought her small *rryl.* "I will play for you with pleasure, but my throat is too thick with smoke to do anything but croak; anyone who still has breath to sing, may sing!"

She went toward the fire. Camilla explained, "A new crew of men has been sent out from Neskaya, and they are on the lines; so there is some leisure in the camp tonight; though all of us may be called out if there is another turn for the worse like this afternoon!"

Magda lay silent, listening to the *rryl's* sound. One or two of the Renunciates had gone to listen to the music, though Camilla stayed near Magda in case she should want anything. Magda shut her eyes and tried to sleep; the older woman had been working hard all day, too hard, and Magda was worried about her. Magda knew it would be no use to try and urge her to work less tomorrow.

But silence had fallen over the camp, and Rafaella had come back to the fire and spread her blankets beside Keitha's, when there was a stir and a flare of torches and the sound of riders. From a distance Magda heard the voice of Damon Ridenow, as she had heard it when he came to their fires, and other voices; then at the center of the camp there was a bustle of sound and several riders were sliding down from their horses. Magda sat up and looked at them; men and women in long bright cloaks, some in the blue and silver of Hastur, others in the same green and black of the cadets of the City Guard. Camilla sat up and said, "Altons of Armida, yes—"

"The *leronyn* from the Tower," someone said.

"Now, perhaps someone will have this fire under control—" another voice said somewhere. "If they have gathered the clouds they can bring rain to drown the fires. . . ."

Magda sat upright to watch. She saw the tall man they had called Ann'dra, and Lord Damon, and a slender woman whose hair blazed like brilliant copper under the blue and silver hood. She looked round quickly and came toward the fire where the Renunciates were camped together.

She said in a clear voice, speaking the pure *casta* of Nevarsin and Arilinn, "Where is the Renunciate who was wounded on the lines today?"

Magda cleared her throat and said, "It is I, but I am better—"

She came and stood by Magda's blankets. At her side was a somewhat taller woman, in a green and black cape; Magda could see that she was pregnant, though she carried it well, almost with careless ease.

The smaller woman in blue said, "I am Hilary Castamir-Syrtis, and it was our land you risked your life to save, as Ann'dra has told us. We owe you a debt, *mestra.* Will you undo the bandages?" she said to Camilla, and the old woman began to untie and unfasten them.

Lady Hilary knelt beside her, and as Ferrika had done earlier, passed the palm of her hand two or three inches above the soles of Magda's feet. "What is your name, *mestra?*"

"Margali n'ha Ysabet," she said.

"Trust me; I will not hurt you," she said, and touched a leather thong about her throat. Magda remembered Rohana's gesture, when Jaelle had been so terribly wounded in Castle Ardais, and it seemed suddenly to Magda that through the layers of leather and silk she could see the blue shimmer of a matrix stone. Lady Hilary closed her eyes for a moment and it seemed to Magda that she could feel a blue shimmer. Abruptly her feet felt as if they had been seared afresh with fire; she gasped with the pain, but it passed quickly and the blue haze was gone.

"Your feet will be healed now, *mestra,* I think you will have little trouble; but the new skin is very tender and you must be very, very careful not to walk on them for a day or two, or break the skin and allow them to become infected. I have other injuries to heal, or I would stay and speak with you; I too have reason to be grateful to the Renunciates. I wish you a good night," she said, and went away, at her side the woman in the green cloak, who had not spoken a word.

Magda looked, by the firelight, at her feet. As she had half expected—she had seen this healing from Lady Rohana when Jaelle was wounded—there was no sign of bleeding nor blackening where fire had seared and bare ground and brambles had torn. Her feet were covered with a layer of grayish scarring with patches, between the scars, of pink thin baby skin, very tender and painful when she touched it with a tentative finger. But it had been healed.

One of the women said scornfully, "They are no proper *Comyn*, and not a proper Tower. Do you know what they call them in Arilinn? Forbidden Tower . . . they work under the ban of Arilinn! They even say—" she lowered her voice as if whispering delicious scandal, and Magda did not hear what she said, but she heard small shocked exclamations.

Camilla said clearly, "What good are the Towers to those of us outside the *Comyn*? Except for these, who will come out of their walls to help and to heal."

"I don't care what you say," one of the men at the next fire said, "it's not right for a *leronis* to go about the countryside with common folk! And both the Lady Hilary and the Lady Callista were thrown out of Arilinn Tower by the old Sorceress and she wouldn't do that without good reason. They'd ought to live quietly at home if they couldn't live decent in the Tower—riding all around the countryside putting out fires and healing the common folk—" he spat, and the sound was eloquent. "We're doing all right with the fire, we don't need their sorcery to come and put it out for us!"

"I say nothing against the Lady Leonie," Camilla said quietly. "Once she was kind to me when I greatly needed kindness. But perhaps the Lady knows little, cloistered as a sacred virgin within her Tower in Arilinn, of the needs of those who must live in the world, and do not know how, or would be too much in awe of them, to seek them out for help or healing."

"I've even heard—my sister is a steward's helper at Armida— that they're teaching the common folk *laran*," said one woman with scorn. "If it can be taught to the likes of us, what good is it? The *Comyn* are descended from the Gods! Why should they come and meddle in our lives?"

Camilla said scornfully, "I cannot talk to such ignorance."

"They're like you Renunciates," said the woman with a concentrated spite. "Won't stay in your place, won't marry and have children, no wonder you want the Hastur kinfolk to come out of *their* proper place too! Want to turn the world upside down, all you folk, make the masters servants and the servants masters! The old ways were good enough for my father and they're good enough for my husband and me! No men of your own, so you want to come out here brazen in your breeches, trying to show off your legs and get them away from us . . . well, *mestra*, I'm telling you, my husband wouldn't touch you with a hayfork, and if he did I'd scalp him! And if I see you waggling your tits at him I'll scratch out your eyes!"

Camilla chuckled. "If all men but your husband vanished from the earth, dame, I would sleep with the house-dog. You are heartily welcome to your husband's attentions for all I care to contest them."

"You Amazons are all filthy lovers of women—"

"Hold!" said an authoritative voice. "No brawling in the camp; fire-truce holds here, too!" It was Ferrika's voice, and the strange woman moved away in the dark. Ferrika said, "Go to sleep, my sisters; 'the man who argues with the braying of the donkey or the barking of his dog will win no cases before the high courts.'"

Silence settled around the Amazons' fire, but Camilla still seemed ruffled as she drew off her boots to sleep.

"I have met with the old *leronis* of Arilinn—I do not say where, but it was when I was very young," she said in a low voice to Magda. "She healed me when I had much need of healing, mind and body—I told you some of this. But the folk of Arilinn know nothing of the needs of common people. If what befell me had happened to a commoner maiden, the Lady would have shrugged and told my folk to marry me off to whatever man would have damaged goods. Because I was one of her own, she had pity on me—" abruptly she broke off. "What has come to me that I babble like this?"

Magda pressed her hand in the darkness. "Whatever you say to me I will never repeat, I promise you, sister."

"That woman called me lover of women as if it were the worst insult she could imagine," Camilla said. "I am not ashamed to hear it spoken, . . . except when I am among women who use it as the worst abuse they can imagine—"

"You are my friend, Camilla, I do not care what you are."

"I think you know I would like to be more than your friend," Camilla said. "I should not say this when you are hurt, but you know I love you. . . and I would dearly love to make love to you; but I am not a man, and my friendship does not depend on it. It is for you to choose . . ." her voice trailed away. Magda felt deeply troubled.

Was this what she wanted then, was this why she had run away from Jaelle—the old children's taunt: *only truth hurts*. Living among women, certainly it was not surprising . . . maybe it was indeed what she wanted; her marriage with Peter had caught on the snag of independence and competitiveness, she had not been content to think of him as husband and lover. Nor had she felt impelled to seek another lover, or to turn to any man. She thought, with deep disquiet, maybe it is a woman I want, I don't know, I do love Camilla, but I never thought of that. . . .

Maybe I ought to take Camilla as a lover, it would make her happy and it wouldn't hurt me, and at least then I would know if that is truly what I want. But do I want to find out? She said gently to Camilla, "We will talk about this when we are back in Thendara, I promise you," and felt warmed by the comforting touch of the older woman.

She lay with her head against Camilla's shoulder, and at last she knew that the older woman was asleep. But she could not sleep. The pain in her feet had all but subsided, but the healing skin itched with maddening intensity, and she knew she must not scratch it. How had Lady Hilary done that? And now she was reading thoughts again. . . .

She listened to the quiet noises of the camp, to the faraway sound that she knew was the roaring of the fire. Could it jump a firebreak as it had done before and suddenly blaze among them, roaring and destroying? They slept here, and others worked along the fire-lines. . . .

After a little it seemed as if she slept, but she was still

conscious of her chilled body, feet itching furiously, as she seemed to look down on the camp from a greyish height; she saw herself lying curled up against Camilla, the other women snuggled close for the warmth, the dying cookfires carefully safeguarded inside rings of stone; then she saw the brilliantly colored cloaks of the men and women, the tall man called An-n'dra, Lady Hilary in her blue cloak with the blazing hair, the dark, diffident Lord Damon, the silent woman who had been pointed out to her as Lady Callista, and they were somehow joined like dancers around a blue blaze like the matrix Hilary had used to heal her feet. . . . They were weaving in a colorful dance weaving in and out and at the same time they knelt motionless and fixed on the matrix . . . Ferrika reached for Magda and drew her into the dance, and then they were dancing among clouds, she was helping Hilary to scoop up the clouds and roll them through the sky to where the fire raged below. . . they felt damp and soft and palpable, like bread dough, under her hands when she punched them down. It felt as if she squeezed them between her fingers and the moisture came oozing out, they grew softer and softer and more pliable, and then rain was trickling from the clouds, trickling down and then pouring, and then flooding. . . .

Magda woke sharply to the drops splashing on her face. At her side Camilla sat up sharply and cried out, "It's raining!" And all over the fields, the men in the camp sent up a great cheer. No fire could stand against this hard, soaking rain.

And I was part of it, she said to herself, confused, and then dismissed the thought. No doubt she had felt the first drops and the whole dream had come out of that. Some of the women were hurrying to pull their blankets into the shelter of the trees, the wagons; Camilla hauled out a waterproof tarpaulin from their pack and spread it over her blankets and Magda's, beckoning Rafaella and Keitha into the shelter, like a small improvised tent. The rain kept pouring down and there were groans of discomfort and cold mixed with the cheering, but better, they all admitted, to be cold and wet than burning up, and this meant crops and livestock and trees would be saved.

Good luck, Magda wondered, weather wisdom, or had the *Comyn* aristocrats with their matrixes created the rain? She had no reason to think the latter except for her bizarre dream.

Or had it been a dream at all? Unlikely that they could have aroused the storm. But on the other hand, it was even more unlikely that Lady Hilary could have healed her burnt feet without even touching her.

Who was she to set limits to other people's powers? A long rumble of thunder drowned out thought and she clung to Camilla, her feet icy in the cold, while someone grumbled, "Damn it, couldn't they have managed rain without downpours and lightning?"

Some people, thought Magda drowsily, were never satisfied.

Chapter 5

There was still no morning-sickness but Jaelle did feel strange and queasy, and had gotten into the habit of lying in bed while Peter shaved and showered and readied himself for work; only when he had kissed her good-bye and gone did she rise and find herself a snack somewhere in their rooms—it was simpler than braving the strange smells of the cafeteria in the early morning.

This morning, by the time she reached Cholayna's office, Monty and Aleki were there, rummaging in files and pulling out printouts.

"There's a fire," Cholayna said. "On Alton lands; I went out with the helicopter. I can't believe they're fighting it by hand!"

"We have been doing it for centuries, long before the Terrans came here," Jaelle said stiffly, "and will be doing it when they are gone."

Peter came in, and Jaelle realized he was dressed for the field; leather breeches, woolly tunic, surcoat and cloak lined with rabbithorn fur, high boots. She envied him. "Ready, Monty? Now remember, Aleki, you're a mute, deaf and dumb; there's no way you could pass yourself off as Darkovan yet with your accent, but it'll give you a chance to observe."

Cholayna thrust a cartridge into the terminal and a fuzzy picture wobbled across the screen; billowing smoke, long lines of men and women scraping bare lines with hoes and rakes and crude tools, some men on horseback directing movement of lines.

"No earth-moving equipment, no tractors, no sprayer planes! We sent out an offer of help—seems like they could use us to spray the flames with foam. But since we heard about that crashed plane in the Kilghards out near Armida, the natives have been nervous about their overflights," Monty said. "Look, there are three villages down that line, you can see them—" He pointed as the picture of the lines of men and women was briefly overlaid by a picture from the weather satellite. Jaelle wondered, not for the first time, if anyone had bothered to tell the Domains about the spy-eye of the satellite in the sky.

Sometimes Renunciates went out on the fire-lines; Magda was housebound, and need not go, though Camilla and Rafaella always went. *If she was in danger, I'd know.*

"Go and check out Aleki's costume, Jaelle, you know better than I do what he ought to need," said Cholayna. "Peter had Monty all ready even before I got the report, and they were going alone, but Aleki pulled rank on them and said he was going, whatever they said." She smiled a little ruefully. "Even if it means leaving you with what he ought to be doing while he's out on the lines!"

"Don't talk as if I was saddling her with the whole department's work," Alessandro Li said defensively. "Language reports, and I want her to check out the satellite printouts and mark the general layout of the Dry Towns. Next week I'll take her on an overflight, if she wants to go—you haven't been up in one of our planes yet?"

"Hell, I'd have taken her if I'd thought she'd want to go," Peter said, "But some other time, all right, Aleki? The horses are ready right outside the gates in the Old Town . . ."

Jaelle was studying the wallscreen, heavy smoke and ashes sweeping over the hills, a blackened swathe left behind. She knew that country, she had ridden through it; every few years, the resin-trees caught and they grew so quickly that new fires came down. Cholayna was frowning and saying something about the destruction of vital watershed.

"Trouble is, there's no rain in sight at all," Peter said. "The people at Armida should be warned about the satellite picture;

the winds are going to sweep across from Syrtis, and Armida itself could go up in flames. Jaelle—"

She wrenched herself away from the picture, so vivid it seemed she could smell the smoke, the acrid smell of ash and the crash of fire. She turned Aleki round, scowled.

"Those boots aren't right. They'll think you're a woman in disguise, or an effeminate. Peter, he's got to have proper boots."

"In hell's name," Aleki protested, "I saw the regulation issue for the field, and I can't walk in the damn things! Do I have to be some striding macho bully, stomping around all over everything? Are the men all as insecure as that?"

"I'm not interested in their psychology," said Peter dryly, "Custom of the country, and all that; those boots would mark you what they call a sandal-wearer anywhere outside the city, and wouldn't look too good even indoors. Go down to Field Issue and get some proper ones. You take him down, Jaelle."

She went down and found him a pair of boots, helped him to haul them on, grumbling all the way. She readjusted the knot of his scarf and warned him again to be deaf and dumb. "Your first trip into the field, you're going to feel very much as I did my first day here," she said. "But it's only a beginning."

On the roof of the copter landing, Peter was arguing with Monty. "If we come in like this, costumes or no, they'll know we're Terrans right away. I think we should ride with that crew down there." He pointed at a group of men saddling up in a street near the HQ.

"They need able-bodied men to fight fire," Monty said. "I don't think they would care whether we were Terrans or *cralmacs* provided we could carry a hoe, and if we go in the copter we can get there sooner and do more work without tiring ourselves out by riding in. The important thing is to help them fight the damned fire! It might even be good public relations, if they knew that the Terran Empire sent able-bodied men to help them—"

"I'd like to remind you both," said Alessandro Li, "that we are still working for Intelligence; this isn't a humanitarian mission. Haldane, who are those people getting ready to ride?

Peter had a strong pair of binoculars tucked in his belt; he raised them and looked down into the street. "Second call-up; the first one, only volunteers went, but this party is evidently taking out all the men they can find, there are old men and little boys no older than twelve in that lineup—I went out one year. And there are three or four *Comyn*, with a few dozen Guardsmen, and at least one *leronis*."

"You mean the lady draped in red?" Monty asked, and Peter nodded.

"*Comyn* again! Damn it, I wish I knew what made the whole countryside jump like frogs whenever they nod their heads!" Aleki said, "but the ones who know won't tell. One of these days, Jaelle, we're going to have a long talk about that, aren't we? Let's get the horses and go. Forget the copter. Don't want anything marking us as Terrans. Intelligence, remember."

Jaelle said swiftly, "I am going too. I have fought before this on the fire-lines—and I need not keep the camp with the women; I am a Renunciate and I can do a man's work."

"Commendable spirit in your lady," said Alessandro Li dryly, "but tell her to stay at home, Haldane, she's more use to us here for language and liaison. If she wants to be helpful, let her get on good terms with what's-her-name, Lady Rohana."

"I need to go. And Magda must be there, if they are calling out all the able-bodied—"

"Able-bodied men," said Monty firmly. "You know as well as I do that they haven't reached the point of calling out women, Jaelle."

Peter interrupted as she opened her mouth to answer, "You are not going out there, Jaelle. There's a full-fledged forest fire raging out there, and you—"

"I have probably fought more fires than you have," she said angrily. "I went first into the lines when I was fourteen—"

"Forget it," said Cholayna. "We don't have time to wait while you get medical clearance—"

"Medical clearance? To go into my own countryside?"

"Right," Peter said. "You're here in Magda's job, and one of the first rules is that nobody—nobody—goes into the field without clearance." The two men were striding toward the elevator; Jaelle said quietly, stepping in after them, "You forget. I am a Darkovan citizen. I am not subject to those regulations—"

"That's what you think." Peter stabbed roughly at a ground-level button. "When we were married, I applied for Empire citizenship for you, so our kids would have it. Besides, by your own Oath, you are here to abide by the terms of your employment. That's one of them. The matter, sweetheart, is closed." He leaned over and kissed the tip of her nose. "See you when we get back, love." He walked quickly away.

Some day, she thought angrily, he was going to throw their marriage, and her Empire citizenship, up at her once too often. She toyed with the notion of going into the hateful surroundings of Medic and getting the damned clearance, to spite them all. They could hardly prevent her . . .

. . . but then they would have her registered as pregnant, and something told her that this one thing she ought to keep from them. For some reason she did not want that on the Terran records. She asked herself if she was only spiting Peter—he would surely want his coming child registered. She started to go, then something inside her said, cold and clear, *No.*

Rationalizing this, she thought of her last visit to Medic, the machines which looked inside and through her, the feeling of being completely depersonalized, her body a machine among other machines, violated. If they knew she was pregnant, it would be worse. She had some days off coming—Peter had explained that to her; she went up to the office and asked Cholayna for the day off to visit the Guild-house.

As she had half expected, Cholayna asked if she might come along. Jaelle went up and dressed quickly, feeling relieved as she slid into her Amazon clothing; leather breeches for riding— they were tight in the waist, she would have to borrow a pair from Rafaella to wear till the baby was born—and proper boots. When she joined Cholayna at the gates, the woman was wearing a heavy weatherproof down jacket which would have been wonderful for the Hellers in winter, but made Jaelle wonder how

Cholayna avoided suffocating in it today—it was really not that cold.

"But I was born on a really hot world," Cholayna said, shivering even in the heavy clothes, and looking in dismay and disbelief at Jaelle's light tunic, over which she wore only the lightest of riding cloaks.

"But it's almost summer," Jaelle said, and Cholayna chuckled.

"Not to me, it isn't."

But Cholayna kept pace with Jaelle, even in the high-heeled sandals in which Jaelle could not have taken four steps without breaking her ankles. Walking beside Cholayna, Jaelle felt like a young girl again, the Amazon fosterling; there had been a time when Kindra had taken employment as a guard for warehouses about the city. When she made her morning rounds, she had sometimes taken her foster daughter with her; it was then that they had had some of their best times together, mother and daughter. It was those months that had made Jaelle an Amazon.

She could have confided in Kindra as she could not in Rohana. Once she had conceived a child, Rohana could not see her, Jaelle, at all, but only the potential mother of a child for the Aillard Domain.

But surely there would be someone in the Guild-house that she could talk to.

They were walking through the marketplace and she saw rounded eyes, curious glances at Cholayna's dark skin. But one would have thought Cholayna had never experienced anything but these shocked or hostile glances; she strode along blithely in her uniform and Jaelle envied the woman her confidence.

I was like that once, when I walked with Kindra and the townspeople stared and jeered at the Renunciates. What has happened to me?

Only on the very steps of the Guild-house did Cholayna hesitate for a moment and ask, "Should I have worn makeup, Jaelle? I could have painted my skin so that I looked like anyone else. I do not want to embarrass you in your own home. . . ."

Jaelle liked Cholayna more for asking, but she shook her

head defiantly. Renunciates themselves were different; if they could not accept Cholyana's differences so much the worse for them!

And indeed, when Irmelin answered the door, she stared for a moment at Cholayna, but quickly collected herself to welcome Jaelle with a hug.

"I know Mother Lauria will want to see you," she said to Cholayna, and showed the Terran woman directly toward the Guild-mother's office. But to Jaelle's inquiries she told her that Rafaella, Camilla and Margali were all out on the fire-lines, they had been gone from the house for several days now.

All of my oath-sisters. There is no one here I can talk to. She supposed Marisela had gone with the others, but Irmelin told her that the woman was in the house, and guessed, of course, why Jaelle wished to see her.

"You're expecting a baby, Jaelle? Why, how nice for you!" Jaelle supposed she should have expected that; she said all the appropriate things, and let Irmelin bring her into the kitchen and sit her down with a cup of hot bark-tea and a piece of fresh buttered bread from the ovens, as if Jaelle were again the twelve-year-old fosterling who had been everybody's pet in the Guild-house.

"I'll fetch down Marisela to you, there's no reason for you to be running up and down all the stairs—"

"Irmi, it will be four moons before running up and down stairs would bother me," Jaelle protested, but just the same, Irmelin's fussing comforted her. At least someone cared; she sat dripping tears into her tea. After a time Marisela came into the kitchen, dipped herself up a cup of tea and sat down, letting it steam in front of her. She smiled at Jaelle, that smile which seldom reached her mouth but only twinkled behind her eyes.

"Well, you look healthy enough, Shaya, is there some reason I should have come down to you?"

"Oh, Marisa, I'm sorry, I *told* Irmelin—"

"No, sister, it's all right, I slept through breakfast and am glad to have some company, with everyone out on the fire-lines."

"Can I get you something?" Marisela started to shake her

head, then looked sharply at Jaelle and said, "Yes. I would like some bread, sliced very thin, please, and honey instead of butter." And Jaelle, busying herself with cutting the bread with the proper knife, and finding the honey crock and spoon and spreading it, found that she no longer wanted to dissolve into tears. She wondered why Marisela was smiling as she sat down again, sliding the plate of bread and honey toward her. The older woman asked, "How far?"

Jaelle counted mentally and told her, and Marisela nodded.

"So that is why you were asking all those soul-searching questions about not knowing our own minds and how to tell whether we are pleasing ourselves or someone else," Marisela said. It was not a question and not sympathetic, and Jaelle felt as if Marisela had flung cold water over her, but she realized she was not entitled to ask for sympathy. No one had bidden her lie with Peter, nor marry him, and she could have made certain she did not get with child. She blinked fiercely, but she no longer wanted to cry. Done was done.

So she told Marisela, making a good, funny story of it, all about the Terran Medic machinery which had inspected her inside and out, and Marisela laughed with her.

"I think we can all agree that you do not need such care as that. You are young and healthy; only if you should begin vomiting, or show any sign of bleeding. Take care what you eat, drink much milk or beer but little wine, get as much fruit and fresh food as you can, and tell the Terrans, if they should ask, that you have seen your own medical adviser. You should come back to the House to bear your child, but the Terrans may not allow it—they think what we know of medical practice is limited and barbarian, and I must admit that to a certain extent they are right and I am not altogether sorry for it. Just the same, two days ago I lost a mother and her child and I would have given all I own for some access to your Terrans' skills—"

"Well," Jaelle said, "Cholayna is in there arranging ways for you to have such help," but Marisela shook her head.

"Ah, no, my dear, it is not as simple as that. It sounds like a perfectly simple thing, and a thing that is all good, that I should be able to save mothers alive to care for their children, and save their children alive so that no mother may weep because half the little children she bears do not live past weaning. But it is not such a good thing as all that."

"Do you dare to say it is a bad thing?"

"Aye, and I do say so," Marisela said, and at Jaelle's indignant stare, she said, "I want to speak with your friend anyway. Shall we go and talk with Mother Lauria? Finish your tea, it is good for you."

Jaelle had grown up thinking of Mother Lauria's office as a sacrosanct place, not to be breached except in emergencies, but Marisela simply knocked and went in, and Mother Lauria smiled at her.

"I was going to send for you, Marisela. Cholayna—" she struggled a little with the name. "Is that how you say it?"

"Near enough," said Cholayna and nodded in a friendly way to Marisela. "So you are the House Medic, as we would say it. It is you who should choose women to be instructed in Medical techniques, or you yourself may come and learn them with the younger women—"

"I should be interested," Marisela said, "and knowledge is always a good thing, but will you teach them only to use their medical sciences or will you teach them when they should not use them?"

"I do not understand," Cholayna said. "The business of a Medic is to save lives, and Mother Lauria was just telling me how you had had to let a woman die because you could not save her or her child. We can teach you ways to save most of them. . . ."

"So that every mother will have a dozen living children?" said Marisela, "and then, how shall they be fed?"

"I am sure you know that we have knowledge of contraceptive techniques," Cholayna said. "So that a woman can put her strength into bearing only one or two children and not spend all her life in bearing them and watching them die."

Marisela nodded. "If the two she does bear are the strongest and best, and we could be sure of that," she said, "but suppose the two who survive are the weakest, and so their children will be weaker yet? Ten, twenty generations down the road, we will be a people of weaklings, kept alive only by sophisticated medical techniques and thus dependent on your technology. If a woman is saved alive when her pelvis is too small, then perhaps her daughters will live to bear more children with this defect, and once again, we are dependent upon more and more medical help to keep them alive in childbirth. Believe me, it hurts my heart to watch women and children die. But when a child is born, for instance, blue and unable to breathe because he has a hole inside his heart . . ."

"That can be repaired," Cholayna said. "Many of our people are living who would have died here at birth . . ."

"And his children will multiply those defects," said Marisela. "Oh, believe me, on the cases where something has gone wrong in the womb and the child is lacking strength, perhaps we should save that child alive, but if it is a defect he will pass to his own sons? Better that one should die now than that a hundred weaklings should sap the strength of our people. And it is like a lottery—the first two children are not always the brightest, the strongest, the best; so often a great leader or genius will be born seventh, or tenth, or even twentieth among the children of his family."

Cholayna said stiffly, "I am afraid I do not like playing God and deciding that women must suffer that way."

"Is it not playing God to decree that they shall *not* so suffer?" Marisela asked. "We once had a breeding program here where we chose to tinker with our genes, to create the perfect people and the perfect race. We bred *laran* into our people and we are still suffering for it. Perhaps when the Goddess decrees that some must die at birth, She is being cruel to be kind."

"I still feel we should not reject the gift of the Terrans when they wish to teach our people their arts," Mother Lauria said, and Marisela nodded.

"Oh, I am sure you are right. But I pray all the Gods that we have the wisdom to know where to end it. There is no virtue in saving some lives which will be a burden to everyone in the household, everyone in the village, everyone in the world. I—I do not want to play God in deciding who must live and who must die, so I leave it to the mercy of the Goddess. If I in my small self have the power to decide that this one must live and this one must die, I can only say, my business is saving lives, I will save alive all I can. That way lies chaos. Perhaps it is better not to have that power."

"I cannot agree that anything which diminishes a woman's power can be right," said Cholayna, and Marisela sighed.

"In theory surely you are right. But sometimes it is a terrible temptation to take the short view and do the immediately humane thing, instead of what might be best for all of humankind over the centuries."

Jaelle asked angrily, "Do you mean you would let people die if you could possibly save them?"

"Alas, no," said Marisela. "I would not, and perhaps that is why I fear that power so much. I hunger for all your knowledge, so that I need never see a woman bleed and die, or a baby struggle to breathe; I hate to lose the fight with that Dark Lady who stands beside every woman at this hour, contending with me for Her due. But my business is to save life when I can, as I said, and I will, I suppose, in the end, stick to my business of saving lives. The Dark Lady is a very ancient and friendly adversary, and she can care for her own."

Cholayna looked at her with interest. She said, "That is a point of view often debated at Head Center. I had not expected to hear it in this House—"

"From a native midwife, or would you call me a witch doctor or sorceress?" asked Marisela, and they smiled at each other in the friendliest way.

But Jaelle was restless as the conversation went far afield into complicated matters of ethics, and was relieved when Cholayna rose to go. Cholayna said, "You may stay as long as you wish, Jaelle, you are certainly entitled to a holiday," but she went for her cloak, telling the older women that she had some work to do. She could surely find some work in Monty's office, since he, and Aleki, had left so much undone when they went to the fire-lines.

But, restless and alone that night in the quarters which seemed so much too big for her, with Peter away, she could not rest. The Guild-house now seemed as unfriendly as the Terran Zone. And her main reason in going there had failed; she had wanted to see Magda, and Magda had been away on the fire-lines, and Marisela and Mother Lauria, friendly as they were, were not really involved in her problems. There was no reason they should be.

She had wanted to, needed to see Magda and make friends again with her. Would it be better to pretend that nothing had happened, or to insist that they talk frankly about it? Perhaps it meant nothing. After all, Magda had had a tremendous load on mind and spirit; all the pressures of the housebound time, hostility because of the fight and the indemnity, the fear of being dismissed from the Guild-house, the pressures of the Training sessions and the endless nightmares . . . was it any wonder Magda had no extra strength to deal with Jaelle's troubles?

Yet it was more than that. Jaelle searched in her mind and found only a confused image of herself picking Kyril's hand off her arm as if it were a crawling bug; intrusive, unpleasantly suggestive of an unwanted intimacy. Yes, and before supper when she had hugged and kissed Magda, the other woman had drawn away uneasily. *Everyone already thinks I am your lover.* We should talk about that; between oath-sisters there should be no such barrier.

It was taken for granted in the Guild-house, but after the usual adolescent experiments, she had never thought about it. For a time when she had first set up the business with Rafaella—they had been lovers, for a time, but it had seemed no more than a way of cementing deep friendship, and Rafaella was at heart far more interested in men; after a few weeks it had simmered down into affection, had in fact never been much more. She had taken it for granted as part of their bonding; had, she now realized, felt that she and Magda should have shared this gesture of trust, of love and openness to one another. But if it was not the custom among Magda's people, as it certainly was not among, for instance, the *cristoforos*, why did she feel so rejected? Was she afraid Magda would come to despise her, and if she could lose Magda's friendship over a thing as simple as that, was her friendship worth having?

She held endless conversations inside her own mind, but once or twice when it seemed she could almost see Magda's face . . . *I shall be reaching her with* laran *if I do not take care.* . . . She tried, in a panic, to slam her mind shut. Now she regretted she had never accepted Rohana's offer, no, her plea, that she should go, even briefly, to a Tower to have her *laran* trained. Now it was too late. Was it too late? And then she would find herself crying again.

She had completely ceased to use the corticator tapes; but she realized that the Language department did not know it, they were complimenting her daily about her growing command of the language.

One evening, when she came into her rooms, she found Peter there, stripping off mud-crusted shirt and trousers.

"No, don't kiss me yet, sweetheart, for God's sake wait until I get out of these things and shower; to put it bluntly, I stink," he said. She sniffed. He certainly did. She supposed her senses had been sharpened by constant access to the level of sanitation in the Terran Zone, where the slightest stain was instantly scrubbed away and disposable clothing was the norm. He thrust his clothes toward the disposal, then wrinkled his nose, bagged them and shoved them into a closet.

"I guess I'd better take them down to be cleaned; they're field clothes and a little grime will make them more authentic," he said, with a wry grin. "How's junior?" He patted her still-flat tummy as he headed for the shower, and she heard his voice trailing off, mostly something about how good it was to be back where he could get hot water and civilization.

The Empire people think civilization and plumbing are the same thing. They are neurotic about smells and dirt, she thought. He should have kissed me, at least! She lay down on the bed, feeling bruised. He hadn't asked about her, only the baby. She felt angry at herself for feeling that way; he was tired, just off the trail, and she was certainly being too sensitive, but like Rohana, once she was pregnant she was not herself, only a sort of walking nest for the damned baby! She buried her face in the pillow. Not an honest feather in it, some damned synthetic stuff. She took a long breath and she smelled again the aseptic, the *Terran* smell of it. It was only the smell. She would not cry. She *would* not.

She could go now, she didn't have to stay here. In half an hour's walk she could be in the Guild-house. But she was sworn; she was legitimately employed to fill Magda's place in the Terran HQ. Magda had not violated her pledge to the Guild-house, under stresses far worse than this; she must at least match Magda's courage.

Would they even *want* her in the Guild-house, swelling daily with a Terran's baby like any drab from the spaceport bars? She could tell herself it was different as much as she wished, but she had wanted Peter, she had wanted to lie with him and now there was a child coming, a child who would never be at home in either world. She was crying now, she did not hear Peter come out of the shower, and when he tried to embrace her she fought and cried hysterically until in the end he had to call a Medic. She spent the rest of the night down on the Hospital floor, drugged into unconscious sleep. There was nowhere else to go.

Part III:

OUTGROWTH

Chapter 1

Although Magda's housebound time would not end till forty days after Midsummer, custom freed the Renunciate novices for the day itself, and Magda came down to breakfast to hear the women discussing their plans for the holiday. Keitha and Magda had been told they might go where they wished during day and the night following; but must be back within the House by dawn.

"What are your plans, Keitha?"

"A midwife cannot make many plans. But before Doria left for Neskaya, she asked me to go this day and see her birth-mother. The woman will not come and see her daughter here, but Rafi says she often asks if Doria is well and content.

"That she does," Rafaella said, sliding down her bowl for porridge. "I think she is afraid Doria will try and make Amazons of her other daughters, but I do not think any of Graciela's other girls have sense enough to take the Oath. She has not seen Doria ten times in the five years before this, but the day Doria was fifteen she began plying her with gifts and offering to find her a husband. Nothing would please her more than to have Dori repudiate her fosterage here and marry the first oaf who offered for her. I do not think she will be glad to see either of us, but whether or no, we will take her Doria's gifts and greetings. And I shall see my youngest son, whom I have not seen in half a year."

Magda remembered that Doria's mother had given her up when she was born, in return for Rafaella's son.

"I too was promised I might see my son," Felicia said, "but I do not know if I can bear it yet, or whether it might be cruel to him. . . ."

"Rafi, you are wanted in the stable," said Janetta, poking her head into the dining hall.

"Well, what is it?" said Rafaella impatiently, "Does one of the horses wish to give me Midsummer greetings?"

"A man who says it is business," Janetta told her, and Rafaella grumbled, threw down her fork and, still munching on a piece of the excellent nut cake which had made its appearance on the table in lieu of ordinary bread and butter, went off toward the stable. Two minutes later Janetta came back and said, "Margali, Rafi wants you too."

Magda had not finished her breakfast, but she was pleased enough at the disappearance of Rafaella's hostility that she went at once; she had tried enough to reassure Rafaella that she would fill Jaelle's place in their business as much as she could, and it was worth being disturbed even at the holiday breakfast. She said, "Save me a piece—" she hesitated; she could hardly call it coffee cake, which would have been the Terran word, and no one had mentioned what they called it; she pointed and Keitha laughed. "I'll guard it with my life!"

Rafaella was talking to a tall man shrouded in a thick cape; he was at the head of a string of horses, among them a few of the fine Armida-bred blacks. Several, too, were the shaggy ponies of the Hellers.

"Margali, I am sorry to ask you to work at Festival, but I did not expect these ponies for another tenday—"

"I too am sorry to disturb you on holiday, *mestra*, but I was in the City now," said the man, and Margali suddenly recognized his voice; he was the big fair-haired man who had carried her out of the fire-lines, *Dom* Ann'dra. *The Terran!* But he was talking about the ponies in an accent better than her own.

"I could not find the ten you wanted, but I have seven here; they are strong and already immune to the hoof-rot, and all have been broken to halter and pack."

Rafaella was going to one after another, examining teeth,

patting soft muzzles. "They are good ones," she said, "but why are you in the City so late in the season, *Dom* Ann'dra? Is your lady traveling with you? And the Lord Damon, will he be in the City for Council Season?"

"No, I am traveling all but alone this year; but since I was coming this way, I was able to escort Ferrika to you." He held out his hand to help down a woman in a heavy traveling mantle who was seated on one of the horses. Over Rafaella's shoulder, as he turned, he recognized Magda and said, "Oh, it is you—I was concerned about you, *mestra*; did your feet heal properly?"

"Oh, yes, quite well," Magda said. "Only my boots were burnt beyond repair: my feet are fine."

Rafaella and Ferrika hugged one another and Rafaella said, "I had hoped you could come earlier in the season, Ferrika—"

The small snub-nosed woman smiled and said, "I too wished to come; but there was need of my services at Armida."

"More children on the estates? Or one of your ladies?"

Ferrika shook her head. She looked grieved. "The Lady Ellemir miscarried a child earlier this year; and her sister stayed to nurse her,—Lady Callista will not take her seat in Council this season—"

"I wonder, then, that you would leave your lady," Rafaella said, but Ann'dra interrupted. "Ferrika is not servant to us, but friend; and Ellemir is well again. But none of us have any heart for merrymaking this year, and there is little to be accomplished at Midsummer, so I came to do what business I must and pay my respects to the Lords of the Council; then I shall be off home again, probably at dawn, I was sorry to disturb your Festival, but I did not wish to stable the beasts in a public compound when they could be in their new home."

"I am grateful to you," Rafaella said. "It takes a tenday or so to quiet them after the long trip; they are far better here in their own stable. Ferrika, *breda*, don't stand out here, go inside and greet your sisters, breakfast is on the table!"

"And holiday nut cake? Marvelous," Ferrika said; and went into the house. Rafaella handed a pony's lead to Magda and said, "Will you take this one into that box-stall down there?"

When she came back Rafaella was writing, propped against the wall. She handed the paper to *Dom* Ann'dra.

"Take this to my patron, *Dom* Ann'dra, and she will arrange to have you paid; the horses are for her, I understand. May the Goddess grant that Lady Ellemir is well again soon."

"Amen to that. Shall I bring the other ponies when I come again?"

"Or sooner, if you have a messenger you can trust," said Rafaella. "And I need a good saddle-horse for an oath-gift to my daughter at Neskaya Guild-house; is one available?"

"Not a good hand-broken horse for a lady, no; we always have too many orders for those," *Dom* Ann'dra said. "I could not promise you one of those for more than two years. But I can let you have a good halter-broken filly if you would like to train it yourself."

"I will not have the time; but Doria should break her own horse anyhow," Rafaella said. "Send it to Neskaya Guild-house for Doria n'ha Rafaella."

Dom Ann'dra scribbled something on the papers he held. "I'll send a man there with it within a tenday," he said. He looked past Rafaella again at Magda curiously, and she almost heard, *What is she doing here?* Well, she thought, I certainly would like to know what *he* is doing here! No doubt he was on field assignment, had probably been so for years; if she went to the Terran Zone she might be able to look him up in Records; Cholayna or Kadarin would certainly know. She helped Rafaella stable and feed the new ponies. When she went back to the hall the porridge was cold, but Irmelin had brought fresh bread and opened a new jar of some kind of conserve, and a second nut-cake which vanished as swiftly as the first.

Ferrika was sitting at Marisela's feet, her head in the woman's lap.

". . . so tragic . . . so many of the noble ladies do not really want children and cannot wait to turn them over to wet nurse and foster mother. But the Lady Ellemir is one of those who, as soon as their arms are empty, already hungers for another babe at her breast. Four years ago, when the Lady Callista could not suckle her child—though I think myself it was more that she did not wish to—Ellemir nursed Hilary along with her own Domenic."

"Was she long in labor this time?"

"Not long, they had hardly time to summon me from the steward's wife," Ferrika said, "but all the more tragic because this time it was almost a matter of a few more days; if she could have carried the child even another tenday it might have lived. A girl, and born alive too, but we could not get her to breathe, her poor little lungs would not open, for all we could do. It was just a little too early. Once I really thought she would breathe and cry . . . a little mewing sound . . ." Ferrika buried her head in Marisela's lap and the older woman patted her hair.

"Perhaps it is just as well; once or twice I have done what seemed a miracle and saved one alive when it seemed hopeless, but then they grow up crippled or partly paralyzed and cannot speak—it was the mercy of the Goddess."

"Tell that to Lady Ellemir!" retorted Ferrika, blinking back her tears. "A girl, it was, perfectly formed, with red hair, and she had *laran* too, she had been real to them for three times forty days . . . I thought they would all go mad with grief. Lord Damon has not left my lady alone for a moment, day or night."

"But think; even with *laran*, if the poor babe had grown up sickly . . . better an easy death and a return to the Goddess, who may send her forth again when the appointed time comes for her to live . . ."

"I know that, really," Ferrika said, "but it was so hard to endure their grief. They had already named her . . ."

"I know, *breda*. But you are here with us, and you must stay until you are refreshed and cheerful again. You have had no holiday for a year and this has been hard on you, too, hasn't it, *chiya*? Come, you must meet our sister Keitha, she works with me, and next year we will send her to the Arilinn College of Midwives. Also she will have Terran training, which will help her perhaps to save some of the ones who might die for no good reason. I want you two to know and love each other as sisters."

As Ferrika embraced Keitha, behind them Camilla said, "How will you spend your holiday, Margali?"

But before she could answer, Rezi, who was on hall-duty, pushed her way quickly through to the fireside.

"Marisela, Rimal the Harp-maker is at the door, his wife is in labor—"

"Oh, no!" Magda said, "On your holiday, Marisela," but the midwife was rising with a good-natured smile. Keitha asked "Will you need me, *breda*?"

"I think so; it is twins and her first confinement," she said, and Keitha made a rueful face and went for her cloak. Marisela chuckled. "Like the beast-surgeon and the farmer, we have chosen a profession where we know no holidays except that the Goddess sends. Finish your breakfast, Keitha, there is no such hurry as all that! Rezi, fetch him some tea and cake in the Stranger's Room and tell him we will be with him as soon as we can." Nevertheless she was heading for the supply cabinet where she kept her midwife's bag, and shortly afterward they heard the door shut behind her. Camilla chuckled.

"Who would be a midwife!"

"Not I," said Magda, reflecting that this was one thing which did not change from Terran to Darkovan; no Medic could ever count on a free holiday, especially in maternity work!

"And what will you do with your holiday, since by good fortune you have not chosen to become a midwife?"

"I am still not sure. Go to the market, certainly, and buy some new boots," Magda said, regarding the ancient and tattered sandals.

"And I," said Mother Lauria, "will stay in the House and write up the year's records, and enjoy an empty house with no one to trouble me! Perhaps I will go to the public dance in Thendara tonight, to listen to the musicians."

"I will certainly go," said Rafaella, "for they have asked me to be there to take a turn at playing for the dancers. And you, Margali?"

"I think so." She had always wanted to attend the public Festival dances in Thendara's main square, but she had not felt she could go alone, and Peter had never been willing to take her. She knew they became rowdy at times, but, as a Renunciate she could take care of herself.

Rezi came in from the hall again, bearing a basket of flowers.

"For you, Rafi," she said, and the women began to laugh and cheer.

"You have a lover so tenacious, Rafi?"

Rezi said, "The lad who brought them is not fifteen, and he asked for his mother," and Rafaella, laughing, hurried out to the hall, snatching up a piece of the festival cake.

"Boys that age are always hungry! Just like girls," she added over her shoulder, laughing.

Magda found herself remembering Midsummer, a year ago. She and Peter had still been married then. She had already known that the marriage was ending, but he had sent her the customary basket of fruit and flowers. It had been the final reconciliation before the quarrel that had smashed the marriage beyond repair. She wondered if he had sent Jaelle flowers this morning. She missed Peter. She was so tired of spending all her time with women!

"And what will you do today?" Camilla asked.

"I think I shall simply walk in the city and enjoy the knowledge that I am free to go wherever I wish," she said, realizing suddenly that she really had no place she wished to go. "But I will certainly buy new boots. And you?"

Camilla shrugged. "There is a Festival supper in the House for everyone who has no place else to dine; I have promised to help cook it, since Irmelin wishes to spend the day with her mother—she is old and blind now and Irmi fears every time she sees her may be the last. But you young ones always want to go out; enjoy yourself, *breda*. And there is a women's dance tonight; I may go to that, for I love to dance and I do not like dancing with men."

Magda thought she might return to the Terran Zone for a visit. But she really had no friends there now. No doubt Peter and Jaelle had plans for this holiday already.

She was coming down with her jacket and the remnants of the burnt boots—it might shorten the wait for a new pair—when Camilla called.

"Margali, a man came asking for you; I sent him into the Stranger's Room. He has a strange accent—perhaps he is one of your kin from beyond the Hellers?"

A slight, dark man, faintly familiar, rose from a chair as she entered. He spoke her Darkovan name with a good accent, though it was not the accent of Thendara. The Terran. Montray's son—what was his name—

"Monty," he said, reminding her. She looked at him appraisingly.

"Where did you get those clothes?"

"Not right?"

"They'll pass in a crowd. But the boots are too well made for a tunic as cheap as that one; anyone who could afford boots as good as that could afford to have had his tunic embroidered, not just trimmed with colored threads. And the undertunic is too coarse."

"Haldane okayed them," Monty said. "I wore them on the fire-lines; and he didn't do with me what he did with Li—he ordered Li to pretend to be deaf and dumb, so I thought I'd pass. . . ."

"Why have you come here?" she asked sharply.

"Jaelle happened to let it drop that you're free to go out today. May I escort you—I see you're dressed to go out—for a little way, have a few minutes conversation with you?"

Well, if this man was in Intelligence there was no reason to offend him because she thought his father a fool.

"You can show me where you bought those boots; they're good and I need a pair made," she said, "and we can talk on the way to the market. Don't talk in front of the women in the hall, they might spot your accent as wrong."

He bowed. It was not really a bad imitation of the proper bow of a Darkovan servant facing a woman of high rank; he wasn't stupid, or unobservant, he simply hadn't had the training she and Peter had had. Or—presumably he was a graduate of the same

Intelligence School on Alpha—he hadn't had the experience. She guessed he was four or five years younger than herself. He followed her at the proper one step behind, through the hallway, and not until they were out of sight of the Guild-house did he come up to walk beside her.

"The Karazin market?"

"I think so," he said, "and if I'm going to walk with you I ought to carry that package, hadn't I?"

She handed him the rolled bundle, but it burst open, and he stared in consternation at the charred soles, and scorched uppers.

"How the devil did you do that?"

"I was caught in one of the break-throughs, where the fire jumped a break."

"I heard there were Renunciates there. Were you hurt?"

"Superficial burns on my feet; they're healed now."

"That explains Jaelle—"

"Jaelle? Did she go into the fire-lines? Oh, I wish I'd seen her—"

"She didn't go; Peter told me she's pregnant," Monty said. "She couldn't have gotten Medical clearance, though she wanted to come and even made noises about it."

Magda said a proper "How nice," but inside she felt a curious sinking cold. So Jaelle would give Peter the son he wanted so much.

"We can go down here and get your feet measured for boots," he said, "and then we can sit and talk awhile—it's not forbidden to sit and talk to me in a public place, is it?"

Magda shrugged. "Not at Festival, certainly. It's not commonplace, but at Festival we do as we please." And if they saw her sitting in a public place with a man, they could hardly think. . . . She cut that thought off in the middle, defiant; let them think what they wished. Again in the person of a mute servant, he handed her package while she arranged with a cobbler to have the soles replaced and bargained for a new pair—he had none to fit her, but if she could return in three hours he would have the soles patched on the old ones and they would serve till the new were ready.

Marion Zimmer Bradley

Magda paid for the work, grateful for the money she had earned helping Rafaella; even after paying her tithes to the House, she had enough for the mended boots and for the new pair. Anyway, she had some back pay in the Terran Zone, banked there, and she should arrange to convert some of it to Darkovan money; she had not needed much in the Guild-house but that was more good luck than good management. Food and clothing were available in return for the help she gave in maintaining the House, and now that Rafaella had accepted her in Jaelle's place and given her work she could do there—sorting loads, packaging travel-food into separate day rations—she had begun to pay her share. When she had finished at the bootstall she walked down the street and Monty caught up again with her.

"Now where can I talk to you?"

"What is this all about?"

"You know that perfectly well," he said, exasperated. "I need a report from you—I told you that when I came there before. We're going to have eight of them down in Medic—Cholayna told me the other day. We need to know more about what makes them tick. You're the only expert we have on Darkovan women."

"Ask Jaelle," Magda said, and he laughed.

"I'm afraid she's a little too prickly for me. In a society like this one, I can see how women who *had* gotten out of it would be a little bit on the defensive—what I can't imagine is how she came to marry Haldane. Can you explain it?"

"Since I think you know that he and I were married once, I suppose that question is purely rhetorical."

"No," Monty said, suddenly serious. "Not at all. Working in the field and seeing the different way men treat women in the Darkovan culture has caused me to re-examine some of my own values. I wonder, sometimes, if perhaps women really prefer a culture where they're looked after. Cared about. Cherished and protected. We make such a big thing of equality, but the women here seem happy enough. Oh, there are exceptions, but seriously, Magda—" he had spoken her Terran name, but she did not correct him, since no one was near enough to hear, "it seems to make sense, to give women supremacy in their own sphere, and not bring them into direct competition; let them have one place where they can be really superior, and keep it separate. Lots of societies work that way. . . . hell, you had anthropology and sociology of culture on Alpha, you know what I'm talking about."

"I don't like the assumptions behind that kind of culture," Magda said sharply. "Why should everything be divided up into what women do and what men do?"

"Well why *shouldn't* they? It happens anyway; it's just that some societies admit it, and others try to pretend it doesn't exist. *Most* women are less competitive, less athletic—why should a society be based on the exceptions? I don't see anything wrong with a man spending his life in, for instance, dresses, but I wouldn't force all men to wear dresses, for instance, so that the few who want to won't feel conspicuous. I remember one nursery school I was in where they wouldn't let the boys play with trucks and spaceships because they said we shouldn't get stereotyped. There were a couple of little girls there who really wanted to play dolls and the nurses kept shoving them at the spaceships and trying to get them to play football."

"So you'd give the girls the dolls and the boys the spaceships, and leave it at that?"

Monty shrugged. "Why not, as long as the girls who want the spaceships and toy trucks get a chance to try them out now and then? But I never got up the slightest interest in playing dolls, no matter how many they shoved into my little hands. At least on Darkover they would have taken it for granted that since I was a boy, I had a right to act like one."

Magda chuckled. "Well, I never had to fight for my chance at a doll or a toy truck. I usually spent my time with paints and listening to my mother play the harp. And dancing. Remember I grew up in Caer Donn."

"I envy you," he said seriously. "A wonderful chance, to grow up in the world you really live in . . . you know my father. He has lived thirty years on Darkover and still can't tolerate the light of the red sun because he lives all the time under Terran-style lights."

"Don't envy me, Monty," she said, matching his seriousness. "It's not an enviable option, to grow up never knowing where you belong, not—not knowing the recognition signals. I was never really Darkovan, and my young friends knew it. And I knew it, Oh, God, I knew it! And when I went to the Terrans it was worse . . . how the devil did I get into all this?"

He smiled. He had, she realized, a nice smile. "I admit I led you into it," he said, "I wanted to hear what made *you* tick. You're *the* expert, you know, on Darkovan culture and language, That doesn't surprise me, I don't think any man has the power of observation about details that a good woman can have."

"I'm glad you admit us to that competence," she said dryly. "I wondered if perhaps you thought my proper sphere of influence was judging suitable clothing."

"Well, that's one of them," he said equably, "and you're living proof that a woman can pass better than a man."

"Well, in a Guild-house, anyway," she said, losing the impulse to argue with him.

"Look, you keep saying you want better understanding between Darkover and the Empire. Start contributing to it, then. Help me understand."

That sounded reasonable. While she was thinking it over, he said, "You have two or three hours to kill, anyhow, while your boots are getting ready. We won't make it a formal report. Just come back to HQ with me, and we can have a drink in my quarters while you put some basic reports on file for me. And show me how to access your other reports, or how to get clearance to work with them, okay? Good God, girl, don't you even know your work is posted as *the* standard of excellence not only here, but all over the Empire? Even when I was still on Alpha I heard about Lorne's work on Cottman Four, and I was hoping I'd be put on assignment with you!"

Flattery, Magda thought; *he's trying to get what he wants. That's all.* But after the discouragement and self-doubt of the last weeks it touched something so deep in her that she could not help feeling warmed and satisfied by the words.

"All right. If I can have a few minutes to get down to the credit transfer department . . ."

"All the time you want," he said amiably, having made his point.

Going in through the Spaceforce-guarded gate, it felt like the times she had come back with Peter from a field assignment, still in field clothes, but ready to take off her Darkovan persona and return to her true self. *I believed then that it was my true self and the Darkovan Margali only a mask. What is the truth?* She was no longer sure.

His quarters were in Unmarried Personnel, not too far from her own old rooms; he found her a seat, asked what she would have to drink.

"Coffee," she said without a moment's hesitation, "if you had to ask me what one thing I missed most, that would be it . . . that, and a hot shower in the morning."

He went to dial it from the comsole. "Pretty primitive in the Guild-house?"

"Oh, no," she said, flicked again on the raw by that assumption. "They have hot baths, hot tubs to soak in, everything . . . it's just that they have a different lifestyle and a different set of priorities. Some things you have to be brought up to; they take it for granted that a nice cold bath is just what you need to wake up in the morning, and hot water is a nighttime indulgence. And I've had to adapt." She laughed, turning the coffee cup between her hands. "I never realized how Terran I was until I *had* to be Darkovan twenty-eight hours a day, ten days a week." She sipped the coffee; it still tasted good to her, despite the sudden strangeness; she wondered if the caffeine in it, now that she was unaccustomed to it, would give her some unexpected high.

"Well, now. What do you need to know? Languages? That's simple—sleep with the corticator tape for at least seven days. Too many people here try to cheat—they can get along after one or two days so they never go back, and that takes time; I grew up on the language, of course, in fact I probably made the tapes you're using, but when I learned the Dry-Town language I slept with it for two full tendays. You have to know it, not on the surface, but where it counts, down in your guts. There was some excuse when we didn't *have* the tapes in full, but now we do. Program the subconscious all the way, not just the superficial language course. You have clearance to use a Braniff-Alpha level corticator, don't you?"

"I've always been nervous about it. I don't like the idea of anything mucking around with my very nerve synapses!"

"It's the only way you can get it on the same level you'd have gotten it when you were a child," she said. "And it's better than being deaf and dumb!"

"That's for sure," Monty laughed. "Now can you put in a report on the Free Amazons—oh, pardon me, Renunciates—"

She corrected his pronunciation slightly, knowing it was temporizing. But a dozen of her sisters would be working here in Medic. She was, in a sense, doing this for the Guild. Monty found her a scribing machine, and Magda sat down to her work.

"The name Guild of Free Amazons, commonly used by Terrans and in the Empire," she began, "is a romantic misconception, based on a Terran legend of a tribe of independent women. The true name of the Guild in their language could be better translated as the Order of Oath-Bound Renunciates," and went on from there, explaining what she knew about the history and original charter of the Amazon movement, which had begun formally in Thendara only about 300 years ago, and for almost half of that time had been a highly secret movement, operating underground, with only a single concealed Guild-house which operated almost like a cloistered convent; only recently, in the last hundred years, had the Amazons begun to operate openly and build other Houses of Refuge.

She heard, for a while, Monty moving around the quarters, then lost consciousness of him as she went on making her report; she translated the text of the Oath and explained some of its more obscure provisions, mentioned some of the taboos and courtesies of the Amazons among themselves and those observed by the common people toward them, including the incredible hostility toward Free Amazons found among the commoner women in the Kilghard Hills. But when it came to speaking of the common accusation that they were haters of men and lovers of women, she found it difficult to keep the detachment of the trained anthropologist. She welcomed, in a sense, the ability to recapture her Terran self, to remain an outsider; but when she began to speak of this she hesitated, played back what she had said, then wiped the last ten minutes and substituted some vague generalities about relationships of the Amazons with men on the fire-lines. Monty came in again while she was finishing this up, and said, "Now I understand how your boots got in such a mess. Tell me—you were out in the edge of the Kilghard Hills, then, as the fire was coming down toward Thendara?"

Magda nodded. He said, "I ordered us up some lunch; dictating is hungry work and your throat must be dry, at least." He set a tray in front of her, and she smelled it appreciatively. *Terran food . . .* she told herself defensively that she had been brought up on Darkovan foods and liked them but that she was enjoying the change, it was nice to have something diffcrent. She had forgotten the completely different textures of synthctic foods, and tasted them exploringly.

He drew up a chair, digging into his own meal, looking appreciatively at the pile of narrow spindles she had piled up. "That's *marvelous*," he said fervently, "You'll get a footnote in history or something, and I won't deny that I'll get a footnote to the footnote for talking you into it!"

She chuckled, shoving aside a tube of apple-flavored synthetic. The stuff, she decided, was as bland and flavorless as she remembered it. "You ought to have a footnote on your own. Or aren't you planning to follow in the Old Man's footsteps?"

Monty's laugh created sudden intimacy between them. "You know, and I know, that my father is no more fit to be Coordinator on a planet like Darkover than that donkey in one of your folk tales—Duran, was it?"

"Durraman," she said. "The one who starved to death between two bales of hay because he couldn't decide which one to bite into first . . ."

"Seriously, it's not his fault, Magda; he wanted to command a Space Station, it was what he was trained for; he got in with the wrong political crowd," Monty said. "My good fortune, of course, this was my world from the moment I could decide. . . . More coffee?"

She shook her head, pushing the tray away. "That *was* good," she admitted, "for a change, anyway."

He glanced at his chronometer, which kept Empire time. "You don't need to hurry; your boots won't be ready for another hour," he said, "but I hate to ask you to do any more dictating; you've done a heroic job already. I can't thank you enough, but you'll find a bonus on your credit when you get back . . . by the way, when *are* you coming back? The Old Man was talking about a special liaison post created just for you. . . ."

"Forty days more to fulfill my obligation to the Guild-house; after that, I'm not sure. I might apply to change citizenship—"

"Oh, don't do that," he said quickly. "Empire citizenship is too valuable for that; Haldane put through for citizenship for Jaelle, so their kid will be born a full citizen. Be as Darkovan as you like, but hang on to your citizenship. Just in case."

Yes, that was the Terran way. Defend against all contingencies, never make a full commitment without leaving a way of escape. Cover yourself. She glanced again at her timepiece. "I should run up to Intelligence HQ, now they've got one, and check in with Cholayna—"

"She's off duty," Monty said, "and I happen to know she went to the Meditation Center and put through a notice not to be disturbed for at least eighteen hours. I suspect she's in an isolation tank or something—she belongs to one of those queer Alphan religions. Very odd lady, though it's good to have someone really competent in Intelligence. Only one drawback; she can't do her own fieldwork. So we have to depend on you. Could I ask a personal favor, Magda?"

"You can always ask," she said, smiling, and suddenly knew that in a sense she was flirting with him, letting the personal part of their communication take over momentarily from the business one, as a way of flattering him . . . was this worthy of an

Amazon? It was the Terran way. She had never noticed it before, but now she knew she was doing it, and heard the harsh voice of Rafaella, *is it so important to you that a man must consider you beautiful?* Rafaella certainly was not the one to talk, she had three sons by three different fathers. . . . at least Camilla, who was a lover of women, was consistent! But through all her doubts it was reassuring, that she could still attract attention, not only professionally, but as a woman.

"You know how to pass as a native. Haldane can do the same thing. I will take the Braniff-Alpha corticators—I will believe it is safe if *you* say so—but can you tell me what I am doing wrong, so that in the Old Town I can pass as a native, as you and Haldane and Cargill do?"

"Why not ask them? They are men and would know what is necessary for a man. . . ."

"No," he said. "I'd trust a woman to spot a man and a man to spot a woman, any day. For instance I think I'd spot you even if you wore Darkovan clothes . . . I mean, when you weren't off guard, as you are here; I think I'd read you in the market, for instance. You don't walk *quite* like them—no, it's your eyes; you don't keep them down, not in quite the same way. You—" he groped for words, "you keep them down but I can tell you're doing it deliberately, not automatically. Is that just being a Renunciate?"

"Maybe, in part. Though you're right I always had some trouble with that. You get into your Darkovan outfit and I'll tell you what you're doing wrong. And while you're doing it, I need to get down to credit transfer . . . oh, damn, I can't go into HQ in this outfit, I'll set off every alarm in the place!"

"One of the women in my office is about your size, and she lives just down the hall; let me go borrow a spare uniform for you."

She acquiesced, warning him not to tell anyone who it was for. She did not want, on her day off, to be flooded with old acquaintances eager to know all the details of her curious field assignment. When he came back with it he stood aside and let her change in his sleeping quarters. She was surprised at how naked she felt in the narrow tunic and tights, after months of the loose, unrevealing Amazon dress. She was conscious of her cropped hair—short even for a Terran, but she brushed it into a fairly smart coiffure; and Monty had thoughtfully asked for a few cosmetics as well so that she could make up properly. As she stepped out he whistled admiringly.

"In that outfit you were wearing, I didn't realize what a smasher you were!"

Again she laughed, realizing how far she had come from such compliments. It felt familiar and strange at once to walk down the HQ halls, knowing that the uniform made her invisible, just another employee with a right to be there. It was different and somehow comforting to drop her individual identity and slip into anonymity.

Soon she would be out of seclusion. Would they want her back here? If so, then she must acknowledge to all her sisters that she was Terran; would they hate her for it? When she got back, Monty was in Darkovan clothing again and she applied herself to critical study.

"Your hair is too short. To look really right, you would have to let it grow down at least to *here*." She brushed a fingertip along his neckline. "Now walk for me . . ." and she watched him seriously. Finally she said, frowning, "I know what it is. You walk too—too lightly, unencumbered. Darkovan men . . . all of them, except beggars and cripples. . . . grow up wearing a sword, and even when they're not wearing it, they're wearing it, if you know what I mean. Here," she said, picking up the Amazon knife she had laid aside. "Belt this on—try walking with it. It's not a sword, of course—"

"It sure looks like one."

"Legally it's not," Magda said.

"By law and Charter no Amazon may wear a sword."

"What *is* the difference?" Monty asked, studying the blade. It did, Magda realized, look very much like what any Terran would call a sword. "About three inches," she admitted dryly, and they laughed together as he belted it on.

"No, you are leaning to one side to compensate. And keep

your wrist a little back so you won't be knocking against the hilt; remember when you first started wearing a wrist-radio and had to learn not to bang it into things? Wrist back— lower—so it won't get in the way but you could draw it at once if you had to. You have to psych yourself into it; you grew up wearing it, you started wearing and training with it when you were about eight, you never went out without it, you would feel as naked if it wasn't there as if you forgot to put your pants on in the morning."

"Good God," Monty exclaimed. "I knew the culture was aggressive, but do they really start their youngsters at eight?"

"The valley men. In the mountains the kids start carrying daggers almost as soon as they can walk, and using them, too. It's just part of the realities of their world; there are plenty of things bigger than they are, out there. And until you can feel that down in your guts, not just know it intellectually, you'll never have more than a superficial understanding of what it's like to be a man on Darkover. Their women are less protected than our men—there were women on the fire-lines and they weren't all Renunciates, either!" After a minute she suggested, "You should get yourself a sword and wear it all the time around your quarters in here."

"How in the world do I sit down in the thing?"

"That's the point," Magda said. "Wear it for six weeks, and you'll know. You'll be able to sit down with it and get up with it and walk with it and work with it and run with it, and slide into a seat in a tavern without bashing the next guy with it."

He followed that, nodded slowly. "Haldane did all that?"

"Damn right, and more; his father actually let him work out with an arms-master with the other boys his age in the village where we grew up. In Empire uniform, he told me once, he feels undressed. We both do." She glanced self-consciously at her long legs in the thin tights. "And I have to change back before I leave." She headed in to the inner room to take off her uniform, adding, "Also, dance as much as you can. Men here start learning it when they're about five. Like everybody else."

"I did hear that," Monty said. "The old proverb—get three

Darkovans together and they hold a dance. I did some work in ballet as well as martial arts before I came back here. . . . studied gravity-dancing on Alpha."

"That explains it," she said. "How you manage to pass at all; you don't walk quite like the average Terran who has no notion of how to move. I noticed that you were graceful. Most Darkovans think Terrans are incredibly clumsy. Dance—they say—is one of the very few wholly human activities; most things are also done by animals, but there's a saying: *only men laugh, only men dance, only men weep*."

"I've noticed that," he said, "the way both men and women move, gracefully. . . . you move like them" he added, "like a feather. . . ."

She was suddenly self-conscious about the way he was looking at her. "I must go and change," she said. "Not even a whore would go out on the streets like this."

He did not look away. "I cannot decide which way I like you better. Darkovan women are so modest, so—" he hesitated, searching for a word, "so womanly. It makes me more conscious of myself as a man. Yet in your Amazon clothing you seem to be trying to negate all that, to be distant. And in uniform—you are very beautiful, Magda," he said, and came over to her. He turned her slowly round and kissed her. "I have been wanting to do that since I first set eyes on you that day in the Guild-house when you were so angry with me. And now when I know you are not some sort of shrew or spitfire but a beautiful woman—and, and, so many things, a colleague and a friend and a woman too—" he stopped talking and kissed her again.

She said after a minute, softly, "Am I really so intimidating?"

"Not now. Don't go and change, Magda, stay with me here awhile. . ." and he drew her against him. Letting him kiss her again, she felt again the curious ambivalence. She liked him. She did not want him to be attracted to her this way. Yet it was reassuring, to know that even through her defenses, she was still desirable—he kissed her bare neck, and she drew away, troubled.

"No," she said in a low voice, "Monty, no. I came here with you for work, not for—not for this."

He did not move away. "It is not true what they say—that the Amazons are haters of men and lovers of women, is it?"

And that is what they say, and now I am wondering is it true? One of the women said it once in Training Session . . . that a woman who gives her love to men is traitor to other women, that men are always trying to reduce us only to something they can, or cannot, have as a sexual conquest, because it means they do not have to take us seriously. He was talking about how my work is the standard of excellence here . . . does he need to seduce me simply to prove that for all that, I am no more than a woman to be taken?

Nevertheless she let him draw her down on the couch, gave herself over to his kisses. She was uneasily conscious of her own response.

I don't want to. I have lived alone and celibate for more than a year, I should be eager. He's a very nice person, but I really don't want to. What's wrong with me? I should never have let it go this far. If she were going to stop him she should have done it swiftly and decisively when he made the first move, she had let him think she wanted it too. It would be cheap and small-minded to stop him now.

It's not as if I were a virgin, for heaven's sake!

After a time he whispered "This is foolish, Magda, kissing like children, with all our clothes on—we're both rational grownup people. You do want me too, don't you?"

Do I? Do I not? Or do I simply want to reassure myself that I am still capable of reacting to a man, that I have not become an alien sexless thing—like Camilla—why am I thinking now of Camilla? That frightened her. She looked up at him and smiled.

"Of course I do," she said clearly, "but I never go to bed with a man before I know his first name."

He laughed down at her with relief and pleasure. His eyes were dark and shining, his face flushed. "Oh, that's all right then," he said, accenting the absurdity, "I don't use it because there's no Darkovan equivalent. That doesn't bother my father

but it does bother me, I don't like having a name no one can pronounce, so I'm Monty. My name is Wade. I really ought to take
a Darkovan given name for myself, I just haven't made up my
mind yet. Isn't that ridiculous? But if that's all it takes—" He
leaned down to her, laughing, and she smiled and let him draw
her down again to the couch.

When she was dressing again, before his mirror, he came
and touched her face gently.

"You are so lovely," he said in a soft voice, "but in those
clothes you look so hard and strange. I hate to see you hide yourself in them, even now that I know it is a lie, that you are not really like that."

She said, laying her hand lightly on his arm, "No, Monty. It's
not a lie. It is—it is *part* of what I am. Can you understand?"

"No," he said, "Never. But I'll try. Shall we have that drink
now?" He was trying to accept her lightness but she liked him a
little better now that she knew it was not entirely casual with
him.

*It was not casual with me either. I liked him and he is a
friend, even if it meant no more than that. Is it wrong to wish to
give pleasure to a friend, even if he is a man?* She sat beside
him, drinking, knowing that he needed somehow to stay close to
her through this strangeness. She wished she could make him
understand that it was strange to her too.

To give myself only in my own time and season . . . the words
of the Oath rang in her head. *But I don't know what that means
anymore. Was I using him for my own needs . . . not sexual
needs, but the need of demonstrating to myself that I could still
attract a man? Is that what the Oath means, to use men for our
needs instead of letting them use us for theirs? Don't we both
have needs?*

"It's hard," he said, fumbling, "to get involved or not to get
involved. I—I don't want to get married. And yet I just can't get
that interested in, in the kind of women I might find in the red-
light district. I played around a little because—because—this
isn't going to make sense—in a way they were Darkover to me.

The only part of it I could have. The real world is a billion light-years away from those girls, and I know it, yet I can—*could* have them, at least in a limited sense, and I couldn't have the rest. Do you understand what I'm saying? And, oh, hell, it suddenly occurred to me, this woman knows, I can level with her. . . . you know, I really *didn't* invite you up here to seduce you, it never crossed my mind—"

"Never mind, Monty. Things happen. As you said, we're both grown up." She sipped from his glass and patted his hand. How absurd that she should be the one to reassure him!

"Perhaps you can show me where to find a sword? I'd like to try that thing you told me about," he said, and she nodded.

"Of course. Although, really, Peter would know more about it. He really knows weapons, and I'm no judge, though I've been taught a little, a very little really, about using them. Peter really *is* an expert."

"All right, I'll ask him, though I really don't know him that well. Actually I know his wife a little better; we work together a lot. Jaelle. You know her, don't you, she's your friend?"

"My oath-mother in the Guild. It's a very special relationship," Magda said, and wondered why the thought filled her with such pain. What had come between them, that they were no longer close friends as they once had been? She did not want to think about that.

"She's a nice little thing," Monty said, "and she seems so isolated here, out of her depth. Oh, competent—very competent. But she looks so sad. She must really be crazy in love with that man, to have left her world for him. A woman who would do that for a man—oh, hell," he broke off, as the door-chime made its discreet announcing burp, "I'll see who that is and try to get rid of them, shall I?"

"Not on my account, Monty, I really have to go and get my boots," she said, as he went to the door.

"Oh, come in, Li. You know Lorne from Intelligence?"

"Cholayna's filled me full of stories about her," Alessandro Li said, bending over her hand. Magda picked up her knife and began to belt it on, fancying that Alessandro Li's eyes followed

her. She flushed, knowing it was foolish. He could not possibly
know what had happened between them and probably would not
care if he did. She said, "Ask Peter about it, Monty. He can get
you a good one, and I understand buying swords is a specialized
business—you have to know what you are doing, and on a
metal-poor planet like this, they are not cheap! But it's a lifetime
investment."

"Thinking of taking up swordplay, Monty?"

"No, but I'll never be able to pass in the field until I learn to
handle them, or at least to look as if I knew how," Monty said.

"Not the kind of thing that would attract me," Li said offhand. "I really do know your work, Miss Lorne, it's a pleasure
to meet you. Jaelle gave me the Darkovan name of *Aleki*, by the
way."

She nodded. "Living here, it's a good idea to have one, to
learn to answer to it and think of it as your name, an automatic
reflex."

"That's what's wrong with Father," Monty said suddenly, "he
can't think of himself as having anything to do with this world.
After—how long? Eleven, thirteen, years, he still feels like an
alien."

"Well, after all," Aleki said, "he *is* alien. It's not healthy—
useful for our work, maybe, but not healthy—to get to thinking
of one's self as belonging to an alien world. I don't think it's
ever right to lose sight of the fact that it's a pretense, a mask. . . .
to let the mask become real. Granted, when we appoint a Legate
here, he should be a man who feels real concern for the natives,
and can identify with them. But he should be a career Empire
man first and foremost. Take Haldane, for instance. He's smart,
he knows this planet backward and forward, and he's got a mind
like the proverbial steel trap. When he's a bit older—of course I
don't have to tell either of you that it's going to depend in part
on my report whether they set up a Legate in here or not, and
when. Haldane's sharp and ambitious—couple of bad spots in
his record, but he's young yet, and he's learning. What about it,
Miss Lorne? Do you think Peter Haldane would make a good

Legate, or are you the right one to ask? You were married to him once, weren't you?"

"I don't know if I am the right person to ask or not," she said, "I like him, but I'm not blind to his faults, if that's what you mean. Of course he'd do better as Coordinator than Russ Montray. Who wouldn't?" But she glanced apologetically at Monty. "Anyone would. *I* would."

"You could have a shot at Coordinator if it were most worlds, but not on Darkover," Aleki said. "It's just one of those things; this society won't accept a woman in the job. If you want a Coordinator's job somewhere else, Lorne, I can put you up for it. Not here, though. But you were telling me what you thought about Haldane—"

"I'm not sure the mistakes he's made are reversible," she said slowly, almost with apology, "or whether they mean a flaw in his imagination. But he's committed to Darkover and wants to stay here."

"I don't know," Aleki demurred, "in a key position like this, you want a man who's unquestionably loyal to Empire, who puts Empire first and the particular planet second—"

Magda shook her head. "If it was up to me," she said, "I'd want a man who thought of the planet first—just to counterbalance all those bureaucrats who are going to put the Empire first; a Legate ought to be a spokesman for the planet itself."

"That's a job for their Senators and other key men in Empire government," Aleki said, "though it's true that they do sometimes think of a Legate as a man to speak up for the world in question. Different theories of how to appoint people, that's all. That's why, even if the Darkovans would accept a woman in the job, you wouldn't make it higher than Coordinator; your service record shows you have a tendency to go native—think from a planetary, not an Empire point of view, and a Legate can't be provincial, planet-minded. Haldane, at least, seems to be working hard to develop a larger point of view." He accepted the drink Monty poured for him. "Oh, thanks."

"No more for me," Magda said, "A Renunciate can't go

around the streets drunk, not even at Festival! More coffee, though; that's wonderful."

Monty indicated the pile of spindles on the table beside the couch. He said, "Miss Lorne came in on her day off and added to our files on the Renunciates."

"And now I am off to spend the rest of the day with the women from the Guild-house—"

"Don't go yet," Aleki said, "I've been wanting to have a talk with you ever since Jaelle mentioned you. I looked up everything about you in Records. While I was out on the fire-lines, I saw some women from Neskaya Guild-house—"

"We were there from Thendara, too," Magda said, "but I didn't see you."

"You wouldn't have noticed me if you did," Alessandro Li said, good-naturedly. "I was supposed to be deaf and dumb, and a servant."

Monty chuckled. "That's just what Magda told me I had better be, walking through the streets this morning!"

"You were in the Kilghard Hills," Aleki said. "Do you know anything about—" he hesitated over the word, "the *Comyn*?"

"All I know is in my report from Ardais," Magda said, conscious that she was evading him, and he scowled. "Not enough. Somehow I think the *Comyn*, whoever or whatever they are, are the key to this whole crazy planet. You know how it is; normally they come to us, begging to join with the Empire—eager for technology, all the benefits of a star-spanning Empire, but these people think their own little frozen ball of mud is the center of the whole damn universe!"

"You can't blame them for that," Magda said. "Doesn't everyone?"

"Not a question of blame. But Darkover is an anomaly and I'd like to know why. I can't ask Jaelle much about the *Comyn*— I gather she's related to some of them. We don't have any men in the field—we heard a rumor around the Trade City, a few years ago, of some kind of power struggle in the *Comyn*. Had to do with something they call the Towers, some kind of rebellion led by a man called Lord Damon Ridenow—and when I went out fighting fire, there he was bossing the whole job."

"Well, you ought to know what's going on out there, then," said Magda, "You've got one of the best men in the field I ever met. I'd never have spotted him, but we were trapped together behind the fire, and I heard him swearing in Terran." And then she was struck with doubt; had she heard him or had she picked it up with that special extra sense she seemed to be developing?

"Best man in the field? What the devil are you talking about?" Aleki demanded, "We don't have *any* men on Alton lands. The only field Intelligence man we have that's really good is Kadarin, and he and Cargill are out in the Dry Towns. Who are you talking about?"

"They call him *Dom* Ann'dra," Magda began, and broke off at the sudden fierce look of triumph on Aleki's face.

"I knew it. I knew it, damn it, for all their talk about contracts and this man being in the legitimate employ of Lord Damon! He's managed to get himself so well in there because he has no known ties with Intelligence—and there's some talk that the Darkovan nobility use psi powers, so we couldn't ever plant an undercover Intelligence man on them! They'd read him, read his mind, but this one, somehow they managed to do a *real* undercover operation; crash his plane out there, have him listed as dead, and now you say this Ann'dra—hell, I *saw* the man, running all over as Lord Damon's special sidekick, and I never spotted him myself as Intelligence!"

"I don't think it's like that at all," Magda said, remembering the man she had met in the stables that morning. This man was one of them, no longer torn between two conflicting worlds; he had found a home. "The Empire has him listed as dead. Maybe he wants it that way."

But Aleki was not listening. "I've got to find out what he knows. Just now, when we're making really crucial decisions about Darkover, he could be the key to the whole thing."

Conflicting Oaths. As much as the Renunciate Oath meant to her, she was in a sense sworn here too. She was Terran, though she did not want to be, and the thought terrified her. She rose decisively.

"I really have to go, Monty." As he rose to escort her, she shook her head. "No, no, I was finding my way around this place when you were still studying for the Service entrance exams!"

She could see that hurt him. Was he so conscious of himself as novice and of her as expert? *He doesn't deserve anything but good from me. I used him and I despise myself for it, and now I'm trying to make him feel small. What a bitch I am!* She let him put his arm round her.

"Are you going to the Festival Ball in *Comyn* Castle?"

"A Renunciate? My *dear!*" She had to laugh. "The people in the castle don't know we exist; they'd invite you people first!"

"Well, that is exactly what they have done," Monty began, and Aleki said, "As it happens I will be there myself; I came here to tell Monty, and that was one reason I was pleased to find you here, Miss Lorne." He handed Monty a sheet of elegant parchment.

"As you can see, it requests the Coordinator, with chosen members of his staff and suite, to attend the Ball as a gesture of good will between Terrans and Darkover," he said. "And people who have lived here a long time, know how to behave properly, dance well and so forth—such as you, Miss Lorne."

"As a matter of fact, I did know," Monty said. "The old man mentioned it. But what with one thing and another, I never got to mention it to you, Magda." His grin struck her as oddly boyish and vulnerable, a side of him she had never seen, hiding behind the hard masks Empire men wore. Peter had shown her this side too, and she wondered if all men had it, even Darkover men like *Dom* Gabriel or Kyril Ardais, hiding behind the imposed roles of their society. *Men are as much trapped in their social roles as women. Aren't they?* But they at least had the benefits of those roles; it was easier to play the role of master than of slave!

Her first impulse was to refuse at once. A Renunciate at Festival Ball, and as part of the Terran delegation? If anyone who had seen her at the Guild-house was there, her careful cover of half a year would go up in smoke.

But they would have to know who she was, sooner or later. She was Terran; why pretend she was not? And it might just be the first chance any Terran woman had ever had—or would ever have—to attend Festival Ball in *Comyn* Castle!

"You can fill me in on everything I need to know," Aleki said, "and keep me from making any real social blunders . . ."

"And my father will be leading the delegation," said Monty, "You owe it to all of us to come and keep him from doing something disgraceful."

"Oh, surely Jaelle—or Peter—"

"I'm not sure Jaelle likes me," Aleki said, "She's civil enough, but I get the feeling somehow that she's fighting me. Haldane resents me, and I don't blame him. His career's here on this world, and I come and then I go but still he knows my report can make or break him. There's no way he's ever going to like me. I'd like to go with someone who's not hostile to me."

She sighed and nodded. "When you put it that way, of course."

"Do you have anything to wear? Or shall I have them requisition something for you?"

"I can do better than that. At Midwinter, Lady Rohana gave me a gown—I wondered when I'd ever have a chance to wear it again."

"Shall I fetch you from the Guild-house?" Monty asked, and she laughed merrily.

"Heavens, no! I can imagine the talk that would cause! I love my sisters, but they have one trait I despise in women—they gossip! I don't grudge them their fun—but I don't want to be part of it either. I'll meet you in the street near the castle."

She gave Aleki her hand; Monty insisted on taking her to the door.

I like him better as a colleague than a lover. I would rather be his friend than his mistress. Reluctantly, she let him take a farewell kiss; she did not want to hurt him.

Walking back through the streets, she remembered that Jaelle had once accused her of being too protective toward men. *Probably true*, she thought, *I'm stronger than most of the men I know, and they're so damned easy to hurt. The Amazons say it's wrong to hurt a woman; why is it right to hurt a man?*

Or have so many of them suffered so much at the hands of men—Camilla, for instance—that they no longer believe men can be hurt at all, but are always superior and invulnerable?

She could feel for Monty—alone and friendless on a strange world—because she remembered when she had been alone on the Alpha colony for training, a stranger from a pioneer world, an exotic, a difficult conquest, there were so many men who had wanted to seduce her because she was alien and different; not because of who or what she was. She had been so lonely. She was lonely now . . .

Men are so weak. Or do I surround myself with men who are weak, because the strong ones would challenge me too much?

There was no one on hall duty, but Rezi came, her hands floury from the kitchen, to let her in.

"Some of our sisters from Bellarmes Guild-house are here for Festival, and you will be going to the women's dance tonight, won't you? Camilla said she was going with you."

Magda thought she really would have preferred the women's dance to the dance in the public square of Thendara, but she shook her head. "I am sorry; I am promised elsewhere. I did not think Camilla would have involved me in her plans without asking."

Rezi made a rueful gesture. "Very well; but do not come and weep in my lap if Camilla is angry with you!"

Magda flared, "I am not Camilla's property nor is she mine!"

Rezi laughed and shook her head. "You and Camilla must settle your lovers' quarrels without me."

Magda went up the stairs frowning. It had never occurred to her that Camilla might expect, or feel she had a right to expect her company at Midsummer. *I should have known. Oath-sisters are family.* If it came to that, she thought she would rather be with Camilla, or even with Rezi whom she really did not know well or like much, than with Monty and Aleki and the whole damned Terran delegation! But she had given her word, and it was important to her work.

She spread her holiday gown on the bed to air; she had showered in the Terran HQ, so she set about brushing up her short hair; while she was at it, Camilla came into the room and stopped short in delighted amazement.

"How pretty you look, *breda*! But that gown is too fine for the women's dance; our sisters from Bellarmes have been on the road for days and have only traveling-wear, and many of the women will be poor widows and the like who would live with us in the Amazon House if they could, but they have children or aging parents they must care for. Festival gowns like that would make them feel very shabby, so we usually do not dress up at all for the women's dances. Besides, dresses like that are only to attract men!"

"Oh, Camilla, I am sorry! But I cannot go to with you to the women's dance, I am expected elsewhere . . ."

Camilla's low voice was filled with ripples of amusement. "And no doubt you have been invited to *Comyn* Castle and Lord Hastur himself will lead you out to dance!"

Magda began weakly to giggle. "I don't know about Lord Hastur," she began, "but the truth is, Camilla . . . oh, you'll never believe this!" She broke off; she could hardly tell Camilla about the Terrans and Alessandro Li's insistence that it was her duty to come.

Fortunately Camilla assumed at once that she had had the invitation through Jaelle, who was her oath-mother; and an invitation from *Comyn* amounted, after all, to a royal command.

"How splendid! You must tell me all about it afterward, *breda*. You have no jewels, but I have a necklace of firestones I can lend you; it is just the color to look beautiful with that dress," she said, and went to fetch it. When Camilla brought it, Magda stared at the precious jewels.

"Camilla, it's too much, I can't take that—"

"Why not? What is mine is yours," Camilla said simply, "and it is for sure I shall never dance at *Comyn* Castle with the Hasturs! It was my mother's; I saw her only once after—" she hes-

itated, "after what I told you; but when she died, it was sent to
me by a messenger. I never wear jewelry; but there is no reason
it should lie forever in a box and not be displayed on the throat
of a beautiful woman for once." She put it round Magda's neck,
and Magda said impulsively, "You are beautiful to me,
Camilla!"

Camilla laughed. "I did not know you suffered also from
poor eyesight with all your other troubles," she said, but she
smiled at Magda, and caught her close in a quick embrace. "The
Comyn ball ends at midnight," she said, "and we will go on in
the public square till dawn. Come and join us afterward."

Magda said impulsively, "I would really rather stay with you.
I only wish I could."

*I would. This isn't a pleasure for me, it's going back on duty.
Camilla's worth any ten of them, and more fun to be with!*

Camilla's face lighted. She said, "Really?" and caught
Magda closer still. She held Magda tight, her face buried in
Magda's hair. She whispered "Margali, Margali . . . you know I
love you . . ." and could not go on. After a minute, when her
voice was steady again, she said, "You are not, like Keitha, a
cristoforo. . . . it does not horrify you . . ." and broke off again.

*I should have expected this. I have been backing away from
it since I came to this House. I discovered this day that it was not
a man I wanted. I did not want Peter, and Monty was no better.
I should have known all along. . . .*

*I gave myself to Monty and I did not care for him. And
Camilla is my sister, my closest friend here, she has cared for me
and stood by me when I was in disgrace, whenever I was alone
here and needed a friend, there she stood, asking for nothing, offering me love and devotion. In the name of the Goddess herself,
how can I blind myself to the truth, how can I give myself to
Monty who is nothing to me, and refuse Camilla this?* She kissed
Camilla's soft greying curls, raised the woman's face and kissed
her on the lips. Camilla smiled at her, breathless, and Magda
said hesitantly, "I—I don't know—no, I am not a *cristoforo*, the
idea does not—does not trouble me in that way, but I—I don't

know, I never thought about it—" she fell silent, fumbling for words.

Never thought about it, that I could love my friends, instead of responding to men who are after all alien to me. . . . She knew that it was more than this, she was not certain, but if she could try to make Monty happy, when he was nothing to her, she was willing—even eager—to turn to Camilla.

"But I don't know—I have never—"

Camilla stopped her confused words with a kiss; but then, taking Magda's face between her hands, she looked at her seriously.

"Do you mean this? Even when you were a young girl, you had no *bredhya . . .* ?"

Numbly, Magda shook her head. *Never. I had no woman friend, not even an ordinary friend, not a lover, till I came to the Guild-house. I did not even know that I wanted a woman for a friend until I discovered myself risking my life for Jaelle.*

It almost seemed to her that Camilla could read her thoughts a little.

"It's all right, love," she said in a whisper. "Love is a simple thing, a very simple thing . . . come and let me show you how simple."

Chapter 2

There was nothing inside the HQ to distinguish Midsummer from Midwinter. The light was the same—no windows to throw back the heavy winter draperies, no smell of baking in the air, none of the street sounds of merrymaking. But when Peter came in, she managed to find a smile for him.

From behind his back, rather self-consciously, he produced one of the baskets of fruit and flowers that vendors sold at this season in the streets. She was touched; he must have gone into the Old Town for it.

"From Midwinter to Midsummer; we have been together half a year, Jaelle. Who could forget that? And when Midwinter comes again, we shall be a family of three." He caught her close in his arms, kissing her, and she felt a flood of warmth for him. He had remembered. But it was not, quite, the old warmth. That was gone forever, and there was only emptiness where it had been. As she nibbled on a piece of the fruit, and went to find something to put the flowers in water, she wondered if this was why Renunciates vowed never to marry *di catenas*; because that first feeling went away so swiftly. . . . He came up behind her, holding her familiarly and whispering in her ear.

"You must find your finest outfit," he murmured, "for dancing tonight, even if you don't do much dancing in your condition—"

"I don't really want to go to the public dance in the square," she demurred. "It's always so crowded, and there are riffraff—

sometimes an Amazon will get into fights with men who want to prove something—"

"Nonsense," Peter said. "I'll be with you; do you think I would let any man lay hands on my wife? Yes, yes, I know, you're strong, your Oath says you can protect yourself, but if you think I'd let a pregnant woman fight . . . anyhow, there's no question of the public dance," he added. "It's a famous first for Darkover, darling, and I'm sure you had something to do with it. An invitation has come from *Comyn* Council for Montray and a delegation from the Terran Headquarters; and of course they specified you and I should make one couple, since you are Darkovan and I have worked so often in the field that I know manners, language, protocol for such things. They are trying to cement good relations by asking certain hand-picked members of the staff—"

"That would certainly leave out Russ Montray," Jaelle said, noting that her tone was acid. Peter shook his head.

"Unfortunately the Coordinator can't be left out, but an unofficial word came that I'm supposed to stick to his elbow and make sure he doesn't do anything too ghastly. And of course Monty will be there. But you're assigned to stick tight to Cholayna, since she's never been in the field here and never will, and she's the only woman here with rank suitable for the Coordinator. I wish we could manage to get Magda from the Guild-house but I don't suppose they'd let her go. Between us we're hoping to keep the Old Man out of trouble."

Jaelle still cringed at the disrespect in his voice. If the man was so incompetent, they should remove him from office, or at least make sure he was a figurehead without power; as *Comyn* Council had done with several recent kings, and she supposed they had done with *Dom* Gabriel—everyone knew Rohana had been the real power behind Ardais, for many years.

Peter directed her eyes to the invitation. "Look, we were specially requested—" and he pointed. "Mr. and Mrs. Peter Haldane. . . ."

Men dia pre'zhiuro . . . never be known again by the name of father, husband or lover . . . "Peter," she said, her voice dangerously quiet, "I am not Mrs. Peter Haldane. I am Jaelle n'ha Melora. I will not say this to you again."

He flinched, but protested. "I know that, love. But the Terrans do not understand, and why does it matter what they call you? It is a legal formality, no more. They probably looked at your name on the payroll lists—don't blame *me* for it."

She let the paper drop with a curious sense of finality. My whole identity gone. Not Jaelle n'ha Melora. Not even Jaelle, daughter of Jalak. Just an attachment of Peter Haldane, wife, mother of his child. . . . *I am no one. Not here. Peter is right. It doesn't matter.*

She saw him relax. "I was sure you'd be reasonable," he said. "That's my good girl." Clearly without speech she heard him say, *I knew you'd see it my way.* "What are you going to wear? You can't go in uniform, or in Amazon breeches. . . ."

"I suppose I shall wear the green gown Rohana gave me at Midwinter," she said, trying to recapture the excitement of their first dance together, but he did not even remember; he shook his head and said "That's been seen; for this you should have something new and special."

"I have dresses at home in the Guild-house, but my own clothes would not fit me now." She looked ruefully at her thickening waist. "But Rafaella and I have always worn one another's clothes, and she is heavier than I; her dresses will fit me perfectly now, and she would be glad to lend me one."

How she had twitted Rafaella when her waist had thickened and she could not wear Jaelle's clothes!

"I can't let you borrow somebody else's used clothes!"

"Piedro, don't be absurd, what are sisters for?"

"My wife does not have to *borrow* clothes, or wear an old, worn dress!"

"Piedro," she said, reasonably, "Rafaella dresses very well, she never wears a Festival gown more than once or twice, and no one here has seen any of them, they might as well be new." It seemed that Piedro was two men again, her lover, and this crazy Terran with his absurd prejudices and notions, standing between her and her beloved Piedro. "Be reasonable, Piedro.

Where in Thendara would we find a dressmaker who would make us a gown on Festival itself? I must either wear my old green gown—though I cannot think of a gown I have worn but once as *old*—borrow one from Rafaella—or wear my old breeches," she finished, laughing. "There is no other choice!"

"I hadn't thought of that. It *is* short notice, isn't it?" He frowned, then his eyes lit up. "I know, we'll go down to Costuming and get them to make up something; it isn't a holiday here. Let me have the green gown—we'll have it copied in some other fabric; do you like blue?"

That took the rest of the day, with barely a moment to snatch a bite of dinner before it was time to get dressed. It seemed to Jaelle that she was always snatching at something in haste—food, hello-good-bye, a shower, piece of paper with important message, a piece of clothing, a minute for lovemaking. She was getting heartily sick of it, but it wouldn't do to be too late; by the time the dress was sent up by messenger, carefully wrapped in plastic sheeting, she was saving seconds, and looking wistfully at the comfortable trail leathers as she brushed out the curls in her hair. As the yards and yards of skirt spilled from the box, Jaelle gasped; it was exquisite, low-cut, trimmed with marl-fur and embroideries. Then, looking more closely, she realized it was not spider-silk, nor fur . . . there was not an inch of honest thread in it. Just chemicals, all artificial, like all Terran clothing. Darkovan made, it would have cost a season's income from a good-sized estate, but it was a sham, a fraud.

"Peter, I can't wear this!"

But he was in the shower and could not hear, and by the time he had turned off the water, she knew she could not refuse. He had spent a week's pay on having it made up so quickly; he could have requisitioned it from Costume as a work expense and turned it back for recycling afterward, but he knew her aversion to recycling things and had paid for it and arranged for her to keep it as a Midsummer-gift.

Yet how could she wear this artificial gown? She would look like a Terran masquerading as Darkovan. . . . *well, that is what I am. Mrs Peter Haldane. Part of the Terran delegation.* As she struggled with the hooks, she wrinked her nose; it didn't smell right. She rummaged in her drawer, bringing out the small silken sachet packet Magda had given her. Her first sewing project, Magda had told her, apologizing for the crooked stitches; the uneven straggling stitchery reminded Jaelle suddenly of Camilla, her first year in the Guild-house, teaching a small bewildered Dry-Town child to sew.

I always thought I would grow up in chains. I had forgotten that. She remembered her first year in the house; maturity had come upon her. In the Guild-house it was a happy celebration, admitting her to the company of women, where in Shainsa it would have meant she would be ceremonially chained. *Yet here I am again in chains* . . . and she was horrified at herself. Kindra had said it so often; it was better to wear chains in truth than to weight yourself with invisible chains and pretend that you are free. *Oh, mother, mother, I wish I could talk to you. . . . I cannot even remember my own mother's face. Only Kindra's* . . .

"What are you doing, *chiya*?" Peter asked, coming out of the shower, naked, and starting to get into his breeches. She showed him the sachet and he nodded.

"I've seen Magda do that; she used to buy all her clothes in the Old Town when she could—she said the stuff from Costume never smelled right—and she never took off a dress without rubbing the seams with sweet spice, and she taught me to do it too." She caught the familiar scent of incense from his cloak as he slung it about his shoulders.

"That's what's wrong with Aleki," Jaelle said abruptly. "His clothes come from Costume; he doesn't smell right in them."

"Right; I knew there was something and I couldn't put my finger on it," Peter said. "I'll mention it to him, shall I? Might come better from a man—you look lovely, *preciosa*. Let's go."

In the walk across the marketplace, though a few members of the delegation complained about the rough cobblestone and holiday footwear, Jaelle began to believe that it was Midsummer; the familiar smells and sounds, the Festival crowds. Even through the lights which blazed in the Old Town she could see the four moons, all nearing full together. Their invitation was accepted at the doorway and she heard musicians already playing. A few professional dancers were already giving displays of dancing, while the guests drifted around the floor, greeting friends; then the first general dance began and Jaelle let Peter swing her out on the floor. The new dress felt lighter than a dress of honest fabric; she felt as if she were floating, as if tensions she had not known she had were dissolving.

She had never before danced in *Comyn* Castle at Festival. She had renounced this heritage, had spent her life among the Renunciates and their simpler Festival celebrations. Yet she might come here again and again, if she did as Rohana asked, and took a Council seat. *And it would please Peter so . . .* in shock, she realized that she was actually considering it, and the shock was followed by a sharp wave of dizziness, almost but not quite nausea.

"*Chiya*, what's the matter?"

She smiled at him, faintly. "It's a nuisance, being pregnant. I need air—"

"Sit here—by the open door. I'll get you a drink," he said, and she sighed with relief as she let herself collapse there. "I don't really want—" she began, but he was already gone, hurrying toward the buffet table.

She was near the balcony doors; and it was very warm. She went out on the balcony, leaning against the stone rail, breathing in the night fog. The multicolored moonlight turned the fog to pearly rainbows. She could smell the heavy scent of flowers, and the soft chirring of insects. It was so pleasant, after weeks of sterile indoor smells and yellow harsh Terran lights. She sat still on the bench. Soon she must go inside or Peter would worry when he could not find her. But it felt so good to sit here and breathe in all the smells of the summer. Momentarily, she dozed, then snapped awake, hearing a voice she could not reconcile with the smells of the Castle garden. Alessandro Li; an angry whisper in Standard.

"I told you he would be here! What luck!"

"Alessandro—Aleki—hasn't Jaelle been able to teach you anything? He is the son-in-law of Lord Alton; you simply cannot approach him and start asking impertinent questions about the private business of the Domain—" It was Magda! What was Magda doing here?

"You don't understand, Magda. This man is the key to everything I was sent here to find out about Darkover. Carr knows—"

"This man is *Dom* Ann'dra Lanart, and that is what you must deal with," Magda said sharply. "I don't know if he's Carr or not—"

"Well, I do; personnel pictures. And who else would he be? You said yourself he was Terran!"

"Pictures be damned," Magda said, and then Jaelle heard Monty's voice.

"He may or he may not be the one you are looking for, Sandro. But you can't approach him here, and that's all there is to it. Dance with him, Magda; that's what we're here for, not to make trouble."

"I'm hardly going to make trouble," Aleki said, but Jaelle could hear that he was angry. "I simply must talk to him; why don't you help me find a way to do it, instead of being so damned stubborn?"

"You are hardly the one to talk about being damned stubborn," Magda said angrily, "Once and for all, get it out of your head, and stop thinking like a damned Terran, with your mind on business even at a Festival ball!"

"Magdalen Lorne!" That was the voice of the elder Montray, being heavily jocular, "Is that any way to talk to your superior, and at a party too? You look smashing. Monty, why didn't you tell me you'd hunted her up and talked her into coming? I might have pulled rank on you, son, and grabbed her for my escort myself!"

"Cholayna," Magda said, and Jaelle could hear the relief in her voice, "How charming you look. Are you here with the Coordinator?"

Cholayna's gentle, neutral voice said, "Not nearly so many stares as I had expected. I don't know whether it is simply good manners, or whether they just expect that Terrans will look freakish."

"If they're so narrow-minded they'd stare at you because your skin color is different," Alessandro Li said, "then to hell with them all. They're just a bunch of ignorant natives after all. Hullo, Haldane, where's your lovely lady?"

"She felt a little faint," Peter said. "I left her by the doors while I went to get her something cool to drink."

Jaelle, knowing this was her cue, picked herself up and went back inside the balcony doors. "I went out for a breath of air. It was very warm in there." She accepted the glass Peter put in her hand and sipped. It was the pale mountain wine, and it made her think of their first dance, at Midwinter. She wondered if Peter remembered. Magda was wearing the rust-colored gown she had worn at Midwinter, with a superb necklace of firestones; Jaelle went to examine this.

"Did Camilla lend you this? It is exquisite," she said. "I have seen it among her treasures; she let me wear it at the party in the Guild-house when I took my Oath. . . ." and as she mentioned Camilla's name, she saw something she could not identify; trouble, unease . . . *fear?* What was troubling Magda? She could still see it, as an uneasy haze, when Monty came and demanded a dance, and as they moved away, she saw the way Monty's hand glided to Magda's bare neck, the way he hovered over her, an intensity almost sexual . . . *what is the matter with me, why am I seeing things like this? It can hardly be a side effect of pregnancy; at least it's not one I ever heard about!*

"We've got to think of a way to get that girl back," said Alessandro Li, "No offense, Haldane, but she's worth any ten other employees in Intelligence; the girl's a genius, we can't let her waste herself in the field like this! She deserves a holiday, certainly, but we can't take the chance she'll go over the wall! That seems to be what happened to Carr; he certainly isn't listed as being on detached or undercover status! Yet every damn time I spotted Carr and tried to move in on him tactfully, Magda would drag me off for another dance."

"But Magda is right," Jaelle said gently. "Even if this Carr is someone you wish to know, there is a right and a wrong way to make someone's acquaintance. Even at Midsummer, you cannot possibly walk up to *Dom* Ann'dra Lanart and say, 'Hi, Andy, what's new?' " Savagely, she mimicked the Terran's accent, and Peter cringed.

"I don't know why not," Montray said. "I wouldn't be that crude, of course, but surely I could speak to an old employee— not that he was ever in my department—and request him to do me the courtesy of coming in to straighten out his legal status. There are standards of manners among Terrans too—even if you do not think so, Mrs. Haldane. I am sorry we have made such a bad impression on you." And as Magda and Monty returned, the Coordinator touched Magda on the shoulder.

"Miss Lorne. I would like to remind you that both Alessandro Li and myself outrank you very much; and I am going to make it an official order. Find us a way to communicate with the man Carr, and do it before we leave here."

She said icily, "May I remind you that at the moment I am officially on leave, and that I am here as a favor?"

"You are here officially under my orders, like every Terran on this planet," said Montray grimly, "and that includes Andrew Carr. I don't know why we are handling this man with gloves; he is, after all, a citizen of the Empire . . ."

"Once and for all, he is *not*," Magda said, "I took the trouble to check his legal status. He is carried on the rolls as *dead*, and legal death carries legal termination of citizenship . . . and legally, termination of citizen's privileges carries also freedom from citizen's duties . . ."

"If you are going to argue legalities," said Montray, "he is a year away from being legally dead; he is *presumed* dead for one more year; after another year he may be legally dead. There is a difference."

"No," Peter said. "On the Darkovan side a man is who he says he is, unless he has committed a crime."

"That's rubbish and you know it," Montray said. "You've spent too much time in the Darkovan sector and you are going native. And you, Miss Lorne, are going to obey orders or you can be shipped offplanet—it's as simple as that."

Magda said, trapped and furious, "If you want a scandal which will insure that we are not only the first Terran delegation invited here, but also the last, you let those orders stand! In a specific matter involving protocol in the field—and you can't deny that we are in the field—a resident expert has a legal right to override even a direct order from a Legate, if said order would damage the reputation and credit of the Terran Empire. And, take it from me, this one would."

Sobered, he stared at her, and Jaelle knew Magda was right. But would either of them back down? At last Li said heavily "What's the proper protocol for approaching him, then?"

"An introduction must be made by a mutual acquaintance," Magda said, "and the one of higher rank must initiate the introduction. The Regent of Alton is not here this year—I have heard that his lady is ill—and *Dom* Ann'dra is here as his personal delegate."

"Can't you see," Cholayna said gently, "that is exactly why we must talk to him before he disappears again. Any Terran who can work himself so strongly into the hierarchy of a Domain—I am not the expert you are, Magda, but I know it is extraordinary."

She said slowly, "If he is a member of the household of the Regent of Alton, your best choice would be to send a man in the field to Armida, and ask for a private interview with *Dom* Ann'dra—not with Andrew Carr—and make certain that the interview was private; then broach your business. Treat him as if he were a field agent whose cover you were reluctant to disturb."

"I hardly have time for that—" Alessandro Li said, but old Montray sighed. "You're right, at that. I guess I'm getting too old for this job, Lorne. And I'm used to having you as my right hand."

"We can arrange that," Cholayna said, "but it will take time. . . ."

"We have plenty of that," Monty said, "Carr—*Dom* Ann'dra, I mean—isn't going to run away. He's evidently well established there and highly visible." He touched Magda's hand and moved closer to her. "And if we stand here arguing all night, the Dark-ovans will surely think we are plotting against them. I suggest we dance. May I—"

Jaelle, watching them closely, saw again the tension between them; but the elder Montray moved in, "Rank has its privileges," he said with heavy-handed jocularity. "My turn for a dance, Magda. I wouldn't step out on this floor with anyone else, but you know how to make me look acceptable."

Peter, also reminded of duty, said to Cholayna, "Would you like to dance?" and left Jaelle talking to Alessandro Li, who promptly asked her for a dance.

"Do you mind if I don't? I'm still a little short of breath," she said. She stood fanning herself, watching the dancers. The music came to an end; her eyes went to where Cholayna and Peter had come to halt, near the buffet.

"Who is the lady who came to speak to Haldane?" Aleki asked suddenly, and Jaelle saw, with surprise, that Lady Rohana had left the line of dowagers and approached Peter and Cholayna.

"She is my kinswoman—my mother's foster-sister," said Jaelle, "Lady Rohana Ardais—"

"And the man beside her?"

"Her son. My cousin Kyril. Yes, I know of the resemblance," she said, and indeed it was stronger than ever; Peter in his Ter-ran dress uniform, his cropped red hair bright in the room, and *Dom* Kyril, his hair slightly longer, curling about his earlobes; *Dom* Kyril bowed stiffly and she saw him say something polite to Cholayna, and all at once it seemed that the space between them in the room melted as if she was standing by Peter's side, and Rohana spoke beside her ear.

Is Jaelle here tonight, Piedro? I was hoping to speak with her about taking her seat in Council—she did tell you that she is now expected to attend Council as one of the few remaining in direct succession to the Aillard Domain, I suppose?

Jaelle felt herself turn white. She had not wanted Peter to know that; she had carefully not spoken of it. The room around her suddenly went fuzzy and dim and Magda was suddenly holding her arm.

"What is it, *breda?* Are you still feeling faint? Perhaps you should not have come to anything as crowded as this," Magda said solicitously. "Please, sit down again, we'll sit here for a little while and talk. I wouldn't think Peter would have dragged you here tonight if you weren't feeling well, as strongly as he feels about having a child. . . ."

Jaelle, through Magda's touch on her shoulder, could feel the other woman's thoughts, the sharp regret, *you are doing what I could not manage to do, giving him that child . . .* "How did you know? Did Marisela tell you?"

Magda shook her head. "No; she did not mention it. Were you in the Guild-house?"

"While you were on the fire-lines, *breda*; I was worried about you," Jaelle said.

"It was not she who told me, it was Monty; I was in the Terran HQ today, making a report," Magda said, and told Jaelle how Monty had come to the Guild-house, and how she had happened to be invited. She left out a certain private half-hour, but Jaelle, with that frightening new awareness, picked it up anyhow, and was shocked. She didn't want to know. Why had Magda told her this? But Magda *hadn't*. She had picked it up from the other woman's mind. *Laran* again. To ward away her uneasiness she said flippantly, "Just like a Terran; working all day even at Midsummer!"

Magda lowered her voice and said, "We'd better speak Darkovan."

"I thought we were," Jaelle said. "Is it normal, Margali, to be so confused? Those machines—I never know, any more, which language I am speaking. . . ."

"That could be one of the side effects of the corticator," Magda began, and stopped, as if frozen; to cover it, she took a couple of wine glasses from a servant circulating with a full tray.

"There is *Dom* Ann'dra," she said, and Jaelle, following her eyes, saw a small group of men in the colors of the Alton Domain, with a tall man, fair as a Dry-Towner, at their center. Was

Magda seriously trying to tell her that this man was the renegade Terran who had supposedly gone down with the plane, and reappeared somewhere in Alton lands, in the service of the Alton Regent? Chewing her lip, Magda said, "I must speak with him, warn him. He said that he would be leaving the city at dawn . . ." and Jaelle no longer bothered to question how Magda knew. But as Magda started to move away from the bench Jaelle tugged at her hand.

"You were just lecturing them on protocol; how can you—"

"But I do know him," Magda said. "He saved my life on the fire-lines. And he came to the Guild-house this morning to bring Ferrika there. . . ."

"I do not know Ferrika at all," Jaelle said. "She took the Oath at Neskaya, but is she not Marisela's oath-daughter? And yet she was traveling with this *Dom* Ann'dra, whoever he is—" Jaelle was frowning, confused, but Magda murmured, "*Breda*—" and Jaelle was touched, knowing Magda rarely used the word with that inflection, "—trust me. I promise I will explain later."

And she moved toward the man she had called *Dom* Ann'dra.

And then Jaelle saw something which made her realize why she could never be Magda's replacement, or even her equal, in the Terran Zone. As she moved into Ann'dra's visual field, Magda was a very proper and ladylike Darkovan woman, except for the short-cropped Amazon curls. Then, for perhaps a half a second, just as Ann'dra's eyes lighted on her, she became transformed into a Terran; it was as if Jaelle could see through the Darkovan lady, who might have been *Comyn* of the second rank, to the woman standing there, as if in the half-naked Terran uniform, a perfect representative of the Empire. And then again she was a correctly courteous Darkovan noblewoman, bowing to a *Comyn* noble and tacitly asking permission to approach him.

Dom Ann'dra bowed over Magda's hand. Jaelle was not close enough to hear any of what they were saying, though it was low-voiced and quick, but she was confused again, surely this man was a *Comyn* noble, how could anyone possibly believe him Terran? Then Magda was back at her side again, and they were drifting together toward the buffet table, and Jaelle found that she had one sharp impression in her mind of *Dom* Ann'dra, *Comyn* or Terran; a tall powerful man, fair-haired, not handsome, but with an impression of immense power and self-confidence. It reminded her of—she searched in her mind for impressions—of the time when she had been presented, as a child, to Lorill Hastur, Regent of *Comyn*. He had been a small, quiet man, soft-spoken, almost diffident—or perhaps that was only good manners. But nevertheless she had the impression, behind the courteous quiet facade, of almost awesome personal power, kept perfectly controlled. It was what she associated with *Comyn*. *Dom* Gabriel had never had it, but then, he had been, since she knew him, an invalid. But that a Terran should have it? Nonsense; it must be only a trick of his great height and enormously powerful frame. The buffet was all but deserted; Jaelle scooped up a cup of some fruit drink but when she put it to her lips it was too sweet and she set it aside almost untasted.

"Look," Magda said, "I think he is leaving." And indeed *Dom* Ann'dra and the man with him were bowing before Prince Aran Elhalyn as if taking formal leave.

"It doesn't make any difference, you know," Jaelle said abruptly. "That man could talk all day to Montray, or to Aleki, without giving anything away that he didn't want them to know."

Magda was filling a small dish at the buffet with an assortment of fruits in cream. It looked delicious, and Jaelle looked at the other colorful delicacies almost wistfully, wishing she could manage to feel hungry enough to try them.

Magda said, "Can't you see? That's why I had to keep them apart. No matter what he told Li, it would be wrong; what's the old proverb, it takes two for the truth, one to speak true and one to hear? Alessandro Li has made up his own mind about Carr; the truth is beyond him. What he wants is an excuse to have the *Comyn* declare Carr *persona non grata* so that Li could wring him out and find out everything he thinks Ann'dra can tell him about the *Comyn*. Then the Altons would have a grudge against the Terrans that would last for generations. And if Carr made up the lies Alessandro expects to hear he'd find some way to twist it . . ." Magda broke off, and Jaelle could almost hear her say, *I am disloyal, disloyal to my own people as I have been disloyal to everyone*, and her dismay stabbed with real pain at Jaelle.

She is my sister, and I cannot help her because I myself am so filled with confusion!

Magda gasped, "God above!" and abruptly she was thrusting through the crowd, muttering apologies. Jaelle, following slowly with her plate in hand, saw that Alessandro Li and Russell Montray, Peter hurrying behind them, were approaching Carr's party near the door. Peter caught at the Coordinator's shoulder, expostulating with him in a whisper, but Montray wrenched loose.

He walked up directly to Carr and said something in a low voice.

Jaelle could not hear what *Dom* Ann'dra said in reply; she saw only the frosty politeness in his voice. Montray said something loud and aggressive this time, and *Dom* Ann'dra's two bodyguards closed in, one on either side, clearly ready to protect their lord from this bumptious alien.

The tension was now plain enough to draw attention from onlookers, as Montray said, clearly enough for Jaelle to hear every word, "Look, I just need to talk to you for a few minutes; I'm sure you don't want to do it in front of everybody here, do you? But I'll do it that way if you leave me no alternative . . ."

Peter grabbed him urgently, physically hauling him backward, and Ann'dra's bodyguards closed in, their intent and threat unmistakable. Suddenly a little murmur ran through the crowd, and Aran Elhalyn, Prince of the Domains, between his aide and young Danvan Hastur, came toward them, the crowd parting with little respectful murmurs to either side. Magda caught Alessandro Li by the shoulder and said something urgent in an undertone, and Li turned and bowed to the nobles. He was speaking Terran Standard and Magda, at his elbow—and Jaelle noticed, it was very clearly the *Terran* Magda again—translated in fluent *casta*;

"Majesty, your pardon is humbly beseeched; this matter will

be attended in private; and we gravely regret any disturbance."
Even before Magda finished speaking, Prince Aran waved a
negligent hand, dismissing the matter, and turned away, and
Alessandro Li said in a savage undertone, "Montray, damn it,
one more word and I'll make damn sure you never get another
post except punching buttons in a penal colony!"

Jaelle wondered how she could hear at this distance. It didn't
matter. Peter came and guided her to the rest of the delegation.
The music had surged up again and a group of cadets in black
and green were dancing some kind of energetic dance with a lot
of stamping and kicking; Prince Aran had withdrawn to watch
them.

Dom Ann'dra and his party were gone. Peter shook his head
and muttered "That tears it. Everybody knows what Montray is.
Nobody has taken official notice of it before now—"

Russell Montray was muttering, "I am going to make an official appeal to Lord Hastur. That man is a Terran citizen and I
demand the right to speak to him officially—"

"Let it alone sir," Monty said quietly, "before you get us all
expelled from here. Haldane knows what he's talking about.
And so does Magda—"

Montray turned on them both in a fury. "And I've had
enough of both of those damned so-called experts, and their insubordination," he snarled, in a grim undertone. "I've put up
with it, and knuckled under to the way you go around bootlick-
ing the natives, just about long enough! Because you think you
are rated *expert,* you think you can get away with anything!
Well, I have heard enough and I mean enough! The minute I get
back to HQ I am going to put through a formal request to have
both of you transferred out, as far as I can, somewhere in the
other end of the Galaxy, and I'll make damn sure neither of you
ever gets clearance to get back! I still have that much authority,
and I should have done it a long time ago! As for you, Lorne, I
want you back on HQ and under orders tonight. Not tomorrow.
Tonight."

"I am officially on leave," Magda began.

"Leave canceled," he snapped. "Recalled to active duty under orders under Section 16-4—"

"To hell with that," Magda said, and to Jaelle it seemed that visible, electrical sparks were flying from her eyes and creating a field of light all round her, "I resign. Cholayna, witness it. I'm sorry, it has nothing to do with you—"

"Magda," said Monty, putting his arm around her waist, "Honey, listen to me. Everybody calm down. Father—" he addressed the angry Montray, "this is neither the time nor the place—"

"I've calmed down and listened for the last time in my life; don't you think I know what everybody here thinks, that I'm just a figurehead and no one has to listen to me? Well, it's about time I stopped listening to that shit! This whole damned planetary administration has been mismanaged for forty years, we've been handling people with gloves and it's about time we made them realize that they can't face up to the Terran Empire that way. There's going to be a new deal around here. I am going to have some new Intelligence people here, people whose main loyalty is to the Empire, and I want a clean sweep of the people who have been mismanaging everything so badly! As for you, Haldane, I knew when you married a native woman that your judgment and loyalty had gone to hell, and I should have fired you right then. And I'm going to be rid of all of you if it's the last thing I do."

"It probably will be, sir," said Alessandro Li. "The way Darkover is being handled at Central is a matter of very high policy," but Montray was too angry to listen.

"Then, damn it, maybe I can get transferred out myself— which I've been trying to do for seven years!" He turned and strode away; Peter said, numbly, "Good God," and turned to Jaelle.

"Darling. Go back with Li and Monty, will you? I've got to get to him before he gets that request sent through Empire channels or we're all in the porridge pot. We can appeal, but by that time—"

Monty put a hand on Magda's arm. "Don't worry about the

Old Man. He'll calm down. Haven't you ever seen him in a tantrum before?"

"I was dealing with his tantrums when you were doing entrance examinations for the Service," Magda said wearily, "but I've just dealt with the last one. I meant it, Monty. I resign. And I have to be back inside the Guild-house by sunrise—"

"I'll go with you and spend the night in the Guild-house," Jaelle said, but Peter seized her shoulders.

"No, Jaelle! Don't fight me now, for the love of God! Go back to the Terran Zone and wait; I've never needed loyalty so much—what kind of wife are you, anyhow? For my sake, for the baby's sake—I'm fighting for all of us!"

The baby. I had forgotten. What can I do? I have no choice now. Alessandro Li said, "Let me escort you home, Jaelle," and she slumped against him. All she wanted was to run through the streets to the Guild-house, run *home*—but it was not her home anymore. Why was she deceiving herself?

Peter had hurried away after the Montrays. She never remembered that walk back through the streets of Thendara, only that they were filled with gaiety, crowds laughing, drinking, dancing, tossing flowers. When she was in her quarters alone, she found small flowers caught in the folds of the imitation dress in which she had danced so gaily.

She found herself thinking, with a bitterness that astonished her, *I hope they do send him offworld, I hope I never have to see him again. Never think again of my failure. My failure? No, his; he loves no one, he thinks only of his own ambition and his own work . . .*

She told herself she was not being fair. Her needs and Peter's had been so different, they had really had no chance; but they had been blinded by passion. She had never known a man before. She had not been prepared for the all-encompassing pull of love—of sex, if she must be perfectly honest with herself. She had been ready for a love affair; and she had not been able to admit that it was no more than that. But they each had needs the other could not meet. He had needed—if he needed anything—a woman content to further his ambition, to be there when he

needed her and patiently stand aside when he did not. He was
not cruel or heartless; he was a kind and good man. But the magical togetherness and blending she imagined had never been
there; or it had been there only a little while and she had imagined that it continued only because she had needed so much to
feel it there.

If she had truly loved him, friendship and kindliness and
shared goals could have come to take the place of that first
blinding passion. They could have accepted this new level of
closeness, enough to build a pleasant life together, as even
Gabriel and Rohana had done. But Gabriel and Rohana, whose
marriage had been arranged, had never been led to expect anything more, and had never been blinded by that first rush of passion. She and Peter had had nothing more, and when that was
gone, nothing was left.

Nothing left—except Peter's child. Poor unwanted child,
perhaps it would be better if it was never born. No, it was not
unwanted; Peter wanted it. And she really had wanted it too, for
a little while. Or perhaps it was her body, ready to exercise its
natural function, which had wanted the child. *Any child. Not just
Peter's.*

Now she could see why Magda and Peter had not stayed together. To Peter a woman was a necessary convenience, a background to his ego. Suddenly she felt sorry for him. He needed
women, but he needed them to be all wrapped up in him in a
way neither of them could be. She was sorry for the thing in
Peter which attracted strong women to take care of him. She
supposed it had been happening all his life, but when he had
them he must weaken and destroy them because he feared their
strength.

It did not matter now. It was over, as this Festival Night was
over.

*But I am sworn, for the legal term of my employment. Be-
cause Peter is false to what he has promised, must I be false too?*
She had at least known enough not to marry him *di catenas.*
Freemate marriage could be dissolved at will; among the Terrans there were a few legal formalities. She was still responsible

for Monty, and for Aleki. And after that disastrous near-meeting with *Dom* Ann'dra, or Andrew Carr, or whoever he was, who knew what either of them would do? By the Amazon Oath she was not liable to any man. . . .

She had been with the Terrans too long. Now the Amazon Oath too seemed too constricting. She had taken the Oath when she was too young to know what it meant. But could she now forswear it because she had outgrown it? That was not the honorable way. Rohana had said, *honor is abiding by those oaths even when it is no longer convenient.* But Rohana, for her own purposes, would bind her to the greater slavery to Council and *Comyn*; she could not trust Rohana completely, any more than she could trust the Terrans.

She did not want to wait for Peter to come in. Nor did she care how his confrontation with Coordinator Montray had come out. He had created the problem for himself and must now deal with it as best he could. He was perfectly competent in his own way, he did not need her help, and if she thought that he did, that was just one more symptom of what had gone wrong between them. There was such a deep sadness in her, because all the sweetness had gone awry. But Kindra had always said; *there is no use fretting after last winter's snow.* And the love they had shared was further away than that.

Quickly she dressed herself in uniform, checking the small communication device built into the collar. How quickly habits grew! She remembered how she had resented this. She would go down to the cafeteria and find something to eat, then go to Cholayna's office and try to work out some new arrangement. The Darkovan women who would soon be coming here to work in Medic would live outside the walls, and come here only to work, surely they would let her do the same. Part of her knew she would miss the conveniences of the Terran way of life.

She was fastening the final tab on her collar when she heard Peter's step. She could see, as he walked in, that he was very drunk. She shivered; once when Kyril was drunk he had tried to molest her and she had had to defend herself. To this day she hated drunkenness. But Peter only flung a surprisingly vicious curse at her.

"Peter, what's the matter? What did you find out from Montray? Where have you been?"

He looked her straight in the eye. "What the hell do you care?" he said, and pushed past her. She heard the shower running.

Part of her wanted to stay and have it out with him when he was sober. Another part did not care. She said "You're right, I don't," knowing he could not hear her over the running water, and went out.

Chapter 3

Magda moved slowly through the streets of the Old Town, Cholayna's words still in her ears; she had promised to wait, to think over her resignation when the older woman could come and talk to her in the Guild-house but she wished she had not. She wished she could flee back to the company of her sisters in the Guild-house and never return to the Terran world at all. The effort to confront old loyalties again had taken its toll of her.

After the half year free of the conflicts between men and women, even the most casual contacts between the sexes now seemed strange and abnormal to her; she found herself examining the least of them for nuances. Of course, that was what the housebound time was all about, to break old habits, to examine life rather than living mindlessly by old patterns laid down in childhood.

She had half promised to meet Camilla at the women's dance . . . was that where her loyalties now lay? Suddenly she was troubled again. She was a trained scientist, a skilled professional, what was she doing here, after a day spent in using the special skills she had trained for. Was she seriously thinking of giving it all up, going back to obey their silly damn rules, mucking out barns, asking permission to step outside the garden? She thought wearily that if she had a grain of sense she would go back to the HQ, put in for transfer—Montray had threatened her with it anyhow—and get right away from a world she desired and hated and of which she could never be a real part.

Would she really be able to give up the Renunciates? Seriously, now, without worrying about things like stables and bathrooms. She had discovered a kind of solidarity which she had never known, a world of women. If that world was small and petty in many ways, built on denial and restraint, by women who thought themselves free but were bound in a hundred small ways, what life was entirely free? And there were amazing freedoms in that life. In all her twenty-seven years she had never found a world so near to fulfilling all her dreams and needs; could she leave it because it was not perfect?

Who was the Terran philosopher who had written that since no man could be free, that man could be counted fortunate who could find a slavery to his liking? The *Comhi Letzii,* the Sisterhood of the Unbound, had at least chosen for themselves.

As I choose. . . .

And there was Camilla to be considered, too . . . she had avoided thinking about Camilla, yet Camilla was one of the reasons, she knew, why she now wished to take flight.

Within a single day, in the sudden freedom of Midsummer, she had broken through her self-chosen isolation; first with Monty—and she was still not sure why she had done that, though it had seemed reasonable enough at the time—and then with Camilla. She had been astonished at herself—even now her mind shrank from confronting all the new things she had discovered about herself. But now she knew why she had fled, in panic, from Jaelle's touch.

I was not ready to know that. I am not ready now.

Even now she could not identify herself as a lover of women, she could never embrace all the narrowness of women like Rezi or Janetta, who considered only women to be fully human, and considered the slightest contact with a male, even father, brother or employer, as treason to their sisterhood. Even Camilla was not like that. But she could not look down on the Rezis and Janettas either, knowing what she knew. And they were her sisters too. She could turn her back on them only by turning her back on the Guild-house forever.

And she could not do that. They had accepted her, given to

her, a stranger, all the sisterhood and friendliness and love she had hardly known how to accept. But now the housebound time was nearly over. Camilla at least must know her real identity. To any or all of the others she could lie, but Camilla deserved honesty from her. Camilla must know the truth, even if her love turned to rejection and revulsion.

It was late; most of the revelry in the open streets had subsided, though in the public squares and gardens, she knew, the dancing and drinking and feasting would continue most of the night. Even now, in dark buildings and entryways, she could sense the warmth and sweetness of the night, where the four moons floated brilliantly overhead and couples enlaced, lovers for an hour or a lifetime, in search of somewhere to end the night together. Peter, she thought, this time without bitterness, and Jaelle. Magda turned her eyes away from the many couples and sighed. It seemed that all of Thendara was coupled this night, and only she was alone. She need not have been alone, Monty would have been happy, if, the troubles of this night ended, she had been waiting for him in his quarters. Then she need never face what was awaiting her in the Guild-house, or at the women's dance . . .

I should have gone with Camilla anyhow. I never should have let Monty talk me into going to the damned Festival Ball. What is it to me, anymore, what the relations are between the damned *Comyn* aristocracy, and the Empire?

Surely this was the street and the house where the women's dance was to be held? But the place was dark, locked, silent and forbidding, and Magda stared at it with dismay. *What do I do now?* Then she heard laughter and voices: down the street light flooded from the open doors of a wineshop whose clientele had spilled over into the street, and instruments were playing; against the light, shadowy forms were dancing in a ring-dance on the uneven cobbles.

It was very late. At one table a knot of Guardsmen were gathered, some of them with women; at another, two tables had been pushed together and Magda recognized many of the women. Mother Lauria was there, and Rafaella, but she got up and went to dance with one of the Guardsmen as Magda approached. Camilla was there with a glass in her hand, and Keitha and Marisela in their working clothes, with the white coifs all midwives wore in the city tied around their hair. Keitha raised her glass and beckoned.

"Come and sit with us, Margali—it is lucky to be born under the four moons, and it seems that half the women in the city are eager to give their babes that luck! But any mother who has not dropped her burden by now is probably too drunk to go into labor this night—let us follow!"

Magda accepted a drink from the pitcher on the table, and one of the young Guardsmen at the farther table came over to them.

"Well met under the four moons, Margali! Do you remember me? We met in the winter past at Castle Ardais, and now I have taken employment here in the city—remember, we knew one another as children at Caer Donn, you had dancing lessons with my sisters—I am Darrill of Darnak; will you come and drink with me?"

She smiled, letting him bow over her hand. "I am sorry, but my sisters are waiting for me—"

He looked at her with comical disappointment. "All night I have traveled around the city looking for you. When you have greeted your friends and quenched your thirst, will you dance with me?"

Magda hesitated, glancing at Camilla, who said, "Dance if you like, child." She smiled up at Darrill, saying, "We are companions of the sword; may I offer you a drink?"

"I think I have already had too much to drink, but will you favor me with a dance, *mestra*?"

Camilla chuckled. "I do not dance with men, brother. But I am sure there are others in our company who would be pleased."

Marisela rose, laughing, and moved toward him. "I have been busy all this day, and have had small chance for merrymaking. But Festival Night must not pass without a dance or two. If my sister will introduce me—I cannot dance with a man whose name is unknown to me!"

Magda laughed and presented Darrill to Marisela who looked flushed, pretty, younger than she was in her blue gown; she pushed the white coif back so that her short copper-colored hair stood out in curls around her face. Darrill bowed and pulled her into the circle-dance that was forming in the street; Janetta pulled Mother Lauria into the circle, too, but Camilla shook her head as they gestured her and Magda to join them.

"You look tired, Margali," said Camilla, "but very pretty. How was the great ball? Were all the great folk of *Comyn* there? And the Lady Rohana? And Shaya, was she there with her free-mate? What sort of man is he?"

"Yes, they were both there," Magda said, wondering how to answer Camilla's question; what could she say to Camilla about Peter Haldane? "But Jaelle looked very tired, I think—she is pregnant, you know."

"Little Jaelle, with a baby of her own!" Camilla said, diverted as Magda had hoped. "Only a season or two ago, it seemed, I cut her hair for her and gave her her first lessons with the knife. I suppose she will return to the House for the birth?"

Some of the partnerless Guardsmen had come up and asked the remaining Amazons to dance; it seemed that another, impromptu party was in the making. Some of the women danced together instead. But a few men remained alone at the table, with one woman—no, Magda realized suddenly, they were all men, what she had thought a woman was only a very slender, extremely young man, with delicate features, who had allowed his hair to grow considerably longer than most men; he had furthermore pinned it back in a way that suggested, though it did not actually imitate, a woman's coiffure. And in this last group, Magda noticed a few Terrans. One was actually wearing the black leathers of Spaceforce.

Of course. It made sense. At Festival, when all classes mingled without prejudice, it would make sense to certain men to get away from the Terran prejudice. *In Darkovan Society it would not matter so much that they are lovers of men. Or even that they are Terran. Outcasts do not look down on other outcasts.* She had seen one of the men on the spaceport that very day. He had taken her ident pass. She thought vaguely that he should have gotten himself Darkovan clothing, not come down here in uniform. Who was she to criticize, who sat here beside a woman who was her lover?

Darrill , son of Darnak, had come back, and Marisela was thanking him for the dance. One of the more effeminate men had risen and said diffidently to Marisela, "I like to dance, but I have no sister and no woman friend. Will you honor me, *mestra*?"

Marisela smiled acceptance. Of course; even at Midsummer men did not dance together in Thendara, except in the all-men circle dances. She wondered why. Why shouldn't men dance together if they wanted to? Women could dance together, in fact it was considered the most suitable thing for women in strange places! She was sure the young man would rather have danced with his friend at the other table than with Marisela. She had seen them holding hands. But they couldn't dance together. How strange, and how sad, that even on this most permissive of nights, men were still more trapped than women. She could wear, and as a Renunciate *did* wear, breeches in public. If this man wore skirts, and he looked as if he would feel and look better in them, he would be lynched. How sad, and how foolish, people were!

Camilla asked, "Will you dance with me, Margali?" and Magda hesitated. She would have liked to. But she could not get up and dance with Camilla in front of those heartbreaking men. Darrell bowed expectantly and Camilla gave her a little indulgent shove.

"Go and dance, child."

Reluctantly—she wished Camilla had forbidden her!—she moved away. It was a dance in couples. She hoped he would not speak of their shared childhood in Caer Donn, he had known her as the daughter of the Terran scholar Lorne, and she did not want that mentioned just yet. But it was obvious he had other things on his mind. He was a good dancer, but he held her just a fraction too close, and she would have refused a second dance, except that they were at the far side of the square and it would have seemed unkind. It was very warm; such unseasonable warmth in

Thendara always predicted severe storm very soon. The smell of
the air told her dawn was not far away. As the second dance
ended she could see the musicians finishing their drinks and
putting their instruments away. Darrill steered her into a darkened doorway and touched her lips. She did not protest, kisses
at the end of a dance did not commit her to anything, but when
he tried to embrace her, murmuring, "I do not want to end this
night alone," she pushed him away.

"All around us, all men and women do honor to the loves of
the Gods—"

No. This was too much. Already this Festival had brought her
more than she wanted of such matters, and she would not, she
simply would not, give herself to him here in the open air as
some of the women were doing, scarcely troubling to shelter
themselves from the eyes of passersby as they took the license
of this night. She hardly knew this man. "No," she said, pushing
him away again. "No, I am honored, thank you, but no, really
no—"

"But you must," he muttered, trying to nuzzle her bare neck;
if she had known how drunk he was she would not have danced
with him at all! His hands were hot and urgent on her bare neck
and he was trying to fumble into her breast. She wished she were
wearing her Amazon tunic instead of the Festival gown. She
knew how to defend herself, but this man was a childhood friend
and she really did not want to hurt him. She shoved him roughly
away, but as his hands clung she followed it with a ringing slap
which made him blink and stare at her stupidly.

"You aroused me and now you refuse me—"

She said in exasperation "I danced with you; you roused
yourself! Don't talk like a fool, Darrill! Are you honestly trying
to claim I deliberately roused you? Why, if that were so, every
woman in Thendara must go veiled like a Dry-Towner!"

He hung his head, with a shamefaced grin.

"Ah, well—no harm in asking."

She was glad to return his smile. "None. Provided you only
ask and do not try to snatch unwilling!"

"You cannot blame me for that," he said good-naturedly and

bent to kiss her bare shoulder, but she moved out of reach; she was not trying to flirt with him! Damn it, after all those months of isolation and celibacy, suddenly men, handsome and eligible men at that, were literally crawling out of the trees! First Monty, now this perfectly nice young Guardsman—if it had not been for Camilla would she have agreed to go with him this night? She would never know. Camilla was there.

She could see against the shadow of one of the buildings, a woman in Amazon clothing—Rafaella, surely—standing in a man's arms, so violently embraced that it was almost a struggle; both were fully clothed but from their movements it was reasonably obvious what was happening. She turned away, embarrassed, and went back to the bench where the last of the women lingered.

Camilla yawned, covering her mouth with a narrow hand. "We must be away to the Guild-house," she said. "The moons are setting, and you and Keitha, child, must be indoors by dawn."

She chuckled. "I could stay out as late as I wished—but by now my only desire is for my comfortable bed."

The owners of the wineshop were now unobtrusively removing every bench as soon as it was vacant, stacking them, eager to call it a night. The Guardsmen who had been dancing, finding their seats gone, wandered away down the street. The group of women were still sharing a final pitcher of wine. Rafaella came back to where Magda sat with Camilla and Keitha— Marisela was exchanging a final word with a young man, and ended by kissing him in a motherly way on the cheek, so Magda supposed he must be a nephew or something of that kind. Rafaella's face was flushed, her hair mussed, the laces of her tunic undone; she bent over Camilla and whispered to her, and Camilla reached up and patted her cheek.

"Enjoy yourself, *breda*. But take care."

Rafaella smiled—she was a little drunk too, Magda realized— and went away, arms enlaced with the man who had been holding her. Keitha's eyes were as wide as saucers. Janetta leaned over from the next bench and said, "Bold creature! Such

indecent ways cast shame on all Renunciates; they will come to
think us no better than harlots! I wish we were still in the ancient
days when no Renunciate might lie with a man, or her sisters
would cast her out!"

"Oh, hush," said Marisela, coming back to the table. "Then
we were denounced as lovers of women, seducers of decent
wives and daughters, luring their children astray because we had
none of our own! All women cannot live as you do, Janetta, and
no one has appointed you keeper of Rafi's conscience."

"At least she could do such things in decent privacy, not before half the city of Thendara," Janetta complained, and
Marisela laughed, glancing around the all-but-deserted square.

"I think they are trying to get us to leave. But we have paid
for the wine, and I for one will sit here and finish it." She raised
her glass. "It is easy for you to talk, Janetta, you have never been
tempted in that way, and for the love of Evanda spare me your
next speech, the one about the woman who lies with a man
being a traitor to her sisters, I have heard it all too often, and I
believe it no more than I did when first I heard it. I care not
whether you, or anyone else, lies down with men, women, or
consenting *cralmacs*, so that I need not hear them argue about it
when I am trying to sleep—or finish my drink!" She raised her
glass and drank.

But I agree with Janetta now more than I ever did, Magda
thought. *Yet here I sit beside a woman who has been my lover,
and for whose sake I refused a man this night.* For that matter,
Camilla had laughed and blessed Rafaella, and why not? She
picked up her own glass, then heard a voice say, "Margali—"
and looked up into the eyes of Peter Haldane.

He was wearing Darkovan clothing; no one but herself,
surely, would have known him for the young Terran among the
delegation at Festival Ball in *Comyn* Castle this night.

Camilla said to Magda, "Finish your drink, child, I shall be
back at once," and with Marisela and Mother Lauria, wandered
away to the latrines, at the back of the wineshop garden. Peter
sank down across from Magda. She had never seen him so
drunk.

She said in the language of Caer Donn, "Piedro, is this wise?"

"Wise be damned," he said. "I've been fighting for my life. Montray was so damned determined I'd be on that ship pulling out just about now for the Alpha Colony, up for discipline before Head Center Intelligence. I finally went over his head, got Alessandro Li to pull rank on him, and Cholayna—where the hell were you, Mag? It was your problem, too. And what were you up to with Monty?"

She said, "I'm sorry you were having trouble, Peter." She was not, definitely not going to discuss her relationship with Monty here, nor with him. "But it is all right, then?"

"Till he starts in on me again. God, I'd give ten years of my life to get that man shipped off Darkover; I swear, if I live, I'll do it. Even his own son knows—" he broke off. "But what are you doing here, Mag? In *this* place?" His horrified eyes fell on the last remaining table except for theirs, where a couple of the men were still drunkenly pawing one another and the effeminate who had danced with Marisela was asleep with his head on the table. Magda noted, with sadness and some pity, that he wore a woman's butterfly-clasp in his long hair.

"Maggie, don't you know what this place *is?*"

She shook her head. He told her. His outrage seemed misplaced.

"At least no one will trouble women alone here. And anyhow, *you're* here."

"Looking for you," he said. "They told me some women from the Guild-house were still here drinking, dancing—wanted to talk to you," he said with drunken earnestness. He saw Camilla's drink on the table and absentmindedly picked it up and drank it. It seemed to thicken his speech immediately. "Need you," he said. "Need you to talk to Jaelle. You're her friend. My friend too. Good friends. Both need you, both of us. Need you to talk to her, tell her what it means. Be a good Terran wife. Back us up. She's having a baby," he informed Magda with drunken seriousness. "My baby, got to get her straightened out so she can help me instead of fighting me all the time. Got to get in good with all the higher-ups so we can bring up our baby here. My son. Only she won't help me the right way. She doesn't know how to handle Terran bureaucrats. You always handled old Montray just fine. Maggie, you talk to her, you tell her—"

She stared at him, not believing what she had heard him say.

"You," she said, "have got to be right out of your mind. Peter! You want me—*me*?—to talk to Jaelle, and tell her how you want her to act as your wife? I never heard such a thing in my life!"

"But you know the kind of trap I'm in, how I need it—"

"Handle it the way I did," she said sharply. "Tell them all to go to hell. If you want to let them push you around, don't come crying to me!"

He grabbed her hand, held it, staring into her eyes with drunken intensity.

"Never should have let you go," he said thickly. "Mistake of a lifetime. Nobody like you, Maggie. You—you got to be the best there is. Only now there's Jaelle. I love her, if only she'd settle down and put her weight behind me, do what she ought to do. And now there's our kid. My kid. F'the sake of that kid, I got to stick to her. Can't quit. Can't bring the kid up like some damned native, out in the outback of nowhere—wish *you'd* had our kid, Maggie, you'd have done it right . . . you got to help us, Mag. My friend. Jaelle's friend. Talk to her, Maggie."

"Peter," she said helplessly. "you're drunk; you don't know how outrageous that sounds. Go home, Peter, and sober up. Things will look different when you're sober, when you've had some sleep—"

"But you've got to *listen* to me!" He grabbed her, pulled her close to him. "I got to make you understand just what a bind I'm in—"

"*Bredhiya*," said Camilla's gentle voice behind her, "is this man annoying you?"

Camilla, tall and somehow formidable, was towering over the slightly built Peter, who was swaying on his feet. Of course Camilla had spoken in the intimate mode which gave the words only one possible meaning. Camilla, too, was more than a little drunk. Peter looked at them both with horror and sudden dismay.

"Damn," he said, "now I understand. Never saw it before. No wonder you wouldn't stay with me, no wonder . . . and I thought you'd come here because you didn't understand. Of course you wouldn't be the one to talk to Jaelle. What the hell would you know about it?" He made a gesture of disgust and revulsion. "So *that* was why you left me, went into the Guild-house. Of course you couldn't be a decent wife to me, to any man—"

She said angrily, "How dare you speak to me that way?"

"How dare *you* speak to any decent person? You?" He wrinkled his nose in wrath. "If I catch you anywhere near Jaelle," he said in drunken wrath, "I'll—I'll break your neck. You stay away from my wife, hear me, I don't want you corrupting her!"

Camilla, of course, had not understood a word of all this, but she could tell perfectly well that he was being offensive. She said, not knowing that Peter could understand—he had, after all, been speaking the last few sentences in Terran Standard— "*Bredhiya,* shall I get rid of him for you?"

"You—" Peter snarled. It was a gutter insult, and Camilla's hand closed on her knife-hilt. It flashed.

"No!" Magda cried out. "He's drunk—he doesn't know—"

One of the men at the other table lurched over, closing his hand on Peter's shoulder. He said with thick earnestness, "No, no, no sense picking a fight here at Festival, brother, no sense talking to the likes of them." He gestured at Camilla and added, "I'm the one you came down here to find, brother. Come on over here with us, we're all friends over here." He put his arms around Peter, breathing heavy camaraderie, wine-laden, into his face. "C'mon, brother, it's late and I'm still all alone, come on, leave all them bitches out of it. Let them go off by themselves if they want to, who needs *them?*" he shoved his own tankard in Peter's face. "Drink up, little brother, drink up."

Peter could not push the man's hand away; he swallowed, coughed on the strong liquor, sank down at the other table, staring up in bewilderment at the man.

"Look, I didn' come down here lookin' for you—" he muttered.

"Aw, come on," said the man, staring down intensely into Peter's flushed face, "what else you come down here for? I know you Terrans, you can't find what you're lookin' for on *your* side of the wall, can you? None of our brothers over there, got to come down here in the City, we get a lot of you fellows. . . . I know all about it, here, have another drink—"

Oh, poor Peter! Magda thought, but somehow she could not resist an unholy glee. Camilla said in an undertone, gathering up their possessions, "Come along, Margali, it's better than a duel at this hour."

Magda stared in dismay at Peter, who had sunk down, semiconscious, too drunk even to express his anger. He slid down, slowly, under the table, and the man who had urged him to drink knelt over him.

"Ah," he urged drunkenly, "don't go passing out on me now, little brother, that's no way to treat a pal. . . ."

Magda did not know whether to laugh or cry, but Camilla urged her gently away. She could not help wondering what would happen to Peter when he woke up there . . . would he get back to the Terran Zone with his virtue intact?

Camilla put her arm around Magda's waist as they walked down the street. "I shall be glad to get home to our bed," she said, yawning. "I am sorry I am too drunk and weary to end the night as is fitting for Midsummer . . . that is no way to treat you at Festival, *bredhiya*. . . .

Magda flushed, snuggling against Camilla's arm round her waist. Through all the aggravations of this evening she remembered the lovemaking of this afternoon, amazed at herself. In Camilla's arms she had discovered another whole new self, a Magda previously unknown to her. She remembered, with a wave of heat, how she had cried out to Camilla in surprise and wonder and delight. Body and mind were all alive with a sudden hunger to know that delight and that wonder again. Why had she never guessed?

"That Terranan . . . how did you come to know him?" Camilla demanded, suddenly suspicious.

"He is—Jaelle's freemate," Magda said, then fell silent before the dawning suspicion in Camilla's eyes; but the older woman said no more. The streets were already filled with greyish-pink light. At the door of the Guild-house she stopped, touched Camilla's hand.

"I swear you shall know everything some day, oath-sister," she said, using the word in the most intimate form. "Not now, Camilla, I beg you, give me a little time."

Camilla stopped in the street and put her arms around Magda, holding her close. "You are my sister, and my beloved," she said. "You are sworn to me and I to you. Tell me what you wish, whenever you wish, and in your own time, my precious. I trust you." She kissed Magda, and suddenly leaned forward and picked her up.

"Come love," she said, "we must be inside before the last moon sets, that is our law." She carried her up the steps and inside the house.

What a bitch I am, Magda thought. I've played hell with two men today—three if you count Peter—and now I'm using Camilla's love and devotion to give myself time—time to think what I can say to her.

But she was overcome with such a wave of fatigue that she could hardly stand on her feet. Without protest she let Camilla lead her up the stairs.

Toward morning, Magda began to dream. She was living in Married Personnel Quarters in the HQ skyscraper, but somehow all the showers and bath sections had been redesigned, and women from the Guild-house were living in little doorless cubicles all along the corridors, so that she wandered in them for hours trying to find a place for a shower unobserved; and through all this she could not allow them to know that she was pregnant nor that she had had a mark tattooed on her back. She was not sure what it said, but it was something like the "Product of the Terran Empire" mark which went on goods imported to fully developed planets and prohibited on Class B undeveloped ones like Darkover. She kept trying to find Jaelle in the confusing quarters, because Jaelle knew Terran writing and could read it to her. It had been done while she was asleep and somehow they had made a mistake while she slept, and tattooed Jaelle with the mark too. And she was pregnant, and she kept thinking how pleased Peter would be, but what would Jaelle think? If she could only find Peter, they could all straighten it out, but he was nowhere to be found in the miles and miles of tiled corridor, because all the Quarters had been redesigned for Darkovans living on the HQ base and he was out somewhere redesigning the Guild-house for Terrans who wanted to explore living on Darkover in native style. "But that would make it no better than a hotel," she heard someone say querulously in her mind, and then she and Jaelle were trying to hold up the roof of the Guild-house while Marisela and someone else whose face she could not see . . . was it the small-freckled Amazon who had bandaged her feet on the fire-lines? . . . could search through a long telescope for *Dom* Ann'dra Carr. Only, though she could see the ground lenses clearly, sparkling blue like Lady Rohana's matrix, the telescope was invisible and kept slipping out of their hands as if it had been greased with glycerine. Then someone was calling her, and Bethany from the Coordinator's office was saying, "Margali? Oh, I think she slept last night in Camilla's room. . . ." and she woke, to hear those very words spoken aloud, followed by a knock on the door.

"Margali? Margali? Camilla, is she there?"

Magda woke, blinking, grasping at absurd troubled remnants of the dream. Camilla, sitting up in bed, was swearing under her breath as she hunted for her stockings.

"What is it? Who wants me?"

"Mother Lauria, downstairs," said Irmelin. "There is a visitor and only you can talk to her, for some reason or other—a woman who has had some terrible skin disease and is all discolored, dark as a *cralmac*'s hide. . . ."

Cholayna, Magda thought, and jumped up, grabbing some

clothes and running to splash her face with the icy water. *What in the devil can she want here? And is Jaelle with her?*

Jaelle was not; Cholayna had come alone, and was talking amiably with Mother Lauria in the Stranger's Room. When Magda came in, Mother Lauria said, "I will leave you alone for a moment; but I hope you will both join me in my office in a little while. Margali, you have not breakfasted; shall I send for tea and rolls in my office? *Mestra*, may I offer you breakfast?"

Cholayna smiled and nodded. "I had forgotten it was a holiday here and that some of you would still be sleeping," she said, as Mother Lauria went away, "and they told me they could not find you in your room, they thought for a minute that you were sleeping out; some of the women slept out of the House on Festival Night." Abruptly and with a flash of memory Magda remembered Rafaella with her hair mussed and her tunic open, showing her breasts, going off with the Guardsman. How was she better than that? She had spent yesterday morning in Monty's arms and this morning they had had to look for her in Camilla's bed. Nonsense; she was a grown woman, it was nothing to Cholayna where she spent her night, or with whom. Magda braced herself, remembering that she had resigned last night. She said bluntly, "Why have you come here? None of it is anything to do with me any more. No, I mean it this time, Cholayna, you can't talk me out of it the way you did when you first came here. What do I owe you now?"

"Not to me," Cholayna said, "but to your sisters, and perhaps to yourself. You have a very rare opportunity, Margali." She said the name in Darkovan, and Magda was astonished. But still distrustful.

"You tell me that, Cholayna? I have heard it all before, and it has brought me nothing but grief—always between two worlds and never at home in either—" Astonished, Magda discovered that her eyes were prickling as if she were about to cry, and she stopped herself, appalled, wondering, *what on earth do I have to cry about? I'm mad, not unhappy!* And then such a surge of misery flooded up within her that she clamped her teeth over the pain, knowing that if she shed a single tear she would cry and cry until she melted like Alice into a pool of tears. She said, tightly, against it, "Everyone who has told me that has wanted to use me one way or the other. When can I be simply myself, do what is good for myself and not for a hundred other people?"

"When you are in your grave," Cholayna said gently, "No one alive lives only for herself. We are all part of one another, one way or another, and anyone who does any action which is not for the common good is little more than a murderer."

"I am not interested in your religion!" Magda almost shouted.

"That is not religion." The other woman's dark face held an eerie calm. "Philosophy perhaps. It is a simple fact; no one can do anything without either helping or harming everyone with whom she has any contact of any kind. Only an animal does not take that into account." Her face softened. "You are very dear to me, Magda. I have never had children; I decided many years ago that they were not for me since I could not rear them among my own people and I would not bring them up haphazardly, crammed into the niches and crannies of a life roving around from world to world. I hoped I had found in you something that women find in their daughters—a sense of continuity—" She stopped, and Magda, ready to throw a rude or angry voice back into the woman's face, was silenced.

She thought, *if I betray Cholayna, then I am false to the real spirit of the Amazon Oath*, and wondered what in the world had brought that into her mind.

She asked sullenly, "What do you want of me, Cholayna?"

Cholayna reached for her hand, then sighed and did not touch her. "At the moment? Only to take no irrevocable decisions. I could have killed Montray; I am not sure it would not have been a good thing if I did, but alas, the habit of non-violence is too strong—and he is not even good to eat!" The joke was not a good one, but she laughed nervously anyway.

"If you feel you must go out of our reach for a time, at least help me to settle, with Lauria, which of your sisters shall work with the Headquarters, learning our ways for the benefit of both worlds."

Part of Magda was angry at Cholayna for presuming to use the special speech of the Amazons, for speaking about her sisters and her duty to them, but there was a curious feel in the room, as if Cholayna were not speaking only in words but somehow communicating with her on a deeper level. She knew things which the older woman had not told her, would never dream of telling her, had probably never told anyone alive, things of which Cholayna was not fully aware herself, and it terrified Magda to know this much about any human being. She thought, she is wide open, without knowing clearly what she meant by the words, and so am I. She sensed the weariness in the long, lean face and body, the pain from the alien sun, the sense that it was very dark here, the longing for the brighter warmth and light of her own world; Cholayna was living in what to her was an eerie half-light. She knew that Cholayna was potentially a lover of women, as much or more than Camilla, but because of the worlds where her life had been spent, it had never surfaced into her consciousness. But this was why she had spent her life in the teaching and training of younger women, in a half-formed hope that one day some one of them would give her, she hardly knew what herself, some returned warmth which she identified with the warmth of her own sun which had been so long denied her. And she did not clearly know this herself, and yet Magda knew it, and her scalp crinkled and icy fingers of dread ran down her back one by one. She did not know what this meant and could not guess. It was like the night she had wakened in Jaelle's arms and the other woman, drawn perhaps by that flooding awareness between them, had kissed her; only this time it could not be dismissed as a random sexual impulse, it was deeper than that. A thing of the spirit? Magda was not comfortable with such ideas and she suspected that Cholayna would be appalled by them.

Yet the emotion was there and she could neither identify nor restrain it. As for rebuffing it, it would have been as unthinkable to slap Camilla when she proffered her love and devotion. Magda lowered her head so that Cholayna would not see the tears in her eyes and said ungraciously, fighting whatever it was that was making her want to cry, "Well, I will do that, of course,

I don't want to leave any loose ends. Mother Lauria is waiting for us."

In Mother Lauria's office the older woman had sent for breakfast; there was a platter of hot bread, smoking and sliced, another plate of the cold sliced Festival cake, raisins studded all through it, left over from the day before; and a huge steaming pitcher of the roasted-grain drink the Amazons drank in lieu of wine or beer. There was also a bowl of hard-boiled eggs and a dish of soft curd cheese. Impelled by a feeling she would never have considered until this morning, Magda said quickly, "You will not want to eat the eggs, Cholayna, since they once had life, but everything else you can eat freely."

"Thank you for warning me, Magda," said Cholayna imperturbably. "I do not expect the world to be arranged for my convenience; I have, perhaps, become too dependent on manmade foods. Perhaps the Alphan scruples are foolish anyway. It was a wise sage who said that it is not what goes into our mouths that defiles us, but what comes forth from them; lies and cruelty and hatred. . . ." She helped herself to the cheese, and took a piece of the cake, and Magda saw her turning it thoughtfully in her mouth.

"Have your people such a saying?" Mother Lauria asked. "Some women in this house make a point of eating only grains and fruits; yet their sage wrote that everything which shares this world with us has life, even to the rocks; and all things prey and feed upon one another and come at last to feed the lowest life of all. So that we should eat reverently of whatever comes to us, bearing in mind that some life was sacrificed that we might live and that one day we will feed life in our turn. Ah, well, another philosopher has written that the morning after Festival makes every drunkard a philosopher!"

She laughed and passed a jar of fruit conserve to Magda, who spread some on her bread, wishing she could explain her feelings in terms of a simple hangover!

"Well, we must decide," said Lauria briskly, finishing the tea in her mug. "I feel that Marisela should be the first."

"I agree, and I doubt not she will teach the Terrans as much as she learns from them," said Cholayna, "but can she be spared here?"

"Probably not, but she must have this chance all the same," said Mother Lauria. "Keitha can do her work, and later have her turn. I would like to send Janetta—Margali, are you as sleepy as that? Should I send you back to bed?"

"Oh, no," Magda said quickly. It had seemed to her for a moment that Marisela was standing in a corner of the office listening to their deliberations and at the same time she knew Marisela was upstairs in her bed, still half asleep, wondering how long she could enjoy this delicious sleep before someone came in search of a midwife and roused her. She was not alone in bed, and Magda recoiled, not wanting to know this about Marisela either. She said hastily, "Janetta is too rigid, she could not, I think, accept Terran ways."

"She is more intelligent than you think her," Mother Lauria said. "There is little here to challenge her mind; I had hoped to send her to Arilinn, but she would never make a midwife, she's not sympathetic enough to women. She herself has decided she wishes for no children, having a certain distaste for the preliminaries. Yet there is no other training available to her; Nevarsin will not train female healer-priests. She is extremely clever, too clever for most of the things ordinary women, even Amazons, are able to do. She has no interest in soldiering, nor has she the physical strength for it. I think she would be very valuable to you; and what she learns would be priceless to us as well."

Magda still felt skeptical, and Mother Lauria continued "You do not know Janni's story. She came from a village where her mother was left widowed with seven children, and had no other skills to keep them, so she became a harlot. She tried to train Janetta to her trade before the girl was twelve. For a year or two Janni was too young and timid to resist; then she ran away to us."

Camilla had said it once; every Renunciate has her own story and every story is a tragedy. *How have I earned my place among them?*

"There is a young woman called Gwennis," Mother Lauria

said. "She is at Nevarsin now, working with some scrolls in the keeping of the brothers—you do not know her, Margali—"

"I do not know her well enough to recommend her for this," Magda said, "but she is my oath-sister, after all—she was in the band led by Jaelle."

"I think she would be a good choice," Mother Lauria said. "The very fact that she volunteered for that work would perhaps make her good at this. And perhaps Byrna; she has an inquiring mind—not to mention that she is still pining for her child and this would be a blessing, give her something new to think about. Cholayna—" she used the Terran woman's name hesitantly, "have you any particular ideas about what age these women should be?"

"I do not think it matters," Cholayna said. "They should, perhaps, not be too young. Your people, I have heard, are trusted with responsibility at an earlier age than ours; but if the Empire people thought them mere children, they might not take them seriously enough, as independent adults. Not younger than twenty, I should think."

"So old?" Mother Lauria asked. Magda was remembering that Irmelin was one of the most bookish women in the House, spending most of her leisure hours in reading or sometimes in writing for Mother Lauria in her office, and suggested her name.

"I think she is too lazy, perhaps, too content with things as they are," Mother Lauria said. "Three years ago, perhaps, but not now. Though if she wishes it, once it is made clear to her how much work it is, she might be given a chance. Certainly she is intelligent enough, and does not shrink from hard work."

"What I would like," Cholayna said, "would be a chance to administer one of the specific intelligence tests to all of your women . . . we have some very good ones which are not culturally biased, measuring only the ability to think abstractly and to learn."

"That might be valuable to us as well," said Mother Lauria. Certainly there are stupid women, just as there stupid men, but the most intelligent of women can be taught as a girl that seeming stupid is her most useful skill when she is among men, and most of them are clever enough to learn to do *that!* The ones who cannot learn that, or will not learn it, are often the ones who come to us. But sometimes we have women who are even afraid to try to learn to read, because they have been taught so well that it is beyond their skills! How, in Evanda's name, anyone can think that a woman who spins and weaves and grows food in her own greenhouse and supervises her servants, teaches her children, and manages all of a family's resources, can be called stupid, I will never know! It is as if we should call a farmer, who can manage crops and animals at all seasons of the year, stupid because he knows nothing of the philosophy of the ancient sages! Women come here thinking themselves stupid, and I do not know how to convince them otherwise. But perhaps, if your tests were presented as games, and I could convince them that there are different kinds of learning . . ."

"Well, certainly we have enough tests, and people to administer them," said Cholayna. "I am thinking of one of the technicians in the Psych department. She might be a good one to send here, not only for your sake but for her own—I think she could learn much from you. She is—" Cholayna hesitated; "I am not sure of your word—Magda, help me? One who has no sexual interest in men—"

"*Menhiédris,*" said Magda, using the politest of many words; ruder ones were used every day in the Guild-house but she was feeling sensitive on that subject just now.

"She would welcome knowing that there was a place in this culture which would not despise her," Cholayna said. "A good many of our cultures are—shall we say far from perfect? It would interest her to know how your society structures such things. She might feel at home among you, more than some others, if you think they could accept anyone from another world. As, perhaps, you have accepted Magda—Margali?"

Mother Lauria said rather stiffly, "I am glad you think there is something where we can teach as well as learn from you," and Cholayna smiled at her with disarming friendliness.

"Oh, you must not judge us by our worst and narrowest, Lauria. It is unfortunate that our Coordinator is a narrow-minded man, the worst rather than the best, a political appointee who has never wished to be here at all. But we have those among us who truly love the worlds where we are assigned, and wish to share them. Magda, for instance—"

Mother Laura's face softened.

"Margali has been truly one of us," she said, "and if there are others of your people who are like her—or like yourself, Cholayna—we would welcome them as friends. And to be just, there are enough of our people who are narrow-minded, who judge your people by the men in the spaceport bars, not your scientists and your wiser men. There are even some who still think your people sky-devils . . . For their sake, I think, Margali, it is time to reveal the truth; who you are and where you came from, so that when they speak disparagingly of Terrans, those who know better may say to them, 'but look, Margali is one of them, and she has lived as a sister to us in this house for a half year,' and show them that their prejudices are foolish . . . what do you say to that, Margali?"

Magda felt dismayed; surely not yet, surely she could not yet face the sudden shock and hostility with which at least a few would greet her . . . and even as the thought crossed her mind it seemed she could almost see the hostile faces, the rejection where there had been friendship, the awkwardness when they knew she had won friendship under false pretenses. . . .

Again Cholayna was taking it for granted that she would again agree to put herself on the line between the two cultures, that again she would choose to be in the vulnerable spot of liaison of her two worlds. How they would despise her when they knew! And Camilla, Camilla would surely hate her. . . .

I never allowed myself to be vulnerable to any man as I have been to Camilla; always before I have been guarded, trying always to be strong and in perfect possession of myself. With Camilla it is different, and I cannot bear that she should judge me harshly, it would be worse than when I lost Peter. One of the reasons he left me, she thought, *was because I was too independent and could not surrender myself and my judgment, and now. . . .*

"Margali?" And suddenly Magda knew that she had lost track of the conversation, that both Mother Lauria and Cholayna were looking at her. She said at random, "What was that you said about Camilla? I am sorry, my mind was wandering," and then she was frightened. How had she known they were speaking about Camilla?

"Are you ill, Margali? You are as white as a shroud," Mother Lauria said, and Cholayna asked, smiling, if she had danced too late last night.

"No one is good for anything on the day after Festival," Lauria said. "This was the wrong time for this visit, perhaps, but you could not know that. All we said, Margali, was that Camilla is in the house and she probably knows the women better than I; when you have trained a girl in swordplay and self-defense, you know all her weaknesses. The same is true of Rafaella, but she slept out last night, Camilla said. Would you run upstairs and ask her to come down to us? Your legs are younger than mine."

Magda was glad to get out of the room, and on the stairs she stopped, gasping, holding herself together by sheer force of will. It was happening again, once again it seemed as if she were like a spider at the center of the web, twitching everywhere and feeling the threads move, upstairs to where Marisela was awake and singing as she splashed her face with the icy water . . . someone is on the steps seeking a midwife, but how had Marisela known that? The same way that I know it? Lady Rohana called it *laran* . . . but she also said I had learned to barrier it, what has happened to my control? She could feel Irmelin downstairs in the kitchen, she could hear Rezi and two other women cursing as they struggled with barn-shovels; the very dairy-animals sensed the disturbances of Midsummer, or was it only that after dancing till very late the inflexible routine of caring for the animals did not fit well with a hangover? *Keitha . . . Keitha is more prejudiced even than I about lovers of women, I was not the only woman to succumb to someone I loved at Midsummer. . . .*

"In Evanda's name, why are you blocking the staircase?" demanded a cross voice behind her, and Magda, shaking, drew herself upright to face Rafaella. She was still wearing her holiday gown, which looked strange in the morning glare, and her hair was mussed, her eyes reddened. It was obvious even to Magda how she had spent the night . . . *or am I reading minds again?*

She moved to one side, with a murmur of apology, but Rafaella stopped and looked at her, taking her brusquely by the arm.

"What in hell ails you? You look as if you were going into labor or something like that!"

"No, no, I'm quite well—Mother Lauria sent me on an errand—"

"Then go and do it," Rafaella said, not unkindly, "but you look as if you, not I, were the one who had spent a sleepless night and drunk too much. Well, I don't suppose we are the only ones; when you have done your errand, you had better spend the rest of the day in bed—preferably alone!" She laughed and went on up the stairs, and Magda, feeling her face flush with heat, managed to recover herself and go on up to Camilla's room. The older woman was awake and half dressed; she heard Rafaella on the stairs and put her head out into the hall.

"So you woke the dawn-birds, Rafi love—was it worth it?"

Rafaella rolled her eyes expressively, then chuckled. "How would you know if I told you? But oh, yes—for once in the year! Now I shall go and sleep!" She disappeared into her room, and Camilla chuckled softly as she turned to Magda.

"Did you come to find me? I supposed that Mother Lauria and the Terran woman would send for me sooner or later. . . ."

Is she doing it too? Magda felt brittle, raw-edged as if she would fly into pieces; one part of her was seized by Rafaella's much too clear surface memories of the night just past, he must have been quite a man, a memory of excitement, pleasant athletic competence, and she was furious with herself because the shared memory sent a flood of sexual heat through her own body, and now Camilla was reading her message before she delivered it. Did they all do it? It had never happened before, Camilla was red-haired, it was not impossible she had some *Comyn* blood; faded now, gingery sand-colored, but when she was a young girl she must have been bright redhead, *Tallo*, they said here, like Jaelle, but as she looked at Camilla it seemed that the gaunt scarred face slid off and what she saw was a lovely child, fourteen or fifteen, shining dark-red curls, a delicate arrogance, a sheltered child treated like a princess . . .

. . . *a lovely child, yes, small good it did me,* then a flood of confused memories tumbling one over the other, *a delicate child suddenly torn away from home into the hands of bandits, the roughest of men, repeated brutal violation, a plaything for the cruellest of them, from hand to hand like a whore, no, worse than a whore, not even a human being, beaten like an animal when I tried to escape . . . lashes ripping flesh from the bones. . . .* Magda had seen the scars on face and body. . . . *I cannot be reading all this,* but her own body was racked with the same, horror, pain . . . and then a flood of denial, dread.. . . .

"No," she managed to gasp, "Camilla, don't—" and again shame washed over her, how could she refuse even to remember when her friend had had to endure all this, when the memory alone was enough to make Magda retch. . . .

"Margali! *Bredhiya* . . ." Camilla caught her as she swayed, and the touch brought another flood of the unendurable, intolerable memories. . . .

Then, abruptly like a slamming door, they were cut off, and it was only the familiar Camilla again, saying gently, "I am sorry, I did not know you were—vulnerable to that."

"I think—I am going mad—" Magda choked. "I am—I keep reading people's minds—"

Camilla sighed. "I suppose—Jaelle has the Ardais Gift, a little; she is a catalyst telepath, and you are so close, she has perhaps awakened your own *laran*. And of course she does not know how strong it is; she has managed to barricade herself so well, she hardly knows she has *laran* at all. And of course I learned long ago to remain barriered, for months at a time I never even think of it; living among the head-blind, one does learn to keep barriers up. I promise you, my dear, I have never tried to read you, never—violated your privacy. A long time ago I made the decision to set all that aside. I have never turned back. This does not happen twice in five years. Forgive me, sister."

"I think—perhaps you should forgive me," Magda managed to murmur. The world was slowly coming back into normal focus, but it seemed that only the thinnest of veils guarded her from that unendurable wide-openness to everybody and everything.

"You have had no training," the older woman said, "and I when I was a girl—after—" she moved her hand, unwilling to speak, and Magda knew what she meant, after the ordeal of which Camilla had spoken only once, after what she had read. . . . *how can she live with such memories?*

"My family could never manage to forget," Camilla said quietly. "I had to learn, or die. But enough of that, love—now we must go down to Mother Lauria. Margali, are you all right?"

Magda managed to nod. Once again she felt a desperate wish to lean on the strength of the older woman. She could not endure what was happening to her, and despite Camilla's words she was not ready to admit that it was, in fact, happening.

She could hear excited voices at the door as she came downstairs, and Marisela's gentle voice soothing the tumult.

"Yes, yes, I understand, my little ones—no, truly, your Mammy isn't going to die, she is going to birth your little brother or sister, that is all. Yes, yes, I will hurry. Irmelin, take our little friends here into the kitchen and give them some bread and honey—things were too confused at home for breakfast this morning, were they not, girls? And you can look into the Guild-house kitchen and see what it is like, you would like to have a look, wouldn't you?" She made a laughing gesture at the women on the staircase, then her eyes met Magda's and her face changed as abruptly as if she had been slapped.

"Ah, Goddess, I did not know—Margali, I know I must speak with you, and yet—" she pressed her hands, distracted, to her head. "I must hurry; in spite of what I said to the little girls, this is the woman's fifth child and there is not much time to spend." She came quickly to Magda and put her hands on her shoulders, looking into her eyes. Magda thought, *she knows what is happening to me. But that is not possible.*

"Promise me, little sister, that you will not do anything rash before you and I can sit down together like sisters and have a good talk, such as we have never had—I am at fault, I should have known better, but promise me, Margali—now I must go and get my bag. But wait, do you really need me as much as that? My duty to a sister comes first; shall I send Keitha to take care of this confinement and stay with you, *breda?*"

But already the overload of sensation and confusion was fading. *I am imagining things,* Magda thought, overtired, *I drank too much last night, and you can believe anything when you have a hangover.* "Of course not, Marisela, go along; look, the children are waiting for you." The little girls had appeared at the door to the kitchen, their faces and pinafores smeared with honey. Marisela still looked uncertain.

"Look after her, Camilla, just while I go up and arouse Keitha—"

"Pah!" Camilla wrinkled her nose with contempt. "You *leroni*, you think you have the answers to everything, don't you? I'll look after her. You attend to birthing babies, which is what you do best!" She laid an arm around Magda's shoulders, and Marisela sighed and turned to the little girls, grabbing up the black canvas sack in which she kept the tools of the midwife's trade.

"Come along, let us get back to your Mammy, my dears."

"Come along, love," Camilla said. "Mother Lauria is waiting," and Magda, pulling herself together, followed her into the office; but it seemed still that she could see the troubled blue eyes of the midwife resting on her back.

Yet inside the office it was as if a button had been pushed and her mind clicked over into another gear, all the way back to normal. Camilla was perfectly barriered . . . *she will not do that incredible thing to me, not as Marisela has done, she is so tightly barriered from years of habit, I do not think Camilla has even read me enough to know I am Terran. But perhaps I should have asked Marisela to stay, perhaps she can help me learn to shut all this out. . . .*

But no. It had never happened, Magda decided, looking from Cholayna's wise brown eyes to Camilla's level gray ones. She was simply imagining things. Camilla was listening to Cholayna's description of what they wanted, giving serious attention to it.

"Gwennis," Camilla said, "Margali, she was among your oath-sisters that night we witnessed your Oath, but perhaps you would not remember her—it is a crime not to know your own oath-sisters. She would be good for this, the very fact that she was willing to go and learn at Nevarsin—"

"If she is Margali's oath-sister," Mother Lauria said, "I would not like to separate them again as soon as Gwennis has come back, by sending Gwennis to the Terran Zone, unless Margali is to go too," and Magda realized, and again it struck her with the difference, Mother Lauria really meant it just like that; her priorities were so different it was still impossible, even after half a year in the House, for Magda really to understand how her mind worked. She really thought it was more important that Magda and Gwennis should remain together, just because of the accident that they had both happened to run into one another that night in the travel-shelter where Magda had taken the Oath, than that Gwennis should have an opportunity to study under the Terrans! Suddenly Magda felt alienation again, *I am so different, here among these strangers,* and fought furiously to shut it out again. It was just a matter of making up her mind not to surrender to it. Camilla was looking at her expectantly, and she said, pulling herself together, "But I really know nothing about Gwennis; I met her only that one night." She knew Camilla, and Mother Lauria too, would be shocked if she confessed that of the women who had been there when she took her Oath, she could remember only Jaelle and Camilla, and she could not even remember which had been Gwennis, and which the other women— Sherna, was it? Roryna? She was not even sure of their names. Yet she was sworn to them.

They spent hours working in Mother's Lauria's little office, but the afternoon sun had begun to grow dim in the room when Mother Lauria stretched and yawned.

"Well, I think we have the proper group—if only the women we have chosen are pleased; if they all refuse then we will have to start again—"

"But they will not all refuse, certainly," said Camilla. "One or two of them might, which is why we have chosen ten instead of five or six. And you, of course, will want to talk to them—. Cholayna," she added, rather shyly. Magda was pleased to see that they liked one another. *But still Cholayna has not mentioned that I am Terran. How will Camilla feel when she knows that? Will she hate me? I love her, I do not want to leave her,* and then Magda realized she must be tireder than she thought; she was seeing pictures again, herself riding away from Camilla, the older woman's sad face . . . when would they meet again, if ever? This was nonsense; she would not leave Camilla, not now. Not for a long time, she hoped, though she was still not sure there would be any kind of permanent commitment.

At one moment, during the long love-play before they slept this morning, Camilla had stopped for a moment, looked at her with heartbreaking intensity. "Margali, I would swear an oath with you; you know that?" and Magda had laughed and kissed her, but inside she thought; *No. I am not yet ready for this. Not yet, if ever.* Something inside had warned her not to say anything rash.

Just like a Terran. Keep control all the time, never just let anything happen . . .

"I think we are all too tired to go on much longer," Mother Lauria said, "and we have done as much as we can before we bring it up in House Meeting, which will be in four days. You can come then and talk to us, Cholayna, and meet these women face to face, and ask them for their own opinions. So—" she rose, briskly, though Magda could see the lines of weariness in the old woman's face. "Cholayna, will you stay and eat dinner in the House? Our women may as well begin to get used to you as our friend."

"It would please me," Cholayna temporized, "but perhaps we

should go a bit more slowly, until they know who I am and why I am here. Once I have been introduced in your House Meeting, and they have a chance to decide for themselves whether they wish to make friends—"

"You are right," Mother Lauria said, "then I shall expect you on the evening of that night; you will dine in the House with us before the meeting?"

"I should be honored," she said. It seemed to Magda that she was a little fearful.

"Remember, Mother Lauria, that Cholayna does not eat meat, or any food which has once had life."

"That can be arranged, easily enough," Mother Lauria said, and Cholayna smiled with relief as she went into the hallway to find her outer coat, a thick fur thing covering her uniform, which was more adapted to the heated corridors of the Headquarters.

Janetta was on hall duty; Mother Lauria introduced her to the Terran woman. Janetta's face lighted—she had been suggested, Magda remembered, for this kind of learning, and evidently Mother Lauria had mentioned it to her.

"Janetta will escort you back through the City," Mother Lauria said. "No, really, Cholayna, it is growing late, and if you lost yourself—there are some quarters where a Terran would not be safe, and some where a woman would have trouble, and you are both. I am sure that you, like Margali, can protect yourself perfectly well, but it would be easier if you had no need to do so; I am sure she has told you that one of the first laws of a Renunciate is that it is better to avoid a situation causing trouble than to get out of it once it has happened."

"I should be honored," said Janetta with quiet formality. She laid a hand for a moment on her knife. "Nothing will happen while she is in my care, Mother."

"But this is ridiculous," Cholayna said, laughing, "Do you really think I need an armed escort?" No, Magda realized, she had not said it, once again she had heard Cholayna thinking those words, then realizing that they would have been offensive, a rebuff of something that was very serious to Janetta; aloud Cholayna said only, "Thank you, Janetta; it is very kind of you, and kind of you, Lauria, to arrange it." The two women stood looking at one another for a moment, then Lauria suddenly laughed and hugged her.

"All Amazons are sisters, and the Goddess grant, one day I may truly welcome you as one of us; till then, you are welcome among us as a kinswoman, Cholayna," she said, and Cholayna, hugging her in return, said seriously, "May it be so, indeed."

Magda, watching, knew she had witnessed something very important, more important than anything Montray had babbled about diplomatic relationships, in its own way just as important as that invitation from *Comyn* Castle to bring a Terran delegation to Festival Ball. *Now indeed I have done the work which I came here to do,* she caught herself thinking, but she shook Cholayna's hand and heard the woman saying that she would see her in a few days from now.

"I like her," Camilla said, as they stood in the hallway watching Janetta escort her down the walk, "as I never thought I would like any woman from another world. Kindra—who was my oath-mother as well as Jaelle's—used to say that a day would come when we would find we had much to learn from the Terrans, and every year I grow more convinced of how wise she was. You knew the Terrans when you were in Caer Donn as a child, did you not, Margali? I could see that you knew one another well." She yawned. "Well, we have spent the whole day at this, but I do not think it was wasted. I had meant to go out for a ride today, I am weary of being housebound, and I thought I might get leave to take you out with me. But it is too late now to ride, I think—look, the night's rain is beginning; Janni will be soaked before she returns!"

"Oh, she won't melt," Mother Lauria laughed. "She is used to being out in all weathers. . . . Margali, how tired you look, my dear! Take her upstairs and put her back to bed, Camilla, and we will send you both up some supper. You won't mind that, will you, my girls?" She winked at them kindly, and Magda thought, abashed, *She knows we are lovers; well, of course, she probably takes it for granted that any woman coming to the house will experiment before the housebound time is past. Even Keitha, who was so scornful* . . . and she remembered how she had sensed, this morning, that Marisela was not alone . . . well, their work had thrown them together, as with Magda and Camilla, only perhaps she was more open to it than the *cristoforo* Keitha—

"And where is Marisela?" Mother Lauria asked, so appropriately that for a moment Magda wondered if the Guild-mother, too, was reading her mind. "I knew she went out on a case this morning; it must have been unusually difficult, poor girl, she will be half dead when she comes home; I think I will make her go up and have supper in bed too! These things always happen, for some reason, the day after Festival—is Keitha still here to look after her when she comes in?"

"No indeed," said Irmelin, who was on hall duty. "I saw her go out with her midwife's bag; a man came for her, and since Marisela was not yet back, she went out with him—"

"She should not go about the city alone," said Mother Lauria, troubled, "Legally she is housebound still; but worse than that, her husband might still try to revenge himself on her, or to catch her outside alone, so that he could get her home and imprison her . . ."

"She knew that," said Irmelin, "but I think this man had spoken in her presence to Marisela; Keitha knew him and said she could not let a woman suffer when there was need of her skill. I think she believes her work as midwife may even be more important than her Renunciate's Oath—"

"There is nothing in either to negate the other," said Camilla, "yet I am her oath-mother and I worry about her; I should go to the man's house and make certain she is all right, perhaps escort her home to be sure she is safe. Marisela would never forgive me if I let anything happen to her. . . ."

"That would be a good idea," said Mother Lauria, relieved, "Irmelin, did she leave word where sho was going?"

"To the Street of the Nine Horseshoes," said Irmelin, and Camilla pulled down a cloak from the ones hanging in the hallway.

"Shall I take Margali with me, Mother?"

"Indeed not," said Mother Lauria severely. "It is bad enough for one novice to go out into the streets on the night after Festival, which Keitha should not have done without asking leave; though I can see how it would seem natural to her to rush off to deliver a child. But not both of them. If you don't wish to go alone, take Rafaella or someone, but not Margali."

Camilla bowed somewhat ironically to the Guild-mother and went out, saying, "I will be back as soon as I know she is safe—"

"No, no, wait and escort her home," said Mother Lauria, "though I am sorry to send you out when you are so tired. But Margali is a big girl and can put herself to bed for once!"

She chuckled, and Magda felt herself blushing. She said, "Don't be silly, I am not as tired as all that; I will go and see if they can use any help in the dining room putting supper on the table, since Keitha is not here."

"You mustn't mind," said Irmelin while they were putting on their aprons and taking down crockery bowls. "It is always so, they like to tease the women who have become lovers—after a few days they will take you for granted, as they do Cloris and Janetta, but if you and Camilla quarrel and stop sharing a bed they will tease you again for a few days, that is all; you heard how they teased Rafi when she went home for the night with a man—and speaking of Rafaella, did I not hear her on the stairs just now?"

"No, she went out hours ago, when you were all in Mother's office," said Rezi, "She said she had a caravan to take out, Shaya had sent for her from the Terran Zone. I had all kinds of questions to ask her, but she had no time for any of them, and Margali—"

"Never mind," said Mother Lauria hastily. "Go after Camilla; take your knife and go swiftly. If it is truly a trap that Keitha has walked into—"

Rezi's face changed. She said, "By the Goddess, I never thought of that! And Keitha is out alone—the Street of the Nine Horseshoes, you said?" She was drawing on her cloak as she spoke. "I'll catch up to Camilla before the end of the street."

The door banged behind her, and Mother Lauria said, "We

need not wait dinner. I am sure there is nothing worth waiting for anyhow; the night after Festival there will be nothing on the table but leftovers."

"Well, there is half a roast rabbithorn," Irmelin said, "and plenty of the gravy and stuffing. And if anyone does not want leftovers there is plenty of good bread and cheese, and after Festival it would do anyone good to fast for a day or two anyhow." The women moved around, finding seats.

Magda was glad Camilla had not gone alone; the woman was not young and they had had a couple of sleepless nights. Yet she wished she could be the one to fight at Camilla's back, if fighting was needed; she envied Rezi, who was sent matter-of-factly to defend her sister. She took up a piece of cheese and nibbled it absentmindedly.

She should have gone with Camilla. Mother Lauria was wrong. Camilla was her oath-sister and her lover; it was her personal responsibility to fight beside her; and Keitha was her oath-sister as well, so that it was her personal responsibility to protect Keitha too. She should have argued Mother Lauria into realizing that it was an obligation of honor.

I have been Terran all this day and now I am thinking like a Darkovan again. . . .

There was a stir in the hallway and loud shouts, and three women came into the dining hall, their outdoor cloaks soaked.

"Ah, how it rains! As if it were trying to make up for good weather on Festival Night, like always," they cried. "Well, we are back, everybody—"

"Sherna! Gwennis! Rayna!" exclaimed Mother Lauria, coming forward to embrace them, and then everyone was up from the table to hug the newcomers, to help them off with their coats, to ask a thousand questions. It was the tall quiet one, Rayna, who recognized Magda first and hugged her.

"Margali! I had heard you were going to Neskaya, but of course Jaelle would have wished to bring you to her own House—where is Jaelle n'ha Melora?"

"Oh, she has taken a freemate, and is living in the Terran Zone—"

"Jaelle? A freemate? Now will I truly believe that Durraman's donkey can fly," said Gwennis, laughing boisterously. "She would be the last woman in the world, I had thought, ever, to give herself over to a man—she has been with Rafaella too much, that is all, Rafi has corrupted her—"

They all crowded to the table, teasing and joking. Sherna demanded, "Where is Camilla?"

"She and Rezi went off—there was some worry about one of our novices," Mother Lauria said, "A fear her husband might try to find her again outside the house; so they went to escort her home." And then the three of them had to be told all about the fight with Keitha's husband and his hired mercenaries, about how Keitha had apprenticed to Marisela and later become her lover, rapid-fire gossip and shared memories and allusions which Magda could hardly follow. They told, too, how Magda had fought for the House and been wounded—by now, Magda realized in surprise, they were not angry with her over the indemnity, but proud of her for defending them so well.

"Cloris, fetch a couple of bottles of the good wine from the cellar," Mother Lauria said. "We will drink to the return of our sisters."

"We have more to drink to than that," said Rezi, coming in, with Keitha and Camilla, all very pale. "As you thought, Mother, it was a trap. Oh, yes, there was a woman in childbirth, but while Keitha was there in the house someone had sent word to Shann MacShann. We found him in the street outside, ready to waylay Keitha when the child was born and she was done with her work."

Keitha looked pale but peaceful, though Magda could see that she had been crying. "I should have been terrified, if my sisters had not been there. As it was, I told him that I should die before I ever came back to him, and laid my hand on my knife, saying that I would turn it either on myself or him, as he chose. So he took himself off, swearing and cursing me and vowing I should wait forever for the return of my dowry; and I told him to keep it for the boys when they were grown. I do not think he will trouble me again. He said at the last, as if it would make me wish to come back, that now he had found a decent woman who would not run away, so if I ever changed my mind—" she smiled faintly, "it was too late. I think he was shocked when I wished him happiness with her. I did not tell him how sorry I was for her, whoever she is."

Camilla hugged Keitha and said "We are all proud of you, *breda*. So now we can drink to his downfall as well. And you will really have something to tell Marisela when she comes back," she added with a sly grin, and Keitha blushed crimson.

The wine was brought and poured, and they all drank, laughing and toasting each other.

"So now we are all here from that night in the travel-shelter except Jaelle," said Sherna, coming over and hugging Camilla and Magda together, "Where is Shaya? Is she out with Rafaella on her travel-business? Did not one of you say she had taken a freemate, of all things?"

"Ah, Goddess! How stupid I am," exclaimed Rezi. "Jaelle was here, and asking for you, Margali—it was hours ago! But you were closeted with Mother in her office and I could not interrupt, and then there was all the hullabaloo about Keitha, and it went right out of my head!"

Magda swung toward her, and suddenly the awareness she had been keeping at bay, all this long day, crashed over her again.

Something is very wrong. Something terrible has happened to Jaelle. . . . there was nothing specific about it, she simply knew, with a knowledge that went deeper than words, that Jaelle needed her, that Jaelle was in deep trouble; and yet when she should have kept herself open to Jaelle, she had barricaded herself and refused to accept the knowledge because she was afraid of it. She looked at Camilla in dismay, knowing that the older woman's superb barriers had kept her locked tight against Jaelle's need.

Danger. Danger, closing in on Jaelle from every direction. Red blood spilled on the sand. The dream and the bond they had shared. She had wakened in Jaelle's arms, her friend needed her,

*but she had fled from it, and now Jaelle was gone, running
away . . . Peter was dead, and now Jaelle was gone . . .*

She could hardly hear her own voice.

"Quick, Rezi! Tell me what happened!"

"Shaya—she came for her horse, and for travel-food, and her
boots—I loaned her my own riding boots; I do not know what
had happened to her own. She had been crying, but she would
not tell me what was wrong, and then she rode away. It was before the rain started."

Magda's throat felt tight. It was not Rezi's fault. She should
have known that Jaelle needed her, and she was shut up in
Mother Lauria's office discussing things that could have been
settled in a moment, playing diplomacy games! But that was not
fair either. Cholayna could not possibly have known. She looked
at the women, still laughing and joking and drinking wine with
the three who had returned from Nevarsin. They were Jaelle's
friends, too. Camilla was her oath-sister. . . .

*Outsiders. They were outsiders. None of them understood.
Jaelle had crossed over some invisible line and she was an outsider just as Magda had always been an outsider here. Even
Camilla had been able to shut it out, cut away Jaelle's trouble
lest it remind her of her own.* Quietly, knowing that no one
would pay the slightest attention, she slipped out of the dining
hall, hurried up the stairs. Before Jaelle was too far out of the
city, she could find her. Quickly she rolled warm stockings,
extra warm underwear, her warmest trousers and tunic, into a
bundle, changed her shoes for her riding boots. She ran down
the back stairs, into the kitchen and made up a package of hard
journey-bread from the barrel, some cheese and cold meat and a
scoop of dried fruit from the bin. She hurried to the stable,
quickly saddled her horse. It was the one she had ridden into the
mountains when she went to rescue Peter Haldane; the one she
had ridden to the fire-lines. She was breaking her housebound
Oath but she hardly thought of that.

She was about to swing into the saddle when she saw that
Camilla was standing at the stable door, watching her.

"You cannot go, Margali," said Camilla in an undertone. "Love, you must not. This is oath-breaking."

Magda let her foot slip from the stirrup. She came to Camilla and laid her hands on the woman's shoulders.

"Camilla, it is a matter of honor," she pleaded, and then, swallowing hard, used the weapon she had told herself she would not use.

"We swore an oath in the mountains, before ever I came here to Thendara House," she said, her voice trembling. They had not, not in words; but she knew now that in the truest sense they had sworn their very lives to one another, when Jaelle lay dying with a bandit's blow, and Magda had chosen to abandon her mission that Jaelle might live. Peter Haldane had never mattered to either of them, against that bond, only Magda had not known it till then.

If I had known, if I had known what Jaelle truly meant to me, she would never have married Peter; only I did not know. It was Camilla who taught me what Jaelle truly meant to me, that the love of sisters means more than any man living in this world. . . .

"We are *bredhyini*, Camilla," she said. "I beg you—if you love me, Camilla—let me go after her."

Camilla's face was white. "I should have known," she said, "and this was why you would not swear to me. I—" she drew a long breath. "It does not matter that we have been lovers," she said after a moment. "What is important is that we shall always be friends and sisters. If it is a matter of honor to you—" she hesitated a moment and said at last, "You are oath-bound not to leave the House save at the command of one of the Guild-mothers. I am an Elder here, Margali. I may command you lawfully to go." She drew Magda to her and kissed her fiercely. "Jaelle is my oath-sister too," she said, "and has been like a daughter to me. Go, Margali n'ha Ysabet, without oath-breaking. I will make it all right with Mother Lauria."

"Oh, Camilla—Camilla, I do love you—"

Camilla kissed her again. "I love you too," she said gently, "in more ways than you know. Go now. Give my love to Jaelle, and the Goddess grant you come through this safely. I do not know when we will meet again, my darling; be it as the Goddess wills, and may She ride with you."

Then Magda was in her saddle, her face blindly streaming tears as she rode past Camilla, and into the cobbled street. She did not know where she was going. Only that she was going after Jaelle, and that they had been moving inevitably toward this very moment, since that night in the travel-shelter in the Hellers.

I have not broken my Oath, Camilla has set me free. Yet she knew that she would have broken her Oath without question and without compunction, as if the Oath were a pair of old shoes that had grown too small and she had burst out of them.

Camilla does not know it, but I am no longer bound by the Guild, even as I am no longer simply a Terran. I have outgrown all these things. I do not know what I am now. Perhaps, when I find Jaelle, when I overtake her where she has gone, she will show me.

She was a Terran. She was a Renunciate. She was Darkovan. She had become a lover of women. She was a *leronis*, for surely what she had been fighting away all this day was *laran*. And now she must use it to follow where Jaelle had gone. But she was no longer simply any one of these things. All her life she had believed she must choose between being Terran and Darkovan, Magda or Margali, Intelligence Agent or Renunciate, lover of men or lover of women, head-blind or *leronis*, and now she knew that she could never describe herself as either one thing or the other, she knew that she was all of these things and that the sum of them all was more than any or all of them.

I do not know who or what I am. I only know that I do what I must, no more and no less.

She rode through the gates of the City, without looking back.

Chapter 4

Jaelle did not even remember, as she went down the long corridor that led from Married Personnel Quarters, why she had such a shuddering disgust for drunkenness; she only knew that at this moment, Peter was loathsome to her. Well, she need not return, except once and briefly. Once their marriage had been formally dissolved—and she knew now that it must be dissolved, that it was as far in her past as the Great House of Jalak of Shainsa—they might let her live off base, as the Renunciate Medic Technicians were to be allowed to do. But if they insisted that she must continue to fill Magda's place—as if she could, as if one person could ever be an exact equivalent for another, they had been mad ever to suggest it—they would have to allow her quarters in Unmarried Personnel. Magda, after all, had lived there.

She passed the cafeteria level. She should eat something. The main cafeteria had food she could manage to eat, and all she could get later would be the tasteless synthetics of the small cafeteria up in Communications. She remembered Marisela telling pregnant women in the House that they must eat whether they felt like it or not . . . they were no longer the masters of their own destinies, they had chosen to carry their children and that was a year-long commitment to the welfare of the child's body even before their own.

So I have become no better than any of Jalak's concubines, just a brood mare to bear the next generation. No better than Rohana, for all my gallant talk about personal freedom.

Somewhere in the back of her mind she could hear Kindra saying that even becoming an Amazon did not exempt a woman from universal emotions, but she cut it off with vicious self-contempt. *So now I must go into that nauseating cafeteria and stuff my disgusting body with food which revolts it, just because my wretched child, Peter's child, which I did not want anyhow, is yelling at my body to feed it. . . .* Coldly she depersonalized the child into an it, a thing, not the daughter Rohana had told her she would bear. . . . *Well, let her yell. Go ahead and cry, baby, nobody's going to feed you now.* She turned decisively away from the sickening smells of the cafeteria, feeling that for a day, at least, she was back in charge of herself.

Upstairs in the Communications office—for, with maddening slowness, the Empire HQ Administration had not yet assigned the Intelligence Personnel to their new office space in Cholayna's division—Bethany looked pink and chipper.

"That's right, it's not a holiday today, is it? Yesterday was some kind of enormous Darkovan holiday, I remember," she said, "and they told me that half of Montray's staff was invited to some enormous affair across the City. Actually in *Comyn* Castle, wasn't it?" She looked impressed, and Jaelle felt like snarling at her; the *Comyn* are not superhuman, they are just ordinary mortals with too much sense of their own damned importance. But she said glumly—after all, Bethany was not responsible for her bad mood—"It's a damn shame you couldn't have gone instead of me. You're prettier than I am and you probably dance just as well, and you'd have enjoyed it. Festival is no treat for me."

Bethany chuckled.

"Peter would have had something to say about that, wouldn't he? Anyhow, I went to bed at a decent hour last night, and from the long faces I see all over the department, there are plenty of you who seem to have danced till dawn. There are a few advantages to being so low down in the scale of hierarchy that you never get invited out to a Royal Command and don't have to stay up all night! Seriously, Jaelle, you look like something the cat wouldn't bother dragging in. . . . can I get you some coffee or something?"

Jaelle thanked her and declined. She didn't know what she needed, but coffee, which was not a Terran luxury she enjoyed, was certainly not that need.

"Maybe you should have put yourself on sick report and gone up to Medic," said Bethany solicitously. "After all, strictly speaking, you worked all night and should put in for overtime." It was, Jaelle imagined, one way of looking at it—she hadn't gone to *Comyn* Castle for her own pleasure, after all. But she only shook her head—the last thing she wanted was to be lectured by Medic about her responsibility to her unborn child— and took her place at the desk which had once been Magda's and was now hers, until she could rid herself of the unwelcome responsibility, and surveyed the unfinished language tapes without enthusiasm.

I still feel as if I ought to be doing something more important than this. But I don't know what.

She worked without stopping for more than an hour until Monty stormed in, swearing.

"Where in the *hell* is Cholayna? She's not up in Intelligence and I can't find her anywhere."

"Maybe she put in for a day of sick leave," said Bethany. "Didn't she go to *Comyn* Castle last night?"

Monty grinned humorlessly. "That's right she did and so, unfortunately, did the Old Man. My father said that listening to barbarian music squawking till the wee hours of the morning wasn't *his* idea of recreation and it wasn't what *he* was being paid for, anyhow. Could you page her in Medic and see if she registered to take the day off, Beth?"

Subtly, as something Magda might have noticed, Jaelle recognized that small matter of protocol. He would not, now that he knew her importance, ask Jaelle to do routine chores like this; while Bethany, whose whole employment was to do small routine errands which higher status employees could not be troubled to do, could be interrupted at any time. She had noticed one thing among Terran woman employees; the scramble to find a position where they were more than small-errand runners for the men. They jealously fought for these marks of status. But they also accepted this as part of the conditions of their employment. Magda was proud of being out of the main centralized office she called the madhouse; it was not a point of view Jaelle shared— if she had to work in an office at all she would rather be with the other women rather than isolated in lonely splendor with the higher-status males. She was beginning to get some vague inkling of Terran social and cultural layering and it seemed foolish to her, but she was also intelligent enough to know that social structuring was seldom rational. Just last night she had had to explain simple matters of protocol and had at least inwardly jeered at the elder Montray because he could not understand why a man who had once been his employee, the man Carr, could not be casually approached without creating the equivalent of a diplomatic incident.

Bethany was using the Communication equipment which defined her job and which it seemed to be a matter of Terran etiquette to avoid using as you went up in the ranks of employment. At last she raised her head and said, "She's not in Medic, Monty, and I even got them to page her in her quarters, in case she was taking a day but was willing to be interrupted on an overtime basis. I got a message saying she'd gone into the Old Town and would be at the Guild-house of Renunciates."

Monty slammed his hand down on the desk, swearing. "Any way to reach her there?"

"I shouldn't think so," Jaelle said. *Now*, she thought with an obscure sense of having been assaulted, *I cannot even take refuge in the Guild-house. Even there I find Terrans, Magda and now Cholayna have been welcomed there.*

"I'm being sent out into the field, and I need Intelligence briefing," he explained quickly.

"Lord Aldaran, way up in the Hellers near Caer Donn—that's where the old spaceport used to be, before it was moved down here to Thendara—"

"I know where the Hellers are," Bethany said waspishly. "Magda and Haldane both grew up there, didn't they?"

"Haldane could help me with this—" Monty began.

"I wouldn't ask him," Jaelle said wryly, "He's up in our quarters, dead drunk and sleeping it off."

Monty said, after a minute, "I heard that he and the Old Man had a flaming row last night and Peter stormed into the City. So he came in drunk, huh? Lucky bastard; I wish I could!"

"What's your problem, Monty?"

"Going into the field," he said. "I told you a little about it— or was it Magda I told? I need to be sure I will not antagonize them, and—" he gave a deprecating smile, "I can't afford to impress them as effeminate. I need to know precisely how to dress and what to do—and what not to do under any circumstances. Magda made a start, but—" he shrugged.

For a moment a very clear picture of Magda and Monty in his quarters rushed over her . . . *why am I suddenly picking up all this? Why can I not push it away as I have always done before* . . . Magda, tying her Amazon knife to his waist, showing him how to move . . . she fought to barricade what she was picking up from Monty, including an overwhelmingly sexual awareness of Magda that filled her, for no reason at all, with bewildering rage. *Why should I suddenly hate Monty because he has taken Magda to bed? Magda/Margali is not my lover. . . .* Fighting to be fair through the staggering wave of resentment that made her feel physically ill, she said, "Of course I can help you, Monty. Come on up to Intelligence and tell me all about your business at Aldaran, unless it's really a secret mission."

"Not a bit of it," Monty responded. "On the contrary, when Aleki heard about it, he was all smiles; he told the Old Man he'd deal with it personally as a Senatorial Representative, and you can imagine, the Old Man would have loved that!" His voice was ironic. "For once, Darkover is predictable—or that's how he saw it. Some bigwig back in Caer Donn—I'll have to look up the details, but his name is—Aldaran of Aldaran and Sca—" his face wrinkled in a struggle. Jaelle, picked it up effortlessly from his mind. "Aldaran of Aldaran and Scathfell, the old Seventh Domain of the *Comyn*; they're not *Comyn* any more."

"At war with *Comyn*?"

"Oh, no. Too far away for wars to make any sense. But they were once the Seventh Domain, and broke away."

"Geographically I can see that makes sense," Monty said as they went into Ingelligence, looking at the map on the walls. This was something Cholayna had done, evidently. Jaelle had not seen it before. "But then, why didn't Ardais break away from the *Comyn* too? It seems, geographically speaking, that the country would be divided between the Lowland Domains—" he pointed, "the Aillards and Elhalyns in the lowlands, Ardais and Aldaran in the Hellers, and Altons, Hasturs in the Kilghard Hills, with the Ridenow 'way over here almost in the Dry Towns—"

"You ask me for the answer to a riddle that no one has ever been able to understand," said Jaelle stiffly, "yet the Aldaran are exiled from *Comyn*—perhaps for some old crime? No one truly knows; yet the Ardais have always been loyal to *Comyn*, though once, I am told, the Aldarans of Scathfell fought to make themselves Lords over Ardais too."

"I don't, of course, expect to understand a thousand years of the History of the Domains overnight," said Monty. "Anyhow, the Aldarans have put through a formal request to the Empire for technological help and assistance; Medic personnel, and—this is where I come in—helicopters and men to fly them. It seems that conventional aircraft are useless over the Hellers—as you may remember from that episode in *Comyn* Castle when we were called there to talk about the Mapping and Exploring plane that went down, they're not even really safe in the Kilghard Hills. Of course what you call hills on Darkover would be pretty formidable mountains on almost any other planet I can think of. But helicopters, and some kinds of vertical take-off-and-landing aircraft, might be usable in spite of the thermal conditions in and around the Hellers, so I am being sent to do a feasibility study. Of course I'm only in charge of protocol and liaison; Zeb Scott's going to handle the aircraft itself. And so I need a last-minute Intelligence briefing—damn Cholayna for taking this particular day off!"

"Cholayna has a right to a holiday, too," Jaelle said, so fiercely that Monty flinched.

"Yes, of course, it's damnably inconvenient for me, that's all," he said. "But perhaps you can help; find me an outfit, tell us how to arrange transport. They'll ship in the aircraft by cargo freight, of course, but we will have to have transport through the hills; foot transport. Your business, Cholayna told me once, was travel escort."

"Yes; my partner, an Amazon, and myself," Janlle said quietly. "Let me send a message to the Guild-house and my partner Rafaella can be arranging the transport." And suddenly she knew the answer to the whole complicated business. Peter could not prevent her from doing the work she had been hired to do in the Terran Zone. She would assign herself on this mission—she had enough authority for that—to guide them into the Hellers to Aldaran. And this would remove her from Peter's presence, which had been so galling to her for so long, and when she came back—which would hardly be before the autumn—she could quietly file for divorce by Terran law.

She took paper and writing stylus and quickly scribbled a note to Rafaella, to be sent to Guild-house at once. "Rafi may still be sleeping. Last night was a holiday and probably Rafaella danced in the dawn. But as soon as she wakes, this will bring her, and she will start assembling people and horses, guides and pack animals. How many men will you have for escort?"

Monty gave her the details. She picked up, dimly, that he was astonished at her efficiency; he had not seen her before this in the special sphere of her competence. They talked about days on the trail, man-days of food, the best purveyor for travel clothing, which she insisted should be of natural leathers and furs rather than the Terran synthetics, and he managed to requisition purchase orders for the supplies they would need. Men had to be chosen too for the mission; Monty had access to Personnel records and knew which of the available men came from cold, inhospitable or mountainous planets and could therefore tolerate and even enjoy an excursion into the worst terrain and worst weather on Darkover.

This work was so familiar to her that by the time she had made out the preliminary listings, and arranged for Rafaella to meet with Monty at noon, she was over the worst of her ill-humor. She checked out his clothing carefully, and even went to her own quarters for the small packets of sachet that she had rubbed into the seams of her dress last night; then, hesitating, stopped to ask herself whether the scents and herbs she had used might not be unsuitable for a man's clothing. She went and sniffed the seams of the holiday gear Peter had flung on the floor, when he came in drunk. No, these were different—or as nearly as she could make out through the overwhelming smell of whisky on them.

"Jaelle!" said Peter behind her, almost apologetic. "Love, you don't have to deal with those things; you're not my valet. Anyhow, in the shape they're in, there's nothing to do but chuck them into the disposal; they're hardly worth cleaning."

She smiled and shook her head. "I'll have them cleaned in the Old Town," she said. "They'll look all the more authentic when you go into the field again. That's why I'm here—Monty's going into the field with a consignment—aircraft for Aldaran or something like that."

"Damn! Of course, as the Old Man's son he'd be in line for any favorable assignment," Peter grumbled.

"If you think he really wants to take this away from you, you are very much mistaken," she said slowly, "though there are other assignments in the field which will bring you more prestige than this. Monty would appreciate having your help in checking out his fitness for Intelligence—Cholayna seems to be taking the day off," she added artfully, and immediately he was the Terran Peter again, eager to seize the slightest advantage.

"Right; I'll go check out his kit," he said. "He'll probably have to requisition the right kind of boots." He turned to go, saying, "Meet me for lunch, will you, Jaelle?" He came back to kiss her, and her heart almost melted then. He was so dear to her. Perhaps all they needed was time, time to adjust, to grow together. . . .

"In the main cafeteria," she specified. "I simply cannot eat the synthetics upstairs," and he nodded, gently patting her tummy.

"Junior doesn't like synthetics? All right; nothing but the best for my boy," he said.

"Peter, Rohana told me it was a daughter—"

"Don't be silly, darling. Even the Terran Medics could hardly be sure about it—you're not even two months pregnant yet. We'll wait for the scientific verification, all right? If you want to enjoy thinking about a daughter, all right, sweetheart—you've got a fifty-fifty chance of being right, after all—but I'm still betting on Peter, Junior! Anyway, I'll see you in the main cafeteria at lunchtime or a little after." He kissed her quickly again with the habitual, reflex glance at the clock, and was gone.

Jaelle smothered her anger and went down to talk with the supply people about horses for the journey. They were eager to supply trucks to carry the heavy equipment across the plains, but she pointed out that there were no suitable roads, and the days in the saddle before going up into the mountains would be valuable in acclimatizing the men to the altitudes of the Hellers. "Have you no knowledge of mountain sickness, if they are transported too swiftly to higher altitudes?"

"We can deal with mountain sickness, we have drugs for it," the Transport Officer said, but Jaelle insisted quietly, "It would be better not to let them depend on drugs, since they will be in the far country and away from your—" she groped for the word, to her surprise found it in the man's mind without trying, "your— lifeline—of medical help."

"You certainly have a point, Mrs. Haldane. I understand from Monty that you're coming into the mountains with us; you know the Hellers?"

"Lady Rohana Ardais is a kinswoman of mine and I have visited her in Ardais lands many times; also, my business partner and I have led expeditions into the Hellers before this," she said. "Rafaella knows every trail in the Hellers."

"We can certainly use someone who does."

"It will not trouble you to work with a woman?"

"Look, Mrs. Haldane," he said, so seriously that for once she did not protest the refused name, "When I have to work with somebody, I don't give a cat's whisker whether it's a man, a woman or a sentient dolphin, providing it knows its job. I've worked on enough planets not to quibble with brains, whatever body they happen to come packaged in. Haven't seen many women on this one, but I understand the Head of Intelligence here is a woman, and I heard scuttlebutt around the Division that they sent a woman here, because there was a woman in the Co-ordinator's office who had practically set up the whole Intelligence operation singlehanded by her fieldwork—you know who Magdalen Lorne was, don't you? I mean, I figured Haldane would have told you, he was married to her once. Or have I spoken out of turn?"

"No," she said. "I know Magda's work," and she wondered again if because of Peter's personal limitations she had been drawn into wronging the Terrans. They had, after all, brought Cholayna here; and had been wise enough to see that the Renunciates would be the best beginning when the people of both planets must work together.

Maybe it is not the Terran in Peter I find objectionable; maybe it is his Darkovan side which insists I must be no more than his wife and mother of his children . . . other Terran men are not like that. And if Cholayna is right I must unconsciously be a child of the Dry Towns and unconsciously wish to belong to a man, claimed as his property. . . .

The thought was so disquieting that she shoved it aside swiftly as the communication speaker interrupted them.

"For Mrs. Haldane; a personal message, a Darkovan woman at the gates." And Jaelle went to hear Rafaella's voice coming over the speaker.

"I understand I am to help you set up an expedition for these Terrans," she said, and Jaelle turned to the Transport Officer with relief.

"Come down and I will introduce you to Rafaella n'ha Doria," she said, and they went down to the Gates.

After a few minutes she could see that the Transport Officer liked Rafaella and would listen to her judgment; so she found them a map, signed Monty's Requisition order for supplies, and went to join Peter in the cafeteria.

He was gentle and solicitous as he chose foods he had seen her enjoy, but her mind was filled with knowledge of what needed to be said, and after a few bites she put down her fork and said what had been on her mind all morning.

"Peter, I'm sorry I sounded harsh the other night. But it's true and we must admit it. Our marriage was a terrible mistake. It's time to end it, dissolve it by whatever means you think suitable, and let it go."

His face crumpled.

"Oh, Jaelle, I was drunk. Can't you forgive me? There are compromises to make in every marriage—now, with a baby coming, is this any time for that kind of decision?"

"I think it is the best time for such a decision," she said, "because everything in my life will change; so this is the right time for that change too."

"And do I have nothing to say about it? It's my son too—"

"Daughter," she corrected automatically and wondered when she had begun believing it.

He fiddled nervously with his fork in a pile of some white mashed root. "Look," he said, "I admit we've both made mistakes—serious ones. But if you'll try and tell me what bothers you, I'll try and change. Jaelle, it's wrong to give up on each other now. Among other things, the kid's going to need a father. And I want my kid to have the advantages of a Terran education—"

"Surely that can be arranged without continuing to live together," she said, not looking at him. Where had it gone, all the love?

"It's a rotten thing to do," he said angrily. "I didn't think you were that kind of person. Use me to get Empire citizenship for yourself and the kid, then walk out on me—"

She started to her feet, eyes blazing, physically holding herself back from flinging her crock of soup into his face. "If you can believe that of me, then there is not even any basis for trying further—"

"Oh, God, Jaelle, I didn't mean it," he said, rising in his turn, stretching across the table to try to enfold her hands in his. She wrenched them angrily away.

"Jaelle, forgive me. Let's try again. Remember how it was at Ardais and how happy we were there?"

She did not want to remember; she felt tears raining down her face. He said, capturing her hands again and holding them to his heart, "Please, Jaelle. Darling, don't cry, don't. Not here; people will think I've been beating you—"

"If you care so much what they think—" she began, then stopped. She owed him this at least, to finish this in decent privacy. She sighed and turned to follow him out of the cafeteria. But the intercom loudspeaker device interrupted them.

"Peter Haldane, Peter Haldane. Mrs. Haldane, Mrs. Haldane. Please report to the Coordinator's office at once. Please report to the Coordinator's office immediately."

Peter swore. "I wonder what the old bastard wants now? For the love of God, Jaelle, stand by me now, don't let him get this to hold over me too!" he pleaded. She did not fully understand but picked up something from his mind, *if he thinks I can't stick out what I begin, if he knows I have nothing to tie me to Dark-over*, and sighed. She said, "I won't make any decision until we have agreed on it, if that's what you mean," and let him capture and hold her hand under his arm.

"I'll never agree to let you go," he said softly. It sounded like the old tenderness. But under the veneer of tenderness she knew that he was considering what this would do to his career and she hardened her heart again. Side by side, but inwardly as far apart as if they were on separate planets, they walked toward Coordinator Montray's office.

Outside the clear glass expanse visible from the office, she could see heavy clouds hanging high in the pass. Before night-fall the city would be shrouded with it and the passes, perhaps, uncrossable. Montray was standing there, staring out into the storm, and again like a flash Jaelle caught the picture in his mind, a brilliant sun, a world of shining water and rainbows, and the pain he never allowed to surface because it would do him no good at all, marooned on this icy dark world where.... "This doesn't look much like Midsummer to me," he said grimly, without turning round, "Tell me, Haldane, you've lived on this planet all your life, do you ever have anything remotely resembling real summer here?"

"I understand that it's much warmer in the Dry Towns and it's much warmer down on the seacoast," Peter said, "only almost no one lives there."

"I'll never understand Head Central," Montray said, and Jaelle picked up the thought, *sending me here*, and wished she could comfort him somehow, but all he said aloud was "We could have built our spaceport there and not even interfered with the natives, which would have suited *us* and suited *them* and we'd all have been happy. Only first they set us down in a place like Caer Donn, and then they move down here—Jaelle, is there any proverb on this planet which means the same as we do when we say *going from the frying pan into the fire?*"

She picked it up in his mind that Magda had been accustomed to play this game with him, and that he missed Magda though he would never let himself say it or think it. She said gently "We would say, *the game that walks of itself from the trap to the cookpot.*" For the first and last time in her life she came close to liking Russell Montray. She wondered if everyone on the face of this world, or any other, covered desperate sadness with his own defenses, harsh cruelty, nasty humor, icy stone-cold refusal to communicate—*are we all barriered from one another that way? Is there never any way to break through it? Peter and I thought we had found a way, but it was only a pretense.* She was struck with such sadness that she wanted to cry, for herself, for Peter, even for Montray, who hated the very world on which he lived and the very air he breathed, and covered it by being hateful. But she was doing it too, she only wanted to cry and here she was covering her real feelings with obedient compliance because crying simply wasn't done in offices like this one. She said, anticipating Peter by only a breath, "Surely you didn't call us down here just to talk about proverbs,

Mr. Montray, we were at lunch," and then before he could answer, before she looked into the darker part of the room, she knew why he had summoned her there, and turned around to say coldly to Rohana "Lady." She bowed.

But she felt tight all over. *She has come to ask me again what I do not want to do.*

Jaelle, no one living can do only what she wants. She could read Rohana's thoughts as if the woman had spoken. *I would have liked to spend my life in a Tower. You would have preferred to be only a Free Amazon. But do you think it is only women? Gabriel would have preferred to spend his life making songs to the lute. And you know better than I what Peter wants and cannot have, and what this man Montray would rather have. . . .*

Is this what it is like to have laran, *knowing so well what everyone else needs that you have no time for your own thoughts and wishes?* And then Jaelle slammed off the awareness, with an effort that turned her pale and cold, while Montray was blandly introducing them to Lady Rohana.

Rohana stretched out her hand and said, "But Jaelle is my kinswoman, Montray, the daughter of a cousin who was raised with me like a sister, and of course I have met her freemate many times. He was my guest last winter." She went on to make some polite question about Peter's health and his work.

"At least I don't have to be out in the storm that's coming," Peter said, looking past Montray out the window. "I don't envy Monty one single bit, starting out for Aldaran in this kind of weather."

"Storm? I don't see any damned storm," said Montray truculently. "Dark and dismal, and nothing like Midsummer, or what I'd call Midsummer on any halfway human-type world—no offense intended, Lady Rohana, but do you *really* like this kind of weather? I suppose you must—"

"Not necessarily," Rohana said, smiling. "There is an old story; at one time the Gods gave mankind control over the weather, but he foolishly asked only for sunny days, and the crops failed, because there was no rain and snow. So a merciful God took away control again. . . ."

"On most civilized planets," Montray said glumly, "we've *got* control of the weather. That story sounds damn simplistic to me. Don't you have crop freezes, and floods, and more blizzards than you really need, and wouldn't it be a blessing if you could have the kind of weather you need for optimum crops and the benefit of your people?"

Rohana shrugged. "It would be difficult to know who could be trusted to arbitrate the weather," she said, "though I am sure you heard of the work done by people from one of the Towers during the forest fire last season, in bringing rain where it was needed. And that is one of the reasons I have come to you. I am sure you already know, for Peter has told you, that you have in your employ a young woman who is potentially material for a Tower. Jaelle—"

She whirled around, feeling trapped and betrayed. She said, spitting her words out angrily, "Rohana, we had all this out before ever I came here. I have no *laran*—"

Rohana said, very quietly, "Look in my eyes and say that, Jaelle."

That is what it is; all these last days, the laran *I barricaded so well all these years, why is it suddenly coming on me now?* "It is my life, and I have renounced that. How dare you come here, Rohana, among the Terrans, and throw this at me now?"

"Because I have no choice, Jaelle. I told you why it is so necessary that you take your rightful place among the *Comyn* and among the Council—and I have come here because I do not want you to say that your husband and the Terrans who have, I believe, some kind of claim on your services, will not allow you to do your duty to your kinsfolk and to the Domains."

Jaelle? A seat in Council? and at once, she knew, Peter was thinking how he could use this to his advantage. *And not even a secret now; my wife on* Comyn *Council and it will not demand secret Intelligence work, since Rohana has openly come here and spoken of it.*

She could no longer read Montray's thoughts; perhaps, for her, it took a moment of close sympathy, which they had shared for a moment but not now. Montray said, "I don't know a lot

about the Council, Lady Rohana, but I know it's been reasonably unsympathetic to our presence here in Thendara—"

"Your presence here in Thendara, Mr. Montray, is a fact, and
there is no use quarreling with facts; we must simply determine
how to make these facts less traumatic for everyone. I freely
admit that there are those on Council who would rather that
Jaelle was neither a Free Amazon nor the consort of a Terran,
but those too are facts, and must be accepted and taken into account. Perhaps I came here merely to assure myself that you are
not preventing Jaelle from doing her duty in this matter—"

"We wouldn't think of it," Montray said quietly. "It's none of
my business, of course, what she does with her life, but I can assure you, if what she needs is time off to take her place on the
Council—"

"This is ridiculous!" Jaelle said angrily. "Why are you
doing this, Rohana, and what can it possibly have to do with
the Terrans?"

"As I said; the Terrans are a fact; and if one of those who
would normally sit on our Council has chosen to use her work
for the Terrans as an excuse for not doing her duty—"

"Once and for all I renounced—"

Rohana cut her off with a gesture; but then she sighed, looking very tired. She said, "You and Magda have spoken with me
about building a bridge between two worlds; doing this by helping to place Darkovan women, Renunciates, in the Terran HQ as
Medical Technicians and bringing the Terran medicine, which is
excellent, into the life of our city. Would this not be even a better way to build a bridge between worlds, by taking a seat in the
Council when you know the Terran ways well because you have
married across the wall between our people? You are not, after
all, the very first—" she smiled faintly, "but of course you are
not supposed to know that."

"Wait a minute," Montray said. "Another Terran—we have
no record of a Terran marriage—"

"Andrew Carr," said Rohana, "your missing person. He married the Lady Callista Lanart, once Callista of Arilinn. I heard
this from Damon Ridenow, Regent of Alton. It is not impossible

that the Lady Callista might one day sit on the Council. And it is certain that some of this man Carr's children and grandchildren will one day do so."

"Wait a minute," Peter said. "Granted, I don't know a great deal about the Council. But one of the things I thought I knew was that women didn't very often sit on it—"

"They don't, except in the Aillard clan, where the line of descent is female; a man who marries into the Aillard clan knows that his daughters, not his sons, will succeed him, and that they will do so by their mother's name, not his own. But there are times when a woman sits on the Council. Several Keepers have done so; The Lady of Arilinn has a Council seat as of right, although Leonie of Arilinn does not always appear. I myself, as Regent for Gabriel, have taken the Council seat, until my son Kyril was declared of age. There was once a period of ten years when the Lady Bruna Leynier sat in Council for the Altons while the Heir to Alton grew to maturity; his father died a few months before he was born, and she, his father's sister, was considered a more suitable Regent than the boy's mother, who was young, and preferred to stay with her child." She shrugged. "I assure you; it is not only that we wish to make a Council seat available to Jaelle, but that we need her. It will not, when they come to consider it clearly, be a bad thing that a Renunciate should sit in Council for a time, a voice for the women of Darkover. Some of the old graywigs will be shocked, but it is not a bad thing for them to be shocked out of their complacency. Change is often desirable, frequently necessary, and always inevitable, so we can only consider which changes are best for our world, and at what rate they should come. And about that, there will always be many different opinions."

Montray had opened his mouth several times while she was talking, and closed it again, not wishing to interrupt her. Jaelle thought, without noticing particularly, that it was almost the first time she had seen Montray choose not to be rude.

He only said, "You knew all along about this man Carr? And I tried to speak with him at Midsummer, and still was prevented—"

"I did not prevent you."

"No," said Montray, with a blazing angry stare at Peter, "it was my own people who did that. Excuse me, ladies." He leaned across and pushed a stud on his desk.

"Beth. Find out for me if Monty's left yet. And tell him to get his—to get himself up here now—immediately, do you hear?"

"I think he's gone," Bethany said over the intercom, "but I'll find out, sir."

"And if he's gone, get His Excellency Li to my office, by the most diplomatic route possible, hear me?"

"Right away, sir."

After a moment, Beth's voice came over the intercom.

"Mr. Wade Montray has already left the city; Spaceforce passed him out more than two hours ago." Jaelle thought, *right after I finished with him.*

Peter said, "It was not the wisest thing, letting him out in this weather, but he's got good people with him and plenty of tents, food, and all that stuff. Weather watch were sleeping on the job, but he'll come to no harm. It's not as if he had gone alone, and with luck he'll be over the pass before it hits full strength. But the folks who were here for Festival from the Kilghard Hills—people from Alton and Syrtis—they are probably going to run into some trouble!"

"Most of them will have stayed for Council," said Rohana, and after a moment the intercom beeped again.

"We haven't been able to locate Alessandro Li, sir. He left a message that he was going to attempt to communicate with Cholayna Ares in her private quarters on a matter of extreme urgency, since she was not in her office today."

Jaelle said uneasily, "I should have been there. You made him my personal responsibility, sir—" and Montray looked at her with unusual kindness.

"He's a grown man, Jaelle. You're only responsible for him if he's off the HQ area, out in the native—the off-base part of Darkover. Don't worry about it. I heard that congratulations are in order, by the way. Check with Medic; you're entitled to all kinds of maternity leave and benefits, you know."

So he knew, too, and it was part of their damned *Records*. Was nothing personal anymore, here? She felt trapped, betrayed, outraged, and behind this all was a creeping sense of guilt. She had accepted personal responsibility for Li, and somehow she had betrayed that, too.

Rohana has done this, in the hopes that when I am on the Council I shall be willing to turn over my child to them for suitable fostering, to bring up my child to Comyn. . . . *so there is no freedom any more, not for me, not even for my daughter. . . .*

I thought, when I went among the Renunciates. I could never be trapped into the life which killed my mother or left her to die. But now it has reached out to seek me even among the Terrans. Trapped, betrayed, she turned angrily on Peter.

"You babbler, can't you keep anything to yourself? Must you tell all my secrets like a braggart in the marketplace, so that all men can pat you on the back for your virility, as if any tomcat could not do the same little trick? You think that between you and Rohana, I will do everything I am told, like a good little Terran—or Darkovan—wife? It won't work, damn it! I am leaving Peter; put *that* into your damned Record. And you, Rohana—" she swung angrily on her kinswoman, "I will see my daughter dead before I see her on your Council."

Rohana turned white. She said, "Jaelle, don't say that! Oh, don't—" and Peter said, "Jaelle, love, listen to me—Lady Rohana, she's been feeling sick, she's upset—" clearly she heard, and she knew Rohana heard. *She's sick and irrational, she's pregnant and women get a little crazy when they're pregnant, but I can talk her out of it, just let me handle her!*

Jaelle swung around, with a stableboy's muttered oath which made Rohana blanch, and stormed out of the office.

She had promised Peter the chance to talk to her about the divorce in private. But he had violated that first; he had brought out their personal business before Montray, even though he had nothing but contempt for the older man; Montray, of all people! She might have been able to forgive him, if he had told some close friend here on the base about their child—men *did* brag of incipient fatherhood, she knew that—but to tell Montray, to put it formally into Personnel Records? *Damned big-mouthed*—she was too angry even to complete the thought. She went into their shared quarters and began slinging clothes into her old saddlebags.

A few things she must settle before she left. She would speak with Cholayna: well, she could do that in the Guild-house. She should formally give over her pledged responsibility for Aleki— Alessandro Li had accepted her word and that was a matter of honor. Then she would go home.

She went to the Intercom. She had resented it; now it seemed a wonderful convenience and she wondered suddenly how she would manage without it.

"Communications, please. Bethany, has anyone managed to locate Alessandro Li?"

"He left a message for you, Jaelle. You should come and pick it up, if you can."

She looked at the nearly packed saddlebags. She was tempted to ignore it. They had, she considered, violated the terms of her employment so often, now violating even her privacy by making her pregnancy part of official record, that she felt that she should ignore it in turn.

But she would not stoop to their level. She had accepted personal responsibility for the well-being of this particular dignitary and she could not abandon him now.

She said, "I'll be right over," and left the bulging saddlebags in the middle of her bed. If he saw them when he came in, Peter would get the message loud and clear. His cozening had not worked; whatever he might now say or do, her decision was irrevocable.

Bethany, in Communications, gave her a troubled smile.

"Oh, Jaelle! Is that your Amazon—excuse me, Renunciate outfit? Are you going out in the field? Oh, yes, of course, you're going after with Alessandro Li, aren't you?"

"What do you mean, Beth?"

"I've been trying to find you all day, but you haven't been in any of the places I expected you. Li left a message here for you early this morning—"

This morning. But she had been with Monty, readying him to leave the city, and then involved in that long and stupid argument with Peter—

"You knew I was up in the Coordinator's office," she remonstrated, and Bethany shook her head.

"Li said *particularly* that this message wasn't to be given where Montray would hear about it until at least a full 28 hours after he had gone. You know what he thinks of Montray."

"This message—"

"I don't understand all of it," Beth said, "but he gave it to me; he said he didn't want it in the computer. That's against regulations, of course, but you know what it's like, the boss is right even when he's wrong. He said he had received some information about this man—" she checked a scribbled note on her desk. "Andrew Carr does that mean anything to you? He was starting out into the Kilghard Hills and would be heading toward Armida, and that you should catch him up on the way. Jaelle, what's the matter? You look sort of funny—"

Into the Kilghard Hills. Into an unseasonable freak storm, into some of the worst and most confusing terrain on Darkover. And alone? She asked, already knowing the answer and hoping that she was simply imagining things, "Who went with him, Bethany? He took some local guides and so forth, didn't he?" No; that had been what she had planned for Monty, that his well-equipped expedition should have the well-trained mountaineering skills of Rafaella and her party. But she could have planned something like that for Li if Peter had not detained her. Li knew that she had those skills and was planning to take her with him as guide and bodyguard; out of Thendara—she need not even return to the Guild-house and admit her failure! But all day she had been delayed, first with Monty, then by the idiotic argument with Peter. What did she owe him? Duty came first, the clear and simple fact that she had sworn to be *personally responsible* for Li and his safety. And he had gone off alone, on strange roads with a dreadful storm brewing—at least she would have persuaded him to wait until the storm had passed.

I've got to follow him; I've got to get away fast, she thought, thanking Bethany for the message in routine words that would not betray her agitation. He was on Carr's trail, and Carr had left the Festival Ball shortly before midnight. He might have checked the weather with his starstone and realized that he must get well away to be safe at Armida—or perhaps some intermediate house of safety, Syrtis or Edelweiss—before the storms broke. Li had delayed till dawn—had he somehow heard Lady Rohana's admission that Carr was married to the Lady Callista? She wondered who the Lady Callista was and why in the world she would have married a Terran. *I can tell you, Lady, you'll be sorry. I tried it and I thought it would work, too. It won't.*

So off he had gone, to try to trace down this missing man, find out more about the *Comyn*, learn what had happened. . . . but he should have waited for her, consulted her. *And I failed him too! Failed in my duty as I have failed at my marriage!*

There was no sense in her first impulse, to rush madly down to the gates after him, try to stop him. He was probably well outside the City. She needed boots and clothing that would protect her in bad weather. Her horse was at the Guild-house, and she could get food there too, and her saddlebags were almost packed.

On a sudden impulse, she squeezed Bethany's hand. She said, "You have been a good friend to me, Bethany. I promise you I will not forget it. I must go, now," and hurried away, not listening to Bethany's shocked question about what she meant.

Cholayna had been her friend too. All Terrans were not like Peter or Montray, wholly self-absorbed and involved only with their ambition—

The little apartment in Married Persons Quarters was still empty; good, she could get away without any further confrontation with Peter. She put a final few things into the top of the saddlebags, extra warm socks for riding, one or two small packages of the Terran synthetics which could be eaten quickly and would give fast energy and protein. She looked with a stab of regret at the bed they had shared. She had been so happy, and now—but she was wasting time. She pulled the straps of the saddlebags tight, and saw Peter standing in the doorway, watching her.

"Jaelle! Sweetheart, where are you going? I thought you said we had to talk—"

"It was you who said that," she replied precisely. "And I found out in Montray's office that you had already done too much talking, without even the courtesy to speak first to me of it. There is really nothing left to say, Peter. I am sorry; I will readily admit that it is my fault that our marriage failed. But now I must go at once. Don't worry, I am not abandoning my duty, but fulfilling it." She started to pick up the saddlebags, but he stepped forward and prevented her, grabbing her arms.

"You must be out of your mind! If you think I'm going to let you go, with a storm coming up, alone, pregnant—no, Jaelle. You're my wife and it's my duty to look after you, and damn it, that doesn't include letting you ride out into the Kilghard Hills. Li can afford to hire all the native guides he could possibly want, but my wife isn't going to be one of them, and that's that."

"I have pointed out to you already," she said, feeling her lips thinning in what she knew might look like a smile but was a grimace of anger, "that our marriage is at an end. I am not *your wife*—I never was *your wife* in that particular tone of voice, as if I were a toy you owned and could do with what you liked. I do not admit your right to prevent me from doing my duty—or anything else I choose to do. Peter, this is foolishness; I am leaving you now, whatever you do, and please do not make a fool of yourself by giving me orders which you know perfectly well I will not obey."

He reached out and tried to wrench the saddlebags away from her. "Will you put that thing down? You shouldn't even be lifting anything that heavy, in your condition. You're not going anywhere, Jaelle. There's no sun, but it must be near sunset, and rain, or even snow will be starting soon."

Yes, and Aleki is alone in it; he may lose his way, or come to

grief on the trail. I do not know how well he planned this trip.
"Get out of my way, Peter. I told you, I am going."

"And I said you're not," he retorted at white heat, "You're
my wife and you don't talk to me that way. Put that thing down,
I told you! Now, sit down, and let's have a drink and discuss this
sensibly. You talk about how sensible the Renunciates are, but
you are behaving like a hysterical pregnant girl, ready to rush off
into a storm without even stopping to think! Does that sound
like a sensible thing to do, Jaelle?"

He went to the refreshment console and dialled her a hot
drink, one he knew she liked. The rich smell, something like
jaco without the bitterness, stole into the room.

"Sit down, drink your chocolate, Jaelle. Try to see this
reasonably."

"You mean, see it your way?" She accepted the chocolate;
she would need her strength with a long ride before her. "Peter,
can't we discuss the formalities of divorce just as well when I
come back? By that time you will have calmed down, and you
will see that this is reasonable. If our child should be a boy—
though Rohana says it is a daughter—I will give it to you to foster; then you will have the son you want. I think that is all you
ever wanted from me anyhow—"

She detected a glimmer in his mind of logical resentment;
women were damned unreasonable creatures, yet a man was at
their mercy if he wanted children, and how else could they have
any immortality? It almost made her pity him.

"Don't be silly, Jaelle. I'm not going to let you divorce me,
not with a baby coming. I owe it to my child at least, to protect
and look after his mother, even if we're not getting along too
well."

"And you think that I am going to sit here in the HQ and
never stir myself out of doors, just because you would rather
have me under your thumb? No, Peter." She set down the plastic cup so forcefully that it fell over and a little trickle of brown
liquid ran across the surface of the table. "I will meet with you
when I come back—in the Stranger's Room in the Guild-
house—and we will talk about our child, if you must. But not

now; and you are delaying me; I want to be on the road before dark." She leaned to pick up her saddlebags. She had to step around him. "I'm sorry, Peter. I wish it could have been different. I—" she started to say *I loved you*, but she was no longer sure of that. She sighed and hoisted the saddlebags to her shoulder.

"No, damn it! Jaelle, you're crazy! Can't you even see how crazy this is?" He grabbed at the saddlebags and dumped them heavily on the floor. His face was flushed with anger.

"Peter, get out of the way, I do not want to hurt you!"

"I tell you, you're not going *anywhere*, not in this weather, not alone, not pregnant!" His lips thinned with wrath. "If I have to, I'll call down to the gates and have Spaceforce stop you, and you'll end up in Medic under protective restraint; I'll tell them you're pregnant and have gone crazy, and they'll lock you up until you behave!"

And he could do it; that was the terror of it, she saw herself in restraints or again drugged out of her senses; he needed only claim that she was out of her mind, meaning that she did not do everything he wanted her, as her husband, to do. She could probably prove herself sane; she was not, as a Terran wife, his property even as she would have been had she married a Darkovan. She could call Cholayna to witness that she was perfectly in her right senses, and explain her sense of obligation. But that would take time, she would have to locate Cholayna, and meanwhile she would be drugged and up in the hospital!

"And to think I believed you loved me!"

"I do love you," he retorted, "but does that mean I have to put up with every crazy idea you get into your head?"

"Peter—ah, Gods, can't you understand a sense of honor, of obligation? Can you think of no one but yourself?"

"And who the hell are *you* thinking of? Certainly not me, or your baby. If you want to convince me you're in your right mind, put down those damned saddlebags, and try making some sense," he demanded.

"Our marriage—it is my fault it failed," she said quietly. "I think you really wanted to marry *di catenas*, and though you knew my Oath prevented it, you thought perhaps if you loved me enough I would change."

You and that damned Oath. For a moment she thought he had said it aloud. There was no talking to him in this mood. What could she do to prevent him carrying out his threat? He was wide open to her; she could feel his rage, his frustration, even grief for the love that had gone awry. Yet it would do no good to walk past him, even to fight her way out of the room, if the moment she was outside he used the intercom and persuaded the Spaceforce guards at the gate that his insane pregnant wife had some lunatic purpose in going out into the coming storm, and should be forcibly prevented for her own good. *My wife. She's pregnant, she's crazy, I have to keep her locked up for her own good* . . . when had those same thoughts battered her before this? *A picture of Jalak, of her mother monstrously swollen in pregnancy . . . no; surely she could not remember her mother, could not remember Jalak, she had been only a child then, without* laran . . . *or had it only been too painful to remember?*

"What you really want," she flung at him, in confusion and agony so great she hardly knew what she said, "is to put me in chains . . . so that I will do nothing you do not want. . . ."

"Ah, God, Jaelle, I don't want to hurt you, but you're not even listening to me," he flung at her, "and if I have to get Medic to put you in restraints I will—" and she saw in his mind a picture of herself. . . . the picture in his mind was only of a quieter Jaelle, perhaps tranquilized, perhaps tied to a bed, but in her mind she saw herself chained, *a picture in her father's mind, the young Jaelle, budding breasts, old enough to be chained like a woman, copper links binding her hands, when she was wounded in the Pass of Scaravel Magda had tied her hands so she would not tear the bandages from her wounds, she had never remembered that till this moment, she heard herself screaming and Magda had quickly untied her. All that night Magda sat by me and held my hands because of my fear of being chained. . . .*

"Don't touch me," she spat out at him, retreating backward, "if you dare—"

He grabbed her hands—and Jaelle exploded, fighting on pure

instinct. Camilla had trained her both in armed and unarmed combat, how to react if any man laid a hand on her unwilling; she had forgotten that this was Peter, she had forgotten everything; she fought as she would have fought the men who would come to chain her on the morning of the day after she had become a woman. She felt the edges of her hands, soft now because she had done so little fighting in the last years, strike something soft, she felt Peter's fear, agony striking through him. . . .

And silence. Silence . . . she looked down at Peter. He was lying on the floor, and his *laran* was silent, nowhere, nowhere . . . she could not feel his presence in the room.

She knew now what she had barricaded from her mind for all these many years; she had begun to have *laran*, begun to reach out with her mind, and then, on that dreadful night when her mother bore her brother Valentine in the desert, surrounded by the Amazons, she had tried to block it out . . . too much, too much pain and terror . . .

Her mother's arms around her, her mother's pain filling her to the brim, stifling her. She could not breathe. Jaelle, Jaelle, it was worth it, it was worth it all, you are free, free . . . oh Jaelle, come here and kiss me . . . and a flood of pain and weakness and then nothing. Nothing. Nothing, her mother was nowhere in the world, was a lifeless body sprawled bloodless on the sand, blood staining the sand as the rising sun stained the rocks red with blood. . . .

And nothing, blankness, mind nowhere as Peter's mind was nowhere, he was lying before her—lifeless? Lifeless? She had killed him, then? She could not see whether he was breathing. She bent toward him, drew her hand back in horror.

She could call a Medic. . . .

And they will say that I murdered him.

The icy cold of shock flowed over her. Dead or no, there was nothing she could do now for Peter, and unless she wished to spend all the rest of her pregnancy in Medic, confined for her own good and the safety of her child—they might not be harsh even on a murderess if she was pregnant, but they would certainly never listen to her explanation that it had been purely an accident.

She must go. She must go at once, before they could stop her. He would not be discovered until the next morning, when someone missed him when he should have reported to work; the Terran obsession with clocks and with being on time for everything, especially work. They would believe he was off duty, closeted with his pregnant wife, if he chose not to appear in the cafeteria they would simply believe that they were sharing a meal in privacy in their quarters.

Resolutely, she hoisted her saddlebags. She could get out of the HQ, they had no instructions to stop her, Spaceforce would let her through. And then the Guild-house for her horse. Perhaps Magda—no; she was housebound. *I must not tempt Margali to break her Oath as I have broken mine.*

And after that, the city gates and the long road to Armida, racing to catch Aleki before the storm broke. She blocked from her mind any thought of the length of the road. *There is no journey of a thousand miles that does not begin with a single step.* And the first step was into this corridor. She hesitated still, listening with her mind for some trace of Peter's awareness, some sign that perhaps he still lived . . . no, nothing. She must go, go at once.

She must get her horse, and food from the Guild-house. But Magda must not be involved.

She closed the room door behind her, slamming down a gate in her mind on the memory of Peter, their love and their failure . . . and now it had ended in murder. But she could still salvage something. Perhaps if she saved Aleki's life it would count for something in honor. *A life for a life to the Terrans. . . .*

On silent feet she went out of the building, across the great plaza, proffering her ident disk to the Spaceforce man at the gates for the last time. She hurried through darkening streets and gusty winds, the weather knowledge of a lifetime telling her that she might, if she hurried, make it before the storm.

Chapter 5

The rain was beginning, mixed with little slashes of sleet, but warmer than most of the nocturnal rains; it was after all, Magda realized, only a day after Midsummer, and the daylight lingered, even though the sun was already hidden in boiling cloud to the west. She pulled the hood of her thick riding cloak over her head; the stiffened brim kept the rain from her eyes. Her horse twitched its head from side to side, protesting this ride in the rain, evidently troubled at the oncoming night and the absence of the warm Guild-house stable, but Magda urged the creature on into the face of the rain.

Two hours north of the City she paused to consider. There was a multitude of roads into the Kilghard Hills, and Jaelle might, or might not, have seen the good aerial map of Darkover which had been made by Survey. The commonest road to Armida itself was to take the Great North Road as far as Hali, and turn off westward, just south of the ruined city, riding along the Lake on the road to Neskaya as far as Edelweiss; then turn southeast toward the fold of the hills where the Great House of Armida lay. This meant good fast roads all the way, and she had heard that a good rider on a really fast horse could, in dire necessity, make that trip in a single day. It would be a very long day indeed, of very hard riding, pushing your best horse to the edge of exhaustion. Riding with the fire-fighting crew they had, of course, had riders good, bad and indifferent, and had been accompanied by pack-wagons and pack animals of equipment and supplies; it had taken the best part of two days and they had not

gone nearly as far as Armida. Also, they had traveled by side
roads, some of them not much better than pack-trails.

Alessandro Li had been out with the fire-fighting crew,
though they had arrived when most of the work was over. He
might have known the road they took better than the North Road.
Jaelle, she supposed, who had actually staffed a travel-service,
would know virtually all the roads through the hills, but which
one she had taken, and which one she thought Li would have
taken, was still conjectural. For the first time since she had taken
flight from the Amazon House, Magda stopped to wonder if she
had done a reckless and foolish thing. Tracking Jaelle into the
hills, when Jaelle herself was distraught and on the trail of a man
who did not know the hills himself, was a blunder twice compounded. As a Terran she could have requisitioned a helicopter
for a search to find Alessandro Li—or at least to make certain he
was not in any danger. But with the cloud-cover and rain, it was
unlikely that a helicopter could see much, and if the wind of the
fierce storm she felt in her bones should actually arise, it might
well blow any helicopter right out of the sky.

As for Jaelle, herself on the trail of Li—perhaps she should
have gone to *Comyn* Castle and thrown herself on the mercy of
someone like Lady Rohana, to trail her with a starstone. . . . and
then Magda wondered if she were going mad. How Jaelle, who
detested everything to do with matrix technology, would react to
such trailing, she could only conjecture.

Yet I have done a foolish thing. Jaelle was in danger; she
knew it; she could feel it, like the oncoming storm, in her very
bones; yet racing off alone into the storm after her, with no hint
even as to which way she had taken, was not the most rational
decision either. At the very least she should have asked the
weatherwise Camilla, a skilled tracker and guide, to accompany
her. *Camilla loves us both . . . and Jaelle is like a daughter to
her.* Yet it had never occurred to her.

Why did I rush off like this alone? Try as she might, Magda
could find no answer except the compelling, *Because I must, because there was no other honorable way.*

She had rushed away from the Guild-house without eating

her dinner. Now she took a handful of dried fruit from the pocket of her cloak and chewed on it, a piece at a time, while she let her horse take a slow jog. Soon she must decide which road to take into the hills. She could follow the present good road, the Great North Road which ran all the way up into the Hellers to end at Aldaran, as far as Hali; but if she did so, she might lose her chance of overtaking Jaelle quickly. She might not be able to persuade Jaelle that Alessandro Li could be trusted on a mission—but she could, at least, ride with her and help to find the man before his ignorance of Darkovan roads and Darkovan weather killed him.

Damn fool girl, rushing off like that. . . . would she, Magda, have done as much for her superior officer? Well, yes; in a sense she had done something nearly as rash when she had taken the road into the mountains, disguised in Free Amazon clothing, though knowing little of the Amazons, to rescue Peter Haldane. And that apparent madness had brought her here; Amazon herself, sworn Renunciate, it had been a mad choice and yet the right one on the road to her destiny. Would she have wished it undone? No, for it had saved Peter's life—and for all the ways in which she was angered by Peter, she still would not have wished him dead—and it had brought her to the Guild-house, which had also been a part of her fate so inescapable that now she could not think of her life without the background of the Oath.

Even though, at this moment, she left the sworn Oath behind her. . . .

No. There was no reason to torment herself with scruples. She had Camilla's permission to go, the permission of a Guild-mother in the House. Magda drew up her horse, in the fading gray light and rain, looking at the crossroads and trying to summon up in her mind—trained in eidetic memory techniques by Terran Intelligence—the picture of the map, the roads than ran into the Kilghard Hills. Where she sat her horse, three roads forked; the Great North Road running northward past Hali and later turning off to Armida, the small trail that led westward up through Dammerung Pass and into the Venza Mountains (at least she could forget about that one), and the road that turned directly into the Kilghard Hills. This road was narrow, steep, twisting and turning along the slopes of several hills—or, to put it correctly in any but Darkovan terms, fairly high mountains. No sensible person familiar with the terrain would take this road to Armida. Yet anyone who had only seen it on the flat surface of a map, since it cut directly across the hypotenuse where the Great North Road and the road from Hali were the two straight legs of a right triangle, might consider it a short cut; and Alessandro Li, as far as she knew, had spent most of his life on civilized planets and probably believed that a road marked on a map was a road as he thought of it; a surfaced artifact. If Jaelle's intention had been only to reach Armida before him, she would have taken the longer, faster, better-surfaced road. But Jaelle's concern was for Li, traveling alone and unprotected on a world whose dangers he would not recognize.

Mentally Magda rehearsed those dangers. Sleet and snow, even at Midsummer, in these latitudes. Hardly banshees, unless he went astray and got on to one of the high passes above the timberline. But that was not impossible, either. And there was the ever-present danger of forest fire among the resin trees; he could set a fire himself, unless he was overwhelmingly careful about camping and cooking his food. And, if he thought of roads in the way most Empire personnel thought of roads from experience on tamer worlds, he could easily lose the trail and be hopelessly lost in country which was, except to the trained eye, trackless wilderness.

Now it would really be a help to be psychic, and know which way Li went, and which way Jaelle went after him. And did she know which way he had gone or was she only guessing? Jaelle makes a point of the fact that she has no really reliable laran, *and again and again she makes it clear that she hates and mistrusts her own* laran.

So I'll just have to psych her out and try to decide how her mind was working when she made the choice.

She was afraid of the hazards of the wild road through the hills. Yet even as she told herself that Li would not have hazarded it but stuck to the better traveled road, a picture came to her mind, Jaelle on her scrubby little mountain pony, her tartan hood bundled over her head, riding head down along a road that clung hazardously to the side of a narrow track overlooking a shadowed valley.

Hallucination? Or a genuine flash of psychic sight? Magda did not know. The picture was gone and try as she might she could not bring it back. Whichever way she chose, she would be guessing; she might as well treat her hunch as valid. She had done so before and never regretted it. Hesitating, trying to see in that strange way, she tried to cast her mind ahead and see if she could bring to mind an image of Jaelle on the better-surfaced Great North Road, hurrying along to catch up with Li—but she only saw again the steep mountain trail. She sighed and tugged at the rein to turn her horse off the main road and on to the narrow trail.

At first the road was only a little narrower, leading past isolated farmsteads with dim huddled shapes of buildings, the soft noises of animals bedded in snug barns for the night, pale firelight past the windows. Once or twice a dog barked with idle curiosity but to her great relief no one ventured into the rain to see what had aroused the creatures. Any solitary traveler on a night like this, the farm people doubtless thought, was bound on his own concerns, and in no way interesting. It made Magda think of that other trip—had it, after all, been less than a year ago?—when she had ridden north after Peter Haldane.

But after a time the road grew softer underfoot, sodden with rain, and began to climb into the hills. Thick trees, smelling of resin and wet needles, overhung the road which was narrower and narrower, until Magda knew that two horses could hardly ride abreast on the trail. The isolated farmsteads were left behind, and somewhere Magda heard the cry of a prowling nightbeast of the cat-kind, hunting. The sound made her shudder; the cat-creatures seldom attacked mankind unprovoked, but if she disturbed one by accident they were savage. Then, too, in these hills there were still the remnants of the wild hominids called by early explorers *catmen*; they were sentient, probably protohuman, and very dangerous. She did not know of any Terran, except Kadarin, who explored in curious places alone, who had ever actually encountered one; but his reports had been quite enough to imbue her with a healthy respect for the creatures. Of all the nonhuman races on Darkover, only the *catmen* were a real threat to *homo sapiens*. And while she had heard that they no longer lived in the Kilghard Hills, only four or five years before this, a nest of them had made war on the folk of the hills, and word had come to the Trade City that many of them had been killed; there might be stray survivors, bitterer than ever against the humans who had all but exterminated them.

Strictly speaking the Terrans should have moved in to prevent genocide, if they are protohuman. Humans are the worst enemy of the protohuman cultures. Why am I worrying about that now? Afar in the hills she heard again the cat-cry and knew why it was in her mind. Well, she had a knife, and had been trained in its use, and she had sworn the Amazon Oath to defend herself and turn to no man for protection. She could probably manage the catlike hunting beasts, and if she let them alone they would certainly let her alone. And since few humans, and no Terrans, had ever encountered a *catman,* why should she imagine she would be the first?

It was completely dark now; her horse had to pick its way, step after step, on the trail which was growing steeper and muddier by the minute. The rain beat down as if something had forgotten how to turn off a celestial spigot somewhere up there.

She began to wonder how long she could continue riding like this, Magda's horse, Lady Rohana's gift, was a good one; but Jaelle's pony was trail-bred and accustomed to these steep paths. She had no idea what Li was riding. Proof, if needed, that she had been insane to rush off without further inquiry. But she had really had no choice.

I am sworn to Jaelle. There is a life between us.

And she wondered, puzzling it out slowly between the careful complaining steps of her horse under her, just what that meant.

Jaelle was her oath-mother; had brought her into the Comhi'-

Letzii. That was a part of it. Jaelle was her friend—they had stood side by side under attack by bandits, they were shield-mates. Yet she could say the same of Camilla, when they had fought together on the steps of the Guild-house. Further, Camilla was her lover. So why should the bond with Jaelle be stronger?

She shied away from that. She was still not comfortable with that idea. But sneaking into her mind through her attempt to turn away from it was the awareness; that too was a part of the bond with Jaelle and though she had not known it at the time—*it was Camilla who made me see it*—it had been there all along.

And Jaelle, who had married my husband, who is to give him the child I cannot. . . . Deliberately she made herself turn away from that thought. What led her after Jaelle was nothing so complex; only that she was sworn to defend Jaelle and Jaelle needed her now, when Jaelle, alone, sick, pregnant, had gone off on some insane impulse . . .

No. That was certainly what an outsider would say, but, knowing Jaelle, she knew that the impulse which had sent Jaelle after Li was as sane as her own.

Li certainly had not known what he was getting into; but Jaelle did know and had made herself responsible for him. She had done what she must, as now Magda, in following her, had done what she must.

She reached the top of the steep path and paused there. To the west there was a break in the clouds; sullen pale light shone there, and the face of the largest moon, intermittent as the swift-moving clouds covered, then blew away from the luminous disk. To the east all was dark and endless, only the deeper black-ness of mountains obscuring part of the sky, and occasional flashes where lightning played around a peak. Here at the height of the pass the wind blew with such ferocity that Magda's horse shuffled around to present its sturdy rump to the wind. The rain was less heavy here, but still coming down with some ferocity. She searched the path below her as far as she could see, hoping against hope to see the small figure she had seen in her . . . was it a vision? But the road down between the hills was shrouded in the impenetrable darkness of the night, and the storm. Somewhere down there wan a flicker of light. A farmstead where someone still sat by an open fire, seen through the window? The flame of a campfire where Jaelle—or Li himself—crouched for shelter? She had no way to know. A bandit pack huddled together in a lean-to, awaiting the cessation of rain?

Damn, I can see where on a planet like this, laran *would be a simple survival skill.* The thought did not seem like her own and she wondered where she had picked it up.

It was pointless to sit there, exposed in the height of the pass. She urged her horse round, sympathizing, with a pat on the neck, to the complaining beast as it faced reluctantly into the storm, and started down the slope. The road was uneven and rutted, rain washing from the heights, leaving only heavy stones and gravel under foot; even at this height most of the snow was melted, and she could smell curious flowery scents and little stings of resin and pollen in the air; the height of summer, flowers and buds everywhere rioting swiftly in the short hill-country summer. When the sun rose she would see flowers everywhere, she supposed, in the brief budding and fruiting season. An image from somewhere swept her mind, a slope covered with blue flowers and drifting golden pollen; something, perhaps, that she had seen on her travels with Peter, when they were in the field together? There was something she ought to remember about that. Well, it would come to her, no doubt.

Could she possibly press on through the night? She had had but little sleep the night before. But her horse was fresh, and for a time at least, since Jaelle was at least two hours ahead of her, she could drowse in the saddle; there was certainly no likelihood that she would pass her in the darkness. Jaelle would never try to set up camp on a steep slope like this. The rushing of water down the hillsides, to valley streams noisy with the swelling rain, was loud in her ears, and the uneven steps of her mount's hooves on the descending road. Not even Alessandro Li would have considered this a main road. Would he have realized it and turned back? No, for if he had, she or Jaelle would have met him—there was certainly, in this high trail, no place to get off the road, and it was barely wide enough for two on horseback to ride abreast. Her hood protected her face from rain, and she was warmly clad, but enough of the wind got under the hood to make her shiver and it took all her attention to stay in the saddle as the protesting animal carefully picked its way among the ruts of the trail.

A gap in the blowing clouds cast fitful light over the trail, and she gasped, pulling her beast against the cliff; normally she was not afraid of heights, but here the road, narrowing to a path, hugged the cliff and water cascaded off the trail in two places where the edge had been carried away by erosion or landslide. Well, both the man and the woman before her had passed this point; there would have been some sign if anyone had stumbled over the cliff in the ailing light. Abruptly cloud covered the moon again and she was left in darkness. Dark or light, this was not a good place to stay; with the rain still pouring, and water rushing down in ruts beside the trail, there could be another landslide. She would have preferred to dismount and lead her horse down the narrowing trail, but there was no place to get off and so she was committed to trust the beast's feet as it edged on, snorting a little.

"Your opinion of this place is just about like mine, fellow," she said softly. "Let's get along out of it. But take your time, old boy. Careful." And in a few minutes they were again safely within a darkness where both sides of the trail rose safely between heavy masses of trees. Again somewhere in the forest she heard some night beast, but she was less afraid of them than of the dreadfully exposed cliff trail which might open up again before her.

They have passed it. I can too, if I must, Magda thought, but while she was under the trees her breath came easier. Really, she should dismount here and wait till daylight. Li was not likely to travel in a strange world in the total dark—she thought he came from one of the planets with brighter suns and he would find this even darker than she did, who had lived here since childhood—and he had after all passed this way some hours even before Jaelle and would have reached the comparative safety of the valley floor and camped there for the night; surely they would come up with him in the morning.

And still the rain cascaded on, flooding down from the heights, pouring in every little rut it could find, toward the valley. Most of the winter's snow must be melting on the slopes, for the rain was warm; she could already see the damage flood had done on the track and on the hillside, and once or twice she had to pick her way around a tree which had fallen during the winter storms and lay blocking the path. If a tree should come down across any point where the trail narrows against the mountainside, there would be no passage at all. . . .

Well, she would, literally, cross that bridge when she reached it. For the moment the trail was safe enough; she felt even the muscles in her scalp relaxing, and her conscious mind caught up with the subconscious enough to realize that she had passed the worst.

No need even to hypothesize *laran*, she told herself logically; the sound of water, wind and erosion, the subliminal cues in the way my horse behaves. That's all it is. Unconscious logic below the conscious threshold. I wonder how much *laran* is this subliminal adding up of unconscious cues?

It doesn't matter what it is. It probably saved my life on that damnable cliff!

She reached inside her cloak for a hunk of bread and another mouthful of dried fruit, and chewed on it. The rain blew crosswind in many places, sometimes soaking a mouthful of the bread before she could get it from fingers to mouth. Just like a man, she thought crossly, to take off into a storm; a woman would have had the sense to look at the weather and wait till it cleared.

Li could not have been expected to know what Darkovan weather was like, and after the winter snows, it must have seemed mild to him. *But he could have had the sense to ask Jaelle. That was what she was there for!*

Chapter 6

When Jaelle woke it was still raining. Fortunately she had managed to get over the pass, and down along the worst of the trail, before the light had faded. She could not imagine why Li had not continued on the Great North Road at least as far as Hali, then turned west. But at least it was past. She did not want to think about what it would have been like to come down that eroded, water-washed cliff trail in the darkness.

Now, even through the rain, she felt a faint smell that tickled her nose. She had not smelled it for a long time, but no one who had ever smelled the *kireseth* flower could mistake the scent. She had no wish to ride through the rain, but it was better than ripening *kireseth* pollen, scattered by the wind.

It was early, but if she got on the road as quickly as she could, she would catch up to Li all the sooner. So far there was no danger which a reasonably good rider could not have avoided, and against all reason she clung to the belief that if harm had already come to him on the trail she would know it.

The rain was definitely slowing. Jaelle groaned and rolled out of her sleeping bag, hauling on her boots. She spread the bag on her saddle—rolling it wet would only cause it to mildew—and wished there were some way to coax a fire. A hot drink would feel very good just now, but there was no way to get it. She sniffed the dried fruit, and shrugged, thrusting it back into the saddlebag.

The ranchers out this way, usually small-holders whose main crop were the scrubby ponies or woollies, tried to keep the *kireseth* clear. But even this close to Thendara, there was a lot of wild, untraveled country, and in such sparsely settled places, there was no way to tell what might have been there. At one time during the night past, she was sure she had heard the cry of one of the catlike predators, hunting, and shivered. In years of traveling she had never met one face to face. But she was afraid of them.

The mist from the damp ground was blowing away in wisps on the erratic breeze. Jaelle swung herself into the branches of a low-growing tree, and climbed a few feet higher, looking across the valley as far as she could. No sign of Li. But he must be somewhere on this road. There was no place to turn off the cliff road, so he must have come down here, and set off across country. If she rode hard, she would surely come up with him in a few hours. There was still another mountain to cross before they reached the edge of the vast Alton lands, and another valley; a bad one, with ravines into which, she supposed, Carr's plane had gone down years before. She didn't suppose Li had come out to have a look at the wreckage of the plane, but she was no longer sure of anything a Terran might do.

She climbed down and into her saddle. She set off at a steady trot that ate up distance, and before the sun was well above the cloud layer she was climbing the steep path at the far side of the valley. Halfway up the mountainside she looked back, out over the valley. For a moment between the trees she thought she caught a sign of a solitary figure on horseback but then it was gone into the greenery again. All around her in the warmth of the day flowers were blooming, taking advantage of the short season; as she rode up the trail her nostrils were filled with their scent and her eyes with their color. Why, she was free again, did it truly matter what she had left behind her?

Piedro . . . perhaps he was not dead after all but only stunned. She must believe that. If he was dead . . . if he was dead, why, then, she had murdered him. . . . but she would not let herself think about that. Not now. It was her duty to find Aleki in this wilderness, to come up with him and escort him to Armida.

She rode swiftly as her pony could carry her, her eyes bent

on the trail to spot any signs that a rider had passed this way, or camped anywhere along here. Her eyes were sharp and she had been trained in tracking; halfway up the side of the mountain she spotted crushed ferns where someone had tethered a horse, a small cooling pile of horse manure, the scrap of paper which once had wrapped some Terran ration packs. Aleki had come this way, then. She had not wasted her time on this dreadful trail while Aleki went off in some other direction. He had passed this way at least three hours before, but she was gaining on him. Surely she would come up with him before nightfall.

The trail narrowed near the top again, and once again the edges of the path were worn away by water and erosion; rills of water were still taking every available rut down the mountain-side, rushing down alongside the trail, taking short cuts down from worn-away dirt between the rocks. Branches of trees had come down during the storm and once or twice she had to dismount and lead her pony carefully around them. The sun was warm, and Jaelle was grateful, for her damp clothes were drying and steaming on her back, but still, at the back of her nose she seemed to smell the ominous haze of *kireseth* pollen. She had been warned about it; under its influence, men and beasts, she was told, went mad, attacked; animals rushed about madly or coupled out of season. She had been told other stories of its influence too. Well, she could not imagine that it would have enough of an effect on her that she would tear off Alessandro Li's clothes and attack him! The idea made her laugh. She was glad to have something to laugh about.

Now she began to descend into the valley. From the top of the trail she thought, again, that she saw a rider. *Peter is dead. They have sent someone to track down his murderer, bring me back to justice.* The smell of the *kireseth* was thick now in her nostrils, and she realized that her head felt muddled. Maybe she had not seen a rider trailing her, she could not see it now, maybe she had hallucinated the whole thing. Now she *knew* her mind was going, for somewhere it seemed that she could hear Magda's voice calling her name.

Jaelle! Breda! But the voice was all in her mind. Magda,

thanks to the Goddess, was safe in the Guild-house. She had destroyed everything else but she had not, *this* time, dragged Magda into her troubles, or involved Magda in Peter's murder.

None of this would have happened if I had not stopped to fight with Peter. I should have ignored him and done my duty as an Amazon would do it, without worrying about any man, any lover. Then I would have gone with Li, I would not be trailing him on this Godforgotten road!

Her thinking was far too muddled. She had better do something about the smell of the *kireseth*. She pulled off her neckerchief and dipped it in the little stream that rushed down alongside the road, then tied it across her face. It would filter out the worst of the pollen. It was uncomfortable, blocking her breathing and clogging her breath, but after half an hour or so she could see a fine layer of yellow grains on the kerchief; so it was filtering out some of the stuff. But what about Li? Had anyone bothered to warn him about the *kireseth* in the hills? What shape was he in?

A rabbithorn loped across the road, leaping high into the air and twisting to land and scoot between her horse's legs. A *rabbithorn?* Normally they would hide in the shrubbery, and never venture out—but she was already fighting her horse, who was rearing up and plunging so hard that she had to cling to its back to keep from sliding off. She tried to quiet the frantic animal, noticing with the edges of her mind that the rabbithorn who had caused all the trouble was sitting quietly at the side of the road. It made no sense at all. She had never seen any wild animal behave like that!

It must be the pollen. Not a true Ghost Wind, perhaps. But enough of the stuff to affect the animals. The rabbithorn was gone. How long had she been sitting there in the saddle, staring at the sky? She pulled off the mask and wet it again. It was caked with the yellow stuff. What had it done to her horse? For that matter, how would it affect Li's horse? She did not even know if he had bought a seasoned mountain animal, or one that would bolt at the first whiff of the stuff!

The road forked, and her horse came to a halt, bending its

head to crop at the green grass in the triangle formed by the roads. She got down to look for water to wet the mask, and look at the marks in the mud. Which way had Li gone?

She had tarnished her Oath so many times. But at least this duty was clear. She had made herself personally responsible for this man. His safety had to be her first priority.

What would the kireseth *do to her child?* She tried frantically to recall midwives' lectures in the Guild-house. They had warned about certain medicines and herbs which could damage even the child in the womb, but she had been so sure she would never want a child, she had only half listened. She looked at the roads ahead. This one must run over the peaks to the South, winding up at Edelweiss, though it was not a direct route. There were farmers living out there, and one or two little villages, and a fulling-mill where cloth was gathered in from cottage weavers who dwelt in little hillside crofts and spun and wove coarse cloth from their own woollies, dyeing it with herbs for the ancient tartan patterns. This road, when it was clear of snow, must lead by twisting hill paths to Armida, and if Li had studied the map and had a good direction-finder, this was the road he should have taken. Leading off to one side of this was a cattle trail, heavily beaten out and flat with *chervine* hoofs. Li would never have taken this one. She swung into the saddle again and started down the road to Armida. Surely now she would come up with Alessandro Li in less than an hour. He must be on this road. She settled her horse into a canter, but something nagged at her mind.

The width and flatness of the cattle trail. Beaten out flat and broad by hoofs. Could Li have thought this was the road? Just because it *was* broad and flat and beaten smooth. . . .

No. Surely he would have seen the hoofmarks and recognized it for what it was. He would have known that nothing on less than four feet had passed that way in at least a tenday.

Or would he? She stopped, pulling on the reins, swinging the animal around. A sharp hallucinatory pattern burst into her mind in the midst of brilliant colors; Aleki, sprawled across the trail insensible. . . .

She must go back and at least check the cattle trail for marks of a solitary horseman passing. Damn the man! Hadn't he sense enough to stay on what was clearly a road? But in the past months, among Terrans, Jaelle had seen many pictures and could now—sometimes—get a flash of what the world looked like through a Terran's eyes. As she looked at the beaten-flat cattle trail, it began to look more and more to her like a main road—more like a road than the two small narrow roads which led off to the other sides. The cattle trail led nowhere, only back into endless, bottomless ravines into which nothing could go but the surefooted *chervines,* into canyons and wide open spaces. But to Aleki it would have looked like a man-made, artificially smoothed road.

Surely they would have warned him in Thendara. But, no. He had probably looked at the aerial map and traced a straight cross-country route to Armida, and it might have seemed to him that this was the road. And if he had breathed enough of the *kireseth* pollen, he might even have *seen* it as a road.

Hallucinated it even, as a Terran-style paved road.

Now she was all but sure. She steered the mount on to the trail. The pony whickered, distrusting the smell of *chervines,* and she had to urge it on, down into the broken country, used only in summer to pasture *chervines* and similar cattle. There must be wild range herds out here, checked only once or twice a year, and cropped now and then for skins or for meat. There were always lush valleys tucked away in this kind of country, though she had never seen this particular stretch before, and there was certainly an inaccessible valley somewhere where the *kireseth* blossomed year by year, undisturbed. The sun was hot on her back, and the light dazzled, flickers of mirage along the trail, like spilled water. It would be all too easy to lose yourself in this country and never get out.

A solitary horseman must have passed this way, not long ago. She hallucinated a brilliantly colored picture, like a small video on one of the security monitors inside the Headquarters, of Aleki, his tall lean figure wrapped in a bright blue parka, his hair blown around his head, leaning over the back of his horse in the rain. He could not now be very far ahead of her on the trail. But it was quickly replaced with an even more brilliant little picture on the inside of her eyelids, Aleki sprawled lifeless (*Like Peter! Like Peter lying dead inside the HQ!*) arms and legs flung wide, his head lolling against a stone while at his side the horse lazily cropped tufts of grass. What to believe? And now she could hear Magda again.

She had better dampen the scarf. Her head felt fuzzy and the air shimmered. Picture succeeded picture, Aleki climbing a steep trail on foot, and for a moment sprawled half naked beneath a strange spiky tree like nothing that had ever grown or ever would grow on Darkover, beside the shores of a strange lake with the tree bending over him and moving in an invisible wind. He was naked, erect, and he reached out for her with an immediacy which made Jaelle start and blink and the picture was gone. *Aleki*? Never! Surely it was the fault of the pollen, or had she picked up some random erotic image from his mind or memory? That meant he must be quite near. But she found that her palms felt sweaty and her heart pounded with something like panic. She had never had the slightest sexual awareness of Alessandro Li, would have said she could never have had, and the fact that she had been capable of seeing that kind of mental picture, even if it was pure hallucination, terrified her. It was not hers. She would not own to it even as a vision.

She rode for more than an hour along the trail, which slowly narrowed, and suddenly divided into six or eight narrow paths, running in every direction down into little ravines.

If Aleki had come along here, surely he would have realized that this was a dead end, that it was not a road at all. Surely his judgment would lead him to turn back. *If he still had any judgment after hours of exposure to* kireseth. He must be lying down there somewhere, dead or incapacitated, or—she remembered the sudden, erotic force of the hallucination—wildly intoxicated with *kireseth* and not knowing what had happened to him. Had anyone warned him about scorpion-ants or greenface leaves? Certainly not. She had believed that she would be with him, to guide his first essay into the field, and had relied on that. She had made herself personally responsible for him. And now she was forsworn again.

I have failed, failed, failed, at everything and with everyone.

She looked at the sky, slitting her eyes to see it through what looked like spiderwebs of color. Clouds were rushing across the sun. The day was far advanced; somehow she had lost time. She looked around wildly, knowing that she could search all her life long in this broken country and never find a solitary man and his horse. He could starve or die out here. She had lost him. Failed again. And the sky looked as if the rain might start again, harder than ever. At least that would settle the *kireseth*, and her mind would clear. Trying to see what was really there through the layers of strange colors, she saw canyon walls rising on either side. There were caves up there. She could try to shelter against the rain, perhaps even build a fire—she had food with her and could brew some bark tea; it might clear her head. If she could manage to climb, or get her pony up the trail. Yet urgency nagged at her. Aleki, lying down in one of those ravines, unconscious but still alive.

If she had only allowed Lady Rohana to train her *laran*. She could have used it to track Aleki, to see which way he had gone. She had been selfish and arrogant, wanting none of the duties and responsibilities of *Comyn*.

If get out of this alive, I will go to Rohana and beg her to teach me. It would have made it possible for me to do my duty. I have always believed I had so little laran, *yet now I know that I could have learned to use what I have. I killed Peter, I sacrificed Aleki's life, because I would not accept what I was.* It seemed that she was looking back over her whole life and finding failures everywhere, from the moment she turned away . . . turned away. . . .

She was standing on desert sand, and the sun was rising . . . *a great patch of blood lay red like the rising sun, and for the first time in her waking life, Jaelle saw, in waking consciousness, her mother's face. And she was caught up in her mother's pain and terror, and with a frantic effort she made it all go dead and silent. . . .*

From that moment I blocked away my laran, *because I could not bear the terrible pain of her death. She died, she abandoned Jalak's house knowing that she would die, so that I would not be brought up in chains. She died that I could be free, and I could not accept that I was the cause of her death.*

She freed me. But I chained myself again with that guilt. . . .

And now I do not know how to open what I closed away.

I killed Peter because I could not bear to remember. I struck out blindly at him, and I killed him. As I killed my mother. . . .

She forced herself to climb into the saddle again, though the effort made her whole body tremble with pain. She ached all over; she had not ridden in so long, and now she had been in the saddle for the best part of three days. This can't be the best thing for the baby, either, she thought. But then it was too late to worry about the baby. She should have thought about the baby before it was conceived. Or before she killed its father.

Oh, stop worrying. You were brought up on Camilla's story of how Rafaella was caught out on the trail and barely had time to get her breeches off before she dropped the baby and rode home. The baby can take care of herself, she's nice and snug inside there. And yet it seemed that somewhere the baby was crying. Poor baby. Nobody wants her. Her father wanted her but her father is dead. What will become of her?

Surely Aleki would have gone back to the main trail, or tried to. But if he had made it back to the trail she would have seen him. No doubt he was lying down in one of the canyons, dead, or drugged with *kireseth*, or thrown by his horse and unconscious . . . she must go down there too, and search for him, it was the least she could do, it was her sworn duty. She ignored the rational voice that told her that the search for a single leaf in a forest of nut trees would be simple by contrast. She rode forward, desperately trying to force her mind ahead to see Aleki.

No. She must get back to the trail, to the main trail. If she reached one of the small villages she could bring out a search party to find him. And yet she could hear Magda calling her. . . .

No. It was the rising wind. Long trails of cloud were stretching across the sky, the trees moaning and whipping around; a branch slapped across her face; she was back on one of the smaller trails leading upward along the canyon wall. Why? What had made her choose this trail? There was only one thought in her mind, that Aleki was somewhere ahead of her, that instead of going down into the hundred little valleys of the canyon floor he had chosen to ride upward, to get a view of the valley and find out where he had lost the road. Intelligent. But if he had been intelligent enough he would never have come out alone, but would have waited for her to guide him, knowing she was sworn on her honor to keep him safe.

But he did not trust her oath either. She was a Darkovan and he looked down at her as a native from the height of his own prejudices. No wonder he had left without her. Now, when it was too late, it seemed she understood him. She had been one of those who had obstructed him from what he perceived as his duty, finding out what had happened to the man Carr, and how that fit into the peculiar patterns which Darkover made, alien to other uncivilized planets when the Empire came in.

But it was my fault, Jaelle. I mentioned Carr in his presence, put Aleki on Carr's trail; I thought Carr was Intelligence, and perfectly undercover, and I spoke out of turn. Truly, it was my fault and not yours. The voice was so clear in her mind that Jaelle actually turned and was confused not to see Magda riding at her side. She could even hear the hoofs of Magda's horse. The trail led upward, and the wind was hot in her face, like the desert wind of that journey from Shainsa that she had never wanted to remember. Kindra and Rohana had carried her little brother, wrapped in the fragments of her mother's cloak. They had tried to get her to carry him, to play with him, she would not touch him. She had never remembered that journey before, but now she remembered lying, a terrified whimpering bundle, in Kindra's arms. She had been bleeding. She had forgotten that. She only remembered that it meant she would be chained, but she could not even manage to tell them of her fears. She was only afraid they would find it out. It went away in a day or two, even before they were in Thendara, and by the time it happened again they were in the Amazon House and she had lost her fear and forgotten that it had happened before; she had learned enough, by then, to be proud that it meant she was a woman. Why did I forget all this until this very day?

My little brother. He must now be twelve or thirteen, I have lost track. . . . I cannot remember ever looking upon his face. He has neither mother, father, nor sister; truly he is orphaned. What was it Rohana said about him? That he was sworn paxman to Valdir Alton. But if live I must go to my brother and get his forgiveness too . . . and for the first time she remembered words Rohana had spoken on that same journey, words barricaded by her own terrible fear.

Don't you want to see your baby brother? You had your mother for twelve years . . . He has none but his sister . . . I could have helped him. I could have been at least a sister to him, if not a mother. I have failed at every human relationship in my life, and now I have killed Peter. It would have been enough to leave him. And now it is too late. Too late for everything.

The sky was filled now with billowing clouds which seemed to move on their own, independent of any wind.

This way, Jaelle. When the rain comes there will be flood down there. Keep your horse climbing. Once again she turned to look at Magda and found her friend was not there. She was hallucinating again. She had failed with Magda too, if she had actually led Magda out to follow her here, into the wild trackless range country, where she would die.

Then she saw them.

She heard their hooves before she saw the riders, sweeping down toward her. *A Legion of mounted men, rank after rank, riding at full gallop, and over them flew* Comyn *banners, rippling in the rainbow wind. The colors of their robes were whirling around their horses' flanks, and they raced across the sky, their hooves pounding on the cloud as if it were the canyon floor. She could hear the pounding, the thunder of a million hooves, digging into the whirling air and sending little sprays of cloud up like dust. Then the Aillard banner stretched across the sky, and now she could see the young woman who rode beneath it.*

She was tall and magnificent, clad in blue with golden hair like a bell of the kireseth *itself, like the painting of Cassilda in the ancient chapel. Yet somehow through and over the blue shimmered the crimson robes of a Keeper. My child, my daughter, did I bear you for this? So terribly young, so perfect in her virgin austerity. And behind her pounded the men of the* Comyn, *led by another* leronis *in crimson, men and women in Tower robes of green and blue and crimson and white, racing on to drive her down, flashing knives pursuing her, driving her up the canyon, the man who rode at her side went down beneath their hooves, she saw his head explode in blood which splashed her robe. . . . She could see the horses now, hear the pounding of their hooves and smell their rank sweat, but she sat frozen, unable to take her eyes from the face of the young girl. . . .*

Pain jarred through her; a cloud of dust—real dust—suddenly choked her and the world came back into focus; from nowhere a rider, kerchief tied across the face, lean and swift, swooped out on the trail, grabbed her elbow, pulled at her horse.

"Quick! This way! Jaelle! Jaelle, wake up, *hurry!* Can't you *see. . . .*" insanely, it was Magda's voice. This was another hallucination, surely, but Magda sounded angry, she had better go with her to keep her happy. Jaelle dug her heels into the pony's flank, pushed on upward on the trail. The thunder of hoofs was still there, but the riders in the sky were gone; the noise was below her, and her horse was scrambling for footing on the steep trail at the side of the gorge. But as Jaelle tried to speak, to protest this madness, the thunder and sound overwhelmed them. *Chervines.* Thousands of them, stampeding down the canyon floor, pounding, flying, a sea of cattle driven by the narrowing ravine into an impassible flood of horns, jammed bodies, hooves, right where she had been sitting her pony in the center of the trail!

The stampede poured past, on and on. Jaelle was shaking. *I could have been killed, I would hove sat there drugged by the* kireseth *vision and let them ride right over me. . . . And Madga. Magda. She is really here and once again she has saved my life.*

The last of the herd roared past, bleating and shoving. A last straggler bawled. A few of the beasts, driven and pushed to the edges, plunged off the trail and out of sight. Then they were gone, though the noise of their passing still shook the ground. And as the sound dulled to a distant thunder, the rain began, pouring as if the heavens had opened and dumped buckets on them.

Magda put out a hand in the sudden downpour. She said, "Up this way. I saw a cave."

The light was already going as they climbed, and by the time they reached it, it was only a darkness against the cliffside, and Jaelle slid, still shaking, from her pony, and led it in. Magda followed her. She said, in a high terrified voice, "I saw you—and you were just *sitting* there—and the *chervines* coming down the canyon like the wind. . . ."

"What made them—stampede like that?" Jaelle heard herself say. "The *kireseth* . . . ?"

"Was that what it was? I didn't know. But there is floodwater above, pouring down into the ravine," Magda said, and put her hand out. "Look."

Down where they had been riding, a wall of water was sweeping down the canyon, almost a river. Would the *chervines* be drowned or would they make it to higher ground? Magda thrust her head out till Jaelle was frightened as she hung over the canyon wall from the mouth of the cave, then pulled back inside.

"The high-water mark is a good four feet below us," she said. "We'll be safe here." She pulled her saddle and saddlebags off the horse. "Well, *breda*, it's better than the pass of Scaravel. At least I doubt if we'll meet any banshees here."

Jaelle's legs would hardly hold her upright. She stood holding on to her horse, unable to move. Magda turned to say sharply, "Better get your saddle off and get into dry clothes if you have any. And have you anything to light a fire? There's plenty of dry wood stacked back there—and look at the fire-ring; this place must be a regular place of resort for herd-men."

But still Jaelle's legs would not move, and finally Magda came and pushed her down on her spread cloak. "Lie down, then. Keep out of my way while I build a fire."

I am shirking again. I have failed my duty. Even Magda, even Magda I have led into my failures. My mother died for me. I failed Rohana when she would have given me my heritage of laran. I failed my brother. And my oath-sisters. And my baby. And Peter . . .

Magda had spread a blanket across the entrance for a windbreak, and was kneeling by the ring of stones, kindling a fire. Her dark hair was soaked, clinging in little wisps to her face. She had stripped off her soaked shirt and undertunic. Jaelle coughed on the smoke as the fire caught and began to blaze upward. A rough chimney had been guided through a hole in the roof of the cave. Soon Magda had a small pot rigged and was brewing bark-tea. She brought a small clay cup of the stuff to Jaelle and held it to her lips. Jaelle tasted it; it was sickeningly sweet and she shoved it away. Magda pushed it against her mouth and said sharply, "Drink it. You're in shock and sugar is the best thing for that."

Obediently Jaelle swallowed, and felt her head clear a little. She said after a minute, "You've saved my life again. How did you happen to turn up just in time?"

"I've only been trailing you for two days," Magda said grimly. "What *possessed* you to take off like that—alone, pregnant, a storm coming up? You must have been crazy."

"That's what Peter said," Jaelle whispered. "He threatened to have me drugged. Chained—"

"Peter would never do that," Magda said incredulously. "Do you think he is a Dry-Towner?" Then she caught the picture in Jaelle's mind, restraints, perhaps tied to a bed in the Hospital floor—she knelt at Jaelle's side and caught the woman in her arms.

"Oh, love, they wouldn't have hurt you—truly they wouldn't—" she whispered. "I can see how afraid you were—but they wouldn't have hurt you, and Cholayna or I could have told them you were not crazy—"

"I killed him," Jaelle whispered, her voice only a thread of horror. "I killed Peter. I left him lying dead in the HQ, on the floor of our bedroom!"

"I don't believe you," Magda said flatly. "I think you are delirious and don't know what you did, or didn't do. For now, get out of those wet clothes. We can't keep a fire in here all night—we have to save the dry wood in case it snows, everything outside here is wet." But Jaelle sat dazed and in the end Magda had to undress her like a child and wrap her in a blanket from her pack. With the embers of the fire Magda toasted some dry meat over the coals, and tried to persuade Jaelle to eat a little, but Jaelle, though she tried, could neither chew nor swallow. Magda got into dry underwear and a dry tunic, hanging her breeches near the coals of the fire.

"I was terrified," she said at last. "You must have been completely out of it—you were sitting in the middle of the trail with all those *chervines* stampeding down the canyon and the floodwater up ahead. And I kept seeing—I know it was only the clouds, but it looked like—well, once I saw all the *Comyn* lords parading down the streets in Thendara with their banners, only this time they weren't parading. They were chasing a girl—a girl with red hair, and she looked like you. Like you, Jaelle, and I thought for a moment it *was* you. And they all went galloping and galloping by over my head, and then I knew it was a real stampede through the hallucination, but you weren't up in the sky dressed in *Comyn* robes, you were down in the canyon right in the middle of the stampede—" She shuddered, and clutched at Jaelle.

"I saw the same thing," said Jaelle almost in a whisper, but the noise of the rain drowned her out and she had to repeat it. She had not realized that the girl in the vision had worn her face. An irrational conviction kept saying, *that was my baby, and the* Comyn *will kill her.*

Magda said at last, "I have heard that *kireseth* can do strange things to people's minds. There is an underground traffic in *kirian* resin in Thendara, you know. The stuff comes up from the Plains of Valeron, and there are people who drink it for the visions it gives. Banned in the Terran Zone, of course, but people do go over the wall for it, the way they do for women. If we were breathing it, that explains . . . well. It's over now." She crumbled pieces of bread into the bark tea and fed it to Jaelle, like a child. Jaelle swallowed obediently. She could not remember when she had eaten last. The food and hot drink cleared away the last remnants of the fuzziness from her mind. Even the overwhelming horror of the murder receded. Maybe Magda was right. Maybe her memory was playing her tricks. If she could remember things she had forgotten since her mother died, how could she trust what she thought she knew? She could not do anything about it now, anyhow.

She said at last, shakily, "I don't understand. How is it that you are here? You are supposed to be still housebound. If you forswore your Oath to save my life—it wasn't worth it, Margali. I am not worth it."

"You're no judge of that right now," said Magda coldly. "Go to sleep. As it happens, I didn't break my Oath. Camilla gave me leave to go. She loves you; you don't seem to have realized that." Her face was so grim that Jaelle could not bear it. Abruptly, in utter exhaustion, she dropped into a bottomless pit of sleep.

When she woke the fire had burned down to a dead pit of coals, the tiniest red eyes in the darkness, and Magda was curled up at her side; but Magda heard her stir and rolled over.

"Are you all right?"

"You saved my life again," Jaelle whispered. "Oh, *breda*, I thought I was so brave, and I am such a coward, and I have failed at everything—you shouldn't have risked your life for me—"

"Hush, hush," Magda whispered, holding her. "It's all right."

"Piedro—you know I killed him—"

"You told me," Magda said softly, but she could hear Magda's thoughts, like colored spiderwebs in the curious darkness, *I don't believe you did any such thing.* "Forget about Piedro."

"Why should I forget him?" she flared, "I'll forget him in my own time and my own way!" She did not know why she was filled with such murderous rage. "It's not for you to say!"

"Jaelle, I only meant—I'm sorry for him. One of these days Montray will succeed in getting him kicked off Darkover—"

It's too late for that. What was it Peter had said about Carr, *Death legally terminates a citizen's responsibilities and privileges.* Now he had no more.

"And you're all Peter has. You and the baby."

"I don't belong to him! And neither does my baby!"

"He thinks—"

"And that was why I hated him, that's why I killed him! He wanted to own me, me and the baby, like things, toys. . . ."

Magda laid a soothing hand over hers. She said, "You mustn't talk like this." *Maybe if she acted like this Peter had reason to think something was wrong with her mind. I wonder— is it even possible that she could have killed him? But even Keitha reached a point where she no longer wanted to kill her husband, but only to turn her back and walk away from him . . . and Jaelle has been a Renunciate all her life. . . .*

"No, I wasn't," Jaelle whispered. "Do you remember how you cried when you took the Oath? I never did. I—it was just confirming something I'd made my mind up to, a long time ago, and I was happy about it. I—I wasn't *renouncing* anything, I never knew till I met Peter that there was anything to renounce—I had forgotten so much, blinded myself to so much—"

Suddenly she was crying, tears raining and raining down her face.

"My mother. I couldn't remember my mother's face, remember that her hands were chained, till Peter tried to put chains on me . . . that was the worst of it, he didn't know what he was doing. But I am a Renunciate, I should have seen it. I should never have let it go so far. Cholayna—" her voice choked on a sob. "I could have killed her too, if I had been wearing a knife I would have drawn it on her, when she reminded me that I was truly a woman of the Dry Towns, but it is true, true, they don't chain us, we chain ourselves." They were still in contact, their minds open to one another. *I thought it was enough to say no to all this, but that is only the beginning. All the women who had*

*come to the Amazons, and fought and cried through the Train-
ing Sessions and left, free, having grown into freedom, but she
had pretended she had nothing from which she must be freed.*
She had never had any idea of the anguished battles they fought.
Now she knew why it took beatings, chainings, the threat of a
fatal pregnancy, to drive a woman away from her husband. She
gripped Magda's wrist and felt the pain in her own arm but
could not let go until Magda gently took her hand and loosened
the fingers.

"They don't chain us. We chain ourselves. Willingly. More
than willingly. We crave chains. . . . Isn't that what it means to
be a woman?"

"Of course not," Magda said, puzzled and shocked. "It
means—to be in command of your own life, your own actions—"

"And your children's lives. I didn't want this child, I did it to
make Peter happy—"

How sick it was, to want to be dominated by him. . . .

"Darling," Magda said softly, "it surely wasn't all like that."

She could see herself through Magda's eyes in the first flush
of passion, the warmth of her first real love. *I was ready for a
love affair, it was no more than that. I would have been saner
and wiser to take you for my lover, Margali. . . . Do you think he
would have risked his life for me even the first time? And you . . .
I knew there was a life between us. . . .*

*You know I love you, Jaelle, and now I know how much, but
you are sick and exhausted. . . . This is no time for this kind of
decision, bredhiya.* She remembered Camilla saying something
of the same kind to her when she had been burned on the fire-
lines. She cradled Jaelle in her arms, rocking her like a small
child.

*Like my mother. I cannot really remember my mother, but she
died to set me free, and I betrayed her by chaining myself
again. . . .*

Magda rocked her, gently, crooning to her. *So Jaelle is to
have a child and she is no more than a child herself. I wish I
could bear it for her.* But when Jaelle's sobbing quieted, she
tucked her under the blankets.

"I'll make you some tea. You need it. Do you think you could eat something?"

Jaelle lay quiet, content to let Magda mother her. She said at last, "Aleki. He must be dead. First the Ghost Wind, and the stampede, and then the flood. . . ."

Magda crawled to the entrance of the cave and pushed the blanket aside. It was raining, and she looked down into the valley; Through Magda's eyes Jaelle saw the brownish, mud-swollen torrent still filling the canyon, dead trees floating, and a dead, bloated *chervine,* belly up and legs sticking straight toward the sky, rolling past.

"He could have found a cave before the flood started," Magda said, "Let's not give up hope yet. There are a lot of caves up along here."

Jaelle surprised herself by saying, "I think I would know if he was dead." At one time, during the *kireseth* madness, she had reached his mind. After that, surely she would have felt him die if he had died.

Magda brought her the tea and she sat up to drink it. She crawled to the door of the cave and looked down at the flood-swollen valley. She said prosaically "Thanks to the Goddess! I brought ten days' trail food; it's going to be some time before we can get out of here."

Magda felt her forehead. "You aren't fit to ride anyway; go back and lie down," she said. "There's nothing we can do so you may as well rest. That kind of hard riding can't have been good for you at this stage of pregnancy. I don't care what Rafaella is supposed to have done, you're probably not as strong as she is, and all this can't have been good for you . . ."

I never wanted this baby! It would be better if it never were born. Knowing I murdered her father—

And she believes that. That kind of obsession—she could worry herself into a miscarriage.

All the better if I did! The flood of guilt and misery was so great that Magda came and pushed her gently back on the blanket. "The best thing you can do is to rest, and not worry."

     *   *   *

But when Jaelle had fallen again into an uneasy, nightmare-ridden sleep, Magda went again to the cave mouth and sat there, watching the endless rain swelling the torrent in the canyon. They could be there for days, a tenday. No one knew they were there. She did not like the feverish look in Jaelle's eyes, the burning, almost delirious intensity of her thoughts. She was taking it for granted now that she would share Jaelle's thoughts if there was close contact between them. Well, Lady Rohana had told her once that she had potentially strong *laran*, and now she knew that Camilla had confirmed it, in her own way, even managing to keep it barriered for her for a long time. Camilla's intentions had been good—in fact, she had done it out of the purest love—but it meant she had had no chance to learn to control it and to grow strong in its use. And now something had intensified it. Contact with Jaelle? Exposure to the *kireseth* resin, strongly psychedelic as it was?

However it had happened, it *had* happened and now she was confronted with it, with an enormous overload of new sensory data that her mind had not yet learned to process. It seemed that she saw all the way around her, as if she had eyes not only in the back of her head but in her scalp too and at several places on her body, so that she saw the back walls of the cave as well as the flooded canyon below her, the small rodents scurrying in the back walls, nocturnal mammals half hibernating in nests of sticks hanging from the ceiling. She could feel Jaelle's body as if it were embedded in her own extended senses—was this what it was like to be pregnant, feeling an *other* within yourself? She could feel pain slumbering somewhere inside Jaelle ready to waken. Reaching deeper, she could feel the sleeping consciousness at a deeper level where the baby curled and sheltered within her womb, drowsing, but aware . . .

I never wanted a child. Was it only that I did not want Peter's child? I thought I did, but somewhere within me I knew I did not. And now I know that what I would feel for a child is what I feel for Jaelle, and more, and I shall never be happy now until I have a child. And that made her smile to herself, almost sadly, *for now I am certain that I am a lover of women, and it is not very likely that I shall manage to get pregnant that way! That is the only disadvantage I can think of. Maybe I should have had a baby before I decided that.* But she laughed inside herself, knowing that when she left the Guild-house she had left that kind of self-definition behind her forever. *No, I do not call myself a lover of women. There are women that I love, that is all, but what may happen in the future—well, I will fly that falcon when her wings are grown.* She wondered why, in spite of their desperate situation, alone, isolated by flood, with Jaelle sick, perhaps desperately sick and perhaps insane, she felt such flooding happiness, as if she and Jaelle and the child were all one with something greater than themselves, something that beat through all the living things around them. Sky and water and falling rain and rushing torrent, trees standing to bathe their leaves in the rain, the earth opening to the flood like a woman to a lover's touch, even the little beasts burrowing in the cave and the tiny bugs in the straw were part of it. Was she still a little drugged with resin of *kireseth?* No, this was something else. She supposed if she were a religious person she would call it an awareness of God, a knowledge that everything around her had life and that she was part of it. Her love for Camilla, her intense love for Jaelle, the passion she had shared with Peter, her brief tenderness for Monty, even the sympathy she had felt dancing with Darrill, son of Darnak, even the way she had mothered old Co-ordinator Montray, the pain she had shared with Byrna giving birth, her own fear on the trail—all these things came together as if, for one moment, she saw her whole life pure and whole. Even as she was aware of it she knew it was beginning to fade, and she knew she must not fight to keep it, for then she would retain only the struggle. She must let it go. But it would be part of her forever.

She built up the fire, then went and lay down beside Jaelle. She, too, was still weary from the long ride, and she must build up her strength for the time when they could get out of here. She hoped Jaelle would be able to ride.

Chapter 7

Four more times night settled down over the cave on the canyon wall; four more dawns rose red, and on the third dawn, when the Bloody Sun rose over the canyons, the rain had stopped and by that night the water had begun to go down. Magda, leading the horses out to graze on the slope, felt relieved, for though they had enough food, the grain she had brought for the horses was beginning to fail. But it would be a considerable time before the canyon was passable, and they were running short of dry wood for fires. Resin-trees would burn, even when wet, but not very well.

Jaelle was sitting up when she came back, and Magda realized that she was dreadfully worried about her. She was rational most of the time now, but she clung to her obsession that she had murdered Peter and Magda would not talk with her about it. Jaelle believed it; that was all there was to it. Magda firmly refused to believe it.

And the short Midsummer season was waning; soon they would need fire to survive. They must be ready to ride out as soon as the canyon waters went down enough so that they could get out even by swimming the horses, and for that Jaelle must be stronger. The fever hung on, and every night she woke screaming from nightmares, so that Magda had to hold and soothe her for a long time before she knew where she was; all her forgotten Dry-Town childhood seemed to be coming back to her, and again and again she woke screaming, believing herself in chains. Magda shared enough of these nightmares, with her new awareness of Jaelle, so that she insisted that they should sleep at opposite ends of the cave.

"We're simply picking up each other's nightmares and reinforcing them," she said, "and we each have enough of our own, I'd think." But it was really too cold and they did not have enough blankets for that, so she slept beside Jaelle, and when the other woman woke shrieking, she would hold her and soothe her back to sleep. Magda was always grateful to see the cave begin to lighten. But during the day, though Jaelle was feverish and in pain—Magda wondered if she had caught some illness on the trail—she was rational enough. *Except for that damned delusion about Peter. Or is it a delusion?*

Yet she was equally sure Aleki was alive. "He's trapped in one of these caves, just like us," she insisted, and as she spoke Magda had a flash of him there, lying alone and filthy, unable to move. *He's hurt. And we've got to get him back to Thendara. If he dies, out here, it's going to cause a full-fledged diplomatic incident.*

"And it's my responsibility," Jaelle said quietly. "I made myself personally responsible for him."

"And I have made myself *personally responsible* for your obligations," Magda said, touching her hand lightly. "I am better fitted now than you to honor that pledge. That is what oathsisters are for."

"I feel a little guilty," said Jaelle after a long silence, "I wanted this mission to fail. And now it has, for we can take him back to Thendara—I didn't want him to get out to Armida and question that man Carr, or *Dom* Ann'dra, or whatever he calls himself—"

Magda smiled faintly. "From what I saw of him, that man Carr can take perfectly good care of himself. Between the two of them, I'd bet on Carr."

"I am not so sure. When Li is on the trail of *Comyn*, he is tenacious, Magda. You don't know how stubborn he is. I—I am *Comyn*, though I never fully realized it before. *Comyn*, but I am free of it through the Renunciate's Oath so I can see Darkover from both sides. *Comyn* and commoner. And I have seen the worlds of the Empire through their little screens. I don't want my world to be like that. And that's what Li—Aleki wants."

"And he will do it, if anyone can," said Magda. "That's what Agents are made of."

"And you are one of them—" Jaelle said hesitantly. "Do you—do you want to help him on his mission? Or will you stand by Darkover?"

Magda took her hands gently. "It's not as simple as that darling. There's no way to say, Darkover against Terra. Neither of them is all good or all bad. Let's be sure he's alive before we start worrying about his mission."

Jaelle should be getting better, if it's only a cold or a chill or some mutant strain of influenza. But she isn't. She did not want Jaelle to know how much she was worried about her.

She herself had recovered after the fatigue of travel and fear. *If this is* laran, *I am one of the fortunate ones. I have escaped threshold sickness,* she thought, not realizing how much she had picked up from Jaelle's mind. She was eager to be on their way. Perhaps it would be better for Jaelle to try to travel, even when she was sick. If they had been in the Terran Zone she would un-hesitatingly have put Jaelle into a hospital. *She's really sick, and she's not getting better. So it's up to me. But tomorrow morning if she can travel at all we've got to get out of here.*

Toward morning, as cold crept into the cave from the snow outside, they began to dream.

Red sun rising over jagged rocks, blood spreading out on the sand. It was worth it, Jaelle. You are free. You are free. And then her mother was gone, was nowhere, like Peter, gone, dead . . .

No, my darling. I am here. And I am free, too. She was stand-ing on the red sand, tall and beautiful, her red hair not braided in the loops of a Dry-Town woman but in a heavy coil caught by a copper butterfly-clasp.

Mother! Mother! Come back, Mother. . . . But she had faded away, had gone to her own freedom. *And I am free too.* The crimson stain of blood on the red sands was gone, but she could still feel all her mother's pain, as the world dissolved around her.

And she was a little girl, lying shivering in the bedroll of the strange old *emmasca*, who was holding her, touching her as she had never wanted to be touched by any woman . . . no, she was Magda, lying in Camilla's arms . . . it was not I. I never thought of Camilla that way. Of course not. Camilla was my mother, one of the ones who mothered me when I had lost my own mother, when I could not remember her at all. And I was the nearest to a child of her own that Camilla had ever had. But Magda was not Camilla's child, she could be Camilla's lover. . . .

But the little girl was still there, a little girl who wanted so much to live . . . *No,* Jaelle said, *it's not possible,* chiya, *you will have to go back. To choose another mother.*

But you have chosen me and I have chosen you, said the little girl. Why could she not see the child clearly, only hear her voice? She was in so much pain. Her mother had felt like this and Jaelle could not barricade away her pain. It was too much. Too much, she was breaking apart, they were torturing her, she was screaming as she had heard screams from Jalak's torture chamber. . . .

Don't cry, mother. I'll wait for you. I'll come back again, when you want me. Such a trusting voice, a child. The little girl, in a blue dress, her golden hair curling like the golden pollen on the bell of the *kireseth* flower. Jaelle could see her walk away, into a gray world, gray silence, and it seemed to her that the little girl who could have been her daughter walked away into gray cloud like the Lake of Hali, farther and farther, and only when she could not see the little girl any more, but only the pale blue shimmer of her gown, did it strike her that this was a true parting. *Another death.*

"No! No! Come back," she cried over and over, but it was too late. The little girl was gone, and she was crying, crying because she hurt so much, so much . . . like the first time she had discovered herself bleeding and was afraid to tell. . . .

"Jaelle!" Magda, very pale, was bending over her. "You were crying in your sleep . . . what's the matter . . . ?"

"Oh, Magda, she's gone, she's dead, I couldn't call her back, I told her I didn't want her and she just went away—"

"Who, Jaelle? You had another nightmare, love. Tell me."

"My mother. No, it was my baby. And she just went away . . ." Jaelle sobbed. "I wanted to name her for you, Margali . . . oh, I hurt all over, I hurt so—"

Magda held and soothed her, believing that she had only had a nightmare, but as she held Jaelle in her arms, she realized that it was more than this. She could feel the pain knifing through the younger woman, and in a clutching terror, she realized what was happening.

I was afraid of this. She has been so sick, and under so much strain. She is miscarrying. And it is so much too early, not more than four months. Not even with the Terrans and their birth-support machines could this one live. And she, Magda, did not have the slightest idea what to do; alone, without even hot water or simple sanitation, in a filthy cave, marooned by flood-water—

Jaelle was twisting and crying out again in pain, and Magda took her hands. "Darling," she said. "Jaelle, darling, you have got to be brave, you have got to stop crying and do what you can to get hold of yourself."

I don't want you to die. And this is no place to have a mis-carriage. And I don't know what to do for her. Oh, Goddess, I need help. I need Marisela or someone like that. And I am all alone with her. And I can't even let her know how frightened I am. She is frightened enough already.

Well, she would simply have to do the best she could. Jaelle's sobs had subsided to a soft whimpering. *I'll try to be brave. Like the time I fell and dislocated my shoulder riding, and Kindra was proud of me because I was so brave. I can be brave for Magda too. Poor Magda, she's been so good to me.*

My poor baby. My poor little girl. I wonder if it hurt her to die?

Magda tried to block out as much awareness of Jaelle as she could. It wouldn't help Jaelle a bit for her to suffer too. She dragged together all the dry wood they had left, and built up the fire as much as she dared. Then she put water to boil—Jaelle would need hot drinks and afterward she would need some strengthening food. She rummaged in her saddlebags and found, among the trail clothing, a couple of clean flannel nightgowns. She did not even remember packing them, but she would put one of them on Jaelle afterward. She laid the other one on top of the cleanest side of the blanket. At least it was clean. Women had been having babies, and miscarrying them, under primitive conditions without Terran-style sanitation, for centuries, she reminded herself.

Yes, and dying of it, too. She told that thought to go away and be quiet, and braced herself to reassure Jaelle, even though she was not quite sure what to do. She was sure there would be a lot of blood. She had picked that up from too many nightmares Jaelle had been having.

"The first thing you have to do," she said, kneeling down to get Jaelle's dirty and blood-soaked travel clothing off her, "is to relax and try to breathe deeply. Come on, Jaelle, you've heard more midwives' lectures than I have. *One* of us ought to remember enough of them so that I don't botch this up too badly."

Chapter 8

Most of the firewood was gone. Magda, dead weary, dragged herself to the mouth of the cave and looked down into the valley. The water had receded still farther during the day. *We could have gotten out today,* she thought, *if Jaelle had been able to travel. If she had held off one more day. . . .*

It wasn't Jaelle's fault. She looked over her shoulder, tenderly, at the dark hump of bedclothes that was Jaelle. At least she was asleep now and it was over . . . at least she thought it was over. She had done her best, but she wasn't a Medic or even a midwife, and her best probably wasn't good enough.

And now she did not know how long it would be before Jaelle was able to travel. That was one extremely sick girl there. *I did the best I could, but there was no way to make sure everything was properly sterilized.* She needed proper food, and a warm bed, and good nursing. Magda put her head in her hands and cried.

And even as she wept she was conscious of rationalizing it to herself. *I'm just overtired, the strain of all this, knowing that Jaelle could still die. I love her, I'd do anything to take care of her, and I may have killed her. This whole thing is my fault. I introduced her to Peter in the first place. If I hadn't been such a rotten person back then, if I'd been able to give Peter a child, if I hadn't been so arrogant and competitive with him. . . . now he is dead and Jaelle may die . . .* she cried and cried, unable to stop herself, and even while the sobs continued to rack her, she remembered Marisela saying that one day she too would be able to weep. . . .

This is supposed to be good for me? Who's crazy?

It's a good thing I learned more than *that* from Marisela, isn't it? After the night past, she could have giggled; and she wiped her nose on her sleeve—there wasn't even a clean rag! and drew a deep breath, trying to assess their situation without hysteria.

Jaelle was sleeping; but she was very weak. Magda thought she had lost altogether too much blood. She needed medical attention, to be sure Magda had not botched handling the miscarriage and everything was clean. At a very minimum she needed dry clean clothes, nourishing food, and warmth. Magda could provide that, foraging for resin-branches which would burn when wet, provided she got them now before the fire was dead out.

Otherwise, she realized soberly, they could both die here.

If Jaelle's fever went down within the next few hours, perhaps she should simply bundle the girl on her horse, even if she had to tie her in her saddle, and pack her out to civilization, where she could organize search parties for Aleki, and Jaelle could get nursing. On the other hand, suppose they encountered some isolated farm where the woman of the place reacted like the woman who had cursed Magda on the fire-lines? That one might have been capable of turning them out to die.

If they stayed here, there was nothing ahead but starvation and cold, but she was still strong. Could she possibly leave Jaelle alone and go for help? Behind her in the cave she heard Jaelle whimper in her sleep, as if the very thought terrified her.

Jaelle, who was so strong. *Yet I have always protected her. My child. My love.*

She would stay with Jaelle, no matter what. Either she would risk taking her out to civilization, now or when Jaelle was stronger, or they would await rescue here.

The weather knowledge of years told her that there was another storm on the way, but it was not yet imminent. Still, she should get in as much fuel as she could.

She bent over Jaelle, intending to whisper to her that she

must not be frightened, she was not going far away; but for the moment the woman was sleeping peacefully and Magda hated to disturb her. Could she possibly reach her mind? During the aftermath of the *kireseth* storm they had spent much time in contact, and had even shared their dreams. Before the miscarriage, however, knowing she could not care for Jaelle adequately if she must also suffer all Jaelle's pain and fear, she had done something, she still did not know what, and blocked her mind from Jaelle's. Could she now reverse this process?

She tried to sink into the sleeping woman's mind; she did not know how well she had succeeded, but she tried to shape her thoughts without disturbing Jaelle's sleep; after that nightmare of pain and fumbling midwifery, Jaelle needed sleep. But she needed reassurance too.

Darling, I have to leave you just for a little while, I have to get wood, or something we can burn. If you wake up and I'm gone, don't be frightened. She repeated it mentally several times, but Jaelle did not stir and Magda wondered if she had reached her at all. Well, with luck she would be back before Jaelle woke, and could have some tea for her, and perhaps some hot porridge. It wasn't what Magda would have chosen but Jaelle had presumably lived on it before this and the stuff supposedly had all the nutritious elements needed—it was the staple travel food of the Amazons, anyhow. The fact that it tasted like stale hot cereal didn't really matter.

She pulled her hooded riding-cloak over her head, thinking that she would have felt more comfortable in Jaelle's Terran style down jacket. But Jaelle was smaller than she was and the jacket would not fit, so it was the riding-cloak or nothing. At least it was warm. She checked on the horses to be sure they had not strayed too far, patted them, gave them the last few bites of grain. Then she began dragging branches of damp resin trees up the slope. It was heavy, hard work and her arms ached, and she broke her nails on the wood. *Damn, if I could only reach an intercom somewhere. Primitive planets are wonderful, I love this one, but damn it, in an emergency like this one, what do you do? Sit marooned and die?*

She could have sent out an alarm and had Terran helicopters out looking for Jaelle before she got over the pass! She could have had a full-scale search and rescue out for Aleki before he was two hours ride out of Thendara! If Jaelle had had half a brain, that was what she would have done, instead of going racing off at night into a storm after him!

But Jaelle had killed Peter—or thought she had, Magda thought, sobered. *It was an accident. But she'd have to convince the Terrans of that.* And she couldn't have helped Aleki very much if she had been locked up in the hospital, or held for questioning.

She dragged an armload of wood to the cave mouth and went down for another one. Halfway up the slope she saw flakes of snow drifting down on to the folds of her cloak; the thick wet flakes, clumped together into little snowballs, almost, which meant it would soon be coming down hard. Some of it would melt when it hit the remaining water in the canyon, but enough would pile up on the slopes to make the trail dangerous.

That settled it. They could not be walled in here; they dared not stay. Somehow she must get Jaelle on her horse and they must make a fight to get to civilization.

The hell with all that stuff about waiting here to be rescued. A Renunciate has to rescue herself! Grimly, she dumped the wood and started getting her things together, what was left of the food. She built up the fire with the last of the dry wood and put their dried meat to boil; she would get them a good hot nourishing meal so they would be better able to travel. She packed what she could, ruthlessly discarding everything but food and blankets. She loaded them into her own saddlebags. She would put Jaelle on the horse, with her saddlebags, and ride Jaelle's pony herself. It was going to be a rough trip enough without extra weight.

If they made it out she would send a search party to seek for Aleki, or his body, in the higher caves.

By the time the soup was done, smelling reasonably edible, she knew she dared wait no longer. Already it was snowing hard, and she hesitated again; if the snow got harder yet, they could be lost in whiteout blizzard. Yet what was the alternative? To be snowed in here until they died? She drank some of the hot soup herself, and ate a handful of nuts, then poured the cooled soup into a cup and bent over Jaelle to shake her awake.

"Jaelle. Shaya, love, wake up and drink some soup. I've got to get you out of here; it's snowing and we've got to try and get out of this canyon while we still can."

Jaelle stared at her vacantly, and Magda's heart sank.

"Kindra?" Jaelle whispered, "It hurts. I'm bleeding. Am I going to die, Kindra?"

"Jaelle!" Roughly, Magda shook her. "Stop that! You're here with me! It's Magda! Wake up, damn it! Here, drink this!" She held the soup to Jaelle's mouth, tilting the cup; Jaelle swallowed a mouthful obediently, then pushed it away; when Magda swore at her, shoving the cup against her mouth, she stared, not knowing what Magda wanted, letting it dribble down her chin. Magda felt like slapping her.

But it's not her fault. She's sick; she doesn't even know who I am. She checked the folds of improvised bandages. Jaelle was bleeding again. *If she loses any more blood* . . . and Magda realized that if she made Jaelle get up and walk now or ride, it would probably kill her. Her face was fire-hot, and Magda had no medicines to give her.

She could be dying. Magda looked at the heavy snow outside the cave and thought, *If we wait another hour or two it might be too late to get out before the storm, but I can't move her now.*

She tucked the blankets around Jaelle again, feeling desperate. Did she have to sit here and let Jaelle die? If only she had a way to reach Lady Rohana, who could use her starstone. . . .

If she had a way to reach Lady Rohana. . . .

But she did. She had *laran*. She was not sure how to use it, but she might reach *somebody*. The blue-gowned red-haired *leronis* who had healed her feet on the fire-lines—what was her name, Hilary? Lady Callista? Ferrika, who was an Amazon herself?

Anybody. But how do you do it? I was a fool. I should have let Lady Rohana teach me. . . .

How do you yell for help with *laran?* And as she formulated the question in her mind, from somewhere the answer formed in her desperation. *You just do it. You just yell, Help!*

Well, help! Help, anybody! Magda crouched on the floor of the cave, covering her eyes with her hands, trying desperately to recapture the sureness of that moment when she had seen the whole world around her as part of herself. *Jaelle is very sick. We are marooned here by floodwater. Jaelle is sick, maybe dying, she's bleeding, we are running out of fuel. . . . Oh, help, somebody, help!*

She repeated this again and again, concentrating with agonizing intensity, trying to visualize the call going out, farther and farther, spreading in widening circles as if she had dropped a stone into the quiet around the cave.

There was a little stir in the air of the cave. Magda looked up. Dimly sketched on the air, she seemed to see faces. Women's faces, none of them familiar.

And then, without real surprise, she saw Marisela's face in the dimness.

You promised me you would do nothing rash until I could talk to you, child. . . .

Magda said aloud, wondering if she was crazy, "I couldn't let Jaelle go off like that alone—"

I suppose you could not. It seemed now that Marisela was standing there, though she was shadowy and Magda felt that she could see the wall of the cave *through* the woman's body. *Is she really here or have I flipped out after all this trouble?* And then Marisela was gone, wholly gone, and Magda was no surer than ever that she had ever seen her. *And if she had been there,* Magda thought in indignation, *well, I must say that wasn't a lot of help, just scolding me for going away alone and vanishing again! She could at least have given me some telepatheic advice about what I ought to do for Jaelle. She's the midwife!* The snow was making a soft swishing sound outside. It was just as well they had not gone into it. She should go out and get the horses inside; they probably could not endure this weather either. Wasn't there some serious disease, tetanus or something, carried by horse droppings? It was probably too late to worry about that. She and Jaelle had been handling horses enough that if she was going to get it, she'd get it. She herself had been vaccinated; she hoped Jaelle had been through a good Medic checkup lately.

There was a soft sound like the calling of crows; she felt a curious swirling in the air and looked up. The snow was suddenly gone; she was standing in a fire-blue haze—she thought of Lady Rohana's starstone—and around her were shadowy figures, dark-robed women; she recognized none of their faces.

She is one of the pivot points of history, said a voice in her mind. She knew it was not really there.

Remember; we dare show no compassion for individuals. We are concerned only with centuries, and some must suffer and die. . . .

Magda thought; I am hallucinating that conversation Mother Lauria had with Cholayna. Only I wasn't even there. It was Jaelle.

There will be no lack of suffering, but neither must die now; she is not important, but the blood of the Aillard is important, for one day the rule of Arilinn must be broken . . .

Then will the Forbidden Tower fail?

All those who work for the hour must fail. But we must think in terms of centuries. . . .

A Terran's child in Arilinn would break their rule and their stranglehold. . . .

Do you dare presume to deny her free will? She chose not to bear the Terran's child, thinking thus to avert suffering; she has not yet learned, and so she will suffer threefold. . . .

This time we will save them both for you. But remember; it is not personal compassion for any individual. It is only that this is a point where destiny intersects with the humane thing to do. We would all rather save lives. But we cannot interfere.

Then the words dissolved into the calling of crows; and Magda found that she was standing motionless in the heavy snow, falling thickly on her face and into her eyes, blurring her vision.

She fought her way through the blinding snow. It was just as well Jaelle had not tried to ride, they could never have gotten back to the main road in this. But the horses were not where she had left them, and in panic, Magda went down farther than she had intended on the slope; her foot slipped on the wet, slushy ground and she rolled down toward the canyon's floor, crying out in protest.

Her riding cloak and breeches were soaked now, and she could see no sign of the horses. In the thick snow she could not see the cave mouth. *Jaelle! I must get back to Jaelle!* Shading her face against the thickening snow she finally made out a tiny thread of smoke where their cave opened, and struggled back up the steep grade, without the horses.

Then before her, Ferrika's snub-nosed face appeared, with eyes blue and compassionate.

Don't be frightened, sister. You have been heard in the Forbidden Tower, and someone will come to you. Don't be frightened.

And Ferrika's face was gone. Magda blinked, remembering the fragments of conversation she had heard, Lord Damon, Regent of Armida, and something about an illegal Tower. Well, they were already in trouble with the Terran authorities, if Jaelle had really killed Peter; they might as well be in trouble with the Darkovan authorities too. From what she had heard this particular Tower wasn't in very good odor with the regular Towers.

Any port in a storm, kid. She blinked, thinking that someone had spoken to her in Terran Standard. *Am I losing my mind? I had better get inside out of the snow!* Jaelle was still lying where Magda had left her, stuporous, her face burning.

Who are you?

You know who I am. I said you had guts enough for three. Make that thirty-three, kid.

Ann'dra—Andrew Carr?

I'm not great at this kind of receiving. I ought to let Callista try to reach you. No time. I saw the smoke. Don't worry. And then a picture in her mind, men turning and riding down the canyons, swarming out from what looked like a great center of blue fire . . . no, she couldn't be right . . . she couldn't expect telepathic reception to come in like television, for heaven's sake! Jaelle was muttering and moaning and throwing herself around, and Magda mended the fire and went and sat by Jaelle and drew the girl into her arms, holding her and rocking her. Jaelle muttered, "Mama? I thought you were dead, Mama. Who are these women? I'm scared, I don't want to go. Oh, Mother, it hurts—" and Magda stroked her hair and tried to soothe her.

"It's all right, Shaya. It will be all right, I promise you. They're coming, they know we're here. It's all right."

Jaelle looked at her quite clearly and said, and her voice was almost rational, "But Amazons don't wait to be rescued. We're supposed to do the rescuing. The way we did before, Margali," and dropped off into vacancy.

Magda patted her cheek. She said gently, "Even Amazons are only human, Jaelle. It's taken me a year to find that out."

But she knew the sick woman could neither hear nor understand her. The fire was dying; she crawled into the blankets and tried to warm Jaelle, holding her closely in her arms. And at last, unbelievably, she slept.

She woke to hear voices. Andrew Carr's voice, calling out in the dialect of the Kilghard hills, halloing wildly.

"Not here—not this one! No, damn it, I tell you there's got to be another cave, there are two sick women out here! Keep looking! Try lower down, along the slope! Eduin, come up here with two men and stretchers, this man has a broken leg!"

They've found Aleki. Thank God, he's alive. A picture came into her mind, as she had seen it before, *Alessandro Li, the elegant Terran diplomat, disheveled, filthy, sprawled on the cave floor, his leg bundled in an improvised splint, looking up with an open mouth as Carr grinned down at him.*

"Alessandro Li, I presume. Heard you've been looking for me," he said, and offered a Terran handshake. Li stammered *"You—you—you—"* and the picture winked out.

Magda crawled out of the blankets. The fire was dead, they could not see the smoke; it was very cold in the cave, but Jaelle was breathing and seemed all right. She pulled her riding cloak

over her head and hurried to the door of the cave. The slopes
were alive with men and horses and she could see a group of
men, crowded around the dark mouth of a cave down the
slope—about half a Terran kilometer, she supposed. She could
see Carr now, a tall man with a shock of fair hair, standing a
good head taller than the other men.

She shouted, knowing he could not hear her over the intervening space but knowing that he could hear her *somehow.*

"Ann'dra! *Andrew!* Up here!"

He started as if galvanized, looked and pointed; raised his
hand to her in a wave, a signal.

Okay, hang on, I see you.

And Magda collapsed in the mouth of the cave, in the mud
and dirt there, and began to cry. She cried and cried, as if she
would never stop, knowing suddenly what Marisela had meant.

Some day you will cry and be healed.

She was almost unaware when a man, quiet and deferential
in the Ridenow colors, came up the slope; but she heard him call
"They're here, *vai dom!* Both of them." He cleared his throat,
"*Mestra*—" and she quickly scrambled to her feet, clutching
some dignity, some remnants of composure. A poor pretense,
she knew; her face was blotched and swollen.

"*Mestra*, are you all right?"

She said quickly, "My friend. She is sick; you will have to
get a stretcher to move her, too. There is nothing wrong with
me."

"We have a stretcher," he said. "Down there. As soon as we
can get him into a horse-litter, we will come up and move her,"
and Magda saw, at the cave mouth farther down the slope, men
carrying a prone form on the litter, carrying it down the hill to
waiting horses and men. And then Andrew Carr was striding up
the slope to the very mouth of the cave.

He smiled at Magda, a good-natured grin, and said quietly so
that the man could not hear, "It's all right. They know I'm Terran and they don't really care. I've been racking my brains to
figure out who *you* could possibly be. Lorne of Intelligence,

aren't you? I knew you by reputation, but I don't think we ever actually met each other—"

And, incongruously, they shook hands.

Then he was bending over Jaelle.

"Miscarried, has she? Well, we'll have her down where they can look after her. Ferrika's still in Thendara for Midsummer, but *Mestra* Allier from Syrtis can look after her. God knows Lady Hilary's had enough of that kind of trouble. We'll take her to Syrtis, and when she's well again we can move her to Armida." He laughed. "Somehow I think you and I have a lot to say to each other. But it can wait."

He bent and scooped up Jaelle in his arms. He was so tall he lifted her like a child. She could see, without knowing why, the picture in his mind of a beloved woman who had recently suffered such a loss, and his compassion and enduring sadness; but when Jaelle cried out in pain and fear he spoke gently to her, and Jaelle quieted at the touch of his hands and perhaps, Magda thought, of his *laran*.

The other man's hand was on her arm.

"*Mestra*, let me help you—"

She started to say, "I can walk," and then realized she couldn't. She let herself lean on him, and stumbled toward the horses in the valley. She should be there when Jaelle recovered consciousness.

Epilogue

Alessandro Li, still holding himself erect between two crutches, managed to give the impression, though he hardly moved his head, of bowing deeply over Magda's hand.

"I am truly grateful to you. Jaelle, I hope your recovery is swift and complete." He spoke a polite phrase which Magda recognized as a formal farewell in his own language, but it was one of the Empire languages of which she had only a smattering. "My Lord—" another of the gestures which somehow implied a deep formal bow, to Damon, "I am thankful for your hospitality."

The Great Hall of Armida, with its massive beams and the huge fireplace, was warm and snug around them; but a chilly draft entered the hall as the doors opened. Outside it was snowing softly. Andrew murmured, "This way, sir," and Aleki followed him, hobbling on the crutches, two or three men on either side. They would escort him to Neskaya, where he would be picked up by Terran helicopter.

Lady Callista said quietly to Magda as the door closed behind him "I hope he will not make trouble in the Empire," and Andrew, striding back into the hall, said, smiling, "He won't."

"How can you know? What he did while he was a guest in this house might be very different—"

Andrew chuckled. "Don't worry about Li," he said. "I know his kind. He'll dine out on the story for the rest of his life, about his hairbreadth escape on a primitive planet, and enjoy being thought the expert on Cottman Four—which means he'll have to tell himself how wonderful it all was."

"But he did promise to get rid of Coordinator Montray," Magda said quietly, "and to put in a Legate who knows the planet and appreciates it. He even offered to put in a word for me if I wanted the job."

"You should take it, if only to spite them," Jaelle said. She was lying on a sofa, wrapped in a frilly soft blue house robe which looked very unlike her. She had some color in her face again, but it had been a long, hard fight against weakness and infection, and even earlier that day, Aleki had tried to persuade her to come back to the Terran Zone so that the Medics could give her a thorough going-over. "We owe you that," he had protested, but Jaelle smiled and told him that by now she was perfectly well again, and Magda had heard the unspoken part of that as well as Jaelle; that she had not the slightest intention of returning to the HQ, now or ever.

Magda did not believe that she was perfectly well—only when she was flat on her back and delirious could Jaelle ever admit any weakness at all—but she was over the worst. She had been desperately ill when they carried her down to Syrtis, and for all they could do for her, she seemed to have lost the will to live.

She had begun to recover only when Magda, knowing at last what was troubling her, gathered with the *leronis*. They called Lady Callista, the Regent, Lord Damon, and Andrew, at their invitation, and gone out in their *laran* circle to seek out Peter Haldane's fate in the Terran Zone. He was alive; he had been found lying in a coma and carried down to the Hospital floor, but now he was recovering.

"You struck him with your mind as well as your hands," Lord Damon had said soberly to Jaelle. "You could easily have killed him; it was only an accident that you did not. Perhaps it was the grace of some God with whom you are on better terms than you know."

And from that day Jaelle had begun to sleep without nightmares and to eat and gain back a little of the weight she had lost.

That hour within the matrix circle—and Magda knew she had taken a full part in it—had somehow made her part of them; Andrew and Callista treated her like a sister and brother, and she felt as if she had known Damon all her life. She felt somewhat less close to the pretty Lady Ellemir, who said forthrightly that for these years while the children were young she wished to give them her full time and attention. She was sitting now at the far end of the hall, the children of the household gathered around her. Magda still did not have them all straight, though she knew that the seven-year-old, curly-haired redhead they called Domenic was the oldest son of Damon and Ellemir, and her only surviving child. Lady Callista had two daughters somewhere between four and seven, one dark and serious— Magda thought her name was Hilary, a name she remembered because of the *leronis* who had healed her feet—and one fair-haired and giggly, but Magda never could remember her name. There were several other children who were explained offhandedly as fosterlings of the House; the smallest of them Callista explained blandly as Andrew's *nedestro* son, which seemed strange—no one could possibly mistake the deep devotion between Callista and Andrew; Magda had never seen such a devoted couple—and the others were small redheads who had, Damon explained with equal casualness, some *Comyn* blood somewhere, had been born to small-holders and farmers, and were being brought up where they could be properly trained when their *laran* surfaced. Magda and Jaelle too were astonished at the way in which this was taken for granted. Ellemir mothered all the children indiscriminately.

"It is pure self-indulgence," she admitted, "but they are little only such a short time, and Callista is my twin—she has *laran* enough for two, so for these precious years while they are so tiny, I take delight in them while I can. We come from a long-lived family; I shall have forty or fifty years to come back into the circle and master my *laran* after they are grown." Now she was telling them all some kind of story, the littlest one on her lap, the others clustered around her knees.

Jaelle sighed as the sound of Alessandro Li's escort died

away outside. She said, "I do not suppose Peter will make any trouble—now—about giving me a divorce. Aleki promised to set it up so that I need not—go back." Her eyes were shadowed, and Magda knew without needing to touch her mind what she was thinking, Jaelle was still easily depressed, and cried easily, but Ellemir had privately assured Magda that it would pass in time.

"I know," Ellemir said sorrowfully, "I have lost three; and the last only this season. Just before Midsummer." Magda remembered Ferrika, crying in Marisela's arms. Having been, though briefly, part of the circle, she understood the bond, and knew Ferrika was a very real part of this matrix circle—the only one on Darkover which was not hidden, guarded, shielded behind Tower walls. And Ferrika, though commoner born, was as much part of it as Lord Damon himself, or his brother Kieran, or the aristocratic Lady Hilary, who was married to Colin of Syrtis. Hilary's one son Felix was somewhere in the circle of children around Ellemir, but Magda had forgotten which one he was.

You never wholly cease to grieve, she had said to Jaelle. *But you learn to live with grief, and find a way through it. And you try again. And you open your heart to other children.*

Jaelle had said, very low, "As Kindra did. And as Camilla does still," and from that day she had begun to sleep without nightmares of the little girl with red hair, walking away into the gray irrecoverable mists of the Overworld.

Now Andrew came and said, "I am going to ride out and see that everything is well with the horses before the storm shuts down. Who wants to come with me, lads?"

All the boys, except the tiny one in Ellemir's lap, raced out after him. They all called Andrew by the word which could mean Uncle, or foster-father, or just as all of them—including her own two daughters—called Lady Callista by the intimate nickname meaning auntie, or foster-mother; but Lady Ellemir was simply "Mama." Not only to her own and Callista's children but to every child on the estate of Armida.

One of the girls grabbed down her cloak and demanded to be

taken too. Ellemir said deprecatingly "Oh, Cassie—" but Andrew only laughed, picking up his younger daughter.

"You shall come if you like, Cassilde n'ha Callista," he said, setting her on his shoulder, and Callista explained, with a laugh, "She is Ferrika's favorite, and Ferrika always said she had the making of a Renunciate! Andrew, you should not call her that, she might take it seriously!"

"Why not?" Damon asked, "We shall need rebels some day," but Ellemir shivered. She said in a low voice, "Don't, Damon. Time enough for that—" and Damon patted Ellemir's shoulder and stood close to her for a moment. It seemed to Magda that she could hear the curious rustle of the dark robes and the far echo like the calling of crows, as if the fates were flying overhead. Then Andrew went out with his brood; Ellemir called a nurse and had the other children taken upstairs to the nursery suite, and Lady Callista came to sit by the fire between Magda and Jaelle, fingering her *rryl*. She said, "Had I ever heard of the Renunciates, I think I might never have gone to Arilinn!"

Damon laughed and said, "They would not have accepted you in a Guild-house, Callie. I was in Council the year Lady Rohana stood before them and pledged herself for Jaelle, that she should be freed—"

Jaelle began dripping tears again, though she bent her head and tried to hide them, and her awareness of failure was painful to everyone in the circle around the fire. But Damon only said quietly, "Well, you must take your own seat there until you choose—what is it you say, *in your own time and season*—to bear a daughter for the Domain of Aillard. And if you do not, no doubt the Hastur-kin will survive, as they have for centuries." But again Magda had the flickering vision of the little girl with red hair, running in a storm of autumn leaves behind the girl Ellemir had called Cassie. She did not understand it, but accepted.

Her *laran*, so recently wakened, was still not wholly under her control. She saw again the curious circle of women's faces under their dark hoods and the sound of the crows calling far away, and her mind slipped away.

We are not concerned with the good of the Comyn, *nor yet of the Terrans, nor of the Renunciates; we must think in terms of centuries. So many of the* Comyn *are loyal only to their own caste, and most of the Towers have become only their instruments, where once they served all for the common good. That is why the Altons and the Forbidden Tower have become our instruments for the moment. They too shall suffer for the moment, although in the centuries they shall attain perfection and enlightenment.*

Magda whispered, almost aloud, *Who are you?*

You may call us the Soul of Darkover. Or the Dark Sisterhood. . . .

"Magda, where are you?" asked Jaelle, and the vision faded swiftly, even as Magda sought to hold on to the awareness, the last fading words, *We are instruments of fate, even as you, sister. . . .*

Callista touched Jaelle's hand. Magda had been among them long enough to know what a rare gesture of intimacy this was. She said, "I was Keeper long enough to know how you feel, Jaelle. I did not share Ellemir's acceptance of the duty to bear children for the Domain—"

"Duty?" declared Ellemir with a touch of annoyance. "Privilege! Anyone who would willingly refuse to have a child— well, I can only imagine she must be mad, or I am very sorry for her!"

Callista smiled affectionately at her twin. It was evidently an old argument between them. "Well, I promised you that you might bring up all of mine, and I have kept that promise," she said, laughing. "I am fond enough of my children, and of yours too, and some day I suppose I will resign myself to give Andrew the son he wants, though it seems unfair that I, who would be richly content if I never had a child, bear them so easily, while you, who would like to have a child in your arms every ten moons—no, don't deny it, Elli—can have them only with so much trouble and suffering."

And loss. . . . They all heard it, but none of them spoke it aloud. But Ellemir said quietly, "The Alton blood is a precious heritage. I am proud to be the instrument of transmitting it."

Jaelle said ruefully, "You sing the same song as Lady Rohana, and to the same tune. And yet you are a potential *leronis*, which must be very like being a Renunciate—having something better to do than other women—"

"I do not see how it can be better," Ellemir said, "A racing mare, no doubt, is proud of winning all her races. Yet if she does not transmit that bloodline she might as well have stayed in her stable eating hay. We need the brood mare as well as the racing filly."

"I will do my duty," said Jaelle quietly. "I know, now, why I must." The women around the fire seemed very close; to Magda it was like the peace that sometimes came at the end of Training Session, when they had argued and cried and fought their way to peace. Callista, she sensed, had fought longer and harder battles than any Renunciate, yet she seemed even more serene.

"And yet you are sworn to Jaelle, Margali," said Callista. "Will it not trouble you if she turns from you to a man—since, as yet, there is no other way to bear a child, and Jaelle has promised this?" Callista was rehearsing in her mind the Oath of the Amazons, wishing there had been some such way for her as a young woman, and at last it burst out of her.

"Andrew and Damon are bound to one another, I think, by a stronger bond than to either of us. Men may swear such oaths. And yet for women, such an oath is always taken, it seems, as a thing for untried girls, and means only, *I shall be bound to you only so long as it does not interfere with duty to husband and children. . . .*"

Jaelle turned and took Magda's hand. Memory flamed between them of the bond tested by the very edge of survival in the canyon; and of a night, during Jaelle's convalescence, when they had turned to one another and each, taking her Amazon knife, had exchanged it with the other; the strongest bond known to women. Close as Rafaella was to Jaelle, and even though they had been lovers for a time, they had never exchanged knives in this way, and Magda knew it was a bond as close as marriage.

"Only one bond is closer," said Ellemir, just audibly.

Callista's fingers began to stray over her *rryl* again, and she said at last, "Can it be that a woman's bond to a woman is not overturned by her commitments to others, just as her bond to a single child is not overturned when she bears another? I thought, when I bore Hilary, though I had not wanted her, that I loved her as I had never loved even Andrew, or you, Elli. And yet when Cassie was born, I loved her no less . . ."

As I love Andrew no less because my bond with Damon is eternal and strong. . . . Magda could hear Callista's thoughts, and Jaelle said softly "Is it possible—that women can love without needing to possess what they love? Every woman knows that one day her child will leave her." And for the first time without pain, she understood her mother's dying words, without guilt.

It was worth it all, Jaelle. You are free. With great pain, Jaelle had seen her own daughter leave her, and had known she would some day have courage to free her, again, to live her own life and bear her own risks.

"Peter—he wanted to possess me and the child," said Jaelle, and Magda nodded, and Callista, her face still bent over the *rryl*, said, "It was a long time before Andrew understood . . . and even now . . ." and could say no more.

Ellemir said softly, "But Damon is not like that." And for a moment all of the women in the circle knew who would father Jaelle's child for the Aillard clan; because he would have no need to possess woman or child, but could leave them free to their own heritage and destiny.

The silence and the crackle of the fire and the soft, absentminded sounds of Callista's hands on her harp were broken by Andrew's laughter.

"No, no! No more! I am not a *chervine* to carry you all on my back! Run to the kitchen and find some bread and honey, and let me talk to the grown-ups! Yes, Domenic, I promised that you and Felix should ride with me tomorrow unless the snow is too bad, and if it is, when it clears! And yes, Cassie, you may come

too! Now, for the love of heaven, run along, all of you. I saw
some apples in the kitchens—go and get them."

The children scattered and Andrew came back into the hall.
He said something to Damon about the stock and pasture shelters for the snow, then joined the women at the fire.

"Play for us, Callie," he said, and she began to sing an old
ballad of the hills. Damon and Ellemir were sitting close together on the foot of Jaelle's couch, and Magda felt a moment
of deep strangeness. It was as if a door had slammed between
herself and the life among the Amazons that she had loved and
sworn to. The Terran life, too, was gone, and she felt cold and
alienated. She was sworn to Jaelle, yet she could see that this
bond held no promises of security, either. And though she knew
the strength of the *laran* circle, she did not know if it would be
enough.

Andrew leaned over, and put a friendly arm around her.

"It's all right," he said, hugging her close with a brotherly
smile, "Listen, girl, do you think I don't know how you're feeling?" Magda's Amazon spirit recoiled at that careless "girl"; I
am a woman, she thought, not a girl, but then she knew it was
only Andrew's way; like Ellemir, he had the habit of protecting.
Like herself, he would have made a good mother.

*Are Andrew and I going to spend the next ten years trying to
decide whose business it is to protect all the rest of us here in the
Forbidden Tower?* Magda wondered, and gasped at the knowledge of how much that implied.

Andrew said gently, "But that's what the Forbidden Tower is
all about, Magdalen." He alone chose to use her full name, without shortening it. "There isn't one of us here who hasn't had to
tear up our old lives like waste paper and start over again.
Damon's had to do it two or three times. It isn't safety, or security. But—" his arms tightened around her for a moment again,
"we've got each other. All of us."

And for a moment, again, Magdalen Lorne heard the faint far
calling as of distant crows—or fates?—and the rustle of wings.

CITY OF
SORCERY

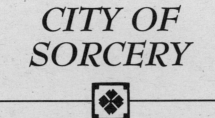

ACKNOWLEDGMENTS

Although every character and event in this novel is entirely my own invention, the theme and structure of the story were suggested by a novel by the late Talbot Mundy; THE DEVIL'S GUARD, copyright 1926 by the Ridgeway Company. I read it in 1945 or thereabout, and have felt for many years that this kind of Ideal Search or Quest novel should be retold in a Darkover context.

Also my grateful thanks to my elder son, David Bradley, for preparation of the final manuscript. David went above and beyond the call of duty in retyping, at an hour's notice, from a very imperfect print, the first chapters into a second word processor after the first one had blown up in my face, losing all the early disks and backups. This is why Darkovans are said to hate technology. And thanks to my secretary, Elisabeth Waters, who gave up the use of *her* word processor for three weeks so that we could finish the book on time.

—M.Z.B.

Chapter 1

The messenger was a woman, and though she was wearing Darkovan clothing, she was not Darkovan, and not accustomed to the streets of Thendara's Old Town at night. She walked warily, reminding herself that respectable women were seldom molested in the streets if they minded their own business, acted and looked as if they had somewhere to go; did not loiter, kept moving.

She had learned this lesson so well that she strode along briskly even through the marketplace, looking neither to one side nor the other, keeping her eyes straight ahead.

The red sun of Cottman IV, informally called the Bloody Sun by Terran Empire spaceport workers, lingered at the rim of the horizon, casting a pleasant red-umber twilight. A single moon, like a pale violet shadow in the sky, hung high and waning. In the marketplace, the vendors were closing the front shutters of their stalls. A fried-fish seller was scooping up the last small crispy crumbs from her kettle, watched by a few stray cats; she scattered the crumbs, provoking a cat-scrimmage underfoot, which she watched, amused, for a moment before she hoisted the kettle on its side, straining the fat through several layers of cloth. Close by, a saddlemaker slammed down the front shutters of his stall and padlocked them shut.

Prosperous, thought the Terran woman in Darkovan clothing. *He can afford a Terran metal lock.* Darkover, Cottman IV to the Terrans, was a metal-poor planet. Other vendors were tying their shutters down with ropes and cords and trusting to the night watchman to notice any unauthorized person fumbling with the ropes. A baker was doing haphazard business selling the last few stale buns in her stall; she looked up as the Terran messenger passed with her quick stride.

"Hey there! Vanessa n'ha Yllana, where are you going in such a rush?" Vanessa was moving so swiftly that she had gone several steps past the baker's stall before she really heard the words. She stopped and came back, smiling tentatively at the plump woman who was making change for a small boy with a bun in his fist.

"Sherna," she acknowledged, "I didn't see you."

"I could have imagined that," said the baker with a grin. "Striding along as if you were on your way to exterminate a colony of banshees, at the *least,* my dear! Have a bun?" When Vanessa hesitated, she urged, "Go on, take one, there's no sense in hauling this lot all the way back to the Guild-house; it's not as if there were enough left for everyone to have one at supper!"

Thus urged, Vanessa picked up one of the leftover buns and bit into it. It was hearty, made with nut-flour to eke out the grain, and sweet with dried fruits. She stood nibbling, moving automatically to one side as the stall-keeper a few feet away began to bumble about with a broom, sweeping the front of his shop.

"Were you going to the Guild-house, or on some other errand?" Sherna asked.

"To the Guild-house," Vanessa admitted. "I should have thought to come here at once so that I could go through the streets with you." Secretly she was annoyed at herself; where had her mind been?

"Good," Sherna said. "You can help me carry the baskets. But tonight is not a Bridge meeting, is it?"

"Oh, no, no, not that I remember," Vanessa said, picking up one of the breadbaskets. "I have a message for Margali n'ha Ys-abet. I cannot see why the Guild-mothers refuse to have a communicator in the Guild-house; it would save sending messengers through the streets this way, especially after dark."

Sherna smiled indulgently. "You *Terranan,*" she said, laughing. "So that the noise of the thing can invade our privacy in season and out, to save a messenger the trouble of walking a few minutes' walk in good weather? Ah, your poor abused feet, my heart aches for the lazy things!"

"The weather isn't always so good," Vanessa protested, but the argument was an old one, habitual between the women, and the protests were good-natured.

Both women were members of the Bridge Society, *Penta Cori'yo,* which had been formed a few years ago, when members of the Free Amazons—*Comhi Letziis,* the Guild of Renunciates—had been the first Darkovans to offer themselves for work in the Terran Headquarters; as medical technicians, as mountain guides and travel-advisers, as translators and language teachers. The Bridge Society offered a home, a place to live, friends among Darkovan women; for Terrans who agreed to live by Renunciate laws, but could not commit themselves fully to the Guild-house, there was even a specially modified form of the Oath. The Bridge maintained homelike quarters for Darkovan women, mostly Renunciates, required by their work to live in the Terran HQ.

It was open to any Darkovan woman who had worked for three of the forty-day moon cycles in the Terran HQ, or any Terran woman who spent the same time within a Guild-house. Sherna n'ha Marya, a Renunciate from Thendara Guild-house, had worked half a year as a translator, helping to compile standard works in *casta* and *cahuenga*, the two languages of Darkover. Vanessa ryn Erin, a graduate of the Terran Intelligence Academy on Alpha, had now been four years on Darkover, and had lived in the Guild-house most of the last year, preparing for field work outside Headquarters.

Sherna handed the last of the sweet buns to a woman with a small child in her arms, another clutching her skirt. "Take them for the little ones. No, no," she protested as the woman began to fumble for coins, "they'd only go into the pail for the hens. So, Vanessa, we managed that well, only two loaves to carry back, and the kitchen-women can make us a bread-pudding with them."

"Are we ready to go back to the Guild-house, then?"

"There's no hurry," Sherna said, and Vanessa had been on Darkover long enough not to protest, despite the urgency of her errand. She helped Sherna tie up the front shutters of the bake-stall in leisurely fashion, and collect the scattered baskets.

There was a sudden flurry of activity at one of the gates visible from the marketplace, and a caravan of pack animals clattered over the stones. A cluster of small children playing king-of-the-mountain from the top of an abandoned stall scampered out of the way. A tall, thin woman, clad in the ordinary garb of a Renunciate, loose tunic and trousers tucked into low boots, carrying an Amazon knife as long as a short sword, strode toward them.

"Rafi," Sherna greeted her. "I didn't know you'd be back tonight."

"Neither did I," said Rafaella n'ha Doria. "These people have been bumbling about the pass for three days. I think the pack animals smelled home, or they'd still be wandering up there looking at the green grass growing and hunting for mushrooms on apple trees. Let me go and pick up my pay. I'd have left them at the city gates, but I'm sure they'd have lost themselves between here and their stables, judging by the way they've behaved all along. And Zandru whip me with scorpions if I ever again accept a commission before it's firmly understood who's bossing the trail! Believe me—I could tell you some stories—" She hurried off to talk briefly with the head of the caravan. Some money changed hands. Vanessa saw Rafaella carefully stop to count it—even the Terran woman knew what an insult that was, in an open marketplace. Then Rafi came back to them; greeted Vanessa with a casual nod, swung the last of the wicker bread-baskets to her shoulder, and the three women set off together through the cobbled streets.

"What are you doing here, Vanessa? News from HQ?"

"Not much," Vanessa said evasively. "One of our planes from Map and Ex is down in the Hellers."

"Maybe there will be work for us, then," Rafaella said. "Last year, when they sent us out on a salvage contract for a downed plane, there was plenty for everyone to do." Rafaella was a travel-organizer, and was in considerable demand among Terrans who must venture into the little-known and trackless mountains of the northern Domains.

"I don't know if that's what they have in mind. I don't think it's where anyone can salvage it," Vanessa said. The women walked along silently through one of the quieter streets of the city, and paused before a large building of stone, turning a windowless front wall on the street. A small placard on the front door said:

THENDARA HOUSE
GUILD OF RENUNCIATES

Sherna and Vanessa were laden with the baskets; Rafaella alone had a free hand to ring the bell. In the front hall, a heavily pregnant woman let them in, closing and locking the door after them. "Oh, Vanessa, is it the night for the Bridge Society? I had forgotten." But she gave Vanessa no chance to answer. "Rafi, your daughter is here!"

"I thought Doria was still busy among the *Terranan*," said Rafaella, not very graciously. "What is she doing here, Laurinda?"

"She is giving a lecture, with the box which makes lighted pictures on the wall, to seven women who are to be trained as healing assistants, beginning next tenday," said Laurinda. "'*Nurses*,' the *Terranan* call them, isn't that a funny word? It sounds as if they were going to work breast-feeding *Terranan* babies, and that's not what they're being trained for at all. Just caring for the sick and bedridden, and looking after wounds and the like. They must be nearly finished now; you could go in and speak to her."

Vanessa asked, "Is Margali n'ha Ysabet within the house? I am here with a message for her."

"You are fortunate," the woman said, "she is to set out tomorrow morning for Armida, with Jaelle n'ha Melora. They would have gone today, before noon, but one of the horses cast a shoe and by the time the smith had done with her work, it was threatening rain; so they put off their departure till tomorrow."

"If Jaelle is still in the house," Rafaella said, "I should like to speak with her."

"She is helping Doria with the lecture; we all know she has worked among the *Terranan*," Laurinda said. "Why don't you look inside and see? They're in the music room."

"I will go and put away my baskets first," said Sherna, but Vanessa followed Rafaella toward the music room at the back of the building, and opened the door, quietly slipping inside.

A young woman, her hair cropped Renunciate style, was just finishing a slide lecture; she ticked off several points on her fingers, clicking off a colored slide as the women entered.

"You will be expected to write accurately; they will expect you to read well, and to remember what you read, and to write it down precisely. You will be given preparatory lectures in anatomy, in personal hygiene, in scientific observation and how to record what you observe, before ever you are allowed even to bring a patient a tray of food or a bedpan. You will work as assistants and aides, helping the qualified nurses to care for patients, from the very first day of your lectures; and as soon as you are taught any nursing procedures you will be allowed to do them at once on the wards. Not until your second half year of training will you be allowed to assist the surgeons, or to study midwifery. It is hard, dirty work, but I found it very satisfying, and I think you will too. Any questions?"

One of the young women curled up on the floor listening raised her hand.

"Mirella n'ha Anjali?"

"Why must we have lessons in personal hygiene? Do those Terrans think that Darkovan people are dirty or slovenly, that they must teach us this?"

"You must not take it personally," said Doria. "Even their own women must learn new and different ways of cleanliness when they study nursing; cleanliness for everyday use, and surgical cleanliness for when they must work around people who are very ill, or who have unhealed wounds, or are exposed to disease germs and contagion, are not at all the same, as you will learn."

Another woman asked, "I have heard that the *uniforms*—" she stumbled over the unfamiliar word, "worn by the Terran workers are as immodest as the wear of a prostitute. Must we wear them, and will it violate our Oath?"

Doria indicated the white tunic and trousers she was wearing. She said, "Customs differ. Their standards of modesty are different from ours. But the Bridge Society has been successful in creating a compromise. Darkovan women employed by Medic wear a special uniform designed not to offend our standards, and it's so comfortable and warm that many of the Terran nurses have chosen to adopt it. And before you ask, the symbol on the breast of the uniform—" She indicated the red emblem, a staff with entwined snakes. "It's a very old Terran symbol indicating Medical service. You will be expected to know a dozen such symbols in order to find your way around the HQ."

"What does it mean?" one young girl, not more than fifteen, asked.

"I asked my own teacher this. It is supposed to be the symbol of a very old Terran God of Healing. No one now worships him, but the symbol has remained. Any other questions?"

"I have heard," said one woman, "that the Terrans are licentious, that they regard Darkovan women as being—being like the women of the spaceport bars. Is this true? Must we carry knives to protect ourselves there?"

Doria chuckled. She said, "Jaelle n'ha Melora lived among them for a time. I will let her answer that."

A small woman with flaming red hair stood up at the back of the room. "I cannot speak for all Terran men, she said, "even among the Gods, Zandru and Aldones have not the same attributes, and a *cristoforo* monk behaves differently than a farmer in the Valeron plains. There are boorish men and roughnecks among the Terrans as well as on the streets of Thendara. But I can assure you that among the Terrans in the Medic Department, you need not fear discourtesy or molestation; their Medics are sworn by oath to treat everyone, patients or professional associates, with proper courtesy. In fact, it may disturb you that they will not seem to take any note of whether you are a man, a woman, or a piece of machinery, but will treat you as if you were novice Keepers. As for carrying knives, it is not the custom among the Terrans, and you will not be allowed to bring any weapons for defense into the Medic Department. But then, the Terrans will not be carrying them either: it is forbidden by their regulations. The only knives you will see anywhere in Medic are the surgeon's scalpels. Are there any other questions?"

Vanessa realized that the questions could go on until the bell rang for the evening meal. She said, from where she stood by the door, "I have a question. Is Margali n'ha Ysabet within this room?"

"I have not seen her since noonday," Doria said, then saw Rafaella in the doorway beside Vanessa.

"Mother," she called, and hurried to Rafaella, enveloping her in an enormous hug. Jaelle, smiling, came to her old friend, and the three women stood for a moment embracing.

"It's wonderful to see you, Jaelle. Damn, how long has it been? For the past three years we've kept missing each other; whenever I'm in Thendara, you're out at Armida, and whenever you come to the city, I'm likely to be somewhere north of Caer Donn!"

"It's only luck this time; Margali and I were supposed to leave at noon," Jaelle said. "I have been away from my daughter for a pair of tendays."

"She must be a big girl now, Dorilys n'ha Jaelle," said Rafaella, laughing. "Five, isn't she, or six by now? Old enough to bring her to the house for fostering."

"There's time enough for that," said Jaelle, and looked away, greeting Vanessa with a nod. "I know I met you a few days ago at the Bridge Society meeting, but I have forgotten your name."

"Vanessa," Doria reminded her.

"I am sorry to break up your lecture," Vanessa said, looking at the young women who were putting away the cushions and scattering about the room, but Doria shrugged.

"It's just as well. All the serious questions had been answered.

But, they are nervous about their new work, and would have kept thinking up silly questions to be answered until the supper-bell!" She went back to the center of the room, and began packing up her slides and the projector. "How fortunate you came. You can return these to Medic for me tonight, and save me a trip through the streets at night. I borrowed them from the Chief of Nursing Education. You'll take them back when you go, won't you? Or are you spending the night?"

"No, I came here with a message for Margali—"

Doria shrugged again. "I am sure she's somewhere in the House. It's nearly time for the supper-bell. You will be sure to see her there!"

Vanessa had been long enough on Darkover, and lived long enough in Guild-houses, to be accustomed to this casual attitude about time. She was still Terran enough to feel that they really should have sent someone to fetch Margali, or at least told her where to go and find her, but she was on the Darkovan side of town, now; resigning herself, she told Doria that she would be glad to return the slide equipment to the Medic Department for her—actually, she felt it was a considerable imposition, and she was a little annoyed at Doria for asking. But Doria was a sister in the Guild, and there was no courteous way to refuse a request of this sort.

"Is there any news yet about the plane that's down in the Hellers?" Doria asked.

Vanessa was saved from answering by a scornful sound from Rafaella.

"Foolish *Terranan*," Rafaella said. "What do they expect? Even we poor benighted souls without the benefit of Terran science—" She made the words sound like a gutter obscenity— "know that it is folly to travel past the Hellers, at any season, and even a Terran should know there's nothing north of Nevarsin to the Wall Around the World, but frozen wasteland! I say, good riddance to bad rubbish! If they send their foolish planes there, they must expect to lose them!"

"I think you are too hard on them, Rafi," Doria said. "Is the pilot anyone I know, Vanessa?"

"She is not a member of the Bridge Society. Her name is Anders."

"Alexis Anders? I have met her," said Jaelle. "They have not recovered the plane? How dreadful!"

Rafaella put an arm around Jaelle's waist. "Let's not waste time talking of the Terrans, *Shaya*, love, we have so little time together these days. Your daughter is such a big girl now, when will you bring her to the Guild-house for fostering? And then perhaps you will come back too."

Jaelle's face clouded. "I don't know if I can bring her here at all, Rafi. There are—difficulties."

Rafaella's quick temper flared. "So it is true. I did not believe it of you, Jaelle, that you would go meekly back to your high-born *Comyn* kindred, when they had cast you off! But then, perhaps it was always certain that the *Comyn* would never let you go, certainly not when you bore a child to one of them! I wonder that no one has yet called your Oath in question!"

Now Jaelle's face, too, bore the high color of anger; she had, Vanessa thought, the temper associated traditionally, by Terrans, with her flaming red hair.

"How dare you say that to me, Rafaella?"

"Do you deny that the father of your child is the *Comyn* lord Damon Ridenow?"

"I deny nothing," Jaelle said angrily, "but what of that? You of all people, to reproach me with that, Rafi! Have you not three sons?"

Rafaella quoted from the Oath of the Renunciates:

"*Men dia pre' zhiuro*, from this day forth, I swear I will bear no child to any man for house or heritage, clan or inheritance, pride or posterity; I swear that I alone will determine rearing and fosterage of any child I bear, without regard to any man's place, position, or pride."

"How dare you quote the Oath to me in that tone and imply that I have broken it? Cleindori is *my* child. Her father is *Comyn*; if you knew him, you would know how little that means to him. My daughter is an Aillard; the house of Aillard, alone among the Seven Domains, has counted lineage, from the times of Hastur and Cassilda themselves, in the mother's line. I bore my daughter for my own house, not for any man's! What Amazon has not done the same, unless she is so persistent a lover of women that she will not let any man touch her even for that purpose." But Jaelle's anger ebbed; she put her arm around Rafaella again. "Oh, let's not quarrel, Rafi, you are almost my oldest friend, and do you think I have forgotten the years when we were partners? But you are not the keeper of my conscience."

Rafaella still held herself spitefully aloof.

"No, that office is now filled by that he-Keeper of the Forbidden Tower—Damon Ridenow, is that his name? How can I possibly compete with that?"

Jaelle shook her head. "Whatever you think, Rafi, I keep my Oath." Rafaella still looked skeptical, but at that moment a mellow-chimed bell sounded through the hall, announcing that in a few minutes supper would be served.

"Supper, and I am still wearing all the muck of the pack animals and the marketplace! I must go and wash, even if I am not to be one of Doria's nurses! Come along up with me, Shaya. Let's not quarrel, after all, I see you so seldom now, we have no time to waste in arguing about what we can't change. Vanessa, will you come with us?"

"I think not, I must look for Margali n'ha Ysabet." Vanessa watched Jaelle and her friend run up the stairs, and went toward the door of the dining room. There was a good smell of cooking, something hot and savory, the yeasty smell of fresh bread just taken from the oven, and a clatter of dishes where the women helping in the kitchen were setting out bowls and cups on the tables.

If Magdalen Lorne, known in the Guild-house as Margali, was in the Guild-house at all, she must pass through here on her way to supper. Vanessa wondered if she would know her by sight. She had met her only three or four times, the last time only a tenday ago at a meeting of the Bridge Society within this House.

At that moment, she looked up and saw Magdalen Lorne coming toward her, along the hall from the greenhouse at the back of the Guild-house. Her arms were full of early melons. At her side, also carrying melons, was a tall, scarred, rangy woman—an *emmasca*, a woman who had undergone the dangerous, illegal and frequently fatal neutering operation. Vanessa knew the woman's name, Camilla n'ha Kyria; knew that she had once been a mercenary soldier, was now a teacher of sword-play in the Guild-house, and knew that she was reputed to be Magdalen Lorne's lover. That still embarrassed Vanessa a little, though not as much as it would have done before she had dwelt for months in the Guild-house and knew how commonplace and unremarkable it was. It no longer seemed to her mysterious and perverse; but she was Terran, and it embarrassed her.

Even before she had come to Darkover, since first she had gone into training for Intelligence work, Vanessa ryn Erin had known of the legendary Magdalen Lorne.

She knew most of the story: that she had been born on Darkover, in the mountains near Caer Donn, before the building of Thendara Spaceport, so that Magda had been brought up with Darkovan children and learned the language as a native. She knew that Magda had been trained, like herself, in the Intelligence School on Alpha, by Vanessa's own chief, Cholayna Ares, who had at that time been head of Intelligence Training, and had only later come to Darkover. She knew that Magda had, for a time, been married to the present Terran Legate, Peter Haldane, and that she had been the first woman to do Intelligence fieldwork on Darkover, one of the very few women who had ever done so. She knew that Magda had been the first to infiltrate the Guild of Renunciates, had even managed to take the Oath, and had quixotically insisted on keeping it, even to serving the full housebound time, which, before the creation of the Bridge Society, had been required in unmitigated form even of Terrans. She knew that, a few years ago, Magda had left the Guild-house and was on some mysterious detached duty at Armida. This she had known of the legend. But she had met the living woman only a few days ago, and still was not accustomed to her. Somehow she had expected her to be larger than life.

In the Guild-house, courtesy demanded that she use only Lorne's Darkovan name.

"Margali n'ha Ysabet? May I speak with you for a minute?"

"Vanessa? How nice to see you." Magda Lorne, Margali, seemed tall, though she was not much over average height; in her middle thirties, with heavy dark hair, cropped short in Renunciate style, shadowing her forehead; she had deep-set, lively gray eyes which rested on Vanessa curiously. "Here, take some of these, will you?" She shoved some of the armload of melons into Vanessa's hands; sniffed, and made a wry face. "Smells like tripe stew. You can have my share. Will I ever forget how I hated it, my first few months here? But maybe you like it, some people do. Never mind, there'll be plenty of bread and cheese, and melons for dessert. Camilla, give her some of those, if you drop them here in the hall we'll be chasing them all over the place—and if any of them smash open, what a mess to clean away! And I, for one, don't feel like scrubbing floors this week!"

Camilla, who was even taller than Magda, loaded Vanessa's arms with some of the melons she was carrying. They smelled sweet and fragrant, with the earthy smell of the greenhouse, but Vanessa resented the intrusion on her mission. Camilla saw her frown.

"What are you doing here, Vanessa? If it is Bridge Society night, I had forgotten."

Vanessa thought, irritably, that if one more person said that to her she would swear out loud. "No—but I have a message for you, Margali, from Cholayna n'ha Chandria." Vanessa used the Guild-house name, and Magda shook her head in puzzlement.

"Damn the woman, what can she want? I talked with her three days ago, and she knew I was leaving. Jaelle and I should have gone this afternoon. In case you'd forgotten, we have children at Armida."

"It's an assignment. She said it was important, possibly a matter of life or death," Vanessa told her.

Camilla said, "Cholayna doesn't exaggerate. If she said *life or death*, she meant it."

"I'm sure of it," Magda said, frowning. "But do you have any idea what It's all about, Vanessa? I don't want to get hung up here. As I said, I'm needed at Armida. Jaelle's daughter is old enough to be left, but Shaya's not quite two years old, and if I stay much longer in the city she'll forget what I look like!"

"I couldn't say," Vanessa evaded, carefully not saying that she didn't know. She had been briefed on why Magda had left the Guild-house, and something from the most secret and classified files had been made available to her about Magda's work at Armida, but not nearly enough to understand it.

She could not imagine any conceivable reason why an Intelligence Agent of Magda's status should want to burden herself with a half-Darkovan child, and like all women who are childless by choice, she judged Magda harshly. Although she admired the legend, she was not yet accustomed to the living reality of the woman. Walking at Magda's side, it confused her to note that Magda was actually an inch or two shorter than she was herself.

"It's not all that late. Have we time for supper here? No, I suppose if Cholayna said life or death, she means exactly that. Let me go and tell Jaelle n'ha Melora that I may not be able to leave at first light, after all." But her face was grim as she started up the stairs.

"Let me tell you, Vanessa, if this is a nonsense of some sort, Cholayna will wish she had never learned the way to the Guild-house. I'm leaving tomorrow, and that's that!"

She smiled suddenly as she started up the stairs, and for the first time, Vanessa sensed, behind the matter-of-fact woman, the powerful personality who had become the legend.

"Oh, well, if it had to come, what better time? At least I'll miss the tripe stew."

Chapter 2

It was pitch-dark now, and raining, spits and slashes of sleet in the nightly rain. The streets were all but empty when Magda and Vanessa finally crossed the square facing the entrance to the Terran HQ and gave passwords to the Spaceforce man in black leather uniform. He was bundled to the neck in a black wool scarf, which was not regulation, and there was a heavy down jacket over the uniform which was not regulation either, but on this particular planet, at night, should have been. Magda knew they winked at it, but that wasn't enough; they should have changed the rules to authorize it.

And they think the Darkovan people are unwilling to change their primitive ways!

Magda did not know most of the new Spaceforce people now. Even a year ago, she would have introduced herself; now it seemed pointless. She would be going back to Armida in the morning; that was where her life was laid now. She had remained accessible to Cholayna to help in the founding and implementing of the Bridge Society, but now it was working well on its own. And now she had a child to bind her further to Armida and the Forbidden Tower. Cholayna Ares, Head of Intelligence on Cottman IV, would simply have to get along without her.

If she thinks she can send me into the field at a moment's notice, she can simply think again.

Magda had lived so long under the Darkovan sun that she flinched at the bright yellow, Earth-normal lights as they came

on inside the main HQ building. But she stepped into the elevator without hesitation. She had acquired a certain impatience
with these Terran conveniences, but she wasn't going to walk up
forty-two flights of stairs to make her point.

At this hour the sector given over to Terran Intelligence was
dark and deserted; only from the office of Cholayna Ares was
there a gleam of light, and Magda realized that if Cholayna
awaited her in the office, instead of sending for her in her comfortable living quarters, there was something very important in
the wind.

"Cholayna? I came as soon as I could. But what in the
world—this one or any other—is so important that it couldn't
wait until morning?"

"I was afraid that by morning you would be gone," Cholayna
answered. "I wasn't eager to send a messenger after you to
Armida. But I would have done it if I'd had to."

Cholayna Ares, Terran Intelligence, was a very tall woman,
with a shock of silver-white hair in astonishing contrast to the
darkness of her black skin. She rose to greet Magda; gestured
her to take a seat. Magda remained standing.

"It's good of you to come, Magda."

"It's not good at all, you didn't give me a choice," Magda retorted irritably. "You said something about life and death. I
didn't think you'd say that lightly. Was I wrong?"

"Magda—do you remember an Agent named Anders? Alexis.
She came here from Magaera two years ago. Basic Training in
Intelligence; shifted here to Mapping and Exploring."

"Lexie Anders? I didn't know her well," Magda said, "and
she made it very clear she didn't want to know me any better.
Later, when I suggested that if she wanted to know how to relate
to the women here, she join the Bridge Society, she laughed in
my face. I must admit I've never especially liked her. Why?"

"I think you were too hard on her," Cholayna said. "She
came here and immediately found herself up against the 'Lorne
Legend.' " Magda made an impatient gesture, but Cholayna
went on, imperturbable.

"No, no, my dear, I'm perfectly serious. You had done more,

on a world where in general it was impossible for a woman to accomplish anything at all in Intelligence work, than Anders had accomplished in her first three assignments. Whatever she did, she found herself competing with you, and in consequence she knew she was outclassed before she began. I wasn't at all surprised when she shifted to M-and-Ex."

"I can't see why she thought she had to compete—" Magda began irritably; but Cholayna brushed that aside.

"Be that as it may. Her plane went down over the Hellers three days ago. We got a message that she was lost, couldn't navigate—something wrong with the computer compass. Then nothing. Dead silence, not even a tracking beam to the satellite. Not even a signal from the black box."

"That seems very unlikely," Magda said. The "black box," or automatic recording device in a mapping plane, was supposed to keep sending out signals for retrieval, at least with the newer models, for at least three years after the plane went down. Magda knew Alexis Anders well enough to know that she would not have allowed herself to be sent out with anything less than the very newest in equipment.

"Unlikely or not, it happened, Magda. The plane was giving out no signals, the black box and tracking recorder were silent, the satellite couldn't trace a thing."

"She crashed, then?" Magda felt cheap; she had not particularly liked Lexie, but she wished now she had not spoken quite so unkindly of the woman—now, presumably, dead.

Of course, there had been Terrans who had survived the crash of a Mapping plane, and found shelter, and in at least one case, Magda knew, a new life, and a new home. But not in the Hellers, the wildest, most unknown, trackless and uninhabited mountains on Darkover; perhaps the worst on any settled or inhabitable planet. It was almost impossible to survive in the Hellers, at least in winter, for more than a few hours, without special survival gear. And beyond the Hellers, as far as anyone knew (and now the Empire knew Cottman IV considerably better than the Darkovans themselves), was nothing; only the impenetrable mountain range known as the Wall Around the World. And beyond the Wall, nothing but barren icy wastes stretching from pole to pole.

"So she's presumed dead, then? Too bad." Anything further would be hypocrisy. Lexie had disliked Magda quite as much as Magda had disliked Lexie.

"No," said Cholayna, "she's down in Medic."

"You recovered the plane? But—"

"No, we *didn't* recover the plane, do you think I would have brought you across the city in a rush like this for a routine rescue or debriefing?"

"You keep telling me what it isn't," Magda said, "but you haven't given me any idea, yet, what this is. . . ."

Still, Cholayna hesitated. At last, she said, quite formally, "Magda, I remind you that you are still a sworn Intelligence Agent, and are covered by the Official Secrets Provision of Civil Service—"

"Cholayna, I can't imagine what you're talking about," Magda began, and now she was seriously annoyed. What was all this rigmarole? She had never questioned her oath to Intelligence, except during the painful identity crisis of her first half-year among the Renunciates. There had then been no Bridge Society to help in this kind of transition. She had been the first.

"You know, I fought to keep you on inactive duty status, instead of accepting your resignation," Cholayna said deliberately. "One of the tenets of Intelligence work, and this applies to all Empire planets, incidentally, not just Darkover, is this: when one of ours goes over the wall—goes native, acquires a native spouse and children—the rule of thumb is that it makes him a better Agent. Although there is always a question in the record about any decision he might make which could possibly create a conflict as to where his personal interest lies. I'm sure you know that."

"I could quote you pages of regulations about it," Magda said dryly. "I was prepared for this. I assume it applies to me because I've had a child, though as far as you know I'm not married. Right? Well, you're wrong."

"Are you married, then?"

"Not in any way you'd recognize under Terran law. But I have sworn the Oath of Freemates with Jaelle n'ha Melora: by Darkovan law, that creates an analogy to marriage. Specifically, it means that if either of us should die, the other has both a legal right *and a legal obligation* to foster and act as guardian of the other's child or children, exactly as a wife or husband would do. Specifically this oath overrides, by law, any claim of the children's fathers. So for all practical purposes, the situation is identical with marriage. Is that clear?"

Cholayna said, her voice hard, "I'm sure Xenoanthropology will find it fascinating. I'll make sure they get it from the records. But I wasn't inquiring into the details of your private life."

"I wasn't giving them." Magda's voice was equally unyielding, although in fact Cholayna was one of the few people alive to whom she might have given such details if asked. "I was apprising you of the legal situation. I assume, then, that those standard assumptions about Empire men with a native wife and children apply to me, and I am expected to behave accordingly."

"You assume wrongly, Magda. Yes, on the books, It's true; but in actual practice—and this is classified information I'm giving you—on the occasions, and incidentally they are very rare, when a woman goes over the wall—classified practice is to deactivate her Intelligence rating immediately. The reasons given for this are numerous, but they all boil down to the same thing. Official Intelligence policy assumes that a man can maintain an objective detachment from his wife and children, more easily than you or I could, because of—Magda, remember I'm quoting, this isn't my personal belief—because of her deeper involvement. Presumably, a husband can detach himself from a wife easier than vice versa, and the children are, again supposedly, closer to the woman who bore them than they are to the man who fathered them."

Magda swore. "I should have expected something like this. Do I have to tell you what I think of the *reish?*" The Darkovan word was a childish vulgarity, which meant literally *stable-sweepings,* but her face twisted in real anger as she said it.

"Of course you don't. What you think of it and what I think of it are very much the same, but what either of us thinks, is completely beside the point. I'm talking about official policy. I was supposed to accept your resignation the first time you handed it in."

"I suppose it's also in those extremely confidential and classified private files that I am reputed to be a lover of women?" Magda asked with a wry twist of her mouth. "I know the *classified* policy regarding lovers of men, among Terrans—legally they're protected by official policies of non-discrimination. Practically, you know and I know that they're hassled on any pretext anyone can find."

"You're wrong," Cholayna said, "or at least it's not true in every case. There's a legal loophole: a man who is living with a wife and children, no matter what his private preference, cannot officially be classified homosexual. In practice, he's covered, and can fight any such action. You covered yourself against any such action when your child was born, Magda. Nobody really cares whether you married the father or not. But by immunizing yourself from *that* kind of persecution, you invoked the other one: now it's assumed that you are completely unsuited to Intelligence work because your loyalty would be to your child or children, and to the man who fathered them. I should, according to the Code, have accepted your resignation the first time you handed it in."

"I would have been perfectly agreeable to that," said Magda.

"I know. Goodness knows, you've given me opportunities enough," Cholayna said. "You've handed it in so regularly every season that I've wondered if it's just your way of celebrating Midsummer and Midwinter! But I still think I'm seeing a little farther than you do. We can't afford to lose qualified women this way."

"Why are you telling me all this?"

"By way of explaining to you why this request is unofficial, and why, just the same, you have to listen to me, and help me. Magda, you have the ultimate weapon over me; you can tell me where to go and what to do when I get there, and according to regulations I have no recourse at all. The legal situation is, you've gone over the wall, and I have no right to call you in. But I'm bucking regulations because you are the one person who might be able to make sense of what's happening now."

"And so, finally, we come around to it," Magda said, "the reason you hauled me out on a rainy night—"

"All nights here are rainy, but that's beside the point, too."

"Lexie Anders?"

"Ten minutes or so before her plane went down, she transmitted a message via satellite; she was approaching the Wall Around the World, and was preparing to turn back. Her final message said she'd spotted something, like a city, which she had *not* found on the radar map. She was descending to five thousand meters to investigate.

Then we lost her, and the plane. Nothing more. Not even the black box, as I said. As far as HQ or the satellites know, the plane vanished, black box and all, right out of the atmosphere of the planet. But Lexie Anders appeared this morning at the gates of the HQ, out of uniform, without her identity cards. And her mind had been wiped. Wiped clean. Complete amnesia. Magda, she can hardly speak Terran Standard! She speaks the native language of her home planet—Vainwal—but on the baby-talk level. So obviously, we can't ask her what happened."

"But—all this is impossible, Cholayna! I don't understand—"

"Neither do we. And that's an understatement. And it's no use questioning Anders, in her condition."

"So why did you send for me?" Magda asked. But she was afraid she knew, and it made her angry. Although as far as Magda had ever known Cholayna had no *laran,* the woman seemed to sense her annoyance and hesitated; then, as Magda had known she would, she said it anyhow.

"You're a psi-technician, Magda. The nearest one we have, the only properly trained one this side of the Alpha Colony. You can find out what really happened."

* * *

Magda was silent for a moment, staring angrily at Cholayna. She should have expected this. It was, she thought, her own fault for not breaking a tie that had ceased to have any meaning. As Cholayna had reminded her, she had tried to resign from Terran Intelligence, and Cholayna had dissuaded her; Magda, she said, was best qualified to build closer communications, ties, a bridge between the world of Magda's birth and the Darkovan world Magda had chosen for her own. Magda had wanted this too: the Bridge Society was living proof of her desire to strengthen that tie. Yet when Magda had left the Guild-house to become part of the only *laran* circle of trained psychics which worked its trained matrix circle outside the carefully surrounded, safeguarded precincts of a Tower, she should have known this problem would again become acute.

It was not that the Empire had no command of psi techniques. Not as common, nor as well developed as they were on Darkover. Few planets in the known universe had the displayed skill, the taken-for-granted potential of telepaths and other psi-sensitive talents which the Darkovans called *laran*. As far as was known, Darkover was unique in that respect.

But these talents, it was now known, were an ineradicable part of the human mind. Although there were still a few determined skeptics—and for some reason, determined skepticism was a self-fulfilling prophecy, so that skeptics rarely developed any psi skills of any kind—where there were humans, there were the psi skills which were part of the human mind. And so there were trained telepaths, though not many, and even a few mechanical psi-probes had been developed which could do much the same work.

"Only there are none on Darkover; none nearer than the Intelligence School on Alpha," said Cholayna, "and we've got to know what happened to her. Don't you understand, Magda? We've got to know!"

When Magda did not answer, she drew a long breath, loud in the room. "Listen, Magda, you know what this means as well as I do! You know there's nothing out there beyond the Hellers, nothing! So she signals she's spotted something out there, and then she goes down. Nothing on the satellite picture, no black box, no plane recorder—nothing. But if there's nothing out there, she's still gone down with her plane. We've lost planes from Map and Ex before this. We've lost pilots, too. But she didn't go down. Something out there grabbed her—*and then gave her back! In this condition!"*

Magda thought this over for a moment. She said at last, "It means there has to be something out there; something outside the Wall Around the World. But that's impossible." She had seen the weather-satellite pictures of Cottman IV. A cold planet, a planet tilted strongly on its axis by the presence of the high himals of the Hellers, the Wall Around the World, amounting to a "third pole." A planet inhabitable only in a relatively small part of one continent, and elsewhere a frozen wasteland with no signs of life.

"You're beginning to see what I mean," Cholayna said grimly. "And you're trained in what the Darkovans call *laran*."

"I was a fool ever to let you know that!" Magda knew it was her own fault for retaining even this fragile bond. When she had outgrown the ties of the Guild-house, she should have done what Andrew Carr had done before her, and allowed the Terrans, perhaps even the Renunciates, to think her dead.

In the Forbidden Tower, she had found a home, a world of others like herself, who belonged nowhere else in worlds that demanded they define themselves in narrow categories. Callista, Keeper, exiled from her Tower because she could give up neither her human love nor the exercise of the powerful *laran* for which she had nearly given her life. Andrew Carr, Terran, who had discovered his own powers and found a new world and a new life. Damon, exiled from a Tower, the only man who had had the courage to demand what no man had been allowed in centuries: he had become Keeper of the Tower they called Forbidden, and fought for the right to establish his Tower in the open. There were others who had come to it, outcasts from the regular Towers, or those who despite talent would never have been admitted to a Tower; and now, among them, herself and Jaelle.

And she had been foolish enough to let Cholayna know something—*anything*, of this. . . .

"You want me to psi-probe her, Cholayna? Why can't you get a technician out from Alpha? You could send a message and have one here in a tenday."

."No, Magda. If she stays like this, she could drop into catatonia and we'd never know. Besides, if there is something out there, we have to know it. *Now*. We can't send another plane up until we know what happened to that one."

" There's nothing out there," Magda said, with more harshness than she intended. "Satellite pictures don't lie."

"That's what I've always said." Cholayna stared at the lighted panels on her desktop; when Magda said nothing, she got up and came around the desk and grabbed Magda's shoulders. "Damn it, something happened to her! I can understand the plane going down. I've never tried to fly over the Hellers myself, but I've talked to some who have. What scares me is how she got back here, and the condition she's in. If it could happen to Lexie, it could happen to anyone. Not a single person in Mapping and Exploring, or anywhere else outside the Trade City, is safe until we know what took her and her plane—and how, and why—*they*—sent her back. You've got to help us, Magda."

Magda walked away from Cholayna, and stared out at the lights of the Spaceport below. Up here, she could see the whole of Terran HQ, and across the city to the Old Town. The contrast was definite, the glaring lights of the Terran Trade City, the dim scattered lights of the Old Town, already all but dark at this hour. Somewhere in that darkness lay the Guild-house and her friends, while out beyond the pass that was just a blacker darkness against the night sky lay the estate of Armida, a little more than a day's ride north, where was her new world. If only she could consult with one of them, with their Keeper Damon, with Andrew, who like herself had fought the battle between his Terran self and his Darkovan world. But they were *there*, and she was *here*, and it was her own unique predicament and her own unanswerable problem.

"I'm the last person Lexie would want mucking around in her mind, believe me."

Cholayna said, and there was no possible answer, "She wouldn't want to stay like this forever, either. She's down in Medic, in Isolation. We haven't wanted anyone else to know what happened."

Some day, Magda thought, it was going to occur to the Terran HQ personnel that there were some things even they couldn't control. She didn't give a fundamental damn whether the Terrans kept up their pretense of omnipotence. But there was a fellow human being, a woman, caught up in the gears. She said, more roughly than she intended, "Let's get on with it, then. But I'm not a trained psi-technician, so don't blame me if all I can do is make things worse. I'll do my best. That's all I can say."

Chapter 3

Magda hated to ring the night-bell at the Guild-house; it meant that someone would have to be roused, come down the stairs and open the bolted door. Yet she preferred that, inconvenient as it was, to accepting Cholayna's offer to find her a place to stay either in Unmarried Personnel Living Quarters, or even in the Bridge Society Hostel, where some of the Darkovan nurses in training had their lodgings.

She stood shivering on the steps, for even in high summer it was chilly at this hour, listening to the clang of the bell inside. Then she heard a long scraping of the heavy bolt, and at last the door opened grudgingly, and a young woman's voice asked, "Who is it? Do you want the midwife?"

"No, Cressa. It is I, Margali n'ha Ysabet," Magda said, and came inside. "I am truly sorry to disturb you. I'll just go quietly up to bed."

"It's all right, I wasn't asleep. Someone came for Keitha just a little while ago. Poor girl, she was out all day, and had just gotten to sleep, and a man came for her, his wife was expecting her first, so she'll be out all night, too. Someone suggested in House Meeting a few moons ago that the midwives should answer all the night bells, because most of the time, night calls were for them."

"That wouldn't really be fair," Magda said, "they deserve to sleep when they can, if only because they lose so much sleep already. I apologize again for waking you. Do you need help with the bolt?"

"Thank you, it really is too heavy for me."

Magda came and helped her to fasten the heavy lock. Cressa went off to the night doorkeeper's room, and Magda went slowly up the stairs to the room she had been given to share with Jaelle during this stay in the House. She paused at the door; then turned away, went to a nearby door and knocked softly. After a moment she heard a muffled response, turned the knob and went inside.

"Camilla," she whispered, "are you asleep?"

"Of course I am, could I talk to you if I were awake?" Camilla sat up in bed. "Margali? What is it?"

Without answering, Magda came and sat on the edge of the bed, where she slumped, letting her head fall wearily into her hands.

"What is it, *bredhiya*?" Camilla asked gently. "What did they ask of you this time?"

"I don't want to talk about it." Her sensitivity was so high— she had been using *laran* at such a level—that she could almost hear Camilla's thoughts as if the woman had spoken them aloud:

Oh yes, of course, it is because you do not want to talk that you come and wake me instead of quietly going to sleep in your own room!

But aloud, Camilla said only, "You missed supper here; did they at least feed you in the Terran Zone?"

"It's my own fault. After all these years using *laran* I should have known enough to demand something to eat," Magda said, "but I wanted to get away, I couldn't wait to get away. Cholayna did offer—"

Camilla's eyebrows went up in the dark. "You were using *laran* in the Terran HQ? And you don't want to talk about it. That does not sound like what I would expect of Cholayna n'ha Chandria." She slid out of bed and drew a heavy woolen wrapper over her warm nightgown, scuffed her long narrow feet into fur slippers. "Let's go down to the kitchen for something hot for you."

"I'm not hungry," Magda said wearily.

"Nevertheless, if you have been using *laran*—you know you must eat and regain your strength—"

"What in all of Zandru's hells do you know about it?" Magda snarled. Camilla shrugged.

"I know what all the world knows. I know what the little children in the marketplace know. I know *you*. Come downstairs; at least you can have some hot milk, after that long walk in the cold. Take your boots off though, and put on your slippers."

"Damnation, Camilla, don't fuss at me."

Again the indifferent shrug. "If you want to sit in wet clothes all night, please yourself. I suppose one of the young nursing trainees would be delighted at the chance to nurse you through lung fever. But it is hardly fair to go clumping around through the halls after midnight in heavy boots, waking everyone who sleeps on the corridor because you're too lazy to pull them off. If you're simply too tired, I'll help you."

Wearily, Magda roused herself to pull off her boots and soaked jacket. "I'll borrow one of your nightgowns; I don't want to wake Jaelle." Somehow she took off the wet clothes and got herself into a heavy gown of thick flannel.

"We'd better take these down and dry them; there will be a fire in the kitchen," Camilla said. Magda was too weary to argue; she put her wet clothes over her arm and followed Camilla.

She was still shivering as they went down the corridors and the silent stairs, but in the Guild-house kitchen the fire was banked, and near the fireplace it was warm. A kettle of hot water was hissing softly on its crane; Camilla found mugs on a shelf while Magda raked up the fire and spread out her wet garments. Camilla poured Magda some bark-tea, then went into the pantry and cut cold meat and bread, laying them on the kitchen table next to the bowls of rolled grains and dried fruits, soaking for the breakfast porridge.

Magda sipped listlessly at the hot bitter tea, too tired to look for honey on the shelves. She did not touch the food, sitting motionless on the bench before the table. Camilla made herself some tea, but instead of drinking it, she came around behind

Magda. Her strong hands kneaded the tight muscles in the younger woman's shoulders and neck; after a long time Magda reached out and took up a piece of the buttered bread.

"I'm not really hungry, but I suppose I should eat something," she said wearily, and put it to her lips.

After a bite or two, as Camilla had expected, the ravenous hunger of anyone who has been working with *laran* took over, and she ate and drank almost mechanically. She finished the bread and meat, and got up to ransack the pantry for some leftover cakes with spice and sugar.

When her hunger was satisfied, she leaned back, tuning the bench round so that she could put her feet up on the rail that guarded the fireplace. Camilla came and sat beside her, putting up her own feet— long, narrow, somehow aristocratic—on the rail beside Magda's. They sat together, neither speaking, looking into the bed of coals. After a time, Magda got up restlessly and put more wood on the fire, causing flames to flare up so that flickering shadows played on the walls of the cavernous kitchen.

She said, at last, "I'm not really a psi-tech, not the way they think of it in the Terran Zone. I'm not a therapist. The work I do at Armida is—is different. What I had to do tonight was to go into someone's mind, someone who's normally head-blind, and try to—" She wet her lips with her tongue and said, "It's not easy to explain. There aren't words."

She looked around hesitantly at Camilla. She had known the woman at her side for years, and had long known that Camilla had, or had once had, *laran*, though Camilla herself denied it. Magda was one of the few people living who knew all of Camilla's story: born of *Comyn* blood—no trace of which was visible now except for the faded, sandy hair which had once flamed with the same *Comyn* red as Jaelle's—Camilla had been kidnapped when barely out of childhood, and so savagely raped and abused that her mind had broken. Magda did not know all of the details; only that for many years Camilla had lived as a mercenary soldier, even her closest associates unaware that she was not the rough-spoken, rough-living man she seemed. After some years of this, Camilla, wounded and near death, had revealed herself to a Renunciate: Kindra, Jaelle's own foster-mother. She had found herself able, in the Guild of Free Amazons, to take up again, painfully and with great self-doubt, the womanhood she had tried so long and so hard to renounce or conceal.

Once or twice, when their barriers were down to one another, Magda had become certain that Camilla retained some of her family's heritage of *laran*, whatever that family might be. She was sure that Camilla bore the blood of one of the Seven Domains, the great families of Darkover, even though she concealed her *laran*.

It was not impossible that Camilla knew, without being told, how difficult the thing was that the Terrans had asked her to do.

"Do you remember meeting Lexie Anders at the special orientation meeting they gave for the new women working in the Terran Zone?"

"I do. She was very scornful of the notion that the *Penta Cori'yo* had anything to offer Terran women. Even when the other women in the Bridge Society pointed out that, after all, Terran women could hardly go to the Spaceport bars for recreation in the City, and that this would give her friends and associates, and a place to go when she could not stand being cooped up in the HQ anymore—"

"And I know, if Lexie doesn't, that that's one reason women employees haven't been very fortunate on Darkover, unless they were brought up here and feel comfortable with the language and the way women are expected to behave," Magda said. "I remember how rude and casual Lexie was at the reception. She made us all feel like—well, like natives, crude aboriginals; that we should all have been wearing skin loincloths and bones in our hair."

"And you had to go into *her* mind? Poor Margali," said Camilla, "I do not imagine her mind is a pleasant place to be. Not even, I should imagine, for her. As for you—"

"It wasn't only that," Magda said. Briefly, she repeated to Camilla what Cholayna had told her about the lost plane, and about Lexie's mysterious reappearance. "—So I told her, I'm not a trained psi-tech, and don't blame me if I make things worse," she said, "and then we went down to Isolation, in Medic, where they had been keeping her."

Magda had not remembered that Lexie Anders was such a little woman. She was loud-voiced and definite, with such an assertive stance and manner that it was shocking to see her lying flat against her cot, pale and scrubbed like a sick child. Her hair was fair, cut short and curly; her face looked almost bruised, the blue veins showing through the skin. More distressing than this was the emptiness in her face; Magda felt that even Lexie's aggressive rudeness was preferable to this passive, childish pliancy.

Magda had learned a little of the dialect of Vainwal during her years in training on Alpha Colony, in the Intelligence School. "How are you feeling, Lieutenant Anders?"

"My name's Lexie. I don't know why they're keeping me here, I'm not sick," Lexie said, in a childish, complaining tone. "Are you going to stick more needles in me?"

"No, I promise I won't stick you with any needles." Magda lifted a questioning eyebrow at Cholayna, who said in an undertone, "The Medics tried pentothal; they thought if this was simply emotional shock, it might help her to relive it and talk about it. No result."

Magda thought about that for a moment. If Lexie Anders had been, at one moment, in a plane about to crash in the frozen wastelands surrounding the Wall Around the World, and in the next moment, was outside the Spaceport gates of Thendara HQ, the emotional shock alone could have reduced her to this condition.

"Do you know where you are, Lexie?"

"Hospital. They told me," she said, laying her curly head down tiredly on the pillow. "I don't feel sick at all. Why am I in a hospital? Are you a doctor? You don't look like a doctor, not in those clothes."

"Then—you don't remember anything that happened?" Magda had once watched Lady Callista deal with a case of shock: a man who had seen four members of his family killed in a freak flood. "Can you tell me the last thing you remember?"

" 'Member—a kitten," said Lexie with a childish grin. "It ran away."

"You don't remember the plane?"

"Plane? My dad flies a plane," she said. "I want to fly one when I grow up. My cousin says girls don't fly planes, but Dada says it's all right, some girls fly planes, they even pilot starships."

"Certainly they do." Magda remembered a brief ambition of her own (about the time she found out the difference between her parents and the parents of the Darkovan children around her, with whom she had grown up) to be a starship pilot. She supposed most tomboy girls had similar ambitions, and briefly it created a bond of sympathy.

"Lexie, suppose I were to tell you that you have forgotten many things; that you are all grown up, and that you did fly a plane; that you are here because your plane crashed. Will you think about that, please? What would you say to that?"

Lexie did not even stop to think. Her small face was already crinkled up in a jeering laugh. "I'd say you were crazy. Crazy woman, what are you doing in a hospital, trying to act like a doctor? Is it a crazy hospital?

Magda's brief moment of liking and sympathy for Lexie evaporated. An unpleasant child, she thought, who grew up into an even more unpleasant woman. . . . Yet she remembered what Callista, training her in the arts of matrix work, had said about this kind of thing:

They abuse us because they are afraid of us. If anyone is rude and unpleasant when you are trying to help them, it is out of fear, because they are afraid of what you will try and make them see or understand. No matter how deeply their reason is hidden, something in them knows and understands, and fears leaving the protection of shock.

(In the Guild-house, before the fire, hours later, Magda again recalled and repeated these words, so deeply absorbed in her own memories that she did not see Camilla's facial muscles tauten, nor the tense nod with which she acquiesced. There were many things Camilla could not, or chose not to remember, of her own ordeal.)

Magda ignored Lexie's rudeness. From around her neck, she took her matrix stone, carefully unwrapping the layers of shielding. She rolled the blue stone, hidden fires flashing from its depth, out into her palm. Lexie's eyes followed the moving colors in the jewel.

"Pretty," she said in her babytalk voice. "Can I see it?"

"In a minute, perhaps. But you must not touch it, or you might be hurt." For an out-of-phase person, particularly a non-telepath, to touch a keyed matrix could produce a serious and painful shock; worse, it could throw the operator of the matrix, keyed to the stone, into shock that could be fatal. She held the psi-sensitive crystal away from Lexie's childishly grasping fingers and said, "Look into the stone, Lexie."

Lexie twisted her face away. "Makes my head ache."

That was normal enough. Few untrained persons could endure to look into a keyed matrix, and Lexie's psi potential was evidently very slight. Magda realized she should at least have asked for a look at Personnel Records on Lieutenant Alexis Anders, to know her determined level of psi ability. They did test Terrans for such things now. It would have been useful to know.

But they had not, and there was no way to do it now. She held the matrix before Lexie's eyes. "I want you to look into the stone, so that we can see what is the matter with you, and why you are in the hospital here." Magda spoke deliberately, her voice friendly but firm. Lexie pouted like a child, but under Magda's commanding voice and posture, finally fixed her eyes on the shifting colors of the stone.

Magda watched until her face relaxed. She was not sure how an ordinary psi-tech would handle this, but for the best part of seven years she had been intensively trained in the uses of a matrix. The words of the Monitor's Oath, demanded of any telepath soon after being entrusted with a matrix, briefly resonated in her mind: *Enter no mind save to help or heal, and never for power over any being.*

Then she made contact, briefly, with Lexie Anders's mind.

On the surface, it was a jumble, a confused child not knowing what had happened. On a deeper level, something shivered and quaked, not wanting to know. Gently Magda touched the child-mind (a hand confidingly tucked into hers, as a little girl holds the hand of an older sister; she let the warmth linger for a moment, wanting Lexie to trust her).

Who are you? It's scary, I can't remember.

I'm your friend, Lexie. I won't let anyone hurt you. You're a big girl now. You wanted to fly a plane, remember? Let's go, let's find the plane. The first time your hands touched the controls. Look at the plane. The controls are under your hands. Where are you, Lexie?

The young woman's hands curved reminiscently as if over the controls she had mastered. . . .

Abruptly the childish plaintive voice lisping the dialect of Vainwal changed; became crisp, accurate, Terran Standard spoken with the precision of those to whom it was an acquired second language.

"Anders, Alexis, Cadet Recruit, reporting as ordered, Ma'am."

It was no use to try to bring her along with verbal commands. Simple hypnotic suggestion would have brought a less traumatized subject to present time; but Magda had already seen how Lexie's conscious intellect and even the unconscious mind refused the level of mere suggestion. With the matrix, Magda could bypass that resistance. Again she slipped into the younger woman's mind, seeking the child who had walked with her hand in hand, trustingly.

Lieutenant Anders. When did you get your promotion?

A tenday after I was moved to Cottman Four. I decided to move over to Mapping and Exploring.

Magda was prepared to ask, directly in Lexie's mind, why the younger woman had made the transfer application. Surely Cholayna had done her, Magda, a monstrous injustice when she had spoken of the 'Lorne Legend' and the inability of Lexie to compete with the more famous older woman. But she stopped herself. Was this truly relevant to Lexie's problem, or was she, Magda, simply indulging a desire to explain and justify herself? Gently she re-established the rapport; but the childish acceptance was gone. She regretted it, regretted the image of the little sister walking beside her, hand in hand.

Tell me about your work in Mapping and Exploring, Lieutenant. Do you like your work?

Yes. I love it. I can work alone and nobody bothers me. I didn't like it in Intelligence. There were too many women. I don't like women. I don't trust them. Always ready to stab you in the back. You can trust a plane. Does what you tell it to, and if anything goes wrong it's your own damn fault. Her face was almost animated.

Slowly, carefully, Magda insinuated herself into Lexie's memory. This was not ordinary amnesia, where selectively the mind chooses to reject an intolerable burden. It was total rejection. Magda's mind intertwined with Lexie's; she had never held the controls of a plane, large or small, but now her hands covered Lexie's and she shared the full-round vision to all points of the compass, the frozen mountains spread below, the precise definiteness of every motion and idea. She was moving farther north, she was about to set a record if the damned plane would cooperate. Her skill was such that the maddening surges of crosswinds and updrafts only bounced her a little where any other pilot would have been battered. Then—

Lexie Anders screamed and sat bolt upright in bed. Magda, knocked out of the rapport, stood staring, her eyes wide.

"I crashed," Lexie said, in her most precise Terran Standard. "The last thing I remember was going down. And then I was here, at the HQ gates. Hellfire, Lorne, are you involved in Medic too? Isn't there any pie on this whole planet you don't have your fingers into?"

"So what did you tell them?" Camilla asked at last.

"I didn't have any reasonable explanation," Magda said. "I

grasped at the usual straws. I told Cholayna that it was just possible that when the plane went down, Anders developed a sudden surge of previously unguessed-at psi-potential, and teleported herself back here. It's not at all unheard-of, under life-and-death threat like that, to find someone doing something they'd never have believed a remote possibility. I did something like that once, myself—not physically but mentally."

She and Jaelle, in a cave on a hillside, with Jaelle desperately ill, after miscarrying Peter Haldane's child. Escape had seemed impossible. Somehow, she never knew how, she had reached out and touched rescue—had called for help and had, somehow, been answered.

"That kind of thing doesn't show up in test labs because you can't fool the subconscious mind; hypnosis, or what-have-you, may make their conscious mind think they're in danger, but down underneath, they know perfectly well there's no real threat." She sighed, thinking of how, for a brief time, she had actually liked the child Lexie had been.

"But you don't believe that explanation," Camilla said.

"Camilla, I knew it was a lie when I said it."

"But why should you lie? What had really happened to Lexie Anders?"

Before she answered, Magda reached for Camilla's hand. She said, "My fourth night in this house, my very first Training Session as a Renunciate, do you remember? That same night there was a meeting of a society called the Sisterhood. Do you remember that I lost track of what you asked me, and you scolded and bullied me for not paying attention to what was going on?"

"Not particularly," Camilla said. "Why? And what has the Sisterhood to do with Lexie Anders?" She reached across the bench and picked up her cold tea, sipping at it.

Magda said, "Let me make you a fresh cup," took both mugs, and poured the tea. She went to refill the kettle.

At last, knowing she was delaying, she said, "During that meeting, I saw—something. I didn't know then what to call it, I thought it was a—a thought-form of the Goddess Avarra. Of course, at the time, I thought I was hallucinating, that it wasn't really there."

Camilla said, "I have seen it too, during meetings of the Sisterhood. You know that the Renunciates were formed from two societies: the Sisterhood of the Sword, who were a soldier-caste, and the Priestesses of Avarra, who were healers. I believe the Sisterhood invokes Avarra in their meetings. Again—what have their religious practices to do with Lexie Anders?"

Magda stood braced against the table, leaning on her fists. Her face was drawn and distant, remembering. She said, and it was no more than a whisper of horror, "Twice more, I saw— something. Not the Goddess Avarra. Robed figures. A whisper of—of a sound like crows calling. Once I asked: *Who are you?*"

Camilla asked, her voice dropping in response to the frozen dread in Magda's, "Did they—was there any answer?"

"None that made any sense to me. I seemed to hear—not quite to hear, to *sense*—the words, *The Dark Sisterhood*. Something—" Magda wrinkled up her face, tensely; it was tenuous, like trying to remember a dream in daylight. "Only that they were guardians of some sort, but couldn't interfere. And just as I was about to reach the point where Lexie relived and remembered the crash, I saw that. Again."

Her throat closed, her voice was reduced to a thready whisper. "Walls. A city. Robed figures. Then the sound of crows calling. And nothing. After that—nothing."

Chapter 4

Camilla turned away and banked the fire. She felt carefully about the legs of Magda's breeches to see if they were dry.

"Leave them for a few minutes more," she said.

"Camilla! You know something of the Sisterhood; what are they?"

Camilla was still fussing with the half-dried clothing.

"If I knew," she said, "I would be like Marisela—sworn to secrecy. Why do you think those people don't make it, whatever it is that they know, part of the regular Training Sessions? Secrets, bah! Once Marisela tried to get me to join them. When I would not, she was very annoyed with me. Weren't you angry when Lexie refused to join the *Penta Cori'yo?*"

That was different, Magda thought, even though she could not define how. She was not accustomed to defending herself against Camilla, not anymore.

"You don't like Marisela?"

"Certainly I like her. But I refused to make her the keeper of my conscience and of course she has never forgiven me for that. But when first she insisted I should join them, she did tell me something of the original purposes of the Sisterhood. Most of it is what you would expect from the Oath, the usual business about women as sisters, *Men dia pre' zhiuro, sister and mother and daughter to all women*—but there is more; it is to give teaching in *laran* to those who were not born *Comyn* and thus are not eligible for training in the ordinary Towers. She even tried to frighten me—threatened me with all kinds of dreadful consequences if I was not willing to swallow her kind of medicine for my ills."

"That does not sound like Marisela," Magda said.

"Oh, believe me, she did not say it in those words. She didn't bully me, or say do what I suggest or you will have to suffer all kinds of things—no, it was more a matter of being afraid for me. More a matter of—*Let me help you, you poor thing, or you cannot imagine how dreadful it will be.* You know the kind of thing I mean." Magda heard the unspoken part of that, *and you know how much I would hate that kind of thing,* just as clearly as she had heard what Camilla had said aloud. She knew Camilla trusted her enough not to take advantage, or she would never have allowed that.

"Among other things, Marisela tried to tell me that an untrained telepath is a danger to herself and to everyone around her." Camilla's scornful look showed what she thought of that.

But that is perfectly true, Magda thought, remembering her own training. And the attempt to block her own *laran* had all but destroyed Jaelle. If Camilla had done so unharmed, it would have taken such iron control, such perfect self-discipline—

But Camilla *did* have both iron control and perfect self-discipline; she had had to have them, or she could never have survived what had happened to her. And if she had the strength to survive all that—not unscarred, but simply to survive—then she had the control and discipline for that too. But Magda was not surprised that Marisela did not believe it.

"At that time—after I was—changed, and recovered," Camilla said, almost inaudibly, "Leonie offered me this. She said something of the same sort—that I had been born into the caste with *laran* and therefore could not survive without that teaching. I honor Leonie—she was kind to me when I greatly needed that kindness. She saved more than my life; she saved my reason. For all that, I would have been more comfortable with the bandits who so misused me; at least, when they violated me, they didn't pretend they were doing it for my own good."

Magda did not say a word. Only twice in the years they had known each other had Camilla referred to the trauma of her girlhood, which had made her what she was; Magda had some idea what it had cost Camilla to say this much, even to her. Abruptly, Camilla jerked the drying tunic and undervest off the rack and began vigorously to fold them.

"Like Jaelle, I was asked to join the Sisterhood. And like Jaelle, I refused. I have no love for secret societies and sisterhoods, and what I know, I reserve the right to tell as I choose, to whomever I choose. I think most of what they believe they know is superstition and nonsense." She pursed her mouth and looked grim.

"Then how do you explain what happened to me, Camilla? Out there in the Kilghard Hills, in that cave. I know what happened, because it happened to me. We were marooned. Jaelle was dying. We would both have died there in that cave in the hills—I cried out for help. And I—I was answered. Answered, I tell you!"

"You have *laran*," Camilla said, "and I suppose the Terran from the Forbidden Tower—what is his name, Andrew Carr? I suppose this Andrew Carr heard you and answered."

"Ann'dra." Magda deliberately used Carr's Darkovan name. "Yes, he has *laran*. But what prompted him to go looking for me in the first place? For all he knew, I was in Thendara, snug in the Guild-house as a bug in a saddlebag. Instead he sent out a search party for us and found us in time to save Jaelle's life."

"Ferrika," said Camilla. "She is a member of the Sisterhood. And so is Marisela. Marisela knew you had gone, and knew the state Jaelle was in. And Ferrika is midwife at Armida—"

"She is more than that," Magda said. "She is a full member of the Tower Circle."

Camilla looked skeptical, and Magda insisted, "She is, I tell you, as much as I am myself."

Camilla shrugged. "Then, there is your answer."

"And the vision I had? Robed women—crows calling—"

"You said it yourself. You were desperate. You believed Jaelle was dying. Desperate people see visions. I don't believe there was anything supernatural about your answer at all."

"You don't believe that a—a cry for help of that kind can be answered?"

"No, I don't."

"Why not?"

Camilla's lips were set in a hard line. "Don't you suppose that I—prayed? I cried out for help with all my strength. Not only for human help, I cried out to all the Gods and to any supernatural forces that might have been hanging around to help me. If they could have heard you, where were they when I cried out to heaven, or even hell, for help? If they heard you, why did they not hear me? And if they heard me, and did not answer—what sort of Gods or helpers were they?"

Magda flinched before the unanswerable bitterness of that.

Camilla went on, without interruption, "You had a vision, *bredhiya.*" She used the word, which meant originally sister, in the intimate inflection which could make it mean *darling* or *beloved,* and was used only in close family intimacy or to a sworn lover.

"You had a vision, a dream; it was your Ann'dra who heard you. Or perhaps, Marisela, who sent word to Ferrika that a sister was in peril." Since that was certainly possible, and was in any case more rational than her own belief, Magda did not try further to convince her. Camilla's face relaxed a little; she went on.

"The Sisterhood, I have heard, was designed to do for women what the *cristoforo* brethren at Nevarsin do for men. But unlike the Nevarsin brotherhood or the *Comyn,* the Sisterhood—so I am told—do not exact piety nor conformity in return for their instruction. There is an old tale, a fable if you will, but some of the *Comyn* believe it, that the *laran* of the Seven Domains is because they are the descendants of Gods." Camilla's scornfully arched eyebrows told Magda what the *emmasca* thought of that. "It did not suit them that the common folk should have this gift, or believe they have it, or be trained to use it if, as sometimes happens, they have it though they were born outside the sacred caste. I do not know what will happen to the *Comyn* when they fully get it through their minds that *laran* appears even in Terrans like your Andrew Carr. To do them credit, if it is brought to the attention of *Comyn* that a commoner possesses *laran*, they will sometimes have him trained—usually in one of the lesser Towers like Neskaya. I don't doubt at all that your Andrew could—"

"You keep calling him *my* Andrew. He isn't, Camilla."

Camilla shrugged. She said, "Do you want more tea? This is cold." And indeed, despite the fire on the hearth, a thin skin of ice had begun to form on Magda's tea. "Or would you rather go up and sleep?"

"I am not sleepy." Magda shivered; the memory of what she had seen in Lexie's mind was still alive in her, and she wondered how she would ever manage to sleep. She got up and poured boiling water into her mug; tilted the spout toward Camilla. The older woman shook her head.

"If I drink any more, I will never sleep! Nor will you."

"Why should I sleep? I had hoped to be away at daybreak, and now I cannot. Cholayna has asked me to stay until this is resolved."

"And of course you must do as Cholayna commands?"

"She is my friend. I would stay if you asked me; why not for her? But I would like to get back to my child."

"A few more days will not weaken the bond, *bredhiya*." Camilla's face relaxed and she smiled. "I would like to see her— your daughter."

"The journey to Armida is not so long as all that, and for all your talk of being old, Camilla, I know perfectly well that you could be off tomorrow to the Dry Towns, or to Dalereuth, or the Wall Around the World itself, if you had some reason! Why not ride back with me when I go, and see my little Shaya?"

Camilla smiled. "I? Among those *leroni*?"

"They are my friends and my family, Camilla. They would welcome you if only as my friend."

"One day, then, perhaps. Not this time, I think. Shaya—we called Jaelle so, as a child. So she is Jaelle's namesake? What does she look like? Is she like you, your daughter?"

"Her hair curls like mine, but not so dark; her eyes are like mine, but Ferrika thinks they will darken as she grows older. To me, she has a look of my father: I know she has his hands. Strange, is it not? We renounce our fathers when we swear the Oath, yet we cannot wholly renounce them; they reappear in the faces of our children."

"Perhaps it is as well I had no daughter. I would not have cared to see in her the face of the man who renounced me before ever I renounced him! Your father, though, seems to have been a remarkable man, and I dare say you have no reason to resent the likeness. But what of *her* father? I had assumed, of course, it was the same Lord Damon Ridenow who fathered Jaelle's child—*Comyn* lords are encouraged to breed sons and daughters everywhere, as my own real father did. It's odd that although my mother was with child by a man far above her own station and was then married off in consequence to a man far below it, still both of them were too proud to accept that I might be pregnant with the child of one of the rogues who—well, enough of that. But as I was saying—it seemed reasonable to me that it would be Lord Damon who fathered your child, as he did Jaelle's."

Magda laughed. "Oh, Damon is not like that. Believe me, he is not. Jaelle chose him for her child's father, but it was *her* choice. Damon is very dear to me, but he is not my lover."

"That Terran then? Your Andrew Carr, Lord Ann'dra? He is of your own people. I could understand that—well, as much as I could ever understand desire for a man."

"At least you do not condemn it, as do so many women of the Guild, as treason to the Oath."

Camilla chuckled. "No, I lived for years among men, as one of them, and I know that men are very like women—only not, perhaps, so free to be what they are. It's a pity there's no Guild-house for them. Jaelle has talked to me, a little, about Damon. But *is* it this Andrew, then?"

"I love Andrew," Magda said, "almost as much as I love Lady Callista. When first I decided that I wanted a child, we talked of it, all three of us."

She knew she could never have explained to Camilla what the bond was like within the Tower. It was nothing like any other bond she had ever known. In many ways she felt closer to Camilla than to any other human being; she wished that she could share this with her, too. But how could she make Camilla understand? Camilla, who had chosen to block away her *laran* and live forever as one of the head-blind. It hurt to feel Camilla's mind closed to her.

The bond of the Forbidden Tower had reached out to take her in; she had become a part, mind and body and heart, of the Tower circle there. Until Jaelle's child was born, she had not really known how much she wanted a child of her own. They had grown so close, all of them, that for a time it had seemed natural that she too should have Damon's child, so that her child and Jaelle's might be truly sisters. Yet even more than with Damon, she shared a close bond with Andrew Carr: like herself, Andrew had found that the world of the Terrans could not hold him.

"In the end, though," Magda said, "Andrew and I decided not. It was really Andrew's choice, not mine. He felt that he would not want to father a child that he could not rear as his own, and I would not give up that privilege to him. I chose my child's father because, though we felt kindness toward one another, he was someone from whom I felt I could part again without too much grief." She was silent, her eyes faraway, and Camilla wondered what she was thinking.

"I will tell you his name, if you ask me, *bredhiya*. He has his own household, and sons of his own; but he promised, if I bore a son and could not care for him, that he would foster him and give him such a start in life as he could. If I had a daughter, he swore he would make no claim on her. His wife was willing—I would not do such a thing without his wife's consent."

"I am curious about this paragon," Camilla said, "but you are welcome to your secrets, my dear." She rose again and felt the legs of Magda's breeches. "Cover the fire. It is time, and past, that we were in bed. Even if you need not ride at daybreak, there are things I must do tomorrow." She put her arm around Magda as they went silently up the stairs; and not until she was on the very edge of sleep did Magda realize that Camilla had really said nothing about the Sisterhood, after all.

A day or two later, she found Marisela, the Guild-house's senior midwife, enjoying a rare moment of solitude in the music room, idly strumming a *rryl*. But when Magda apologized for her intrusion and would have gone away again, Marisela set down the small lap-harp, and said, "Please don't go. I haven't really anything to do with myself, and I was only killing time pretending I could play. Do sit down and talk to me. We never see each other these days."

Magda sat down and watched as Marisela put the instrument into its case.

"Remind me to tell Rafaella that a string has broken; I took it off, but could not replace it. Well, Margali, do you just want to chat, or do you want to ask me something?"

Magda asked, "Do you remember when I was first in the house, during my housebound time? In my first Training Session, I saw a vision of the Goddess Avarra. I know it came from the Sisterhood. And now again I have encountered—Marisela, will you tell me something about the Sisterhood?"

Marisela fiddled with the clasps on the instrument case.

"There was a time," she said after a moment, "when I felt you were ready for the Sisterhood, and would willingly have had you among us. But when you left the Guild-house, you went elsewhere for the training of your *laran*. For that reason, I do not feel free to discuss the secrets of the Sisterhood with you. I can tell you nothing, my dear. I am sure you are as well among the Forbidden Tower as with us, and if there was ever a time when I resented your choice, it was long ago. But I am sorry. I may not talk of this to an outsider."

Magda felt a sense of total frustration. She said, "If these people who call themselves the Dark Sisterhood reached out to me, how can you say I am an outsider? If they spoke to me—"

"If they did," repeated Marisela. "Oh, no, my dear, I am sure you are not lying, but when this happened, you were under great stress. This much I can say: the Sisterhood are those who serve Avarra; we on the plane which we call physical life, and they, the Dark Ones, on the plane of existence known as the Overworld. I suppose—in such extremity—if you have the talent of reaching out into it, they might hear you from the Overworld and relay a message. You are strongly gifted with *laran*; you may have reached Those Who Hear, and they may have answered you from where they dwell." Deliberately, she changed the subject.

"But now, tell me what you have been doing with yourself these last few years. I haven't really had a chance to talk with you since your daughter was born. Is she well and thriving? Was she a big, strong baby? You told Doria that she was weaned—how long did you feed her yourself?"

"Something less than a year," Magda replied, not really sorry to abandon the frustrating topic, and perfectly willing to satisfy the midwife's professional interest. When she began to cut her teeth, I was quite ready and glad to say to her, if you are big enough to bite, you are big enough to bite bread!"

With an unexpected pang of homesickness she missed her daughter, the small wriggling body in her arms, snuggled sleepily in her lap, struggling to escape being combed or dressed, scampering naked from the bath. . . . "She is very strong and seems to me very intelligent and quick, very independent for two years old. She actually tries to put on her own clothes. Of course she can't yet; gets stuck with her tunic over her head and yells for her nurse to come and get her loose. But she tries! She says *Mama*, but she doesn't always mean me, she says it to Jaelle, to Ellemir—"

"I have never met the Lady Ellemir, but Ferrika and Jaelle have spoken of her. I always thought you would have no trouble in bearing children. Did you have a difficult time?"

"I had nothing to compare it with. I thought it hard," Magda said, "but not nearly as bad as it was for Jaelle."

"I have never had a chance to ask Jaelle about it. Was it difficult for her? I expected that if she had one child, she would want another."

"She did; but Ferrika advised against it. Cleindori is thriving; she was five last Spring Festival."

"What a very peculiar name for a child, to name her after the *kireseth* flower!"

"Her name is Dorilys; it is a family name among the Ardais, I understand, and Lady Rohana was Jaelle's foster-mother. But she is golden-haired, and her nurse dresses her always in blue, so that Ferrika said one day, she looks like a bell of the flower all covered in golden pollen. She is so pretty no one can deny her anything, so of course she's dreadfully spoiled; but she has such a sweet disposition, it seems to have done her no harm. She is very quick and clever, too, already the other girls pet and spoil her, and the boys all treat her as a little queen."

"And I dare say you do homage, too," Marisela said, laughing, and Magda admitted it.

"Oh, she has always been my special darling. When Shaya was born, I expected Cleindori to be jealous, but she isn't. She insists that this is her very own little sister, and wants to share everything with her. When Shaya was only two months old we found her trying to dress the baby up in her own best Holiday tunic, and I have forgotten how many times we had to remind her that it was very nice to be generous, but that Shaya could not eat spice-bread or nut-cake till she had her teeth!"

"Better that the natural rivalry should take that form, than jealousy," remarked Marisela. "She has decided to rival you as mother, instead of Shaya as baby." It was not the first time Magda had been surprised at the woman's psychological insight. It had been a salutary lesson for Magda, who had thought for a long time that a non-technological culture would have no advanced psychological knowledge. But of course, if Marisela belonged to the Sisterhood, whose special province was to train the *laran* and psi skills of those outside the normal system of the Towers, it was not at all surprising. Magda's own awareness of mental processes had increased a thousandfold when she began to explore her *laran*.

"And the father," Marisela asked, "did he follow custom and stay with you for the birth?"

"He would have done, if I had asked him," Magda said, "but since he agreed to make no claim, it was Jaelle I asked to be with me; Jaelle, and Lady Callista." She had never told anyone—although Marisela would certainly have understood—that in the profound helplessness and power of birth, it had somehow been Camilla she had wanted with her. She would never tell that to anyone, not even to Camilla. Instead, she changed the subject.

"But tell me now what our sister Keitha is doing. I understand she studied midwifery both at Arilinn and with the Terrans—"

"And she will go next month to Neskaya, to teach the midwives the new skills she learned from the Terrans; and after that, to Nevarsin, to establish a Guild-house of midwives in that city. The *cristoforo* brethren do not like it, but there is nothing they can do. They can hardly say that they wish women to die in childbirth when they can be saved, can they?"

Magda agreed that they could not, although they might like to; but the choice of subject was an unfortunate one, as it reminded her of what Camilla had said of the Sisterhood: that they had been formed to do for women, in the darkest years of the Ages of Chaos, what the *cristoforo* brethren had done for men— to keep a little learning alive despite Chaos and ignorance. And it also reminded her that Marisela had refused to tell what she knew.

Chapter 5

"There's no reason you should have to stay here," Magda said. "This is my problem, and Cholayna doesn't need you. You could go back to Armida and to the children."

Jaelle shook her head. "No, *breda*. As long as you have to stay, do you think I would leave you here alone?"

"It's not as if I were exactly alone," Magda pointed out to her. "I have Cholayna, and everybody in Bridge if I need them, not to mention a whole Guild-house full of our sisters. I'd really feel better about it if I knew you were with the children, Shaya."

Jaelle n'ha Melora laughed. "Margali, of all the arguments you might have given me, that is the one least likely to make any impression! How much time do I spend with either of the children? I should be there to give her an admiring hug at bedtime? As long as Ellemir is there, and her nurse, and Ferrika—with a whole houseful of nurses and nannies, with Ellemir to supervise them and Andrew to spoil them, I doubt if they know we are gone."

This was true, more or less, and Magda knew it. If anything, Jaelle was far less domestic, and less interested in little children, than was Magda herself. Jaelle loved Cleindori—as who did not?—but since the little girl had been weaned, spent little time in her daughter's company.

She thought again, as she had thought before, that Jaelle had really changed very little since they had met: a small, slight woman with hair only slightly faded from its early tint of new-minted copper; she had the fragile look of many *Comyn*—

Damon had it, and Callista—but Magda knew it was deceptive, and concealed the delicate strength of ancient forged steel.

In many ways, Jaelle is the strongest of us all. They say the Aillard women have always been the best Keepers; perhaps the post of Keeper was designed for their kind of strength. But Jaelle's strength was not *laran.* Perhaps they did not yet know what her true strength would be.

We are both at the age, Magda thought, *at which a woman should have decided what she wants to do with her life. I have outgrown first love, first marriage, early ideals. I have a child, and have recovered my strength and health. I have work I love. I have made some decisions—I know many of the things I do not want to do with my life. I have developed my* laran *and I know that my love and my strongest emotions are given to women. But I am not yet really sure what it is given to me to do with my life.* And this disturbed her so much that she had no heart to argue with Jaelle.

"Stay if you wish. But I can't imagine wanting to stay in the City when you could be out in the country, at Armida."

Jaelle looked up toward the skyline, where the Venza Mountains overshadowed the pass that led down into the city. "You feel it too? I would like to be out again on the trail. I have done my duty to clan and family, and when Dori is only a little older, I shall send her to be fostered as a daughter of Aillard. And then—oh, Magda, aren't you eager to be in the field again, traveling in the mountains? Rafaella wants me to come back to work with her; she's talking about some new special project for the Terrans, but won't tell me any details until I promise I'll join her. It would be hard to leave the Tower, and I would miss it, but—couldn't I take a year away, just to travel again? It's been so long! I never spent so long in one place in my whole life as I have spent at Armida! Five years, Magda!"

Magda smiled indulgently. "I'm sure they would give you leave to spend a year in the mountains if you wished."

"I heard the other day that there is an expedition going to climb High Kimbi. It's never been climbed—"

"And probably never will be," Magda said. "Not by either

of us, in any case. You know as well as I do they wouldn't have women along, not even as guides. If there are still men who think women unfit to be part of anything facing danger or demanding courage, they are the men who go out climbing mountains."

Jaelle snorted. "I led a trade caravan over the Pass of Scaravel when I was not yet eighteen!"

"*Breda*, I know what you can do on the trail. And Rafaella is listed in Intelligence Services as the best mountain guide in the business! But there are still men who won't use women guides. The more fools they."

Jaelle shrugged philosophically. "I guess if we want to climb High Kimbi, or Dammerung Peak, we'll have to organize our own expedition."

Magda laughed. "Forget the *we* part, Jaelle. *You* would have to do it. That one trip across Scaravel was enough to last me a lifetime." Even remembering, she shivered at the thought of the cliffs and chasms of the Pass of Scaravel.

"Talk to Camilla. She'd probably be delighted to go out and climb anything inaccessible you can find."

"And knowing you, you'll be right beside her." Jaelle laughed. "You talk about being timid, but when you're actually in the field—I know you better than you know yourself."

"Whether or no," Magda said, "for the moment we are in Thendara, and here we will stay, for the next few days, at least."

"We should relay a message to Armida, though. They'll be expecting us," Jaelle reminded her. "They should be told that we are all right—not murdered by bandits on the trail, or something of that sort."

"No," Magda said morosely, "only murdered here in Thendara, by bureaucratic nonsense! Shall we get in touch with them tonight?"

"You do it, Magda, you're a far better telepath than I am.

"But they will want to hear from us both," Magda said, and Jaelle nodded soberly.

"Tonight, then, when it's quiet."

*   *   *

But that night there was an Oath-taking in the house. Although neither the new Renunciate nor her oath-sisters were
known to Magda or Jaelle, they could not in decency absent
themselves from such festivities in their own house. Afterward
there was a party with cakes and wine; Magda, knowing what
lay ahead of her, drank sparingly. She spent most of the evening
with Camilla and Mother Lauria, and found herself agreeing
how very young the new Renunciates appeared. It seemed that
the woman who had taken the Oath tonight, and her friends
who had witnessed the Oath, were just children. Had she and
Jaelle ever been as young as that? Apart from the oath-mother,
an older woman was always chosen to witness the ceremony,
and it seemed incredible to see Doria, whom Magda remembered as a girl of fifteen sharing her own housebound time, described as an older woman.

Rafaella was there, and spent much of the latter part of the
evening talking with Jaelle; Magda did not begrudge Jaelle the
company of her old friend and partner, but, watching Rafi drinking heavily of the pale wine from the mountain vineyards, she
hoped Jaelle would not be led into drinking. It was late before
they could get away to the room they shared—but that was just
as well. The atmosphere was quieter at night, with most people
sleeping; much matrix work, in the Towers and outside them,
was done between sunset and sunrise.

"What was Rafi talking about?"

"Some new project from Mapping and Exploring—a survey
in the mountains. She wanted me to promise I'd come." Jaelle
looked regretful as she pulled off her low indoor boots and untied the laces of her tunic. Magda sat on the bed to remove her
own.

"Did you promise?"

"How could I? I told her I would have to consult you, and
also the folk in the Tower. I do not think she knows we have
sworn oath as freemates, and I had no opportunity to tell her."

"Perhaps it is as well not to tell her."

"You told Camilla."

"But Camilla is not jealous. Rafaella and I have worked out

a pact for mutual co-existence—we even manage to like each other most of the time—but she is jealous of our closeness, Jaelle."

"Rafi and I were never lovers, Margali. At least, not since I was a little girl. She was really not much more. And now, at least, Rafaella is certainly a lover of men. What may have been between us when we were young girls does not seem that important to me, and I cannot believe it is important to her." Jaelle shivered, standing barefoot on the icy floor, and quickly pulled her nightgown over her head.

"That is not what she is jealous of." Magda wondered why Jaelle could not see it. "What she envies is that we work together, that we share *laran*. And that is closer than any other bond." She hurried into her warm nightgown and warmer robe, for the Guild-house was not well-heated at night. "Will you monitor, Jaelle, or do you want me to do it?"

"I will. That's about my level of skill." Jaelle had no illusions about her competence working with *laran*. She had spent half a lifetime blocking away her psychic gift, submitting to the training only when the *laran* could not be excluded from her consciousness. Now, she knew, she could achieve only the minimal level of training: sufficient to keep her from being, in the phrase so often used about untrained telepaths, a menace to herself and everyone around her.

Jaelle was, and was glad to be, an integral part of the group of telepaths and psi workers, loosely allied, who worked outside the ordinary structure of matrix workers on Darkover, and in defiance called themselves the Forbidden Tower. But she would never achieve sufficient competence to call herself matrix mechanic or technician. Sometimes when she watched Magda, born a Terran, and now the most skillful of technicians, she was painfully aware that she had cast away that birthright, and could now never recover it.

They were both wearing warm, fur-lined robes, fur-lined slippers. Magda wrapped herself in an extra blanket. Psychic work withdrew heat from the body. If the worker stayed out too

long on the astral planes known collectively as the Overworld,
it could result in painful chill.

Jaelle took her matrix from the tiny leather bag round her
neck, and carefully stripped away the protecting silks. The blue
stone, no larger than the nail of her little finger, glinted with pallid fires.

She spoke aloud, though it was not really necessary; from
the moment Magda had taken out her matrix, they had been in
contact.

"Match resonances—"

Magda was aware first of the physical heat and mass of
Jaelle's body, though she did not look at the other woman; her
eyes were fixed within the matrix, seeing only the moving lights
in the stone. She sensed the living energy fields of Jaelle's body
near her, the pulsing spots where the life currents moved. Then,
delicately, she moved to match the vibration of her stone to
Jaelle's, feeling it as a point of—was it heat, light, some indefinable energy moving in the room? Nothing so tangible as
these. She felt her heartbeat altering slightly, pulsing with the
ebb and flow of the energies of the matched stones, knew that
the very blood in her veins and arteries moved in cadence with
the other woman's.

She sensed, like a hand passing over her body, the monitoring touch of Jaelle, scanning her to make certain that all was
well in her body before she withdrew her consciousness from it,
aware of everything, even noticing the graze on her ankle where
she had skidded the other day on a pebble, the slight clogging of
her sinuses— she must have encountered something in the HQ
today to which she was mildly allergic; she noticed it, as Jaelle
moved energies to clear the condition.

Neither spoke, but she picked it up as Jaelle finished:
Ready?
I'm going out.

Magda let her consciousness slip free of her body and looked
down, seeing herself lying apparently unconscious on the bed
they shared. Jaelle, blanket-wrapped, sat beside her. With total
irrelevance, she thought. *That old robe of mine is really getting*

too old and grubby, I shall have to have a new one before long. What a pity I hate sewing so much. She could have requisitioned a new one from Supplies, in the Terran HQ, but she had lived in the Guild-house too long to see that as a workable solution.

Then she was up and out of the room, finding herself alone in the gray and featureless plain of the Overworld. After a moment, Jaelle stood beside her. As always in the Overworld, Jaelle seemed smaller, slighter, more fragile, and Magda wondered, as she had wondered before, whether what she saw was a projection of the way Jaelle saw herself, or whether it reflected the way in which, for some reason, she had always felt protective, as if Jaelle were younger and weaker than herself.

Around them stretched grayness in every direction, colorless and without form. In the distance, figures drifted. Some of them, Magda knew, were their fellow pilgrims on the non-physical planes of existence; some had merely strayed from their bodies in dreams or meditation. She could see none of them clearly as yet, for she had not yet marked her own path with will and purpose.

Now, in the clearing dimness as what looked like fog dispersed, she could see faint landmarks in the gray. First, foremost, she saw a shining structure, rising tall on the plain, which she knew to be the landmark made on these planes by the thought-form called the Forbidden Tower—shelter from the nothingness of the astral world. Her home, the home she had found for her spirit, shared with those who meant more to her even than the Sisterhood of the Guild-house. She still observed meticulously every provision of the Renunciate Oath; she was a Free Amazon not only in word but in spirit. But the Guild-house could no longer contain the fullness of her being.

With the speed of thought—for what she imagined in the Overworld was literally true—she was standing beside the Tower itself. Simultaneously she was inside it, in what appeared to be, complete in every detail, the upstairs suite in the Great House of Armida. She had come so late to this work that she had never quite accustomed herself to how time and space behaved on this plane.

All four of the rooms were empty—she could see them all at once, in a way she did not understand—but somewhere, there was the blue glow of a matrix where someone of the Tower kept watch. And then, without a moment of transition, Callista Lanart-Carr was beside her.

Magda knew rationally that Callista was not as beautiful in body as she looked in the Overworld. In this case at least she was seeing Callista through the eyes of the spirit and through the eyes of her love and veneration for this woman who was at the center of the heart and spirit of the Forbidden Tower. In reality (but what, after all, was reality, and which was the illusion?)— on the material plane of existence, Callista Lanart-Carr, once Keeper at Arilinn, was a tall, frail-looking woman, her red hair faded almost to silvery gray, though she was not much past thirty; her body was sagging from the three children she had borne, and her face was lined and careworn. Yet on this plane, at least for Magda, Callista had the radiant beauty of early youth.

Magda knew that she did not speak, but speech and sound were irrelevant here. It seemed to her that Callista cried out a joyful greeting.

"Magda! Jaelle! Oh, we have been expecting to see you—

And suddenly they were surrounded by the others of the Tower circle, Ellemir and Andrew and Damon, summoned quickly from dreams or sleep. Damon's brother Kieran was there too, and Kieran's son Kester, and Lady Hilary Castamir-Syrtis, who like Callista had once been Keeper in Arilinn. It seemed to both Magda and Jaelle that for a moment they were encompassed in an instant love-feast of greeting, made up of all the kisses and embraces and tenderness they had ever known, without time or the limits of the body, and it lasted (in reality, Magda knew, a split second or less) a long time.

At last, reluctantly, the intensity of loving communion ebbed (although Magda knew in some deeper reality that it would always be a part of her, always renewed and reassuring), and Ellemir said, "But my dears, we expected to have you here more than a tenday ago. I know the weather in Thendara is harsh sometimes, but I have heard of no storms, even in the pass. What has happened?"

With a humorous question from someone—Kester?—wanting to know what pleasures of the big city kept them away, friends, lovers—something like a swift reprimand for this intrusion from Damon—Ellemir's ill-concealed wonder that anything could keep two mothers from their children—Andrew's special enfolding of Magda in something that was very private between them, a bond of shared experiences stronger than love—

"Cholayna had need for me, and Jaelle stayed to keep me company," Magda told them, and swiftly shared the knowledge of the downed plane in the Hellers. Something might have drifted through into the Overworld.

She felt Andrew's surge of anger like a dull flame of colors, crimson and burnt orange, surrounding the outline of his body; she could sometimes see this even when they were both in their bodies. Here it was unmistakable.

"They should not have asked it of you, Magda." *Damn the Anders woman, nothing was worth doing that to you. That is like the Terrans, their damnable Need to Know, regardless. They have no idea of human needs—*

"That's too strong, Andrew. Cholayna made a point of telling me I could refuse."

Andrew dismissed that. "You should have refused. I'll bet you didn't find out anything worth knowing."

"I did bring Lexie back," Magda defended herself. "She might have stayed like that indefinitely! And there was more." On an impulse, she shared quickly with Callista the image with which she had come away from Lexie's mind.

Robed figures, deep hoods. The sound of crows calling, drifting through a silence deeper than the depths of the Overworld. . . .

Momentarily she could sense that Callista did not find it new, not quite.

I have encountered strange leroni *in the Overworld, now and again*, Callista's memory reached them all at once. *Not often, and only a glimmering. Once when I was very ill*—her mind edged away from the ordeal in which she had been made Keeper at Arilinn—*and again when I was trapped in the other planes of the Overworld and could reach nothing familiar. I remember the calling of strange birds, and dark forms, and little more. Your friend—Alexis?—if, in extremity, she teleported herself from the crashed plane, she may have crossed some strange places in the Overworld. I truly do not think it was more than that, Margali.*

"But what of the crashed plane? And no trace of it found—"

"I have a theory for that, too," said Damon, and the familiar sensation of warmth, strength, protection *(their Keeper, closer than a lover, the figure around whom the Forbidden Tower had gathered, the only one in all the Domains who had had the courage for this, to restore Hilary and Callista to full strength in spite of the laws which forbade a failed Keeper from ever again taking up her* laran, *their shelter and their strength and their lover and their father all at once)* . . .

Again the disparity from what Magda knew as "reality" and how Damon appeared here in the Overworld: in real life, a small, dark-haired, insignificant-looking man with fading hair and tired eyes, showing his age—he was a good twenty years older than Andrew, who was somewhat older than Ellemir or Callista. But here where the things of the spirit were made manifest, Damon appeared to be a tall, strong and imposing man, who gave the impression of a warrior. It had taken a warrior to resist the power of Leonie Hastur, the Keeper of Arilinn, who ruled all the Towers in the Domains with the same iron hand with which her twin brother, Lorill Hastur, ruled the Domains. Damon had won from Leonie, in a psychic battle against terrible odds, the right to establish what was now called, defiantly, the Forbidden Tower.

"I have a theory about the disappearance of your plane," Damon said. "If the Anders woman truly summoned up, from latency in her mind, a new psi skill and teleported herself—and that's not impossible, I saw Callista do it when we were imprisoned among the *catmen*—the pure energy had to come from somewhere. She did not, of course, have a matrix," Damon added. The matrix stones were crystals which had the curious property of transforming thought-waves into energy without transition by-products.

"Somehow, as she summoned the strength to translocate, to teleport herself, she used the kinetic mass of the Terran airplane for the energy requirement. That energy couldn't have come from nowhere, after all. In effect, she disintegrated and atomized the plane and utilized that immense energy for the strength to make the teleportation possible. No wonder they couldn't locate the plane, even with satellites. It doesn't exist anymore. It's disintegrated."

"I think that's a little far-fetched, Damon," Andrew argued. "Where would she get the strength, let alone the knowledge, to do that? If she was a trained psi-tech, even from some other world and some other tradition, I suppose she might have managed it. But a complete novice—possibly head-blind? I can't imagine it. She would have needed help."

"Maybe she had help, from those stray *leroni* Callista mentioned; she might have crossed someplace in the Overworld, and there found such help," suggested Kieran.

"Does it matter?" Ellemir asked practically. She was always the pragmatic one. "It's gone, and I suppose it doesn't matter how or why unless the Terrans get a bee in their bonnet about mounting a salvage operation to try to find if there's a record in—what did you call it, the black box?—of whatever it was she spotted beyond the Wall."

"They'd have a lot of fun with that," Andrew said, with dry irony. "I used to work for M-and-Ex. There's nothing out there, nothing at all."

"Let them look," Lady Hilary said with the equivalent of a shrug. "It will keep them busy and out of trouble. Some of the Terrans may be very nice people—" and her affectionate look encompassed both Magda and Andrew. "But what do we care what foolish quests they may attempt? When are you coming back to us, dear sisters? We miss you. And the children—"

She broke off, for the little group where they were gathered had suddenly been enlarged by two others.

Kiha Margali—it was like a gentle tug at Magda's arm, and

Cassilde, a girl of fourteen, fair-haired and blue-eyed, was immediately enfolded in Magda's embrace.

And Magda felt the surprise in the circle. None of them had known that Callista's eldest daughter had gained access to the Overworld. Young children did not, as a usual thing, have much *laran*—although Cassilde was approaching the age at which any latent *laran* she might have would be surfacing at any time.

Am I dreaming, Mother? Kiha—am I dreaming? Or are you all really here?

"Perhaps you are only dreaming, *chiya*," Damon said gently, and again his thought, wordless, embraced them all, *But she is old enough, we must begin teaching her properly*.

But even as their warm welcome enfolded young Cassie, there was a cry and a clamor for attention.

Mama! Oh, I called you, and see, you have come—

Jaelle enfolded Cleindori in her arms, but the child's confusion astonished them all. Cassilde, at the very verge of puberty, might well have gained access to these non-material planes of thought and spirit; that Cleindori could have done so at five years old was preposterous.

Cassie, my darling, even if you have skill for this, you should not attempt it until you learn the proper way to safeguard yourself, Callista admonished her, gently; and Andrew added, in his kindest and most fatherly tone, *Even if you can come here, child, you should not bring Cleindori with you*.

"I didn't," Cassie began, and simultaneously Cleindori clamored, "Cassie didn't bring me, I came all by myself, I love Auntie Ellemir, love her lots, but I wanted you, Mama, and you stayed away so long, so long! I called you and you came, and I can *too* come here without Cassie bringing me, I come here lots, I can even bring Shaya here, *look!*" Cleindori was crying with loud anger.

And Magda saw her two-year-old daughter, night-gowned, her dark hair tousled from the pillow; she said sleepily, "Mama?"

Half-unbelieving, Magda took the child into a close embrace. Although, their bodies were separated by two days' journey, it felt as if she were holding the actual child in her arms, the snuggling warmth of the little body, the small sleepy head on her shoulder. Ah, she had missed her, how she had missed her! But Shaya, at least, was here only in a dream. She would wake tomorrow, remembering that she had dreamed of her mother; Magda hoped she would not cry.

"Now this is enough!" said Ellemir, with firm authority. "We see what you have done, Cleindori, but this is not allowed. Take Shaya back to bed at once. And you, Cassie, you should go back to bed, too, you are not strong enough to stay out of your body this long. Tomorrow, I promise you, if no one else here will teach you to do it properly, I will do so myself. But for now, you must go back."

Cassie vanished. But Damon took Cleindori gently from her mother's arms. "Listen to me, daughter, I know you are only a very little girl, but since you have done this, we must acknowledge that you are old enough to do it. Do you know where you are, *chiya*?"

"It's the gray world. I don't know what you call it. I think it's the place I go when I dream, isn't it?"

"That and more, little one. Have you been here before?"

Cleindori struggled to find words. "I don't remember when I couldn't come here. I always came here. I think I was here with Mama and Shaya before I was born. When Auntie Ellemir told me about how babies came, before Shaya was born, I was surprised, because I thought they came from the gray world. Because I used to talk to Shaya before she was a baby. She was all grown up here, and then suddenly she was a baby and couldn't talk to me anymore except when we were *here*."

Merciful Evanda! Magda thought. In childish words, Cleindori had explicated a metaphysical theory that was beyond her, and probably beyond all of them; except perhaps, Callista and Damon, who had studied these things.

Damon certainly understood. He hugged the small girl close and said, "But in that world down there, my darling, you are only a little girl, and your body is not strong enough for you to spend much time here. Do you remember Aunt Margali telling you that Shaya could not eat nut-cake till her teeth were grown? Well, *your* body is not grown enough for this, Dori. You must stay in it until you know just how to leave it. You must come here only in dreams, little one; and especially you must not try to bring Shaya here until she is able to come and go without your help. Remember how you watched the chickens pecking their way out of the shell, and you wanted to help?"

She nodded soberly. "I did try to help one, and it died."

"Then you know why you must not help Shaya do anything she is too young to do. She too may stray to this level in dreams. You may ask her to try to dream with you. But no more."

"But when we're dreaming we can't stay here long enough."

"No, but you can stay here as long as you are able, and it will not harm you. But you must not come here except in dreams, my daughter. Will you promise me that?"

She looked into Damon's eyes, and Magda, still deeply in rapport with Damon, saw the child's eyes, and they were not like a child's eyes at all.

Then Cleindori said with unusual meekness, "I promise, Dada."

"Then both of you, back to sleep," said Damon with a gently banishing gesture, and both children vanished into wisps of dream. Extending her awareness, Magda could see the children in their cots, side by side, fast asleep.

Damon sighed. "She is *too* precocious! I knew it must come, but I never guessed it would come so soon!" But before either of them could see further into his thought, he enveloped them all again in his concern and kindness. "You must stay in Thendara as long as you are needed. Believe us, we have been taking better care of the children than you might think, from *this*!"

The gray world was breaking up now into wisps of fog. As Magda felt herself withdrawing from it, knowing that soon the Overworld would merge into normal sleep, and tomorrow this whole encounter would seem hardly more than a dream. For a moment, she felt all of them close and encircling her. In the wispy grayness she saw and briefly embraced Ferrika (the midwife had been out at the far end of the estate, waking and dozing by the bed of a woman in labor, and could not withdraw her waking consciousness even to greet her sisters), and also Colin of Syrtis, Lady Hilary's husband (a brief, sweet moment, momentarily rousing again a passion that had burnt away to embers even before Shaya was born) and then once again, for a sudden long moment, suspended between time and space, she came face to face with her daughter.

A dream. . . .

But of course there is some reality where Shaya is not a child at all. I must always remember that—remember that she is more than just the baby I held in my arms and nursed and cherished. Mothers who forget this do dreadful things to their children, she thought. And then it was all gone into the formless grayness and she was slipping down into her empty half-frozen body.

She crawled closer to Jaelle, hugging the other woman in her arms for warmth. For a moment, roused on a level that was not physical at all, as such work often left her aroused and excited, it seemed to her that she would like to make love to her free-mate, all the tender little rituals of touching and reaffirming what was so strong between them. But Jaelle was already deeply asleep.

We do not need that now, when we can have this, she thought, feeling again the exultation of the moment when they had all been around her with that closeness stronger than any other known bond.

And then, with a longing that was both sweet and sad, she wished that she could share this bond too with Camilla.

Do we make love, Camilla and I, because we cannot share this? And why has she refused this for so long? A little ruefully, she remembered what Damon had told Cleindori, and realized that it was a lesson she too must remember.

As she drifted down into sleep, real sleep, Magda thought, I hope I can remember all this when I wake up!

Chapter 6

A few days later, Cholayna asked if Magda would address a group of women recruits to HQ services. She was glad to accept: at least it gave her the illusion that she was doing something useful.

She had never been really comfortable with public speaking—few Intelligence Agents were; their training essentially prepared them for work outside the public eye. The newcomers to Darkover struck her as being very young; it was hard to remember that most of them were older than she had been when she was first sent into the field with Peter Haldane.

Two of the young women recruits were from Communications; Magda had worked there for a time, while it was still too difficult for women to operate independently as Intelligence Agents on a world with such rigidly structured gender roles as Darkover. Two were from Spaceforce itself. She wondered if these women had known, before they came here, that they could operate only inside the HQ Sector itself. Three were from Mapping and Exploring, and three more from Intelligence, Magda's own service.

"And now," Cholayna said after a few preliminary remarks, "I have brought someone here to speak to you all. I'm sure you already know her by reputation; she practically wrote, single-handed, all the documentation for fieldwork on this planet. Magdalen Lorne of Terran Intelligence."

Magda was nervous enough not to have noticed who was in the audience, but as she made her way forward through the group of women she heard a small, almost scornful sound. She wondered, with a certain resignation, why Lexie Anders had chosen to attend this session. These women knew her only in terms of the "Lorne Legend," for which she was not responsible. Whatever she had done, at the time she had done it, she had only been doing what any of them might do; simply muddling her way, from day to day, as best she could, through whatever she was given to do. She wondered, a little bitterly, how many other "Legends" were simply victims of luck and circumstances.

She spoke only briefly, saying she could hardly give an impersonal assessment of Darkover; it was her home world, and she had been fortunate enough to be allowed to remain. She did warn them about some of the difficulties they would encounter as women working here, and ended by inviting them to attend the meeting of the Bridge Society. She answered several questions about languages and dress from the young Intelligence workers; but when the women from Mapping and Exploring asked technical questions about the planet, she said pleasantly, "I'm sure Lieutenant Anders can tell you more about that than I. Anders is an expert in that field. Lexie—would you take over?"

She felt, as Alexis came up from the back of the room, that she had done her duty. If Lexie still held any grudge against her, it was Lexie's own problem, not hers. There would always be people who didn't like you and that wasn't always your fault.

She left Lexie to answer the technical questions, and went down to the main cafeteria for something to eat. Every now and then she had a craving for foods she could find only in the Terran Zone. She was looking about for a seat, tray in hand, when a voice said behind her, "We don't often see you here, Mag. You're looking well. What brings you today?"

"Cholayna asked me to talk to a group of her young recruits," Magda answered, turning to face the Legate. "Hello, Peter, it's nice to see you."

"If I'd known you were going to be here, I'd have asked you to stop by my office; I'm glad I ran into you." Peter Haldane took her tray and led the way to an isolated table for two. Magda, about to protest, shrugged and held her peace. Whatever the Legate had to say to her, better he said it here, informally, than officially in his quarters.

There was constraint in his voice as he asked, "And Jaelle—is she well?"

"Oh yes, certainly." After her own marriage to Peter had ended, Peter and Jaelle had been married, briefly and disastrously, for half a year. For a long time after that, Magda had not felt comfortable with Peter. She and Jaelle, after all, had chosen one another in a way that excluded Peter himself, and not many men could tolerate or understand that. . . .

But that had all been a long time ago. Peter now seemed her earliest friend, one who shared an otherwise irrecoverable childhood. Like herself, he had grown up with Darkovans before the Terran HQ had been built in Thendara. In the intervening years, she had come to feel that their early marriage had been because Peter had seemed the only person alive that she could talk to, and vice versa. Everybody else either of them knew was either Terran or Darkovan, defined by that difference.

That had not, in the end, been enough to build a marriage on. Nevertheless, she felt they should manage to remain on good terms, despite the different directions their lives had taken.

Peter, like herself, had suffered all the pains of divided loyalties. That would, she hoped, give him a greater understanding of the Terrans over whom he must now serve as Legate. He had always belonged in the career diplomatic service anyhow and never, really, in Intelligence; and Magda had known it before he had.

Like Lexie, he was always competing with me, she thought, and since no one had ever accused Peter Haldane of having any trace of *laran*, she was shocked when his next words were, "You know Lieutenant Anders, don't you, Mag?"

"Certainly I do," she said, abandoning her attempt to finish a dish of custard. "Why do you ask?"

"I suppose Cholayna's kept you up to date on the way she set us all by the ears here, with her plane going down?"

She lifted her eyebrows at him. "Then it wasn't your idea to have Cholayna call me in as a psi-tech for her?"

His blank look was answer enough. "You? A psi-tech? It would never have occurred to me. I gather from that, then, that you know all about it?"

"I know the plane went down and that she ended up here. Even with a mind-probe, that's all I found out. Is there something more I should have known?"

Peter answered with another question. "Then she hasn't come to you with her latest wild idea?"

"Peter, I'm the last person Lexie would have come to. She's never liked me. I've hardly spoken to her, except that night Cholayna called me in. All I know is what I found out then."

"Well, in a word—Anders is convinced there's a real city out there. She's sure what she saw before the plane went down was not a hallucination, or a radar angel or mistaken ground signal, but a real city. Why not? Every developed planet in this Galaxy has an installation which TI can, if necessary, conceal from radar and sky-spies. Why not this one?"

Magda thought that over for a minute.

"I can't imagine it," she said. "You know, and I know, the Darkovans have nothing like that."

"You mean, nothing like that *as far as we know*."

"No, I mean *nothing like that*! Peter, I've been working in a matrix circle now for six years. If there was anything like that in the Domains, believe me, I would know."

"What about *outside* the Domains?"

"Your own satellite reports tell you, that's impossible! Ask anyone in Comm or M-and-Ex."

He bit his lip. "Nothing, you mean, that can be detected. How do we know we can detect everything? The available technology on Cottman Four couldn't handle it, no. But that means nothing. Unofficial sources from outside Empire Civil Service could have set up a base here for some reason—mining, perhaps, or—"

"I can't believe it, you're talking Space Pirates!" Magda said, almost laughing.

Predictably, he reacted with annoyance. "Must you always make fun of everything *you* didn't think of?"

"If I was making fun, Peter, it wasn't of you," she said, now completely serious. "It's only—I can't believe anything like that could have been set up there without being discovered by satellite, or space sensors; it's hard to believe it could be done at all, though I suppose nothing's impossible. Is that what Lexie believes?"

"Yes. And she wants to mount an expedition to find it. I thought she might have come to you because you were working in Intelligence here, and because she knows your Free Amazons are the best mountain guides on the planet."

"As I said, Peter. I'm the last person she'd come to."

"But if she did—"

"I'd tell her the idea's completely mad. We have years of satellite observations to tell us there's nothing—all right, nothing observable—outside the Domains. And I'll bet there's nothing, period. That area must have been uninhabitable since—well, I'm no expert on geology and crustal movement, but—certainly for a geological eon. Probably since the Hellers rose out of the sea bed. As for mounting any kind of expedition, the logistics of it would be all but impossible, even *with* all the resources of Terran Intelligence behind it. Jaelle could tell you better than I what the difficulties would be, but I know enough to know it's impossible, and so do you." They had, after all, been in the field together, traveling as Darkovans. "To begin with— you'd have to cross the Hellers, and when you get beyond Nevarsin, the country's all but unknown. We have no operatives in Intelligence who know the trails, or the languages. There are *catmen* tribes up there, and—and God knows what else. Banshees—perhaps nonhuman cultures—I don't think it could be done, at all. Certainly I wouldn't try it."

Peter looked skeptical. "If she should come to you, that's what you'll tell her?"

"Believe me, Peter, she won't. Anyhow, Anders isn't Intelligence, she's Mapping and Exploring." Legally, Intelligence was responsible only to the Terran Empire Head Center, while Mapping and Exploring was under the sole authority of the Legate of the planet. "She'd have to get your permission, not Cholayna's. Even if you thought Cholayna would do something like that behind your back, Peter, she'd send one of her own operatives, not Lexie."

She did not know if Peter was convinced, but he had reason to know she had always told him the truth. She hoped he knew she always would. They exchanged a few more commonplaces and parted in friendly fashion. But as Magda walked across the city to the Guild-house, she wondered if that was why Lexie had chosen to attend her lecture.

A few days later, as Magda was leaving the HQ, Doria joined her at the Gates.

"Are you going to the Guild-house? I will go with you. I have a message from my mother for Jaelle n'ha Melora."

"Let me take it for you," Magda said, glancing at the sky. "It will save you a long walk in the rain."

Doria colored slightly. "I am sorry—Rafaella said I was to give it only to Jaelle herself."

Magda shrugged. There was a time when she and Rafaella had actually been friends, but she could never count on the other woman's friendliness. She would become accustomed to thinking of her as friendly, even presume on it a little—then discover without warning that Rafi was behaving as if she disliked her. But since she genuinely respected and admired Rafaella, she accepted her as Jaelle's friend, if not her own.

The two women set off side by side, walking swiftly, the hoods of their capes drawn against the rain. "Are you staying much longer in the City, Margali?"

"I hope not. There is really not much for me to do here. I know Jaelle would like to go back to work with Rafi, and Rafaella would like that too, but that would have to be her own decision."

They turned into the square where the Guild-house stood. Doria was about to ring the bell when the door opened and Keitha stormed down the steps, swearing aloud.

"Keitha, what's the matter?"

"Doria? Oh—well—it's not your fault, but when I see your mother again—"

"What? What *is* the matter, Keitha?"

"I leased a horse from Rafaella, since I have none of my own, and sometimes, when I am summoned to a confinement outside the City walls, I must have one. I wanted to make it a formal arrangement, but she said, no, she had a dozen ponies in the stable, eating their heads off, not getting enough exercise, and I was welcome to use one whenever I needed one to ride."

"And you are angry with her for that?"

"No," said Keitha, "but I asked her to lease me one formally, just so this wouldn't happen! Now all her horses are gone, and I must hire one in the market or go afoot."

"Take mine," Magda said, "you know which it is, Keitha, the black." It had been a gift from Shaya's father. "I won't be wanting it tonight."

"Thank you, oath-sister." Keitha hurried back into the house, and Magda and Doria watched her run toward the back door leading to the courtyard and stables. Doria whistled in surprise.

"What, all Rafaella's horses gone? I can't understand this! She must have had a—a large commission, unexpectedly, if she couldn't leave a horse for Keitha! It was really very thoughtless of her not to warn Keitha before-hand." Frowning, Doria went in search of Jaelle, while Magda went to hang her cloak, by now thoroughly soaked, on one of the drying racks in the kitchen.

By the time she had dried the wet cloak and hood, the women were already coming into the dining room, so Magda stayed to help put bowls and mugs on the table. When everyone had been served, she slipped into her customary seat beside Jaelle.

"Did Doria give you her message?"

"Yes, but I cannot imagine what can be in her mind," Jaelle said. She looked troubled. "It was the last thing I expected after all these years. We aren't children anymore."

"What is wrong, Jaelle?" With her freemate so troubled, it was more than Magda could do to keep her resolve to stay entirely out of it.

"The message was only a few words, not even written down: *There is a letter for you in the old place.* Magda, that goes back a long way—to when I was only a little girl, Kindra's fostering. Kindra used to take me with her on long trips, and Rafi and I wouldn't see each other for long periods of time. So we used to have a secret, private letter drop at the old saddlemaker's in the Street of the Four Winds."

Magda shrugged. "Why not? I suppose most children do that sort of thing at one time or another."

"Rafaella wasn't a child, she was older than I—but, well, I thought it wonderful that an older girl would play games with me. Rafi and I have always been—close. You know that."

"Indeed I do," Magda said. The sympathy she felt was very real. As a Terran child, isolated among Darkovans, she had always been an outsider.

"But now we are not children, we are not even young girls, I am a grown woman with a child of my own, and Rafaella is older than you are! Why should she revert to this childish nonsense?"

"Oh, Jaelle," Magda said, "don't worry so about it. Perhaps she wants to confide in you, or to assure herself that you are still close enough to her to do something silly and childish for her. A way of—re-establishing that old closeness. She doesn't trust me not to come between you."

"And that *is* silly and childish," Jaelle said, still looking pale and troubled. "We're *not* children, and does she truly think she can come between freemates? I am ashamed of her, Magda. She can hardly want me as a lover after all these years. But if she does not understand that I will always be her friend—then she is sillier than ever I thought her."

"Don't worry," Magda reassured her, "you'll see, she simply has something she wants to tell you privately."

"But she ought to know I *always* respect her confidences," Jaelle fretted. "I am really afraid she's gotten herself into trouble of some sort—"

Magda shrugged. "I wouldn't think so. If she felt free to leave the city and take all her horses, leaving poor Keitha to borrow mine—"

"*What?*"

"Jaelle, didn't you know?"

"No, all day I have been recopying some old archives for

Mother Lauria. The paper on which they are written is disintegrating, because the ink they used in those days was so acid. They are only about a hundred years old, but they are falling to pieces. And I've nothing else to do here. So I've been shut up all day in the library—"

Briefly, Magda told the story.

"It's really not like Rafi to be so thoughtless. What can she be thinking of?" Jaelle's smooth forehead drew into lines of puzzlement. "I think I should go at once to the saddlemaker's, Magda."

"Tonight? You're out of your mind," Magda said. "Listen to the rain and wind out there!" It sounded like one of the summer gales which blow down through the pass from the Venza Mountains, striking Thendara with rain and high winds and sometimes, even in high summer, sleet or snow. Jaelle frowned, listening to the wind slamming the shutters against the windows.

"Whatever it is, Rafi is out in it." She pushed aside the untouched piece of nut-cake on her plate and went toward the hall. Magda followed.

"You can't go out alone in this weather on some hen-brained notion of Rafaella's—"

Jaelle turned and caught her arm. "Come with me, then. I have a feeling that this may mean trouble, Magda—more trouble than Rafaella being jealous or wanting to play girl's games."

With a sigh of resignation, Magda nodded, and caught up the cloak she had so painstakingly dried. Camilla appeared in the hallway behind them.

"Going out? In this weather? Are you both quite mad?"

Jaelle told her what had happened. Her face was pale and drawn.

"Camilla, come with us. You are Rafi's friend too."

"As much as she will allow," Camilla said. Sighing, she took down a battered old cape. "Let's go."

Wind and rain slammed into the hall as the three women went out into the night.

Chapter 7

The rain poured down as the three women walked swiftly toward the marketplace. Magda was angry at herself for having allowed the hostilities between them to go on for so long. Jaelle's small triangular face was hidden under her hood, but it seemed to Magda that she could see pale anger there.

Camilla strode beside them, gaunt and silent, and the rain sloshed in puddles under their feet and flapped their capes around their faces. The marketplace was empty, pools of icy water making a miniature landscape of lakes and small rocky shores. Stalls, tightly locked and boarded, rose like islands over those shores.

"She's not here. The saddlemaker's stall is closed," Camilla said. "Come home, Jaelle, there's nothing that can't wait till tomorrow."

"I know where the saddlemaker lives." Jaelle spun abruptly on her heel, heading toward a dark side street. Camilla and Magda exchanged a single despairing glance and followed her.

Magda felt she would like to shake Rafaella until her teeth rattled. She was also angry at Jaelle, who was for catering to Rafaella by tearing off into the Old Town at this godforgotten hour.

The wind was icy, even through their capes, striking hard down the back of her neck. Magda spared a thought for Keitha, riding outside the city. But Keitha would be warm inside a house, with a good fire they would build up for heating water. Magda had never had the slightest wish to be a Medic or even a

Renunciate midwife, but at least tonight Keitha knew where she was going and why and what she was going to do when she got there. And that was more than the others knew.

Jaelle stopped before a small weatherbeaten house, spoke briefly to someone who came to answer the bell, and after a time, a fattish old woman came to the door.

"Why, it's our little Jaelle, and all grown up, aren't you? Yes, your partner left you a letter, and I brought it home here, afraid, I was, someone would put it away somewheres I couldn't find it. Now, dear me, where'd I leave it?" The woman dug in several of her capacious pockets like an owl trimming her feathers, hunching herself and digging about. "Ah, here we are—no, that's an order for Lady D'Amato's saddle. This—ah, yes, here you are, *chiya*, won't you come in, and your friends too, and have some sweet cakes and cider by my fireside, like you used to?"

She held out a somewhat grimy fold of paper, sealed with a colored wafer.

"No, I thank you, I must try and catch up with Rafi before she is too far out of the city," Jaelle said, and turned away, her mouth set into a grim line. Magda could see her scanning the letter's front, but it was too dark to see or read.

"Here." Camilla seized Jaelle's shoulder, steered her toward the spill of light from the open door of a wineshop on the corner. The place was humming with talk, crowded with mercenary soldiers and Guardsmen, but though some greeted Camilla with a nod and a word or two, none of them attempted to hinder the tall *emmasca* as she led her friends to a table at the rear. A thick-bodied lamp was swinging over the table. Camilla quieted Jaelle's attempt at protest with a word.

"They know me here. No one will bother us. Sit down and read your letter, Shaya." She jerked her head at the round-bodied woman who hurried toward them. "Just wine punch, and privacy at this table, Chella." Camilla flung a coin on the table, and as the woman scurried off to obey her, said deliberately to Magda, "She's not much now, but you should have seen her ten years ago. Skin like rich cream, and the softest neck I ever tried

to bite. Her hair was long enough to sit on, then, and the color—
it made you want to hang it with silver, and believe me, she
knew it. But she's a good soul for all that."

The woman, coming back with the hot wine, giggled softly
and ran her fingertips lightly across Camilla's hand. Camilla
smiled up at her and said, "Another time, Chella. My friends and
I need to talk. Make sure nobody gets any notion that we want
company, will you, Chella?"

Jaelle tore open Rafaella's letter and moved it under the light.
As she read, she frowned, and finally said, "She's gone raving
mad." She tossed the letter to Magda.

Reluctantly, Magda took the letter and read:

Dearest Shaya,

I've been trying to get you to come back to work with me
long enough. Now it's time to stop talking about it, and do
something. I'm leaving this at the old place as a way of reminding you of the good times, but this is bigger in every
way. There might even be a chance at the special expedition
we used to talk about. Lieutenant Anders thinks she is using
me for the big discovery she thinks *she* can make. It's the
other way round, really. But I'll give the woman value for
her money, and so will you.

Remember when we were girls, Kindra's old legends of
the secret city far away in the Hellers, where an ancient Sisterhood watches over the affairs of humankind? There's a
chance it may not be legend after all. Remember the legends
used to say that if you found your way there, and you were
sufficiently virtuous, they would teach you all the wisdom
of the universe. I wouldn't give a *catman*'s tooth for wisdom, and I probably don't have the virtue to qualify, either.

It could be a dangerous business, but the legends all
agree on one thing: they won't, or aren't allowed to interfere
in human affairs, and if you find them, they aren't allowed,
by their laws, to kill. Their city is supposed to be filled with
copper and gold and rare old books of wisdom. They say all
the wisdom of the *cristoforos* came from them, but the

cristoforos only got a little of it. Yet everyone says the *cristoforos* are the custodians of all wisdom!

So I don't have to tell you what I'm doing. The Terran woman wants information for HQ, which she says will make her famous. As for me, I'm betting on some of that copper coin and gold. Forget the wisdom. If I get there, and get out again, I guarantee I'll have something a lot better than some old books and fancy words. But I need your help. I can't do this alone, and there aren't that many women in the Guild-house now that I can rely on, except you.

I need trade supplies, extra-warm clothing, and a few more horses and pack animals. Try to persuade a couple of the Guild-sisters to come along, too—not goody-goodies like Doria or Keitha, but someone who can travel hard, live rough, chew leather and take orders. And whatever you do, *don't* run and blab all this to Margali! For once, love, keep something good to yourself. Remember your old partner— and bring all the horses and trade goods you can get your hands on. It will be a rough trip, but believe it, it will be worth your while. Think of making your daughter independent of her father, even if he *is Comyn!*

I'll wait for you for three days where we had to slaughter the *chervines* that time with Kindra. Don't fail me! Get on the road at once, so we can be over the Kadarin before the weather breaks.

I know you, and I know how you must be longing to be on the road again. I'll be waiting for you, oath-sister! With my love,

Rafi

Magda dropped the letter on the table and took up the smoking cup of hot wine punch that the bar woman had set before her.

She said, "It's not Rafi who's gone mad, it's Lexie Anders."

"Most likely both of them." Camilla picked up the letter, raised an eyebrow toward Jaelle. "May I?"

"Please do."

As she read, Camilla snorted. At last she said, "Legends! Why doesn't she go off looking for the Hidden City, the one with the spice-bread trees all hung with candied fruit . . . I thought Rafi had more sense."

"She's going to get herself into terrible trouble," Magda said. "Of course the responsibility is Lexie's, but that doesn't mean Rafaella can get away with this. Even if such a place had ever existed—"

"Oh, it may well exist," said Jaelle unexpectedly, and Magda turned on her.

"You never said that when Callista and I were talking about strange *leroni* from other parts of the Overworld—"

"To be perfectly truthful, Magda, I hadn't associated the two. I never thought of the Sisters of Wisdom as robed figures with calling crows. When I was a little girl in the Guild-house, and first heard of the Sisterhood, I used to wonder if they came from the Hidden City. Kindra talked of it to me a time or two, when we were traveling together—a city inhabited by wise-women, perhaps descended from the old Priestesses of Avarra. The city is said to be on an island, or it was, once, when the climate was different from today's. If you find it, they have to take you in. They can tell you everything you need to know—how to make a fortune, if that's what you want, or mystical wisdom about the purpose of your life, if *that's* what you want. Kindra said she had met women who had been there, so it never occurred to me that it was a legend. If you put all the stories together, there may well be something to them. That doesn't mean I think the place is *accessible*. According to Kindra, they would do everything they could to keep anyone from finding it. Everything except kill, Camilla's right about that part of the legend. And if you actually *did* find it, they were obligated—oh, none of this makes any sense, I can't imagine why the Terrans should meddle with any of it, or why Rafi would have anything to do with it if they did!"

Magda, heartsick, said, "I'm afraid that's my fault. Lexie, I think, would do anything, anything at all now, to get ahead of me, to make her mark in Terran Intelligence in a way I couldn't hope to equal. I swear I never intended to set myself up as a legend, I wasn't trying to grab *any* glory! She accused me of wanting it all, once, saying I didn't leave anything for anyone else to accomplish—"

"Oh, the woman's a fool," Camilla said, "you did what was set in front of you. If she can't understand that you aren't competing with her—"

It was something very different that was troubling Jaelle. "If she does this, Rafaella will end by being blackballed by the Terrans. She would never work for them again. And what will happen to Lieutenant Anders, Magda, if she does this against official advice?"

"The best she could hope for would be to be shipped off-world," Magda said. "At worst, she could be thrown out of the Service, and serve her right. Unless she made such a major discovery that they'll—that must be what she's hoping for, to make a discovery for M-and-Ex that's so spectacular they'll overlook her disobeying Standard Orders. That's not unknown in the history of the Service, either. Peter told me she was thinking of doing this, but I told him it could hardly *be* done, even with all the resources of the Empire behind her."

"Evidently," Camilla said, "she's *not* trying it with them behind her. Which is just as well, Terrans aren't welcome in the Hellers, and a big expedition wouldn't find anything, except, probably, more trouble than they could manage. But half a dozen women, well-provisioned, with good luck and good weather, might manage it. Kindra always said she'd like to try it, Jaelle, but when she took you in as a fosterling, she waited for you to grow up, and died before she ever had the chance." After a minute, Camilla added, "Rafaella would know about that. Rafi was her kinswoman. I'm surprised that she'd try to take a Terran on such a trip, though."

"I'm not," Magda said. "The Terrans have the resources, the money, maps and so forth, to mount expeditions like that. If, in all these years, Rafi hasn't found any women, even in the Guild-house, who were willing to try, I'm not surprised that when a woman of the Empire brought it up, she'd be excited about the possibility. I *am* surprised Lexie dragged Jaelle into it. And I'd want more evidence that it was real, not just an old story."

But had Lexie been able to provide more evidence than Magda had read in her mind? Magda realized, with sudden horror, that she was jealous; that she was thinking, *This should not have been brushed aside by the Terrans, this should have been given to me, Magda Lorne!* She was, after all, the first woman to do underground fieldwork on Darkover. If something this big was in the wind, what right did they have to let Lexie take over? Magda was shocked at herself. This was the very kind of thing which had precipitated Lexie Anders's hostility in the first place. And far from sending Lexie off on an exciting chase for a legendary city, Peter Haldane had specifically refused to authorize any such thing.

Or had he? Maybe calling Magda in with a blunt prohibition from the Legate's office would be the perfect cover-up for Terran Intelligence to go out looking for the same thing. Was it even ethical for Magda, sworn to the Guild-house, to see Terrans led into the heart of the most carefully guarded women's secret on Darkover?

No, this was nonsense, she was only giving credence to Marisela's absurd intimations of mystical sisterhoods and cosmic secrets.

"I don't know why I am worrying about it," she said. "It's impossible. Suicide. Even with luck and good weather—neither of which are easy to find in the Hellers—it can't be done."

And even if it were possible, even if Cholayna sent for her and asked her to take it over, she would have refused. "Totally impossible," she repeated, again, hunting for conviction in the words.

"I don't know about that," Camilla said. "Assuming Kindra was right, and there really is such a place—if it has ever been done, *ever*—it could be done again. But I don't think Rafi could do it. *You* might, Jaelle. Or might have, once. I don't know if you've still got it in you, after seven years of soft living out at Armida."

Magda said angrily, "That's not the point, is it? Of course, that's what Rafaella wants to do, to lure you to go with her, drag you into the trouble that she and Lexie are making for everyone. She's counting on your sense of loyalty and your friendship. She thinks you'll go off after her the way you pursued Alessandro Li when he took off into the hills on his own. Then she can get you back, which is what she wants—"

"I thought you said you were not competing with her, Magda. Should I let her go alone, to get into trouble in the Hellers, or die there?"

"Then—you're going to do what she wants."

"She was my partner for all those years. But there's no reason to drag you into it, Magda."

"Do you think I'll let you go by yourself, and make trouble for yourself with the Terrans, and—" She stopped, looking into Jaelle's glowing eyes. She said, "That isn't the point, either, is it? You *want* to go! Don't you? You want to be back on the road, and any excuse is good enough."

"Magda—you don't understand—" Jaelle sighed, and said, "I haven't any right to want to go. But it drives me mad that Rafi is free to go and I am not. Besides—"

"You are free to do whatever you think you should do," Magda said, realizing almost in despair that Jaelle was almost echoing her own thoughts. She added, "I should have been straight with Lexie. I should have told her about my own experiences with these people. Whether or not they're real, or from some other plane of existence, if I had been willing to share that with her, tell her how and why I encountered them, perhaps she would have understood—"

Magda now felt she understood. Lexie, like herself, had encountered these mysterious ones, the same dark-robed Sisterhood who had reached out to rescue herself and Jaelle. It was they who had sent Lexie back, as they had sent help to her . . . She knew Camilla did not believe it, but she had been there, and Camilla had not. But Lexie had had the courage to go in search of them, and she had not.

"The legend is very specific," Camilla said wryly, "that if you go looking for them and you are not qualified for admission, you'll wish you'd never heard of them. Somehow I don't think Rafaella's desire for riches is qualification enough. I'll bet on Rafi to bluff her way in, maybe. But not to get out again."

"Can't you see?" Jaelle's eyes were bright. "Those two, they aren't the right ones to go."

"And we are? Oh, come, Shaya—"

"I don't think it's coincidence that all this has happened," Jaelle argued. "In any case, Rafaella has put the safety of their expedition in my hands. She has asked me to catch up to her with more horses, trade goods, warm clothing—I can't abandon her."

"And—perhaps if I tell Lexie what I know of these— these mysterious ones, she'll have a better chance." Magda hesitated. "And I have access to other information she could not get, special security information, what little *is* known about the country in the Hellers beyond Nevarsin—"

And yet, in her heart, Magda knew Lexie would never see it that way. To Alexis Anders, the well-meant attempt to help would be no more than the *Lorne Legend* standing in the way again.

Hellfire, Lorne, is there any pie on this planet that you don't have your fingers in?

"Neither of you are being honest," Camilla said wryly, "yet both of you feel yourselves summoned to this mysterious city. As for me—my motives are perfectly clear." She glared at them and said, "I will go to this mysterious City of Sorceresses, but I at least am honest about my reasons. These people are supposed to be able to tell you the purpose why you were born, and—" She looked around, daring anyone to challenge her. "I have reason to question the Fates. If the Goddess has demanded of me that I suffer these things, then do I have no right to demand of the Goddess that she, or these mysterious women who pretend to do her will, account to me for my life? I choose to seek out this mysterious city, and there demand of the Goddess why she has treated me as a toy."

And despite the angry, half-flippant way in which Camilla phrased her words, Magda knew that they were a threat. And in any confrontation of that sort, Magda would bet on Camilla to come off best.

Jaelle shoved her chair back; thrust the letter, which had been lying on the table, into the pocket of her breeches. "When do we start?"

Magda felt as if she had been caught in the track of one of the Terran earth-moving machines, the kind used to transform a green hill, lush with trees and plants, into leveled, bare ground, a stripped place where a spaceport could rise, or anything happen. Jaelle had never taken her protest seriously at all. Yet she had tried, fairly tried, to assess the rights and wrongs of this. Or had she?

"She said she'd wait three days," Magda said. "I'll go in the morning to the HQ and get maps from Intelligence; I have access to satellite overflight pictures, and the computer time to have them blown up into scale maps."

"And I'll make arrangements for horses and trade goods," Camilla said. "I have contacts now. You don't."

And the children? Magda thought. Yet she had been wondering, only the other day, why there seemed nothing now worthy of her energies. She found herself remembering an old Terran proverb: *Be careful what you pray for, you might get it.*

The rain had stopped when they came out of the wineshop, and Magda looked up to the skyline, where the high ragged teeth of the Venza Mountains rose clear. A small moon was just setting over one of the peaks.

They would be going up that way, then northward, past the Kadarin and into the deeps of the Hellers, to Nevarsin and beyond. She had never been so far into the unknown wilds. Her two companions were, with the skill of experienced mountain guides, already planning the stages of the journey.

If there was one thing she had learned when she left the Guild-house for the Forbidden Tower, it was never to assume that her life was settled or would follow an orderly track from now on. She listened to Camilla, scowling and talking about the difficulty of finding mountain-hardened horses at this season, and realized that she was also mentally rummaging through her wardrobe for the warm clothes she would need long before they got into the Hellers.

Chapter 8

At first light, Camilla went off to see about horses, pack animals and saddles.

Magda, who could do nothing until regular work hours in the HQ, went into the dining room, where cold sliced bread and hot porridge were laid out for breakfast. As she ate, she tried to think what she should do first.

As an Agent in the field, she had had access to the most sophisticated fly-over photographs, and to the elegant equipment which could, from a photo taken at eighty thousand meters, generate a map sophisticated enough to distinguish a resin-tree from a spice bush.

There were few Darkovan maps. Few traders came and went in the Hellers, and when they did, they followed trails their grandfathers had known. Beyond Nevarsin, little was known: a frozen plateau, wilderness. The maps from photograph work would help. But not, Magda thought, enough.

Jaelle came down, already dressed for the road, in riding breeches and boots. Magda had never before seen her wearing the long Amazon knife, like a short sword, of a mercenary or soldier. She slid into the seat beside Magda.

"I'll go and see about trail food," she said. "And you should have a riding cape. You'll need it when we get into the mountains; no jacket is ever really warm enough. Do you suppose we can get some Terran sleeping bags? They're better than what we can find in the market."

"I'll arrange it." Extra warm socks, she thought, special

gloves, sunburn cream, sunglasses. . . . A little group of women, readying themselves for work in the market, came in and dipped up bowls of porridge. Sherna raised her eyebrows at Jaelle.

"Dressed for riding? You're away, then?"

"As soon as we can get away. Taking a caravan north."

"If you see Ferrika at Armida, give her my greetings." Sherna finished her porridge and went into the kitchen for the loaves for the bake-stall. She turned back to ask Magda, "Are you going with Jaelle, oath-sister?"

Magda nodded, feeling raw-edged; she knew it was all meant kindly, but one of the few things she still found difficult about Guild-house living was the way everyone intruded on your private life.

She had never seen Jaelle at the work for which her freemate had been trained. She was astonished at the swift efficiency with which Jaelle plotted packloads, ran down lists of items.

"Maps, sleeping bags, perhaps some packaged high-energy Terran rations, they'd be better when we get into the mountains. Camp stoves and concentrated fuel tablets. I'll leave everything from the Terran Zone to you."

"I may have to tell Cholayna—"

Jaelle sighed. "If you have to, you have to. She's met Rafaella, hasn't she?"

"Rafaella is listed with Mapping and Exploring, and in Intelligence, as the best of the available—" Magda flopped, swallowed down "*native*" and finished, "Darkovan guides. Not the best of the *woman* guides, just the best of the guides. She's worked before this with mapping expeditions. Naturally Cholayna knows her. She probably recommends her to all of the bigger expeditions."

Jaelle nodded. "Rafi told me once that she likes working with Terrans. They get the best equipment and they never try to argue about the bills. They either agree to pay, or tell you it's too much and go somewhere else. They don't bargain just for the fun of bargaining. Also, they tip better."

There were, Magda thought, not a few Darkovans like that: working for the Terrans, secretly despising them. Since her first year in the Guild-house, she had had the same curious relationship, compounded almost in equal parts of affection and dislike, with Rafaella.

She said, "Sherna told me the other day that she dislikes trading with Terrans for that very reason—they take all the fun out of being in business. They won't bargain, just yes or no, take it or leave it."

"I know what she means," Jaelle said, "the Terrans have no sense of humor. Neither does Rafaella. That's why she gets along so well with them."

"Why should anyone carry their sense of humor into the marketplace?"

"It's a game, love. It all comes out about the same—maybe a few *sekals* difference, but everybody gains face and everybody thinks they get the best of the bargain."

"I can't see the fun in that sort of thing. I like to know what I'm being asked, and say yes or no to it, not play games for hours every time I want to buy a basket or a pair of boots!"

Jaelle touched her freemate's wrist affectionately. "I know. You're a lot like Rafi, you know? I suspect that's why you two don't get along very well." She pushed away her porridge bowl. "Don't forget sunglasses. We'll be traveling on ice once we're halfway through the Hellers, even at this season."

As she made her way through the City, Magda reflected that Jaelle and Camilla seemed to be taking it for granted that they were going on; that there was no question of catching up with Lexie and Rafaella to bring them back from this unsanctioned expedition, but to join it.

It's my fault. I shouldn't have told her what I had found out about the Sisterhood. That was what started it. She too had wanted to know what was behind the mystery. The difference was that she would never have thought of going off on her own to find it.

I'm not adventurous. Maybe that's why I shouldn't have come between Jaelle and Rafaella. Jaelle has never been quite content to settle down in one place.

She gave her ident numbers to the Spaceforce man at the

gate, and caught herself sounding almost furtive. *What's the matter with me, I have clearance here, I'm an accredited Agent, and for all anybody knows I'm going about my regular duties! Actually, it is my business to stop Lexie going off into unmapped, unexplored parts of Darkover without authorization!*

In the hostel of the Bridge Society, she had begun keeping a few Standard uniforms: the access codes wired into the collars allowed her to come and go in the Headquarters building without constant identity and security rechecks. She greeted the young Darkovan nurses getting ready for the day shift there, went quickly to the locker she kept, and changed into uniform—the dark tunic and tights with the red piping which cleared her for any area except Medic and Psych. Monitors clicked ACCEPT as she went swiftly along the corridors to the major Mapping room. She found a free terminal and requested a satellite picture taken during overflight past Nevarsin. She could read the picture well enough to purse her lips and whistle silently at the terrain.

And Lexie believes there is some sort of city out there which has managed to screen itself from satellite or radar imaging? The woman's insane.

If the mysterious city of the Sisterhood existed—and Magda had an open mind about that—it must be in some inaccessible part of the Overworld. Yet ever since she had known Jaelle, she had heard tales of Kindra n'ha Mhari, Jaelle's foster-mother, who had guided Lady Rohana into the Dry Towns. She had been a legendary explorer and mercenary. If she said she had known women who had actually been inside this legendary city, who was Magda to say it didn't exist?

She touched controls which would generate, from the satellite photograph, a somewhat more detailed computer-diagrammed map, one which would not require her own expertise with Terran formulations to decipher. She studied it on the screen for a time, requesting slight clarifications here and there until it resembled the Darkovan maps she had seen in Rafaella's collection, then asked for a hard copy. The laser-

directed burst-printer moved silently, and in under half a minute
the map slid out. She took it and studied it again for a long time,
seeking errors, comparing it with other pictures on the screen;
making absolutely certain that it was the very best that she could
get.

In her early years with Intelligence, Magda had traveled with
Peter Haldane over much of the Seven Domains, and into the
foothills of the Hellers. She had made some of the early maps
herself, though Peter had been better at that; her own gift was
with languages. As she looked at some of the roads (on any
planet but Darkover, they would have been classified as cattle
trails), memories began resurfacing from that half-forgotten
time . . . How young she had been then, how boundlessly energetic. Had she and Jaelle actually crossed the Pass of Scaravel,
almost four thousand meters high? *Yes*, she thought grimly,
Jaelle has the scars to prove it. And once, she and Peter had
gone in disguise to the City of Snows, Nevarsin of the *cristoforos*. . . . After a moment, she sighed and turned again to the
terminal, requesting yet another review of available maps northward from Nevarsin.

She studied the few narrow tracks that led into the wilderness. The plateau was over two thousand meters high; the passes
might be expected to be short on oxygen; certainly there would
be banshees—those blind, flightless carnivores that moved with
a terrible tropism toward anything that breathed, and that could
disembowel a horse with a single stroke of those dreadful claws.
In the unexplored areas marked in cross-hatching on the maps,
there would be unknown dangers. Some of the passes were far
higher than Scaravel; most of what was shown was covered in
the pale blue cross-hatching that meant, *Unexplored—no hard
data*. If what they were looking for really existed, it would be
somewhere there.

Needles in haystacks, anybody?

There must be more to the legends than that. If women Kindra knew had come and gone, it must be possible, not easy but
possible, to track down information, to buy it, bribe those who
knew—

But that would all have to be done on the Darkovan side. She had pretty well exhausted Terran sources at this point. She got supply on the terminal, requisitioned sleeping bags, solid fuel for camp stoves, sunglasses and sunburn cream—none of these items was at all unusual; any agent of Mapping and Exploring, Survey or Intelligence who was going into the field requisitioned the same things. Even if they hadn't been credited to Magda's personal account instead of being requested without charge as *work related expenses*, they would hardly have blipped a CAUTION flag at Auditing. Still, as a personal expense, she would never, ever have to explain why she had wanted them.

She wondered if Lexie, too, had covered her tracks in this way. Alexis Anders, like herself, had been trained in the Intelligence Training School on Alpha; but Lexie was younger than she was, and had considerably less experience in this sort of thing.

After a minute, Magda opened up the terminal again and entered the access code for Personnel.

As she had expected, she was challenged twice; but her clearance levels were such that she was able to determine that Anders, Alexis, M&E Special Duty Pilot, had put in for vacation time and had requisitioned certain mountaineering equipment. *Very interesting*, Magda thought as she cleared the screen.

She would have to make the trip down to Supply to pick up the things she had requested, even though payment had already been automatically deducted from Magda's credit at HQ. Indeed, it had nearly cleared her account: detached-duty pay was not very good. Only the bonuses Cholayna had arranged for her recent work with the Bridge Society had enabled her to pay for them at all.

Well, it'll be worth it. That's what matters.

She specified the kind of packaging she wanted, queried the prices of some other items—Jaelle could probably get them cheaper in the Old Town—and prepared to return to the Bridge Hostel to change into what, when she was in the Terran Zone, she still automatically thought of as *field disguise*. As she shut down the terminal, she looked round to see Vanessa ryn Erin standing in the doorway of the room.

"I thought it was you. What did you want with Lexie's records, Magda? Curiosity isn't a valid reason for snooping in Personnel Files, you know. I'd thought better of you."

"If you talk about snooping, what were you doing snooping on what *I* was doing?"

"Personnel is my job, Magda. Not yours. Come on—explain." Vanessa paused, gazing coolly at Magda. "I'm dead serious. I can have you psy-probed for less cause than this."

Magda, who detested lying, had meant to tell her the truth; but now she realized that, to protect herself, not to mention Jaelle and Camilla, it would be better to think up a good lie, one that would satisfy Vanessa's conspiratorial imagination; and, like many people who are almost compulsively truthful, Magda couldn't think of one. It made her angry. She thought, *I can't just stand here blinking my eyes like a little girl caught with my hands in the cookie jar!* And of course, she did exactly that.

At last she said; "I wanted to know what Lexie was doing. I saw her at the Bridge Society meeting, but after an ordeal like that, I was curious to know if she was really well again." Then it occurred to her what she should have said in the first place. "She seems to have gone off with Jaelle's partner: we needed to know which way they'd gone. Jaelle missed a message from Rafaella, and—"

"As you discovered, she has put in for vacation time," said Vanessa. "When I spoke to Cholayna, though, I got the impression she'd given Lexie an assignment, which was how she got the equipment on a cost-free basis. She hired a Renunciate guide, and she's going into the Kilghard Hills to study women's folk dancing."

"So that's—" Magda stopped herself. She said flatly, "I don't believe it."

"Why not? It's nice, easy work, a good way to get what amounts to a paid vacation. We've all done that kind of thing." For the next half year, Magda regretted that she had not simply allowed Vanessa to believe that. It was such a simple explanation, and would have saved an enormous amount of trouble—if Vanessa had actually believed it.

Instead, she drew a long breath of disbelief and indignation.

"What kind of hare-brained imbecile do you think me, Vanessa? There are Renunciate guides, yes, who would accept a commission to take a Terran woman alone into the hills to study folk dancing, or ballad styles, or the *rryl*, or the basket-weaving of the forge folk. But Rafaella? It was Rafaella who led the Mapping expedition to Scaravel! It's Rafi they ask for when they want someone to coordinate ninety men, five hundred pack *chervines* and half a dozen half-trained mountain guides! Come *on*, Vanessa! Do you honestly think Rafaella n'ha Doria would accept a commission to take one Terran woman on a little Sunday excursion to scribble down the differences between a *secane* and an Anhazak ring-dance? Possibly, just possibly, if they were lovers and wanted an excuse to get away together. I can't think of any other reason. Knowing Rafaella, I don't believe it for a minute—though I don't know anything about Lexie's love-life, come to think of it; but I'd bet you a week's pay she's completely heterosexual. Or didn't you see the look on her face when I introduced Jaelle to her as my freemate?"

Vanessa shrugged. "I hadn't thought much about it. I just thought she wanted to get into the hills. After all, Magda, Lexie *did* train as an Intelligence Agent. I thought, after the crash, this could have been the only assignment she could get. She knew she'd need a Renunciate guide, and I suppose she simply asked for the best one on the list."

"And Rafaella accepted, just like that? Nonsense."

Vanessa burst out, angry, defensive, "I didn't stop to think about it at all until I got a buzz that someone was snooping in her file! After what she's been through, Lexie's certainly entitled to put in for vacation! It's not a crime to hire a guide who's over-qualified, is it? As long as she can pay Rafaella's fees! Maybe Rafaella just wanted some easy money, or to get the better of a foolish off-worlder who's willing to pay four times the—" Vanessa stopped dead, and said, thoughtfully, "Or maybe Cholayna assigned her to study folk dances as a cover, and she's going into the field to do something much more important and serious—"

"Now," said Magda, "you're just beginning to catch up with me."

"But—would Cholayna do that without consulting Personnel, to certify that Lexie was fit—stable enough, for that kind of thing? That's the point, Magda. That's *my* job! With a breakdown and amnesia so recently—I'd demand a consult from Medic and Psych before she went out again. And so would Cholayna! Although Cholayna does tend to—make up her own mind, about people—" She stopped, and Magda, knowing what she was reluctant to say, said it for her.

"You were remembering that *I* was supposed to have been fired, or allowed to resign—weren't you, Vanessa? Of course. And there are plenty of times when I wish she hadn't fought for me. And damn it, *this is one them!* The fact is, Vanessa—I think Lexie's pulled a fast one, and she may just have pulled it on Cholayna, too."

Suddenly it occurred to her that she was sharing with Vanessa a secret that was not hers to share, one that belonged to Jaelle and Camilla. If her purpose was to keep Rafaella out of trouble, or keep Lexie from getting into a part of Darkover where Terrans were not entitled to go, what she had just said was inexcusable.

But Vanessa's anger was not, as Magda had thought, directed at her. It frightened Magda that she could so clearly see what Vanessa was thinking: Vanessa was a Terran, head-blind, she was not even supposed to be able to read Vanessa's mind; yet there it was, clear as could be: *Lexie has a right not to join Bridge Society if she doesn't want to, but she has no right to try to manipulate all of us because she thinks we're fools who have gone native—or something like that! Doesn't she understand that Magda and Cholayna are my sisters, and that if she puts something over on them, she's tangling with me as well?*

But aloud, Vanessa said only, "Let's go up and ask Cholayna."

Chapter 9

Almost since she had known her, Magda had wondered about Cholayna's secret of relaxation. Cholayna never seemed actually to be doing anything, whether you went into her office in the HQ, or whether you sought her out in the special offices of the Alpha Intelligence School. Yet judging by results, one would suppose she spent all her time in frenetic activity.

Today was no exception: Cholayna was lying back in a comfortable chair, her narrow feet higher than her head, her eyes closed. But as Magda and Vanessa came into the office, she opened them and smiled.

"I thought this would be your next stop," she said. "What do you want with the satellite maps, Magda?"

This was why I told Jaelle that I might have to tell Cholayna what was going on. She always knows.

Vanessa, however, allowed Magda no chance to answer.

"I don't suppose you'll tell me, if it's Classified," she said, "but is Lexie's assignment, studying folk dances, a cover for some kind of official Intelligence maneuver?"

Cholayna looked mildly startled. "No, it's just a bit of xenoanthropology. I had to okay it because any time a Terran goes into the field—which in effect means anywhere more than ten kilometers outside the Old Town—Intelligence is supposed to clear it, make sure they won't step officially on anyone's toes. I could see that after the shock she'd had, she wouldn't be much good as a pilot without a fairly extended rest. So I okayed it.

There isn't, after all, a great deal of formal Intelligence work here—why do you think I *picked* this place? I spend ninety-nine percent of my time preparing undercover ops for work in linguistics and xenoanthropology. Which Magda set up before I ever got here." She smiled at Magda, who returned the smile. Vanessa looked suspicious, but Magda was enough of a telepath to know when she was being told the truth.

"So it's not a cover for that expedition Peter Haldane says she wanted to lead into the Hellers?"

"Oh, that." Cholayna chuckled. "Lexie admitted she'd been fairly spaced when she came back, didn't know what she was doing for the first few days. In fact, she wanted me to make sure what she said to him didn't go into her permanent record. She knows Peter and I are old friends. Then she said she needed a good rest, and would like to get out into the mountains. Don't think I don't know when I'm being worked for a free vacation on company time, but Lexie's competent, and she's entitled to the same perquisites as the rest of us. So I told her to find herself a qualified guide from the Bridge Society, and cleared it for her with Xeno-An."

Magda opened her mouth, but again Vanessa spoke first.

"You see, Lorne? You see? I told you so—"

Cholayna put her feet down on the floor. "*What* is going on?"

"Cholayna—what would you say if I told you that the guide Lexie engaged was Rafaella n'ha Doria?"

"Knowing what Rafaella charges," Cholayna said, "I would say that Lexie made a very poor bargain. I know at least half a dozen women who would take her on such a trip for half—no, a quarter of Rafi's standard charge—"

But then she stopped. It was frightening: Magda actually felt the information penetrate through the outer layers of Cholayna's lazy good nature. For the first time since her Training School days she saw the sharp intelligence behind that façade.

"In the name of a million fire-eating demons, what are those two up to?" Cholayna sat back a little, eyes narrowing.

"I think," said Vanessa, "that Lexie has found a way of getting the expedition she wanted, without going through the formalities. At the very least—it makes a fool of you and your department, Cholayna."

Cholayna's face tightened, and the bushy silver eyebrows bristled above her dark eyes. "I should have known. I trained Lexie and I ought to know when she's being devious! So, that's why you wanted the maps. But what do you suppose they're looking for?"

Magda handed her the letter. Cholayna glanced at it, very briefly, then tossed it back across the desk, "Hmm. Looks like an exceptionally private sort of letter. But knowing you, you wouldn't show it to me without a good reason. Why don't you just tell me *that,* instead?"

Magda detailed the contents of the letter.

Cholayna frowned. "Chasing fairy tales doesn't sound much more like Lexie, actually, than studying folk-dancing."

"Oh, it's more than that. Lexie saw them—or thinks she did—and under the same type of circumstances that *I* saw them." Drawing a long breath, Magda explained what she had seen in Lexie's mind when she had probed it: robed women, voices, the calling of crows. Cholayna listened, tapping her long fingers restlessly against the glass surface of her desk.

Magda finished: "I always believed that, if they existed, they existed only in the Overworld. But Camilla said that Kindra knew women who had been there. Marisela knows something about them, too, but she won't tell."

"And you're going after them?" Cholayna sat up briskly. "All right. I'll arrange clearance for all the maps you need. Get Supply, Vanessa, it won't take me more than—" She consulted a chronometer. "Half an hour to be ready to ride."

Magda stared. "Cholayna, you can't—"

"*Can't* isn't a word you use to me," Cholayna reminded her, but she was smiling. "Think, Magda! If Alexis Anders's theory is correct, and some other planetary influence has set up a radar-impervious, satellite-blinding station here, it's not only my business to know about it, we could all be fired, or worse, and Peter and I could be court-martialed if we didn't know about it. What do you think I'm here for? And if you're right, and it's some secret of the Sisterhood—do you think I want some spoiled brat from Map and Ex, someone so arrogant about this planet that she wouldn't even join Bridge, meddling with it? Quite apart from the diplomatic difficulties—if any non-Darkovans are going to be meddling in the Sisterhood's business, better you and me than Lexie, hmm?"

This was all so true that there was nothing Magda could say. Still, she remonstrated.

"You knew when you came here that you couldn't work in the field, Cholayna. Riding with us, you wouldn't even be safe, everyone would know you were not native." Almost alone among planets settled by man, Darkover, one of the "Lost Colonies," had been settled by a commune from the British Isles and was almost exclusively caucasoid.

Cholayna replied, "Out in the wilderness, what does it matter? They'll think, if we meet anyone who thinks anything at all, that I'm deformed, burnt or tattooed by Dry-Town slavers, perhaps; or—as some of the women in the Guild-house thought at first—that I have a terrible skin disease. Or that I'm nonhuman." Cholayna shrugged. "Talk to Supply, Vanessa. I should check Magda's supply list first, there's no sense in duplicating. Do you have enough sunburn cream and extra sunglasses?"

Once, Magda had barely escaped being caught in a stampede of the wild *chervines*, antlered analogues of deer, used as pack or dairy animals, who roamed the Kilghard Hills. She felt something like this now. She wondered what Camilla and Jaelle would say.

Cholayna excused herself, and went swiftly to her quarters; came back with a surprisingly small pack of personal possessions.

"Everything else, except boots, I can get from Supply. They'll be waiting for me at the gate. Let's go. Maps ready, Vanessa? I spoke to my subordinate; she's ready for indefinite takeover. I told her it was Cosmic Top Secret, and not to mention it to Haldane until I had been gone a tenday. She probably thinks she can wriggle her way in enough to become indispensable while I'm gone, and I'm sure she thinks I care one millicredit. Let's go." She slung the pack over her arm.

"Wait," said Vanessa. "I'm going, too."

"Don't be foolish, Vanessa. You can't—"

"It's you who's being foolish," Vanessa said, "but you haven't any monopoly on it. First: I have been climbing since I was sixteen years old. I led an all-woman climbing team in the first ascent of Montenegro Summit, on Alpha. That was one of the factors in sending me here; I know all about severe climates. And you've got to admit that when it comes to climate, Darkover is something really unusual—*especially* in the outer Hellers. Second: I am also a member of Bridge, and what Lexie is trying to do makes a mockery of everything Bridge has done on Darkover, so it's as much my business as hers, or yours. And third—" She held up a hand as Cholayna tried to interrupt her. "If you want to be perfectly technical about it, Personnel has a right to pass on anybody's psychological and physical fitness to go into the field. Just try to leave without me. I'll make sure— no, the Legate will make sure, neither of you get out of the HQ gates."

"This is a fingernail's breadth from blackmail," Cholayna murmured.

"Damn right." Vanessa stared, facing her down. After a moment, Cholayna burst out laughing.

"Shall we all be mad together, then? Ten minutes, Vanessa. We'll meet you at Supply."

Cholayna kept the parka hood of her down jacket, with its priceless ruff of offworld fur, drawn close about her face as they crossed the city. The assigned meeting place was a tavern they knew; at this hour it was half-filled, a few Guardsmen enjoying a noonday pot of beer or a dish of boiled noodles. A smaller circle of Guardsmen were standing at the front, playing darts, but after a moment Magda saw Camilla's tall, lean figure at the center of the group, knife in hand.

"Come on," one of them shouted, "prove it, put your money where your bragging mouth is!"

"I hate to take your money," Camilla said in her gentle voice, and let the knife fly. It landed directly in the center of the dart, slicing feathers from the haft, which split, driving into the board to wedge so tight against the dart's metal pin that a hair could not have been threaded between them. There were gasps of amazement. Laughing gaily, Camilla picked up a dozen coins lying on the bar and shoved them into a jacket pocket before she went to retrieve her knife. She saw Magda at the door, and went to meet her.

"Showing off again, *bredhiya*?" Magda asked.

"They never will believe a woman can throw a knife faster and straighter than they. When I was a mercenary, I used to earn all my drinking money that way," Camilla said, "and this time, I needed some money. I cleaned myself out buying travel supplies this morning. Good thing I brought two extra horses." As simply as that, she accepted Cholayna's and Vanessa's presence, and led them to a back booth where Jaelle waited.

"I ordered soup and bread for all of us. We might as well have at least one hot meal before we get on the trail." She barely glanced at Cholayna as she added, "It doesn't meet your criteria for edibility, Cholayna, I know you try not to eat anything that ever moved of its own accord, but you'll have to get used to that on the road, anyhow."

It was as if she had known all along that Cholayna and Vanessa would be coming with them. Perhaps she had. Magda knew that she would never ask, and that Camilla would never tell her.

Chapter 10

It was still early afternoon when they left the city behind, and before sunset they had crossed Dammerung Pass. It was neither especially high nor steep, but as they began to descend, Camilla, who had set a stiff pace, looked appraisingly at the two Terran women.

"You're in fair shape, Vanessa. Cholayna, you're reasonably soft, but no worse than these two—living soft at Armida all these years, having children—nothing worse for your wind! You'll harden up fast enough on the trail."

They took the road north, traveling at the fastest pace the pack animals could sustain. In the last lingering red light, Cholayna threw back her hood; she looked happy, and later said to Magda as they rode side by side, "I'd forgotten what this was like! After seven years behind a desk in Administration, and fifteen years teaching before that, I thought I'd never get out in the field again. I hadn't really realized what it would mean, coming to Darkover. I stayed because I thought I was doing good work, especially with the Bridge Society. But it's good to be back in the field. It's been so damned long."

She must have been one hell of a Field Operative, if they gave her a post in Training School, Magda thought, and not for the first time, wondered just how old Cholayna was; but it would not have occurred to her to ask.

The sun set, and the swift-falling night which gave Darkover its name dropped across the Venza Mountains. There was no rain; Camilla, taking advantage of the rare good weather, pushed the pace as hard as she could. It was nearly midnight when she signaled a halt. They set up camp quickly by lantern light, and Cholayna kindled a small fire to heat water for hot drinks, though they ate only bread and cold meat from their packs.

"We can get fresh food in the villages for a few days, and save the trail food," Camilla said, chewing a handful of dried fruit. "After that we'll be in the hills; and villages where we can get provisions may be three or four days' ride apart."

"How do we know which way we are going, or shouldn't I ask?" Vanessa's voice was quiet in the darkness beyond the fire; it was Jaelle who answered.

"Margali told you about the letter? Rafaella said she would wait three days at the place where we slaughtered the *chervines*. She knew I would remember that. It was years ago; we were young girls, traveling with Kindra. We ran out of food and water and killed the animals rather than leave them to starve. The fresh meat let us get along without water. But it was a near thing. I haven't been that hungry since, and I hope I never am again."

She cast a quick look at the dark sky. "We'd better turn in. This weather may hold another day, but when it breaks, it's likely to break for good. North of Dammerung Pass, we'll be in the foothills. I'd rather not spend a tenday holed up in a snow cave! And, if we want to catch up with Rafaella, they're traveling lighter than we are."

Jaelle had done this work for years; there had been many times when her life, or the lives of a dozen other people, had depended on her judgment about the weather. Without discussion, Vanessa went to help Camilla with the horses, while Cholayna started pulling out the sleeping bags.

They slept in a ring, feet to the last coals of the dying fire. Magda, looking into the unusually clear night at the rarely seen stars of the Darkovan sky, wondered what Rafaella would say, if they did catch up, about having the Terrans with them.

As if Magda had spoken aloud, Jaelle said, "She did tell us to bring along a few people who could travel hard, live rough—"

"And take orders," Magda said wryly. She couldn't see either Vanessa or Cholayna doing that.

And what if they did not catch up to Rafaella? Only a dangerous trip through the wildest unknown country on Darkover, where Darkovans themselves never went, seeking a city that might not even exist. Her back ached and she was no longer accustomed to hard riding. She thought of Shaya, and had a sudden picture in her mind, like a vision, of her child peacefully sleeping at Armida.

What am I doing here? I have a family now, a child, a home and work I love, and here I am heading into wild country chasing a dream, a legend, wild geese. . . . The memory of Damon's eyes, Callista's chiding face, seemed to reproach her. *Why have I involved myself in this madness? I should have left it to Jaelle—Rafi's her partner, Rafi doesn't even like me. And Cholayna's career is at stake, it makes sense for her to be here.*

In the morning, she decided, she would tell them all firmly that it wasn't her business at all, and set off toward Armida and her loved ones and, most of all, her daughter.

Yet, as she fell asleep, she couldn't help but feel again the excitement of the unknown trail ahead, leading up into territory where no Terran had ever set foot, and quite probably no woman except the unknown *leroni*. That night her dreams resounded with the calling of crows.

Four days north from Thendara, the weather broke, and by noon heavy flakes began drifting slowly from the sky, each one as big across as Jaelle's palm. Jaelle swore softly as she rummaged in her pack for mittens and a warm hood.

"I'd hoped we'd get across Ravensmark Pass before the snow set in. There's always nasty going along those ledges. I should have taken the longer route through Hammerfell, but I gambled on the weather, hoping we could gain a day and catch up with Rafaella. Somebody told me in the last town that some of the road was washed out over Ravensmark in the summer floods. In good weather it wouldn't matter. In this—" She stopped and stood, watching, as if trying to see through the thick flakes.

Vanessa asked, "Should we go back then and catch up on the road to Hammerfell?"

Jaelle shook her head, causing a loose strand of auburn hair to tumble from her hood. "Too late for that. We'd lose two days now. And we have no way of knowing which way they took. Magda, have you any idea?"

Magda caught what she was thinking; she was doing it all the time now, almost automatically. She ought to be accustomed to it by now; she remembered how she had used her *laran* to track Jaelle through hills like these, years ago. But she shook her head.

"I'm not close enough to either of them for that."

"But you actually probed Lexie's mind," Jaelle protested, "that might make a bond."

"I'm not sure I want a bond like that," said Magda wearily; but she closed her eyes and tried to see Lexie; and for a moment, she had a fleeting glimpse of Lexie, her head covered with a Darkovan hooded cape, leaning forward over a pony's neck . . . Snow seemed to blot out the vision, she did not know whether it was the snow falling now, or some other storm in some other place, could not tell whether it had been memory or imagination or a true picture from her *laran*.

She said, doubtfully, "I think I saw—they have been delayed by a storm? I'm not, sure." Even with the whole of the Forbidden Tower matrix circle around her, she knew the same uncertainty would have remained: present—where Lexie was now—or a flash from past or future.

"I'd do as well guessing," she sighed, "and you could make a better guess about Rafaella than I could."

"I've been trying to do that," Jaella told her, "but I don't like it. We were so close, for so long, it's as if I was using that closeness to spy on her. And she has no *laran* at all, she would never understand."

Magda heard also what Jaelle didn't say; this was not the first time her *Comyn* birth, the heritage of *laran* they could never share, had come between them, disrupting their long partnership, even their brief time as lovers. Rafaella could have forgiven Jaelle everything except this, that she had returned to bear a child to a *Comyn* lord—had taken a place in that mysterious world in which Rafaella could have no part. Magda thought Rafaella could even have forgiven Jaelle for that, if Jaelle had had to leave all of her Renunciate world behind. What she could never forgive was that Magda, a Terran, had followed Jaelle where Rafi herself could not.

"Trying to track them with *laran* is foolishness," Vanessa said, so impatiently that for a moment Magda wondered if she had been thinking aloud. Then she remembered what Jaelle had actually said, about trying to follow Rafaella with the psychic bond between them.

"Maybe one of you can do it, maybe you can't, I don't see why you should waste time trying. Is it important to know if they came this way?"

"Only to know how near they are to the meeting place she left the message about," Jaelle said. "If they had good luck and good weather, traveling light, they could be at Barrensclae already—that's where we slaughtered the *chervines*—and we've got three days to catch them there."

"How far is it?" Camilla asked. "I'm not familiar with the place."

"In good weather? Ten hours, once we cross Ravensmark. In this? Your guess is as good as mine. A day, ten days, never. If we hit avalanches, we might not make it at all."

"Avalanches?" Cholayna craned her neck up toward the pass, invisible in the flying snow. "How high *is* Ravensmark?"

"Eleven thousand forty,"

"Meters? Good God! You can't call that a *pass*! That's a mountain all by itself."

"No, eleven thousand forty feet—"

"What's that in civilized numbers?" Vanessa demanded.

"I can't be bothered to figure all these numbers for you," Jaelle snapped, "I have important things to worry about, such as how in the names of all the goddesses we're going to get these horses across here if the road's been washed out from the summer floods! There's a long stretch where the road has never been good for more than one pony's width, a washout there could mean losing half our baggage. Do you want to hike through the Hellers in a backpack and no spare boots? I don't."

"I've probably climbed worse," Vanessa said. "Believe it or not, Jaelle, there are other planets with snow and high mountains in the Empire. If you're not able to get over a pass without your mystical psychic powers—"

"Now listen here—" Jaelle began.

"Hold it! Both of you," Camilla ordered. "If we're going to stand here arguing about what we're going to do, let's use the time for something practical while we wait. Vanessa, hunt out the grain. We'll feed the animals. Then if we decide to start over the pass, they at least will be well fed and in good shape. Jaelle, have you been over Ravensmark before this?"

"Twice. It's easier this way. Coming down from the North, you're more exposed to the wind. But this direction isn't exactly a picnic. I really am worried about washouts, and with snow in the pass—if Vanessa is really as experienced as she claims, she wouldn't take it lightly either."

"I never said I was taking it lightly," Vanessa quibbled, "but I do feel, the worse it is, the more sense it makes to get over it before the snow gets any deeper. If Jaelle doesn't feel comfortable leading the way, I'll try."

"I know the way, and you don't," Jaelle said. "If it can be led at all, I'll lead it. I'm not worried about getting across myself, on foot. The *chervines* can make it, it's their kind of country, after all. And I think the ponies probably can. But I tell you, those ledges are narrow. Even at the best, you don't cross Ravensmark on horseback. It makes Scaravel look like the Great North Road. Even with washouts, I'd try it in decent weather. But if we get a hard freeze, and there's glare ice—I'm not actively suicidal, and I don't imagine you are."

"That bad, huh?" Vanessa looked at Jaelle in silence for a minute. When at last she spoke, to Magda's relief, there was not a trace of argumentativeness in her voice.

"What are our options, then? If the risk is that great—what alternatives do we have?"

Jaelle considered this for a moment. She looked at the thickening snow, and said, "If we don't cross it tonight, it probably can't be crossed at all until after next spring-thaw. That's why it's the least traveled pass in these hills. Once there's glare ice on those ledges, I wouldn't cross it for all the copper in Zandru's tomb. We'd have no choice except to go back, and go round by Hammerfell."

"*Can* we cross it tonight?"

"I think I could get across in daylight," Jaelle mused, "though I might have to lead the horses across one by one. If you're used to mountain-style ice-climbing, you probably could. And I'd bet on Camilla. I'm not sure about Magda, but she did get across Scaravel in the dead of winter, and I wasn't any help even when the banshee found us. But—" She turned and looked at the one remaining woman.

Cholayna looked straight into Jaelle's eyes. "I'm not afraid."

"That has nothing to do with it. It's not your courage I question. It's your balance, your skill, your head for heights. Magda has no head for heights at all, but she knows I do, and she'll take orders. What about you? Ravensmark is about the worst trail you can imagine, and then some. Vanessa has done some climbing for the fun of it, so I know she won't panic when the going gets rough—and believe me, it's rough enough that I get scared myself, and I don't usually scare. If you lose your nerve when we're in the neck of the pass, along those ledges—what then? We won't be able to turn around and go back, not at that point. Once we're halfway over, it's too late. I think we're going to have to go around. I honestly can't be sure you'll make it, and I don't want to risk all our lives on your nerves."

Cholayna opened her mouth to protest, and shut it again. At last she said, "Fair enough. I'm the weak link. Do you want me to turn back, and let the rest of you go on? Because what you're saying is, the rest of you can make it without me. And if you turn back and go around—there wouldn't be much chance of catching up with them in time—right?"

"If we go round by Hammerfell," Camilla said, "I doubt we'd catch up with them this side of Nevarsin."

"And if we—or you—go on, you have a good chance?"

"A chance," Jaelle said. "Not a good chance. There's that, too. I could risk all our lives and push across Ravensmark, and we might *still* lose them. I don't know if it's worth pushing you all this way for such a bare chance. I'm no gambler—never have been."

"Forget about me," Cholayna said. "What do you want to do?"

Jaelle turned on her angrily. "That's not a fair question! How can I forget about you? You're here! Do you think I want your death on my conscience?"

"I shouldn't have come, should I?"

"Too late to worry about that now," Camilla said, while Jaelle hesitated, too polite to answer. "Done is done. I can see why you wanted to come, why you had to. Sending you back alone would be just as dangerous as trying to drag you across Ravensmark, so forget about it. Just shut up and let Jaelle think what's right to do."

Cholayna shut up. It must, Magda thought, have been the first time in twenty years that Cholayna had been treated like a nuisance, a liability. It was Jaelle who must make the final decision. Quietly she went to the saddlebags, dug out rations and shared out handfuls of dried fruit and meat bars.

"Whether we cross or go back, we won't have time for a meal in the neck of the pass. We fed the horses, which makes sense. Eat." She handed Jaelle some of the meat-and-dried-fruit mixture, and Jaelle put some of the stuff, absentmindedly, into her mouth and chewed.

Cholayna nibbled on a raisin, and Camilla said, "Eat some of the meat, too. Whatever we do, in this cold you need something solid."

Cholayna sighed, put the dried meat into her mouth with visible distaste. What Camilla had said was right, and Cholayna knew it, but Magda, watching her struggle to keep from spitting out the detested and unfamiliar food, felt considerable sympathy for her. Cholayna Ares was used to giving orders, not taking them; and while she might be willing to take them on important things which were obviously a question of all their lives, she would, sooner or later, refuse to take orders about personal matters.

Vanessa looked at the sky, from which the color was already beginning to fade as the snow thickened. "So what are we going to do? If we're going to try to cross, we'd better not waste any more time. And if we're not, shouldn't we get under cover?"

Magda knew that Jaelle had no taste for making such decisions. Yet they were all turning to her, demanding it. She wished she could shelter her friend in her arms and protect her. But for better or for worse, the decision was Jaelle's.

Jaelle finished the mouthful of dried meat and fruit, swallowed once or twice, and sighed. "I don't know what to say. I swear I don't! Vanessa, what do you think?"

"I'm not as familiar as you are with the place. I'm not familiar with it at all. If you want to try, I'll follow. We can give it a good try."

"Magda, what do you say?"

"I'm willing to take the risk, if you think it can be done."

"I know that," Jaelle said, and now she sounded irritable. "I'm asking what you think Cholayna's chances are of making it, and whether it's worth pushing on, with the risks what they are; or if we should play it safe, turn around and head for Hammerfell. Or would you take her round by Hammerfell, and Van and I go over, try to catch up, and wait for you at Barrensclae?"

"Maybe you should ask Vanessa," Magda temporized, half joking. "Personnel is *her* job. I think we should all go ahead, or all go back together and go round. If she goes back, I shall have to go with her. What about it, Cholayna? Do you want to try? I see no point losing three days or so, but only you know if you're willing to risk it. But if Jaelle thinks I can make it, you probably can."

"I'll try," Cholayna said, with the ghost of a smile. "And I promise not to lose my nerve. Or, if I do, I'll keep my mouth shut about it."

Jaelle shrugged. "All right. Let's go before the snow gets any thicker and has a chance to freeze. If we can get through before there's ice on the ledges, it will be a lot more workable. One word of advice—and this goes for you too, Magda. Keep your eyes on the trail and don't look down."

Chapter 11

At first the road led upward between hills, steep but not yet menacing. The snowflakes had grown smaller, no longer hand-sized, but the smaller flakes came down thickly, and Magda knew this meant the snow would continue to fall. There were still a few hours of grayish daylight.

Jaelle led the way, muffled in cloak and hood, thick scarf tied over her face; Camilla came after, with two *chervines* broken to a tandem rein; then Cholayna, at the center, on the smallest and most sure-footed of the mountain ponies. Magda came behind her, riding a horse and leading one of the *chervines*. Vanessa, mountain-wise but unfamiliar with the trail, brought up the rear.

As the trail led upward, it grew fainter and steeper. Parts of it were trodden deeply into old mud, rocks lining the path underfoot, and patches of last winter's snow clinging beneath the thick tree-hedges that lined the road. It was very silent, even the animal's hooves sounding muffled underfoot, and the snow continued to fall. Upward and still upward; now there were places where the trail all but disappeared between trees and rocks. The *chervines* did not like it, and whickered uneasily as they picked their way. After an hour's riding—though it seemed like more—Camilla signaled a halt, got down and took the two tethered-together pack animals off the tandem rein.

"They won't be able to make it like this. Cholayna, you take the lead rein on this one. He'll follow the other, she's his mother and they've worked together for years. He won't run off and get lost, but he needs a rein to follow." She climbed back into her saddle. Her face was muffled in a scarf and heavily smeared with cream against the burning of the wind. Cholayna had the same cream on her face; it looked grotesque against the darkness of her skin, as if she were checkerboarded black and white.

When they started upward again, the path was so steep and so narrow that the *chervines* were lurching upward as if they were climbing steps. Magda kept feeling that she would slip backward off her horse as the animal's quarters strained up under her saddle. She thought, *We'll never make it.* A few minutes later, Jaelle signaled a halt. Her figure was blurred through the thickening snow, which was no longer melting as it fell but sticking to the ground, still no more than a thin white sifting; rocks and mud showed patchy black through snowy lace.

Jaelle slid to the ground, hanging the reins on the saddle; she came back, picking her way down over the rocks in the narrow space between the trail's edge against the mountain, and the horses and pack animals. She spoke to Camilla as she edged past, and Camilla dismounted and came after her. Magda heard her say to Cholayna: "It's too steep even for your pony. You'll have to get down. Walk close to your horse and hold his bridle. He'll find the way better than you can." She steadied the older woman as she clambered out of the saddle. "Is the altitude bothering you?"

"Not yet, just a little short of breath."

"Well, take it easy. There's no point hurrying. There's bad going ahead, but no danger here. Are you all right, Magda?"

Magda could feel her heart pounding with the altitude, but so far she was in no trouble. She was not so sure about Cholayna, but so far the Terran woman was keeping the pace well enough, and they were gaining height so slowly that there was time to adjust to the altitude. Her ears felt tight, and she yawned, feeling them pop.

"How are you doing, Vanessa?" Jaelle faced the younger woman at the back of the line.

"So far, so good. What are we? About halfway up?"

"Close enough. The hard going starts up there." Jaelle pointed and Magda sighted up along the path to where a crag hung over the narrow path and, as far as she could tell, the road disappeared and dropped off to nowhere.

Vanessa surveyed it, frowning. Jaelle said, "There are steps. Broad enough and low enough, the horses and *chervines* can make them if the snow doesn't get any more slippery. It's one of the bad spots. I'm going on ahead; let my horse follow if she will, but wait till I signal if it's all right. I want to be sure there are no nasty surprises up here, while it's still light enough to see." She turned and went upward along the narrow trail, half disappearing from sight as the pathway dipped; they could see her red cap bobbing along, then nothing.

Camilla said tensely, "I should have gone up with her."

"She knows what she's doing," Magda said. After a minute or two, Jaelle reappeared and beckoned them forward. Camilla took the lead reins of one *chervine*, letting her horse follow as he would; Cholayna the other. Magda dismounted, taking the reins of horse and *chervine*, one in either hand, until the trail grew so narrow that she was forced to go ahead, leading her horse and letting the mountain-bred *chervine* pick his way as he could. Once she found herself edging a tight curb, looking over a dizzy cliff into gulfs of space. The trunks of tall trees thrust up below at crazy angles on the mountainside, and she looked down into their topmost branches. She clutched the lead rein tight and was careful not to look down again.

Ahead of her, where the trail made its sharpest turn, she saw Camilla holding out her hand to Cholayna.

"Hang on. Let the horse go. She'll find her way all right. Don't look down. It's a little steep here. One long step up. That's right. Fine." Cholayna's legs disappeared around the corner. Camilla's voice came, reassuring her.

"It's a bit slippery, Margali. Careful."

She set her boots down with extra care, scrambling for a hold; rounded the blind corner and found herself on broad, low rock steps. One of them crumbled away perilously close to a sheer drop of at least fifty feet and then vanished into blurred snowy treetops. A little dizzy, her ears ringing, she heaved herself to her feet, scrambled up another step and found herself on

firm ground, her horse lunging upward after her. She came up
on the broad rock plate above, where the wind of the heights tore
at her hair. She struggled to re-tie her hood, hearing Cholayna's
harsh breaths close behind her. Vanessa pulled herself nimbly up
beside them.

"Whew! That's a mean one. And you say it gets worse?"

"Unless there are bad washouts, we can probably handle it,"
Jaelle said, "but let's get along. There's not more than an hour of
daylight left, and the snow's beginning to stick. There are some
places we couldn't possibly manage in the dark."

The upward path was less steep now, but wound close to the
side of the mountain, just wide enough for a woman or a pony.
Cholayna, at Camilla's advice, walked on the inside of the trail,
hugging the rock cliff and clinging to the pony's bridle. Magda
would have liked to do the same; she edged as close to the cliff
as she dared and did not look down. Once she heard a *kyorebni*
scream, and the great carrion-bird loomed close to them; the
pony lunged with fright and Magda struggled with the rein, trying to quiet the animal, herself terrified by the huge beating
wings, the evil glinting eye which looked for a moment straight
into hers, and then was gone; she saw the bird careening off into
the wind below her and quickly turned her head and stared at the
solid rock of the cliff.

Vanessa, behind her so close that Magda could feel her
body's warmth, muttered, "What in hell was that?"

Magda said briefly, in Terran Standard, "Lammergeier. Near
as makes no difference."

They bent their heads against the wind. It was strong now,
whirling the snow in stinging, biting needles. Every step now
strained the muscles of Magda's thighs painfully against the upward slope, and the snow, half an inch thick now under her boot
soles, was wet enough to slip underfoot. She could hear the animals panting hard, their breath like hers, coming in white
clouds against the white snow.

Upward and upward; then she heard Jaelle's shout:

"Washout ahead. Hug the cliff and let the horses find their
own way!"

Ahead, she saw Cholayna inching her way past a giant's bite taken out of the edge of the roadway, so that the path narrowed to a few inches. Trying to steady her breathing, Magda flattened herself against the cliff and placed each footstep with extra caution, closing her eyes against the temptation to look down into the dizzying expanse of snow beneath, blotting out the valley below. She felt Vanessa's hand on her elbow, steadying her.

"All right, Miss Lorne?"

How absurd that sounded, in these wilderness surroundings. She thought, I'll have to speak to her about that, and concentrated on placing her feet with care. The *chervine* picked its way carefully along, shaking its antlers against the thick snow.

Her heart was thumping now. *No more than thirty-four hundred meters, that's not all that high, I must be in worse condition than I thought. And we're not even near the top yet.* Her world had narrowed, the precarious rocky road under her feet, the soft snorting of her horse, the soft clicking of the *chervine*'s hooves muffled by snow. Somewhere above them a rock rattled loose and bounced over the trail ahead and Camilla called back softly, "Careful. Look out for falling rocks along here."

Her eyes blurred; she felt herself swaying, perilously close to the edge. No—she was not dizzy, what was she picking up? Cautiously she made her way along the cliff until she was beside Cholayna. The woman's dark face was gray-white, and when Magda took her gloved hand, it seemed that she could hear the manic thumping of Cholayna's heart.

"Altitude getting to you?"

"Just a little. Not—used to—heights like this." Cholayna, too, kept her eyes averted from the drop edge; although Camilla kept looking over, with curiosity and interest, and Jaelle plodded along at the very edge in a way that sent shivering spasms through the muscles of Magda's thighs and buttocks. Vanessa strolled along as unconcernedly as if she were on an escalator in the Terran HQ.

Magda said to Cholayna in an undertone. "I don't care for this kind of trail myself. You don't *have* to look over the cliff, though. Hang on here if you want to." She felt Cholayna's hand clutching at hers and tried to feel calm, to quiet Cholayna's panic. "It's safe enough. Just don't look over the edge."

"I keep feeling—I'll slip and go over—" Cholayna whispered.

"I know. I get it too. It's not much farther now," Magda added, though she did not have the faintest idea how far it was to the top. "Just take it one step at a time. It's wider than an ordinary staircase and that wouldn't bother you. You're doing fine."

She heard the other woman sigh. "It's all right. It got to me for a minute, that's all. I hate being the weakest link this way."

"Well, if it weren't you, it would be me," Magda said. "All right, now?" She turned her attention to her chervine, but continued to watch, unobtrusively, as Cholayna moved slowly upward through the gathering dark.

I hope we get there before it's much darker, she thought, gritting her teeth against the cold that made her cheekbones ache. Already she could barely see the path under her feet, though the whiteness of the snow made it easier to see where the path actually vanished. Once her foot dislodged a loose rock at the very edge of the trail and she heard it rattle down for what seemed an endless time before it was out of earshot. One step, then another, steeper one, then another and another.

She edged round another sharp switchback where the trail was almost invisible. She bumped softly into Cholayna, motionless before her.

"I can't see the trail anymore!" the older woman gasped.

Neither could Magda, really. "Follow the horse. She can see better than you can." But she wondered how far Jaelle thought they could go on in this dim twilight, with the wind high enough that it was coming at their faces almost horizontally, mixed with needles of sleet.

She could not really see ahead, but she could feel the animals gathered around her on a widening of the ledge, a hollowing out of the overhanging cliff into something like shelter. Vanessa came up with them and they stood gathered in a circle.

Jaelle said, "No way we can get over tonight. We have to bivouac somewhere, and this is the safest place."

Vanessa asked, "Do we have lights with us?"

Jaelle shook her head. "No use, in this. The trail's just too bad underfoot. We'll have to risk snow-freeze on the ledges. In daylight, when we're all fresh and strong, we'll try again. Listen to that!" she added. The wind was howling down from the crags above them, and from somewhere came a long, eerie scream— the cry of a banshee. Magda shivered, remembering her only encounter with such a creature, in the Pass of Scaravel. She hoped this one was a good long way off.

Jaelle said, "Let's get set up. No room for a proper camp, but the overhang gives us some shelter. *Chervines* on the outside. They're more sure-footed than horses."

Magda got a fire lighted to melt snow for hot drinks, though there was no space for much cooking. By the time the drinks were ready, the sleeping bags were spread in the shelter of the ledge. The cold was so fierce, snow hissing past the lantern in white streaks, that they crowded together close under piled blankets, Magda and Vanessa to either side of Cholayna. The older woman's fingers were stiff and shaking as she took off her boots, and her feet looked pale and swollen. Vanessa took them in her lap to warm them in her hands.

Cholayna began to protest. Vanessa said, "Cholayna, I'm an old hand in the mountains and know more about feet and frostbite than you've ever heard of. Drink your tea."

"I'm not thirsty. I don't think I can swallow."

"All the more reason. Go on, you have to. At this altitude, you have to force fluids, because the body tries to shut down peripheral systems to protect the torso, which is why your feet start to freeze. That's right, wiggle those toes as much as you can! Your body starts to eat its own muscle tissue, you see, that means forcing fluids so your kidneys don't shut down, That's the first lesson in surviving high altitudes—not that this is so high, but it's higher than you're used to. Drink that up, and eat." She handed Cholayna a bar of dried fruit, sticky with nuts and honey. Dutifully, Cholayna tried to eat, but Magda could see that she was too weary to chew. She took Cholayna's ration and soaked the dried fruit in the hot tea, making it softer and easier to swallow, a trick she had learned long ago on the trail. She loaded the tea with extra sugar and gave it back to Cholayna.

"Just get it down—don't bother about how it tastes."

"Same to you, Magda," Jaelle reproved dryly. "You've forgotten yours. Finish that before you lie down."

Magda nodded, acknowledging the reproof. She was too tired to rummage in her pack for clean socks, but she did it anyway, and took her boots into the bottom of the sleeping bag. Jaelle and Camilla slid a filled water bottle inside their bag, keeping it from freezing with body heat. They spread extra blankets over all the sleeping bags, huddling together to conserve the last bits of warmth.

Vanessa had chosen the outside edge; Cholayna between her and Magda, with Jaelle and Camilla curled up against them. Magda was too tired to sleep; one by one she heard the other women drop off with soft-breathing slumber, but she lay awake, hearing the soft rasping of Cholayna's breath, Jaelle coughing a little in her sleep. She could sense Camilla's shivers: she was the thinnest of them, with the least body fat; and though Magda knew the *emmasca* was tougher than copper wire, she resolved to speak to her about warmer clothes. At higher altitudes this would be serious, and Camilla had a great deal of emotional investment in proving her own toughness; she might not want to dress more warmly than, say, Vanessa, who had, though she was slenderly made, the normal extra layer of fat on a human female. Camilla didn't, and had a phobia about calling attention to the fact.

Magda turned over cautiously without disturbing the women to either side, and wondered if she was going to sleep at all. She should really try. She composed herself mentally for some of the disciplines she had learned in matrix work; then decided that she would, before she slept, check in briefly with the Forbidden Tower circle—her family. They should know where she was, and that she would not be returning home as soon as she had promised.

Although if we do get over this damnable pass tomorrow, and catch up to Lexie and Rafaella, I'm going back to Shaya as soon as I can!

Jaelle was deeply asleep. *No need for her to come along.*

Briefly, Magda monitored her body, checking to be sure the circulation was adequate in fingers and toes; there was always a small but distinct danger involved in leaving the body under these conditions.

Then she was out of her body and standing in the gray and faceless plain of the Overworld, swiftly looking round for the landmark of the Forbidden Tower, sending out a silent call to Callista.

But there was no sign of the Tower. And then, in the grayness, a strange and unfamiliar face slowly took shape before Magda's eyes.

It was a woman's face, old, with deep-set eyes under eyebrows that were all white; a wrinkled forehead beneath braided hair as white as the eyebrows. Devoid of the benevolent peace Magda always associated with wrinkles and age, this woman glared—and although there were no words, Magda felt the angry challenge.

Go back. You may not pass here.

"By whose authority do you challenge my freedom of the Overworld?" Magda called up in her mind a clear picture of the Tower and of Damon, its Keeper.

The old woman threw back her head and emitted what Magda could only characterize as a series of yelps, though after a moment she knew they were intended as mocking laughter.

That one doesn't cut any ice out here, you'll have to do better than him to get by out here! You ought to turn around and go right back, girl, get back to your baby, you had no business leaving her anyhow! What do you girls think you're at anyway, climbing around out here? Heh-eh-eh! Think you're tough and strong? Proud of yourself for getting up this little hill, heh? You haven't seen anything yet, chiya! (The word was tinged with scathing contempt.) *Pack of girls and a couple of old ladies without the honesty to admit they're too old to take it anymore!*

Oh no, you won't get through when the going gets rough! Suppose you think you know the way, the passwords? Well, try it, just try it, that's all. Heh heh heh, heh-eh-eh-eh-eeeee!

With her head thrown back, the white braids jiggling with scornful laughter, the horrible old crone shook her fist at Magda. Magda knew that she was betraying her fear, for in the Overworld it was impossible to conceal one's real feelings; nevertheless she said firmly: "Old mother, you cannot deny me my place here."

And what are you doing out here, leaving your child and all?

Magda's instinct to answer, *What business of yours is it?* was tempered by some knowledge of the laws by which the Overworld worked. You could not avoid a challenge; nor was this her first, though never had she faced anything like this hideous old woman. So she answered, "I am following a call of duty and friendship."

Hah! You're no friend to either of them that's gone ahead; you don't have the guts to do what they do, jealous, that's all.

Magda considered this and answered, "That doesn't matter. My friends are worried about it, and I am going for their sake."

Heh-eh-eh! Not good enough! I knew it! What you have to do on this quest, you have to do for your own reasons, can't follow no one else out here. See? I knew it. Get back! She raised her hand, and it seemed that a bolt of blue fire struck Magda between the breasts. Pain lanced through her heart, and she felt herself falling, falling. . . .

The gray world was gone. Magda shivered inside her sleeping bag, back in her body . . . Or had she ever left it? Had she not simply fallen asleep, the whole encounter been a bizarre dream dramatizing her own mental conflicts about this strange and unwanted quest? She could hear Cholayna moaning softly in her sleep, and Jaelle muttering, "no, no," and wondered if her friend was having nightmares about ledges and cliffs.

Should she try to go back at once into the Overworld? She had been told that such a failure should immediately be challenged again, that it was like being thrown from a horse: you must at once mount and ride again. But had she ever been in the

Overworld at all, had she not simply fallen asleep? She knew it was unwise to attempt psi work when you were overtired or ill, and the ordeal of the climb and her tremendous fatigue made it unsafe.

Firmly summoning the disciplines she had been taught, she began to count herself quietly down into sleep. She could not afford to lie awake with the crossing of Ravensmark before them tomorrow.

Chapter 12

Jaelle crawled to the edge of the rock overhang and looked out. "Snowing harder than ever," she said grimly. "I don't think we're going anywhere in this!"

"I have to go out anyhow. I'll check the animals," Camilla said, climbing over her. When she returned, she was scraping at her boot distastefully. "Step carefully when you go out; with ten animals out there, it's like a stable."

"Well, there's a snow shovel in one of the loads, if you feel like shoveling it clean," Jaelle said, and went out. She came back grimacing. "Snowing like Zandru's sixth or seventh hell. And guess what?"

Vanessa, kneeling at the back of the ledge to light a fire, turned to rummage in her own pack. She tossed a small packet at Jaelle and said, "Be my guest. There's an old maxim on women's climbing expeditions: whatever's going to happen will happen at the worst possible time. You're lucky. Usually it happens just above seven thousand."

"It's not the worst possible time," Magda said, "it could be a nice clear morning and you'd have to go out and lead the pass. Crawl back in your sleeping bag, Shaya, and I'll make you a hot drink."

Complying, Jaelle said, "I don't suppose you brought any golden-flower tea?"

"Whatever that is, I don't think so," Vanessa said, "but I have some prostaglandin inhibitors in my medikit." She dug out some tablets while Magda was making porridge, heavily fortified with fruit and extra sugar. Cholayna got a heavier sweater from her pack and pulled it on. She was shivering.

"I'd like a good stiff drink."

"At this altitude? You'd be roaring drunk before you could drink three sips!" Vanessa said. "Try a caffeine tablet instead." She handed them around with the porridge; only Camilla refused.

"Does it look as if it would clear any time today?"

"I've no idea," Jaelle said. "I know what's worrying you: if we get two or three feet of snow, we're really in trouble. The pass isn't the kind we can get through with snow up to our knees or worse." They could all hear what she did not say aloud, that going back past the narrow ledges of the washed-out area would be as dangerous as trying to go ahead. And with every hour that passed, their chances of overtaking Rafaella and Lexie grew less.

They ate porridge, and afterward Vanessa and Camilla repacked the stacked loads. The sky remained gray, but the snow grew no heavier. It seemed to Magda that it was slowing, if not stopping.

Camilla said once, staring out over the cliff edge, "There are devils in this place. Was I the only one to suffer Alar's own nightmares?"

"It's the altitude," said Cholayna. "My head is splitting. I dreamed I was in that damned city Lexie was talking about, and there were a dozen women with horns and tails and false-face masks like the demons of my ancestral tribes, all trying to make me crawl through a needle's eye before I could come in. They said I was too fat, and they were squeezing me through and burning off what hung outside the edges."

"Bad dreams are the rule at this altitude," Vanessa said. "I dreamed about *you*, Cholayna. You were telling me that if we ever got back I'd have to take a demotion of three grades for insubordination."

Jaelle chuckled. "I dreamed my daughter was a Keeper, and she was telling me that because I had deserted her, I'd never be competent enough to work on my own. Then she was trying to give me lessons in monitoring, only instead of a matrix it was a *chervine* turd and I had to turn it to stone."

They all laughed, except Camilla, who frowned and stared at her clenched knuckles. "What I dreamed I will not say. But there are devils in this place." "Altitude and cold," said Magda briskly. "You're too thin. Another layer of heavy underwear ought to take care of it."

Hours crawled by. Toward noon, there was a vagrant glimmer toward the south, and Jaelle said, "I think the sun's trying to come out. We ought to get along if we can."

"Want me to break trail?" Vanessa offered, as they crawled out of their sleeping bags.

"No, thanks, really, I'm fine. Your pills are wonder workers, I never felt better. Truly, Vanessa, I'm not just trying to stay ahead. If I need help, I'll say so, I promise. But I know the way and you don't. I can manage. Believe me, if I get chilled or over-tired, I'll let you take the lead, but even with me leading, a lot of the landmarks aren't going to be visible." She slung her pack over the pony's back. "Let's get the loads on. Cinch them well, the footing's likely to be bad."

There was a thick heavy silence around the ledge as they cinched loads and packs. In the damp heavy air, even the small sounds made by the animals seemed unreal. The snow was firm and crunching softly underfoot, and not as slippery as Magda had feared. She looked back down the trail they had come up. It seemed to her that they were very high, but above them the trail went on, curving around rocks and disappearing.

Jaelle put one hand on her pony's rein; she had tethered the *chervine* to it so that the pack beast had no choice but to follow. Camilla took the reins of the next three animals, and began climbing after Jaelle. Here the trail was steep but by no means impassable.

Magda gestured to Cholayna to go before her, and waited until the Terran woman was several steps up the trail before setting her animals on the way and beginning to climb. Up and up the trail led, and as they climbed the sun came out. There was a clear view, where the trail curved, of a whole range of hills beyond; the path led steeply upward, against the sharp rock cliff, to a notch between two peaks.

"Ravensmark," Jaelle said, pointing, and started up toward it.

Magda climbed. She felt fresh and strong, but though she climbed steadily for hours, the pass seemed no nearer. About every hour, Jaelle called a halt for rest, but even so she was tiring, and after three or four rests, she called Vanessa forward to take the lead.

"As soon as we're through the pass, I'll lead again. There's a nasty bit just below the top, on the other side."

Vanessa nodded assent. Jaelle dropped back beside Camilla, who looked like a thundercloud.

"Want to take the rear? I don't feel up to it," Jaelle said, and Camilla went quietly back along the trail to take up the rearguard, pausing to ask how Cholayna was doing.

"It helps to be able to see where we're going."

Magda felt she would rather not see. She kept her eyes away from the edges.

As Camilla passed Magda on her way, she paused to draw a deep breath. "We'll be past the worst soon. From there, it's downhill."

Magda was almost too short of breath to nod her gratitude for that. With the sun out, it was more cheerful, but the snow was beginning to melt and the going was more slippery. For the final steep haul upward to the pass, she had to stretch herself to the utmost; she could hear her breath whistling loudly in her lungs as she struggled up the last bit to stand between Jaelle and Cholayna in the throat of the peaks.

Jaelle swore under her breath; pointed.

"That used to be the trail," she said. Now the pathway downward was buried beneath tons of rock and shifting gravel, half hidden in the snow.

"Washout, rockslide, the gods alone know what else under there. Old rotten ice from the peak must have crashed down on it in the spring rains, and that part of the trail is gone for good."

"So what do we do now?" Vanessa asked. "Can it be crossed at all?"

"Your guess is as good as mine. Lightweight, climbing, I could get across it. The *chervines* could probably get down. Look—" She pointed. "Down past that clump of trees, the trail's fairly good again. At least there *is* some kind of trail! The rockslide covered about five hundred meters, more or less, with rocks and rubble. It's steep, and it looks nasty. It's probably not as bad as it looks—"

"Unless all this loose snow starts sliding down again. It looks as if there might be loose rocks, too, which could start avalanching down when we set foot on it," Camilla said, coming to join them. "No wonder we had nightmares back there." The women stood looking down, while Magda and Cholayna, knowing they could contribute nothing to the discussion, stood silent, looking down at the chaos of snow, rock and old ice heaped up below them where once there had been at least the semblance of a trail.

At last Vanessa suggested, "Jaelle, you and I could rope up and scout the way down on foot. At least we'd know then whether it's solid enough underfoot to bring the animals down after us. With the snow this deep, it's likely to be frozen hard enough underneath that it won't start sliding too fast. That was a damned hard freeze last night."

Jaelle thought that over for a minute, then she said, "I don't see any alternative. Unless someone else has a better idea?"

Nobody did. It was clearly obvious that the only other choice was to turn around, retrace their steps over Ravensmark and detour through Hammerfell. They had certainly lost any chance of catching up with Rafaella at Barrensclae.

"If we'd known," Jaelle said grimly, rummaging through a load, looking for her ice axe, "we could have taken the Great North Road directly to Nevarsin."

"And if the Duke of Hammerfell had worn a skirt," Camilla said, "he might have been the Duchess."

"Jaelle, hindsight is always twenty-twenty vision," Cholayna reminded her. "We did the best we could. The important thing is that we're here, and so far we're safe."

Jaelle said, with a twitchy small grin, "Let's just hope we can still say that tonight. Vanessa, give me the rope. Do you want to lead down, or shall I?"

"I don't see that it makes any difference. We can both see where the road ought to be, and isn't. I'll start." She snapped the buckle of a body harness around her waist, tested the free passage of the rope through it, and took a firm grip on her ice axe.

"A few feet of slack. That's right." She placed her feet gingerly on the snow and rubble and started to pick her way down; went over the edge, slid, and the rope went tight. Magda heard Cholayna's breath go out in a gasp, but after a minute Vanessa called up, "I'm all right, lost my footing. Tricky here. Let me find a solider step. Hang on tight."

Presently her head reappeared, climbing up.

"This way won't go. There's a drop-off of forty meters just below here, I'll have to scout over this way." She went slowly leftward, picking her footing with caution. This time she managed to keep her feet under her; after a time, it began to look rather like a trail. Jaelle handed the rope to Magda.

"You and Camilla belay me from here." She started after Vanessa, picking her way carefully in the rut of Vanessa's trail. Camilla came and stood behind Magda, ready to hold the rope hard if either of the women below them should slip. They were out of sight now. Magda, Camilla holding her firmly round the waist, felt her breath coming hard. Part of it was fear; the rest was helplessness. She was no good here: she had no climbing skills, no mountain-craft. All she could do was hang on and trust her freemate.

"That's enough," Camilla said softly—or had she spoken aloud? Was it the silence, the isolation of the mountain trail, where no other minds intruded, that meant that Magda did not need to shield against the low-level telepathic jangle of cities and crowds, and so made it seem that she was almost constantly in communion with Camilla's mind? She didn't know, and her mind was on something else anyhow. But she leaned back against Camilla's hands, firmly bracing her and holding her weight, as the rope stretched taut, holding the climbers below. Her throat and nose were painfully dry; the cold dryness of the heights dehydrated sinuses and mucous membranes, and all she could think of was how much she wanted a drink. It must have been harder still for Jaelle and Vanessa, fighting ice and loose rock below.

The rope slackened, and for a moment Magda panicked, fearing a broken rope, a fall. . . . Then a ringing call came up from somewhere below them.

"It's all right. It will go this way. I'm coming up." It was Jaelle's voice, and after a long time she reappeared, climbing carefully up from below.

Vanessa came after, bent over and breathing hard.

"I want a drink," she said, and Cholayna found the water bottle and passed it to the climbers.

When Jaelle had recovered her breath, she said, "It's all right; not even very steep. There's one bad place where there's loose rock; we'll have to lead the horses over one at a time, very carefully, so they don't slip. It would be damned easy for any of us to break a leg there. But everywhere else it's solid underfoot, and we kicked away what we could of the loosest stuff. Below there, the trail starts again. It's narrow, but it's *there*. I think we can make it. But I'm going to take Cholayna across that stretch myself." She took another drink, gasping. But at Camilla's concerned look, she said only, "I'm fine, don't fuss," and Magda knew better than to display any concern.

"Hunt out some bread and cheese; we should eat lunch here," Vanessa said, "and if anyone has any little personal things to attend to, do it here. There's no place below to step off the trail."

"As I recall," Cholayna joked, "there's no trail to step off of."

Jaelle carefully redistributed loads on the pack animals as they munched a few mouthfuls of bread and cheese. At last they were ready to start down. Jaelle took the leading reins off of the *chervines'* bridles.

"They'll follow the horses. But they can find the way better than we can." She started down. "Let me get about forty feet along the trail and then come after me, Magda. Then you, Camilla, and Cholayna. I'll come back for the extra horses.

Vanessa, you stay behind in case anyone gets into trouble, all right?"

"Right."

Magda picked up her horse's reins and started down the narrow trail Jaelle was re-making—no more than a scattering of foot- and hoof-prints. The snow was hard, and the snorting of the *chervines* picking their way along after her sounded loud. She placed each foot carefully; her horse whinnied and tried to hang back, and she felt nervous about pulling on the rein.

"Come along, there's a good girl." She patted the horse's nose, encouraging her gently. When they had gotten a little farther down the trail, she heard Camilla's and Cholayna's footsteps behind her; then again the loose, crowding *chervines*. One of them bolted up around the newly rutted trail in the snow; the small bells on its load jingled wildly as the spooked beast galloped downward. Magda hoped the straps on its load would hold and that they would be able to catch it at the bottom. She heard Camilla's breath jolt out hard in a curse; looked back and called, "You all right?"

"Turned my foot on a stone. All right now."

With a quick look behind, Magda saw Camilla was walking unevenly, but there was nothing to be done about it for the moment. They were lucky it was not worse. She felt a stone roll under her own foot, and narrowly escaped turning an ankle as she jolted down hard and unevenly. The horse scrambled more than once to stay balanced.

Jaelle was waiting a few steps ahead. "This is the beginning of the bad patch. I'm going across with my horse. Wait till I call you, then come across, slowly and carefully, understand?" Her face was patched red and white with exertion and there was a narrow band of sunburn across her nose. Magda was glad to rest for a moment; she watched Jaelle picking her way, leading the horse . . . Then Jaelle was across, and waving her ahead. She came across, feeling with her boots for firm patches, twice feeling rocks slip and roll down beneath her. She found that she was holding her breath as if even breathing hard would dislodge the loose gravel and ice. Once she slid to her knees with a little shout and found herself suddenly looking over a sheer cliff; but she mastered the queasy nausea, clawed herself backward and upright again, and went on. It seemed there were no sounds, not even of her own breathing, until a hand, extended, met hers, and she was safe beside Jaelle.

"All right, love?"

"Fine." Magda could hear little but her own breathing.

"Tether your horse. I'm going back across for Camilla's. You come along and lead Cholayna's—or— can you manage that?"

Magda's breath caught at the thought of crossing that hellish stretch of loose rubble and rock not once more, but twice. But Jaelle thought she could do it. She nodded. "Let me catch my breath a little, first."

Jaelle hobbled the horses; hung their reins across the saddles. "I'll go first. Watch where I step. I've been across it four times now. Looks worse than it is, love."

Magda was still shaky, but this time the crossing was easier. They waited for Camilla and Cholayna to arrive at the far edge of the loose rocks; everyone waved at everyone else, and then Magda and Jaelle crossed again with the horses. Almost all of the *chervines* were across by now, though they lurched and nearly fell, scrambling up again on their thin hocks, tossing their heads and whickering in distress. But they all arrived safely, Vanessa last, white-faced, clinging to the rein of her horse.

"What's wrong, Vanessa?" Cholayna asked.

"Ankle." Now they could see that she had been supporting as much of her weight as she could holding on to the horse; abruptly she let go and sank to the ground. Camilla came and tried to pull off her boot, but in the end they had to cut through the heavy leather to remove it. The ankle was swollen, with a great purplish-red patch on the ankle-bone.

"This is worse than a sprain," Camilla said. "You may have knocked a chip of bone out of the ankle."

Vanessa made a wry face. "I was afraid of that. Probably needs X-raying, but there's no good thinking about that here. There are spare boots in my rucksack—"

"You'll never get them on," Magda said. "Take my spares,

they're four sizes bigger. Never thought I'd be grateful for having big feet."

Vanessa let out her breath in a gasp as Cholayna came to examine the foot.

"Wiggle your toes. Fine. Does it hurt when I do this?"

Vanessa's answer was loud, profane, and affirmative.

"Nothing broken, I'd say. Just a really bad bruise and a lot of swelling. Are there elastic bandages in that medikit?"

"There's one in my pack," Jaelle said. She went and found it, gave it to Cholayna and said, "It probably needs bathing and all kinds of things, but there's no good trying to stop and make a fire here, so bandage it up and we'll round up the *chervines*." The beasts were scattered all up and down the next half mile of the downward trail. "Camilla, you turned an ankle too, didn't you? Is that okay? Any other casualties?"

Camilla's ankle, examined, proved to be only strained a little; nevertheless, Jaelle told her to bandage it up and give it a rest.

"Magda will help me round up the *chervines*. We're not more than a couple of hours from Barrensclae. With Avarra's mercy, we'll be able to ride most of the way from there."

While they were catching and quieting the scattered pack animals, Magda spotted a scrap of something which had no business on that trail. She caught it up and called softly to Jaelle.

"Look here."

Jaelle took the brightly colored scrap of plastic from her; yellow, with a torn letter at one edge. "Packaging?"

"From standard high-altitude emergency rations, yes."
"Lexie's?"

"Who else? Anyone who saw this, though, must have known she wasn't going out to study folk dancing. At least now we know they *did* come this way."

Jaelle nodded and thrust the scrap into a pocket. "Maybe they lost time here, too. Let's go and find out if they're still waiting for us. They do need the things we're bringing—extra warm clothes, trade goods—they'll do better in the Hellers if they wait."

"Then you'll be going on, if we do catch them? You actually think they'll find that—city?"

"Don't you, Magda?" Jaelle looked surprised and hurt. "You're coming too, I thought—?"

"I suppose so," Magda said, slowly and not at all sure. She could deal with Rafaella, who had been both friendly and unfriendly and would probably only accept her for Jaelle's sake, and then only if it was her best hope of continuing the search. But Lexie? Magda could hear her now.

Hellfire, Lorne, are there any pies on this planet you don't have your fingers in?

Chapter 13

Barrensclae was well named, Magda thought; a high plateau, without grass or trees, rocky rubble lying loose, and a few stone ruins where once there had been houses and stockpens. She wondered why it had been abandoned, what had impelled the farmers who had lived here to pull up and go away. Or had they all been murdered by bandits in one of the blood-feuds that still raged in the hill country?

She put the question to Jaelle, who shrugged.

"Who knows? Who cares? It can't have been much or we'd have heard a hundred different stories already."

Camilla said, with a grim smile, "If they just went away on their own, it may have been the only sensible thing they ever did. I'd be more interested to know why they ever thought of settling here in the first place."

Cholayna said the obvious: "If Lexie and Rafaella were ever here, they're not here now."

"They might be hunting. Or exploring." Jaelle rode slowly toward the abandoned stockpen, near a house which still had some semblance of roof clinging to the old stones. "We slaughtered the *chervines* here, and slept three nights in that house. If Rafi left a message, it would be here."

Camilla looked at the sky, lowering gray; the night's rain would begin soon. "We'll spend the night anyway, I suppose. No sense going much farther, and Vanessa's ankle needs looking after. There's something like a roof on this, too. I suggest we look inside and see if we can camp there."

"Any reason we shouldn't?" Vanessa asked. "I mean, the original owners seem to be *very* long gone. What could stop us?"

"Oh, just little things, like—no floor, mold, bugs, snakes, rats, bats." Camilla ticked them over on her fingers, laughing. "On the other hand, we might just find Rafaella's pack animals and their various belongings stored there, in which case—"

Magda was not sure whether she hoped they would find the women there or that they would not. When they managed to swing the heavy door inward from the hinges, the place was suspiciously clear of all the things Camilla had warned against: the old stone-paved floor was dusty but not filthy, and there seemed to be nothing lurking about.

"This place *has* been used recently," —Cholayna remarked. "They were here, and not long ago."

"I wouldn't be so sure," Jaelle warned, "anyone could have used this place. Travelers, bandits—it's possible they were here, but we can't be sure."

It looked to Magda like a good place for bandits: she remembered encountering bandits in a travel-shelter once, years ago. She had not thought about bandits on this trip, and wished she had not had the idea brought to her attention just now.

There was no point in letting it worry her. Camilla could certainly manage three times their weight in bandits, and would probably rather enjoy the opportunity to try. "That's not what's worrying me," Jaelle said. "There are only two of them, and one a *Terranan* greenhorn."

"Don't you believe it," Cholayna said. "Lexie had the same unarmed combat training as Magda. And Rafaella's no weakling."

"Bandits travel in packs," Jaelle said: "Fair fights aren't what they're noted for." Just the same, she brought in her saddlebags and dumped them on the stone floor. "Cholayna, why don't you make a fire so we can look after Vanessa's ankle."

Before long the fire was blazing, and Cholayna was making what use she could of the medikit. She still suspected that

Vanessa had knocked a chip of bone loose from her ankle, but there was nothing they could do about it here.

"At least there's no shortage of ice," Cholayna said, looking out into the snow. "Cold packs until the swelling goes down; after that, hot and cold alternately. A proper medic would put it in a cast, but it's probably not dangerous without one. It's going to make walking hard for a few days, but since Jaelle says we can probably ride most of the way from here, it could be worse. At least you're not in danger of being lamed for life if you don't get proper Terran treatment."

Unasked, Magda pulled out the cooking kit and started making soup from the dried meat in their supplies. A hearty aroma began to steal through the old stone house. Toasting did wonders for the hard journey-bread, too. Soup, cooked grain-porridge, and a kettle of hot bark-tea—it was the first real hot meal they had had since leaving Thendara, and it greatly revived their spirits.

When they finally crawled into their sleeping bags, Magda soon knew all the others were sleeping peacefully. Still she lay awake, troubled without knowing why. She could not help feeling that this whole trip was somehow a reflection of her failures—with Lexie, Vanessa, Cholayna, and, perhaps especially, Rafaella. Somehow, she had made Lexie feel that she must compete with what some people in the HQ insisted on calling the "Lorne Legend"; had said the wrong things to Vanessa and Cholayna or they would not have been here; without meaning to, she had come between Jaelle and Rafaella . . . . But whatever the unknown dangers of the road, Jaelle was right, they could not turn back.

The next morning, Vanessa's ankle was swollen to the size of a peck basket, and she was running a fever. Cholayna dosed her with salicylates from the medikit, while Magda and Camilla repacked the loads to redistribute weight and Jaelle went out to search the terrain for any signs of the passage of the other women. She came back late in the day with the carcass of a *chervine* calf slung over her back.

"We can all use fresh meat. Vanessa particularly needs the extra protein." She set about skinning and butchering the carcass with an expert hand; Cholayna turned her eyes away, but Vanessa watched with fascination.

"Where did you learn to do that?"

"Leading mountain expeditions. We don't have a lot of fancy packaged rations available," Jaelle said, "and hunting skills are one of the first things you learn to feed yourself in the wilds. I could bring down a full-grown animal before I was fifteen years old, and if you're killing your own meat, you have to be able to skin it and cut it up and dry it for the trail, too. We'll eat as much of this fresh as we can. I'll roast a haunch for supper, but it's too small to dry properly. What we can't eat, we'll put out for the *kyorebni* before we leave." She looked regretfully at the delicate dappled skin of the little animal. "Hate to waste this hide, I could get a nice pair of gauntlets out of it if we had the time to tan it."

Cholayna shuddered and kept her eyes even more averted than they had already been; but she said nothing. It must, Magda thought, be difficult for her all round, taking orders when she was accustomed to giving them, and resigning herself to being the oldest and the weakest. This assault on her ethical principles—Magda knew Cholayna had never eaten meat, or anything which had once lived, before this—must be the final trial. But she had kept silent about it, which could not have been easy.

By the next morning, the worst of the swelling was gone from Vanessa's ankle, and Jaelle, looking uneasily at the sky, said they should press on. Cholayna felt that Vanessa should rest her ankle for another day, but Jaelle was uneasy about the weather and studied Magda's maps for a long time, seeking an easier route.

"We'll head straight north, but we'll go around by the trail instead of going straight over the ridge. They have enough of a start on us now that it's very unlikely we'll catch up with them this side of the Kadarin; more probably not much before Nevarsin," Jaelle said.

With horses and *chervines* well rested, they started again, along trails that did not need to be negotiated on foot. There were flurries of snow as they rode, and it was damp and cold; they all dug out their warmest sweaters and underclothing. At night the sleeping bags were dank and clammy, and even Cholayna drank the hot meat-soup gladly.

On the third afternoon, the trail began to rise again, each hill steeper than the last, and finally Jaelle said that on the upward slopes they must dismount and walk to spare the horses the extra weight—except for Vanessa, who was still unable to bear her weight on the injured ankle.

"I can walk if I have to," said Vanessa, brandishing the thick branch Camilla had cut for a walking stick that morning. "I don't need special treatment, either!"

"Believe me, Vanessa, I'll tell you if it's necessary for you to walk. Don't try to be heroic," Jaelle added. "If we end up carrying you, we'll never get through."

They were slogging up the fourth or fifth of these hills— Magda had lost count in the dreary dripping fog—when her foot turned under her, and she lost her footing, fell full length and slipped backward, sliding down the steep path, scraping against rocks, ice and tough roots in the way. She struck her head, and in a flash of pain, lost consciousness.

. . . she was wandering in a the gray world; she heard Jaelle calling her, but the hideous old woman was there, laughing . . . wherever she turned, though she ran and ran, always the old crone was there with that terrible screaming laughter that was like the cry of some wild bird, arms outstretched to shoo her back, force her away . . . suddenly Camilla was there, knife drawn to protect her, facing the old woman; her knife struck blue fire . . .

There was something wet on her face; cold moisture was seeping into her collar. She raised her hand—it felt heavy and cold—to push it away and it turned into a damp cloth. It was like fire on her forehead, which felt as if it had been split with an axe.

Camilla's face looked down into hers; she was pale, and it

seemed to Magda that she had been crying. *Nonsense*, she thought, *Camilla never cries*.

"*Bredhiya*," Camilla murmured, and her hand clasped Magda's so tightly that she winced, "I thought I had lost you. How do you feel?"

"Like hell. Every bone in my body feels as if it had been beaten with a smith's hammer," Magda muttered. She discovered that she was undressed to the waist. "Hell, no wonder I'm cold! Is this standard treatment for shock?"

She tried to make a joke of it, but Jaelle bent over her and said, "I undressed you to make sure you didn't have any internal injuries. You scraped all the skin off one arm down to the elbow, and you may have cracked a rib. Try to sit up, if you can."

Magda pulled herself carefully to a sitting position. She moved her head cautiously and wished she hadn't. "What did I hit, a mountain?"

"Just a rock, Miss Lorne," Vanessa said. It sounded so absurd; Magda had meant to protest before this. Vanessa asked, "Are you cold?" and put her shirt onto her. Her arm, she discovered, was bandaged heavily over some slick and foulsmelling ointment.

Camilla draped a warm cloak around her. "It will be easier than trying to get your jacket on over the bandages and won't rub the sore spots so much," she said, pulling Magda's jacket around her own lean frame. "Do you feel sleepy?"

Magda tried again to shake her head and didn't. "No. Sleepy is the last thing I am."

"Do you think you can go on?" Jaelle asked. "There's no place to camp here, but if you can't—"

Magda managed to pull herself upright with Camilla's help. Her head was still splitting, and she asked for some of Cholayna's painkillers, but Cholayna shook her head.

"Not until we know how serious your concussion is. If you're still wide awake when we stop for the night, you can have some. Till then, nothing that might depress your breathing."

"Miserable sadist," Magda grumbled; but she too had had basic emergency training, and knew about head injuries.

"Look on the bright side," said Cholayna, "now you get to ride uphill along with Vanessa, while the rest of us slog along on foot."

Magda found it almost impossible to haul herself into her saddle, even with Camilla's help, and when the horse began to move, she wished she were walking; the motion was nearly intolerable. The snow was wet now, half rain and half snow, and clung thickly, soaking through her cloak. She rode in dreary misery, every footfall of her horse jolting as if the beast were actually stepping on her head; and the uphill path was so steep that again she felt as if she were slipping backward off her saddle. Without being asked, Camilla came close and took the reins from her hand.

"*Bredhiya*, you just hang on, I'll guide your horse. Just a little further now. Poor love, I wish I could carry you."

"I'm all right, Camilla. Really I am, it's only a headache. And I feel so foolish, falling like that and delaying all of you this way."

"Look, here we are at the top of the ridge. Now we can all ride again, and if you can't sit in your saddle, *bredhiya*, you can ride double with me. My horse will carry two and all you need to do is lean against me. Do you want to do that?"

"No, no, really, I'm all right," Magda said; and though she knew it was unfair, the older woman's solicitude embarrassed her—partly because she knew that it must be embarrassing to the other women, especially Vanessa, who could not understand the bond between them. "*Please* don't fuss over me so, Camilla. Just let me alone, I'm fine."

"Please yourself, then." Camilla touched her heels to her horse's side, and went to the head of the line beside Jaelle. As soon as she was gone, Magda regretted her words and wished Camilla was still beside her; what, after all, did it matter to her what anyone thought, after all these years? Discouraged, her head aching, she clung to the reins and let her horse find his own way down the hill.

As she rounded a turn in the downhill road, past a huge stand of conifers, she could see lights below. A little village huddled in the valley, just a crossing of the narrow road; first an outlying farm or two, then a forge and a stream dammed for a mill, with a granary warehouse, a windmill and a few small stone houses, each surrounded by a patch of garden.

"I wonder if there is an inn in this place?" Camilla asked.

Children and women and even a few men had come out to the roadside to watch as they passed; a sure sign, Magda knew from her years in the field, that the place was so isolated that the appearance of any stranger was a major event.

Jaelle asked one of the women, heavy-set, imposing, in clothing somewhat less coarse than the rest, "Is there an inn where we can spend the night and command supper?"

She had to repeat the question several times, in different dialects, before she could make herself understood, and when the woman finally answered, her own dialect was so rude a patois of *cahuenga* that Magda could hardly understand her. She asked Camilla, who had returned to ride beside her, "What did she say? You know more of the mountain languages than I do."

"She said there is no inn," Camilla said—speaking pure *casta* so that they would not be understood if they were overheard. "But there is a good public bathhouse, she said, where we could bathe. She also offered us the use of a barn which is empty at this time of year. They look like a fine lot of ruffians to me, and I would just as soon not trust any of them, but I don't know what alternatives we have."

Vanessa had heard only part of this. "A bathhouse sounds like exactly what we need most. I'm sure my ankle, and your arm, can use a good long soak in clean hot water. And bathhouse or no, these people look dirty enough that I'd rather sleep in one of their barns than their houses. Or, for that matter, their inns. Lead me to the bath!"

The woman who had appointed herself their guide led the way, a small procession of children following. Cholayna said, "I had not expected to find amenities like this outside Thendara."

"There are hot springs all through the mountains," Magda

said. "Most little villages have bathhouses, even if every house must fetch water for drinking from a common well. And they have separate soaking rooms and tubs for men and women, so you need not worry about differing customs of modesty."

Vanessa shrugged. "I am used to mixed bathing and bath-houses on my own world. It wouldn't bother me if the whole village bathed in one big pool, as long as they changed the water occasionally."

"Well, it would bother me," Camilla said, and Jaelle chuckled.

"Me, too. I was brought up in the Dry Towns, after all."

She turned to haggle with the woman, who seemed to be the proprietor of the bathhouse and a sort of headwoman of the village, over the bathhouse fee. It seemed exorbitant to Magda, but, after all, this village was very isolated, and the hire of the bath-house to occasional travelers was, no doubt, their only source of coined money. At least, Jaelle told her, she had managed to secure the place for their exclusive use that evening, and had arranged with the headwoman for a cooked hot meal to be brought to them; the fee also included use of the barn to stable their animals and spread their sleeping bags. Because it was a stone barn, with no stored hay, they had permission to make a fire there. They went to deposit their goods, unsaddle the horses and off-load the pack beasts before they went to the bath.

"How is your head, Magda?" Cholayna asked. "How do you feel?"

"Better for the thought of a bath."

"Wide awake? Then you can have some pain pills," Cholayna said, and dug some tablets out of the medikit. "Is something wrong, Camilla?" For the woman was standing over their loads, scowling.

"I do not trust these people," said Camilla, still speaking *casta*, although they seemed to be quite alone. "It looks like the abode of bandits. If we are wise, we will not all go to bathe at once; we should not leave all our goods unguarded."

"Most hill-folk are so honest, you could leave a bag of copper unguarded in the center of the square, and find it there untouched when you returned half a year later," Jaelle reminded her, "except that they might have put up a little shelter over it so that the bag would not be destroyed by the winter rains."

"I'm perfectly aware of that," Camilla said testily. "But have you been to this particular village before? Do you know these people, Shaya?"

"Not really. But I have been in many, many mountain villages very like this one."

"Not good enough," said Camilla. "All of you, go off to bathe. I will stay here and guard our goods." And though they argued, she would not be moved from this stance. Finally it was agreed that Jaelle and Vanessa would go and use the bath first, and that Magda, Cholayna and Camilla would bathe in a second shift, which meant that one person in each party would be unwounded, healthy, and skilled in the use of weapons.

"I am still not pleased," Camilla grumbled, as Jaelle and Vanessa went off to the bathhouse, carrying clean clothing over their arms. "These people would cut our throats for the scented soap! The idea might well be to split up our party so that we cannot defend ourselves properly. We should have camped outside the village, and set guard."

"You have a terribly suspicious nature, Camilla," Cholayna reproved gently, kneeling on the floor to light a fire. "I for one will be delighted to get a bath!"

"And so should I, in any decent place. Or do you think I am fonder of dirt than a Terran? But here, I would feel safer sleeping in the muck of the road."

"Camilla," said Magda quietly, out of earshot of the others, as they looked for fresh clothing in their packs, "is this a premonition, is this your *laran*?"

The woman's face was tight-lipped and closed. "You know what I think of that. If it were so, would not you or Jaelle have known it, you who are *leroni* of the Forbidden Tower? It needs no *laran* to know that a ruffian will be a ruffian. *Laran!*" she snorted again, crossly, and turned away.

Magda felt troubled, for she respected, with good reason, Camilla's intuitions; but the party was already split, and her head and injured arm ached dreadfully, so that she felt unwilling to forgo the prospect of a bath. She felt she would even endure an onslaught by bandits if she could get a bath and a good hot meal first.

Chapter 14

There was a little sound in the corner of the room. Within seconds Camilla had her knife out and rushed to the hidden space behind the door; she came back dragging someone by the wrist: a woman, not young, her dark hair braided carelessly down her back. She was no different from any of the people of the village except, Magda noticed, that she seemed personally clean.

"Who are you?" Camilla growled, gripping the woman's wrist so hard that she flinched and squealed, and emphasizing her words with a flourish of her knife, "What do you want here? Who sent you?"

"I didn't mean any harm," the woman said, with a little yelp of fright. "Are you—are you Shaya n'ha M'lorya?"

The name *Jaelle* was a Dry-Town name, very uncommon in the Kilghard Hills. Magda herself called Jaelle, mostly, by the *casta* version of her name, and had given it to her daughter.

"I am not," Camilla said, "but I am her oath-sister; and this—" indicating Magda, "her freemate. Speak! What do you want with her. Who are you?"

The woman's eyes swiveled furtively to stare at Cholayna. Magda thought, *No doubt she has never seen anyone with a black skin before this, maybe she has just come to gawp at the strangers. But then how would she know Jaelle's name?*

"My name is Calisu'," the woman said. "There are no Renunciates in our village. The headman won't have it. But some of us are in—in sympathy." She pulled the loose hair away from her ear, revealing a small earring; the secret sign, Magda knew, recognized for hundreds of years, of women in sympathy with the Guild-houses, who for one reason or another could not legally commit themselves. Lady Rohana herself had worn such a hidden ornament, and Magda was sure not even *Dom* Gabriel had known why. Seeing it, Camilla's grip loosened somewhat.

"What do you want? Why were you sneaking around like that?"

Calisu'—the name, Magda remembered, was a dialect version of Callista—said, "Two Renunciates passed through our village ten days ago. They asked for the village midwife, saying one of them suffered from cramps, and when they came to me, asked if—if I wore the earring."

That was Rafaella's artifice. Not in a thousand years would Lexie have thought of that.

"And then they wanted me give this message to Shaya n'ha M'lorya. But if'n you're her freemate, I can give it to you? If they find me here—"

"You can give the message to me," Magda said.

"She said—they'll meet wi' you at Nevarsin Guild-house."

Camilla said, "But there isn't—"

Magda kicked her shins and she fell silent. Calisu' wrenched her arms free from Camilla's grip, scuttled toward the door and was gone.

Camilla strode after her. She struggled with the ancient mechanism, which was rusted and could not be properly bolted shut again. Finally she sighed, and said, "Put some of the loads in front of it, so we'll hear if someone tries to get in again. I was afraid this would happen. No, no, not you, you shouldn't be lifting things with your head—"

"I seldom do," said Magda, "that's not my *laran*. I'm sad to say I have to use my hands." But she stepped back and let Cholayna and Camilla pile loads in front of the side entrance. Camilla said moodily, "You heard her. What does it mean? There is no Guild-house in Nevarsin, it's a city of *cristoforos*. How can we meet them when—"

"Shaya will understand," said Magda. Her head was splitting

in spite of Cholayna's pain pills, and she wished that Jaelle would return so that she could go and have a bath and lie down.

Listlessly she found clean underclothing and thick socks, a heavy sweater and woollen breeches to sleep in. Jaelle and Vanessa came in; they had even washed their hair, and Jaelle's coppery locks were curled up in tight, damp, frizzy ringlets.

"Just what the weary traveler needs," Jaelle said, elaborately stretching her arms and yawning. "Now, when that meal comes—I saw it cooking; smelled it. Roast fowl on the spit, and mushrooms in a casserole with redberry sauce." She licked her lips greedily. "This is a better place to stop than I thought. Go along, you three, get your baths. But don't be too long or we'll eat all the mushrooms. I wonder if this village makes a good mountain wine?"

"If not," Cholayna joked, "I shall complain to the head-woman."

The bathhouse was an isolated stone building, from which issued wisps of steam. When they went inside, the bath attendant gave them little three-legged stools to sit on and asked with rough deference if the ladies had their own soap and sponges. She scrubbed them well, clucking at Magda's injured arm, and even managed not to stare too long or too inquisitively at Cholayna. Then she ushered them down the steps into the stone-lined pool filled with steaming hot water. Magda sighed with pure pleasure, feeling the scalding heat drawing the pain from her wounded arm, and lay back so that she was covered to the neck.

"Feels good," Camilla agreed, and Magda remembered that she too had hurt her ankle, though not as seriously as Vanessa.

"Are you really all right, *breda*?"

"Nothing hot water and a good night's sleep wouldn't cure. *If* I felt safe about getting it here," Camilla muttered, softly so the bath attendant wouldn't hear. "Careful, let's not say anything serious, it may be her business to carry tales. No, I trust *none* of them, no farther than I could kick a statue uphill."

Under the surface of the water, Magda sought Camilla's hand and pressed the long fingers between her own. She was ashamed of how she had behaved in the afternoon. Had she really been willing to hurt Camilla's feelings because of what Vanessa might think? Why should it matter? She sat holding Camilla's hand, silently, and in the quiet comfort of the bath, she slowly began to pick up her friend's fear, her suspicion.

She could understand both. In the days when she and Peter Haldane, then married, had explored from the Kilghard Hills to the Plains of Arilinn, they had encountered their share, or more, of bandits and outlaws. They had had more than enough narrow escapes—although they had survived, when others had not. Those had been the days when the so-called "Lorne Legend" was in the making. Poor Peter, in a sense it was unfair; it might as well have been called the "Haldane Legend", for he had done as much as she in the matter of gathering information about territories and boundaries, recording linguistic variables and social customs—all the basic information for Intelligence. The difference was that Magda had done it on a world, and in a milieu, where women found it almost impossible to go into the field at all, let alone accomplish anything meaningful there; and so Magda had gotten most of the credit and all the attention.

But Peter had had his reward: he had become Legate, and he was a good one, concerned, fair, committed to the world he loved. She had chosen another path, and different rewards.

"Magda? Don't fall asleep here, there is a good supper waiting for us."

"No, I'm not asleep." Magda pulled herself upright in the steaming water, blinking. She felt almost dangerously relaxed.

Camilla squeezed her hand underwater, and said in a whisper that could not be heard inches away, "*Z'bredhyi, chiya.*" Magda returned the pressure and whispered, "I love you, too." But because they were not alone, she turned to Cholayna and said aloud, "I suppose they are waiting for us, they may not serve supper till we're all there. I suppose we should get out, but I could stay here all night."

Cholayna looked at her fingers, beginning to wrinkle like dried fruit in the steaming water. "We'd end up a great deal smaller, I think." She pulled herself to her feet, and the bath attendant brought a towel to wrap about her. Camilla followed, and Magda saw that in the hot water, the old scars on her back and side were clear white, standing out against her fair skin reddened by the heat. She saw the bath attendant notice them, and Cholayna actually opened her mouth to speak. Magda could almost hear her: *In the name of the secret gods, what happened to you?* before she realized that neither Cholayna nor the attendant had said a word. In the peace and relaxation of the bath, once again she was picking up unspoken thoughts.

Reluctantly, Magda hauled herself out of the hot, relaxing bath, and wrapped herself in the thick towel provided by the attendant. It felt wonderful to dress in clean clothes from the skin out.

"Now for some of that good roast fowl, and maybe the mountain wine Jaelle was talking about."

Cholayna pursed her lips. "I don't want to sound like a nervous foster-mother, Magda, but if you really have concussion, you shouldn't drink any wine. How is your head?"

Magda, though the hot water had relaxed the muscles of her neck and she felt much better, admitted that the headache was still there, a dull hard pounding despite the pain pills.

Camilla said, "She's right, Margali, you really should stick to tea or soup till we're sure about your head," and Magda, inching her sweater over the throbbing bump on her skull, shrugged.

"I'll have to make do with good hot food and fine company, then. Lucky Vanessa, she only bashed her ankle, she can have a hangover if she wants to. I really could use a drink, but I'll defer to your medical knowledge."

It was a shock to go out into the cold again. The fierce wind had blown the snow into deep drifts; they hurried across the narrow space between the buildings. In places the snow had drifted so high that it came up over their boot-tops, icy, chilling the new warmth of their feet. They were glad to see the blazing fire inside the barn allotted to them. The building was so large that it was not exactly warm, but at least they were out of the wind.

Vanessa and Jaelle had made the beds up, and the place looked clean and inviting, almost homelike; though it was

hardly like their own homes, with horses and *chervines* stabled
at the other end. An ample supply of hay had been brought in for
them, which gave a clean healthy smell to the surroundings. Almost at once, serving women began to parade in with dishes and
smoking platters; in addition to the roast fowl, there was a
haunch of roasted *chervine* with its sizzling layer of good-
smelling fat, and rabbithorn stewed in wine. There were long
rolls of bread, hot from the oven, with plenty of butter and
honey, a savory casserole of mushrooms and bland but nourishing boiled whiteroot, and the promised redberry sauce.

"Why, this is really lavish!" Cholayna exclaimed.

"It ought to be. Enjoy it. We paid enough for it," Jaelle said,
as they gathered around, sitting on piled-up loads and packs,
digging in with a good appetite—all except Cholayna. The older
woman ate some of the boiled whiteroot, and tasted the redberry
sauce with appreciation, but after valiantly trying to eat the piece
of roast fowl Jaelle had carved for her, she turned pale and put
her plate aside.

"What's the matter, *comi'ya?*" asked Camilla.

Cholayna said faintly, "It looks—still looks too much like
the—the living animal. I'm sorry, I—I tried. When it's just a—
a bar, or a slice, I can manage it, but—but this is a *wing!*"

"You need the protein," Vanessa said. "Hunt out some emergency rations. You can't make a meal on mushrooms and redberry sauce."

"I—I'm sorry." Cholayna apologized again, and found the
load containing the packaged Terran rations. This was forbidden
in the field, lest some unauthorized observer should catch sight
of the obviously alien packaging, but Magda had not the heart to
reprimand her; she looked so sick. Cholayna had had a hard few
days, and she supposed that if you really applied the rules
strictly, even the elastic bandage on Vanessa's ankle would be
against the laws of Intelligence work.

*On the other hand, if the Head of Intelligence for Darkover
can't break a rule when there's hardly even anyone to know she's
done so—*

"Never mind," Camilla was saying, "have some of the wine,

at least. It's very good. They certainly aren't skimping on us, I'll say that for them! Shaya, tell me—there isn't a Guild-house in Nevarsin, is there?"

"Goodness, no!" Jaelle laughed, raising her winecup to be refilled for the third time. "Keitha used to talk about starting one there, remember? There is a hostel where some women lived while they were copying some of the old manuscripts from the Monastery of Saint Valentine, years ago, but that would hardly count." She frowned. "Why, Camilla?"

"There was a message." She told about Calisu', her earring and her relayed words, and Jaelle frowned.

"Rafi evidently thought it would mean something to me, but—oh, wait!" She broke off and said, "When we were girls, traveling with Kindra, there was a place where we used to lodge. It wasn't an inn; women can't go to public inns in the Hellers unless they are properly escorted by their menfolk. There was an old dame who made leather jackets and boots to sell—that was where I learned to make gloves and sandals, in fact."

"Oh, of course," Camilla said. "I went there once, and one of the young girls taught me to embroider gloves with beads! I remember old Betta, and all her wards and foster-daughters!"

"She took in all the female orphans she could find in the city, and brought them up to work for her, but instead of getting them married off, as virtuous *cristoforo* matrons do with their girl apprentices, this old dame used to teach them a trade and encourage them to set up businesses for themselves. Some of them went off and got married anyway, but some of them are still in business and living in the old woman's house, and others, old Betta sent them south with us to the Guild-house. Kindra used to say, when there *was* a Guild-house in Nevarsin, we should get Betta to run it for us. I think she's dead, but four of her adopted daughters are still running the place, and Guild-women were always welcome there. Certainly, that is where Rafi would lodge."

She drained the winecup, looked wistfully at the bottle, and sighed.

"Oh, finish it if you want to," Camilla chuckled. "You can drink Margali's share."

"Yes, have it by all means," Magda said; her head was spinning and she felt dizzy, though she had not even touched the wine. Jaelle resolutely pushed it away.

"I would have a head worse than hers tomorrow if I drank any more, already I'm falling asleep where I sit. Let's get to bed."

And in fact the dishes were all but empty; the bones of the roast fowl were scattered, only a few scraps of gravy remaining on the platter which had held the roast *chervine*. After the fatigue of the day, the bath and the heavy meal, Magda was sure they would sleep well tonight. Her head still throbbed, and she wobbled when she got up to go to her sleeping bag.

Camilla protested. "Aren't we going to set watch?"

Vanessa yawned hugely. "Not I. An offense to these good people's hospitality. I'm going to—" Another vast yawn split her words. "Sleep."

Jaelle, drawing off her boots, looked up seriously at Camilla. "Truly, do you think we should set a watch, Aunt?" She used the old affectionate word of her childhood, and it made Camilla smile; but the other woman said, "Truly, I do. Even if most of these people are good, trustworthy and hospitable, it is possible there are rogues among them. I will stand first watch myself."

"I will let you, then," Jaelle said, and went to crawl into her sleeping bag. Almost before the others had their boots off, she was fast asleep and snoring. Magda thought, *She must be even more tired than we realized. Of course all the weight of the trip has been on her. I must try to bear more of the responsibility.*

She felt so dizzy, her head pounding, that she asked Cholayna for another of the pain pills, and Cholayna gave it to her, rather reluctantly. "You really should not. After a bath and a meal like that one, I am sure you will sleep well enough without it."

"I won't take it unless I find I cannot sleep," Magda promised. Cholayna pulled off her boots, wrapped her pale halo of hair into a crimson scarf, and crept into her sleeping bag. Camilla, yawning, settled down on one of the loads, her knife across her knees. Vanessa lowered the light of the lantern to its lowest point. "Camilla, wake me after an hour or so. You need sleep, too. We should try to make an early start."

"In this?" Camilla gestured, and in the silence they could hear the rattle of snow blowing against the frame of the building and the wind howling around the corners. "We'll be lucky to get out of here by day after tomorrow."

"Well, maybe it will stop during the night."

"Maybe Durraman's donkey could really fly. Go to sleep, Vanessa. I'll watch for a few hours, at least."

Vanessa's sleeping bag—now that they were not in the wilds, they were using the Terran single bags rather than the doubled ones from the Guild-house—was spread next to Magda's. After a moment, Vanessa asked softly, "Are you asleep?"

"Not nearly. I thought I'd fall asleep right away, but my head really aches. I think I'm going to take Cholayna's pill after all."

"Miss Lorne—may I ask you something? Something really personal?"

"Of course," Magda said, "but only if you stop calling me Miss Lorne. Vanessa, we are sisters of the Guild-house. What would please me most would be if you would call me Margali. It really is my name, you know, it's not just an alias, or the name I use in the field. My parents named me Margali. I was born on Darkover, in these mountains; though I've been away from them for a long time. No one ever called me Magdalen till I went to the Intelligence School on Alpha. I worked so long for the HQ that I'm quite used to Magda now, but I really prefer Margali."

"Margali, then. I—I have some trouble understanding women as freemates. Jaelle is your freemate, yes? But you and Camilla—"

"Camilla is my lover, yes," said Magda deliberately. "The Oath of Freemates is something else. Jaelle and I swore that oath, which is legal for women, so that we could be guardians of one another's children. Jaelle and I—perhaps no one brought up under Terran laws could understand. We have been lovers, too; but Camilla and I—I said you wouldn't understand."

"I don't. I would like to understand. What—what is it like, to love a woman?"

Magda laughed. "What is it like to love? To love anyone?"

Vanessa was asleep at her side. Jaelle still snored softly; she had, Magda reflected, drunk far too much. Cholayna, though coughing a little, was fast asleep. But Magda could not sleep, though she felt as sick and dizzy as if she had finished the bottle of wine herself. She wanted to take Cholayna's pill, but was restrained by the thought that if her concussion was serious, she probably should not. From where she lay, she could see Camilla, the long knife resting across her knees; but even as she watched, Camilla's head sagged forward; she started, pulled herself upright with a jerk—then sagged again, asleep.

And suddenly, as if she had read it printed in letters of fire, Magda knew. She never knew whether it was *laran* or something else, but she knew.

The wine had been drugged. And probably some of the food as well.

Cholayna didn't eat much of their food. She may not be drugged. I should wake her at once and tell her.

But Magda could not make herself move, feeling sicker and dizzier than ever. She thought, in terror, *I am drugged too!* She tried to force herself to move, to wake, to scream out to Camilla, to Cholayna.

But she could not move.

Chapter 15

Magda fought against the sluggishness of her brain, struggling to move. She tried to reach out with *laran* to Jaelle—*Shaya, wake up, we have been drugged, it's a trap, Camilla was right!* She tried to pull herself upright, to crawl over to her freemate and shake her from her drugged and drunken sleep; Jaelle had drunk more of the drugged wine than any of them.

And no wonder. She has carried the fullest weight of this trip, all the way, and now when she has relaxed, now that she will let herself sleep, I may not be able to wake her at all.

Jaelle was probably so deeply drunk and drugged as to be unrousable. If she could reach Camilla, though, and waken her. . . . Magda fought against her weakness and dizziness, her throbbing head and sickness, concentrating on the pain. She gave thanks to the Goddess that she had not swallowed Cholayna's last sleeping pill, or she would now be sleeping alongside her drugged friends; and the folk of this village would be able to come and steal their loads, and perhaps cut their throats, at their leisure . . . or whatever else they might have in mind.

Cholayna had drunk little of the drugged wine, eaten almost none of the food. She might be the easiest to rouse . . . Magda tried to raise her head, clench her fists, anything. Pain lanced through her forehead like blinding knives, but she did force her head a little up from the packload which served her as pillow. Bracing herself with her hands, feeling so sick she was sure she would vomit, she managed to pull herself up inch by inch to a sitting position.

"Cholayna," she whispered hoarsely, but the Terran woman neither stirred nor answered, and Magda wondered if her voice was audible, if she had really even moved at all, whether this was one of those dreadful nightmares where you are convinced that you have gotten out of bed and gone about some business or another while in actuality, you are still motionless, fast asleep . . . Magda managed to get her fist up to her forehead and struck herself on the temple. The resulting flood of pain convinced her that it was real.

Think! she admonished herself. At Cholayna's advice, she had drunk none of the drugged wine, and they would hardly have drugged every dish; probably she had had relatively little of the drug, and Cholayna even less. *If I can only reach her!*

If only Cholayna were one of the Terrans who were gifted with *laran*! As far as Magda knew, she was not. Struggling against weakness, sickness and tears, Magda somehow crawled over Vanessa; deep in drugged sleep, Vanessa muttered in protest.

"Damn it, lie down and go t' sleep, le'me sleep . . ."

She was closest, easiest to reach. Magda tried to shake her, but could manage only a weak clutch at Vanessa's shoulder, and her voice was no more than a thick whisper.

"Vanessa. Wake up! Please, *wake up!*"

Vanessa stirred again, turning over heavily, dragging sleepily at her heavy, makeshift pillow as if to pull it over her face, and Magda, her *laran* wide open, sensed the way in which the other woman retreated further down into dreams.

They had been ready-made victims for the people of this place. That dreadful washed-out pass, the unpeopled wilderness of Barrensclae—and then a hospitable village, a bathhouse, good food and plenty of wine. Most travelers would sleep the sleep almost of the dead at the end of such a trail, even without whatever devilish drug the villagers used to make sure.

Vanessa was sleeping almost as heavily as Jaelle. She had drunk plenty of the drugged wine, after the long ordeal of traveling on her damaged ankle. It would have to be Cholayna, then. Even in her desperate struggle, head throbbing and her body and brain refusing to obey her, Magda felt a surge of hysterical laughter bubbling up at the thought of what Vanessa might think if she woke up suddenly and found her, Magda, sprawled over her like this. But she could not make her limbs obey her enough to get up and walk or go round, and so she had no choice but to crawl over her.

If I can just get her awake at all, I'll take my chances on whether she screams rape, Magda told herself sternly; but although Vanessa muttered, and swore in her sleep, and even struck out feebly at Magda once or twice, she did not wake. Now, however, Magda was close enough to grab Cholayna's shoulder.

"Cholayna," she whispered, "Cholayna, wake up!"

Cholayna Ares had eaten little, and had drunk almost nothing, but it had been a long and exhausting trip and she was sleeping very heavily. Magda shook the older woman, weakly, and struggled to make herself heard for several minutes before Cholayna abruptly opened her eyes and looked at Magda. Now fully awake, Cholayna shook her head in disbelief.

"Magda? What's the matter? Is your head worse? Do you need—"

"The food—the wine—*drugged!* Camilla was right. Look at her, she would never sleep on watch that way—" But Magda had to fight to even make her tight, shaky whisper heard; it sagged and wobbled in the worst possible way. "Cholayna, I mean it! I'm not—drunk, not crazy—"

Something in Magda's urgency, if not in her words, penetrated; Cholayna sat up, looking swiftly about the barn. Once again Magda, shaking and unable to coordinate what was happening, saw the emergence of the woman who had been put in charge of training Intelligence Agents.

"Can you sit up? Can you swallow?" Cholayna was on her feet in one swift movement, hunting in her pack for a capsule. "Now, this is just a mild stimulant; I hate to give it to you, really, you may have a concussion, but you're conscious and they're not. Try to swallow this."

Magda got it into her mouth, managed to force the capsule down, dimly wondering what the effect of Terran stimulants would be when mixed with whatever drug the villagers had used. *This could kill me, she realized. But then, that's probably better than what the villagers have in mind. . . .*

Steadying Magda with one arm, Cholayna stepped toward Camilla, sitting on the packload fast asleep with her knife across her knees. She bent, shaking her roughly.

Camilla came awake fighting, striking out with the blunt end of the knife; but blinking, recognized Cholayna and pulled back. "What the—?" She shook herself like a wet dog. "In hell's name, was *I* sleeping on watch?"

"We were drugged. Certainly in the wine, maybe in some of the food too. We'll have to be on guard for—whatever they have planned," Cholayna explained. Magda's head was clearing; it still throbbed, but the ordinary pain was manageable, as long as she did not have to cope with the dizzy blurring of thought and motion. Cholayna offered Camilla some of the same stimulant she had given to Magda, but Camilla, fisting sleep from her eyes, refused.

"I'm fine, I'm awake. Zandru's buggering demons! I suspected something like this, but I never thought the food would be drugged! The more fool I! I wonder if that midwife— Calisu'—I wonder if they sent her to soften us up and disarm our suspicions?"

Cholayna was opening her medikit again. "I wonder," she said, "if Lexie and Rafaella are lying somewhere with their throats cut."

Magda shuddered. She had not even thought of that. She said, "I don't think a woman who wore the earring would have done that to her sisters—" But after she said it, she realized she could not be sure the earring had not been stolen.

Cholayna had found an ampoule in the medikit, but cursed softly. "I can't use this, Vanessa's allergic to it, oh *hell!*"

"How else would she know about the Nevarsin Guild-house?"

"She may not have known there wasn't one, though; or that Jaelle would interpret it that way. It may have been like saying 'at the fish markets in Temora'; anybody could assume there'd be one on the seacoast. What do they say—'It needs no *laran* to prophesy snow at Midwinter.' The whole thing could have been made up out of whole cloth, except for Shaya's name."

"Only one thing's sure," Cholayna said, "we weren't drugged out of rustic kindness, to give us a good night's sleep. Let's stop talking and see if we can wake up the others. Magda—do you know Jaelle's endorphin type?"

"Her what?"

"You don't, then," Cholayna said in resignation.

Camilla was shaking Jaelle, furiously but fruitlessly. Jaelle fought and mumbled, opened her eyes but stared without seeing, and finally Camilla hauled her and her sleeping bag into a corner.

"She might as well be in Hermit's Cave on Nevarsin Peak, for all the good she'd be in a fight right now!"

"It's just luck we're not *all* in the same state."

"Cholayna," Camilla said, "if I ever say one more word about your chosen diet, ever again, kick me. Hard. Can we get Vanessa part way awake?"

"I can't," Cholayna said.

"Could she fight, anyway, with her ankle the way it is?" Magda asked.

"Well, it's up to us," Camilla said. "Let's try and move her where she won't be hurt if it comes to fighting. No, Margali, not you, sit down a minute longer while you can. You know you're as white as a glacier?"

Cholayna shoved Magda down on the packload where Camilla had slept, and together they hauled Vanessa out of the way behind the stacked loads.

"Are there bolts on the doors that we can draw? It might slow them down a little."

"I checked that even before we had dinner," Camilla said.

"No wonder they have us in a barn instead of an inn. No one expects to be able to make a barn secure."

"Do you think the whole village is in on this?"

"Who knows? Most of them, probably. I've heard about robbers' villages," Camilla said, "but I thought it was a folk tale." They were all speaking in strained whispers. Camilla went to the main door and opened it a crack, cautiously peering out. The wind and snow tore into the room like a live animal prowling; the door almost got away from her and she had to manhandle it shut with all her strength.

"Still snowing and blowing. What hour of night *is* this?"

"God knows," Cholayna said, "I don't have my chronometer. Magda warned me not to bring any item obviously of Terran manufacture that isn't openly sold in Thendara or Caer Donn."

"It can't be very late," Magda said, "I hadn't been fast asleep at all. Not more than an hour can have gone by since we turned in. I should think they'll wait a while longer to be sure."

"Depends on what drug they gave us, and how long it takes to do whatever it does, and how long it lasts," said Camilla. "We might want to keep half an eye on Shaya and Vanessa, just in case they start choking to death." Magda shuddered at the matter of factness of Camilla's voice as she went on, "If it's fast acting and short-lived, they'll be here any minute. If we're really lucky, they'll trust it completely and send one man to cut our throats, and we can arrange something else."

She made a grim, final gesture with her knife. "Then, while they're waiting for him to come back and give the signal to pile up the loot, we high-tail it out of here. But if we're not lucky, the whole village could come in with hammers and pitchforks." She strode to the concealed entrance where Calisu' had come in to give her message. The wind was not so high here, but still it tore through the room. Camilla looked out into the blowing snow, and drew a harsh gasp of consternation; Magda expected her to slam the door shut, but instead she darted out and, after a moment, beckoned.

"Here's the answer to one question," she said grimly, and pointed.

Already covered by a layer of drifted snow, the woman Calisu' lay on the ground, her dead eyes staring at the storm. Her throat had been cut from ear to ear.

Camilla slammed the door and swore. "I hope the headman's wife goes into labor tomorrow with an obstructed transverse birth! Poor damned woman, they may have thought she warned us!"

"Are we going to leave her body lying there?"

"Got to," Camilla said. "If they find it gone, they'll know we *are* warned. Hellfire, Magda, you think it matters to her anymore where her body lies?"

"Do you think it's early enough that we could simply escape—sneak out of here before they come?" Cholayna suggested.

"Not a chance, not with Jaelle and Vanessa still dead to the world. One *chervine* bleat and they'd be on us. They're probably sitting around in that inn they told us didn't exist, whetting their knives," Camilla said gloomily. She stood with her hands on her hips, scowling, thinking it over. "Stack all the loads against the back door—" She pointed. "Slow them down. We'll be ready for them at the front. Magda, are you all right?"

"I'm fine." Whether it was Cholayna's stimulant or the adrenalin of danger, Magda had no idea, but she felt almost agreeably braced at the thought of a fight. Camilla had her knife out. Magda made sure that her dagger was loose in its sheath. It had been a long time since she had faced any human enemy, but she felt it would be a good and praiseworthy deed to kill whoever had cut the throat of the harmless midwife.

She began to help Cholayna stack the loads, but Cholayna stopped. "I have a better idea. Get the loads *on* the animals. Have them all backed up against that door. Then, when they come at us, if Jaelle and Vanessa are awake by then, we can ride out right over them! If not—we can get free, as soon as the first attackers are out of the way."

"Not much hope of that," Camilla said, "but you're right; we have to be able to get the hell out of here without stopping to load and saddle up the animals. We'll do that, but keep an eye on that front door, because that's where they'll come."

"Stack up a few loads against it," Magda suggested.

"No, they'll know we're warned then, and come at us with knives ready. If they come in here thinking we're all asleep and ready for the slaughter, we can get the first couple of them before they have much of a chance at us. Anything that shortens the odds against us is fair under these circumstances."

Camilla started hoisting loads onto *chervines,* while Magda saddled her pony and Jaelle's. Cholayna went to help Camilla with the packloads, taking away everything before the door, and Magda knew, with a shiver down her spine, that Camilla was clearing the space for a fight. She had seen Camilla fight; had fought once at her side. . . . Her head still throbbed faintly, but otherwise everything seemed blindingly lucid, everything she saw sharp-edged and fresh. She started to put a saddle on Camilla's horse, realized it was Vanessa's saddle which was larger, and made the exchange, saying to herself, *I'll be saddling up* chervines *next if I'm not careful.*

The horses were saddled; the pack animals loaded. *If they do kill us, at least they'll have some trouble getting at our stuff, she thought,* and wondered why she thought that it mattered.

Camilla hunkered down where she could face the door, her fingers just resting on her sword. The Renunciate Charter provided that no *Comhi-Letziis* might wear a sword, only the long Amazon knife, by law three inches shorter than an ordinary sword; but Camilla, who had lived for years as a male mercenary, wore the sword she had worn as a man, and no one had ever challenged her.

She grinned at Magda. "Remember the day we fought Shann's men, and I said you had dishonored your sword?"

"Will I ever forget?"

"Fight as well as that and I'm not afraid of any bandit in the hill country."

Cholayna, half-smiling, leaned against the wall nearby. "Do you hear something?" she asked suddenly.

Silence, except for the high whistle of the blowing snow and wind roaring around the eaves of the building. Some small animal rustled in the straw. After the frantic activity of the last few minutes, Magda felt let down, her heart bumping and pounding, the metallic taste of fear in her mouth.

Time crawled by. Magda had no idea whether it was an hour, ten minutes, half the night. Time had lost its meaning.

"Damn them, why don't they come?" Cholayna's voice came tight through her teeth.

Camilla muttered, "They may be waiting till we put out that last light. But Zandru whip me with scorpions if I'm going to fight in the dark, and if we have to wait till morning, so be it. I'd just as soon they never came at all."

Magda wished that if there was going to be a fight, it would come and be over with; but at the same time, she was remembering in sharp-edged detail her first fight beside Camilla, feeling the appalling pain of the sword slicing along her thigh and laying it open. She was, quite simply, terrified. Camilla looked so calm, as if she actually relished the notion of a good fight.

Maybe she does. She earned a living as a mercenary for God-knows-how-many-years!

Then, in the silence, she heard Cholayna's breath hiss inward, and the Terran woman pointed at the door. Slowly, it was pushing inward, the wind howling around the edges. A face peered around the edge; a round, scarred, sneering face. Immediately the bandit saw the light, the cleared space and the women awaiting him, but even as his mouth opened to give a warning yell, Cholayna leaped in a *vaido* kick, and his face burst, exploding blood; he fell and lay still.

Camilla bent to drag the man, unconscious or a corpse, out of the way; another bandit rushed in after him, and she ran him through expertly. He fell, with a short hoarse howl. The man who pushed in after him got his neck broken by a swift slam of Magda's hand.

"You haven't forgotten *everything*, anyway," Cholayna whispered approvingly.

There was a lull, and then the man whose belly Camilla had split groaned and began screaming again. Magda cringed at the terrible cries, but did nothing. He had been ready to cut all their throats as they slept. She owed him no pity; but as Camilla stepped toward him, her knife raised to silence him once and for all, he fell back again with a gurgle, and the barn was almost silent again.

There are certainly more of them out there, thought Magda, sooner or later they'll rush us all at once. They had been lucky: Magda had killed her man, and the one Cholayna had kicked, though possibly not dead, had at least had all the fight knocked out of him. . . .

The door burst open, and the room filled with men, yelling like so many demons. Camilla ran the nearest one through, and Magda found herself fighting with her knife at close quarters. Cholayna was in the center of a cluster of them, fighting like some legendary devil or hero, kicking with frequently deadly accuracy. Magda's next opponent ran in over her dagger and drove her backward, off-balance; she felt his knife slice into her arm and kicked out wildly, then slammed her other elbow into the base of his throat and sent him flying aside, unconscious. She could feel hot blood trickling down her arm, but another bandit was on her already, and there was no time for pain or fear.

One of them, running toward the horses, literally stumbled over Jaelle; he bent swiftly with his dagger, and Magda flung herself on him from behind, shrieking a warning. She pulled her knife across his throat with a strength she had never imagined having, and he fell, half-beheaded, across Jaelle—who woke, staring and mumbling uncomprehendingly.

As quickly as that, it was all over. Seven men lay dead or unconscious on the floor. The rest had retreated, possibly to regroup, Magda did not know which or, at the moment, care.

Jaelle muttered, plaintively, "What's going on?"

"Cholayna," Camilla ordered, "get into your pack, try to get one of those pills of yours down Jaelle and Vanessa! That was just the first onslaught, they'll be back."

Jaelle blinked and Magda saw her eyes come into focus.

"We were poisoned? Drugged?"

Cholayna nodded, imperatively gesturing for Jaelle to

swallow the stimulant capsule. Forcing it down, Jaelle exploded, "Damn them! They had the nerve to *haggle* with us over the price of the food and wine, too!" She got out of her sleeping bag, tried to haul Vanessa to her feet; then gave it up, and grabbing up her knife, Jaelle came to join Camilla. She still looked groggy, but the stimulant was taking effect.

Magda thought, *We were lucky with the first fight, and Cholayna is one hell of a scrapper for her age! Nevertheless, there's no way the four of us—even if Vanessa could be waked in time—we can't kill off an entire village! We'll die here . . .* But was that so, she wondered; now that the villagers knew the women would be no easy pickings, could they bargain for their lives? Looking at Camilla's face, she knew the swordswoman would entertain no such notions; she was prepared for a fight to the death. What other defenses did they have?

They would probably rush them all at once. Magda was aware of pain now in her wounded arm, and her head was beginning to throb. The man Camilla had gutted began, unexpectedly, his terrible moaning again; Camilla knelt and quickly cut his throat.

Cleaning the knife on the dead man's ragged coat, Camilla stood up, fingering her sword. Magda felt she could almost read her mind, knowing the mercenary's code of honor. Camilla was more than ready to die bravely. *But I don't want to die bravely*, Magda thought. *I don't want to die at all. And I don't want Cholayna's and Vanessa's lives on my conscience if I don't! Is there any alternative—?*

Then, with a dreadful sense of *déjà vu*, she saw a face peer round the door, as if they had returned to the very beginning of the fight.

Think, damn it, think! What good is it having laran *if it can't save your life* now!

A bandit rushed at her, knife upraised. She struck hard, felt him crumple away under her—but they were outnumbered. Desperately she reached out with her *laran*, remembering an old trick; suddenly seeing, like an image painted behind her eyes, the fireside at Armida, and Damon telling them about a battle fought with *laran*, long ago.

Jaelle! Shaya, help me!

Jaelle was fighting for her life with a bandit in a red shirt. Magda reached desperately, wove an image, saw the bandits recoil; above them in the barn a demon wavered, no Darkovan demon but an ancient devil out of Terran myth, with horns, tail, and a mighty stink of sulphur . . . The line of men broke and surged back. Then Jaelle linked with her, the minds of the freemates locking into one; and suddenly a dozen fanged demons armed with swords faced the bandits. The villagers faltered again, fell back yet again, and then with a howl, turned and ran. Some even threw down their weapons as they went.

Vanessa chose that moment to sit up. Staring about the barn with bewilderment, she saw the demons, emitted a strangled squeak and buried her head in the blankets.

The stink of sulphur still lingered, Cholayna ran quickly to Vanessa, urging her to get up. Camilla said, "That ought to hold them for a while! Not for long, though.

Let's get out while we can!"

Swiftly they scrambled to their horses, Vanessa still shaking her head and mumbling dizzily. Magda checked her bleeding arm. Nothing, she supposed to worry about; though blood was still oozing slowly from the cut. *If a vein was severed*, she told herself, *it would be a steady flow, and if the artery had gone, I'd have bled to death already*. She tore a strip from the bottom of her undertunic once she'd clambered into her saddle; she tied the bandage swiftly, anchoring it with her teeth to keep both hands free.

Clumped together on their horses, *chervines* on lead reins, they moved toward the door. Jaelle said, "Wait—" and Magda felt the touch of her *laran*, "let's make sure they don't get in here for a good long time. . . ."

Magda looked over her shoulder at the face and form of the Goddess, dark robe glittering with stars, jeweled wings overshadowing the dark spaces of the barn, her face haloed and her eyes piercing, sorrowful, terrifying. She did not envy the villager who tried to use that barn again, even for an innocent purpose. Where had she found the image in her mind? On the night of that first meeting of the Sisterhood?

They rode together out of the barn into the wind and blowing snow. A few villagers huddled together, watching them go, but made no move to stop them. Maybe they still saw the demons she and Jaelle had created.

All at once, Magda was fearfully sick and dizzy. She held to her saddle with both hands, trying to avoid falling from her horse. Her wounded arm—the same arm she had scraped raw in the fall, she realized for the first time—stung with pain, and her head throbbed as if every pulse of her blood were a separate stone hurled at her forehead; but she clung to the saddle, desperately. The important thing was to put as much space as humanly possible between themselves and that miscrable, damnable village. She tried to hang on with one hand and pull her scarf over her face to protect her eyes a little from the stinging wind—without much luck. She bent forward, huddling her face into the neck of her jacket, riding in a dark nightmare of pain. She hardly heard Camilla's voice at her side.

"Margali? *Bredhiya*? Are you all right? Can you ride?"

Isn't that what I'm doing? Would it make any difference if I said I couldn't? she tried to say, irritably; but her voice would not obey her. She felt that she was fighting the reins, fighting the horse that would not obey her. Later she knew that she had fought and tried to hit Camilla when the older woman lifted her bodily from her horse and into her arms. Then Magda's mind went dark and she fell into a dark dream of screaming demons pinioning her to a cattle-stall while a banshee-faced *kyorebni* tore with a fierce beak at her arm and shoulder; then it pecked out her eyes, and she went blind, and knew no more.

Chapter 16

*S*he was wandering in the gray world; alone, formless, without landmarks. She had wandered there for a hundred thousand times a hundred thousand years. And then, into a universe
without form and void, there were voices. Voices curiously
soundless, echoing into her throbbing brain.

I think she's coming around. Breda mea, bredhiya, *open your
eyes, speak to me.*

No thanks to you, if she is. This was Jaelle's voice, and it occurred to Magda in the formless grayness that the emotion
which formed and inhabited and throbbed in Jaelle's voice now
was anger; right-down, gut-level, honest wrath. *You say that you
love her so much, yet you do nothing to help. . . .*

There is nothing I could have done. I am no leronis, *I leave
that to you. . . .*

*I have heard you say that before, Camilla, and I believe it no
more than I did then. If it is your fancy, as it may well be your
privilege, to say at all times that you were born without* laran
*and to maintain it when it harms none but you, so be it; but with
her very life at stake—*

*Her life? Nonsense; the goddess be thanked, she breathes,
she lives, she's waking—*breda, *open your eyes.*

Camilla's face came out of the grayness, pale against a clear,
cold starry dark. Magda said her name shakily. Behind Camilla
she could now see Jaelle; and then the fight and its aftermath
came back to her.

"Where are we? How did we get away from—from that place?"

"We're far enough away that it's not likely they'll come after us," Cholayna said, somewhere out of Magda's sight. "You've been unconscious for four or five hours."

Magda raised her hand and rubbed her face. It hurt. Camilla said, "I am sorry, Margali—I had no alternative. You would not let me take you off your horse to carry you before me on my saddle—you seemed to think I was another of those creatures from the village." She touched, tenderly, the sore spot at the point of Magda's jaw. "I had to knock you out. While you were healing her, Shaya, couldn't you have done something about that?"

"You don't know anything about it." Jaelle's lips were still tight and she was not looking at Camilla.

Her fingers strayed to the narrow crimson seam of the knife scar along her own face. She said, "I have repaid you for this, at least." Years ago Magda had discovered her own *laran* in helping Lady Rohana to heal it. Then she asked, "How do you feel?"

Magda sat up, trying to assess how in fact she did feel. Her head still ached; apart from that, she seemed quite all right. Then she remembered.

"My arm—the knife—"

She looked curiously down at her arm. It had been skinned raw in the fall, later laid open by the bandit's knife, but there was only a faint pale scar, as if long healed. Jaelle had called upon the force of her *laran* to heal the very structure of the cells.

"What else could I do? I slept through most of the fight," Jaelle said lightly. "And Vanessa didn't really get herself awake until we were an hour outside the village; I don't think she really believed there had been a fight until she saw your arm, Margali."

"Was anyone else hurt?"

"Cholayna's nose was bloodied, but a handful of snow stopped that," Camilla said, "and one of the bastards cut open my best holiday tunic, though the skin was not much more than scratched under it. Jaelle's ribs will be sore for a tenday where you squashed that bandit against her chest." Magda vaguely remembered, now, trying to pull a bandit off Jaelle and cutting his throat in the process.

It was blurred, like a nightmare, and she preferred that it should stay that way.

"We were lucky to get out of there all alive and well," Jaelle said. "Camilla, I owe you an apology."

"Nine times out of ten you would have been right and the place as safe as a Guild-house," Camilla said gruffly.

"And still you insist you have no *laran*?"

Camilla's pale narrow features flushed with anger. "Drop it, Shaya" she said, "or I swear by my sword, I will break your neck. Even you can go too far."

Jaelle clenched her fists and Magda felt the anger again surging up in both of them, like tangible crimson lines of force woven into the air between the women. She strained to speak, to break the tension, but realized that she could hardly sit up, hardly manage a whisper.

"Camilla—"

Jaelle let her breath go. "Hellfire, what does it matter? You heard the warning, kinswoman, call it what you will. I don't doubt it saved all our lives. That's what matters. Vanessa, is the tea ready?" She set a steaming mug in Magda's hand. "Drink this. We'll rest here till it's light enough to see our way."

"I'll stand guard," Vanessa offered. "I think I have had enough sleep for a tenday!"

"And I will stand guard with you," said Jaelle, sipping from another mug. "These three have a fight behind them, and they deserve some rest. We'll off-load the beasts till morning, too. Cholayna, is there any dried fruit?"

Cholayna gestured toward a saddlebag. "But you can hardly be hungry, after that meal—I didn't think any of us would be hungry for three days!"

But Magda knew, watching Jaelle gnaw on dried raisins, the fierce hunger that succeeded the depletion of *laran*. Camilla took a handful of the raisins too.

"You girls stand watch. You missed the real fun," she said, spreading her blankets beside Magda and Cholayna. Magda suddenly felt anxious about Camilla.

She was not a young woman, and that had been a dreadful fight. And Camilla had been so worried about her that she had probably not troubled to look after herself. Yet she knew if she inquired, Camilla would make it a point of honor to insist there was nothing wrong with her.

Cholayna, lowering herself to her spread blankets, hesitated.

"Shall I cover the fire? It might show us up to—to anything that's prowling in the woods."

"Leave it," said Jaelle. "Anything on four legs, the fire would scare them away. Anything on two legs—Goddess forbid—we might as well see what's coming after us. I don't want anyone— or anything—sneaking up on me in the dark." She laughed, nervously. "This time Vanessa and I will do the fighting and let *you* sleep."

Magda did not feel sleepy, but knew she should rest. The healing skin on her arm itched almost to the bone. The fire sank lower. She could see Vanessa, seated on a saddlebag; Jaelle was somewhere out of her sight, but Magda could *feel* her pacing boundaries of their camp, protecting it, as if she spread brooding wings over it . . . *dark wings of the Goddess Avarra, sheltering them. . . .*

For so many years she had thought of Jaelle as younger, fragile and vulnerable, to be protected as she would have protected her child; yet from the first Jaelle had assumed leadership of this journey, taken responsibility for seeing all of them safe. Her freemate had grown; it was time for Magda to stop thinking of Jaelle as less than her equal.

She is as strong as I, perhaps stronger. It is high time for me to realize that I cannot, I need not, carry all the weight alone. Jaelle, if I let her, will do her share. And more. . . .

They took the road northward, cutting across wild country by little-known trails toward the Kadarin, avoiding main roads and villages. After five days of travel they came on a better-traveled road; Jaelle said that she would rather keep away from main roads, especially with Cholayna with them. "Even this far north, gossip may have run into the hills that among the Terrans in Thendara there are some with black skins, and I would as soon answer no questions about what we are doing with a Terran in our company. Renunciates raise enough question in these hills, without a Terran woman as well. Vanessa could pass for a mountain woman, some of the forge-folk have animal eyes. Nevertheless we must ford the Kadarin, and for that we must go to one of the main fords or ferries; last spring's floods have made the less-traveled fords too dangerous."

"I'll risk anything you will," Vanessa said.

"Never mind; Cholayna, just keep your hood around your face and don't answer any questions. Pretend you're deaf and dumb."

"I should have stayed in Thendara, shouldn't I? I'm just endangering all of you," said Cholayna with a touch of bitterness, but Jaelle made an impatient gesture.

"Done is done. Just keep your wits about you and obey orders, that's all I ask."

And for a minute Magda wondered if her freemate was actually glad to see the Terran woman, Head of Intelligence, for a change taking orders rather than giving them, if Jaelle was pleased to have Cholayna under her command. Then she absolved Jaelle, mentally, of that pettiness. She herself might have felt that way, at least for a moment; Jaelle was all too obviously only worrying about the safety of the group.

And in fact there was probably less danger for any of them, even if Cholayna *was* recognized as Terran, at the large populated fords and ferries, than in some remote village where the Kadarin could be forded in secret. They had had enough of remote villages for one trip.

Half a dozen caravans were at the ford before them, and Camilla, who was wearing a short down jacket, her ragged gingery hair and scarred gaunt features hardly identifiable as a woman's, made some excuse and rode along the stacked-up groups awaiting the ferry. She came riding back looking disappointed.

"I had hoped to see Rafi here, with the Anders woman, perhaps."

Jaelle shook her head. "Oh, no. They are a long way ahead of us, kinswoman."

Camilla tightened her mouth and looked away, her eyes veiled like a hawk's. "That's as it may be; there is always the chance. Are we going to ford, or pay the ferryman?"

"Ford, of course. I don't want anyone getting a good look at Cholayna; there's a proverb in these hills, inquisitive as a ferryman's apprentice. What's the matter, afraid to get your feet wet?"

"No more than yourself, *chiya*. But I thought we were in a hurry."

"We'd have to wait an hour for the ferryman, with all those people ahead of us; we can ford as soon as that man and his dogs and his *chervines* are all across," Jaelle said, watching the badly organized group ahead of them, a pair of young boys urging dogs and *chervines* into the water with sticks and menaces, women in riding-skirts clinging to their saddles and squealing; something frightened one of the nervous riding-beasts in midstream, and one of the women was out of her saddle and floundering in the water; it was an hour before the ford was clear again, and Jaelle paced the bank restlessly. Magda could see that she was itching to get out there and show the men how a well-organized caravan forded a river. Their mission permitted no such indulgence.

"Never mind," Magda said as they started leading their pack animals into the trampled mud at the near edge of the ford, "you can get out there and show them how a Renunciate guide takes her crew across."

Jaelle grinned, abashed. "Am I as transparent as that?"

"I've known you a long time, *breda mea*."

They went in orderly fashion, Jaelle leading with the foremost of the pack animals on a lead rein, then Magda, Vanessa, Cholayna muffled like a *leronis* in Magda's spare riding-cape, and Camilla bringing up the rear. They had, she reflected, forded the Kadarin more easily than if they had waited for the ferry, which was now caught in one of the eddies of the ford, while the ferryman and his sons, swearing and shouting, were trying to pole it free.

They left the ferry behind, and the Kadarin, and rode away into the mountains.

At first the slopes of the foothills were gentle, and they rode on well-marked trails, every slope leading between deep canyons filled with conifers and cloud. Jaelle led, setting the fastest pace the horses could endure. This was home country for the *chervines,* and they headed into the fiercest winds with pure pleasure.

Gradually the hills began to rise higher, the passes now leading between naked rock. Jaelle was careful not to be caught above the treeline after dark, but at night, cuddled in their doubled sleeping bags for warmth, Magda shivered at the savage shrilling cry of banshees in the frozen passes, a cry which could, she remembered, paralyze any prey within range.

"What in hell is that?" Vanessa quavered.

"Banshee. You read about them, remember? They probably wouldn't come below the treeline except in a specially hard winter when they were starving. This is still summer, remember?"

"Some summer," Cholayna grumbled. "I haven't been warm since we forded the Kadarin."

"So eat more," Magda suggested. "Calories are heat, as well as nourishment." Cholayna was tolerating the pace, the cold and the altitude better than Magda had hoped; *she must have been one hell of a Field Agent*. Though as the passes grew steeper, more like *chervine* trails to climb, and they were forced to dismount and walk or climb up the steeper slopes—past Nevarsin they might have to abandon the horses altogether, and ride *chervines*—the Terran woman's face seemed pinched, her eyes daily deeper sunken in her head. Camilla was hardened to rough travel, and Vanessa sometimes acted as if the whole trip was something she had organized for the fun of it; her own special climbing holiday. This attitude sometimes got on Magda's nerves, but since Vanessa's mountaincraft had helped them over some of the worst stretches, she supposed Vanessa was entitled to enjoy herself.

Ahead of them lay the Pass of Scaravel, more than seven thousand meters high. On the fifth day past the Kadarin, they camped on the lower slope of the road up into Scaravel after daylong travel in thin flurrying snow that cut visibility to a few horse-lengths ahead. Camilla and Vanessa had grumbled about this, but Magda was just as well pleased; she could keep her eyes on the trail and was not confronted at every turn with the sight of bottomless chasms and dizzying drops off sheer cliffs. The path was slippery in the snow, but not really dangerous, she thought, only dimly realizing how hardened she had grown to roads that would have had her sweating blood only a few tendays ago.

"There's still light," Vanessa argued, "it's less than three or four kilometers to the top. We could still get across."

"With luck. And I'm not trusting to luck any more," Jaelle said testily. "There are banshees above the treeline here, as I have good cause to remember. Want me to introduce you to one in the dark? It's easier to get over in daylight. And we could all do with some rest and hot food."

Vanessa glared and for a moment Magda was sure she would continue the argument, but finally she turned away and began to unsaddle her horse.

"You're the boss."

"I want all the loads unpacked and redistributed before we start out tomorrow," Jaelle ordered. "We've used up a considerable amount of supplies; and the less weight the animals have to carry, the easier to get across Scaravel—and through the mountains beyond. There are passes beyond Nevarsin which make Scaravel look like a hole in the ground."

Magda came to help with the loads, while Camilla started a fire in the camp stove and Cholayna began unpacking rations. They had fallen into a regular camp routine by this time. Soon a good smell of cooking began to steal through the camp.

"Snowing harder," Camilla said, surveying the dark sky. "We'll need the tents. Come and help me set them up, *breda*."

They had made it a habit that whenever they set up tents they should alternate, changing tentmates every camp; Magda would have preferred sharing quarters permanently with either Camilla or Jaelle, but she understood Jaelle's insistence that they should not divide themselves into cliques or teams; that this had been the ruin of many expeditions. Tonight Magda was sharing the smaller tent with Vanessa, while Camilla, Cholayna and Jaelle were in the larger one. Vanessa, changing her socks before dinner, dug into her personal pack and began to attack her hair with a brush.

"I think I'd face bandits again for a chance at a bath," she said. "My hair feels filthy and I'm grubby all over."

Magda agreed with her that this was one of the greatest hardships of the trail. "There will be a women's bath-house in Nevarsin, though," she said, "and perhaps we can find a washerwoman for some clean clothes."

"Ready to eat, you two?"

"Just brushing my hair," Vanessa said, tying a cotton scarf over her head. Camilla was ladling stew onto plates and handing it round; they sheltered under the tent flaps, sitting on saddlebags, to eat. Magda was hungry, and cleaned up her stew quickly, but Cholayna was simply pushing the food around on her plate.

"Cholayna, you are going to have to eat more than that," Camilla said. "Really, you must—"

Cholayna exploded. "Damnation, Camilla, I am not a child; I have been looking after myself for the best part of sixty years, and I simply will not be badgered this way! I know you mean well, but I am sick and tired of being endlessly ordered about!"

"Then you should act as if you knew how to look after yourself as a grown woman," Camilla snarled. "You are behaving like a girl of fifteen on her first excursion from the Guild-house! I don't care how old you are or how experienced in other climates or among the Terrans, here you do not know how to care for yourself—or you would be doing it. And if you cannot be trusted to eat properly, then someone must make sure that you do it—"

"Hold it, Camilla—" Jaelle began, and Camilla turned on her.

"Don't *you* start! I have been holding back from saying this for a tenday now. It is not fair; if Cholayna neglects herself and gets sick, she can endanger us all—"

"Even if this is true, it is not your place to say it—" Jaelle began, but now Camilla was in a rage.

"At this point I care nothing whose place it may be! If the leader says nothing, then I will. I have been waiting for days for you to do your duty and speak to her about this, but because this Terran woman was once your employer you have not had the courage or the common sense to speak a single word. If that is how you see your duty as head of this expedition—"

"I do my duty as I see it," Jaelle said, at white heat, "and I am not a girl to be lessoned by you—"

"Listen to me, both of you," Cholayna interrupted. "Settle your places in the pecking order somewhere else, and don't use me as your excuse! I am trying to eat as much as I can of your damned filthy food, but it's not easy for me, and I don't need reminding all the time! I will do the best I can; leave it at that, will you?"

"Just the same," Vanessa said, "what they said is true, Cholayna. You act as if they had no right to say it. But on an expedition like this, politeness is not as important as the truth. If you get sick, the rest of us will have to look after you. I have told you before that at these altitudes you simply must force fluids and calories."

"I am trying, Vanessa, but—"

Magda joined in for the first time. "Even if what you say is true, Vanessa—and you too, Camilla—do you have to be so hard on her? Remember, this is Cholayna's first trip into the field in many years, and her first experience with this kind of climate—"

"All the more reason, then, that she should be guided by those of us with experience—" Camilla said, but Jaelle interrupted her:

"Do you think it is going to do her any good if you simply stand there and scream at her like a banshee? I don't think I could eat a bite with you standing over me and yelling at the top of your voice!"

Magda held out her hand in a conciliating gesture.

"Shaya, *please*—"

"Damnation, Margali, will you at least keep out of this? Every time I try to settle something, you want to get into it. If Camilla and I cannot talk without you trying to jump into the gap, as if you were afraid something would slip by without your having a hand in it—"

Magda shut her mouth with an effort. It was so much like what Lexie had said: *Hellfire, Lorne, is there any pie on this planet you don't have your fingers in?* Was this truly how she appeared to people? She started to say, I was only trying to help, and realized, if it wasn't obvious, that she wasn't.

Cholayna had picked up her plate and was making an effort to force down the cold, greasy meat stew.

Can't they even see that if she tries to eat that, and she's already half sick, it's going to make her worse? Jaelle at least should be able to see that. She opened her mouth again, knowing that she risked another setdown for interfering, but Camilla reached for the plate.

"Let me heat that up for you, Cholayna, or if you'd rather, we still have plenty of the dried porridge-powder, which may be easier for you to eat. I'll mix it with plenty of sugar and raisins. There's no sense wasting good meat on anyone who doesn't appreciate it and probably can't digest it properly anyhow. Does anyone want to share the rest of the stew with me while I make up some porridge for Cholayna?"

"And I've been thinking," Vanessa volunteered, "it might be a good thing to save the special Terran high-altitude rations for her. They're almost entirely synthetics, but they're very high-calorie, high-fat, high-carbohydrate, and they won't upset her; the rest of us can make do on the dried meat and fruit from natural sources. Here," she added, handing over the porridge-powder into which Camilla had stirred sugar and raisins, and Cholayna accepted the mixture gratefully.

Magda could see that she had to force herself to eat, but at least it was simpler to force herself when it was simply disinclination to the effort of chewing and swallowing, not an attempt to overcome decades of training, both in custom and ethical preference.

It frightened her to be so aware of what Cholayna was thinking. There had been times, in her early training in the Forbidden Tower, when she had found herself unable to cut out the thoughts and emotions of her colleagues. But they had all been strong telepaths. Cholayna was head-blind and a Terran, and there should be no such involuntary spillage of emotions.

And Camilla, too, had seemed to know—and Magda stopped herself there. No one should know better than she herself that beneath Camilla's rough-talking exterior was a singularly sensitive, even a motherly woman. There was surely no need to postulate that the stress of this trip, or something else she had no way of identifying, was bringing out latent *laran* in Camilla, or even Cholayna.

Jaelle said sheepishly to all of them at large, "I'm sorry. I can't imagine what got into me. Camilla, forgive me, kinswoman. I meant what I said but I should have been more tactful about it. Margali—" She turned to Magda and held out her arms. "Forgive me, *breda mea*?"

"Of course!" Magda hugged her, and after a moment Camilla came to join them; then Vanessa and Cholayna were there and the five of them were joined in a group embrace that washed away all the anger.

"I can't imagine why I started yelling," Camilla said. "I didn't mean to, truly, Cholayna. I don't want you to get sick, but honestly, I didn't mean to keep on at you about it."

Vanessa said, "This kind of group tension on an expedition is to be expected. We should be on guard against it."

"Maybe," Camilla said wryly, "the Sisterhood is testing us for our worthiness to be admitted to that place?"

"Don't laugh. We are—" Jaelle looked at them seriously.

"The legend says that we *will* be tested ruthlessly, and—we—"
she swallowed, searching for words, "Can't you see? We are
searching for Sisterhood, and if we cannot keep it among ourselves—" her voice trailed away into silence.

At least, Magda thought as she crept into the tent she shared
with Vanessa, they were all speaking again. Magda rejoiced; it
would be hard enough to cross Scaravel even with their utmost
cooperation.

Chapter 17

Jaelle pointed through a light flurry of falling snow.

"The City of Snows: Nevarsin," she said. And Magda picked up her thought—they were almost frighteningly open to one another now—*Will we find Rafaella and Lexie there? And if we do not, what then?* It was beyond belief that Jaelle, at least, would be willing to turn around and go home again. In her mind this journey took on unreal and dreamlike proportions, it would go on forever, farther and farther into the unknown, in pursuit of robed figures, the sound of crows calling, the shadow of the Goddess brooding over them with great dark wings. . . .

Camilla's horse bumped gently into hers. "Hey, there! Are you asleep on your feet like a farmer at spring market, gawking at the big city?"

Nevarsin rose above them, a city built on the side of a mountain, streets climbing steeply toward the peak, where the monastery rose, naked rock walls carved from the living stone of the peak. Above the monastery were only the eternal snows.

They entered the gates of Nevarsin late in the day, and found their way through snow-covered streets, which angled and climbed and sometimes were no more than flights of narrow steep steps, up which their horses had to be urged and their *chervines* led and sometimes manhandled upward. Everywhere there were statues of the *cristaforo* prophet or god—Magda knew little about the *cristaforo* sect—the Bearer of Burdens, a robed figure with the Holy Child on his shoulders surmounted by what could have been a sun or a world or perhaps merely a halo. Bells rang out at frequent intervals, and once as they climbed toward the top of a narrow street, they met a procession of monks, robed in austere garments of sacking, barefoot in the snow-covered streets. (But they seemed as comfortable, their feet as pink and healthy, as if they were dressed for a more amenable climate.)

The monks, chanting as they came—Magda could make out very little of the words of their hymn or canticle, which was in an obscure dialect of *casta*—looked neither to left nor to right, and the women had to move their horses and pull them to one side of the street, dismounting to hold the reins of the pack animals. The monk at the head of the procession, a balding old man with a hook nose and a fierce scowl, looked crossly at the women, and Magda supposed he did not approve of Renunciates.

So much the worse for him, then; she was going about her own business just as he was, and really with far less trouble to other people; at least their band was not expecting everybody to get out of the middle of what was, after all, a public thoroughfare.

There were a great many of the monks, and by the time they had all passed by, dusk was falling, and the snow was coming down heavily.

"Where are we going, Jaelle? I suppose you know?" Camilla asked.

"Nevarsin is a *cristoforo* city," Jaelle said, "and as I think I told you, women are not welcome at public-houses or inns unless properly escorted by husbands or fathers. I told you about the place; Rafi and I used to make jokes about the Nevarsin Guild-house. They may be there waiting for us."

The house, a large one built from the local stone, was in the remotest corner of the city, and inside had the good smell of freshly worked leather. Inside, the great door opened on a huge courtyard ("Dry-Town style," Jaelle whispered to Magda as they were shown inside), where young women in heavy workman's aprons and thick boots were running about. They stopped to greet the strangers with hospitable bows. The mistress of all these women, a small tough old woman with arms like a black-smith's, came out, looked at Jaelle with a huge grin, then wrapped her in a smothering embrace.

"Ah, Kindra's fosterling!"

"Arlinda, you look no different than when I last saw you—can it have been seven years ago? More than that?"

"It was seven years; Betta had just died, Goddess give her rest, and left the place in my hands. How good to see you, there is always room here for Renunciates to lodge! Come in, come in! Suzel, Marissa, Shavanne, lead their horses into the stable, run and tell Lulie in the kitchen that there will be three, no, four, no, five guests for dinner! Give their horses hay and grain, and their *chervines* too, and haul all their packloads into the strong-room; I will give you a receipt, no, *chiya*? Just so there's no question. You came across Scaravel? Mercy me, you look thin and tired, and no wonder, after such a trip! What can I do for you first? Hot wine and cakes? A bath? A meal within ten minutes, if you are famished?"

"A bath would be heaven," Jaelle said, to enthusiastic sec-onding murmurs from all four of the others. "But I thought we would have to go out to the women's bathhouse—"

"My dears, we *are* the women's bathhouse now, it was going downhill, no towels, the attendants with their hands out for tips all the time, and pimps hanging around for so many of the women of the streets that the respectable family men wouldn't let their respectable family women go to it anymore! So I bought it on the cheap, and let it be known that I wanted the street girls certified clean by one of the women's doctors here. And if I caught them making assignations here, out they went. And I chased off all the pimps for good and all. I let the good-time girls know in no uncertain terms that if they wanted baths here, they'd better behave on these premises like apprentice virgin Keepers! And do you know, I think they were glad of it, to be treated just like family women, no difference between them and the wives and daughters of gentlefolk." She shouted. "Suzel, take these ladies to the best guest-chamber, and then straight to the baths, bath's on the house, no charge; these are old friends!"

She drew Jaelle aside but they all heard her whisper, "And when you're bathed and rested, deary, I have a message for you from your partner. Not now, not now, go and have your bath and I'll send some hot wine for you in your guest room."

Jaelle looked pale and strained. "I beg of you, Arlinda, if Rafi is here, send her to me at once. We have traveled from Thendara in the greatest haste we could manage, hoping to overtake her. Don't play games with me, dear cousin."

Arlinda wrinkled up her face, wrinkled and tanned like her own saddle leather. "Would I do that to you, deary? Oh, no, Rafi's not here; they were here three days and went on only yesterday morning. The one who'd been sent to meet them from you-know-where came for them and they left with her."

Jaelle slumped forward and for a minute Magda thought she would faint. She put her arm out and Jaelle leaned on it hard. Through the touch of her freemate's hand Magda could feel misery and dismay.

To come so far, and to miss them by so little . . .

But she recovered herself swiftly. She said with gentle dignity, "You spoke of a message, but if they have gone on before us, it certainly can wait until my companions are bathed and rested. I thank you, cousin."

Arlinda's establishment was nothing if not efficient. In a few seconds, so it seemed to Magda, they had been shown to rooms, given receipts for their packloads and had their personal sacks brought to their assigned room, which was large and light and as clean as if it were a department of Terran Medic. There was a laundry on the premises too, and their soiled and travel-grubbied clothing was whisked away with the promise that it would be returned the next morning. All these things were accomplished by young, energetic, friendly girls, mostly between fifteen and twenty, who scurried around briskly, but with the utmost gaiety, and showed no sign whatever of being driven or intimidated. When Camilla was slow to change her garments (Camilla, because of the scars on her mutilated body, always hesitated to bare herself among strangers) they tactfully offered her a bath-wrap to wear while her clothing was being washed, whisked away to fetch it for her, and had her clothes off and the fresh wrap on her body almost, it seemed, while Camilla was grumbling at them that she could manage perfectly well without it.

"Now I know," said Camilla, wrapping herself in the bath garment, which was faded and wrinkled but smelled cleanly of soap, "Why Kindra used to call this place the Nevarsin Guildhouse."

"It's certainly more efficiently run than many in the Domains," Magda agreed. One of the young women, beckoning to conduct them to the bath, halted a little and she addressed herself directly to Jaelle.

"You are the leader of this band, *mestra*?"

"I am."

"The tall woman with white hair. She is—does she—is the skin disease from which she suffers contagious in any way? If so, *mestra*, your friend must bathe by herself and may not come into the common pool." Her voice was a little embarrassed, but quite firm, and Jaelle answered in the same way.

"On my honor, she suffers from no contagious ailment. Her skin is that way from birth; she comes from a far country where all men and women have such coloring."

"Well, I never! Who'd have believed it!" the girl blurted in wonder. Cholayna, who had stood behind Jaelle wondering what was going to happen, said, "It is true, my girl. But if your customers in the bathhouse will be bothered or afraid that they will catch something, I am willing to bathe alone, as long as I have a bath somehow."

"Oh, no, *mestra*, that won't be necessary, our mistress has known Jaelle a long time, her word's good," the little girl said, kindly if not tactfully. "It's just that nobody here's ever seen nobody like you, so we didn't know, so we had to ask because of the other customers, you see? No offense meant, none at all."

"None taken," Cholayna said graciously (how she managed it, naked in a bathwrap. Magda never knew). As they went on into the bath cubicles assigned to them, Cholayna said to Magda in an undertone, "I had never thought how strange it would be, in a part of the world where everyone looks very much alike.

But then, there are other planets like this, though not many. Skin as pale as Camilla's would be almost as unusual on, say, Alpha, as I am here. What material is this?" she asked, fingering the bathwrap, "It can't be cotton, not in this climate; or do they grow it in the south near Dalereuth?"

"It is the fiber of the featherpod tree; they grow everywhere in the hills. Woven podwool like this is costly; it is commoner to treat it like felting or papermaking, because the fibers are short. But when it is woven this way, it takes the dyes so beautifully that many people think it worth the trouble and cost. In the old days, podweavers were a separate guild, who kept their craft secrets by living in their own villages and never marrying outsiders at all."

Then the bath attendants came in; the child must have passed on the word about Cholayna, for there was not even any undue staring as they soaped and scrubbed all the women; even Camilla's customary defensiveness relaxed when no one paid the faintest attention to the scars covering her body, and she laughed like a young girl as the attendants rinsed them under a hot spray before sending them out into the hot pool. Magda sank into it gratefully, though the water was too hot at first for Vanessa, who yelped aloud as she stepped in.

"You sound like a pig ready for butchering, Vanessa! You'll get used to it," Jaelle advised, lowering herself into the steaming water. It smelled faintly sulfurous and seemed to soothe out all the sores and aches of riding. The women leaned back on the stone shelf in the water, sighing.

"It feels too good to be true," Cholayna said. "The last time we were this comfortable, they had us drugged and poisoned!"

"After this, I feel as if I could handle my weight in bandits," Magda laughed.

Jaelle said seriously, "We are as safe here as in our own Guild-house, and much safer than we should have been in any of the public bathhouses, some of which are run by pimps and such people."

"In Nevarsin? Where the holy monks rule everywhere?" Camilla was frankly skeptical.

"The holy monks are much too holy to think of such things as laws to protect women traveling alone," Jaelle said wryly. "In their opinion, virtuous women do not use such luxuries as public bathhouses where strangers might see their naked bodies, and if a woman frequented such a place she would deserve whatever came to her—disease, unwelcome attentions of whatever kind. There was a time, when the *cristoforo* rule of Nevarsin was absolute, that there were laws to close all the public bathhouses. A few stayed open outside the law, and of course, being run by lawless men, they were lawless places; and the monks used the conduct at such places to justify their closing them . . . *see, baths are wicked places, look at the kind of people who attend them!* Fortunately the laws are more sensible now, but I understand the monks are still not allowed to attend public bathhouses, nor are pious *cristoforo* women."

Camilla snorted. "If the monks' bodies are as filthy as their thoughts, then they must be a dirty lot indeed."

"Oh, no, Camilla, they have their own baths, I am told, within the monastery. And many homes also have baths on the premises. But of course those are only the richer folk, and the poorer sort of people, especially poor women, had no respectable place for a clean bath until some women opened them. And of course, the early ones were not overly respectable, as Arlinda told us; she has done the women of this city as much service as any Guild-house." "She should be made an honorary Renunciate," Camilla said, sinking down to her chin in the hot water.

Jaelle lowered her voice so that the small group of pregnant matrons at the far end of the hot pool might not hear.

"I think she is more than that. Did you hear what she said about Rafaella? *The woman sent from you-know-where* . . . what, do you think, could that be, if not some envoy from the place we are looking for? One of the things mentioned in the old legend was this: if you came far enough, you would be guided. Rafaella and Lexie have come far enough, perhaps, to encounter that guidance. It may be that the message Rafi left me was about the guides sent from—that place."

Camilla's voice was openly scornful.

"And when we get there we will find ourselves among the spicebread-trees and the rainbirds who build nests of scented woods to roast themselves for the hungry traveler?" But Jaelle was perfectly serious.

"I do not know at all what it is that we will find. The legend says that what each person finds is different, and suited to his needs. There was an old story my nurse used to tell me—oh, I was very little then, a tiny child in the Great House of Shainsa." Magda could hardly keep from staring at her freemate. Only once before in all the years she had known her freemate had Jaelle referred, even fleetingly, to her childbood in the Dry Towns, and never to anyone in her father's house there. She could tell from Camilla's eyes that this was equally astonishing to her.

"The story said that three men went out to seek good fortune," Jaelle said, in a faraway voice, "and one married a beautiful wife with much gold and treasure, and thought he was fortunate. And the second found an abandoned homestead where he pruned the trees and they grew fruits and mushrooms for him, and he tamed wild cattle, and fowl, and as he labored night and day to build his farm by the hard work of his hands, felt himself the most fortunate of all men. But the third, they say, sat in the sun and watched the clouds, and heard the grass grow, and listened to the voice of God, and said, Never was any man so fortunate and favored as I."

There was a long minute of silence. Then Cholayna said, determinedly practical, "As long as I find Alexis Anders alive and unharmed, I have already enough notes on this country and have seen enough strange things that I should be the most ungrateful of women to complain if I find nothing more."

"I would hope for a mountain to equal Montenegro Summit," said Vanessa, "but one can't have everything."

"Be careful what you pray for," Jaelle laughed, "you might get it. There are mountains here, I tell you, much higher than Scaravel—though, after this, I could live richly content if I knew

I would never again travel above the treeline. Margali, what do you want from that city of legends, should we be guided there?"

"Like Cholayna, I'll be content to find Lexie and Rafaella safe and well. Somehow I can't imagine either of them being very interested in ancient wisdom—"

"And as for legends," Vanessa said cheekily, "you yourself are the legend against which they are measuring themselves, you, Lorne—"

Magda flinched as if Vanessa had struck her. She needed no reminding of that—that in a sense she was to blame that these two women, who should have been her friends, had risked this desperate and dangerous journey.

For all that, would I have wished this road untraveled? I have tested my own strength and found myself stronger than I ever believed. Would I wish this undone?

Leaning back in the clouds of steam, her body at ease in the hot bath, she realized that it did not matter a particle whether she wished all this undone. It *had* happened; it was a part of her, whether for good or bad did not matter either. It was up to her to learn what she could from the experience, and pass on to the next thing in her life.

Just as she suddenly knew that she felt free of the "Lorne Legend" which had pursued her for so long. No one, least of all Magda, had required of Alexis Anders that she try to equal or surpass Magda's achievements. *It had been Lexie's own doing, not hers!* Magda felt as if a burden heavier than the *chervine* packloads had fallen from her back and dissolved in the hot water. She would still help Lexie when she found her; the younger woman had gone into deeper waters than she was trained to handle. Magda was obligated to do anything she could to help her. But only as her vow required her to be . . . in the words of the Renunciate Oath . . . *mother and sister and daughter to all women.* Not from guilt, not because it was her fault Lexie had done this rash and stupid thing. She sighed, a long sigh of pure relief.

"I am getting soggy," Vanessa said. "I think I will get out, and try some of that hot wine they offered us."

"Enjoy yourself," Jaelle said, "but I must have Rafaella's message as quickly as possible."

Clean clothing was as great a luxury as the bath; Magda had saved one set when she let the laundry women take away hers for washing. Food had been brought and smelled most appetizing; but Jaelle hurried off to Arlinda for Rafaella's message.

"Forgive me, *breda*. But Arlinda has known me since before I took Oath as a Renunciate, and she may talk more freely with me alone than with someone else to hear. Save me some of the roast rabbithorn I can smell on those platters."

Magda conceded the good sense of this, but felt troubled as she watched Jaelle go off alone. Her Amazon trousers had gone for cleaning and she was wearing her old fur-lined bathrobe; she looked small and vulnerable, and Magda wished she could protect her. But Jaelle was not a child to be protected. She went back and watched the others taking covers off dishes with frank greed. Even Cholayna succumbed to a dish of boiled whiteroot seasoned with cheese and pungent spices, with a great dish of four kinds of mushrooms and a side platter of stuffed vegetables. Although she did not touch the roast rabbithorn, she did eat some of the stuffing of dried apples and bread soaked in red wine.

Magda set aside a haunch of the rabbithorn and plenty of the stuffing and vegetables for Jaelle. All through the meal she kept expecting the door to open and her freemate to return, but they had cut into the dessert by the time Jaelle came back.

"I thought I would never eat redberry sauce again, after that place," Vanessa said, dribbling the sweet red stuff across the surface of a smooth custard. "But I find it tastes as good as it did then, and this time, at least, I am sure there is no noxious drug in it." They all turned to look as Jaelle came in.

"We saved you plenty of dinner," Vanessa said, "but it's probably cold as a banshee's heart."

"Banshee heart, boiled or roasted, is a dish I would never cook," said Cholayna, "but if the rest is too cold, we can probably have it heated up in the kitchens."

"No, that's all right. Cold roast rabbithorn is served at all the .

best banquets," Jaelle said, as she came and sat down and helped herself to rabbithorn and mushrooms. It seemed to Magda that she looked cold and constrained.

"What was Rafi's message, love?"

"Only to come after her as fast as I could manage," Jaelle said, "but there was another message which Arlinda gave me." But after this she was silent so long that Vanessa finally asked belligerently, "Well? Is this some great secret?"

"Not at all," Jaelle said at last. "Tonight, so Arlinda told me, one will come, supposedly, from that place, and she will speak with us. And I could tell, from the way Arlinda spoke, that she was afraid. I cannot imagine why, if the Sisterhood is as benevolent as I have always heard, a woman like Arlinda would have anything to fear from her. What Arlinda has managed to do, in a city like Nevarsin, is all but unbelievable. Why should the Sisterhood frighten her?" Jaelle poured herself some of the spiced wine, and sipped at it, then shoved it away.

"So, we are to be tried," said Camilla. "That is a part of every search, Shaya, love. The Goddess knows you have nothing to fear. Do you truly think they will find us wanting?"

"Oh, how am I to know that, how do I know what they require?" Jaelle munched cold rabbithorn, as uninterested as if it were packaged field rations, her face stolid and closed-in, betraying nothing. "They will judge me in the name of the Goddess and I do not know what to say to them."

Camilla said, and to Magda she sounded fiercely defensive, "You are what you are, *chiya*, like all of us, and none of us can be otherwise. As for me, I have no more reverence for these women of the Dark Sisterhood than for their Goddess, who thrust me unasked and uninvited into a world which has treated me as I, who am no more than human, would not have treated the meanest of creatures. If their Goddess wishes me evil, I will demand of her why, since when it befell me I was too young to have done anything to deserve it; if she wishes me well, I will ask why she calls herself a Goddess when she was powerless to prevent evil. And when I have heard her reply, then I will judge her as she or her representatives think to judge me!" She poured herself another glass of wine. "Nor should you fear anything from these women who presume to speak in Her name."

"I don't fear," Jaelle said slowly. "I wonder why Arlinda fears, that is all."

Cholayna had spread out her sleeping bag—the single one of Terran make—on the floor, and, using her saddlebag and her pack as a pillow, was leaning back, writing in a little book. She had, Magda thought, admirably recovered the habits of a Field Agent. Vanessa was meticulously combing and sectioning her hair for braiding.

Magda was debating following either example, and had started to get her sleeping bag out of its pack when one of the young apprentices came in, carrying an embroidered leather hassock, an elaborate guest-seat. Behind the girl came Arlinda herself. Although Magda expected that Arlinda would take that seat, she did not; she backed against the wall and sat down there, legs crossed beneath her heavy canvas apron, her brawny arms akimbo, bristling all over with expectation.

Then a woman came into the room, and they all looked up at her.

She was not exceptionally tall, but she seemed somehow to take up more space than she physically occupied in the room. It was a trick of presence; Magda had met a few people who knew how to use it, but they were seldom women. She had dark-auburn hair, twisted into a tight coil at the back of her head and fastened there with a copper pin or so. She was dressed in clothing of rather better quality than anyone Magda had seen at the baths or in the leather-worker's shop so far, and it fitted her well, something unusual for women in this chilly city of *cristoforos* where women were expected to efface themselves. Her eyes were pale gray, looking out with an imperious commanding presence from under her piled hair.

She took the elaborate seat quite as if it was the expected thing. Magda glanced at Arlinda and noticed that the brawny woman's arms showed signs of gooseflesh, as if she were cold.

What in the name of all the gods on all the planets in or out of the Empire has she got to be afraid of? Magda had not believed anything could make this old Amazon—better fitting the name than any Renunciate—afraid.

"I am the *leronis* Acquilara," she announced. She looked them over, one by one. "Will you tell me your names?"

With one accord they waited for Jaelle to speak.

"I am Jaelle n'ha Melora," Jaelle said slowly. "These are my companions." One by one she repeated their names. "We are from Thendara Guild-house in that city."

Acquilara heard them without motion, not a flicker of muscle moving in her face or a flicker of her eyes. An imposing trick, Magda knew. She wondered how old the woman was. She could not guess. Her face was less lined than Camilla's; yet the boniness of her fingers, the texture of her skin, told Magda this was not a young woman. When she moved, it was with an air of complete deliberation, as if she moved only when she had decided to move and never for any other reason.

She swiveled her head to Cholayna and said, "I have known a woman with your skin color. She was poisoned in childhood with a metallic substance. It is so with you, is it not." It was not a question but a statement. She sounded very self-satisfied, as if waiting for them to acknowledge her cleverness in solving such a riddle.

But Cholayna spoke with equal composure. "It is not. I have known such cases of heavy-metal poisoning, but my skin was this way at birth; I am from a far country where all men and women are like me."

The eyes of the *leronis* flickered and jolted abruptly to Cholayna again. Her face was so motionless otherwise that Magda knew they had really taken her by surprise. *We were meant to be impressed and we spoiled that for her.* Arrogance was a part of the woman. Somehow Magda had expected that envoys from the mysterious Sisterhood would be like Marisela, benevolent and unassuming.

Was this some form of test? The words formed in her mind without volition. She looked at her freemate, trying to send her a warning; *Be careful, Jaelle!*

But she knew Jaelle had not received the warning, her brain

felt dead, the air in the room an empty void that would not carry thought. *So we have had a demonstration of her powers, if not the one she expected.*

Arlinda was still cowering by the wall, and Magda looked at the old Amazon with displeasure, not at Arlinda for her fear, but at the arrogant *leronis* for imposing it. Why should an envoy from the Sisterhood try to terrify them? Suddenly Magda remembered the old woman of her dream in Ravensmark Pass. But she was more afraid of this Acquilara than she had been of that old woman.

Acquilara began again.

"I have heard that you are searching for a certain City."

Jaelle did not waste words. "Have you been sent to take us there?"

Magda knew, without being sure how she knew, that Jaelle had displeased the woman. Acquilara shifted her position; after her stillness this motion was as surprising as if she had leaped up and yelled aloud.

"Do you know what you are asking? There are dangers—"

"If we were afraid of the dangers," Jaelle retorted, "we would not have come so far."

"You think you know something of dangers? I tell you, girl, the dangers you have met on the road—banshees, bandits, all the demons of the high passes—they are nothing, I tell you, nothing beside the dangers you still must face before you are taken into that City. It is not I who impose that test on you, believe me. It is the Goddess I serve. You call upon that Goddess, you Renunciates. But will you dare to face Her, if She should come?"

"I have no reason to fear her," Jaelle said.

"You think you know something of fear?" Acquilara looked at Jaelle with contempt, and turned to Camilla.

"And you. You are seeking that City? What for? This is a City of women. How shall you, who have renounced your womanhood, be admitted there?"

Camilla's pale face flushed with anger, and Magda suddenly thought of the Training Sessions in the Guild-house, when the young women, newly admitted to the Guild, were incited to anger and put on the defensive, to force them to clarify their real thoughts; to get beyond what they had been taught as young girls that they ought to think and feel. Were they being subjected to some such process now, and why? And why at the hands of this woman, this *leronis*, if she was a *leronis* at all?

"Why do you say I have renounced my womanhood, when you find me in the company of my sisters of the Guild-house?" Acquilara seemed to sneer.

"Where else could you swagger and play the man so well? Do you think I cannot read you as a woodsman reads the tracks in the first snow? Do you dare deny that for years you lived among men as a man, and now you think you can become a woman again? Your heart is a man's heart—have you not proven that by taking a woman lover?"

Magda watched Camilla's face, angry and pained. Surely this woman was a *leronis*, or how could she strike so precisely at Camilla's defenses? Yet she, who had been Camilla's lover so long, knew better than anyone alive how unjust it was. Sexless as Camilla's mutilated body might seem, the body of the *emmasca*, Magda knew better than any other that Camilla was all woman.

"You, who have denied the Goddess in yourself, how will you justify yourself to Her?"

Camilla was on her feet, and her hand was gripping her knife. Magda wanted to jump up, physically prevent her from whatever rash thing she might contemplate; yet she sat as if paralyzed, unable to move a muscle to warn or prevent her friend.

"I will justify myself to the Goddess when she justifies herself to me," Camilla said. "And I will justify myself to her, not to her envoy. If you were sent to guide us to that City, then guide us. But don't venture to test us; that is for her, not her lackeys." She stood over the *leronis*, and for a moment it was a contest of arrogance.

Magda was never sure what happened next. There was a flash, something like blue fire, and Camilla reeled backward; she fell, rather than sat down, on her sleeping bag.

"You think you know the Goddess," stated Acquilara, and

now her voice was all contempt. "You are like the peasant women who pray to the bright Evanda to make their garden bloom, and their dairy animals to drop their calves without blight, and to bring them handsome virile lovers and healthy babies. And they pray to the sheltering Avarra to ease their pains of birth and death. But they know nothing of the Goddess. She is the Dark One, cruel and beyond the comprehension of mortal women, and Her worship is secret."

"If it is secret," Vanessa said—all this time she had sat silent on her sleeping bag, listening but not speaking—"why do you tell us about it?"

Acquilara rose abruptly to her feet.

She said, "You girls—" the term was frankly one of contempt now, and included even the mature Cholayna in its scorn—"you think you will use the Goddess? The truth is that She will use you in ways you cannot even begin to contemplate. She is cruel. Her only truth is Necessity. But like all of us, you are grist for Her mill, and She will grind you up in it. Your friend saw this, and she has begged a place for you. Be ready when she calls you!"

She turned her back without looking round, and strode out of the room. The apprentice picked up the seat without a word and followed her.

Arlinda was still cowering against the wall in an agony of fear.

"You should not have angered her," she whispered, "she is very powerful! Oh, you should not have made her angry."

"I don't care if she's the Goddess herself," Jaelle said, brusquely, "she rubbed me the wrong way. But if she's got Lexie and Rafaella, we've got to play along with her, at least for a while."

Vanessa had resumed combing her hair and was now braiding it into half a dozen small braids, for tidiness. "Do you think she has Lexie and Rafaella, then?"

Jaelle turned to Arlinda. "Did Rafi go with her?"

Arlinda shook her head and mumbled, "Nay, how am I to

know of her comings and goings? She is a *leronis*, a sorceress, whatever she wills, so she will do. . . ."

Magda was shocked, even horrified. Arlinda had seemed so strong, so hearty and tough, and now she was mumbling as if she were a senile old woman. Soon after, she kissed Jaelle good night and went away, and the women of the party were left alone.

"Better get to bed," Jaelle said. "Who knows what might be up for us in this place? Keep your knives handy."

Vanessa looked at her in shock. She said, "I thought you said we were as safe here as in the Guild-house, with Arlinda—"

"Even a Guild-house can catch fire or something. Arlinda's changed from when I knew her ten years ago. Sitting shaking in a corner while the old beldame bullies her guests—ten years ago she'd have slung Aquilara, or whatever that so-called *leronis* calls herself, out into the street on her backside."

"You don't think she's a *leronis*?" Magda asked.

"Hell, no, I don't." Jaelle lowered her voice, glancing cautiously around as if she thought Acquilara might be lurking unseen in a corner.

"She took a lot of pains to impress us with how much she knew about us already. About Camilla having lived as a man, for instance. Anything she *could* have used against us, she would have used to put us at a disadvantage." Jaelle stopped and glanced from Cholayna to Vanessa.

"But she couldn't even guess that you three were Terrans. What the hell kind of *leronis* is *that?*"

Chapter 18

"**Y**ou're right." Magda frowned, trying to decide what this might mean. "She misses things that even Lady Rohana would have picked up. This 'great *leronis*' would appear to be rather lacking in mental abilities, although," she added grimly, "she obviously has some physical ones."

Camilla was still sitting on her bedroll looking stunned. Magda went to her.

"*Breda*, did she hurt you?"

For a frightening minute Camilla did not reply and Magda had a brief memory picture of Arlinda, maundering suddenly like a senile old woman. Then Camilla drew a long breath and let it out.

"No. Not hurt."

Vanessa asked, "What precisely did she do to you, Camilla? I could not see. . . ."

"How should I know? That devil-spawn in the shape of a woman but pointed her finger at me, and it seemed that my legs would no longer hold me up; I was falling through an abyss torn by all the winds of the world. Then I found myself sitting here without wit to open my eyes or speak."

Vanessa said, "If *that* was a representative of your Sisterhood, I do not think very highly of them."

Cholayna, in her guise as a professional, was doing a mental analysis. "You say, Jaelle, that she hasn't the mental abilities one would expect from most of the *Comyn*. The physical abilities she displayed could be duplicated by a stunner. She seemed to rely on presence and the old 'I know what you're thinking' trick. She reminded me of someone running a confidence game."

"You're right," Vanessa agreed. She drew herself up and solemnly intoned, "Trust me, dear children! I am the personal representative of the One True Goddess; I see all, know all; you see nothing, know nothing." She dropped the pose and looked thoughtful. "She said we would be *called*. What do you suppose she meant by that?"

"I have no idea," said Jaelle, "but I would go nowhere—not out of this house, not to the next room, not to the *cristoforo* heaven itself—at *her* call."

"I don't see that we have a choice," Cholayna said. "If she, whoever and whatever she is, has Anders and Rafaella, or even knows where they are. . . ."

Jaelle nodded bleakly. "Right. But we'll hang on here as long as we can. For the moment we should get some rest, be ready for whatever it is they may be planning for us. Want me to take first watch?"

Cholayna put away the little book in which she had been writing. Vanessa tied her braided hair into a scarf and snuggled down in her sleeping bag. Camilla backed herself up against the one wall of the room where there were no doors, and said to Magda in an undertone, "I feel like a fool; yet for the first time in many years I am afraid to be alone. Come and sleep here beside me."

"Gladly," Magda said, positioning her sleeping bag so that Camilla lay protected between her and the wall. "I'm sure that creature—I refuse to call her *leronis*— would send us nightmares if she could manage it."

The fire burned low; Jaelle had kept one of the lamps lit, and she was sitting up on her sleeping bag, hand ready to her knife. Magda touched the hilt of her own knife . . . Jaelle's knife; years ago, they had exchanged knives, in the age-old Darkovan ritual binding them to one another. It was familiar now as her own hand.

She thought, now that we are safe here I should try and let them know, in the Forbidden Tower, that we are safe. And I would like to know that the children are well and content. She composed herself for sleep, one hand touching the silken bag at her throat where her matrix rested. Drowsing, she let her mind start to range outward. An instant later she was in the Overworld, looking down through grayness at her apparently sleeping form, the motionless bodies of her four companions.

But although she tried to move outward, into the gray world, seeking the landmarks of the Forbidden Tower, something seemed to hold her in the room. She hung there motionless, vaguely sensing that something was wrong. She found herself glancing toward each of her companions in turn, tensed for flight but held there by some force she could not overcome. She was not accustomed to this, and while, out of her body, she was free of physical sensation, she felt an anxiety, a hovering fear that simulated real pain.

What could be wrong? All seemed normal; Jaelle, sitting quietly alert; Vanessa and Cholayna, the older woman lying on her side, her face hidden in the pillow and only the pale shock of hair visible, Vanessa burrowed under her blankets like a child. Camilla was asleep too, tossing and turning unquietly and muttering to herself, her face twisted into a frown. Magda silently damned Acquilara in every language she could think of.

Softly at first, then louder, she heard a small sound in the silence of the Overworld; it was the calling of crows. Then she could see them, hooded forms, misty images gradually becoming more defined. For an instant she had a formless sense of well-being. *Yes, this is the right path. We are doing what we were born to do.*

Then the uneasiness came back, stronger than before; the crows squawked their alarm cry, raucous, shrilling through the Overworld. Then a sharper scream rang through the room which was not really the room at all. Hawks! From somewhere, dozens of hawks were in the room, angling, stooping down on the crows in every direction. A great wave of emotion, combined of anger, frustration, and jealousy, emanated from the hawks—it reminded Magda of the Terran legend of Lucifer and his fallen angels, cast out from heaven and forever trying to keep others from what they had lost for themselves.

A pair of hawks, feathers falling, speckled with blood, made a dive at Camilla, and Magda snapped back into her body as Camilla woke screaming.

Or had there been any sound at all? Camilla was sitting bolt upright in her sleeping bag, her eyes wild, her arms outstretched to ward off some invisible menace. Magda touched her shoulder, and Camilla blinked and truly woke.

"Goddess guard me," she whispered. "I saw them; ten thousand devils . . . and then you came, Margali, with . . ." she stopped and frowned, and at last said in a confused whisper, "*Crows?*"

"You were dreaming, Kima." The rarely used, rarely permitted nickname was the measure of Magda's disturbance.

Camilla shook her head. "No. Once before you spoke of the emissaries of the Dark Lady as taking crow form. I am not sure I understand it. . . ."

"I don't either." But as she spoke Magda had a sudden vision of Avarra, Lady of Death, mistress of the forces which break down and carry away that which is past usefulness; crows, scavengers and carrion birds, cleaning up the debris of the past.

Hawks; raptors, preying on the living. . . .

Vanessa mumbled in protest, burrowing deeper into her sleeping bag. Magda glanced with compunction at her companions. She should not disturb them. She got up and went to the fireside, kneeling beside Jaelle.

She asked in a whisper, "Did you see anything?" and Jaelle started from an unquiet doze.

"Ayee—! What a guardian I am! We could all have been murdered in our beds here!" She made a nervous gesture at the fire. "I saw in the flames . . . women, robed and hooded, with the faces of hawks, circling about us . . . Margali, I do not like your Sisterhood."

Magda beckoned Camilla forward.

"We saw. Both of us. I think the hawks are—are Acquilara's crew, if that makes any sense to you, and that they have nothing to do with the *real* Sisterhood. But the real ones are near us. They will protect us, if we listen. But if we listen to Acquilara and her threats and summonings. . . ."

"Yes," said Camilla gruffly, "I too have had a warning. If we stay here, we might better have died at the hands of the robbers. It is not our bodies in danger this time; they strike at the inner bastions of our minds. Our souls, if you will. It is not Arlinda or her girls that I fear, but they have somehow let this place be opened . . ." she stopped and said in confusion, "I do not know what I am talking about. Is this what you two mean when you speak of *laran?*"

Jaelle looked from one to the other, dismayed. She said, "What do you suggest that we do?"

"Get the hell out of here," Camilla said, "not even waiting for daylight."

"A poor return for hospitality," Jaelle said, hesitant.

"Hospitality indeed," Camilla said dryly, "loosing such a sorceress—I will not give her the honorable title of *leronis*—upon us."

But Jaelle was still troubled.

"Cholayna was so far right," she said. "If Acquilara has Rafi—and Lieutenant Anders—I do not see how we can afford to leave them in her power. If she can guide us to them—"

"I think she lied, to deceive us into following her," Camilla said.

"But in the name of the Goddess herself, for what reason?" Magda asked. "What would she want with us, and why would she try to deceive us anyhow?"

"I don't know," Camilla said, "but I wouldn't believe a word she said. If she told us Liriel was rising on the eastern horizon I would look at the sky to be certain."

For seven years it has distressed me that Camilla would not use the laran *to which she was born. Now when she does I am trying to argue with her,* Magda thought. Yet from Jaelle she picked up the very real concern; on their actions in the next few hours, the very lives of Lexie and Rafaella could depend.

She thought, *damn them both*, and quickly retracted the

thought. She had known for years that a thought was a very real thing. She did not have the *laran* of the Alton Domain, where a murderous thought could kill, but she realized wearily that she did not want any harm to come to Rafaella, who was Jaelle's oldest friend. She felt that she would like to box Lexie's ears, but she did not really want to see her hurt or killed. What they had done was unwise, foolish, and tiresome, but death or damnation would be too great a penalty.

What then was the answer?

"Just supposing that she told the truth—even if her purpose could have been to confuse us like this," Magda said, "and that she really does have Lexie and Rafaella? What do we do then?"

"Wait perhaps till she comes back, and I will guarantee to get it out of her," Camilla said; she put her hand on her knife, then let it fall, her face grim. "I was not so good at getting it out of her that way, was I?"

Jaelle said, "No. We can't fight her like that. I think that kind of fighting would be the worst thing we could do. She would be able to use the—the emotion of it against us. Do you know what I am trying to say, Magda?"

"She could make us fight among ourselves. Against each other. That may be all the mental power she has, but I am sure she could do that or something worse. Look what she seems to have done to Arlinda."

"But in the name of all the Gods and Goddesses there ever were," demanded Camilla, "what would her *reasons* be? You cannot tell me that she came into our lives, lied to us and sent her demons against us, just for amusement! Even if she has a bizarre sense of humor and a taste for lying, what could she possibly hope to gain? Evil she may be, but I cannot believe in the evil sorceress who indulges in wickedness and mischief-making for no reason whatsoever. What does she think she can get from us? If it was theft she had in mind, she would not need to resort to this rigmarole. It would be simpler to bribe Arlinda's dogs and watchwomen."

"Maybe," said Jaelle tentatively after a long time, "it's a way of keeping us away from the real ones. The real Sisterhood."

Camilla said scornfully, "I can just about manage to believe in one Sisterhood of wise priestesses watching over humankind in the name of the Dark Lady. *Two* of them would strain my credulity well past the limit, Shaya."

"No, Camilla. Seriously. The legends all say we will be tested. If they are what people say, they must have enemies. Real enemies, or why would they be so secret in their doings? To me it is not hard to believe that there might be—well, others, a rival Sisterhood, maybe, who hate everything they stand for and will stop at nothing to try to keep anyone from getting through to them. And the real Sisterhood let it go on because it—well, it makes it harder for the serious aspirants to get through to them. I mean, I can't imagine they would want to be bothered with the kind of people who would listen to Acquilara, or her kind."

"You have missed your profession, Jaelle. You should be a ballad-singer in the marketplace; never have I heard such inventive melodrama," Camilla said.

Jaelle shrugged. "Whether or no," she said, "it leaves our main question still unanswered. Whatever this Acquilara may be, liar, thief, mischief-maker or representative of some rival Sisterhood, the problem facing us is still the same. Does she have Rafaella and Lexie, or was she lying about that too? And if she does, what can we do about it, and how can we tell the difference? If either of you has any answer to *that* question, melodrama or no, I will listen with great willingness. I am reluctant to leave here without knowing for certain whether Rafaella is in that woman's hands."

It always came back to that, Magda thought in frustration. They were beginning to go around and around without getting anywhere, and she said so.

"You might as well get some sleep, Jaelle. Camilla and I are not likely to sleep much after that—" she hesitated for a word, reluctant to say *attack*; it might have, after all, been a dream shared among the three of them and born of their mistrust and fear of this place. But Jaelle picked it up.

She said hesitating, "It is not really late. If we had not all traveled so far, none of us would try to sleep this early. Arlinda's apprentices may well be awake, perhaps drinking or dancing in their common-room, or even lounging in the bath, and I will go and try to talk with them. Perhaps one of them spoke with Rafi while she was here."

"A fine idea. Let me go with you, *chiya*," Camilla suggested, but Jaelle shook her head.

"They will speak more freely to me if I'm alone. Most of them are my age or younger, and there are two or three of them I used to trust. I'll see if they're still there and if they'll talk to me." She slid her feet into boots, said, "I'll try to be back before midnight," and slipped away.

Chapter 19

When Jaelle had left them, the night dragged. Magda and Camilla talked almost not at all, and then brief commonplaces of the trail. Magda grew sleepy, but dared not lie down and close her eyes for fear of renewed assault by whatever had attacked her before. She knew it was reasonless, but she was for some reason terrified of seeing again those diving hawks; and although Camilla put a brave face on it she knew Camilla felt much the same.

Cholayna slept restlessly; Magda feared that the Terran woman was undergoing, at the least, evil dreams, but she did not wake her.

Cholayna needed rest. She could certainly survive bad dreams, but there were other worries. She suspected, from the sound of her breathing, that Cholayna was beginning to suffer a few of the early symptoms of mountain sickness. How would the older woman survive the dreadful country past Nevarsin? They had only begun to get into the really high plateau.

Cholayna was tough, she had already survived Ravensmark and the robbers, and had come across Scaravel, exhausted, frostbitten, but still strong. Still, she should ask Vanessa, who knew more about mountains and altitude than any of them, to keep an eye on Cholayna.

As if Vanessa wouldn't, without my telling her! I'm doing it again; trying to protect everyone. That's not my job and I should realize it; other people have a right to run their own risks and take their own chances.

Around them the pulse of the night was slowing; the faint street noises died almost to nothing. She did not know how to read the faraway chime of the monastery bells, but they had rung softly several times, a distant and melancholy sound, before Jaelle came back into the room. Camilla, motionless before the fire, raised her head.

"Well?"

Jaelle came close, dropped on the floor before the fire.

"I found a couple of old friends," she began. Her voice was quiet; partly, Magda felt, not to waken Vanessa and Cholayna, but partly because Jaelle feared being overheard by something that was not in the room at all.

"One of them was a girl I knew when I used to come here with Kindra. I was no more than twelve years old then, but Jessamy remembered some of our games. She recognized Rafaella at once when they came here. They were lodged in this very room."

"They were here; I thought so," Camilla said. "But why didn't they wait for us? And was Anders with her?"

"So Jessamy said. Apparently Lexie had a slight case of frostbite, and they stayed here an extra day, so she would be in better shape to travel. Jessamy didn't talk with Rafi about anything personal, or in private, but Rafi told her that I would be coming—in fact, Jessamy thought they'd intended to wait here for me. Which is why she was so surprised when Rafi left without bidding her good-bye, or even leaving the customary way-gift."

"That's not like Rafaella," Camilla said. "I've traveled with her in the mountains. She has always been generous with tips—it's good business. Up here, everything runs that way—greasing the wheels, so to speak. Even if she was running short of money, she would have been apologetic, made what gifts she could, and many promises. I wonder what happened?"

"Jessamy said Arlinda was not disturbed—they had paid for their lodging, after all, and she never inquires into what tips the girls get. But Rafaella has stayed here before with explorers and climbers and as you say, Camilla, she's always been generous with tips. Jessamy was not complaining or criticizing Rafi, but she did mention that Rafaella must have been in great haste. She didn't even remember the women who repaired saddle-tack and doctored one of their ponies."

Camilla's mouth was grim. "If you wanted evidence, there it is for you. Rafi wouldn't do that kind of thing, not if she ever expected to come back here and get decent service. For one reason or another, they left in a hurry, when they'd been expecting to wait here for us. What more do you want? Probably that Acquilara, or whatever she calls herself, spirited them away in the middle of the night."

"If she was here to speak with us, she didn't go with them," Magda protested.

"Unless she has taken them somewhere and hidden them," said Jaelle. "And if they went willingly, how do you explain Rafaella leaving without the proper way-gifts and courtesies?"

"Might she have intended it as a signal to us that she did *not* go willingly?" Camilla asked.

"And if Acquilara has hidden them nearby," Magda said, "then we can simply wait here, and she will lead us to them. That's what she intends. She said so."

"I know not what you may choose to do," Camilla said, "but I go nowhere in that creature's company. *Nowhere*, understand me? I would not trust her behind me—not even if she was bound and gagged."

"If she has Rafaella and Lexie—" Magda began.

"If Rafaella was such a fool as to trust that evil sorceress, then she deserved whatever—"

"Oh, stop it, both of you," Jaelle pleaded. "This is not helpful. I cannot imagine Rafi trusting that woman at all."

"Jaelle, do you think I am not troubled about her, about both of them? If Camilla feels she cannot trust that woman Acquilara, then if she sends for us, if she says Rafi and Lexie are with her, then perhaps you and I—"

"I trust Camilla's intuition," Jaelle said. "Perhaps tomorrow I shall seek out the woman who doctored their ponies, give her the tip which I know Rafi would have given her, and try to find out who saw them leave, and who was with them."

"That seems reasonable. It will do Cholayna no harm to have an extra day's rest," Magda said.

"I am worried about her too," Camilla said. "If only for her sake, it would be as well if our journey ended here in Nevarsin. The country past here—you know what it is like."

"Only too well. I was born in Caer Donn," Magda reminded her. She yawned, and Camilla said predictably, "If you are sleepy, Margali, go and rest. I will keep watch with Jaelle."

Magda was still reluctant to sleep; yet she knew she would not be able to travel on the next day unless she rested. That was even more true of Camilla, who was not young, and already showing signs of travel-fatigue, but who seemed even more fearful of sleep in this place than she was herself. No more than Cholayna could she travel on without rest.

Camilla's *laran* seemed to be surfacing after all these years when she had attempted to block it, and suddenly, with a pang of dreadful loneliness, Magda thought, *I wish Damon were here. He could show me what to do for Camilla.* It was too heavy a burden to bear alone.

Yet Damon was far away in the Kilghard Hills, and for some reason or other she seemed barred from the familiar access to the Forbidden Tower by way of the Overworld. She had tried, and she knew, deep in her bones, that to try again would bring down upon them the renewed attack of . . . *hawks?*

Damon could even handle that. He is our Keeper.

And then she remembered something Damon had said; *any halfway competent technician can, in necessity, do the work of a Keeper.* Anything she felt she must call upon Damon to do, she could handle for herself. And now she must.

"You must sleep, Camilla. What would you tell me in such case? I am afraid too, *bredhiya*," she added, using the term of endearment deliberately, a way of saying, *trust me.* "All the same, you must sleep. Jaelle and I will ward this room and guard it so that no sorceress or evil influence can come in here, even in dreams. Shaya, help me."

Deliberately, she unwrapped her matrix, watching Camilla's face; the older woman's eyes followed the matrix, looked away.

"Do not try to look into the matrix, you are not trained to it. It will make you ill," she said. "That time will come. For now, don't try—"

"I? A matrix? The Goddess forbid—"

"As long as it is the Goddess who forbids and not your own fear, Kima." Again, deliberately, she used the nickname she had never before spoken in the presence of a third party. "What if it is the Goddess leading you to this? Trust me; I know what I am doing. But turn away your eyes from the matrix for now." She edged her tones gently with what they called *command-voice* and Camilla, obedient and startled by her own obedience, looked away.

"Jaelle—?"

Together they matched resonances until they were working in unison. For an instant the rapport flared, burned between them, a closeness, an intimacy beyond speech or sex, indescribable.

If Camilla could only share this. . . .

Neither of them was sure which mind originated the thought, or which answered, regretfully:

No. She's not ready. Not yet.

As their matrixes flared into resonance, there was a moment of blue fire in the room. Camilla jerked up her head, startled, but it was so brief, Magda knew, already Camilla was wondering if she had really seen it at all.

If the hawks are awaiting any movement out of this room— then the true Sisterhood must also be watching over us. They will help us to seal the room. . . .

They cannot interfere. But we have that power. . . .

Jaelle's touch was like a hand clasped in hers, a hand that gripped an Amazon knife that glowed with blue fire. Although Magda knew that she did not move from where she knelt by the fire, her matrix between her fingers, somehow she was walking beside Jaelle, circling the room, a line of blue-white fire trailing them in the wake of the knife. She closed the circle; together, they raised their joined hands in an arch (although they never moved) and between their hands a web of pallid fire ran back and forth.

The old woman was there, with her yelping laughter. So, so, so, you think you can keep me out, silly girls?

Mother, not you. But our friends must rest and shall not be pecked by hawks while they sleep.

Blue fire flamed from the matrixes, weaving like a fiery shuttle, until the room was enclosed in a shimmering dome. Magda ran her consciousness round and round, seeking any chink in their protection. For an instant Acquilara's face was there, menacing, terrible as Magda had seen it for an instant through her pretended good nature and scorn, flaming with rage.

So she is warned, she knows that we know she is not what she seems. . . .

Did you really think we could do this kind of work without warning her?

The hawk was there . . . it was diving for her eyes . . . Magda instinctively thrust her matrix toward it, interposing a shield of fire. The hawk's feathers burst into flame and Magda recoiled from the heat, from the sudden terrible screaming; she felt her fingers go limp and her matrix drop from her hand. Fire and a smell of burning . . . *feathers?* . . . flamed in the room; then her matrix was in her hand . . . had she ever loosed it at all, or was that an illusion?

The fire in the grate had burned to an even bed of coals. The room was silent and peaceful, void of magic, just a quiet room where five weary women could sleep. A few dishes from their supper were still on the table at the center; Jaelle went to the table, brought back a slice of bread, speared it on the end of her knife and held it companionably over the blazing fire. While it toasted, Camilla fetched the last bottle of wine and they shared it, passing it from mouth to mouth.

All Jaelle said was, "Did you see the old woman?"

"I was afraid of her the first time. Now I know she will not harm us," Magda said, swallowing her share of the wine. For the first time she had no hesitation. Now they were safe. Jaelle split the toasted bread into halves, passed the second to Magda, and they munched in silence. At Camilla's questioning look, Jaelle said, "Food closes down the psychic centers. Are you hungry?"

"For some reason, yes, though I thought I had eaten so much at that fine supper that I would not be hungry for days," Camilla said. She bit into a piece of fruit then flung the core into the fire. For an instant Magda smelled a whisper of burning feathers; then only the fruity smell of the burning apple core.

They slept without dreams.

Magda was wakened by the sound of coughing; deep, heavy, racking coughs, that shook Cholayna's slender body as if by some external force. Vanessa was already at her side with the medikit, checking her, but Cholayna broke away and hurried into the latrine next door, where they could hear her vomiting.

"Bad," Vanessa said briefly. "What's the altitude of this city?"

"Jaelle has the maps. She can tell you; I don't know offhand." Magda understood without being told. Maybe one in forty or fifty people suffered severely at high altitudes. About half of these, given rest and time to acclimate slowly to the new altitudes, got better. Some few developed pulmonary edema, pneumonia, or even cerebral hemorrhaging if they went higher. There was no way to tell how Cholayna would react, except to wait.

Camilla, waking, heard and said, "She has the mountain sickness. I will go and see if in Arlinda's kitchen they have blackthorn tea. If not, almost any tea or fluid will do, but she must drink as much as she can."

"Stop worrying," said Cholayna, appearing in the door. "That dinner last night was too rich for me after days and days of travel rations, that is all."

"Nevertheless," said Vanessa, "you have shown all the symptoms, coughing, queasiness and vomiting. Unless there has been a miracle and you are pregnant at your age, you have a well-developed case of altitude sickness; believe me, Cholayna, that is nothing to take lightly."

Cholayna's eyes were sunk deep in her head. She tried to smile and couldn't manage it.

"I've done it again, haven't I? Delayed you, been the weakest link in the chain—"

"We took all this into account when we agreed to let you come," said Camilla brusquely. "But you must rest today, and your body may adapt itself to the thin air here. I will go and fetch tea, and not forget to tip the kitchen women, which may serve more than one purpose."

Magda had not thought about that. Perhaps Rafaella had spoken with one of the kitchen workers; if Lexie had been suffering from frostbite they would have needed medicines and special hot drinks for her.

Raising her eyes, she crossed glances with Jaelle, who said, "I am going out to the stable. Now that I think of it, one of the ponies looks a bit lame on one side. I will find the woman who helped Rafaella and give her the tip I am sure my partner would have wanted her to have, if she had not been in so great a hurry when she left."

That was an errand only Jaelle could do, and it was best left to her. Camilla went off to the kitchen, and when Jaelle had dressed and gone, Magda persuaded Cholayna to get back into her sleeping bag and rest. Camilla came back with a steaming kettle and half a dozen little packets of herbs stowed about her person.

"They told us that breakfast would be coming along in a few minutes," she said, "and I smelled a nutcake baking. One of them told me that they had baked one for our Guild-sisters when they lodged here." She poured boiling water over the herbs.

"This is blackthorn; it is a stimulant to the heart and will also make red blood; it will help you acclimate to the mountains," she said, kneeling beside Cholayna.

"Drink it now and rest. Perhaps by tomorrow your body will be accustomed to the heights here and you can go on with us."

Cholayna drank the bitter tea without protest, only wrinkling up her nose a little at the taste. She asked weakly, "And if I do not?"

"Then we will wait until you are able to travel," Magda said promptly. The excuse that one of their companions was too ill to travel would at least ward off any insistence by Acquilara or any of her cohorts that they should immediately follow the sorceress.

Any further discussion was cut short by the arrival of their breakfast, on several trays which took two girls to carry. Magda tipped the women generously, and sat down to the array of hot fresh bread, scones and nutcakes, plenty of butter, honey and apple nut conserves, boiled eggs and fragrant mushroom sausages. Vanessa and Camilla ate heartily; but Cholayna was too queasy to eat anything. Magda persuaded her to swallow a little bread and honey with her tea, but it was no use coaxing Cholayna to eat the unfamiliar food; she probably could not keep it down anyhow.

Jaelle did not return. No doubt she had decided to breakfast with the apprentices in the stable, to try to find out what they knew. The women who cleared away the breakfast trays were soon succeeded by women bringing back their clean laundry. Camilla went away with them, invited to visit the glove-maker's shops. Magda settled down to mend socks; she liked sewing no better than ever, but she liked wearing socks with holes in them, especially in this climate, even less. Vanessa followed suit, and the women sat quietly mending their clothes.

Cholayna, propped up on her pillows, was writing in her little book. The fire crackled cheerfully on the hearth; the women had brought what looked like an endless supply of firewood. It was peaceful in the room; Magda felt that her nightmares had been no more than that.

But Cholayna's heavy coughing broke the peace of the room. What would Jaelle find out? What would happen if Acquilara summoned them before Cholayna was able to travel? She made some more of the special tea for Cholayna and urged her to drink as much as she could.

"Cholayna, if you are not better in a day or two, it may mean that you are one of the people who simply cannot acclimate properly to the mountains. Now that we know where Lexie and

Rafaella are, would you trust me to go on in your place, and let Vanessa take you back to Thendara? You would not have to cross the passes, except Scaravel; you could go by the Great North Road, which is well-marked and well-traveled all the way. I do not want your illness on my conscience—"

"There is no question of that, Magda. I chose to come, no one compelled me, and you are in no way responsible."

"All the same," Vanessa chimed in, "altitude sickness is serious. Tell me, have you any blurring of vision?"

"No, no, nothing of the sort," Cholayna said impatiently. "I am tired and the food is not agreeing with me very well. A day's rest will put me right."

"I certainly hope so," Magda said, "but if not, your only recourse is to go down to a lower level; you will not recover while you stay in Nevarsin. And beyond Nevarsin it is worse, much worse. Couldn't you trust me to do what I can for Lexie?"

Cholayna reached out her hand and touched Magda's. It was a gesture of real affection. "It is not a question of trust, Magda. How long have we known each other? But I trained Alexis, too. I cannot—no, I *will* not abandon her now. You of all people should understand that." She smiled at Magda's look of frustration.

"Let's wait and see. Tomorrow I may be able to travel. I know that some people acclimate more slowly than others. I'm not as fast as Vanessa, that's all."

"But if you don't? At least promise me that you'll agree to go back then," Vanessa said.

"If I do not, then we will decide that then. I make no promises, Vanessa. You are not yet my superior—"

"If I certify you unfit for duty—"

"Leave it, Vanessa," Cholayna said gently. "None of us are here on the same terms as we were in the HQ. I take your advice as mountain expert and I will do whatever you say to try and make up for my slowness in acclimation, Even to drinking that nauseating old-wives remedy Camilla brought me."

"It contains something analogous to—" Vanessa mentioned a Terran drug with which Magda was not familiar—"and they have been using it in these mountains for centuries for just such cases of altitude sickness. Don't be narrow-minded."

"It's not narrow-minded to say I would prefer a couple of capsules of something familiar, rather than this horrid brew." Nevertheless Cholayna swallowed the tea Vanessa handed her, grimacing. "I am doing my best. You were born in these mountains, Magda; and you, Vanessa, have been climbing since you were in your teens. Give me time."

"You're a stubborn-old bitch," Vanessa grumbled, and Cholayna smiled at her. She said, with equal affection, "And you are a disrespectful brat."

The bells in the city rang in the distance. Cholayna had fallen into a light doze. Vanessa was restless.

"If only there were something I could *do*!"

"Camilla and Jaelle can do anything that can be done, better than we can, Vanessa. All we can do is wait, and take care of Cholayna." This too was not easy for Magda. In her years as a Field Agent, she had grown accustomed to handling everything herself so that it would be done her way. The very act of submission, of sitting back and letting someone else do what needed to be done, was foreign to her nature.

It was high noon; Cholayna had wakened, and they had persuaded her to drink more of the blackthorn tea, when Jaelle came back, coming into the room and tossing her old jacket on the chair.

"I talked to the woman who mended Lexie's saddle, and it seems that they left very suddenly—as she put it, at weird-o'-the-clock in the morning, when everyone was sleeping. She happened to be sitting up in the stables to doctor a sick pony. She said the monastery bells had just rung for the Night Office, which is just a few hours after midnight—my brother was educated in Nevarsin and he told me."

"Was Acquilara with them?" Magda demanded.

"No one was with them, at least no one that Varvari saw," Jaelle said, "they saddled and loaded their horses themselves.

And she knew which route they were taking because she heard Rafi talking about the dangers from banshees in the pass."

"Two possibilities, then," said Vanessa. "One, Acquilara scared them away. Two, they arranged to meet her somewhere else. I'm sorry, Jaelle, I don't see that this gets us much further on."

"At least we know they left the city," Jaelle pointed out. "We could hardly search Nevarsin from house to house. It may not be easy to look for them in the wilderness, but at least there are not so many people to get in the way of the search. And we know that they went northward over Nevarsin Pass, rather than turning southward again, or taking the road to the west, across the plateau of Leng. I have always heard that road was impassable and haunted by monsters next to whom banshees are household pets."

"That sounds like the Darkovan equivalent of 'here there be dragons,'" murmured Cholayna.

"Nevarsin Pass, and banshees, are dragon enough for me," said Jaelle, the pragmatic. "Sixteen thousand feet; higher than Ravensmark. The road's probably somewhat better, but the question is, is this a bad year for banshees? It depends on a fairly complicated ecological study, or so Kindra used to tell me; if there are enough ice-rabbits, the banshees are well fed above the timberline, and stay up there. If some lichen or other is in the wrong part of its life cycle, there is some kind of population crash among ice-rabbits, the she-rabbits are barren, and the banshees starve, so that they come down below the treeline and look for larger prey. And what I know about the life-cycle of the ice-rabbit could be painlessly carved on my thumbnail. So we'll just have to take our chances."

"We're going to follow them over the Pass, then?" Cholayna asked.

"I am. I'm not so sure about *we*," Jaelle said. "It's a commitment for me. *You* don't look fit enough to go to the monastery for Evening Prayer, let alone to sixteen thousand feet to fight off the banshee."

"We had this all out while you were away," Cholayna said.

"It's a commitment for me too, Jaelle. Rafaella was only following the lead Alexis gave her. Where you go, I go. That's
settled."

Jaelle opened her mouth to protest, but something in the tone
of Cholayna's voice stopped her.

"All right. Get what rest you can, and try to eat a good dinner. We'll be leaving early."

Chapter 20

The afternoon dragged slowly. Jaelle went off again to settle their account with Arlinda, and (she told Magda privately) to make the tips and way-gifts Rafaella had not made.

"I suspect she avoided the usual gifting because she felt that might tip off some spy here that she was leaving," Jaelle said. "It's fairly obvious, first, that Arlinda is petrified with fear of Acquilara, and second, that there must be spies, or members of Acquilara's Lodge, or whatever they are, among the women who live here."

"Then don't you run the risk, when you're making these gifts, that you'll warn the very people Rafi was trying to avoid?"

"Can't be helped," Jaelle said. "Rafaella might need to come back here some day; or I might. I'll tell them I'm making the gifts Rafaella would have made if she had had time and ready money. Maybe they'll believe it; maybe they won't. Have you a better idea?"

Magda didn't. She repacked her personal pack with clean and mended clothing; Camilla went to the market, taking Vanessa with her, to purchase extra grain-porridge and dried fruit for Cholayna, since it seemed unlikely she would be able to eat much of the dried-meat bars which were the regular trail ration. She also bought a supply of the blackthorn tea which had done Cholayna so much good.

Jaelle also presented Arlinda with a full packload of the trade goods she had brought for Rafaella. "Rafi won't need them past here; there's nothing to trade and almost nobody to trade with," she said, "though I kept a load of things we might use for gifts or bribes if there are any villages up here; sweets and candies, small tools, mirrors and the like. And the Guild-house needs to be on good terms with Arlinda's establishment; it's the only decent place for Renunciates to stay in Nevarsin."

"I'm not so sure of that, if Arlinda's being watched or dominated by Acquilara's people," said Camilla, packing the fresh supplies into a saddlebag. "We ought to trade off the horses here, and take only *chervines* into the high country. Horses don't have the stamina."

"Cholayna and Vanessa can't ride *chervines*," said Magda, "and I'm not sure I could. The mountain horses can go almost anywhere a *chervine* can go. I suspect if we reach any country too rough for a horse, it will be too rough for us."

While they were loading the saddlebags, Camilla drew Magda aside for a moment and gave her a pair of embroidered gloves, made of the fine leather from the shops covered by Arlinda's establishment. Ever since they had been lovers, Camilla had enjoyed surprising her with little gifts like this, and Magda's eyes filled with tears.

"But these are expensive, Camilla, you shouldn't—"

"I found a few mountain men in the taverns who liked to play at darts and would not believe any woman, even an *emmasca* who had been a mercenary soldier, could throw a knife as well as they could. And when their pride, and their love of gambling, had prompted one man to wager more than he could pay, I generously accepted these in settlement of the debt. I suppose he had bought them for his wife or his lady friend, but she will have to teach her man not to gamble on his masculine pride!" She chuckled, low in her throat. "They are foolish and frivolous for this mountain city—your hands would freeze in them—but you can wear them when we return to a gentler climate!"

And for a moment Magda felt cheered, aware of optimism again; they *would* return to the comparatively benign climate of Thendara. She had hardly realized till this moment how much her world had narrowed to ice, cold, frostbitten fingers, frozen boots. The thin, frivolous little beaded gloves reminded her of flowers, sunshine, a world where it was possible to dance in the streets till dawn in Midsummer; not this austere monastic city where snow lay in the streets all year round.

She pressed Camilla's hand, and Camilla put an arm around her waist. Jaelle looked up and saw them, and as the kitchen-women entered with the dinner they had ordered, Magda saw her frown slightly, as when she was planning some bit of mischief. Then she embraced Vanessa deliberately and leaned over to kiss her on the mouth. Vanessa looked startled, but Magda heard— though she was too far away to hear and knew she was reading the thought behind the whisper, "Play along, silly! Or do you think I am seriously trying to seduce you?"

Vanessa blinked in surprise, but did not protest; she put up her arms around Jaelle, who kissed her long and hard, then turned languidly to the women unloading trays and dishes.

"Don't disturb us till the fifth hour after the monastery bells ring for Morning Prayer," she said, and went on to describe an elaborate breakfast, and pay for it, adding a generous tip. When the women went away, full of promises about the expensive delicacies Jaelle had ordered, Vanessa pulled herself free of Jaelle, her face crimson.

"Have you gone mad? What *will* they be thinking?"

"Exactly what I want them to think," Jaelle said, "that we will be long lying abed tomorrow, in various combinations. It will never occur to them to suspect that we are intending to leave the city before the bells ring for Night Office; they won't know we are gone until they bring that fancy breakfast when the sun is high."

"And if Acquilara's spy is not among the kitchen workers but among the girls in the stable?" Vanessa asked.

"Then I will have embarrassed you for nothing," Jaelle said. With a mischievous shrug, she pulled her close and kissed her again. "Did you really object as much as all *that?* I saw no sign of it."

Vanessa only giggled. A few days ago, Magda thought, she would have been angry.

At least she no longer feels that we are a threat to her.

*   *   *

Another leisurely bath; then a plentiful supper, served in their rooms, and they settled down to sleep as long as they could. But for Magda sleep was slow in coming, even though, with the room sealed against intrusion, she had no fear of nightmares. She was lying between Jaelle and Camilla; after the older woman slept, she tossed and turned and finally Jaelle whispered, "Can't you sleep either? What's the matter? It's going to be a rough trip, but even Cholayna seems better; I think she can make it. You're not still worrying about that old witch Acquilara, are you? I think we've shaken her off. I think Lexie and Rafaella managed to get free of her too."

"I'm not so sure, Shaya. What bothers me is—who *are* they? What would they want with us, and why?"

"I thought you had a theory about that. That they probably wanted to keep us away from the *real* Sisterhood."

"But again, why? What would they get out of it? Just for sheer love of mischief-making? I cannot believe that. It must take as much talent and energy to run whatever it is this Acquilara is doing as it takes us to gather and work with the Forbidden Tower."

"So?" Jaelle asked. "Perhaps it is simply hatred and jealousy of the powers of the Sisterhood; she does not seem to have very many powers herself, in spite of what she managed to do to Camilla."

"But even if she hated the Sisterhood . . . no, Jaelle. *We* have a reason to exist, Jaelle. Damon, Callista, Andrew, Hilary, all of us—we're working to bring the good of *laran* to people born outside the Towers, people who don't wish to deny their gifts, but will not live in the Towers, cut off from the real world. We're trying to bring *laran* into the world, prove that it's not necessary to be born *Comyn*, or aristocrat, or even Darkovan, to have and to use these gifts. We have purpose in what we're doing, but it's hard work, sometimes even painful work. I can't believe she'd go to that much trouble, just to impress us."

"I don't know what her motive could be, Magda. Does it matter? I want nothing to do with her, *or* with her powers, and I do know this much, that if you go on thinking of her you will pick her up telepathically, and all our precautions will be useless."

Magda knew Jaelle was right, and she tried to compose herself to sleep as best she could. She thought of her faraway home, of putting her little girl to bed at Armida; Shaya in her nightgown, her soft dark curls tousled. She had not known she remembered so many of the Darkovan folk songs and hill ballads that it had been her mother's lifework to collect, until she began singing them to Shaya as lullabies. Elizabeth Lorne, she knew, had loved her work, and had died thinking that her daughter Magdalen cared nothing for it, knew nothing of it. *How pleased she would have been to hear me singing to Shaya those old ballads from the Hellers and the Kilghard Hills which she so loved. Some day when Shaya is grown, she shall see her grandmother's collected songs and ballads—eight volumes of them, or something like that—in Records, and know a little about her work.*

Perhaps Shaya would be a musician; she remembered that her dark-haired daughter could already carry a tune, clearly and sweetly, even before she could talk plain.

Cleindori in the Overworld; I was surprised when Aunty Ellemir told me where babies come from. I thought they came from the gray world. What a fascinating light on the relationship of sex education to metaphysics. *She was all grown up, and then she was a baby and I couldn't talk to her, except here in the Overworld.* The Overworld was barred to Magda now, because of the sorcery of Acquilara; or she could reach her child, hold her once more. *If I should die on this trip,* she thought, *if I should never see Shaya again.*

But if what Cleindori said is true, and I have no reason not to believe it, then death might not make any difference either. Curious, that I should learn faith from a child five years old.

She was sliding off to sleep, hearing in the distance the reassuring sound of the calling of crows.

It seemed only moments later that Jaelle woke her.

"The monastery bells have just rung the Night Office. Wake

Cholayna; there is bread and dried fruit from supper, which we will eat on the trail." Jaelle was pulling on long wool leggings under her breeches. Magda got into her clothes swiftly, bending to whisper to Cholayna. The Terran woman was sleeping heavily, and it occurred to Magda that if they had wanted to leave her behind, they could have stolen away and left her here sleeping, to be wakened only when the kitchen women came in with the unnecessary breakfast.

No. She is our sister, too. We have to be honest with her, Magda thought, but sighed, wishing Cholayna had agreed to remain here in comparative safety or return to Thendara with Vanessa. She almost wished she were heading south herself, to Armida and her family of the Tower and to her child, even to Thendara and her sisters of the Guild-house. She pulled on an extra layer of warm sweater, wordlessly handed Camilla another.

"I'm all right, Margali, don't fuss so!"

She stared Camilla down, and the older woman, grumbling, pulled it over her head. Camilla was so thin, she would be glad of the warmth when they got into the pass.

Cholayna was shivering in the chill of the big room; they had allowed the fire to burn down. Wasting fuel and warmth were a major crime in the Hellers. The breakfast they had ordered would be eaten by somebody, and would be none the worse for being consumed by someone other than the travelers who had paid for it, but keeping a blazing fire all night was a waste the mountain-bred Magda and Camilla could not condone, even though it meant they must sleep under all their blankets. A thin skin of ice had formed over the pitcher of water at the table where they had eaten their supper, and frost rimed the single high, narrow window of the room.

Jaelle muttered in an undertone, "My brother told me once that the novices in the monastery sleep naked in the snow, wearing only their cowls, and run barefoot. I wish I had their training."

"I suppose it is one of your psychic powers," Vanessa said.

"Valentine says not; only use and habit, and convincing the mind to do its task of warming the body."

Cholayna raised a skeptical eyebrow. "I am not convinced. Hypothermia has killed and continues to kill many people. How can they overcome that?"

"Val would have no reason to lie to me; he says that one of the tests for the higher degrees among the monks is to bathe in a mountain stream from the glacier on Nevarsin Summit, and then to dry, with his body heat, the cowl he wears. He has seen it done."

"A conjuring trick to impress the novices with their power?"

"What reason would they have for that?"

"Nevertheless," Vanessa said, "I heard it too when I went into Mapping and Exploring. It has been told before this, in the old days on Terra; before the Empire. Some of the men who lived on the high plateaus, at four thousand meters or more, had lung capacity greater than those who lived at sea level, and their bodies were so adapted that they became ill in the lowlands. I do not doubt that the Nevarsin brethren can learn to do these things. The human animal is amazingly adaptable. Many people would consider your native planet, Cholayna, too hot for human habitation. I visited there once and thought I would die with the heat. Man is not intended to live where the ambient temperature of the air is normally higher than blood heat."

"Maybe not," said Cholayna, forcing on her narrow boot over three layers of thick socks, "but I would rather be there than here." She pulled her heavy windbreaker over her jacket. "Ready?"

Carrying their personal packs over their shoulders, they stole through the quiet halls, and down a long corridor, away from the living quarters, into the stables. The heavy doors creaked, but there was no other sound, except for Cholayna, who went into a sudden spasm of coughing.

"Quiet," Jaelle snarled, half-aloud, and Cholayna tried to muffle the sound in her sleeve, without much success, her whole body shaking with effort.

Their horses and *chervines,* and their loads, reduced considerably from what they had been when they left Thendara, were stacked in a corner of the same stable.

Jaelle whistled softly with relief. "I suspect Arlinda understood what I meant when I talked with her. Last night, these were stowed away in another set of cupboards in a different stable."

Saddling up her horse, Magda found herself next to Vanessa. She asked in an undertone, "What do you think? Is Cholayna fit for travel?"

"Who can tell? But I checked her as best I could; her lips are a healthy color and her lungs seem to be clear; that ghastly cough is just throat irritation from the dry air and wind at these heights. All we can do is to hope for the best."

They hoisted loads on to the backs of *chervines,* and in whispers settled their order of march. Jaelle, who knew the city well, was leading; Camilla, who knew it almost as well, bringing up the rear. Magda delayed at the end to help Camilla shove the heavy stable door together and brace it; but they could not bolt it from the inside, and finally Camilla whispered, "Wait, Margali, I will be with you in a moment." She slipped back inside; Magda heard the heavy bolt slide. She waited in the street so long that she had begun to wonder if Camilla had been captured by one of Acquilara's spies in the house. *We should have left the door alone*, she thought, but just as she was about to try and follow Camilla inside, the tall *emmasca* reappeared from a window. She slid down, turned briefly to blow a kiss, then hurried down the street after Jaelle.

Magda ran after her. "Camilla, what—"

"Let's not waste any more time; I heard the monastery bell. Let's go." But she snickered as she hurried after Jaelle.

"I wonder what they'll think when they find us gone and the stable still locked from the inside?"

There was no way to silence the hooves of the horses and *chervines* on the cobbled streets, but leading them was quieter than riding. Still they struck hard, the metal shoes of the horses drawing flinty sparks in the cold. It was icy and clear; stars blinked above the darkened city, and high above, the only faint lights were from the dimmed windows of Saint Valentine's monastery. Bells rang loud in the predawn stillness.

As they climbed the rocky streets, the stars paled above them, and the sky began to flush with the dawn. Magda could see her own breath, the breath of her companions and of the animals, as little white clouds before her. Her hands were already cold inside her warm gloves, and her feet chilly in her boots, and she thought, regretfully, of that breakfast Jaelle had ordered and never intended them to eat.

Upward and upward, the streets growing steeper and steeper; but Magda had been on the road so long now that she was hardly short of breath at the top of the steepest hills, and even Cholayna was striding along at the quick pace Jaelle set.

The northern gate was at the very top of the city, and the road beyond led over the very summit of Nevarsin Pass. At the gates were two men, *cristoforos* by their somber clothing, though not monks, who opened the wide gates to let them through.

"You are abroad early, my sisters," one of them said as he stepped back to let their animals pass through.

"We follow two of our sisters who came this way the morning before last," said Camilla in the exceptionally pure *casta* of a mountain-bred woman. "Did you perhaps let them out this very gate two mornings ago, as early as this, my brother?"

The *cristoforo* guard blew on his bare knuckles to warm them. His breath too was a cloud and he spoke through it, scowling disapprovingly at the *emmasca*.

"Aye, it was I. One of them—a tall woman, dark-haired, a soldier like you, *mestra*, with a *rryl* slung over her shoulder—was she your sister?"

"My Guild-sister; have you news of her, brother, in the name of him who bears the burdens of the world?"

He scowled again, his disapproval of *emmasca* and Renunciate contradicting the inborn freemasonry among soldiers, *cristoforo* or no. And there was no halfway polite way to refuse a request in the very name of the *cristoforo* saint.

"Aye. She had another woman with her, so small I thought for a moment she was travelin' with her daughter like a proper woman. A little thing, wrapped up so I couldn't see much of her but the big blue eyes."

Lexie. So they were still together and Lexie safe and well as recently as two days ago. Magda heard Cholayna's soft sigh of relief. They might even overtake them somewhere in the pass.

"She asked me—the tall one, your sister—if it was a bad year for banshees. I had to tell her, yes, a terrible one; we heard one howling right outside this gate a tenday ago in the last storm. Go carefully, sisters, try to get over the high part before the sun's down again," he warned them. "And saints ride with you. Aye, you'll need them if you take this road by night." He stepped back to let them through, closed the heavy city gate behind them.

Ahead the road led upward, stony and steep, ankle-deep in snow, with heavy drifts to right and to left. Jaelle mounted and signaled to the others to do likewise, and they climbed into their saddles. From the heights far above, like a warning, they heard the shrill distant cry of a banshee.

"Never mind," said Jaelle, "the sun will be up long before we reach the pass, and they're nocturnal. Let's go."

Chapter 21

Three days later, Magda sat on a packsaddle looking at a dried-meat bar in her hand. She was almost too weary to think about eating it; the effort necessary to chew and swallow seemed more than she could imagine.

The harsh winds of Nevarsin Summit had blown away such extraneous fears as the thought of sorceresses or psychic attack; none of them had had a moment to think about anything but the raw mechanics of survival. Narrow ledges, a snowstorm which blew away their last remaining tent and left them to huddle in a hastily scooped hole in the snow, fierce winds which stripped away the last pretense of courage or fortitude, and always in the night the terrible paralyzing cries of the lurking banshee.

Camilla put a cup of tea into her hand. How could Camilla, at her age, remain so strong and undamaged? Her eyes looked red and wind-burned, and the tip of her nose had a raw patch of frostbite, but the few hours of sleep they had managed in the snow had revived her. She sat down on another packload, and slurped her own tea, into which she had crumbled the dried meat and bread, but she didn't say anything. At this altitude there was no breath for extraneous words.

"Is Cholayna all right this morning?"

"Seems to be. But if we don't get down to a lower height, I wouldn't like to guess what might happen. She was coughing all night long." But not even Cholayna's coughing could have kept Magda awake last night, after the nightmare of the descent from the pass after dark, by moonlight on the surface of the snow:

kyorebni looming suddenly from the dizzy gaps of space almost at their feet, wheeling and screaming and then disappearing again: washed-out patches of trail where even the *chervines* balked and had to be coaxed to step across, and the horses had to be dragged or manhandled, fighting backward, their eyes rolling with terror at the smell of banshee in the crags.

Jaelle had brought them all across, undamaged, without losing a horse or a pack animal or even a load; unhurt. Magda looked at the familiar slight form of her freemate, slumped across a packload, a handful of raisins halfway to her mouth. Her red curls were uncombed and matted under her fur-trimmed hood, her gray eyes sore and wind-burned like Camilla's and her own. Magda wondered at the strength of will and courage in that small body. There had been moments in the pass when Magda herself, a strong young woman in superb physical condition, had wanted to lie down like one of the ponies, without breath or courage for another step; heart pounding, head splitting, face and body numbed with frost. She could only imagine what it had been like for Cholayna, but the older woman had struggled along bravely beside her, uttering not a single word of complaint. It was Jaelle, Magda realized, who had kept them all going.

Magda followed Camilla's example and crumbled the meat bar into her boiling tea. The taste was very peculiar, but that didn't seem to matter. It was astonishing how, at this altitude, she could actually feel the hot food and fluid heating her all the way down, restoring a feeling of warmth to her exhausted and chilled limbs. When she finished the mess she dug into the ration sacks and got out another bar, this one of ground-up nuts and fruits stuck together with honey, and gnawed at it. Cholayna was resolutely spooning up a similar mixture dissolved in her tea.

Vanessa said, "I ought to take my boots off and look at that wretched ankle. But it's too damned cold. Where are we going now, Jaelle?"

Jaelle glanced back at Nevarsin Peak, rising behind them. "The main road branches off toward Caer Donn. If there were any mysterious and unknown cities in that area, one of us would have run across it before this." She fumbled with gloved fingers for the map, and pointed; removing gloves unnecessarily at this altitude was to court freezing. "This little settlement isn't marked on any of the Darkovan maps. It showed up from the satellite picture, and this—" she traced with her outstretched finger—"looks something like a road."

"Something *like* a road," Cholayna groaned. By now they all knew what unmarked roads in this area were like.

"I know, but I can't imagine any other road Rafaella could have taken," Jaelle said. High in the pass, they had come across an abandoned packload, all but empty, with Rafaella's mark on it. "They must be running low on food and grain for the ponies . . . they know we are following them. Why don't they wait for us?"

Magda couldn't imagine, unless Lexie and Rafaella had been given some special guidance to that unknown city of the legend. From the summit of Nevarsin, in a brief moment of blazing sun between storms, she had looked across an endless view of mountain ranges, trackless peaks, toward the remote and inaccessible icewall known as the Wall Around the World. She had glimpsed it only once before and then, from a Mapping plane, and never in her remotest dreams had it occurred to her that she would ever travel toward it on foot.

"More tea, anyone?" Camilla asked, and divided the remaining brew into the four mugs held out to her before stowing the kettle and scattering snow over the remaining fire; sheer habit of years on the trail, for there was certainly nothing here to burn.

Vanessa slung packloads on *chervines,* pulling the straps tight and double-checking them, and Cholayna began helping Jaelle with the saddles. Abruptly she bent over in a renewed fit of coughing, clinging to the saddle-straps and bracing herself against the horse's side. Vanessa's eyes on her were calculating; Magda knew she was wondering if the older woman could make it. But there was nothing to be done. After a moment Cholayna, eyes streaming and the tears already freezing on her cheeks, straightened up and rummaged in her pack for the compass with which she checked the map and the road.

"This way," Jaelle decided. "Let's go."

For a time, then, the road led downhill, then swerved away into an ill-marked trail leading upward between two long slopes. The sun rose higher and higher, and Magda felt sweat streaming down her body under her jacket, and freezing there.

They had ridden about three hours, and Jaelle passed the word back to look for a good place for a rest. The road was steep and narrow; the horses were struggling upward alongside an old glacier, pale with rotten ice. The trail curved, and led across a long snow-laden slope. As they set foot on it, there was a scream as a dozen birds flapped and flew upward in a streaming flight; then a roar like sudden thunder. Jaelle, in the lead, pulled her horse up sharp.

Then, from somewhere above them, tons of rock and ice cascaded down a deep-carved gully in the mountainside. The horses reared upward, neighing. The very mountain seemed to shake beneath them. The pack animals jostled together and their horses crowded close; Camilla leaned over and clutched at Magda, and they clung together as the avalanche roared down and down and down and went on forever.

At last it was silent, though the air was full of crushed ice and dust, and the sound of screaming went on and on. Jaelle's pony had collapsed, struck by a falling boulder. Camilla slid from her horse and hurried, picking her way across the rock-strewn trail. Jaelle, shakily upright, was kneeling beside the stricken pony. Magda looked swiftly around to her companions. Vanessa was hugging herself, arms tight wrapped to her chest, her face very white. Magda could hear Cholayna's breath wheeze in and out as she hung over her pony without even the strength to cough. Silence, except for the screaming of the hurt animal and the shrill cries of the disturbed birds still wheeling in the air.

At last Vanessa said shakily, "They say you can never hear the one that has your name on it. If you can hear it, you're still alive." She picked her way fastidiously over the debris of rock and ice which was all that was left of the trail, to kneel at Camilla's side by the pitiably screaming pony.

"Leg crushed," she said, "nothing to be done."

Jaelle's eyes were streaming tears, which froze on her cheeks, as she struggled to get out her knife. Camilla said, "Let me," and for an instant laid her free hand over Jaelle's. It was almost a caress. "Hold her head, Shaya."

Jaelle held the pony's head in her lap; the struggling animal quieted for an instant, and Camilla's dagger swept down and swiftly severed the great artery in the neck, A few spurts of blood, a final struggle, and quiet. Camilla's lips were set as she tried to brush away the blood from her riding-cape.

"Get the saddle off her. You have ridden stag-ponies before this. Put it on the *chervine* with the white face; he's the gentlest and most trustworthy," she said briskly, but Magda knew her sharpness concealed real concern. As Vanessa got the saddle off the swiftly freezing corpse (the pony's leg had been crushed under a great rock, it was a miracle Jaelle had not been thrown and killed) Magda went to Jaelle, who looked almost stunned. She took a tube of cream and smeared it over the frozen tears on her freemate's face. Mingled with the splashed blood of the pony, it looked grotesque, but it would keep her cheeks from frostbite.

"Are you hurt, *breda*?"

"No." But Jaelle was limping, and leaned heavily on Magda. "Something hit me in the shins when the pony fell. I don't think the skin's broken, just a bruise." But she threatened to cry again. "Oh, Dancer!" That was the horse's name. "Damon gave her to me, the year Dori was born. When she was a colt she followed me around like a puppy. I broke her to the saddle myself. Oh, Magda, Damon will be so angry that I didn't take better care of her."

The words were meaningless; she was hysterical and Magda knew it. Jaelle was in shock; they were all in shock.

"Get the other saddles off, Camilla, and we'll brew tea; Jaelle needs it after that. We all need it."

At her urging, they moved upslope from the corpse of the

pony, around which the *kyorebni* were already wheeling and fighting. Vanessa began to build a fire. Magda sat Jaelle down on a saddle load and surveyed what had once been a road. It had been all but obliterated above them. Nevertheless they were lucky to be alive, to have lost only one mount.

Magda pushed Jaelle down on a load. With the trail gone, there would have to be reconnaissance ahead. But neither Jaelle nor Cholayna was in much shape to forge on for their route. Tea was brewed and drunk; Camilla got the saddle of the dead horse, and tried to fit it on the smallest and most tractable *chervine,* but the difference in size and contour, even when the bony back of the *chervine* was padded with a small blanket, made it an almost impossible proposition.

"I have ridden *chervines* bareback in my day, but I don't intend to try if there's any alternative; that backbone-ridge always splits me in two," Jaelle complained. With hot tea and some sweets from the packloads, some color had come back into her face, but her shin was skinned raw and bruised bone-deep.

"When we come to another village, we will try to trade for a riding-*chervine,* or at least a proper saddle for this one," Camilla said. Magda finished her food, and stood up wearily.

"It's up to us, Vanessa, to scout ahead and see whether there is a trail anywhere up there." She scanned the map. It was past noon and the day was still fine, but long, narrow, hook-ended clouds were beginning to blow across the sky from the north, and Magda knew, they all knew, what that presaged: high wind at least, perhaps storm and deep snow.

The map showed something like a settlement or a village. She prayed it would not be a village like the last one they had discovered in emergency.

"Put your leg up and rest it while you can, Jaelle. Vanessa and I will scout ahead." Cholayna, she thought, looked worse than Jaelle, her breath coming in heavy rasping wheezes. Yet there was no way to return, and no shelter near. They must simply go ahead and hope they found shelter. Magda was not superstitious, but it seemed that the pony's death was an ill omen.

They had had too much good luck on this long trek, and if that good luck had deserted them, who might be next?

Camilla said, "Let me go with you—"

"You've got to stay here and look after Cholayna and Jaelle. Vanessa is mountain-wise and I'm the most able-bodied one now." Magda smiled faintly. She said, "You have the hard part; it's going to be cold here, not moving. Get out sleeping bags and wrap up in them. At least Vanessa and I will keep warm moving."

Jaelle said, "In all of Kindra's old stories, it was made clear that the way to the secret city of the Sisterhood was guarded. I wonder if we are being tested."

Cholayna said, wrapping a sleeping bag around herself and Jaelle, "I find it hard to believe that they have that much power. Weather, perhaps—I can just manage to believe that. Avalanche? No, I think perhaps that must be marked up to—" she interrupted herself with a prolonged paroxysm of coughing, finishing, half strangled, "to the general cussedness of things. Camilla, is there any more of your witches' brew?"

Magda was oddly reluctant to turn her back even on the makeshift camp. It was her first experience with being roped up, but one look at the debris-strewn, rocky, icy surface above and below them convinced her to let Vanessa make her fast to the rope. They hugged the glacier, picking their way carefully along the heaps of loose rocks, at the imminent risk of breaking an ankle or worse. From the glacier above, walls of ice seemed to tilt forward and hang over them.

Magda was breathless with the altitude—they must, she thought, be somewhere above five thousand meters. The whole of the slope seemed to be strewn with newly fallen snow and old ice. There were several buttresses of rock widely separated by gullies filled to the brim with loose stone and unstable boulders. There seemed no hint of a trail, no suggestion that anyone had ever traveled this way before.

As they climbed, the whole of the great plateau was revealing itself. They were nearing the vast wall of ice which guarded the summit marked on the map; they crossed the gullies in rushes, wary of fresh rockfalls from above, seeking the safety of the natural stone buttresses which stood out from the slopes, clear of the danger.

"Too damned much loose rock and ice this way," said Vanessa, pausing to wipe her face in the shelter of one of the huge boulders. "If we bring everybody up this way, we're going to have to stay awfully close together, which probably means roping the horses and *chervines* and bringing them up in clusters. Not good. And I don't like the look of that."

She pointed, and Magda, already breathless, felt her heart stop in her throat. They were far to one side, and safe, but the great glacier, an overwhelming mass of tortured formations of ice frozen in the very act of toppling over, loomed high above the other slope, the very end of a great bed of ice sitting almost atop the summit they must cross.

Magda knew little of glaciers; the rock slope was a gentle gradient, but she knew that the ice was in slow, inexorable motion, moving, though imperceptibly, down the slopes they must somehow cross or climb. As the great masses of ice, under immeasurable pressure, reached the edge of the summit, they must break asunder and roar their way down into the valley. Such was the avalanche which had killed Jaelle's pony and nearly taken Jaelle with it. How could they know how soon the next point of inequilibrium would be reached? Were their comrades even safe where they were now?

They hurried across another gully of broken stone and razor-sharp flakes of loose shale which cut at their boots. The sun had gone behind the thickening layer of cloud, and Magda, looking down, could only see a small reddish dot, the sleeping bag Cholayna had wrapped round herself and Jaelle. Looking upward and across the valley, they could see, on the next slope, a few rectangular grayish shapes.

"Now is that the village marked on the map, or is it just a cluster of stone blocks like these?" Magda wondered aloud.

"God knows; and I'm not in Her confidence," Vanessa said. "But at the moment I'd take out a nice mortgage on my soul for a helicopter: I wonder if this might have been what Lexie saw from the plane?"

"No way of telling. And I don't like the look of the sky," Magda said. "If it is a village we'll have to make directly for it. There's nothing else that even looks like shelter, and I don't like the idea of letting Cholayna spend another night in the open. Vanessa, I'm worried, really worried about her."

"You think I'm not? We'd better pray that place *is* a village or settlement of some sort. I don't think it's what Lexie saw; it's marked on the maps. But it looks a little too regular to be a rock formation. Anyway we've got to try for it. The way that sky looks, we have no choice. I don't want to bivouac in *that*."

"Who would?" Magda turned to descend the way they had come, but turned to look at Vanessa, who was standing at the very edge of the cliff in a way that made Magda's arms and legs prickle with cramping apprehension.

Vanessa said in an undertone, "God, Lorne, just *look* at it. It makes the mountains of Alpha look like foothills. I was proud of collecting Montenegro Summit. I've never seen anything like this. No matter how this comes out, just the chance to see this—" She broke off, and looked at Magda.

She said softly, "You don't understand at all, do you, Lorne? To you it's just difficulties and dangers and hard travel and rough going, and you can't even see it, can you?"

"Not the way you do, Vanessa," Magda confessed. "I never wanted to climb mountains for their own sake. Not for the love of it."

Unexpectedly, Vanessa reached out and put an awkward arm around her. "That's really something. That you keep going, like this, when it doesn't even mean anything to you. Lorne, I'm— I'm glad we've got to know each other. You're—you're what they always said you were." Her cold lips brushed Magda's cheek in a shy kiss. Abruptly, she turned away.

"We'd better get back down, and tell them what we found. If anything. I'd feel damned funny to climb all the way up to that cluster of gray stuff and find it was just a bunch of rotten old square rocks!"

"Funny isn't exactly the word for what I'd feel," Magda agreed, "but it's the only halfway repeatable word for it."

Going down was easier, though they picked their way carefully to avoid a fall. As it was, Vanessa stumbled and was saved by the rope from a long fall down a debris-strewn slide; putting out her hand to save herself she wrenched her wrist painfully.

The sky was wholly clouded over now, and a cutting wind had begun to blow; Magda was shivering, and halfway down the slope they stopped, sheltering behind one of the rock buttresses to dig out the emergency rations from their pockets and suck on honey-soaked dried fruit. Magda's face felt raw in spite of the cream she had smeared on it. As the sky darkened it was harder to place their feet. How, in heaven's name, were they going to bring horses and *chervines,* not to mention the ailing Cholayna, up this way? She had no chronometer, but it could not be so late in the day as that sky presaged. Did that mean one of the blizzards, roaring down out of the impassable north?

"How far away would you say that place was?"

"A few kilometers; if we could ride, a couple of hours, no more. Climbing, God only knows," Vanessa said. "Maybe when we get past the bad part, we can put Cholayna on a horse and lead it across, at least." She drew the strings of her hood closer around her face.

It seemed to Magda that the wind was growing fiercer, that it held the very smell of heavy snow. She told herself not to borrow trouble; things were bad enough as they were. As they approached the spot where they had left the others, her mind was tormented with sudden fears; suppose the campsite was deserted, Jaelle and Cholayna and Camilla gone, snatched into oblivion by the hand of the sorceresses who had perhaps led Lexie and Rafaella into some doom in these mountains. . . .

But as they picked their way carefully down the last slope they could see a flash of orange against the rock and snow, Camilla's old riding-cape, and the gleam of a campfire. Then they stumbled into the camp and Camilla thrust mugs of boiling tea into their hands; Magda collapsed on a spread sleeping bag.

Nothing, it seemed, had ever tasted so good to her burning throat.

Revived a little by the hot drink, warmed (but not enough), she asked, "How is Cholayna?"

Jaelle tilted her head to where Cholayna was sleeping between piled sleeping bags and blankets. Even from where they sat Magda could hear the rasp of her breathing. Vanessa went and bent her head to listen to the sound at close quarters.

Camilla asked, "Well?"

"Not very well at all," said Vanessa, tight-lipped. "There's fluid in her bronchial passages; I don't know enough to know if it's spread to her lungs. But we've got to find shelter for her before very long. Let's just pray that what we found will *be* shelter."

And I didn't want Vanessa to come. What would we have done without her?

Quickly they told what they had discovered, saddled up ponies and loaded the *chervines,* roping them together. Cholayna, rousing quickly from her light sleep, protested that she was able to walk with the rest, but they insisted she should ride and set her on her horse Magda took the reins, and they started upward. For the first stretch, at least, they need not be roped up.

But a few hundred feet above the spot where they had camped after the avalanche, the rocks and ice were so loose under foot that Vanessa insisted on getting out the ropes and roping them all together.

"I'm sorry, Cholayna; you'll have to get down. I don't trust any horse's footing here. If you could manage to ride a *chervine*—"

"No need of that." Nevertheless, Cholayna clung to the *chervine's* saddle-strap to haul herself along; it was the elderly female, the most tractable of all the animals, and although it whickered uneasily, it did not protest as Cholayna held tight. The other *chervines* followed their leader; the horses, too, had to be trusted to pick their own way over ice and rubble. Magda knew it would be a miracle if all the animals got across undamaged. Once Camilla's foot slipped and only the taut-stretched rope kept her from rolling down the long rocky slope; she hauled herself to her feet, swearing breathlessly in a language Magda hardly understood.

"Hurt, Camilla?"

"Only shaken up." She was favoring one foot, but there was nothing to be done about it here. Slowly, they forced their way up the long slope, under the lowering sky, pregnant with undelivered clouds of snow. It was deliberate, hard going; Magda, who had covered this upward route already once today, felt her knees would hardly hold her up; she heard her own breath deepen and roughen, whistling loudly in and out. Her head throbbed and her ears ached, but there was no longer any feeling in her face. She drew up her scarf over her nose in a rude mask, but the warm breath condensed and froze so that her face was soon covered in an ice-mask.

Her world reduced itself to this; one step, then another. Yet outside the little circle described by the sound of her own breathing, she was aware somehow of her companions, could feel the stab of pain in Jaelle's bruised leg, the knife-edge of pain through Camilla's foot every time she set it down, knew that the ankle Vanessa had hurt early in the trip was still paining her in this cold, felt the dull pain in Cholayna's chest. She fought to shut it out, knowing that she could do nothing for the others except to hoard her own strength so that she needed no help from them. She knew that Vanessa was crying softly with weariness and pain. She too had climbed this route once already today.

Just one step and then another. Nothing outside this.

It was a long nightmare. They had been climbing forever and they would go on climbing forever. *I will take ten more steps*, she bargained with herself, *and then I will give up.* And at the end of ten steps; *I will take ten more steps, only ten more, I will not think any farther than that.* She could just manage, breaking it up into these little segments, carefully not thinking farther than this, *seven, eight, nine, ten steps, then I will lie down and never get up again. . . .*

"Magda," it was Vanessa's voice, very soft. "Can you help Cholayna?" Looking up, outside the circle of her own preoccupation, she found that Cholayna had let go the *chervine's* rein and sunk down in the snow. Vanessa was struggling with one of the horses, fighting to lead it over the rubble, and with one part of her brain Magda wondered why she bothered, while a small detached part of herself knew that if they lost any more horses they would never make it to that village they had seen.

She made her way to Cholayna's side, bent and took the woman by the arm.

"I'll help you. Lean on me."

Cholayna's face was a mottled mess of cream and half-frozen pale patches against her dark skin, her eyes reddened and sunken in her face. Ice clung to loose strands of her hair. Her voice was only a harsh whisper.

"I'm never going to make it. I'm only holding you back, You others go on. Leave me here. No reason the rest of you shouldn't get across. But I'm done, finished."

Magda could *feel*, inside her own mind, the depth of Cholayna's weary despair, and fought against making it part of herself.

"You're only tired. Lean on me." She bent to slip her arm under Cholayna's shoulders. Part of her was angry, she had barely strength enough for herself, but the other part knew that this was a final struggle. "Look, we're only a little way from the summit, you can ride from there."

"Magda, I can't . . . I can't. I think I'm dying . . ."

And for a moment Magda, looking at Cholayna, believed it; she half released Cholayna's hand . . . then something, anger, a final spurt of adrenalin, flooded her with rage.

"Damn it, don't you *dare* pull that on me! You bullied us into letting you come when I told you you couldn't make it, I *told* you you couldn't travel past Nevarsin, you wouldn't let us send you back from there! Now you haul your stubborn old rear end up out of that snow, or I'll kick you to the top myself! You've got to do it, I haven't the strength to carry you, and the others are worse off than I am! Get *up*, damn you!" She heard herself, half incredulous. But the anger was flooding her to the point where she actually raised her arm to strike Cholayna.

Cholayna's breathing rasped in and out for a moment, then she stirred, wearily. Magda held out a hand and Cholayna dragged herself upright, clinging to the outstretched arm for a moment. She said between her teeth, "If I had the strength I'd—" but the words evaporated in a spasm of heavy coughing. Magda put an arm round her.

"Here. Lean on me."

"I can manage," said Cholayna, forcing herself to stand without Magda's support, glaring at her with her teeth bared like an animal. She took an unsteady step, another. But at least she was walking. Magda put her arm around her again, and this time Cholayna did not draw away from the offered support.

Jaelle was in the lead; Vanessa struggling with the horses just behind her. Camilla had caught up with the roped *chervines,* and was clinging to a saddle-strap as Cholayna had done for so long, and Magda longed to go to her; yet she knew Camilla could, if she must, manage without her help, and Cholayna needed her.

Somewhere below them there was the thunder of an avalanche and the mountain shook. Magda gasped and Cholayna clutched at her; but it was far below, and subsided after a few moments.

We've got to get across this stretch; it could all go, any minute!

"Look," Jaelle called wildly from a few dozen steps above them. "Look, Vanessa! Across the slope, up there! Do you see? Lights! Lights, over there! It's the settlement marked on the map! It's really there, and we've found it!"

Magda drew in a breath of relief. It hurt her dry throat, and the icy air burned in her lungs, but it had come just at the right time. Now they could go on. It did not even matter that it was starting to snow. With Cholayna clinging to her arm, they struggled up the last steps to the peak, and they all clustered there, staring at the faint glimmer of lights across the valley. From here it was downhill, and at least part of the way, they could ride.

Chapter 22

Partway down the slope, it began to snow; they rode through the deepening dusk as the snow thickened, Cholayna and Camilla riding, Jaella leading on foot with Magda and Vanessa behind her. The extra horses and the *chervines* came after, jostling on the narrow downhill trail. From the position of the lights, Magda could tell that they were well above the valley's floor, and she hoped there would be a road or trail upward. She did not know how Cholayna would fare on another mountain path.

As they went down, the road was lined more thickly with trees, sometimes blotting out the distant lights. The snow fell more and more heavily, and the wind began to rise.

Suppose we cannot reach the village in this snow; suppose it becomes a full blizzard? Suppose they will not take us in, or they are a village of robbers like that one past Barrensclae? But Magda was really too weary to care, to think any further than those welcoming lights. Lower and lower they descended, sheltered somewhat from the fierce wind and snow by the twisted trees lining the road, and there was a faint smell of resins; Magda was so chilled that it was a long time before she could be sure she smelled anything. Down and still down, and then she was certain she smelled smoke and the faint far smell of food cooking, so delicious that it made her eyes stream. The lights flickered faintly far above them, but they seemed too near to be across the valley, as if they were floating in the air.

Magda could no longer see the lights. Then she bumped

softly into Camilla's horse, and all the animals jostled together at the foot of a cliff. It was as dark as the inside of a pocket.

"Somebody, strike a light?" It was Camilla's voice. Cholayna was coughing. Jaelle fumbled in the dark and then there was a tiny flare. Gradually, by its light, Magda began to see why they had been so abruptly halted.

They were clustered at the foot of a cliff which rose sheer before them. Someone a long time ago had cut steps into the sheer face, too steep, too far apart, for climbing, as the original designers had been not quite human.

But beside the steps hung a long rope, with a handle, a plain chunk of wood wrapped in greasy rope. With a quick glance round, Jaelle pulled at it, and heard, a long way above them, the sound of a bell.

Then for a long time nothing happened at all. At least they were in the shelter of the cliff, and out of the wind; but the cold was still fierce and biting. Jaelle and Vanessa stamped about, striking their boots hard against the rock underfoot. Magda knew she should do the same, but had not the necessary strength of will to force herself. Cholayna was coughing and wheezing again, huddled in her down jacket, a thick scarf muffling her face and the sound of her breathing. Magda shivered and waited.

"Do you hear anything, Jaelle? Should you ring the bell again?"

"Something. Up there." Jaelle stepped back away from the cliff, trying to look through the thick darkness and whirling snow. Now they could all hear it, a rough scraping sound.

Jaelle struck another light; then into the tiny circle of flame, crossed with thick-falling flakes of snow, a booted foot descended, then another, quickly followed by trousered legs and a body wrapped in what looked like an assortment of thick heavy shawls. This was surmounted by a face half concealed by matted, ice-rimed white hair, thick and wild, snow lingering on the bushy white eyebrows.

"Ye'll have to lave yer riden' beasts down yere," said a

rasping voice in thick mountain dialect. "We got na way to bring dem up. Be ye men or women, strangers?" And in the last sputtering light of the match Magda saw that the deep-sunken eyes were clotted with thick white film. Nevertheless for a shocking instant Magda thought it was the old woman she had seen in the Overworld.

"I am Jaelle n'ha Melora, a Renunciate of Thendara Guild-House," Jaelle said, "and these four women are my oath-sisters. We are all travel-weary and one of our number is ill. We beg shelter for the night."

"Ay, usn'll shelter ye the night, na worrit to that," said the blind woman. "Shelter ye even be ye men, but men sleep in by the stable wi' dey beasts. This be the hermitage of Avarra, daughters. Men here be curst if dey try to enter, but ye may come up and sleep sound. Bide here just."

She tilted her head upward and gave out a long, shrill, wordless call that resonated in the snow-filled air for a long time. For a minute Magda thought it was a word in her nearly incomprehensible dialect, then realized it was a signal. It was followed by a harsh scraping sound and then, on a rope, swaying from side to side, a dark shape descended. After a minute Magda realized that it was a great heavy basket, woven of something like wicker, bumping against the edge of the cliff as it came down.

The blind woman gestured.

"Get ye in, girlies. Usn'll stable dey beasts." And indeed as the basket descended farther, Magda could see inside the slender shape of what looked like an adolescent boy but was probably a girl, wrapped in shapeless garments like those of the woman.

Camilla asked, "Shouldn't I stay with the horses?"

The blind woman swiveled her head round quickly at the voice; came and felt about Camilla's head and shoulders, her narrow body.

"Here, ye, be ye woman? Tha' hands be more fit for sword and tha' got nae tits—"

That settled one question, thought Magda dispassionately; this was not the hidden City of the Sorceresses; the woman had

no *laran*. Her throat ached with awareness of Camilla's humiliation, but Camilla said quietly: "I am *emmasca*, old mother, and
made so as a young girl. Yet I was born a woman, and so I remain. Is there a law of this place that a woman may not bear a
sword?"

"Hrrmmphh!" It was an untranslatable sound; Magda did not
know whether it was contempt or simply acceptance. The blind
woman stood with her hands still on Camilla's shoulders. Then
she said, "Na, na, her above shall judge ye, I be not one to do
dat. Get ye in." She signaled toward the basket; the young girl
climbed down out of it and held it tilted for Camilla to climb in,
followed by the others. The blind woman steadied Cholayna
with both hands as she clambered shakily into the basket, then
sent up that long reverberating shriek of a signal again. It was
answered by a similar cry from above, and then the basket began
to move upward.

During that terrible bouncing, swaying ascent, up and up on
creaking pulleys invisible in the dark above them, the rope jig-
gled and the basket bumped heavily against the cliff, jostling
loose and beginning again the slow creaking ascent. The wind
buffeted the basket, setting it swaying and spinning with sickening lurches every few feet. Cholayna peered over the edge
with frank curiosity, trying to pierce through the darkness, but
Magda clung with both hands to the edge of the basket and hid
her eyes in her cloak.

Cholayna murmured, "Fascinating!"

Magda noted, with wonder, that although the Terran
woman's breath was still rasping, her voice weak and shaky, she
had recovered her curiosity and interest in what was happening
around her. She murmured to Magda, "Do you suppose this is
the City of the Sorceresses?"

Magda whispered back, "I don't think so." She explained
why.

"But the old blind woman is only a kind of gatekeeper or
something like that. The people inside might be quite different,"
Jaelle murmured under her breath.

Magda didn't answer. The motion of the basket was making her sick.

How high up is this place anyway? she wondered. It seemed to her that the basket had been making its slow, bumpy way upward for at least half an hour, though she knew realistically it could not possibly be so high. *The next time I volunteer to go on a journey in the mountains*, she told herself, *I shall try to remember that I suffer from acrophobia.*

But even the apparently endless journey bumped and wobbled and swayed at last to stillness. There were lights, mostly crude torches of tar, which flared and smoked and smelled to high heaven. They were held by women, mostly clothed in coarse skirts and shawls, their hair ragged and uncombed.

"If these are the chosen of the Goddess," whispered Vanessa in Terran Standard—not to be overheard or understood—"I do not think much of them. I never saw such a filthy crew."

Magda shrugged. "Not much fuel or water here for washing. The first thing they did in the robbers' village was to offer us a bath; you can't judge by that."

A pair of the women steadied the swaying basket so that the occupants could climb out. Magda was grateful for the darkness around the torches so that she need not see the long dizzy drop up which they had come.

"Tha' all well come to Goddess's holy house," said one in that barbarous dialect. "May Lady shelter ye safe. Get ye in fra' the snow and wind." Surrounding them, they guided them up a long steep cobblestoned path, into the shadow of a cluster of buildings. The hiss of the storm blew around between the buildings and howled in the cornerstones, but in their lee they were out of the falling snow and sheltered from the wind. Magda remembered seeing the gray cluster of stones from the distance and guessed at their size; they were not built on human scale at all, any more than those steps down which the blind woman had clambered alone in the darkness of the storm.

Their guides thrust them along a sort of corridor between two of the immense buildings, and abruptly through a great door, into a room where a fire was burning; a tiny fire in a stone fireplace, which hardly lighted the immense dark spaces and corners of the room.

Near the fire, a dark figure shrouded in coarse shawls and veils crouched in the hearth. The women shoved them forward.

"*Kiya,*" said one, using the word of courtesy used for any female relative of a mother's generation, usually meaning in context something like Aunt, or foster-mother. "Here be strangers, and a sick one for your blessin'."

The woman before the fire rose and slowly put back the hood from her face. She was a tall old woman, her face swarthy, with wide-spaced eyes under slender gray eyebrows, and she turned her eyes from one to the other of them slowly.

"A good evening to you, sisters," she said at last. She spoke the same mountain dialect as the other women, but she spoke it slowly, as if the language was unfamiliar to her. However, the pronunciation was clearer and less barbarous. "This is the holy house of Avarra, where we live in seclusion seeking Her blessing. All women are welcome to shelter at need; ye who share our search are blessed. What can this person offer thee the night?" Her voice was deep contralto, so deep it hardly sounded like a woman's voice at all.

Jaelle said, "We seek shelter against the storm; and one of us is ill."

The woman looked them over, one by one. Cholayna coughed in the silence; the old woman beckoned her forward, but Cholayna seemed too weak and lethargic to see the gesture, far less obey it, so the woman went to her.

"What ails thee, sister?" But she did not await an answer. "One knows from thy cough; thee is from lowlands and the mountain air sickens thy breath. It is so?" She came and opened Cholayna's jacket, laying her gray head against Cholayna's chest. She listened a moment, then said, "We can cure this, but thee will not travel for a handful of days."

She beckoned to Vanessa. "And thy fingers be frozen, and chance be thy feet as well. My sisters will bring thee hot soup and hot water in a little time, and show ye all a place to sleep safe and dry." Her eyes went to Jaelle and it seemed they sharpened with sudden interest.

"Thy name, daughter?"

"I am Jaelle n'ha Melora—"

"Na', thy true name. Once this one who bespeaks thee dwelt in lowland country and she does well know a Renunciate may call herself to her liking. Thy name of birth, *chiya*."

"My mother was Melora Aillard," Jaelle said. "I do not acknowledge my father; am I a racehorse to be judged by the blood of my sire and dam?"

"Plenty, girl, will judge thee by less than that. Thee does wear thy *Comyn* blood in thy face like a banner."

"If you know me for a Renunciate, old mother, you know I have renounced that heritage."

"Renounce the eyes in thy head, daughter? *Comyn* thee is, and with the *donas*"—she used the archaic word, meaning *gift* rather than the more common term *laran*—"of that high house. And thy brother-sister there?"

She beckoned to Camilla, and said, "Why break laws of thy clan, half-woman?" The words were sharp, but for some reason they did not sound offensive, as the question of the blind gatekeeper had been. "Will thee entrust this old one with thy birth name, Renunciate?"

She looked straight into Camilla's eyes.

Camilla said, "Years ago I swore an oath never again to speak the name of those who renounced me long before I renounced them. But that was long ago and in another country. My mother was of the Aillard Domain, and in childhood I bore the name Elorie Lindir. But Alaric Lindir did not father me."

Magda barely managed to stifle a gasp. Not even to her, not even to Mother Lauria, had Camilla ever spoken that name. That she did so now betokened a change so deep and overpowering that Magda could not imagine what it meant.

"And thee has *donas* of the Hastur clan?"

"It may be," said Camilla quietly. "I know not."

"Well ye are come to this house, daughters." The tall woman inclined her head to them courteously. "Time may be for this one to speak wi'ye again, but this night thy needs are for rest and warmth. Make known to these whatever else may be given." She beckoned to the women who had brought them, gave a series of low-voiced instructions in their peculiar dialect. But Cholayna swayed and leaned against her, and Magda did not listen to what she said.

"Come ye wi'us," said one of the women, and led them through the drafty corridors again, then, and into an empty, spacious, echoing old building, stone-floored, stone-walled, with birds nesting in high corners and small rodents scurrying in the straw underfoot which had been laid for warmth. The only furnishings were a few ancient benches of carven stone, and a huge bedstead, really no more than a stone dais. One of the ragged crew laid a fire in the grate and touched her torch to it.

"Be warm an' safe yere," she said in her crude dialect, at the same time making a surprisingly formal gesture. "Usn' will bring ye hot soup from the even' meal, an' medicines for thy frozen feet an' for the sick one." She went away, leaving the women alone.

"They are more generous with fire for us than they were with that old woman, their priestess or whoever she was," Vanessa remarked.

"Of course," said Jaelle, "they are mountain folk; hospitality is a sacred duty to them. The old one who welcomed us—she has probably taken vows of austerity: but they would give us of their best, even if their best was half a moldy pallet and a handful of nut porridge."

"Jaelle, who *are* these people?" Vanessa asked.

"I haven't the faintest idea. Whoever they are, they have saved our lives, this night. If someone told me that Avarra, or the Sisterhood, guided us to them, I would not argue the point." She looked round and saw that Cholayna had collapsed on one of the benches.

"Vanessa, bring the medikit," she said, then hesitated, looked sharply at Vanessa, who had slumped down at once on another of the stone benches and was huddled over, in pain.

"Can you walk?"

"More or less. But I think I have frozen my feet," Vanessa confessed. The words were almost an apology. "They don't hurt. Not quite. But—" she clamped her lips together, and Jaelle said quickly, "You'd better get your boots off and attend to them as quickly as you can. How did you come to do that?"

"I think there may have been a hole in one of my boots—it was cut on the rocks," Vanessa said, as Jaelle helped her off with her boots. "Yes—see there?"

Jaelle shook her head at the cold white toes. She said, "They told us they'd be bringing hot water in a few minutes. Go near the fire, but not too close. No, don't rub them, you'll damage the skin. Warm water will do it better." She glanced around, at Cholayna lying collapsed and oblivious on the stone dais, at Camilla, who was pulling at her boot carefully, and finally pulled out a knife to slit it.

"How many of us are out of commission? Cholayna's probably the worst," Jaelle said. "Magda, you're one of the more able-bodied ones right now. Get her into a sleeping bag—as close to the fire as possible. The old woman said she would send medicines, and hot water, and hot soup—all of which we can certainly use."

"Now, *that* one—I would willingly believe *her* a *leronis*," Camilla said, cutting the boot away to reveal a foot dreadfully swollen, with purplish blood-colored blisters and patches of white. Magda glanced up and saw it, shocked; she wanted to go to her, but at the moment Cholayna was even worse, semi-conscious, her forehead, when Magda touched it, burning hot. As Magda touched her she muttered, "I'm all right. Just let me rest a little. It's so cold in here," and she shivered, deep down.

"We'll have you warm in a few minutes," Magda said gently. "Here, let me pull off your coat—"

"No, I want it on, I'm cold," Cholayna said, resisting.

"Keep it, then, but let's get out of those boots," Magda said, easing Cholayna down on her sleeping bag and bending to help her pull them from her feet. Cholayna tried to protest, but her weakness overcame her; she sank back, only half conscious, and let Magda take off her boots and her outer clothes and wrap her in blankets.

"Hot soup and some of that blackthorn tea will help her, if we can't get anything better," Magda said. She did not confess her real fear, which was that Cholayna was in the early stages of pneumonia. "What other injuries do we have? Jaelle, that leg you hurt when Dancer fell on you; you've been walking on it. How bad is it? No, let me see it, at once."

Jaelle's shin was bruised and bloody, but nothing seemed to be broken. It was, however, unlikely that she would walk in comfort for several days; she had already overstrained the damaged muscles and tendons. In addition, there were Vanessa's frozen feet, and patches of white on her hands as well. Camilla's foot was swollen and painful; Magda suspected that one or two of the small bones in the foot were broken.

Magda herself had a patch or two of frostbite on her face, but, although her nose was streaming and her sinuses ached, and she felt she would like to lie down and sleep for at least three days, she seemed to be the only one who had no serious illness or injury at the moment.

Presently the old doors creaked open. Snow and wind blew distantly into the room as a pair of women came in, carrying a couple of great cauldrons of water, with basins and kettles and bandages, and a third followed them with a great pot of steaming soup, which she promptly hung over the fireplace. They smiled shyly at the strangers but did not speak and went away at once, ignoring Magda's attempt to thank them in what she knew of the mountain dialect.

Magda, who was the only one who could walk properly, set herself to get into their saddlebags and ladle hot soup into mugs—first Jaelle and Camilla and Vanessa. Then she got Vanessa's feet into a basin of steaming water—at this altitude, she remembered, water boiled at a temperature quite tolerable to frostbitten or frozen skin.

"This is going to hurt. But keep on with it, otherwise you could—"

"Could lose toes or even fingers. I spent three years learning about altitude injuries and sickness on Alpha, Margali, I know what's at stake here. Believe me." She sipped soup, holding the mug in her uninjured hand—the other was in the hot water—and Magda saw her jaw tighten with pain, but she said with assumed nonchalance, "Damned good soup. What's in it, I wonder?"

"Might be better not to ask," Camilla said. "Ice-rabbit, probably; that's about the only game you find at this altitude, unless somebody's figured out how to cook a banshee."

Magda propped Cholayna's head up and tried to get her to swallow some of the hot soup, but the older woman was unconscious now, her breath rattling through her throat so loudly that Magda had a panicky moment of wondering if Cholayna was really dying.

"If she does have pneumonia," Vanessa said, so quickly that Magda wondered if Vanessa was reading her thoughts, "there are some wide-spectrum antibiotics in the medikit. Hand it here—I'm a little tied down at the minute." She rummaged in the tubes and vials. "Here. This ought to do. I don't think she can swallow, but there's a force-injection dispenser which you can give without any special medical knowledge—"

But before Magda could get the injection device loaded, the door opened again, and, warded by two reverential young women, the old woman who had welcomed them in the entrance chamber came in.

By the flickering firelight she seemed anyone's idea of a witch. But, Magda thought, not the ordinary Terran notion of a witch; something older, more archaic and benevolent, a primitive cave-mother of the human race, the ancient sorceress, priestess, clan-ruler in the days when "mother" meant at once grandmother, ancestress, queen, goddess. The wrinkles in her face, the gleam of the deep-sunken eyes beneath the witchlike disorder of her white hair, seemed wise, and her smile comforting.

She went with ponderous deliberation to Cholayna and squatted down on the dais beside her. Peripherally Magda noted that she was the first person on all their travels who had not shown the faintest surprise at Cholayna's black skin. She touched Cholayna's burning forehead, bent to listen again to her breathing, and then looked up at Magda, bent anxiously beside them. Her smile was wide and almost, Magda noticed, toothless, but when she spoke her voice was so gentle it made Magda want to cry.

"Thy friend be hot wi' the lung-sick," she said, "but fear none, *chiya*, this we can help. Get thee some soup for thysen', thee is so busy with thy friends' ills thee has not tended tha' own. This one is wi' her now; go thee and eat."

Her eyes were stinging; but Magda said, "I was about to give her some medicine, old mother—" she used the title in the most respectful mode—"then I will go and eat."

"Na. Na," said the old woman, "this be better for her than thy outland medicine; strangers here come wi' the lung-sick, but this will help her more." She pulled, from somewhere about her wrapped garments, a small vial and an ancient wooden spoon. Swiftly, she raised Cholayna's head on her arm, pried her mouth open and poured a dose between her lips. "Eat," she said to Magda, gently but with such definiteness that Magda reacted like a child scolded; she went quickly to the big pot and dipped herself a mug of soup. She sat on the bench beside Vanessa and raised it to her lips. It tasted wonderful, hot and rich and comforting, though she had no idea what was in it.

"I don't care if it *is* stewed banshee," she said in an undertone.

Vanessa whispered, "Magda, should we just let that old tribeswoman pour God-knows-what-kind of folk remedies down Cholayna without even asking what they are?"

"They couldn't survive in a place like this without knowing what they're doing," Magda whispered back. "Anyway, I trust her."

She turned to watch what the old woman was doing now; with her two attendants, they were raising Cholayna, piling thick bolsters behind her so that she was half-sitting, and spreading blankets over her for a crude sort of tent, under which they introduced one of the steaming kettles, while one of their number moved a burning brazier under the kettle, so that it was an improvised steam tent. Already, or so it seemed to Magda, between the steam and the old woman's unknown drug, Cholayna's breathing was easier.

The woman took a stick from the fire and with the burning tip lighted a curiously colored candle; it had a strong, astringently pungent smell as its smoke stole into the room.

Then she went to where Magda sat beside Vanessa, checked the hot-water basin where the latter was soaking her feet, and nodded.

"The daughters ha' brought thee bandages and medicine; when the skin is all pink again, bandage wi' this ointment. Use it also for thy bruises," she added, stopping beside Jaelle and Camilla. "It will help the skin heal clean. As for thy friend—" she gestured toward Cholayna—"while that candle burns, keep the pot on a hard boil, that she may breathe hot steam, and here be herbs to strew in the water. The candle will make thy breathing easier as well. When candle burns down, gi' her one more spoon of this——" she produced the small bottle and spoon " and let her sleep covered warm. Sleep thee also; she will do well enough now."

For a brief moment she bent and peered into Magda's face, as if something she saw there puzzled her; then she straightened up and said, to all of them, somehow even including the semiconscious Cholayna, "'Varra bless 'ee all, the night an' ever," and went away.

Vanessa turned the little bottle in her hand, studying it. It was lumpy greenish glass, hand-blown, with many flaws. She worked out the stone stopper and breathed the strong herbal smell.

"Obviously, a powerful decongestant," she ventured. "Listen; already Cholayna's breathing easier. And the steam tent is more of the same. About the candle, I couldn't say, but it does seem to make it easier to breathe."

"How are your feet?" Magda asked.

Vanessa grimaced, but passed it off lightly. "Hot water does miracles. I was lucky. This time." Magda, who had experienced frostbite in the Kilghard Hills many times during her travels and knew the agony of returning circulation, took that for what it was worth.

"Don't forget the ointment she gave you, when you bandage them."

"Thanks. But I think I'll stick to the antibiotics in the medikit."

"I've had experience of both," Jaelle said, reaching out for the small jar the old woman had left, "and I think I'll use this. Magda, you're up, will you get me another mug of soup?" And as Magda complied, she added, "The Priestesses of Avarra are legendary; according to Kindra, they have been healers for centuries and have a long tradition in healing arts. Some of them have *laran*, too."

And as if that reminded her of that surprising first interview with the old woman, Jaelle turned to Camilla, who was trying to wrap her foot in bandages. She took the foot into her own lap and took over the bandaging.

"So, you are my kinswoman, Camilla?"

Camilla said, very softly—and to Magda's astonishment she spoke in almost the identical mountain dialect—"Truly, did thee not know, *chiya?*"

Jaelle shook her head mutely. "Rohana said something once which made me suspect; though I do not think she knew it was you. Just that a daughter of Aillard had—had disappeared, under mysterious circumstances—"

"Oh, yes," Camilla said grimly, "the fate of Elorie Lindir was a scandal for at least half a year in the Kilghard Hills, till they had something else to wonder at, some other poor girl raped and forgotten, or some Hastur lord acknowledging some other bastard—why, think you, did I live so long as a man, save that I sickened at the gossip of housebound ladies—? Rohana is not so bad as most, but those snows were melted twenty winters past. Leave it, Shaya."

"You are *her* kinswoman too, Camilla." She stretched her hand to Magda and said, "I hate to keep ordering you around like this, but you can walk and I can't; can you get a couple of pins from my personal kit?"

"It's all right, *breda*," Magda said, found the pins and gave them to Jaelle, who pinned up Camilla's bandages, then got her own bruised leg up on the bench. "One of you, bandage this, will you?"

Magda moved it into her lap and began smoothing the old woman's herbal ointment on the torn and lacerated skin.

Camilla said, with a sudden undertone of fierceness, "I will claim kin with Lady Rohana when she claims kin to me!" She rose, tested her weight on the bandaged foot, wincing, and went to shake out her sleeping bag by the fire.

"Shall I stay awake to tend Cholayna's steam kettle or will you?" The flat tone of her voice closed the subject completely.

"I will,"· said Magda, but Jaelle shook her head.

"You've been looking after all of us all day. Go to bed, Magda, I'll look after her now. When that candle burns out—it can only be an hour or two—I can sleep too. At least we needn't keep watch all the time; here we are under Avarra's protection, and all the Renunciates are under her wing."

Magda wanted to protest, but her eyes seemed to be closing of their own accord. She nodded agreement and spread out her sleeping bag beside Camilla's. The fire burned low; outside she could hear the hissing of the thick snow, the wind howling like ten thousand screaming demons around the old buildings.

At the very edge of sleep, Camilla's head lying on her shoulder, she thought again how little she knew this woman she loved. The astonishing words rang in her mind.

My mother was of the Aillard Domaih, and my childhood I bore the name Elorie Lindir.

And thee has donas *of the Hastur clan?* And Camilla's even more astonishing words: *It may be.*

Chapter 23

The blizzard lasted for three days.

For the first day Magda did little but sleep; after the exhaustion of the long journey, the stress and fear, her weary body and wearier mind demanded their toll, and for a night and a day and most of another night she spent the hours asleep or in a state of incomplete somnolence, rousing only to eat or drink. They were all in much the same state.

"We thought at first that you too had taken the lung-fever," Camilla told her later, "but that old *leronis* said no, it was only weariness and cold. And, the Goddess be praised, she was right."

This morning Magda had had the energy to wash (at an icy indoor pump where the water was a little above freezing) and to change her underclothing and socks, and to brush her hair.

"How is Cholayna this morning?" she asked.

"Better," Camilla told her, "her fever is down, and she has eaten a little soup. She is still very sick, but her breathing is easier. And she spoke to me in *cahuenga*, which at least meant she knew who I was. What a relief after the last two days of her speaking only in some language none of us could understand, and not recognizing any of us!"

"How are the others?"

"Jaelle has climbed down the cliff—in this snowstorm!—to make sure the pack animals are all right. It is not that she does not trust the women here; but I think she wanted the exercise."

Camilla chuckled, and Magda laughed weakly with her. Jaelle always wearied quickly of inaction.

"And Vanessa?"

Camilla pointed; Vanessa was sleeping near the fire, only a few curls of dark hair showing above the top of her sleeping bag.

"Her feet are still very sore and painful, and two toenails came away last night when she changed the bandages, but it is fortunate it is no worse. My feet were almost as bad, but they are healing better. I think it is because Vanessa used only your Terran medicine, while Jaelle and I used what that old *leronis* gave us."

Magda finished the coarse, burnt-tasting porridge, put the bowl away, and slid down wearily.

"I am not sleepy now. But my whole body feels as if I had been beaten with wooden cudgels."

"Rest, then, *bredhiya*," Camilla said. "No one is going anywhere in *that*." The storm was still raging unabated outside; it seemed to Magda that it had raged through her sleep for the last hours and days.

Jaelle came in presently, her outer garments covered with snow, snowflakes clinging to her eyebrows and to her auburn curls.

"You're awake, Margali? Good. I was beginning to worry about you. I climbed down the cliff this morning, and back up, though they said I could ride up in the basket with the grain sacks. It was wonderful even in the snow; when it is not snowing, they tell me, one can see all the way to Nevarsin Peak on the one side, and to the Wall Around the World on the other."

Magda wondered at her freemate's idea of fun. She remembered that only a few weeks before her daughter was born, Jaelle had insisted on accompanying Damon to the far ends of Armida for the horse-roundup, saying that she knew perfectly well that she had time enough to return before her child was born. She had been in the saddle again before Cleindori was forty days old. Magda herself had been tired and lethargic all during her pregnancy, content to stay indoors and allow Ellemir and Callista to cosset her.

But before she had much time to reflect on it, the door opened and the ancient wise-woman who had welcomed them and brought medicines for Cholayna, came in. She barely nodded to the women but went directly to Cholayna, knelt and felt her forehead; bent her head to listen to her heart and the sounds of her breathing.

"Thee is stronger this morning, daughter."

Cholayna awoke, looked at the wild hair and ragged clothing of the ancient woman, and struggled to sit up. Magda came quickly to her side, so that Cholayna could see that she was not alone and at the mercy of a stranger.

Cholayna demanded weakly, "Where are we? What is happening?"

The old woman spoke a few soothing words but they were in the strange mountain dialect and Cholayna did not understand them.

"Who are you? What is going on?" As the old woman brought out the bottle of medicine and spoon, gesturing to Cholayna to open her mouth, she demanded shakily, "What's this, what are you giving me?" She moved her head from side to side in panicky denial. "What is it? Magda, help me, tell me, isn't anyone listening to me?"

There was real terror in her face, and Magda knelt quickly at her side, taking Cholayna's hands in hers.

"It's all right, Cholayna, you have been very ill, but she has been nursing you. I don't know what she is giving you, but it has made you better. Take it."

Cholayna opened her mouth docilely enough and swallowed the medicine, but she still looked confused. "Where are we? I don't remember coming here."

Questions flooded from her in Terran Standard as she struggled to sit upright, staring wildly about her.

Magda reassured her quickly in the same language.

"Cholayna, no one will hurt you. These people have been very good to us . . . we're safe here—"

"Who is this strange woman? Is she one of Acquilara's

people, did they follow us here? I—I think I have been dreaming; I thought Acquilara had captured us, brought us here—"

"Tell un, must not talk, lie down, rest, be warm," the old woman commanded. Magda laid her hand over Cholayna's wrist, gently forcing her back on the pillows.

"You mustn't talk. Lie still and rest, and I'll explain."

Coughing, Cholayna let herself sink back. Her eyes followed the attendants as they rigged again the improvised steam tent. She listened to Magda's simplified explanations, without question; Magda suspected she was simply so weak that she took everything for granted.

At last she whispered, "Then these are not Acquilara's servants? You are sure of that?"

"As sure as I have ever been of anything," Camilla reassured her. "She has been coming in every few hours to make sure your fever was under control. But now you really must lie down and rest, don't think of anything except getting well."

Cholayna closed her eyes again weakly, and the old woman raised her head, glaring at Camilla.

"A name was spoken that is forbidden in 'Varra's holy house. What ha' ye to do with that one?"

"Who? Acquilara?"

The old woman gestured angrily. "Silence! Speak not the names of evil omen! This one said, when thy sickness and weariness should be healed, thy story would be heard. Now perhaps is the very time for that hearing; what do ye in these wilds where no women come save in search of Her blessing?"

"Margali will tell thee, Grandmother," said Camilla in the mountain dialect. Magda wondered when she had learned it, and saw in Camilla's mind there was a flash of memory, a year spent as an abused and beaten child, enslaved in a bandit encampment. . . .

"We come in search of Her blessing too." Magda found in her memory the night when first she had seen the image of Avarra during the first meeting of the Sisterhood. "We seek a City said to be inhabited by the Sisterhood of the Wise. Two of our companions were seeking it, and had gone before. We thought, when we saw your lights in the wilderness, that perhaps we had found that place, and perhaps our comrades also."

"This one has read thy mind and memory in thy weakness, granddaughter. We are only sheltering in the shadow of Her wings, *chiya*, and are not of Her Sisterhood. Yet thy search does make thee sacred here, where thy companions have *not* come."

The old woman's hand fell on Magda's shoulder. "Yet tell, what of that other name *she* spoke now twice?"

"She came to us by night, promised that she could lead us to our comrades."

"And why did thee not follow her?"

"It seemed to us," Camilla said slowly, "that truth was not to be found in her mouth, and that to follow such a guide was worse than to wander unguided."

"Yet thy companion cried out to her in her unknown tongue—"

"Cholayna was afraid of her," Magda corrected sharply. "Read *her* mind and memory if you can, Old Mother, and you will know I speak truth."

Jaelle asked Magda in Standard, "What's the trouble?"

"She says Rafi and Lexie haven't been here. Which may mean they have fallen into—" she started to say, Acquilara's hands, then looked at the old woman's face and didn't. "I fear, then, that the two we seek may have fallen into the hands of those we count as enemies."

The old woman looked from one to another of them, then said slowly, "Thy friend is better, but still very sick. Watch thee by her a handful of days more," and went away.

Camilla and Jaelle looked at Magda and demanded, "Now what was *that* all about?"

The old woman did not return that day, nor the next, nor the next. Silent attendants came in three times a day, bringing them food: rough porridge morning and noon, thick and nourishing soup in the evening. The enforced rest was good for all of them; Magda recovered her strength, Vanessa's frozen feet healed, and even Cholayna began to sit up for a time during the day.

On the fifth or sixth morning—Magda had lost count of the days, as they slid by with nothing to distinguish them—the snow stopped and the sound of silence woke Magda; the wind was no longer wailing and screaming around the buildings. She stepped out into a bright world, the sun dazzling on roofs and the sky so clear that it seemed she could see across an endless landscape of snowy peaks and valleys far below them.

Perhaps Cholayna would be able to travel soon. Magda began mentally sorting through their possessions for gifts they could make to the old woman and to the Sisterhood in return for their hospitality. She trembled at the thought of the return journey down the cliff in the basket. And how much farther must they go? Perhaps the old woman could tell them something about Lexie and Rafaella; at least she seemed to know something of Acquilara's people and despised them.

Cholayna was sitting up this morning, and had actually eaten some porridge. She looked better, healthier; she had asked for water to wash her face and dug into her personal pack for a hairbrush; but she was too weak to sit up for so long, so Vanessa had come and taken the brush, and was trying to ease the tangles out of the shock of pale hair.

"I can see that you are feeling better," Magda said, kneeling beside her, and Cholayna smiled.

"I am beginning to feel halfway human again; I can breathe again without knives through my chest! And the snow seems to have stopped. Tell me, Magda, how long have we been here?"

"Five or six days. As soon as you are well enough to travel, we will go on. I think perhaps these people know something of the City. Perhaps, if we ask in the right way, they will tell us."

"But what is the right way?" asked Vanessa.

"One thing we know," Camilla said, joining them, "they aren't in league with—" she stopped, and Magda could read in Camilla's mind the memory of the exaggerated anger the old woman had displayed when she spoke Acquilara's name.

It was as if someone not present spoke, not in words:
The name of evil can summon it and be used as a link . . .

"They aren't in link with that woman who came and tried to

bully us in Nevarsin, in Arlinda's house," Magda said. "They have an unholy horror of her very name, though, so they evidently know what's going on."

"I wish *I* did," Vanessa complained. "That old woman gives me the creeps! Inhuman!"

Jaelle protested, "She saved Cholayna's life, and you could have been permanently lamed. Don't be ungrateful!"

"I know what Vanessa means, though," Canrilla said. "Have you noticed, Margali? I don't expect Vanessa to understand it, she doesn't know the language as well as you do; you learned it in Caer Donn as a child. You noticed she never says *I* at all; just stands aside and speaks of herself as someone else. I don't begin to understand it."

"I don't know if it's ever possible to understand an alien religious practice," Cholayna said thoughtfully. "Perhaps we should just be grateful that she's well-disposed toward us."

"We need more than that, though," Jaelle said. "We've come to the end of the trail. I don't know of anything beyond here and there's nothing on the maps. If they can't tell us where to go on, I don't know where we can go."

"And the old woman hasn't been near us for days," Camilla said. "When you spoke—" again the hesitation, "a certain name, you seemed to put her off. She'd been so friendly before that, and then—nothing. Not a sign nor a sight of her." Her smile was bleak.

"Maybe when she found out that some of us had *laran* she decided we could find our own way from here."

"But," Magda said, "that would mean there's something to find. And that it would be possible to find it from this place."

That night when the attendants came in to rig Cholayna's steam tent again—they indicated by signs that she should sleep in it, even if she could breathe well enough during the day—Jaelle went with them down to see to the animals again. When she came back, she beckoned them all close to her.

"Tomorrow, they said, someone will come to talk with us. I gathered, from what the blind woman—her name is Rakhaila, by the way, that's Hellers dialect for Rafaella—from what she said, there are women here who come and go from—" Jaelle hesitated—"the place we may be looking for. I have a feeling we should be ready to leave at a moment's notice."

"Cholayna's not able to travel yet," Vanessa protested.

"That's another thing we have to talk about. I think perhaps we must send Cholayna back; or leave her here to recuperate further. From something Rakhaila said, this could lead us out beyond the Wall Around the World. There's no way Cholayna's fit enough to make that kind of trip."

Cholayna said doggedly, "We had this all out before. I can manage. I'll do it if it kills me."

"That's what we're afraid of, you stubborn old wretch," Vanessa said. "What good would it do to kill yourself on the trip? Would that do Lexie any good, or you?"

But Magda was not so sure. "We've come this far together. I don't think it would be right to abandon Cholayna here. I think we all go together, or none of us." She did not know why she was so certain.

But when Cholayna had been settled for the night, Jaelle touched Magda's arm.

"*Breda*, we need to talk. Come outside with me for a minute."

They went out into the long corridor between the buildings. Jaelle led the way to a spot at the very edge of the cliff. The pulleys and baskets hung there awaiting the journey down.

"The steps aren't so bad," Jaelle said. "I've been down them twice now."

"Better you than me," Magda said. "Well, Jaelle, do you remember in Thendara you were saying you wanted a year off to go to the mountains? You've had your adventure, haven't you?"

Above them the sky was sprinkled with the stars of a rare, clear Darkovan night. Jaelle looked away north, to where, Magda knew, the Wall Around the World rose, the end of the known world of the Domains. She said, "Maybe it's only beginning."

Magda smiled indulgently. "You're enjoying this, aren't you?"

It was almost a joke; but Jaelle was completely serious. She said, "Yes. Terrible as this trip has been, I loved every minute of it. I wish I hadn't dragged you along, because I know you've hated it—"

Magda said, "No." She surprised herself with the word. "I wouldn't have wanted to miss—parts of it."

The sudden sense of self-mastery when she had accomplished what she had never believed she could do. Cholayna and Vanessa, friends only in the limited sense of co-workers; now, she knew, they were as close as the sisters she had never known. Would she have wanted to miss that? And in a very real sense it was *her* quest. From the day she had first seen the robed figures in their circle, first heard the sound of calling crows, she had known that she must follow them, even if the search led over the roof of the known world.

For a moment she knew this, then practicality took over again. "Would you go off to this City out of Kindra's legends, and stay there?"

"I don't know if they'd have me. I think you have to—well, to study and prepare yourself a long time first. There seems to be a college of this kind of wisdom and I'm still in kindergarten. But if I decided I wanted to try preparing to be worthy of it? Or if anything happened that I *couldn't* go back. On a trip like this, one false step—we've all come that close to the edge, Margali. If I didn't make it back, you'd look after Cleindori for me, wouldn't you?"

Magda smiled gently. "I'd have to get in line for the chance, after Damon, and Ellemir, and Lady Rohana . . . about all I could do for her would be to sponsor her if she decided she wanted to work for the Terrans, and considering that she's Heir to Aillard, I doubt she'd be given that option. But if you mean, would I love her as my own—do you doubt our Oath, freemate?"

Jaelle touched the hilt of Magda's knife which she wore at her belt. "Never, *breda*."

"We should go in," Magda said. The great violet disk of Liriel was rising, almost at full; the largest of the four moons.

The bluish crescent of Kyrddis hung almost at the zenith of the sky. Stars were beginning to shine through the clear pallor of the falling night, and an icy wind was beginning to blow over the heights, a veritable jet-stream of a wind which tore at their hair and buffeted them toward the cliffs. Magda clung to a frost-rimed wall to keep her balance against the fierce gusts. It was not dark; all round them the growing light of the moons was reflected from snow everywhere.

"Are you cold? Have some of my cloak," Jaelle said, putting it round her with her arm around Magda. Magda smiled as they snuggled together under it.

Jaelle said seriously, "I need to talk to you alone, just for a few minutes. I wish I didn't have to go back at all, Magda. I'm not needed in the Forbidden Tower. My *laran* isn't that strong; never has been. I'm hardly a competent monitor, and you—a Terran!—you are as powerful a technician as Damon himself. They love me, perhaps, but don't *need* me. In a very real sense I've never been needed anywhere. People don't need me, don't cling to me the way they do to you. Even my daughter comes to you for mothering, instead of me; she sees it too, Magda, the thing that makes people come to you. I've never known—where to go, or why."

Magda listened, appalled. Ever since she had known Jaelle she had envied what she thought was the younger woman's confidence, sense of purpose, the intensity with which she flung herself into things with a wholeheartedness Magda herself had never known. It had never occurred to her that Jaelle felt this way.

"That's not true, Shaya. You're so much stronger than I am in so many ways. You're braver than I am. You don't hold back and panic, and hash everything over in your mind all the time—"

"Oh—courage," Jaelle said, faintly smiling. "Damon told me once that he thought courage, a soldier's kind of courage, the kind I have, just means I haven't enough imagination to be afraid. Damon himself admits he's a horrible coward, physically, because he has too much imagination. And I have so little. No imagination, not half the brains you have or half the sensitivity either. Maybe what I need is the kind of wisdom they have, these sorceresses of that legendary City. I'm like Camilla. Maybe I need to go and ask them why I was born and what life is all about for me."

"There are times I've felt the same way, Jaelle. But we both have ties. Duties, responsibilities—"

Jaelle moved restlessly away from Magda. She was pacing at the very edge of the cliff in a way that made Magda wince. Courage? Or a lack of imagination, knowing she would not fall, so why did she need to worry about what could happen if she did?

"Oh, Margali, can't you see? There's no *reason* for me to go back. In a sense it seems my whole life has been leading up to this, a chance to find out what's real, what's under the surfaces of life. To make some *sense* of it all. Maybe these *leroni* of the Sisterhood know the answers and can tell me. Or help me find out."

"Or maybe they only claim they can. Like Acquilara. To give themselves importance. And it's all tricks."

"No. Can't you see the difference? Acquilara's full of arrogance and—and hates you and me because we really *have laran* and she doesn't though she wanted us to think she did. I'm thinking of—well, Marisela. She doesn't argue about why life happens, or try to convince or convert anyone, she just does what she needs to. I want to know what it is that she knows. The legend says if you get there under your own energies they have to take you in, and if they don't I'll sit on their doorstep until they do."

The idea had its attractions; *to know what life was truly all about, to fling yourself straight at the source of wisdom and demand to know.* Yet there were other duties, obligations, responsibilities.

"Would you really go after this kind of wisdom and leave me alone, Shaya?"

"You wouldn't be alone, Margali. You're not the kind of person to be alone. And anyway, you have Camilla—"

Magda gripped her hands tight.

"Jaelle—*bredhiya*, my love, my freemate, do you really think it's the same thing?" Love wasn't like that, Magda knew, it couldn't be pigeonholed that way. "I simply cannot believe you are jealous that Camilla and I—"

"No, oath-daughter." It was rare that Jaelle called her that now, but it came from the first of their many pledges to one another. "Never jealous, not that. Only—" Jaelle held her hands tightly; in the reflected moonlight, snow-light, her face was very pale, her great dark-lashed eyes somber in the pale triangle of her face. It seemed for a moment that a flood of memories reached out and enfolded them.

Jaelle looking up at her like a trapped animal, awaiting the knife-stroke of the hunter; she had saved Jaelle from bandits who would have killed them both, but now Jaelle in turn was prisoner, not the captor who had forced the Amazon Oath on her unwilling; now with a single stroke of her knife Magda could free herself, she need not even kill. She need only walk away, leaving the wounded Jaelle to die of exposure.

Jaelle, in the cave where together they had faced floodwater, death, abandonment, starvation. Jaelle, for whom her laran *had wakened. The exchange of knives, the Oath of Freemates.*

Jaelle, close to her in the Tower circle, bonded by the matrix link, closer than family, closer than sex, closer than her own skin . . .

Jaelle, clinging to her, her face covered with the sweat of hard labor, the night Cleindori was born; rapport between them so close that years later, when Shaya was born, even the stress of birth was not new to her; less conscious of agony than of fierce effort, terror, triumph and delight; Cleindori in a very real sense her own child, since she too had struggled to bring her to life. . . .

Whatever path she chose, always it seemed that Jaelle had been there before, and she only a clumsy follower in her steps. Even now. . . .

Then the rapport fell away (how long had it lasted? A lifetime? Half a second?) and Jaelle said quietly, "No, *bredhiya mea, viyha mea*, not jealous of Camilla. No more than you are jealous of Damon."

But there had been a time, Magda remembered, when she *had* been jealous of Damon, painfully, blindly, obsessively jealous of Damon. She could not bear that either, any more than she could bear, after she and Jaelle had come together as if destined, that any man could give Jaelle anything she could not. Now she was ashamed of that brief jealousy, her fear that Jaelle could love her less because she loved the father of her child. She had fought through and triumphed, still loving Jaelle, and loving Damon just as much *because* he could give Jaelle the one thing she could not, for all her love.

"The one thing that could make me hesitate would be leaving you, Margali. Even Cleindori has a dozen who would be glad to rear her if I could not. But you have something to return for. I don't. What do I have ahead of me but to go back, take the Aillard seat in Council when Lady Rohana is gone? And why should I want to do that? In the Renunciates, and also in the Forbidden Tower, we are working so that the Domains need not depend on Councils, and *Comyn*, who try to keep *laran* in their own hands for their own good. The Hasturs who rule the Council don't want independent subjects, thinking for themselves, any more than they want independent women."

"Then isn't it your job to take that Council seat and help them change the way they think?"

"Oh, Magda, *breda*, don't you think I've been through all that in my mind? I can't change the Council because, at heart, the Council doesn't want to change. It has everything it wants the way it is: power, the means to work for its own greed. Now when people don't work for it of their own free will, it bribes them with promises of power of their own, and an appeal to *their* greed."

She turned and paced restlessly along the cliff, her face starkly moonlit. "Look what they did to Lady Rohana! They said to her, 'It doesn't matter to you that you are not free; you have power instead, and power is more important than freedom.' They bribed her with power. I am so afraid that they will do that to me, Magda, find out what I want most, and bribe me with it—I simply cannot believe that all the *Comyn* are corrupt, but they have power, and it makes them greedy for more. Even the Towers are playing the game of power, power, power, always over other people."

"Maybe that's simply the way life works, Jaelle. I don't like it either. But it's like what you said about bargaining, haggling in the market; it makes each party think he's getting the better of the other." Magda's smile was strained. "You said you liked haggling."

"Only when it's a game. Not when it's real."

"But it is a game, Shaya. Power, politics, whatever you call it—it's simply the way life works. Human nature. Romantics among the Terrans think the Darkovans are immune to it because you aren't part of an interstellar Empire, but people *do* operate because of profit, and greed, as you say—"

"Then I don't want any part of it, Magda. And I know they will try to bully me into taking that Aillard seat in Council, and within ten years I should be as bad as any of them, using power because they have convinced me that I am doing good with it. . . ."

"I think you would be incorruptible, Jaelle—" Magda began, but Jaelle shook her head with a wise sadness.

"Nobody's incorruptible, not if they let themselves be tricked into trying to play those power games. The only thing to do is to stay outside them. I think maybe the *leroni* of Avarra, the Sisterhood of the Wise, could show me how to stay outside. Maybe they know why the world works that way. Why good and evil work the way they do."

Jaelle turned restlessly, her cloak flying.

"Look at Camilla. She has a right to hate—worse than Acquilara. Did you hear her say she was a Hastur, at least that she had Hastur *laran*? And look what they did to her! But she's such a good person, such a *loving* person. And Damon, too. Life has treated him badly—but he still can love. The world is so rotten to people, and people keep saying it isn't fair—"

Magda murmured, "The *cristoforos* say it: 'Holy one, why

do the wicked flourish like mushrooms on a dead tree, while the righteous man is everywhere beset with thorns . . . ?' "

"Magda, did you ever think? Maybe the world isn't *supposed* to be a better place? Maybe it goes on the way it does so that people can *choose* what's really important." Jaelle spoke passionately, striding to and fro into the face of the wind, her auburn curls flying from under the hood of her cloak. She had forgotten the cold and the jet-stream wind.

"Let the Council, and the Terrans, play power games with each other. Andrew walked out and did what he could somewhere else. Let the Towers have their political struggles, under that horrible old hag Leonie Hastur—I don't care what Damon says, he may love her, but I know she is a tyrant as cruel and domineering as her twin brother who rules the Council! Between the Council, and the Towers, where is there a place for the use of *laran?* But Hilary and Callista found another way, even though the Towers were corrupt. Let women wear chains in the Dry Towns, or be good wives in the Domains, unless they have the courage to get out of it—real courage, not my kind that's just lack of imagination. Courage—to get out of the Dry Towns, or their own chains, the way my mother or Lady Rohana did, or the way you did when you found the Guild-house—"

"But your mother didn't get out of it, Jaelle. She died." For years, Magda knew, Jaelle had concealed this knowledge from herself.

"Sure she died. So did yours. So will you and I some day. Since we're all going to die anyhow, no matter what we do or don't do, what sense does it make to go around scared all the time, crawling, and putting up with a lot of rotten stuff just to hang on a little longer? Look at Cholayna. She could have stayed nice and safe in Thendara, or accepted your offer to send her back from Nevarsin. Even if she died here, wouldn't it have been better than turning back at Ravensmark and knowing she'd failed in what she set out to do? Living is taking risks. You could have stayed in the Guild-house and obeyed orders. My mother could have stayed in the Dry Towns and worn chains all her life. She might have died when Valentine was born even though, but she'd have died in comfort, and I'd still be there. In chains." She looked pensively at her bare wrists.

"It's all there is, Magda. We can't change life. There's too much greed and profit and—and *safety*. Human nature, like you said. We can only get out of it. Like Damon when he founded the Forbidden Tower. He could have been *blinded*—his *laran* burned out, because he wouldn't back down and promise to use his *donas* only in the way the others, the ones with the power, said he should. But if he'd done that he'd have been blinded anyway; he'd have done it to himself. And he knew it."

Magda knew Damon's story. She knew she did not have that kind of strength. *Except, sometimes, when Jaelle forces me to follow her into some mad challenge . . .*

"So don't you see, Magda? I can go back and play dreary games of power in the Council, or I can go *ahead*, to whatever these *leroni* can teach me—"

"You said that courage was needed to set up the Forbidden Tower, and we have a place there—"

"That was Damon's trial of integrity, Margali. Not mine." Jaelle turned and faced her freemate. "Only I can't go if it's going to hurt you *that* much. That's the one thing that could stop me. I won't do it over your—your dead body."

There was such a lump in Magda's throat she could hardly speak. She didn't have to; she gave Jaelle her hands again.

Shaya, my love, my treasure, do what you must do.

And you'll come too, Margali?

Suddenly Magda knew that Jaelle's quest had become her own. But she had, perhaps, stronger ties. A weakness, now, not a strength, but:

I don't know. I must see Cholayna safe. I brought her here and I cannot abandon her now. I'm not sure, Jaelle. But I won't try and hold you back.

"I had hoped we could go together," Jaelle said aloud as they turned back toward the buildings. "Margali, we must go in, we'll freeze." And indeed it was growing colder, the cold no longer bracing and stimulating but deadly. "I suppose you're right; if you're not ready, it wouldn't be right for you. But, oh, *breda*, I want to say, we go together or not at all. I couldn't bear to leave you behind."

But always, Magda thought, Jaelle was that one step ahead of her.

"Lead on," she said lightly, "and I'll follow as far as I can. But just now I'd prefer to follow you in out of the cold."

Chapter 24

Magda was dreaming. . . .

There was a circle of robed figures around a fire; dark hooded figures, gathered around something that lay at their center. Magda could not see what it was, nor see what they were doing to it; only that there was a sound like the screaming of hawks, and with every cry of the hawks there was a pitiable crying, so that for a moment Magda thought in horror, *it is Shaya, they have my little Shaya there, they are hurting her.* The fire at the center shot up and surged high, and Magda could see that it was no child, but the naked figure of a woman, lying bound in their circle.

Magda tried to rush forward to her, but it seemed that she was held in place by invisible bonds; chains like the chains of a Dry-Town woman.

"For the love of God, help me, Lorne! You got me into this, now you have a duty to get me out of it!"

It was Lexie's voice. She had known all along somehow that it was Lexie lying there helpless, and that she had been responsible for the act or omission that had landed Lexie there.

She struggled against her bonds, but the hawks went on screaming. She could see what they were doing now; with every surge upward of the flame, the hawks swirled, borne on the currents of fire, and swooped over Lexie's inert figure, and with every downward swoop they tore into her naked flesh, carrying away great dripping hunks of blood and skin, while Lexie screamed, terrible screams that reminded Magda horribly of the time she and Jaelle had been marooned in a cave with rising floodwater, and Jaelle had miscarried Peter Haldane's child. She had been delirious, not fully aware what was happening much of the time, and in her delirium she had screamed like that, as if she were being torn asunder, and Magda had not been able to help her. They had come so close to dying there.

And now it was Lexie screaming. And it is my fault; she was competing with me, and that was how she got into this.

Again Magda strained against her bonds to rush forward to Lexie, but there was a curious blue fire in the air, and in that evil glow she could see the face of the black sorceress Acquilara.

"Yes, you always want to ease your own conscience by being so ready to help other people. But now it is your task to learn detachment; that her troubles are not of your making, and that she must take the consequences of her own actions," Acquilara explained callously. It sounded so rational, so reasonable, and yet the screams tore at her as if every stroke of the razor talons and cruel bloody beaks fell on her own heart.

"Yes, that is what they are doing," Aquilara went on explaining. "They will tear and tear at that false and sentimental conscience of yours which you think of as your heart, until it is gone from your breast." And Magda, looking down, saw a great bleeding hole opening in her chest, from which a screaming hawk carried away a piece of flesh . . .

No. Think. This is a dream. Slowly a sense of reality penetrated Magda's mind; slowly, slowly. She felt herself pull free, free of the invisible bonds, raised her arms, jerked herself up, and found herself sitting bolt upright in her cold sleeping bag. Her heart was still pounding with the nightmare. She heard Jaelle cry out, and reached over to shake her freemate awake.

"Shaya, Shaya, are you having a nightmare too?"

"Zandru's hells," Jaelle whispered, "it was a dream, a dream, I was only dreaming—Acquilara's sorceresses. They were torturing Rafaella, and they had chained me up to Rafi's big *rryl* and were making me play ballads on it, and she was screaming—ah, how she was screaming, like a girl of fourteen in childbirth—and the demons all kept yelling, 'Louder, play louder, so we cannot hear her scream . . .' " She shuddered and buried her head against Magda's shoulder.

Magda stroked Jaelle's soft hair, comprehending what had happened. Even the themes in the nightmares they had shared had been all but identical.

She wondered if Camilla and the others were suffering nightmare too. She was almost afraid to try to sleep again. "I thought this place was guarded," she said, "that even the names of that witch and her people could not be spoken here. . . ."

"I think that was only while we were sick and exhausted," Jaelle ventured. "Now that we are well again, and there are decisions to be made, nightmares can move in our minds, those demons—" she hesitated, said tentatively ". . . torturing us?"

But Magda could not attend to the question. A wave of horror swept through her, making her physically ill with its impact.

She was lying on the ground, chained hand and foot at the center of a ring of robed and hooded figures . . . no; they were men, scarred bandits, wielding knives, naked, their gross hairy bodies and erect phalluses touching her everywhere, intruding into her everywhere, and they were like razors, like knives shearing off her breasts, invading her womb, tearing her womanhood from her. One of them, an evil hawk-faced man with a scar, held up the body of a naked, bleeding child, a fetus half-formed, shrieking, "Here is the Heir to Hastur that she may never bear!" *Slowly, slowly, the face of the bandit changed, became, not gross and scarred, but noble, pale, detached, the face of the sorceress Leonie . . . No; it was a man's face. The face of the regent, Lorill Hastur.* "How can I acknowledge as my own child a girl who has been so treated, so scarred?" *he asked coldly, and turned away. . . .*

"Magda!" Jaelle clutched at her in horror; Magda freed herself from the terrible paralysis of nightmare. Once before during the waking of her own *laran* she had become a part of Camilla's nightmares. A dreadful time; and the worst of it had been Camilla's horror and shame, that she could not barricade these memories and horrors from her friend and lover.

She bent over Camilla and shook her awake.

"You were crying out in your sleep, love. Were you having a bad dream?"

Magda had seen this before: how Camilla struggled up from the paralysis of terror. With shaking hands, she wiped the sweat of nightmare from her face, fighting to compose herself.

"Aye," she whispered at last. "My thanks for waking me, oath-sisters." She knew, and she knew they knew, what she had been dreaming. But she could trust them to ask no questions, and she was grateful.

The next morning, Cholayna's color was good, and her breathing so easy that the women who came to bring the breakfast porridge dismantled the steam tent and took it away. Cholayna sat up and dressed herself, all except her boots, saying she felt perfectly well.

But Magda knew this raised again the question they had been avoiding while Cholayna's life was in danger, and she found herself dreading the debate. Cholayna could face no more rough weather and exposure.

Yet how likely was it that she would agree to go back, and could she turn over the search for Lexie to Vanessa and Magda? *Would* she? Magda doubted it.

So they carefully avoided the subject, and Magda felt the enforced silence fraying away at her nerves. It was a fine bright day, and Vanessa went out to walk along the cliffs, trying to scan out a route ahead. Magda walked with her a little way.

"Tell me, Vanessa, did you have bad dreams last night?"

Vanessa nodded, but she turned her face away, her cheeks crimson, and did not volunteer to say what she had dreamed, and Magda did not ask. They were under attack again; the Sisterhood of the Wise was most effectively guarded by the Sisterhood of the Dark or so it seemed . . . or could it be that the two were inextricably intertwined? Her own nightmare and Jaelle's had come from their own inner demons and flaws, not from anything anyone had imposed on them from the outside.

But Camilla? This was no nightmare based on something she had done wrong, no background of mistake or cruelty or omission coming back to haunt her, as with Jaelle and Magda, but something done to an innocent child who had no way deserved any of it. . . .

Jaelle had asked the unanswerable question: *Why do the wicked flourish?* But even the *cristoforos* had no answer to that question; they framed the question itself in poetic language and called it a mystery of their God.

Vanessa was involved at the moment not in philosophical speculations, but practical realities.

"We'll have to go on from here, on foot. A couple of *chervines* might make it, but I can't imagine taking a horse over those trails."

"Do you think Cholayna can make it?"

"Hellfire, Lorne, I'm no mind reader. But she'll insist on trying, and I don't think I'd be able to stop her. You want to try convincing her? No? I thought not."

When they went back to the building where they had spent the last few nights, Camilla was on her feet, bowing to someone in the lee of the fireplace. Magda and Vanessa came in, and Jaelle said, as if completing an introduction she had begun, "and these are our companions Vanessa n Erin and Margali n'ha Ysabet."

Magda came around the fire and saw a small, slight young woman, with her hair in a long braid down her back, as the countrywomen around Caer Donn wore it. She wore a simple knee-length tunic, dark saffron-color, embroidered at neck and sleeves with a childish pattern of leaves and flowers, and simple unadorned brown riding breeches. Otherwise she wore no jewelry or ornament except for a plain copper ring in her left ear.

She said, "My name is Kyntha." She spoke the ordinary *casta* of the hill country, but slowly and carefully.

"I have been sent for, and I must go soon. Tell me why you have come into this country, so far beyond Nevarsin?"

Jaelle leaned forward and whispered so softly that no one else could hear, "This is the woman Rakhaila told me about." Aloud she said, "We came after friends of ours. Now we have cause to think they have met with catastrophe, or captivity."

Kyntha said nothing, and Jaelle dug into a pocket and pulled out Rafaella's letter, which had started them on their travels.

"I do not know if it is the custom in your country for women to read and write—"

"I can read, yes," said Kyntha, stretching out her hand for the letter. She read it slowly and carefully, her lips moving as if it were in some other language.

Then she said, "What do you want of me? If it is the Sisterhood of the Wise that your friend seeks, I think you know she failed before she started."

"Can you help us rescue her?" Jaelle asked.

"No." It was flat, final, left no room for discussion or argument, and had more impact than a dozen protestations or excuses.

"Nevertheless, for the sake of our friendship, I must attempt it," said Jaelle.

"If you must, you must. But beware of being dragged into the causes which she set in motion. And if you save her from the effects of her own folly, what then? Will you safeguard her all her life lest she fall again into error?"

Vanessa began, "If she has trespassed unwittingly on your sacred Sisterhood, would you punish her for ignorance?"

"Does the snow punish the child who strays into it without cloak or hood or boots? Is the child less frozen for that?"

That was, Magda thought, another conversation-stopper. At last Jaelle asked, "Can you help us find the way to the City where the Sisterhood dwells?"

Kyntha said, even more deliberately:

"If I knew the way to that place, I should be sworn never to tell. I think you know this much. Why then do you ask?"

"Because I know that there are some who have come and gone," Jaelle said, "and why should I look for a key to a strange lock when, perhaps, knocking politely on the door will gain me entrance?"

Kyntha smiled fleetingly for the first time.

"Some have gained entrance there. It is not for me to say you would not be welcomed. Who told you of that place?"

"My foster-mother, for one," Jaelle said. "Though I never thought I would seek it. But now it seems to me that the time has come."

"And your companions? Do you speak for them?"

Jaelle opened her mouth, then shut it again. Finally she said, "No. I will let them speak for themselves."

"Good." Kyntha looked at each of them in turn, but there was a perceptible silence. At last Cholayna said, "I have no wish to trespass upon your City. My interest is in one of the young women mentioned in the letter."

"Is she your daughter or your lover? Or is she a child that you seek to keep her from the consequences of her own actions, daughter of Chandria?" Magda was surprised that Kyntha, after the hasty mass introductions, remembered Cholayna's name.

"None of those. But she was my student; I trained her. I accept responsibility for her failure."

"Arrogance," Kyntha said. "She is a grown woman. The choice to fail was her own, and she is entitled to bear her own mistakes."

Vanessa interrupted in an argumentative tone, "If it is forbidden to help a friend in your city, I hope I may never go there. Dare you tell us that it is forbidden, or unlawful by your rules, to help a friend?"

Kyntha's eyes met Vanessa's for a long moment. Then she said in the same serious manner, "Your motives are good. So with the child who wanted to help the tigercat move her kits to a warm and cozy den in his own bed. You do not know what you are doing, and you will not be spared because your motives were admirable."

Her eyes moved on to Camilla. "Do you seek the City, or are you here only from an ill-conceived desire to share the fate of your friends?"

"If you scoff at friendship, or even at love," Camilla retorted, "then I care not what you think of me. My reasons for seeking that city are my own, and you have not yet convinced me that I should entrust them to you. What evidence have I that the key is in your hands?"

"Good," Kyntha remarked. "There are many who know the way to that place, but some of those who offer to show you the way do not know it as well as they think they do. It is not impossible that permission would be granted for you, and perhaps for this one—" she indicated Jaelle with a faint movement of her head. "I don't know. If it is ordained that you shall be allowed to seek that end to your journey, then you may be guided or even helped. But many have been offered help and turned back, and some who persevered could not finish the journey, for one reason or another. You must be wise and wary." She turned to Magda and said, "And you?"

"Twice I have encountered the Sisterhood, or so I believe," Magda said. Kyntha's eyes on her were oddly compelling; Magda felt it would be unthinkable to lie before those eyes. "Once they saved my life and the life of my freemate. One of these women who in your words, *trespassed*, has also, in great crisis and at the point of death, encountered this same Sisterhood. Therefore I believed that I—and perhaps she too—had been summoned. How do you know that we have *not* been summoned, but assume immediately that either of us has chosen to trespass?"

"Because I read her companion's letter," Kyntha replied. "Even if she had been summoned, anyone who could concur in the motives of that letter would never find the place they sought. It would be for her, at that particular time, and in that particular company, an act of trespass. As for you, I have no way of knowing whether you have in fact been summoned, or whether you suffer from a delusion. If you have in truth been summoned, help will be forthcoming. And you will be left in no doubt."

Silence. At last Jaelle said, "May I ask you a question?"

"Or a dozen. I cannot promise to answer, though. I was not sent to you for that, and I am not learned or wise."

"Are you a member of that Sisterhood?"

"If I should claim to be so, how would you know I told you the truth? Anyone might make such a claim."

Camilla interrupted, "There are those among us with *laran*. Enough, at any rate, to know a liar from a sooth-teller." Her voice was bard, but Kyntha only smiled. Magda got the definite impression that she liked Camilla.

"Another question," Jaelle said. "We met with—" She hesitated, and Magda guessed she remembered they were not to speak Acquilara's name. "With one who presumed to try and give us commands in the name of the Goddess. Tell me, was she one of your Sisterhood?"

"Why do you question your own instincts, Shaya n'ha Melora? Will you let me counsel you a little, as much as I may?"

"Certainly," said Jaelle.

"Then this is what I advise you. Be silent. Speak to no one of your objective, and never, thrice never, name the evil you distrust. It would be simpler for your little daughter to cross Ravensmark Pass in her silken indoor slippers and armed only with a wooden spoon against the banshee, than for you to enter into that place in the wrong company. And there are some who, if you are summoned, will attempt to stop you out of jealousy, or from the sheer love of mischief-making. If help is sent to you, trust your instincts." She bowed, somehow including all of them in the gesture.

"I wish you good fortune, whether you believe it or not," she said, and without any more fuss or any kind of leavetaking, went away.

"Well," said Cholayna, when it was obvious that she would not return, "what are we to make of *that?*"

"I've no idea," Jaelle said. "But I wouldn't count on hospitality from these people much longer. We've had our warning, we're rested and well again, now it's up to us to decide whether we are going on, or back."

"I am not going back," said Camilla. "I gather from what she said that the city we seek is near, and as for a city of Avarra's Sisterhood, it would be safer to assume it is nearer Avarra's holy house, than farther. She said nothing of sending us back."

"And I think perhaps she was sent to determine how determined we are," said Jaelle. "She certainly did her best to discourage us."

"That wasn't the idea I got at all," Magda protested. She thought Kyntha had been admirably straightforward. "However, if she's gone to make some sort of report to her superiors, maybe we ought to wait until the report's gone through and the verdict delivered. She said help might be forthcoming, even guides."

"I gather we all agree on one thing, that she was sent, and that she is not a member of—the *other* crew," Vanessa said. "She acted, though, as if there was no question of letting me, or Cholayna, near the place. Just you two and maybe Magda." She looked, mildly startled, at Magda. "I noticed she treated you as if you were one of the Darkovans yourself."

Magda felt she should have noticed that herself. *Yes surely, she had a right to be considered among the Darkovans.* But did she really, or was that merely a flattering assumption? And why was she worrying about this, questioning her own motives, at this late date? She had surely gone too far to turn back now.

"I think we should leave as soon as we can, then," said Jaelle.

"I think we should wait to see if the help they hinted at is offered," Magda demurred.

"I don't agree," said Camilla, "and do you know the reason why? She said she could give us no help in rescuing Lexie and Rafaella. She treated Cholayna and Vanessa as if they were slightly unwelcome intruders, in spite of the kindness and hospitality they had been offered. My guess is this: if we wait for their help, it will come at the price of sending you two—" she nodded at the two Terrans, "back at once, and on abandoning all hope of rescuing Rafaella. I'm not ready to do that."

"Nor I," said Magda. "I think we should pack at once, and go as soon as we possibly can." She added, diffidently, "None of us has been ready to try this, but I believe it's our last resort; I am willing to try to follow Lexie and Rafaella with *laran*, no matter in whose hands they may now be. You, Jaelle?"

"I would be afraid of picking up—that *other*," Jaelle said, troubled, but Camilla shook her head.

"If they're in *her* hands, as I have begun to suspect, we have no choice. I see Lexie and Rafaella, and I see—*her*. Shaya, is this what happens when you call it *laran*?"

But there was no leisure to answer the question. First a couple of the attendants came in, scurrying. Then the old woman who had tended Cholayna walked in with kindly assurance, and took her seat among them.

And behind her came a small sturdy woman at whom they blinked for a moment, disbelieving. If the Terran Legate himself had walked in, Magda could not have felt more amazement, more disruption of everything she had expected.

"Well, this looks like a meeting of the Hellers branch of the Bridge Society," the woman said. "Isn't anyone even going to wish me good day?"

But they were all too astonished to speak. It was Cholayna, at last, who croaked, in a voice still hoarse and rasping, "I should have known. Hello, Marisela."

Chapter 25

"Marisela! How did you get here?" demanded Jaelle.

"Same way you did; riding when I could, walking when I couldn't, climbing when I had to," Marisela said. "Of course, since I knew where I was going, I took the straight road as far as Nevarsin.

"You might have told us," Camilla said.

"Yes," said Marisela dryly, "I could have held your hand every step of the way. Don't be a fool, Camilla. What I said to Margali is still true, I was not and am not free to discuss the affairs of the Sisterhood with outsiders, and that includes their abode, and the necessary search, unaided, to reach them."

"If they demand this much effort to reach them," Camilla asked, "how do we know it is worth this kind of suffering?"

"You don't. No one forced you to come. Be very clear about that, Camilla. At any moment you could have turned back to safety and to known rewards and everything you have claimed for yourself from life. There is no reason to renounce any of it, and for you, less reason than most. Yet I notice that none of you chose to turn back."

"This is all beside the point," Vanessa said. "Whatever psychic search you are talking about, Camilla, our interest is only in finding Lexie and Rafaella."

But it was Marisela who answered.

"Are you very sure of that, Vanessa? I notice you have not turned back, either. Have you gained nothing from this trip yourself? Is your search entirely unselfish?"

"I wish you'd stop talking in riddles," Vanessa complained. "What's that got to do with it?"

"Everything," said Marisela, "think carefully, now. Because on your answer may depend whether or not you are allowed to go on. Friendship may carry you far, and please don't think I am deriding the good instinct to help your friends. But in the long run, Vanessa ryn Erin—" Magda was startled and shocked that she used, not the Guild-house name by which Vanessa was known there, and in the Bridge Society, but Vanessa's Terran, legal name—"In the long run, nothing matters but your own motives for this quest. Have you gained nothing?"

"Is that wrong?" Vanessa asked aggressively.

Marisela hesitated and looked for a moment at the old priestess in her bundled rags, seated impassively on the stone dais. The old woman raised her eyes and looked sharply at Vanessa. For a moment Magda expected that she would attack, with those quick harsh words she could use and demolish Vanessa with some sharp answer. But the ancient's voice was surprisingly gentle.

"She does not question thee about right or wrong, little sister. Thee seeks right, us knows that, or thee would be outside in the storm, whatever thy need; shelter is not offered here to those who actively seek to harm their fellow beings. Thy sister asks thee, of many good things, has thee found something which is thy own and to thy liking? Speak sooth now and fear nothing."

"I can't believe that you are asking me this," Vanessa said impatiently. "Yes, one of the reasons I came on this trip was because I wanted to see these mountains, wanted a chance to climb some of them, and I knew I'd never get the chance otherwise, and I was prepared to put up with a lot for that chance. That doesn't mean I wasn't sincere about helping to find Lexie and Rafaella."

"I didn't know you were so fond of her," Marisela observed.

"*Fond* has nothing to do with it," Vanessa said angrily. "She's not my lover or my bosom friend or confidante, I'm not—well, I know it's the custom here and there's nothing wrong with it, but I'm not *interested* in women as lovers. But we were in Training School together, and she's in trouble. She needs friends, and she doesn't have many. I suppose if I was in trouble she'd give me a hand. Or what else is all your talk about sisterhood—and I don't mean all this stuff about secret Sisterhoods and societies, either—what's it supposed to mean, if I can't try to help out a friend? And Rafaella, well, she's a mountaineer. I *respect* her. Can't you understand that kind of thing?"

The old woman was smiling, but Vanessa took no notice of her. Marisela nodded to Vanessa, almost a formal gesture of recognition.

She said, "Rafaella and I were housebound together in Thendara Guild-house; it seems a long time ago. I am worried about her myself; she was one of the reasons I came so far. She has a right to her own search, even if what she seeks is riches, but I was afraid she was getting into deep waters where she could not swim, thinking only that she was doing legitimate business. I knew Jaelle was concerned about her, and if it was only a question of bad weather and a rough trail, Jaelle, with you to help her, could have been left to the search. But there were other things involved and I hoped to keep her from getting into them without a clear idea of what she might be facing." She sighed heavily. "So, you have not caught up with her?"

"As you can see, we have not," Camilla said dryly. "As if you did not know, being a *leronis* . . ."

"I'm no more omniscient than you are, Camilla. Until I actually came here, I still hoped. But if she was not safe *here* during that great storm, there are two possibilities; either she is safe *somewhere else* . . ." she spoke the words with a careful intonation and a hesitant glance at the old woman, and Magda knew suddenly that she was speaking of Acquilara and her followers, "or she is dead. For there was no other shelter and nothing could have lived unsheltered in these hills. I can't bear to think they could be in the hands of—" She blinked angrily, and Magda noticed she was trying hard to stifle uncontrollable tears.

The old woman bent toward her and said soothingly, touching Marisela's hand, "Thee may hope she is safe dead, granddaughter."

Cholayna, who had been following all this with close, concentrated attention—Magda, who had been through the same kind of training, knew what effort it would take her to follow this conversation in the language they were using, though Cholayna had had the best and most effective language training in the whole of the Empire—spoke up for the first time.

"Marisela, I'm like Vanessa, I can't believe I'm hearing this. Are these people so jealous that they'd really hope Lexie and Rafaella are *dead*, rather than involved with some religious heresy? I've heard of religious bigotry, but this beats anything I ever heard of! I'm not ungrateful to these people. They saved my life, saved Vanessa from being lamed for life—they saved us all. But I still think that's *terrible!*"

It was the old woman who spoke, slowly, as if—she were trying to make Cholayna understand across an insurmountable barrier.

"Thee is ignorant. This old one canna' give thee a lifetime wisdom in a few minutes on this floor. But if thee canna' imagine worse than simple dyin' thee is worse than ignorant. Are there na' things thee would die rather than do? Those whose names we would not speak—" she stopped, frowned, shook her head in frustration almost tangible.

"How to say to thee? Would thee rather die, or torture a helpless child? Would thee rather die, or betray thy innermost honor? It is their joy, those ones, to see others do that which they thought they would rather die than do, out of their weak fear of dyin', because they know nothing an' believe less about death." Her head shook with wrath. "An', an', to speak their name is to invite them into thy mind. Think this old one hates thee, that she takes that risk for thee and thy ignorance, sister, to try an' teach thee a crumb's worth of wisdom."

Magda looked at Jaelle, and for one blazing instant, whether it was *laran* or something deeper, it all came together in her mind. It was all one with what Jaelle had said the night before: *We're all going to die anyway.*

Magda was remembering dreadful things done, in the history of the human race, by men to their fellow men—and women—

because they so feared death: guards who had forced their fellow creatures to death in concentration camps; the immense slaughter of war where the killer justified himself by fear of being killed in turn; infinite terrible betrayals out of that most ignoble fear—*I'll do anything, anything, I don't want to die . . .* It was bad enough to do these evils because in some demented way you thought they were good, like the religious monsters who burned, hanged or slaughtered others to save their souls. But what possible justification could there be for anyone who did these things because the alternative was personal death? In a single blazing moment, Magda felt a fierce joy. It suffused her with a flush, an almost physical rush of total awareness, knowing how strong was life and how little death had to do with it.

In a great rush she felt totally involved and caught up in it; aware of her intense love for Jaelle, *of course, this was why I risked my life for her;* her wholly different love for Camilla. Love reached out for no reason even to encompass that ridiculous old woman, *she doesn't even know Cholayna and she is risking what she thinks of as a very real spiritual death for her, she fears she's inviting Acquilara and her crew into her very head to play games with her, and because she loves us. . . .*

They could only kill me, and that wouldn't matter. Dying hurts, but death won't.

And then she snapped out of it, astonished at her own thoughts. There was no question—nobody had asked her to die for anything! *What's wrong with me? I don't want to die any more than anyone else, why am I indulging myself in heroics?*

And then she wondered if it had all been imagination; for Cholayna was saying, with polite strained patience, that she didn't really think the question had any application here.

"No one has offered me that choice. And with all respect, I find it hard to believe that these rival sisterhoods, or whatever they are, will behave like some old legendary dictator or brainwashing expert and offer them a choice between death or dishonor. How absurdly melodramatic!" Then Cholayna bent toward the old woman, very serious.

"Whenever I hear anyone say there are things more important

than life or death, I find myself wondering whose life they are planning to risk. I find it is seldom their own."

The old woman's toothless smile was gentle, almost despairing.

"Thee means well, but thee is ignorant, daughter of Chandria. 'Varra great thee lives long enough that thee may one day learn wisdom to match thy good strength and will."

Marisela stood up, as if gathering up the scattered threads of her discourse.

"It's time to go, while the weather holds, and the only way to go is to get going. Are you ready to leave?"

Jaelle said quietly, "I told you, Magda. We were warned to be ready."

Camilla thrust her hands into the pocket of her tunic, and demanded, "Go where?"

"To the place you have been seeking. Where else?"

"To the City of—"

"Hush," Marisela said quickly, "don't speak it aloud. No. I am serious. Word and thought have power."

"Oh, in the name of the Goddess, or of all Zandru's demons, Marisela, spare me your mystical rubbish!"

"Do you dare to tell me that? You know better, however you have tried to barricade it, *Elorie Hastur*."

Camilla actually laid her hand on her knife.

"Damn you, my name is *Camilla n'ha Kyria*—"

Marisela stared her down.

"And still you say names have no power, Camilla?"

Camilla folded herself abruptly into a seat, her voice gone.

Magda began matter-of-factly to gather their possessions. The enforced stay of days in that room had made it a gypsy-camp clutter, though they had tried to keep what order they could. The old woman rose stiffly; Marisela stooped to assist her. Camilla strode toward her.

"Grandmother of many mysteries! Is a question permitted the ignorant?"

"How else shall they be instructed?" asked the old woman mildly.

"How did you know—" she stopped and swallowed and finally said, "all that?"

"To those who see beyond surfaces, little daughter—" her voice was infinitely gentle, "it is written in thine every scar, every line of thy face. In the energies which surround thy body it can be read as clearly as a hunter of the wild *chervine* reads the spoor of his game. Fear not; thy friend—" she nodded at Marisela, "broke not thy confidence. This one swears it."

"She couldn't," said Camilla brusquely. "She didn't have it." She stared quizzically at Marisela, and Magda could almost hear the words: *did she read me too, does she know everything about me?*

Then she asked, her voice abrupt and harsh, but speaking clearly in the mountain dialect the old woman spoke, "Thee makes it thy task to search out old names and buried pasts. May I then ask thine own, Mother?"

The toothless smile was serene.

"This one has no name. It was forgotten in another life. When thee has reason to know, *chiya*, thee will read it clear as I read thine. Avarra bless thy long road, little one. Few of thy sisters have had such trials. How shall the fruit grow unless the blossoms are pruned from the tree?"

She smiled benevolently, and closed her eyes as if falling into the sudden light sleep of senility. Marisela looked at Camilla almost in awe, but didn't speak.

"How soon can we get out of here? It's a fine day; let's take advantage of it."

In a surprisingly short time they were ready to leave. The sky was cloudless, but the wind blew across the heights as they approached the cliff. They went in two shifts, and Magda, edging unobtrusively back to wait for the second, watched with horror as the basket jerked and wobbled and bumped against the cliffs. The rope looked too small to hold it, though it was a mighty cable of twisted fibers almost three fingers thick. She turned away her eyes, knowing if she did not she would never have the courage to get into the contraption.

Jaelle, Cholayna and Camilla, with Marisela, had gone in the first load. As the basket came bumping back to where she stood with Vanessa and the old blind woman Rakhaila, Magda recoiled; coming up in the dark was one thing, but in broad daylight, she could not, she *could not* force herself to step into it.

Rakhaila felt her cringe, and guffawed.

"Haw! Haw! Ye rather climb down cliff, missy? I be old an' blind, an' I do so every livin' day. Steps be right yonder." She gave Magda a push toward the edge, and Magda cried out and fell to her knees, grabbing for safety; in another moment she might have stumbled over that terrifying edge.

Vanessa caught her arm. She whispered, "It's perfectly strong, really. There's nothing to be afraid of, Magda, they've evidently been going up and coming down here for centuries and it's never failed them yet." She steadied Magda's arm as she managed, carefully turning her eyes away from the narrow dizzying gap between basket and ground far below, to step over the edge, and sink in, her eyes on the floor of the basket, strewn with bits of straw and grain.

Where do they get their food and grain up here? Does it all have to be hauled up in this one basket? she asked herself, knowing that it was just a way to keep herself from being afraid. And then she was sourly amused at herself.

All my fine theories about not being afraid of death, and here I am almost wetting my breeches with fright because of a primitive elevator that's probably just as safe as the ones in the Terran HQ!

Acrophobia, she reminded herself, was, by definition, not a *rational* fear. But surely it hadn't been nearly as bad as this when she first crossed Scaravel with Jaelle seven, no, eight years ago. And she remembered positively enjoying her first trip to Nevarsin with Peter when they had both been in their twenties.

With unbelievable relief she felt the basket touch ground and scrambled out.

"You're going with us, Marisela?"

"Of course, my dear. But I don't know all the ins and outs of the trail; Rakhaila will guide us. The horses will have to stay here. We'll take one pack animal and leave everything else for the return journey."

Wondering vaguely how a blind woman could guide them on a confusing trail which even Marisela could not find, Magda volunteered to lead the pack *chervine* for the first stretch. Down here the wind was not the jet stream of the heights, but still blew so strongly that old Rakhaila's matted hair blew out behind her magnificently as she set off in the teeth of the gale.

The snow was slushy under foot, and the wind cut hard; but Magda, wrapping her woolly scarf over her face, was grateful that it was not freezing. Vanessa, she noticed, was still limping a little. She followed Rakhaila close; behind her came Jaelle, then Camilla with Cholayna at her side; at least at the start, Cholayna set off fresh and strong and rested, and her breathing was good. Perhaps she had managed to acclimate to the altitude by now. They would not have let her go, she told herself, if there had been any sign of continuing pneumonia.

They set off along a trail which led across the knife-edge of a ridge, with a long drop to either side. Magda, leading the *chervine* behind Cholayna and Camilla, looked to the right, where the slope was gradual and gentle, and did not make her dizzy. The trail was just wide enough for one, but looked quite well-traveled; where the snow had melted Magda could see that it had been beaten down hard as if by generations of feet.

Behind Magda and the *chervine* was Marisela bringing up the rear. The fierce wind prevented much talk, and they went on at a smart pace.

An hour on the trail; part of another. The five days of rest had done Magda good; her heart no longer beat furiously with the altitude. Lower down she could see the tops of trees. A good place for banshees, she thought dispassionately, looking out over the icy wastes below her, on either side of the ridge, but even they would have starved to death centuries ago.

Rakhaila flung up her arm with a long shrill cry and they came to a halt.

"Rest ye here; eat if ye ha' need." Rakhaila herself, thought Magda, looked as if she had been battered into stoicism by all the winds of a hundred years; as they got out the camp stove and brewed tea she hunkered by the trail, immobile, looking like a random bunch of rags, and when Camilla offered her a mug of the brew she shook her head contemptuously.

Camilla muttered, "Now *there's* an Amazon who makes us all look like puppies!" She gnawed on a half-frozen meat bar.

Cholayna had one of the cakes made from ground-up nuts and fruit stuck together with honey; she munched at the stuff with determination.

Magda heard her ask Camilla: "Do you really think they are dead?"

"Marisela isn't given to exaggeration and I've never known her to lie. If she says they're probably dead, she means it. Or else, as she said, they're in the hands of Acquilara, or whoever else is hanging around."

"And we're still looking for this, whatever it is, this City of Sorceresses? I think we ought to try and trace where the *others* have gone, try to find out where Acquilara could have taken them. If they're being held for ransom, we can pay it. And if they want to fight, well, I'll try that too."

Rakhaila's old filmed eyes turned to Cholayna. She said, "Ha' ye a care what ye ask, sister; the goddess may gi' it to ye."

"I'll take that chance, if you will guide me there," said Cholayna quietly. "Marisela can take these others on to the City, or wherever they prefer to go. *Will* you guide me to whatever place Marisela believes our friends are being held?"

Rakhaila only gave a contemptuous, "Haw!" and turned away.

Jaelle and Camilla were sitting on their packs, eating meat bars. Magda heard them talking about Kyntha.

"She said, 'Never name the evil you fear.' Does that mean such things as weather? Is it wrong to discuss the storm that's coming?" Jaelle asked.

"Wrong? Of course not. Wise? Only if you can do something to avoid it. Certainly it is sensible to discuss precautions you can take. Apart from that, it only creates a self-fulfilling fear of something that can't be helped. Don't talk of how terrible the storm might be; think of what you can do to ride it out undamaged."

"Then why did she tell us not to talk about Acquilara or even mention her name?" Marisela smiled. Magda noticed it was the same cheerful, dimpled smile she used when she was instructing the young Renunciates in the Guild-house.

"I have spent too much of my life as a teacher," she remarked, "I must be getting old; I am glad that there are wiser heads than mine to instruct you two. In brief, naming them could attract their attention; thoughts, as we know, have power."

"But who *are* they, Marisela? I can just manage to believe in one benevolent Sisterhood demonstrating some interest in the affairs of women—"

"Of humankind, Camilla. Our sisters and our brothers as well."

"But the idea that there is a rival organization dedicated to doing harm to humanity strains my belief!"

Marisela looked troubled. She said, "This is not the wisest place to discuss their doings. Let me say only that—Jaelle, you must have heard this among the Terrans as I heard it when I was in nurse's training there—*for every action there is an equal and opposite reaction.*"

"So they are a reaction to the good sorceresses, and do evil?"

"Not that simple. I can only say that they care not enough to do evil to humankind; they want what they want, that is all. They want power."

"Is that a bad thing?" Jaelle argued. "You are always telling the young girls, in Training Session, that women have a right to claim power—"

"Power over *themselves*, my dear! That kind of power is in accord with the Sisterhood. We have only one aim; that in the fullness of time, everyone who comes to this world shall become everything that he or she can be or do or accomplish. We do not fall into the error of thinking that if only people would do this or thus, the world would thereby be made perfect. Perfection is for individuals, one at a time, we do not determine the way they choose to live. Nevertheless, when the Sisterhood sees long-term trends and dangers, they nurture—how shall I put it—tendencies which will break these patterns and give people a chance to live another way." She smiled gently at Camilla and said, "I do not know; perhaps it was a part of the pattern that you should not have grown up to be the powerful Keeper you were so obviously born to be."

"Keeper? I?" Camilla snorted indignantly. "Even had I grown to womanhood in my father's house—my *real* father, that is, and after this I should be a fool if I did not suspect who he was . . ."

"Right. Can you imagine yourself in the sorceress Leonie's position?"

"I would rather—" Camilla began, drew a long breath, and said on a note of surprise, as if she had just this moment thought of it, "I would rather have wandered the roads all my life as a bandit's sword-mate!"

"Exactly," said Marisela, "but had you been reared in the silks and privileges of the royal house of Hastur, I doubt you would have felt that way, but would willingly have followed Leonie into Arilinn. Ah, Camilla, Camilla love, don't fall into the error of thinking this was your destiny, ordained in stone before you were born. But if some God or well-meaning saint had put forth his hand to save you from your fate, where would you be today?"

Of course, Magda thought. It was the totality of her life that had made Camilla what she was.

Camilla asked, "Did you know? Before this?"

"I knew of you, till this very day only what you chose to tell me, Camilla, and what once I read in your mind and heart when you were—broadcasting; believe me, I have never invaded your privacy. What you *were* is of no interest to me."

Jaelle said aggressively, "I suppose now you will say that the

Sisterhood chose to save my life and Magda's for some reason—"

"I am not privy to all their reasons! Shaya, child, I am only one who serves them, one of many messengers. I am free to guess, no more. Perhaps they felt some long-term purpose would be served that the daughter of Aillard should bear a child lest her *laran* be lost to the world forever. Perhaps they wished some psychic gift of the Terrans to be strengthened in the Forbidden Tower and thus brought Magda there after she had decided she wished for a child, so her little Shaya would be reared among those who would foster her *laran*. Perhaps some one of them succumbed, as I do even when I know it might be better not, to the simple wish to save a life. Who can tell? They too are only human, and make mistakes, though they can see further than we do. But no one is perfect. Perfectable, maybe, in the fullness of time. Not perfect."

"Yet after they went to all the trouble of saving Lexie's life they let her fall into the hands of—Acquilara? I'm sorry, Marisela, I just can't believe that."

"I never asked you to believe anything," said Marisela, suddenly indifferent, and rose to her feet. "Except that just now, I believe Rakhaila wants us to move on, and my legs are cramped from sitting down. Can I help you pack the kettle?"

As they went on Magda had plenty to think about. If what they said about *laran* in those of Terran blood was true, she thought, I am surprised that I was not somehow pushed into having Andrew's child; heaven knows, he has about the strongest *laran* of any Terran I have ever known. But evidently they allow total free will. They left me to destiny. And I have heard that the Syrtis are an old Hastur sect; so Shaya is kinswoman to Camilla by blood as well as to Jaelle by the laws of a freemate's oath.

That was reassuring. *If anything happens to me, Shaya will have kinfolk who will care for her. She and Cleindori are sisters indeed.*

Jaelle said, "I'll take the *chervine* now for a bit, *breda*," and Magda relinquished the rein, moving forward to walk at Marisela's side. The path was leading upward now, edging alongside a mountain trail with long switchbacks, hugging a stone cliff from which, sometimes, loose rocks bounced downward; but the trail at this point was covered with an overhang and Rakhaila strode confidently along it as if she could see every step of her way.

"Want to walk on the inside?" Marisela asked. "As I remember, heights bother you." ·

"A little," Magda said, and accepted, and they strode along side by side for a time, without talking. At last Magda asked:

"Marisela, these—I won't name them; you know who I mean—" the picture of Acquilara was in her mind, in the curious bluish glow of her nightmare, "May I ask just one thing? Why would anyone—want to go that way? Are they the ones who, maybe, tried to—to look for the *real* Sisterhood and failed? And this was easier?"

"Oh, no, my dear. It takes much, *much* more strength and power to do evil than to do good, you see."

"Why is that? I heard that evil was just being weak, taking the path of least resistance—"

"Goodness, no. That's just being weak, fearful, selfish . . . in a word, human, imperfect. If being weak were a crime we'd all stand before the judges. That's excusable. Terrible sometimes, but certainly excusable. The thing is, people who are good, or are *trying* to do good the best way they can, they're working with nature, see? To work up the power to do positive evil, you have to go *against* nature, and that's much, *much* harder. There are resistances, and you have to work up momentum against the whole flow of nature."

This was a new idea to Magda, that good was simply fulfilling nature's plan and evil was anything which worked against it. She was sure she did not entirely understand it, for Marisela was a midwife and a nurse and, taken to extremes, this could be interpreted as a prohibition against saving lives, which Marisela had spent her whole life doing. She decided she would have to talk further about it some time with her friend. She was never to have the chance.

They were taking a long dip now, along the steep trail, into a long valley below the timberline. Before they dipped into the trees, Marisela called softly to Rakhaila to halt a moment, and pointed upward. Across the valley was a long line of steep ice cliffs, shining in the crimson brilliance of the sun.

"The Wall Around the World," she said.

They drew together, watching, stunned. Vanessa drew a long, overawed breath. But all she could find to say was, "They look—bigger than they do from a plane in M-and-Ex."

That was an understatement. They seemed to go on forever, far past sight. Magda thought, God, we're not going over *that*, not on foot, are we?

Rakhaila gestured impatiently and set off at a swinging pace that took her out of sight among the trees. Camilla and Jaelle followed, but Cholayna dropped back beside Magda and Vanessa.

"I shall be glad to be going downhill," she said.

"Tired?"

"Not as much as I thought I should be." Cholayna smiled at her. "In a way I am more glad than ever that I came, if I could only stop worrying about Lexie."

"This must have been what she saw," said Vanessa. "It was worth it, just to see this. And we're going across it!" She made a small sound of incredulous delight.

"And in line of duty too," Cholayna said dryly. "Who was talking about rewards and wangling a working holiday, Vanessa?"

It was a pleasure Magda could gladly have dispensed with, but she would not spoil Vanessa's enjoyment. They were between the trees now, some growing at crazy angles on the slope below, others hanging thickly over the trail, darkening the bright sunlight; but it gave some shelter, too, from the wind. Rakhaila, with Camilla and Jaelle, were out of sight. Marisela turned back to gesture toward the three Terrans to hurry, and for a moment her face, smiling gaily, was frozen for Magda in sudden horror and then blotted out in a shower of blood. Her eyes were still staring; in a split second of shock Magda remembered reading somewhere that the eyes of a corpse could see for some twenty seconds after death.

Then somewhere Acquilara's gloating laugh echoed in her ears and she was dragged backward and down without a chance to struggle. She heard Cholayna's smothered gasp, the only sound she could hear—Marisela had died without a chance to scream.

I had no chance either, she thought, insanely aggrieved, before the world became dark and silent.

Chapter 26

The first thing she remembered was, *Dying hurts, but death won't.* But it did, she thought. Her arms and back felt battered, and she was sure at least one leg had been skinned.

I thought, if I died, I'd find myself in the Overworld. Cleindori said she was there before she was born. Or was that a child's dream?

Too bad. It was a beautiful idea. She was sure now that the reality would be less pleasant. But where was Marisela? If they had been killed together, shouldn't they be together now?

After a long time there began to be an orange glow, and from the distance she heard a voice.

"You bungled it, as usual. I especially wanted the other one alive, the midwife."

Acquilara's voice. *Of course. What else?*

"Shall we kill this one now, then?"

"No. I can find a use for her."

After a measurable interval Magda thought, *but they're talking about me.*

The next thought came also after a perceptible time. *If they are considering killing me, then, obviously, I'm not dead.*

And then she did not remember anything more for a long time.

When she woke again she was afraid she was blind. Darkness surrounded her, and silence except for a faraway dripping of water. Magda listened carefully, and after a time she heard soft raspy breathing. There was someone else beside her, sleeping. *Sleeping*, she thought indignantly, when Marisela has been killed, when I have been captured and beaten. How can they sleep? Then she remembered she had been sleeping or unconscious herself for a considerable time. Maybe she wasn't blind. Maybe it was dark where she was, she and the other sleeper. She didn't know . . . her eyes were closed.

As soon as that thought occurred to her, she opened her eyes.

She was lying in a cave. Above her great pale stalactites stabbed down from the roof, shadowing each other for as far as she could see, like pillars of some great Temple. In the distance there was a glow of fire flickering and throwing strange images and shadows.

She was covered with a thick fur blanket, but not tied up, as far as she could tell. That made sense. Who could run away, where could anyone go in this climate? She turned over; by the dim flickering light she could make out two blanket-wrapped forms sleeping beside her on the floor. Captors? Or fellow captives? There was not really enough light to recognize anyone. She felt at her waist and found that her dagger was gone.

"Shaya?" she whispered, and one of the motionless bundles stirred.

"Who is it? Is there someone else here?"

"Vanessa, it's Magda," she whispered. "Did they get all of us?"

"They have Cholayna. She hasn't stirred; I think they may have hit her too hard." Magda could tell that Vanessa had been crying. "I can't hear her breathing. Oh, Magda, they killed Marisela!"

"I know. I saw." Magda's throat was tight. Marisela had been her friend since almost the very first day in Thendara Guildhouse; they had worked together to found the Bridge Society. She could not believe the suddenness with which that innocent life had been snuffed out.

Why, why?

She said they were evil. She was right. I cannot remember

that Marisela ever harmed anyone, or so much as spoke an unkind word; not in my hearing, anyhow.

And now they might have killed Cholayna as well. She crawled closer to Vanessa. "Are you hurt, *breda*?" She wondered why she had never called Vanessa by this simple sisterly word before this.

"I'm—not sure. Not badly, I think, but there's a lump on my head. They must have hit me just hard enough to put me out. As far as I can tell most of my reflexes are intact. Everything works when I wiggle it."

Magda's eyes stung. How practical, and how like Vanessa. "Are any of the others here?"

"If they are, I can't see them. They could—" again Vanessa's voice quavered and Magda knew she was crying again, "they could all be dead, except us. If they'd kill Marisela—"

Magda hugged her gently in the dark, "Don't cry, *breda*. It's terrible, *they're* terrible, but we can't do her any good now with crying. Let's just make sure they don't have a chance to do any more killing. Did they take your knife?"

Vanessa managed to stop crying. *She can cry for Marisela*, Magda thought. *I can't. Yet I loved her.* She knew she had not yet really begun to feel the loss. And she faced the knowledge that Jaelle and Camilla might be dead as well. All the more reason to care for Vanessa, and Cholayna if she was still alive. She repeated softly, "Did they take your knife? They took mine."

"They have the knife I was wearing in my belt. I have a little one in my coat pocket and as far as I know they haven't got that one, not yet,"

"Look and see," Magda whispered back urgently, "and I'll see if Cholayna is—is breathing."

Vanessa began groggily searching her pockets, while Magda crept toward the inert bundle that was Cholayna Ares.

"Cholayna!" She touched the woman's hand warily. It was icy cold. The chill of a corpse? Then it occurred to Magda that it was very cold in the cave—though not nearly as cold as outside in the wind—and her own hands were nearly freezing. She fumbled to open Cholayna's coat, thrust her hand inside and felt warmth, living warmth. She bent her head close, and could hear, very faintly, the sound of breathing.

Perhaps asleep, perhaps unconscious but Cholayna was alive. She relayed this information to Vanessa in a whisper.

"Oh, thank God," Vanessa whispered, and Magda feared that she would begin to cry again.

She said hastily, "We can't do anything until we know what kind of shape she's in. I'll try to wake her."

With a possible head injury she did not dare shake her. She murmured her name repeatedly, stroked her face, chafed the icy hands between her own, and finally Cholayna stirred a little, with a painful catch of breath. She opened her eyes and stared straight at Magda without recognition.

"Let go of me—! You murdering devils—" It was obvious that Cholayna was trying to scream at the top of her voice; but the scream was no more than a pitiful whisper. It was equally obvious to Magda that if she did manage to scream, she would alert their captors, who could not be far off. She hugged Cholayna in her arms, trying to restrain the woman's struggles, saying softly and insistently, "It's all right, Cholayna. Be quiet, be quiet, I'm here with you, Vanessa's here, we won't let anyone hurt you." She repeated this over and over until at last Cholayna stopped fighting her and recognition came into her eyes

"Magda?" She blinked, put her hand to her head. "What's happened? Where are we?"

"Somewhere in a cave," Magda answered in a whisper, "and I think Acquilara and her crew have us."

Vanessa crept close to them in the dark. "I have my little knife. Are you all right, Cholayna?"

"I'm still in one piece," Cholayna said. "I saw them kill Marisela; then they hit you over the head, Magda, and grabbed me; I think I may have stabbed one of them before they got the knife away from me. Then that damned bitch Acquilara hit me over the head with a ton of bricks, and that's all I remember."

"And then we woke up here," Vanessa summed up, clutching at them both in the darkness. "Now what?"

Magda laughed, mirthlessly. "Well, you tried to bribe

Rakhaila to bring you here. She *said*, be careful what you pray for, you might get it . . . and here we are. Right in Acquilara's stronghold. At least, if Lexie and Rafaella are still alive, we're in a prime position to rescue them. Or ransom them."

Cholayna nodded; her dark face contorted in an expression of pain and she clutched her head again and held still.

"Who knows? Sooner or later, they're sure to come back for us; if they thought we were all dead, they would hardly have wasted blankets on us. I don't see Marisela laid out here awaiting proper burial, or anything so charitable."

Magda shuddered. "Oh, don't," she implored.

Cholayna leaned toward her and held her close. "There, there, I know you loved her, we all loved her," she said, "but there's nothing to be done for her now, Magda. Though if ever I get that filthy sorceress at the end of my knife . . . but now we have to think of ourselves, and what we can do to get out of here. What about Jaelle and Camilla? Do you know if they are alive or dead?"

Magda could remember nothing more than Marisela falling in a shower of blood. Then nothing.

"I saw you fall, Magda, and Cholayna," Vanessa repeated. "Jaelle and Camilla were out of sight, round a bend in the road; they may have gotten clean away, and never known we were gone until they stopped on the trail and we didn't catch up."

"Do you know how long ago that was?" Cholayna asked. But neither of them had the slightest idea of elapsed time, or even whether it was night or day. Nor did they know how many their opponents were, nor how they were armed, nor what their plans might be, or whether Jaelle and Camilla were dead.

Yet Magda had an almost totally irrational conviction . . . "I think I would know if they were dead," she said. "I think, if either of them had been killed, I am *sure* I would know."

"Being sure isn't evidence," Vanessa said, but Cholayna interrupted her.

"You're wrong. Magda has had very intensive psi-tech training. Not the kind they give in the Empire, but probably even more effective. I'd say her feelings *are* evidence, and evidence of a very high order."

"You may be right," Vanessa conceded after a moment, "but I don't see how that helps us much, since they obviously don't know where we are, or how to rescue us."

It was enough for Magda at that moment, after seeing Marisela murdered before her eyes, to be certain that both her lover and her freemate had escaped that fate. Yet she and her two Terran compatriots were in the hands of a cruel and unscrupulous woman, possibly one with some kind of *laran*—she remembered how Acquilara had struck down Camilla with a look.

She would as soon kill us, too, as look at us!

Vanessa felt the shudder and her arms tightened about Magda.

"Are you cold? Here, put my blanket round you. We might as well relax while we can; for all we know it could be early evening and they'll get a good night's sleep before they come to fetch us here. We may as well try and do likewise."

They huddled together, silent, under the blankets. Magda could pick up the dread and apprehension of the other women, the pain that crept, with the cold, into Cholayna's bones and muscles, as if in her own body. She wanted to shelter her, to protect them both, yet she was powerless.

Time crawled by; they never knew how long. Perhaps an hour, perhaps two. Magda kept falling into little dozes, where she would hear incoherent words at the very edge of hearing, see blurs of light that turned into strange faces, then jerk awake and know that none of this had happened at all, that she was still huddled between Cholayna and Vanessa in the dark and cold of their prison. She thought it was another of these tiny dreams when she began to see a light, but Vanessa stiffened at her side and whispered, "Look! They're coming!"

There was the light of a torch, bobbing up and down as if being carried, waist-high. It moved closer. It was no illusion. It was not fire on the end of a long stick. It was a small, brilliant flashlight, and in another minute she could see who was carrying it.

Lexie Anders bent over them and said, "All right, Lorne, get up and come with me. Do you see this?" Briefly, she showed Magda something that made Magda gasp; this was breaking every lawful arrangement between Terrans and Darkovans.

"It's a stunner," Alexis explained. Magda could see all too well what it was.

"For your information, it has a lethal setting. I would rather not be forced to use it, but I swear that if you try to make trouble, or attempt any silly heroics, I will. Get up. No, Van, you stay where you are, I don't choose to try to handle you both at once."

"Anders, in heaven's name, are you working with these people?" Cholayna sounded outraged. "Do you know what they are? Do you know they killed Marisela in cold blood?"

"That was a mistake," said Alexis Anders. "Acquilara was very angry about it. Marisela got in the way, that was all."

Cholayna said with hard anger, "I'm sure Marisela would be glad to know that."

"It wasn't my doing, Cholayna, and I refuse to feel guilty about it. Marisela had no business to interfere."

"Interfere? Going about her lawful business . . ." Magda cried.

Lexie moved the stunner. "You don't know a damn thing about it, Lorne, you don't know what's at stake here or what Marisela was involved in. So keep your mouth shut and come with me. If you're cold, you can bring the blanket."

Magda crawled slowly out from between Vanessa and Cholayna. Cholayna put out a hand to hold her back.

"For the record, Anders. Insubordination; defection; intrusion into closed territory without authorization; possession of an illegal weapon in violation of agreements between the Empire and duly constituted planetary authorities. You *do* know you're throwing your career away—"

"You're a stubborn old bitch," said Lexie. Shocked, Magda remembered Vanessa saying the same thing; but she had said it affectionately. "You don't know when you're beaten, Cholayna. You can still get out of this alive; I'm not bloodthirsty. But you'd better keep your mouth shut, because I don't think Acquilara is particularly tolerant of Terrans. I warn you, shut up and stay shut."

Another peremptory gesture with the stunner. Magda touched Cholayna's hand, saying in an undertone, "Don't put yourself on the line for me. This is between us. I'll see what she wants."

When she rose to her feet, she found that she was shaking all over. Was it the stunner pointed menacingly at her, was it the cold, was it simply that they must have struck her on the exact site of the previous concussion? She saw the glint of satisfaction in Lexie's eyes.

She thinks I am afraid of her and for some reason that pleases her. Well, let Lexie continue to think that. Magda realized that while she was a little bit afraid that the stunner in Lexie's hand might go off by accident, she was not at all afraid of Lexie herself.

She didn't turn a hair when Cholayna was throwing that list of indictments at her. That means one of two things. Either she's resigned to throwing her career away—or she has no intention of leaving Cholayna alive to testify against her.

Lexie waved the stunner again.

"This way."

She took Magda across the great cave filled with stalactites, gestured to her to walk down a slippery ramp, wet with falling water from somewhere, and pushed her through into another cave.

This one was lighted by torches stuck in the wall and smoking upwards; randomly Magda noted the direction of the smoke and thought, *there must be air coming in somewhere from outside.* At the center was a fire burning; at first Magda wondered where they got wood for fire, then realized from the smell it was not a wood fire at all, but a fire of dried chervine dung; a stack of the dried pats was at one side of the fire. Around the fire was a rough circle of hooded figures, and for an instant of awful disillusionment Magda thought, *is this the Sisterhood?*

Then a slender familiar figure rose from beside the fire.

"Welcome, my dear," she said. "I'm sorry my messengers had to use so much force. I told you to be ready when you were summoned, and if you had listened to me, you could have saved us a great deal of trouble."

Magda drew a deep breath, trying to compose herself.

"What do you want, Acquilara?"

Chapter 27

But Acquilara did not do business that way. Magda should have known.

"You are hurt; let us bandage your wounds. And I am sure you are cold and cramped. Would you like some tea?"

Magda sensed that to accept any offers from the black sorceress would be to yield to her power. She started to say proudly, *No, thank you, I want nothing you can give.* She never knew what stopped her.

The most serious obligation she had now was to stay as strong as possible, so that she could get away, could help get Vanessa and Cholayna out of this. She said deliberately, "Thank you." Someone handed her a foaming cup of tea. It was faintly bitter, and smelled of the dung-fire, and a lump of butter had been stirred into it, which gave it a peculiar taste, but added, in the bitter chill, to its strengthening quality. Magda drank it down and felt it warming her all through. She accepted a second cup.

Two women came from the ring around the fire to help bandage her wounds. On the surface they were somewhat more prepossessing than the women of the hermitage of Avarra; they seemed clean enough and wore under their long, hooded cloaks the ordinary dress of village women from the mountains, long tartan skirts, thick overblouses and tunics, heavy felted shawls and boots. The bandages they used were rough, but seemed clean. Magda realized that skin had been stripped from her leg—she never knew how it happened, though she surmised that in the fight she must have rolled down a slope covered with sharp rocks. There were abrasions on her face too; she had not noticed them before.

With the scrapes and bruises salved and bandaged, she did feel better, and the tea, even with its faintly nauseating taste, had strengthened her so that she felt prepared to meet whatever might come next.

"Feeling better?" Acquilara was almost purring. "Now let us sit down together and discuss this like civilized women. I am sure we can come to some agreement."

Agreement? When you have murdered my friend, imprisoned my companions, and for all I know you may have killed my free-mate and my lover? Never!

But Magda had more common sense than to say this aloud. If this woman was half the *leronis* she claimed to be, she would sense Magda's antipathy and know how little likely Magda would be to accede to her plan.

"What do you want with me, Acquilara? Why have you, as you put it, summoned me?"

"I am the servant of the Great Goddess whom you seek—"

Magda started to say, *Nonsense, you're no such thing*, but decided not to antagonize her.

"Very well then, tell me what your Goddess wants with me."

"We should be friends," Acquilara began. "You are a powerful *leronis* of the Tower called Forbidden, which has refused to play into the hands the Hasturs, or to submit to that terrible old *teneresteis* Leonie of Arilinn, who keeps all the people of the Domains paralyzed under the iron rule of the Arilinn Tower. As one who has helped to free our brothers and our sisters, you are my ally and my comrade and I welcome you here."

And Marisela? But Magda said nothing. Perhaps if she waited long enough Acquilara would tell her what really was going on. As Camilla had pointed out, even an "evil sorceress" did not go to all this trouble simply to amuse herself.

"Your friend has told me that you are from another world, and she has said something about the Empire," Acquilara began over again. Magda's eyes strayed to Lexie where she stood in the corner. She had put the stunner out of sight. "You are a powerful *leronis*, but you owe nothing to the *Comyn*. And among your companions are two others of *Comyn* blood. Am I not right?"

"You have been correctly informed," she said. *Casta* was a stiff language and Magda wasted none of its formality.

"Nevertheless, I cannot imagine what all this has to do with the fact that you have murdered one of my friends and imprisoned others."

"I told you, Acquilara, you wouldn't get anywhere with her that way," said a voice from the shadows where Lexie stood. Rafaella n'ha Doria did not have a stunner, or any weapon Magda could see except for the usual long knife of a Renunciate.

"Let me talk to her. In a word, Margali, she knows you have had *laran* training in your Forbidden Tower, or whatever it may be. But you are Terran. On the other hand, Jaelle, born *Comyn*, has renounced her *Comyn* heritage, and as a Renunciate she is free to use her powers as she will."

She stood waiting for Magda to confirm what she said; instead, Magda burst out in anger.

"I would not have believed it if they had told me, Rafi! You, whom she loves as a sister, to sell her out this way! And Camilla, too, calls you her friend!"

"You don't know what you are talking about," Rafaella said angrily. "Sell her out? Never! It is you who have induced her to betray herself, and I am trying to remedy that." She came all the way forward and stood facing Magda.

"You have not even let Acquilara tell you what she is offering. No harm is intended to Shaya, or even to Camilla—"

"That is the red-headed *emmasca*?" Acquilara nodded with satisfaction. "She has *Comyn* powers, perhaps Alton, perhaps Hastur, there is no way of telling but to test her. That's easily enough done. She may balk a little at the testing, but there are ways of handling that."

The words of the Monitor's Oath flashed through Magda's mind: *enter no mind save to help or heal and only by consent.* These people had never heard of this obligation. The thought of

Camilla, forced unwilling to enter, undesired, that painful open-ness, made her shake with rage. At that moment, if she had had a weapon, she could cheerfully have killed Rafaella.

Did Rafaella even know what she was proposing or how painful it would be?

"Listen to me, Margali," said Rafaella earnestly. "We are sis-ters in Bridge Society—perhaps we haven't been as good friends sometimes as we might, but just the same, we're work-ing for the same objectives, aren't we?"

"Are we? I don't think so. It seems to me that if your motives are the same as the Bridge Society you would have brought your proposal to Cholayna, or to me, or even to Jaelle or Camilla her-self. Lieutenant Anders—" she used Lexie's official rank delib-erately, "is *not* a member of Bridge. Why go to *her*?"

"It was she who came to me with this proposal. And if you do not know why she would not come to you or to Cholayna with it—I should have known, of course, you would never admit anything could be done, in Bridge, or in the Empire, without your being a part of it." Rafaella's words were an angry torrent, but a brief gesture from Acquilara cut her off.

"Enough. Tell her what the proposal is. I am not interested in your personal grievances against her."

"Jaelle has had some training in the Forbidden Tower but these women can complete her training until she is more pow-erful than Leonie of Arilinn. Camilla, too, will be trained to the maximum of which she is capable. If she truly has Hastur blood, she may be the most powerful *leronis* for many years. Real power awaits them—"

"What makes you think that is what they are looking for?"

It was Acquilara who answered. "For what else did they come into these hills in search of the old crow-goddess in her abandoned shrine? Was it not to seek the full potential of what powers they might one day have? They may not know it, but that is what they were doing. This is the end of every quest; to be-come what you are, and this means power, real power, not phi-losophy and moral lectures. From the crow-people they will get austerities without number, and at the end, a pledge never to use or indulge their powers. They will be told that the end of all wisdom is to know and to refrain from doing, for actually *doing* anything would be black sorcery." Acquilara's face was savage with contempt. "I can offer them better than that."

"While if they are taught here by Acquilara," said Rafaella, "at the end of their training they will be sent back to Thendara, armed with the means to make some real changes in their world, to turn it to their own real advantage. Jaelle on the Council, as she could have been, *should* have been all along. And Camilla—there's no end to what Camilla might do. She could rule all the Towers in the Domains."

"That's not what Camilla wants."

"It is what, as a Hastur, she ought to want. And when I am done with her, she will want it," said Acquilara with unshakable confidence.

This woman had power. Magda could feel it in her very stance, her gestures. Acquilara gestured to Lexie to go on.

"You are very naïve, Lorne," Lexie added. "That is why you have meddled in so many things and never achieved anything real. Have you seen your file in personnel at HQ? I have. Do you know what they say of you? You could be in a real position of power. . . ."

Magda found her voice.

"I can't presume to tell you what Camilla and Jaelle want," she said, "but I can tell you that power, in that form anyhow, is not what I want."

"And I can tell you that you are a liar," Lexie said. "For all the talk, there is really only one real game, only one thing anyone wants, and that is power. Pretend, be a hypocrite if you like, deny it, lie about it, I know better; that is what *everybody* wants."

"Do you judge everybody by yourself?"

"Unlike you, Lorne, I don't pretend to be better than everybody else," Lexie said, "but it doesn't matter. When the new cooperation between Terran and Darkovan begins, it will take a whole new turn; and this time it will not be Magdalen Lorne's name at the head of it, but Alexis Anders's."

"Is that what you want more than anything else, Lexie?"

"It's what you wanted and what you got, isn't it? Why say it's unworthy of me?" Lexie demanded.

Again Acquilara brought the talk to a halt with one of those imperative gestures. Magda, watching her carefully, realized that she was uncomfortable whenever the focus of the discussion moved away from herself.

"Enough, I say. Magdalen Lorne—" like all speakers of *casta* she mangled the pronunciation of the name, diminishing her dignity; she knew it and tried to look all the more imposing, "promise me that you will help me to convince Jaelle n'ha Melora and the other *comynara*, the red-haired *emmasca*, to work with me, and I shall find a use for you too among us. It would be a good thing to have a Terran Intelligence worker as one of us. This would be a truly powerful *Penta Cori'yo*, not a ladies' lodging society and dinner club. Once our influence was entrenched in Thendara, it would be easy to have you as Head of Terran Intelligence—"

"What makes you think that is what I want?"

"Damn it, Acquilara, I told you more than once, that is not the way to get anywhere with Lorne," Lexie interrupted.

"You presume on your importance, *terranis*," snarled Acquilara. "Don't interrupt me! Well, Magdalen Lorne, think it over."

"I don't need to," Magda said quietly. "I'm not interested in your proposition."

"You cannot afford to refuse me," Acquilara said. "I am making you a very generous proposal. *Terranan* are not popular in these hills. I need only reveal who you are in any village to have you torn to pieces. As for your friend, the woman with the black skin, what would they think of her? A pitiful freak, to be exposed on the hills for the banshee and the *kyorebni*. Yet if you are one of us, you are under my powerful protection anywhere in these hills."

She motioned to two of the women.

"Take her back, and let her think it over. Tomorrow you will give me your answer." She signaled to Lexie.

"Guard her with your weapon."

One of the women stepped up to Acquilara and whispered to her. She nodded.

"You are right. If she is as powerful a *leronis* as we've heard, then she will lose no time in warning the *comynaris*. Give her some *raivannin*."

Raivannin! Magda thought in consternation. It was a drug which paralyzed the psi facilities and *laran*; sometimes it was used to immobilize a powerful telepath who was ill or delirious and could not control his or her destructive powers. She sought, quickly, to leap into the Overworld, to align herself with Jaelle, to cry out a warning, *Jaelle, Camilla, beware* . . . a few words. A few seconds of warning. . . .

She had underestimated these people. Someone seized her— not physically; no hand touched her—but she discovered that she was ice-cold, she could not move or speak. She felt she was falling, falling, though she knew she stood motionless; her body and mind were buffeted by raging ice, wind, as if she stood naked in a blizzard. . . .

She heard Lexie say, "Let me take care of her. I can set the stunner to keep her out for a few hours."

"No, she needs freedom for the decision," said Acquilara smoothly. Suddenly Magda was seized by two powerful sets of hands and held motionless, physically this time. Rafaella forced her mouth open and poured something icy and cloyingly sweet down her throat.

"Hold her about half a minute," Acquilara said from out of the darkness. "It's very fast-acting. After that she'll be safe enough."

An incredible flush of heat pulsed across Magda's face, making her sinuses pound and a hot flare of pain fill up her head. Only a moment, but she wanted to scream aloud with its impact. Then it ebbed slowly away, leaving her feeling dull and empty, and suddenly deaf. She blinked, letting herself lean on the women who were holding her; she could hardly find her balance; all the peripheral awarenesses were gone, she was shorn and blinded, naked in her five senses, she could see and hear and touch, but how little, how inadequate the world seemed; nothing, nothing outside herself, the universe dead . . . even her ordinary senses felt dulled, there was a film over her sight, sounds came dulled as if from far away, and even the cold on her skin seemed remote as if she had been dipped in something heavy and greasy, insulating her from the world.

Raivannin. It had sheared away all her expanded senses, leaving her head-blind. A powerful dose; once she had taken it when she was ill and Callista felt she should be shielded from a Tower operation; but it had only blunted her awareness of the matrix work going on around her, so that she could shut it out if she chose. Nothing like this total insulation, this closing and clogging of her senses.

"You gave her too much," said one of the women holding her—even her voice sounded indistinct, or was this the way ordinary voices sounded, un-enhanced by the psychic awareness of their meaning? "She can hardly stand up. She may never recover her *laran*, after a dose like that."

Acquilara shrugged. Magda realized, in despair, that she could not even hear the malice and falseness in Acquilara's voice any more, it sounded like anybody's voice, she even sounded pleasant, how did the head-blind ever know whom to trust?

"Small loss. We can manage without her, and she might be easier to handle that way. Take her away, back to the others."

Chapter 28

As the women hauled her away from the ring of firelight and back to the first cave where she had waked in captivity, Magda was conscious only of despair. She could not even warn Jaelle or Camilla.

She tried to convince herself that she should not be worrying. Jaelle and Camilla did not know where she was, or even where to look. Now that she was drugged with *raivannin* they could not even hunt for her with *laran*.

And if Acquilara tried to persuade them to join her plans, they could always refuse. There would be no way to force them, and no danger that Jaelle or Camilla would find Acquilara's offer tempting enough to be worth deserting their own principles. So why was she worrying?

They dumped her unceremoniously in the first cave and went away. Magda huddled down on the floor in misery.

Lexie is certainly intending to kill Cholayna or have her killed, or she would not have dared to speak that way to her.

Cholayna raised her head as Magda slumped down on the floor.

"Magda, are you all right? What did they want?"

"To make me an offer, of no particular interest to me," Magda said dully. "Nothing's wrong. I told them, in essence, to go to hell. Go to sleep, Cholayna."

She had made a fatal error of strategy. She should have pretended to play along, pretended to be impressed with Acquilara's plans; then they would have left her free, and she could have put herself in touch with Jaelle or Camilla with her *laran*. Now it was too late.

"You're shaking all over," said Vanessa. "I don't think you're all right at all. What did they do to you, really? Here, come under my blanket, get yourself warm. You look like hell."

"Nothing. Nothing you'd understand. Let me alone, Vanessa."

"Like hell," said Vanessa, pulling Magda by main force under her blanket and wrapping it around her. She took Magda's hands in hers and said, "They're burning hot! Come on, Lorne, what did they do to you? I've never seen you like this before!"

Magda felt dulled, exhausted, and yet she just wanted to cry and cry until she dissolved in tears. Vanessa's hands on hers felt like a stranger's hands, no sensation but the raw physical touch. What must it be like to have only this to share with another person, however dear; how could you tell friend from stranger or lover? And she could be like this forever. It would have been better to die. She let herself fall against Vanessa, and to her despair and shame she was aware that she was sobbing helplessly.

Vanessa held her and patted her back.

"Sssh, sssh, don't cry, it's going to be all right, nothing's so bad it can't be helped. We're here, right here . . ." and Cholayna, hearing them, arose and took Magda's burning hands in hers, rubbing them.

"Come on, tell us, what did they do to you? You'll feel better if you tell us, whatever it was. Let us help you."

"There's nothing anyone can do," Magda muttered, despairing, through her sobs. "They—they drugged me. With *raivannin*."

"What the hell is that?"

"It—it shuts down—*laran*. So that—I couldn't—it's like being deaf and blind—" Magda felt her own words stumbling on her tongue, lifeless, conveying nothing of her real personality or her true thoughts, dead noises, like the mouthings of an idiot.

Cholayna put her arms around Magda, holding her tight. "What a ghastly thing to do! Can't you see, Vanessa? It was so

that she couldn't warn Jaelle, or even reach her—do you understand? What a *fiendish* thing to do to anyone with psychic talent!
Oh, Magda, Magda, my dear, I know I can't really understand
what it means to you, I can't really *imagine* it, but I can understand just a little what it must mean to you!"

Magda was completely discomposed; but, held warmly and
comforted between her friends, she managed after a time to stop
crying.

"It might even be a help somehow," Vanessa said in a whisper. "I notice that when they brought you back they didn't bother
to send Lexie and her stunner. They evidently thought that with
your *laran* inoperative you couldn't be dangerous to them. I get
the feeling that they didn't even bother to worry about us—me
and Cholayna—because we *didn't* have any kind of psychic
powers."

Magda had not thought of that. She had been, she realized, so
deeply in shock that she had not thought of anything.

Have I, she wondered, come to rely so deeply on my *laran*
that I forget everything else? That's not right, either.

"You're right," she said, pulling herself together and sitting
upright, wiping her tears on her sleeve. What Vanessa said was
true; they were unguarded. Something might be done. Without
food, packs, or maps, and not even knowing whether it was daylight or dark outside, escape would be difficult; but it need not
be impossible.

Vanessa had her knife, a small affair, razor sharp, with a
blade as long as her hand; it folded up, and perhaps they had not
even recognized it as a knife. Cholayna was unarmed.

"But I'm not afraid of anyone I can see," she said grimly,
making a gesture Magda recognized; she too had been trained in
unarmed combat. Magda had not, until they were attacked in the
robber's village, used it to kill; but she had been impressed with
Cholayna's fighting skill.

"It must be night outside," she said, making an effort to rally
her ordinary strengths. They might have disabled her *laran*, but
after all, she had lived almost twenty-seven years without any

hint that she possessed it; there was more to Magdalen Lorne than just *laran*.

"Acquilara told them to guard me—at first—so that I could think over my answer till tomorrow; I had the idea they were winding things up for the night. Sooner or later, even this crew must sleep; they're not some sort of Unsleeping Eye of Evil, they're just women with some nasty powers and nastier ideas about using them. If we're going to make a move, it should be while they're sleeping."

"We might not even have to kill them," Cholayna said. "We might be able to sneak out past them. . . ."

"If we knew the way out," Magda said, "and I suspect there will be guards, unless they are dangerously over-confident—"

"They just might be," Cholayna said. "Think of it, Magda, the psychology of power. This cave is isolated in the most godforgotten part of these isolated and godforgotten mountains. No one knows the way here. No one ever comes here at all. They probably guard it psychically from the rival crew, the Wise Sisterhood, but I'd bet a month's pay that there won't be any *physical* guards at all. They've immobilized you. They'll take precautions about the rival Sisterhood tracking them down by *laran*. But they don't even bother to guard Vanessa and me. Just you, and just your *laran*."

Cholayna was right. So they had only two problems: to wait until Acquilara and her cohorts were sleeping, so that they could find their way out of the cave (she had felt a draft of outside air blowing from the outer cave where they had challenged her, so it must be nearer the exit) and second, how to survive outside.

The second was the most important. Vanessa was already ahead of her: "Supposing we do get out? We don't have food, outer clothing, survival equipment—"

"There's sure to be food and clothing somewhere in these caves—" Cholayna protested.

"Sure. Want to go to Acquilara and ask her to give us some?"

"Another thing, even more important," said Cholayna with a quiet determination, "Lexie. I'm not going to leave without her."

"Cholayna, you saw," Vanessa protested. "She held a gun on us. Rescue, hell, she's *one* of them!"

"How do you know that there wasn't a gun, or something worse that we couldn't see, being held on *her?* I'd want to hear from her own lips that she wasn't coerced before I'd abandon her here," Cholayna said. "And Rafaella—did you see her, Magda, is she alive?"

"Alive and well," said Magda grimly. "She held me while they poured the drug down my throat. And I'll guarantee nobody had a gun on her, or anything like that. She explained to me at considerable length what Acquilara was doing and why Jaelle and Camilla ought to be convinced to join them rather than the Sisterhood. I wasn't convinced, but she seemed to be. I honestly don't think we ought to waste time trying to rescue them, I got the impression that they were exactly where they wanted to be and it would be no use at all to try to persuade them to leave."

"I can't believe that of Alexis," said Cholayna in despair. "But then, I would never have believed she would hold a stunner on me, either."

Even without *laran* Magda could feel Cholayna's sorrow. How hard it must be, to accept that Lexie was not a prisoner here, but a willing accomplice.

But Cholayna brought herself sternly back to duty, and was searching her pockets. She brought out from the depths a wrapped package.

"Emergency field rations. We need the fuel." She broke the bar into three parts. "Eat."

Magda shook her head. "They gave me some hot tea with butter in it; I'm all right. You two share it." She accepted only a mouthful of the dry, flavorless, but high-calorie ration, chewing it slowly. *I'll never complain about the taste of this stuff again, after butter-flavored tea smelling of dung-fire.*

Vanessa opened her little knife, had it ready. They folded up the blankets and slung them across their backs; they might need them as basic shelter, if they found their way out of the caves. Their eyes had adapted so well to the faintest of light within this cave that they could see the glow that came from the outer cave which was apparently the meetingplace and headquarters of Acquilara and the women of her cult.

Magda was wondering: Acquilara's people, where do they come from? Do they live here all year round, or meet here occasionally? They can't live in these wilds, because there's nothing to live on.

There was no reason to waste time now in speculation. Magda didn't care if they came here out of necessity, imitation, or sheer perversity, or because like Vanessa they had a passion for climbing mountains.

They stole noiselessly toward the orange glow of the fires in the outer cave. Magda was aware of the dungfire smell, of a flow of cool air on her cheek—these caves were well ventilated. This might in part explain why there was so little marked on the map in the Hellers, if some inhabitants lived in caves. But people needed more than simple shelter; they needed fire, clothing, food or some place to grow it. If there were many people living in this area, there would be more signs than this. She did not for a single moment believe Lexie's theory about a city in these wastelands, made invisible to observers by some unknown technology. A few isolated hermits, withdrawn here for spiritual purposes, perhaps. Not any great population.

There were a couple of intermediate caves, one with steps leading downward into a vague glow. Probably torchlight somewhere, Magda thought. She had once seen a geological survey indicating that there were several active volcanoes in the Kilghard Hills—which would have been obvious anyway from the presence of hot springs all through the countryside. There must be dormant ones here too, but nobody would be living in them.

Vanessa whispered, "We should search these caves. There might be storerooms of food and clothing."

"Can't risk it," Cholayna said in an undertone. It was surprising, Magda thought, the way in which Cholayna, without discussion, had become their leader. "We could stumble on all them, sleeping down there. We need to get out fast and not be weighed down. We'll manage somehow. Straight out, fight our way if we have to; don't kill unless there's no alternative, but don't mess around, either." She adjusted the blanket she had strapped across her back, making sure her arms and legs could move freely, and Magda remembered how she had dealt with the robbers in the village.

Another few steps and they were in the rear mouth of the main cavern, or at least what Magda supposed to be so; the great cavernous room where she had spoken to Rafaella and Lexie under Acquilara's eyes. She looked at the ring of scattered coals which had once been a fire, and shuddered, here they had held her . . . *drugged her, a violation worse than rape, afflicting her very selfhood.* . . .

"Steady." Vanessa gripped her shoulder. "Easy, Lorne, you're all right now."

Vanessa did not understand, but Magda firmly took hold of herself. They had stopped her, wounded her, but she was alive and still in possession of her senses, her self, her integrity.

Yet if Acquilara was right, if they overdosed me to the point where I am permanently blinded of laran. . . .

I can live without it. Camilla chose to live without it. She bemoaned the thought that she might never share with Camilla what she shared with Jaelle, with her companions in the Tower, but if she must, she could accept that. *Camilla lost more than that.* She looked warily around the great cave.

At first it seemed empty. They had withdrawn to whatever deeper caves they used, whether for sleeping or for whatever mysterious rites occupied their time. *When they're not murdering or drugging people. I don't care if they're all down there consorting sex with demons or banshees. I wish them joy of it. So long as it keeps them busy while we get the hell out!*

"But there must be guards somewhere, even if it's only at the outside doors," Vanessa whispered. "Be careful! Can you tell where that draft's coming from, Magda?"

She turned her head from side to side, trying to decide from which direction the air flowed. Now *laran* would have been useful, though clairvoyance was not her most outstanding talent. Cholayna touched her arm silently and pointed.

Someone was sleeping on the floor, at one side of the cavern, by the light of the guttering torches. A woman's form, wrapped in a blanket. One of Acquilara's sorceresses. A guard, at least. Vanessa had her knife out. She started to bend over, her hand poised for the stroke, but Cholayna shook her head, and Vanessa shrugged and obeyed.

Magda had identified the airstream. She hesitated a moment; some such caves, she knew, were ventilated by long chimneys of rock, and taking that direction might lead them into an impassable labyrinth. But they had to risk something. Anyhow, it was most likely that a guard would be posted, even if she was sleeping, across the doorway an escaping prisoner must take to reach the outside world. She pointed.

One by one they stepped carefully over the sleeping form of the woman. But if Magda had hoped that the next cave would lead to the outside world with a blaze of daylight and a few steps to freedom, she was doomed to disappointment, for the next cavernous chamber was larger than the last, totally empty, and all but lightless.

Chapter 29

They could wander in these caves for days; except that Acquilara's gang would find them sooner or later, more likely sooner, and bring them to a quick and messy end. Acquilara had wanted to use her, but she did not deceive herself that there would be any kindness or forbearance shown.

Not drugging, this time. Death.

Vanessa was making her way very slowly around the walls, feeling every inch with outstretched hands before her. She slipped, recovered, let herself down on one knee and beckoned. They came on tiptoe to join her. She had fallen over a cluster of large sacks, one or two of which had been opened and folded over at the top.

One held dried fruit; the second held a kind of grain, millet, probably intended as food for pack animals. At Cholayna's gesture they filled their pockets from the sacks. It might mean, in that bitter cold outside, the narrow razor edge of separation between life and death.

Beyond the piled sacks rose a long stairway; dimly they made out that the steps were carved in part from the soft limestone, filled in with a kind of rock and cement and smoothed over just enough to climb without falling. The steps were wet, slippery and treacherous, and Magda hesitated to set foot on them.

"Do you think this is the way out? Or does it go farther into the caves?"

"Let's find out first." Cholayna began slowly groping her

way around the rest of the wall. Magda tried, automatically, to reach out with her *laran*, to try to see past the opening of the stairs, but there was only a dull ache.

In her . . . eyes? No. In her heart? *I can't identify what's missing, but I'm only half there.* She banished the thought, forcing herself to go slowly around the dripping walls. Back at the feed sacks she bumped gently into Vanessa.

"There's a big door over there," Cholayna murmured. "I'd like to get out of here before that guard over there wakes up and we have to kill her."

"I think it's the stairway that leads out," Vanessa argued. "I can feel air blowing from up there."

"I'm not so sure. Think, Vanessa. Could they have carried all of us down these stairways without at least one of us waking up?" Cholayna sounded persuasive. Vanessa said, "You're the boss."

"No. It's too serious for that. You and Magda have a stake in this too. Magda, what's your best hunch?"

Grimly Magda reminded herself that Cholayna had no idea how that question would seem a wounding prod of her loss; Cholayna meant it at strict face value.

"Don't have any just now, remember? But I'd like to have a look at that doorway before we try climbing the stairs."

"But hurry," Cholayna fretted, and Magda began silently feeling her way. It was very dark. She could hardly make out her spread fingers before her face. Vanessa murmured something and slid away into the darkness. After a heart-stopping time she came back, carrying one of the low-sputtering torches.

"I had to step right over her. I took this one. It seemed to have more time left on it than the others, but none of them looked all that great. I wish I could find where they keep their stash of fresh ones."

"That's another thing," Cholayna said between her teeth. "Unless we find our way out damn fast, we're going to need light; we could, literally, wander the rest of our lives in these caves."

"Hold this," Vanessa said, thrusting the low-burning torch

into Cholayna's hands and slipping away again. After another long time and some curious soft scraping sounds, she returned, breathless, her arms filled with the torches. One or two had a coal or so on the end; the others had been extinguished.

"Sorry I was so long about it," she whispered. "I had to pull them down off the wall. Now we'd better get moving—one look at the place and anybody will know we passed through. Let's move."

Cholayna reached out and gripped her wrist. She said, "Good thinking. But get one thing straight, Vanessa: from this very minute, we stick together, we don't get separated. Understand? You may know mountains; I know something about caves. You stick close; better yet, we stay in physical contact all the time. If one of us gets lost or separated we can't even yell to find each other!"

"Oh. Right," Vanessa said, sobered.

Magda took the burning torch from Cholayna's hands. "I won't go out of sight. But I'm going up to see where these steps lead. There's no sense of all of us coming if it's a blind chimney, or another empty chamber."

"I doubt it's blind; the stairs look too well-used for that," said Cholayna, bending low to scan the marks on the roughly floored surface.

Holding the torch before her, Magda slowly climbed the steps.

She looked back at Cholayna, standing at the foot of the crude stairway. It was not blind. It led into some kind of chamber above, and there was light there. Daylight, already? She thrust her head up over the edge and instinctively recoiled.

She thrust the torch behind her to conceal its light. At least two dozen women lay sleeping in the chamber above; Magda could see at the far end of the room Lexie Anders's curly blond head. She did not see Acquilara. Slowly she began to withdraw down the steps, placing each foot carefully on the stair below.

The woman nearest the stairhead opened her eyes and looked straight at Magda.

It was Rafaella n'ha Doria.

*   *   *

Magda never knew how she stifled a yell. She withdrew swiftly down the stairs, and Vanessa, watching her precipitate retreat, snatched out her knife and stood braced.

But nothing happened. Silence; no outcry, no rousing of the legions, no outraged hordes pouring down the stairs with weapons raised. *Was she fast asleep? Didn't she see me? Did she decide to let me go for Jaelle's sake or because we used to be friends?*

Then, stealthily, Rafaella came down the stairs. Vanessa held her little knife at the ready, but Rafaella gestured to her to put it away and motioned them all to a safe distance from the stairway.

"You can put it away, Vanessa n'ha Yllana," she said. "If you are leaving, I'm going with you."

"You had me fooled," Magda said in an undertone.

"Oh, don't deceive yourself," Rafaella said sourly. "You haven't converted me to the rightness of your cause, or anything like that. I still think Jaelle would be better advised to work with them than with that other crew. But I don't like what they've done to Lexie and I don't want them doing it to me."

"Do you by any chance know the way out?"

"I think I can find it. I've been in and out twice since the storm." Rafaella led the way swiftly through the other large doorway and into a chamber strewn with rubble and rocks. Phosphorescent fungus shed an eerie light from the walls, and the torchlight wavered on giant formations of limestone, pale and gleaming like bone, folded and layered most marvelously. "Careful here. It's wet and dripping all through here, but at least the water's pure and good drinking, and there's plenty of it." She scooped up a handful from a little stream that ran downhill beside where they were climbing.

"If you get lost again in here remember to follow the stream *uphill.* If you follow it down it leads *way* down—I've only been down three or four levels; they say there are at least ten levels below this, and some of them are filled with old books and artifacts from a time—they must be thousands of years old. Lexie went down and saw a few of them and said there had evidently been a time of very high technology on Darkover, though none of it looked Terran. Which surprised her. She said Darkover was once a Terran colony, but this was completely different. Then Acquilara told her that it was *before;* that there was a whole civilization before humans colonized this world. You're the specialist, Margali, all that stuff would interest you, and Mother Lauria would go crazy over it, but it's not for me."

At the far end of this chamber lay a gleam of light—not daylight, but a faint glimmer somehow different in quality from the guttering torchlight. From it they could all feel a faint breath of the terrible chill outside. Magda shivered, buttoned up her heavy jacket, drew on her gloves. Vanessa arranged her blanket snugly over her shoulders like a mountain man's plaid. Four abreast, they moved stealthily toward the entry.

Magda always swore that for what happened next there was no natural explanation. Vanessa said she came from the staircase and they never stopped arguing about it. Magda saw a faint blue flare, a shrill faroff shrieking like a hawk, and Acquilara stood in the doorway before them.

"Are you leaving us? I'm afraid I can't relinquish your company so soon." She raised her hand, and Magda realized there were women warriors all around the entrance chamber. They struck the torches from Cholayna's hand, knocked Vanessa to the ground, took her knife, then dragged them along with Magda and Rafaella back into the chamber of fires, where all four of them were held securely.

The room filled up with women, some of them, Magda was sure, hastily roused sleepers from the chamber above.

"I am too lenient," Acquilara said. "I can tolerate no traitors. *Terranan*—"

Lexie came forward through the crowd.

"I underestimated her strength and intelligence," Acquilara said, indicating Magda. "Once she is broken, we can find a use for her. But I must make an example of what happens to those who mock my clemency. This one betrayed us."

She went to Rafaella and took the knife from her belt; handed it to Lexie.

"Prove yourself loyal to me. Kill her."

Cholayna cried out sharply. "Lexie! No!"

With brutal deliberation Acquilara backhanded Cholayna across the mouth. "It should be you, freak," she said. "*Terranan*, I wait."

Lexie barely glanced at the knife and dropped it.

"To hell with your tests of loyalty. If you need them, to hell with *you*." She let the knife lie where it had fallen.

Magda thought Acquilara would strike Alexis down where she stood; she had defied her, risked letting the sorceress lose face before her women. Acquilara stood frozen for a moment, then evidently decided to salvage what she could from the incident.

"Why, *Terranan*?"

"She knows the mountain roads. She is competent. She will be needed to escort them back to Thendara when the time comes; by that time she will know better than to defy or disobey. Killing her would be waste. I abhor waste." Lexie spoke coldly, without the slightest emotion.

Now is she telling the exact truth, or is it some latent loyalty in Lexie? After all, they traveled over the mountains together, and they must have some kindness and respect for one another after sharing an experience like that. Magda ached for the touch of *laran* which would make it possible to know.

Soon they found themselves back in the cavern from which they had come. Rafaella was dragged along with them, and unceremoniously dumped there. Their hands were tied, and Acquilara ordered her women to go around and take their boots off, one by one.

Cholayna protested. "You have not even told us why we are your prisoners. And without our boots we will surely freeze."

"Not if you stay in these caverns, where the temperature all year round is sufficient to keep water from freezing," Acquilara said. "Only if you try to leave them will you suffer the slightest harm. I should really take all your outer garments as well."

But she did not carry out that threat; she even left the

blankets. She also posted a pair of guards, armed with knives and daggers, at the door of the chamber. She would not, Magda thought, underestimate them again.

Cholayna wrapped her blanket around herself, clumsily, using her long, prehensile toes, and told the others to do the same. "We need to keep warm, stay as strong as we can."

"Jaelle—they didn't kill her, did they?" Rafaella asked, shrugging into her blanket as best she could with her hands tied.

"As far as I know she got clean away. And I hope she stays so."

"By the paps of Evanda, so do I, I swear it! I would not have harm come to her for all the metal in Zandru's forges. I truly believed we would find—" she broke off. "I did not know the *Terranan* woman was quite so bloodthirsty. For a moment I thought Lexa' really would kill me."

"I had hoped not," Cholayna said gravely. "I cannot believe that of her."

Rafaella said, "I don't suppose this is what Lexa' really meant by a *City of Wisdom*. Still, if we could get at the ancient artifacts under the mountains, I dare say your Terrans would call it a fortune."

"I wouldn't mind seeing them," Cholayna said, "but I'd prefer to get out of here with a whole skin. I don't know if we can manage another escape attempt. Still, if any kind of chance comes we should be ready." She wriggled around, lying close to Magda. "See if you can manage to get my hands loose, Magda. Vanessa, see what you can do for Rafi's."

"The guards—" Magda gave an uneasy glance over her shoulder.

"Why do you think I suggested we all do a lot of moving around getting ourselves wrapped up in blankets and so forth? The guards won't pay any attention if we move discreetly and behave as if we were still tied up."

Magda started slowly easing the knots loose. They had been well tied, and it took a long time, but she had nothing else to do anyhow. At last she slipped free the last cord, then thrust out her own wrists, to let Cholayna fumble with her bonds.

"It must be daylight outside," said Vanessa, lying full length and shamming sleep while Rafaella picked at a difficult knot.

Daylight. If she had had sense, or *laran*, not to go up those stairs, to take the doorway, they could by now have been miles away.

Rafaella asked, "This Acquilara. Do you think she is a powerful sorceress?"

"She's not much of a telepath. I don't know what else she has or doesn't have, and right now I'm in no position to judge," Magda said.

"Laran!" Rafaella's voice was scornful, but suddenly Magda was aware of the overpowering reason behind Rafaella's jealousy. It took no psychic powers to read; since Jaelle's childhood, Rafi had known Jaelle to be a daughter born into the powerful caste of *Comyn*, who ruled all the Domains, all Darkover, with their powers. Nevertheless, Jaelle had chosen the Guildhouse over her *Comyn* heritage, blotting out the great distance that would otherwise lie between Rafaella and Jaelle. They had been friends, partners; even, for a brief time in their girlhood, lovers.

And then Magda, who was not even Darkovan and should have had no more *laran* than Rafaella herself, had come between them, and it had been Magda, the alien, who had lured Jaelle back to her *laran* and to her heritage.

I should have had imagination enough to see this before.

"*Laran* or no," Cholayna said, "I know one thing about this Acquilara: she is a psychopath. Any little thing can touch her off, and then she can be dangerous."

"You think she's not dangerous now? Would a sane woman have tried that business of trying to make Lexie kill Rafaella?" Vanessa asked.

"A sane woman might well have tried it. But a sane woman would not have been diverted so easily from it," Cholayna warned, "I am more afraid of her than of anything so far on this trip."

The day, or night, dragged on, and they had no way of marking it. What did it matter? Magda wondered. It was unlikely that they would get out of this one. Either Acquilara would kill them in a fit of psychotic frenzy, or they would escape, to be followed by a swift death from exposure, or a slow one from starvation. She only regretted that her *laran* should die before she did. She would have liked to be able to reach Callista, Andrew, and especially her child. The Forbidden Tower would mourn her, never knowing how she had died. Perhaps it was as well they should not know.

She wondered if it was an ethical question peculiar to women. There were some, even in the Guild-house, who would have said that she should not, with family responsibilities and a child to raise, have undertaken such a dangerous mission. Terran HQ, at least in Intelligence, usually reserved such missions for unmarried men with no families.

But Intelligence was a special volunteer service. In Mapping and Exploring, in Survey, for instance, a man's marital status did not affect what he was expected or allowed to do. Was it so much worse to raise motherless children than fatherless ones? She longed for Shaya and wondered if she would ever see her again. If Jaelle had gotten clean away, Jaelle would look after her daughter. If Jaelle had been killed too—well, at least the children were safe.

"I don't suppose they'll bother to send in anything to eat," said Vanessa, "but I still have a pocketful of the stuff we got out of those sacks. Here. . . ." She passed it from hand to hand, out of sight of the guards. "We might as well eat and keep up our strength."

Magda was chewing prosaically on a raisin when it happened, a flare like a light exploding in her brain and Callista's voice:

. . . *as an Alton one of my talents is speech to the head-blind.* . . .

It was as if she were speaking in the next room, but perfectly clear. Then it was gone, and nothing would bring it back; Magda reached out desperately, trying to touch Jaelle, Camilla, to reach for the Overworld and the Forbidden Tower . . .

But her mind was still filled with the insidious inhibiting

power of *raivannin* and she had no idea how that voice had gotten through to her.

If I could only pray. But I don't believe in prayer. She didn't, she thought, even believe in the Goddess Avarra, even though she had seen the thought-form of the Sisterhood. She tried to summon that image, the brooding goddess with wings, the robed figures, to fill her mind with the sound of calling crows, but she was all too aware that it was only an image, mind and memory, nothing like the sureness of contact with her *laran.*

She slumped in her blanket, munching wretchedly on dried fruit, which, like everything else in these caverns, smelled of the dung-fires they burned here.

She looked up, and Camilla stood before her.

But not the real Camilla. She could see the wall through her body, and her eyes blazed with supernatural fires. Her hair, in the real world faded and sandy, seemed alive with the brightest of copper highlights. Not Camilla. Her image in the Overworld. Yet Magda's head was still filled with the sick fuzzy strangeness of *raivannin.* So she was not seeing Camilla with her *laran.* Somehow Camilla had come to her. Then she saw, standing next to Camilla—but her feet were not quite touching the floor of the cave, and she was surrounded by a curious dark aureole—the slight, modest young woman who had come to the hermitage to speak with them.

She heard the words with her ears. They were not in her head.

"Try not to hate them," Kyntha said, matter-of-factly, "this is not a spiritual recommendation, but a very practical one. Your hate gives them entry to your mind. Tell the others."

Then she was gone and Camilla was standing before her again.

Bredhiya, she said, and vanished.

Chapter 30

It had happened. She could not use her *laran* to cry out to Camilla; drugged with *raivannin* she was head-blind, insensitive, unreachable. Jaelle, alone, without helpers from the Tower, was all but powerless. And so Camilla had made the breakthrough, done the thing that she had been avoiding all her life.

Magda felt a confusion beyond words. On one level she was filled with pride for Camilla, that she had overcome her dread and distaste for this long denied potential. On another she was almost immeasurably humbled that Camilla would do this for her sake, after so many years of denial, of rejection. On yet another, she felt pain that was almost despair. *Camilla would never have come to this, except for me. It would have been better to die than to force this on her.*

She was so filled with mixed joy and sorrow for her friend, that for a moment she did not realize what it meant. Camilla had found her, by *laran*. One way or another this meant rescue was on the way, and they must be ready.

She crawled toward Cholayna and whispered, "They've found us. Did you see Camilla?"

"Did I—*what?*"

"I saw her. She appeared to me. No, Cholayna, I wasn't hallucinating. I saw Kyntha, too. It means that since I could not search for her, she came looking for me, and it means an attempt at rescue. We must be ready."

Vanessa listened with a skeptically raised eyebrow.

"Talk about psychological defense mechanisms! I suspect you're out of your mind temporarily, Lorne, and no wonder— giving you all kinds of strange drugs, without the slightest reason—"

"You haven't been on this planet as long as I have," Cholayna said, overhearing this. "It happens and it's no delusion, Vanessa. I didn't see anything. I didn't expect to. But I don't doubt Lorne did and we should be ready."

"They won't get us away without a commotion of some sort," Vanessa said. "Not without our boots."

Rafaella, who had been dozing, sat up, and the good news was relayed to her in a whisper.

"And Jaelle? What of Jaelle?" she asked. "Any word?"

Magda said dryly, "Not going to try persuading her this time that Acquilara's gang would be more useful in the long run? Changed your mind about what kind of solid citizens they are?"

Rafaella's face was white.

"Damn you, Margali, is it any wonder I didn't want you in this? You always have to twist the knife, don't you? And you of course, you never make mistakes, you're always so right, so perfectly absolutely smug-faced *right!* All these people who are so damn awed by you because you never do anything wrong— some day Jaelle's going to realize what you're doing to her, what you do to everybody you say you care about, and break your neck, and I hope I'm there to see it and cheer!"

She turned her back on Magda and buried her head in her blanket. Her body shook, and Magda realized she was crying.

For a moment Magda was almost too shocked to draw breath. *Rafaella and I have quarreled before, but I always thought she was still my friend. Is that what I am like? Is that how people see me?*

Vanessa had heard; more, she had seen Magda's face. She leaned close to Magda. "Never mind," she said in a voice that could not be heard a foot away, "she always calms down sooner or later. Remember her own judgment of people's just turned out not to be so great, after all. She gambled on Anders and lost."

It's as if this whole thing had been my fault, my fault Lexie Anders did what she did, my fault Rafaella followed her.

She remembered what Kyntha had said. *Try not to hate.* Her mind was still clouded, but she knew that she did not hate Rafaella. *I'm angry with her. That's different.*

Lexie? That was more difficult. However she tried, she could not exonerate Lexie from the blame for this whole miserable expedition.

"What is it?" Cholayna whispered, and Magda remembered that Kyntha had said, *Tell the others.*

"I'm trying hard not to hate Lexie." She repeated what Kyntha had said. Her feelings about Rafaella were her own affair, and she could not share them with Cholayna, but Lexie was another matter.

"You can leave the hating to me," Vanessa said implacably. "She's come so close to getting us all killed—"

"But she didn't kill Rafaella," Cholayna argued. "Not even with a knife in her hand, and an admiring audience standing around watching."

Rafaella stuck her head out from under her blanket. "I knew she wouldn't. I know Lexa' pretty well by now." Magda was astonished at herself, realizing that even in this adversity she still thought like a linguist, noting that Rafaella said *Lexa'*, using the Kilghard Hills dialect, rather than the *Lexie* that the rest of them, the Terrans, used.

"She would never have killed me," Rafaella insisted. They might all have been sitting around in the music room of the Guild-house, arguing a point in Training Session for the young Renunciates. "She wouldn't have killed Margali, not even when she had the gun—blaster? Stunner—on her."

If she can forgive Alexis that, *how can I possibly keep on hating her? How can I keep on being angry with Rafi? We've quarreled before. Yet she'd speak up for me just the way she did just now for Lexie.* She wanted suddenly to hug Rafaelia, but she knew the other woman was still angry with her.

Well, she has a right to be. What I said was *nasty, under the circumstances.*

But if she can forgive Lexie, then I should be able to stop hating her. Magda made herself remember Lexie at her best; explaining Survey work to the young women for the Bridge Society; Lexie in Training School on Alpha, sharing experience with the younger students; Lexie, regressed to her early years . . . *a little fair-haired girl, Cleindori's age. I walked hand in hand with her like a younger sister.* . . . She sought the sympathy she had found for her then.

I don't know if it will do any good. But I'm trying.

Vanessa said grimly, "I can just manage not to hate Lexie, if I have to. But don't try asking me not to hate that woman Acquilara. That's carrying good will too far. She'd have killed us all—"

"But the fact is that she *didn't* kill us," Cholayna said. "She even left us the blankets. 'One who does good, having an infinite power to do evil, should have credit not only for the good she does but for the evil from which she refrains.'"

"What in hell are you quoting?"

"I don't remember; something I read as a student," Cholayna said. "Remember, too: the woman's psychotic. She can't help herself."

"I've never believed in diminished responsibility," said Vanessa, frowning.

Magda wondered: did this in any way exonerate Acquilara, who was at least guilty of searching for power by any means she could grab it? Jaelle had defined that as evil. She didn't know.

"Listen! What's going on?" asked Cholayna, suddenly raising her head. At the far end of the cavern there was a stirring, women running in and out. Alexis Anders came up to one of the guards; they spoke urgently for a few minutes. Then the guards hurried toward the prisoners.

They held out four pairs of boots.

"Get into them! Hurry, or it will be the worse for you!"

"What are you going to do with us?" Vanessa demanded.

"No questions," said one of them, but the other had already said, "You're being moved. Hurry up."

They hurried into their boots, afraid the guards would lose

patience and force them to move without the boots. The guards prodded them to their feet with long sticks, urged them ahead. Cholayna found an opportunity to whisper to Vanessa and Magda, "If you're right about Camilla organizing a rescue, this could be it. Keep alert and seize any chance to fight our way out!"

Magda tried to get her bearings—which way was she being taken into the labyrinth? The darkness made her nervous, with no light but that from the smoking torches, making wavering images on the uneven shapes of the walls. Something sticking to her sock inside her boot hurt her foot. She recognized the slippery stairway up which they had tried to escape.

Cholayna was breathing hard. She was not, after all, long out of bed after pneumonia. Rafaella grabbed her rudely around the waist. "Lean on me, Elder." The respectful Guild-house term rang strangely here.

Vanessa bumped into her from behind. Magda felt the younger woman's breath on her neck as she whispered hastily, "I'm going to try and get that stunner away from Lexie. It could even the odds against us."

Magda's first impulse was to protest—she had lived long enough as a Darkovan to be appalled at the thought of any weapon effective beyond arm's reach. Also, Terran law prevented high-tech weapons on low-tech planets. But Alexis Anders had already used, displayed, the weapon here. And they were desperately outnumbered, four or five to forty or more. And—the final convincer—she didn't think her protest would stop Vanessa anyway. She muttered back, "Get me to testify at the courtmartial when we get back."

But at first, when they were herded into a corner of the upper chamber, she did not see Lexie at all. She heard shouting, noise, commotion below, but they were in the dark, lighted only by one torch on the walls, sending out tarry choking smoke, and another wavering in the hands of an old woman, who stood against the cavern wall.

Then there was a clash like the sound of metal and Magda

saw a press of people crowding around the head of the staircase. She could not see what was going on.

The Sisterhood do not kill. That was the one thing that was in all the legends, both Jaelle and Camilla had repeated that. Would they fight even for a rescue? Someone was screaming on the staircase. There was a new glare of freshly lit torches, and by their light Magda saw Camilla at the stairhead fighting.

It was time to act. She dashed at one of their guards; shoved her so hard that the woman toppled toward her, and she grabbed the sword out of her belt; as the woman scrambled up, she knocked her down again with a kick she had learned on another world. Her own violence spun her around and she saw that Cholayna and Rafaella were trying to follow her example, but she had no time to see what happened, as she ran toward Camilla, shouting. Where was Jaellc? In the torchlit shadows it was all but impossible to tell friend from enemy.

Camilla grabbed her hand, pulling her down the stairs, and they ran together. Somebody rose up in front of them and Magda struck out with the edge of her hand. She did not think to use the snatched-up sword instead. They ran right over her. Camilla was shouting, in a ringing voice that echoed through the caverns:

"*Comhi-Letzii!* Here. Gather here!"

Somebody came up and grabbed Magda; she almost struck her down before she realized it was Jaelle, in a thick pointed cap shoved down over her bright hair.

"They're here." Magda gabbled at her, breathless. "Rafi. And Lexie. Rafi's all right. She's on our side. Lexie has a stunner. Be careful. I think she'd use it."

Acquilara's women were crowding down the staircase. Magda heard Vanessa scream and whirled. Lexie had the stunner and was holding it almost in Cholayna's face, in an attitude of wordless threat.

Cholayna's foot swept up in a *vaido* kick and the stunner went flying, scooting over heads like a soaring ball. Magda ran for it, sliding, snatching it up before Acquilara's hands closed on it. Acquilara had a knife; Magda kicked it out of her hand.

A woman with an evil scar halfway across her face closed

with her. Magda kicked, fought, scrabbled, thrust the stunner inside her own tunic. It felt icy cold against her bare skin and she was suddenly terrified that Alexis had taken off the safety catch and it would go off. Where was Lexie? Frantically, Magda sought her in the flickering torchlight, where women were pushing and crowding and screaming. Cholayna. Where was Cholayna? Magda pushed back through the press of people to find her. Cholayna was lying on the ground and for a frightful moment Magda, seeing Alexis Anders standing over her, thought that Lexie had struck her down.

But Cholayna's rasping breath could be heard halfway across the cavern. She struggled to rise, and realization swept over Magda. Cholayna was poorly acclimated to the altitude; she had been fighting like a woman half her age. Lexie was unarmed.

I have the stunner! And she hasn't been checked out for the field here—she's had unarmed-combat training, but against a knife—unarmed, Alexis was holding off two women with knives who were trying to get to Cholayna. Magda thrust frantically through the crowd toward them. *Rafaella was right*—Vanessa grabbed Cholayna, hauling her to her feet. The three of them backed off, slowly, toward the daylight that could be seen at the edge of the big chamber. The knife-bearers made a final rush, and Lexie went down in a sprawl of bodies.

Magda fought her way toward them, and saw Camilla rise upward, throwing off assailants. Vanessa dragged Cholayna up to her feet, gasping, leaning heavily on her arm. Camilla's face was pouring blood from a slash on her forehead.

Lexie Anders lay motionless on the floor of the cavern, and for a moment Magda thought she was dead. Then she stirred, and Vanessa leaned down and grabbed her. She fought her way up, clinging numbly to Vanessa's arm.

She wouldn't let them kill Cholayna, I knew it. How badly is she hurt?

Magda's throat was hurting, and she paused a moment, painfully catching her breath. Then she ran across the big chamber to where Cholayna and Camilla found shelter, with Vanessa supporting Lexie. Now Magda could see the great splotch of blood on the back of Lexie's tunic. It looked bad. They were enormously outnumbered. Rafaella and Jaelle were back to back, trying to hold off another threatening rush by Acquilara's women, who were all armed with knives and looked as if they would have no hesitation about using them. For the moment they were hanging back, but any second they might attack again.

The slash across Camilla's forehead poured blood into her eyes turning her face into a bloody mess. Magda reminded herself that all head wounds, even minor ones, bled like that and if it was that serious Camilla would not still be on her feet. Still the sight terrified her, and she ran to join them. In this lower chamber they could dimly see daylight from the cave-mouth, but, before that, there seemed to be dozens of women with knives. Cholayna's breath was still coming so hard that Magda wondered how she stayed on her feet. Vanessa, herself limping, was holding Lexie upright, half conscious.

Then as if from nowhere in a glare of light—*torchlight? No, too bright!*—half a dozen strange women, hugely tall, veiled in dark blue, with high-crowned vulture headdresses suddenly appeared. They bore great curved swords with gleaming edges, such swords as Magda, who had made something of a study of weapons, had never seen on Darkover anywhere, swords that glittered with a supernatural light. Magda knew they could not possibly be real. Acquilara's women retreated. Even the one or two who had courage to try to rush up against the glare of those lighted swords fell back, cowering and screaming as if wounded to the death, but Magda could see no blood. Were they entirely illusion, then?

A familiar voice said, "Quick! This way!" and rushed her, a hand on her shoulder, across the lower chamber toward the daylight outside. Magda flinched at the paralyzing chill, the gust of wind, but Kyntha said in her ear, "Hurry! The fighters are illusion; they cannot hold long!" She pushed Magda along what looked like a concealed trail leading between the cliff wall and the caverns.

A swift glance behind her showed Magda that all her companions were gathered in that crevice, Camilla still trying to wipe blood from her eyes. Magda hurried back toward her, shaking Kyntha's hand from her elbow. The wind flung her, slipping and sliding, toward the edge of the cliff; she brought herself up, terrified, clutching at the wall.

Camilla was all right. Where was Jaelle? Cholayna's breath, rasping and harsh, could be heard even over the shouts from inside the caverns. Vanessa was limping. Two of the tall women in vulture headdresses were guarding the rear, covering their escape. *Where was Jaelle?*

Magda saw her now, behind the vulture-crowned women warriors. Illusion? How could it be? She hurried back toward her freemate. Suddenly there was a dreadful glare of pallid light, like ultraviolet, and Acquilara rose up behind them. She had a dagger, and struck out at Vanessa, who was at the rear. One of the tall, robed women in the vulture headdresses was there with her blazing sword, but Acquilara made some strange banishing gesture and the woman in the vulture headdress exploded into blue light.

Jaelle flung herself at Acquilara, her sword out. Magda started to rush to her freemate's side, her hand on her sword. The path was narrow, but she thrust herself through the others, uncaring.

Acquilara pointed. Another of the robed, vulture-crowned women warriors—*illusion?*—flared horribly into blue light and was gone. Magda tried to rush her.

"No! No!" Magda never knew whether Jaelle screamed the words aloud or not, "I'll hold her back! Get the others away!" She flung herself on Acquilara with the knife.

Acquilara feinted with her long knife, and Jaelle brought up her arm in guard. Her sleeve was covered with blood. Then the sorceress's knife came up, and Magda rushed forward—

And stopped, sick and dizzy with terror of the cliff edge before her. Jaelle's knife went into Acquilara's breast, and the sorceress shrieked, a frantic dying howl of rage, and jumped at Jaelle. Her arms locked around Jaelle's neck.

Then the two slid together, slowly, slowly, with the dreadful inevitability of an avalanche, toward the edge, together slipped over the edge and fell. Magda screamed, rushed toward the cliff-edge; Camilla's strong arm snatched her back as she tottered, shrieking, on the very brink.

From below came a rumble, a great shattering sound like the end of the world, and a thousand tons of rock and ice ripped away from the cliff and roared down to bury them both a long, long way below.

Camilla's cry of horror and grief echoed her own. But even while Magda still heard the shaking of the avalanche, Kyntha pulled them away.

"Come! Quickly!" And as Magda turned back to where Jaelle had fallen, Camilla shouted, "No! Come! Don't make her sacrifice useless! For the children—for *both* the children—*bredhiya*—"

But it was already obvious that the fight was over. With Acquilara gone, the remnants of her group were scattering, throwing down their arms, screaming in terror, like an anthill kicked over. The phantom women warriors rose up over them, triumphant.

Cholayna had sunk to her knees, gasping, unable to breathe. Magda looked back at them, numbly.

Jaelle. Jaelle. The fight was over, but too late. What difference did it make, now, if they all died? *My own cowardice. I couldn't face the cliff. I could have saved her. . . .*

She was too numbed even to cry. But in the icy blast of the wind, the last sound she had expected to hear broke her out of her frozen despair.

In all the years she had known her she had never known Camilla to weep.

Chapter 31

Camilla's eyes were swollen almost shut with unaccustomed tears. She had refused to let the old blind woman, Rakhaila, tend her wounds, the slash across her forehead, the knife wound in her hand that had nearly severed the sixth finger on her right hand.

Magda sat close to her, in the upper room in the cliff-top retreat of Avarra, where Kyntha had taken them when the battle was over. All the way up in the basket she had forced herself, self-punishing despite the vertigo, to look down into the dizzying chasm.

Too late. Too late for Jaelle.

Less than an hour after the fight was over, she had felt the numbness leaving her; the *raivannin* was wearing off, her *laran* reasserting itself. Now, as she held Camilla, she felt the redoubled pain, her own and Camilla's anguish. She had longed for so many years to share this with Camilla; and now it was only loss and bereavement they could share.

"Why couldn't it have been me?" Magda was not sure, again, whether Camilla's words had been spoken aloud or not. "She was so young. She had everything to live for, she had a child, there were so many who loved her . . . you at least tried to save her, but I couldn't even *see*. . . ." She struck, with a furious hand, at the slash on her forehead, a dreadful matted mess of hair and frozen blood.

"No, Camilla—truly, *bredhiya*, you have no reason to reproach yourself. It was my—my cowardice—" Again, in despair, Magda relived the moment when she had held back, in fear of the unguarded cliff-edge. Could that moment have saved Jaelle?

She would never know. For the rest of her life she would torment herself, in nightmares, about that memory. But whether or not—she forced her mind away from her own anguish, it was too late for Jaelle, nothing she did could change that now, but Camilla was still living, and it seemed that Camilla's grief was worse than her own.

"Kima, *bredhiya*, love, you must let me care for this." She went and fetched hot water from the kettle over the fireplace, sponged away the frozen blood, revealing an ugly, but not dangerous slash.

"It needs stitches," she said, "but I cannot do it, and I do not think Cholayna can. Not now, at least."

"Oh, leave it, love, what difference does it make? One more scar," said Camilla. Passive, uncaring, she let Magda bandage the wounded hand. "I did not even know they had kidnapped you— Acquilara and her crew—imagine, it was the blind woman who insisted we turn back, to find you gone. And Jaelle—" Camilla's throat closed and her grief threatened to overwhelm her again. "Jaelle—tried to follow you with *laran*, and was not strong enough, she could not find you. So she—" Camilla bowed her scarred head on her hands and cried again, while Magda heard in her mind that shattering scene. Jaelle, crying, begging. . . .

I can't, Camilla. I am not strong enough. Only you can find them. They could be anywhere in these mountains, dead or alive, and if we do not find them soon they will starve, freeze, die . . .

I am no leronis. . . .

Will you cling to that last lie to yourself until they are all dead? Is there no end to your selfishness, Camilla? For myself I do not care, but Magda—Magda loves you, loves you more than anyone alive, more than the father of her child, more than her sworn freemate. . . .

As she heard those words in her mind, Magda felt that she too would be overcome again with weeping. Had it been true? Had Jaelle gone to her death believing that Magda loved her less?

Then, resolutely, Magda forced herself to abandon that lacerating train of thought. She told herself firmly: Either Shaya knows better now, or she is someplace where it makes no difference to her. She's gone beyond my reach. Painful as it was, she could do nothing more for Jaelle. She brought her full awareness back to Camilla.

"So she persuaded you—and you came for me! But where did Kyntha come from?"

"I do not know. Jaelle—" Camilla swallowed and resolutely went on—"Jaelle said to me, *I am a catalyst telepath, I have little skill myself, but I am told I can awaken it in others.* She touched me, and it was as if—as if a veil fell from me. I saw you, and I *knew* . . . and I came to you."

"She saved us all." But not herself. Magda knew she would never cease to grieve; nor would Camilla. She had only begun to feel the pain that would come back to haunt her at odd hours for the rest of her life, but for now she must put it aside. When she thought of Jaelle now she saw the Jaelle she would always remember, her wild hair streaming behind her, in the wind of the heights, turning to say, "*I don't want to go back.* . . ."

She shared the picture with Camilla, saying softly, "She told me that. She didn't want to go back. I think she knew, I think she saw her life as a finished thing. . . . She had done all she wanted to do."

"But I would so gladly have died instead—" Camilla said, choking.

Rafaella's hand fell on her shoulder. "So would I, Camilla. The Goddess knows—if there is a Goddess—" She had been crying, too; she bent and hugged Camilla hard.

Kyntha was standing beside them. Her voice was compassionate, but matter-of-fact as always.

"Food has been prepared for you. And your companions' wounds have been cared for." She bent to examine Camilla's forehead.

"If you wish, I can stitch it for you."

"No. Not necessary," Camilla said. Wearily she rose and followed Kyntha to the end of the room near the fireplace. Magda hung back a little, looking curiously at Kyntha. She said, "You do not speak the mountain dialect of these women. Where did you come from?"

Kyntha looked a little chagrined. "I can speak it when I must, and here I try to remember to do so, but I am—young and imperfect as yet. I grew up on the Plains of Valeron, and served five years in the Tower at Neskaya before I found a more meaningful service, Terran."

"You know?"

"I am not blind; Ferrika is known to me, and Marisela was my sworn sister in service to Avarra. There was a time when I too thought that I would cut my hair and swear the vows of a Renunciate. Do you think we come out of mysterious cracks from the underworld? Come and have some soup."

One of the women tending the kettle put a mug into her hand. She thought, *how can I eat, with Jaelle. . . .*

But she forced herself to drink the soup, which was hearty and thick with beans and something like barley. It seemed to melt, a little, the icy lump at her heart.

One of the beshawled attendants she had seen in her previous stay in this place was kneeling by Vanessa, rebandaging her injured leg. Rafaella seemed uninjured, though Magda had seen her in some close-quarters fighting, and her heavy cloak was cut and slashed and badly torn. Cholayna had been propped up on pillows; Magda knelt beside her.

Cholayna stretched out her hand toward Magda.

"I'm all right. But oh, I'm sorry about Jaelle, I loved her too, you know that—"

Magda's eyes filled. "I know. We all did. Let me get you some soup." It was all she could do. She looked at Lexie, lying on a pallet made of coats and spare blankets, still unconscious.

"Is she—"

"I don't know. They've done what they could for her, they say." Cholayna's voice was tight. "Did you see? They—those women—I was down. They were kicking me to death. Lexie saved me. That was when they stabbed her."

"I saw." So Rafaella had been right about Lexie. Magda knelt and looked at the younger woman, pale, like a sick child, her feathery fair hair lying on her childish neck. Her eyes were closed and she was breathing in long shuddering gasps.

Rafaella came and stood behind her. She whispered, almost inaudibly, and it was like a prayer, "Don't die. Don't die, Lexa', there's been too much dying." She raised her eyes to Magda and said defiantly, "You never knew her. She was a—a good friend, a good trail-mate. She fought like a mountain-cat to get us over Ravensmark after the landslide. I—I never thought I'd ask this of you, but you're—you're a *leronis*. Can you heal her?"

Magda knelt beside Alexis Anders. There had been too much death. She reached out to Lexie's mind, trying to reach the child she had sensed there for a moment, thrusting gently for contact—

Lexie's eyes opened; she turned over a little, her breath rasping in her throat. At the back of her mind Magda took notice: *lungs pierced. I doubt if Damon and Callista with Lady Hilary to help them could heal this.* Yet she knew she must try.

Lexie's eyes held awareness for a moment. She whispered, "Hellfire! You again, Lorne?" and her eyes closed, deliberately. She turned her head away.

"I can't reach her," Magda whispered, knowing it was the truth. "I am no magician, Rafaella. This is far beyond my powers."

For an instant Rafaella's eyes met her own, acknowledging the truth in what Magda said. Then, still defiant, she turned her back and moved past her. Magda had not seen; the old nameless priestess sat there in her bundle of shawls, her toothless, creased face regarding them all silently. Rafaella knelt before the ancient shamaness and said, "I beg you. *You* can heal her. Help her, please. *Please.* Don't let her die."

"Na', it canna' be done," said the old woman. Her voice was gentle, but detached.

"You *can't* just let her die . . ." Rafaella cried.

"Does thee not believe in death, little sister? It comes to all; her time comes sooner than ours, no more than that." The old woman patted the seat beside her, almost, Magda thought, as if encouraging a puppy to curl up at her side. Rafaella numbly sunk down in the indicated place.

"Hear 'ee, that one dying *chose* her death. Chose a good death, saving her friend from dying before her time—"

Cholayna turned as if galvanized. She cried out, "How can you say that? She was so young, how can she be dying before her time when I, I am old and still alive, and you helped me—"

"This one told thee before, thee is ignorant," said the old priestess. "That one dying there, she chose her death when even for a moment she allied herself wi' the evil."

"But she turned back! She saved me," Cholayna cried, and burst into a fit of coughing, half strangling with it, tears running down her face. "How can you say she was evil?"

"Was not. Better to die turning away from evil, than die with it," said the old woman. "Rest thee, daughter, thy sickness needs not these tears and cries. Her time was on her; thine will come, and mine, but not today or tomorrow."

"It's not right!" Rafaella cried out in despair. "Jaelle died saving us all; Lexie tried to save Cholayna. And *they* died, and the rest of us lived—any of us deserved death more than Jaelle: *they* deserved to live—"

The old priestess said very softly, "Oh, I see. Thee thinks death a punishment for wrong-doin' an' life the reward for good, like a cake to a good child or a whip to a naughty one. Thee is a child, little one, an' thee canna' hear wisdom. Rest thee all, little sisters. There is much to say, but thee canna' hear in thy grief."

She rose creakily from her seat; the old blind woman, Rakhaila, came to her and offered an arm, and she tottered slowly from the room.

Kyntha remained a moment, staring at them with resentment. Then she said, "You have grieved her beyond words. You have brought blood here, and the deaths of violence." She stared with distaste at Lexie. "Rest and recover your strength, as she has bidden you. Tomorrow there are decisions which must be made."

*   *   *

Lexie died just before sunset. She died in Cholayna's arms, without recovering consciousness. As if they had known, four of the old woman's attendants came in silently and took the body away.

"What will you do with her?" asked Vanessa apprehensively.

"Gi' her to the holy birds of Avarra," said one of the women, and Magda, remembering the high vulture-headdresses of the women warriors of illusion, knew that their Sisterhood paid reverence to the *kyorebni*, whose task it was to deal with matter which had outlived its usefulness. She explained this quietly to Vanessa and Cholayna, and Cholayna bowed her head.

"It does not matter to her now. But I wish she had not come so far to die. Poor child, poor child," she murmured.

Vanessa rose and put on her heavy coat. "I'll go and watch. I can do that much for Personnel. No, you stay here, Cholayna, if you go out in this cold you'll have pneumonia again and hold us up another ten days. It's my job, not yours."

They seemed to know what she intended, and waited for her.

Rafaella rose and said roughly, "My coat's torn to pieces. Lend me yours, Margali, you're about my size. I'll go, too. We were comrades; if she'd lived, we would have been—friends."

Magda nodded, with tears in her eyes.

"No, Camilla, you stay here, she was nothing to you. We loved her."

Camilla and Magda came by instinct to kneel by Cholayna's bed, holding her hands as Alexis Anders' body was borne away by the priestesses. After a long time Rafaella and Vanessa came back, silent and subdued, and had nothing further to say that night. But Magda heard Rafaella crying far into the night, and after a long time Vanessa got up and went to her, lay down beside her, and Magda heard them whispering to one another till she fell asleep.

Magda woke before the others, and lay listening to the soft hiss of the snow outside the building. Jaelle was gone; their search was ended. Or was it? They had found Lexie and Rafaella; Lexie was dead. Jaelle, who had come to seek a legendary city, had preceded her into death. Marisela, who knew the City and the Sisterhood, was dead too. Were they nowhere, lonesome spirits on the wind, or were they together, seeking something tangible? Magda wished she knew. She could not even guess.

The Sisterhood. They know. Marisela knew. If Jaelle had lived, Magda now knew, they would have sought that knowledge together; perhaps with Camilla, whose quest was to demand of the Goddess, if there was in truth a Goddess, the reasons for her life and her suffering. Now she had another grievance against the Goddess who had taken Jaelle from her. If she could find or fight her way in, Magda knew Camilla would go on.

And Magda should go with her. It was her destiny. But as she listened to Cholayna's hoarse breathing, Magda knew she was not free to follow. Cholayna might already have pneumonia again, and would not be fit to travel for many days. She could not follow them to the City; she would not be admitted. A search for wisdom was not her destiny; she would return to the Terran HQ, as Vanessa must. And she, Magda, must take them back.

She had a swift vision of Jaelle—head bent against the wind, face against the storm, leading—leading the way on some madcap adventure—

Now Jaelle had gone before her again, where she could not follow. She must persuade Camilla to go on; but Magda must go back with her Terran compatriots.

Day dawned fully, and after they had cooked and eaten some breakfast, the old woman came back, ceremoniously seating herself on the stone dais, accompanied by the blind woman Rakhaila and by Kyntha.

"Did ye all sleep well? Medicines 'ull be given thee, sister," she added to Cholayna, then turned to Kyntha.

"Thee shall speak, what must be said."

Kyntha faced them. There was an odd ceremoniousness in her voice. She spoke the mountain dialect this time, though she spoke it slowly.

"Thy sister Marisela should ha' said this to ye all. Her duty, which I do with grief. Thee has come to seek the Sisterhood, and

Marisela was leading thee to a place where thee might be questioned as to thy will. We ha' no heart to make thee travel again that path, so I ask thee here. What does thee seek?" She turned toward Camilla.

Camilla said, harshly, "Thee knows I seek those who serve the Goddess, that I may ask them—or Her—what Her purpose is for me."

Kyntha said gently, "She answers not such questions, sister. It will be thy own task to gain wisdom to hear her voice."

"Then where do I start looking for this wisdom? In your City? Take me there."

Blind Rakhaila erupted with a guffaw.

"Jes' like that, thee says? Haw!"

"Thee has lived a life of much suffering and travail, seeking wisdom," Kyntha said. "Yet look on Rakhaila here. She is older still; she has endured as much as thee; yet she has not been admitted there. She is content to dwell at the outer gates as servant to the beasts who carry the servants of the Sisterhood."

"Has she asked it?" Camilla said. "There are different paths to the Sisterhood; furthermore, I think you have the duty to do so, because I have demanded it. Do your duty, my sister, that I may do mine."

The old shamaness beckoned to Camilla. She patted the seat beside her, as she had done with Rafaella the day before.

"To one who asks, all is answered," she said. "I bid thee welcome, granddaughter of my soul."

Magda felt a sharp pain at her heart. Jaelle had gone before her, with Marisela. Now Camilla had outstripped her and was to be taken from her.

Kyntha said to Rafaella, and her voice was not harsh, but faintly sarcastic, "Now you know the City is no place of riches and jewels, do you still wish to go there?"

Rafaella shook her head. She said, "I accepted a lawful commission. It is ended badly; my companion is dead. But I do not regret the search. I have no desire to be a *leronis*. I leave that to others."

"Go, then, in peace," Kyntha said. "I have no authority over you." She turned to Vanessa. "And you?"

Vanessa said, "With all due respect, I think it's all moonshine. Four moons' worth of moonshine. Thanks, but no thanks."

Kyntha smiled. "So be it. I respect you for your loyalty in following others where you had no interest in the quest—"

"You're giving me too much credit," Vanessa said. "I came because there were mountains to climb."

"Then, I say to you, you have had your reward and you are welcome to it," Kyntha said. Then she bowed to Cholayna.

"Sister from a far world, you have all your life sought wisdom beneath every strange sky. You hold life in reverence and you seek truth. The Sisterhood has read your heart from afar. If it is your will to enter, you too may come, and seek wisdom among us."

For the first and last time, Magda felt the touch of the Terran woman's thoughts; she could not read them as words, but she touched the expanded sense of their import, the knowledge that in her own way Cholayna had sought this all her life.

Then Cholayna sighed, with infinite regret.

"My duty lies elsewhere," she said. "I think you know that. I cannot follow my wishes in this matter. I have made another choice in this life, and I will not turn away from it."

Again Kyntha bowed, and turned at last to Magda. "And you? What is your will?"

Magda knew her own sigh was an echo of Cholayna's. She said, "I would like to come to you. I wish—but I too have duties, responsibilities—I am sorry. I wish—".

But she knew she must return with Cholayna and Vanessa, to the world on the far side of those mountains. If this wisdom was meant for her, then some day she would have another chance, and be free to take it. If not, it was not worth having. She must return to her child, to Jaelle's child as well. . . .

Kyntha took a single step toward her. She put her hand under Magda's chin and lifted it. She said, "This is the place of truth! Speak!" It was like a great gong. "The tides of thy life are moving. *What is thy truest will?*"

Magda heard what Andrew had said to her, when she came to the Forbidden Tower. *There isn't one of us here who hasn't had to tear their lives up like a piece of scrap paper and start over. Some of us have had to do it two or three times.* Far off it seemed that she could hear the calling of crows.

Would she ever return? She dismissed that. If she should never return, then that was her destiny. She had abandoned the Guild-house when the time came for that, and returned to build a Bridge Society between her two worlds. Jaelle had ruthlessly run ahead, knowing she had worn out the challenges of the past, looking ahead. Magda would have courage to follow.

"I would like to follow Camilla to the City. But I have a duty to my companions—"

A brief silence in the room. Then Rafaella said roughly, "Isn't that just like you, Margali? You think I'm not fit to take Cholayna and Vanessa back to Thendara? You stay here and do what you damn please. I'm the mountain guide. Who needs you?"

Magda blinked. Rough as the words were, what she heard in them was pure love; what Rafaella had said was, *sister*.

"Hell, yes. Lorne. That's settled. When Cholayna's able to travel, you go." Vanessa went and stood beside Rafaella. "We decided that last night when you were asleep."

Almost disbelieving, Magda looked round. The ancient sorceress beckoned to her. She went and numbly sat on the dais beside her, feeling Camilla's cold hands in hers.

The end of a quest? Or a beginning? Did all quests end like this, a final step upward to the pinnacle of a mighty mountain, which gave way to reveal a new and unknown horizon?

MARION ZIMMER BRADLEY

THE DARKOVER NOVELS

☐ DARKOVER LANDFALL	UE2234—$3.99
☐ HAWKMISTRESS!	UE2239—$4.99
☐ STORMQUEEN!	UE2310—$6.99
☐ TWO TO CONQUER	UE2174—$4.99
☐ THE HEIRS OF HAMMERFELL	UE2451—$4.99
☐ THE SHATTERED CHAIN	UE2308—$5.99
☐ THENDARA HOUSE	UE2240—$5.99
☐ CITY OF SORCERY	UE2332—$6.99
☐ REDISCOVERY*	UE2529—$6.99
☐ THE SPELL SWORD	UE2237—$3.99
☐ THE FORBIDDEN TOWER	UE2373—$6.99
☐ STAR OF DANGER	UE2607—$4.99
☐ THE WINDS OF DARKOVER & THE PLANET SAVERS	UE2630—$4.99
☐ THE BLOODY SUN	UE2603—$4.99
☐ THE HERITAGE OF HASTUR	UE2413—$4.99
☐ SHARRA'S EXILE	UE2309—$5.99
☐ EXILE'S SONG	UE2734—$6.99
☐ THE SHADOW MATRIX	UE2812—$6.99
☐ TRAITOR'S SUN	UE2810—$24.95

*with Mercedes Lackey

Prices slightly higher in Canada   **DAW:110**

Payable in U.S. funds only. No cash/COD accepted. Postage & handling: U.S./CAN. $2.75 for one book, $1.00 for each additional, not to exceed $6.75; Int'l $5.00 for one book, $1.00 each additional. We accept Visa, Amex, MC ($10.00 min.), checks ($15.00 fee for returned checks) and money orders. Call 800-788-6262 or 201-933-9292, fax 201-896-8569; refer to ad #120.

EXILE'S SONG

A Novel of Darkover

by Marion Zimmer Bradley

Margaret Alton is the daughter of Lew Alton, Darkover's Senator to the Terran Federation, but her morose, uncommunicative father is secretive about the obscure planet of her birth. So when her university job sends her to Darkover, she has only fleeting, haunting memories of a tumultuous childhood. But once in the light of the Red Sun, as her veiled and mysterious heritage becomes manifest, she finds herself trapped by a destiny more terrifying than any nightmare!

- A direct sequel to *The Heritage of Hastur* and *Sharra's Exile*
- With cover art by Romas Kukalis
- ☐ **Hardcover Edition**   UE2705-$21.95

KRISTEN BRITAIN
GREEN RIDER

"The gifted Ms. Britain writes with ease and grace as she creates a mesmerizing fantasy ambiance and an appealing heroine quite free of normal clichés."
—*Romantic Times*

Karigan G'ladheon has fled from school following a fight that would surely lead to her expulsion. As she makes her way through the deep forest, a galloping horse plunges out of the brush, its rider impaled by two black arrows. With his dying breath, he tells her he is a Green Rider, one of the legendary magical messengers of the King. Giving her his green coat with its symbolic brooch of office, he makes Karigan swear to deliver the message he was carrying. Pursued by unknown assassins, following a path only the messenger's horse seems to know, she unwittingly finds herself in a world of deadly danger and complex magic, compelled by forces she does not yet understand. . . .

0-88677-858-1 $6.99

Prices slightly higher in Canada   **DAW: 109**

Penguin Putnam Inc.   Bill my: ☐Visa ☐MasterCard ☐Amex_____ (expires)
P.O. Box 12289, Dept. B   Card#_____
Newark, NJ 07101-5289

Please allow 4-6 weeks for delivery.   Signature_____
Foreign and Canadian delivery 6-8 weeks.

Bill to:

Name_____

Address_____City_____

State/ZIP_____

Daytime Phone #_____

Ship to:

Name_____ Book Total $_____

Address_____ Applicable Sales Tax $_____

City_____ Postage & Handling $_____

State/Zip_____ Total Amount Due $_____

This offer subject to change without notice.

The Palm Canyon of Arizona. (Photograph by Robert A. Darrow.)

Lyman Benson

is now Professor of Botany at Pomona
College, and formerly was affiliated
with the University of Arizona as
Assistant Professor of Botany. Besides
being author of THE CACTI OF
ARIZONA, he has written more than
thirty technical articles for various
botanical journals, including the first
edition of THE TREES AND
SHRUBS OF THE SOUTHWEST-
ERN DESERTS (under the title of
*A Manual of Southwestern Desert
Trees and Shrubs,* now out of print).
His interest in the desert goes back
to boyhood; his grandfather, Anderson Benson, was one of the wandering
party of starving '49'ers who discovered Death Valley. Dr. Benson, a native Californian, took his A.B., M.A.,
and Ph.D., at Stanford University.

Robert Darrow

is Professor of Ecology in the Department of Range and Forestry at the
Texas Agricultural and Mechanical
College. He received his Ph.D. from
the University of Chicago and is
author and co-author of a number of
technical studies. Much of the data for
the distribution maps in this book was
obtained by intensive botanical ex-
ploration by Dr. Darrow in the deserts
of Arizona and adjoining regions.

Trees and Shrubs
of the
thwestern Deserts

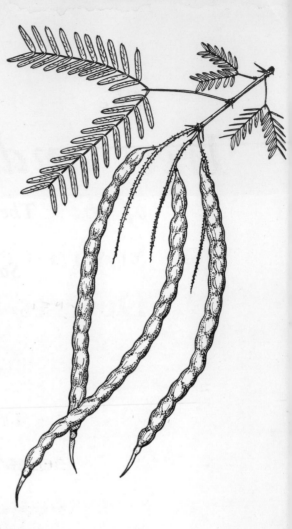

LYMAN BENSON
(Systematic Botany)

Professor of Botany, Pomona College

Formerly Assistant Professor of Botany,
University of Arizona

ROBERT A. DARROW
(Geographical Distribution and Economic Notes)

*Professor of Range Management, Agricultural
and Mechanical College of Texas*

Formerly Professor of Botany,
University of Arizona

THE UNIVERSITY OF ARIZONA · THE UNIVERSITY OF NEW MEXICO
PRESS . . . . . TUCSON   PRESS . . . . ALBUQUERQUE

Published March 15, 1954

The
Trees and Shrubs
of the
Southwestern
Deserts

LYMAN BENSON
and
ROBERT A. DARROW

First published by
THE UNIVERSITY OF ARIZONA
Under the title:
A MANUAL OF SOUTHWESTERN
DESERT TREES AND SHRUBS

Line Drawings by
LUCRETIA BREAZEALE HAMILTON

Published by
The University of Arizona Press, Tucson

and

The University of New Mexico Press, Albuquerque

Botany

Second Edition

1954

Copyright 1945
University of Arizona

Copyright 1954
The University of New Mexico Press

LIBRARY OF CONGRESS CATALOG CARD NUMBER: 53-7210

PREFACE

FIRST EDITION

This work continues a series on the flora of Arizona and the
Southwest. The first publication of the group is University of
Arizona Biological Science Bulletin No. 5, *The Cacti of Arizona*
(Univ. of Ariz. Bull., Vol. XI, No. 1). The present work is
intended to constitute a semipopular or semitechnical manual
for identification of trees and shrubs growing in the deserts
of the southwestern United States without the intentional aid of
man. They include all the woody plants, and only the "bushy"
types, which are more or less transitional between shrubs and
herbs, are excluded. However, a few relatively small bushes of
especial interest are discussed.

The text is designed for use in identification of trees and
shrubs. The matters of more general interest, including the
geographical distribution of species and their values to man
or to other animals, appear in larger type in order that they
may have greater prominence. A few outstanding diagnostic
characters of each plant or group of plants are given in likewise
larger type in order to facilitate recognition of families, genera,
and species. Although determination of the names of plants
by use of the keys and descriptions given in smaller type is the
only thoroughly accurate method, it is hoped that many plants
may be recognized by merely consulting the illustrations or
by looking up in the index well-established English, Spanish,
or Indian names.

The floristic or vegetational types included are the creosote-
bush (sometimes known locally as greasewood) desert and the
desert grassland; and the geographical limits may be summed
up roughly as from Palm Springs, California, to El Paso, Texas.
A more detailed description follows:

CALIFORNIA. The Mojave Desert, including the Death Valley
region, and the Colorado Desert, part of which is known more
commonly as the Imperial Valley.

NEVADA. The southern tip, including portions of Nye and

Lincoln counties, and all but the higher mountains of Clark County.

UTAH. The Virgin River Valley about St. George.

ARIZONA. The lowest level of the Grand Canyon and all the territory west and south of the Mogollon Rim and the White Mountains.

NEW MEXICO. The territory from Albuquerque southward, west of the White and Sacramento mountains.

TEXAS. El Paso County, specifically. The manual should be usable also for all of Trans-Pecos Texas, including the Big Bend region, but for territory outside El Paso County a few trees or shrubs will not be found.

New names and new combinations of names have been published in articles in the *American Journal of Botany* for March and July, 1943. A complete list of synonymous scientific names and of type collections is given in the Appendix, p. 365.

LYMAN BENSON

May 1, 1944

SECOND EDITION

The first edition of this book, published as a MANUAL OF SOUTHWESTERN DESERT TREES AND SHRUBS, was in print for less than two and one-half years, and requests from many sources indicate the need for a new printing. The necessary changes are relatively few, and the second edition is only slightly revised.

LYMAN BENSON

February 14, 1953

ACKNOWLEDGEMENTS

Gratitude is expressed to the directors and curators of the following institutions for the privilege of examining specimens of special groups of plants: Dudley Herbarium, Stanford University, California; University of California, Berkeley, California; Gray Herbarium, Harvard University, Cambridge, Massachusetts; New York Botanical Garden, Bronx Park, New

York City; United States National Herbarium, Smithsonian Institution, Washington, D.C.; U.S. Field Station, Sacaton, Arizona;* Herbarium of Forrest Shreve, Tucson, Arizona.* The authors are grateful to Dr. Thomas H. Kearney, Mr. R. H. Peebles, and Mr. A. A. Nichol for data on the distribution of species.

Photographs have been furnished by the following individuals, and the appreciation of the authors is expressed to them: A. A. Nichol, D. M. Crooks, L. M. Pultz, J. M. Webber, R. H. Peebles, K. W. Parker, Herbert A. Anderson, R. B. Streets, Elbert L. Little, Jr., William P. Martin, E. T. Nichols, Forrest Shreve, W. S. Phillips. Several photographs are furnished through the courtesy of the Southwestern Forest and Range Experiment Station, Forest Service, U.S. Dept. of Agriculture. Photographs taken by Mr. Peebles and Mr. Webber are used through the courtesy of the Bureau of Plant Industry, Soils, and Agricultural Engineering, U.S. Dept. of Agriculture.

The four collaborators who kindly supplied the texts on special plant groups have proposed few changes to be incorporated into the second edition. It is a pleasure to acknowledge the outstanding contributions of the individuals who prepared the original data on the following families or genera:

The Family Amaryllidaceae by
ELBERT L. LITTLE
Forest Service, United States Department of Agriculture

The Family Euphorbiaceae by
LOUIS C. WHEELER
Department of Botany, University of Southern California

The Family Labiatae by
CARL EPLING
Department of Botany, University of California, Los Angeles

The Genus *Lycium* by
C. LEO HITCHCOCK
Department of Botany, University of Washington

*Now in University of Arizona Herbarium.

TABLE OF CONTENTS

ix

INTRODUCTION

VEGETATION OF THE SOUTHWESTERN DESERTS

The Southwestern deserts of the United States occupy the lowest elevations from the eastern slopes of the southern Sierra Nevada and the mountains of Southern California to the Rio Grande and the Pecos River in New Mexico and Texas (see map, Fig. 2). Altitudinal limits vary from below sea level in the Salton Sea Basin and the Death Valley region upward to 3,500 feet along the western margins of the California deserts and to approximately 5,000 feet in the southern Sierra Nevada, southern Nevada, southwestern Utah, and New Mexico. The desert belt is nearly continuous through the region, and it is broken only here and there by the higher mountains and plateaus, which support grassland, woodland, or forest.

The vegetation of the deserts is wholly unlike any other in the United States. The perennial plants are adapted in various ways to the rigorous climate, and among the adaptations are bizarre and unusual growth forms. Low, infrequent rainfall, coupled with high temperatures and rapid evaporation, makes survival impossible for any but plants capable of conservation of moisture and endurance of long drought periods. The cacti, the elephant tree, jatrophas, and other plants have enlarged, succulent stems which take up and store quantities of water in the brief rainy periods, and it is utilized in the prolonged periods of dryness. Similarly, the leaves of other plants, including the century plants or agaves and to a limited degree the saltbushes and their relatives growing in alkali flats, are adapted to the storage of water.

Nonsucculent perennial plants are adapted to the desert climate by various devices tending to reduce water loss. The creosote bush, acacias, mimosas, desert broom, and ephedras or Mormon tea conserve moisture by reduction of leaf area, and complete elimination of leaves is achieved in the various crucifixion thorns (*Canotia, Holacantha,* and *Koeberlinia*). Other plants, including the palo verdes, ocotillo, and jatrophas, have an abundance of leaves in the rainy seasons, but they are

1

deciduous with the advent of drought. In most of these plants the stems are green, and they take over much or all of the manufacture of food normally performed by the leaves. Outstanding examples of photosynthetic (food-manufacturing) stems are in the palo verdes, cacti, crucifixion thorns, and ephedras. Most of the trees and shrubs have a copious supply of waxes and resins on their surfaces, and these make loss of water exceedingly slow.

The desert vegetation at most seasons consists of trees, shrubs, and succulents, but in the spring and summer rainy season numerous annual plants appear for brief periods. These herbaceous plants are able to withstand drought only in the seed or resting stage.

The vegetation varies markedly in structure (growth form) and composition (species) from one place to another. In most areas shrubs constitute the principal life form, but in south-central Arizona shrubby and columnar cacti are important and striking. Trees occur along the principal drainages or "washes," and, in the higher parts of the desert, small trees, including palo verdes, desert ironwood, Joshua tree, and crucifixion thorns, give the landscape an appearance of woodland.

DESERT CLIMATE AND PHYSIOGRAPHY

Development of a desert-type vegetation is the result of climate. High temperatures, low and infrequently distributed rainfall, low atmospheric humidity, high evaporation, and cloudless days with high light intensity restrict the character and number of plants capable of survival.

The deserts of the earth in both hemispheres are in the belts of tropical calms or horse latitudes at about 20 to 30 degrees. The dryness in these areas is due to movement of warm air masses poleward from the equator. This air descending in the horse latitudes creates an area of high pressure and low rainfall. With the lack of prevailing winds little moisture is brought in from the oceans, and most of the rain is from the local convectional storms characteristic of desert climate.

The portion of the desert within the United States is at the northern edge of the belt of tropical calms, and in the wintertime as climatic zones are shifted southward, it is barely within the zone of prevailing westerly winds. Consequently, the southern Sierra Nevada and the high mountains of southern California have an important effect upon winter climate, since they form a barrier which deprives the prevailing westerlies of much of their moisture.

The western edge of the desert in the lee of the southern California mountains receives only the scant moisture brought over the mountains by the winter winds, and summer rains are rare. Eastward in the desert the ratio of summer to winter rain increases. West and north of Tucson, Arizona, winter rain exceeds that of summer, but eastward and southward summer rain is predominant.

Summer rainfall occurs usually in local torrential convection showers, and often it is concentrated over the mountain masses. Flash floods are a common result of these heavy summer storms, and walls of water rush down the normally dry washes. With the accompanying high temperatures and rapid evaporation, only a small portion of the precipitation becomes available to plants. Winter rainfall, on the other hand, is associated with the eastward passage of cyclonic storm centers originating in the Pacific Northwest or over the Pacific Ocean. Winter storms are usually slow, steady, and of several days' duration. With the lower temperatures and reduced evaporation rate, most of the water enters the soil as it falls and thus becomes available for plant growth.

Annual precipitation in the Southwestern deserts varies from about 2 to 20 inches, but the greater portion of the desert receives less than 10 or 15 inches. Most of the months of the year are practically without rainfall.

Desert temperatures have extreme daily and monthly ranges. Maximums of 100 to 120 degrees are common in the summer, and an extreme maximum of 134 degrees is reported officially from Death Valley. Over much of the desert, minimum winter temperatures do not fall below 20 to 25 degrees, while in the lower elevations of the Salton Sea Basin and along the Colorado River freezing temperatures are infrequent or unknown. Daily variations of 30 to 50 degrees or more are resultant from the low degree of cloudiness and the aridity characteristic of the desert climate.

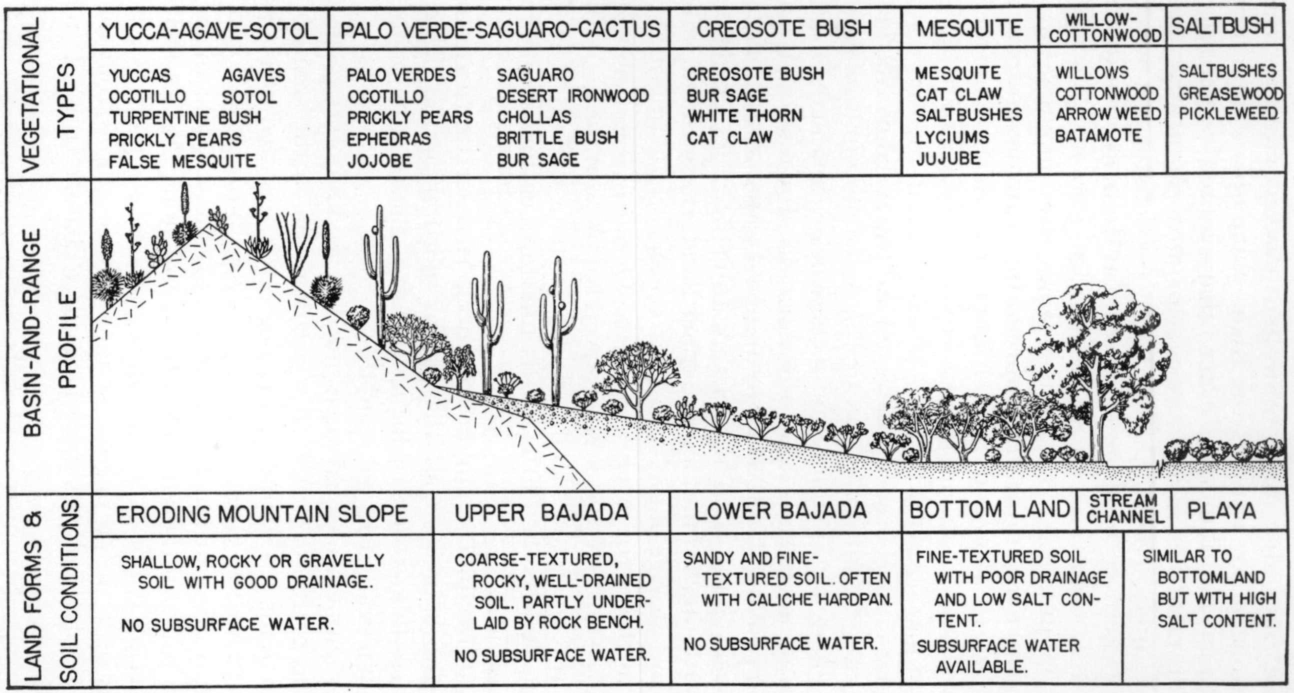

VEGETATIONAL TYPES	YUCCA-AGAVE-SOTOL	PALO VERDE-SAGUARO-CACTUS	CREOSOTE BUSH	MESQUITE	WILLOW-COTTONWOOD	SALTBUSH
	YUCCAS AGAVES OCOTILLO SOTOL TURPENTINE BUSH PRICKLY PEARS FALSE MESQUITE	PALO VERDES OCOTILLO PRICKLY PEARS EPHEDRAS JOJOBE SAGUARO DESERT IRONWOOD CHOLLAS BRITTLE BUSH BUR SAGE	CREOSOTE BUSH BUR SAGE WHITE THORN CAT CLAW	MESQUITE CAT CLAW SALTBUSHES LYCIUMS JUJUBE	WILLOWS COTTONWOOD ARROW WEED BATAMOTE	SALTBUSHES GREASEWOOD PICKLEWEED

BASIN-AND-RANGE PROFILE

LAND FORMS & SOIL CONDITIONS	ERODING MOUNTAIN SLOPE	UPPER BAJADA	LOWER BAJADA	BOTTOM LAND	STREAM CHANNEL	PLAYA
	SHALLOW, ROCKY OR GRAVELLY SOIL WITH GOOD DRAINAGE. NO SUBSURFACE WATER.	COARSE-TEXTURED, ROCKY, WELL-DRAINED SOIL. PARTLY UNDER-LAID BY ROCK BENCH. NO SUBSURFACE WATER.	SANDY AND FINE-TEXTURED SOIL. OFTEN WITH CALICHE HARDPAN. NO SUBSURFACE WATER.	FINE-TEXTURED SOIL WITH POOR DRAINAGE AND LOW SALT CON-TENT. SUBSURFACE WATER AVAILABLE.		SIMILAR TO BOTTOMLAND BUT WITH HIGH SALT CONTENT.

Fig. 1.—Idealized profile through a desert mountain range and basin, showing the vegetational types and soil conditions developed on the various land surfaces. The trees and shrubs are typical of the Arizona Desert.

Physiographically, the Southwestern deserts, together with the sagebrush desert of the Great Basin, make up a unit known as the Basin and Range Province, characterized by isolated, roughly parallel mountain ranges separated by nearly level basins or intermountain plains. Large portions of the desert consist of enclosed areas with no external drainage. Although most of the region has potential drainage into major water-courses, the prevàiling climatic conditions permit only a small contribution from the desert proper to the permanent streams.

A schematic representation of basin and range topography is shown in Fig. 1, and this diagram illustrates the land surfaces and soils found commonly in the desert and outlines the plant communities as they are represented in central and southern Arizona.

The characteristic topographic feature of the desert is the alluvial fan, outwash slope, or bajada of erosional material deposited at the base of each mountain range by water rushing down the slopes after torrential summer rains. Formation of these fans or slopes has been described as "a mountain burying itself in its own debris." Material derived from mechanical weathering and active erosion of the rocky mass of the mountain is deposited in successive layers on a sloping alluvial apron skirting the mountain. The textural series is graduated with the coarse fragments nearest the mountain and the finer material at the outer edge of the bajada. On the surface of the alluvial fan, drainage may result in formation of a treelike (dendritic) pattern of gravelly or sandy washes accentuated by the plants growing along them as a result of extra moisture.

Between the mountain ranges there is either an ephemeral principal drainage (large wash) or an undrained basin or playa (alkali flat or "dry lake"). Usually the finer-textured soils of these low-lying areas accumulate high concentrations of salts and become strongly alkaline. In some of the larger basins and along the main drainages the water table is near the surface, and in many instances the plant growth (at least around the margins where the salt concentration is not too high) is luxuriant.

DESERT VEGETATION

The distinctive climatic and physiographic conditions of the Southwestern deserts give rise to a complex vegetation essentially similar in general appearance from one end of the desert to the other and with some of the more conspicuous species occurring everywhere. The more nearly level bajadas and the intermountain plains bear uniform stands of shrubbery in which the creosote bush (*Larrea divaricata*) is the outstanding perennial plant (Pl. III *A*). Individual large shrubs are widely spaced and more than half the ground is bare. Smaller shrubs, such as the bur sages (*Franseria dumosa* and *Franseria deltoidea*), are associated with creosote bush on the plains, and the monotony is broken only by the larger acacias, palo verdes, and mesquites along the minor drainages. In the more arid portions of the desert most or all of the plants may be restricted to the washes, and the intervening level areas may be covered with interlocking fragments of volcanic gravel and small rocks forming desert pavement (Pl. IV *B*).

The upper bajadas and the eroding mountain slopes support a richer flora, for the coarser soils allow deeper infiltration of rain water. Where rainfall is more abundant, the slopes support a sort of woodland of Joshua trees, giant cacti or saguaros, crucifixion thorns, palo verdes, and desert ironwood. Smaller shrubs and perennial herbs, particularly of the pea and sunflower families, are abundant, and annual plants, including grasses, mask the barren rocky soil during the rainy seasons. Rocky slopes at the upper edge of the desert support a vegetation rich in large members of the lily and amaryllis families, notably the yuccas, agaves, or century plants, nolinas, and sotols.

FLORISTIC REGIONS OF THE SOUTHWESTERN DESERTS

The Southwestern creosote-bush deserts fall into the following categories arranged according to species composition and general structure of the vegetation (cf. Fig. 2):

    a. Mojave Desert

    b. Sonoran Desert

       (1) Colorado Desert

         (a) Salton Sea Basin

         (b) Colorado Basin

       (2) Arizona Desert

    c. Chihuahuan Desert

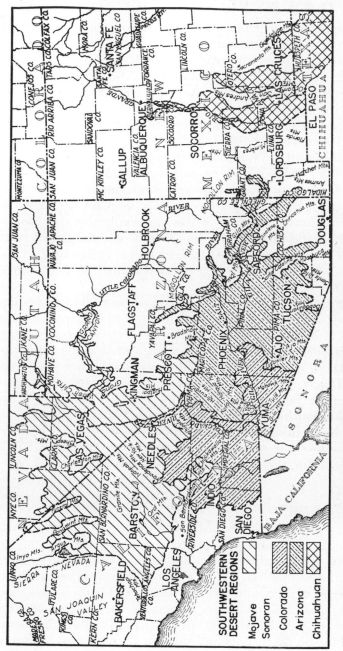
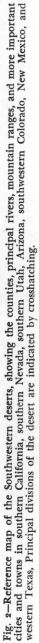

Fig. 2—Reference map of the Southwestern deserts, showing the counties, principal rivers, mountain ranges, and more important cities and towns in southern California, southern Nevada, southern Utah, Arizona, southwestern Colorado, New Mexico, and western Texas. Principal divisions of the desert are indicated by crosshatching.

a. MOJAVE DESERT. The Mojave Desert is bordered on the
west by the southern Sierra Nevada and the continuation of
the axis in southern California and on the south by the Little
San Bernardino and Eagle mountains. Northward it reaches
the edge of the Great Basin and eastward it extends to the
Virgin River Valley about St. George, Utah, to a point in the
Grand Canyon near the mouth of the Little Colorado River,
to the Grand Wash Cliffs, and to the Harcuvar Mountains
just south of Bill Williams River, Arizona. The range of altitude is from 1,500 to 3,000 or sometimes 5,000 feet.

The Little San Bernardino and Eagle mountains in California have not been a positive barrier to plant migration as
have the higher mountains to the westward, and the Mojave
Desert flora and that of the northern Colorado Desert have
tended to mingle. Likewise, about Owens Valley and in the
Death Valley region there is a gradual transition to the sagebrush of the Great Basin.

Primarily the Mojave Desert consists of a series of undrained
basins separated by mountain ranges with broad, gently sloping
bajadas. The basins are large, nearly level, and have strong
concentrations of salt; locally they are called "soda lakes" or
"borax lakes." Although the Colorado River cuts across the
Mojave Desert, the Mojave River is the characteristic stream.
It rises in the San Bernardino Mountains and ends in a series
of dry lakes south of Death Valley. Death Valley is the extreme
example of an undrained basin, since it is as much as 280 feet
below sea level. It receives water from the Amargosa River,
which heads in the Charleston Mountains of Nevada. With
few exceptions the mountain ranges between the basins of the
Mojave Desert are of insufficient altitude to support any but
desert vegetation.

The vegetation of the Mojave Desert is predominately
shrubby. Annual flowering plants are abundant during the
winter and spring rainy season, and they differ markedly from
those of the Sonoran Desert to the southward. There are only
a few species of cacti, and most of them are inconspicuous, low-
growing types. Around the periphery of the desert and here
and there on the higher hills, but particularly along the desert
slopes of the Sierra Nevada and the San Bernardino Mountains

and at Grand Wash Cliffs in Arizona, the fantastic Joshua tree
is abundant; it is one of the few trees in the Mojave Desert.
In areas of higher rainfall the mixture of shrubby species is
rich, but on the broad intermountain plains often it is restricted
to creosote bush and bur sage (*Franseria dumosa*). Blackbrush
(*Coleogyne ramosissima*) is dominant on the highest slopes
to the north and east, and it is associated with many plants
characteristic of the Great Basin sagebrush desert.

Approximately one fourth of the plants of the Mojave Desert flora are
endemic or essentially so. Shrubby endemics or near endemics are the
following:

Joshua tree...................................*Yucca brevifolia*
Parry saltbush..................................*Atriplex Parryi*
Indigo bush....................*Dalea Fremontii* var. *Saundersii*
Mojave sage................................*Salvia mohavensis*
Bur sage.................................*Franseria eriocentra*

In Death Valley the extremes of temperature and the low annual rainfall
(less than 2 inches) provide unfavorable conditions for perennial plants.
This low-lying basin flanked on either side by high mountain ranges has
afforded a desert environment probably for a longer period than has the
surrounding area. As a consequence of this isolation, several local endemic
shrubs occur about the valley. Among these are the following:

Death Valley ephedra.............*Ephedra californica* var. *funerea*
Bailey greasewood.............*Sarcobatus vermiculatus* var. *Baileyi*
Tetracoccus.............................*Tetracoccus ilicifolius*
Death Valley sage..............................*Salvia funerea*

The flora of the Mojave Desert is related in some degree to the Great
Basin desert flora to the northward. Many genera are common to both
deserts, and several species of shrubs occur in both areas. Among these are
the following:

Nevada ephedra..............................*Ephedra nevadensis*
Green ephedra................................*Ephedra viridis*
Utah agave.....................................*Agave utahensis*
Shadscale................................*Atriplex confertifolia*
Winter fat......................................*Eurotia lanata*
Spiny hop sage.................................*Grayia spinosa*
Blackbrush..............................*Coleogyne ramosissima*
Nevada dalea................................*Dalea polyadenia*

Affinity of the Mojave Desert flora with that of the San Joaquin Valley
and adjacent areas is shown by shrubs and other plants which have migrated

through the low gaps in the Greenhorn and Tehachapi mountains at Walker and Tehachapi passes. Among the shrubby species are the following:

Green ephedra...............................*Ephedra viridis*
Spiny saltbush..............................*Atriplex spinifera*
Desert saltbush......................*Atriplex polycarpa*
Western honey mesquite.........*Prosopis juliflora* var. *Torreyana*
Screw bean................................*Prosopis pubescens*
Cooper lycium...............................*Lycium Cooperi*

The Providence, Clark, and Charleston mountains in the eastern Mojave Desert are noteworthy for a number of species of limited distribution and for others with affinities with the Sonoran Desert and its adjacent regions. Some shrubby species occurring in these ranges which are typical of the Sonoran Desert or adjacent areas are:

Crucifixion thorn.........................*Canotia Holacantha*
Wright lippia................................*Lippia Wrightii*
Menodora.....................................*Menodora scabra*

b. SONORAN DESERT. The Sonoran Desert centers in Sonora west of the Sierra Madre Occidental in Baja California and northern Sinaloa, Mexico, but it has an important extension north of the International Boundary. In the United States it occurs in the Imperial Valley, along the Colorado River, and in central and southern Arizona.

Physiographically the Sonoran Desert is similar to the Mojave Desert but has fewer large undrained basins.

The vegetation is characterized by a relatively high percentage of trees and large shrubs, and this is particularly the case in the Arizona Desert where the summer rainfall is high. Large cacti are abundant, and they dominate the landscape in many areas. Annual herbs are predominant in the spring, and in the eastern part of the desert they are well developed after the summer rains, as well.

As in all the deserts, the creosote bush is the characteristic species of the intermountain plains, and often it is accompanied by the bur sages, *Franseria dumosa* and *Franseria deltoidea*. It occurs on loose, sandy soils in the more arid regions, but in parts of central Arizona it is characteristic of caliche. Vegetation of the lower basins is essentially uniform throughout the desert, but the plants of the higher slopes vary considerably from place to place. These differences are marked in the eastern and western portions of the Sonoran Desert in the United States, and the subdivisions are known as the Colorado and Arizona deserts.

(1) *Colorado Desert.* The low-lying Colorado Desert includes the Salton Sea Basin, or Imperial Valley, in California and the Colorado River Basin. The depressions below 1,500 feet in the eastern parts of San Bernardino, Riverside, and Imperial counties, California, and below 1,000 feet on the lower Gila River drainage in Arizona are included in the Colorado Basin.

Physiographically, the Colorado Desert consists of the large, enclosed Salton Sea Basin, which is as much as 250 feet below sea level, and several smaller basins and lateral drainages bordering the Colorado River. The Salton Sea Basin is a former extension of the Gulf of California, which has been cut off in recent times by Colorado River delta deposits; the ancient shore line is conspicuous above the Salton Sea. A considerable portion of the area is below sea level, and as a result of marine deposits the salt content of the soil is high. Sand dunes are frequent, and the best-known and largest ones are in California immediately west of Yuma, Arizona. These are the setting for many of the "Foreign Legion" moving pictures.

Extreme contrast in types of desert habitat is a resultant of the varied desert topography. For example, along the Colorado and Gila river bottom lands the growth of willows, cottonwoods, mesquite, screw bean, and arrow weed is luxuriant, but nearby the arid desert vegetation is composed of widely scattered creosote bushes, blue palo verde, desert ironwood, and a few other leguminous shrubs. The low-lying Colorado Desert provides a suitable habitat for such frost-sensitive plants as desert ironwood and the smoke tree and other daleas. The greatest variety of tree and shrub species occurs along the western and northern borders of the Salton Sea Basin, where the rainfall is relatively high.

The California fan palm is found in isolated groves in desert canyons and in moist alkaline places above the old shore line of the Salton Sea Basin, and its isolated occurrence is mute evidence of its antiquity and its once greater abundance and wider distribution under more moist conditions.

Tree and shrub species largely confined to the Colorado Desert and the adjacent regions include the following:

California fan palm........................*Washingtonia filifera*
Parry nolina.........................*Nolina Bigelovii* var. *Parryi*
Bigelow nolina...............................*Nolina Bigelovii*
Desert apricot.............................*Prunus Fremontii*
Dalea..........................*Dalea Fremontii* var. *simplifolia*
California lote bush............................*Condalia Parryi*
Vasey sage...*Salvia Vaseyi*

The number of shrubs occurring in the Colorado and Mojave deserts but not in the Arizona Desert is relatively small. It includes the following:

California ephedra...........................*Ephedra californica*
Desert holly............................*Atriplex hymenelytra*
Desert almond.............................*Prunus fasciculata*
Spiny senna.......................................*Cassia armata*

The area including the Gila, Tinajas Altas, Cabeza Prieta, Tule, and Growler mountains of extreme southwestern Arizona are considered here to be a portion of the Colorado Desert, but they exhibit several distinctive species of limited distribution in the United States. Several of these do not occur in the Californian portion of the Colorado Desert, as for example:

Argythamnia................*Argythamnia Brandegei* var. *intonsa*
Jatropha....................................*Jatropha cuneata*
Kearney sumac..............................*Rhus Kearneyi*

Affinity of this area with the California portion is shown by the presence of such shrubs as the following:

Bigelow nolina...............................*Nolina Bigelovii*
Desert agave.....................................*Agave deserti*
Hoffmanseggia.....................*Hoffmanseggia microphylla*
Elephant tree..........................*Bursera microphylla*
Hollyleaf ragweed.............................*Franseria ilicifolia*

(2) *Arizona Desert.* The portion of the Sonoran Desert east of the immediate Colorado River and lower Gila River drainages is the Arizona Desert. Altitudinally, this desert ranges from 1,000 feet on the western border to between 3,500 and 4,000 feet on the northern and eastern borders, where the higher elevations of the Mexican Plateau form a topographic limit.

The outstanding topographic feature of the Arizona Desert is a series of elongated mountain ranges about 3,000 to 4,000 feet high, and these are separated by broad intermountain plains with relatively few enclosed basins. Potential drainage is provided for most of the area by the Bill Williams and Gila rivers, perennial streams draining the Mexican Plateau and the edge of the Colorado Plateau or Mogollon Rim.

The Arizona Desert differs from the other Southwestern deserts in its richness in arboreal and succulent plants. Here the well-known giant cactus, or saguaro, attains its maximum size and density, although sparsely populated stands occur along the lower Colorado River drainage, and a few individuals are native on the California side of the river. On the eroding mountain slopes and the upper bajadas the saguaro is associated with small trees, such as the palo verdes, the desert ironwood, and the crucifixion thorns and with a host of other cacti and shrubs of the legume and sunflower families. (Pl. II; IV *A;* V.) At and above the upper limits of the saguaro, where minimum winter temperatures become effective in limiting the distribution of frost-sensitive plants, the vegetation on rocky slopes is dominated by shrubby members of the lily and amaryllis families, such as yuccas, agaves, bear grass, and sotol and by leguminous shrubs, such as acacias and mimosas. On the broad intermountain plains, the ubiquitous creosote bush dominates the landscape except along the drainage patterns which are marked by larger shrubs and trees, such as mesquite, cat claw, and blue palo verde. In the major canyons and washes skirting the higher mountains along the eastern and northern borders of the Arizona Desert there are mixed groves of larger trees, such as Arizona sycamore, Arizona ash, Arizona walnut, and Fremont cottonwood.

The Arizona Desert flora is partly isolated from the remaining portions of the Southwestern deserts by the low elevations of the Colorado River on the western border and by the higher portions of the Mexican Plateau between southeastern Arizona and southwestern New Mexico, these separating the Arizona and Chihuahuan deserts.

Isolation from the Colorado Desert is shown by a large number of important species which occur in both the Chihuahuan and Arizona deserts but which do not range into the lower elevations of the Colorado Basin. Tree and shrub members of this group include:

Palmilla or soapweed..............................*Yucca elata*
Bear grass...................................*Nolina microcarpa*
Arizona walnut...................*Juglans microcarpa* var. *major*

White thorn.................................*Acacia constricta*
Western soapberry..........*Sapindus Saponaria* var. *Drummondii*
Desert honeysuckle......................*Anisacanthus Thurberi*
Desert elderberry................*Sambucus cerulea* var. *mexicana*
Jimmy weed........................*Haplopappus heterophyllus*

Shrubs of wide distribution within the Arizona Desert, but absent from both the Colorado and Chihuahuan deserts, include the following:

Thornber yucca....................*Yucca baccata* var. *brevifolia*
Schott agave......................................*Agave Schottii*
Limberbush............................*Jatropha cardiophylla*
Hop bush.....................*Dodonaea viscosa* var. *augustifolia*
Bur sage....................................*Franseria deltoidea*
Canyon ragweed.........................*Franseria ambrosioides*

The following shrubs are of more limited distribution in the Arizona Desert, and probably they are remnants of formerly widespread types:

Kofa Mountain barberry...................*Berberis Harrisoniana*
Gila sophora................................*Sophora formosa*
Bitter condalia.............................*Condalia globosa*
Mexican bluewood.........................*Condalia mexicana*
Ashy jatropha..............................*Jatropha cinerea*
Desert olive............................*Forestiera phillyreoides*
Jacobinia..................................*Jacobinia candicans*

c. CHIHUAHUAN DESERT. The lower Rio Grande drainage, the Tularosa Basin, and the Pecos Valley in New Mexico and western Texas include the northernmost extensions of the Chihuahuan Desert. The relatively small area of the desert included in this book is similar in general physiography to that of the other regions, and it is restricted to the foothills and lower alluvial outwash plains in the immediate Rio Grande drainage. One of the largest undrained basins of the creosote-bush desert is the Tularosa Basin, between the Organ and Sacramento mountains, which includes the well-known White Sands National Monument where there are extensive deposits of gypsum sands. Upper altitudinal limits of the Chihuahuan Desert lie at approximately 4,500 to 5,000 feet.

Perennial vegetation of this desert consists largely of shrubby forms, and there are few trees except along the major drainages. Cacti are not so conspicuous as in the Arizona Desert, but smaller forms occur with dense stands of yuccas and agaves on

Plate II.—Deserts: Arizona Desert in two views—palo verde-cactus vegetational type colored by spring annuals with the California poppy, *Eschscholtzia californica*, predominating. The larger plants include foothill palo verde, *Cercidium microphyllum*, giant cactus or saguaro, *Cereus giganteus*, creosote bush, *Larrea divaricata*, bur sage, *Franseria deltoidea*, prickly pear, *Opuntia Engelmannii*, and chollas, *Opuntia fulgida* and *Opuntia acanthocarpa*. (Photographs by E. T. Nichols.)

Plate III.—Deserts: *A*, creosote-bush desert. Extensive areas throughout the Mojave and Sonoran deserts support pure stands of creosote bush on mesas or intermountain plains; *B*, Mojave Desert. Joshua tree, creosote bush, *Acampto-pappus*, and other shrubs occur on the higher slopes fringing the desert. (Photographs: *A* by A. A. Nichol; *B* by Robert A. Darrow.)

Plate IV.—Deserts: *A*, Arizona Desert—palo verde-cactus type. On rocky foothill
and upper bajada slopes occur mixtures of saguaro, foothill palo verde, chollas,
prickly pears, brittle bush, jojobe, and bur sage; *B*, barren desert pavement
typical of the drier parts of the desert, with plants such as saguaro, foothill
palo verde, ironwood, brittle bush, and chollas restricted to the drainages.
(Photographs by Robert A. Darrow.)

Plate V.—Desert: palo verde-cactus type—above, saguaro, *Cereus giganteus,*
foothill palo verde, *Cercidium microphyllum,* prickly pears, *Opuntia,* and bur
sage, *Franseria deltoidea;* below, organ pipe cactus, *Cereus Thurberi,* foothill
palo verde, and brittle bush, *Encelia farinosa.* (Photographs: above by E. T.
Nichols; below by Robert A. Darrow.)

the rocky mountain slopes. Annuals are important components of the vegetation only during the summer rainy period.

Creosote bush, in association with allthorn or crucifixion thorn (*Koeberlinia spinosa*) and blackbrush (*Flourensia cernua*), dominates the level intermountain plains and lower bajadas. Along the major drainages, the creosote-bush type is replaced by western honey mesquite (*Prosopis juliflora* var. *Torreyana*), Wislizenius cottonwood (*Populus Fremontii* var. *Wislizenii*), and other stream-bank trees and shrubs, and on the higher rocky slopes there are complex associations in which yuccas, agaves, and sotols mingle with a variety of shrubs and perennial grasses.

Separation of the Chihuahuan Desert flora from the remaining portion of the creosote-bush desert is effected by the Sierra Madre Occidental of Mexico and the northern extensions of the Mexican Plateau which form the Continental Divide on either side of the International Boundary. These low elevations between the upper Gila River and the Rio Grande drainages in southeastern Arizona and southwestern New Mexico provide the only definite break in the continuity of the western North American mountain axis north of the tropics, except for a gap in southern Wyoming. Similarities in the flora of the Arizona portion of the Sonoran Desert and the northern extensions of the Chihuahuan Desert are evidence of past migration of desert plants through this wide mountain gap, although at present the creosote-bush desert does not form a continuous belt over the Continental Divide.

Species which bridge this gap and range widely through the Southwestern deserts include such important ones as the following:

Mexican tea.....................................*Ephedra trifurca*
Boundary ephedra.................*Ephedra nevadensis* var. *aspera*
Banana yucca.....................................*Yucca baccata*
Four-wing saltbush..........................*Atriplex canescens*
Cat claw...*Acacia Greggii*
Ratany.......................................*Krameria parvifolia*
Western honey mesquite..........*Prosopis juliflora* var. *Torreyana*
Ocotillo....................................*Fouquieria splendens*
Arizona ash...................................*Fraxinus velutina*
Arrow weed....................................*Pluchea sericea*

For other species characteristic of the Chihuahuan Desert, the Continental Divide has acted as a physiographic barrier in limiting distributions to the lower elevations along the Rio Grande and southward. Representative shrubs in this group are:

Torrey yucca	*Yucca Torreyi*
Sotol	*Dasylirion leiphyllum*
Lechuguilla	*Agave lecheguilla*
White crucillo	*Condalia lycioides*

Isolated areas of Chihuahuan Desert flora occur in the San Pedro and Sulphur Springs valleys of southern Arizona at elevations normally suitable for the development of a desert grassland type. These islands of Chihuahuan Desert flora within the desert grassland are almost entirely restricted to limestone hills and shallow favorable soils developed from limestone. Shrubs found in these areas, with limited distribution in Arizona, include the following:

White thorn	*Acacia constricta* var. *vernicosa*
Shrubby senna	*Cassia Wislizenii*
Arizona star leaf	*Choisya dumosa* var. *arizonica*
Mortonia	*Mortonia scabrella*
Allthorn or crucifixion thorn	*Koeberlinia spinosa*
Blackbrush	*Flourensia cernua*

Vegetational Types Adjacent to the Southwestern Deserts

At its upper elevational limits the creosote-bush desert makes contact with several vegetational types. On its western border it merges with the special types of chaparral and of oak woodland occurring in the southern California mountains; and along the eastern slopes of the Sierra Nevada from the vicinity of Owens Lake to Tehachapi Pass, the pinyon-juniper belt replaces the chaparral as the neighbor of the desert. In the transitional zone, shrubby oaks and junipers mingle with the characteristic desert shrubs. Along the northern desert limits in California and southern Nevada there is a gradual transition to the sagebrush desert of the Great Basin. Many species of the Mojave Desert are represented in the southern part of the Great Basin, and a definite relationship in origin of portions of the two floras is indicated. In northwestern Arizona the creosote-bush desert merges with a grassland type, which includes many species characteristic of the Great Plains short grass, while in southeastern Arizona, southern New Mexico, and western Texas the higher basal elevations support a desert grassland to which a considerable number of shrubby species are contributed by the bordering desert. At 3,000 to 4,000 feet elevation in the mountainous complex below the Mogollon Rim in central Arizona, a mixture of chaparral and oak woodland and pinyon-juniper woodland species mingles with a rich element of the desert flora.

These adjacent vegetational types will be discussed briefly, since many of the desert trees and shrubs included in this work are distributed in one or more of these adjoining types.

Desert Grassland

Despite affinities to the flora of the central prairies and the southwestern type of oak woodland and chaparral, the desert grassland (Pl. VI; IX *A, B*) bridges the gap between the Arizona and Chihuahuan deserts, and the trees and shrubs of the grassland are included here.

The desert grassland occurs immediately above the creosote-bush desert at 3,000 to 6,000, or more commonly 3,500 to 5,000, feet elevation in southeastern Arizona, southwestern New Mexico, and western Texas. It merges at its upper limits with the oak woodland and chaparral and the pinyon-juniper woodland.

Climatic conditions within the desert grassland are more favorable to plant growth than in the desert. Precipitation is between 10 and 20 inches annually, and more than half the rain falls during the summer months of July, August, and September. This summer rainfall occurs principally in the form of local convectional storms, and it varies considerably on a geographical as well as on a seasonal basis. Higher precipitation rates are recorded for the grassland areas immediately adjacent to the high mountain ranges of southern Arizona than at corresponding elevations in the nearly level plains of southern New Mexico.

The deep, well-drained soils of the level elevated portions of the Mexican Plateau favor the best development of grassland vegetation, but a limited development is found on the steeper slopes. The northward extension of the desert grassland is favored by the close spacing of the mountains below the Mogollon Rim in central Arizona. Land surfaces are similar to those found in the desert, but the denser vegetation of the mountain ranges reduces the extent of erosional and depositional forces active in reducing the general relief to base level. Drainage is effected for most of the area by the Gila River and Rio Grande tributaries, together with several smaller streams which flow southward across the International Boundary into the Gulf of California; for example, Whitewater Draw and Black Draw in southeastern Arizona. Several extensive undrained basins are found in this area; among the larger ones are Sulphur Springs Valley in Arizona, and Animas Valley in New Mexico.

A rich mixture of grasses, principally gramas, three-awns, beard grass, tobosa, and curly mesquite, constitutes the matrix of the vegetation of the desert grassland. At higher elevations dense sods of blue, hairy, and slender gramas and curly mesquite are characteristic, and there is a variable admixture of shrubs, including yuccas, bear grass, acacias, and mimosas. At lower elevations the grasses are largely of the bunch type; for example, tobosa grass, Rothrock grama, bush muhly, and poverty grass. The proportion of shrubs in these low-lying areas is definitely higher, particularly where past overgrazing has reduced the density of the perennial grasses. Large acreages of this overgrazed desert grassland are now dominated by velvet or western honey mesquite accompanied by burroweed (*Haplopappus tenuisectus*) and snakeweeds (*Gutierrezia Sarothrae* and *Gutierrezia lucida*). Plate VI shows some of the higher grassland in southern Arizona where invasion of mesquite and other shrubs has occurred.

Oak Woodland and Chaparral

There are two distinct areas of oak woodland and chaparral (brush) vegetation near the Southwestern deserts. One type occurs in California and Baja California, Mexico, and the other in central and southern Arizona and New Mexico.

The oak woodland and the chaparral of California are found in the Coast ranges and the mountains of southern California and in the western foothills of the Sierra Nevada bordering the Great Valley at from 1,000 to 3,000, or southward up to 5,000, feet elevation. Contact with the creosote-bush desert is made by this chaparral type along the western borders of the Mojave and Colorado deserts, where some intermingling of chaparral and desert species occurs.

California oak woodland and chaparral develop under a climate of warm, almost completely dry summers and mild, wet winters. Annual rainfall is from 10 to 30 inches, and practically all of it falls between October and April.

The oak woodland is dominated by various species of evergreen and deciduous oaks, madroño (*Arbutus Menziesii*), California laurel (*Umbellularia californica*), California buckeye (*Aesculus californicus*), Digger pine (*Pinus Sabiniana*), and some other evergreen and deciduous trees. At lower elevations or on particular soil types, especially in the southern California mountains, the chaparral is best developed, and it consists largely of densely branched, leathery-leaved shrubs, such as manzanita (*Arctostaphylos*), scrub oak, buckthorn (*Rhamnus*), Christmas berry (*Photinia arbutifolia*), and chamiso (*Adenostoma fasciculatum*). For the most part the chaparral flora is sharply distinct from the adjoining desert flora, although several shrubs range widely through both types; for example, chaparral yucca (*Yucca Whipplei*) and burro fat (*Cleome Isomeris*).

The Arizona and New Mexico area of chaparral and oak woodland exhibits a close similarity in general appearance to that of California, but it differs markedly in tree and shrub species as well as in climatic conditions. Winter precipitation predominates in the characteristic chaparral parts of the Arizona area, although in southeastern Arizona and southwestern New Mexico, where the woodland type prevails, summer precipitation exceeds that of winter. The annual rainfall for the area approximates 14 to 18 inches.

In the central mountainous portion of Arizona below the Mogollon Rim, the vegetational cover includes such shrubs as turbinella oak (*Quercus dumosa* var. *turbinella*), buckthorn, manzanita, and mountain mahogany (*Cercocarpus*). The more isolated mountain ranges of southern Arizona and New Mexico support a woodland type of vegetation with various kinds of evergreen oak, junipers, and shrubby components of the chaparral type. A few of the desert grassland shrubs, such as bear grass, wait-a-minute bush (*Mimosa biuncifera*), and feather dalia (*Dalea formosa*), range upward into the chaparral type, and a few species which center in the woodland belt extend downward

into the desert or desert grassland. Among these are the following: mountain yucca (*Yucca Schottii*), Parry agave (*Agave
Parryi*), and red barberry (*Berberis Nevinii* var. *haematocarpa*).

Pinyon-Juniper Woodland

Pinyon-juniper, or juniper-pinyon, woodland occurs along
the eastern slopes of the Sierra Nevada and the Cascade mountains, on the mountains and higher plateaus of the Great Basin,
and on the Colorado Plateau in Utah, Colorado, Arizona, and
New Mexico at elevations generally between 2,000 and 3,000
feet northward and between 5,000 and 7,000 feet southward.
In most localities it occupies a belt above the sagebrush desert,
but in a few areas in California and Arizona it makes direct
contact with the Southwestern deserts.

The moderately cool climate, with 12 to 15 or more inches
of precipitation falling mostly as snow during the winter
months, favors the development of an open woodland vegetation. The small, densely branched trees are scattered in open
orchardlike stands with an intervening ground cover of grasses
and small shrubs. Several species of pinyon pines and junipers
make up the dominant cover, and other small trees and large
shrubs, such as algerita (*Berberis*) and cliffrose (*Cowania*),
may be important constituents.

Sagebrush Desert

Sagebrush desert occupies the lower elevations throughout
the Great Basin and adjacent areas from the eastern slopes
of the Sierra Nevada and Cascade mountains to Wyoming and
Utah. On its southern limits there are types transitional to
the creosote-bush desert.

Climatic conditions of this desert differ in several respects
from those of the creosote-bush desert. Annual precipitation
in the major portion of the area is between 5 and 10 inches in
the winter months and is distributed chiefly in the form of
snow. The lower temperatures and higher rainfall make this
desert an area of less extreme drought conditions than the
Southwestern deserts.

Sagebrush-desert vegetation is comprised principally of small
shrubs with scattered perennial grasses and herbaceous plants

in the open spaces between the dominant shrubs. The ever-present sagebrush (*Artemisia tridentata*) occupies a role similar to that played by the creosote bush in the Southwestern deserts, and it covers large areas as the principal shrub species. Other important plants are shadscale (*Atriplex confertifolia*), rabbit brush (*Chrysothamnus*), spiny hop sage (*Grayia spinosa*), and other species of sagebrush (*Artemisia*).

Short Grass Plains

Extensions of the short grass plains into northern Arizona and New Mexico make contact with the Mojave Desert in Coconino and Mohave counties, Arizona, and with the Chihuahuan Desert in southern New Mexico. These short grass areas occur between 4,500 and 6,500 feet elevation, and they are characterized by lower temperatures and less precipitation than is the desert grassland, which occurs at somewhat lower elevations.

Perennial plants in this short grass vegetation consist primarily of such grasses as gramas, three-awns, drop-seeds, and galleta, with a variable admixture of small shrubs and a few small cacti. Overgrazing in this type has resulted in a general depletion of the grass cover and replacement by a number of shrubs unpalatable to livestock, including snakeweed (*Gutierrezia*) and rabbit brush (*Chrysothamnus*). Among the shrub components of this grassland which range into the creosote-bush desert are winter fat (*Eurotia lanata*) and four-wing salt-bush (*Atriplex canescens*).

USE OF THE DISTRIBUTIONAL MAPS

In addition to the detailed descriptions of geographical distribution of each species and variety given in the text, the known range within the area treated in this book for many of the more important plants is shown on distributional maps. On each base map the geographical range of creosote bush (*Larrea divaricata*), the most characteristic and widespread plant of the Southwestern desert, has been incorporated to serve as a general outline of the desert region. The area above or outside the range of creosote bush is represented by open crosshatching; areas above 7,000 feet are shown by closely spaced crosshatching. The dotted line represents the 1,000-foot contour line.

The floristic regions and geographical features mentioned in the detailed discussions of distribution may be located by reference to Fig. 2.

MEDICINAL VALUE OF PLANTS

Many of the Southwestern desert plants, including the trees and shrubs, have value as medicinal plants, and the native peoples have made use of them for centuries. In many cases the medicinal use is beyond question, since it has been established by laboratory investigation; but in others it is slight or doubtful, or the plants are of no value at all. It is to be hoped that research may be applied increasingly to determination of pharmaceutical worth and that in the course of time it may be possible to exploit to the fullest the properties of the unique and relatively little-known flora of the Southwest.

To those who would make use of native plants for medicinal purposes, a few words of caution are necessary. First, some of the plants are harmful and some are even strongly poisonous. Second, medicinal values are discovered only rarely by random application of plant material to a particular individual illness, and the following point commonly is overlooked. Most ailments are overcome, not by application of cures, but ultimately by the resistance developed within the blood stream and tissues of the human body. Often the medicines applied by the physician aid the process of recovery by destroying some or all of the invading organisms or by reducing their effect, thus relieving the severity of the symptoms or the danger of the earlier stages while the body is mobilizing its own defense mechanism.

Many popular remedies owe their human following, as do quacks, to the prevalent notion that a cure is necessary to recovery from any ailment, and most maladies are thought to be overcome by application of the last remedy in the series; that is, the one tried just before natural recovery. This fact is responsible for the use of many herbs in primitive medicine

Plate VI.—Desert grassland: *A*, with scattered bear grass and velvet mesquite on the slopes and with live oak and rabbit brush along the drainages; *B*, with scattered velvet mesquite and palmilla or soapweed. Various species of *Acacia*, *Calliandra*, and *Mimosa* occur in such grasslands. (Photographs: *A* by Robert A. Darrow; *B* by U.S. Forest Service.)

Plate VII.—Ephedra and California fan palm: *A*, Mexican tea, *Ephedra trifurca*; *B*, boundary ephedra, *Ephedra nevadensis* var. *aspera*; *C-E*, Palm Canyon near Palm Springs, California; *F*, Palm Canyon, Kofa Mountains, Arizona. (Photographs: *A* by D. M. Crooks; *B-F* by Robert A. Darrow.)

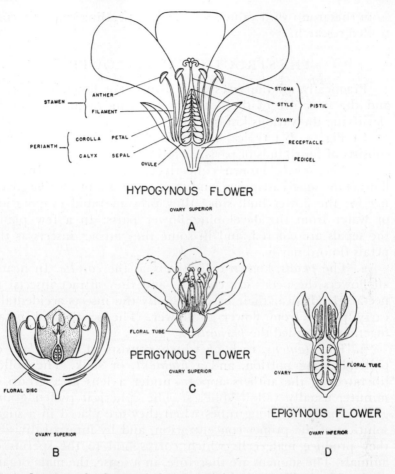

Fig. 3.—Structure of a flower: *A,* a typical flower with all the parts hypogynous (below the ovary); *B,* a flower with the stamens on a floral disc; *C,* a flower with the sepals, petals, and stamens on a floral tube (perigynous); *D,* a flower with these parts upon a floral tube and apparently upon the ovary (epigynous), the tube attached to the ovary wall and appearing to be a part of it.

and for the acceptance of health fads among those supposedly not so primitive.

In view of the relatively few cases in which the medicinal values of Southwestern desert plants actually have been demonstrated, the writers have attempted to maintain the utmost caution, and undoubtedly many useful plants have been excluded from the group with value in medicine, pending carefully controlled research.

THE STRUCTURE OF A FLOWER

Practically all the trees and shrubs are flowering plants, and the structure of the flower is the fundamental factor in classifying the various kinds.

In Fig. 3 *A* a typical flower is shown. Fundamentally it consists of four kinds of parts, as follows:

1. The *sepals,* known collectively as the *calyx.* In most flowers the sepals are green, and they serve as a protective covering for the flower bud, since they prevent rapid evaporation of water from the developing flower parts. In a few plants the sepals are colored, and in some they attract insects as the petals do ordinarily.

2. The *petals,* known collectively as the *corolla.* In nearly all flowers the petals are colored, and they attract insects[1] to nectar glands near their bases. Usually the insects accidentally carry pollen from flower to flower. The sepals and petals together are called the *perianth.*

3. The *stamens,* each of which consists of an *anther,* or pollen-bearing portion, and a *filament,* or stalk. The pollen liberated by the anthers appears under a lens as a group of minute, usually yellow spheres. The spherical pollen grains grow rapidly into long tubes when they are placed in a sugar solution of the proper concentration, and by internal division they produce male cells which correspond to the sperms of animals. The stamens are therefore, in a sense, the male organs of the flower. Flowers which have only stamens and no pistils are known as *staminate flowers.*

4. The *pistil* or *pistils,* each of which consists of a basal *ovary,* a median *style,* and a terminal *stigma.* The ovary contains *ovules,* which, after fertilization, develop into *seeds;* the style is a hollow passageway; the stigma is a collector of pollen. Pollen, once it is transferred by insects or wind to the stigma of a flower, develops in a warm, sticky sugar solution in the

---

1. It is to be noted that many insects have color vision, while the majority of other animals, except the birds, are incapable of seeing color but rather live in a world of white, black, and various grays.

way described above, and the long pollen tube grows down through the passageway in the style into the large cavity of the ovary. There it grows into an opening (micropyle) in one of the ovules, and its male cells or sperms are discharged. The male cells effect fertilization, which is followed by development of an embryo. The ovule forms a protective covering about the embryo, and the whole is known as a seed. Eventually, after germination of the seed, the embryo develops into a new plant. Since the ovule contains female cells, the entire pistil is, in a sense, a female organ. Flowers having pistils and no stamens are called *pistillate flowers*.

The four principal structures noted above are the appendages of the stem which form the flower, and each is thought to be fundamentally a specialized leaf. The stem apex to which these parts are attached is known as the *receptacle,* and the stalk of the flower (above the nearest joint or node of the stem) is called the *pedicel*. The stalk of a cluster of flowers is known as a *peduncle*.

In the flower in Fig. 3 *A*, the sepals, petals, and stamens are attached to the receptacle below the ovary and they are described as *hypogynous* (below the ovary: hypo-, below; gynoecium, female, or in this case pistil or ovary). Since the ovary is above them, it is called *superior*. The entire flower may be called hypogynous. Even though the stamens and more rarely the petals may be produced from a *floral* or *hypogynous disc* (Fig. 3 *B*), the flower is considered here to be hypogynous (but with a hypogynous disc).

THE FLORAL TUBE OR CUP

Most flowers are fundamentally like those in Fig. 3, *A* or *B,* but others are like those in *C* and *D,* being characterized by a *floral tube* or *floral cup*.

In *C*, the floral tube or cup arises from the margins of the receptacle and surrounds the ovary. The nature of this tube is in dispute. Some believe it is derived from the receptacle, and they call it a hypanthium; others believe it is derived largely from the bases of the sepals, and they call it a calyx tube. Probably in some instances it may be formed one way and in some the other, and the name floral tube is adopted here to

avoid taking sides in the controversy. In the flower shown in
C, all the other parts (sepals, petals, and stamens) are perigynous with respect to the ovary. The entire flower may be
spoken of as *perigynous,* and the ovary as *superior.*

In *D*, the flower is essentially like the one in *C*, but *the
floral tube is joined to the wall of the ovary.* Consequently, the
sepals, petals, and stamens appear to be upon the ovary, or
epigynous, while the ovary itself may have the appearance of
being sunken into the stem (pedicel) under the flower. The
ovary is called *inferior*, since it seems to be below the other
parts.

To summarize, the sepals, petals, and stamens may be
described as (1) hypogynous, below the ovary, (2) perigynous,
around the ovary, or (3) epigynous, upon the ovary. In the
hypogynous type there is no floral tube, and in the perigynous
type the tube is free from the ovary. In both these types the
ovary is superior. In the epigynous type the floral tube is joined
to the ovary, and the ovary is inferior. In Fig. 4 fruits formed
from hypogynous (*B 1*), perigynous (*A 1*), and epigynous
(*C 1*) flowers are shown, although this is not the primary purpose of the plate.

FRUITS

Sepals, petals, and stamens are thought to be specialized
leaves. A pistil may be either a single specialized leaf or two
or more leaves united to one another. A pea pod is formed
from a single specialized leaf or *carpel* and is developed from
the only pistil in the flower. Fig. 4 *A 1* shows three pistils of a
perigynous flower. Each of these has developed into a fruit
resembling a pea pod, but the three are separate from one
another. As shown in the cross section of one of them (*A 2*), the
seeds are in two rows. Fundamentally, these rows of seeds are
on the upper side of the carpel, or specialized leaf. The upper
side of the leaf is on the inside of the pistil, and the lower or
back side of the leaf is on the outside. The midrib of the leaf
is represented in the cross section by the dot at the top; the
edges are turned together and fused. Since the seeds are on
the upper side but at the margins, they are inside the ovary
but in rows along the point of joining of the margins.

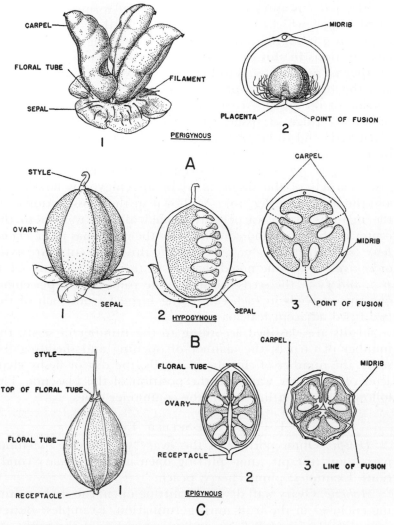

Fig. 4.—Union of carpels (specialized leaves each forming all or part of a pistil):
A 1, three carpels of the (perigynous) flower of *Crossosoma* developed into separate fruits (follicles), *2*, cross section of one carpel; *B 1*, three carpels of the (hypogynous) flower of a violet forming a single 1-chambered fruit (capsule), *2*, longitudinal section, *3*, cross section, showing union of the edges of the carpels; *C 1*, three carpels of the (epigynous) flower of a plant of the amaryllis family joined to form a 3-chambered fruit (capsule) surrounded by the adherent floral tube, *2*, longitudinal section, *3*, cross section, showing the margins of the three carpels turned inward to the center of the ovary, each carpel forming a seed chamber (lines point to the backs of 2 carpels). (x 1²/₃.)

Fig. 4 *B 1* is an external view of a fruit formed from three fused carpels which compose the single pistil of a hypogynous flower; *B 2* is a longitudinal section of the same fruit; *B 3* is a cross section. In this case, the three carpels are joined to one another in such a way as to form an ovary with a single cavity, and the fused margins of the carpels (leaves) are along the outside of the pistil. At each of the points of joining, a seed-producing ridge of tissue (*placenta*) has been formed. The placenta is said to be *parietal,* since it is on the margin of the ovary.

Fig. 4 *C 1-3* is prepared from a fruit formed from three fused carpels of the single pistil of an epigynous flower (cf. also the flowers in Fig. 16). As shown in the cross section *C 3,* the margins of the carpels are folded all the way in to the center of the ovary and consequently the ovary has three *chambers* (seed chambers) or *cells* and the three placentae are *axile* or *central.* It will be noted that in all the cross sections (*A 3, B 3, and C 3*) the seeds are in double rows on the placentae, one row of seeds in each case being formed from each of the two fused adjacent leaf margins.

Fruits are classified according to the number of seeds, the number of carpels, the manner of opening and shedding the seeds, the number of chambers or cells, the dry or fleshy character of the ovary wall, and the position of the placenta. The following brief outline covers the commoner types.

Usually One-Seeded Types

Drupe. Outer portion of the ovary wall fleshy, the inner part stony (the pit), not splitting open under ordinary conditions. Examples: plum, cherry, peach.

Achene. Ovary wall dry, not splitting open, the seed remaining enclosed in the fruit until germination. Examples: buttercup, cliffrose (Fig. 28 *E 1*), and any member of the sunflower family.

Two- to Many-Seeded Types

1. With one carpel, the ovary wall not fleshy at maturity

Follicle. A pod which splits open along only one side, the midrib of the carpel—that is, the side opposite the seeds. Examples: larkspur (*Delphinium*), milkweed, *Crossosoma* (Figs. 4 *A;* 26 *A 1, 3*).

Legume. A pod which splits open along both sides, (1) the midrib of the carpel and (2) its fused margins. Example: pea pod. It is to be noted that some fruits popularly called pods are not formed from a single carpel and that they are capsules.

2. *With more than one carpel or, when the fruit is fleshy, sometimes with only one*

Capsule. Ovary wall dry, splitting open along definite lines and shedding the seeds. Examples: yuccas of the dry-fruited type (Fig. 16 *C, E*), penstemon, snapdragon, tobacco.

Berry. Ovary wall fleshy, ordinarily not splitting open, at least not along regular lines. Examples: currant (formed from an inferior ovary), Joshua tree (Pl. X *B;* Fig. 21 *B 1, C, E 4*), banana yucca (formed from a superior ovary), grape, gooseberry, banana. It is to be noted that the fruit of a blackberry is not a berry but an aggregation of tiny drupes each of which has exactly the same structure as a plum. A strawberry is an aggregation of achenes (the "seeds") on an enlarged, fleshy receptacle which turns red.

ARRANGEMENT OF FLOWERS AND FRUITS

The following are illustrations (Fig. 5) and descriptions of *inflorescences*—that is, arrangements of flowers or fruits.

Axillary arrangement. The flowers are arranged one above each leaf on the upper part of the stem. The angle between the leaf and the stem above it is called the *axil*. The leaves are as large as the leaves on the rest of the stem.

FIG. 5.—Inflorescences.

Raceme. The flowers are arranged spirally along a leafless or essentially leafless branch, which usually is elongated. The raceme elongates as the flower buds at the apex develop (*left*).

Spike. A spike is similar to a raceme, but the flowers have no pedicels—that is, they are *sessile* (*right*).

Corymb. The flowers are arranged like those of a raceme, but the pedicels of the lower flowers are progressively longer stalked, and the inflorescence forms a flat-topped cluster. The terminal bud is the last to form a flower. At an intermediate stage the buds are in the center of the cluster, the fruits on the outside (periphery), the reverse of the arrangement in a cyme (cf. below).

Fig. 5.—Inflorescences. (Continued.)

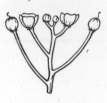

Panicle. This is a group of racemes, spikes, or corymbs aggregated into a single inflorescence. A panicle may be *racemose,* like the one at the *right,* or it may be *spicate* or *corymbose.* Sometimes it is called a *compound* raceme, spike, or corymb.

Cyme. The terminal bud of the main stem forms the first flower, and all the later flowers are from lateral buds lower on the stem. As illustrated, there are two types:

Type A. The cyme is flat-topped, because the lower flowers have progressively longer pedicels. The cluster resembles a corymb, but at an intermediate stage of development, the buds are on the outside and the fruits in the center because the terminal flower bloomed first.

Type B. The main stem terminates in a flower, and it is replaced by two branches which form an apparent fork of the main stem. After reforking perhaps several times, each ultimate branch ends in a flower.

Umbel. A number of approximately equal pedicels arise at the end of a branch, and each of these bears a flower. Some plants have *compound umbels*—that is, umbels of umbels.

Head. Like an umbel, but the flowers without pedicels, and consequently congested at the end of the stem. The best-known flower heads are of the sunflower family *(left)* in

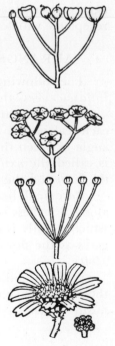

which there may be two kinds of flowers, the outer ones simulating petals and the inner ones other flower parts and the whole surrounded by an *involucre* of *bracts* (specialized leaves) resembling sepals.

Numerous compounds of types and intergradations of types may be found in actual practice, and some floral arrangements are so nondescript as to be called merely *clusters*.

STEMS

Stems may be classified as *herbaceous* or *woody*. A woody stem is one which persists for more than one season and which usually is increased in girth year after year by the action of the *cambium,* a layer of tissue which adds to the wood and bark. This book is not concerned with *herbs* nor with *vines,* even though some vines have woody stems.

The external structure of a stem is relatively simple. At the apex is a *bud,* which may be actively growing or dormant, depending upon the season. During the winter, the buds of most shrubs are dormant and are covered by brownish or grayish structures called *bud scales* (Fig. 19 *B 3*). These are actually specialized leaves. The older portion of the stem is divisible more obviously into two parts, the *nodes,* or joints, and the *internodes* between them. Leaves are produced only at the nodes, and in the plants with which we are concerned there is always at least potentially a branch or bud (embryonic branch) just above each leaf.

Many of the desert trees and shrubs, if not most of them, have thorny stems, and in many instances thorn types are of use in classification. Thorns[2] are of two types, as shown below in the text and in Fig. 6:

2. Use of the word "thorn" here is not technical, and it means nothing more than the popular word "sticker." The use of the term "spine" in the sense employed in this book is based upon similar usage by various botanists, including Asa Gray and B. Daydon Jackson, and it appears in *The Encyclopedic Dictionary,* by Robert Hunter, et al. In *Webster's Dictionary,* and in many other works, thorn is used for pointed branches, a restricted botanical usage. Webster further restricts the term spine in a botanical sense to nonvascular structures and particularly those formed from leaves or their margins or stipules. The various authors agree on use of the word "prickle" to refer to outgrowths of the cortical tissues of stems.

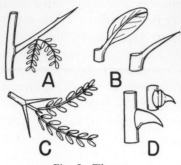

Fig. 6.—Thorns.

Spines are, in reality, either specialized branches *(A)*, leaves *(B)*, or stipules *(C)*, paired appendages at the base of the stalk (petiole) of a leaf, and they are in part continuations of the main woody tissue of the stem. *Prickles* are mere outgrowths of the soft tissues of the outer part of the stem and not of the internal woody portion. The prickle *(D)* of a rose, which is essentially the same as a prickle of a cat claw, of a mimosa, or of any of several other desert plants, is a good example of the type. It will be recalled that merely pushing on the side of a rose prickle is enough to dislodge it and that the scar left on the surface of the stem is not a deep one. There is in the scar no evidence of connections with the vascular bundles (woody conducting tissues) of the stem.

LEAVES

As shown in Fig. 7 *A,* a *simple* leaf consists of three parts, the *blade,* or large, flat portion, the *petiole* or stalk, and the expanded *leaf base* at the point of attachment to the stem. At the sides of the leaf base there may or may not be accessory structures called *stipules*. These are remarkably diverse in form. *Compound leaves* are those in which the blade is not a single structure. They are of two types, *palmate* *(B;* cf. also Pl. VII *E, F)* and *pinnate* *(C)*. A palmate leaf has the divisions of the blade spreading from a single point of attachment as do the fingers of a human hand, and a pinnate leaf has a featherlike arrangement

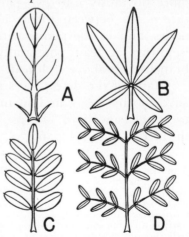

Fig. 7.—Leaves: simple and compound.

with *leaflets* produced along two sides of an elongated axis, or *rachis.* Pinnate leaves may be further subdivided into simply *pinnate* types (as shown in *C*) , *bipinnate* types (*D*) (with the *primary leaflets* pinnate—that is, made up of *secondary leaflets*) , *tripinnate* types (with the secondary leaflets subdivided into *tertiary leaflets*) , *quadripinnate* types (with tertiary leaflets divided into *quaternary leaflets*) , and so on. The rachis of the smallest pinnate leaflet in the series is called the *rachilla.* Sometimes the primary leaflet is called a *pinna* and the smallest (simple) leaflets of a bipinnate, tripinnate, or quadripinnate leaf are called *pinnules,* but these terms are not used in this book.

INDENTATION OF LEAVES

Simple leaves and leaflets are not necessarily *entire* like the one in Fig. 7 *A,* and they may be "cut in" more or less along the margins. If the indentation is shallow, the leaves are said to be toothed. The following are the more common types of teeth (Fig. 8) :

Dentate. With the angular teeth standing out at right angles to the margin of the leaf (*left*) . The diminutive is *denticulate*—that is, with small teeth.

Crenate. With low, rounded teeth spreading more or less at right angles or directed somewhat forward (*center*) . The diminutive is *crenulate.*

Serrate or *saw-toothed.* With sharply angular teeth directed forward (*right*) . The diminutive is *serrulate.*

If leaves are more deeply indented, they are referred to by the following terms, according

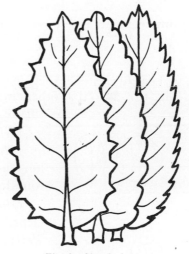

Fig. 8.—Simple leaves: margins.

to the depth of indentation (*lobing,* broad sense) (Fig. 9) :

Lobed. With the indentation running inward less than

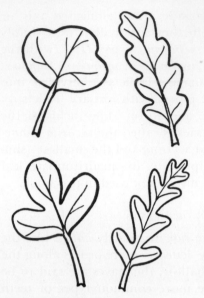

Fig. 9.—Simple leaves: lobed and parted types.

halfway to the midrib. Leaves may be either *palmately (upper left)* or *pinnately lobed (upper right)*, according to the direction of the "cutting."

Cleft. With the indentation running inward about halfway to the midrib (either palmately or pinnately).

Parted. With the indentation running inward more than halfway to the midrib (*lower right*) or, if the leaf is palmately parted (*lower left*), to the base of the blade.

Divided. With the indentation running inward almost all the way to the midrib or to the base of the blade. A divided leaf is almost palmate or almost pinnate, and it is referred to as *palmatifid* or *pinnatifid*.

SHAPES OF LEAVES

Leaf blades or leaflets may have any of the following shapes (Fig. 10), as well as others not common among desert trees and shrubs.

Orbicular. Practically circular (*left*).

Elliptic. One and one half times as long as broad, broadest at the middle, rounded at both ends (*right*).

Obovate. The same as ovate, but attached to the petiole at the smaller end (*left*).

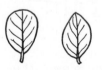

Ovate. Egg-shaped; one and one-half times as long as broad, narrower apically, rounded at both ends (*right*). See "ovoid."

Lanceolate. Four to six times as long as broad, broadest near the base, tapering to a sharp angle at each end *(left)*.

Oblanceolate. The same, but broadest near the apex *(right)*.

Oblong. Approximately a rectangle but the corners rounded *(left)*.

Linear. Eight or more times as long as broad, the sides parallel or nearly so *(right)*.

Cordate. Shaped like a valentine, the petiole joined to the blade in the notch *(left)*.

Obcordate. The same, but the petiole joined at the point *(right)*.

Reniform. Kidney- or bean-shaped; broader than long, the petiole attached at the indentation *(left)*.

Sagittate. Arrowhead-shaped, the petiole attached at the notch *(right)*.

Hastate. With a broad base and a pair of basal divergent lobes *(left)*.

Cuneate. Wedge-shaped; triangular with two sides equal, the third shorter, the petiole attached at the sharp angle *(right)*.

Deltoid. An equilateral triangle, the petiole attached to one side *(left)*.

Spatulate. Like a spatula; apex enlarged, base narrow and elongated *(right)*.

Peltate. Nearly circular but with the attachment in the center; like a coin balanced upon a pencil eraser. The best-known example is a garden nasturtium leaf.

Fig. 10.—Simple leaves: shapes.

THE BASE AND APEX OF THE BLADE

The bases and apices of leaf blades may correspond to any of the following more common types:

Rounded. Forming an arc of a circle.

Obtuse. Forming an obtuse angle.

Acute. Forming an acute angle.

Attenuate. Drawn out into an elongated point or tapering into an elongated base.

Truncate. "Chopped off" abruptly.

Cordate. Applied only to the leaf base; indented as in the base of a cordate leaf.

Auriculate. With two expanded, rounded basal lobes resembling the lobes of a human ear.

Notched. Emarginate with a sharp notch; *retuse* with a broad shallow notch.

PETIOLES

Leaves having petioles are referred to as petioled. When the petiole is not developed the leaf is called sessile.

POSITIONS OF LEAVES ON THE STEM

When each node of the stem produces a single leaf, the leaves are *alternate;* when each node produces two leaves, they are *opposite;* when each node produces three or more leaves, they are *whorled* or in *cycles* or *verticils.*

MISCELLANEOUS TERMS

Appressed. Turned upward and lying flat—e.g., hairs bent inward and upward against a stem or leaf.

Arborescent. Treelike.

Basifixed. Attached at the base—e.g., an anther with the filament attached to its base. See "versatile."

Bract. A specialized leaf subtending a flower or a cluster of flowers. Most bracts are smaller than the other leaves and are green, but some may be large and colored, as in the cultivated poinsettia.

Ciliate. With a fringe of hairs along the margin like eyelashes of an eyelid.

Deciduous. Falling away—e.g., leaves falling from a tree in the autumn.

Deflexed. Turned downward.

Dehiscent. Splitting open along regular lines.

Distinct. Separate.

Glabrate. Becoming bald in the course of time. Man is not glabrous but glabrate.

Glabrous. Bald—that is, without hair from the beginning.

Globose. Practically spherical.

Indehiscent. Not splitting open, at least not regularly so and not along regular lines.

Mucro. A sharp but rather soft point at the apex of a leaf, fruit, or other structure.

Mucronate. With a mucro.

Mucronulate. With a small mucro.

Obovoid. Ovoid but attached at the small end.

Ovate, see under "ovoid."

Ovoid. Egg-shaped; one and one-half times as long as broad, rounded at both ends, broadest toward the base. Three-dimensional. Ovate answers the same general description, but it refers to flattened or essentially two-dimensional structure.

Papillate. With low, more or less rounded projections (*papillae*).

Petiolule. The petiole of a leaflet of a compound leaf.

Recurved. Curved into a hook, the tip directed backward.

Spathe. A large bract covering an entire inflorescence, white or colored but not green.

Spicate. Arranged in a spike. See "arrangement of flowers and fruits" above.

Spiniferous. Spine-bearing, spiny.

Sub-. A prefix meaning almost, nearly, practically, or just about. (A great favorite of botanists.)

Turgid. Bulging, not flattened.

Versatile. Attached at the middle—e.g., a versatile anther is one with the filament attached to its middle. See "basifixed."

SYSTEMS OF MEASUREMENT

In the brief popular diagnoses of plants in this book the English system of linear measurement (yards, feet, and inches) is used, but in the more technical descriptions and in the keys the metric system replaces it. The scales shown below should

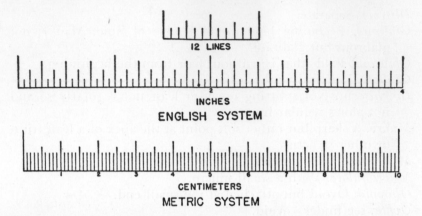

facilitate measuring plant parts according to either system. The principal unit of the metric system is the *meter* (*m.*), which is a little more than 39 inches and which is reckoned here as 3 feet when rough translations to the English system are given. One-tenth meter is a *decimeter* (*dm.*); 1/10 decimeter or 1/100 meter is a *centimeter* (*cm.*); 1/10 centimeter or 1/1000 meter is a *millimeter* (*mm.*). A decimeter is about 4 inches; a centimeter is about 2/5 inch; a millimeter is 1/25 inch. An old English unit of measurement is a *line* (1/12 inch), and lines are used in some botanical books. Translation from millimeters to lines and vice versa is easy, since a line is about 2 millimeters.

SCIENTIFIC NAMES

The scientific name of a plant or animal is constructed as is the name of a person, but with the surname first. The name of the blue palo verde is *Cercidium floridum.* The foothill palo verde is *Cercidium microphyllum.* The two are related to each other as are lions and tigers, and the closeness of relationship is expressed by their membership in the genus *Cercidium* just as cats are in the genus *Felis.* (The plural of genus is genera; this word and general are derived from the same root.) The names *floridum* and *microphyllum* represent species or kinds of *Cercidium.* (The plural of species is species, and the word is derived from the same root as specific.) Another palo verde, the Mexican palo verde or horse bean, is related to the

Plate VIII.—Dry-fruited yuccas: *A, palmilla* or soapweed, *Yucca elata*, with old open capsular fruits of the previous season; *B*, palmilla in flower; *C*, close-up of a young palmilla showing the fibers on the leaf margins; *D*, Spanish bayonet or chaparral yucca, *Yucca Whipplei*, in flower. (Photographs: *A* by R. B. Streets; *B* by Robert A. Darrow; *C* by A. A. Nichol; *D* by L. M. Pultz.)

Plate IX.—Yuccas: *A*, palmilla or soapweed, *Yucca elata,* showing flowers and old fruits; *B*, Great Plains yucca, *Yucca glauca,* with unopened fruits; *C*, Torrey yucca, *Yucca Torreyi,* with old flower stalks. (Photographs by J. M. Webber, Bur. of Pl. Ind.)

blue palo verde and the foothill palo verde, but it is much less closely related to either of them than they are to each other. It is *Parkinsonia aculeata,* a species of another genus in the same family.

Genera are made up of species; families are made up of genera; orders are made up of families; classes are made up of orders (which may or may not be grouped into subclasses under the class) ; divisions are made up of classes; the plant kingdom is made up of divisions. In a list, with the desert apricot as an example, these appear as follows:

Kingdom.............................Phyta or plant
Division..................Spermatophyta or seed plants
Class.................Angiospermae or flowering plants
Subclass...................Dicotyledonae or dicotyledons
Order.........................Rosales or rose order
Family......................Rosaceae or rose family
Genus.........................Prunus or plum genus
Species...................Fremontii. The desert apricot

All the trees and shrubs in the desert are Spermatophyta or seed plants, either of the class Gymnospermae (cone plants) or the class Angiospermae (flowering plants). The flowering plants are of two groups (subclasses), Monocotyledonae (mono-cotyledons) and Dicotyledonae (dicotyledons). The orders are not given in this book, since their organization for the flower-ing plants is not fully understood, and consequently it is in dispute. Families, genera, and species are described in detail. In many cases the species include not only the *typical variety,* but other *varieties* with formal scientific names.

POLICY IN CLASSIFICATION

The policy employed in this book is conservative. In particu-lar many entities considered by others to be species are reduced to varietal status.

The writer has presented a detailed discussion of his philoso-phy of genera, species, and varieties in the following article: Lyman Benson. "The Goal and Methods of Systematic Botany," *Cactus and Succulent Journal* 15: 99-111. July, 1943. (Cf. particularly pp. 101-103.) In the article mentioned, an attitude of complete neutrality has been maintained, for, on purely logical grounds, as long as populations recognized by scientific names are natural, a conservative or liberal or any intermediate policy in delimiting them must be of equal value. The choice must be based, therefore, upon (A) conformity to prevailing practice through the world as a whole for naming the entire plant kingdom, as far as this can be determined, and (B) practical considerations.

A. The writer has adopted a conservative policy in all his publications partly because it is most nearly in harmony with world-wide prevailing practice. A local "liberalism" endemic in the United States in the period from about 1900 to 1930 is reflected in many of the older works touching on the flora of the Southwestern Deserts. This policy has been abandoned or modified by the great majority of botanists in even this country, but there is bound to be some variation in degree of conservatism from book to book according to the policies of the authors (as well as the data available to them). The policy adopted in THE TREES AND SHRUBS OF THE SOUTHWESTERN DESERTS is the approximate equivalent of that in such standard botanical books as Gray's *Manual of Botany* and Jepson's *Manual of the Flowering Plants of California*.

B. Conservative policy with respect to recognition of species is followed here for the following practical reasons as well:

1. A great many fairly well-marked natural populations are lacking in characters of sufficient stability to make their use in keys practical. The writer believes that these populations of less stability are considered more effectively as varieties than as species. This removes the necessity of attempting to segregate them in keys, and it leaves for separation within the keys only the major populations with relatively clear and stable diagnostic characters. This saves the reader no end of frustration in determining the species. If he is interested in identifying the variety, this may be accomplished by comparing the descriptions, but it must be remembered that the characters more frequently are inconsistent in their association. When a species is represented by several varieties, these are differentiated in a key.

2. Lack of organization of species into varieties and consideration of each local element as a separate species makes carrying over of knowledge from one region to another very difficult. It gives the flora of each locality the aspect of being a local independent unit rather than a phase of the general flora of the continent and of the world as a whole. If one is concerned with the flora of only a limited geographical region, the necessity for reconciling the plants with those of another area is not encountered, and the use of a trinomial (e.g. *Prunus virginiana* var. *demissa* for the chokecherry of the Pacific States) seems cumbersome as compared with *Prunus demissa*. However, for anyone who has known elsewhere a closely similar plant (e.g. *Prunus virginiana* var. *virginiana,* the chokecherry of the East, Middle West, and Southeast), it is helpful to know that the plant he encounters in a new situation is similar to what he knows already but that it does differ in some not wholly stable characters present through a particular geographical region. If the Pacific Coast chokecherry, for example, appears under the binomial *Prunus demissa,* there is no ready correlation with knowledge of the flora of other regions. Before the writer are half a dozen books written by members of the American "liberal" school. Each of them covers one or another of the states or larger portions of the Western States. In each of them one or two chokecherries are described, but in none of them is there any statement of close relationship to *Prunus virginiana.* In some books *Prunus demissa* appears; in some *Prunus melanocarpa* occurs; in some both are mentioned. Were it not for the fact that these are among the relatively few plants with well-established English names, all evidence of the transcontinental inter-relationships of the chokecherries would be obliterated. Obviously there is room for difference of opinion, but to the writer it seems far better to consider these incompletely differentiated geographical units as follows: *Prunus virginiana* var. *melanocarpa* of the Rocky Mountains and the borders of the Great Basin; *Prunus virginiana* var. *demissa* of largely the Pacific Slope but penetrating far inland in some areas. Such a policy makes "variety" a strong and useful category (or taxon) of value in improving organization.

CHANGES IN THE RULES FOR NAMING PLANTS

According to the revision of the International Rules of Botanical Nomenclature adopted at Stockholm in 1950, the name of the typical variety repeats automatically the specific epithet, e.g. *Mortonia scabrella* var. *scabrella*. Specific and varietal epithets may be all decapitalized or those formed from personal, generic or aboriginal names may be capitalized. There is no rule, and although the trend at Stockholm was toward decapitalization there was no decision. The author's practice remains unchanged. In this book, where not specified otherwise, reference to only the genus and species (e.g. *Ephedra nevadensis*) is to the typical variety (understood) or, where indicated, to the species as a whole including all its varieties.

POPULAR NAMES

The application of popular names to plants is far more confused than the use of scientific names, because there are no definitely established rules to be followed. It is not unusual for several plants to be designated by the same English name or for one plant to have several such names. In this book well-established English, Spanish, and Indian names are included when they are available. Since they are conspicuous, most of the trees and major shrubs have vernacular names, but most plants do not. As far as possible, only well-known names have been adopted, and in most cases adoption of "synthetic" alleged "common" names has been avoided.

HOW TO USE THE KEYS FOR PLANT IDENTIFICATION

Although many of the trees and shrubs may be recognized from the illustrations and some of them may be found by looking up the common names, accuracy in identification may be achieved only by means of the keys and descriptions. Only a little effort is required to learn the proper means of determination, and its application to a small group like trees and shrubs is not difficult. The information made available to the individual who is patient enough to attempt it will be an adequate reward for the effort.

The key is actually a process of elimination similar to the parlor guessing game which begins usually with the question, "Is it in the mineral, vegetable, or animal kingdom?"

In the following illustration of the method of using keys, the desert apricot is chosen as an example. This plant has the same fundamental flower structure as any apricot, plum, prune, peach, cherry, or almond, and the fruit, too, is essentially the same. The desert apricot is figured in Fig. 28 *A,* and a flower of essentially the same type is shown in Fig. 3 *C.* Comparison of these figures with the characters in the key should aid in following the outline below:

Turn first to the key to the classes and subclasses on page 45. In this key there are two leads beginning with the number 1. These are opposed to each other, and a choice must be made between them. The fruit of the desert apricot is almost identical in structure with that of a cultivated apricot, and it contains one seed; flowers are present; the stems are not jointed and not striate (lined lengthwise) , and the leaves are well developed and alternate. Therefore the desert apricot "fits" the second of the two leads numbered 1, and it checks exactly with the second of the subordinate leads numbered 2.

As indicated on page 45, the next step is to turn to the Dicotyledoneae on page 94. Here there is a recapitulation of the characters of the group, followed by a key to the families on page 94. In this key there are two leads numbered 1 and opposed to each other. The first is on page 94; the second is on page 96. The flowers of the desert apricot have both stamens and pistils, and the plant fits the second lead of the pair. Under this lead are two subordinate leads numbered 2. The fruit is a drupe and not a legume, so the apricot fits the second member of the pair. Directly under this lead is another pair numbered 3, and, since the petals are separate, the plant fits the first lead, and it is necessary to choose between the two subordinate leads numbered 4. The flower in Fig. 3 *C,* which is similar to that of the desert apricot, has been used as a typical example of a perigynous flower, so the apricot fits the second lead numbered 4, page 97. Under this are two leads numbered 5, and the apricot fits the first one, since there are obviously more than ten stamens. The next choice, between the two subordinate leads numbered 6, will give the family. Since stipules (see p. 32) are present, at least when the leaves are young, since the fruit is a typical drupe (see p. 28), and since the leaves are not entire but toothed, the second lead fits the apricot, and it is in the family Rosaceae or rose family, page 139.

The description of the rose family is followed by a key to the genera, page 139. The apricot fits the second of the leads numbered 1, since the pistil is a single carpel (p. 26), since the leaves fall away each autumn as they do in its cultivated counterpart, and since the plants are shrubs rarely more than 3 meters (9 feet) high. The plant fits the second number 2 lead, for there is only one pistil in the flower, and apricots have no tails. The second lead 3 is chosen because the fruit is a drupe, the petals are white, there are five sepals, and the leaves are alternate. The genus, then, is *Prunus*.

On page 147 there is a key to the species of *Prunus*. The flowers of the apricot have obvious stalks (pedicels), and the leaves are glabrous. Therefore, the plant fits the first of the leads numbered 1. In the choice between the leads numbered 2, the white petals, the greenish calyx and floral tube, and the more or less heart-shaped leaves somewhat more than half an inch (12.5 mm.) broad place the desert apricot as *Prunus Fremontii*. This species is described and discussed on page 147.

CLASSIFICATION OF SOUTHWESTERN DESERT TREES AND SHRUBS

1. Seeds produced at the ends of branches and subtended by cycles of scales arranged in 2's or 3's, not covered by an ovary wall and therefore not a part of a fruit, the entire structure (seed and subtending scales) similar to a pine cone; flowers none, the male organs (sporophylls) produced in cones composed of cycles of scales, each sporophyll resembling the stamen of a flowering plant in its appearance and in its basic structure; our single desert genus composed of jointed shrubs with scalelike leaves in whorls of 2 or 3 at the nodes of the striate stems, not at all resembling the conifers in the mountains. (Fig. 11; Pl. VII *A, B*.)

Class I. GYMNOSPERMAE (p. 46)

1. Seeds produced in the ovary, which matures into the fruit or seed vessel; flowers present, each composed typically of sepals, petals, stamens, and 1 or more pistils, sometimes without petals, more rarely without either sepals or petals, sometimes unisexual—that is, with either stamens or pistils as the case may be and with or without sepals and/or petals; plants not jointed with 2 or 3 scale leaves in a whorl at each stem joint, the stems usually not striate. (Pls. I; VII *C* to XXXIV; Figs. 14 to 84.)

Class II. ANGIOSPERMAE (p. 54)

2. Principal veins of the leaves parallel to one another; sepals, petals, and usually the other flower parts in 3's or multiples of 3 (Pl. X *A*); stem with the vascular bundles (fibers containing fine, tubular cells which conduct food and water) scattered irregularly through the pithy tissue, not increasing in girth by formation of annual layers (rings) of wood; seed leaf (cotyledon) 1 in the embryo in the seed. (Pls. I; VII *C* to XVI; Figs. 14 to 16.)

Subclass A. MONOCOTYLEDONEAE (p. 54)

2. Principal veins of the leaves branching out from the midrib or the base of it not parallel, forming a network—that is, netted-veined; sepals, petals, and usually the other parts of the flowers in 2's, 4's, or 5's; stem with the vascular bundles in a cylinder (ring), the cambium adding a new cylinder each year or each growing season; seed leaves (cotyledons) 2 in the embryo in the seed, these usually visible above ground and after germination of the seedling plant. (Pls. XVI to XXXIV; Figs. 18 to 84.)

Subclass B. DICOTYLEDONEAE (p. 94)

45

CLASS I. *GYMNOSPERMAE*. CONE-BEARING PLANTS

The gymnosperms (Mormon or Mexican tea) occurring in the Southwestern deserts are utterly unlike the cone-bearing trees (pines, firs, spruces, etc.) growing at higher altitudes. Neither are they similar to flowering plants. They are surviving relic species of a group once more widespread and variable, the order Gnetales, which is related on the one hand to the conifers but distinct from them, and on the other hand to the flowering plants but distinct from them also. At present there are three types of plants in the group, as follows: (1) *Gnetum,* a tropical group of perhaps fifteen species occurring in both hemispheres and characterized by paired ovate or elliptic leaves much like those of an ordinary dicotyledonous flowering plant; (2) *Welwitschia,* with a single species (*Welwitschia mirabilis*) confined to a district on the west coast of South Africa where the average annual rainfall is less than 1 inch, a curious plant consisting of a heavy base and two broad, ribbon-like leaves several feet long and a few inches broad but often frayed to strips by action of the wind as it sweeps them across the barren ground; (3) *Ephedra* or Mormon or Mexican tea, a group of about fifty species occurring largely in the dry regions about the Mediterranean Sea, in Asia, in western North America, and in South America.

The naked seeds (not enclosed in an ovary) are the outstanding feature which places the Mormon tea with the gymnosperms or cone-bearing plants. The anthers are essentially the same as those in stamens of a flowering plant, or they correspond also to the spore-bearing scales in the male cone of a pine tree. Some of the microscopic details of the life history match those of the conifers, while some are in closer harmony with the flowering plants.

Ephedra is well known in the Southwestern deserts, and many supposed medicinal uses are ascribed to it. Various racial groups assign it remarkable value as a cure for venereal and other diseases, and it would be a great contribution to medicine and a simplification of pharmacy if one plant might have all its alleged virtues. A Chinese species yields the important drug, ephedrine, which is well known as a shrinking agent for tissues of the nasal passages when they are inflamed by colds. The drug is not available from the native species in the American deserts in sufficient quantities to be worth while, and a better source is available since ephedrine is produced synthetically.

Family 1. *EPHEDRACEAE*. Ephedra Family

1. *EPHEDRA*. Mormon Tea; Mexican Tea

Ephedra is a scraggly shrub rarely more than 4 or 5 feet high, (Pl. VII *A, B*) , and the intricate network of brittle, practically leafless green, yellow-green, or blue-green branches is the outstanding feature of the plant. In the springtime, the male plant becomes a conspicuous and beautiful mass of yellow clusters of anthers, and the green (later darker) seeds are an obvious but less conspicuous feature of the female plant (Fig. 11; Pl. VII *A, B*) .

Branches finely grooved and ridged, jointed, producing scale leaves a few millimeters long, united in pairs or 3's at each node, the leaves united or sometimes separate; stalked anthers (microsporophylls) produced in clusters at the ends of longer common stalks which are developed among scalelike bracts arranged in pairs or 3's in a conelike structure, the cones clustered at the nodes of the stem; ovules produced singly or in pairs, each solitary ovule or group of 2 or 3 ovules subtended and largely enclosed by a conelike group of scalelike bracts (scales) arranged in pairs or 3's, the ovule with a terminal elongated tubule through which the pollen tube enters, the ovule and tubule together resembling in appearance the ovary and style and stigma of a flowering plant pistil but actually corresponding to one of the ovules or seeds within the flowering plant ovary or within the cone of a conifer.

The staminate (male) and ovulate (female) cones are produced in the springtime. (Fig. 11 *E 1-4* and other figures on the same plate.)

KEY TO THE SPECIES

1. Scale leaves and scales of the cones in 3's (Fig. 11 *D 2*); seeds solitary or rarely 2 or 3 in some cones, the cones not stalked.

    2. Staminate* and ovulate cones obviously unequal in size (Fig. 11 *A 2, 3; D 3, 4*), the staminate 5-7 mm. long, the ovulate 10-12 mm. long; scales of the ovulate cones in many pairs, largely membranous and translucent, 7-9 mm. in diameter, the stalks of at least the upper ones slender, 2-3 mm. long; seeds wrapped in scales, not protruding.

        3. Leaves 8-12 mm. long, shredded or separated in age, the free apices 2-3 mm. long, forming sharp points, not recurved in age;

*Use of the term "staminate" is open to question.

seeds smooth; branches tipped each with a spine; stalks of the individual anthers or at least of some of them 0.6-1 mm. long.

1. *Ephedra trifurca*

3. Leaves 3-4 mm. long, not markedly shredded in age, the apices usually becoming recurved and spreading widely; seeds roughened by narrow, short, crosswise ridges; branches not forming obvious sharp points; stalks of the individual anthers mostly 0.3-0.5 mm. long. 2. *Ephedra Torreyana*

2. Staminate and ovulate cones of about equal size, 8-9 mm. long; scales of the ovulate cones in 5-6 pairs (Fig. 11 *B 1*), not strongly membranous, 3-6 mm. in diameter, not markedly stalked; seeds not wrapped in scales, protruding 1-3 mm. beyond the scales.

3. *Ephedra californica*

1. Scale leaves and scales of the cones in 2's; seeds in pairs or solitary, the cones stalked or not stalked.

2. Twigs few, divergent, averaging about 2 mm. in diameter, glaucous (bluish) in the grooves; leaves falling completely away, the bases gray. 4. *Ephedra nevadensis*

2. Twigs numerous, tending to be parallel like the straws of a broom, averaging 1-1.5 mm. in diameter, green, not glaucous, with rough papillae on the ridges; bases of the leaves persistent, conspicuously brown. 5. *Ephedra viridis*

1. *Ephedra trifurca* Torr. MEXICAN TEA. (1) Scalelike leaves of the stem in 3's, $^1/_3$ to $\frac{1}{2}$ inch long; (2) seeds very long and slender, smooth, wrapped in many scales; (3) scales of the cones conspicuously membranous-margined, the centers reddish tan, the margins light colored. (Fig. 11 *D*; Pl. VII *A*.)

Branches slender, elongated, each ultimately tipped with a weak spine, the twigs mostly about 1.5 mm. in diameter, green to yellow-green; leaves 8-12 mm. long, the upper 2-3 mm. of each free, forming a slender, sharp point, the united portion becoming frayed and dull gray in age, not curving downward; staminate cones broadly ovoid to nearly spherical, 5-6 mm. long, stalks of the individual anthers at least 0.6-1 mm. long; ovulate cones not stalked, about 10-11 mm. long, the scales in many cycles of three, conspicuously membranous except at the centers, nearly circular, 7-8 mm. in diameter, the bases notched, stalked, the stalks 2-3 mm. long, the other scales ultimately spreading widely; seed reddish tan, the body narrowly ovoid, 4-6 mm. long, 3 mm. in diameter, tapering into a beak 4-6 mm. long.

Mesas, plains, and sand hills in the desert and the desert grassland from sea level to 5,000 feet elevation. California along the Mojave River in the Mojave Desert near Barstow and Dag-

gett and in the Colorado Desert (rare) ; Arizona from the Bill
Williams River drainage in southern Mohave County to Yuma
County and eastward to southern Yavapai County and to Greenlee and Cochise counties; New Mexico along the Gila River
drainage and along the Rio Grande Valley from Albuquerque
southward; Baja California and eastward and southward in Mexico (Fig. 12 *1*) .

2. *Ephedra Torreyana* S. Wats. TORREY EPHEDRA; MORMON
TEA. (1) Scalelike leaves of the stem in 3's, $^{1}/_{6}$ to $^{1}/_{8}$ inch long;
(2) seed roughened by short, narrow, crosswise ridges, beaked,
the narrow beak as long as the body, wrapped in scales; (3)
scales of the cones yellow on the thin, membranous outer parts,
pinkish to reddish tan in the centers, the upper scales of the
ovulate cones stalked. (Fig. 11 *A*.)

Branches rather large, the bulk of the twigs about 2 mm. in diameter,
green or yellow-green, perhaps sometimes glaucous; leaves with the apices
recurved in age, 3-4 mm. long, brown with the edges light, thin, and membranous; staminate cones nearly spherical or ovoid, about 5-7 mm. long,
the scales nearly circular, 2-3 mm. long, stalks of the individual anthers
0.3-0.5 mm. long; ovulate cones not stalked, 10-12 mm. long, the scales
in many cycles of three, conspicuously membranous except in the centers,
the blades 6-8 mm. long, 7-9 mm. broad, the stalks of the upper ones about
2 mm. long; seed obscured by the scales, light colored, the body narrowly
ovoid, 4-5 mm. long, the beak or attenuation about the same length.

Sandy or gravelly plains and mesas in the sagebrush and creosote-bush deserts at 2,000 or commonly 4,000 to 6,000 feet elevation. Southern Nevada, nearly reaching the California border in
Nye and Clark counties; central and southern Utah; southwestern Colorado; Arizona from northern Mohave County southeastward to northern Yavapai County and eastward along the
Colorado and Little Colorado river drainages; New Mexico on
the San Juan River and the Rio Grande drainages from Santa
Fe southward; western Texas; Chihuahua, Mexico. (Fig. 12 2.)

3a. *Ephedra californica* S. Wats. var. *californica*. CALIFORNIA
EPHEDRA. (1) Scalelike leaves of the stem in 3's, $^{1}/_{8}$ to $^{1}/_{6}$ inch
long; (2) seeds smooth except for the fine lines formed by the
elongated walls of the cells which form its outer covering, not
beaked; (3) scales of the cones brown, not stalked or membranous-margined. (Fig. 11 *B*.)

Branches rather large, the bulk of the twigs about 2 mm. in diameter, green, with minute patches of bluish white wax (glaucousness) in the grooves; leaves with recurved apices, mostly about 3-4 mm. long, brown, the edges at first lighter than the middles; staminate cones not stalked, ovoid, about 8 mm. long, the scales in 5-6 cycles of three, brown but somewhat glaucous, stalks of the individual anthers 0.2-0.4 mm. long; ovulate cones ovoid, the scales brown but partly glaucous, from broadly triangular to nearly circular, 3-6 mm. long; seed brown, ovoid, relatively broad, 8-9 mm. long.

Dry plains and slopes in the desert or in the grassland at 500 to 3,000 feet elevation. California in the innermost South Coast ranges from Panoche Pass to the Temblor Mountains and northeastward to the Greenhorn Mountains, Kern County, southward to San Diego County, eastward to the Death Valley region, the Mojave Desert, and the Colorado Desert; Baja California, Mexico.

3b. *Ephedra californica* S. Wats. var. *funerea* (Cov. & Mort.) L. Benson. DEATH VALLEY EPHEDRA

Scales of the ovulate cones more membranous; seed smooth or somewhat roughened, elongated-pyramidal, drawn out into a beak, 7-9 mm. long, 2-4 mm. in diameter. Synonym: *Ephedra funerea* Cov. & Mort.

Washes and mountain sides in the desert at 2,000 to 3,000 feet elevation. From the Funeral and Black mountains on the east side of Death Valley, California, to the south end of the Charleston Mountains in adjacent Nevada.

4a. *Ephedra nevadensis* S. Wats. var. *nevadensis*. NEVADA EPHEDRA. (1) Scalelike leaves of the stem in 2's, the bases gray, falling away in age; (2) seeds in pairs (solitary in the variety), the ovulate cones stalked; (3) twigs few, divergent, averaging $1/_{12}$ inch in diameter, bluish in the grooves.

Branches rather stout, not spiny, brittle, smooth, bluish green; leaves 2-4 mm. long; staminate cones ovoid, 5-7 mm. long, the anthers unusually large, nearly 1 mm. long, the individual stalks 0.1-0.3 mm. long; ovulate cones with stalks 5-15 mm. long, ovoid, 6-7 mm. long, the scales in about 3-5 pairs, firm, not membranous, green in the middles, tan to whitish on the broad margins, broadly ovate, 2-5 mm. long, not stalked; seeds broadly boat-shaped, the flat "deck" of each facing the other member of the pair, dark greenish lead color, 5-7 mm. long, about 2.5-3 mm. broad, not beaked.

Sandy or rocky plains and slopes in the sagebrush and creosote-bush deserts at 2,000 to 6,000 feet elevation. Southeastern

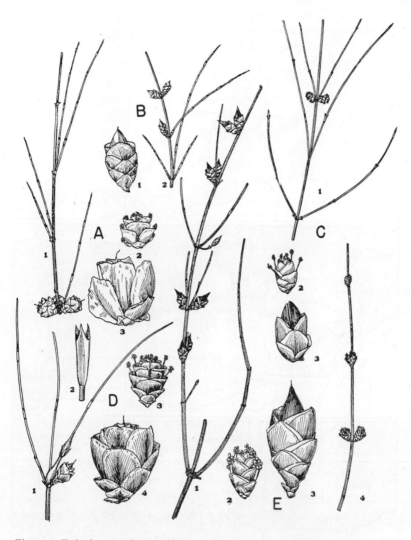

Fig. 11.—Ephedras or Mormon teas: *A*, Mormon tea, *Ephedra Torreyana*, *1*, branch with whorls of 3 scalelike leaves and a whorl of 3 ovulate cones, *2*, staminate cone, *3*, ovulate cone; *B*, California ephedra, *Ephedra californica*, *1*, ovulate cone, *2*, branch with ovulate cones; *C*, green ephedra, *Ephedra viridis*, *1*, branch with staminate cones, *2*, staminate cone, *3*, ovulate cone with 2 seeds; *D*, Mexican tea, *Ephedra trifurca*, *1*, branch with an ovulate cone and with swellings (galls) caused by insects, *2*, a whorl of 3 united leaves, *3*, staminate cone, *4*, ovulate cone with only the tip of the seed visible; *E*, boundary ephedra, *Ephedra nevadensis* var. *aspera*, *1*, branch with ovulate cones, *2*, staminate cone, *3*, ovulate cone, *4*, branch with staminate cones. (Branches x $^1/_3$; separate cones x $1^1/_3$.)

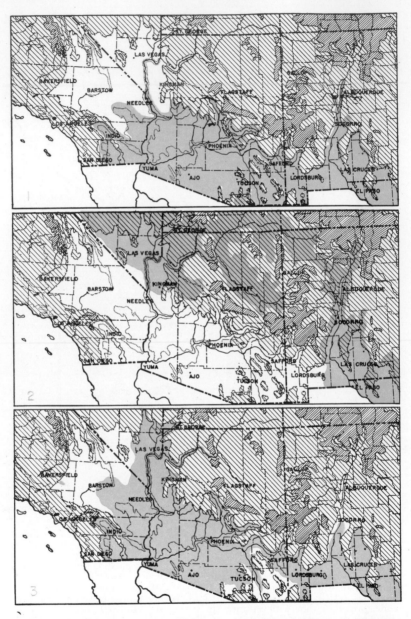

Fig. 12.—Distributional maps: *1*, Mexican tea, *Ephedra trifurca; 2*, Mormon tea, *Ephedra Torreyana; 3*, boundary ephedra, *Ephedra nevadensis* var. *aspera*.

Oregon; California east of the Sierra Nevada as far south as the Mojave Desert; Nevada; western and central Utah; Arizona in west-central Mohave County. (Fig. 13 *1*.)

4b. *Ephedra nevadensis* S. Wats. var. *aspera* (Engelm.) L. Benson. BOUNDARY EPHEDRA (Fig. 11 *E*; Pl. VII *B*)

Branches smooth or with minute rough usually yellowish papillae on the ridges, yellow-green, not glaucous or with a wash of glaucousness on both the grooves and ridges just above each node; ovulate cones not stalked or short stalked; seed usually solitary, about 8-9 mm. long, narrowly ovoid, drawn into an apical conical point, smooth except for the minute longitudinal lines of the cell walls of the epidermis or sometimes roughened.

Desert flats and slopes at mostly 1,000 to 4,000 feet elevation; sometimes in the desert grassland up to 5,000 feet. California in the eastern Mojave and Colorado deserts; southern Nevada in Clark and Lincoln counties; southwestern Utah; Arizona in the Mojave and the Sonoran deserts; New Mexico along the Gila and Pecos river and Rio Grande drainages; western Texas; Mexico. (Fig. 12 *3*.)

5a. *Ephedra viridis* Cov. var. *viridis.* GREEN EPHEDRA. (1) Scale leaves of the stem in 2's, the brown bases conspicuous and persistent; (2) seeds in pairs; (3) branches many, dense, tending to be parallel like the straws of a broom, bright green, slender, averaging $^{1}/_{16}$ inch or less in diameter. (Fig. 11 *C*.)

Branches not spiny, with rough papillae on the ridges; leaves 2-3 mm. long, the bases and middle portions conspicuously dark brown, the rest light green and tending to be membranous, all but the bases falling away in age; staminate cones nearly spherical, 3-4 mm. in diameter, the anthers relatively large, 0.5 mm. long and 0.5-0.6 broad, practically lacking individual stalks; ovulate cones with stalks 2-6 mm. long, ovoid, 5-7 mm. long, the scales in about 3-5 pairs, not membranous, green at the middles, lighter colored and thinner toward the margins, ovate, 2-5 mm. long, not stalked; seeds more or less boat-shaped, the flat "deck" of each facing the other member of the pair, dark greenish lead color, 5-7 mm. long, about 2-2.5 mm. broad, not beaked.

Rocky or sandy slopes and plains of the sagebrush desert, the higher creosote-bush desert, the desert grassland, and the oak woodland at 3,000 to 7,000 feet elevation. California east of the Sierra Nevada from Lassen County southward to the mountains of Inyo County, westward through the mountains of Kern

County to eastern Ventura County, southward to the mountains of San Bernardino County; northern and central Nevada and southward to the Charleston Mountains; western Utah and on the Green and Colorado river drainages eastward; Arizona from northern Mohave to northern Yavapai and Apache counties; northwestern New Mexico in San Juan County. (Fig. 13 *3*.)

5b. *Ephedra viridis* Cov. var. *viscida* (Cutler) L. Benson. NAVAJO EPHEDRA

Stems somewhat stouter and shorter than in var. *viridis,* sometimes sticky; ovulate cones with stalks usually 5-10 mm. long.

Sandy and rocky plains of the short grass prairie, the sage-brush desert, and the pinyon-juniper woodland at 4,000 to 6,000 feet elevation; rarely in the creosote-bush desert at 3,500 feet. Southeastern Utah east of the Colorado River; southwestern Colorado; Arizona on the Navajo Indian Reservation and south-westward to Oak Creek Canyon and Montezuma Castle National Monument; northwestern New Mexico and as far eastward as Santa Fe. (Fig. 13 *2*.)

CUPRESSACEAE. CYPRESS FAMILY. The members of this family commonly are indicators of the flora of higher levels. However, two members of the family occur sometimes in the desert. *Cupressus arizonica* Greene, Arizona cypress, occurs along east-central Arizona mountain canyons commonly in the oak belt, but here and there, as at Sabino Canyon, near Tucson, it follows down the streams into the desert. *Juniperus monosperma* (Engelm.) Sarg., a juniper, is common in the middle elevations of Arizona, New Mexico, and Texas, and occasionally it occurs on the higher hills of the desert, as, for example, west of Pantano and in Davidson Canyon, southeastern Pima County, Arizona, or in the desert grassland. Both cypresses and junipers are recognized readily by their minute, scalelike, appressed leaves, which completely clothe and obscure the small branchlets, and they are distinguished with ease by their cones. The woody cypress cone resembles a small walnut, and it contains many seeds; the juniper cone is berrylike, usually fleshy, and usually with 1-3 seeds.

CLASS II. *ANGIOSPERMAE*. FLOWERING PLANTS

SUBCLASS A. *MONOCOTYLEDONEAE*. MONOCOTYLEDONS

The more obvious distinctions between the monocotyledons or "monocots" and the dicotyledons or "dicots" are simple and well known. They are summarized in the following table:

Monocotyledons	*Dicotyledons*
1. Principal veins of the leaves parallel to one another; as, for example, in a corn leaf.	1. Principal veins of the leaves branching out from the midrib or the base of it, not parallel, forming a network—that is, netted-veined. Examples: apple, orange.
2. Sepals, petals, and usually the other flower parts in 3's or multiples of 3 (Pl. XI *A*).	2. Sepals, petals, and ordinarily the other parts of the flowers in 2's, 4's, or 5's (Fig. 26 *A* 2).
3. Stem with the vascular bundles (fibers containing fine, tubular cells which conduct food and water) scattered irregularly through pithy tissue, not increasing in girth by formation of annual layers (rings) of wood.	3. Stem with the vascular bundles in a cylinder (ring), the cambium adding a new cylinder of wood each year or each growing season. (Much of the desert has both winter and summer rain, which may be erratic with long intervening drought periods between storms, and so two or more rings may be formed in a single year.)
4. Seed leaf (cotyledon) one. (A corn or wheat "seed," for example, is not divided readily into two conspicuous parts, the cotyledons, as are most dicot seeds.)	4. Seed leaves (cotyledons) two. (A pea or bean seed is divided readily into two large cotyledons, which form the bulk of the embryonic plant. In some plants —for example, beans or cotton— these seed leaves enlarge, become green, and emerge from the seed coat at germination time. In others—for example, the garden pea—they remain in the seed coat while the young plant lives on the stored food.)
Examples: lilies, irises, orchids, grasses (including corn), sedges, rushes, tule, yuccas, bear grass, sotol or "desert spoon," century plants, palms.	Examples: peach, pear, apricot, manzanita, oak, walnut, cat claw, mesquite, palo verde, ocotillo, sunflower, dandelion, tobacco, tomato, mint, buttercup, larkspur, poppy, mustard, sycamore.

The monocotyledons are rarely trees or shrubs, and the curious large species occurring in the Southwestern deserts are

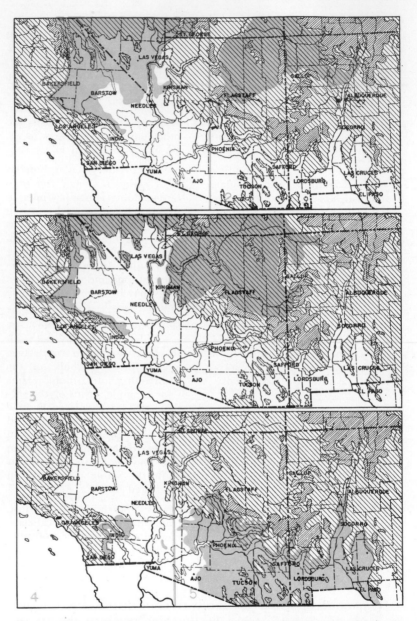

Fig. 13.—Distributional maps: *1*, Nevada ephedra, *Ephedra nevadensis; 2*, Navajo ephedra, *Ephedra viridis* var. *viscida; 3*, green ephedra, *Ephedra viridis; 4*, California fan palm, *Washingtonia filifera; 5*, palmilla or soapweed, *Yucca elata*.

among the few woody members of the group, which consists largely of herbs. Only three families are represented by woody members, as follows: *Palmae* or palm family, *Liliaceae* or lily family, and *Amaryllidaceae* or amaryllis family.[3] (Pls. I; VII C to XV; Figs. 14 to 16.)

KEY TO THE FAMILIES

1. Leaves palmately parted or cleft or pinnate; fruit 1-seeded, the outer portion fleshy or in age a dry husk, the inner portion (seed) exceedingly hard, the embryo small, produced at the side of the seed; trees with unbranched stems; flower cluster enclosed at first by a large yellow bract (spathe). (Pls. I; VII *C-F*.)   Family 2. PALMAE (p. 57)

1. Leaves simple, linear, or lanceolate, the margins sometimes minutely toothed or obviously prickly; fruit many-seeded or, rarely, 3-seeded; flower cluster not enclosed by a spathe.

    2. Ovary superior (Pls. V *A*, XI *A*); leaves not succulent. (Pls. VIII to XII; XIV; Figs. 14, 15 *center, right*.)   Family 3. LILIACEAE (p. 59)

    2. Ovary inferior (Pl. V *D;* Fig. 16 *A 3-5, B 4, D 1*); leaves succulent or sometimes not so. (Pls. XIII; XIV, *left;* XV; Fig. 16.)
        Family 4. AMARYLLIDACEAE (p. 75)

Family 2. *PALMAE*. PALM FAMILY

The palm family occurs in the tropics throughout the world, and some of the species are native to subtropical North America, including various parts of Mexico. Only one genus, *Washingtonia,* is native in the Southwestern states, and it is restricted to isolated colonies of a few, or rarely as many as one hundred, trees growing in canyons in the desert mountains in California and Arizona. These plants grow at the northern limits of palms at the present day, but their rarity and the discontinuous nature of their distribution may indicate either greater abundance and more nearly continuous distribution in the past or transportation of the seeds from place to place by Indians to whom the palms were useful for food, shelter, or fiber. (Pls. I; VII *C-F*.)

1. *WASHINGTONIA*. FAN PALM

The fan palms are distinguished readily from the commonly cultivated date palms by the arrangement of the leaf blades. In the fan palms the blade is nearly circular in outline, and the

3. A few woody plants in the grass family have been introduced in the deserts, but these are not included in this work. Some of the plants discussed in this book—e.g., the century plants—are not, strictly speaking, trees or shrubs.

divisions extend only half or two thirds of the way to the base, being arranged palmately (like the fingers of the human hand). In the date palms the blade is greatly elongated and divided all the way to the midrib, with the separate leaflets pinnately arranged (like the segments of a feather) along the elongated axis.

1. *Washingtonia filifera* (Linden) Wendl. var. *filifera*. CALIFORNIA FAN PALM. (1) Trunk 20-40 or 50 feet high or sometimes taller, 1-4½ feet in diameter at the base; (2) leaf divisions with long fibers fraying from their edges. (Pls. I; VII *C-F*.)

Bark gray, shallowly fissured in age after the fall of the long-persistent dead leaves or leaf bases; leaf blades about 1-1.5 m. in diameter, palmately cleft or parted into numerous linear lobes, the bases slightly cordate, the petioles 1-1.5 m. long, 4-7 cm. broad, the bases broader, with prickles along half or all of the margins; flowers bisexual, produced in numerous elongated (2-5 m. long), drooping series of panicled spikes (5-12 panicles in a series), the spathes (bracts) yellowish, 3-5 dm. long, 3-5 cm. broad, the lower ones larger and apparently empty; sepals united; petals united into a funnel-shaped corolla; stamens attached to the petals; fruits nearly black, ellipsoidal, about 8 mm. long, the solitary seed tan or brown, ellipsoidal, 6 mm. long.

Moist soil along alkaline streams or in canyons or rincons (recesses) of the desert mountains at 500 to 3,000 feet elevation. California in scattered groves along the northern and western portions of the Salton Sea Basin of the Colorado Desert and on the southern margin of the Mojave Desert; Arizona in canyons of the Kofa Mountains, Yuma County; Baja California, Mexico. (Fig. 13 *4*.)

The most striking grove of palms in Arizona, or perhaps anywhere in the Southwest, is in Palm Canyon in the Kofa (S.H.) Mountains. This canyon is reached by turning eastward on a road leading from the main highway about 19 miles south of Quartzite. At the foot of the mountains, it is necessary to hike now only about ½ mile into Palm Canyon, which is the conspicuous gash in the western side of the mountain range. About halfway up the canyon, a trail leads to the left (north) up a steep side canyon where the largest group of palms is plainly visible. The trees occur along this tributary canyon for some distance, and they are to be found here and there in the main canyon and in other side canyons. Palm Canyon is notable not only for its palms but also for a number of other rare and localized plants and for its steep topography and its reddish rock. Several bedding grounds of the desert bighorn sheep are at the base of the conspicuous cliff near the trail on the south side of the main canyon across from the chief grove of palms. The palms occur also in at least one other canyon in the Kofa Mountains, besides Palm Canyon and its tributaries.

The palms in the Kofa Mountains have relatively slender trunks (cf. Pl. I) as do some of the native plants in California (cf. Pl. VII *C-E*). The circular horizontal ridges on the trunk (Pl. I) are also reminiscent of var. *gracilis,* cf. below.

The largest and most extensive native stands of the California fan palm are in Palm Canyon near Palm Springs, California, and in Thousand Palms Canyon, near Indio. Where the trees are undisturbed by fire or vandals, the densely thatched, tall trunks provide a deep shade comparable to that in humid forest regions.

This well-known tree of the Southwestern deserts has been long under cultivation in California and throughout the world.

Washingtonia filifera (Linden) Wendl. var. *gracilis* (Parish) L. Benson. Trunks mostly 15-25 m. (about 50-80 feet) high, 3-6 dm. (8-16 inches) in diameter above the bases; petioles more densely spiny in young trees; leaf blades 0.8-1 m. in diameter, less deeply parted in mature trees, not fraying along the margins or only slightly so, shining-green; ligule at the top of the petiole shorter and broader. Native of Baja California and Sonora long cultivated in California and now cultivated throughout the Southwest and in other parts of the world. Cf. notes on the palms in the Kofa Mountains under var. *filifera. (Washingtonia robusta* Wendl.)

Family 3. *LILIACEAE.* LILY FAMILY

The plants in the lily family which qualify as trees and shrubs (and some of those included here really do not) are scarcely reminiscent of lilies. They are bizarre desert or near-desert types, the appearance of which may recall palm trees or greatly overgrown herbs with great rosettes of basal leaves and slender flowering stems. All of them belong to the same group within the lily family, and they are a compact unit perhaps not closely related to any other desert plants. The group shows some similarity to the agaves, or century plants, here considered to be in the Amaryllidaceae or amaryllis family, and union of the two groups as a family separate from other groups has been proposed. It is possible that such a grouping is justified, but the authors are not prepared to make such a change without a great deal of additional study. The present treatment is the classical one and perhaps, though not necessarily, the better one. (Pls. VIII to XII; XIV *center, right*; Figs. 14 and 15.)

Commonly herbs developed from bulbs, corms, or rootstocks, but rarely trees or shrubs or ponderous plants developed from a thick subterranean caudex (stem base). Leaves (of this group) linear, elongated, in dense rosettes. Flowers usually bisexual, rarely unisexual; perianth practically always of 3 sepals and 3 petals, usually not differentiated from one another in appearance or apparent structure; stamens 6, hypogynous (sometimes attached to the perianth). Ovary superior, 3-celled, with central placentae; styles united, the stigmas separate or united.

KEY TO THE GENERA

1. Margins of the leaves not prickly, sometimes with minute, sharp teeth.

　　2. Flowers all bisexual—that is, stamens and pistils in the same flower; sepals and petals at least 15 mm. long, each with several veins; seeds several or many in each of the 3 cells of the ovary. (Pls. VIII to XI; XIV *center, right*; Fig. 14.)　　　　　　　　　　　1. YUCCA

　　2. Flowers of various plants either staminate, pistillate, or bisexual; sepals and petals not more than 4 mm. long, each with a single vein; seeds 2 or 3 in each of the 3 cells of the ovary. (Pl. XII *C, E, G.*)
　　　　　　　　　　　　　　　　　　　　　　　　　2. NOLINA

1. Margins of the leaves with conspicuous, stout prickles; staminate and pistillate flowers on different plants. (Pl. XII *A, B, D, F.*) 3. DASYLIRION

1. *YUCCA*. SPANISH BAYONET

(1) Flowers ½ to 3 inches long; (2) leaf with smooth or finely toothed margins or with the margins separating into long threads, not prickly on the margins but with a sharp point at the end. (Pls. VIII to XI; XIV *center, right*; Fig. 14.)

Shrubs, trees, or heavy-based plants each developed from a ponderous, thickened, sometimes branched caudex (stem base) below ground. Leaves linear, sharp-pointed and usually daggerlike, the margins sometimes with minute teeth, usually separating into elongated fibers. Flowers bisexual, in panicles 0.3-3 m. long, large, perfect (bisexual); perianth 1.5-7.5 cm. long, the sepals and petals thick, white, or greenish or tinged with purple, lavender, or magenta; filaments thickened above. Fruit a capsule (dry and splitting open) or spongy or even fleshy, with numerous seeds in each of the three cells.

The yuccas are among the most striking desert plants, and they are one of the groups most frequently associated with the desert in art and popular literature. They are the source of a fair quality coarse fiber, which is developed in the leaves, and they have long been used as a source of soap. The trunks and leaves contain important chemicals now coming to be used in medicine and in regulation of the human body.

Pollination of the yucca flower is accomplished by the yucca moth, a type which flies at dusk during the yucca flowering season. At this time the white yucca flowers are readily visible, and the insects are attracted to them. The following account of the pollination procedure is quoted from Mr. J. D. Laudermilk. The full discussion appears in the *Desert Magazine* for December, 1942, and in the *Cactus and Succulent Journal* for June, 1943.

Fertilization of the yucca flower goes like this: *Pronuba* [the yucca moth] first goes to a mature flower and climbs up a stamen. Here she collects some pollen. She works this up into a tiny ball which she tucks under her chin. She visits several flowers, perhaps three or four. By this time the pollen ball is bigger than her head. Now she goes to another flower and opens up negotiations. Her operation here is that of laying her eggs. She begins by inserting her ovipositor, a long, thread-like apparatus with a sharp point, straight through the wall of the pistil, about a third of the way down from the top or stigma. She lays 20 or 30 eggs. Each egg is put directly into an ovule. After each egg is laid she carefully pulls out her ovipositor and climbs up to the stigma where she makes payment by ramming in some pollen grains. This insures that the flower which now has a consignment of eggs is going to be fertile and set seed. As the eggs hatch and the grubs grow, so does the yucca capsule. Since the grubs eat only a few seeds in any case, the plant will have plenty left.

The height of the flowering season for the yuccas, as for the cacti, is the month of May, but some species, for example, *Yucca elata,* flower in June and others in April. Unfortunately many of the plants do not come into flower, since cattle eat the young flowering stems of some species. Wherever the area is fenced or the plants are tall, white sprays of yucca flowers are to be found in abundance.

KEY TO THE SPECIES

1. Fruit drying and splitting open at maturity, the opened capsules persistent on the old inflorescence through the winter. (Pl. VIII *A*.)

2. Leaves not toothed, fibers separating and remaining attached to the margins (Pl. VIII *C*); stigma with 6 notches, not a simple knob, with perforations, not with papillae. (Section CHAENOCARPA.)

   3. Trunk of the mature plant 2-5 m. high, usually with 2 or 3 branches; inflorescence an open panicle elevated on a stalk of equal length; (Pls. VIII *A, B*; IX *A*; XIV *right*) stigma white.

                                              1. *Yucca elata*

   3. Trunk none above ground level, unbranched; inflorescence a raceme or slightly paniculate, not stalked; stigma green. (Pl. IX *B*.)   2. *Yucca glauca*

2. Leaves finely toothed on the margins, the teeth sharp and effective, spreading, fibers not separating from the leaf margin; stigma a simple knob, with numerous elongated papillae. (Section HESPEROYUCCA.) (Pl. VIII *D*.)   3. *Yucca Whipplei*

1. Fruit not splitting open, fleshy or spongy, not persisting on the inflorescence through the winter. (Pl. X *B*.)

   2. Leaf margin with fine, spreading, effective teeth, fibers not separating from it; tree up to 10 or even 20 m. high, the trunk branching and rebranching repeatedly in old individuals; sepals and petals curved inward, greenish, thick and fleshy; inflorescence 3-5 dm. long, a very dense panicle; style none. (Section CLISTOCARPA.) (Pl. X.)

                                              4. *Yucca brevifolia*

   2. Leaf margin not toothed, fibers often but not necessarily separating from it; trunk none above ground or the plant with 1 or several sparingly branched stems 0.5-3 or rarely 6 m. high; sepals and petals not curved markedly inward, white or tinged with lavender or purple, not markedly thick and fleshy. (Section SARCOCARPA.)

      3. Margins of the leaves not separating into fibers or in age producing a few very fine fibers; (Pl. XI *E*) branches of the inflorescence densely hairy.   5. *Yucca Schottii*

      3. Margins of the leaves eventually separating into fibers (Pl. XI *B*); branches of the inflorescence either glabrous or with a few hairs.

         4. Ovary at flowering time remarkably long and slender, the pistil over all 2.3-8 cm. long, the length several times the diameter.

            5. Sepals and petals usually 6-9 cm. long; pistil at flowering time usually 4-6 or 7 cm. long.   6. *Yucca baccata*

            5. Sepals and petals 2-4 cm. long; pistil at flowering time 2-3.5 or sometimes 4 cm. long.   7. *Yucca Torreyi*

         4. Ovary at flowering time short and barrel-shaped or short-cylindroidal, 0.8-1.2 cm. long (Pl. XI *A*).   8. *Yucca schidigera*

1. *Yucca elata* Engelm. PALMILLA; SOAPWEED. (1) Trunk 6-15 feet high, usually with 2 or 3 branches, clothed with the old drooping leaves of previous seasons; (2) leaves 10-18 or 24 inches long and ⅛ to 5/16 inch broad, only 1/32 inch thick, flexible, the margins with fine separated fibers; (3) fruit splitting open. (Pls. VIII *A-C;* IX *A;* XIV *right.*)

Leaves sharp-pointed, not glaucous; flowers in an open panicle about 0.5-1 m. long, the naked stalk about the same length; sepals and petals white, narrowly elliptic-acute, 3-4 cm. long, 1.5-2 cm. broad; stamens 1.5-2 cm. long, slender; style nearly white; fruit dry, 4-6 cm. long, 2-3 cm. in diameter. Synonym: *Yucca angustifolia* Pursh var. *radiosa* Engelm. Segregation as a species rather than a variety of *Yucca glauca* is questionable.

Common on deep, well-drained soils of plains and washes in the desert and the desert grassland at 2,000 to 6,000 feet elevation. Arizona from Salome, northern Yuma County, southward to Ajo, Pima County, and eastward to the Verde, Salt, and Gila river drainages; New Mexico on the Gila River and the Rio Grande drainages from Albuquerque southward; western Texas; Sonora and Chihuahua, Mexico. (Fig. 135.)

The palmilla is the common treelike yucca of large areas in southern Arizona and southern New Mexico, where it often forms pure stands on the grassy plains. The young flower stalks are sought by cattle as a choice food available during the drought period of May and June, and for this reason only the tallest plants produce flowers in most areas. The name "soapweed" may be traced to the large quantity of soapy material in the roots and stems. A slice of the trunk or root cut straight across is not only soapy, but the ends of the fibers form an effective soft brush. Indians formerly used the palmilla for both soap and fiber, and the leaves are still an important source of basketry material. As an emergency source of coarse fiber, the plant is now important. In drought periods, cattlemen sometimes shred or chop the leaves to provide an emergency food for livestock.

2. *Yucca glauca* Nutt. GREAT PLAINS YUCCA (Pl. IX *B*)

Trunk none or very short, the rosette of leaves on the ground; flowers in a nearly stalkless raceme or the inflorescence sometimes with a few branches and therefore a panicle; flowers tending to be closed into a sphere; sepals and petals greenish white, sometimes tinged with brown, up to 5 cm. long;

style and stigma green; margins of the seeds reported to be narrower than in *Yucca elata*. Synonym: *Yucca angustifolia* Pursh.

Common in the short-grass prairie of the Great Plains and occasional westward in usually modified form in the sagebrush desert and the pinyon-juniper woodland. South Dakota to Texas; northern, central, and especially eastern New Mexico. Plants known as *Yucca angustissima* and *Yucca Baileyi* are found from central Nevada to southwestern Colorado and northwestern New Mexico, and they may be merely transitional forms between this and *Yucca elata*. In Arizona they occur in northern Mohave and Yavapai counties and eastward north of the Mogollon Rim. Intermediate types between these forms and *Yucca elata* are found along the southern limits of the range in Arizona. A plant with leaves 12-14 mm. broad occurs in northern Mohave County, Arizona, near St. George, Utah (Peebles & Parker 14753). Another type with short leaves and coarse leaf fibers has been collected in the Little Colorado River Gorge, Coconino County, Arizona (Kearney & Peebles 12819). The species in this group need further study.

3. *Yucca Whipplei* Torr. SPANISH BAYONET; QUIJOTE PLANT; CHAPARRAL YUCCA. (1) Fruit splitting open at maturity and disseminating the seeds (to be observed on old flower stalks of the preceding season); (2) leaves with fine but very sharp spreading teeth which saw the hands of anyone pulling them unwarily. (Pl. VIII *D*.)

Stem subterranean, the leaves in solitary or clustered rosettes, 1 or more of the rosettes commonly flowering each season, in some geographical races dying after flowering of the solitary rosette and in some sending up branches with other leaf rosettes; leaves 2-8 dm. long, 1-2 cm. broad, about 3-6 mm. thick, glaucous, the apical point of each remarkably sharp; flowers in an open panicle of racemes, thin and the flower stalk 2.4 m. high, the panicle alone about 1-2 m. long, 3-4 dm. in diameter; sepals and petals white, broadly lanceolate, 3.5-6 cm. long, 1-2 cm. broad; stamens 1-1.5 cm. long, slender; fruit dry, 3-4 cm. long, 1-2 cm. in diameter.

Mountain slopes and mesas in the chaparral and in the desert from near sea level to about 4,000 feet elevation. California in the inner South Coast ranges from Monterey and San Benito counties and the foothills of the Sierra Nevada near Kings River southward to the mountains of southern

California and on desert slopes and mountains of the Mojave Desert; Arizona along the Colorado River system from Grand Wash Cliffs to the mouth of Kanab Creek, Mohave County; Baja California, Mexico. (Fig. 15 *1*.)

The chaparral yucca forms a conspicuous element in the chaparral-covered slopes of southern California where it attains its greatest size and abundance. On the slopes of the mountains bordering the Mojave Desert, plants are smaller in stature, being considered by some botanists as of the variety *caespitosa*. The widely separated occurrence of the chaparral yucca in the Grand Canyon region is indicative of the great age of the species and of a broader continuous distribution in antiquity.

The species includes a number of geographical forms, and these have been worked out thoroughly in a remarkably interesting and original study by Lee Haines, who has assigned them names as subspecies. These groups are based upon the ability of the individual to persist and reproduce after the first flowering and fruiting season as a result of branching underground or branching at ground level. These characters are not consistently associated with other features, except to some extent with size of the flower stalk in one or two cases, and, according to the policy followed in this work, the geographical types are not worthy of formal names.

Yucca Newberryi McKelvey, Yuccas S. W. U.S. (2): 49. 1947, is a form with poorly developed placental wings in the capsules occurring in Arizona along the Colorado River from Lake Mead to the Grand Canyon. It needs further evaluation.

4. *Yucca brevifolia* Engelm. JOSHUA TREE. (1) Plant is a tree as much as 30 (rarely to 50) feet high with the stem sometimes 2-4 or 5 feet in diameter at the base, being rebranched many times in older individuals; (2) the minute, sharp, firm teeth of the leaf margins. (Pl. X.)

Leaves short, 1-3.5 dm. long, tapering gradually, 7-13 mm. broad toward the bases, sharp-pointed; inflorescence not stalked, 2-4 dm. long, very dense, a panicle of racemes; sepals and petals thick and fleshy, greenish, incurved so that the flower is practically spherical, 2-3 cm. long, about 8-10 mm. broad; stamens 1-1.5 cm. long, the filaments stout, greatly enlarged just below the anthers; fruit rather dry and spongy at maturity, ellipsoidal, 6-9 cm. long, 4-5.5 cm. in diameter, not splitting open.

Desert plains and gravelly alluvial fans at 2,000 to 5,000 feet elevation. California from the Haiwee Reservoir south of Owens Lake southward through the mountains along and in the Mojave Desert (but occasionally on the flats) to the Iron and Eagle mountains, Riverside County, and eastward to the Grapevine Mountains near Death Valley; Nevada from Goldfield, Esmeralda County, to Lincoln and Clark counties; southwestern Utah; Arizona south of the Colorado River in Mohave County and southeastward to southwestern Yavapaia County. (Fig. 14 2.)

The Joshua tree is one of the best-known plants of the desert, and pictures of it are used in nearly all elementary botany texts. It ranks with the saguaro, or giant cactus, as a symbol of the desert, and it is the most distinctive plant of the Mojave Desert, just as the saguaro is the most characteristic type of the Sonoran Desert in Arizona. At a few points near Bill Williams River in west-central Arizona, these two monarchs of the desert are to be found together, but this is a rarity. The age of the largest Joshua trees is not known, since they do not form annual rings in the stem as do dicotyledonous trees and gymnosperms, but these weird plants are among the oldest living things in the desert, and some of them attain enormous size, as is indicated in the popular description above. The short, toothed leaves die back and eventually drop off, exposing a true corky bark, a character not possessed by other native yuccas. The light, pliable wood is suitable for surgeons' splints, and it can be cut into veneer sheets for wooden novelties.

A dwarf or miniature form of the Joshua tree occurs here and there in the eastern portion of the Mojave Desert in California east of Baker and eastward to the southern tip of Nevada and the Virgin River Valley in Arizona and adjacent Utah (west of St. George). Some trees are small, mostly only 3-4 m. (9-12 feet) high, and they branch in the first meter (yard) above the ground and rebranch several times above. The leaves of some individuals are short, most of them about 1-2 dm. (4-8 inches) long. In many areas this form is defined poorly and trees with long and short leaves occur side by side.

5. *Yucca Schottii* Engelm. MOUNTAIN YUCCA. (1) Fruit fleshy at maturity, not splitting open, not persisting on the

flower stalk through the winter; (2) pistil at flowering time less than 1 inch long, about 3/16 to 1/4 inch in diameter; (3) margins of the old leaves not separating into fibers; (4) inflorescence hairy; (5) confined to southeastern Arizona and the adjacent corner of New Mexico. (Pl. XI *E*.)

Stems 1 or a few, unbranched or slightly branched, 1-5 m. high; leaves mostly 4-8 dm. long, 3-5 cm. broad, about 1-2 mm. thick; flowers in a rather dense panicle of racemes about 3-6 dm. long, somewhat overtopping the leaves, not stalked or only shortly so; sepals and petals white, broadly lanceolate or narrowly elliptic-acute, about 3 or sometimes 4 cm. long, 1-1.5 cm. broad; stamens about 1.5 cm. long, the filaments slender; fruit green and fleshy, 10-14 cm. long, about 4-5 cm. in diameter.

Hillsides and canyon slopes in the upper desert grassland and the oak woodland at 4,000 to 7,000 feet elevation. Arizona from eastern Pinal County to Santa Cruz County and eastward to Cochise County; New Mexico in southern Hidalgo County; Mexico. This is the only yucca occurring above the lower edge of the oak woodland. It is rare in the desert grassland, but it occurs in this vegetational type in some localities; as, for example, at Box Canyon in the Santa Rita Mountains. (Fig. 14 6.)

6a. *Yucca baccata* Torr. var. *baccata*. BANANA YUCCA. (1) Fruit fleshy at maturity, not splitting open, not persisting on the flower stalk through the winter; (2) pistil at flowering time 1¾ to 3 inches long; (3) margins of the old leaves with fibers separating from them. (Pl. XI *D*.)

Stems 1-several, subterranean or lying on the ground; leaf rosettes clustered or solitary at ground level; leaves 4-8 dm. long, 3-5.5 cm. broad, about 2 mm. thick, with usually coarse and often short fibers separating along the margins; flowers in a rather dense panicle of racemes 5-8 dm. long, not standing much above the highest leaves, short-stalked; sepals and petals white or cream, lanceolate to oblanceolate, most frequently 6-9 cm. long, usually 1.5-2 cm. broad; stamens 2-4 cm. long, the filaments slender; fruit 12-18 cm. long, 5-6 cm. in diameter.

Common on hillsides and plains in a variety of soils in the upper desert, the desert grassland, the pinyon-juniper woodland, and the oak woodland at 2,000 to 7,000 feet elevation. California in the New York, Clark, and Providence mountains in the eastern Mojave Desert; Nevada in Clark and Lincoln counties; Utah along the Virgin and Colorado river drainages; northern Arizona and southeastward below the Mogollon Rim to the

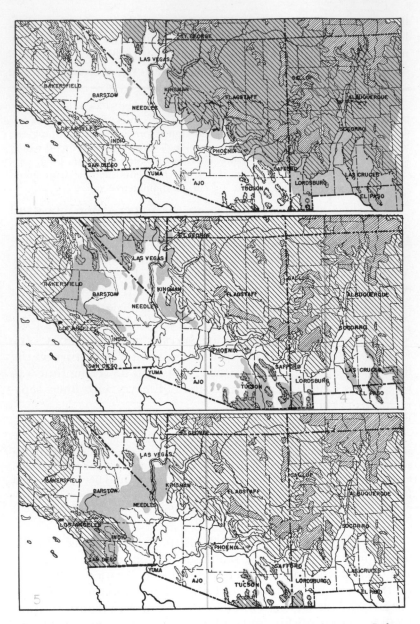

Fig. 14.—Distributional maps: *1*, banana yucca, *Yucca baccata;* *2*, Joshua tree, *Yucca brevifolia;* *3*, Thornber yucca, *Yucca baccata* var. *brevifolia;* *4*, Torrey yucca, *Yucca Torreyi;* *5*, Mojave yucca, *Yucca schidigera;* *6*, mountain yucca, *Yucca Schottii.*

mountainous portion of the Gila River drainage; New Mexico; southeastern Colorado; western Texas; Mexico. (Fig. 14 *1*.)

Banana yucca is the common broad-leaved yucca in much of Arizona and New Mexico. The large fleshy fruits are an important food among the Indians, especially the Navajos who eat them raw or roasted, and often these fruits are dried, ground, and made into small cakes to be used during the winter. Leaf fibers of this species are used in basketry.

6b. *Yucca baccata* Torr. var. *brevifolia* (Schott) Benson & Darrow. THORNBER YUCCA; BLUE YUCCA (Pls. XI *B*; XIV *center*)

Stems 1-several, erect, the longer ones usually 1-2 m. high, often branched; fibers of the leaves fine and threadlike; inflorescence without a stalk or with a stalk up to 3 dm. long. Synonyms: *Yucca brevifolia* Schott, not Engelm.; *Yucca Treleasei* Macbride, not Spreng.; *Yucca Thornberi* McKelvey; *Yucca arizonica* McKelvey; *Yucca confinis* McKelvey.

Hills, mesas, and flats in the upper part of the desert, the desert grassland, and the lower portion of the oak woodland at 3,000 to 4,500 feet elevation. Arizona from the Quijotoa Mountains in the vicinity of Sells, Pima County, to Gila and Cochise counties; Hidalgo County, New Mexico; northern Sonora, Mexico. Intergrades to the typical variety occur in southern Gila and southern Graham counties, Arizona. The plants occurring in the moist region about Nogales and Patagonia tend to be large, and some of them have stalked inflorescences. Those on the dry creosote-bush plains northeast of Douglas and the flats southeast of Warren are shorter, and some do not develop trunks. The angle of divergence of the upper swollen portion of the filament, a character sometimes used to segregate species in this group, is dependent upon the age of the flower, and all types may be found in a single inflorescence. (Fig. 14 *3*.)

7. *Yucca Torreyi* Shafer. TORREYI YUCCA (Pl. IX *C*)

Trunk 1-5 m. high; sepals and petals 2-4 cm. long; pistil at flowering time 2-3.5 or 4 cm. long; fruit usually 10-14 cm. long.

Mesas, slopes, and plains in the desert and the desert grassland at 3,500 to 5,000 feet elevation. New Mexico on the Rio Grande drainage in Grant and Doña Ana counties and in the Sacramento Mountains; Texas as far southeastward as Devil's River and Uvalde. (Fig. 14 *4*.)

According to a letter from V. L. Cory, this plant should be treated as a distinct species, and in his opinion it is related rather closely to *Yucca Treculeana* Carrière, a point of view taken earlier by McKelvey. The writers are not familiar with the plant as it occurs in the field, and it is not possible to present an accurate evaluation of its status in the present publication.

8. *Yucca schidigera* Roezl. MOJAVE YUCCA. (1) Fruit fleshy at maturity, not splitting open, not persisting on the flower stalk through the winter; (2) pistil at flowering time less than 1 inch long, ⅜ to nearly ½ inch in diameter; (3) margins of the old leaves with fibers separating from them; (4) California to southern Nevada and Mohave County, Arizona. (Pl. XI *A, C.*)

Stems 1-several, slightly branched or unbranched, 1-5 m. high; leaves mostly 0.5-0.6 sometimes 1.3 m. long, 1.5-3.5 cm. broad, about 1 mm. thick, broadest at the middles; flowers in a rather dense panicle of racemes about 3-6 dm. long, not standing much above the highest leaves, not stalked or shortly so; sepals and petals white or cream, tinged often with lavender or purple, lanceolate or broadly so, 3-5 cm. long, 1-1.8 cm. broad; stamens 12-16 mm. long, the filaments slender; young ovary abruptly tapering into the style above; fruit fleshy, 5-8 cm. long, 3-4 cm. in diameter. Synonym: *Yucca mohavensis* Sarg.

Rocky or gravelly mountain slopes and in the desert and in the chaparral at 1,000 to 4,000 feet elevation. California in the interior valleys and chaparral-covered slopes from Los Angeles County to San Diego County and in the southern Mojave Desert from Victorville eastward to the New York and Providence mountains, also in the northern and western portions of the Salton Sea Basin of the Colorado Desert; Nevada in southern Clark County; Arizona in Mohave County north and west of Kingman. (Fig. 14 *5.*)

The California Indians have made much use of the Mojave yucca as a source of fiber for ropes and coarsely woven blankets and as a source of soap. The fleshy fruits are eaten raw or roasted as are those of banana yucca.

2. *NOLINA*. NOLINA

(1) Flowers not more than 1/6 inch long; (2) leaf with smooth or minutely sharp-toothed margins or with the margins separating into long threads. (Pl. XII *C, E, G.*)

Large plants resembling *Yucca* in appearance or plants with the aspect of large, coarse grasses. Stem subterranean or above ground and unbranched, not more than about 2 m. high. Leaves linear, elongated, sharply pointed but not necessarily spine-tipped, sometimes appearing grasslike, flexible. Flowers very numerous, in dense racemes in open or dense panicles; bisexual, staminate, or pistillate flowers occurring on various individuals; perianth not more than 4 mm. long, the sepals and petals thin, white or greenish; stamens shorter than the perianth, the filaments short but slender. Fruit a capsule, appearing inflated, with 3 winglike compartments bursting irregularly; ovules 2 in each cell, not all developing.

KEY TO THE SPECIES

1. Leaves 9-18 mm. wide, flat or nearly so; plants not appearing grasslike (Pl. XII *C*), the stems of older individuals 0.5-2 m. high; fruit about 10-15 mm. broad.

  2. Edges of the leaves not markedly saw-toothed, only slightly roughened, the blades flat; panicle branches and pedicels slender; sepals and petals about 2 mm. long; fruit about 10 mm. broad; seeds light gray. 1. *Nolina Bigelovii*

  2. Edges of the leaves distinctly saw-toothed, the blades concave; panicle branches and pedicels stout, the panicle strongly congested; sepals and petals about 4 mm. long; fruit about 12-15 mm. broad.
  1a. *Nolina Bigelovii* var. *Parryi*

1. Leaves about 3-8 mm. wide, channeled on the upper surfaces; plants resembling large, coarse grasses (Pl. XII *E, G*), the stems wholly subterranean; fruit about 6 mm. broad; seeds brownish.
2. *Nolina microcarpa*

1a. *Nolina Bigelovii* (Torr.) S. Wats. var. *Bigelovii*. BIGE-LOW NOLINA. Leaves flat, ⅝ to 1¼ inches wide, the edges not toothed or only slightly so, separating into fibers. (Pl. XII C.)

Trunk up to 1 m. high; leaves about 7-12 dm. long, flat, the margins not toothed, slightly roughened, separating into elongated fibers; panicle dense, perhaps 6-8 dm. in length, the stalk 3-8 dm. long, the branches and pedicels slender; sepals and petals about 1.5-2 mm. long; stamens about 1 mm. long; fruit about 8 mm. long, about 10 mm. broad, notched at both ends, the walls thin and membranous; seeds pale gray, about 3 mm. long.

Rocky or gravelly hillsides or canyon walls in the desert at 500 to 3,500 feet elevation. California in the Old Woman Mountains in the Mojave Desert and in the mountains bordering the Colorado Desert; Arizona in Mohave, Yuma, and Yavapai counties and in the vicinity of the Grand Canyon; Baja

California and Sonora, Mexico. Flowering in June and July. (Fig. 15 5.)

1b. *Nolina Bigelovii* (Torr.) S. Wats. var. *Parryi* (S. Wats.) L. Benson. PARRY NOLINA. Leaves nearly flat ⅜ to ¾ inch broad, the edges markedly toothed, the teeth rough, the leaf margin not separating into fibers.

Similar to the typical variety; the trunk up to 1-2 m. high; pedicels and branches of the panicle stout, the panicle densely congested; sepals and petals about 4-5 mm. long; fruit 12-15 mm. long, 13-15 mm. broad, seeds brownish, about 4 mm. long.

Rocky hillsides and slopes in the desert and in the chaparral at 3,000 to 7,000 feet elevation. California from Ventura County to San Diego County, reaching the Colorado on the northern edge of the Salton Sea Basin and in San Diego County; Arizona near Kingman and southward toward the mouth of Bill Williams River; Baja California, Mexico. The Arizona plants need further study.

1c. **Nolina Bigelovii** (Torr.) S. Wats. var. **Wolfii** (Munz) L. Benson, comb. nov. (cf. p. 418). Leaves flat, 1-1½ inches wide, the edges markedly toothed, not separating into fibers; plant much larger than either of the other varieties (cf. below).

Trunk 1-4 dm. high; leaves up to 2 m. or more in length; panicle up to 6 m. long, including the stalk; sepals and petals about 5 mm. long; fruit about 12-15 mm. long, 12-15 mm. broad; seeds brownish, 3-3.5 mm. long. *Nolina Parryi* S. Wats. subsp. *Wolfii* Munz. Change of status is technical.

Desert hillsides and slopes at higher altitudes; juniper-pinyon woodland and the upper portion of the Mojave Desert at 3,000 to 6,000 feet. California in the Kingston Mountains, Little San Bernardino Mountains, Eagle Mountains, and the southern portion of the San Jacinto Mountains; just above and in the Mojave and Colorado deserts.

2. *Nolina microcarpa* S. Wats. BEAR GRASS; SACAHUISTA. Leaves channeled, ⅛ to a little less than ⅜ inch wide, the margins with minute teeth, the tips frayed. Plant resembling a large, coarse grass. (Pl. XII *E*, *G*.)

Stem wholly subterranean, the leaf rosettes on the ground; leaves averaging about 1 m. in length; panicle rather open but the branches dense, standing perhaps 1-2 m. above the ground, the stalk elongated, the branches and pedicels slender; sepals and petals about 2 mm. long or a little

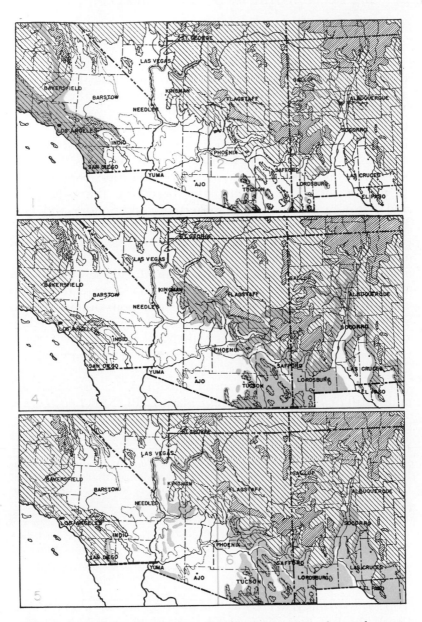

Fig. 15.—Distributional maps: *1*, Spanish bayonet or chaparral yucca, *Yucca Whipplei*; *2*, Schott agave or amole, *Agave Schottii*; *3*, *Dasylirion leiophyllum*; *4*, bear grass, *Nolina microcarpa*; *5*, Bigelow nolina, *Nolina Bigelovii*; *6*, sotol or desert spoon, *Dasylirion Wheeleri*.

longer; fruit about 5 mm. long, about 6 mm. broad; seeds brown, spheroidal, 2-2.5 mm. in diameter.

Gravelly or sandy, well-drained soil of slopes and mesas in the upper desert, the desert grassland, and the oak woodland at 3,000 to 6,000 feet elevation. Arizona from the Hualpai Mountains, Mohave County, and Havasu Canyon, Coconino County, southeastward through the mountains below the Mogollon Rim to Pima County (from the Baboquivari Mountains eastward) and to Cochise County, also in an isolated area in southern Navajo and southern Apache counties; New Mexico in the mountains and high plains bordering the Gila River and Rio Grande drainages; western Texas; Sonora and Chihuahua, Mexico. Flowering in June and July. (Fig. 15 4.)

The Indians obtain fibers from the long, slender leaves and use them for weaving baskets and mats. Cattle graze only sparingly on the leaves in normal seasons, but during severe drought the flower stalks and portions of the leaves are eaten. Even though the plant is reputed to be poisonous under certain growth conditions, bear grass is used for emergency feeding of livestock when forage is exceedingly scarce.

3. *DASYLIRION*. Sotol

(1) Leaf margin with conspicuous prickles; (2) staminate and pistillate flowers on different plants. (Pl. XII *A, B, D, F.*)

Large plants resembling *Yucca* or *Nolina Bigelovii* in appearance, the stem subterranean or extending above ground for a short distance. Leaves linear, elongated, not spine-tipped. Flowers very numerous, in dense racemes in dense elongated panicles, stalked. Perianth about 2-2.5 mm. long, the sepals and petals thin, whitish; stamens longer than the perianth, the filaments slender. Fruit 3-winged, the solitary seed enclosed in the central portion.

KEY TO THE SPECIES

1. Prickles of the leaf margins directed upward; fruit 6-8 mm. wide; leaves rather glaucous.   1. *Dasylirion Wheeleri*

1. Prickles of the leaf margins directed downward or mostly so; fruit 3-5 mm. wide; leaves not glaucous.   2. *Dasylirion leiophyllum*

1. *Dasylirion Wheeleri* S. Wats. SOTOL; DESERT SPOON. Prickles on the leaf margins forward-directed, the prickles 1/16 to ⅛ inch long. (Pl. XII *A, B, D, F.*)

Leaves about 1 m. long, rather glaucous; panicle 1.5-2.5 m. long, usually 2-3 dm. in greatest diameter, the stalk perhaps 1 m. long or more; fruit 7-9 mm. long, 6-8 mm. broad; seed 3-angled.

Rocky or gravelly hillsides and slopes in the upper desert, the desert grassland, and the oak woodland at 3,000 to 5,000 feet elevation. Arizona from the Mazatzal Mountains and the Roosevelt Lake watershed, Gila County, to the Baboquivari Mountains, Pima County, and to Greenlee and Cochise counties; New Mexico on the Gila River drainage and the Rio Grande drainage from Socorro County southward, and eastward to the White Mountains, Lincoln County; western Texas; Sonora and Chihuahua, Mexico. Flowering in early summer. (Fig. 15 6.)

The Indians roasted and ate the young flower stalks and they used leaf fibers for coarse ropes and mats. In extreme drought cattlemen split the trunks for livestock food. In recent years the sotol has become known as "desert spoon," or among the uninformed as "spoon flower," from the use of the leaf bases for decorative purposes.

2. *Dasylirion leiophyllum* Engelm. ex Trel.

Leaves not glaucous, the prickles turned backward (downward); fruit narrow, 7-9 mm. long, 3-5 mm. broad.

Hillsides in the desert and the desert grassland. Southwestern New Mexico from Hidalgo County to Luna County; western Texas; Mexico. (Fig. 15 3.)

Family 4. *AMARYLLIDACEAE*. AMARYLLIS FAMILY

By ELBERT L. LITTLE, JR.*

Plants mostly succulent herbs, or some perhaps to be called shrubs, often with bulbs or horizontal underground stems, usually without erect stems other than the conspicuous flowering stalks. Leaves basal, narrow, the margins entire or with prickles. Flowers bisexual, regular; perianth with 6 equal segments or lobes; stamens 6, inserted in the floral tube opposite the perianth segments; ovary inferior, 3-celled; style 1, slender; fruit a capsule with numerous seeds. In the Southwest represented by a few herbaceous species and the following genus of large succulent shrubs. (Pls. XIII; XIV *left;* XV; Fig. 16.)

*Forest Service, United States Department of Agriculture.

1. *AGAVE*. Century Plant

The genus *Agave,* from a Greek word meaning admirable or noble, is known by the same common name, agave (pronounced usually a-gah-ve). It includes the plants variously named century plant, maguey, mescal, lechuguilla, and amole. The native agaves vary greatly in size from nearly as large as the ornamental century plants down to the size of a head of lettuce. Though usually scattered and seldom abundant, agaves are very conspicuous plants, especially when in flower on the rocky slopes of foothills, mountains, and canyons of the Southwestern deserts and the zones just above the deserts.

Agaves resemble *Yucca, Nolina,* and *Dasylirion* in some ways, but they may be distinguished from these other large Southwestern monocotyledons by the inferior ovary and by the following combination of characteristics: (1) there is no trunk (in our species); (2) the plant consists of a cluster of leaves spreading out at ground level from a very short central subterranean stem; (3) the leaves are evergreen, usually succulent, thick, usually long and narrow, with a distinct, very sharp-pointed terminal spine and with spines or threads along the margins; (4) after several years the plant rapidly produces a relatively tall flower stalk and then dies. (Pls. XIII; XIV *left*; XV; Fig. 16.)

Succulent shrubs (or herbs), often growing in colonies by formation of underground sprouts. Leaves usually many and crowded, arranged in a cluster or basal rosette on the ground around a very short stem, evergreen, succulent, tough, long, narrow, thick, each ending in a sharp, stout terminal spine, with prickles or threads along the margins. Flower stalks relatively large and tall, branched or unbranched, bearing numerous succulent flowers varying from greenish to yellow, whitish, or pink; floral tube usually funnel-shaped, perianth segments 6, equal; stamens 6, inserted in the floral tube, the filaments greatly elongated, the anthers attached at the middles; style elongated at maturity, slender; stigma slightly 3-lobed; ovary green. Fruit a brown 3-celled capsule, usually cylindroidal, containing many thin, flattened, black seeds in 2 rows in each cell.

The genus *Agave* contains about 250 species native in tropical and subtropical America, and it is most abundant in Mexico. The shrubby agaves extend into the United States only in the Southwest (New Mexico and Texas and as far north as California, Nevada, and Utah) and in southern Florida. Arizona, with eight species, has more than any other state. Nine species are native within the area of this book. Another, *Agave Shawii* Engelm., of Baja California, Mexico, is rare in occurrence near San Diego, California. Two additional shrubby species (*Agave Harvardiana* Trel. and *Agave glomeruliflora* [Engelm.] Berger, synonym *Agave chisosensis* C. H. Muller) are native in southwestern Texas, and four (including two escaping from cultivation) occur in southern Florida. Three or four herbaceous species (with bulbs and with annual leaves without spines and therefore sometimes placed in a separate genus, *Manfreda*) are found in Texas, and one of these (*Agave virginica* L.) has a wide range in southeastern United States. *Agave* may be related closely to *Yucca*, of the family Liliaceae, but is generally and conveniently placed in the family Amaryllidaceae because of the inferior ovary.

Agaves furnish many important products in tropical America, and they were utilized in various ways by the Indians of southwestern United States.[4] Among the products are fiber, food, drink, soap, and medicine. The leaves of certain species are the source of commercial fibers, such as sisal hemp, henequen, and ixtle. These fibers are used especially for cords, ropes, sacking, and brushes. Agaves are grown for their commercial fibers on plantations in more than forty tropical countries.

Indians prepared the sweet food, mescal, from the central stems (crowns or heads) of the larger species, such as *Agave Palmeri, Agave Parryi,* and *Agave utahensis*. After the leaves were removed, the white crowns were baked in a pit lined with stones previously heated. The Mescalero Apaches of southern New Mexico derive their name from this use of mescal as food. Pulque, the national drink of Mexico, is fermented from the sap collected in a cavity hollowed out of the center of a plant of a large Mexican species when it begins to flower. The distilled alcoholic drinks, mescal and tequila, and industrial alcohol also are made from the central stems and leaf bases. A soapy substance (containing saponin) is obtained from the

4. A detailed account of the uses of Agave by Southwestern Indians is contained in the following publication: Edward F. Castetter, Willis H. Bell, and Alvin R. Grove. *The Early Utilization and Distribution of Agave in the American Southwest.* New Mexico Univ. Bull., Biol. Ser., 5 (4) :1-92 *illus.* 1938.

stems of certain smaller agaves called amoles, and it is used as soap.

The name century plant, given to the large agaves, is derived from the mistaken belief that the plants flower after one hundred years. Plants transferred to cooler climates may rarely bloom or may require many years to mature under the unnatural conditions of greenhouses and gardens. The age at flowering varies, but probably ten to twenty years or less is common for the wild agaves.

Agaves are prized as ornamentals for lawns and rock gardens because of their odd, succulent leaves, their symmetrical shape, and their rapidly growing flower stalks. A large collection of these succulents, including representatives of tropical American species, may be seen at the Boyce Thompson Southwestern Arboretum, near Superior, Arizona. The larger century plants, or magueys, cultivated as ornamentals in the Southwest wherever the winters are mild, are introduced from tropical America. In southern Arizona and southern California the common century plants with erect, concave, bluish green leaves belong mostly to the species *Agave expansa* Jacobi. Those with spreading or blending brighter green leaves, sometimes with white stripes near the margins, are *Agave americana* L., a species which has become naturalized from cultivation in southern Texas and southern Florida.

The native species of *Agave* are among the plants protected by law against destruction, mutilation, or removal in Arizona and New Mexico and in many counties of California. Unrestricted collecting might greatly reduce the numbers of these outstanding desert succulents in the more accessible areas or might even exterminate the rarer species. One species slightly outside the range of this book has suffered essentially this fate. *Agave Shawii* Engelm. (mentioned above), a species of the large, cabbagehead type, is found along the Pacific Coast in northern Baja California, Mexico, and in 1896 was reported to be abundant in southern California near the International Boundary south of San Diego. By 1935 it was thought to be extinct in the originally limited portion of its range within the United States, but in 1937 one colony was reported to be present in California. The fate of this species north of the

Plate X.—Joshua tree, *Yucca brevifolia: A*, a flower cluster at the end of a branch, the flowers remaining essentially closed by the incurving of the sepals and petals; *B*, a cluster of fleshy fruits; *C*, a large old tree with a trunk diameter of 2 or 3 feet at the base. (Photographs: *A* by Herbert A. Anderson; *B*, by R. B. Streets; *C*, by William P. Martin.)

Plate XI.—Fleshy-fruited yuccas: *A*, Mojave yucca, *Yucca schidigera*, close-up view of flower; *B*, Thornber yucca, *Yucca baccata* var. *brevifolia*; *C*, Mojave yucca; *D*, banana yucca, *Yucca baccata*, in flower; *E*, mountain yucca, *Yucca Schottii*, in flower. (Photographs: *A-D* by A. A. Nichol; *E* by Robert A. Darrow.)

Plate XII.—Nolinas and sotol: *A, B, D, F*, sotol or desert spoon, *Dasylirion Wheeleri*; *C*, Bigelow nolina, *Nolina Bigelovii*; *E, G*, bear grass, *Nolina microcarpa*. (Photographs: *A, C, D, F* by Robert A. Darrow; *B, G* by William P. Martin; *E* by A. A. Nichol.)

Plate XIII.—Century plants: *A*, Huachuca agave, *Agave Parryi* var. *huachucensis*, showing the young flower stalk; *B*, desert agave, *Agave desertii*, showing young plants which have not yet flowered and the flower stalk and dying leaves of an older plant which has just flowered; *C*, small-flowered agave, *Agave parviflora*, showing the small leaf clusters and the white markings on the leaves; *D*, Palmer agave or mescal, *Agave Palmeri*; *E, F*, Parry agave, *Agave Parryi*. (Photographs: *A* by A. A. Nichol; *B, E* by R. B. Streets; *C, D* by Robert A. Darrow; *F* by E. T. Nichols.)

boundary emphasizes the necessity of protecting these interesting native succulents from destruction by commercial collectors and others.

The species of *Agave* are distinguished mainly by differences in leaves and flowers. Though the flowers may be collected during only a short period of the year, dead flower stalks with dry fruits, seeds, and usually some old dried flowers can be found with the evergreen leaves at almost any time. It is not always possible to identify plants, especially young ones, from leaves alone. As some species of *Agave* have limited geographical distribution, the locality may be of assistance in naming incomplete specimens (Figs. 15 2; 17). The following key is based as far as possible upon leaf characters.

KEY TO THE SPECIES

1. Leaves with threads along the margins (Fig. 16) (or also with minute teeth near the bases), small and very narrow, 5-40 cm. long and less than 2 cm. wide; plants small, 1-5 dm. in diameter, resembling *Yucca;* flower stalks unbranched.

    2. Each leaf less than 10 times as long as the width at middle; flowers whitish to pink or green, less than 25 mm. long; stamens inserted at the base or near the middle of the portion of the floral tube above the ovary. (Fig. 16 *A 4, 5.*)

        3. Leaves 5-10 cm. long above the bases; marginal threads coarse, short, 1 cm. long; flowers pink or whitish; floral tube cylindrical, the perianth segments less than half as long as the floral tube; stamens inserted at the base of the tube; range localized along the Arizona-Sonora boundary west of Nogales, Arizona. (Fig. 16 *A.*)   1. *Agave parviflora*

        3. Leaves 8-25 cm. long above the bases; marginal threads fine, 1-5 cm. long; flowers white, greenish tinged; floral tube funnel-shaped, the perianth segments about twice as long as the floral tube; stamens inserted near the middle of the tube; range localized in central Arizona. (Fig. 16 *D.*)   2. *Agave Toumeyana*

    2. Each leaf more than 20 times as long as the width at middle; flowers light yellow, 30-50 mm. long; stamens inserted in the upper fourth of the portion of the floral tube above the ovary.

        3. Leaves only 6-10 mm. wide at the middles, 20-30 cm. long (Fig. 16 *B 1*); very common in southern Arizona, extreme southwestern New Mexico, and Sonora, Mexico. (Fig. 16 *B.*)

                                        3. *Agave Schottii*

3. Leaves 13-18 mm. wide at the middles, 25-40 cm. long. (Fig. 16 *F*); very rare and localized in the Santa Catalina Mountains, Arizona.
3a. *Agave Schottii* var. *Treleasei*

1. Leaves with spines along the margins, relatively large or small but more than 20 cm. long and more than 2 cm. wide.

2. Flower stalks unbranched (Pl. XV *D*); flowers less than 35 mm. long, in groups of 2-4 along the vertical flower stalks; capsules 15-30 mm. long. (Fig. 16 *D*.)

3. Spines of the leaf margins connected by a continuous, detachable, horny border 1 mm. wide; plants growing in large colonies; flowers and capsules attached to flower stalks by short pedicels less than 1 cm. long; flowers greenish or yellowish white, sometimes tinged with purple; stamens inserted at the top of the floral tube; southeastern New Mexico to southwestern Texas and northern Mexico.   4. *Agave lecheguilla*

3. Spines of the leaf margins separate (or with a few spines near the tip of the leaf connected with the terminal spine); plants usually single or in small colonies; flowers and capsules on conspicuous, elongated pedicels 2-3 cm. or more long; flowers yellow; stamens inserted near the middle of the tube; eastern California to southern Nevada, southwestern Utah, and northwestern Arizona.   5. *Agave utahensis*

2. Flower stalks branched (Pls. XIV *left*; XV *A-C*); flowers more than 35 mm. long, numerous in clusters on the large lateral branches; capsules 30-75 mm. long. (Fig. 16 *C, E*.)

3. Leaves of mature plants relatively broad, usually widest above the middles and abruptly narrowed at the tips, less than 5 times as long as the width at the middles (Pl. XIII *A, E, F*); leaves grayish- or bluish-green, numerous and crowded, curving upward to form a rounded, cabbagelike cluster 5-12 dm. or more in diameter; flower stalks stout, the branches much flattened; flower buds red, the flowers greenish yellow tinged with red; stamens inserted at the top of the oral tube.

4. Leaves about 4 times as long as broad, plants 5-10 dm. in diameter; widely distributed in central and southeastern Arizona, southern New Mexico, southwestern Texas and Chihuahua, Mexico.   6. *Agave Parryi*

4. Leaves about 3 times as long as broad; plants 8-12 dm. or more in diameter; localized in the vicinity of the Huachuca Mountains, southeastern Arizona, and probably in adjacent Sonora, Mexico.   6a. *Agave Parryi* var. *huachucensis*

3. Leaves of mature plants narrow, gradually narrowing toward the tips, more than 6 times as long as the width at the middle

(Pl. XIII *B, D*); leaves bright green, widely spreading; flower stalks slender, the branches rounded or slightly flattened; flower buds greenish, the flowers yellow or greenish.

4. Leaves 20-45 cm. long (Pl. XIII *B*); cluster of leaves 4-7 dm. in diameter; stamens inserted at the top of the floral tube; desert mountains of southern California, western Arizona, and northern Baja California, Mexico. (Pl. XIV *left.*)
7. *Agave desertii*

4. Leaves 30-100 cm. or more in length (Pl. XIII *D*); cluster of leaves 6-15 dm. in diameter; stamens inserted near the middle of the floral tube.

   5. Terminal spines of the leaves short, 12-15 mm. long; flower stalks elongating in early winter and bearing flowers and many bulbils in the spring; very rare and localized in central Arizona.   8. *Agave Murpheyi*

   5. Terminal spines of the leaves long and slender, 20-50 mm. long; flower stalks elongating in the spring and bearing flowers (and rarely bulbils) in the summer; common.

      6. Marginal spines of the leaves many, about 10-20 mm. apart; branches of the flower stalks horizontal, widely spreading, bearing flowers in open clusters; perianth greenish, tinged with purple and yellow; southeastern Arizona, southwestern New Mexico, and Sonora, Mexico.   9. *Agave Palmeri*

      6. Marginal spines of leaves few, about 20-30 mm. apart; branches of the flower stalks ascending, shorter, bearing crowded clusters of flowers; perianth golden yellow, not purple-tinged; central Arizona.   9a. *Agave Palmeri* var. *chrysantha*

1. *Agave parviflora* Torr. SMALL-FLOWERED AGAVE. The smallest *Agave* native in the United States. (1) Cluster of leaves being less than 6 inches in diameter at maturity and no larger than a head of lettuce; (2) leaves only 2-4 inches long, with conspicuous, white, zigzag markings, with small teeth near the base and with white threads ½ inch long on the margins; (3) flower stalks unbranched and only 3-6 feet high; (4) flowers small, only ½ inch long, pink or whitish; (5) localized distribution in the mountains along the Arizona-Sonora boundary west of Nogales, Arizona. (Fig. 16 *A;* Pl. XIII *C.*)

Plants single or by vegetative propagation forming colonies 3-5 dm. in diameter; leaves many, dark green, linear-lanceolate, 9-14 mm. broad, the terminal spine 5 mm. long, the margins of adjacent leaves in the bud adhering later as diagonal white lines about 2 mm. broad on both sides of the mature leaves; flower stalks very slender, bearing flowers in clusters of 2-6 on short peduncles; floral tube pink or whitish, becoming darker purple on drying, cylindrical, 5-6 mm. long, 4-5 mm. in diameter; perianth segments rounded, 2 mm. long, less than half as long as the floral tube; stamens inserted at the base of floral tube; the filaments white, turning purple, 10-14 mm. long; anthers greenish, becoming yellow, 4-6 mm. long; style greenish, becoming purple, 11-12 mm. long at maturity; ovary 6-7 mm. long; fruits light brown, spheroidal to slightly elongated, 7-10 mm. long, 5-8 mm. broad; seeds 3 mm. long, by 2 mm. broad, 1 mm. thick.

Mountain slopes with shallow, gravelly or rocky soils in the desert grassland and the oak woodland at 4,500 to 5,000 feet elevation. Arizona in and near the Pajarito Mountains along the International Boundary in Santa Cruz County and in adjacent Sonora, Mexico. Flowering in June and July. (Fig. 17 *3*.)

The numerous small, dark green leaves with white markings and stout white threads and the odd pinkish flowers make the plants especially attractive.

2. *Agave Toumeyana* Trel. TOUMEY AGAVE. (1) Leaves 3-10 inches long, 1/2 to 7/8 inch wide, with white zigzag markings and with small teeth near the bases and white threads 1/2 to 2 inches or more in length along the margins; (2) flower stalks unbranched and 3-10 feet high; (3) flowers white, greenish tinged, 5/8 to 1 inch long; (4) localized in central Arizona. (Fig. 16 *D*.)

Plants usually in clusters, with the rosettes of spreading leaves 15-40 cm. in diameter and 10-30 cm. high; leaves many, bright green, curved or straight, narrowly lanceolate, 10-22 mm. wide, the terminal spine 6-15 mm. long; leaf margin with minute teeth near the base and with fine white marginal threads 1-5 cm. or more in length; borders of adjacent leaves forming white marks on both leaf surfaces; flower stalks 10-30 dm. high, slender, bearing flowers in clusters of 2-7 on short peduncles; perianth segments 8 mm. long, about twice as long as the funnel-shaped floral tube; stamens inserted near the middle of the floral tube or slightly above; anthers yellowish green to tan, 7-8 mm. long; style white, 15 mm. long at maturity; ovary 10-12 mm. long; fruits brown, usually 2-4 in a cluster, short-cylindrical or almost spheroidal, 9-12 mm. long, 7-8 mm. in diameter; seeds 3 mm. long, 2.5 mm. broad, 1 mm. thick.

Rocky slopes in the mountains in the upper part of the desert and along the lower edge of the chaparral belt at 3,000

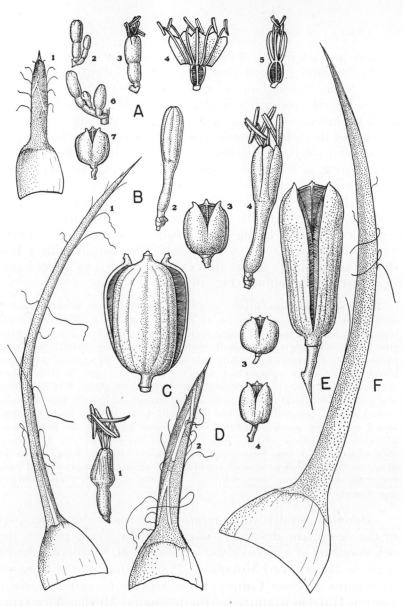

Fig. 16.—Century plants and amoles: *A*, small-flowered agave, *Agave parvi-flora*, *1*, leaf, *2*, *6*, flower buds, *3*, flower, *4*, flower laid open, *5*, flower in longitudinal section, *7*, fruit; *B*, Schott agave or amole, *Agave Schottii*, *1*, leaf, *2*, flower bud, *3*, fruit, *4*, flower; *C*, fruit of Parry agave, *Agave Parryi*; *D*, Toumey agave, *Agave Toumeyana*, *1*, flower, *2*, leaf, *3*, *4*, fruit types; *E*, fruit of Palmer agave or mescal, *Agave Palmeri*; *F*, leaf of Trelease agave, *Agave Schottii* var. *Treleasei*.

to 5,000 feet elevation. Rare and localized in central Arizona in the Mazatzal, Superstition, Pinal, and Galiuro mountains, in the Sierra Ancha, and in nearby areas. The total range is within a circle 100 miles in diameter in Maricopa, Gila, and Pinal counties. Flowering in June and July. (Fig. 17 2.)

One of the least-known agaves in the Southwest because of its rare and localized distribution. This species has been under investigation as a possible commercial source of the rare drug cortisone.

3a. *Agave Schottii* Engelm. var. *Schottii*. SCHOTT AGAVE; AMOLE. (1) Plants small, resembling *Yucca,* growing crowded together in mats covering large areas; (2) leaves very narrow, 8-12 inches long, 1/4 to 1/2 inch wide, the margin with a few slender threads; (3) flower stalks unbranched, 5 to 9 feet high; (4) flowers light yellow. (Fig. 16 *B.*)

Plants spreading vegetatively, 30-40 cm. in diameter at maturity; leaves bright green, curved, and 6-10 or 12 mm. wide at the middles, gradually tapering from the expanded bases; terminal spine 6-12 mm. long, the margins sometimes with a few minute teeth at the bases, especially in young plants, the leaf surfaces with white markings from the margins of adjoining leaves; flower stalks unbranched, slender, 15-27 dm. high, bearing many crowded paired flowers; flowers 30-45 mm. long; ovary green, 8-10 mm. long and 5 mm. wide; floral tube 10-20 mm. long, constricted at the base, broadly funnel-shaped; perianth segments light yellow, 12-15 mm. long, 5-6 mm. broad, spreading; stamens inserted in the outer fourth of the floral tube; filaments pale yellow, 18 mm. long; anthers light yellow, 7-12 mm. long; style whitish, 32-36 mm. long at maturity; ovary 8-10 mm. long, 5 mm. in diameter; fruits brown, almost spherical or slightly elongated and sub-cylindroidal, 10-15 mm. long, 8-10 mm. in diameter; seeds 4 mm. long, 3 mm. broad.

Abundant on dry, rocky mountain slopes in the upper part of the desert, the desert grassland, and the lower part of the oak woodland at 3,300 to 6,500 feet elevation. Southern Arizona from the Baboquivari Mountains, Pima County, to the Dragoon Mountains, Cochise County; New Mexico in extreme southwestern Hidalgo County; northern Sonora, Mexico. Flowering from May until August. (Fig. 15 2.)

This species, as well as certain other agaves and yuccas, is known as amole, because the short stem, or crown, is used extensively as soap by Indians and Mexicans in the Southwest.

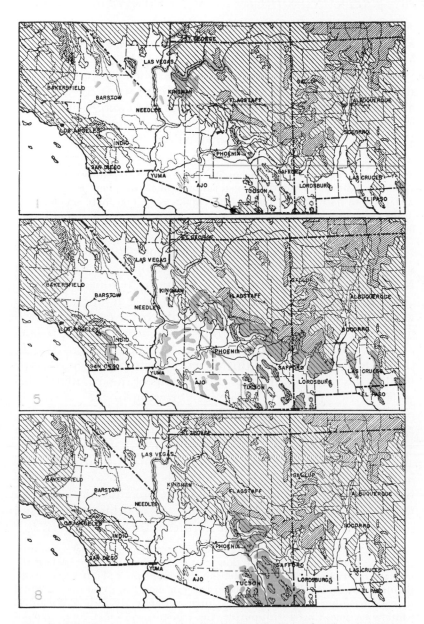

Fig. 17.—Distributional maps: *1*, Utah agave, *Agave utahensis; 2*, Toumey agave, *Agave Toumeyana; 3*, small-flowered agave, *Agave parviflora; 4*, lechuguilla, *Agave lecheguilla; 5*, desert agave, *Agave desertii; 6*, Huachuca agave, *Agave Parryi* var. *huachucensis; 7*, Parry agave, *Agave Parryi; 8*, Palmer agave or mescal, *Agave Palmeri* (including var. *chrysantha*).

As they form a dense cover over rocky hillsides, the plants are also of value in erosion control. They are grown occasionally as ornamentals in southern Arizona.

3b.　*Agave Schottii* Engelm. var.*Treleasei* (Toumey) Kearney and Peebles. TRELEASE AGAVE. (1) Leaf 10-16 inches long, about 1 inch wide at the lowest green portion and ⅝ inch wide at the middle; (2) restriction to a rocky slope in the Santa Catalina Mountains near Tucson, Arizona. (Fig. 16 *F*.)

Plants 40-50 cm. in diameter and 30-40 cm. high at maturity; leaves dark green, 25-40 cm. (8½ to 16 inches) long (to 50 cm. in cultivated plants), 13-18 mm. wide at the middles, the terminal spines 10-15 mm. long, the leaf surfaces with no white markings; flower stalks 20-35 dm. high, smaller than in the typical variety, some stalks appearing apart from the cluster of leaves; flowers 35-50 mm. long.

This variety is rare and localized, being confined to a rocky southern slope in a poorly accessible area of the Santa Catalina Mountains in Pima County, southeastern Arizona. It is associated with *Agave Schottii* and *Agave Palmeri* at an elevation of about 6,500 feet in the lower part of the oak woodland. It was discovered in 1896 by J. W. Toumey, then professor of botany at the University of Arizona, and it has been collected rarely since. Only a few plants of this variety were found when the type locality was revisited in 1940. Descendants of the original plants collected by Professor Toumey are growing in the University of Arizona succulent garden.

4. *Agave lecheguilla* Torr. LECHUGUILLA. (1) Leaves with gray continuous, detachable, horny borders bearing spines; (2) leaves only about 10-30 in number, narrow, usually only 8-16 inches long and 1-1½ inches wide; (3) flower stalks unbranched, 6-13 feet high; (4) flowers greenish or yellowish white, sometimes tinged with purple; (5) southwestern Texas, southeastern New Mexico, and northern Mexico.

Plants in colonies, forming large mats; leaves light green, each terminal spine 20-50 mm. long, extending downward 4-12 mm. along the back of the leaf, the horny borders 1 mm. wide, the marginal spines about 2 cm. apart, pointing downward; flowers in clusters of 3 or more, 25-40 mm. long; floral tube short, funnel-shaped, 2-3 mm. long; perianth greenish or yellowish white, sometimes tinged with purple; the segments 15-18 mm. long; stamens inserted at the top of the floral tube; filaments purple, greatly exserted, 30-35 mm. long; anthers 13-16 mm. long; style 30-40 mm. long; ovary 10-14 mm. long; fruits brown, cylindroidal, 15-25 mm. long, 12-15 mm. in diameter; seeds 4-5 mm. long, 3 mm. broad.

Abundant on arid mesas and limestone cliffs in the desert up to about 5,000 feet elevation. Southeastern New Mexico; southwestern Texas; northern Mexico from Chihuahua to Tamaulipas and Zacatecas. It is a dominant species of the vegetation on thousands of square miles of limestone hills in southwestern Texas from the Franklin Mountains near El Paso east to the Guadalupe Mountains in southeastern New Mexico, the Pecos River, and the western and southern portions of the Edwards Plateau and south to the Big Bend area. It is common around El Paso, and it extends to the border of New Mexico north of that city. It is likewise conspicuous on the limestone hills at Carlsbad Caverns National Park, in southeastern New Mexico. Flowering from May to July. (Fig. 17 4.) The specific name is taken with slight modification in spelling from lechuguilla, the Mexican common name which is the diminutive of lechuga, lettuce.

The fiber ixtle, used for ropes, brushes, and bagging, is made from the leaves of this and related species. Because of its abundance, this native species has possibilities as an emergency source of fiber from wild plants. However, under normal conditions it is doubtful whether fiber from wild or cultivated agaves in the United States could compete financially with fiber from foreign countries, where production costs are lower. The short stem is used as a substitute for soap called amole. This species is a popular ornamental in succulent gardens in Texas.

Lechuguilla plants are poisonous to livestock and produce a disease known as lechuguilla fever, goat fever, or swellhead. Losses among sheep and goats occur when the animals are forced to eat these spiny plants on overgrazed ranges or in periods of drought.[5] This widespread desert species is regarded locally as a pest and a hazard to man and beast. The daggerlike leaves may cause severe sharp and lingering pain when a terminal spine comes in contact with an ankle and it may cause serious injury to horses' feet.

5. *Agave utahensis* Engelm. UTAH AGAVE. (1) Leaves narrow,

5. Frank P. Mathews. *Lechuguilla* (Agave lecheguilla) *Poisoning in Sheep, Goats, and Laboratory Animals,* Tex. Agric. Exp. Sta. Bull. (554) :1-3 *illus.* 1937.

6-15 inches long, with marginal spines; (2) flower stalks of the unbranched type but with the flowers borne on peduncles 1 inch or more long instead of on very short peduncles or pedicels as in other species with unbranched flower stalks; (3) flowers yellow. (Pl. XV D.)

Plants single or in small colonies, the cluster of leaves about 25-40 cm. in diameter and up to 35 cm. high at maturity; leaves bright green, narrowly lanceolate, 15-35 cm. long, gradually narrowed upward from the bases or sometimes broadest near the middles, 2-5 cm. wide, the terminal spines 20-50 mm. long or much elongated, the margins with usually small spines; flower stalks slender, 15-40 dm. high; flowers in clusters of 2-4 or more at the ends of the peduncles, 2-3 (to 5) cm. long, each 22-35 mm. long; floral tube 4-5 mm. long; perianth segments yellow, 10-15 mm. long; more than twice as long as the floral tube; stamens inserted near the middle of the floral tube; filaments about 18 mm. long; anthers 10-12 mm. long; style about 28 mm. long; ovary 10-12 mm. long; fruits light brown, cylindroidal, 18-30 mm. long, 10-12 mm. in diameter; seeds 4 mm. long, 3 mm. broad. Synonym: *Agave kaibabensis* McKelvey.

Desert and mountainous areas at 3,000 to 7,500 feet elevation. California in the Granite, Providence, and New York mountains in the Mojave Desert; southern Nevada in the mountains of Clark and Lincoln counties; southwestern Utah; northwestern Arizona in Mohave and Coconino counties on the Colorado River drainage. This species is found along the rocky cliffs at the Grand Canyon National Park, in northern Arizona, where it is observed by visitors along both rims as well as by those who go deeper into the canyon. Flowering from May until July. (Fig. 17 *1*.)

A form in eastern California and southern Nevada, differing chiefly in having the terminal spine elongated and slender (5-10 cm. long), has been designated as *Agave utahensis* var. *nevadensis*. Further field study is needed to determine whether *Agave scaphoidea* Greenm. and Roush, described from a specimen collected at St. George, Utah, is specifically distinct from *Agave utahensis*. The characters by which *Agave scaphoidea* was separated, slight differences in leaf margins, lateral and terminal spines, and in size of flowers, vary greatly.

Agave utahensis is the most northern of all the species of *Agave,* with the exception of the herbaceous species, *Agave virginica* L., of the southeastern United States. *Agave utahensis* is suitable as an ornamental, but probably it is not so hardy as certain other species, including *Agave Parryi,* which endure colder climates at higher elevations in the mountains. *Agave utahensis* grows at low elevations in warm desert areas.

Plants of this species were used by Indians as a source of fiber and food.

6a. *Agave Parryi* Engelm. var. *Parryi.* PARRY AGAVE; MESCAL. (1) Plants growing in colonies, large, rounded, each suggesting an enormous cabbagehead 2-3 feet or more in diameter; (2) leaves numerous, crowded, usually forming a rounded, compact cluster by curving upward closely together instead of spreading widely, grayish- or bluish-green, 10-16 inches long, 2½ to 4 inches wide, about four times as long as broad, spiny-margined; (3) flower stalks large and stout, branched; (4) flower buds red, the flowers greenish yellow but tinged with red. (Pls. XIII *E, F*; XV *A.*)

Plants spreading by underground sprouts, 3-6 dm. high; leaves obovate or oblong, with an abrupt or acute tip, 25-40 cm. long above the bases, 6-10 cm. broad, 3-5 cm. thick at the bases, thinner and concave at the middles, 5-8 mm. thick, the terminal spines 20-30 mm. long, each with a prominent groove on the upper side; lateral spines many; flower stalk 3-5 m. high, 6-10 cm. in diameter at the base, with many flattened, widely spreading branches on the upper half; flowers numerous, crowded, large, 5-7 cm. long; floral tube broadly funnel-shaped, 10-15 mm. long, 13-14 mm. in diameter at the mouth; perianth segments 16-20 mm. long, narrow; stamens inserted near the top of the floral tube; filaments yellowish green, 35-50 mm. long, more than twice as long as the perianth segments; anthers deep yellow, 20-24 mm. long; style light green to almost white, 55-75 mm. long; ovary elongated, almost cylindrical, 25-40 mm. long, 7-8 mm. in diameter; capsules broadly cylindroidal, light brown, 30-50 mm. long and 20-25 mm. in diameter; seeds 8-9 mm. long by 6 mm. broad. Synonyms: *Agave neomexicana* Woot. & Standl.; *Agave Parryi* Engelm. var. *Couesii* (Engelm.) Kearney & Peebles.

Common in the mountains at higher elevations than the other species of *Agave* (actually above the area included in this book); the oak woodland and chaparral at 4,500 to 8,000 feet elevation, the colonies usually scattered in openings in the woods. Arizona from Yavapai County and southern Coconino County southeastward below the Mogollon Rim to the Santa Catalina Mountains, Pima County, and the Chiricahua Mountains, Cochise County; southern New Mexico; northern Chihuahua, Mexico. (Fig. 17 7.) Flowering in June and early July.

Because of its large size, grayish leaves, cabbagelike shape, and large flower stalks with showy, reddish-tinged flowers, this species should be popular as an ornamental. In addition, probably it is the hardiest of all the native shrubby agaves, as it endures the coldest climate. These agaves grow where they are covered by snow in winter and where the temperature sometimes drops to zero for short periods. On the warmer slopes, a few plants are found at 8,000 feet elevation in mountains of southern Arizona and at 7,000 feet in northern Arizona (near Flagstaff). Because of its large size and wide distribution, this species was important to Southwestern Indians as a source of food, fiber, and other products.

6b. *Agave Parryi* Engelm. var. *huachucensis* (Baker) Little. HUACHUCA AGAVE; CENTURY PLANT. (1) Large colonies of crowded plants covering areas 25 feet or more in diameter; (2) large size, with the cabbage-shaped plants becoming 3½ feet or more in diameter and 2½ feet high; (3) leaves large and especially broad, about three times as long as broad, 14-16 inches or more long, and 5-6 inches or more wide; (4) localized distribution in the Huachuca Mountains and on near-by plains along the Arizona-Sonora border. (Pls. XIII *A*; XV *C*.)

Plants multiplying by underground sprouts; leaves broadly oblong and acute-pointed, more than 5 cm. thick near the bases and up to 1 cm. thick at the broadest parts; terminal spine about 25 mm. long; marginal spines many; flower stalks 4-6 m. high, 10-13 cm. in diameter at the bases, bearing flowers 55-85 mm. long; perianth segments up to 30 mm. long; fruits 45-75 mm. long.

Characteristic of openings in the oak woodland at elevations of 5,000 to 8,000 feet, but with scattered, isolated colonies of smaller plants occurring here and there in the desert grassland at slightly lower elevations. Confined to an area less than 30 miles in diameter in southeastern Arizona; Huachuca Mountains and adjacent plains along the Mexican Boundary in Santa Cruz and Cochise counties, Arizona; probably in adjacent Sonora. Flowering from June until August. Occasionally planted as an ornamental in southern Arizona. (Fig. 17 6.)

7. *Agave desertii* Engelm. DESERT AGAVE. (1) Flower stalks branched; (2) leaves spiny-margined, narrow, widely spreading, but smaller than in the other species having this combination

of characters, about 8-18 inches long, 2-3 inches wide; (3) restriction to desert mountains of southern California, western Arizona, and northern Baja California, Mexico. (Pls. XIII *B*; XIV *left*.)

Plants in large colonies or solitary, about 4-7 dm. in diameter; leaves grayish green, sometimes transversely banded, lanceolate, widest at about the middles, concave, terminal spines 20-45 mm. long, slender, marginal spines 1-3 cm. or more apart; flower stalks slender, 2-6 m. high, with branches on the top quarter or third; flowers 35-40 mm. long; floral tube funnel-shaped, 5-8 mm. long; perianth segments yellow, 15-16 mm. long, 7 mm. wide at the bases; stamens inserted at the upper end of the floral tube; filaments yellowish green, 30-45 mm. long; anthers 18-20 mm. long; style about 4 cm. long; ovary light green, 18-30 mm. long and 7 mm. in diameter; fruits brown, cylindroidal, 35-45 mm. long and 15-17 mm. in diameter; seeds 5 mm. long, 4 mm. broad. Synonym: *Agave consociata* Trel.

Common on rocky or gravelly slopes in the desert mountains at 500 to 3,500 feet elevation. California on the western edge of the Salton Sea Basin of the Colorado Desert and in the Whipple and Providence mountains in San Bernardino County; Arizona from the mountains of southern Mohave County southward to Yuma County and eastward to western Yavapai and western Pima counties; Baja California and probably northern Sonora, Mexico. Flowering in June. The specific name means "of the desert." (Fig. 17 5.)

The crowns of this species were pit baked by various Indian tribes.

8. *Agave Murpheyi* Gibson. MURPHEY AGAVE. (1) Leaves 1½ to 2 feet long, narrow, 2½ to 4 inches wide, broadest above the middles, with many spines along the margins, the terminal spine unusually short, about ½ inch long; (2) flower stalks branched, elongating in November, the plants dormant in midwinter, bearing flowers in the spring; (3) bulbils, or young plants, commonly produced vegetatively on the flower stalks with the flowers; (4) rare and localized in central Arizona.

Plants in colonies about 1 m. or more in diameter; leaves widely spreading, numerous, bright green, narrowly oblanceolate, concave; flower stalks about 3.5 m. high, bearing near the top a group of about 16 branches as much as 21 cm. long, these arising at angles of about 45 degrees; flowers 6 cm. long; floral tube 15 mm. long, 13-17 mm. wide, perianth segments pale greenish yellow, slightly tinged with red, 17 mm. long; stamens inserted at the middle of the floral tube; filaments greenish yellow, about 45 mm. long; anthers pale brownish yellow, 25 mm. long; style 5 cm. long; ovary 25 mm. long; fruits dark brownish black, more or less cylindroidal but narrower toward the bases, 6 cm. long, 25 cm. in diameter; fertile capsules few; additional bulbils formed after flowering; seeds 9 mm. long, 6 mm. broad.

Rocky desert hills at 2,000 to 2,500 feet elevation in central Arizona; known from only four localities in Maricopa, Gila, and Pinal counties. Flowering in late March and April.

Descendants of the type plant are growing at the Boyce Thompson Southwestern Arboretum, near Superior, Arizona. This rare plant, discovered only a few years ago, is too little known for adequate evaluation of its status as a species. It is of interest because of its early flowering and its odd production of many bulbils.

9a. *Agave Palmeri* Engelm. var. *Palmeri.* PALMER AGAVE; MESCAL; CENTURY PLANT. (1) Plant large, this being the largest *Agave* native in the Southwest and the one most resembling the cultivated century plants; (2) leaves numerous, spreading widely, large, 1-3 feet or more long, 2-4 inches wide, spiny-margined; (3) flower stalks tall, branched but relatively slender, 10-23 feet high; (4) flowers greenish, tinged with purple and yellow. (Pls. XIII *D*; XV *B*.)

Plants usually single and scattered, or with a few smaller lateral sprouts; varying greatly in size; leaf cluster 6-15 dm. or more in diameter, 4-12 dm. high; leaves bright green, linear oblanceolate, thick and rigid, straight, concave, the terminal spine 2-4 cm. long, the marginal spines about 10-20 mm. apart; flower stalks 6-12 cm. in diameter at the bases, the branches slender, horizontal, widely spreading, flowers in open clusters, 40-55 mm. long; floral tube 10-15 mm. long; perianth segments 10-15 mm. long, as long as the floral tube or slightly shorter; stamens inserted near the middle of the floral tube; filaments 30-50 mm. long, purple-tinged; anthers 12-18 mm. long, yellowish green; style 4-6 cm. long, purple-tinged; ovary green, elongated, 20-30 mm. long and 7 mm. broad; fruits dark brown, elongated, narrowly cylindroidal or broadest at the tops and gradually narrowed toward the bases, 40-65 mm. long, 15-17 mm. in greatest diameter or only 5-6 mm. wide at the bases; seeds relatively small for the size of the plant, 5-6 mm. long, 4 mm. broad.

Scattered but common locally in rocky foothills and on mountains in the upper part of the desert and in the desert grassland and the oak woodland at from 3,500 to 6,500 feet elevation. Widely distributed in southeastern Arizona, southwestern New Mexico, and adjacent Sonora. Flowering in June and July. An especially large form is common in the Mule Mountains near Bisbee, Arizona. (Fig. 17 *8*.)

Agave Palmeri has been remarkably useful to the Southwestern Indians, who baked the central stems or crowns to prepare food (mescal) and who made the long fibers of the leaves into ropes and other products. The species may have some economic possibilities at present. The United States Forest Service has made a study of the growth, propagation, and harvesting of *Agave Palmeri* in the Coronado National Forest in southeastern Arizona and has found that (1) plants might be suitable for the manufacture of alcohol and (2) the long, stout fibers of the elongated leaves appear to be superior to the fibers of most other native agaves and yuccas. However, the plants are not abundant, and the number of wild individuals probably is not sufficient for extensive commercial development. Moreover, the location of the scattered plants in poorly accessible mountainous areas would make costs of harvesting and transportation high. Although the plants could be cultivated or planted on the desert hillsides, the rate of growth is slow. Costs would be greater than those of the competing foreign products, and they might be prohibitive.

9b. *Agave Palmeri* Engelm. var. *chrysantha* (Peebles) Little. GOLDEN-FLOWERED AGAVE; MESCAL; CENTURY PLANT. (1) Marginal spines of the leaves fewer, averaging about 1 inch apart; (2) flower stalk with shorter (and ascending) branches and more crowded flowers; (3) flowers golden yellow, not purpletinged; (4) restricted to south-central Arizona, northwest of the main range of the typical species.

Plants not reaching the maximum size for the typical species; cluster of leaves 6-10 dm. in diameter, 4-8 dm. high; leaves bluish green, proportionately broader than in *Agave Palmeri,* 30-85 cm. or more long, 5-12 cm. broad, terminal spine 30-50 mm. long; flower stalks 4-7 m. (12-21 feet) high, the branches crowded on the top third of the stalk, flowers as many as 100 to 300 in a cluster, floral tube greenish yellow; filaments pale yellow; anthers yellow; style pale orange-yellow to almost white; fruits crowded.

Desert mountains, foothills, and canyons at 3,000 to 6,000 feet elevation. South-central Arizona in Maricopa, Gila, Pinal, and Pima counties; occupying a rectangular area extending 50 miles east and 100 miles south from the center of the state, including the Sierra Ancha, the Mazatzal, Superstition, Pinal, and Santa Catalina mountains; the characteristic *Agave* of the Apache Trail and the Miami-Superior Highway. Plants showing recombinations of the characters of *Agave Palmeri* and var. *chrysantha* have been found in the Rincon Mountains. Flowering in June and July. (Fig. 17 *8,* where it is included with *Agave Palmeri.*)

SUBCLASS B. *DICOTYLEDONEAE.* DICOTYLEDONS

Dicotyledons comprise the bulk of modern higher plants, and this group of flowering plants has been distinguished (p. 55) from the monocotyledons by a table of characters. For the most part, the dicotyledonous trees and shrubs are not so extraordinary in appearance as are the large monocotyledons, but it is to be remembered that this is merely a way of saying that most plants are dicotyledons and that they have been adopted arbitrarily as a standard because they are common. Some groups of desert dicots have become modified or specialized into quite as weird types as the yuccas and the century plants. The cacti are the most outstandingly modified group, but, since they have been treated rather extensively elsewhere[6] they are omitted from this work. The ocotillo is the closest approach to the cactus family in degree of specialization, but many other groups approach the ocotillo. Almost all the outstanding desert trees and shrubs are spiny, are greatly reduced in leaf area (and therefore reduced in evaporation surface), and have other specialized means of withstanding the rigors of a dry, hot climate.

KEY TO THE FAMILIES

1. Flowers or most of them unisexual, the staminate and pistillate on the same or different plants, sometimes some of the flowers bisexual (one alkali shrub of Family 8 with bisexual flowers, the plant recognized by its succulent, leafless branches). (Fig. 22 *C.*)

    2. Staminate flowers and sometimes the pistillate flowers in catkins (soft spikes or racemes of small flowers without petals, each flower subtended by a scalelike bract). (Figs. 18; 19.) ("AMENTIFERAE")

6. Benson, Lyman. *The Cacti of Arizona,* ed. 2., 1950, Univ. of Arizona Press at the Univ. of New Mexico Press. Albuquerque.

3. Leaves simple; pistillate flowers in catkins; calyx none in either the staminate or the pistillate flowers, both types sometimes subtended by a cup- or saucer-shaped disc (cottonwoods) (Fig. 19 *B*) or by nothing but a scalelike bract (willows) (Fig. 18); fruit a capsule with many seeds, each with a tuft of cottony hairs, the ovary superior.   Family 5. SALICACEAE (p. 102)

3. Leaves pinnate; pistillate flowers solitary or in clusters of 2 or 3; calyx present, the sepals 3-6, usually 4; fruit a walnut, the seed solitary and very large, glabrous, the ovary inferior and the sepals therefore produced near its apex (at the top of the husk, which is the floral tube). (Fig. 19 *A*.)   Family 6. JUGLANDACEAE (p. 110)

2. Staminate and pistillate flowers not in catkins.

   3. Leaves alternate.

      4. Plant scurfy (with white scales resembling dandruff on the stems and leaves). (Fig. 22.)
              Family 8. CHENOPODIACEAE (p. 117)

      4. Plant not scurfy.

         5. Fruit not winged and not a berry, about 12 mm. in diameter.

           6. Flowers hypogynous (Fig. 3 *A*) and not with a hypogynous disc.

              7. Ovary 1-celled, not a capsule in fruit; petals none.

                8. Inflorescence not a chain or series of ball-like clusters of flowers; leaves entire or toothed; shrubs or small trees up to 10 or 12 m. high; fruit a "berry" (actually drupelike) 4-6 mm. in diameter, solitary, yellow or orange at maturity. (Fig. 21 *B, E*.)   Family 7. ULMACEAE (p. 113)

                8. Inflorescence a series of ball-like clusters of staminate or pistillate flowers; leaves palmately lobed or cleft, very large; trees commonly 15-25 m. high, the bark conspicuously white except sometimes on the lower portion of the trunk; fruits dry, elongated, finally separating from the clusters (balls). Fig. 26 *C, D*.)
                    Family 11. PLATANACEAE (p. 136)

              7. Ovary 2-4 celled (1-2 celled in a genus with petals), the fruit a capsule with 1 seed pendant from the top of each cell, the seeds large. (Figs. 52 *A-D*; 54.)
                Family 19. EUPHORBIACEAE (p. 227)

           6. Flowers either perigynous (Fig. 3 *C*) or with a hypogynous disc. (Fig. 3 *B*.)

7. Fruit dry; bark white on the outside, the outer layers peeling off as thin sheets, the next thin layers green, the inner layers thick and red; small trees with thick, short trunks, which become irregularly swollen and massive; odor pungent; leaves pinnate. (Fig. 49 *A*; Pl. XXIII.)
Family 18. BURSERACEAE (p. 225)

7. Fruit fleshy; bark not as above; shrubs.

8. Fruits (of our only unisexual-flowered species) solitary or 2 or 3 together (Fig. 28 *A*); style 1; carpel 1; stems spiny. (Figs. 26 *B*; 28.)
Family 13. ROSACEAE (p. 139)

8. Fruits numerous in dense clusters; styles 3; carpels 3; stems not spiny.
Family 21. ANACARDIACEAE (p. 248)

5. Fruit either dry and with 3 conspicuous wings or berrylike and about 12 mm. in diameter. (Fig. 57; Pl. XXIX *right*.)
Family 24. SAPINDACEAE (p. 255)

3. Leaves opposite.

4. Fruit subtended by the persistent, rapidly growing sepals (which become 20-25 mm. long) resembling an acorn; leaves simple, entire, elliptic, thick, 2-5 cm. long, 1-2 cm. broad. (Fig. 56 *C*.)
Family 20. BUXACEAE (p. 247)

4. Fruit not subtended by a rapidly growing calyx, the sepals minute, usually 1-2 mm. long, the fruit either dry with a conspicuous, elongated, flat terminal wing or fleshy and resembling a small olive; leaves, when both simple and entire, oblanceolate, 1.5-2.6 cm. long, 3-5 mm. broad. (Pl. XXVII; Figs. 62; 66 *A, B, D, E*.)
Family 31. OLEACEAE (p. 272)

1. Flowers all bisexual.

2. Fruit a legume (pea pod), splitting open along both margins (or rarely not opening), formed from a single carpel, commonly several-seeded, rarely a 1-seeded but more than 1-ovuled spiny bur; sepals 5, the number sometimes obscure because of union; petals 5, the corolla, at least somewhat irregular. (Figs. 29-48; Pls. XVII-XX.)
Family 14. LEGUMINOSAE (p. 148)

2. Fruit not a legume or spiny bur, when a "pod" formed from a single carpel, splitting open along only 1 margin.

3. Petals separate or rarely none.

4. Flowers hypogynous (Fig. 3 *A*) and not with a hypogynous disc.

5. Stamens 10 or fewer, usually separate.

6. Carpels 1 or 2, the fruit a berry or a capsule.

    7. Anthers opening by special pores, each provided with a lid; sepals 6 in 2 series; petals 6 in 2 series; leaflets with spines on the lobes; fruit a berry, formed from 1 carpel. (Fig. 21 *C, D.*)

        Family 9. BERBERIDACEAE (p. 131)

    7. Anthers splitting open; sepals 2 or 4; petals 4 or else 6 in 3 unequal series; leaflets not spiny; fruit a capsule with a special stalk above the receptacle, formed from 2 carpels. (Fig. 21 *A.*)

        Family 10. CAPPARIDACEAE (p. 134)

6. Carpels 5, separating when the fruit becomes mature. (Pl. XXI; Fig. 49 *A.*)

        Family 15. ZYGOPHYLLACEAE (p. 216)

  5. Stamens far more than 10, united into an elongated column. (Fig. 60 *D, F.*)   Family 26. MALVACEAE (p. 263)

4. Flowers either perigynous (Fig. 3 *C*) or with a hypogynous disc.

  5. Stamens more than 10, spirally arranged; flower perigynous.

    6. Stipules none; each flower producing 3-5 separate non-woody follicles; leaves bluish, simple, entire, glabrous. (Fig. 26 *A 1-3.*)   Family 12. CROSSOSOMACEAE (p. 137)

    6. Stipules present at least when the leaves are young; in our species each flower producing a cluster of 5 woody, united follicles (therefore a capsule), a single achene, 5-6 achenes each with a long feathery tail, or a drupe; leaves, when simple and entire, densely hairy beneath, not bluish. (Figs. 26 *B*; 28.)

        Family 13. ROSACEAE (p. 139)

  5. Stamens 10 or fewer; flower usually with a disc.

    6. Carpels of the fruit divergently spreading, not winged.

      7. Plant glandular and aromatic; stems not markedly or not at all spiny; leaves well developed, at least at flowering time. (Figs. 50 *B;* 52 *E, F.*)

        Family 16. RUTACEAE (p. 219)

      7. Plant not glandular or aromtaic; stems rigid, green, divergent, the larger ones spine-pointed; leaves reduced to minute scales. (Fig. 50 *A;* Pl. XXII *A, B.*)

        Family 17. SIMAROUBACEAE (p. 224)

    6. Carpels of the fruit not divergently spreading, in one species the 3 wings on the carpels spreading away at right angles to one another.

7. Bark white on the outside, the outer layers peeling off as thin sheets, the next thin layers green, the inner layers thick and red; small trees with thick, short trunks which become irregularly swollen and massive; odor pungent; leaves pinnate. (Fig. 49 *A;* Pl. XXIII.)   Family 18. BURSERACEAE (p. 225)

7. Bark not as above; shrubs, or, if treelike, the trunk not swollen or massive.

8. Leaves or leaflets of our species not more than 1.5 cm. long, or if longer, ovate or oblong; fruit a capsule, a 1-seeded dry structure, or berry- or drupelike and not more than 5 mm. in diameter.

9. Ovary 1-celled; fruits drupelike and in dense clusters or capsular and in dense spikes.

10. Leaves minute and scalelike but green, 1-1.5 or 2 mm. long; flowers and fruits in dense spikes, the fruit a capsule. (Fig. 60 *E.*)
Family 27. TAMARICACEAE (p. 267)

10. Leaves large and well developed; flowers and fruits in dense clusters but not in spikes, the fruit drupelike.
Family 21. ANACARDIACEAE (p. 248)

9. Ovary more than 1-celled.

10. Leaves well developed but often rather small; branches spine-pointed or not spiny, usually not conspicuously the green photosynthetic part of the plant.

11. Stamens alternate with the petals; petals produced under the stamen-bearing disc, therefore hypogynous; seeds winged. (Fig. 56 *A.*)
Family 22. CELASTRACEAE (p. 249)

11. Stamens opposite the petals; petals produced on the stamen-bearing disc, therefore perigynous; seeds not winged. (Fig. 60 *A-C;* Pl. XXIV *A, B.*)
Family 25. RHAMNACEAE (p. 258)

10. Leaves reduced to mere scales; branches spine-pointed, green and therefore photosynthetic, the chief food-manufactur-

ing part of the plant. (Pl. XXII *C, D;*
Fig. 56 *B, D.*)

Family 23 KOEBERLINIACEAE (p. 252)

8. Leaves or leaflets 4-11 cm. long, linear or lanceolate; fruit (of our species) either a berry 10-13
mm. in diameter or a 3-winged structure (samara) 1.5-2 cm. in horizontal diameter. (Fig. 57.)

Family 24. SAPINDACEAE (p. 255)

3. Petals united; sepals united; stamens united to the petals or, in
Family 28, to the floral tube.

4. Plants succulent; clusters of spines produced in definite areoles on the surface of the stem; leaves none or succulent and
ephemeral, appearing on new segments (joints) of the stem
but disappearing within a few months; sepals and petals
numerous, gradually intergrading, united below into a single
tube; ovary inferior, the flower epigynous; style 1, the stigmas
several; stamens perhaps 50 to several hundred.

Family 28. CACTACEAE (p. 268)

4. Plants not succulent; spines, when present, not produced in
clusters in areoles; leaves usually persistent but sometimes
ephemeral, not succulent; sepals and petals not intergrading,
united into 2 separate tubes; styles and stigmas 1-2; stamens
2-19.

5. Ovary superior; flowers hypogynous.

6. Corolla regular, the individual petals the same shape
and size and spreading uniformly from the top of the
tube.

7. Stamens more than 5, or 5 fertile and 5 sterile and
petal-like.

8. Stamens usually 14-19, all fertile; corolla without
lobelike appendages, red; spines formed from
the midribs of the first season's crop of leaves,
the remainder of each blade falling away; plants
with wandlike branches 2-9 m. long arising from
a trunk a few dm. long, spiny their entire
length. (Pls. XXV; XXVI; Fig. 65 *A.*)

Family 29. FOUQUIERIACEAE (p. 270)

8. Stamens 10, 5 fertile and 5 sterile and petal-like;
corolla with lobelike appendages between the
petals, white; spines formed from the tips of
branches; plant with a main trunk and much
shorter branches. (Fig. 66 *C.*)

Family 30. SAPOTACEAE (p. 271)

7. Stamens not more than 5.

    8. Fruit a capsule formed from 2 divergent, spherical carpels, these thin-walled and each part opening by a horizontal slit; corolla funnel-shaped, yellow. (Pl. XXVII; Figs. 62; 66 *A, B, D, E.*)   Family 31. OLEACEAE (p. 272)

    8. Fruit not with 2 divergent, spherical portions, the capsule opening lengthwise by slits, at least at the apex.

        9. Flowers in dense, axillary clusters, forming an interrupted spikelike inflorescence.

        Family 32. LOGANIACEAE (p. 280)

        9. Flowers not in dense axillary clusters, not forming an interrupted spikelike inflorescence.

            10. The 2 carpels only partly united, the ovaries separate (and of course 1-celled), with a single style and stigma arising from the two; seeds of our species with tufts of hair; leaves opposite or whorled; fruits greatly elongated, follicles.

                11. Anthers not united to the stigma; petals not with hoods; pollen not in waxy masses; stems freely branching, the branches not wandlike, leafy; seeds of our shrubby species with a tuft of hairs on each end, cylindroidal. (Fig. 64.)

                Family 33. APOCYNACEAE (p. 281)

                11. Anthers united to the stigma; petals each with an accessory hood arising above; pollen in waxy dumbbell-shaped masses; our species with wandlike branches arising from the root crown, leafless or with a few threadlike leaves; seeds with a tuft of long hairs on one end, flattened. (Pl. XXIV *C;* Fig. 65 *B, C.*)

                Family 34. ASCLEPIADACEAE (p. 281)

            10. The 2 carpels completely united, the ovary 2-celled; seeds glabrous; leaves alternate; fruits not elongated, capsules or berries. (Fig. 69 *B, C;* Pl. XXVIII.)

            Family 37. SOLANACEAE (p. 299)

6. Corolla irregular, the individual petals of different shapes or sizes or spreading from the corolla tube at distinctly different angles and arranged in 2 groups, the upper usually of 2 and the lower of 3 petals.

7. Fruit consisting of 2 or 4 nutlets each with 1 seed, these separating at maturity, each continuing to enclose the seed.

8. Nutlets of our shrubby species 2, the ovary at flowering time not lobed, the style arising from the apex. (Fig. 72 *E*.)

Family 35. VERBENACEAE (p. 286)

8. Nutlets 4, the ovary lobed or divided from the beginning, the style arising among the lobes or divisions. (Figs. 66 *E*; 69 *A*; Pl. XXIX *center*.)

Family 36. LABIATAE (p. 288)

7. Fruit a 2-celled capsule, splitting open and liberating the many seeds.

8. Capsule not stalked; seeds many; flowers of our species either yellow, white, or white-tinged or lined with lavendar; stamens 4, with a fifth sterile filament.

9. Seeds not winged; seed-bearing structures (placentae) produced on the middle of the partition which divides the ovary into two chambers; capsules ovoid, 8-10 mm. long. (Fig. 72 *D*.)

Family 38. SCROPHULARIACEAE (p. 309)

9. Seeds winged; seed-bearing structures (placentae) produced on the side of the ovary wall at the junction of the partition and the outer wall; capsules greatly elongated, 6-20 cm. long. (Fig. 71.)

Family 39. BIGNONIACEAE (p. 311)

8. Capsule stalked (the stalk formed from ovary tissue); seeds few, 2-10; flowers of our species red or varying in *Anisacanthus* from red with an admixture of blue to orange or yellow. (Pl. XXIX *left*; Fig. 72 *A-C*.)

Family 40. ACANTHACEAE (p. 316)

5. Ovary inferior; flowers epigynous.

6. Flowers not in dense heads, or when so, not surrounded by 1 or more series of scalelike bracts (an involucre),

all of one type; fruit not an achene, more than 1-seeded; sepals green, not specialized, sometimes very small or none; stamens separate; styles 1-2; stigmas 1-5, not sweeping the pollen from the anthers.

7. Fruit dry, splitting into two 1-seeded parts; leaves simple and entire.　Family 41. RUBIACEAE (p. 319)

7. Fruit a berry in our species, rarely dry in others, never splitting into two 1-seeded parts; leaves of our species pinnate, the leaflets saw-toothed.

Family 42. CAPRIFOLIACEAE (p. 320)

6. Flowers in dense heads, each of which is surrounded by 1 or more series of scalelike bracts (an involucre), the heads composed of ray flowers (with corollas flattened out and resembling individual petals) or disc flowers (corollas tubular) or both, the entire head usually resembling a single flower, the ray flowers simulating petals and the disc flowers simulating the other parts; fruit an achene formed from 2 carpels; sepals specialized as a pappus of scales or bristles which usually aid in dissemination of the fruits, sometimes wanting; stamens united by the anthers but not by the filaments; style 1; stigmas 2, the hairs on the outside serving as a brush which sweeps the pollen from the inside of the anther tube as the style elongates. (Pls. XXX-XXXIV; Figs. 74-84.)

Family 43. COMPOSITAE (p. 321)

Family 5. *SALICACEAE*. WILLOW FAMILY

The willows and cottonwoods are well known throughout the northern hemisphere, and the names alone may be sufficient to enable nearly everyone to recognize them. In the deserts both willows and cottonwoods are confined strictly to watercourses or water holes or other places where fresh water is near the surface, and this strictness of the limits of distribution is helpful in their recognition. Early in the spring the plants may be recognized by the catkins of flowers which appear before, or with, the leaves. Later the characteristic lance-shaped leaves are a means of identification for the willows, and the broadly heart-shaped ones are a distinguishing feature of the cottonwoods. (Figs. 18; 19 *B;* Pl. XVI *C, E.*)

Trees or shrubs. Bark (of our species) deeply fissured or sometimes checkered, rough. Leaves alternate, simple, entire, or toothed. Flowers unisexual with the staminate and pistillate flowers on different plants, hypogynous, produced in catkins (soft or drooping spikes or racemes). Sepals and petals none, the stamens or the pistil composing the entire flower, the receptacle produced into a cup or saucer below the flower parts in the cottonwoods but not in the willows. Stamens 2 to about 50 or more, the anthers yellow. Pistil green, solitary, formed from 2 or 3 carpels, becoming a capsule in fruit. Seeds with tufts of soft hair, which aid in their dissemination by wind.

KEY TO THE GENERA

1. Leaves lanceolate to linear-lanceolate; flower not subtended by a cup- or saucerlike disc; buds not sealed with resin, each with a single scale; bractlets of the individual flowers persistent; stamens 2-9 in each flower; fruits much longer than broad. (Fig. 18.)   1. SALIX

1. Leaves about as broad as long; flower subtended by a cup- or saucerlike disc; buds sealed with resin, each with several scales; bractlets of the individual flowers falling as soon as the flower opens; stamens 30-75 or more in each flower; fruits spheroidal or ellipsoidal. (Fig. 19 *B*; Pl. XVI *C, E*.)   2. POPULUS

1. *SALIX*. WILLOW; SAUZ; SAUCE

The willows are common throughout the Northern Hemisphere, and, although a few species are outstanding inhabitants of desert stream banks, they are less abundant in the desert than in the temperate regions to the northward. (1) Elongated (linear to lanceolate) leaves; (2) individual flowers (in each case a single pistil or a cluster of stamens) not produced in small cups or discs. (Fig. 18.)

Trees or shrubs or rarely minute plants (alpine species). Juice bitter. Leaves lanceolate to linear, rarely broadly lanceolate or ovate or obovate in species not occurring in the deserts, entire or serrulate or denticulate. Buds each with a single scale, not sealed with resin. Each flower subtended by a scalelike bract, which falls away in our species. Flower with 1 or sometimes 2 small nectar glands; insect pollinated. Stamens 1-10. Stigmas 2 or in 2 pairs.

KEY TO THE SPECIES

1. Stamens 3-9, rarely 2 in some of the flowers of the catkin (Fig. 18 *A* 2); leaves glabrous at maturity, with some hair while they are young, serrulate or entire; trees.

   2. Leaves the same color or essentially so above and beneath, serrulate; twigs yellow or pale gray, never reddish or purplish; stamens 4-6.

      3. Fruiting catkins, or nearly all of them, 4 or commonly 5-8 cm. long, the fruits lanceolate in side view, spaced well apart;

staminate catkins 3.5 or commonly 4-8 cm. long; styles distinctly developed; stigmas very short.   1. *Salix nigra*

3. Fruiting catkins 2-3.5 cm. long, the fruits ovate-attenuate in side view, crowded together; staminate catkins mostly 3-4.5 cm. long, rarely longer; styles practically none; stigmas not exceedingly short. (Fig. 18 *A*.)   2. *Salix amygdaloides*

2. Leaves distinctly green above and bluish (glaucous) beneath; twigs red to purple; stamens 3; fruiting catkins 2-3.5 cm. long, the fruits dense in the catkin; leaves oblanceolate at maturity, most of them broadest at the middles and tapering to the ends, entire.
                                                3. *Salix Bonplandiana*

1. Stamens 2; leaves with long, silky, appressed hairs at maturity, denticulate or entire (Fig. 18 *B 1, 3, 4*); shrubs or rarely (in our range) trees.
                                                4. *Salix exigua*

1a. *Salix nigra* Marsh. var. *vallicola* Dudley. WESTERN BLACK WILLOW. (1) Leaves glabrous at maturity, green above, the same color beneath, broadest at the bases, finely saw-toothed; (2) twigs yellow or pale gray; (3) pistillate catkins mostly 2-3½ inches long at fruiting time, the fruits spaced well apart, slender, lanceolate in side view.

Trees up to 10 or 15 m. high; trunk up to about 1 m. in diameter at the base; bark rough and fissured, dark; leaves linear-lanceolate, 6-14 cm. long, 7-17 mm. broad, attenuate; staminate catkins 3.5 or commonly 4-8 cm. long; stamens 4-6, the filaments hairy below; scales (bracts) yellow, rather densely hairy, the hairs long and soft; pistillate catkins with the yellow scales falling away; styles distinctly present; stigmas 2, notched, very short and broad. Synonym: *Salix Gooddingii* Ball.

Along streams and watercourses in the desert, the desert grassland, and the oak woodland at 200 to 4,000 feet elevation. California in the Great Valley, coastal southern California, and the Mojave and Colorado deserts; southern Nevada; Arizona along the Colorado River to the Grand Canyon and in the central and southern portions; southern New Mexico along the Gila River and Rio Grande drainages; western Texas; Mexico. In the deserts this species is most abundant along the lower Colorado River, where it forms dense stands on the fertile flood plains.

2a. *Salix amygdaloides* Anderss. var. *Wrightii* (Anderss.) Schn. SOUTHWESTERN PEACH WILLOW. (1) Leaves glabrous at maturity, green above, practically the same color beneath,

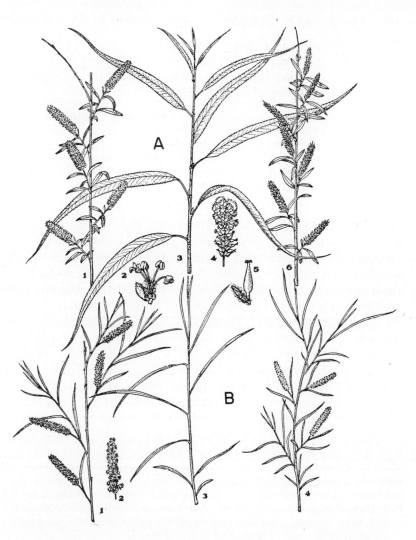

Fig. 18.—Willows: *A*, Southwestern peach willow, *Salix amygdaloides* var. *Wrightii*, *1*, branch with young leaves and catkins of staminate flowers, *2*, single staminate flower composed of stamens alone and subtended by a scalelike bract, *3*, branch with mature leaves, *4*, catkin with mature fruits releasing the hairy seeds, *5*, pistillate flower consisting of a single pistil and subtended by a bract (scale), *6*, branch with young leaves and catkins of pistillate flowers; *B*, sandbar willow, *Salix exigua*, *1*, branch with young leaves and catkins of pistillate flowers, *2*, catkin of fruits, *3*, branch with mature leaves, *4*, branch with young leaves and catkins of staminate flowers. (x ⅓ except *A 2, 5* x 4.)

broadest at the bases, finely saw-toothed; (2) twigs yellow to pale gray; (3) pistillate catkins dense, only 1-1½ inches long at fruiting time, the individual fruits plump, the main portion of each egg-shaped (ovoid), the tip narrow. (Fig. 18 *A*.)

Usually a small tree up to 7-10 m. high; trunk usually 3-6 dm. in diameter; bark rough and fissured; leaves linear-lanceolate, 6-13 cm. long, 7-15 mm. broad, attenuate; staminate catkins mostly 3-4.5 but rarely 5.5 cm. long; stamens 4-6, the filaments hairy below; scales (bracts) yellow, with long, soft hairs; pistillate catkins with promptly deciduous yellow scales; styles practically none; stigmas 2, deeply notched, not exceedingly short.

Along streams and watercourses in the desert, the desert grassland, and the oak woodland at 2,000 to 5,000 feet elevation. Arizona on the Gila and Santa Cruz river drainages in the southeastern part of the state; New Mexico on the Gila River drainage and on the Rio Grande drainage from Albuquerque southward; western Texas; Mexico. This willow may be seen in Sabino Canyon and along the larger watercourses about Tucson. The Arizona plants are referred by Ball to species 1.

3a. *Salix Bonplandiana* H. B. K. var. *Toumeyi* (Britt.) Schn. TOUMEY WILLOW. (1) Leaves glabrous at maturity, green above, distinctly bluish beneath, the upper and lower surfaces in marked contrast to each other, broadest at the middles or above, the margins not saw-toothed; (2) twigs red or purple.

A small tree up to 10-12 m. high; trunk usually 2-5 dm. in diameter; bark dark gray, rough and fissured or checkered; leaves oblanceolate or most of them broadest at the middles and tapering to both ends, or narrowly oblong or broadly linear; acute; staminate catkins mostly 3-4.5 but rarely 5.5 cm. long; stamens 3 or some flowers with only 2, the filaments hairy below; scales (bracts) yellow, with long, soft hairs usually restricted to the basal portion; pistillate catkins with deciduous yellow-gray scales; styles practically none; stigmas broad and short.

Varietal status is somewhat doubtful.

Along streams and watercourses in the upper desert, the desert grassland, and the oak woodland at 2,500 to 5,000 feet elevation. Arizona from Yavapai County southward to Pima and Santa Cruz counties and eastward to Greenlee and Cochise counties; southwestern New Mexico in southern Hidalgo County; northern Mexico.

Salix laevigata Bebb. RED WILLOW. Similar to *Salix Bonplandiana* var. *Toumeyi* but differing as follows: Branches yellowish to reddish brown; leaves lanceolate at maturity, but often oblanceolate before they are fully developed, usually serrulate; catkins mostly 5-8 cm. long at maturity; stamens 4-6; fruits well spaced at maturity, the stalks 2-4 mm. (instead of 1 mm.) long. Along streams and watercourses in the oak woodland and the pinyon-juniper woodland and sometimes at the upper edge of the desert—for example, in South Fork Valley, Kern County, and in Owens River Valley, Inyo County, California. California in the Coast ranges, the Sierra Nevada foothills, coastal southern California, and the western edges of the Mojave and Colorado deserts; southern Nevada; southwestern Utah; Arizona in the Grand Canyon region and along the mountains of the upper parts of the Bill Williams and Gila river drainages as far south-eastward as the Pinal and Huachuca mountains; Mexico.

4. *Salix exigua* Nutt. SANDBAR WILLOW. (1) Shrub 2-5 m. high; (2) leaves with long, dense, appressed, silky hair at maturity; (3) stamens 2 in each flower of the catkin. (Fig. 18 *B*.)

Bark smooth or somewhat roughened at the bases of the largest stems, gray; twigs reddish, soon turning gray; leaves linear but acute at both ends, gray-green or silvery on both sides, 5-10 cm. long, commonly 3-6 but sometimes 2 or 10 mm. broad, entire or denticulate, only the midrib prominent; filaments hairy below; staminate catkins 1.5-2 cm. long; scales (bracts) yellow, hairy; pistillate catkins variable, 1.5-4 cm. long; fruits moderately dense to well spaced, each lanceolate in side view, glabrous or sparsely so; style none; stigmas short.

Along streams and bottom lands in the desert, the desert grassland, the pinyon-juniper and oak woodlands, and the lower yellow-pine forests from sea level to 5,000 or 7,000 feet elevation. British Columbia and Alberta and thence southward through the Great Basin, the deserts, and the Great Plains to Mexico; throughout our range.

Salix sessilifolia Nutt. var. *leucodendroides* (Rowlee) Schn. Stigmas divided into linear or oblong lobes, 3-4 times as long as broad; ovary densely silky-hairy (sericeous). Along streams and arroyos at 100 to 2,500 feet elevation. California from Santa Clara County southward to San Diego County; along the western margins of the Mojave Desert and the bed of the Mojave River; western edge of the Colorado Desert. Not essentially a desert plant.

Salix argophylla Nutt. COYOTE WILLOW. Leaves densely silky with appressed fine hairs; stigmas short and thick; ovaries and capsules with long, slender hairs. Stream beds and bottom lands. Eastern Washington to northwestern Montana, northeastern Utah and the east side of the Sierra Nevada, California; South Coast ranges and Kern County (Bakersfield, *Cohen 431*) to coastal southern California; occurring in the desert along streams of the southern Sierra Nevada entering Owens Lake (Olancha, *L. Benson 11199;* Independence, *L. Benson 5917, 5918*).

Salix taxifolia H.B.K. YEW WILLOW. Similar to *Salix exigua* but differing as follows: Trees up to 10 m. high; trunk diameter up to 5-7 dm; bark rough and fissured; leaves at maturity 2-3 or rarely 3.8 cm. long, 2-4 mm. broad; pistillate (female) catkins 1-1.5 cm. long; capsules densely appressed-hairy, silky; stigmas 0.5-0.7 mm. long, slender. Streams in the oak woodland and rarely in the desert and the desert grassland at 3,500 to 6,000 feet elevation. Arizona in the Santa Catalina and Santa Rita mountains, Pima County, and from Sycamore Canyon near Ruby, Santa Cruz County, eastward to Cochise County, appearing on the desert in the great southwestern recess of the Rincon Mountains and near Tucson; New Mexico in southern Hidalgo County; western Texas near El Paso and in the Big Bend region; throughout Mexico; Guatemala. The resemblance of the leaves to yew leaves is remarkable.

2. *POPULUS.* Cottonwood; Poplar; Aspen; Alamo

The cottonwoods are among the most commonly planted desert shade trees, since they grow rapidly and since it is possible to plant large branches in the ground with likelihood that they will root and grow if sufficient water is available; trees from such plantings develop rapidly and provide an abundance of shade in a short time. The catkins of the staminate (male) trees drop about when the leaves appear, and they do not produce the well-known "cotton" (tufts of hairs on the seeds) which is one of the drawbacks of pistillate (female) cottonwoods. On the other hand, since it is light and wind-carried, the pollen may be responsible for hay fever among persons sensitized to it. (1) Heart-shaped, egg-shaped, kidney-shaped, or more or less triangular leaves, often with an elongated point at the tip of each; (2) individual flowers each consisting of a single pistil or of a mass of stamens subtended by a cup, saucer, or ring of tissue. (Fig. 19 *B*; Pl. XVI *C, E.*)

Large trees. Leaves cordate-ovate, cordate, reniform, broadly ovate, deltoid, dentoid-cordate, or in some mountain and eastern species lance-olate, in our species nearly as broad as long to broader than long, serrate or dentate or in some species entire, usually attenuate. Buds sealed with resin, each with several scales. Stamens about 30-75 or more. Stigmas very large, dilated, 2-4, entire or lobed. Fruit spheroidal, ellipsoidal, or ovoid.

1a. *Populus Fremontii* Torr. var. *Fremontii*. FREMONT COT-TONWOOD. The only cottonwood in the deserts west of the eastern margin of Arizona. (Fig. 19 *B*; Pl. XVI *C, E*.)

Trees up to 17-25 m. high; trunk as much as 1 m. or more in diameter; bark rough and fissured, light gray or brownish or whitish; twigs yellow, soon becoming pale gray, glabrous or glabrate, sometimes densely hairy at first; leaves variable in shape as described above, the attenuation at the apex of each variable in size and shape, entire to deeply serrate, some-times hairy, especially at first; staminate catkins mostly 3-8 cm. long, the flowers well spaced; stamens about 50-60, protruding from the cup at maturity; pistillate catkins mostly 5-9 cm. long; pedicels variable, mostly 1-3 mm. long; disc exceedingly variable, 1.5-5 mm. in diameter; fruit variable in shape and size, ovoid to broadly ovoid or nearly globular, sometimes ellipsoidal or narrowly so, usually 4-12 mm. long, splitting along 3 lines.

Streams, bottom lands, and water holes from sea level to 6,500 feet elevation. California in the Coast ranges, the Great Valley, the Sierra Nevada foothills, coastal southern California, and the Mojave and Colorado deserts; west-central and southern Nevada; southwestern Utah; Arizona on the Colorado and Little Colorado river drainages and everywhere south of the Mogollon Rim; southwestern New Mexico on the Gila River drainage; northwestern Mexico.

The Fremont cottonwood varies somewhat in the size of the disc below the fruits, the shape of the leaf apex, and the hairi-ness of the young stems, but the species is not nearly so variable as the many scientific names applied to it would indicate. The Arizona form has a much longer point at the apex of the leaf than does the California type, but this does not seem to be associated consistently with other characters.

The cottonwood, or alamo, is abundant wherever sufficient underground water is available, and it is an indicator of a water supply not far below the surface. It fringes the banks of streams, and it was an unfailing supply of water within digging depth for the early desert travelers. In the winter when the trees are leafless, the yellow-green foliage of a mistletoe with particularly large leaves becomes apparent on many of the trees.

1b. *Populus Fremontii* Torr. var. *Wislizenii* S. Wats. WIS-LIZENIUS COTTONWOOD

Leaves markedly attenuate, but no more so on the average than in some forms of the typical species; pedicles of both staminate and pistillate flowers elongate and slender, at least some of them equaling or exceeding the length of the fruit, the fruit rather narrowly ellipsoidal, disc small, 1.5-2 mm. in diameter at fruiting time.

Southern Utah; southern Colorado; New Mexico; western Texas; northern Mexico. The Wislizenius cottonwood is the counterpart of the Fremont cottonwood in a range farther eastward.

Family 6. *JUGLANDACEAE*. Walnut Family

Only one walnut is native to the Southwestern deserts, and, since it resembles the well-known black walnuts of the eastern, southeastern, and middle western states and of California, it is readily recognized by the traveler. The tree occurs primarily in canyons in the mountains, but well-developed specimens are not uncommon along the same watercourses where they descend into the deserts. The pinnate leaves, the drooping catkins of staminate flowers appearing before the leaves, and the "black walnut" fruit are adequate for recognition. (Fig. 19 *A*.)

Trees or shrubs. Leaves alternate, pinnate, the leaflets ovate to lanceo-late. Flowers unisexual, pistillate and staminate on a single plant, epigy-nous; sepals 3-6, usually 4; petals none, stamens yellow, 10-40, enclosed by a calyx usually 3-4 mm. in diameter; pistil 1, green, the ovary inferior, the sepals (4 in our species) appearing at the top of the husk (floral tube), the stigmas 2; fruit a walnut with (in our species) a thick, somewhat fleshy husk which soon dries and covers the hard shell tightly; seed 1, large, 2-parted and convoluted.

1. *JUGLANS*. Walnut; Butternut; Nogal

1a. **Juglans microcarpa** Berlandier var. **major** (Torr.) L. Benson, comb. nov. (cf. p. 414) . ARIZONA BLACK WALNUT (Fig. 19 *A 1-3*.)

Broad, rounded tree up to 15-17 m. (about 50 feet) high, the trunk up to 1 m. (1 yard) in diameter; bark dark, fissured; leaflets in about 5-7 pairs, with a terminal leaflet, each lanceolate, sometimes broadly so, about 4-10 cm. long, 1-2.4 cm. broad, attenuate, saw-toothed on the margins; nut deeply grooved, spherical or nearly so, the husk densely hairy, 2.5-3 cm. in diameter at maturity. Synonym: *Juglans rupestris* Engelm. var. *major* Torr.

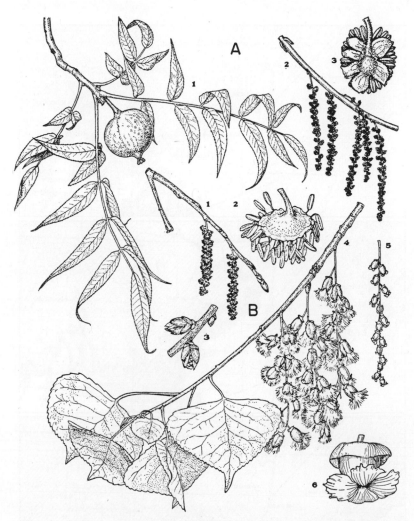

Fig. 19.—Walnut and cottonwood: *A*, Arizona black walnut, *Juglans micro-carpa* var. *major*, *1*, branch with pinnate leaves and a fruit (walnut) enclosed in the husk (floral tube), the dry, shrunken sepals and stigmas still visible at the apex, *2*, leafless branch with catkins of staminate flowers, *3*, single staminate flower composed of calyx and stamens; *B*, Fremont cottonwood, *Populus Fremontii*, *1*, leafless branch with catkins of staminate flowers, *2*, staminate flowers each composed of stamens and a disc, *3*, portion of branch showing the buds, each covered by several sticky resinous scales, *4*, branch with leaves and fruits, the fruits shedding the hairy seeds, *5*, catkin of pistillate flowers, *6*, pistillate flower composed of a single pistil (with greatly expanded stigmas), subtended by a disc. (x ¹/₃ except *A* *3* x 4 and *B* *2, 6* x 3.)

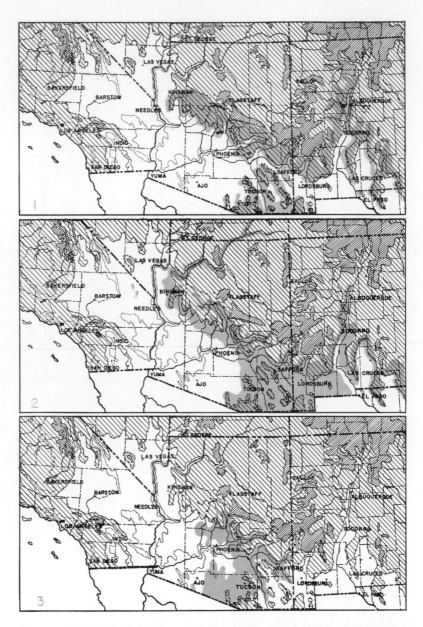

Fig. 20.—Distributional maps: *1*, Arizona black walnut, *Juglans microcarpa* var. *major;* 2, western hackberry, *Celtis laevigata* var. *reticulata;* *3*, desert hackberry, *Celtis Tala* var. *pallida.*

Rocky or sandy soil along streams and in canyons in the upper desert, the desert grassland, and the oak woodland at 3,500 to 7,000 feet elevation. Arizona from the Hualpai Mountains, Mohavc County, southeastward bclow thc Mogollon Rim to the mountains of the central and southeastern parts of the state, thence westward to the Baboquivari Mountains, Pima County; New Mexico on the Gila River and Rio Grande drainages; western Texas; Mexico. (Fig. 20 *1*.)

The familiar walnut family is poorly represented in the western United States, and this is the only member of the group within our range. A single species and a variety occur in coastal California. The Arizona black walnut seldom occurs in pure stands, and commonly the trees are scattered along canyons. The small nuts are edible and were a source of food for the Indian tribes.

FAGACEAE. Beech Family

The family is represented by oaks, readily recognized by their acorns, despite remarkable differences from the well-known types of the East and Middle West. The oaks, like the junipers and cypresses (p. ??), are indicators of the flora characteristic of higher regions than the desert and the desert grassland. However, individuals of any of several species may occur here and there in the transitional areas between the oak woodland and the desert types. In Arizona and New Mexico the Emory oak, *Quercus Emoryi* Torr., and the Mexican blue oak, *Quercus oblongifolia* Torr., occur in canyons and along watercourses at the uppermost edge of the desert and the desert grassland, and through most of the desert the scrub oak, *Quercus dumosa* Nutt. var. *turbinella* (Greene) Jepson, occurs barely in the upper portion of the desert; for example, at Horse Tanks in the Castle Dome Mountains and at Palm Canyon in the Kofa Mountains, Yuma County, Arizona. *Quercus pungens Liebm.*, a low-growing type, occurs on the limestone hills between Bisbee and Douglas, Arizona.

Family 7. *ULMACEAE*. Elm Family

No elms are native to the southwestern deserts, but the family is represented by two outstanding woody plants, the western and the desert hackberry. The former is a tree occurring along watercourses and subirrigated washes, and the latter is a spiny desert shrub bearing practically no obvious resemblance to the elms, except in the juvenile leaves of very young individuals. The hackberries are distinguished readily from all the other desert trees and shrubs lacking petals by the yellow to orange "berries" and the simple, alternate, egg-shaped (ovate) or elliptic leaves, which have either undivided or saw-toothed margins. (Fig. 21 *B, E*.)

Trees or shrubs. Leaves alternate, simple, ovate or elliptic, entire to serrate, alternate, commonly asymmetrical at the bases. Flowers unisexual, the staminate and pistillate on a single plant, some transitional flowers bisexual, hypogynous, greenish yellow; sepals 4 or as many as 9, united; petals none; stamens 4-6; pistil 1, formed from 2 carpels, the styles 2; ovary 1-celled; fruit a nut, a winged structure (samara) or, in our species, an orange or yellow berry.

1. *CELTIS*. Hackberry; Palo Blanco

Bark gray, blue-gray, or gray-brown, commonly with protruding knobs, somewhat furrowed or cross checked or in shrubby species rough bark not necessarily formed at all. Flowers minute, 1-3 mm. in diameter, in cymose clusters, or solitary, produced on the new growth of the season; staminate flowers (consisting of a calyx and stamens) produced first and therefore at the base of the young branch; pistillate flowers (consisting of a calyx and a pistil) produced later and appearing on the upper part of the new leafy branch; bisexual flowers sometimes produced between the unisexual types. Fruit a "berry" (actually drupelike), in our species yellow or orange at maturity, the seed solitary (therefore not a true berry).

KEY TO THE SPECIES

1. Branches not producing spines; leaves asymmetrical at the bases, oblique, reticulate-veiny on the under surface, usually pale beneath, deciduous in the autumn, reappearing the following spring; small trees of living-stream bottom lands, canyons, and subirrigated washes, rarely shrubby in drier situations. (Fig. 21 *B*.)   1. *Celtis laevigata*

1. Branchlets partly or completely specialized as spines; leaves with rounded symmetrical bases, not oblique except in juvenile types, thick, not reticulate-veiny, persistent through the winter; shrubs of the desert floor or also in washes and canyons but not restricted to well-watered situations. (Fig. 21 *E*.)   2. *Celtis Tala*

1a. *Celtis laevigata* Willd. var. *reticulata* (Torr.) L. Benson. WESTERN HACKBERRY. (1) Trees of washes and streams, restricted to areas with a constant water supply; (2) spines none; (3) leaves deciduous in the autumn or winter, reappearing the following spring, strongly veiny beneath, pointed, the bases asymmetrical, one side distinctly larger than the other. (Fig. 21 *B*.)

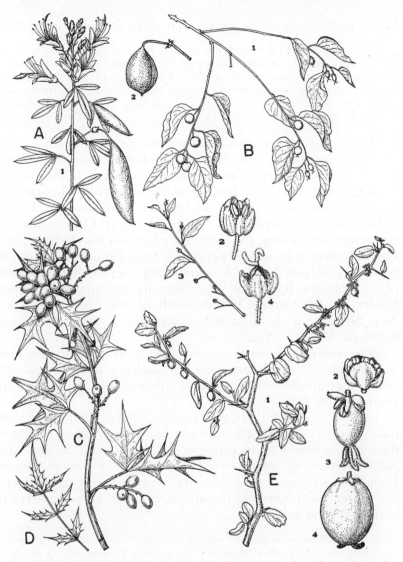

Fig. 21.—Burro fat, hackberries, and barberries: *A*, burro fat, *Cleome Isomeris*, *1*, branch with flowers and fruits (of the elongated type), *2*, fruit of a shorter inflated type showing the long stipe above the receptacle; *B*, western hackberry, *Celtis laevigata* var. *reticulata*, *1*, branch with fruits, *2*, staminate flower, *3*, young branch with immature leaves and with pistillate flowers (above) and staminate flowers (below), *4*, pistillate flower; *C*, Kofa Mountain barberry, *Barberis Harrisoniana*, branch with (blue-black) fruits; *D*, red barberry, *Berberis Nevinii* var. *haematocarpa*, leaf; *E*, desert hackberry, *Celtis Tala* var. *pallida*, *1*, branch with flowers and fruits, *2*, staminate flower, *3*, perfect (transitional) flower composed of calyx, stamens, and pistil, *4*, pistillate flower composed of calyx and pistil (now developed into a fruit). (x ^{1}/$_3$ except separate flowers x 5 and separate fruit in E *4* x 2^1/$_3$.)

Trees 10-16 m. (30-48 feet) high, the trunk usually 2-4 or 6 dm. in diameter; bark well developed, with corky ridges; spines none; leaves ovate-attenuate or ovate-acute, mostly 3-6 cm. long, 1.5-4 cm. broad, entire or occasionally serrate (saw-toothed), rather thick, strongly reticulate and usually pale beneath; flowering branches elongating rapidly; fruit spherical, 8-9 mm. in diameter.

Along watercourses and in canyons of the upper desert, the desert grassland, and the oak woodland at 2,500 to 6,000 feet elevation. Eastern Washington and adjacent Idaho, southward through the Great Basin and the deserts to Mexico and southeastward to Colorado, Oklahoma, and western Texas; California in the Greenhorn Mountains, Kern County, and in the mountains along the western edges of the Mojave and Colorado deserts from Independence, Inyo County, southward; Nevada; southern Utah; Arizona along the northern portion of the Colorado River and its tributaries and along the upper border of the Arizona Desert south of the Mogollon Rim; New Mexico on the Gila River and Rio Grande drainages; northern Mexico. (Fig. 20 2.)

The fleshy fruits were eaten formerly by the Indians, and occasionally the trunks are used now as fence posts. A leaf-gall insect often produces a globular semiwoody gall in the central portion of the leaf.

2a. *Celtis Tala* Gillies var. *pallida* (Torr.) Planch. DESERT HACKBERRY. (1) Shrub 3-8 or 10 feet high occurring on the open floor of the desert or in canyons and washes but in any case not restricted to well-watered situations; (2) short lateral branches specialized as spines; (3) leaves persisting through the winter, not pointed at the apices, rounded and symmetrical at the bases. (Fig. 21 *E*.)

Rough bark none or present only at the very base of the plant; spines developed as sharp-pointed branches, these often bearing leaves or short branches of their own; leaves elliptic or tending to be ovate, 2-3 or rarely 6 cm. long, 1-1.8 or rarely 5 cm. broad, entire or mostly with rounded upward-directed lobes or teeth (crenate-serrate), thick, not veiny and reticulate or noticeably pale beneath; berry ovoid or ellipsoid, about 6-7 mm. long, 5-7 mm. in diameter.

Common on gravelly or well-drained sandy soils of the desert and the desert grassland at 2,000 to 4,000 feet elevation. Arizona in the Arizona Desert and adjacent desert grassland from the Verde and Hassayampa river drainages southward to the Ajo Mountains, Pima County, and eastward; western Texas; northern Mexico. Typical *Celtis Tala,* distinguished by markedly toothed leaves, less hairy branches and leaves, and shorter spiny branches, occurs from tropical and subtropical America to Argentina. (Fig. 20 *3*.)

The desert hackberry is an attractive evergreen shrub with a dense habit of growth, and it is excellent cover for Gambel's quail and other birds. The fruits are eaten by a large variety of birds and mammals, but the spiny twigs make the plant of little value to livestock.

Family 8. *CHENOPODIACEAE.* GOOSEFOOT FAMILY

The bulk of the members of the goosefoot family is characteristic of alkaline habitats, but some members occur as weeds in ordinary cultivated soil or in waste places about towns. Examples are lamb's-quarter and various other goosefoot species *(Chenopodium)*. Some, like the Russian thistle, which covers many miles of more or less open country in semiarid regions, are tumbleweeds. A few, including chard, spinach, and beets, are garden vegetables. Predominantly the members of the family are herbaceous but in the deserts there are a number of significant shrubs. The family is recognized best by the scurfy character of the leaves and branches, which in nearly all species are covered by white scales resembling dandruff. In a few species of herbs these scales are few and scattered, and when the plants are young the scales may not be developed as scurf, since the scales are formed, at least in some instances, from protruding cells which later dry up. (Fig. 22.)

Leaves alternate or sometimes opposite, simple, usually entire. Flowers hypogynous, small and inconspicuous, in most species bisexual, but in all except one of the shrubs unisexual (in some the pistillate flowers without sepals and enclosed each in a pair of tightly appressed and usually fused bracts); sepals usually 5, sometimes fewer or none, green or scurfy; petals none; stamens 5, rarely reduced to 1-4; pistil 1, the ovary superior, 1-celled, 1-ovuled; styles or stigmas 2-3. Fruit an achene or a utricle, the styles persistent, the embryo in the seed curved as in all related families.

KEY TO THE GENERA

1. Pistillate flowers and the fruits enclosed each in a pair of bracts which enlarge greatly after flowering, the bracts appressed and commonly united. (Fig. 22 *A 2, 3; B 3; E 2, 3; F.*)

   2. Bracts of the fruit glabrous; margins of the leaves not rolled tightly downward; hairs not star-shaped.

      3. Margins of the bracts not united from base to apex, not forming a sac, sometimes not united at all. (Fig. 22 *A, B, E, F.*)
1. ATRIPLEX

      3. Margins of the bracts united from base to apex, the apical opening minute.
2. GRAYIA

   2. Bracts of the fruit with many long hairs, which form the conspicuous feature of the inflorescence (Fig. 22 *D*); margins of the leaves rolled tightly downward (revolute); hairs of the branches and leaves star-shaped. (Fig. 22 *D.*)
3. EUROTIA

1. Pistillate flowers and the fruits not enclosed each in a pair of bracts, the bracts when present solitary and not greatly enlarged after flowering time.

   2. Leaves well developed; branches not swollen into fleshy joints; fruit not bordered by a winglike platform; flowers unisexual.
4. SARCOBATUS

   2. Leaves scalelike; branches swollen into fleshy joints; fruit subtended by a horizontally spreading winglike disc formed from the calyx; flowers bisexual. (Fig. 22 *C.*)
5. ALLENROLFEA

1. *ATRIPLEX.* Saltbush

Fruit enclosed in a pair of bracts, the bracts united only part way from base to apex or not united at all, glabrous. (Fig. 22 *A, B, E, F.*)

Herbs or shrubs. Flowers in clusters or spikes, unisexual, the staminate and pistillate on the same or different plants; stigmas 2.

In addition to the following species, *Atriplex acanthocarpa* (Torr.) S. Wats. and *Atriplex obovata* Moq. may be somewhat woody. Both (the former somewhat doubtful in identity, however) have been collected near Safford, Arizona, and eastward to Texas and southward to northern Mexico.

KEY TO THE SPECIES

1. Each bract of the pair surrounding the fruit with a wing down the middle of the back, the whole thus forming a 4-winged structure since the wing-like edges of the members of the pair are fused. (Fig. 22 *A.*)
1. *Atriplex canescens*

1. Each bract of the pair surrounding the fruit with winglike margins but not with a wing down the middle of the back. (Fig. 22 *B 3; E 2, 3; F.*)

   2. Bracts surrounding the fruit not with marginal or dorsal projections like the fingers of a glove. (Fig. 22 *B 3; E 2, 3.*)

3. Bracts of the fruit 2-4 mm. in length, the winglike border of each lateral. (Fig. 22 *E* 2, 3.)

4. Bracts nearly circular in outline (Fig. 22 *E* 2, 3) or sometimes slightly broader than long but then broadest below; leaves 1.5-3 cm. long, not cordate, with short petioles; shrubs 5-10 feet high and 8-15 feet in diameter. (Fig. 22 *E*.)
2. *Atriplex lentiformis*

4. Bracts fan-shaped or broadly so, broadest apically; leaves 8-16 mm. long, cordate at the bases, without petioles; shrubs 2-4 dm. high.
3. *Atriplex Parryi*

3. Bracts of the fruit 5-20 mm. in length, the winglike border of each terminal. (Fig. 22 *B* 3.)

4. Branches forming spines after the leaves fall away; leaves not lobed.

5. None of the leaves with conspicuous divergent (hastate) lobes at the bases; bodies of the bracts forming a fan- or wedge-shaped thickened structure around the fruit.
4. *Atriplex confertifolia*

5. Most of the leaves with conspicuous divergent (hastate) lobes at the bases; bodies of the bracts forming a cylindrical thickened structure around the fruit. 5. *Atriplex spinifera*

4. Branches never spiny; leaves lobed or deeply toothed (Fig. 22 *B* 2, 3), the lobes or teeth divergent. (Fig. 22 *B*.)
6. *Atriplex hymenelytra*

2. Bracts surrounding the fruit with marginal and often dorsal projections like the fingers of a glove. (Fig. 22 *F*.)   7. *Atriplex polycarpa*

1. *Atriplex canescens* (Pursh) Nutt. var. *canescens*. FOUR-WING SALTBUSH; WINGSCALE; CHAMISO. The species is characterized by the large four-winged structures (pairs of bracts) around the fruits. (Fig. 22 *A*.)

Shrubs 1-2 m. (3-6 feet) high, distinctly woody, irregular in outline and more or less flat-topped; bark exfoliating in age; leaves mostly oblanceolate but the apices often blunt, mostly 2-4 cm. long, 2-7 mm. broad, thick, glabrous; staminate and pistillate flowers on different plants (except in one specimen); bracts of the fruit 6-14 mm. long, the free tips usually about 1 mm. long, the wings protruding past them, usually not toothed but sometimes so.

Moderately alkaline slopes and plains of the creosote-bush desert, the desert grassland, the sagebrush desert, and the oak woodland from sea level to 7,000 feet elevation. Eastern Oregon to North Dakota and southward to Mexico; California at Burbank, Arlington, and San Diego in coastal southern California and in the Mojave and Colorado deserts; central and southern Nevada; Utah; Arizona; New Mexico; northern Mexico. The most widely distributed species of *Atriplex* in the United States; adapted to a variety of soil and climatic conditions. The extensive root system makes plant remarkably drought resistant.

The highly nutritious foliage makes this plant one of the most valuable forage types for range livestock wherever it occurs in abundance.

Atriplex canescens var. *laciniata* Parish occurs from the California and Arizona deserts to Baja California and Sonora. It has leaves 12-25 or rarely 30 mm. long and the wings of the fruiting bracts are fimbriately cleft to divided.

1a. *Atriplex canescens* (Pursh) Nutt. var. *macilenta* Jepson.

Large shrub 1-2 m. high; leaves linear or linear-oblanceolate, 2-5 cm. long, 1-3 mm. broad; fruiting bracts variable in shape and size but mostly 4-8 mm. long, the free tips 1-3 mm. long, commonly longer than the wings, the margins usually but not necessarily toothed or lobed or even deeply parted. *Atriplex canescens*. var. *linearis*.

Alkaline flats and mesas in the desert from sea level to 2,500 feet elevation. California in the Colorado Desert; Arizona along the Gila River drainage as far eastward as Florence and Tucson; Baja California and Sonora, Mexico. This variety is restricted to more strongly alkaline soils than is the typical variety, and it is associated often with *Atriplex polycarpa*. (Fig. 23 2.)

Atriplex canescens (Pursh) Nutt. var. *macilenta* Jepson, collected in the southern part of the Colorado Desert in California. According to Jepson, "wings much reduced, ¾ to 1½ lines (1.5-3 mm.) broad, coarsely toothed." The plant was unknown from specimens, and evaluation of its status was not attempted until this book was in press. Study in August, 1953, by Mr. Grant D. Brown, of the type specimen of var. *macilenta* Jepson shows that the epithet *macilenta* must replace *linearis,* cf. above.

1b. *Atriplex canescens* (Pursh) Nutt. var. *Garrettii* (Rydb.) L. Benson. GARRETT SALTBUSH

Low shrub 2-5 dm. high; leaves elliptic-oblong to elliptic-obovate, 1-3 cm. long, 1-1.3 cm. broad, petioled; fruiting bracts 6-12 cm. long, the free tips usually 2-3 mm. long, commonly protruding beyond the wings, the wings usually lobed or parted.

Plains and mesas in the sagebrush desert at 3,700 to perhaps 5,000 feet elevation. Southeastern Utah; southwestern Colorado; northern Arizona at the Navajo Bridge and Lee's Ferry on the Colorado River. (Fig. 23 *3*.)

2a. *Atriplex lentiformis* (Torr.) S. Wats. var. *lentiformis*. QUAIL BRUSH; LENS SCALE. (1) Large shrubs of bushy aspect, mostly 5-10 feet high, 8-15 feet in diameter; (2) bracts of the fruits small, not more than 1/6 inch in diameter, circular or nearly so, smooth on the backs. (Fig. 22 *E*.)

Branches smooth, whitish or pale gray, spreading at broad angles, sometimes becoming spiny after the leaves have fallen; leaves ovate or tending to be a little hastate, sometimes ovate with a truncate base or triangular-ovate, 1.5-3 cm. long, 1-2 cm. broad, bluish green or green, noticeably scurfy, of moderate thickness, short-petioled; staminate spikes 1-3 inches long, about 2 mm. in diameter, consisting of compactly placed balls of flowers; bracts of the fruit circular or sometimes tending toward oblong or slightly broader than long, 2-3 mm. in diameter, the marginal wing of variable size, the margins usually with minute teeth, the backs smooth, united about half their length.

Alkaline flats and plains in the desert and the desert grassland at 300 to 2,000 or sometimes 3,000 feet elevation. California in the eastern portions of the Mojave and Colorado deserts; southern Nevada; southwestern Utah; Arizona along the Colorado, Bill Williams, and Gila river drainages as far eastward as the Salt River Valley; Baja California and southeastward into Sonora, Mexico. (Fig. 23 *5*.)

This variety is replaced by *Breweri* west of the main mountain axis of California.

Quail brush is the largest of the native saltbushes, and it grows in soils with a high alkali content and with ample supplies of surface water. The large leafy shrubs provide food and cover for a variety of wild birds and mammals and are an important source of forage for range livestock. The Indians used the leaves and young shoots as greens.

2b. *Atriplex lentiformis* (Torr.) S. Wats. var. *Griffithsii* (Standl.) L. Benson. GRIFFITHS SALTBUSH

Twigs sharply angled, the angles irregular; leaves oblong or oblong-lanceolate, 1.5-2 cm. long, 4-7 mm. broad; bracts of the fruit cordate-reniform, about 4 mm. long, 5 mm. broad, the wing large and conspicuous for this species.

Alkali flats surrounded by desert grassland at about 4,000 feet elevation. Arizona at Willcox Playa, Cochise County. Not known elsewhere. (Fig. 23 6.)

2c. *Atriplex lentiformis* (Torr.) S. Wats. var. *Torreyi* (S. Wats.) McMinn. TORREY SALTBUSH; NEVADA SALTBUSH

Twigs sharply and irregularly angled; leaves about like those of the typical species or more oblong; bracts of the fruit rounded or elliptic, 3-4 mm. in diameter, not united.

Alkaline flats and salt flats in the desert at about 2,000 to 3,000 feet elevation. California from Owens Valley to the northern and western parts of the Mojave Desert; west, central, and southern Nevada; southwestern Utah. This shrub occurs on extremely saline soils where subsurface water is available.

In a recent thesis prepared at the Pomona College Herbarium, Mr. Grant D. Brown has raised *Atriplex Torreyi* to specific status and placed var. *Griffithsii* under it as a variety (unpublished).

3. *Atriplex Parryi* S. Wats. PARRY SALTBUSH. (1) Small shrubs about 1 foot high; (2) bracts of the fruits small, not more than 1/6 inch in diameter or at least not more in length, fan-shaped, smooth on the backs.

Branches spiny, not angled; leaves rounded-ovate to more or less reniform, the bases cordate or somewhat so, 8-14 mm. long, 8-16 mm. broad, without petioles; bracts of the fruit united more than half their length, fan-shaped, 3-4 mm. long, slightly broader than long, with a few rounded apical teeth.

Alkali flats in the desert at 2,500 to 3,500 feet elevation. California from the lower Owens Valley to the Mojave Desert and the Death Valley region; southern Nevada in Esmeralda and Nye counties. (Fig. 23 *1*.)

4. *Atriplex confertifolia* (Torr. & Frem.) S. Wats. SHADSCALE; SPINY SALTBUSH. (1) Bracts of the fruits large, 8-20 mm. long, not contracted beneath the terminal wings, forming a fan-shaped or wedge-shaped structure, smooth on the backs; (2) old branches becoming spiny; (3) leaves not cordate at the bases.

Shrubs 3-8 dm. high; branches smooth, not angled, strongly woody and at length with dark gray bark; straw colored; leaves nearly circular to elliptic, ovate, or oblong, sometimes acute at the apices, 1-2 cm. long, about 1 (or sometimes 2) cm. broad, relatively thin at first but thickening at maturity, gray-scurfy especially at maturity, the bases attenuate, petioles present; bracts of the fruit thickened around the true fruit, each prolonged and broadened into a much larger triangular wing above, 8-20 mm. long and nearly as broad, resembling vegetative leaves in appearance.

Alkaline mesas and plains in the sagebrush desert, the creosote-bush desert, and the desert grassland at 2,500 to perhaps 5,000 or 6,000 feet elevation. Eastern Oregon to Montana and South Dakota and southward; California in Owens Valley and the Mojave Desert; Nevada; Utah; Arizona on the Colorado and Little Colorado river drainages in Mohave, Coconino, Apache, and Navajo counties and on the Gila River drainage in Graham County; northwestern New Mexico on the San Juan River drainage; west Texas near the Rio Grande; Chihuahua, Mexico.

Shadscale is found in nearly pure stands on alkaline soils in northern Arizona and in the Great Basin, and it is an important browse plant for range livestock. In most parts of the Southwestern deserts it is not abundant enough to be important. The plants become rigid and spiny and nearly leafless during the winter.

5. *Atriplex spinifera* Macbr. SPINY SALTBUSH. Similar to *Atriplex confertifolia* but distinguished by the following characters: (1) leaves, except the upper ones, each with a pair of divergent (hastate) lobes at the base; (2) bracts of the fruit united into cylindrical structure around the fruit, with a slight constriction just under the bases of the wings; (3) branches more nearly erect.

Alkaline plains in the grassland of the San Joaquin Valley and in the deserts at 300 to 3,000 feet elevation. California in the San Joaquin Valley and in the western Mojave Desert as far eastward as the Mojave River, near Daggett. Closely related to the shadscale.

6. *Atriplex hymenelytra* (Torr.) S. Wats. DESERT HOLLY. (1) Bracts of the fruits large, 6-11 mm. long and of equal breadth; (2) branches not forming spines; (3) leaves broadly triangular-ovate, mostly about an inch long and an inch broad,

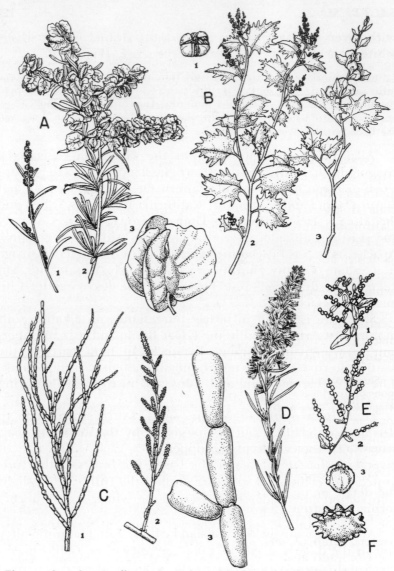

Fig. 22.—Goosefoot family: *A*, four-wing saltbush or chamiso, *Atriplex canescens*, *1*, flowering branch of staminate plant, *2*, fruiting branch of pistillate plant, *3*, fruit; *B*, desert holly, *Atriplex hymenelytra*, *1*, staminate flower, *2*, flowering branch of staminate plant, *3*, fruiting branch of pistillate plant; *C*, pickleweed or iodine bush, *Allenrolfea occidentalis*, *1*, vegetative branch, *2*, branch with spikes of the bisexual flowers, *3*, vegetative branch enlarged; *D*, winter fat, *Eurotia lanata*, fruiting branch; *E*, lens scale, *Atriplex lentiformis*, *1*, branch with staminate flowers, *2*, branch with fruits, *3*, fruit; *F*, desert saltbush, *Atriplex polycarpa*, fruit. (x ¹/₃ except *A 3* x 2 and *B 1*, *E 3*, and *F* x 4.)

with divergent, sharp lobes or teeth all around, thick, silvery white from the numerous scales of the scurf. (Fig. 22 *B*.)

Low shrubs 0.5-1 m. high; branches smooth, silvery; leaves 1.5-4.5 cm. long, and of equal or slightly greater breadth, more or less hollylike, the petioles short but well developed; bracts thickened and fan-shaped around the fruit, spreading into a very broad pair of wings above, the margins free, the backs smooth.

Gravelly washes and alluvial plains in the desert from perhaps 500 to 3,000 feet elevation. California in the Mojave and Colorado deserts; southern Nevada; southwestern Utah; Arizona in the western Mojave and the Colorado deserts; Baja California and southeastward in Mexico. (Fig. 23 *4*.)

This interesting saltbush is well known to desert travelers as desert holly. Its silvery, hollylike leaves are used for decorative purposes in the Christmas season, and sometimes they are ornamented with sparkling materials.

7. *Atriplex polycarpa* (Torr.) S. Wats. DESERT SALTBUSH; CATTLE SPINACH. (1) Bracts with fingerlike projections on the margins; (2) leaves small, only about ¼ inch long, without petioles (stalks) , often in dense clusters (fascicles) . (Fig. 22 *F*.)

Shrubs usually about 1 m. high, rounded; branches smooth, the bark soon splitting; leaves oblong but the apices acute or nearly so, about 5-7 mm. long, usually 1.5-3 mm. broad, rather thick, markedly scurfy; bracts of the fruits, or most of them, with irregular projections or crests from especially near the bases of the backs, these resembling the fingerlike lobes on the margins, silvery-scurfy with very dense scales.

Alkaline plains and occasionally rocky or gravelly slopes in the desert or in grassland at 400 to 3,000 feet elevation. California in scattered localities in the San Joaquin Valley and in the Mojave and Colorado deserts; southern Nevada; southwestern Utah; Arizona in Bill Williams River drainage and in the Colorado and Arizona deserts; Baja California and southeastward in Mexico. (Fig. 24 *1*.)

This is an abundant plant, and it is valuable as forage for livestock. In southern Arizona it occurs in pure stands or with mesquite or creosote bush through large, somewhat alkaline areas, and sometimes it grows on rocky slopes free from alkali.

2. *GRAYIA*. Hop Sage

Small shrubs similar to the saltbushes but readily distinguished by the practically complete union of the pair of bracts surrounding the fruit, these having only a pinhole opening at the summit.

Branches spiny; bark gray. Leaves alternate, entire. Staminate flowers with no bracts; sepals usually 4; stamens 4 or 5; pistillate flowers with no calyx. Fruit enclosed in a bag or sac formed from two fused bracts flattened from side to side, each bract with a wing on the back, the edges not showing the line of union.

1. *Grayia spinosa* (Hook.) Moq. spiny hop sage

Shrub 0.5-1 m. high; branches usually forming spines after the leaves fall away; leaves oblanceolate but with the apices obtuse, mostly 10-25 mm. long, 2-4 mm. broad, somewhat fleshy, scurfy at first; pistillate flowers in spikes; fruiting bracts forming a sac 6-14 mm. in diameter.

Alkaline plains and slopes in the sagebrush desert and the creosote-bush desert at 2,500 to 7,000 feet elevation. Eastern Washington to Wyoming and southward through the Great Basin; California in Owens Valley and the Mojave Desert and at scattered localities in the Salton Sea Basin of the Colorado Desert; Nevada; Utah; Arizona in western Mohave County and at Keam's Canyon in Navajo County. (Fig. 24 *3*.)

This is a valuable forage plant in the Great Basin and in the higher parts of the Mojave Desert, where it is found in abundance. It is named in honor of Asa Gray, one of the leaders in establishing systematic botany in America.

3. *EUROTIA*. Winter Fat

Shrubs resembling the hop sage and the saltbushes but readily distinguished by the numerous long white hairs growing from the bracts of the fruit and completely obscuring them. The hairs are about 3/16 inch long, and they are the conspicuous feature of the inflorescence. In old herbarium specimens, all the hairs of the plant turn reddish tan, as they do in some other groups of plants. (Fig. 22 *D*.)

Branches densely hairy with star-shaped hairs, not spiny. Leaves narrow, covered with star-shaped hairs, the margins rolled backward (revolute). Staminate flowers without bracts; sepals and stamens 4; pistillate flowers

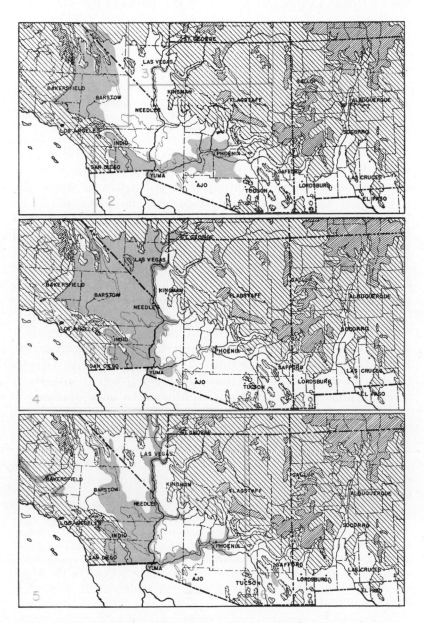

Fig. 23.—Distributional maps: *1*, Parry saltbush, *Atriplex Parryi; 2,* narrow-leaved saltbush, *Atriplex canescens* var. *linearis; 3,* Garrett saltbush, *Atriplex canescens* var. *Garrettii; 4,* desert holly, *Atriplex hymenelytra; 5,* quail brush or lens scale, *Atriplex lentiformis; 6,* Griffiths saltbush, *Atriplex lentiformis* var. *Griffithsii.*

with no sepals, each enclosed by two bracts which are united more than half their length, the apices spreading, the sac becoming angular in fruit, with 2 short apical horns.

1. *Eurotia lanata* (Pursh) Moq. WINTER FAT (Fig. 22 *D*)

Shrubs 2-8 dm. high, leaves linear or linear-lanceolate, 1.5-3 cm. long, mostly 2-3 mm. broad; sac formed by the bracts elliptic, about 5-6 mm. long, 3.5-4.5 mm. broad.

Slopes and plains in the sagebrush and creosote-bush deserts, the desert grassland, and the oak woodland at 2,500 to 7,000 feet elevation. Eastern Washington to Saskatchewan and southward to Mexico; California east of the Sierra Nevada from Lassen County to the Mojave Desert and in the upper San Joaquin Valley; Nevada; Utah; Arizona on the Colorado and Little Colorado river drainages at elevations above 4,000 feet and in the desert grassland in eastern Pima, Graham, and Cochise counties; New Mexico through the San Juan and Gila river and Rio Grande drainages; western Texas. (Fig. 24 2.)

Winter fat derives its name from its importance as a highly nutritious winter forage on sheep ranges. Throughout most of its range it is considered a valuable food for range livestock. In the Great Basin and to a limited extent in northern Arizona the species occurs in pure stands which may cover thousands of acres. In some areas it has been eliminated by close grazing.

4. *SARCOBATUS.* GREASEWOOD

(1) Fruit not enclosed by a pair of greatly enlarged bracts, subtended by a spreading winglike disc or platform which develops from the calyx; (2) leaves well developed, elongated, fleshy.

Fair-sized shrubs; branches more or less spiny after the leaves have fallen. Leaves alternate, linear, not petioled. Staminate and pistillate flowers on the same plant or different plants; staminate flowers in dense terminal spikes; sepals none; stamens 2-5, subtended by overlapping bracts specialized as stalked scales; pistillate flowers usually solitary in the upper leaf axils; calyx adherent to the ovary, saclike, developing a winglike border at fruiting time.

1a. *Sarcobatus vermiculatus* Torr. var. *vermiculatus.* GREASE-WOOD; BLACK GREASEWOOD

Shrub 1-1.5 m. high; branches numerous and dense; bark light colored, white or tannish; leaves 1-3 cm. long, 1-2 mm. broad, thickened and somewhat succulent, usually glabrous; wing of the calyx about 10-12 mm. in diameter at fruiting time.

Alkaline flats in the sagebrush and creosote-bush deserts at 2,000 to 5,000 feet elevation. From the Great Basin to Alberta, Canada, and southward to California and western Texas; California east of the Sierra Nevada from Modoc County to the Mojave Desert; Nevada; Utah; Arizona along the Little Colorado River drainage and in the Salt River Valley in Maricopa and Pinal counties; New Mexico on the San Juan River and upper Rio Grande drainages.

This is the true greasewood of the Great Basin, and it is not to be confused with the creosote bush to which the same common name sometimes is applied in southern Arizona. It forms the principal cover on many alkali flats in the Great Basin, but in our area usually it is scattered. It is browsed to some extent by livestock, but it may poison sheep if it is their only food during the spring months.

1b. *Sarcobatus vermiculatus* Torr. var. *Baileyi* (Cov.) Jepson. BAILEY GREASEWOOD

Plant smaller; branches more spiny; bark gray; leaves usually hairy, 8-14 mm. long. The plant is not known to us, and the characters are adapted from Jepson.

Gravelly and alkaline soils in the sagebrush and creosote-bush deserts. Along the western edge of the Great Basin and somewhat southward; California in Modoc and Inyo counties; southern Nevada in the western portions of Esmeralda and Nye counties.

5. *ALLENROLFEA*. PICKLEWEED

Shrubs restricted to alkali flats, readily recognized by the leafless branches with swollen, fleshy joints. Plants resembling the better-known genus of salt-marsh herbs, *Salicornia*, but readily distinguished by the woody habit and by the alternate instead of opposite branches and scale leaves. (Fig. 22 *C*.)

Branches green, manufacturing the food of the plant, the leaves reduced to mere scales. Flowers bisexual, in dense, swollen spikes, each subtended

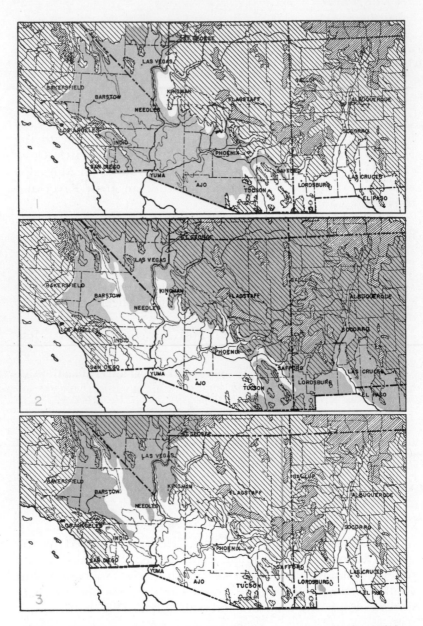

Fig. 24.—Distributional maps: *1*, desert saltbush or cattle spinach, *Atriplex polycarpa*; *2*, winter fat, *Eurotia lanata*; *3*, spiny hop sage, *Grayia spinosa*; *4*, agritos, *Berberis trifoliolata*, not showing the Arizona locality.

by a fleshy bract; sepals 4 or 5, more or less joined to one another; stamens 1-2; fruit membranous, naked.

1. *Allenrolfea occidentalis* (S. Wats.) Kuntze. PICKLEWEED; IODINE BUSH (Fig. 22 *C*)

Profusely branched shrub about 1 m. high; scale leaves scarcely more than raised ridges below the nodes, each with a broad point or angle at the apex; spikes not stalked, some very short, others 1-2 cm. long, of somewhat greater diameter than the branches; calyx rather spongy at fruiting time.

Moist alkaline flats and plains in the sagebrush and creosotebush deserts and in the desert grassland. California along the western side of the San Joaquin Valley from Contra Costa County to Kern County and eastward to flats southeast of Bakersfield, also in Death Valley region and in the Colorado Desert; Nevada; southwestern Utah; Arizona along the immediate drainages of the Little Colorado and Gila rivers; New Mexico along the Rio Grande drainage from Socorro southward and in the Tularosa Basin; western Texas; Mexico.

The plant is abundant in strongly alkaline soils with subsurface water. It tolerates more alkali than any other desert shrub, and it provides but little forage for livestock. The name iodine bush is derived from the color of the dried sap of the crushed stems.

Family 9. *BERBERIDACEAE.* BARBERRY FAMILY

Plants of the barberry family are recognized readily by their evergreen, palmate or pinnate leaves with spiny-toothed leaflets.

Shrubs or herbs. Leaves alternate, compound; stipules none. Flowers bisexual, hypogynous; sepals, petals, and stamens 6 in 2 series; petals separate; anthers opening through pores, each of which has a lid opening upward; pistil 1, formed from a single carpel. Fruit a berry, a capsule, or a dry, leathery structure. (Fig. 21 *C, D*.)

1. *BERBERIS.* BARBERRY; ALGERITA

Shrubs, the wood remarkable for its yellow color. Leaves evergreen, pinnate or else palmate with 3 leaflets, glabrous; leaflets toothed, lobed, or parted, the teeth or lobes ending in stout, exceedingly sharp spines; rachis in most species jointed. Flowers conspicuously yellow, in racemes, the sepals and petals both colored, the sepals petal-like; petals concavoconvex; filaments sensitive to the touch. Fruit a spheroidal berry, red or blue-black or blue, the blue types usually with a bluish white bloom (glaucous). (Fig. 21 *C, D.*)

KEY TO THE SPECIES

1. Leaves palmate, with 3 leaflets, these not stalked, the petiole showing no evidence of being jointed for a missing pair of leaflets. (Fig. 21 *C.*)

2. Berries blue-black; filaments toothed at the apices. (Fig. 21 *C.*)
   1. *Berberis Harrisoniana*

2. Berries red; filaments not toothed.   2. *Berberis trifoliolata*

1. Leaves pinnate, with 5 or more leaflets or with only 3 leaflets but with a joint below them at the point where the petiole joins the rachis; berries red. (Fig. 21 *D.*)   3. *Berberis Nevinii*

1. *Berberis Harrisoniana* Kearney & Peebles. KOFA MOUN-TAIN BARBERRY. (Fig. 21 *C.*) (1) Leaflets 3; (2) berries blue-black; (3) plants localized in the Kofa and Ajo mountains, Arizona.

Shrub up to 1 m. high; leaves palmate, with 3 leaflets, the petiole continuous below the leaflets; leaflets not stalked, all alike, elliptic or ovate or obovate in outline, 2.5-4 cm. long, 2-3 cm. broad, cleft or parted, with 5 strongly divergent parts, each of these ending in a stout, sharp spine, thick and leathery, relatively rigid; flowers in corymblike racemes; larger sepals and petals about 6 mm. long; filaments 2-toothed at the apices; berries spheroidal or slightly elongated, blue-black, apparently glaucous, 5-6 mm. in diameter.

Rocky desert canyons at about 2,500 feet elevation. Arizona in Palm Canyon in the Kofa Mountains, Yuma County, and in Pitahaya Canyon in the Ajo Mountains, Pima County.

This is probably a relict species, the surviving fraction of a population once more widespread. Both the known localities are in proximity to outlying stations of the widely distributed, dissimilar barberry, *Berberis Nevinii* var. *haematocarpa*.

2. *Berberis trifoliolata* Moric. AGRITOS. (1) Leaflets 3; (2) berries red; (3) southern New Mexico, western Texas, and the Rincon Mountains in eastern Pima Couny, Arizona.

Similar to *Berberis Harrisoniana;* leaflets proportionately narrower and more glaucous; filaments not toothed; berry red.

Slopes and mesas in the desert and the desert grassland. Arizona at the Colossal Cave State Park barbecue area (*L. Ben-*

son 11325, 11539) ; New Mexico in southwestern Luna County; western Texas; northwestern Mexico. The station in Arizona is one inhabited by at least two other localized colonies of species absent or rare elsewhere in the state—a grass, *Tridens eragrostoides* (*L. Benson 9174, 9801*) and the leguminous tree *Lysiloma microphylla*, described in this book. (Fig. 24 *4*.)

3a. *Berberis Nevinii* A. Gray var. *haematocarpa* (Woot.) L. Benson. RED BARBERRY; ALGERITA. (Fig. 21 *D*.) (1) Leaflets 5; (2) berries red.

Shrub 1-2 m. high; leaves pinnate, the leaflets 5, or sometimes the lower pair not developed, but the junction of the rachis and petiole evident as a joint where the leaflets might have been produced; leaflets not stalked, the terminal (greatly elongated) one appearing so but actually produced at the terminal joint of the rachis, the lateral ones usually 1.5-3 cm. long, 1-2 cm. broad, cleft into 5-9 lobes, these more or less divergent, ending in sharp spines, the leaflets thick and leathery, glaucous, not reticulate beneath or scarcely so; racemes few-flowered, the pedicels remarkably long and slender; petals 6-8 mm. long; berries red, 8-10 mm. in diameter, juicy.

Slopes and mesas in the upper desert, the desert grassland, and the oak woodland at 3,000 to 5,000 feet or rarely to 7,500 feet elevation. Arizona in the mountainous area below the Mogollon Rim from the Hualpai Mountains, Mohave County, to Greenlee and Cochise counties and from the Kofa Mountains, Yuma County, and the Ajo Mountains, Pima County, eastward; New Mexico in the mountains of the Gila River and Rio Grande drainages, occurring as far north as Albuquerque; western Texas; Mexico. (Fig. 25 *1*.)

The red barberry is common on the upper desert slopes and in the chaparral in central Arizona, where the fruits are used for jellies and preserves. The Indians of this region prepared a yellow dye from the bark and the roots.

The California plants referred to in the first edition of this work are *Berberis Nevinii*.

Berberis Fremontii Torr., FREMONT BARBERRY, occurs on "mt. slopes: e. Mohave Desert; Colorado Desert . . . ," according to Jepson. In Arizona it appears to be confined to areas in the oak woodland and chaparral just above the desert. The species is distinguished from *Berberis Nevinii* var. *haematocarpa*, as follows: terminal leaflets usually 1.5-2.5 times as long as broad (instead of 3-10 times); berries blue-black, soon becoming dry; leaves usually more reticulate beneath than in var. *haematocarpa.* Slopes and mesas in the desert grassland and the pinyon-juniper woodland at 4,000 to 7,000 feet elevation; occasional in the upper part of the desert. California in the mountains of the Mojave Desert; southern Nevada; southern Utah; southwestern Colorado; Arizona from eastern Mohave County and northern Yavapai County eastward to Apache County; northern New Mexico.

Family 10. *CAPPARIDACEAE.* Caper Family

The plants of this group are strongly and heavily scented herbs or rarely shrubs. The burro fat, which is the most common shrub in our range, is readily recognized by: (1) its long-stalked, inflated pods, the stalk being produced above the receptacle of the old flower; (2) the numerous yellow flowers, each with 6 or 9 long, protruding stamens. (Fig. 21 *A*.)

Leaves palmate or simple; stipules none. Flowers bisexual, hypogynous, in racemes or racemose clusters, the racemes often leafy; receptacle enlarged into a torus (platform or rim) in our genera; sepals 2 or 4; petals 4 or 6, yellow in our species; stamens 6 or 9 in our genera, protruding far beyond the petals. Fruit usually a many-seeded capsule, but in one genus drupe-like and 1- or 2-seeded, opening along 2 lines or rarely remaining closed.

KEY TO THE GENERA

1. Plant glabrous, not scaly; fruit a several-seeded, inflated, long-stalked capsule; stamens 6; sepals and petals 4. (Fig. 21 *A*.) 1. CLEOME

1. Plant, especially the young leaves and branches and the sepals and fruits with dense, round, fringed scales; fruit drupelike, 1-2-seeded, not splitting open; stamens 9; sepals 2, petals 6. 2. ATAMISQUEA

1. *CLEOME*

Shrubs, the parts not scaly or hairy. Leaves palmate, the leaflets 3. Receptacle forming a torus. Sepals 4, united below; petals 4; stamens 6. Fruit a several-seeded, inflated, long-stalked, slightly leathery capsule, 1-celled. (Fig. 21 *A*.)

1. *Cleome Isomeris* Greene. BURRO FAT (Fig. 21 *A*)

Rounded shrub 1-1.5 m. (about 3-5 feet) high; leaflets oblanceolate or broadest at the middles, about 1.5-3 cm. long, 4-7 mm. broad, with a short, sharp point; petals 1-1.5 cm. long; stamens about 2 cm. long; pod typically oblong, about 4-6 cm. long, 1-1.5 cm. broad, the stipe 1.5-2 cm. long. Synonym: *Isomeris arborea* Nutt. The monographic study of Mr.

Plate XIV.—Century plant and yuccas: *left*, desert agave (century plant), *Agave desertii; center*, Thornber yucca, *Yucca baccata* var. *brevifolia; right*, palmilla or soapweed, *Yucca elata*. (Photographs: *left* by R. B. Streets; *center* and *right* by William P. Martin.)

Plate XV.—Century plants: *A,* Parry agave, *Agave Parryi; B,* Palmer agave or mescal, *Agave Palmeri,* showing plants which have not flowered and two old plants in the center, one with an erect fruiting stalk and dying leaves, the other fallen over; *C,* Huachuca agave, *Agave Parryi* var. *huachucensis* in flower; *D,* Utah agave, *Agave utahensis,* in flower, showing the relatively compact and simple inflorescence. (Photographs: *A, B* by Elbert L. Little, Jr.; *C* by William P. Martin; *D* by Robert A. Darrow.)

Hugh Iltis, Missouri Botanical Garden, indicates that this species should be classified with the woody species of *Cleome*.

Dry slopes and mesas in the desert, or in the grassland, chaparral, or oak woodland at 200 to 3,000 feet elevation. California in the South Coast ranges from Monterey County southward, in coastal southern California, in the Greenhorn and Tehachapi mountains in Kern County, in the western Mojave and Colorado deserts and eastward as far as the Eagle Mountains; Baja California and Sonora, Mexico.

The fruit varies from globose-inflated to broadly linear and scarcely inflated. Globose fruit is occasional in coastal southern California, and it is the only type found in the San Joaquin Valley. Some pods are even retuse. The typical form, which is more or less ellipsoid but acute at both ends, is the common type of coastal southern California, and it occurs sparingly on the western margins of the Mojave and Colorado deserts. The form described as *Isomeris arborea* var. *angustata* is the dominant one on the deserts, and it is restricted to them. Its pods are greatly elongated and markedly flattened instead of strongly inflated. They vary from lanceolate to broadly linear. Despite the weak tendency toward geographical segregation of the forms, the pod characters apparently are not associated with any other characteristics, and therefore, according to the policy of the writer, the geographical types are not worthy of formal names.

2. *ATAMISQUEA*

Shrubs; young leaves and branches and the sepals and fruits with dense, round, fringed scales (lepidote). Leaves simple. Receptacle forming a torus. Sepals 2; petals 6, in unequal pairs; stamens 9. Fruit drupelike, somewhat fleshy; seeds 2 or, by abortion, 1.

1. *Atamisquea emarginata* Miers

Shrubs or sometimes small trees usually 2-3 m. (6-9 feet) tall; branches at first golden, later dirty gray; leaves linear to linear-oblong, 1-2.5 cm. long, 3.5-4.5 mm. broad, leathery; flowers about 7-8 mm. in diameter, in dense, leafy racemes on short new branches.

In the desert at about 1,000 to 1,500 feet elevation in our range. Arizona at Quitovaquito in the Organ Pipe Cactus

National Monument, Pima County; Baja California and east-ward in northern Mexico; Chile and Argentina.

Family 11. *PLATANACEAE*. SYCAMORE FAMILY

The sycamores are the largest trees in the deserts. The palmately lobed to cleft leaves are the largest to be encountered, and the irregularly branched, leaning, white trunks form a remarkable tree skeleton long to be remembered. The sycamores may be recognized also by the chains or series of ball-like clusters of small staminate or pistillate flowers or later of fruits. (Pl. XVI *A, B, D;* Fig. 26 *C, D.*)

Trees of great size, the trunks irregular and branching irregularly. Leaves simple, nearly circular in outline, but palmately lobed to palmately parted into 3-7 principal segments, the bases rounded or somewhat cordate; stipules large and conspicuous, united around the node into a circular platform as much as 2 cm. in diameter, protecting the bud in the leaf axil. Flowers hypogynous, unisexual, produced in dense, spherical heads borne along a usually elongated axis, the flowers of any one axis usually all of the same sex; heads of staminate flowers usually red or reddish or yellow and red; stamens few in each flower, consisting of elongated wedgelike anthers and traces of filaments; sepals scalelike; pistillate flowers green below, but the protruding styles and stigmas tending to be red or purple; pistils 1 or several per flower. Fruit a nutlet, the fruits forming dense, spheroidal heads 1-2 cm. in diameter.

1. *PLATANUS*. SYCAMORE; PLANE TREE

1a. *Platanus racemosa* Nutt. var. *racemosa*. CALIFORNIA SYCA-MORE (Fig. 26 *C*)

Trees 10-35 m. (roughly 30-110 feet) high; trunk 6-20 dm. in diameter; bark mostly smooth and white; leaves 10-25 cm. (4-10 inches) long, of about the same breadth, mostly lobed to cleft, the lobes acute or usually so, markedly and densely hairy at maturity, the leaf base rounded, truncate, or obtuse; clusters (balls) of flowers usually not stalked, lying against the main axis of the inflorescence.

Rocky or sandy soil along watercourses in grassland or in oak woodland or rarely in the desert at 100 to 4,000 feet elevation. California on the coastal side of the Sierra Nevada axis from the lower Sacramento River southward and on the desert slopes of the San Gabriel Mountains at Rock Creek and (in modified form) elsewhere along the western sides of the

Mojave and Colorado deserts; Baja California to Sinaloa, Mexico.

1b. *Platanus racemosa* Nutt. var. *Wrightii* (S. Wats.) L. Benson. ARIZONA SYCAMORE (Pl. XVI *A, B, D;* Fig. 25 *D*)

Leaves mostly cleft or parted, the lobes attenuate, the upper sides nearly glabrate and the under sides not conspicuously hairy at maturity, the leaf base usually rather deeply cordate; heads (balls) of flowers markedly stalked, the stalks up to 2-3 cm. (1 inch) long.

Common along watercourses and streams in the upper desert, the desert grassland, and the oak woodland at 1,000 or commonly 2,500 to 6,000 feet elevation. California in Andreas Canyon on the desert side of the San Jacinto Mountains and in forms tending toward typical *Platanus racemosa* at other points on the western sides of the Mojave and Colorado deserts; Arizona from the Burro Creek drainage, southeastern Mohave County, southeastward to Pima and Cochise counties; New Mexico along the Gila River drainage; northern Sonora and Chihuahua, Mexico. (Fig. 25 2.)

Family 12. *CROSSOSOMACEAE.* CROSSOSOMA FAMILY

Crossosoma is recognized with ease by its small entire, bluish leaves, its white flowers nearly an inch in diameter, and its group of 2 to 5 fruits developed from each flower. There are only two species in the family, and these are in the single genus. One occurs on the islands off the coast of southern California; the other is confined to the Southwestern deserts. (Figs. 4 *A;* 26 *A.*)

Shrubs. Leaves simple, entire, alternate; stipules none. Flowers bisexual, perigynous, terminal on new twigs of the season; sepals 5, green, turned downward; petals 5, white; stamens 15 to about 50, spirally arranged on the floral tube. Fruits 2-5 from each flower, follicles, several-seeded.

1. *CROSSOSOMA*

1. *Crossosoma Bigelovii* S. Wats. CROSSOSOMA

Shrub 0.5-2 m. (1½ to 6 feet) high; leaves oblanceolate or broadest at the middles, 10-18 mm. long, 3-9 mm. broad, each with a short apical point, glabrous; petals about 10 mm. long, stalked; stamens about 15-20; fruits mostly 3 or 4, 6-11 mm. long, 3-5 mm. broad, 2-5-seeded. (Figs. 4 *A;* 26 *A.*)

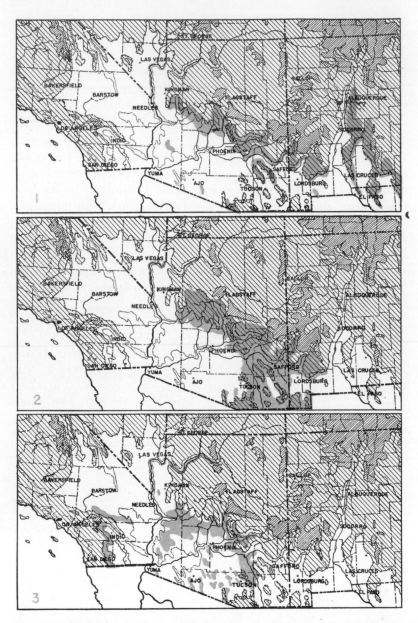

Fig. 25.—Distributional maps: *1*, red barberry, *Berberis Nevinii* var. *haematocarpa*; *2*, Arizona sycamore, *Platanus racemosa* var. *Wrightii*; *3*, crossosoma, *Crossosoma Bigelovii*.

Rocky canyon walls and cliffs in the desert and the desert grassland at 1,500 to 4,000 feet elevation. California at isolated stations in the Mojave Desert (Black Range near Death Valley; Ord Mountains; Sheep Hole Mountains; Warren's Well) and along the western edge of the Salton Sea Basin in the Colorado Desert; Arizona in the Grand Canyon region and from the Ute (Black) Mountains, Mohave County, to Yuma County and eastward in the Arizona Desert to Roosevelt Lake and the San Pedro River drainage; Mexico. (Fig. 25 *3*.) The type in the eastern part of the range is var. *glaucum* (Rydb.) Kearney & Peebles. The fruits are broader and more glaucous.

One of the earliest flowering and most attractive shrubs in the desert in Arizona.

Family 13. *ROSACEAE.* Rose Family

The rose family is one of the largest plant families, and it includes more cultivated fruits than any other. These fruits are of diverse types, among which are strawberries, blackberries, raspberries, peaches, plums, prunes, cherries, apricots, almonds, apples, pears, loquats, and quinces. The family is rich in ornamentals, including the spiraeas, roses, pyracanthas, cotoneasters, haws, flowering quinces, and the Christmas berry or "holly berry" of California. The family is not so well represented in the deserts as it is in other areas, including the mountains just above the deserts, but some of its members, including the Arizona rosewood and the desert peach, apricot, and almond, are of special interest. (Figs. 26 *B;* 28.)

The family as represented in our range is best distinguished from the other families in the desert group by the perigynous flowers, the numerous stamens, and the stipules of the leaves.

Herbs, shrubs, trees, or vines. Leaves alternate, nearly always with stipules (the best mark not only of the family but of the order Rosales, although even this character is missing from some groups). Flowers nearly always bisexual, perigynous or epigynous, regular; sepals 5; petals 5; stamens numerous, spirally arranged on the floral tube. Fruits solitary to numerous, achenes, follicles, solitary drupes, aggregated drupelets, berries, or in one case follicles united to form a 5-celled capsule.

KEY TO THE GENERA

1. Pistil formed from 5 carpels, the fruit consisting of 5 partly united follicles forming a capsule; leaves evergreen, most of them 4-10 cm.

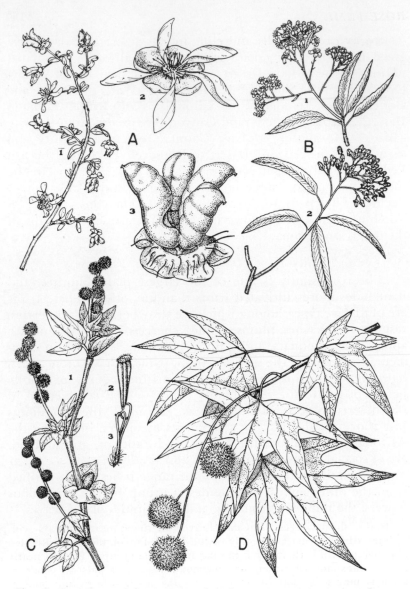

Fig. 26.—Crossosoma, Arizona rosewood, and sycamores: *A*, crossosoma *Crossosoma Bigelovii*, *1*, branch with flowers and fruits, *2*, flower (perigynous), *3*, clusters of fruits (follicles) formed from a single flower, still subtended by the floral tube, calyx, and filaments; *B*, desert rosewood, *Vauquelinia californica*, *1*, branch with flowers, *2*, branch with fruits; *C*, California sycamore, *Platanus racemosa*, *1*, branch with young leaves and stalkless balls of pistillate flowers (above) and staminate flowers (below), *2*, single stamen, showing the large anther and minute filament, *3*, pistillate flower with 3 pistils; *D*, Arizona sycamore, *Platanus racemosa* var. *Wrightii*, branch with stalked balls of fruit. (x $^1/_3$ except *A* 2, 3 x 1$^2/_3$ and *C* 2, 3 x 3$^1/_3$.)

long, linear to lanceolate, alternate; trees up to 4-8 m. high, the trunks 1-2 or 3 dm. in diameter, the plant not spiny. (Fig. 26 *B*.)

1. VAUQUELINIA

1. Pistil or pistils formed each from a single carpel, the fruit an achene or a drupe; leaves deciduous, not more than 1 cm. long or, if up to 3 cm. long, ovate or rounded; shrubs 1-2 or rarely 3 m. high or sometimes large shrubs up to 5 m.

    2. Pistils 5-10 per flower, each forming an achene with a long, feathery, silvery tail (the style). (Fig. 28 *C-E*.)   2. COWANIA

    2. Pistil 1 per flower, the fruits not with elongated, feathery, silvery tails. (Fig. 28 *A*, *B*.)

        3. Fruit an achene; petals nearly always none; sepals 4, yellow, conspicuous; leaves opposite or in fascicles above the opposite scars of the leaves of the first growing season of the branch. (Fig. 28 *B*.)   3. COLEOGYNE

        3. Fruit a drupe; petals present, white or lavender to reddish purple; sepals 5, not yellow or else not conspicuous; leaves alternate, often fascicled but above alternate scars. (Fig. 28 *A*.)

    4. PRUNUS

1. *VAUQUELINIA*

Small spineless trees 12-25 feet high. (1) Leaves long, narrow, mostly 1¾ to 4 inches long and with stout saw teeth on the margins; (2) flowers white, in dense terminal clusters; (3) fruits 5-celled. (Fig. 26 *B*.)

Leaves simple, evergreen, linear to linear-lanceolate. Flowers in dense panicles, these flat-topped to somewhat rounded, each flower about 8-9 mm. in diameter, perigynous; sepals green; petals white. Fruit consisting of 5 rather woody partly united follicles, each of which splits open rather tardily.

1. *Vauquelinia californica* (Torr.) Sarg. ARIZONA ROSEWOOD (Fig. 26 *B*)

Bark dark; leaves mostly 4-10 cm. long, mostly 9-15 mm. broad, the larger ones linear but some of the smaller ones lanceolate; petals elliptic, about 3 mm. long, 2 mm. broad; stamens about 15 or 20; fruits densely hairy, about 6 mm. long.

Hillsides and canyons in the upper desert and the lower oak woodland at 2,500 to 5,000 feet elevation. Arizona from the Sierra Estrella and the Superstition Mountains, Maricopa County, to the Ajo Mountains, Pima County, and southeastward to the Whetstone Mountains on the western edge of Cochise County; reported from the Guadalupe Mountains in the southeastern corner of Arizona; Baja California and Sonora, Mexico. (Fig. 27 2.)

2. *COWANIA*. Cliffrose

Shrubs or reported to be sometimes small trees, not spiny; leaves small, simple and entire to pinnately lobed, leathery, often glandular, the margins revolute. Flowers solitary, produced at the ends of small lateral branchlets. Floral tube enlarged gradually upward; sepals and petals 5; stamens numerous, perigynous, as are the sepals and petals. Fruits 5-10 per flower, each achene with a long, feathery, silvery tail (the style) several times as long as the body of the achene. (Fig. 28 C-E.)

KEY TO THE SPECIES

1. Plants not glandular, woolly; leaves entire or a few 3-cleft at the apices (Fig. 28 *C 3, 4*); bark ashy gray; petals about 4 mm. long; fruits with tails about 2 cm. long. (Fig. 28 *E*.)   1. *Cowania subintegra*

1. Plants usually markedly glandular on the branches, leaves, pedicels, and flowers; leaves 3-5-parted (Fig. 28 *C 1, 2*); bark reddish brown; petals about 6-9 mm. long; fruits with tails 3-5 cm. long. (Fig. 28 *D*.)
                                        2. *Cowania mexicana*

1. *Cowania subintegra* Kearney. BURRO CREEK CLIFFROSE (Fig. 28 *C, E*)

Shrubs less than 1 m. high, the base of the stem up to 3-5 cm. in diameter, but this portion ending just above the ground level; twigs more or less persistently woolly, densely so at first, with no straight, spreading hairs; bark ashy gray, the young branches not reddish brown; leaves entire or some of them 3-lobed or -cleft, not gland-dotted or sticky; pedicels, floral tubes, and calyces woolly, not glandular; sepals about 4 mm. long, 2-3 mm. broad; petals white, about 4 mm. long, 2.5 mm. broad; fruits with tails about 2 cm. long.

Gravelly slopes formed from a peculiar white rock in the upper desert at about 3,500 feet elevation. Arizona in the Aquarius Mountains about a mile and a half west of Burro Creek at its intersection with the Mohave-Yavapai county line. Known only from the original collections, *Darrow & Crooks 3* and *Darrow & Benson 10891* (type).

This is probably a relict species. Its nearest relative is *Cowania ericaefolia*, which occurs in Texas.

2a. *Cowania mexicana* Don var. *Stansburiana* (Torr.) Jep-

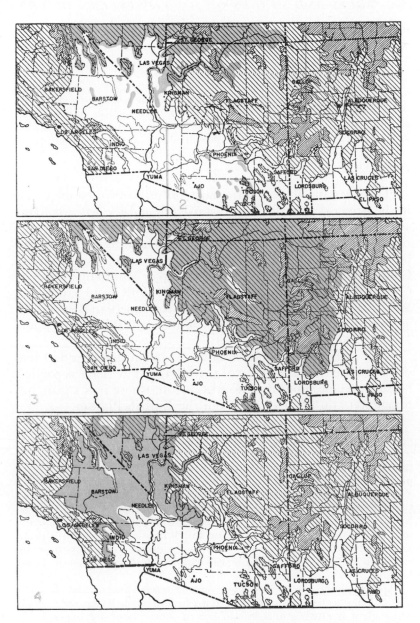

Fig. 27.—Distributional maps: *1*, blackbrush, *Coleogyne ramosissima; 2*, Arizona rosewood, *Vauquelinia californica; 3*, cliffrose, *Cowania mexicana* var. *Stansburiana; 4*, desert almond, *Prunus fasciculata.*

son. CLIFFROSE; QUININE BUSH. (1) Shrub large, scraggly, with hairy twigs; (2) leaves glandular or resinous, with 3-5 narrow lobes; (3) flowers white, ¾ inch wide, the calyx glandular. (Fig. 28 *C, D*.)

Twigs with some straight, spreading hairs, not woolly or woolly only around the leaf axils, with stalked glands; bark reddish brown; leaves all pinnately 3-5-parted into linear lobes, the margins and the upper surface with conspicuous, sticky, glandular dots; pedicels, floral tubes, and calyces with stalked glands; petals 6-9 mm. long, 4-6 mm. broad; fruits with tails 3-5 cm. long.

Hillsides and slopes particularly on soils of limestone origin in the upper desert, the desert grassland, and the oak woodland at 3,500 to 8,000 feet elevation. California in the Death Valley region and in the Clark and Providence mountains in the Mojave Desert; southern Nevada; Utah; Arizona throughout the Colorado Plateau and from the Hualpai Mountains, Mohave County, southeastward below the Mogollon Rim to Santa Cruz and Cochise counties; New Mexico on the San Juan River drainage and west of the Rio Grande; southern Colorado; northern Mexico. (Fig. 27 *3*.)

The cliffrose is an important browse plant for deer and livestock despite the bitter taste of the foliage. The plant is particularly abundant about the Grand Canyon, where it is a principal forage item on the deer ranges of the Kaibab Plateau.

Fallugia paradoxa (Don) Endl., APACHE PLUME, occurs just above the desert grassland. It may be distinguished by the presence of 5 narrow bractlets attached to the floral tube and alternating with the sepals and by the purplish color of the tails of the fruits. Rocky or gravelly slopes and alluvial plains in the upper desert, the desert grassland, and the oak woodland at 3,500 to 7,500 feet elevation; rare in the desert. California in the Old Dad, Clark, and Providence mountains in the eastern Mojave Desert; southern Nevada; Utah; southern Colorado; Arizona throughout the Colorado Plateau and in the upper portions of the Bill Williams and Gila river drainages, southward to Santa Cruz and Cochise counties; New Mexico on the San Juan and Gila river and the Rio Grande drainages; western Texas; Mexico.

Apache plume derives its name from the resemblance of the cluster of long-tailed, purplish, feathery fruits to the headdress of the Apache Indians. Although it is rated as only low to fair in forage value for livestock, the species is an important browse plant where it is abundant. It is valuable also for erosion control.

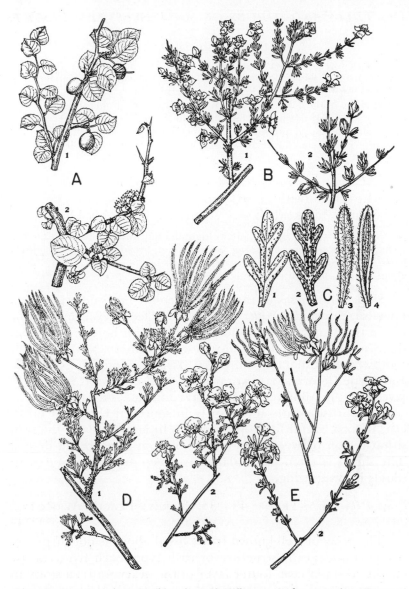

Fig. 28.—Desert apricot, blackbrush, and cliffroses: *A*, desert apricot, *Prunus Fremontii*, *1*, fruiting branch, *2*, flowering branch; *B*, blackbrush, *Coleogyne ramosissima*, *1*, flowering branch, *2*, fruiting branch; *C*, upper and lower sides of leaves; *1, 2*, cliffrose, *Cowania mexicana* var. *Stansburiana*, *3, 4*, Burro Creek cliffrose, *Cowania subintegra*; *D*, cliffrose, *1*, fruiting branch, *2*, flowering branch; *E*, Burro Creek cliffrose, *1*, fruiting branch, *2*, flowering branch. (x $^1/_3$ except *C* x $2^2/_3$.)

3. *COLEOGYNE*. Blackbrush

Shrubs. Leaves opposite, as may be seen by the branches (which are opposite) or by the fact that leaf fascicles of the current season are produced above the opposite scars of the original leaves of the first growing season of the branch, deciduous, simple, linear or linear-oblanceolate, entire, the margins rolled downward. Flowers yellow; sepals 4; petals nearly always none; stamens 20-40, produced on a special outgrowth of the receptacle, therefore perigynous. Fruit an achene (dry, 1-seeded, not splitting open). (Fig. 28 *B*.)

1. *Coleogyne ramosissima* Torr. blackbrush. A densely branched shrub with linear, opposite leaves and dark gray bark, which turns black when wet (hence the name blackbrush).

Shrub 0.5-1.5 m. (1½ to 4½ feet) high; densely and intricately branched, spiny; leaves less than 1 cm. long, about 2 mm. broad, covered with forked hairs (appearing to be simple hairs attached by the middles), gray; sepals about 7-8 mm. long, of two forms. (Fig. 28 *B*.)

Slopes and mesas in the upper creosote-bush desert and the lower sagebrush desert at 3,000 to 5,000 feet elevation. California in the Mojave Desert and on the western border of the Salton Sea Basin of the Colorado Desert; southern Nevada; Utah; southwestern Colorado; northern Arizona along the Colorado and Little Colorado river drainages and southward in the Mojave Desert in Mohave and Yavapai counties. (Fig. 27 *1*.)

Blackbrush occurs abundantly in southern Utah and northern Arizona, and it forms pure stands in large areas in the transition region between the creosote-bush and sagebrush deserts. The shrub is eaten particularly by sheep and goats and withstands heavy grazing.

4. *PRUNUS*. Prune; Plum; Cherry; Peach; Apricot; Almond

The array of well-known fruits listed above is not surprising if one considers the structure of each type. Each fruit consists of a fleshy outer coat (outer layer of the ovary wall), a stony inner coat or "pit" (inner layer of the ovary wall), and a nearly always solitary seed. In all but the almond, the fleshy layer is edible, but in the almond it is the seed which is eaten, and the fleshy outer layer is a mere husk which dries up and separates from the pit. (Fig. 27 *A*.)

Trees or shrubs, the bark remaining smooth for many years; our species spiny. Leaves deciduous, simple, mostly lanceolate to ovate or obovate, sometimes nearly circular, finely saw-toothed. Flowers white to red or purple, clustered or solitary on short spur branches, sometimes developed before the leaves, perigynous. Fruit a drupe—that is, as described above.

KEY TO THE SPECIES

1. Flowers pediceled, 10-22 mm. in diameter, all bisexual; leaves glabrous.

    2. Petals white; calyx and floral tube apparently green or greenish yellow; leaves ovate, cordate-ovate, or nearly circular, the larger ones 15-20 mm. broad. (Fig. 28 *A*.)   1. *Prunus Fremontii*

    2. Petals red or pink; calyx and floral tube red; leaves oblanceolate or a few lanceolate, 4-7 mm. broad.   *Prunus Andersonii*

1. Flowers practically without pedicels, 5-8 mm. in diameter, tending to be unisexual with the staminate and pistillate flowers on different plants; leaves hairy on both sides, oblanceolate. 2. *Prunus fasciculata*

1. *Prunus Fremontii* S. Wats. DESERT APRICOT. (1) Flowers white, with stalks; (2) leaves broad, ovate, cordate-ovate, or nearly circular, resembling (on a small scale) the leaves of the cultivated apricot. (Fig. 28 *A*.)

Shrub or rarely a small tree, 1-3 or 5 m. high; leaves ovate, cordate-ovate, or nearly circular, the larger ones 1.5-3.2 cm. long, 1.5-2 cm. broad, crenulate-serrulate, glabrous, green on both sides, the veins reddish; flowers mostly solitary, sometimes 2 or 3 together, 10-13 mm. in diameter; floral tube and calyx apparently greenish yellow; petals white, about 5 mm. long; fruits obliquely ovoid or elliptic-ovoid 10-13 mm. long.

Rocky canyon slopes and mesas in the desert at 1,000 to 1,500 feet elevation. California on the mountain slopes of the western edge of the Salton Sea Basin of the Colorado Desert; Baja California, Mexico.

Prunus Fremontii S. Wats. var. *pilulata* Jepson is characterized by Jepson as follows: "Leaf blades orbicular, more or less truncatish or subcordate at base, 5 to 8 lines long; fruit (immature) subglobose, a little flattened, a little broader than long, 4 lines long." It occurs on the west side of the Colorado Desert in California in Sentenac Valley and at Mountain Springs. The plant is not known to the writers.

Prunus Andersonii A. Gray. DESERT PEACH. (1) Flowers red or pink, with stalks (pedicels); (2) leaves narrow, glabrous. Shrub 1-2 m. high; leaves oblanceolate or a few lanceolate, the larger ones 15-20 mm. long, 4-7 mm.

broad, glabrous, minutely saw-toothed, rather bluish, the veins red; flowers bisexual, either solitary or clustered, 12-22 mm. in diameter; floral tube and the sepals red; petals red or pink, narrowly obovate, stalked, 7-10 mm. long, 3-5 mm. broad; fruits flattened-obovoid to -ovoid, 12-14 mm. long, covered with dark brown hair. Hillsides and slopes in the creosote-bush and sage-brush deserts and in the pinyon-juniper woodland at 3,500 or commonly 5,000 to 7,000 feet elevation. California along the eastern slope of the Sierra Nevada from Modoc and Lassen counties to Walker Pass, Kern County, and in South Fork Valley below Walker Pass as far westward as Onyx; along the western edge of Nevada. The only occurrence in the creosote-bush desert is in South Fork Valley, and here the plant is associated with the Joshua tree rather than with the creosote bush, which is at lower levels.

2. *Prunus fasciculata* A. Gray. DESERT ALMOND. (1) Flowers white, practically lacking stalks, not more than $1/3$ inch in diameter, in the other species at least $2/5$ inch in diameter; (2) leaves narrow, finely hairy on both sides.

Intricately branched shrub 1-2 or sometimes 3 m. high; leaves oblance-olate, mostly 9-18 mm. long, 2-3 or 4 mm. broad, with a few saw teeth, green above and below; flowers tending to be unisexual with the staminate and pistillate flowers on different plants; floral tube and the calyx yellow-ish; petals white, about 2-3 mm. long; fruits ovoid-acute, with a dense velvety coat of light brown hairs, 8-10 mm. long.

Hillsides and mesas in the creosote-bush and sagebrush deserts and in the oak woodland and pinyon-juniper woodland at 2,500 to 6,500 feet elevation; below 4,500 feet in Arizona. California in the Mojave Desert and along the western edge of the Salton Sea Basin of the Colorado Desert, as well as in the mountains of San Luis Obispo and Santa Barbara counties; Nevada in southern Nye County and in Clark and Lincoln counties; southwestern Utah; Arizona in the Grand Canyon region and in the Mojave Desert southeastward through south-western Yavapai County to Wickenburg, Maricopa County. (Fig. 27 *4*.)

Family 14. *LEGUMINOSAE*. PEA FAMILY

The pea family (about 13,000 species) is the second largest of the three hundred families of flowering plants, exceeded in num-ber of species by only the sunflower family (20,000 species) . The orchid family includes about 10,000. In the Southwestern deserts each of three plant families comprises roughly 10 to 15 per cent of the flora. These are the grass family, the sunflower family, and the legume or pea family. The leguminous trees and shrubs are the most outstanding element of all. They are not bizarre in appearance as are the yuccas and century plants, but they form the backbone of the desert vegetation, as may be seen from the following list of a few of the better-known members of the family: cat claw and other acacias, fairy duster, mesquites, screw bean, mimosas, palo verdes, cassias or sennas, smoke tree, ironwood, coral bean. Many of the species are of use to man, and many provide food for range livestock or for wild mammals and birds. Removal of this group of plants from the desert would, as one man put it, cause a "terrific stink of dead animals." Economically, the pea family is one of the three or four most useful, not only in the deserts but throughout the world. (Figs. 29 to 32.)

Recognition of the pea family is relatively easy, since the well-known pea pod is the oustanding character of the family, and it occurs in nearly all the members. This pod type (legume) may be distinguished from other similar-appearing fruits by the presence of only one double row of seeds and by the fact that the pod splits open along both edges instead of along only one; as, for example, in *Delphinium* (larkspur) or in *Crossosoma* (Fig. 26 *A*). Such a pod is called a legume, and the name of the family is derived from this structure. Oddly enough, however, the pods of a few leguminous plants are not strictly legumes. The "beans" of mesquites, screw beans, and peanuts do not split open, and in *Krameria* the fruit is a 1-seeded, spiny bur which remains closed (indehiscent).

Trees, shrubs, herbs, or twining vines; leaves usually pinnate or bipinnate or more finely dissected, rarely simple or palmate; stipules almost always present; flowers hypogynous or sometimes perigynous in the Caesalpinoideae; corolla regular or irregular; petals 5, separate or rarely united; stamens 10 or rarely fewer; pistil 1, formed from a single specialized leaf (carpel), with a single double row of seeds (or ovules) along one margin, splitting open along both margins, or rarely indehiscent.

The *Leguminosae* are made up of four groups of related genera, which may be distinguished by the following list or by the key below it:

1. ACACIA SUBFAMILY. Flowers regular, very small, crowded into dense spikes or heads; corolla inconspicuous, the stamens the obvious part of the flowers; leaves bipinnate. (Figs. 29 *B*; 30 to 37; Pls. XVIII *lower right*; XIX *A*; XX *B*.) Technical name, Mimosoideae.

2. BIRD-OF-PARADISE SUBFAMILY. Flowers slightly irregular (strongly irregular in the redbud, or Judas tree, which is recognized by its simple leaves 1-2½ inches in diameter), large, usually not crowded; stamens (except in the bird-of-paradise) much less conspicuous than the yellow corolla, never more conspicuous; banner (upper petal) not usually strongly differentiated from the others except sometimes in color; folded inside the two adjacent petals in the bud; the petals separate from one another, none of them united to form a keel; leaves pinnate or bipinnate. (Figs. 29 *C*; 38 to 40; 42; 43 *D*; Pls. XVII; XVIII *lower left*; XIX *C*; XX *A*.) Technical name, Caesalpinoideae.

3. RATANY SUBFAMILY. Pod a 1-seeded, spiny bur which does not split open; leaves simple and narrow, stipules none; flower strongly irregular; sepals more conspicuous than the petals or stamens. (Figs. 29 *D;* 43 *A-C*.) Technical name, Kramerioideae.

4. BEAN SUBFAMILY. Flowers strongly irregular; corolla the conspicuous part of the flower, differentiated (as for example in a sweet pea flower) into a banner (upper petal), 2 wings (lateral petals), and a keel formed from fusion of the two lower petals and enclosing the stamens and the pistil; banner enclosing the wings in the bud. (However, in *Eysenhardtia* the corolla is white and practically regular. The plant may be recognized by the brown or tan sunken glands dotting the leaves, stems, and flowers.) (Figs. 29 *A*; 45; 47; Pls. XVIII *upper figs.*; XIX *B*.) Technical name, Papilionoideae.

KEY TO THE SUBFAMILIES

1. Corolla regular or slightly irregular, not papilionaceous (butterflylike or actually sweet pealike); that is, the 5 petals not differentiated into a banner, 2 wings, and a keel formed from two petals united by their adjacent margins and enclosing the stamens and the pistil. (Fig. 29 *B-D*.)

   2. Fruit a legume, nearly always splitting open, usually several seeded; leaves pinnate or bipinnate, with stipules; calyx smaller than the corolla, regular or practically so; stamens 10 or rarely 7.

      3. Flowers crowded into dense spikes or heads; corolla regular, inconspicuous, less than 5 mm. long; stamens the conspicuous part of the flower, exceeding the petals in length but not more than 7 mm. long. (Figs. 29 *B*; 30 to 37; Pls. XVIII *lower right*; XX *B*.) Subfamily 1. MIMOSOIDEAE

      3. Flowers not crowded into very dense spikes or heads, usually 1 cm. or more in diameter or length; corolla slightly irregular (strongly irregular in *Cercis*, which is recognized by simple,

Plate XVI.—Sycamore and cottonwood: *A, B, D,* Arizona sycamore, *Platanus racemosa* var. *Wrightii, C, E,* Fremont cottonwood, *Populus Fremontii.* (Photographs: *A-D* by Robert A. Darrow; *E* by R. B. Streets.)

Plate XVII.—Palo verdes in flower: *above*, blue palo verde, *Cercidium floridum*, along a wash; *below*, foothill palo verde, *Cercidium microphyllum*, on a hillside. (Photographs: *above* by Walter S. Phillips; *below* by Robert A. Darrow.)

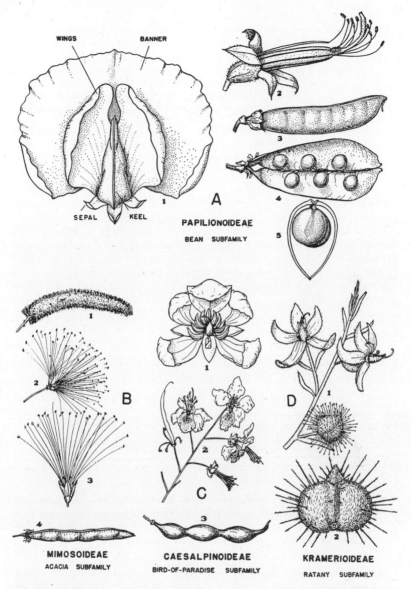

WINGS   BANNER

SEPAL   KEEL

A

PAPILIONOIDEAE

BEAN SUBFAMILY

B

D

C

MIMOSOIDEAE

ACACIA SUBFAMILY

CAESALPINOIDEAE

BIRD-OF-PARADISE SUBFAMILY

KRAMERIOIDEAE

RATANY SUBFAMILY

Fig. 29.—Subfamilies of the pea family: *A*, bean subfamily, *Papilionoideae*, *1*, end view of flower, *2*, side view of flower with petals removed, *3*, fruit, *4*, fruit open along the back, *5*, cross section of pod; *B*, acacia subfamily, *Mimosoideae*, *1*, typical dense flower cluster, *2*, flower cluster of fairy duster, *3*, flower of fairy duster, *4*, pod; *C*, bird-of-paradise subfamily, *Caesalpinoideae*, *1*, flower, *2*, inflorescence, *3*, pod; *D*, ratany subfamily, *Kramerioideae*, *1*, branch with flowers, fruit, and characteristic simple leaves, *2*, burlike fruit. (*A, D* 2 x 1$^1/_3$; *B* *1* x $^1/_3$; others x $^2/_3$.)

cordate-reniform leaves), with a banner somewhat differentiated from the other petals and folded inside the two adjacent petals in the bud; corolla the conspicuous part of the flower, the stamens rarely several cm. long and equally conspicuous (bird-of-paradise), but not distinctly more conspicuous. (Figs. 29 *C*; 38 to 40; 42; 43 *D*; Pls. XVII; XVIII *lower left*; XIX *C*; XX *A*.)
Subfamily 2. CAESALPINOIDEAE

2. Fruit not a legume, indehiscent, spiny, 1-seeded (with 2 ovules at flowering time); leaves simple, linear, without stipules; calyx much larger than the corolla, irregular, reddish purple; corolla irregular, very small; stamens 4, restricted to the upper side of the flower. (Figs. 29 *D*; 43 *A-C*.)
Subfamily 3. KRAMERIOIDEAE

1. Corolla strongly irregular, papilionaceous (butterflylike or actually sweet pealike); that is, the 5 petals differentiated into a banner, 2 wings, and a keel formed from 2 petals united by their adjacent margins and enclosing the stamens and the pistil (Fig. 29 *A*). (However, in *Eysenhardtia* [Fig. 45 *A* 2] the flowers are white and practically regular. The plant may be recognized by the many tan or brown sunken glands on the leaves, stems, and flowers.) (Figs. 29 *A*; 45; 47; Pls. XVIII *upper figs.*; XIX *B*.)
Subfamily 4. PAPILIONOIDEAE

Subfamily 1. *MIMOSOIDEAE*. ACACIA SUBFAMILY

(1) Small flowers in dense heads or spikes; (2) filaments of the stamens the conspicuous feature of the flowers. (Figs. 29 *B*; 30 to 37; Pls. XVIII *lower right*; XIX *A*; XX *B*.)

Trees or mostly shrubs, rarely herbs. Leaves bipinnate, Calyx bell- or top-shaped, the sepals united. Petals separate or united. Pods linear to oblong or oblanceolate, splitting open except in *Prosopis*. Seeds several.

KEY TO THE GENERA

1. Stamens 20 or more, the anthers minute, 0.2 mm. square. (Figs. 29 *B 2, 3*; 30 *A 1*, *C 1*; 34 *D 2*.)

2. Stamens separate; pods not with heavy, cordlike margins much thicker than the rest of the pod (but with a tendency in that direction in *Acacia constricta*, which has bright yellow flowers in heads); spines or prickles present, except in *Acacia angustissima*. (Figs. 30; 32 *A, B*; 37 *lower right*.)   1. ACACIA

2. Stamens united at the bases; pods with heavy, cordlike margins much thicker than the rest of the pod; spines or prickles not present.

3. Stipules green and leaflike (Fig. 32 *C 1*), falling after the leaves are mature; pods 1-2 dm. long, 1-2 cm. broad; secondary leaflets in 25-33 pairs; large shrubs or sometimes small trees 1-2 m. high (in Arizona). (Fig. 32 *C*.)   2. LYSILOMA

3. Stipules brown and scalelike; pods 3-7 cm. long, 4-6 mm. broad; secondary leaflets in 4-13 or 17 pairs; small shrubs up to 1.5 mm. high or practically herbaceous plants. (Figs. 29 *B* *2-4*; 34 *D*; Pl. XIX *A*.)   3. CALLIANDRA

1. Stamens 10 or fewer, the anthers oblong, 0.4 mm. long or longer. (Figs. 36 *D*; 27 *C 1*.)

2. Pods separating into 1-seeded fragments, leaving the margins as a separate, persistent skeleton (Fig. 34 *B* 2); spines none, broad-based prickles present; petals not each with an apical hairy spot on the inner side; primary leaflets in 3 or more pairs except rarely in a few leaves; anthers not with stalked glands; flowers in heads or sometimes in spikes, lavender to purple or white; shrubs not more than 2 m. high. (Fig. 34 *A-C*.)   4. MIMOSA

2. Pods not splitting open or shedding the seeds, with fleshy partitions between the seeds; spines present, produced in pairs at the nodes, nearly cylindrical; each petal hairy at a spot just below the apex on the inner side; primary leaflets in 1-2 pairs; anther with a stalked gland at the apex, but this often falling away in dried specimens; flowers in elongated spikes, creamy yellow; large shrubs or trees 2-10 m. high. (Figs. 36; 37; Pl. XX *B*.)   5. PROSOPIS

1. *ACACIA*. ACACIA

The acacias are well known in cultivation, since many species, especially those native in Australia, are grown in the Southwest as shade or ornamental trees. (1) Stamens more than 10 (usually 20-100) in each of the minute flowers in the dense spike or buttonlike head; (2) stamens separate. (Figs. 30; 32 *A*, *B*; Pl. XVIII *lower right*.)

Trees or shrubs. Spines or prickles present, except in *Acacia angustissima;* spines, when present, developed from stipules and occurring in pairs at the nodes; prickles, when present, arranged irregularly. Primary leaflets in 1 or 2 or commonly in 3-many pairs; secondary leaflets commonly numerous, sometimes in as few as 5 or 6 pairs. Corolla of separate or united petals; anthers minute, 0.2 mm. square. Pod flat or turgid, linear, splitting open along the not particularly prominent margins.

KEY TO THE SPECIES

1. Flowers in cylindrical spikes (Figs. 30 *C* 2; 32 *B* 2; Pl. XVIII *lower right*) or in heads with a tendency to be racemose; filaments of the stamens white or tinged with pink or lavender or else creamy yellow, not a bright, nearly golden yellow; stems not with a pair of stout, rigid spines at each node, either with a pair of weak, more or less

flexible spines at each node (Fig. 32 *B*) or with prickles irregularly disposed on the stem (Fig. 30 *C 2*) or none; petals separate.

2. Flowers in cylindrical spikes 2-4 cm. long and 10-12 mm. in diameter (Figs. 30 *C 2*; 32 *B 2*); stems with a pair of weak spines at each node or with prickles disposed irregularly; pods 9-19 mm. broad (Figs. 30 *C 3*; 32 *B 1*); seeds broader than long.

   3. Prickles disposed irregularly on the stem, similar to rose prickles or to a cat's claws, broad at the bases and curved above, about 3-5 mm. long (Fig. 30 *C 2*); spines none; flowers creamy yellow; pods mostly 6-13 cm. long, 10-19 mm. broad, often constricted between the seeds; primary leaflets in 2-3 pairs (Fig. 30 *C 2*); secondary leaflets in 4-6 pairs, each leaflet oblong-obovate, 3.5-7 mm. long, 1-3.5 mm. broad. (Fig. 30 *C*; Pl. XVIII *lower right*.)
                                          1. *Acacia Greggii*

   3. Prickles none, the stipules forming two slender, weak spines at each node of the stem; flowers white; pods 5-8.5 cm. long, 9-12 mm. broad, not constricted between the seeds; primary leaflets in usually 5-10 pairs; secondary leaflets in about 20-30 pairs, each oblong but with an acute tip, about 2-3 mm. long, approximately 1 mm. broad. (Fig. 32 *B*.)   2. *Acacia millefolia*

2. Flowers in heads with a tendency to be racemose; stems with neither spines nor prickles; pods 7-9 or 10 mm. broad, not constricted between the seeds; seeds markedly longer than broad. (Fig. 32 *A*.)
                                     3. *Acacia angustissima*

1. Flowers in nearly hemispherical heads (Fig. 30 *A 3*); filaments of the stamens a bright nearly golden yellow; stems with a pair of stout, rigid spines at each node (Fig. 30 *A 3*); petals united (Fig. 30 *A 1*); seeds longer than broad.

   2. Pod flattened, constricted between the seeds (Fig. 30 *A 2*), not woody, splitting promptly, the seeds in one row; common. (Fig. 30 *A*.)   4. *Acacia constricta*

   2. Pod nearly cylindroidal, not constricted, woody, splitting tardily, the seeds in 2 rows; rare in California and Arizona. (Fig. 30 *B*.)
                                   5. *Acacia Farnesiana*

1. *Acacia Greggii* A. Gray. CAT CLAW. (1) Prickles, similar to the claws of a cat, scattered irregularly along the branches; (2) pale yellow flowers in dense, cylindroidal spikes 1½ to 2 inches long and ½ inch in diameter; (3) pods ribbonlike, somewhat twisted, usually 2½ to 5 inches long and ½ inch broad. (Fig. 30 *C*; Pl. XVIII *lower right*.)

Large shrubs or small trees up to 7 m. high; prickles dark brown or gray, broad-based, curved, 3-5 mm. long; primary leaflets in 2-3 pairs;

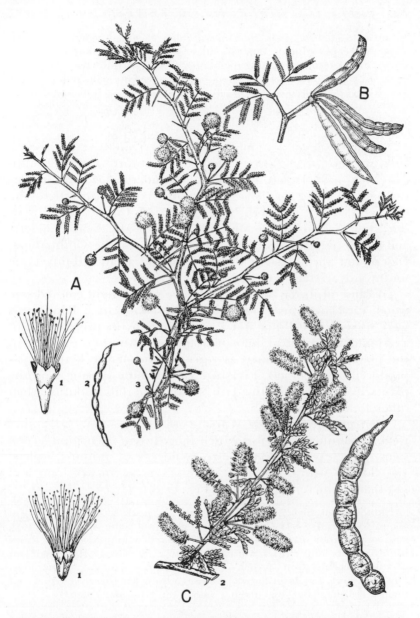

Fig. 30—Thorny acacias: *A*, white thorn, *Acacia constricta*, *1*, flower, *2*, fruit, *3*, flowering branch showing the pairs of spines at the nodes; *B*, huisache, *Acacia Farnesiana*, fruiting branch; *C*, cat claw, *Acacia Greggii*, *1*, flower, *2*, flowering branch showing the prickles irregularly arranged along the stem, *3*, fruit or pod. (x $^1/_3$, except separate flowers x $5^1/_3$.)

secondary leaflets in 4-6 pairs, cuneate-oblong, 4-7 mm. long, 1.5-3 mm. broad, glabrous; stipules thin, scalelike, falling away while the leaf is young; calyx green, 2 mm. long; petals green, with narrow, creamy margins, separate, 3 mm. long; stamens about 50, the filaments pale yellow, about 6 mm. long; pods often constricted between the seeds; seeds dark, biconvex, nearly circular but a little broader than long, about 7-8 mm. long, 8-10 mm. broad.

Along washes and on mesas in the desert and desert grassland from sea level to 5,000 feet elevation. California in the southeastern Mojave Desert from Daggett and the Ord Mountains eastward to the Providence Mountains and southward to the Colorado Desert; southern Nevada in Clark County; southwestern Utah; Arizona in the Mojave, Colorado, and Arizona deserts and in the desert grassland; New Mexico in the Chihuahuan Desert and the adjacent desert grassland from Albuquerque southward; western Texas; Mexico. (Fig. 31 *1*.)

Because of its dark-colored heartwood and light-colored sapwood, cat claw is used for trinkets and souvenirs. Ripe seeds were used by the Pima and Papago Indians in preparation of a ground starch meal known as pinole. Another product of the plant, cat claw honey, is rated as one of the better types produced in the desert. Livestock browse only sparingly on the plants except during the late spring and fall months when other forage is sparse.

2. *Acacia millefolia* S. Wats. SANTA RITA ACACIA. (1) Spines weak, insignificant, 1/8 to 1/4 inch long, two at each joint of the stem; (2) leaves dissected into hundreds of minute leaflets; (3) flowers white, crowded in spikes 1-1½ inches long and less than ½ inch in diameter. (Fig. 32 *B*.)

Shrubs 1-3 m. high; primary leaflets in 5-10 pairs; secondary leaflets in about 20-30 pairs, each leaflet oblong with an acute tip, about 2-3.5 mm. long, approximately 1 mm. broad, with a few appressed hairs; calyx white, 1 mm. long; petals white, separate, 2 mm. long; stamens about 50, the filaments white, 5 mm. long; pod linear-oblong, 7-9 cm. long, 9-13 mm. broad, glabrous; seeds reddish brown, flat, nearly circular but slightly broader than long, about 7 mm. long, 8-10 mm. broad.

Rocky canyon slopes and ridges in the upper desert grassland and the lower oak woodland between 4,000 and 5,500 feet elevation. Arizona in the Rincon, Santa Rita, Empire, Whetstone, and Mustang mountains, Pima County, and in the hills east of Douglas, Cochise County. Occurring most commonly on limestone ridges.

The finely divided bright green foliage and the white flower clusters make the plant desirable for ornamental plantings.

3a. *Acacia angustissima* (Mill.) Kuntze var. *hirta* (Nutt.) Rob. FERN ACACIA. (1) Spines or prickles absent; (2) flowers white, tinged with pink or lavender, in compact heads about ½ inch in diameter. (Fig. 32 *A*.)

Low shrubs or bushes or sometimes scarcely woody, the plant usually less than 1 m. high; twigs deeply grooved, often hispid or hirsute (with long hairs); primary leaflets in usually 6-14 pairs, acute at the apices; secondary leaflets in 20-33 pairs; each leaflet linear-oblong, 3-6 mm. long, usually 1 mm. or less broad, with a few appressed hairs along the margins; stipules scalelike, brown, 2-3 mm. long, ciliate; flower "heads" actually with a tendency to be racemose, produced in the leaf axils or sometimes in terminal racemes or panicles; calyx green, 0.7 mm. long; petals green, separate, 2.5 mm. long; stamens 100 or more, the filaments white or tinged with pink or lavender, 6-8 mm. long; pod brown, linear-oblong, 4-7.5 cm. long, 7-9 or 10 cm. broad, glabrous; seeds mottled, gray with brown, dark brown, or black, oblong, 3.5-4 mm. long, 2.5-3 mm. broad, thick.

Hillsides, mesas, and canyon slopes in the upper desert, the desert grassland, and the oak woodland at 3,000 to 6,000 feet elevation. Arizona from the Verde River drainage near Camp Verde, Yavapai County, southward along the Salt and Gila river drainages to Gila and Greenlee counties and to Cochise County, westward to Pima County; New Mexico in southern Hildalgo County; eastward to Texas, Missouri, and northern Florida; Mexico. (Fig. 33 *1*.) Some of the types occurring at higher levels, especially in the Huachuca Mountains, Arizona, are not evaluated here.

3b. *Acacia angustissima* (Mill) Kuntze var. *cuspidata* (Schlecht.) L. Benson

Primary leaflets in 2-5 pairs; secondary leaflets in 9-18 pairs, obtuse at the apices.

Arizona at Blue River in the White Mountains, near Tucson, and in the Chiricahua Mountains; occasional in southern New Mexico and in western Texas; Mexico.

4a. *Acacia constricta* Benth. var. *constricta* WHITE THORN. (1) Spines in pairs at the nodes of the stems (stipular), usually white, on some stems and particularly on rapidly grown shoots the spines as much as 1-1½ inches long and ⅛ inch in diameter, on other parts of the plant only ⅛ to ½ inch long, entirely absent on some plants; (2) flowers almost golden yellow, in "buttons" or heads about ²/₅ inch in diameter; (3) pods elongate, flattened, constricted between the seeds, 2½ to 5 inches long, about ³/₁₆ inch broad. (Fig. 30 *A*.)

Spreading shrubs commonly 0.5-2 or sometimes 3 m. high; lower branches spreading near ground level, the outline of the plant hemispheroidal; primary leaflets in commonly 3-7 pairs; secondary leaflets in about 6-16 pairs, each leaflet oblong, 1.5-2 mm. long, 0.7 mm. broad, with a few hairs on the margins; calyx yellow, 1-1.5 mm. long; petals yellow, united into a tube, 2-2.5 mm. long; stamens 30-40, the filaments golden yellow, about 4 mm. long, the anthers yellow; pods light reddish brown, glabrous; seeds mottled, black and gray, smooth, oblong, about 5 mm. long, 2 mm. broad.

Common along washes and on slopes and mesas in the desert and the desert grassland at 2,000 to 4,500 or rarely 6,250 feet elevation. Arizona in the Arizona Desert and in the adjacent desert grassland; New Mexico along the Gila River drainage in the Chihuahuan Desert and from Socorro County southward; western and southern Texas; Mexico. (Fig. 31 2.)

As a forage plant, white thorn has negligible value, due partly at least to its spiny character and the sparsity of the foliage. The pods are browsed by livestock, and during the late spring drought periods cattle and jack rabbits may make some use of the young twigs. According to Professor Thornber, the plant is sometimes poisonous to livestock in the late autumn. The Papago Indians used the seeds of white thorn and those of other desert legumes as a constituent of the starchy ground meal known as pinole. White thorn flowers make a definite contribution to the annual production of desert honey.

4b. *Acacia constricta* Benth. var. *vernicosa* (Standl.) L. Benson

Whole plant, including the twigs, leaves, and pods, glandular and sticky; primary leaflets in 1 or 2 pairs; secondary leaflets in 6-10 pairs, dark colored from the secretion of the dotlike glands on the surface, glabrous; (as pointed out by Wiggins) calyx irregularly parted.

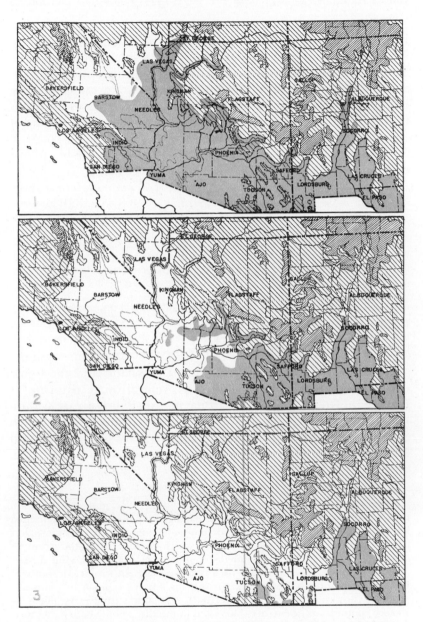

Fig. 31.—Distributional maps: *1*, cat claw, *Acacia Greggii*; *2*, white thorn, *Acacia constricta*; *3*, huisache, *Acacia Farnesiana*; *4*, *Acacia constricta* var. *vernicosa*.

Rocky hills and mesas, particularly those of limestone origin; in the upper desert and the desert grassland at 3,500 to 5,000 feet elevation. Arizona from near Vail, Pima County, to the San Pedro and Sulphur Spring valleys, Cochise County; eastward through northern Mexico to western Texas. Characteristically a plant of the Chihuahuan Desert reaching its northern limit on favorable limestone soils in the southeastern corner of Arizona and along the San Pedro River. (Fig. 31 *4.*)

5. *Acacia Farnesiana* (L.) Willd. HUISACHE. The plants closely resemble those of white thorn in leaf, twig, and flower characters. (1) Plant much larger than *Acacia constricta,* a large shrub or small tree; (2) pods are nearly cylindroidal, woody, 2-2½ inches long, and about ¼ to ⅜ inch in diameter. (Fig. 30 *B.*)

Shrubs or sometimes small trees occasionally 10 m. high; spines 3-6 or 12 mm. long, stipular, paired at the nodes; primary leaflets in usually 3-6 pairs; secondary leaflets in about 10-20 pairs, each leaflet linear-oblong, 3-6 mm. long, about 1 mm. broad, with some mostly marginal hairs; flowers in dense heads about 1 cm. in diameter; calyx about 1 mm. long; petals united almost their whole length, 2 mm. long; stamens about 20; the filaments bright yellow, about 4 mm. long; pods dark brown or with some purple pigment, splitting open only tardily.

Hillsides and canyons of the desert grassland and the lower oak woodland at 3,500 to 5,000 feet elevation. California at Otay, San Diego County; Arizona in the Baboquivari Mountains, Pima County, and at Sycamore (Bear) Canyon near Ruby, Santa Cruz County; common in southern Texas; common in Mexico and the New World tropics; southward to Chile. (Fig. 31 *3.*)

The following is quoted from Standley:

The wood is used for many purposes. The bark and fruit contain tannin and are used for tanning and dyeing, and the bark is often used for making ink. The viscous juice of the pods is employed in some places for mending broken china. The gum which exudes from the trunk is employed locally in making mucilage; it is very similar to gum arabic. The leaves are of value as forage for stock, especially in winter. In southern Europe the plant is cultivated extensively for flowers (known in commerce as cassie flowers), from which perfume is manufactured. As much as 100,000 pounds of them are harvested annually about Grasse, France. In tropical America the flowers are often laid among linen to impart their perfume to it.

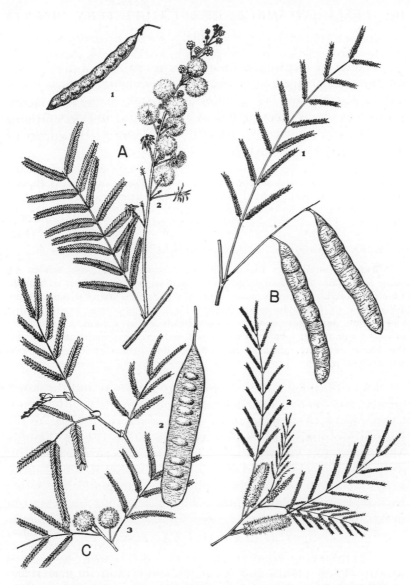

Fig. 32.—Thornless acacias and lysiloma: *A*, fern acacia, *Acacia angustissima*
var. *hirta*, *1*, pod, *2*, branch with heads of (white, pink, or lavender) flowers;
B, Santa Rita acacia, *Acacia millefolia*, *1*, fruiting branch, *2*, branch with spikes
of (white) flowers; *C*, lysiloma, *Lysiloma microphylla*, *1*, leafy branch showing
the large, green stipules (represented by scales or spines in *Acacia*) , *2*, pod,
3, branch with heads of (white or cream) flowers. (x $^1/_8$.)

2. *LYSILOMA*. Lysiloma

A genus of shrubs and small trees resembling *Acacia* in appearance and in having more than 10 stamens in each of the flowers of the head. (1) Stipules green, leaflike, present on the young leaves; (2) pods 4-8 inches long, $^2/_5$ to 1 inch broad, with cordlike ridges along the margins; (3) bases of the filaments of the stamens united. (Fig. 32 *C*.)

Trees or shrubs. Spines none. Primary leaflets in 1 or 2 or commonly 4-15 or rarely 25 pairs; secondary leaflets commonly numerous. Flowers in dense heads or spikes, small; corolla tubular, the petals united; stamens more than 10, the anthers minute, 0.2 mm. square. Pod flat, linear or oblong, the sides separating from the thickened margins.

1. *Lysiloma microphylla* Benth (Fig. 32 *C*)

Shrubs or small trees 1-3 m. high in Arizona; primary leaflets in 4-9 pairs, secondary leaflets in 25-33 pairs, each leaflet oblong, 4-5 mm. long, 1.5-2 mm. broad, with only a few appressed marginal hairs; stipules green, asymmetrically ovate-lanceolate, 5 mm. long, about 2 mm. broad, falling away when the leaf is mature; flower heads about 1.5 cm. in diameter; calyx 1.5 mm. long; petals white, tipped with green; stamens about 25-30, the filaments white, about 8 mm. long, the anthers yellow-green; pod oblong, glabrous.

Rocky hillsides and slopes in the upper desert and the desert grassland at 2,800 to 4,000 feet elevation. Arizona near Chimney Creek on the western slopes in the great recess (rincon) of the Rincon Mountains, Pima County; Baja California and Sonora, Mexico, to the West Indies. The isolated occurrence of this widespread species in Arizona is undoubtedly of relict status, since, according to Professor Thornber, the plants are killed back by frost of colder winters. The species may be dying out in Arizona.

3. *CALLIANDRA*. Calliandra

One species of *Calliandra*, the fairy duster, is among the most striking desert plants, and it catches the eyes of most travelers in Arizona. The group is recognized by: (1) absence of spines or prickles; (2) more than 10 stamens (united at the bases in contrast to *Acacia*) in each of the small flowers of the head; (3) minute, brown, scalelike stipules (in contrast to the larger green ones of *Lysiloma*). The scientific name refers to the

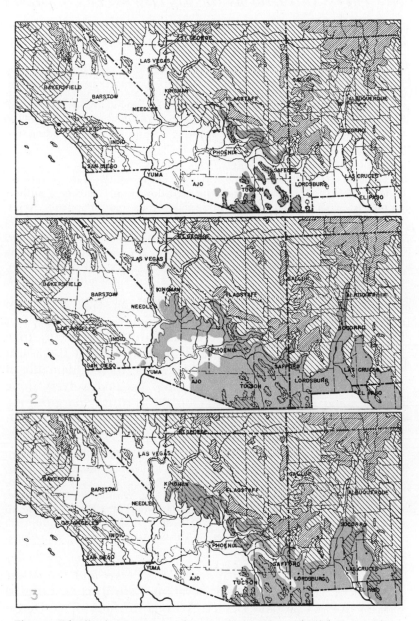

Fig. 33.—Distributional maps: *1*, fern acacia, *Acacia angustissima* var. *hirta;* *2*, fairy duster, *Calliandra eriophylla; 3*, wait-a-minute bush, *Mimosa biuncifera.*

"beautiful stamens," which, as in all the acacia tribe, are the outstanding feature of the flowers. (Figs. 29 *B* 2-4; 34 *D*; Pl. XIX *A*.)

Small shrubs or nearly herbaceous. Primary leaflets in 1-6 pairs; secondary leaflets in 4-17 pairs, strongly asymmetrical at the bases. Flowers in heads; petals united; stamens 20 or more, the filaments united at the bases, the anthers minute, about 0.2 mm. square. Pod flat, oblanceolate, with cordlike, thickened margins, splitting lengthwise and shedding the seeds.

KEY TO THE SPECIES

1. Filaments 15-25 mm. long, lavender or rarely white; pods velvety on the sides; hairs of the stamens appressed downward (retrorse); anthers purple; seeds 6-7 mm. long; calyx and corolla reddish purple. (Figs. 29 *B* 2-4; 34 *D*; Pl. XIX *A*.)   1. *Calliandra eriophylla*

1. Filaments 10-12 mm. long, white or perhaps creamy yellow; pods glabrous; hairs of the stems few, spreading or appressed upward; anthers yellow or cream colored; seeds 3-5 mm. long; calyx and corolla green.
2. *Calliandra Schottii*

1. *Calliandra eriophylla* Benth. FAIRY DUSTER; HUAJILLO; FALSE MESQUITE. A low, bushy shrub about 1 foot up to 3 feet high. (1) Heads of pink or reddish purple flowers 1¼ to 2 inches in diameter, much larger than in the rest of the acacia subfamily, the size of the heads being due to the filaments of the stamens, which are ⅝ to 1 inch long; (2) pods velvety along the sides and more or less hairy on the cordlike margins, 1½ to 3 inches long and ³/₁₆ to ¼ inch broad. (Figs. 29 *B* 2-4; 34 *D*; Pl. XIX *A*.)

Twigs gray, densely covered with soft hair appressed downward; primary leaflets in usually 3 pairs; secondary leaflets in usually 7-9 pairs, each leaflet 2-3 mm. long, 0.8-1.3 mm. broad, appressed-hairy; calyx reddish purple, about 2 mm. long, appressed-hairy; corolla reddish purple, 5-6 mm. long, appressed-hairy; filaments lavender or reddish purple to sometimes white, anthers purple; pod with a slender apical point 5-6 mm. long; seeds lead gray, smooth, oblanceolate-obovate, 6-7 mm. long, 3 mm. broad.

Common on slopes and mesas of the desert and the desert grassland at 2,000 to 5,000 feet elevation. California at scattered stations in the Colorado Desert; Arizona in the Mojave Desert on the Bill Williams River drainage in southern Mohave and western Yavapai counties and in the Arizona Desert and the

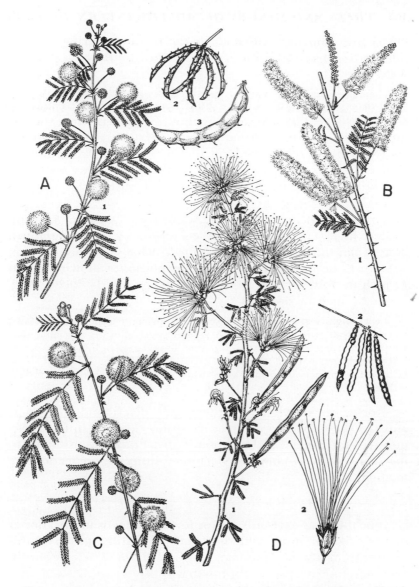

Fig. 34.—Mimosas and fairy duster: *A*, wait-a-minute bush, *Mimosa biuncifera*, *1*, flowering branch, *2*, cluster of pods, *3*, pod; *B*, Wright velvet-pod mimosa, *Mimosa dysocarpa* var. *Wrightii*, *1*, flowering branch, *2*, fruits separating into 1-seeded sections; *C*, Graham mimosa, *Mimosa Grahamii*, flowering branch; *D*, fairy duster, *Calliandra eriophylla*, *1*, branch with pods and the conspicuous heads of (lavender to magenta) flowers, *2*, flower. (x $^1/_3$, except *A 3* x $^2/_3$ and *D 2* x 1.)

desert grassland; New Mexico in the Chihuahuan Desert and the desert grassland from Albuquerque southward; western Texas; Mexico.

The fairy duster is one of the most valuable browse and erosion control plants of the Southwest. The shrubs may be closely cropped by livestock without injury because of the capacity of the plant to spread by means of underground sprouts. In experiments conducted at the Santa Rita Experimental Range, fairy duster plants were found to be highly palatable to captive mule and whitetail deer but of little forage value to jack rabbits. (Fig. 33 2.)

2. *Calliandra Schottii* Torr. SCHOTT CALLIANDRA. A shrub 2-4 feet high. (1) Secondary leaflets mostly $\frac{1}{4}$ inch long, much larger than those of the fairy duster, in which they are minute; (2) flower heads apparently white or possibly yellowish, about $\frac{3}{8}$ inch in diameter; (3) pods glabrous, $1\frac{1}{2}$ to $2\frac{1}{2}$ inches long, about $\frac{1}{4}$ inch broad.

Twigs slightly angled, thinly short-hairy; primary leaflets in 1-2 pairs; secondary leaflets in 4-6 pairs, each asymmetrical obovate, 3-7 mm. long, 1.5-4 mm. broad, with hairs 0.2-0.3 mm. long or glabrous; calyx green, bell-shaped, about 1 mm. long, glabrous; corolla green, 2.5-3 mm. long, glabrous; filaments 10-12 mm. long, white or possibly yellowish; anthers yellow.

Rocky canyon slopes of the upper desert and the desert grassland at 3,000 to 4,000 feet elevation. Arizona in the Baboquivari and Santa Catalina mountains, Pima County, and in the Chiricahua Mountains, Cochise County; Sonora and Chihuahua, Mexico.

4. *MIMOSA*. CAT CLAW; SENSITIVE PLANT

The mimosas have only 10 (or fewer) stamens in each flower of the spike or head, and they may be distinguished by this feature from *Acacia, Lysiloma,* and *Calliandra*. They are shrubs and therefore not to be confused with *Desmanthus,* and they are readily differentiated from the mesquites and screw beans by presence of rose-type prickles instead of spines and by the presence of more than two pairs of primary leaflets in each compound leaf. As cat claw, this genus is not to be confused

Plate XVIII.—Coral bean, blue palo verde, and cat claw: *upper left,* coral bean, *Erythrina flabelliformis,* showing the flowers which appear before the leaves; *upper right,* coral bean, open fruit showing the seeds; *lower left,* blue palo verde, *Cercidium floridum,* close-up view of flowers; *lower right,* cat claw, *Acacia Greggii,* flowering branch. (Photographs except *lower right* by Robert A. Darrow; *lower right* by R. B. Streets.)

Plate XIX.—Fairy duster, coral bean, and hoffmanseggia: *A*, fairy duster *Calliandra eriophylla*, upper portion of plant in flower; *B*, coral bean, *Erythrina flabelliformis*, showing the pinnate leaves each with three large leaflets; *C*, hoffmanseggia, *Hoffmanseggia microphylla*, showing the raceme of buds, flowers, and fruits. (Photographs: *A* by E. T. Nichols; *B*, *C* by Robert A. Darrow.)

with *Acacia Greggii*. The species are of limited value as browse plants, but the seeds are eaten by game birds. (Fig. 34 *A-C*.)

The genus is the more noteworthy for the species *Mimosa pudica*, the sensitive plant of tropical regions, which is grown in the United States as a greenhouse curiosity. When touched, the leaflets fold rapidly together in pairs, and finally the whole compound leaf drops. Recovery requires a few minutes.

Shrubs (or some species not occurring in the Southwest, herbs). Prickles present but few and scattered in some species; spines none. Primary leaflets in 3 or more pairs; secondary leaflets in 4-12 pairs. Flowers in spikes or heads; petals united; stamens separate, the anthers oblong, about 0.4 mm. long. Pod flat, linear-oblong, splitting open or the 1-seeded segments disarticulating and leaving the cordlike margins of the pod.

KEY TO THE SPECIES

1. Flowers in heads (Fig. 34 *A, C*); pods not disarticulating into 1-seeded units (Fig. 34 *A 2, 3*).

   2. Prickles in pairs or solitary at the nodes of the stem, not on the internodes, rarely 1 or 2 on the rachis of each of a few leaves; pod 3-4 mm. broad; primary leaflets 2-4 mm. apart.
   1. *Mimosa biuncifera*

   2. Prickles occurring along the internodes and on the rachis of the leaves as well as at some of the nodes; pod 5-8 mm. broad; primary leaflets or nearly all of them 5 mm. or more apart.
   2. *Mimosa Grahamii*

1. Flowers in spikes (Fig. 34 *B 1*); pods disarticulating into 1-seeded units which fall away leaving the cordlike margins of the pod as a skeleton (Fig. 34 *B 2*).

   2. Secondary leaflets 3-5 mm. long, 1-1.5 mm. broad; pods about 3 mm. broad, velvety; prickles numerous, distributed irregularly on the stems and rachises. (Fig. 34 *B*.)   3. *Mimosa dysocarpa*

   2. Secondary leaflets 8-16 mm. long, 5-10 mm. broad; pods 8-10 mm. broad, glabrous; prickles few and remote.   4. *Mimosa laxiflora*

1. *Mimosa biuncifera* Benth. WAIT-A-MINUTE BUSH; CAT CLAW. (1) Prickles arranged mostly in pairs at the nodes of the stem, but some nodes with only a single prickle, the axes of the compound leaves rarely with prickles and then with only 1 or 2 on each of a few of the leaves; (2) flowers white and pink or lavender, arranged in buttonlike heads about $^3/_5$ inch

in diameter; (3) pods brown or reddish brown with only a few marginal prickles and almost glabrous, 1¼ to 1⅝ inches long, ¹/₆ to ⅛ inch broad. (Fig. 34 *A*.)

Shrubs usually 2-6 feet high; twigs grooved and ridged, rather densely short-hairy; primary leaflets in usually 4-7 pairs; secondary leaflets in 6-13 pairs, linear-oblong, 2-3 mm. long, about 0.5 mm. broad, hairy but not densely so; calyx brownish, top-shaped, 2 mm. long, finely and rather densely hairy; corolla pale green, 3.5-4 mm. long, finely hairy; filaments white, 5-8 mm. long; anthers pale yellow; seeds dark brown, almost black, smooth, oblong-ovate, 3-4 mm. long, 2 mm. broad.

Common in canyons and on hillsides in the desert, the desert grassland, and the lower oak woodland at 3,000 to 6,000 feet elevation. Arizona in the Hualpai Mountains, Mohave County, in the mountains below the Mogollon Rim, and in southeastern Arizona from the Baboquivari Mountains of Pima County eastward; southern New Mexico on the Gila River and Rio Grande drainages south of Socorro County; western Texas; Mexico. (Fig. 33 *3*.)

Wait-a-minute bush, or cat claw, forms dense, nearly impenetrable thickets which offer food and shelter to wild life but little sustenance to domestic livestock. Captive whitetail deer, however, were found to relish this species.

2. *Mimosa Grahamii* A. Gray. GRAHAM MIMOSA. (1) Prickles either in pairs or solitary at the nodes and distributed irregularly along the stem, as well as along the central axes (rachises) of the compound leaves; (2) heads of flowers buttonlike, ½ to ¾ inch in diameter; (3) pods with few prickles along the margins, ½ to 1½ inches long, ¼ to ¹/₃ inch broad. (Fig. 34 *C*.)

Low bush 3-6 dm. high; all parts densely hairy or glabrous; twigs grooved and ridged; primary leaflets in 4-8 pairs; secondary leaflets in 8-12 pairs, each leaflet oblong or ovate-oblong, 2-6 mm. long, 1-2.5 mm. broad; flower heads in the leaf axils, calyx purplish red-tinged, 1-1.3 mm. long; corolla purplish red-tinged, 4 mm. long; filaments creamy white, 7-9 mm. long; anthers pale yellow.

Hillsides and canyons in the upper desert grassland and the oak woodland at 4,000 to 6,000 feet elevation. Arizona in the mountains along the Mexican border in Santa Cruz and Cochise counties; New Mexico in southern Hidalgo County; Sonora and Chihuahua, Mexico. A rare species often occurring in heavily shaded canyons.

3a. *Mimosa dysocarpa* Benth. var. *dysocarpa*. VELVET-POD MIMOSA. (1) Prickles broad, thin, yellowish, curvcd, arrangcd irregularly along the stem and along the axes of the compound leaves; (2) plant markedly hairy, the twigs and pods velvety; (3) spikes of purple flowers about 1 inch long and ½ inch in diameter; (4) pods prickly, 1-2 inches long, ¼ inch broad, constricted between the seeds, the 1-seeded segments falling separately leaving the cordlike margins of the pod.

Shrub 1-2 m. high; twigs 5-ridged; prickles 5-8 mm. long, the larger ones sometimes as much as 3-4 mm. broad 1 mm. above the bases; primary leaflets in 5-10 pairs; secondary leaflets in 6-12 pairs, oblong or narrowly oblong, 3-5 mm. long, 1-1.5 mm. broad, hairy on both sides, not glaucous; spikes in the leaf axils; calyx purple, 1.5 mm. long, densely and finely appressed-hairy; filaments purple, 7-9 mm. long; anthers pale yellow; seeds light brown, angular, acute at both ends or barely obtuse at the bases, 3 mm. long, 2.2 mm. broad.

Mountain canyons largely in the oak woodland or at the lower edge of the yellow pine forests at 5,500 to 6,500 feet elevation. Arizona in the Chiricahua Mountains; southwestern New Mexico; southern Texas; Mexico. Flowering in summer. (Fig. 35 2.)

Less common in Arizona than var. *Wrightii*.

3b. *Mimosa dysocarpa* Benth. var. *Wrightii* (A. Gray) Kearney & Peebles. VELVET-POD MIMOSA (Fig. 34 *B*)

Prickles few, straight, narrow; secondary leaflets glabrous on the upper surfaces or with the hairs soon falling away, glaucous above; spikes 4-6 cm. (about 1½ to 2½ inches) long; pods without prickles or with only a few.

Hillsides and slopes in the desert grassland and the oak woodland at 4,000 to 6,000 feet elevation. Arizona from the Baboquivari, Tucson, and Santa Rita mountains, Pima County, to Santa Cruz County and the Mule Mountains, Cochise County; Mexico. More common than the typical variety. (Fig. 35 *1*.)

Velvet-pod mimosa is less abundant than its close relative wait-a-minute bush, but the plants are more palatable to livestock. The showy flowers make this a desirable species for ornamental plantings.

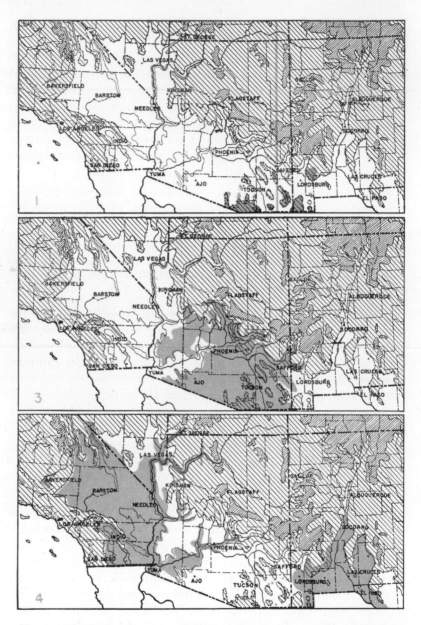

Fig. 35.—Distributional maps: *1*, Wright velvet-pod mimosa, *Mimosa dysocarpa* var. *Wrightii*; *2*, velvet-pod mimosa, *Mimosa dysocarpa*; *3*, velvet mesquite, *Prosopis juliflora* var. *velutina*; *4*, western honey mesquite, *Prosopis juliflora* var. *Torreyana*.

4. *Mimosa laxiflora* Benth. GARABATILLO. (1) Prickles few and scattered but stout; (2) secondary leaflets much larger than those of any other Arizona *Mimosa,* as much as $^1/_3$ to $^2/_3$ inch long and $^1/_5$ to $^2/_5$ inch broad; flowers light reddish lavender, later turning white, produced in spikes; (3) pods without spines or hairs, about 2 inches long and $^3/_8$ to $^7/_{16}$ inch broad, constricted between the seeds and disarticulating, leaving the rather thin cordlike margins as a curious skeleton, individual segments of the pods membranous and with reticulated veins.

Shrub, prickles few and remote, stout; twigs 5-angled with cordlike ridges; primary leaflets in 3-4 pairs; secondary leaflets in 3-6 pairs, obovate, the larger ones 8-16 mm. long, 5-10 mm. broad, glabrous or glabrate; flowers in spikes 2-3.5 cm. long; filaments lavender or white; pods about 5 cm. long, 9-11 mm. broad; seeds black, shining, nearly circular, biconvex, 2-3 mm. in diameter.

Canyon slopes and along washes in the desert at about 2,500 feet elevation. Arizona near Quijotoa and Sells on the Papago Indian Reservation, Pima County; Sonora to Sinaloa and Chihuahua, Mexico.

5. *PROSOPIS.* MESQUITE; SCREW BEAN; TORNILLO

The mesquites and screw beans are spiny trees or large shrubs. The flowers of our species are inconspicuous, creamy yellow spikes 1¼ to 3½ inches long and $^2/_5$ to ½ inch in diameter. They may be distinguished from *Acacia, Lysiloma,* and *Calliandra* by having only 10 stamens instead of 20-100 in each of the small flowers of the spike and from *Mimosa* by having straight, nearly cylindroidal spines instead of prickles similar to rose prickles. The mesquites have straight pods and the spines are not attached to the stalks of the compound leaves; the screw beans or tornillos have tightly coiled pods and the spines attached to the stalks of the compound leaves. (Figs. 36; 37; Pl. XX *B.*)

Spines paired at the nodes, developed either from branches or from stipules. Primary leaflets in 1 or 2 pairs; secondary leaflets in 5-21 pairs. Corolla with separate or united petals, each petal with a hairy spot at the apex of the inner side; stamens 10, separate, each anther bearing a stalked apical gland; pistil stalked, woolly, the stigma a deep cup or hollow cylinder. Pod flattened or coiled, not splitting open, with fleshy partitions between the seeds.

The mesquites and screw beans are among the dominant and most significant plants in the Southwest, and they rank high among the trees and shrubs which give unique character to the desert. Especially the mesquites are of value as range food plants, because the highly nutritious seeds and the young shoots are eaten by cattle and many other animals. Mesquites are important as bee plants, and at one time they were of great value as timber trees in desert areas where no other lumber was available. They are still much used for fence posts and for firewood, and, since the wood is hard and reddish and capable of taking a high polish, it is used for trinkets and novelties. A gum which exudes from the stem is collected and sold for the manufacture of gumdrops and mucilage. The seeds were used by the Indians and by the white pioneers for making flour, and as a source of bread they were one of the staple desert foods.

The mesquites have pods, which, contrary to the usual development in the pea family, do not split open. Cattle eat and digest the fruits and some of the seeds and distribute the rest of them on the ranges. Many areas formerly not occupied by mesquites now have an abundance of the plant for this reason, the seeds having been introduced on the open range from the vicinity of streams, washes, and waterholes. In some areas the young mesquites restrict the grazing of cattle, excluding them from grasses and other food plants, and control measures are necessary to prevent loss of availability of forage.

KEY TO THE SPECIES

1. Fruit not a tightly coiled compact spiral of uniform diameter (Figs. 36 *A*; 37 *A, B*); stalked, beaked; petals separate from one another (Fig. 36 *D*); spines developed as sharp-pointed branches, not joined to the petiole of the leaf (Figs. 36 *B*; 37 *B*); seeds 5 mm. long or longer. MESQUITES. (Section *ALGAROBIA*.) (Figs. 36; 37 *A, B*.)

   1. *Prosopis juliflora*

1. Fruit a tightly coiled compact spiral of uniform diameter (Fig. 37 *C 2, 4*), not stalked, not beaked; petals united firmly into a tube (Fig. 37 *C 1*), the petals sometimes separating rather readily; spines developed as modifications of stipules, joined to the base of the petiole of the leaf (Fig. 37 *C 3*); seeds 3-4 mm. long. SCREW BEANS or TOR-NILLOS (Section *STROMBOCARPA*). (Fig. 37 *C*.)

   2. *Prosopis pubescens*

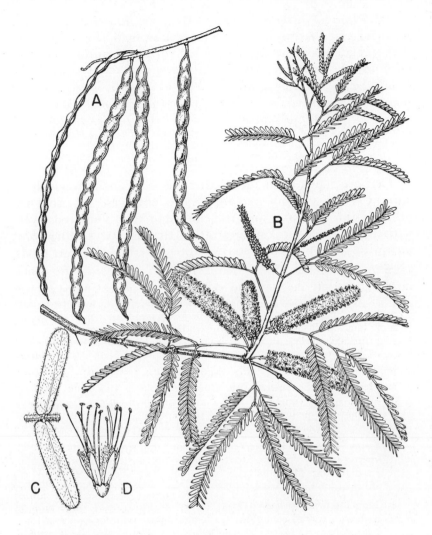

Fig. 36.—Velvet mesquite, *Prosopis juliflora* var. *velutina:* A, axis of an old flowering spike now bearing fruits; B, branch with bipinnate leaves (1 or 2 primary leaflets) and spikes of flowers; C, pair of secondary leaflets enlarged, showing the hairs; D, flower, showing the 10 stamens and the separate petals, each hairy on the inner side at the apex. (x $^1/_3$, except C x $2^1/_3$ and D x 4.)

1a. *Prosopis juliflora* (Swartz) DC. var. *juliflora*. MESQUITE. Mexican and West Indian plant distinguished from the most closely related Southwestern type, the velvet mesquite (*Prosopis juliflora* var. *velutina*), by the following characters:

Plant essentially glabrous, the ovary woolly at flowering time but the hairs promptly falling away as the fruit develops; stigma 0.3-0.35 mm. long (instead of 2 mm.); petiolule 0.3-0.6 (instead of 0.2-0.3) mm. long; secondary leaflets 4-6 times as long as broad; petioles 0.3-0.8 mm. in diameter; primary leaflets usually in 1 pair; seeds 5 (instead of usually 7) mm. long; anther gland usually 0.2 (instead of 0.1) mm. in diameter.

Certain plants from the vicinity of the Chiricahua Mountains, Cochise County, Arizona, have characters of *Prosopis juliflora* var. *juliflora,* and it is possible that they are representative of the typical species rather than of its varieties. The mesquites in the southwestern United States belong to three varieties segregated by the following key:

1. Plant markedly short-hairy to velvety in practically all its younger parts; secondary leaflets oblong or narrowly oblong, 3.5-4 times as long as broad, spaced 2.5-5 mm. apart; beak of the fruit 2-6 or rarely 11 mm. long; pedicels (stalks) of the individual flowers about 0.7 mm. long; primary leaflets in 2 pairs in perhaps half of the leaves. (Fig 36.)
   1a. Var. *velutina*

1. Plant glabrous or essentially so, sometimes with scattered hairs; secondary leaflets linear or narrowly linear-lanceolate, 7-11 times as long as broad, spaced commonly 6-18 mm. apart; beak of the fruit usually 8-23 mm. long; pedicels (stalks) of the individual flowers usually 0.8-1 mm. long; primary leaflets in 1 pair, a few in 2 pairs. (Fig. 37 *A, B.*)

   2. Larger secondary leaflets 15-23 mm. long, 7-9 times as long as broad, spaced usually 6-7 mm. apart; petioles 1-6 cm. long, mostly 0.5 mm. in diameter; filaments 3-5.5 mm. long; seeds obovate, about 1.5 times as long as broad. (Fig. 37 *B.*)   1b. Var. *Torreyana*

   2. Larger secondary leaflets 25-45 or 63 mm. long, 9-11 times as long as broad, spaced commonly 9-18 mm. apart; petioles 5-13 cm. long, 0.8-1.1 mm. in diameter; filaments 5-7 mm. long; seeds usually narrowly ellipsoidal, about twice as long as broad, occasionally obovate. (Fig. 37 *A.*)   1c. Var. *glandulosa*

1b. *Prosopis juliflora* (Swartz) DC. var. *velutina* (Woot.) Sarg. VELVET MESQUITE. (1) Hair dense, short, covering practically the entire plant including the seed pods; (2) leaflets 3.5-4 times as long as broad; (3) pods with beaks only $^{1}/_{12}$ to

·¼ or very rarely ½ inch long; (4) primary leaflets in 2 pairs in perhaps half the leaves. (Fig. 36; Pl. XX *B*.)

Trees up to 17 m. high or less commonly shrubs after the early years; trunk as much as 1 m. or more in diameter; spines developed from pointed branches, separate from the petioles, 1-3 or 8 cm. long; secondary leaflets oblong, spaced 2.5-5 mm. apart on the rachilla; the larger ones 7.5-13 mm. long, 2-4 mm. broad; petioles 0.8-1.2 mm. in diameter; petals separate; pods 8-20 cm. long, 6-10 mm. broad, stalked, the beak 2-6 or rarely 11 mm. long; seeds obovate, 5 or commonly 7 mm. long, 1.5 times as broad as long.

Common along washes and in bottom lands and on slopes and mesas in the desert, the desert grassland, and occasionally the lower oak woodland at 1,000 to 4,500 feet elevation. California near the Grantville School, San Diego River, San Diego County (a single tree); Arizona on the Little Colorado River at Tanner's Crossing, Coconino County, and from the Kofa and Castle Dome mountains, Yuma County, and the upper Bill Williams River drainage, Yavapai County, through the Arizona Desert and the desert grassland of the upper Gila River drainage and from the Tule Desert, Yuma County, eastward to Guadalupe Canyon in southeastern Cochise County; New Mexico along the Gila River in Grant County; El Paso, Texas; Mexico. On the periphery of its range in the upper Verde River valley near Sedona (Coconino County) and in the San Simon and Sulphur Spring valleys, Cochise County, the variety *velutina* is definitely shrubby, and it resembles var. *Torreyana* in its dune-forming habit. (Fig. 35 *3*.)

The characters segregating the velvet mesquite and the western honey mesquite are somewhat unstable, as may be expected in plants considered as varieties, and var. *velutina* intergrades with var. *Torreyana* in many localities in Arizona. Field observation has revealed evidence of recombination of the characters of the two varieties where their ranges overlap.

1c. *Prosopis juliflora* (Swartz) DC. var. *Torreyana* L. Benson. WESTERN HONEY MESQUITE. (1) Smaller secondary leaflets ³/₅ to ⅞ inch long, 7-9 times as long as broad, spaced usually ¼ inch apart; (2) seeds obovate, 1.5 times as long as broad. (Fig. 37 *B*.)

A large shrub or sometimes a tree with a short trunk as much as 6 dm. in diameter; glabrous or nearly so; primary leaflets in 1 pair or rarely in 2 pairs in a few leaves; secondary leaflets in 9-17 pairs, linear, acute, 15-23 mm. long, 2-2.5 or rarely 3 mm. broad, sometimes with scattered, usually appressed hairs, spaced mostly 6-7 mm. apart; petioles 1-6 cm. long, 0.4-0.6 mm. in diameter; filaments 3-5.5 mm. long; pods glabrous, the beak 4 or commonly 8-20 mm. long; seeds brown or reddish brown, 6-7 mm. long, 4-5 mm. broad.

Common in washes and bottom lands and on sandy alluvial flats and mesas in the desert and the desert grassland at elevations below 3,000 feet in the desert and at 4,000 to 5,000 feet in the desert grassland. California in Cuyama Valley, San Luis Obispo County, in alkali flats of the upper San Joaquin Valley between Bakersfield and Taft, in the southern part of coastal southern California, and in the Mojave and Colorado deserts; Nevada in southern Nye County and in Clark County; southwestern Utah; Arizona along the Colorado River in the Grand Canyon region and southward through the Mojave Desert, and the Colorado Desert eastward along the Gila River to the Hassayampa River as far upstream as Wickenburg, Maricopa County, but absent from the rest of the state except for isolated colonies in Cochise County; New Mexico in the Chihuahuan Desert and the adjacent desert grassland; Texas along the Rio Grande and eastward along the Gulf of Mexico to Corpus Christi; Mexico. (Fig. 35 *4*.) Flowering abundantly in April and continuing to flower sporadically until autumn. The plant is replaced on the plains of Texas and Oklahoma by var. *glandulosa*. The name is for John Torrey, one of the first students of the mesquites and screw beans.

In sandy flats, dunes commonly develop about shrubs of this variety (and sometimes of the other varieties), finally leaving only the tips of the branches exposed. In some of the higher areas once valuable grassland has become useless as mesquite-centered dunes have developed.

This well-known plant was confused for about one hundred years with *Prosopis juliflora* var. *glandulosa* (Torr.) Cockerell, from which it is clearly different in its extreme form. The inconstancy of characters is evident from herbarium specimens as well as from the examination of living plants in the

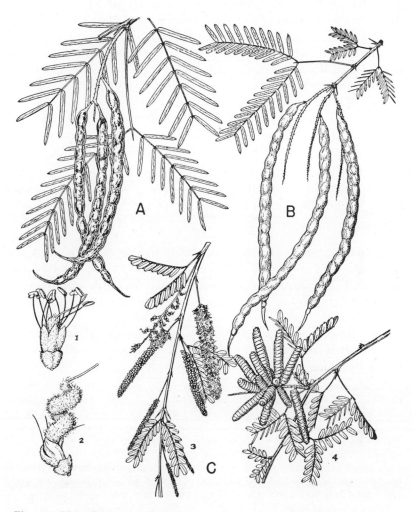

Fig. 37.—Mesquites and screw bean: *A*, honey mesquite, *Prosopis juliflora* var. *glandulosa*, branch with leaves and pods; *B*, western honey mesquite, *Prosopsi juliflora* var. *Torreyana*, branch with leaves and pods; *C*, screw bean or tornillo, *Prosopis pubescens*, *1*, flower, showing the 10 stamens, the united petals characteristic of the screw bean, and the sepals, *2*, young fruit beginning to coil, *3*, branch with leaves and spikes of flowers and flower buds, the leaves with stipular spines attached in pairs to the petioles, *4*, branch showing the mature pods or "screw beans." (x $^1/_3$, except *C 1*, *2* x $2^2/_3$.)

field. Along the Rio Grande in the vicinity of El Paso, Texas, these two varieties of *Prosopis juliflora,* as well as var. *velutina,* grow together, and, judging by herbarium specimens, there occurs a perplexing series of intermediate forms and of plants with recombinations of the characters of all three mesquites or of any two of them.

1d. *Prosopis juliflora* (Swartz) DC. var. *glandulosa* (Torr.) Cockerell. HONEY MESQUITE. (1) Larger secondary leaflets 1-2 or 2½ inches long, 9-11 times as long as broad, spaced commonly ⅜ to ¾ inch apart; (2) seeds usually ellipsoidal, about twice as long as broad. (Fig. 37 *A*.)

A large shrub or a small tree 3-9 m. high; glabrous; primary leaflets in 1 pair or rarely 2 pairs, linear or narrowly linear-lanceolate; petioles 5-9 or 13 cm. long, 0.8-1.1 mm. in diameter; filaments 4 or 5-7 mm. long; pod glabrous, the beak 10-13 mm. long.

Plains, washes, and bottom lands in the desert, the desert grassland, and the short grass prairie. New Mexico from Silver City and Deming northeastward and eastward; plains from southeastern Colorado to southcentral Kansas, Louisiana (Shreveport), and Texas; northeastern Mexico.

2. *Prosopis pubescens* Benth. SCREW BEAN; TORNILLO. (1) Pods tightly coiled; (2) bases of the spines united with the stalks (petioles) of the leaves. (Fig. 37 *C*.)

Small trees or large shrubs 2-10 m. high, the trunks sometimes 2-3 or even 4 dm. in diameter; bark flaky-fibrous or stringy; stipules developed into white or pale gray stout spines 0.2-2 cm. long, these joined to the petiole; primary leaflets in 1 pair or sometimes in 2 pairs; secondary leaflets of the larger leaves in 5-8 pairs, each of the larger leaflets oblong or sometimes elliptic-oblong, 7-11 mm. long, 2.5-4 mm. broad, usually 2.5-3 times as long as broad, finely and rather sparsely appressed-pubescent on both surfaces, spaced 3-5 mm. apart; spikes 4-5.5 cm. long, the lower portions often lax; calyx 1 mm. long, very finely hairy externally; petals united, 2-3 mm. long, finely short-hairy dorsally, filament 4-5 mm. long; anthers 0.5-0.7 mm. long; pod 2.5-5 cm. long over all but tightly spirally coiled, the coil about 4-5 mm. in diameter, markedly hairy, without a stalk or beak; seeds tan, nearly ovoid but somewhat asymmetrical, 3 mm. long, 2 mm. broad, 1.5 times as long as broad.

Bottom lands along desert streams and water holes. California in the vicinity of San Bernardino and along the major watercourses in the Mojave and Colorado deserts; southern

Nevada; southwestern Utah; Arizona along the Colorado, Bill Williams, Gila, and Santa Cruz rivers; New Mexico along the Rio Grande from Socorro southward; Texas along the Rio Grande as far southeastward as Devil's River; Baja California, Sonora, and Chihuahua, Mexico.

Subfamily 2. *CAESALPINOIDEAE*. BIRD-OF-PARADISE SUBFAMILY

The bird-of-paradise subfamily is characterized by relatively large, slightly irregular (strongly irregular in *Cercis,* the redbud or Judas tree) flowers with readily discernible petals. Except in the bird-of-paradise, a plant escaped here and there from cultivation, the stamens are much less conspicuous than the petals, and even in the bird-of-paradise they are no more conspicuous than the corolla. The upper petal or banner does not differ greatly from the others except sometimes in color, and it is folded inside the two adjacent petals in the bud. There is no union of petals to form a keel. (Figs. 29 *C*; 38 to 40; 42; 43 *D*; Pls. XVII; XVIII *lower left*; XIX *C*; XX *A*.)

Trees or shrubs or a few species bushy or even herbaceous. Leaves pinnate or bipinnate, sometimes reduced to a single pair of leaflets or in one genus (*Cercis*) simple. Calyx spreading like a saucer. Petals separate. Stamens 10, rarely some sterile. Pods linear to oblong or oblanceolate, splitting open. Seeds several to many.

KEY TO THE GENERA

1. Leaves pinnate or bipinnate; flowers slightly irregular, yellow or at least partly so (in our species), appearing after the leaves in most species.

    2. Leaves bipinnate; anthers splitting lengthwise and so disseminating the pollen, versatile—that is, attached to the filament at a point above its base.

        3. Filaments red, 6-10 cm. long, as conspicuous as the yellow (in our species) corolla and calyx, which are about 3-3.5 cm. in diameter.   1. CAESALPINIA

        3. Filaments not red, not more than 2 cm. long, less conspicuous than the corolla and calyx.

           4. Spiny trees or shrubs 2-16 m. high, the main branches 1 dm. or more in diameter; sepals reflexed (turned downward); branches remaining green and photosynthetic for many years, rough bark formation not occurring or postponed until the

stem is 1-2 dm. in diameter; leaf bipinnate, the petiole and primary rachis practically undeveloped.

5. Flowers in racemes 9-20 cm. long; primary leaf rachis ending in a spine; rachillae of the primary leaflets persistent and green after the secondary leaflets have fallen, 2-5 dm. long, forming conspicuous streamers; banner (upper petal) in our species turning red as it withers. (Figs. 29 *C 2, 3;* 38.)   2. PARKINSONIA

5. Flowers in racemes 2-5 cm. long; primary leaf rachis not ending in a spine; primary rachillae not persistent after the fall of the secondary leaflets, not forming streamers, 0.5-2.5 cm. long; banner (upper petal) not turning red as it withers. (Figs. 29 *C*; 39; 40; Pl. XVIII *lower left.*)
                                                  3. CERCIDIUM

4. Spineless shrubs not more than 1.5 m. high, the stems not more than 1 cm. in diameter; sepals not reflexed (turned downward); leaf with a well-developed petiole and primary rachis and with a terminal primary leaflet. (Pl. XIX *C*; Fig. 42 *C*.)   4. HOFFMANSEGGIA

2. Leaves pinnate, with no terminal leaflet; anthers not splitting open, disseminating the pollen through terminal pores, basifixed—that is, attached to the filaments by the bases. (Fig. 42 *A, B.*)
                                                     5. CASSIA

1. Leaves simple, reniform; flowers strongly irregular, lavender, appearing in the spring before the leaves; shrubs 2-3 m. high. (Fig. 43 *D.*)
                                                       CERCIS

1. *CAESALPINIA.* Bird-of-Paradise

The species commonly escaped from cultivation may be recognized by the long, red filaments of the stamens. These are 2½ to 4 inches long and as conspicuous as the yellow corolla and calyx, which are about 1¼ inches in diameter. A species with red flowers is occasional in cultivation.

Trees or fairly large shrubs, the branches remaining more or less green for several years. Spines none. Leaves bipinnate; primary leaflets in about 6-12 pairs, the petiole and rachises well developed; secondary leaflets in mostly 5-7 pairs in our species. Flowers in racemes averaging about 1 dm. long, the pedicels and calyces glandular, all but the upper glands stalked. Sepals not reflexed, yellow. Petals yellow, rather narrow. Stamens 10, the filaments greatly exceeding the other floral parts; anthers versatile, splitting open. Pod flat, not constricted between the seeds, splitting open with almost explosive force and ejecting the seeds, which sail through the air for many yards.

1. *Caesalpinia Gilliesii* (Hook.) Wall. BIRD-OF-PARADISE

Small tree 2-4 m. high; secondary leaflets oblong, 4-5 mm. long, 2-3 mm. broad; sepals larger than the petals; petals 2.5-3 cm. long; pod 5-8 cm. long, about 1.5 cm. broad. Synonym: *Poinciana Gilliesii* Hook.

Native of Argentina and Chile, established in somewhat alkaline situations and in washes in southeastern Arizona and southern New Mexico. Commonly cultivated as an ornamental tree. Flowering from May until September but especially in the early summer.

This plant is not to be confused with *Strelitzia,* also known as bird-of-paradise and related to the banana.

2. *PARKINSONIA.* PALO VERDE

This genus of palo verdes is well known in cultivation in Southwestern cities and towns. There are only two species, *Parkinsonia aculeata,* which is common in the American tropics and subtropics, and *P. africana,* restricted to South Africa. The Mexican palo verde is distinguished readily from *Cercidium* by the long, narrow "streamers" (rachillae of the primary leaflets), which are present at all times of the year, and by the fact that the uppermost petal (banner) turns red as it withers. The palo verdes of both genera (*Parkinsonia* and *Cercidium*) are recognized easily, since they are large trees with no rough bark except on the main trunk or some of the largest branches. All the smaller branches and most of the larger ones remain green and capable of manufacturing food (photosynthesis). Palo verde means "green tree" or "green stick." (Figs. 29 *C* 2, 3; 38.)

Trees up to 15 m. high; main trunk often several dm. in diameter. Spines present in pairs at each of the nodes and a spine terminating the primary leaf rachis. Leaves bipinnate; primary leaflets in 1-3 pairs, crowded, both the rachis and the petiole practically obsolete; secondary leaflets numerous. Flowers in racemes 9-20 cm. long. Sepals reflexed. Banner yellow spotted with red, turning red in age. Stamens 10, all functional; anthers versatile, splitting lengthwise. Pod bulging, strongly constricted between the seeds.

1. *Parkinsonia aculeata* L. MEXICAN PALO VERDE; HORSE BEAN (Figs. 29 *C* 2, 3; 38)

Secondary leaflets narrowly elliptic-oblong, 3-6 mm. long, 1-1.5 mm. broad; flower about 2 cm. in diameter; sepals about 7 mm. long; banner

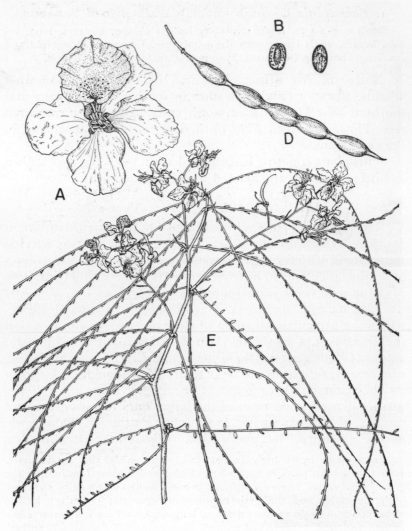

Fig. 38.—Mexican palo verde or horse bean, *Parkinsonia aculeata: A*, flower greatly enlarged, showing the reddish banner differentiated from the other four petals; *B*, seed in two views; *D*, pod; *E*, branch with leaves and flowers, showing the elongated streamers (rachillae or axes of the primary leaflets) bearing small secondary leaflets. It will be noted that the primary rachis (axis) of each leaf is exceedingly short and that it ends in a spine. The stipules are likewise spinose. (x ¹/₃, except *A* x 1¹/₃, *B, C* x ²/₃.)

Plate XX.—Palo verde and mesquite: *A*, blue palo verde, *Cercidium floridum,* growing in the bed of a sandy wash; *B*, velvet mesquite, *Prosopis juliflora* var. *velutina,* growing in desert grassland. Originally the mesquites were practically confined to bottom lands and washes, but in recent years they have spread into adjacent grassland areas. (Photographs by Forrest Shreve.)

Plate XXI.—Creosote bush, *Larrea divaricata: A,* a single bush with relatively dense foliage; *B,* a desert flat with a nearly pure stand of creosote bush; *C,* well-spaced creosote bushes, showing the hillocks which form under the plants (partly as the result of accumulation of wind-blown material, while dust is blown away between plants) ; *D,* sand dunes invading an area in which a few creosote bushes still survive; *E,* creosote bushes on nearly level sandy soil near the base of an alluvial fan or bajada; *F,* creosote bush and white bur sage, *Franseria dumosa,* associated with each other at the lower edge of a bajada. (Photographs by Robert A. Darrow.)

yellow spotted with red, turning red as it withers, nearly circular, 10-11 mm. in diameter, the claw (stalk) about 5 mm. long; other petals golden yellow, similar in size and shape, the claws 2-3 mm. long; anthers 2 mm. long, elliptic, red-margined; pod several-seeded, 5-10 cm. long, 9-12 mm. broad, short-stiped, sharp-pointed.

Gravelly or sandy alluvial fans and canyons in the desert and the desert grassland at 3,000 to 4,500 feet elevation. California as an introduced plant near El Centro and elsewhere; Arizona as a native plant at Horse Tanks in the Castle Dome Mountains, Yuma County, and in the foothills of the Coyote and Baboquivari mountains, Pima County, and as an escape in various parts of the state, notably in the Santa Cruz River valley near Tubac and Amado; New Mexico here and there as an escape but not abundant; Texas to Florida; Mexico to the West Indies and South America.

This attractive tree is used extensively in cultivation in the Southwest, and it is ubiquitous about towns and farms throughout our range.

3. *CERCIDIUM*. PALO VERDE

The common native palo verdes belong to *Cercidium*, a genus of eight or ten species occurring largely in the Southwestern states, Mexico, and Central America. One species grows as far southward as western Peru, and another is restricted to Argentina and Paraguay. The genus is differentiated readily from *Parkinsonia* by the absence of long, narrow streamers (rachillae of the primary leaflets) . (Pls. XVII; XVIII *lower left*; XX *A*; Figs. 39; 40.)

Trees up to 10 m. high; main trunk up to 3-5 dm. in diameter; branches remaining photosynthetic for many years, as described in *Parkinsonia* above, rough bark formation either not occurring or postponed until the trunk is 2 dm. or more in diameter. Spines developed either as pointed branches up to 5 cm. or more in length or as short solitary spines at the nodes of the twigs. Leaves bipinnate; primary leaflets in a single pair, the petiole either obsolete or up to 3-6 mm. long, the rachis not spiny; secondary leaflets in 1-7 pairs in our species. Flowers in racemes 2-5 cm. long. Banner not turning red as it withers. Sepals reflexed. Stamens 10, all functional; anther versatile (attached at or near the middle), splitting lengthwise. Pod bulging or flat, strongly or slightly constricted between the seeds.

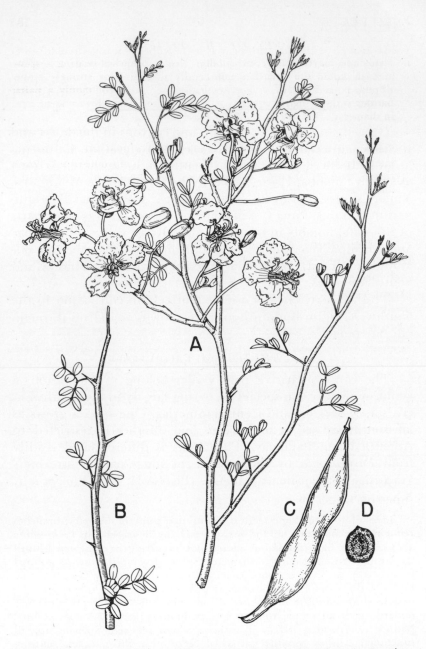

Fig. 39.—Blue palo verde, *Cercidium floridum*: *A*, flowering branch; *B*, spiny branch showing the bipinnate leaves with secondary leaflets in 1-3 pairs and the short spines, one at each node; *C*, pod; *D*, seed. (x ²/₃.)

KEY TO THE SPECIES

1. Stems and leaves blue-green; smaller (leafy) branches bearing a spine at each node, the branches not rigidly spreading or strongly spine-tipped; pods flattened: secondary leaflets in 1-2 or commonly 3 pairs; banner yellow, slightly spotted with red at the base; flower 18-20 mm. in diameter. (Pls. XVII *A*; XVIII *lower left*; Fig. 39.)

1. *Cercidium floridum*

1. Stems and leaves yellow-green; smaller (leafy) branches not bearing lateral spines at the nodes, rigidly spreading and spine-tipped; pods turgid, bulging strongly at each seed and constricted between the seeds; secondary leaflets in 4-7 pairs; banner white or cream; flower as a whole pale yellow, 10-13 mm. in diameter. (Pl. XVII *B*; Fig. 40.)

2. *Cercidium microphyllum*

1. *Cercidium floridum* Benth. BLUE PALO VERDE. (1) Branches and leaves blue-green; (2) spines ¼ inch long, one at each node of each leafy twig; (3) pods flattened; (4) flowers bright yellow, ¾ or ⁴/₅ inch in diameter, the banner (upper petal) yellow with a few red spots, not becoming red as it withers. (Pls. XVII *A*; XVIII *lower left*; XX *A*; Fig. 39.)

Small trees up to 10 m. high; branches and leaves blue-green; secondary leaflets in 1-2 or commonly 3 pairs, narrowly obovate, 5-8 mm. long, 2-3 mm. broad; petioles 3-6 mm. long; sepals about 4 mm. long; banner blade circular, 6-8 mm. in diameter, the stalk (claw) 3-4 mm. long; other petals yellow, ovate-attenuate, 7-9 mm. long, 4-5 mm. broad; anthers 1 mm. long; pod about 1-4 seeded, oblong or usually oblanceolate or irregular, flattened, usually 4-8 cm. long, 9-15 mm. broad, not markedly stiped or beaked. Synonyms: *Parkinsonia Torreyana*. S. Wats. *Cercidium Torreyanum* Sarg.

Along washes in the desert plains and in canyons and sometimes on slopes in the desert grassland from sea level to 4,000 feet elevation. California throughout the Colorado Desert; Arizona in the Mojave Desert south of Kingman, Mohave County, and in the Colorado and Arizona deserts and the adjacent desert grassland eastward to near Duncan, Greenlee County; Baja California and Sonora, Mexico. (Fig. 41 *1*.)

The blue palo verde is one of the most attractive trees in the desert, and each tree becomes a mass of yellow flowers in late March or in April, depending upon the altitude. The plant is characteristic of washes and other areas with a substantial underground water supply, and often it grows in washes only a short distance from its relative, the foothill palo verde, which inhabits the slopes. It flowers earlier than *Cercidium microphyllum.* The beans of the palo verdes, and especially of this species, were used by Indians as food.

2. *Cercidium microphyllum* (Torr.) Rose & Johnston. FOOT-HILL PALO VERDE. (1) Branches and leaves yellow-green; (2) spines developed as pointed branches up to 2 inches or more in length; (3) pods bulging, strongly constricted between the seeds; (4) flowers pale yellow, about ½ inch in diameter, the banner (upper petal) white or cream. (Pl. XVII *B*; Fig. 40.)

Small trees up to 6 or 8 m. high; secondary leaflets in 4-7 pairs, ellip-soidal, 2-3 mm. long, 1-1.8 mm. broad; petioles none; banner circular, about 5 mm. in diameter, the stalk (claw) about 3 mm. long; other petals creamy yellow, ovate-attenuate, 5-6 mm. long, 3.5 mm. broad; anthers yellow or orange, 2 mm. long; pod 1-4-seeded, elongate, 4-9 cm. long, about 9-10 mm. broad, with a long stipe and a pronounced beak. Synonym: *Parkinsonia microphylla* Torr.

Common on the plains and in the foothills of the desert from 500 to 3,500 feet elevation. California near the Colorado River in the Whipple Mountains, San Bernardino County; Arizona along the Bill Williams and Big Sandy rivers in Mohave County, in the Colorado and Arizona deserts, and eastward to the Coolidge Reservoir and to Benson, Cochise County; Baja California and Sonora, Mexico. (Fig. 41 2.)

The foothill palo verde is a common tree in the Arizona Desert, and it is abundant on rocky bajadas and alluvial fans fringing the desert mountains. It is associated commonly with the saguaro, or giant cactus, desert ironwood, ocotillo, chollas, prickly pears, and hedgehog cacti. At the northern limits of its range the species is replaced by one of the crucifixion thorns, *Canotia Holacantha,* a similar tree. The relatively small size of the trees is accounted for by slow growth and by frequent death of portions of the larger branch systems during drought. According to Dr. Shreve, some of the trees are as much as four hundred years old.

The foothill palo verde was of great importance to the Indians, who used it for fuel and food. It has limited value as a browse plant for livestock.

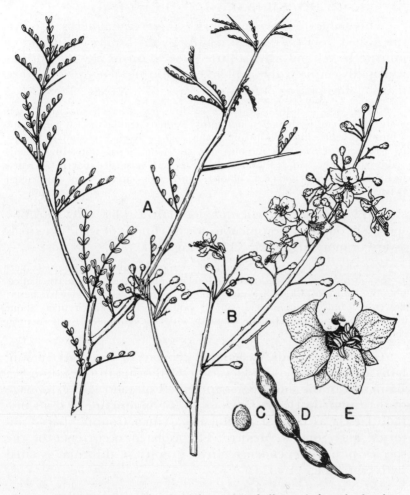

Fig. 40.—Foothill palo verde, *Cercidium microphyllum: A,* branch showing bipinnate leaves with 4-7 pairs of secondary leaflets and with practically no petioles (stalks) and showing the spines formed as pointed branches; *B,* flowering branch, practically leafless at this season; *C,* seed; *D,* pod; *E,* flower, showing the white banner differentiated somewhat from the four other petals. (x ²/₃, except *E* x 2.)

4. *HOFFMANSEGGIA*. Hoffmanseggia

This genus includes small shrubs or perennial herbs. It is distinguished from *Cassia* most readily by the bipinnate instead of pinnate leaves and, with a little closer scrutiny, by the anthers which disseminate the pollen by splitting lengthwise rather than by the opening of terminal pores. (Pl. XIX *C*; Fig. 42 *C*.)

Shrubs with wandlike branches or low perennial herbs. Stems not more than 1 cm. in diameter, not spiny. Primary leaflets in 1-6 pairs, with a terminal leaflet, the petiole and rachis well developed; secondary leaflets in 4-18 pairs. Flowers in racemes 1-15 cm. long. Sepals spreading. Petals yellow or yellow and red. Stamens 10; anthers versatile—that is, attached near the middles. Pod flat, oblong, linear, or curved, not constricted between the seeds.

1. *Hoffmanseggia microphylla* Torr. The only shrubby species in our area; conspicuous for its clumps of wandlike stems a yard or more high. (Pl. XIX *C*; Fig. 42 *C*.)

Stems less than 1 cm. in diameter, remaining green; primary leaflets 3, the terminal one 1.5-2 times as long as the others; secondary leaflets oblong or elliptic-oblong, 2-3 mm. long, 1-1.5 mm. broad, somewhat hairy; flower 5-6 mm. in diameter, yellow; pod narrowly semicircular, about 2 cm. long, 7-8 mm. broad, covered with stalked glands, the margin short-hairy.

Gravelly or sandy washes and canyons of the desert mountains at 500 to 2,000 feet elevation. California in the Salton Sea Basin and in the lower portion of the Colorado River drainage of the Colorado Desert; Arizona in the mountains of the Colorado Desert as far east as Mohawk, Yuma County; Baja California and Sonora, Mexico. The isolated occurrence of the species near Independence, Inyo County, California, is cited by Jepson. (Fig. 41 *3*.)

5. *CASSIA*. Senna; Partridge Pea

This genus includes bushy shrubs and perennials. It is distinguished from *Hoffmanseggia* by the pinnate instead of bipinnate leaves and by the dissemination of the pollen from the anthers through terminal pores instead of by longitudinal splitting (except in *Cassia leptadenia*) . (Fig. 42 *A, B*.)

Bushy shrubs or perennial herbs, not spiny except in *Cassia armata*. Petiole and rachis well developed; leaflets in 1-18 pairs, with no terminal

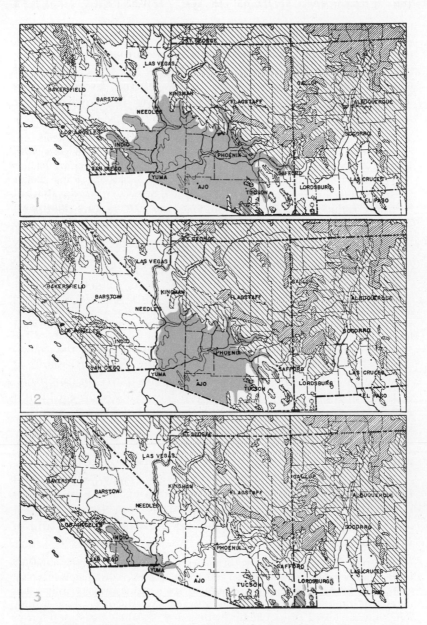

Fig. 41.—Distributional maps: *1*, blue palo verde, *Cercidium floridum;* *2*, foot-hill palo verde, *Cercidium microphyllum;* *3*, hoffmanseggia, *Hoffmanseggia microphylla;* *4*, shrubby senna, *Cassia Wislizenii.*

leaflet. Flowers in racemes. Sepals spreading. Petals yellow. Stamens 10, commonly 3 of them sterile; not splitting lengthwise. Pod flat or turgid, linear-oblong, not markedly constricted between the seeds.

KEY TO THE SPECIES

1. Shrubs 1-3 m. high; branches with brown or gray bark, not grooved; leaf rachis about 0.5 mm. in diameter, not prolonged beyond the leaflets and not spiny; flowers 3-4 cm. in diameter; pods strongly flattened, 7-10.5 cm. long. (*PALMEROCASSIA.*) (Fig. 42 *A*.)

1. *Cassia Wislizenii*

1. Bushes 0.3-0.6 m. high; branches green or yellow-green, without bark, grooved; leaf rachis 1 mm. thick, fleshy, prolonged beyond the leaflets and ending in a weak spine; flowers about 1.2 cm. in diameter; pods nearly as thick as broad, 2.5-4.5 cm. long. (*XEROCASSIA.*) (Fig. 42 *B*.)

2. *Cassia armata*

1. *Cassia Wislizenii* A. Gray. SHRUBBY SENNA. The only large shrub in the genus within our area; 4-9 feet high. (Fig. 42 *A*.)

Branches with rough bark; leaflets in 2-3 pairs, elliptic, mucronate, 5-9 mm. long, 3-5 mm. broad, rather thick but not fleshy, with a few long hairs; rachis not prolonged beyond the leaflets; flowers 3-4 cm. in diameter, in racemes; petals yellow; stamens 10, the upper 3 sterile, minute; pod linear, the margins cordlike, 7-10.5 cm. long, 6-7 mm. broad.

Rocky hills of the upper desert and the desert grassland at 4,000 to 5,000 feet elevation; occurring principally on limestone. Arizona in the vicinity of Bisbee and Douglas, Cochise County; New Mexico in southern Hidalgo and southern Luna counties; southern Texas; Mexico. (Fig. 41 *4*.)

The large flowers of this fair-sized shrub make it unusually attractive, and it is common in cultivation about Bisbee.

2. *Cassia armata* S. Wats. SPINY SENNA. (1) Low bushes 1-2 feet high; (2) branches, green, grooved, thick, more prominent than the leaves, which are inconspicuous; (3) tip of the leaf axis developing into a weak spine; (4) branches tapering almost into spines. (Fig. 42 *B*.)

Conspicuously green bushes; branches 2-3 mm. in diameter, tapering in the last 4-6 cm. to a diameter of about 1 mm., conspicuously 10-14-grooved, clothed with downward-pointed scale hairs; leaflets in 2-3 not necessarily opposite pairs, asymmetrically elliptic-orbicular, about 5 mm. long, 4 mm. broad, thick, fleshy, with a few scalelike hairs; leaf rachis thick and fleshy, about 1 mm. in diameter, prolonged 15-25 mm. past the leaflets; flowers about 12 mm. in diameter, solitary or in pairs in the axils of the upper alternate or opposite leaves, the inflorescence having the appearance of a raceme; petals yellow; stamens 10, the 3 upper ones sterile and minute; pods light tan, oblanceolate to lanceolate, not curving, turgid, somewhat constricted between the seeds, 2.5-4.5 cm. long, 4-7 mm. broad, 3-6 mm. thick.

Sandy soil or gravelly washes of the desert plains and hills at 500 to 3,000 feet elevation. California throughout the Mojave and Colorado deserts except on the lower Colorado River drainage; southern Nevada in Clark County; Arizona in western Mohave County; Baja California, Mexico. (Fig. 44 *1*.)

The shrub is leafless during most of the year, and the bulk of its food is manufactured in the branches.

CERCIS. Redbud or Judas Tree

Cercis occidentalis Torr. western redbud; judas tree. (Fig. 43 *D*.) Large shrubs 2-7 m. high; not spiny; glabrous; bark relatively smooth, gray; roots exceedingly long and difficult to clear from the soil; leaves simple, reniform, 5-10 cm. long, 4-9 cm. broad, the basal notch 1.5-2 cm. deep or the sinus rarely closed; flowers in 2-5-flowered racemes or clusters in the leaf axils, the slender pedicels about 1 cm. long; corolla pink or lavender, strongly irregular, appearing to be like the Papilionoideae but with the banner enclosed by the wings and the keel petals not united; banner much shorter than the other petals, 4-5 mm. long; wings 6-7 mm. long; keel petals about 12-13 mm. long, conspicuously exceeding the wings; stamens 10, all fertile; anthers minute, splitting lengthwise; pod flat, tan or pinkish lavender, oblanceolate, 5-8 cm. long, 1.3-2.5 cm. broad, not constricted between the seeds, with conspicuous broad margins.

Hillsides in the chaparral and the oak woodland and along streams at the upper edge of the desert; 500 to 3,000 feet elevation on the coastal side of the California mountain axis and 4,000 to 6,000 feet elevation in the desert regions. California in the Coast ranges and the Sierra Nevada foothills and in the Laguna and Cuyamaca mountains, San Diego County; southern Utah; Arizona in the following scattered localities: Grand Canyon, Pagumpa Spring in Mohave County, Superstition Mountains in Pinal County, Baboquivari Mountains in Pima County (according to Goodding) ; western Texas.

The redbud is a large, rounded shrub with many branches from the base. It is 6 to 15 feet high and of about the same diameter. The genus is distinguished readily from all other mem-

bers of the pea family treated in this work by its simple, kidney-
or bean-shaped leaves. It is segregated easily from all the other
members of the bird-of-paradise subfamily by the strongly irregular pink and lavender flowers, which superficially resemble
those of the sweet pea.

Subfamily 3. *KRAMERIOIDEAE*. RATANY SUBFAMILY

(1) Bur-like pods 1-seeded, spiny, not splitting open; (2)
leaves narrow, simple, with no teeth or divisions; (3) flowers
irregular, red-to-purple, somewhat smaller than a dime, produced singly on short branches or in the leaf axils. (Figs. 29 *D*;
43 *A-C*.)

Shrubs or herbs less than 5 dm. high. Leaves simple, entire, linear, these
and the younger branches densely appressed-hairy; stipules none. Calyx
much larger than the corolla, irregular, reddish purple. Corolla irregular,
the petals 3-5, reddish purple or partly yellowish. Stamens 3-5, only those
on the upper side of the flower developed; anthers opening by terminal
pores. Fruit a dry, indehiscent bur with barbed spines, 1-seeded.

The group, despite its distinctive character, is closely related
to the Caesalpinoideae.

1. *KRAMERIA*. RATANY

KEY TO THE SPECIES

1. Spines of the fruit each bearing an apical group of 3 or 4 flat barbs
   arranged like the ribs of an umbrella (Fig. 43 *B* *1-2*); sepals lanceolate,
   the lower one 8 or usually 10 mm. long, the other 6 or usually 8 mm.
   long; larger leaves usually 1.5-2 mm. broad. (Figs. 29 *D* *1*; 43 *B*.)
   1. *Krameria Grayi*

1. Spines of the fruit each bearing barbs laterally along the distal part,
   these near but not restricted to the apex of the spine (Fig. 43 *C* *1-2*);
   sepals 5-8 mm. long; larger leaves usually not more than 1.2 m̃m. broad.
   (Figs. 29 *D* *2*; 43 *C* *1-2*.)   2. *Krameria parvifolia*

1. *Krameria Grayi* Rose & Painter. WHITE RATANY. Low
shrubs usually about 1-2 feet high. Cluster of 3 or 4 barbs at the
tip of each spine of the burlike pod resembling the ribs of an
umbrella and not scattered along the spine as in the other
species. (Figs. 29 *D* *1*; 43 *B*.)

Plant usually densely and intricately branched; leaves linear or linear-
oblanceolate, the larger ones 9-12 or 14 mm. long, 1.5-2 mm. broad; flowers

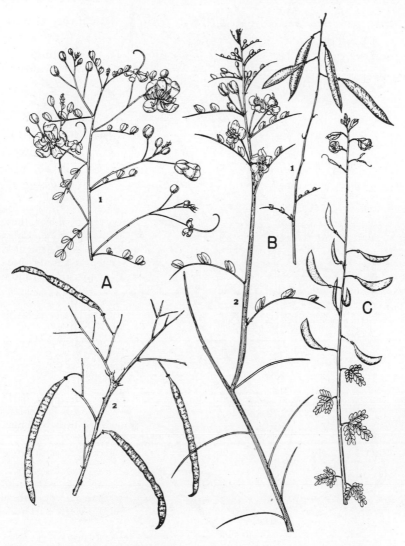

Fig. 42.—Cassias and hoffmanseggia: *A,* shrubby senna, *Cassia Wislizenii, 1,* branch with pinnate leaves, flowers, and flower buds, *2,* branch with pods after the leaves have fallen; *B,* spiny senna, *Cassia armata, 1,* branch with fruits, *2,* branch with leaves, flowers, and weak spines formed as pointed branches; *C,* hoffmanseggia, *Hoffmanseggia microphylla,* branch with buds, flowers, fruits, and bipinnate leaves. (x ¹/₃.)

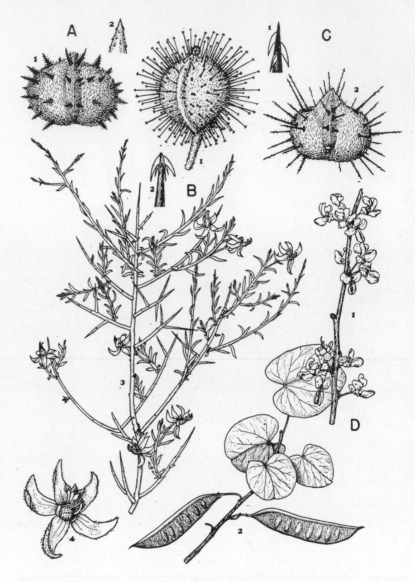

Fig. 43.—Ratanies and redbud: *A, Krameria secundiflora, 1,* fruit, *2,* enlargement of a spine tip of the fruit; *B,* white ratany, *Krameria Grayi, 1,* fruit, *2,* enlargement of a spine tip of the fruit, showing the cluster of barbs all at the same level, *3,* flowering branch, *4,* flower, showing the large sepals, the small petals, the 3-5 stamens, and the pistil; *C,* ratany, *Krameria parvifolia, 1,* enlargement of a spine tip of the fruit, *2,* fruit; *D,* redbud, *Cercis occidentalis, 1,* flowering branch, *2,* fruiting branch. (*A 1, B 1, 4, C* 2 x 2; *A 2, B 2, C 1* x 26; others x $^1/_3$.)

10-13 mm. in diameter; lower sepal 8 or usually 10 mm. long, the others 6 or usually 8 mm. long; petals spatulate, about 3 mm. long, 1 mm. broad; bur with slender spines, the length of each apical barb exceeding the diameter of the spine.

Sandy or rocky soils of the desert foothills or alluvial fans at 500 to 4,000 feet elevation. California from the Mojave Desert south of the Mojave River to the Colorado Desert; southern Nevada in Clark County; Arizona in the Mojave Desert south of Kingman, in the Colorado Desert, and in the Arizona Desert as far eastward as the Roosevelt Reservoir and Tucson; western Texas; Baja California to Chihuahua, Mexico. (Fig. 44 5.)

White ratany is more abundant in the desert than *Krameria parvifolia,* and it is common on the lower desert mesas. The plants are partly parasitic upon the roots of their neighbors, including bur sage (*Franseria*) and the creosote bush. The shrub is a favorite browse plant, and the prickly pods are disseminated by grazing animals. According to report, the Pima Indians used the powdered roots of this species for treatment of sores.

2. *Krameria parvifolia* Benth. RATANY. A low shrub usually not more than 1 or 1½ feet high, often spreading to a greater diameter, commonly compact because of the browsing of young shoots by cattle. Spines of the bur slender, each with several barbs scattered along its upper portion. (Figs. 29 *D* 2; 43 *C*.)

Shrub 2-5 dm. high; calyx, pedicels, and leaves sometimes with conspicuous dark, stalked glands; leaves linear or linear-oblanceolate, the larger ones 6-12 or rarely 14 mm. long, mostly 0.7 to 1 mm. or sometimes 2 mm. broad; flowers about 10 mm. in diameter; sepals 5-8 mm. long, about 2-5 mm. broad; petals linear (almost filiform), 3 mm. long, the terminal portion of each ovate-oblong and about 0.3 mm. broad; bur with slender spines, the length of each of the several barbs exceeding or equaling the diameter of the spine. Synonyms: *Krameria glandulosa* Rose & Painter; *Krameria parvifolia* Benth. var. *imparata* Macbr.; *Krameria imparata* Britt.

Rocky slopes and gravelly plains in the desert and the desert grassland at 500 to 5,000 feet elevation. California in the deserts from the Death Valley region and Victorville southward and eastward; southern Nevada; southwestern Utah; Arizona in the Grand Canyon region, in the Mojave, Colorado, and Arizona deserts, and in the desert grassland; New Mexico in the Chihuahua Desert and the desert grassland; Baja California and southwestward in Mexico. An isolated occurrence at San Diego is reported by Abrams. (Fig. 44 6.)

This species is an important browse plant for range livestock, and the significance is increased by the fact that the associated vegetation often includes few other palatable plants. The shrubs are resistant to grazing, and they sprout readily from their shallow root systems. After a few years each plant becomes a dense, rounded, spiny mass from which the new year's tender growth protrudes. In Mexico brown and yellow dyes are prepared from the stems and roots. The plant is also a root parasite.

Krameria secundiflora DC. (Fig. 43 *A*.) (1) Herbs, spreading along the ground; (2) spines of the fruit thick, hairy, with the barbs shorter than the diameter of the spine. Synonym: *Krameria lanceolata* Torr. The identity of the original material of *Krameria secundiflora* is in doubt, however. Elevation 4,000 to 7,000 feet in the desert grassland and the oak woodland of southeastern Arizona and southern New Mexico; eastward to Kansas and Florida; Mexico.

Subfamily 4. *PAPILIONOIDEAE*. Bean Subfamily

The bean or pea subfamily is by far the largest and, in the world as a whole, the most significant subfamily of the pea family. However, the development of its shrubby or arboreous members in the Southwestern deserts does not rival the other three subfamilies taken as a unit or, necessarily, the acacia and bird-of-paradise subfamilies individually. (Figs. 29 *A*; 45; 47; Pls. XVIII *upper figs*; XIX *B*.)

The bean subfamily is characterized by flowers of the butterfly type, and its technical name is derived from that of the butterfly family in the animal kingdom (Papilionidae). This flower is characterized by outstanding irregularity of the corolla, which consists of 5 petals disposed as follows: (1) the banner (or standard) on the upper side of the flower and usually much larger (but sometimes smaller) than the other petals and folded outside them in the bud; (2) the wings, next to the banner at the sides of the flower; (3) the keel, a boatlike structure formed from 2 petals united along one edge. The banner and the wings are the chief insect attracters. The keel encloses the stamens and the pistil. In some members of the subfamily, for example,

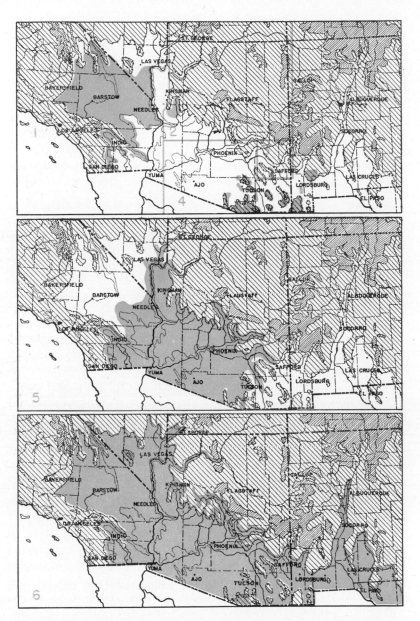

Fig. 44.—Distributional maps: *1, spiny senna, Cassia armata*; *2,* Arizona sophora, *Sophora arizonica*; *3,* Gila sophora, *Sophora formosa*; *4,* coral bean, *Erythrina flabelliformis*; *5,* white ratany, *Krameria Grayi*; *6,* ratany, *Krameria parvifolia.*

the Spanish broom, a heavy insect alighting on the keel forces it and the stamens and pistil downward, but the reproductive organs, having greater resiliency than the keel, soon spring upward, sending a little cloud of pollen into the air about the insect. A few members of the group, e.g., *Eysenhardtia,* have nearly regular flowers.

Trees or shrubs or mostly herbs or bushy plants. Leaves pinnate or simple in our plants but occasionally palmate in others. Flowers of our genera in racemes. Stamens 10, rarely fewer, commonly united into a single tube (monadelphous, or in one brotherhood) or 9 united and 1 free (diadelphous, or in 'two brotherhoods). Pod linear to oblong or oblanceolate, splitting open. Seeds several to many.

KEY TO THE GENERA

1. Flowers bright red, the banner 2-5 cm. long, lanceolate in side view (Pl. XVIII *upper left),* the wings and the keel much shorter, about equaling the calyx; leaflets 3, triangular but the angles rounded off, broader than long, 4-7 cm. long, 5-10 cm. broad (Pl. XIX *B);* seeds red, ellipsoidal, 10-14 mm. long (Pl. XVIII *upper right).*

1. ERYTHRINA

1. Flowers not red; leaflets more than 3 (or the plant leafless), not triangular, longer than broad, not more than 3.5 cm. long or 2 cm. broad.

    2. Leaves, branches and flowers not dotted with sunken glands; plants leafy.

        3. Stamens separate; leaves with a terminal, unpaired leaflet; leaflets silky, the mass of hairs markedly shiny, especially when the leaf is young, later somewhat silky on at least the underside; flowers purple; seeds red. (Fig. 45 *D.)*   2. SOPHORA

        3. Stamens 10, 9 united; leaves with no terminal leaflet, all the leaflets paired or nearly so (Fig. 45 *B 1, C 1);* leaflets with scattered hairs, or at least not silky or shiny; flowers lavender or else yellow tinged with lavender; seeds brown.

            4. Trees; petals lavender; pods 7-8 mm. broad, not constricted between the seeds; leaflet not terminated by a short, slender point; spines produced in pairs at the nodes of the branches; calyx and pedicel densely hairy, not glandular. (Fig. 45 *B.)*

3. OLNEYA

            4. Shrubs; petals yellow, tinged with lavender or purple; pods about 5 mm. broad, constricted between the seeds; leaflet tipped with a short, slender point; spines none; calyx and pedicel with sparse hairs and stalked glands. (Fig. 45 *C.)*

4. COURSETIA

2. Leaves, branches, and flowers dotted with sunken glands, at least beneath (Figs. 45 *A*; 47); the secretion of the gland commonly arising above the surface of the leaf, however; one species usually leafless, all its branches ending in spines (Fig. 47 *D*).

3. Petals all about the same shape and size, white (Fig. 45 *A* 2); pods turned downward but in erect racemes, flat, narrowly oblong, far longer than the calyx, 12-18 mm. long (Fig. 45 *A* 1); leafy, spineless shrub or small tree; stamens separate.

5. EYSENHARDTIA

3. Petals markedly unequal, the corolla distinctly papilionaceous (Fig. 29 *A* 1); pods not turned downward, turgid, ovate or short-oblong, not, or only a little, exceeding the calyx, not more than 10 mm. long; low shrubs or a practically leafless, ashy gray small tree or large shrub (Fig. 47 *D*); stamens united into a single group. (Fig. 47.)

6. DALEA

1. *ERYTHRINA*. CORAL BEAN; CORAL TREE

The coral bean is a small or medium-sized shrub readily recognized in the early summer by its leafless spiny branches with terminal racemes of brilliant red flowers about 1-2 inches long and perhaps ¼ inch in diameter, in midsummer by its nearly triangular leaflets 1½ to 3 inches long and 2-4 inches broad, and in late summer and autumn by its thick pods 6-10 inches long and ½ to ¾ inch broad and its bright red poisonous seeds about ½ inch long and ⅜ inch wide. (Pls. XVIII *upper figs.*; XIX *B*.)

Branches thick, the bark light tan; spines short, solitary, or paired at the nodes. Leaflets 3, broader than long. Calyx cylindroidal, the teeth not developed. Banner 2-5 cm. long, straight, folded, nearly lanceolate in side view, 10-12 cm. broad when unfolded; wings and keel barely equaling the calyx. Stamens 10, 9 united. Pod 1.5-2 cm. broad. Seeds red, large, ellipsoidal.

1. *Erythrina flabelliformis* Kearney. CORAL BEAN; CHILICOTE

Leaflets triangular but the angles rounded off, 4-7 cm. long, 5-10 cm. broad; calyx 7-9 mm. long, 4-5 mm. in diameter, a warty gland present at the apex of the lower side. Stamens as long as the banner. Pod 15-25 cm. long, about 1 cm. thick. Seeds 12-14 mm. long, about 10 mm. broad. (Pls. XVIII *upper figs.*; XIX *B*.)

Rocky canyon slopes and washes of the higher desert mountains, the desert grassland, and the oak woodland at 3,000 to

5,000 feet elevation. Arizona from the Baboquivari and Santa Catalina mountains, Pima County, eastward to Cochise County; New Mexico in southern Hidalgo County; Mexico. (Fig. 44 *4*.)

The coral bean is commonly a large shrub with brittle, spiny, short-lived branches growing from a large tuberous root, but in Mexico, under more favorable conditions, the species attains tree size. The brightly colored beans (Pl. XVIII *B*), from which the plant derives its name, are used often in making necklaces and novelties. Livestock browse occasionally on the foliage, but it is reported that the stems and seeds are poisonous to stock. *Erythrina Corallodendron, Erythrina Crista-Galli,* and other species are common in cultivation. *Erythrina flabelliformis* is cultivated as coral tree in southern California.

2. *SOPHORA*. Sophora

The shrubby species of Sophora are distinguished readily from the other leguminous trees and shrubs of the bean sub-family, except *Dalea,* by the shiny, silky surface of the rather large leaflets and by presence of a terminal, unpaired leaflet. The stamens, or at least 9 of the 10, are united in all the other genera. The seeds are red, and a species occurring in Texas and Mexico, *Sophora secundiflora,* is known as coral bean, but it is not to be confused with *Erythrina. Sophora* has no spines. (Fig 45 *D*.)

Shrubs 1-2 m. high. Twigs densely white-hairy but soon become almost black, later, after the hairs have fallen away, becoming light colored. Leaflets 7 or 9, or in some leaves fewer or up to 13, ovate-lanceolate to lanceolate or narrowly oblong, shiny and silky, especially when young, and later particularly so on the lower surface, thick and leathery. Calyx 7-11 mm. long, the teeth short, silky. Flowers purple, 15-23 mm. long. Pod 10-17 cm. long, 10-12 mm. broad, flat, silky when young, the hairs persistent, especially on the constricted portions between the seeds. Seeds flattened.

KEY TO THE SPECIES

1. Flowers 20-24 mm. long; banner oblong-obovate, 19-23 mm. long; stalks (claws) of the keel less than half as long as the fused blades.
   1. *Sophora arizonica*

1. Flowers mostly 14-17 mm. long; banner broadly ovate, 17-20 mm. long; stalks (claws) of the keel somewhat more than half as long as the fused blades. (Fig. 45 *D*.) 2. *Sophora formosa*

1. *Sophora arizonica* S. Wats. ARIZONA SOPHORA. Most readily distinguished from *Sophora formosa* by the larger flowers, about ⅞ inch long.

Larger leaflets 8-15 mm. broad, obtuse; flowers 20-24 mm. long, the banner oblong-obovate 19-23 mm. long, the keel with short stalks less than half as long as the fused blades; seeds averaging about 1 cm. long.

Sandy washes in the desert plains and foothills at 2,000 to 4,000 feet elevation. Arizona on all sides of the Hualpai Mountains in Mohave County. This and *Sophora formosa*, to which it is very closely related, are highly localized Arizona endemics. (Fig. 44 2.)

2. *Sophora formosa* Kearney & Peebles. GILA SOPHORA. Flowers about ⅝ inch long. (Fig. 45 *D*.)

Larger leaflets usually 6-10 mm. broad, tending to be acute; flowers mostly 14-17 mm. long, the banner broadly ovate, 17-20 mm. long, the keel with stalks somewhat more than half as long as the fused blades; seeds averaging about 9 mm. long.

Desert mesas and hills at 3,000 to 4,000 feet elevation. Arizona at the northern and northeastern end of the Graham (Pinaleno) Mountains in Graham County. (Fig. 44 3.) As pointed out by Kearney and Peebles, the nearest relative of this species is *Sophora arizonica*, known only from the Hualpai Mountains in Mohave County about 250 to 300 miles away (Fig. 44 2). The limited distribution of the two plants may indicate that both species are surviving relics of a once more widespread and variable population. Recognition of *Sophora formosa* as a species distinct from *Sophora arizonica* may, of course, become dubious if additional material is discovered.

3. *OLNEYA*. DESERT IRONWOOD

The desert ironwood is a tree 10-30 feet high, most readily distinguished at flowering time (June) by its lavender, pea-type flowers, but at any season it is recognized by the blue-green color of the leaves. The bark is gray with a tendency to be stringy, and its development on all but the smaller branches affords a ready means of distinction from the blue palo verde, which is also blue-green and restricted to washes.

Fig. 45.—Kidneywood, desert ironwood, coursetia, and sophora: *A*, kidneywood, *Eysenhardtia polystachya, 1,* branch with odd-pinnate leaves and a raceme of fruits, *2,* leaf and raceme of flowers; *B*, desert ironwood, *Olneya Tesota, 1,* branch with even-pinnate leaves and fruits, *2,* branch with flowers; *C*, coursetia, *Coursetia glandulosa, 1,* branch with even-pinnate leaves and flowers, *2,* branch with fruits; *D*, Gila sophora, *Sophora formosa, 1,* branch with odd-pinnate leaves and flowers, *2,* branch with fruits. (x $^{1}/_{3}$.)

Twigs green or partly gray or tan, the smaller ones densely short-hairy. Leaves developed in dense clusters from the axillary buds at the nodes of the small branches; leaflets all paired. Corolla papilionaceous. Stamens 10, 9 united. Style flattened, long-hairy on the upper part. Pod brown, thick walled, 7-8 mm. broad, turgid, not constricted between the seeds. Seeds brown, ellipsoid-oblong.

1. *Olneya Tesota* A. Gray. DESERT IRONWOOD; PALO FIERRO (Fig. 45 *B*)

Leaflets in 2-10 pairs, obovate-oblong, obtuse, thick, finely appressed-hairy, the hairs very inconspicuous at maturity; calyx firm, 5-6 mm. long, gray-velvety, the lobes 2-3 mm. long; corolla 12-14 mm. long; pod 2-7 cm. long; seeds 1-6, about 10 mm. long, 7-8 mm. broad.

Gravelly or sandy mesas or rocky foothills of the desert from sea level to 2,500 feet elevation. California in the Colorado Desert; Arizona in the Colorado and Arizona deserts, as far eastward as the lower Verde River and vicinity of Tucson; Baja California and Sonora, Mexico. (Fig. 46 *1*.)

The ironwood is one of the most outstanding trees of the desert. Its heavy wood makes excellent fuel, and it is used for desert souvenirs and other novelties. It is so hard that sawing it is exceedingly difficult, and it dulls cutting instruments. The wood has been used by the Indians for arrow points and tool handles. The mature seeds were gathered and roasted to be eaten without further preparation or to be ground into pinole.

The lower limits of temperature tolerance are similar for ironwood and citrus trees, and the presence of ironwood often is considered as an indicator of a proper climate for the citrus group.

4. *COURSETIA*. COURSETIA

Shrubs 3-6 feet high, with a number of points in common with the desert ironwood, e.g., with no unpaired terminal leaflet and with similar flower structure. Since the ironwood is distinctly a tree with blue-green leaves, spines, and lavender petals, while *Coursetia* is a shrub with green leaves, no spines, and yellow petals only veined or tinged with lavender, there is no danger of confusion. (Fig. 45 *C*.)

Small branches light gray or with some tan. Leaflets tipped with a short, slender point, the rachis prolonged beyond the leaflets. Calyx parted, calyx and pedicels with stalked glands. Stamens 10, 9 united. Pod brown rather thick walled, rather turgid, markedly constricted between the seeds. Seeds brown.

1. *Coursetia glandulosa* A. Gray. COURSETIA (Fig. 45 C)

Leaflets in mostly 5 pairs, elliptic-oblong, 5-7 (rarely 15-20) mm. long, 2-3 (rarely 6-8) mm. broad, appressed-hairy; calyx 5-7 mm. long; corolla 11-13 mm. long; pod 2-5 cm. long, about 5 mm. broad; seeds 2-7, about 3 mm. in diameter.

Rocky canyons and gravelly alluvial fans in the desert foothills and the desert grassland at 2,000 to 4,000 feet elevation. Arizona from the Kofa and Mohawk mountains, Yuma County, eastward to the Superstition Mountains, Maricopa County, and the Santa Catalina and Baboquivari mountains, Pima County; Mexico. (Fig. 46 6.)

Sometimes the stems are covered with a lac which has been utilized by the Indians as a supposed remedy for colds and fevers. This lac and that on the creosote bush bear resemblance to common shellac obtained from India. The lac is deposited by an insect. That on *Coursetia* is orange.

5. *EYSENHARDTIA*. EYSENHARDTIA

(1) Flowers white, almost regular; (2) pods narrow, about ½ inch long, produced in great numbers, turned downward in the raceme; (3) glands sunken, on the leaves, stems, and flowers (especially on the calyx.) The secretion of the gland rises above the adjacent surface of the leaf or other part. (Fig. 45 *A*.)

Twigs brown, tan, or gray. Spines none. Terminal leaflet unpaired, obtuse. Calyx narrowly top-shaped, toothed. Corolla nearly regular, white. Stamens 10, separate. Pod green, becoming tan or brownish, thin-walled, 1-18 cm. long, 2-3.5 mm. broad, flat, not constricted between the seeds. Synonym: *Viborquia*.

1. *Eysenhardtia polystachya* (Ort.) Sarg. KIDNEYWOOD (Fig. 45 *A*)

Leaflets in mostly 10-20 pairs, narrowly oblong, 10-20 mm. long, 3-6 mm. broad, rather thick, very finely and inconspicuously hairy; calyx 5-6 mm. long.

Hillsides and canyons of the upper desert grassland and the lower oak woodland at 4,000 to 5,000 feet elevation. Arizona

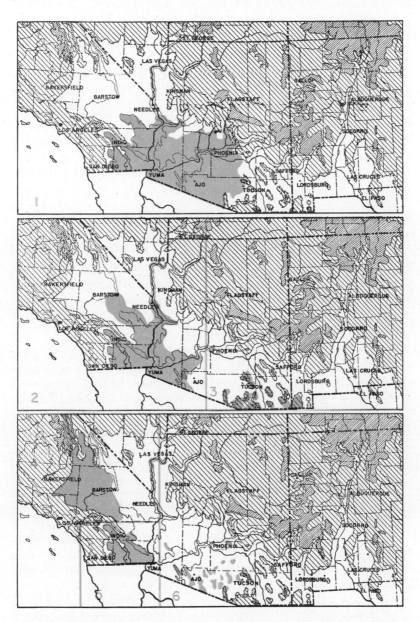

Fig. 46.—Distributional maps: *1*, desert ironwood, *Olneya Tesota*; *2*, smoke tree, *Dalea spinosa*; *3*, kidneywood, *Eysenhardtia polystachya*; *4*, indigo bush, *Dalea Fremontii* var. *Saundersii*; *5*, mesa dalea, *Dalea Schottii*; *6*, coursetia, *Coursetia glandulosa*.

from the Baboquivari Mountains, Pima County, eastward to Cochise County; New Mexico in southern Hidalgo County; Mexico. (Fig. 46 *3*.)

Kidneywood derives its name from the diuretic properties of the wood, which is used in many localities in Mexico for kidney and bladder diseases. Infusions of the heartwood in water exhibit fluorescence, and they have been utilized as dyes.

The gland-dotted herbage (Fig. 45 *A*) has a distinctive resinous odor, and most classes of livestock seek it eagerly for forage. Wild animals eat it, too, and it is particularly palatable to deer.

6. *DALEA*. Parosela; Dalea

Dalea is recognized by the sunken glands on the calyx and the leaves. The secretion of the gland fills up the depression and rises above the surface of the leaf. In *Eysenhardtia*, which has similar glands, the flowers are white and nearly regular, but in *Dalea* the flowers are very irregular and purple or lavender. Also, the pods are short and ovoid or oblong, and they scarcely protrude beyond the calyx. (Fig. 47.)

Small trees or shrubs. Twigs green, brown, tan, gray, or silvery-hairy. Leaves pinnate with a terminal unpaired leaflet or sometimes simple. Flowers in racemes or spikes. Calyx bell- to top-shaped, toothed. Stamens 10, united into a single group. Pod ovate or oblong, barely exceeding the calyx or enclosed by it; seeds few. Synonym: *Parosela*.

KEY TO THE SPECIES

1. Small tree or sometimes a large shrub, practically leafless, the few simple leaves falling away before flowering time (June or July); all the branches ending in sharp, effective spines; calyx with a single circle of large, conspicuous, reddish tan glands; plant silvery or ashy with dense, appressed hair; flowers dark purple, 5-10, in a rather loose raceme 1-1.5 cm. long, the pedicels only about 1 mm. long. (Fig. 47 *D*.)   1. *Dalea spinosa*

1. Shrubs or bushes with numerous leaves; the branches not spiny or the smaller ones or some of them sharp-pointed but not particularly effective as spines; calyx with small, relatively inconspicuous glands distributed irregularly. (Fig. 47 *A-C*.)

    2. Racemes or spikes 2-12 cm. long, the flowers well spaced, dark bluish purple (Fig. 47 *A*); twigs or most of them sharp-pointed and more or less spinelike; pod protruding beyond the calyx (Fig. 47 *A 2*); calyx not long-hairy, the lobes not markedly slender.

3. Flowers in racemes 4-12 cm. long (Fig. 47 *A*); leaves, branchlets and calyces not densely hairy, the relatively sparse hairs long or woolly; thorns relatively few; leaflets narrow, not decurrent on the rachis.

 4. Leaves simple, entire (not lobed, parted, or divided in any way), linear; plant green, not markedly hairy except on the very youngest parts.   2. *Dalea Schottii*

 4. Leaves pinnately parted or pinnate (only the upper ones simple in *D. Fremontii* var. *simplifolia*); plant with short, straight, appressed hairs. (Fig. 47 *A*.) 3. *Dalea Fremontii*

3. Flowers in spikes 2-3.5 cm. long; leaves, branchlets, and calyces densely hairy, the hairs forming an ashy, felty, and conspicuous mat; thorns slender, long and numerous; leaflets mostly one-third to two-thirds as broad as long, often decurrent on the rachis.
             4. *Dalea arborescens*

2. Spikes 1-1.5 cm. long, the flowers crowded (Fig. 47 *B, C*), magenta to lavender; pod enclosed in the calyx, calyx lobes long-hairy (Fig. 47 *B 2*), slender, or in *Dalea scoparia* narrowly triangular.

 3. Petals not attached to the stamens; bracts (subtending scale leaves below the flowers) not present; hairs of the young twigs dense, directed downward or spreading (if spreading, the whole plant covered with a dense, white felt); pointed, somewhat spinelike branches present on the plant, but the points usually ineffective and the branches usually flexible; glands of the branches reddish to tan or yellow and translucent, those of the leaves dark; apical portion of the pod not fringed with long hair.

  4. Leaves pinnate; free portion of the sepal narrow and elongated, the apical gland small and inconspicuous, light colored; glands of the stem reddish tan, those of the leaves black.

   5. Plant green, the hairs of the young branches directed downward; leaflets mostly obovate or broadly so, the terminal one broader than the others and practically circular.
           5. *Dalea polyadenia*

   5. Plant covered with a dense, white felt of hairs spreading at various angles; leaflets obovate or narrowly so, the terminal one oblanceolate and sharply acute at both ends. (Fig. 47 *C*.)   6. *Dalea Emoryi*

 4. Leaves simple, linear, few; free portion of the sepal narrowly triangular, tipped with a conspicuous dark gland; glands of the stem yellow and translucent, those of the leaflets darker or some of them partly yellow; plant green, hairs of the young branches directed downward. 7. *Dalea scoparia*

3. Petals (all but the banner, which stands alone) attached to the united stamens; bracts present; hairs of the young twigs sparse, directed upward (appressed) or spreading; pointed branches none; glands all dark or sometimes some of those on the stem lighter colored; apical portion of the pod fringed with long hair.

    4. Bracts ovate-attenuate, hairy on only the margins; leaflets glabrous; spikes reduced to heads, the axes only 1-2 mm. long; flowers 2-6 per spike, 15 mm. long. (Fig. 47 *B.*)

                                              8. *Dalea formosa*

    4. Bracts linear-lanceolate, densely long-hairy on the margins and the backs; leaflets hairy; spikes not reduced to heads, the axes about 1 cm. long; flowers numerous, about 10 mm. long.

        5. Leaflets mostly 11-17, linear-oblong or sometimes oblanceolate, usually not folded in dried specimens, thinly hairy, not silky or only slightly so.　　　　9. *Dalea Wislizenii*

        5. Leaflets 5-7, cuneate-obovate but mostly folded in dried specimens and appearing narrower, covered with short, appressed, shiny hairs and appearing silky. 10. *Dalea pulchra*

    1. *Dalea spinosa* A. Gray. SMOKE TREE. This small tree (sometimes shrubby when young) is distinguished readily by its smoky to silvery aspect and its compact mass of leafless branches, all of which end in sharp spines. (Fig. 47 *D.*)

Trees 2-8 m. high; leaves few, simple, oblanceolate, 6-9 mm. long; racemes 1-1.5 cm. long, few-flowered; calyx about 4 mm. long, ridged, with a circle of conspicuous reddish brown sunken glands; corolla dark purple, 9-10 mm. long; pods ovate, largely enclosed in the calyx, not splitting open; ovules 4-5; seeds 1 or 2.

Gravelly or sandy washes in the desert from below sea level to 1,000 feet or rarely 1,500 feet elevation. California in the Colorado Desert, occurring as far northward as the vicinity of Baker, San Bernardino County; Arizona, throughout the Colorado Desert; Baja California and Sonora, Mexico. (Fig. 46 *2.*)

The smoke tree is named for the ashy gray color of the branches, which makes the plant appear like a cloud of smoke in the distance. In early summer the trees become conspicuous for their profusion of bright purple or indigo flowers. The plant is used sometimes as an ornamental, but it is restricted to frost-free areas.

    2. *Dalea Schottii* Torr. MESA DALEA. Bush 2-7 feet high, distinguished from the smoke tree by the following characters: (1)

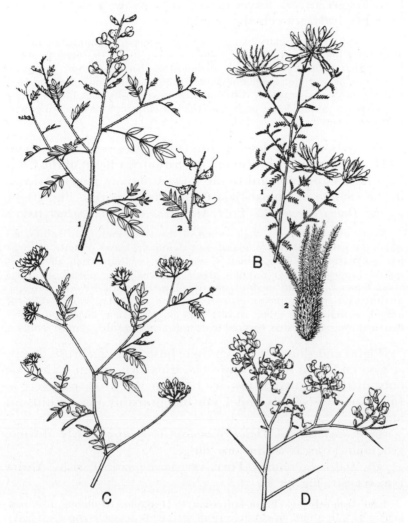

Fig. 47.—Daleas: *A,* indigo bush, *Dalea Fremontii* var. *Saundersii, 1,* leafy branch with flowers, *2,* pods showing the large glands on the surface; *B,* feather dalea, *Dalea formosa, 1,* leafy branch with flowers, *2,* calyx completely enclosing the pod, showing the dark glands on the surface; *C,* white dalea, *Dalea Emoryi,* leafy branch with heads (congested racemes) of flowers and of fruits enclosed in the calyces; *D,* smoke tree, *Dalea spinosa,* showing leafless, spiny branches with (purple to indigo) flowers. (x $^1/_3$, except *B* 2 x $2^1/_3$.)

branches green; (2) leaves numerous, narrow; and (3) thorny branches, leafy, scarcely sharp at all.

Plant only slightly hairy except on the young parts; glands not numerous; leaves linear, 1.5-3 cm. long, about 1 mm. broad, the margins rolled backward (revolute), the exposed portion of the back with short, appressed hairs; racemes 5-7 cm. long, not dense; calyx about 5 mm. long, ridged, with rather small, irregularly distributed glands; corolla dark bluish purple to indigo, 10-12 mm. long; pods more or less elliptic, 8-12 mm. long, with red glands, usually single seeded.

Gravelly or sandy desert plains from below sea level to about 500 feet elevation. California in the Salton Sea Basin of the Colorado Desert and eastward to the lower Colorado River; Arizona in the vicinity of Yuma; Baja California, Mexico. (Fig. 46 5.)

3a. *Dalea Fremontii* Torr. var. *Fremontii*. FREMONT DALEA

Shrub usually 0.5-2 m. high; some of the twigs ending in spines, the spines not particularly sharp; glands not abundant; leaves pinnate, the leaflets 3-5, narrowly oblong, about 6 mm. long, separate from the rachis, sparsely appressed-hairy; racemes about 7-12 cm. long, not dense; calyx about 6 mm. long, with small glands distributed irregularly; calyx lobes, as in all the varieties except var. *pubescens*, broad, dissimilar, shorter than the united portion of the calyx; corolla dark purple, 1 cm. long; pods ovate, flattened from side to side, covered with conspicuous brown glands; ovules 2.

Plains and slopes of the creosote-bush and sagebrush deserts at 2,000 to 3,000 feet or more elevation. Known in California only in the vicinity of Owens Lake in the Mojave Desert in Inyo County; Nevada and Utah but probably not within our range.

Five varieties of *Dalea Fremontii* occupy nearly distinct geographical areas within our range.

3b. *Dalea Fremontii* Torr. var. *Saundersii* (Parish) Munz. INDIGO BUSH (Fig. 47 *A*)

Leaflets mostly 7-9, elliptic-lanceolate to lanceolate or oblong, 6-13 mm. long, 2.5-3.5 or 4 mm. broad, free from the rachis, sparsely appressed-hairy, the rachis often densely hairy; calyx about 4 mm. long, not markedly ridged; pods 8-12 mm. long, 5-6 mm. broad.

Desert slopes and plains at 2,000 to 6,000 feet elevation. California from the Owens River valley to the Mojave Desert as far east as Victorville and to Death Valley region. (Fig. 46 *4*.)

3c. *Dalea Fremontii* Torr. var. *minutifolia* (Parish) L. Benson. JOHNSON DALEA

Leaflets linear to narrowly lanceolate, 6-20 mm. long, 1-3 mm. broad, free from the rachis, appressed-hairy, sometimes densely so; calyx perhaps more strongly ribbed, usually only slightly hairy outside; pod about 8 mm. long.

Desert slopes and plains at mostly 2,000 to 5,000 feet elevation. California in the Mojave Desert from the Death Valley region to the Ord and Cottonwood mountains and southward to the vicinity of Indio in the Colorado Desert; southern Nevada in Nye and Lincoln counties; southwestern Utah in Washington County; Arizona in the Mojave Desert and eastward along the Colorado River to the vicinity of Toroweap Valley. (Fig. 48 *1*.)

3d. *Dalea Fremontii* Torr. var. *pubescens* (Parish) L. Benson

Calyx lobes all alike, awl-shaped, that is, very narrow, but broadest at the bases and tapering outward, as long as the united portion of the calyx; otherwise similar to var. *minutifolia*. Synonyms: *Dalea amoena* S. Wats. *Parosela Johnsonii* (S. Wats.) Vail var. *pubescens* Parish.

Desert slopes and canyon sides at 500 to 4,500 feet elevation. Southern Nevada; southern Utah; Arizona in Mohave and Coconino counties. Rare or at least not well known.

3e. *Dalea Fremontii* Torr. var. *simplifolia* (Parish) L. Benson

Leaflets 1-7 (the upper ones near the inflorescence simple), not distinct from the rachis (decurrent), often joining one another, linear, 8-15 mm. long, 1-2 or 3 mm. broad; calyx appressed-hairy outside; corolla about 8 mm. long; pod about 8 mm. long. Synonyms: *Dalea californica* S. Wats.; *Parosela californica* (S. Wats.) Vail var. *simplifolia* Parish.

Desert plains and canyons at 1,000 to 3,500 feet elevation. California in the northwestern portion of the Colorado Desert and on the eastern slope of the San Bernardino Mountains. (Fig. 48 7.)

4. *Dalea arborescens* Torr. MOJAVE DALEA. (1) Large shrub; (2) hairs dense, felty, ashy, covering the leaves and branchlets and the calyx of each flower; (3) plant localized in the Mojave Desert.

Glands not numerous; leaves pinnatifid—i.e., the leaflets not quite dissected apart, the leaf divisions mostly ovate to elliptic, 4-8 mm. long, 3-5 mm. broad; spikes 2-3.5 cm. long, not dense; calyx 6-7 mm. long, striate, with small, obscure glands distributed irregularly; corolla dark purple, 10-12 mm. long; mature pods not available.

Hills and plains in the desert at 2,000 to 2,500 feet elevation. California at Benton, Mono County, and near the Mojave River in the vicinity of Barstow, Mojave Desert. A rare species apparently distinct from *Dalea Fremontii*. (Fig. 48 *3*).

5. *Dalea polyadenia* Torr. NEVADA DALEA. (1) Flower clusters about ½ inch long; (2) twigs green, hairy, bearing conspicuous brown glands; (3) plant occurring in the Mojave Desert and northward.

Shrub 0.5-2.5 m. high; some of the twigs ending in spines, the spines not particularly sharp, the branches covered with conspicuous large, reddish brown to orange glands, green but densely short-hairy, the hairs turned downward; leaves pinnate, the leaflets 7-13, obovate to nearly circular, 3-5 mm. long, 2.5-4.5 mm. broad, rather densely but not conspicuously appressed-hairy, with sparse black glands; spikes 8-12 or 15 mm. long, very dense; calyx covered with long, woolly hairs, the lobes very slender and long-hairy; corolla lavender or magenta, 7-8 mm. long; pod shorter than the calyx.

Mesas and sandy slopes of the creosote-bush and sagebrush deserts at 2,000 to 6,000 feet elevation. California east of the Sierra Nevada in Mono and Inyo counties and southward to the Mojave River and eastward to the Death Valley region; western to southern Nevada in Clark, Nye, and Lincoln counties; southwestern Utah. (Fig. 48 *6*.)

6. *Dalea Emoryi* A. Gray. WHITE DALEA. (1) Densely branched bush with white felty branches and leaves; (2) plant occurring in sandy areas in the Colorado Desert. (Fig. 47 *C*.)

Bush or bushy shrub 0.4-1 m. high, the branches very dense and inclined to fork, covered with a dense white felt of spreading hairs; twigs narrowed down to points but too soft to be considered as spines; some of the main branches often elongated; leaves pinnate, the leaflets 3-9 or sometimes only 1, the terminal one narrowly oblanceolate, sharply acute at each end, usually 10-14 mm. long, the lateral ones obovate or narrowly so, mostly 4-8 mm. long, 1-3 mm. broad, densely felted with spreading white hairs; glands of the stem, petiole, and rachis reddish tan, those of the leaflets black; spikes about 1 cm. long, 1.5 cm. in diameter, very dense; calyx with dense long, spreading hairs, these turning from white to reddish brown in old herbar-

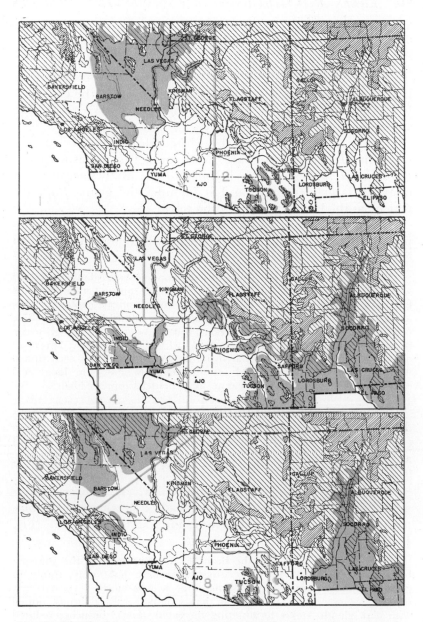

Fig. 48.—Distributional maps: *1*, Johnson dalea, *Dalea Fremontii* var. *minutifolia*; *2*, Wislizenius dalea, *Dalea Wislizenii* var. *sessilis*; *3*, Mojave dalea, *Dalea arborescens*; *4*, white dalea, *Dalea Emoryi*; *5*, feather dalea, *Dalea formosa*; *6*, Nevada dalea, *Dalea polyadenia*; *7*, *Dalea Fremontii* var. *simplifolia*; *8*, Gregg dalea, *Dalea pulchra*; *9*, broom dalea, *Dalea scoparia*.

ium specimens, densely covered with red glands in the grooves; free portion of the sepal long, narrow, and hairy; corolla magenta, 5-6 mm. long; pod shorter than the calyx.

Sandy desert plains from below sea level to 500 feet elevation. California in the Colorado Desert; Arizona in the Colorado Desert eastward as far as Aztec, Yuma County; Baja California and Sonora, Mexico. (Fig. 48 *4.*)

In the vicinity of Yuma, the white dalea and other species, including *Dalea Schottii,* are hosts for a tiny parasite plant, *Pilostyles Thurberi,* which belongs to the Rafflesiaceae. This family is largely tropical, and it includes the genus *Rafflesia,* which has the largest flowers in the world.

7. *Dalea scoparia* A. Gray. BROOM DALEA. (1) Leaves simple, ¼ to ¾ inch long; (2) plant restricted to sandy soils in New Mexico and western Texas; rare in Arizona.

Bush perhaps 1 m. high, green but the younger twigs densely covered with downward-directed hairs; branches flexible, some of them pointed but not spinose; leaves few, simple, entire, linear, mostly 4-10 or 15 mm. long; glands of the stem with a clear, translucent yellowish secretion, those of the leaves appearing much darker; spikes about 1 cm. long, 1 cm. in diameter, dense; calyx densely covered with long, somewhat appressed or matted stiff hairs, the lobes narrowly triangular, long-hairy, each tipped with a conspicuous dark gland; corolla magenta, 7-8 mm. long; pod enclosed in the calyx, elliptic, 3 mm. long, densely appressed-hairy.

Dunes and sandy soils of the desert and the desert grassland. Arizona at Leupp, eastern Coconino County, and Willcox, Cochise County; New Mexico about Deming, Luna County, and abundant in the Rio Grande Valley; western Texas; Mexico. (Fig. 48 *9.*)

8. *Dalea formosa* Torr. FEATHER DALEA. (1) Flower clusters with 2 to 6 flowers forming small "heads"; (2) leaves glabrous, with 7-15 leaflets; (3) shrubs low, intricately branched. (Fig. 47 *B.*)

Low shrub, 2-4 dm. high, the branches distinctly woody, the youngest branches with sparse long, spreading hairs; bark light gray, spines or pointed branches, none; leaves pinnate, the leaflets mostly 7-15, narrowly obovate, 2-3 mm. long, mostly less than 1 mm. broad, glabrous, dotted with dark glands; spikes terminating the small, lateral branches reduced practically to heads, the axis 1-2 mm. long, the flowers 2-6 per spike, each flower enclosed by a special, gland-dotted ovate-attenuate bract which is

Plate XXII.—Crucifixion thorns: *A, Holacantha Emoryi,* with clusters of the persistent fruits; *B, Holacantha Emoryi,* close-up view of a single branch with fruits; *C, Koeberlinia spinosa,* close-up view of flowering branches; *D, Canotia Holacantha,* a tree growing on an alluvial fan. (Photographs: *A* by R. H. Peebles; *B, D* by A. A. Nichol; *C* by Robert A. Darrow.)

Plate XXIII.—Elephant tree, *Bursera microphylla: A,* a single tree in a desert wash; *B,* close-up view of the swollen trunk and main branches showing the white bark. (Photographs by Robert A. Darrow.)

hairy only on the margin; calyx with dense long, spreading hairs, the lobes long and slender, covered also with long, spreading hairs; corolla reddish to magenta, about 15 mm. long, the wings and the keel attached to the stamens, the banner free and standing off by itself; pod obovate, about 3 mm. long, largely glabrous, but densely fringed with long hair on the apical margin, enclosed in the calyx.

Gravelly or rocky slopes in the upper desert, the desert grassland, and the oak woodland at 3,000 to 6,000 feet elevation. Southwestern Utah; Arizona in the mountains below the Mogollon Rim from Yavapai County southeastward to eastern Pima, Santa Cruz, and Cochise counties; New Mexico on the Gila River and Rio Grande drainages, occurring as far north as Santa Fe; eastern Colorado to Texas; Mexico. (Fig. 48 5.)

This small shrub is used sometimes as an ornamental, and it is attractive at flowering time. Feather dalea is considered as fairly good browse for range livestock, and it is eaten by native animals. It is known to be especially palatable to deer.

9a. *Dalea Wislizenii* A. Gray var. *sessilis* A. Gray. WISLIZE-NIUS DALEA. (1) Leaves thinly hairy, with 11-17 leaflets; (2) spikes with many flowers; (3) plant occurring in southeastern Arizona.

Shrub similar to *Dalea formosa*; leaflets mostly 11-17, mostly linear-oblong but sometimes oblanceolate, usually not folded in dried specimens, thinly hairy, not silky or only slightly so; spikes terminating both long and short branches, not reduced to heads, the axes about 1 cm. long, many-flowered; bracts linear-lanceolate, densely long-hairy on the margins and the backs; flowers about 1 cm. long.

Hillsides and canyons of the upper desert and the desert grassland at 3,000 to 5,000 feet elevation. Arizona from the Baboquivari and Santa Catalina mountains, Pima County, eastward to the mountains of Graham, Greenlee, and Cochise counties; Mexico. (Fig. 48 2.)

10. *Dalea pulchra* Gentry. GREGG DALEA. (1) Leaves gray, silky-hairy, with 5-7 leaflets; (2) plant occurring in south central Arizona.

Shrub similar to *Dalea formosa* and especially to *Dalea Wislizenii* var. *sessilis,* from which it differs chiefly as follows: leaflets 5-7, cuneate-obovate, but mostly folded in dried specimens and appearing narrower, covered with short-appressed, shiny hairs and appearing silky. Long considered as *Dalea Greggii* of Mexico; the recent segregation apparently valid.

Rocky or gravelly slopes and canyons in the upper desert and the desert grassland at 3,000 to 5,000 feet elevation. Arizona from the Baboquivari Mountains, Pima County, eastward to western Cochise County; Mexico. (Fig. 48 *8*.)

This shrub is suitable for ornamental plantings, and its silvery leaves and rose-purple flowers are unusually attractive. It has some forage value for livestock, but usually it is not sufficiently abundant to be important.

The recently-described *Dalea tentaculoides* Gentry evidently occurs in the oak woodland at higher altitudes than the area covered in this manual.

Family 15. *ZYGOPHYLLACEAE*. Caltrops Family

The caltrops family receives its name from the spiny fruits of *Tribulus,* the puncture vine, bullhead, or caltrops. In the Middle Ages caltrops—that is, 4-spined iron structures—were scattered on the ground to check the charge of horsemen. The five segments of the fruit of the plant caltrops are somewhat similar to the iron caltrops. The puncture vine is one of the best-known southwestern weeds, and it has spread rapidly along highways because the spiny fruit segments penetrate readily a variety of objects including the tires of automobiles (which they sometimes puncture) . (Pls. III *A*; XXI; Fig. 49 *A*.)

Other plants of special interest are the so-called "summer poppy," *Kallstroemia grandiflora,* and a near shrub, *Fagonia chilensis,* common in the portions of the deserts near the Colorado River. The outstanding plant of the family, in so far as the Southwestern deserts are concerned, is the creosote bush, and this plant is the one, above all others, characteristic of the desert. Its range practically outlines the desert, and no other plant is as accurate an indicator.

An outstanding character of the family is the fruit, which consists of 5-12 segments (carpels) which separate at maturity. The hypogynous flowers, the curious pinnate leaves with only 2 leaflets and these joined, the petals arranged like the blades of an electric fan, and the 5 segmented woolly fruits are adequate to distinguish the only true shrub in our area, the creosote bush.

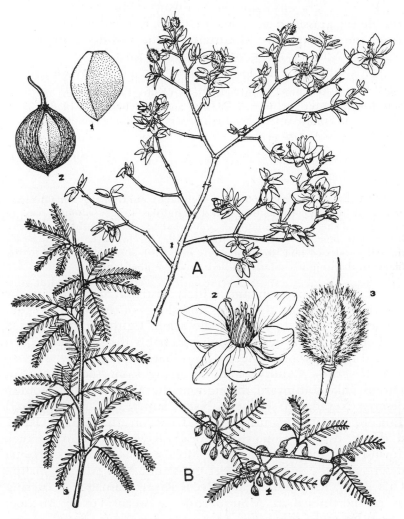

Fig. 49.—Creosote bush and elephant tree: *A,* creosote bush, *Larrea divaricata,*
sometimes known locally as "greasewood," *1,* branch with pinnate leaves each
consisting of two fused leaflets and with flowers, *2,* flower, *3,* fruit, showing the
style and the 5 densely hairy carpels of the ovary, which separate at maturity;
B, elephant tree, *Bursera microphylla, 1,* seed, *2,* fruit splitting open, *3,* leafy
branch, showing the pinnate leaves, *4,* branch with fruits. (x ¹/₃, except *A 2, 3*
and *B 1, 2* x 2.)

Herbs or shrubs. Leaves opposite and pinnate or palmate with 3 leaflets; stipules present. Flowers bisexual, hypogynous, solitary; sepals 5; petals 5; stamens 10.

1. *LARREA*. Creosote Bush

Resinous, ill-smelling shrubs. Leaves pinnate but consisting of only 2 leaflets and these jointed, varnished. Flowers solitary, terminating the short branches; petals yellow, turned sidewise and resembling the blades of an electric fan. Fruit nearly spheroidal, separating into 5 woolly segments. (Pls. III *A*; XXI; Fig. 49 *A*.)

1. *Larrea divaricata* Cav. creosote bush (Pls. III *A*; XXI; Fig. 49 *A*)

Shrub usually 1-2 m. (3-6 feet) high; root crown heavy; main stems arising at an angle from the ground, wandlike, limber, about 1 cm. in diameter on the average, simple or somewhat branched, bushy at the tips; leaflets 6-10 mm. long, 3-4 mm. broad, sessile, the broad bases of the pair united; petals 6-9 mm. long; stamens each with a scale attached to the filament, the scale irregularly slashed; fruit 7-8 mm. long.

The most common and widely distributed shrub in the desert; occurring on the plains and slopes of the foothills from sea level to about 4,000 feet elevation. California at isolated stations west of the deserts, where probably the seeds have been carried in the wool of sheep (Poso Flat, Kern County; Aguangua, Riverside County) and occurring from the vicinity of Owens Lake southward throughout the Mojave and Colorado deserts; Nevada in southern Nye County and in Clark and Lincoln counties; southwestern Utah on the Virgin River drainage; Arizona along the Colorado River from Kanab Creek downstream and throughout the Mojave, Colorado, and Arizona deserts and the adjacent desert grassland; New Mexico on the Gila River, Rio Grande, and Pecos River drainages; occurring as far northward as Albuquerque; western Texas; Mexico; Argentina and Chile. (Fig. 51 *1*.)

The plant varies in leaf width, venation, and hairiness, and in size of the scales of the filaments. The North American plants may constitute one or more varieties of *Larrea divaricata*, described from a South American type, but differences are slight.

The creosote bush occurs in the driest and hottest portions of North America. It forms pure stands in many of its ranges, particularly on sandy or gravelly mesas and slopes. In southern Arizona and New Mexico it may occupy sandy or heavy soils underlain by the calcareous hardpan known as caliche. It is adapted to many soil types, but usually it is absent from markedly saline soils.

The small, resinous leaves impart a strong creosotelike odor which is evident particularly after a rain. The abundance of the species and the odor have led to application of such local names as hedionilla or "little bad smeller." The plant is called also gobernadora, and in southern Arizona the commonest name is "greasewood," a name applied to many plants and better reserved for the widespread shrub of alkaline places in the Great Basin and in portions of the creosote-bush desert, *Sarcobatus vermiculatus*.

The creosote bush is fed upon by only a few insects and occasionally by jack rabbits. However, in some parts of Mexico the flower buds pickled in vinegar are considered to be a choice food item. Standley reports that poultices of creosote bush are applied to bruises and sores and that decoctions of the leaves have antiseptic properties. In primitive medicine the decoctions are taken internally for tuberculosis and gastric complaints. Like other ubiquitous plants with peculiar odors or flavors, creosote bush has tended to become a cure-all.

The excretions of the lac scale (*Tachardiella*) are deposited sometimes in great quantity on the stems, and the Indians utilized them for mending pottery and for waterproofing baskets. According to Mr. Lloyd Mason Smith these are common near Palm Springs. In most areas they are uncommon. Globular leafy galls about as large as marbles or walnuts are common on the stems. These are produced by the creosote gall midge (*Asphondylia*).

Family 16. *RUTACEAE*. Citrus Family

This family, often called the rue family, is best known for the genus *Citrus*, which includes the oranges, lemons, citron, and grapefruit. The desert shrubs are readily distinguished by the glandular aromatic nature of the stems and leaves and the deep division of the fruits into divergent carpels. (Fig. 50 *B*; 52 *E, F*.)

Fig. 50.—Crucifixion thorn and turpentine broom: *A*, crucifixion thorn, *Hola-cantha Emoryi*, one of the three types in the Southwestern deserts, *1*, character-istic spiny, leafless branch, *2*, branch with dense fruit clusters, *3*, flowering branch, *4*, fruit with several carpels which separate at maturity, *5*, single flower showing the several stigmas, the densely hairy stamens, the petals, and the shorter sepals; *B*, turpentine broom, *Thamnosma montana*, *1*, the curious bi-spherical fruit covered with minute glands, *2*, branch with fruits, *3*, flowering branch with several of the dark bluish purple flowers. (x $^1/_3$, except *A 4, 5* x 2; *B 1* x $2^2/_3$.)

Shrubs or small trees. Plant with dotlike glands secreting aromatic oils (as in the orange), glabrous. Leaves alternate, simple or palmate. Flower with a disc; sepals and petals 4-5; stamens usually 4-5 or 8-10; carpels 2-12 or more, united firmly; style 1.

KEY TO THE GENERA

1. Fruit consisting of 2 spheres, each of which divides crosswise, shedding the seeds; leaves simple, linear, not persisting after flowering time; petals purple. 1. THAMNOSMA

1. Fruit with 5 divergent carpels, each splitting vertically at the top; leaves palmate, the leaflets linear, persistent; petals white. 2. CHOISYA

1. *THAMNOSMA*. TURPENTINE BROOM

Herbs or shrubs, the branches elongated, barely spiny at the apices or not spiny. Leaves small, linear, falling away soon after flowering time. Fruit with 2 divergent, spheroidal segments, each dividing crosswise, shedding the seeds. (Fig. 50 *B*.)

1. *Thamnosma montana* Torr. & Frem. TURPENTINE BROOM; CORDONCILLO. Distinguished from other small shrubs by the yellowish green, gland-dotted branches and small purple flowers. (Fig. 50 *B*.)

Shrub 3-8 dm. high, profusely branched; leaves ephemeral, 4-8 mm. long, 1 mm. broad; sepals 4, green, forming a saucer 3-4 mm. broad; petals 4, dark blue-purple, 8-10 mm. long, erect; stamens 8, the anthers dark blue-purple; each half of the fruit 5-8 mm. in diameter, gland-dotted.

Rocky or gravelly slopes and mesas in the desert at mostly 2,000 to 4,000 feet elevation. California in the Mojave Desert from Death Valley and Barstow southward and along the western and northern edges of the Salton Sea Basin of the Colorado Desert; southern Nevada; southwestern Utah; Arizona along the Colorado and Little Colorado rivers in the Grand Canyon region, in the Mojave Desert, and in the Arizona Desert as far eastward as eastern Pinal and Gila counties; Baja California and Sonora, Mexico. (Fig. 51 2.)

Like most other strong-scented plants, this leafless shrub is reputed to have medicinal properties.

An herbaceous or slightly woody species, *Thamnosma Texana* (A. Gray) Torr., grows at middle altitudes from eastern Arizona to Texas and Mexico.

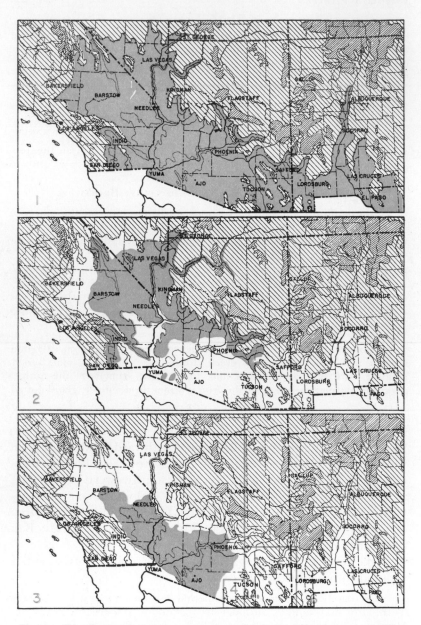

Fig. 51.—Distributional maps: *1*, creosote bush, *Larrea divaricata*; *2*, turpentine broom, *Thamnosma montana*; *3*, crucifixion thorn, *Holacantha Emoryi*; *4*, *Choisya dumosa* var. *mollis*; *5*, Arizona star leaf, *Choisya dumosa* var. *arizonica*; *6*, star leaf, *Choisya dumosa*.

2. CHOISYA

Shrubs, the branches not spiny. Leaves palmate, the leaflets linear, persistent. Fruit with 5 divergent, glandular carpels, each carpel with a knob or point in the upper portion of the middle of the back. (Fig. 52 *E, F.*)

1a. *Choisya dumosa* (Torr.) A. Gray. var. *dumosa*. STAR LEAF; MEXICAN ORANGE. Distinguished by the palmate (star-shaped) leaves, the leaflets narrow, glandular on the margins and petioles. (Fig. 52 *E.*)

Branchlets and petioles short-hairy, the hairs appressed or spreading, abundant but not obscuring the surface beneath them, those of the pedicels long, spreading; leaflets 5-13, 1-4 cm. long, 1-3 mm. broad; petioles half as long to fully as long as the leaflets; flowers relatively small, the petals 5-8 mm. long; stigmas tending to remain separate, each about 0.2-0.4 mm. in diameter; each of the 5 carpels of the fruit about 6 mm. long, sparsely spreading-hairy, the persistent style and the warty projection of the back low and inconspicuous, the glands prominent.

Sandy or rocky soils of slopes and canyons in the upper part of the desert, the desert grassland, and the oak woodland at 4,000 to 7,000 feet elevation. New Mexico on the Rio Grande drainage; western Texas; northern Mexico. (Fig. 51 *6.*)

When they are crushed, the gland-dotted leaflets are heavily aromatic, and their fragrance resembles that of the foliage of the related citrus fruits. The plant is worthy of cultivation as an ornamental, since both the bright green foliage and the flowers are attractive. Livestock do not browse the species, and it is reputed to be poisonous.

1b. *Choisya dumosa* (Torr.) A. Gray var. *arizonica* (Standl.) L. Benson. ARIZONA STAR LEAF (Fig. 52 *F*)

Branchlets and petioles obscured by the dense, appressed, silvery hairs; leaflets 3-5, 2.5-5 cm. long, 1-3 or (Aravaipa Canyon) 4.5 mm. broad; petioles $1/_{10}$ to $1/_2$ as long as the leaflets; flowers relatively large, the petals 10-13 mm. long; stigmas forming a knob about 1 mm. in diameter; carpels about 7 mm. long, appressed-hairy, the apical and dorsal points long and prominent, the glands inconspicuous.

Rocky or gravelly slopes in the upper desert, the desert grassland, and the oak woodland at 4,000 to 5,500 feet elevation. Arizona in the mountains of eastern Pima, southern Graham, and Cochise counties; northern Sonora. Commonly occurring on limestone soils. (Fig. 51 5.)

Choisya dumosa (Torr.) A. Gray var. *mollis* (Standl.) L. Benson. Branchlets and petioles with rather long spreading hairs resembling those found on parts of the similar organs of *Choisya dumosa;* leaflets 3-5, 2-4.5 cm. long, 3-5 mm. broad; petioles about half as long as the leaflets or somewhat longer; flowers relatively large, the petals 8-10 mm. long; stigmas transitional between the two preceding types; carpels similar to those of the typical variety.

This variety occurs above our range in the oak woodland at about 5,000 feet elevation. Arizona in the mountains of Santa Cruz County west of Nogales; Sonora, Mexico. (Fig. 51 4.)

Family 17. *SIMAROUBACEAE.* QUASSIA FAMILY

This family is well known in the subtropics and tropics, but in the Southwest it is represented by only the tree of heaven (*Ailanthus*), which occasionally escapes from cultivation and grows along streams or in other fairly well-watered situations, and by one of the three crucifixion thorns. The crucifixion thorn is recognized by lack of leaves and by its large, rigid, spine-pointed, finely hairy branches ranging from $1/6$ to $1/3$ inch in diameter and its large clusters of long-persistent fruits (lasting several seasons), each having from 5 to 10 divergent parts. (Fig. 50 *A*; Pl. XXII *A, B*.)

Shrubs or trees; not glandular or aromatic, the branches very densely and finely hairy at first. Leaves alternate, various. Flowers with discs, bisexual or sometimes unisexual; sepals 3-5; petals 3-5; stamen-bearing disc 10-lobed. Fruit various.

1. *HOLACANTHA.* CRUCIFIXION THORN

Small trees with rigid, spine-pointed, intricately arranged branches. Branches densely and finely hairy at first. Leaves scalelike, ephemeral. Flowers unisexual, the staminate and pistillate flowers on different plants, produced in dense clusters; sepals about 5-8; petals 5-8; stamens about 10-15, the filaments densely hairy. Carpels 5-10, separating into as many drupelike structures. (Fig. 50 *A*; Pl. XXII *A, B*.)

1. *Holacantha Emoryi* A. Gray. CRUCIFIXION THORN; CORONA DE CRISTO (Fig. 50 *A*; Pl. XXII *A, B*)

Tree 2-4 m. (6-12 feet) high; branches very stout; flowers about 6-8 mm. in diameter; sepals hairy, reddish purple-tinged, about 1 mm. long; petals densely hairy on the backs, reddish purple on the upper sides, about 3 mm. long; fruit segments (carpels) ovate, markedly flattened, about 6 mm. long.

Fine-textured alluvial soils of desert valley at about 500 to 2,000 feet elevation. California in the lower elevations of the Mojave Desert near Daggett and along the low-lying valleys of southeastern San Bernardino County and the Colorado River drainage; Arizona on the lower Gila River drainage as far eastward as Florence, Pinal County; northern Sonora, Mexico. The plant occurs normally on alluvial bottom lands, but in the more arid parts of the desert frequently it occurs on unstabilized sand dunes. (Fig. 51 3.)

This is one of the three crucifixion thorns occurring within the Southwestern deserts. The others are *Canotia Holacantha* and *Koeberlinia spinosa.*

Family 18. *BURSERACEAE.* Torchwood Family

The torchwood family is known best for plants of the genus *Boswellia,* which yield frankincense, and the aromatic properties of the two species of the family occurring in the Southwestern deserts are marked. The leaves of the commoner of the two native species, the elephant tree, yield copal, which is burned by the Indians as incense used in religious ceremonies. (Fig. 49 *B;* Pl. XXIII.)

Small trees or shrubs. Leaves alternate, pinnate, the leaflets small. Flower with a disc; sepals 3-5, united; petals 3-5; stamens 6-10. Ovary superior; carpels 2-5; style 1; fruit dry, 1-5-celled, only 1 ovule maturing into a seed.

1. *BURSERA*

Leaves deciduous, in our species odd-pinnate. Flowers solitary or paniculate. Carpels 3, the fruit 3-angled, splitting open along the angles; seed 1, large; ovary wall fleshy but becoming dry and leathery. (Fig. 49 *B;* Pl. XXIII.)

KEY TO THE SPECIES

1. Lateral leaflets ovate to oblong, mostly 0.5-1 cm. long; flowers solitary or in small, short-peduncled clusters.   1. *Bursera microphylla*

1. Lateral leaflets lanceolate or ovate-lanceolate, mostly 1.5-4 cm. long; flowers several in a cluster below a tuft of new leaves at the end of a short branch.   2. *Bursera odorata*

1. *Bursera microphylla* A. Gray. ELEPHANT TREE; TOROTE; COPAL. (1) Shrubs or small trees with reddish brown twigs and massive, papery-barked trunks; (2) leaves pinnate, aromatic; (3) fruit 3-angled, leathery, 1-seeded. (Fig. 49 *B*; Pl. XXIII.)

Small tree usually 2-5 m. (6-15 feet) high in Arizona but sometimes up to 10 m. (about 30 feet) high in Mexico; trunk proportionately massive, irregular and short perhaps because of frequent freezing back in the early years, 2-7 dm. in diameter at the base; bark white on the outside, the outer layers peeling off as thin sheets, the next thin layers green, the inner thick layers red, the plant reported to have "bloodlike juice" in the bark, at least at certain seasons; leaves with about 8-16 pairs of leaflets, the leaflets linear or linear-oblanceolate, 5-10 mm. long, 1-2 mm. broad, smooth-margined; some of the flowers unisexual; sepals and petals 5; stamens 10; fruit more or less ellipsoidal, but somewhat angular in cross section, 7-8 mm. long, 5-6 mm. thick.

Rocky desert slopes mostly at 1,000 to 2,000 feet elevation. California on the west side of the Salton Sea Basin of the Colorado Desert between Fish and Carrizo creeks; Arizona in the mountains south of the Gila River from Yuma County to the Sierra Estrella, Maricopa County, and to western Pima County; Baja California and Sonora, Mexico. (Fig. 53 *1*.)

This distinctive tree is characteristic of extremely arid regions. Its stout, sharply tapering trunk and branches have given rise to the name elephant tree. The bark of the twigs is reddish brown, but on the older branches and the main trunk it becomes light colored and papery in the outer thin layers, green in the next thin layers, and red in the inner thick layers. The bark is used in Mexico as a source of dye and tannins. Like the rest of the family, the tree contains abundant aromatic oil.

2. *Bursera fagaroides* (H.B.K.) Engler. The plant is distinguished readily from *Bursera microphylla* by the large, lanceolate, ovate-lanceolate, or narrowly elliptic leaflets usually 1.5-4 cm. long and by the subapical clusters of flowers or fruits on short side branches ending in clusters of leaves. Synonym: *Bursera odorata* Brandegee.

Dry situations on limestone hills at about 4,000 feet elevation. Arizona near Fresnal at the west base of the Baboquivari Mountains, Pima County; Baja California and Sonora, Mexico.

Family 19. *EUPHORBIACEAE*. Spurge Family

By Louis Cutter Wheeler*

Herbs, shrubs, or trees, often with milky juice. Leaves alternate, opposite, or whorled, simple or rarely compound; stipules present and separate or united, or absent. Flowers unisexual; calyx present or absent; corolla present and petals separate or united, or absent; stamens 1 to indefinitely numerous; ovary superior, 3-chambered or sometimes 1-4 chambered; ovules pendulous, 1 or 2 per chamber; styles as many as the chambers, distinct or variously united, often divided. Fruit a capsule, each carpel usually splitting open by two elastic valves, sometimes tardily splitting open or even remaining closed. Seeds carunculate (with a protrusion near the attachment point) or not carunculate; seed coat crustaceous; endosperm copious, oily; embryo straight or curved. (Figs. 52 *A-D*; 54.)

The descriptions of the family, genera, and species apply to all the plants belonging to each group which occurs in the area. The statements of distinctions, as well as the keys, apply only to those woody members of the family included in the present treatment. This will explain seeming contradictions between certain generic diagnoses and the keys and statements of distinctive characters.

KEY TO THE GENERA

1. Leaves not lobed.
    2. Plant with star-shaped hairs. (Fig. 52 *C 3*.)
        3. Leaves not lobed or scarcely so; flowers unisexual, the staminate and pistillate flowers on the same plant; staminate flowers with the parts in 5's, with petals; anthers turned inward and downward in the bud; stamens 12-17; carpels not carinate (not with a ridge down the back); seeds carunculate. (Fig. 52 *C*.)

        2. CROTON

        3. Leaves crenate, flowers unisexual, the staminate and pistillate flowers on different plants; staminate flowers without petals; sepals 3-4; stamens 3-7; anthers erect in the bud; carpels with an obvious ridge down the back (carinate) when they are young, this persisting at the apex at maturity; seeds not carunculate. (Fig. 52 *D*.)   4. BERNARDIA
    2. Plant glabrous or with simple or forked hairs (these often appearing like simple hairs attached at the middles).
        3. Flowers with petals; filaments united into a column; stamens 8-10; flowers in racemes, cymes, or dense clusters or solitary.

* Department of Botany, University of Southern California, Los Angeles, California.

4. Petals separate; flowers in racemes; anthers about as broad as long; pistillate and staminate flowers on the same plant, imparting a purple color to water on boiling; leaves elliptical to lanceolate, the margins irregularly and often bluntly saw-toothed; seeds not carunculate, angled; ovary densely hairy.
3. DITAXIS

4. Petals joined for about three fourths of their length (Fig. 54 *B 3*); flowers in cymes or dense clusters or solitary; anthers distinctly longer than broad; pistillate and staminate flowers on different plants, without water-soluble pigments; leaf blades obovate-cuneate, spatulate, cordate-reniform, or cor-date-deltoid with an acuminate apex, the margins entire or crenate-dentate; seeds carunculate, without angles; ovary glabrous. (Fig. 54 *A, B.*)
7. JATROPHA

3. Flowers without petals but sometimes produced in cyathia resembling simple perfect flowers, the involucre of the cyathium resembling a short floral tube and bearing petal-like appendages on the margin; filaments free or, if united near the base, stamens 2.

4. Pistillate and staminate flowers on different plants; ovules 2 in each chamber of the ovary; styles 3-4, not divided. (Fig. 52 *A, B.*)
1. TETRACOCCUS

4. Pistillate and staminate flowers on the same plant; ovule 1 in each chamber of the ovary; styles 3, forked, or dissected into threadlike segments, or 2 and undivided.

5. Styles 3, dissected into threadlike segments, or 2 and entire; inflorescence spikelike.

6. Foliage and branchlets glandular-hairy; stamens 6-8; carpels 3; styles 3, dissected into threadlike segments; inflorescence beset with numerous stalked glands; pistillate flower subtended by leaflike bracts, which continue growth after flowering; juice not milky. (Fig. 54 *F.*)
5. ACALYPHA

6. Foliage and branchlets glabrous; stamens 2; carpels 2; styles 2, undivided; pistillate flowers subtended by bracts which do not grow after flowering; juice milky. (Fig. 54 *C.*)
9. SAPIUM

5. Styles 3, each forked; inflorescence a cyathium simulating a perfect (bisexual) flower.
10. EUPHORBIA

1. Leaves palmately lobed. (Fig. 54 *D 2, E 2.*)

2. Leaves peltate; staminate flowers borne below the pistillate; stamens numerous, the number indefinite; filaments united into a treelike

structure; stigmas red, linear, recurved, with minute projections; ovary with long projections (papillate); fruit (capsule) spiny.

6. RICINUS

2. Leaves not peltate; staminate flowers borne above the pistillate; stamens 8-10; filaments separate, attached around a fleshy central disc; stigmas pale, broad, thin, flat, and fanlike; ovary and capsule essentially smooth or at least not conspicuously rough. (Fig. 54 *D*, *E*.)

8. MANIHOT

1. *TETRACOCCUS*

(1) Ovules 2 in each chamber of the ovary; (2) styles 3 or 4, undivided. (Fig. 52 *A*, *B*.)

Shrubs, leaves simple, alternate or opposite, with petioles, without stipules. Pistillate and staminate flowers on different plants; petals none. Staminate flowers in dense clusters on short spurlike side branchlets or crowded in heads or racemelike panicles; sepals 5-12; stamens 5-12; filaments separate, attached beneath the lobed central disc. Pistillate flowers 1 to 3 together; sepals 5-6 or 8; ovary 3-4-chambered; styles spatulate; fruit a capsule, splitting open; seeds 2, or, by abortion, often 1, carunculate.

KEY TO THE SPECIES

1. Leaves entire, oblanceolate to spatulate; staminate flowers in small umbels of a few on short lateral spurs; pedicels 2-5 mm. long; pistillate flowers almost lacking pedicels; ovary and capsule with 3 chambers; styles 3. (Fig. 52 *A*.)   1. *Tetracoccus Hallii*

1. Leaves dentate, narrowly ovate-acute to ovate and even elliptical; staminate flowers very numerous, in stalked heads or racemiform panicles, on pedicels 0.5-1 mm. long; pistillate flowers on peduncles 6-10 mm. long; ovary and capsule with 4 chambers; styles 4. (Fig. 52 *B*.)
2. *Tetracoccus ilicifolius*

1. *Tetracoccus Hallii* T. S. Brandegee. (1) Leaves (except on the current year's growth) in little clusters; (2) stems leafy nearly throughout; (3) branches divergent, spreading almost at right angles. (Fig. 52 *A*.)

Rigid branched shrub 0.5-2 m. tall; leaves alternate on the season's branches, fascicled on very short spurs on older branches, 4-12 mm. long, entire, oblanceolate to spatulate, tapering to a very short petiole, practically glabrous to sparsely appressed-hairy; staminate flowers 1-5 on each spur branchlet, the pedicels 2-5 mm. long; sepals 5-8; stamens 5-8, filaments glabrous; pistillate flowers 1-3 on the spurs, with the 5-6 sepals appressed-hairy, the disc irregularly lobed, the margin slightly slashed; ovary appressed-hairy, usually 3-, rarely 2- or 4-chambered; styles equaling the chambers in number, the appressed-hairy tips spreading; fruit scarcely

Fig. 52.—Euphorbia family and star leaf: *A, Tetracoccus Hallii, 1,* branch with leaves and fruits, *2,* staminate flower consisting of sepals and stamens, *3,* pistillate flower consisting of a pistil and calyx; *B, Tetracoccus ilicifolius,* branch with fruits and hollylike leaves; *C,* Sonora croton, *Croton sonorae, 1,* branch with leaves and fruits, *2,* flowering branch, the upper part of the spike with staminate flowers and the lower with 1-3 pistillate flowers, *3,* star-shaped hair from a leaf or a young branch, *4,* staminate flower with sepals, petals, and stamens; *D, Bernardia incana, 1,* staminate flower with sepals and stamens, *2,* branch with leaves and fruits; *E,* star leaf or choisya, *Choisya dumosa, 1,* fruit with the five carpels separating at maturity, *2,* branch with leaves and a flower cluster; *F,* Arizona star leaf, *Choisya dumosa* var. *arizonica,* branch with leaves and flowers (the longer, more numerous leaflets are to be noted). (x ¹/₃ except *A 2, 3* x 1¹/₃; *C 3* x 16; *C 4* x 7; *D 1* x 8; *E 1* x 1.)

Plate XXIV.—Gray thorn and desert milkweed: *A,* gray thorn, *Condalia lycioides* var. *canescens; B,* close-up view of a branch with fruits; *C,* desert milkweed, *Asclepias subulata,* showing the rushlike, leafless stems, the flower clusters, and the pods. (Photographs: *A, B* by A. A. Nichol; *C,* by Robert H. Peebles.)

Plate XXV.—Ocotillo, *Fouquieria splendens: A,* relatively young ocotillos in leaf; *B,* large ocotillo in flower; *C,* ocotillos flowering during a dry spring, the stems remaining leafless; *D,* ocotillos with well-developed leaves during a wet season; *E,* ocotillo branch with the leaves of the first season of growth. The petioles and lower midribs of these leaves form the persistent spines, and leaves of succeeding seasons are produced in a dense fascicle from the axillary bud above each spine. (Photographs by Robert A. Darrow.)

stalked, 8-9 mm. long, sparsely appressed-hairy, ovoid to ellipsoidal, the base depressed; seeds laterally compressed when 2 seeds mature, usually 1 per chamber by abortion, compressed-pear-shaped (grape-seed shape), about 7 mm. long.

Hillsides and mesas in the desert at 500 to 2,500 feet elevation. California in the mountains along the northern edge of the Colorado Desert; Arizona from the Rawhide Mountains, Mohave County, to the Castle Dome Mountains, Yuma County; to Coahuila, Mexico. Flowering from March until May. Fertile seeds seem to be produced infrequently. (Fig. 53 *4*.)

2. *Tetracoccus ilicifolius* Cov. & Gilman. (1) Leaves opposite, with sharp teeth (dentate) ; (2) branches produced during the current season, reddish brown; (3) ovary and capsules with 4 chambers. (Fig. 52 *B*.)

Shrubs 0.3-1.5 m. tall; leaves evergreen, leathery; leaf blades narrowly ovate-acute to ovate and even elliptical, 10-23 mm. long, glabrous at maturity; petioles 1-2 mm. long; staminate flowers borne in heads or racemiform panicles, very numerous, pedicels 0.5-1 mm. long, sepals lanceolate, 7-12, stamens 7-12, filaments hairy at the base; pistillate flowers solitary on bibracteate peduncles 6-10 mm. long, sepals woolly, 8 in 2 series of 4 each, the disc irregularly lobed; ovary woolly, 4-chambered; styles 4, the tips turned inward; fruit rusty-woolly, nearly spheroidal, about 8 mm. long; seeds usually 2 in each chamber, 5-5.5 mm. long, laterally compressed, narrowly oblong, smooth, shiny, tan, the caruncle pale.

Crevices in lava and on limestone cliffs. Mountains of the Death Valley region, Inyo County, California; Death Valley Canyon and Tetracoccus Peak in the Panamint Mountains; Tin Mountain in the Cottonwood Mountains; Falls Canyon in the Grapevine Mountains. Flowering in May and June. (Fig. 53 *3*.)

2. *CROTON*. CROTON

The genus *Croton* yields the dangerously drastic purgative and vesicant, croton oil, which is obtained from the seeds of a tropical species, *Croton Tiglium*. Other species also are known to be poisonous. The cascarilla bark of commerce, employed in medicine as a tonic, is produced by the Bahaman species, *Croton eluteria*. The plant with glossy varicolored leaves of many shapes frequently cultivated as "croton" is really *Codiaeum variegatum,* a distantly related member of the spurge family.

The genus most likely to be confused with *Croton* is *Bernardia,* and some distinctions are given under that genus. The shrubby members of the two genera may be distinguished by the presence of petals in the staminate flowers of *Croton* and their absence in *Bernardia.*

Herbs or shrubs. Leaves alternate, simple, petioled; stipules minute or well developed. Inflorescence racemose; the staminate flowers above and the pistillate below when both staminate and pistillate are on the same plant; staminate flowers with 4-5 sepals and petals, or the petals absent; stamens several to many; pistillate flowers with 4-5 sepals and petals but the petals usually rudimentary or absent; ovary 3- or sometimes 2-chambered, the ovules solitary, styles 3 or sometimes 2, once to four times forked. Fruit a 3- or sometimes 1-seeded capsule. Seeds carunculate. (Fig. 52 *C.*)

KEY TO THE SPECIES

1. Stipules minute; style branches 6; margins of the leaves devoid of stalked glands.   1. *Croton Sonorae*

1. Stipules obvious, lacinate; style branches about 12; margins of the leaves bearing stalked glands.   2. *Croton ciliato-glandulosus*

1. *Croton sonorae* Torr. SONORA CROTON (Fig. 52 *C*)

Shrub 0.6-2 m. tall; branches whitened with close star-shaped hairs, these falling away in age; leaves deciduous; leaf blades ovate-lanceolate to ovate, long-acuminate, 15-35 mm. long, with scattered star-shaped hairs above, with more numerous similar hairs beneath, especially on the veins, margin subentire; petioles 2-11 mm. long, densely hairy; racemes terminal, 1-5 cm. long, the flowers scattered, staminate throughout or often with 1-3 pistillate flowers below; staminate flowers few to numerous; pedicels glabrous; sepals 5, almost glabrous except for a tuft of simple hairs at the tips; petals 5, slightly exceeding the sepals, marginally hairy on the basal half or two thirds with simple glistening white hairs, with a tuft of simple hairs at the tips; stamens 11-17, filaments usually glabrous, about twice as long as the sepals; pistillate flowers very shortly pedicelled; sepals 5, nearly glabrous; petals 5 about equaling the sepals or none; ovary densely covered with star-shaped hairs, 3-chambered; ovules solitary; styles 3, slender; once-forked, glabrous except for a few star-shaped hairs near the bases; fruit sparsely covered with star-shaped hairs, 3-lobed, oblong-globose, about 6 mm. long; seeds about 5 mm. long, brownish gray, lenticular-ellipsoidal, the caruncle low, transversely elongate.

Mountains in the desert at 2,000 to 3,000 feet elevation. Arizona on Table Top Peak, Pinal County, and on Quijotoa Mountain, at Topawa, and in the Ajo Mountains, Pima County; southward in Mexico to Oaxaca. Flowering in August.

2. *Croton ciliato-glandulosus* Ortega

Shrub 0.5-1 m. or perhaps taller; branches tomentose (woolly), glabrate in age; leaves deciduous, the foliage scented; leaf-blades ovate or ovate-lanceolate, acute, 2-6.5 cm. long, tomentose, the margins stipitate-glandular especially at the base, otherwise subentire; petioles 1-3.5 cm. long, more or less tomentose; stipules divided into several to many filiform gland-tipped segments; racemes terminal, the flowers loose in anthesis, pistillate flowers below, staminate flowers above; staminate flowers several to numerous, pedicels tomentose; sepals 5, tomentose outside; petals 5, slightly exceeding the sepals, ciliate toward the base; stamens numerous, filaments glabrous; pistillate flowers short-pedicelled; sepals 5, tomentose outside, glabrous inside, margins glandular-ciliate; petals none; ovary densely tomentose, 3-chambered; ovules solitary; styles 3, each divided into usually 4 branches, stellate-pubescent below; capsule stellate-pubescent, 3-lobed, globose, about 6 mm. long; seeds 5-6 mm. long, brownish gray, lenticular-ellipsoidal, the caruncle low, transversely elongate.

Mountains in the desert at 3,600 feet elevation. Arizona near Ruby at the mouth of Sycamore Canyon, Santa Cruz County (*Darrow & Haskell 2215*); southward through Mexico to Guatemala and Honduras and eastward to Cuba.

3. *ARGYTHAMNIA*

(1) Branches pithy inside; (2) a water-soluble purple pigment present in at least the staminate flowers; (3) hairs on the young leaves lying parallel with the surface and attached in the middle like the blade of a pick (i.e., malphighiaceous).

Herbs or shrubs. Leaves simple, alternate, without stipules. Pistillate and staminate flowers on the same plant, borne in bracteate axillary racemes, or sometimes solitary; sepals 5; petals 5 or sometimes wanting in pistillate flowers; glands 5, alternating with the petals; stamens 8-12, usually 10; filaments united below into a column (androphore); anthers in two whorls, the lower of 5 or 6, the upper of 3, 5, or 6; ovary 3-chambered, ovules solitary; styles 3, bifid, distinct or partly connate. Fruit a dehiscent, 3-seeded capsule. Seeds not carunculate.

1. **Argythamnia Brandegei** Millsp. var. *intonsa* (I. M. Johnston) Ingram, comb. nov. (Cf. p. 394.)

Shrub 1-2 m. tall with a few coarse, widely spreading, elongate, pithy branches; leaf blades elliptic or elliptic-lanceolate to lanceolate, 4-12 cm. long, sparsely rough-hairy with malphighiaceous hairs especially beneath when young, sometimes glabrous or nearly so at maturity, the margin irregularly and often obscurely bluntly serrulate; petioles 1-2 cm. long;

flowers in bracteate axillary racemes, the staminate above, several, the pistillate below, few; sepals of the staminate flowers lanceolate, usually glabrous; petals rhombic-lanceolate, equaling or slightly exceeding the sepals, joined at the base to the androphore, with a line of sparse hairs on the outside along the midvein; stamens usually 10, anthers in 2 whorls of 5 each; sepals of the pistillate flowers broadly lanceolate, exceeding the petals, almost glabrous; petals lanceolate, sparsely hairy on the outside; ovary densely clothed with erect hairs, styles united for about half their length, divided to about the middle; fruit sharply 3-angled, about 7 mm. long, glabrate; seeds brownish, triangular-pyramidal, 4-5 mm. long, the base truncate, the apex acute. Synonym: *Ditaxis Brandegei* (Millsp.) Rose & Standl. var. *intonsa* I. M. Johnston.

Gravelly soil in canyons or on rocky slopes in the desert at 500 to 2,000 feet elevation. Yuma County, Arizona, at the Experimental Farm near Yuma and in the Gila and Tule mountains; Baja California, Mexico. Flowering from April until July. (Fig. 53 5.)

The varietal name means "unshaven," and it refers to the hairs present on at least the ovary.

4. BERNARDIA

This genus may be distinguished from its nearest relative (in Arizona), *Croton,* with which it shares the character of possessing star-shaped hairs, by the following characters: (1) leaves crenate rather than entire or nearly so; (2) staminate and pistillate flowers on different plants, the sepals of the staminate flowers 3-4 rather than 5, the stamens 3-7 rather than 11 or more, the anthers erect in bud rather than turned inward. (Fig. 52 *D*.)

Shrub. Leaves deciduous, alternate, with petioles and stipules. Flowers apetalous. Staminate flowers in lateral racemes. Pistillate flowers terminal, solitary or in pairs. Ovary 3-chambered; ovules solitary; styles 3, forked. Fruit a 3-seeded capsule. Seeds without caruncles.

1. *Bernardia incana* C. V. Morton (Fig. 52 *D*)

Shrub 1-2 m. tall; branches glabrate; leaves mostly in clusters on short lateral branchlets; leaf blades ovate to elliptical or to orbicular-obovate in some of the smaller ones, 5-22 mm. long, closely felted beneath with fine star-shaped hairs, less densely felted above; petioles 1-2.5 mm. long; stipules about equaling the petioles, tapering, fleshy and purplish at the bases; staminate flowers in slender lateral racemes up to 2 cm. long but usually less than 1 cm. long; stamens 3-7, the filaments separate; pistillate

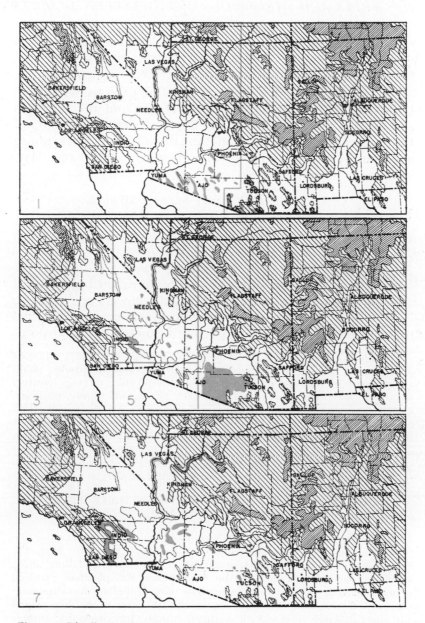

Fig. 53.—Distributional maps: *1* elephant tree, *Bursera microphylla;* 2 narrow-leaved cassava, *Manihot angustiloba;* 3, *Tetracoccus ilicifolius;* 4, *Tetracoccus Hallii;* 5, *Argythamnia Brandegei* var. *intonsa;* 6, limber bush, *Jatropha cardiophylla;* 7, *Bernardia incana.*

flowers terminal, solitary or in pairs; sepals 5; ovary 3-chambered, ovules solitary; styles short, warty; capsule nearly spheroidal, densely felted with star-shaped hairs, 3-lobed, about 9 mm. in diameter; seeds grayish brown, almost spheroidal to ovoid-globose, 4.5-6 mm. long.

Rocky canyons in the desert at 2,000 to 3,500 feet elevation. California in the southern Mojave Desert and the northern and western parts of the Colorado Desert; Arizona in the Grand Canyon and from Mohave and Yuma counties to Wickenburg and southeastward to Bisbee. Flowering in April and May. (Fig. 53 7.)

5. *ACALYPHA*. Three-Seeded Mercury

Some species of *Acalypha* are cultivated for either the showy red chenillelike pistillate spikes or for their varicolored foliage. A single shrubby species occurs in Arizona.

(1) Style branches red, resembling frayed silk thread; (2) bracts beneath each pistillate flower blunt-toothed, glandular; (3) staminate inflorescence spikelike, the flowers are crowded, each with 6-8 stamens; (4) anther cells 2, separate, attached to the filaments only at their tips (like a wind sock at an airport). (Fig. 54 *F*.)

Herbs or shrubs. Leaves alternate, simple, petioled; stipules small. Inflorescence of terminal or axillary spikes or spikelike racemes; entirely staminate, staminate above and pistillate below, or wholly pistillate. Flowers apetalous, pistillate and staminate flowers on the same plant. Staminate flowers several to numerous in the axil of each bract, pedicelled; sepals 4; filaments separate. Pistillate flowers sessile, 1-2 in the axil of each accrescent foliaceous bract; sepals 3; ovary 3-chambered; ovules solitary; styles 3, separate, dissected into filiform segments; capsule usually 3-seeded, splitting open. Seeds small, ovoid, with small caruncles.

1. *Acalypha Pringlei* S. Wats. PRINGLE'S THREE-SEEDED MERCURY (Fig. 54 *F*)

Glandular-pubescent straggling shrub 0.6-1 m. tall, the branches glabrate; leaf blades ovate-cordate to ovate-cuneate, 1.5-5.5 cm. long, the margins crenate-serrate, stipules nearly linear but tapering, falling away; staminate spikelike racemes in the axils below the pistillate racemes, slender, stalked, often with 1-3 pistillate flowers below the staminate; staminate flowers numerous in the axils of each bract which they exceed and conceal; sepals covered with scattered, minute, tapering hairs; anthers longer than the filaments, vibrio- or spirillum-shaped; pistillate spikes terminal and in the upper axils, few- to several-flowered, stalked, stipitate-glandular (with stalked glands) throughout, but especially on the margins of the bracts; bracts in fruit reniform-cuneate, up to 5 mm. long by 10 mm. wide, with 7-20 crenate-dentate segments; upper half of the ovary stipitate-glandular; styles red, up to 7 mm. long; capsule about 2 mm. long, with numerous erect slender fleshy projections on the upper half bearing the stipitate glands; seeds ovoid, about 1.7 mm. long, brownish gray, caruncles a low median terminal ridge.

Ravines, washes, and rocky foothills in the desert at 1,500 to 3,500 feet elevation. Arizona at Gunsight Pass, in the Quijotoa Mountains, and in the Ajo Mountains, Pima County; Sonora, Mexico. Flowering in June and August.

According to Kearney, this shrub ". . . is conspicuous when in full leaf, contrasting with most of the associated species in the light green of its foliage. . . . There is considerable variation in the size of the leaves and in the length and color of the staminate inflorescence."

6. *RICINUS.* CASTOR BEAN

The castor bean is cultivated commonly both as an ornamental and for the seeds, which yield castor oil. The plant varies from an annual herb to a shrub or a tree, depending largely upon climate. The color of foliage varies greatly, and many horticultural forms are dull red to purplish or approaching bronze. The brightly colored nearly ripe clusters of fruits are used sometimes for bouquets, but their disquieting habit of projecting their seeds forcibly, when the capsules burst, limits their usefulness for interior decoration.

(1) Leaves large, peltate, palmately lobed; (2) juice not milky; (3) pods spiny, borne at the tips of the branches; (4) stamens extremely numerous (in the staminate flowers).

Herbs, shrubs, or trees. Leaves alternate, petioled; stipules united, membranous, falling away. Flowers without petals, in terminal racemes or panicles, the pistillate above, the staminate below. Calyx of the staminate flower usually 5-lobed, persistent; filaments united into a treelike androphore. Pistillate calyx 2-5-lobed, falling away; ovary spiny, 3-chambered, each chamber 1-ovuled; styles 3, forked, with rough projections, red. Seeds prominently carunculate.

1. *Ricinus communis L.* CASTOR BEAN

Herb, shrub, or tree 1-10 m. tall; stem and branches hollow, brittle; leaf blade suborbicular in outline, up to at least 0.8 m. in diameter, usually with 7-10 palmate lobes, the margins bluntly and often glandularly saw-toothed; petioles stout, usually exceeding the blades, hollow, bearing substipitate glands at both ends on the upper sides; stipules sheathing, leaving a circumferential scar; staminate calyx membranous; fruit (capsule) splitting open (sometimes tardily), slightly 3-lobed, very shortly oblong and truncate to subglobose, 1.5-2.5 cm. in diameter; seeds mostly mottled gray and brown, oblong to suborbicular in outline, compressed from back to front, 1-2 cm. long, the seed coat hard, brittle; endosperm very oily.

Established here and there in the desert washes and near streams. (Specimens largely lacking because of the contempt of collectors for this large, coarse, ill-scented plant.) Probably native of Africa but widely dispersed at an early date. Flowering in summer.

Probably the entire plant, and particularly the seeds contain the phytotoxin or toxalbumin *ricin* which, if it enters the bloodstream, may, after an incubation period of several days, cause violent symptoms ending in death. A mere trace of the substance of the seed placed in the eye may cause serious irritation, possibly resulting in blindness. Ricin is destroyed by prolonged heating. Happily this poisonous principle is absent from the extracted oil. In addition to its notorious but relatively minor use as a purgative, castor oil is assuming increasing importance in chemical industry in the production of pliable plastics, and high octane gasoline. The remarkable resistance of the oil to decomposition by high temperatures has resulted in a demand for it for use as a lubricant for jet motors. Dehydration produces a drying oil the use of which in paints and varnishes is increasing, and sulfonation produces wetting and emulsifying agents. Development of suitable horticultural varieties with indehiscent capsules has made mechanical harvesting practical in consequence of which the crop is assuming increasing importance in the Southwest.

7. *JATROPHA.* Jatropha

A few species are cultivated in tropical America. The seeds are known to be purgative or even emetic in several species. The juice is generally rich in tannin and this accounts for its use in dyeing, tanning, and as a fairly harmless cure-all in primitive medicine for treating superficial maladies. The prevailing common name in Mexico is "sangre de drago" (dragon's blood), which frequently is corrupted by the illiterate.

(1) Ovary 1- or 2-chambered; (2) fruit tardily splitting open or even remaining closed, 1- or 2-seeded; (3) staminate and pistillate flowers on different plants, borne in cymes or fascicles or solitary. (Fig. 54 *A, B.*)

Perennial herbs, shrubs, or small trees. Leaves simple, alternate, stipules small or none. Calyx of the staminate flower 5-lobed; petals 5, more or less joined into a tube; stamens 8-10, filaments united below into a column; anthers in 2 whorls, the lower of 5 and the upper of 3-5; calyx of the pistillate flower 5-lobed; petals 5, more or less joined; ovary 1-3-chambered; ovules solitary, styles 1-3, entire or shortly forked. Seeds carunculate.

KEY TO THE SPECIES

1. Leaf blades about as broad as long, widest near the bases, mostly 2 cm. or more long at maturity; petioles 1 cm. or more long.

    2. Leaf blades glabrous, cordate-deltoid, the apices acuminate, the margins crenate-dentate; ovary 1-chambered. (Fig. 54 *B.*)
                1. *Jatropha cardiophylla*

    2. Leaf blades short-hairy at least beneath, reniform-cordate, the margins entire; ovary 2-chambered.   2. *Jatropha cinerea*

1. Leaf blades obovate-cuneate to spatulate, 5-18 mm. long, petioles about 1 mm. long; ovary 1-chambered. (Fig. 54 *A.*)   3. *Jatropha cuneata*

1. *Jatropha cardiophylla* (Torr.) Muell. Arg. LIMBER BUSH. (1) Leaf blades heart-shaped-triangular (cordate-deltoid), tapering at the tips and mostly over $^4/_5$ inch long, margin with rounded teeth, petioled; (2) petioles $^2/_5$ inch long or longer; (3) hairs totally absent except on the flowers. (Fig. 54 *B.*)

Low shrub; leaves mostly fascicled on short spur branchlets; leaf blades 1.5-7 cm. long; stipules minute; staminate flowers in cymes terminal on the spur branchlets; calyx about one third as long as the corolla; petals joined into a tube, about 4 mm. long, more or less hairy inside on the lower third; stamens mostly 10, the filaments united for about half their length, anthers in 2 whorls of 5 each; glands 5, free; pistillate flowers 1-3 at the tips of the spur branchlets, pedicellate; calyx about one third as long as the corolla, deeply 5-lobed, the 3 outer lobes glandular-toothed; petals joined into a tube about 7 mm. long, glabrous; style entire; stigma irregularly lobed; fruit 1-seeded, not splitting open or possibly opening tardily, 17-20 mm. long including the persistent thickened style; seeds globose-ellipsoidal, about 1 cm. long.

Fig. 54.—Euphorbia family: *A. Jatropha cuneata*, *1*, leafy branch with a fruit, *2*, old branch with the leaves restricted to short spurs; *B*, limber bush, *Jatropha cardiophylla*, *1*, fruit, *2*, leafy branch with staminate flowers; *3*, staminate flower; *C*, Mexican jumping bean, *Sapium biloculare*, *1*, leafy branch with a spike of flowers, all but the lower ones staminate, *2*, seed, *3*, staminate flower, *4*, fruit; *D*, narrow-leaved cassava, *Manihot angustiloba*, *1*, inflorescence with young fruits, *2*, leaf, *3*, *4*, seed; *E*, Arizona cassava, *Manihot Davisiae*, *1*, staminate flower, *2*, leaf; *F*, Pringle three-seeded mercury, *Acalypha Pringlei*, *1*, pistillate flower with bracts pulled backward to show the pistil, *2*, branch with spikes of pistillate flowers (above) and staminate flowers (below) . (x ¹/₃ except *B 1*, *C 2*, *4*, *D 3*, *4*, *E 1* x ²/₃; *B 3* x 2; *C 3* x 10; *F 1* x 1²/₃.)

Arid rocky south slopes in the desert at 2,000 to 3,000 feet elevation; frequently growing under other bushes. Arizona from southern Maricopa County to Pima County; Sonora, Mexico. (Fig. 53 6.)

The plant is called limber bush for its flexible branches, or sangre de drago for the reddish sap of the roots, which supply tanning and dyeing material. The roots contain over 5 per cent of tannic acid, dry basis. Both this and the related species *Jatropha cuneata* are reported to be used in Mexico for medicinal purposes. The plant contains some rubber.

2. *Jatropha cinerea* (Ortega) Muell. Arg. ASHY JATROPHA. (1) Leaves between kidney- and heart-shaped; (2) leaves felted with fine hairs at least beneath, petioled; (3) capsule 2-seeded and much broader than long, slightly winged on the backs of the two lobes.

Shrub or small tree 1.3-6 m. tall; leaves mostly fascicled on spur branchlets; leaf blades reniform-cordate on the spur branchlets, sometimes more or less 3-lobed on vigorous shoots of the current season, 1.5-6.5 cm. long, glabrate, the margin entire; stipules minute; staminate flowers in cymes terminal on the spur branchlets; calyx about one third as long as the corolla; petals united into a tube, 7-9 mm. long, hairy inside on the lower third, margins of lobes hairy; stamens mostly 10, the filaments united for about half their length; anthers in 2 whorls of 5 each; glands 5, free; pistillate flowers 1-3 at the tips of the spur branchlets, pedicellate; calyx about one third as long as the corolla; petals joined into a tube, sparsely appressed-hairy outside, about 7 mm. long, the lobes hairy on the margins; pistil glabrous; ovary 2-chambered, ovules solitary; style with a bulge about halfway up, forked, the stigmas irregularly fungoid-lobed; capsule very tardily splitting open, usually 2-seeded (sometimes 1-seeded by abortion), transversely narrowly reniform-cordate to broadly oblong in outline, tipped by the persistent style, 20-23 mm. wide, 12-15 mm. long; seeds 10-12 mm. long. (*Jatropha canescens* [Benth.] Muell. Arg. in Kearney & Peebles, Fl. Pl. & Ferns of Arizona.)

Dry plains and hillsides in the desert at 1,000 to 1,500 feet elevation. Arizona at Quitovaquito, Pima County; Baja California to Sinaloa, Mexico. Flowering from June until September.

"A decoction is employed as a mordant in dyeing. The juice is astringent and is used as a remedy for warts and sore throat, and for hardening the gums" (Standley).

3. *Jatropha cuneata* Wiggins & Rollins. (1) Leaves small,

5-18 mm. long, entire, widest near the apices; (2) petiole barely 1 mm. long. (Fig. 54 *A*.)

Shrub or small tree 1.5-2.5 m. tall, semisucculent, the bark slightly wrinkled when dry, the sap clear, flowing freely from wounds; leaves alternate, on the older branches borne in fascicles on stubby spur branchlets, obovate-cuneate to spatulate, often emarginate, 5-18 mm. long, entire, glabrous or nearly so, tapering to a petiole about 1 mm. long; stipules minute, linear, falling away; staminate flowers terminal on the spur branchlets, fascicled or in short, few-flowered cymes; calyx about one third as long as the corolla; petals joined into a tube, about 7 mm. long; stamens 10, in 2 series of 5 each, the filaments united for one third to one half their length; pistillate flowers solitary on the tips of the spur branchlets, pediceled; calyx about one half the length of the corolla; petals joined into a tube about 7 mm. long; pistil glabrous; ovary 1-chambered; style entire, stigma with two approximate lobes; fruit not splitting open or opening tardily, 1-seeded, 10-17 mm. long including the persistent thickened style, slightly asymmetrical; seeds 9-13 mm. long, globose-ellipsoidal, with a thin coat of granular blackish substance beneath the membranous outer coat. Long known as *Jatropha spathulata* (Ortega) Muell. Arg.

Rocky slopes in the desert at 1,000 to 2,000 feet elevation. Arizona in southern Yuma and southwestern Pima counties (Tinajas Atlas to the Growler Mountains) ; Baja California and Sonora, Mexico. Flowering in July and August.

8. *MANIHOT*. Cassava

Manihot esculenta Crantz, the source of cassava and tapioca and a native of Brazil, now is cultivated widely in the tropics of both hemispheres. The Ceara rubber tree, *Manihot Glaziovii* Muell. Arg., also native of Brazil, is the second or third most important rubber tree after *Hevea* for use on plantations.

(1) Leaves palmately divided almost to the bases of the blades; (2) stamens separate, 10, attached around a central disc; (3) calyx of the staminate flower slightly inflated in bud. (Fig. 54 *D, E*.)

Glabrous shrubs with milky juice. Leaves with 5-7 divisions, long-petioled, with stipules. Inflorescence terminal, racemose. Flowers apetalous, the staminate and pistillate flowers on the same plant. Staminate flowers several to many, on the outer end of the raceme; calyx 5-lobed, slightly inflated in bud; stamens 10, alternately long and short, attached in the indentations of the lobed central floral disc. Pistillate flowers few to several at the base of the raceme; sepals 5, distinct, falling away early; ovary seated on a floral disc, 3-chambered; ovules solitary; styles 3; seeds carunculate.

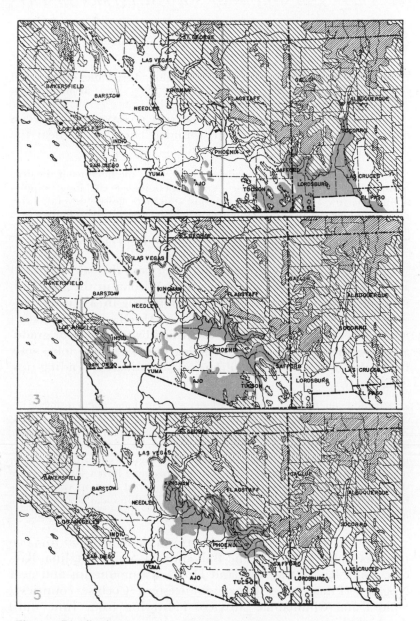

Fig. 55.—Distributional maps: *1*, Mexican jumping bean, *Sapium biloculare;* *2*, *Rhus microphylla;* *3*, Utah mortonia, *Montonia scabrella* var. *utahensis;* *4*, jojoba, *Simmondsia chinensis;* *5*, crucifixion thorn, *Canotia Holacantha.*

KEY TO THE SPECIES

1. Divisions of the leaves broadly lobed toward the tips. (Fig. 54 *E.*)
   1. *M. Davisiae*

1. Divisions of the leaves lobed only at or below the middles, narrow and tapering at the tips. (Fig. 54 *D.*)   2. *M. angustiloba*

1. *Manihot Davisiae* Croizat. ARIZONA CASSAVA. This species may be identified by the broad, rounded lateral lobes near the tips of the primary lobes of the leaves. (Fig. 54 *E.*)

Shrubs or semishrubs; leaf blades 3-11 cm. long, the margins of the divi sions, except for the lateral lobes, entire; petioles 3-8 cm. long; stipules minute, narrow and tapering, deciduous; staminate flowers several; calyx 11-12 mm. long, sepals united about half their length; pistillate flowers few; mature capsules or seeds not seen. [*Manihot carthaginensis* (Jacq.) Muell. Arg. in Kearney & Peebles, Flowering Plants and Ferns of Arizona.]

Mountain canyons in the upper desert and the oak woodland at about 3,500 to 4,000 feet elevation. Arizona in the Baboquivari and Santa Catalina mountains. Flowering in August.

2. *Manihot angustiloba* (Torr.) Muell. Arg. NARROW-LEAVED CASSAVA. This species is identified by the linear or gradually tapering primary lobes of the leaves with lateral lobes only below the middle and these often with acuminate ascending tips. (Fig. 54 *D.*)

Shrubs 0.5 m. or more tall; leaf blades 8-15 cm. long, the margins of the divisions, except for the lobes, entire; petioles ½ to ²/₃ as long as the blades; stipules linear, small, deciduous; staminate flowers several, calyx 10-12 mm. long, sepals united about half their length; pistillate flowers few, sepals lanceolate, distinct; ovary globose; styles and stigmas combined, about 1 mm. long, styles united below, the stigmas broadened into a somewhat fan-shaped structure, with a broad, thin, minutely lobed margin; capsule globose, about 13 mm. long; seeds broadly lenticular-ellipsoidal, about 11 mm. long, tan, mottled with white streaks.

Canyons in the desert and desert grassland at 3,000 to 5,000 feet elevation. Arizona in the Baboquivari, Santa Catalina, Rincon, Santa Rita, Patagonia, and Huachuca mountains and near Nogales (Pima, Santa Cruz, and western Cochise counties); Sonora and Chihuahua, Mexico. Flowering from June until August. (Fig. 53 2.)

9. *SAPIUM.* Mexican Jumping Bean

Several species of *Sapium* growing in northern South America produce good to excellent rubber, which often is not distinguished in commerce from that produced by *Hevea,* the Brazilian rubber tree, the foremost producer of rubber. The combination of milky juice and flowers in spikes is found in no other woody member of the family in this area. (Fig. 54 *C.*)

Trees or shrubs with milky juice. Leaves simple, alternate, stipulate. Flowers borne in terminal spikes, the staminate above, the pistillate below; corolla none; staminate flowers in fascicles of several, each fascicle subtended by a bract; calyx 2-lobed; stamens 2; filaments united at the bases; pistillate flowers 1 or 2 per spike, each solitary in the axil of a bract, calyx deeply 2-lobed, slightly succulent; fruit a capsule, splitting open.

1. *Sapium biloculare* Pax. mexican jumping bean (Fig. 54 C)

Shrub or tree 2-6 m. tall; glabrous; leaves deciduous, blades serrulate, leathery, prevailingly lanceolate but varying to oblong-lanceolate, 2-6 cm. long; petioles 1.5-4 mm. long; stipules triangular, inequilateral; spikes 2.5-6 cm. long, progressively elongating during the flowering period, the axis with groups of few to several sessile glands just below and on both sides of each fascicle of flowers; staminate flowers fragrant with the "odor of plum blossoms," some not stalked and some shortly pedicellate, the various flowers in one fascicle blooming successively, the flowers mingled with linear bracteoles; calyx membranous, 2-lobed; stamens 2, the filaments united at the bases; pistillate flowers 1 or 2 at the base of the spike, ovary 2-chambered, each chamber 1-ovuled; styles 2, longer than the ovary, entire, recurving, with slight rough projections; fruit splitting open, 2-lobed, deltoid-cordate in outline viewed from the broad side, 1.1-1.2 cm. wide; seeds not carunculate, mottled brownish gray, depressed-globose, the inner face often flattened, 6-8 mm. in greatest dimension.

Rocky slopes and along watercourses in the desert at 1,000 to 2,500 feet elevation. Arizona from the vicinity of Gila Bend southwestward across the Papago Reservation to Tinajas Atlas; Sonora and Baja California, Mexico. Flowering from March until November. (Fig. 55 *1.*)

The juice of the plant is poisonous. It is used as a fish poison, and it is reputed to have been used as an arrow poison; hence the Spanish name "hierba de la flecha" (herb of the arrow). Smoke from the burning wood and sleeping under the tree are

said to cause sore eyes, but it is difficult to believe that the tree
is so poisonous that it exhales an effluvium or miasma which
would afflict the unwary sleeper. "Hierba mala" (bad herb) is
another Spanish name recorded in literature.

This is one of the species which produces "jumping beans"
(erroneously supposed by many to be legumes). The propelling
agent is the larva of a moth, *Carpocapsa saltitans* Westwood,
which, by its violent movements, makes the seed move. The
term Mexican jumping bean is applied to two plants: *Sapium
biloculare,* which occurs in Sonora and Baja California, Mexico, and *Sebastiana Pavoniana,* the better-known and more
widely distributed species.

10. *EUPHORBIA.* Spurge

The spurges are known well in cultivation, and included
among them is the common poinsettia, a native of Mexico.
Many cactuslike African species are prized in rock gardens. The
latex (milky juice) of many species is more or less poisonous
or corrosive by virtue of a protein-dissolving enzyme. Rubber
varying in grade from excellent to very poor is obtained from
several species. The genus was named in honor of Euphorbus,
physician to Juba II, King of Mauretania, but the name is also
quite possibly, at least partly, a pun meaning "well fed" in allu-
sion to the succulent nature of many species. The only woody
spurge in this area may be distinguished readily from other
members of the same family by the apparently perfect flowers
which are really small but very complex inflorescences.

Annual or perennial herbs or shrubs. Leaves simple, alternate, opposite,
or whorled. Staminate and pistillate flowers in the same inflorescence, a
cyathium simulating a simple flower; pistillate flower solitary in the center
of the cyathium, pedicellate, naked, ovary 3-chambered, each chamber 1-
ovuled, styles 3, usually forked; staminate flowers in 5 fascicles, opposite the
lobes of the involucre, 1 to several per fascicle, naked, each consisting of a
single stamen with a short filament jointed to a long pedicel and commonly
subtended by a bracteole; the flowers of the cyathium surrounded by a
hypanthium- or calyx-like involucre bearing on its margin 1-5 nectariferous
glands of various shapes alternating with the lobes of the involucre, petaloid
appendages often extending from beneath the glands. Fruit a 3-chambered
capsule, 3-seeded, splitting open elastically, usually nodding.

1. *Euphorbia misera Benth.* CLIFF SPURGE

Shrub 0.5-1.5 m. tall; branches mostly thick, often tortuous, glabrate at maturity; branchlets short, with many nodes or joints, scurfy, sparsely short-hairy; leaves sparsely short-hairy, the petioles 2-5 mm. long, the blades 5-15 mm. long, oval-oblong to obcordate-cuneate, entire; cyathia solitary, borne on the branchlets, long-peduncled; involucres open-campanulate (bell-shaped), 3 mm. in diameter, hairy; glands maroon, transversely oval to oblong, 1.5-2 mm. long, petal-like appendages usually conspicuous, white, glabrous, crenulate to bluntly toothed; staminate flowers 30-40; capsule glabrate, roundly 3-lobed, depressed-globose, 4-5 mm. long; seeds white, without caruncles, ovoid, 3 mm. long, covered with shallow irregular concavities.

Occasional on seaward bluffs and desert mesas at low elevations. California from the coast of Orange and San Diego counties and the vicinity of Whitewater, Riverside County, south to Baja California, Mexico. The occurrence of the isolated station in the Whitewater region at the northwesterly end of the Colorado Desert of a plant otherwise maritime, at least in California, is puzzling. The plants may have persisted from the not-so-remote day when the Gulf of California extended nearly to this station. (Cf. p. 11 in the introduction.)

Family 20. *BUXACEAE.* Box FAMILY

The box family is represented by a single species, the jojoba or goat nut, in the western United States. This desert shrub is recognized readily by its opposite (paired), elliptic or elliptic-oblong, thick, bluish leaves, and by the fruits which resemble acorns. (Fig. 56 *C*.)

Shrubs with leaves persisting the entire year. Flowers of our species unisexual, the staminate and pistillate flowers on different plants, on peduncles from the leaf axils, hypogynous, the staminate yellowish green, in congested small panicles, the pistillate green, solitary in the leaf axils; sepals about 5, separate, usually somewhat unequal, markedly so in the pistillate flowers, greatly enlarged in fruit; petals none; stamens about 10-12; pistil 1, the styles and stigmas 3; ovary superior, 1-celled, the fruit splitting along 3 lines, essentially a capsule but 1-seeded.

1. *SIMMONDSIA.* JOJOBA

1. *Simmondsia chinensis* (Link) Schn. JOJOBA; GOAT NUT (Fig. 56 *C*)

Desert shrub 1-2 m. (3-6 feet) high, spreading widely; leaves 2-5 cm. long, 1-2 cm. broad; fruit about 1.5-2.2 cm. long. Synonym: *Simmondsia californica* Nutt.

Rocky or gravelly, well-drained slopes in the upper desert and the chaparral at 1,500 to 5,000 feet elevation. California near San Diego and in the mountains bordering the Salton Sea Basin of the Colorado Desert; Arizona in the Arizona Desert from the Kofa and Castle Dome mountains, Yuma County, eastward to the chaparral-covered slopes of southern Yavapai and Gila counties and from the Ajo Mountains of Pima County eastward to western Cochise and Greenlee counties; Mexico. (Fig. 55 4.)

This important desert plant has a variety of common or local names applied because of its many uses. In California, where it is an important browse plant, it is known as goat nut; in Arizona it is known as jojoba, and it has been called coffeeberry, a name commonly used for *Rhamnus*. Cattle, goats, and deer relish the foliage and young twigs, and since the plant often constitutes the principal cover on rocky mountain slopes it is an important browse plant. The seeds are palatable and the Indians ate them raw or parched. They were boiled also to provide a well-flavored drink similar to coffee. A liquid wax somewhat resembling sperm oil is contained in the seeds, and it may prove to be of commercial value.

Family 21. *ANACARDIACEAE*. CASHEW FAMILY

Trees or shrubs. Juice with an abundance of resins, sometimes milky or acrid, in some species toxic. Flowers with discs, small, usually in dense clusters, bisexual or sometimes all or some unisexual; flower parts in 5's, the stamens either 5 or 10, but the carpels 3. Fruit drupelike, 1-celled, often hairy; styles 3.

1. RHUS. SUMAC; POISON IVY; POISON OAK; LEMONADE BERRY

Leaves of most species pinnate but in a few simple and leathery, sometimes trifoliolate. Flowers bisexual or unisexual; stamens 5. Fruit hairy.

KEY TO THE SPECIES

1. Leaves pinnate, deciduous, not markedly leathery, hairy; flowers appearing before the leaves; plants somewhat spiny.   1. *Rhus microphylla*

1. Leaves simple, evergreen, markedly leathery, glabrous; flowers appearing with the new leaves; plant not spiny.   2. *Rhus Kearneyi*

1. *Rhus microphylla* Engelm.

Shrub usually 1-2 m. high; branches somewhat spiny; leaves pinnate, the leaflets mostly in 3-4 pairs, with or without a terminal leaflet, each elliptic-oblong, 6-18 mm. long, 3-7 mm. broad, appressed-hairy on both faces, but the hair tending to fall away from the upper surface; flowers about 3 mm. in diameter, in exceedingly dense panicles produced along the branches; petals white; fruit ovoid, about 6 mm. long, red, somewhat hairy.

Gravelly or sandy mesas and slopes in the upper desert and the desert grassland at 4,000 to 6,000 feet elevation. Arizona from the Rincon Mountains in eastern Pima County to southern Greenlee and Cochise counties; New Mexico in the Chihuahuan Desert and the adjacent desert grassland, occurring as far north as Socorro; western Texas; Mexico. (Fig. 55 2.)

2. *Rhus Kearneyi* Barkley. KEARNEY SUMAC

Large shrub or small tree; leaves simple, ovate to elliptic-oblong, 2.5-6 cm. long, remarkably leathery, entire, the extreme margins rolled downward and inward, practically glabrous; inflorescence terminal, a short, congested compound spike; flowers about 5 mm. in diameter; petals white; fruit oblong, compressed, constricted at each end, about 1 cm. long, 6-8 mm. in diameter, hairy.

Arid slopes in the desert at about 1,000 to 1,500 feet elevation. Arizona at Tinajas Atlas, Yuma County.

This species is related closely to another simple-leaved species, *Rhus ovata,* occurring in Arizona and California.

Family 22. *CELASTRACEAE.* BITTERSWEET FAMILY

The family is best known in the United States for *Euonymus,* including the spindle tree and the burning bush; *Pachystima,* including the Oregon box; and *Celastrus,* including the bittersweet. *Glossopetalon spinescens*[7] (*Forsellesia spinescens*), a spiny shrub with the aspect of a desert plant, occurs along the upper margin of the desert but essentially in the pinyon-juniper belt, and it is not included in this work. The single true desert species in the family is recognized by leaves which are thick and leathery, nearly circular to elliptical, and about ¼ to ½ inch long. They are turned conspicuously upward along the

7. Cf. Harold St. John. Proc. Biol. Soc. Wash. (55) : 109-12. 1942.

branches, and the spiral arrangement includes such short turns that some of the leaves appear whorled. (Fig. 56 *A*.)

Shrubs. Leaves simple, alternate. Flowers with discs, regular; sepals, petals, and stamens 4-5 or rarely 6, the stamens on a floral disc, alternate with the petals. Carpels 2-5, the aril of the seed often prominent.

1. *MORTONIA*. Mortonia

Small shrubs. Flowers in small terminal cymes; sepals, petals, and stamens 5; carpels 5 but the fruit with a solitary seed, dry, hard, not splitting open. (Fig. 56 *A*.)

1a. *Mortonia scabrella* A. Gray. var. *scabrella*. MORTONIA (Fig. 56 *A*)

Shrub 0.5-1 m. (1½ to 3 feet) high; leaves 5-8 mm. long, 3-6 mm. broad; flower clusters 2-4 cm. long; flowers 4 mm. in diameter; petals white, 2 mm. long; stamen-bearing floral disc lining the calyx tube; fruit short-cylindroidal, 4 mm. long, 2 mm. in diameter, somewhat roughened longitudinally.

Rocky or gravelly slopes and mesas in the upper part of the desert and the desert grassland at 3,000 to 5,000 feet elevation. Arizona in southern Gila County, along the San Pedro River drainage in eastern Pima County and in Cochise County, and in the foothills of the Chiricahua Mountains; extreme southern New Mexico; western Texas; Mexico.

This species is one of a group characteristic of the Chihuahuan Desert flora, which occurs in the southeastern corner of Arizona and especially along the San Pedro River. It often forms nearly pure stands on soils derived from limestone. It has no economic value except for erosion control.

1b. *Mortonia scabrella* A. Gray var. *utahensis* Cov.

Leaves 10-15 mm. long, 6-12 mm. broad; flower clusters larger than in the typical variety, up to 8 cm. long; flowers 5-7 mm. in diameter; fruits 5-6 mm. long. Synonym: *Mortonia utahensis* (Cov.) Rydb.

Rocky slopes and canyon bottoms in the desert. California in the Panamint Mountains near Death Valley and near Kingston in the eastern Mojave Desert; southern Nevada; southern Utah on the Virgin River drainage and in Rainbow Bridge Canyon; Arizona at Havasu Canyon, Coconino County, and Horse Spring, Mohave County. (Fig. 55 *3*.)

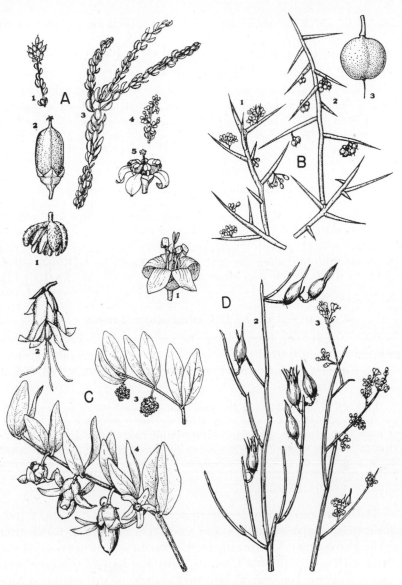

Fig. 56.—Mortonia, crucifixion thorns, and jojoba: *A*, mortonia, *Mortonia scabrella*, *1*, branch with leaves and fruits, *2*, fruit, *3*, leafy branch, *4*, flower cluster, *5*, flower; *B*, crucifixion thorn, *Koeberlinia spinosa*, *1*, leafless branch with flowers, *2*, branch with fruits, *3*, fruit; *C*, jojoba or goat nut, *Simmondsia chinensis*, *1*, staminate flower, *2*, pistillate flower, *3*, branch with clusters of staminate flowers, *4*, branch with fruits; *D*, crucifixion thorn, *Canotia Holacantha*, *1*, flower, *2*, leafless branch with fruits, *2*, branch with flowers. (x ¹/₈ except *A* 2, 5 x 2²/₃; *B* 3, *C* 1, 2, *D* 1 x 1²/₃.)

Family 23. *KOEBERLINIACEAE*. Crucifixion
Thorn Family

Shrubs or trees, not glandular or aromatic, the branches either hairy or with lines of wax flakes. Leaves very small, scalelike, alternate, ephemeral. Flower with a disc; sepals 5; petals 5; stamens 5 or 10. Carpels 5, forming a beaked, 5-celled capsule in fruit, splitting along 5 or 10 lines, or carpels 2 and the fruit a berry. (Pl. XXII *C, D*; Fig. 56 *B, D.*)

KEY TO THE GENERA

1. Branches remarkably limber before drying, not strongly divergent, glabrous, with minute flakes of white wax in the grooves; fruit, including the beak, about 2 cm. long, the body narrowly ellipsoidal, reddish tan; ovary 5-celled. (Pl. XXII *D*; Fig. 56 *D.*)   1. CANOTIA

1. Branches rigid, strongly divergent (often at right angles), hairy when young; fruit including the beak 4-6 mm. long, the body spheroidal, black, shiny, 3-4 mm. in diameter; ovary 2-celled. (Pl. XXII *C*; Fig. 56 *B.*)   2. KOEBERLINIA

1. *CANOTIA*. Crucifixion Thorn

(1) Small tree resembling the palo verde, with ascending yellowish green branches and trunk; (2) fruit a woody capsule.

1. *Canotia Holacantha* Torr. CRUCIFIXION THORN (Pl. XXII *D;* Fig. 56 *D*)

Tree 2-6 m. (6-18 feet) high; branches remarkably flexible when fresh, the spine-pointed ones 2-3 mm. in diameter, more or less nearly parallel, at least not divergent, glabrous, with minute flakes of white wax in the grooves; flowers in small clusters along the branches, the parts glabrous; sepals 2 mm. long; petals 5-6 mm. long; stamens 5; fruit 12-14 mm. long, with a beak 7-8 mm. long, splitting open along 10 lines, persistent only until the following spring.

Hillsides and slopes of the upper desert and the lower portion of the chaparral at 2,000 to 5,000 feet elevation. California in the Providence Mountains in the southeastern portion of the Mojave Desert; southern Utah in Rainbow Bridge Canyon; Arizona at Havasu Canyon, Coconino County, in the southern Mojave Desert, and in the northern part of the Arizona Desert and the adjoining chaparral as far eastward as the San Carlos Reservoir. (Fig. 55 5.)

This is the most abundant of the three crucifixion thorns in the Southwestern deserts. In the northern portion of the Gila

River drainage, *Canotia* replaces the foothill palo verde as a dominant plant on the rocky foothills and the upper bajadas. The leafless, thorny branches provide scant forage for livestock, and the principal value of the plant is for erosion control.

2. *KOEBERLINIA.* CRUCIFIXION THORN

1a. *Koeberlinia spinosa* Zucc. var. *spinosa* CRUCIFIXION THORN. (1) Spreading shrub with stout, divergent, dark green branches; (2) fruit a black berry. (Pls. XXII *C;* Fig. 56 *B.*)

Rounded shrub 1-1.5 m. (3-4½ feet) high; branches rigid, strongly divergent, the spine-pointed ones 2-5 cm. long, 2-3 mm. in diameter, yellow-green, glabrate; flowers in small clusters on the branches, the parts glabrous; sepals 1 mm. long; petals 4 mm. long; stamens 5, the filaments broadened; fruit a berry, black, shining, 3-4 mm. in diameter; flowering in late summer.

Sandy or gravelly mesas in the upper desert and the desert grassland at 2,400 to 5,000 feet elevation. Arizona in the Tucson Mountains, Pima County, and on the San Pedro and Gila River drainages above Winkelman; New Mexico on the Gila River drainage and on the Rio Grande drainage from Sierra County southward; western Texas; Mexico. (Fig. 58 2.)

This crucifixion thorn occupies medium- to fine-textured soils of broad intermountain plains of the Chihuahua Desert and related outlying areas in southeastern Arizona. It forms dense, low thickets or sometimes individuals occur separately. Commonly it is associated with creosote bush and blackbrush, *Flourensia cernua.* Jack rabbits browse on the twigs, but the plant is of little or no value to livestock.

1b. *Koeberlinia spinosa* Zucc. var. *tenuispina* Kearney & Peebles.

Shrub up to 3.5 m. high; spines 5-10 cm. long, 1.5-2 mm. in diameter, dark green; sepals 1.5-2 mm. long; petals 4-6 mm. long; flowering in March and April.

Rocky foothills and upper bajada slopes in the desert at 1,500 to 2,000 feet elevation. California in the Chocolate Mountains in the eastern part of the Colorado Desert; Arizona from Yuma County to eastern Maricopa County (Kofa, Castle Dome, Eagle Tail, and Little Horn mountains) ; Sonora, Mexico. (Fig. 58 *1.*)

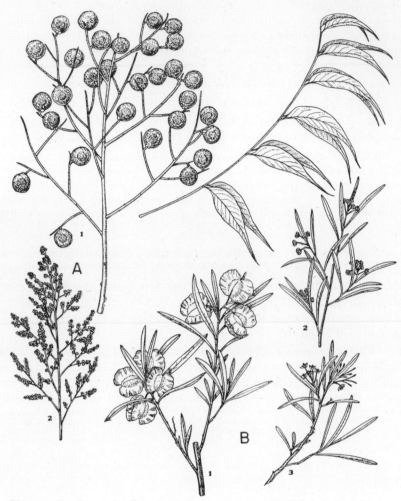

Fig. 57.—Soapberry family: *A*, western soapberry, *Sapindus Saponaria* var. *Drummondii*, *1*, branch with an inflorescence of the translucent amber fruits and a pinnate leaf (detached), *2*, inflorescence at flowering time; *B*, hop bush, *Dodonaea viscosa* var. *angustifolia*, *1*, branch with leaves and the 3-winged fruits, *2*, leafy branch with staminate flowers, *3*, leafy branch with pistillate flowers. (x ¹/₃.)

Family 24. *SAPINDACEAE*. Soapberry Family

The soapberry family is known in various parts of the United States for its members, the balloon vine or heart seed, as well as for the soapberry. (Fig. 57, Pl. XXIX *right.*)

Trees, shrubs, or sometimes vines, commonly vinelike in the tropics. Leaves commonly alternate, without stipules, simple, palmate, or pinnate. Flowers often unsymmetrical, sometimes some of them unisexual, sometimes the staminate and pistillate flowers restricted to different plants; sepals and petals commonly 4 or 5; stamens usually more numerous but ordinarily not twice as many. Fruit a berry or of a capsular type, but more or less divided in some groups so that a winged fruit (samara) is formed, as in *Dodonaea.*

KEY TO THE GENERA

1. Leaves pinnate; fruit a berry with a translucent outer fleshy portion (or turning black in dried specimens); petals present; perigynous. (Fig. 57 *A.*)   1. SAPINDUS

1. Leaves simple; fruit with 3 wings (a samara); petals none; hypogynous. (Fig. 57 *B*; Pl. XXIX *right.*)   2. DODONAEA

1. *SAPINDUS*. Soapberry

(1) Leaves large, pinnate; (2) fruit berrylike, with a remarkable amber or yellowish, translucent flesh, ½ inch in diameter. (Fig. 57 *A.*)

Trees or shrubs, most of them tropical or subtropical. Wood yellow. Flowers perigynous, some of them unisexual; sepals 5; petals usually 5; stamens 8-10. Fruit 1-seeded.

1a. *Sapindus Saponaria* L. var. *Drummondii* (Hook. & Arn.) L. Benson. WESTERN SOAPBERRY; CHERIONI (Fig. 57 *A*)

Small trees 2-5 m. (6-15 feet) high or in favorable situations taller; bark gray, rough; leaflets about 13-19, narrowly lanceolate-attenuate, 4-11 cm. long, 1-2 cm. broad, not toothed; flowers in large, dense panicles 4-5 mm. in diameter, the sepals and petals with short hairs along the margins, the stamens with long hair on the filaments. Synonym: *Sapindus Drummondii* Hook. & Arn.

Along watercourses and canyon sides in the upper portion of the desert, the desert grassland, and the oak woodland at 2,500 to 6,000 feet elevation. Arizona near Hackberry, Mohave County, and in the mountains below the Mogollon Rim from Yavapai

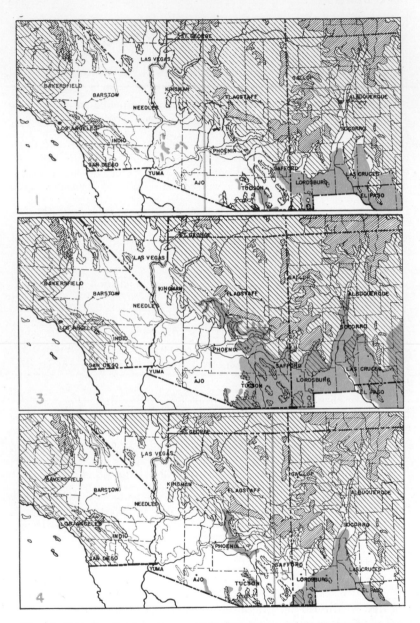

Fig. 58.—Distributional maps: *1*, crucifixion thorn, *Koeberlinia spinosa* var. *tenuispina*; *2*, crucifixion thorn, *Koeberlinia spinosa*; *3*, western soapberry, *Sapindus Saponaria* var. *Drummondii*; *4*, hop bush, *Dodonaea viscosa* var. *angustifolia*; *5*, white crucillo, *Condalia lycioides*.

County southeastward to Pima and Cochise counties; New
Mexico on the Gila River drainage and on the Rio Grande
drainage from Albuquerque southward; western Texas; eastward to Kansas and Louisiana; northern Mexico. (Fig. 58 *3*.)

The brilliant amber-colored fruits are rich in saponins, and
in Mexico they are used for laundry soap. Saponins are poisonous, and digitalis extract is one of them. It is believed that the
fruits of the soapberry are poisonous, and in parts of Mexico
the natives stupefy fish by throwing the crushed fruits into the
water. Cattle seldom browse the plants.

2. *DODONAEA*. Hop Bush

The following characters apply to the Southwestern Deserts
species: (1) Leaves simple, narrow; (2) fruit a 3-winged structure (samara) more than ½ inch in diameter. (Fig. 57 *B*; Pl.
XXIX *right*.)

Shrubs or sometimes small trees. Leaves alternate, oblanceolate to
linear, entire or toothed (rarely pinnate in some foreign species), resinous
and either sticky or varnished. Flowers hypogynous, unisexual, the staminate and pistillate flowers on different individuals; sepals 3-5; petals
none; stamens usually 5-8, the stamen-bearing floral disc not developed.
Fruit a capsule, but the segments each produced into a wing, rarely not
so in foreign species; carpels 3 or 4.

1a. *Dodonaea viscosa* Jacq. var. *angustifolia* (L. f.) Benth.
DODONAEA; HOP BUSH (Fig. 57 *B*; Pl. XXIX *right*)

Shrub 1-3 m. (3-9 feet) high; leaves linear-oblanceolate, 5-9 cm. long,
4-8 mm. broad, sticky; flowers yellowish green, about 5 mm. in diameter;
stamens about 8, the anthers exceedingly large, about 2 mm. long, the
filaments slender, 0.5 mm. long; fruit about 11-13 mm. long, 15-20 mm.
in diameter including the wings, the 3 seeds brown, ellipsoidal to ovate,
somewhat flattened, about 3.5 mm. long.

Canyons and rocky or gravelly slopes in the upper desert and
the desert grassland at 2,000 to 4,000 feet elevation. Arizona
from the Verde River in southern Yavapai County southward
in scattered localities to Pima and Santa Cruz counties; Florida;
Baja California and southeastward in Mexico; widely distributed through the warm countries of the world. (Fig. 58 *4*.)

The dark green foliage and the colorful hoplike fruits make
the plant worthy of consideration as an ornamental. The winged

fruits have not only a resemblance to hops, but they have been used as a substitute in making yeast and beer. Various medicinal preparations have been derived from the leaves and bark, but the amateur medicine man should have caution, since the plant contains saponins which are poisonous. In some countries they are used as fish poison.

Family 25. *RHAMNACEAE*. BUCKTHORN FAMILY

In California and the Southwest the two best-known genera of the Rhamnaceae are *Rhamnus* (coffeeberry), species of which yield the laxative cascara, and *Ceanothus,* best developed in coastal California and known as mountain lilac. Two genera, *Condalia* and *Colubrina,* are characteristic of the deserts, and *Sageretia* occurs in the desert grassland and the oak woodland above it. The family is recognized by the fact that the stamens and petals are both on the floral disc and opposite each other (Cf. Fig. 60 *A 3, C* 2). (Fig. 60 *A-C;* Pl. XXIV.)

Shrubs or small trees. Leaves simple; stipules present but soon falling away. Flowers usually perigynous, in umbels or umbel-like clusters, the inflorescence sometimes compound; sepals, petals, and stamens 5 or sometimes 4, the petals sometimes none, each petal forming a hood which commonly covers or subtends the adjacent stamen; carpels 3 or sometimes 2; fruit a 3-celled usually 3-seeded capsule or berrylike and 1-seeded; ovary superior or sometimes partly inferior by union of the lower part with the floral disc and the calyx tube.

KEY TO THE GENERA

1. Ovary superior; fruit fleshy, berrylike or drupelike.
    2. Fruit with a single stone with 1 or 2 internal compartments; leaves not green and shining. (Fig. 60 *A, B;* Pl. XXIV *A, B.*)   1. CONDALIA
    2. Fruit with 3 stones; leaves green and shining.   2. SAGERETIA
1. Ovary partly inferior; fruit dry, a capsule, 3-chambered, 3-seeded. (Fig. 60 *C.*)   3. COLUBRINA

1. *CONDALIA*

Fruits berrylike, the calyx and the stamen-bearing disc not joined. (Fig. 60 *A, B.;* Pl. XXIV *A. B.*)

Shrubs. Branches spiny, divergent. Leaves alternate, entire. Flower clusters (umbels) in the leaf axils; sepals 5; petals 5 or sometimes none; stamens 5; carpels 2, only 1 seed developing but 2 ovules sometimes present; fruit berrylike.

KEY TO THE SPECIES

1. Petals present; leaves 8-18 mm. long, ovate, obovate, or elliptical.

    2. Fruit without a beak, the pedicel 2-4 mm. long; flowers in a stalked cluster; branches with patches of hair when young or in a variety densely short-hairy at all times. (Fig. 60 *A*; Pl. XXIV *A, B*.)

        1. *Condalia lycioides*

    2. Fruit with a short beak, the pedicel 8-14 mm. long; flowers in stalkless clusters; branches glabrous.   2. *Condalia Parryi*

1. Petals none; leaves 4-6 mm. long (to 15 mm. in *C. mexicana*), narrowly obovate, cuneate, or spatulate.

    2. Fruits pedicelled; branchlets slender, rather flexible, moderately spiny; leaf veins prominent.

        3. Shrubs; berry not bitter. (Fig. 60 *B*.)   3. *Condalia spathulata*

        3. Small trees; berry bitter (even in dried specimens).

        4. *Condalia globosa*

    2. Fruits not pedicelled; branchlets stout, rigid, spiny; leaf veins inconspicuous.   5. *Condalia mexicana*

1a. *Condalia lycioides* (A. Gray) Weberb var. *lycioides*.
WHITE CRUCILLO; LOTE BUSH

Scraggly shrubs 1-3 m. high; branches and leaves glabrous or with only patches of hair; spines up to 1 dm. long, standing at right angles to the larger branches; leaves narrowly elliptical to narrowly ovate or narrowly oblong, 8-15 mm. long, 5-7 mm. broad, relatively thin, the veins rather prominent and somewhat reticulate; umbel with a peduncle; sepals about 2 mm. long, triangular, hairy on the backs; petals about 1.5 mm. long, white; fruits blue-black, with a bloom (glaucous), ellipsoidal, not beaked, about 7-8 mm. long, the pedicel 2-4 mm. long. Synonym: *Zizyphus lycioides* A. Gray.

Mesas and slopes of the desert and the desert grassland at mostly 1,500 to 4,500 feet elevation. Arizona in southeastern Cochise County (Douglas and San Bernardino) ; New Mexico from southern Grant County to Doña Ana County and southward; western Texas; northeastern Mexico. Essentially a plant of the Chihuahua Desert, barely entering southeastern Arizona. (Fig. 58 5.)

1b. *Condalia lycioides* (A. Gray) Weberb. var. *canescens* (A. Gray) Trel. GRAY THORNE (Fig. 60 *A;* Pl. XXIV *A, B*)

Branches and leaves densely short-hairy; leaves elliptical to ovate, 8-19 mm. long, 5-9 mm. broad, thicker than in the typical variety.

Mesas and slopes of the desert and the desert grassland at mostly 1,000 to 4,000 or sometimes 5,000 feet elevation. California in the mountains along the northern border of the Salton Sea Basin; Arizona in the Grand Canyon region, in southern Mohave County, and in the Arizona Desert as far eastward as the vicinity of the Chiricahua Mountains, Cochise County; Baja California, Mexico, to Sonora and perhaps southward.

The fruits are a favorite of birds, including Gambel's quail and the band-tailed pigeon. At one time the Indians used them as food. The Pima Indians of southern Arizona used decoctions of the roots as a remedy for sore eyes, and the bark of the roots of this and the typical variety has been used in parts of Mexico as a substitute for soap. (Fig. 59 *1*.)

2. *Condalia Parryi* (Torr.) Weberb. CALIFORNIA LOTE BUSH

Shrub 1-3 m. high; branches and leaves glabrous; leaves obovate to oblong or elliptic, 8-18 mm. long; umbel without a peduncle; petals present; fruit 8-15 mm. long, with a short beak 1-2 mm. long, the slender pedicel 8-10 mm. long. Synonym: *Zizyphus Parryi* Torr.

Canyons and foothills of the desert below 3,000 feet. California along the northern and western borders of the Salton Sea Basin of the Colorado Desert; Baja California, Mexico. (Fig. 59 *2*.)

The large fruits formerly were ground into a coarse meal and used as food by the Cahuilla Indians of Southern California.

3. *Condalia spathulata* A. Gray. MEXICAN CRUCILLO. (1) Leaves narrow, gradually expanded upward, about ¼ inch long; (2) berry sweet, edible. (Fig. 60 *B*.)

Compactly and densely branched shrub usually 1-1.5 m. high, the branching sometimes so dense as to give the plant a resemblance to a small juniper when seen from a distance; leaves commonly narrowly cuneate to spatulate, about 4 mm. long, 1-2 mm. broad; petals none; fruits about 3 mm. long.

Sandy or gravelly well-drained mesas and slopes in the desert and the desert grassland at 2,500 to 4,500 feet elevation. California at scattered stations in the eastern part of the Salton Sea Basin of the Colorado Desert; Arizona from the Silver Bell, Comobabi, and Baboquivari mountains, Pima County, eastward to the Arizona Desert and the desert grassland south of the

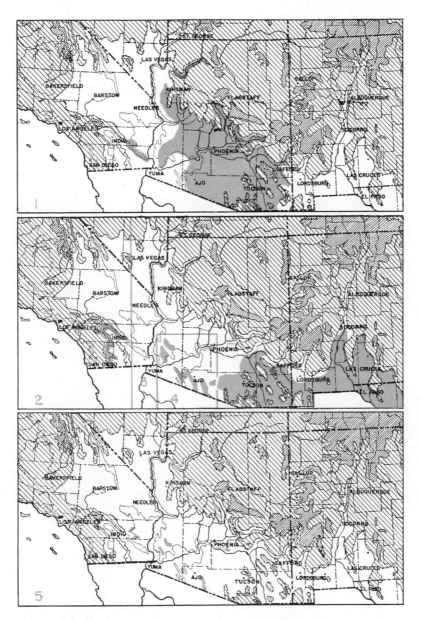

Fig. 59.—Distributional maps: *1*, gray thorn, *Condalia lycioides* var. *canescens*; *2*, California lote bush, *Condalia Parryi*; *3*, Mexican crucillo, *Condalia spathulata*; *4*, bitter condalia, *Condalia globosa*; *5*, California colubrina, *Colubrina texensis* var. *californica*.

Gila River; New Mexico on the Gila River drainage and in the Chihuahuan Desert from Sierra County southward; western Texas; Mexico, including Baja California. (Fig. 59 *3*.) The disjunct distribution in the deserts of California and Arizona is striking. The closely related species *Condalia globosa* occupies the intermediate area.

4. *Condalia globosa* Johnson. BITTER CONDALIA

Similar to *Condalia spathulata* but a small tree 2-5 m. high; veins of the leaves less crowded; berry bitter, the taste becoming noticeable and soon overwhelming after chewing, as distinctive in dried specimens as in fresh.

Sandy washes in the desert at 1,000 to 2,500 feet elevation. Arizona in the Kofa and Castle Dome mountains, Yuma County, and in the Growler and Ajo mountains and the Sierra Blanca, western Pima County; Sonora and Baja California, Mexico. (Fig. 59 *4*.)

5. *Condalia mexicana* Schlect. MEXICAN BLUEWOOD

Similar to *Condalia spathulata* and *Condalia globosa* but a shrub with very stout, rigid, spiny, spreading branches; leaves 10-15 mm. long, 3-5 mm. broad, with relatively inconspicuous veins; fruit with practically no pedicel.

Rocky canyons and gravelly slopes in the upper part of the desert, the desert grassland, and the oak woodland at 3,000 to 4,500 feet elevation. Arizona in the Baboquivari Mountains, Pima County, at Sycamore Canyon near Ruby, Santa Cruz County, and in the hills east of Douglas, Cochise County; Mexico.

2. *SAGERETIA*. SAGERETIA

(1) Fruit berrylike, containing 3 stones; (2) leaves green, shiny.

Spiny shrubs with spreading branches; petals present, white; fruit fleshy, the ovary superior.

1. *Sageretia Wrightii* S. Wats.

Shrubs 1-4 m. high; leaves opposite or nearly so, obovate to elliptical, mostly 10-15 mm. long, 8-10 mm. broad, thin, serrulate; fruit dark colored, nearly black.

Hillsides and canyons in the desert grassland and the oak woodland at 3,500 to 5,500 feet elevation. Arizona from the Superstition Mountains, eastern Maricopa County, and the Baboquivari Mountains, Pima County, eastward to Greenlee and Cochise counties; western Texas; Mexico.

3. *COLUBRINA*. COLUBRINA

Fruits capsular, spheroidal, 3-grooved, the calyx and stamen-bearing floral disc attached to the ovary, which is about one-quarter inferior (Fig. 60 *C*).

Trees or shrubs. Branches strongly divergent, some of them forming slender spines. Bark gray. Leaves alternate, entire or saw-toothed. Flowers in small, dense clusters in the leaf axils; free portions of the sepals falling away at fruiting time; petals present.

1a. *Colubrina texensis* (Torr. & Gray) A. Gray var. *californica* (I. M. Johnston) L. Benson. CALIFORNIA COLUBRINA (Fig. 60 *C*)

Shrub 1-2 m. (3-6 feet) high; young branches densely short-hairy; leaves elliptical to obovate or nearly oblong, 8-16 mm. long, 6-10 mm. broad, finely hairy, entire; flower clusters forming a narrow, leafy panicle; flowers about 3-4 mm. in diameter; fruits light brown, nearly spheroidal, 7-8 mm. in diameter, the walls hard. Synonym: *Colubrina californica* Johnston.

Rocky or gravelly slopes in the desert at 2,000 to 3,000 feet elevation. California in the Eagle and Chuckawalla mountains, Riverside County; Arizona in the Kofa and Castle Dome mountains, Yuma County, the Ajo Mountains, Pima County, and the Santan Mountain, Pinal County, and at Fish Creek Canyon on the Apache Trail, Maricopa County; Baja California and probably Sonora, Mexico. (Fig. 59 5.)

This is a relict type of interest for its occurrence in widely separated areas.

Family 26. *MALVACEAE*. MALLOW FAMILY

The mallow family is common in cultivation, and the hollyhock, hibiscus, okra, and cotton are among its best-known members. The common cheese weed or mallow is likewise well known, especially for its segmented fruits which resemble sec-

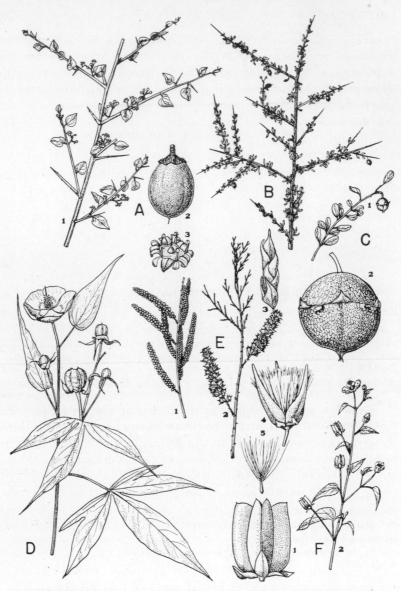

Fig. 60.—Buckthorns, tamarisk, and mallows: *A*, gray thorn, *Condalia lycioides* var. *canescens*, *1*, branch with flowers, *2*, fruit, *3*, flower; *B*, Mexican crucillo, *Condalia spathulata*, branch with fruits; *C*, California colubrina, *Colubrina texensis* var. *californica*, *1*, branch with fruit, *2*, fruit; *D*, desert cotton, *Gossypium Thurberi*, branch with flowers and fruits; *E*, Tamarisk, *Tamarix gallica*, var. *pycnostachys*, *1*, branch with spikes of flowers and buds, *2*, branch with spikes of fruits, *3*, enlarged portion of a branch, *4*, fruit, *5*, seed; *F*, Pringle abutilon, *Abutilon Pringlei*, *1*, fruit, *2*, branch with flowers and fruits. (x ¹/₃ except *A* 2, 3, *C* 2 x 1¹/₃; *E* 3 x 4; *E 4, 5, F 1* x 2²/₃.)

tions cut from a round cheese. The family is distinguished by its showy hypogynous flowers with five conspicuous petals and with the stamens united into a tube around the several styles. Most of the members are herbaceous, and in the Southwestern deserts only the desert cotton or thurberia is a particularly significant shrub, although some species of *Abutilon* (besides the one included here) and of *Horsfordia* might be considered as worthy of discussion. (Fig. 60 *D, F.*)

Herbs or sometimes shrubs or somewhat shrubby plants. Hairs of the plant commonly star-shaped because of their branching. Leaves alternate, simple, commonly palmately lobed to divided; stipules none. Flowers bisexual, hypogynous; sepals 5; petals 5, the bases usually joined to the base of the conspicuous stamen tube; stamens many; carpels 3, 5, or commonly 8-15, united, but usually separating at fruiting time; not so in our genera, however.

KEY TO THE GENERA

1. Stamens produced along the upper part of the filament tube for a distance of about 1 cm., the stamens not more numerous at the apex of the tube than below it; leaves palmately 3-parted or -divided, averaging nearly or more than 1 dm. in diameter; involucre of 3 conspicuous bractlets just below the saucerlike calyx; seeds woolly, at least at first. (Fig. 60 *D.*)   1. GOSSYPIUM

1. Stamens produced only at the apex of the filament tube, crowded; leaves entire or toothed or obscurely lobed, in our only truly shrubby species not more than 2-3 cm. long; involucre none, the calyx parted, not saucerlike; seeds not woolly. (Fig. 60 *F.*)   2. ABUTILON

1. *GOSSYPIUM*. COTTON

Herbs or shrubs, most of them tropical or cultivated in warm climates. Leaves lobed to divided. Flower subtended by an involucre of 3 bracts (specialized leaves) just below the calyx; calyx chopped off abruptly at the apex, scarcely showing evidence of the 5 sepals; stamens separating from the stamen tube and producing anthers at various levels on the upper portion of the tube. Fruit a capsule which splits along 3 or 5 lines; seeds woolly or short-woolly but the hair falling away early (glabrate). (Fig. 60 *D.*)

1. *Gossypium Thurberi* Tod. DESERT COTTON; THURBERIA; ALGODONCILLO. (1) Leaves palmately 3-parted or -divided, 2-4 inches long; (2) petals white or lavender, 1 inch long; (3) capsules dark brown, 3- to 4-celled. (Fig. 60 *D.*)

Shrub commonly 1-2 m. (3-6 feet) high or, according to Professor Thornber, sometimes up to 4 m. (12 feet) with a trunk diameter of 1 dm.

(4 inches); bark rather smooth, gray-brown; leaves palmately 3-parted or -divided, the divisions lanceolate-attenuate, each of them 6-12 cm. long, 1-3 cm. broad, green above, somewhat paler beneath, minutely hairy on only the edges; flowers in groups of about 2-3, 5-7 cm. in diameter; bractlets 3, lanceolate-attenuate, 10 mm. long; calyx a saucer 7-8 mm. broad; petals white and lavender to magenta, 2.5-3.5 cm. long, 2-3 cm. broad; stamen tube 12-15 mm. long, less than 1 mm. in diameter; capsule nearly spheroidal, 1-12 mm. in diameter, 3-celled, splitting along the middle of each section; seeds short-woolly, glabrate. Synonym: *Thurberia thespesioides* A. Gray, not *Gossypium thespesioides.* (Benth.) F. Muell. Also known incorrectly as *Ingenhouzia triloba* DC.

Rocky or gravelly mountain slopes and canyons in the desert and the desert grassland at 2,500 to 4,500 feet elevation. Arizona from the Bradshaw Mountains, southern Yavapai County, to the Superstition Mountains, Maricopa County, and to Santa Cruz and Cochise counties; Mexico. (Fig. 61 *1.*)

This species is a host for a cotton boll weevil, and it has been largely eradicated in areas where it occurred near cultivated cotton. The fibers are too short to be of use.

2. *ABUTILON*. Indian Mallow

Herbs, shrubs, or suffrutescent plants. Leaves entire to toothed or slightly lobed. Flower not subtended by an involucre; calyx lobed to divided, the individual sepals obvious; stamens crowded at the apex of the stamen tube, the rest of the tube bare. Fruit a nearly globose or in our species a truncate, cylindroidal capsule, the carpels united, the number variable, 5 or more; seeds glabrous. (Fig. 60 *F.*)

Several species of *Abutilon* are transitional between herbs and shrubs.

1. *Abutilon Pringlei* Hochreutiner. PRINGLE ABUTILON. (1) Leaves simple, densely hairy, mostly less than 1 inch long; (2) petals white or lavender with a basal red spot; (3) capsules tan, 5-celled. (Fig. 60 *F.*)

Shrub 0.5-1.5 m. high; bark gray, somewhat roughened; branchlets covered densely with fine star-shaped hairs; leaves cordate or mostly very narrowly cordate, somewhat attenuate, those on the mature branches mostly 1-2 cm. long, sometimes (especially on young shoots) up to 3 cm. long, 7-15 or 20 mm. broad, finely and densely covered with star-shaped hairs; flowers 10-15 mm. in diameter; petals 6-8 mm. long, white, pinkish, or lavender, each with a red spot at the base; fruit prismatic-cylindroidal, about 8 mm. long, 6-8 mm. in diameter.

Rocky or gravelly slopes in the desert and the desert grass-land at 2,000 to 3,500 feet elevation. Arizona from Yavapai County to Pima County; northern Sonora, Mexico.

Family 27. *TAMARICACEAE*. Tamarisk Family

Shrubs or trees. Leaves green, scalelike, appressed or spreading some-what. Flower small, in dense racemes or spikes. Sepals and petals 4-5; stamens 4-5 or 8-10; petals and stamens produced on a hypogynous disc; styles 3-5. Fruit a capsule, 1-celled, the seeds attached at the base; seeds each with a tuft of hairs. (Fig. 60 *E*.)

1. *TAMARIX*. Tamarisk

Despite the absence of native species, the genus *Tamarix* is one of the best known in the Southwest, particularly because of the introduction by Professor Thornber of the most commonly cultivated species, *Tamarix aphylla* (L.) Karst. (*Tamarix articulata* Vahl.) This tamarisk, known as athel, has been cultivated in every Southwestern state, and it is common as a hedge or avenue plant. In somewhat alkaline bottom lands—for example, at Indio and across the river from Yuma—the tree becomes a handsome one notable for its drooping branchlets. In some places it has become a large tree; for instance, on the school grounds at Florence, Arizona. Occasionally it has become established outside of cultivation. The wood is light colored, with a beautiful grain, and it is capable of taking a high polish. It has been proposed for use as a source of furniture and of fence posts.[8] (Fig. 60 *E*.)

1a. *Tamarix gallica* L. var. *pycnostachys* Ledeb. TAMARISK; SALT CEDAR (Fig. 60 *E*)

Shrub 1-3 m. high, forming rounded masses several meters in diameter where conditions are favorable; leaves narrow, tapering from base to apex, 1-2 mm. long, less than 0.5 mm. broad; flowers pink, 1.5 mm. long, 1.5 mm. in diameter, crowded in racemes about 2-3 cm. long and 4 mm. in diameter.

According to Elizabeth McClintock (Jour. Calif. Hort. Soc. 12: 76-83. 1951), the species introduced in the deserts is *Tamarix pentandra,* but specific status is dubious. The varietal combina-

8. Cf. G. E. P. Smith. *Creosoted Tamarisk Fence Posts and Adaptability of Tamarisk as a Fine Cabinet Wood.* Univ. of Ariz. Coll. of Agr. and Agr. Exp. Sta. Tech. Bull. (92) :223-54. 1941.

tion used here is chosen only tentatively, for the classification problem is a difficult one which cannot be solved in the Western Hemisphere.

Stream beds and irrigation ditches. Naturalized here and there in California from Lake and Colusa counties southward; abundant along the major watercourses in the deserts from California to western Texas; native from the Balkans eastward to the Himalaya Mountains in Asia.

Family 28. *CACTACEAE*. Cactus Family

Plants succulent trees, shrubs, or herbs, the stems greatly swollen; clusters of spines produced in definite, special areoles on the surface of the stem; leaves none or succulent and ephemeral, appearing on the new segments (joints) of the stem but disappearing within a few months; sepals and petals numerous, gradually intergrading, united below into a short or elongated common tube; ovary inferior, the flower epigynous; style 1, the stigmas several; stamens from perhaps 50 to several hundred; fruit a fleshy berry covered with areoles or sometimes drying up at maturity.

The family is not included in this work. The reader is referred to *The Cacti of Arizona*, by Lyman Benson. Second Edition. University of Arizona Press and University of New Mexico Press. 1950.

Family *GARRYACEAE*. Silk Tassel Family

Garrya flavescens S. Wats. Shrub often 3-4 m. high; leaves opposite, simple, entire, ovate or elliptic, acute at both ends, appressed-hairy, the hairs silky, rather sparse, sometimes glabrous; flowers unisexual, staminate and pistillate flowers on different plants, arranged in drooping catkinlike structures; petals none; staminate flowers with the sepals linear, united at the bases; stamens 4, the filaments separate; pistillate flowers with the sepals united and free portions practically undeveloped; ovary inferior; styles and stigmas 2; fruit a berry. Mountainsides and canyons in the desert, the chaparral, and the pinyon-juniper woodland at 2,000 or mostly 4,000 to 7,000 feet elevation. California west of the chief mountain axis from San Benito and Fresno counties southward and eastward to the Granite, Clark, and Providence mountains in the Mojave Desert; southern Nevada in the Charleston Mountains; southern Utah; Arizona from the Hualpi Mountains, Mohave County, to Coconino County and southeastward under the Mogollon Rim to Cochise County; western Texas; Northern Mexico. Occurring in the desert in Palm Canyon, Kofa Mountains, Yuma County, Arizona, probably persisting there as do some oaks and other plants because of the perpetual shade on the south side of the canyon and the probably constant

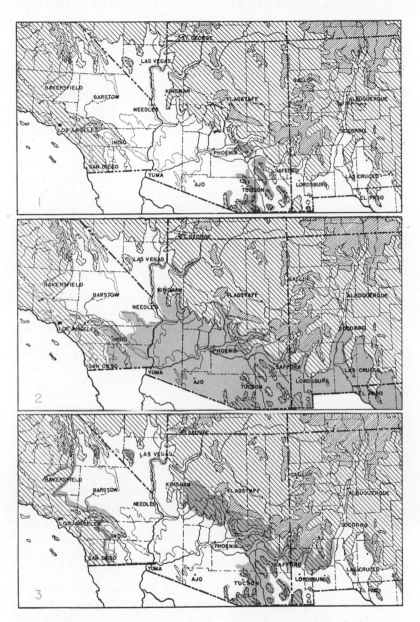

Fig. 61.—Distributional maps: *1*, desert cotton, *Gossypium Thurberi*; *2*, ocotillo, *Fouquieria splendens*; *3*, Arizona ash, *Fraxinus velutina* including var. *coriacea* on the western margin of the range.

underground water supply. The plant is characteristic of the extreme lower edge of the pinyon-juniper belt and of the higher levels.

Garrya Wrightii Torr. occurs at the edge of the Desert Grassland from southeastern Arizona to Texas and northern Mexico.

Family 29. *FOUQUIERIACEAE*. Candlewood Family

The candlewood family is a small one, since it contains only one genus of 3 species (according to the most conservative count or 8 according to a more radical interpretation). The boojum tree or cirio of Baja California and Sonora, Mexico, is cultivated occasionally as a curiosity, since it has an inverted carrot-shaped or columnar trunk and only very small branches and consequently has a weird appearance. Some of these trees are in the traffic island just northeast of the Chemistry-Physics building on the University of Arizona campus. The best-known plant of the group is the ocotillo discussed below. (Pls. XXV; XXVI; Fig. 65 *A*.)

Shrubs or small trees with a short or elongated massive trunk and either large wandlike branches or (when the trunk is long) relatively small branches. Spines numerous, each formed by hardening of the persistent petiole and midrib of a leaf of the first season of growth (Pl. XXV *E*); leaves of succeeding seasons produced in clusters in the axils. Flowers in terminal panicles, cream colored or red; sepals 5, unequal, overlapping; petals 5, united; stamens mostly 14-19, sometimes fewer. Fruit a capsule, incompletely 3- or 4-celled; seeds several.

1. *FOUQUIERIA*. Ocote; Ocotillo

1. *Fouquieria splendens* Engelm. OCOTILLO; COACHWHIP. (1) Shrubs with slender spiny branches arranged in fan-shaped clusters or inverted cones; (2) flowers red, in dense panicles at or near the ends of branches. (Pls. XXV; XXVI; Fig. 65 *A*.)

Trunk a few dm. long, the wandlike, spiny branches 2-9 m. long, 2-6 cm. in diameter; spines 1.5-3 cm. long; leaves obovate, sessile or practically so, 1.5-5 cm. long, 1-3 cm. broad, glabrous; flowers in dense terminal panicles; sepals reddish; corolla red, 16-20 mm. long; stamens red, mostly 14-19, protruding well beyond the corolla; style divided into 3 or 4 elongated portions; fruit 16-18 mm. long, splitting along 3 or 4 lines.

Rocky, exposed slopes or gravelly or sandy plains from sea level to 5,000 feet elevation. California in the extreme southwestern Mojave Desert and in the Colorado Desert; Arizona in the lower part of the Grand Canyon region, in the southern Mojave Desert, and in the Colorado and Arizona deserts and the adjacent desert grassland; New Mexico southward; western Texas; Baja California and southeastward in Mexico. Flowering in April or May and sparingly after the summer rains. (Fig. 61 2.)

The ocotillo is one of the most distinctive shrubs in the Southwestern deserts, and it is one of the types which give outstanding character to the region. The spreading inverted cone of spiny branches comes into leaf during each rainy season, and the foliage is shed in the intervening dry spells. When drought periods are broken suddenly by torrential summer rains, the ocotillos may come into full leaf within a few days. The formation of spines from the petioles and midribs of the leaves may be observed upon growing branch segments.

The ocotillo serves many useful purposes. It is used for fencing of yards and enclosures, the full-sized stems being planted as cuttings, and it is used as building material, particularly for support of thatched roofs of ramadas and other structures. The southern California Indians used the flowers as a source of food. The stem contains deposits of waxy materials from which a commercial belt dressing is prepared.

Family 30. *SAPOTACEAE*. Sapodilla Family

The family is known best for the tropical tree, *Achras Zapota*, the sapodilla. This is not only an important fruit tree, but it yields the chicle of chewing gum, which is obtained from the latex or milky juice of the stems. The exudate of our species of *Bumelia* is chewed by children. (Fig. 66 *C*.)

Trees or shrubs with milky juice. Leaves alternate, simple, usually leathery; stipules none. Flowers relatively small, in axillary clusters; sepals 4-12, in whorls, in our genus 5 and unequal; petals in our genus 5, united, in one cycle; corolla with or without appendages; stamens as many as the petals, attached to the corolla tube; staminodia (sterile stamens) usually present and alternating with the developed stamens. Fruit drupelike or berrylike.

1. *BUMELIA*

Trees or shrubs, commonly spiny, the spines formed from pointed branchlets. Flowers white or sometimes greenish, produced in our species on short spur branches terminated by leaf clusters. Sepals 5, of different sizes; petals 5, with 2 appendages between the pairs of petals; staminodia resembling petals; fruit drupelike, 1-seeded. (Fig. 66 *C*.)

1a. *Bumelia lanuginosa* (Michx.) Pers. var. *rigida* A. Gray. CHITTAMWOOD. (1) Small tree with brown spiny branches; (2) leaves elliptical or oblanceolate, leathery, covered with loosely matted white or tan hair especially on the under surface. (Fig. 66 *C*.)

A small tree 2-4 m. high, the trunk usually 1-2 dm. in diameter; bark gray; twigs brown and spiny; leaves oblanceolate, 2-4 cm. long, mostly 1-1.7 cm. broad, leathery; flowers about 10-15 in a cluster, each 2-3 mm. in diameter; petals, appendages, and staminodia white; fruit ellipsoidal, in the material available about 8-10 mm. long.

Fine-textured or sandy soils along watercourses and washes in the upper part of the desert, the desert grassland, and the oak woodland at 3,000 to 5,000 feet elevation. Arizona from the Baboquivari and Santa Catalina mountains, Pima County, eastward to scattered localities in Cochise County; southwestern New Mexico; western Texas; northern Mexico.

The wood is used sometimes for cabinet work and tool handles, and, as stated above, gum exudations from the stem are used locally as chewing gum.

Family 31. *OLEACEAE*. Olive Family

The family includes the olive, privets, lilacs, ashes, and jasmines. Inclusion of the ash trees, which have no petals, may seem curious, but some species of ash have united petals, and the flowers of these species are not unlike those of other groups in the family, including the lilacs *(Syringa).* (Pl. XXVII; Figs. 62; 66 *A, B, D, E.*)

Trees or shrubs. Leaves usually alternate but sometimes opposite. Flowers in dense clusters or in panicles, bisexual or unisexual and the staminate and pistillate on either the same or different individuals. Stamens 1-4. Flowers hypogynous, the ovary superior, 2-chambered. Fruit various, in our genera either 1-winged and dry (a samara), drupelike (similar to an olive), or a bispheroidal capsule, which splits horizontally in each section.

KEY TO THE GENERA

1. Trees growing along streams or subirrigated washes; leaves pinnate, several cm. long; petals none, staminate and pistillate flowers in dense

clusters on different individuals; fruit 1-winged and dry (a samara). (Pl. XXVII; Fig. 62.)   1. FRAXINUS

1. Shrubs growing on the floor of the desert or in washes; leaves simple, not more than 2.5 cm. long; petals present or absent; fruit not winged.

   2. Petals none, flowers small; fruit similar to a small olive; shrub 2-5 m. high. (Fig. 66 *D, E*.)   2. FORESTIERA

   2. Petals present, corolla more or less funnel-like; fruit a bispheroidal capsule, each portion opening by a horizontal slit; bushes not more than 1 m. high. (Fig. 66 *A, B*.)   3. MENODORA

1. *FRAXINUS*. Ash

(1) Trees of stream banks and subirrigated washes; (2) leaves large, pinnate; (3) flowers without petals in our species, appearing before the leaves, the yellow staminate and the green pistillate flowers on different individuals; (4) fruit with a single large terminal wing. (Pl. XXVII; Fig. 62.)

Trees or shrubs. Flowers unisexual, the staminate and pistillate flowers on different plants or in some species all or some of the flowers bisexual; sepals greenish yellow or green, very small; petals usually none but in some species 2 and united; stamens usually 2. Fruit cylindroidal to flattened, the wing elongated .

1a. *Fraxinus velutina* Torr. var. *velutina*. ARIZONA ASH; FRESNO (Pl. XXVII; Fig. 62)

Trees 3-12 m. high; bark fissured, gray; twigs not markedly angled; leaflets in 2-3 pairs, with a terminal leaflet. lanceolate, oblanceolate, elliptical, or elliptic-oblong, 4-7 or 10 cm. long, 2-3 or 4 cm. broad, with or without a petiolule, sometimes markedly attenuate at the base, sometimes not, saw-toothed, dentate, or entire, densely short-hairy or glabrous, rather thin or sometimes thick and leathery (exceedingly variable in all respects, hence the large number of synonymous names); staminate flowers in remarkably dense clusters about 2-4 cm. in diameter, the stamens 2 or sometimes 3 per flower, the conspicuous yellow anthers elongated, the filaments almost obsolete, the calyx yellowish, vestigial; staminate flowers fewer and less congested, green, the stigmas longer than the ovaries, the calyx green, irregular, well developed; fruits in dense clusters, the bodies mostly 9-12 mm. long, 2-3 mm. broad, the wings of each about 15-20 mm. long, 4-6 mm. broad. Synonyms: *Fraxinus Toumeyi* Britt.; *Fraxinus Standleyi* Rehd.; *Fraxinus velutina* Torr. var. *Toumeyi* (Britt.) Rehd.

Along the major drainages in the desert, the desert grassland, and the oak woodland at 2,500 (or rarely lower) to 6,000 feet elevation. California in the mountains along the western borders of the Mojave and Colorado deserts; southern Nevada; southwestern Utah; Arizona in the lower Grand Canyon region and south of the Mogollon Rim from eastern Mohave County to the Baboquivari Mountains, Pima County, and eastward; New Mexico on the Gila River and Rio Grande drainages from the vicinity of Socorro southward; western Texas; Mexico. One of the most prominent stream-bank and canyon trees in the desert; restricted to areas with a permanent water supply, at least underground. (Fig. 61 *3*.)

1b. *Fraxinus velutina* Torr. var. *coriacea* (S. Wats.) Rehder

Similar to var. *velutina;* leaves thick; ridges radiating from the guard cells of the leaf stomata forming a pattern of larger size and more diffuse content; leaflets distinctly petioluled.

Coastal southern California and the mountains bordering the desert; along streams extending into the upper edge of the Mojave Desert in California; Charleston Mountains, Nevada; northern edge of Baja California, Mexico.

Recent study by P. A. Munz and J. D. Laudermilk has demonstrated the validity of this segregation (El Aliso 2: 49-62. 1949).

Fraxinus Gooddingii Little, GOODDING ASH, has been distinguished from other species of the genus occurring in Arizona (except the GREGG ASH, *Fraxinus Greggii*, with which it has been confused) by the following characters: (1) leaves evergreen or nearly so, usually persisting until flowers appear in the spring; (2) twigs slender, mostly less than 2 mm. in diameter, tawny with fine wool when they are young; (3) leaf rachis with narrow wings; (4) leaflets small, only 1-2.5 cm. long; (5) fruits relatively small, 1.2-2 cm. long. According to the author of the species, it is distinguished from *Fraxinus Greggii* by the following characters: (1) twigs, buds, and petioles covered densely with fine tawny wool, the hairs with several branches; (2) leaflets more numerous, 5-9 but commonly 7 instead of 3-7 or sometimes 1, elliptical (and broader and thinner than in *Fraxinus Greggii*), usually acute at the apices, the margins not revolute; (3) wing of the fruit decurrent nearly to the base. The plant is known from the region of Sycamore Canyon and Peña Blanca west of Nogales, Santa Cruz County, Arizona, and from the region of Rio Bavispe in northeastern Sonora, Mexico (*Edwin A. Phillips 736*).

Fraxinus anomala Torr. SINGLE-LEAF ASH. Shrubs; twigs markedly angled, glabrous; leaflets 1-3, the terminal leaflet nearly circular or broadly ovate. Canyons and hillsides in the lower pinyon-juniper woodland or occasionally

Fig. 62.—Arizona ash, *Fraxinus velutina*, *1*, branch with mature leaves and clusters of the winged fruits, 2, staminate flower with calyx and stamens, 3, pistillate flower with calyx and pistil. (*1* x ¹/₃; 2, 3 x 6²/₃.)

along the upper margin of the desert. California in the Panamint and Providence mountains of the Mojave Desert; southern Nevada in the Charleston Mountains; southern Utah on the Virgin and Colorado river drainages and occurring as far north as Labyrinth Canyon; western Colorado; northern Arizona from the Grand Canyon to the northern Navajo Reservation; northwestern New Mexico.

2. *FORESTIERA*. ADELIA

Recognized by: (1) leaves simple; (2) petals none; (3) large shrubs; (4) fruit resembling a small olive (Fig. 66*D, E*).

Flowers very small, unisexual, the staminate and pistillate flowers on different plants; sepals none or minute; petals none; stamens 2-4.

KEY TO THE SPECIES

1. Leaves oblanceolate, more or less persistent, 15-26 mm. long, 3-5 mm. broad, not toothed, moderately hairy above and below, the edges rolled inward (revolute); anthers purple; fruit about 5 mm. long, 3 mm. in diameter. (Fig. 66 *E*.)   1. *Forestiera phillyreoides*

1. Leaves obovate to oblong, promptly deciduous, 12-14 mm. long, 8-20 mm. broad, finely toothed, glabrous, the edges not rolled inward; anthers yellow; fruit 5-8 mm. long. (Fig. 66 *D*.)   2. *Forestiera neo-mexicana*

1. *Forestiera phillyreoides* Benth. DESERT OLIVE (Fig. 66 *E*)

Shrub 1-4 m. (3-12 feet) high; leaves oblanceolate, 15-26 mm. long, 3-5 mm. broad, green on both surfaces, moderately hairy on both sides, the edges rolled inward (revolute), entire, more or less persistent through the winter; anthers purple; fruits ellipsoid-cylindroidal to narrowly obovoid, about 5 mm. long, about 3 mm. in diameter.

Rocky canyon walls and slopes in the desert at 2,500 to 4,500 feet elevation. Arizona from the Kofa Mountains, Yuma County, and the Sierra Estrella, Maricopa County, to the Ajo and Tucson mountains, Pima County; Mexico. (Fig. 63 2.)

2. *Forestiera neo-mexicana*. A. Gray. DESERT OLIVE (Fig. 66 *D*)

Leaves glabrous, obovate to oblong, promptly deciduous, 12-40 mm. long, 8-20 mm. broad, the edges not rolled inward (revolute), toothed; anthers yellow; fruits more or less ellipsoid, 5-8 mm. long.

Along streams and on hillsides and mesas in the upper desert, the desert grassland, and the oak woodland at 3,000 to 7,000 feet elevation. California in the South Coast ranges from Alameda County to Santa Barbara and Kern counties and to Los

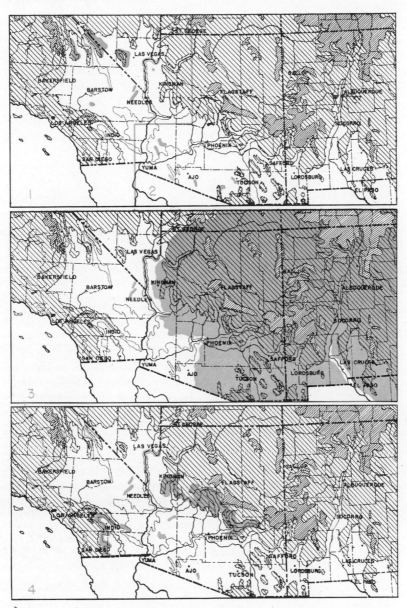

Figure 63.—Distributional maps: *1*, ground thorn, *Menodora spinescens*; *2*, desert olive, *Forestiera phillyreoides*; *3*, menodora, *Menodora scabra*; *4*, broom menodora, *Menodora scabra* var. *glabrescens*.

Angeles and San Bernardino counties, in the western Mojave Desert, and on the northern border of the Salton Sea Basin of the Colorado Desert; southern Utah; southwestern Colorado; Arizona on the Colorado Plateau, in the Hualpai Mountains, Mohave County, in the mountains below the Mogollon Rim but above the desert border, and occurring in the desert near Burro Creek on the boundary between Mohave and Yavapai counties; New Mexico on the Gila, San Juan, and Rio Grande drainages at 5,000 to 7,000 feet; western Texas.

3. *MENODORA*. MENODORA

(1) Leaves simple; (2) petals present, yellow, forming a conspicuous funnel-shaped corolla; (3) small shrubs or bushes; (4) fruit a bispheroidal capsule, each portion opening by a horizontal slit. (Fig 66 *A, B*.)

Leaves alternate or opposite. Flowers bisexual; sepals 5-15, linear, green; petals 5; stamens 2; seeds usually two in each chamber of the ovary.

KEY TO THE SPECIES

1. Plant not spiny; larger leaves 15-30 mm. long; lobes of the yellow corolla averaging 2.5-4 mm. broad, the length of each considerably exceeding the length of the tube. (Fig. 66 *A*.)   1. *Menodora scabra*

1. Plant markedly spiny; larger leaves 6-12 mm. long; lobes of the white corolla about 1.5 mm. broad, the length of each not exceeding the length of the tube. (Fig. 66 *B*.)   2. *Menodora spinescens*

1a. *Menodora scabra* A. Gray var. *scabra*. MENODORA. (1) Plant not spiny; (2) larger leaves $^3/_5$ to $1^1/_5$ inches long. (Fig. 66 *A*.)

Shrub 3-8 dm. high; branches not spiny; plant either finely and roughly hairy or glabrous; leaves lanceolate to oblong-lanceolate, 4-8 mm. broad, entire, green, opposite or alternate, those on the upper part of the stem somewhat reduced; flowers in open terminal clusters, the clusters on opposite-leaved branches, somewhat cymose; sepals 7-12 or 15, sometimes fewer in some of the flowers; petals yellow, united into a funnel-shaped corolla, the corolla 10-14 mm. long and 11-15 mm. in diameter, the lobes much longer than the tube, 2.5-4 mm. broad; fruit 6-9 mm. long, each portion 5-7 mm. broad. Synonyms: *Menodora laevis* Woot. & Standl. *Menodora scabra* A. Gray var. *laevis* (Woot. & Standl.) Steyermark.

Rocky or gravelly slopes and mesas in the desert, the desert grassland, and the oak woodland at 1,500 to 7,000 feet elevation.

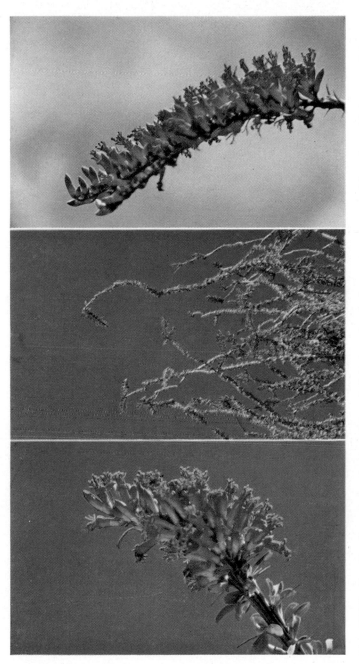

Plate XXVI.—Ocotillo, *Fouquieria splendens: left* and *right*, branches in flower; *center*, mass of branches with leaves and flowers. (Photographs: *left* by E. T. Nichols; *center* by Robert A. Darrow; *right* by Walter S. Phillips.)

Plate XXVII.—Arizona ash, *Fraxinus velutina: A,* branches of a staminate tree in flower; *B,* large tree in full foliage. (Photographs by Robert A. Darrow.)

California in the New York and Providence mountains in the southeastern Mojave Desert; southern Utah; southwestern Colorado and at Canyon City, Pueblo County; throughout Arizona below 7,000 feet except in the Colorado Desert; New Mexico throughout the Gila River, Rio Grande, and Pecos River drainages; western Texas; Mexico. (Fig. 63 *3*.)

This is an important browse plant in nearly all its range, and it is included here for this reason despite its suffrutescent character.

1b. *Menodora scabra* A. Gray, var. *glabrescens* A. Gray. BROOM MENODORA

Plant glabrous; upper leaves markedly reduced, the upper portion of the stem often nearly naked; sepals 5-6 or sometimes 8. Synonym: *Menodora scoparia* Engelm.

Dry slopes and mesas in the upper desert and the oak woodland at 3,500 to 5,000 feet elevation. California on the western border of the Salton Sea Basin of the Colorado Desert and in the Providence Mountains in the eastern Mojave Desert; Arizona in the Kofa and Ajo mountains and from the Mojave Desert near Kingman southeastward in the mountains below the Mogollon Rim to Cochise County; Baja California and Sonora, Mexico. Probably the plant occurs in extreme southern Nevada and in southwestern New Mexico. (Fig. 63 *4*.)

2. *Menodora spinescens* A. Gray. GROUND THORN. (1) Branches markedly spiny; (2) leaves ¼ to ½ inch long. (Fig. 66 *B*.)

Low shrub, usually 3-7 dm. or occasionally 1 m. high; finely hairy; leaves oblanceolate to nearly linear, 1-2 mm. broad; sepals 5 or sometimes more; petals white, forming a tubular-funnelform corolla 8-14 mm. long and about 7-8 mm. in diameter, the lobes not exceeding the length of the corolla tube, about 1.5-3 mm. broad; fruit deeply divided, about 6 mm. long, each division about 6 mm. in diameter.

Rocky slopes and mesas in the desert mountains at 3,500 or 4,000 to 5,000 feet elevation. California in the northern and eastern parts of the Mojave Desert; Nevada from southern Mineral County to southern Lincoln County; Arizona in the Mojave Desert 21 miles southeast of Boulder Dam *(L. Benson 10153).* (Fig. 63 *1*.)

Family 32. *LOGANIACEAE*. Logania Family

Shrubs, trees, or herbs or sometimes twining plants. Leaves opposite, entire or toothed. Sepals 4-5, united; petals 4-5, united, the corolla regular; stamens 4-5, joined to the petals. Fruit a capsule, a berry, or a drupelike structure.

1. *BUDDLEJA*. Butterfly Bush; Summer Lilac

Shrubs or sometimes small trees. Hairs usually star-shaped. Leaves entire or serrate or dentate. Flowers in dense heads or cymes or in dense clusters in the leaf axils. Sepals, petals, and stamens 4. Fruit a capsule.

KEY TO THE SPECIES

1. Leaves 5-15 cm. long, 1.5-3 cm. broad, not markedly hairy, thin, the margins not rolled downward, not with raised veins beneath.
   1. *Buddleja sessiliflora*

1. Leaves 1-3 cm. long, 3-6 mm. broad, markedly and densely short-hairy, thick, the margins rolled downward, the veins raised on the lower surface. 2. *Buddleja utahensis*

1. *Buddleja sessiliflora* H. B. K.

Shrub or a small tree, 1.5-6 m. high; leaves broadly lanceolate to narrowly elliptical and acute at both ends or narrowly lanceolate, 5-15 cm. long, 1.5-3 cm. broad, attenuate into the petioles, thin, saw-toothed, glabrous or only rather sparsely hairy at least within our range, the veins not raised on the lower surface; flowers in terminal spikelike groups of dense axillary clusters, greenish yellow or apparently purple or blue; fruits about 3 mm. long.

Hillsides in the upper part of the desert. Arizona in the Quinlan and Santa Catalina mountains, Pima County; Mexico.

2. *Buddleja utahensis* Cov.

Shrub; leaves oblong, or oblanceolate or lanceolate, 1-3 cm. long, 3-6 mm. broad, markedly and densely short-hairy, thick, the margins rolled downward, the veins raised on the lower surface, sunken on the upper.

Rocky slopes often on limestone in the creosote-bush and sagebrush deserts. California in the Panamint and Grapevine mountains in the Death Valley region and in the Kingston Mountains in the eastern Mojave Desert; southern Nevada; southwestern Utah; Arizona in northern Mohave County.

Buddleja scordioides H. B. K. is reported to occur within our range, but we have seen no evidence of its occurrence.

Family 33. *APOCYNACEAE*. Dogbane Family

Mostly perennial herbs, sometimes shrubs or suffrutescent plants; juice milky or somewhat so, containing some rubber. Leaves opposite, simple, entire. Flowers bisexual; petals 5, united, convolute in the bud, the corolla regular; stamens 5, united to the corolla tube, alternate with the petals, each with a basal sterile appendage, all standing close to the stigma but free from it. Pistil 1, the ovaries 2 and separate, the styles and stigmas united. Fruits 2 per flower, elongated, follicles. (Fig. 64.)

1. *HAPLOPHYTON*. Cockroach Plant

(1) Suffrutescent sprawling bushes with slender green branches; (2) leaves small, opposite, with fine appressed hairs; (3) corolla yellow; (4) fruit of paired slender follicles resembling young branches; (5) seeds with a tuft of hair at each end.

1. *Haplophyton Crooksii* L. Benson. Arizona Cockroach Plant (Fig. 64 *A*)

Leaves lanceolate, 15-27 or rarely 32 mm. long, 4-8 or 10 mm. broad; seeds black, 6-7.5 mm. long, somewhat grooved and ridged, the ridges not continuous, interrupted here and there and sometimes so short as to give the effect of pebble-grained leather.

Dry canyon sides in the desert and the desert grassland at 2,000 to 4,500 feet elevation. Arizona in Pinal County (Devil's Canyon near Superior and the Dripping Springs and Galiuro mountains), in Pima County (Baboquivari, Quinlan, and Santa Catalina mountains), in Santa Cruz County (near Patagonia); "New Mexico"; Texas in El Paso County and at Boquillas; southern Chihuahua, Mexico.

Haplophyton cimicidum (Fig. 64 *B*), the cockroach plant or hierba de la cucaracha, is abundant in Mexico from Guaymas, Sonora, southeastward and in Guatemala, and it is used as an insecticide. A decoction of the vegetative parts of the plant is mixed with corn meal and used as a poison for cockroaches. *Haplophyton Crooksii* is toxic to insects, and it may have commercial possibilities.

Family 34. *ASCLEPIADACEAE*. Milkweed Family

The true milkweeds are characterized by unique points of flower structure. Each of the five petals may have an accessory hood arising at about the point where the individual petal sep-

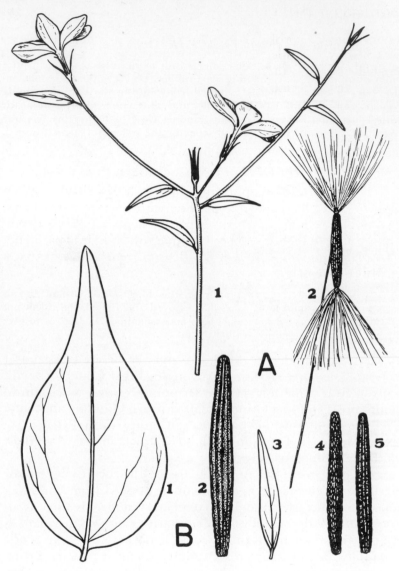

Fig. 64.—Cockroach plants: *A*, Arizona cockroach plant, *Haplophyton Crooksii*, *1*, branch with flowers, *2*, young seed with a tuft of hairs at each end and with the long stalk (funiculus), *3*, single leaf, *4, 5*, mature seeds; *B*, cockroach plant, *Haplophyton cimicidum*, a native of Mexico and Central America from which *Haplophyton Crooksii* is newly distinguished, *1*, leaf, *2*, mature seed. (*A 1* x ²/₃; leaves *A 3*, *B 1* x 1¹/₃; seed *A 2* x 2²/₃; seeds *A 4, 5*, *B 2* x 5¹/₂.)

arates from the corolla tube, and sometimes 1 or more horns are attached to the upper side of the hood. Oddly (as in the related dogbane family), there are 2 separate ovaries, but there is only 1 style, and it terminates in a single stigma. In the milkweeds, the 5 stamens are united to the edges of the stigma, and the whole structure forms a body resembling a pentagonal table (Fig. 65 C). The table top is highly polished, and when an insect lands upon it at least one leg is likely to slip down into one of the five grooves along the edge and to come up with a dumbbell-shaped mass of pollen hanging on one of the hooklike structures of the tarsus.

The only shrubby plants in the milkweed family in our area are recognized by their wandlike spineless and leafless branches, which arise in a cluster. (Pl. XXIV C; Fig. 65 B, C.)

Herbs, vines, or rarely shrubs with milky juice containing small or significant quantities of rubber. Leaves opposite or sometimes whorled. Flowers in umbels; sepals 5, united; petals 5, united; pollen united by wax into a pear-shaped mass within each anther cell, the pear-shaped mass joined by the narrow end to the similar mass formed in the nearest anther cell of the adjacent anther, thus forming a dumbbell-shaped mass; fruit a follicle (2 per flower); seeds with a tuft of silky hair.

1. *ASCLEPIAS*. Milkweed

KEY TO THE SPECIES

1. Hoods of the corolla about twice as long as the united stamens, style, and stigma. (Pl. XXIV C; Fig. 65 B.)   1. *Asclepias subulata*

1. Hoods of the corolla about half as long as the united stamens, style, and stigma. (Fig. 65 C.)   2. *Asclepias albicans*

1. *Asclepias subulata* Decn. RUSH MILKWEED; DESERT MILKWEED (Pl. XXIV C; Fig. 65 B)

Woody-stemmed plant, the stems wandlike or rushlike, in clusters (the clusters often dense), 1-3 m. (3-9 feet) high, 3-8 mm. in diameter; leaves ephemeral, rarely a few persisting, 2-3 cm. long, threadlike, less than 1 mm. broad; flowers cream color or dull yellow; hoods of the petals very long, twice as long as the stamens and style, tightly folded, enclosing the rather broad horn; fruits 8-13 cm. long, usually about 9-12 mm. in diameter; hairs of the seeds white, silky, about 2-3 cm. long.

Sandy or gravelly plains and rocky slopes in the desert from sea level to 2,500 feet elevation. California in the Colorado Des-

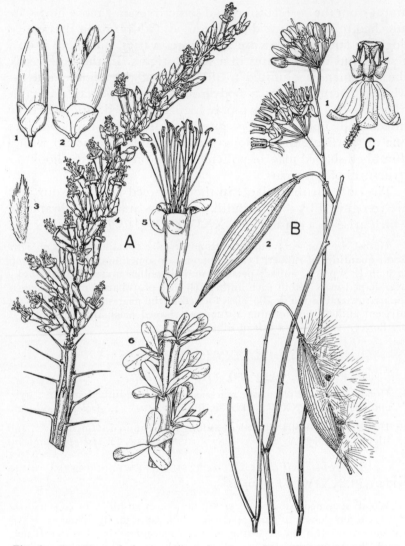

Fig. 65.—Ocotillo and desert milkweeds: *A*, ocotillo, *Fouquieria splendens*, *1*, fruit with the calyx at the base, *2*, fruit split open, *3*, seed, *4*, flowering branch, *5*, flower showing the sepals, petals, and numerous stamens, *6*, leafy branch, the leaves produced in clusters above the spines; *B*, desert milkweed, *Asclepias subulata*, *1*, leafless branch with an umbel of flower buds and an umbel of flowers, *2*, branches with fruits; *C*, wax milkweed, *Asclepias albicans*, single flower showing the much shorter hoods than in the desert milkweed at the left. (x $^1/_3$ except *A 1-3, 5, C* x $1^1/_3$.)

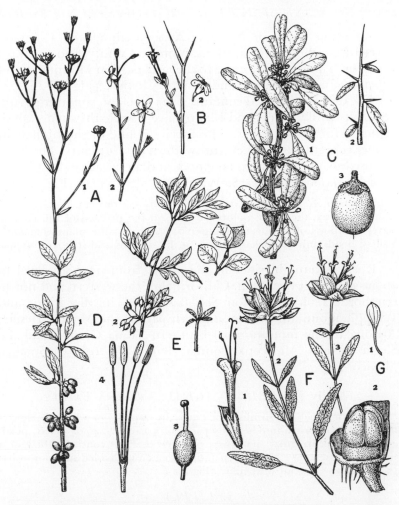

Fig. 66.—Menodoras, chittamwood, desert olives, and salvias: *A*, menodora, *Menodora scabra*, *1*, branch with the peculiar bispherical fruits, *2*, branch in flower; *B*, ground thorn, *Menodora spinescens*, *1*, branch in flower, *2*, flower; *C*, chittamwood, *Bumelia lanuginosa* var. *rigida*, *1*, branch in flower, *2*, spiny branch, *3*, fruit; *D*, desert olive, *Forestiera neo-mexicana*, *1*, branch with mature fruits, *2*, branch with young fruits, *3*, twig with another leaf type, *4*, staminate flower, *5*, pistillate flower; *E*, desert olive, *Forestiera phillyreoides*, twig with leaves; *F*, Mojave sage, *Salvia mohavensis*, *1*, flower showing the calyx, the united petals, the protruding portions of two connectives and their half-anthers, and the style and stigmas, *2, 3*, branches with leaves and flowers, the flowers with conspicuous white to blue bracts; *G*, audibertia, *Salvia carnosa* subsp. *argentea*, *1*, leaf, *2*, fruit with most of the calyx cut away, showing the typical four nutlets of the mint family. (x ¹/₃ except *B* 2 x ²/₃; *C* 3 x 1¹/₃; *D* 4, 5 x 10; *F 1* x 1; *G* 2 x 4²/₃.)

ert; extreme southern Nevada; Arizona along the Colorado River below the Ute Mountains, Mohave County, and eastward along the Gila River drainage to the Superstition Mountains and Superior; Baja California and Sonora, Mexico. (Fig. 67 2.)

The desert milkweed contains an appreciable amount of rubber in its milky juice, and plants have been cultivated experimentally for their rubber. The species is one of the highest in rubber content among the Southwestern desert plants. The latex was used by the Indians as an emetic and a purgative.

2. *Asclepias albicans* S. Wats. WAX MILKWEED (Fig. 65 *C*)

Similar to *Asclepias subulata;* stems usually 2-3 or 4 m. high, covered with white wax, the plant glabrous except on the pedicels of the flowers; leaves in whorls of 3, linear, falling away early and the plant commonly leafless; hoods only about half as long as the stamens and style and stigma.

Rocky mountain sides in the desert from near sea level to about 2,000 feet elevation. California on the western and northern borders of the Salton Sea Basin and in the Pinto and Whipple mountains in the southern part of the Mojave Desert; Arizona in the mountains of southern Yuma County and the Sierra Estrella, Maricopa County; Baja California to Sinaloa, Mexico.

Family 35. *VERBENACEAE*. VERBENA FAMILY

Herbs or sometimes shrubs. Leaves usually opposite or whorled. Flowers in spikes or congested into heads; sepals 4 or 5, calyx 2-, 4-, or 5-cleft; petals 4 or 5, united, irregular; stamens 4 or rarely 2. Fruit consisting of 2 or 4 nutlets formed from 2 carpels, separating from an undivided superior ovary; in some cases the fruit drupelike. (Fig. 72 *E*.)

1. *LIPPIA*

Calyx 2- or 4-cleft; flowers in short spikes or heads; fruit consisting of 2 nutlets. (Fig. 72 *E*.)

1. *Lippia Wrightii* A. Gray. WRIGHT LIPPIA. (1) Shrub with slender, fibrous-angled twigs; (2) leaves small, toothed, opposite, strongly veined, aromatic; (3) flowers small, in elongated spikes. (Fig. 72 *E*.)

Shrub 1-1.5 m. (3 to 4½ feet) high; stems 4-angled; leaves opposite, ovate to orbicular or sometimes broader than long, 6-13 mm. long, 4-10 mm. broad, crenately toothed, green above, strongly veiny and white-hairy be-

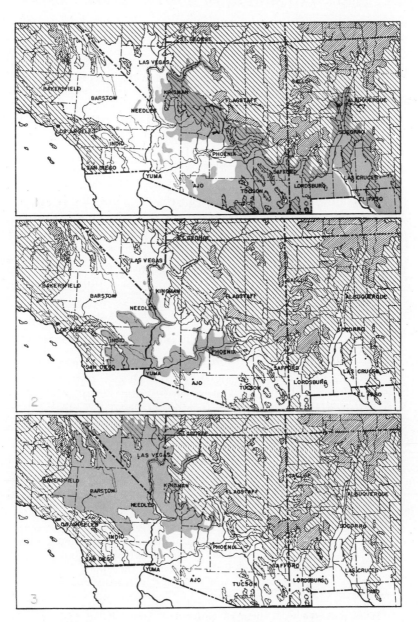

Fig. 67.—Distributional maps: *1*, Wright lippia, *Lipia Wrightii*; *2*, desert milkweed, *Asclepias subulata*; *3*, bladder sage, *Salazaria mexicana*.

neath; flowers in more or less dense elongated spikes 2-7 cm. long and 4-5 mm. in diameter; calyx about 2 mm. long, short-cylindroidal, densely hairy; petals about 4 mm. long, the corolla tube about 1 mm. or less in diameter; the calyx at fruiting time splitting readily so that one half covers each nutlet, the inner exposed face of the nutlet showing many minute white papillae, the back smooth and brown.

Rocky or gravelly slopes and canyons in the upper part of the desert, the desert grassland, and the oak woodland at 2,000 to 6,000 feet elevation. California at Twenty-nine Palms and in the Providence Mountains in the southeastern Mojave Desert; southern Nevada; Arizona in the Mojave Desert as far eastward as the Grand Canyon region and in the Arizona Desert and the adjacent mountains; New Mexico on the Gila River drainage and on the Rio Grande drainage from Socorro southward; western Texas; Mexico. (Fig. 67 *1*.)

Lantana horrida H. B. K. is reported by Kearney and Peebles to be established or native near Sells, Pima County, Arizona.

Family 36. *LABIATAE*. Mint Family

By Carl Epling *

The mint family is well known for its abundant species with their many characteristic essential oils. Desert representatives are numerous and, like the desert representatives in other families, distinctive. The family is characterized by the usually strongly irregular corolla formed from 5 united petals and by the fruit, which is composed of 4 small (1-seeded) nutlets separating from one another at maturity. The style arises from a point low among the four lobes of the ovary (Fig. 66 G 2) . (Figs. 66 *F, G*; 69 *A*; Pl. XXIX *center*.)

Herbs or less commonly shrubs or suffrutescent plants. Stems (at least the young ones) commonly but not always square. Leaves opposite, simple. Sepals 5, the calyx usually with 2 sepals forming an upper lip and 3 a lower but the sepals sometimes all similar; petals 5, united, the corolla usually with 2 lips and strongly irregular, the 2 petals of the upper lip sometimes forming a hood (galea); stamens 4 or sometimes 2, usually in 2 pairs of unequal length; style 1; stigmas 2; ovary 4-lobed, usually deeply so.

* Division of Botany, College of Agriculture, University of California, Los Angeles.

KEY TO THE GENERA

1. Stamens 2; staminodia (sterile stamens) sometimes present.
    2. Anther cells separated in each of the stamens by a long connective, the external end of the curved connective bearing a functional pollen sac, the other end included in the corolla and the pollen sac reduced in size or absent; sepals usually appearing to be in 3's. (Fig. 66 *F, G*.)   2. SALVIA
    2. Anther cells adjacent to one another and parallel; sepals obviously 5.
                                               3. POLIOMINTHA
1. Stamens 4; staminodia none.
    2. Calyx greatly inflated and bladderlike in fruit, the individual sepals not developed as teeth beyond the united portion of the calyx; corolla bluish violet and white, 1.5-2 cm. long, the upper lip strongly hooded and arched, the stamens and style not protruding; plant tending to be spiny, the spines weak and ineffective. (Pl. XXIX *center*.)   1. SALAZARIA
    2. Calyx not greatly enlarged and not inflated in fruit, the individual sepals developed as teeth beyond the united portion of the calyx; corolla lavender or toward magenta, 5-7 mm. long, the upper lip 2-lobed, the stamens and style protruding; plant not spiny. (Fig. 69 *A*.)   4. HYPTIS

1. *SALAZARIA*. Bladder Sage

(1) Branches somewhat spiny, naked, spreading widely; (2) calyx pouch-shaped, equally 2-lipped, becoming a bladder; (3) corolla bluish violet and white, hooded. (Pl. XXIX *center*.)

Subspinose shrubs with divaricate (spreading) branches and inconspicuous leaves; flowers in the axils of small bractlike leaves; calyx lips entire, rounded, the tube inflated at maturity and bladderlike; corolla tubular, the spreading portions relatively short, the lateral lobes more or less joined with the upper lip to form a hood which includes the stamens and style; stamens 4, paired; nutlets roughened.

1. *Salazaria mexicana* Torr. BLADDER SAGE; PAPER-BAG BUSH (Pl. XXIX *center*)

Intricately branched bushy shrubs as much as a meter tall, with densely short-hairy branches and spinescent branchlets, the leaves glabrous, oblong, or elliptical, 1-1.5 cm. long, entire; flowers opposite in the axils of the upper diminished leaves; calyces pouchlike, 6-8 mm. long, usually purple; corollas 16-20 mm. long, the tube white, the lower lip deep bluish violet; mature calyces papery, globose, as much as 2 cm. in diameter, pearly or rose color.

Foothills and washes in the desert at 1,000 to 3,500 feet elevation; reaching the margin of the pinyon-juniper belt. California in the Mojave and northern Colorado deserts; southern Nevada; Arizona in the Mohave Desert as far eastward as Toroweap Valley, in the Arizona Desert as far south as the Castle Dome and Tinajas Atlas mountains, Yuma County, and eastward to the Agua Fria drainage, Yavapai County, and Cave Creek, Maricopa County; western Texas; northern Mexico. (Fig. 67 *3*.)

This is an important shrub in the Mojave Desert and sometimes forms nearly pure stands.

2. *SALVIA*. Sage

The salvias, or sages, comprise a group of more than 500 species widely distributed in the temperate and warmer regions of North and South America. Several species are of importance for their culinary and medicinal properties, and a larger number of forms are prized as ornamentals. The sages are not to be confused with sagebrush, *Artemisia tridentata*, a member of the sunflower family, which occurs in the Great Basin but not in the Southwestern deserts. (Fig. 66 *F, G*.)

(1) The single pair of stamens in which the connective is remarkably developed and bears usually only one pollen sac; (2) the usually 2-lipped calyx. (Fig. 66 *F, G*.)

Each stamen of *Salvia Greatae* and *Salvia funerea* has two pollen sacs borne on the tips of a V-shaped subsessile connective (or one thrust back into the corolla tube). In the other species only the outer-pollen sac is developed. The calyces of *S. funerea* are 5-toothed. In technical characters some species are, therefore, similar to *Poliomintha*, but they can be distinguished readily by the spiny leaves.

Shrubs or half shrubs with the leaves variable in form, either obovate or linear-oblong and entire, more or less deltoid and usually toothed, or hollylike with sharp or spinose teeth; flowers numerous, in dense globose glomerules disposed in interrupted or sometimes continuous spikes, or the glomerules sometimes terminal and solitary, or the verticils few-flowered and paniculate, or the flowers even solitary above the opposite bracts, the bracts usually persistent, sometimes falling away early in *Salvia Pinguifolia;* calyces mostly 2-lipped, the upper lobes being united into a single sometimes spinose or bristlelike tooth, the lower pair dissimilar and usually free or more or less equally 5-toothed; corollas blue, violet, rose,

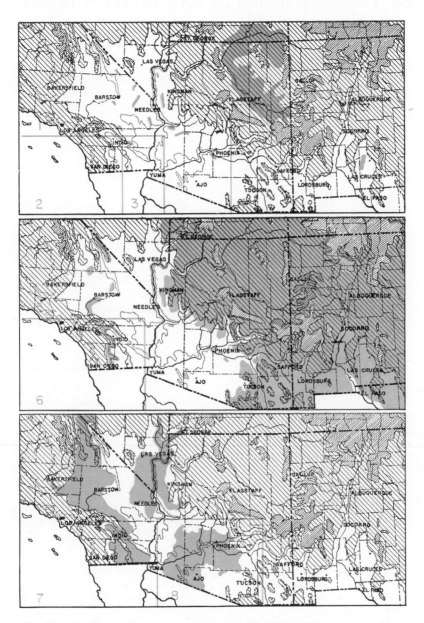

Fig. 68.—Distributional maps: *1*, Mojave sage, *Salvia mohavensis; 2*, Santa Rosa sage, *Salvia eremostachya; 3*, Salton sage, *Salvia Greatae; 4*, bush mint, *Poliomintha incana* (Cushenberry Springs in California omitted) ; *5*, pale lycium, *Lycium pallidum; 6*, Vasey sage, *Salvia Vaseyi; 7*, Cooper lycium, *Lycium Cooperi; 8, Lycium macrodon.*

rose-purple, or white, strongly 2-lipped, the upper lip usually shorter than the lower, much reduced and flaplike in one species, usually plane (flat) but hoodlike and enclosing the stamens and style in two species; stamens 2, either included in the galea, or more commonly thrust out from the tube, each bearing usually only one pollen sac, but provided with two in two species, the connective being the conspicuous part of the stamen in either case, the filament short or obsolete.

KEY TO THE SPECIES

1. Upper lip of the corolla hoodlike (galeate), enclosing the stamens and all but the tip of the style.

 2. Calyces hairy but short, simple hairs, the lower teeth expanded and ovate at maturity.   1. *Salvia pinguifolia*

 2. Calyces densely white-woolly with branched hairs.   2. *Salvia Parryi*

1. Upper lip of the corolla not at all hoodlike, plane (flat) (reduced to a small flap in one species); stamens thrust out from the tube.

 2. Calyx 5-toothed; leaves spiny or, if entire, the tips spinose; hairs branched.

    3. Calyx teeth deltoid, acute or obtuse, subequal; connectives 1.5 mm. long; Funeral and Panamint Mountains near Death Valley.   3. *Salvia funerea*

    3. Calyx teeth lanceolate-spinose; connectives 2.5 mm. long; shrubs of the Orocopia Mountains near the Salton Sea.   4. *Salvia Greatae*

 2. Calyx 3-toothed.

    3. Leaf blades entire, oboate, oblanceolate or spatulate, similarly clothed on both sides with minute appressed hairs. (Fig. 66 G.)   5. *Salvia carnosa*

    3. Leaf blades crenulate, mostly linear-oblong, deltoid-oblong, or oval, similarly clothed with minute hairs on both surfaces in two species, but such leaves not obovate.

      4. Leaves silvery, similarly clothed on both surfaces with minute appressed hairs, smooth and soft.

        5. Flowers numerous in each whorl, the clusters nearly spheroidal, remote from one another; corolla tubes 11-14 mm. long; calyx teeth bristlelike.   6. *Salvia Vaseyi*

        5. Flowers few in each whorl, the clusters near one another, forming a panicle; corolla tubes 5-7 mm. long; calyx teeth acute or obtuse; upper lip of corolla an inconspicuous flap.   7. *Salvia apiana*

      4. Leaves green, deeply wrinkled on the upper surfaces, the lower surface bearing stiff, small hairs.

5. Middle lobe of lower lip of the corolla entire, 3-4 mm. long; flower clusters commonly terminal and solitary, the whitish bracts conspicuous. (Fig. 66 *F*.)

8. *Salvia mohavensis*

5. Middle lobe of lower lip of the corolla erose (gnawed), forked, 5-6 mm. long; glomerules of flowers several in an interrupted spike. 9. *Salvia eremostachya*

1. *Salvia pinguifolia* (Fern.) Woot. & Standl. (1) Corolla blue, hoodlike—that is, galeate; (2) hairs not branched; (3) leaves similar in outline to those of the quaking aspen, *Populus tremuloides*; (4) corolla tubes 4-6 mm. long.

Shrubs about 1.5 m. tall; leaf blades 2-5 cm. long, broadly deltoid-ovate, broadly cordate or cuneate at the base, coarsely crenate-serrate, the lower surfaces minutely hairy, frequently silvery; flowers 3 in the axil of each of the tardily deciduous bracts, disposed in lax spikes 3-8 cm. long; flowering calyx 6.5-7 mm. long, the lower teeth 3.5-5 mm. broad at maturity; anther connectives about 6.5 mm. long.

Oak woodland and the upper edge of the desert grassland at 2,500 to 7,000 feet elevation. Arizona from the Superstition Mountains and the Sierra Estrella, Maricopa County, to eastern Pima County and to Greenlee and Cochise counties; eastward across New Mexico to the Franklin Mountains, Texas, and southward to the Sierra Santa Eulalia, Chihuahua, Mexico.

2. *Salvia Parryi* A. Gray. PARRY SAGE. (1) Corolla hoodlike, blue; (2) hairs treelike, branching, minute; (3) leaves white-woolly.

Half shrubs 20-50 cm. tall, branching at the base and densely white-hairy throughout; leaf blades deltoid, or ovate-lanceolate, 1-4 cm. long, 1-2 cm. broad, obtuse, rounded or truncate at the base, crenulate, both surfaces with short white wool; flowers usually 6 in the axil of each persistent or tardily deciduous bluish bract, the clusters more or less crowded into spikes 5-15 cm. long; flowering calyces 4-5 mm. long, densely white-woolly, 6-7 mm. long at maturity; corolla tubes 5-5.5 mm. long.

Hillsides and rocky slopes of the desert grassland and the oak woodland at 3,500 to 5,000 feet elevation. Arizona along the International Boundary in Santa Cruz and Cochise counties; southwestern New Mexico; northern Mexico.

3. *Salvia funerea* M. E. Jones. DEATH VALLEY SAGE. (1) stamens each bearing 2 anthers, one of which is thrust out from the

corolla tube but not beyond the lips of the corolla, the other included within the tube; (2) calyx teeth 5, subequal, deltoid, blunt; (3) leaves ovate, hollylike with one or two stout spinose teeth on each margin (infrequently entire, but spine-tipped) ; (4) calyces white-woolly, at maturity resembling globose pellets.

White shrubs as much as 1.5 m. tall, leaf blades 1.5-2 cm. long, elliptical or ovate, spinose at the apices, provided with one or two stout spinose teeth on each margin, infrequently entire; flowers prevailingly in 3's in the axils of the leaves, crowded into leafy spikes 5-8 cm. long; flowering calyces densely white-woolly, 4.5-6 mm. long; corolla violet, its tube 9-11 mm. long; filaments 1.5-2.5 mm. long, the connective 1.5-2.5 mm. long.

Rocky canyon slopes in the desert. California in narrow canyons tributary to Death Valley.

4. *Salvia Greatae* Brandegee. SALTON SAGE. (1) Stamens each bearing two anthers which are thrust out from the corolla tube beyond the upper lip; (2) calyx teeth spinose; (3) leaves ovate, hollylike, with 2-3 stout spinose teeth on each margin.

Fragrant, usually densely short-hairy shrubs as much as 1 m. tall; leaf blades 2-3 cm. long, mostly spiny-toothed, the lowermost entire; flowers numerous in the axils of diminished leaves, the glomerules 3-6 cm. distant; flowering calyces 11-12 mm. long, whitened with branched hairs, or glandular; corolla rose color, its tube 9-11 mm. long; filaments 1 mm. long, the connective 2.5 mm. long, V-shaped.

Rocky desert canyons of California in the Orocopia Mountains and the Chocolate Mountains east of the Salton Sea, Riverside County (at Salt Creek Wash near Dos Palmas and in the narrow canyons behind Hidden Spring). (Fig. 68, 3.)

5a. *Salvia carnosa* Dougl. subsp. *carnosa*. AUDIBERTIA. (1) Leaves silvery, entire, obovate, spatulate or oblanceolate, the surfaces alike in color and similarly covered with minute silvery appressed hairs; (2) corolla tubes 5-10 mm. long; (3) calyces 5-7 cm. long.

Erect or sometimes sprawling shrubs usually less than 1 m. tall; leaf blades mostly 1-2 or rarely 3-4 cm. long, obovate or spatulate, infrequently linear-oblong, rounded at the apices or sometimes notched, both surfaces silvery with minute appressed hairs; flowers many, in dense glomerules which are disposed in compact but interrupted spikes, the bracts conspicuous, usually rose color or violet; flowering calyces turbinate; corolla blue.

Plate XXVIII.—Fremont lycium, *Lycium Fremontii,* in fruit. The thick leaves are noteworthy. (Photograph by Robert A. Darrow.)

Plate XXIX.—Beloperone, bladder sage, and hop bush: *left*, beloperone, *Beloperone californica* in flower, showing the leafless flowering branch, and the leafy sterile branch; *center*, bladder sage, *Salazaria mexicana*, in flower and in fruit, the fruit enclosed by the inflated, bladderlike calyx; *right*, hop bush, *Dodonaea viscosa* var. *angustifolia*, showing the 3-winged fruits. (Photographs by Robert A. Darrow.)

The subspecies[10] *carnosa* occurs on plains and rocky slopes in the sagebrush desert and pinyon-juniper woodland in eastern Washington; eastern Oregon, southwestern Idaho, and California along the Klamath River near the Pacific Highway. It does not occur in the Southwestern deserts.

KEY TO THE SUBSPECIES

1. Leaf blades oblanceolate or linear, 2-4 mm. broad.   5b. Subsp. *Mearnsii*
1. Leaf blades obovate or spatulate, rarely oblanceolate, mostly more than 4 mm. broad.
  2. Leaf blades usually oval or elliptical, rarely obovate, rarely oblanceolate, prevailingly 1.5-3, rarely 4 cm. long.   5a. Subsp. *carnosa*
  2. Leaf blades usually rotund or spatulate, abruptly narrowed to the petioles, mostly 4-15, rarely 20 mm. broad.
    3. Bracts usually glabrate except for the ciliate (hair-fringed) margins; glomerules of flowers mostly 2-3.
      4. Glomerules of flowers mostly 1.5-2.5 cm. in diameter, generally crowded. (Fig. 66 G.)   5c. Subsp. *argentea*
      4. Glomerules of flowers mostly about 1.5 cm. in diameter, usually 0.5-1.5 cm. distant, on slender peduncles.
                                                          5d. Subsp. *Gilmani*
    3. Bracts long-hairy on the outer surfaces; glomerules of flowers mostly 3-4.   5e. Subsp. *pilosa*

5b. *Salvia carnosa* Dougl. subsp. *Mearnsii* (Britt.) Epl.
Alluvial plains in the desert and the desert grassland. Arizona at Sedona, Coconino County, and at Jerome Junction and Camp Verde, Yavapai County.

5c. *Salvia carnosa* Dougl. subsp. *argentea* (Rydb.) Epl. (Fig. 66 G)
The creosote-bush desert and ranging into the pinyon-juniper belt in the southern Great Basin. Idaho in Owyhee County; Utah; Nevada; Arizona in Mohave and Coconino counties. This subspecies grows near or with subsp. *pilosa* in the Charleston Mountains, Nevada, and seemingly maintains its identity there.

10. Subspecies as employed here by Dr. Epling is essentially the same as variety in the rest of this work. Under the International Rules of Botanical Nomenclature, as revised at Stockholm in 1950, the typical subspecies or variety is named by repetition of the specific epithet.

5d. *Salvia carnosa* Dougl. subsp. *Gilmanii* Epl.

Lower margin of the pinyon-juniper woodland. California in the Panamint Mountains, Inyo County; Nevada near Goldfield, Esmeralda County, and in the Valley of Fire, Clark County.

5e. *Salvia carnosa* Dougl. subsp. *pilosa* (A. Gray) Epl.

Found chiefly on the Mojave Desert at the lower limits of the pinyon-juniper woodland at 2,000 to 7,000 feet elevation; ranging into the creosote-bush and sagebrush deserts. California in Lassen, Inyo, Kern, Los Angeles, San Bernardino, and Riverside counties; Nevada in Esmeralda and Clark counties; Arizona in Mohave County.

6. *Salvia Vaseyi* (Porter) Parish. VASEY SAGE. (1) Leaves silvery, crenate, deltoid, the surfaces of the same color and similarly covered with minute appressed white hairs; (2) flower glomerules distant, compact, globose, forming moniliform spikes (constricted here and there) ; (3) calyx teeth bristlelike.

Rounded snowy shrubs as much as 1 m. tall; leaf blades prevailingly deltoid-ovate, truncate at the base or abruptly cuneate, crenulate; flowering calyces 8-10 mm. long, excluding the bristles on the teeth which may be 3-5 mm. long; corolla white, its tube 11-14 mm. long, the upper lip 3-4 mm. tall.

Alluvial plains and slopes in the desert. California in Morongo Valley in the southern Mojave Desert and along the western border of the Salton Sea Basin in the Colorado Desert; doubtless in Baja California, Mexico, but not recorded from that state. (Fig. 68 *6*.)

7. *Salvia apiana* Jepson. BEE SAGE. (1) Leaves silvery, crenate, elliptical or oval, both surfaces of the same color and similarly covered with ovate appressed hairs; (2) flower clusters few-flowered, the panicle much branched; (3) upper lip of the corolla flap-like, 1-2 mm. long, greatly exceeded by the elongate lower lip.

Rounded snowy shrubs, the flowering panicles as much as 3 m. tall, leaf blades crenulate; flowers few in each glomerule, disposed in narrow elongated panicles as much as 1.5 m. long, the lateral branches relatively short; flowering calyces 5-7.5 mm. long, the teeth acute or blunt, not bristle-tipped; corolla white or speckled with lavender, its tube 5-7 mm. long.

Along the coast and ranging into the alluvial plains and slopes in the chaparral and along the upper limits of the desert. California, in the coastal mountain ranges from Santa Barbara County to San Diego County, eastward to the western border of the desert; Baja California, Mexico, almost as far south as Rosario.

This is one of the important honey plants of Southern California, and it is a prominent constituent of the chaparral. The seeds have been an important source of food for the Indians of the region.

8. *Salvia mohavensis* Greene. MOJAVE SAGE. (Fig. 66 *F.*) (1) Leaves more or less deltoid, green, deeply wrinkled, crenulate; (2) flower glomerules commonly solitary and terminal, subtended by usually whitish bracts; (3) lower lip of the corolla 3-4 mm. long, entire.

Low, rounded shrubs as much as 1 m. tall or more, but usually less; leaf blades mostly 1.5-2 cm. long, truncate at the base, more or less hispidulous (with short, stiff hairs) on both surfaces; flowering calyces 7-12 mm. long; corolla pale blue, its tube slender, flaring near the throat.

Rocky canyon walls and slopes in the desert. California, in the eastern Mojave Desert from the Little San Bernardino Mountains to the Providence and New York mountains; extreme southern Nevada; Arizona, from Mohave County and northern Yuma County eastward to the Sierra Estrella, Maricopa County; Pinacate Mountains, Sonora, Mexico. (Fig. 68 *1.*)

9. *Salvia eremostachya* Jepson. SANTA ROSA SAGE. (1) Leaves deltoid-oblong, green, deeply wrinkled, crenulate; (2) flowers in crowded glomerules; (3) lower lip of the corolla with "gnawed" (erose) margins, forked.

Intricately branched shrubs about 1 m. tall; leaf blades mostly 1.5-3.5 cm. long, 4-10 mm. wide, mostly truncate at the base, more or less hispidulous on both surfaces, flowers relatively few in dense glomerules disposed in short interrupted spikes; flowering calyces about 11 mm. long; corolla blue or rose color, its tube cylindrical, somewhat curved, 14-17 mm. long.

Desert canyons. California at the eastern base of the Santa Rosa Mountains near Borrego in the Colorado Desert near the line between Riverside and San Diego counties. (Fig. 68 2.)

3. *POLIOMINTHA*

(1) Leaves silvery, entire, covered with a minute feltlike coat of wool; (2) stamens in a single pair, the two anther sacs of each side-by-side upon a thickened, broadly deltoid connective; (3) calyx almost equally 5-toothed, cylindrical, long-hairy, the orifice with a ring of hairs.

Small snowy shrubs or half shrubs covered with dense feltlike hair; leaves narrowly elliptical or linear-oblong, entire; leaves 1-3 in the axils of the upper diminished leaves; calyx subequally 5-toothed, the orifice hirsute-annulate (ringed with hairs); corolla 2-lipped.

1. *Poliomintha incana* (Torr.) A. Gray. BUSH MINT

Half shrubs as much as 1 m. tall, snowy throughout with dense, minute, feltlike hair; branches strict, slender; leaves narrowly elliptical or linear-oblong, or linear-lanceolate, mostly 10-20 mm. long, ascending or erect, entire; cymules 1-3 flowered, disposed in the axils of the upper diminshed leaves, sometimes subspicate; calyx tubes 3.5-4.5 mm. long, pilose with silky spreading hairs, the teeth subequal, about 2 mm. long; corolla tube 6-9 mm. long.

Sandy plains and slopes in the desert and the grasslands at 4,000 to 6,000 feet elevation. California at Cushenberry Springs in the Mojave Desert; southern Utah; Arizona on the Colorado Plateau in Coconino, Apache, and Navajo counties; New Mexico on the Rio Grande drainage and in the Tularosa Basin; western Texas; Chihuahua, Mexico. (Fig. 68 *4.*)

4. *HYPTIS*

(1) Hairs branching; (2) cymules of flowers subglobose, usually pedunculate; (3) calyx teeth equal, narrow, tapering; (4) middle lobe of the lower lip of the corolla dipper-shaped. (Fig. 69 *A.*)

Shrubs with branching hairs and ovate, serrate leaves; flowers in globose, usually pedunculate but sometimes sessile cymules, subtended by linear bracts; flowering calyces top-shaped, equally 5-toothed, the teeth narrow and tapering, nearly as long as the mature calyx tube which is cylindrical; corolla tube cylindrical, the upper lip notched; stamens 4, thrust out from the tube and more or less declined along the lower lip.

1. *Hyptis Emoryi* Torr. DESERT LAVENDER (Fig. 69 *A*)

Grayish shrubs as much as 3 m. tall; leaf blades generally 1-2 cm. long, usually ovate, serrate, both surfaces covered with short wool, as well as ashy or white with shorter hairs; cymules borne in the axils of the upper diminished leaves, sometimes crowded into cylindrical spikes; tubes of flowering calyces 1.5-2.2 mm. long, densely white-woolly, calyx teeth 1.2-3 mm. long, rarely 4 mm., the mature calyx tube 3.5-4 mm. long, rarely 5 mm.; corolla tubes 3-4.5 mm. long.

Washes and foothill slopes in the desert from sea level up to 4,000 feet elevation. California in the Colorado Desert; Arizona in the Mojave Desert south of Oatman and in the Colorado and Arizona deserts; Baja California and Sonora, Mexico.

Desert lavender is often called bee sage because of its value as a honey plant. The tall, lavender-scented shrubs are restricted largely to lower alluvial plains and warm rocky slopes of the desert foothills where they provide suitable forage for range livestock.

Family 37. *SOLANACEAE*. Nightshade Family

The nightshade family is remarkable for the number of cultivated plants it includes, and it is one of the most valuable economic groups. It includes food plants (tomato, potato, eggplant, red or cayenne pepper, ground cherry), medicinal and narcotic plants (belladonna, tobacco, henbane, mandragora), and ornamentals (petunia, salpiglossis). (1) Petals united, forming a regular corolla; (2) sepals united, only the tips free, persistent in fruit; (3) ovary usually forming a 2-celled capsule in fruit, but sometimes a berry. (Fig. 69 *B, C*; Pl. XXVIII.)

Herbs or shrubs. Leaves alternate, usually simple but sometimes pinnate. Sepals, petals, and stamens 5, the stamens attached to the corolla, alternate; ovary superior, the 2 placentae thick, central; style 1.

KEY TO THE GENERA

1. Fruit a capsule (dry and splitting open); plant not spiny; corolla of our species tubular and not spreading at the apex. (Fig. 69 *B*.)
   1. NICOTIANA

1. Fruit a berry (fleshy and not splitting open); plant spiny; corolla funnel-shaped. (Fig. 69 *C*; Pl. XXVIII.)
   2. LYCIUM

1. *NICOTIANA*. Tobacco

Sticky, strong-scented herbs or one species a tree. Leaves simple, entire, large. Corolla funnel-shaped or in our species tubular. Seeds small, numerous. (Fig. 69 *B*.)

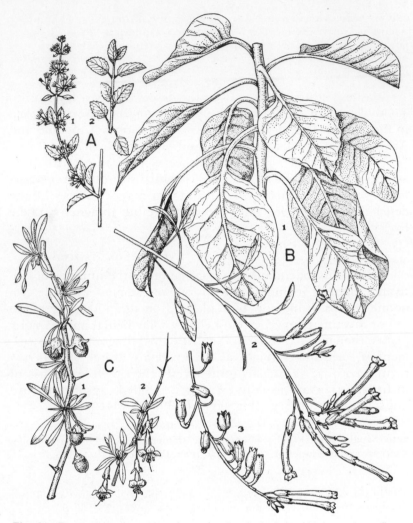

Fig. 69.—Desert lavender, tree tobacco, and pale lycium: *A*, desert lavender, *Hyptis Emoryi*, *1*, branch in fruit, the fruits (nutlets) enclosed by the calyces, *2*, vegetative branch; *B*, tree tobacco, *Nicotiana glauca*, *1*, leafy branch, *2*, flowering branch with yellow tubular flowers, *3*, fruiting branch with terminal flowers; *C*, pale lycium, *Lycium pallidum*, *1*, branch with leaves, spines, and fruits, *2*, flowering branch. (x ¹/₃.)

1. *Nicotiana glauca* Graham. TREE TOBACCO. (1) Tree usually 6-12 feet tall; (2) leaves ovate, bluish green, persistent, 2-4 inches long; (3) corolla yellow, tubular, about 1½ inches long. (Fig. 69 *B*.)

Tree 2-7 m. (6-21 feet) high; leaves evergreen, ovate or narrowly so, 4-13 cm. long, 2-9 cm. broad, green but glaucous, glabrous, the petioles 2-7 cm. long; flowers in panicles at the ends of the branches; calyx green, cylindroidal, about 11-13 mm. long; corolla yellow, about 3-4 cm. long, about 4 mm. in diameter, constricted a little at the throat; fruit ovoid, about 1 cm. long.

Roadsides, stream beds, and near cultivated areas at low elevations. Naturalized in the Southwest; California in the Coast ranges and the Great Valley, in southern California, and through the deserts; Arizona in the Colorado and Arizona deserts; New Mexico in the Chihuahuan Desert; western Texas; Mexico; native of Argentina and Chile.

Tree tobacco is planted as an ornamental. The tubular flowers are attractive to hummingbirds.

2. *LYCIUM*. DESERT THORN

By C. LEO HITCHCOCK *

The species of *Lycium* are known commonly as desert thorn or wolfberry, although one species, *L. halimifolium,* is the rather frequently cultivated matrimony vine, an excellent plant for training over fences and lattice work. The genus is distributed widely in the Old and New worlds, and it is to be distinguished from our other shrubs of the nightshade family by the thorny woody branches, the small, somewhat funnel-shaped corollas, and the berrylike fruit. (Fig. 69 *C*; Pl. XXVIII.)

Shrubs or vines. Branches usually sharp-pointed and thus thorny. Leaves usually fascicled, from nearly cylindroidal to flat, fleshy, deciduous. Calyx tubular, the lobes short to longer than the tube. Corolla white, lavender, or greenish, tubular to campanulate or salverform, the 4- or 5-lobed limb (spreading part) often rather abruptly reflexed. Stamens 4 or 5, longer or shorter than the corolla, the filaments hairy at the bases. Stigmas capitate or nearly so. Ovary superior, 2-celled, several-seeded, the fruit a berry, usually juicy and red, less commonly dry and hardened and with as few as 2 seeds. The flowers of some species are dimorphic, the stamens of some flowers being much longer than the styles, those of other flowers being enclosed by the corolla and much surpassed by the styles.

* Department of Botany, University of Washington, Seattle.

KEY TO THE SPECIES

1. Young twigs woolly; fruit constricted crosswise, the upper portion dry, brown or greenish.

    2. Calyx 6-8 mm. long, the lobes linear, at least as long as the tube; fruit 2-4-seeded; corolla glabrous on the outside.

    1. *Lycium macrodon*

    2. Calyx 8-15 mm. long, the lobes triangular to ovate, usually shorter than the tube; fruit 6-20-seeded; corolla usually hairy on the outside.

    2. *Lycium Cooperi*

1. Young twigs glabrous or only sparsely hairy; fruit not constricted crosswise, many-seeded and more or less fleshy or only 2-seeded when mature.

    2. Corolla tube 12-20 mm. long, flaring markedly above, greenish with purple veins; leaves 1-4 cm. long, glaucous (with bluish powdery wax particles on the surface), about 1 cm. in diameter. (Fig. 69 C.)

    3. *Lycium pallidum*

    2. Corolla tube usually not more than 15 mm. long, not flaring markedly above; leaves often less than 1 cm. long, greenish; fruit red, usually either less than 1 cm. in diameter or otherwise dry and 2-seeded.

        3. Margins of the corolla lobes densely and closely woolly; leaves glabrous.

        4. *Lycium Torreyi*

        3. Margins of the corolla lobes not densely and closely woolly, sometimes with a fringe of short hairs (ciliate); leaves often densely hairy.

            4. Calyx and young leaves conspicuously hairy.

                5. Lobes of the calyx from one half as long to as long as the tube.

                    6. Corolla lobes ¹⁄₃ as long to equal the corolla tube.

                    5. *Lycium brevipes*

                    6. Corolla lobes less than ¹⁄₃ as long as the corolla tube.

                    6. *Lycium Parishii*

                5. Lobes of the calyx less than one half as long as the tube.

                    6. Flowers pendulous; calyx 2.5-6 mm. long; filaments densely hairy; stamens often exserted 2-3 mm.; corolla lobes pale lavender.

                    7. *Lycium exsertum*

                    6. Flowers not pendulous; calyx 4-8 mm. long; filaments glabrous or but sparsely hairy; stamens usually included in the corolla; corolla lobes purple. (Pl. XCV.)

                    8. *Lycium Fremontii*

4. Calyx and young leaves sparsely hairy to glabrous.

    5. Fruit 2-seeded, hardened; corolla usually 4-lobed, the tube 1-3.5 mm. long, the lobes one half as long to as long as the tube.   9. *Lycium californicum*

    5. Fruit several-seeded, fleshy; corolla 4- or 5-lobed, the lobes $^1/_6$ to $^1/_3$ as long as the tube, the tube 4-18 mm. long.

        6. Corolla funnelform, flaring markedly at the top, 4-7 mm. long; calyx 1-2 mm. long.   10. *Lycium Berlandieri*

        6. Corolla tubular-funnelform, not flaring markedly at the top, 7-14 mm. long; calyx 1.5-3 mm. long.

                              11. *Lycium Andersonii*

1. *Lycium macrodon* A. Gray. (1) Young twigs woolly; (2) ovary constricted crosswise, the portion above the constriction being hardened and bearing the fertile seeds; (3) calyx bell-shaped with linear lobes longer than the tube (the only species in Arizona with such lobes).

Spiny, hairy shrubs 1-3 m. high, the young twigs woolly; leaves linear-spatulate or broader, 6-30 mm. long, 2-5 mm. broad, with petioles 1-2 mm. long, densely short-hairy; calyx bell-shaped, 6-8 mm. long, the lobes 5, linear, about twice as long as the tube; corolla 9-12 mm. long, the tube greenish white, the lobes white or pale lilac, glabrous on the outer surfaces; stamens equal to or slightly longer than the corolla; styles shorter than the stamens; fruit constricted slightly below the middle, the lower portion semifleshy but without fertile seeds, the upper half hardened, with 2-4 large fertile seeds.

Alluvial outwash plains and moderately alkaline soils of the desert at 500 to 2,000 feet elevation. Arizona in the Colorado Desert and the adjacent portions of the Arizona Desert in Yuma, Maricopa, Pinal, and western Pima counties; Sonora, Mexico. (Fig. 68 *8*.)

2. *Lycium Cooperi* A. Gray. COOPER LYCIUM. (1) Young branches woolly and the leaves or even sometimes the calyx and corolla densely hairy; (2) fruit constricted crosswise near the top, wholly dry and bony.

A stout, spiny, rounded shrub 1-2 m. high; leaves spatulate to oblanceolate, 10-30 mm. long, 4-10 mm. broad, usually densely hairy but glabrate; calyx bowl-shaped to oblong or more or less bell-shaped, 8-15 mm. long, usually glandular-hairy with the hairs later falling away, the lobes triangular to lanceolate, from one half as long to equal to the tube; corolla greenish white with lavender veins, usually withering-persistent, 8-15 mm. long, nearly cylindroidal, often hairy on the outer surface; stamens and style subequal to the corolla; fruit 5-9 mm. long, yellow-green, hardened, transversely constricted above the middle, the lower portion several-seeded, the upper portion 2-seeded. (The form known as *Lycium Shockleyi* A. Gray has hairy corollas.)

Alluvial plains and foothill slopes of the creosote-bush desert and the sagebrush desert at 400 to 6,000 feet elevation. California in sand dunes south of Bakersfield and at White Wolf Grade near Arvin and South Fork Valley in Kern County, in the Owens River valley, in the Mojave Desert, and in the Salton Sea Basin of the Colorado Desert; Nevada in Mineral and Esmeralda counties and southward; southwestern Utah; Arizona in the Mojave Desert in Mohave and northern Yuma counties. (Fig. 68 7.)

3a. *Lycium pallidum* Miers var. *pallidum.* PALE LYCIUM. (1) Leaves large, glaucous (bluish white) ; (2) corollas large, greenish; (3) fruit large, bluish red. (Fig. 69 C.)

A spiny spreading shrub 1-2 m. high; leaves spatulate, elliptical, or ovate, 10-40 mm. long, 3-15 mm. broad, almost glabrous, glaucous-green; calyx broadly bell-shaped, 5-8 mm. long, glabrous, glaucous-green, the lobes lanceolate or broader, equal to or longer than the tube; corolla funnel-shaped, 12-20 mm. long, flaring markedly above, greenish with purple veins, the lobes $^1/_5$ to $^1/_3$ the length of the tube; stamens and styles subequal to or longer than the corolla; fruit red, more or less glaucous, rather juicy, many-seeded, about 1 mm. broad.

Plains and slopes in the creosote-bush desert, the desert grassland, the sagebrush desert, and the oak woodland at 3,000 to 7,000 or rarely 8,000 feet elevation. California in the central Mojave Desert from the Death Valley region southward to the Mojave River; southern Nevada adjacent to Death Valley; Utah in the Virgin and San Juan River basins; southern Colorado near Trinidad and on the San Juan River drainage; Arizona, throughout the state excepting the Colorado Desert and the lower portions of the Mojave and Arizona deserts; New Mexico throughout the Rio Grande and Gila River drainages below 7,000 feet; western Texas; southward to San Luis Potosi, Mexico. (Fig. 68 5.)

This is the most widespread species of the genus, and it occurs most abundantly above the desert. Where they are locally abundant, the thorny shrubs provide some forage for livestock.

The berries of this species are eaten by wild fowl and other animals, including man. They are quite bitter, however.

3b. *Lycium pallidum* Miers var. *oligospermum* C. L. Hitchcock

Corolla rarely over 20 mm. long; berry 6-7 mm. in diameter, usually with only 4-5 seeds.

California in the Mojave Desert; southern Nevada.

4. *Lycium Torreyi* A. Gray. TORREY LYCIUM. (1) Calyx short, cup-shaped; (2) corolla lobes woolly on the margins; (3) berry red, fleshy.

A spreading to erect spiny shrub 1-3 m. tall, glabrous; leaves spatulate or oblanceolate, 10-50 mm. long, 3-15 mm. broad, very fleshy; calyx broadly tubular, 2.5-4.5 mm. long, the lobes triangular, one quarter to one half the length of the tube; corolla 8-15 mm. long, narrowly obconic, greenish lavender to whitish, the lobes bordered with fringe of tiny, tangled, branched hairs; stamens subequal to the corolla, the style slightly longer and exserted; fruit fleshy, red, ovoid, 6-10 mm. long, 8-30-seeded.

River bottoms and alluvial flats in the desert at 1,000 to 3,500 feet elevation; frequently in rather alkaline soil, often forming solid stands of considerable extent. California in the Mojave and Colorado deserts and the Death Valley region; southern Nevada; southwestern Utah; Arizona along the Colorado River below Havasu Canyon, along the lower Gila River, and in New Mexico along the Rio Grande; western Texas; Mexico. (Fig. 70 *1*.)

The berries of this species are juicy, rather sweet, and therefore more palatable than the fruits of the other species.

5. *Lycium brevipes* Benth. (1) Leaves hairy, at least when they are young; (2) calyx lobes 3-5, linear to triangular, ½ as long to as long as the calyx tube; (3) corolla lobes one third as long to as long as the corolla tube, spreading; (4) stamens protruding about $^1/_3$ to $^1/_5$ of an inch beyond the corolla; (5) fruit red, juicy, $^1/_6$ to $^1/_4$ inch long.

Spiny shrubs 1-3 m. high, either permanently hairy or hairy on the young growing parts; leaves 5-30 mm. long, 3-10 mm. broad; calyx 2-6 mm. long; corolla pink to violet, the tube 4-9 mm. long; fruit many seeded. Synonym: *Lycium Richii* A. Gray.

Washes and flats in the desert from near sea level to about 1,500 feet elevation. California in coastal southern California and in the Colorado Desert; Baja California to Sonora, Mexico.

6. *Lycium Parishii* A. Gray. PARISH LYCIUM. (1) Leaves and calyx hairy, the leaves small; (2) calyx lobes broad, half as long to longer than the tube; corolla lobes less than one third as long as the corolla tube.

A spreading, spiny, hairy shrub 1-3 m. high; leaves elliptic or spatulate, 3-10 mm. long, 1-4 mm. broad (larger on suckers or young branches), hairy and sometimes ashy in appearance; calyx bell-shaped, 2.5-6 mm. long or longer, densely hairy, the lobes oblong-ovate, from half as long to longer than tube; corolla purplish, the lobes darker than the tube, their margins with short hairs; stamens and styles usually exserted (protruding); berry ovoid, red, fleshy, 4-6 mm. long, 7-12-seeded. Synonym: *Lycium Pringlei* A. Gray.

Washes, alluvial fans, and open mesas in the desert from sea level to 1,500 feet elevation; commonly under mesquites. California originally in San Bernardino Valley, and at Vallecitos and Mountain Palm Spring in the Colorado Desert; Arizona in the Colorado Desert and the adjacent Arizona Desert; Sonora, Mexico. The original collection was made near San Bernardino, and apparently the species was represented there by a single plant no longer living.

7. *Lycium exsertum* A. Gray. (1) Leaves fairly large, densely hairy; (2) calyx between tubular and bell-shaped, densely hairy, the lobes nearly half as long as the tube; (3) corolla large, tubular; (4) flowers pendulous; (5) stamens or styles protruding; (6) filaments hairy (glabrous in the next species).

Somewhat spiny shrubs 1-3 m. high, the young branches glandular; leaves spatulate or broader, 5-20 or rarely 40 mm. long, 3-5 or rarely 10 mm. broad, finely hairy and somewhat glandular; calyx 2.5-6 mm. long, the lobes a third or half as long as the tube; corolla whitish to dirty white or purplish, 6 to 10-14 mm. long, obconic; flowers of two forms, the stamens usually exserted 2-3 mm., less commonly enclosed in the corolla or even rudimentary, their bases densely hairy; styles usually shorter than the functional stamens, rarely protruding 2-4 mm.; fruit red, fleshy, ovoid, 20-30-seeded.

Washes and alluvial outwash plains in the desert at 2,000 to 4,000 feet elevation. Arizona near Kingman, Mohave County, and in the Arizona Desert from Yuma County to Graham and Cochise counties; Baja California, Sonora, and Sinaloa, Mexico.

8. *Lycium Fremontii* A. Gray. FREMONT LYCIUM. Similar to *Lycium exsertum* but differing in the following characters: (1)

stamens and styles protruding less; (2) flowers usually not pendulous; (3) calyx tube more elongate. (Pl. XXVIII.)

Freely branching spiny glandular-hairy shrubs 1-3 m. tall; leaves spatulate, 10-25 mm. long, 3-6 mm. broad, short-hairy, sometimes densely hairy; calyx densely hairy, tubular, 4-8 mm. long, the lobes triangular, about 1 mm. long, the lobes one quarter to two fifths the length of the tube, the margins finely hairy; flowers of two forms, the stamens equaling or much shorter than corolla, sparsely hairy at the bases; styles subequal to the corolla or very short and enclosed in the corolla; fruit fleshy, red, 4-9 mm. long; seeds 40-60. Synonym: *Lycium gracilipes* A. Gray.

Alluvial plains in the desert from near sea level to 3,000 feet elevation. California on Santa Rosa Island, near San Diego, and in the Colorado Desert; Arizona in the Colorado and Arizona deserts; Baja California and Sonora, Mexico. Flowering from January until April. (Fig 70 2.)

9. *Lycium californicum* Nutt. CALIFORNIA LYCIUM. (1) Fruit hardened, 2-seeded; (2) leaves small; (3) corolla short, the lobes about equal to the tube.

Small, somewhat spiny, spreading shrubs up to 1.5 m. high; practically glabrous; leaves linear and cylindroidal to spatulate, 2-12 mm. long, 1-3 mm. broad, glabrous or glabrate; calyx bell-shaped, about 2.5 mm. long, finely hairy; corolla white to lavender, the tube 2-3 mm. long and about as broad, lobes 4, fringed with short hairs; stamens and style protruding from the corolla; fruit hardened, greenish brown, 2-seeded, dry, 2-4 mm. long. Synonyms: *Lycium carinatum* S. Wats.; *Lycium californicum* Nutt. var. *arizonicum* A. Gray.

Coastal slopes and desert mesas from sea level to 3,000 or 3,500 feet elevation. California on Santa Catalina, San Clemente, and San Nicholas islands, and from Santa Monica to San Bernardino and San Diego; Arizona in an area centering around Sacaton, Pinal County, and in adjacent portions of Maricopa and Pima counties, also at Lowell, Cochise County. Flowering from December to March.

10. *Lycium Berlandieri* Dunal. BERLANDIER LYCIUM. (1) Leaves linear or linear-spatulate, glabrous or glabrate; (2) calyx very short; (3) corolla small, flaring markedly at the top.

Shrubs, somewhat spiny, reclining or spreading, glabrous or hairy, up to 2.5 m. high; leaves finely hairy or glabrous, linear or nearly so, 10-25 mm. long, 1-2.5 mm. broad, calyx cup-shaped, 1-2 mm. long and as broad, irregularly 3-5-lobed, the lobes about one third the length of the tube; corolla pale lavender, 4-8 mm. long, the tube narrow at the base, the lobes one sixth to one third the length of the tube; flowers often of two forms; stamens usually protruding, rarely enclosed by the corolla; styles usually at least as long as the stamens; berry nearly spheroidal, about 4 mm. in diameter, red, fleshy, many-seeded. Synonyms: *Lycium Berlandieri* Dunal var. *longistylum* and var. *brevilobum* C. L. Hitchc.

Alluvial plains and rocky foothills in the desert and the desert grassland mostly at 2,000 to 3,000 feet elevation. Arizona in the Tule Mountains, Yuma County, and in the Arizona Desert and the adjacent desert grassland; New Mexico in the Chihuahuan Desert and the adjacent grassland; western Texas; Baja California and southeastward in Mexico. Flowering intermittently through most of the year according to local conditions.

11a. *Lycium Andersonii* A. Gray var. *Andersonii*. ANDERSON LYCIUM. (1) Leaves fleshy, nearly terete when fresh, almost glabrous; (2) corolla narrow, tubular, sometimes fringed with short hairs but not with woolly hair on the margins (compared with *Lycium Torreyi*) ; (3) fruit red, fleshy.

A spiny rounded shrub 1-3 m. high; leaves 3-15 mm. long, 1-2 or 3 mm. in diameter; calyx cup-shaped, 1.5-3 mm. long, irregularly 4-5 lobed, the lobes about one fourth the length of the tube; corolla narrowly tubular, flaring somewhat above, 7-14 mm. long, dirty white or pale lavender, the lobes 5 or sometimes 4, 1.5-2.5 mm. long, often with marginal hairs; stamens and styles equal to the corolla or protruding 2-3 mm.; fruit red, juicy, ovoid, 3-8 mm. long, many-seeded.

Washes, mesas, and foothills of the chaparral and the creosotebush and sagebrush deserts. California from Santa Monica to San Diego and San Bernardino, in Mono County and the Owens River valley, and in the Mojave and Colorado deserts; southern Nevada from Mineral to Clark and Lincoln counties; western and central Utah; Arizona on the Colorado River drainage from Lee's Ferry southward and throughout the deserts; New Mexico at scattered stations (Tularosa; Deming; Playas Valley) ; Baja California and Sonora, Mexico. Flowering from January to May.

11b. *Lycium Andersonii* A. Gray var. *deserticola* (C. L. Hitchc.) Munz

Leaves 20-35 mm. long, 1-2 mm. broad.

California in the Providence Mountains in the southwestern Mojave Desert and in the Salton Sea Basin of the Colorado Desert; Arizona in the Colorado Desert from Yuma County to Maricopa County.

11c. *Lycium Andersonii* A. Gray var. *Wrightii* A. Gray. WRIGHT LYCIUM

Leaves elliptic-spatulate, 3-8 mm. long; corolla 5-8 mm. long, usually 4-lobed; stigma usually protruding 2-3 mm. beyond the corolla.

Arizona in the Arizona Desert and the adjacent desert grassland from Maricopa County to Greenlee and Cochise counties; northern Sonora, Mexico. Often growing with the typical variety.

Family 38. *SCROPHULARIACEAE*. FIGWORT FAMILY

This family includes many well-known herbaceous plants—among them mulleins, toadflax, snapdragons, Chinese houses, figworts, monkey flowers, pentstemons, veronicas, Indian paintbrushes, owl clovers, and elephant snouts—but there are only a few shrubs. In the deserts the only one of any considerable size is a yellow-flowered pentstemon. (Fig. 72 *D*.)

Herbs or sometimes shrubs or trees. Leaves commonly opposite, simple, usually entire or toothed. Sepals 5; petals 5, united, almost always irregular; stamens 2 or 4, with or without the rudiment of a fifth or rarely with the fifth stamen fully developed. Fruit a 2-celled capsule with the seed-bearing structures (placentae) along the middle of the partition. Seeds many, small.

1. *PENSTEMON*. BEARDTONGUE

Herbs, somewhat woody plants, or sometimes distinctly shrubs. Leaves opposite. Flowers nearly always in racemes, rarely in cymes or panicles; sepals 5, united; petals 5, united into a usually but not always long tube, from almost regular to strongly irregular (as in our species); stamens 4, the remnant of the fifth with a long filament but without an anther, often hairy (this part the "beardtongue"). (Fig. 72 *D*.)

1a. *Penstemon antirrhinoides* Benth. var. *microphyllus* A. *Gray*. BUSH PENSTEMON. (1) Leaves elliptical to ovate, ½ inch long, opposite; (2) corolla yellow, irregular (resembling that of a snapdragon) ; (3) stamens 4 fertile and a sterile bearded filament. (Fig. 72 *D*.)

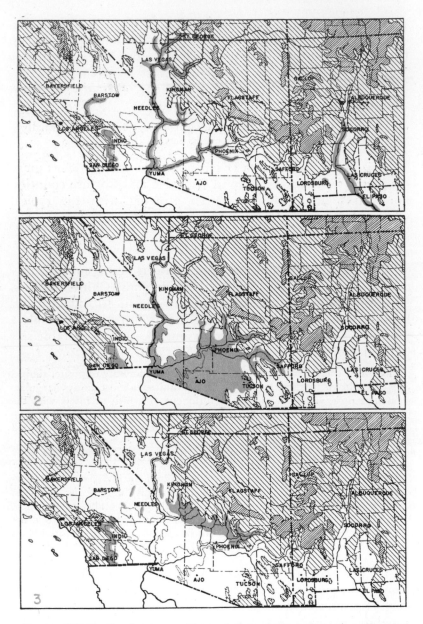

Fig. 70.—Distributional maps: *1*, Torrey lycium, *Lycium Torreyi*; *2*, Fremont lycium, *Lycium Fremontii*; *3*, bush penstemon, *Penstemon antirrhinoides* var. *microphyllus*.

Plate XXX.—Snakeweed and burroweed: *A*, snakeweed, *Gutierrezia lucida*, the most common species in our range, a bad weed on overgrazed range lands; *B*, burroweed, *Haplopappus tenuisectus*, important as a poisonous plant and as a range weed invading overgrazed grasslands. (Photographs by U.S. Forest Service.)

Plate XXXI.—Burroweed and snakeweed: *A*, overgrazed grassland taken over by burroweed, *Haplopappus tenuisectus*; *B*, overgrazed grassland with scattering palmillas or soapweeds (*Yucca elata*) now dominated by snakeweed, *Gutierrezia Sarothrae*. (Photographs by U.S. Forest Service.)

Shrub 0.5-1.5 m. (1½ to 4½ feet) high; leaves ovate, elliptic-lanceolate, narrowly elliptic, or oblong, 8-13 mm. long, 4-8 mm. broad, somewhat hairy; flowers solitary or in small cymes on short side branches; sepals united half their length, about 6-7 mm. long; corolla yellow, strongly irregular, the free portions of the petals as long as or longer than the united parts, 15-20 mm. long; sterile filament densely long-hairy on one side in the apical portion, resembling a toothbrush; fruit ovoid, 8-10 mm. long.

Rocky or gravelly slopes of the desert mountains below 5,000 feet. California in the Old Woman, Old Dad, and Providence mountains in the southeastern Mojave Desert and along the northern and western borders of the Salton Sea Basin of the Colorado Desert; Arizona in the southern Mojave Desert and in the Arizona Desert as far eastward as Roosevelt Lake and southward to the Sierra Estrella, Maricopa County; Baja California, Mexico. (Fig. 70 *3*.)

This plant might well be cultivated as an ornamental. Typical *Penstemon antirrhinoides* has been cultivated successfully in southern California. Livestock browse the plants sparingly where the species is locally abundant.

The generic name has been spelled *Pentstemon*.

Family 39. *BIGNONIACEAE*. Bignonia Family

Trees or shrubs, rarely herbs, sometimes vines. Leaves opposite, in most genera compound. Flowers large and showy, the corolla strongly irregular and 2-lipped. Seed-bearing structures (placentae) on the outer wall of the ovary at the point where the partition joins the wall; seeds winged. A well-known genus cultivated in the Southwest is *Catalpa*. (Fig. 71.)

KEY TO THE GENERA

1. Leaves simple, entire, linear, alternate; flowers of our species white, lined or tinged with lavender or reddish purple. (Fig. 71 *B*.)

1. CHILOPSIS

1. Leaves pinnate, the leaflets toothed, opposite; flowers of our species yellow. (Fig. 71 *A*.)   2. TECOMA

1. *CHILOPSIS*. Desert Willow

(1) Leaves simple, not toothed, narrow; (2) flowers white-tinged or lined with lavender or reddish purple; (3) pods narrow, scarcely flattened, 4-8 inches long. (Fig. 71 *B*.)

Large shrubs or small trees. Leaves linear, alternate. Flowers in racemes; sepals united; petals forming a somewhat flattened tube, the 2 upper petals

Fig. 71.—Trumpet flower and desert willow: *A*, yellow trumpet flower, *Tecoma stans* var. *angustata*, *1*, branch with pinnate leaves and flowers, *2*, single pod (capsule) ; *B*, western desert willow, *Chilopsis linearis* var. *arcuata*, *1*, branch with simple leaves, flowers, and young fruits, *2*, pod (capsule) , *3*, seed with two tufts of hairs. (x ¹/₃.)

erect, the lower 3 forming an unusually conspicuous platform upon which insects land; stamens 4 with a remnant of another. Wing of the seed with long hairs.

1a. *Chilopsis linearis* (Cav.) Sweet var. *linearis*. DESERT WILLOW. (1) Vegetative (nonflowering or -fruiting) branches somewhat woolly (in the varieties glabrous or practically so) ; (2) leaf veins prominent (in the varieties obscure or at least usually not prominent.)

Branchlets not sticky-glandular; leaves straight, not curved, tending to diverge from the branch.

Washes in the desert. New Mexico at Mangas Springs near Silver City and south of Roswell; Texas; Zacatecas and perhaps elsewhere in Mexico. Distinction of var. *glutinosa* (with sticky branchlets) from this entity has not been checked adequately, and it seems doubtful.

1b. *Chilopsis linearis* (Cav.) Sweet var. *arcuata* Fosberg. WESTERN DESERT WILLOW (Fig. 71 *B*)

Large shrub or a small tree 2-8 m. (6-24 feet) high; branchlets not sticky, usually glabrous; leaves simple, linear, curved into an arc, 8-14 cm. long, 2-4 mm. broad (commonly narrower than in the other types), green, glabrous; racemes mostly 3-6 cm. long, the stalks of the flowers short; calyx 7-9 mm. long, the calyx 2-lipped; corolla about 3 cm. long; fruits (pods or capsules) 1-2 dm. long, about 5 mm. broad, splitting into 2 walls and the partition; seeds with long hairs at each end.

Washes in the desert and the desert grassland at 1,500 to 5,000 feet elevation. Coastal southern California as far west as Redlands and occurring in the Mojave Desert east of Daggett and on the northern and western borders of the Salton Sea Basin of the Colorado Desert; southern Nevada; southwestern Utah; Arizona in the Mojave Desert and eastward to the Grand Canyon region and in the Arizona Desert and the adjacent desert grassland; New Mexico in the Chihuahuan Desert and the adjacent grassland south of Albuquerque; Baja California and southeastward in Mexico. (Fig. 73 *1*.)

The desert willows have been used widely as ornamentals, as they are prized for their graceful habit and large, attractive, sweet-scented flowers.

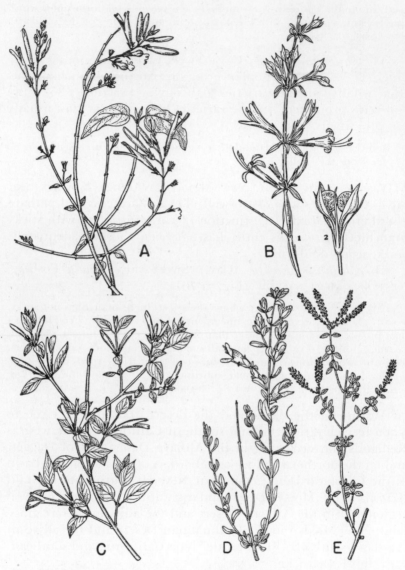

Fig. 72.—Beloperone, anisacanthus, jacobinia, penstemon, and lippia: *A*, California beloperone, *Beloperone californica*; *B*, chuparosa or anisacanthus, *Anisacanthus Thurberi*, *1*, branch with bracts and flowers, *2*, fruit opening and exposing the two seeds; *C*, jacobinia, *Jacobinia candicans* var. *subglabra*; *D*, bush penstemon, *Penstemon antirrhinoides* var. *microphyllus* with leaves, flowers and fruits; *E*, Wright lippia, *Lippia Wrightii*. (x ¹/₃ except *B* 2 x 1.)

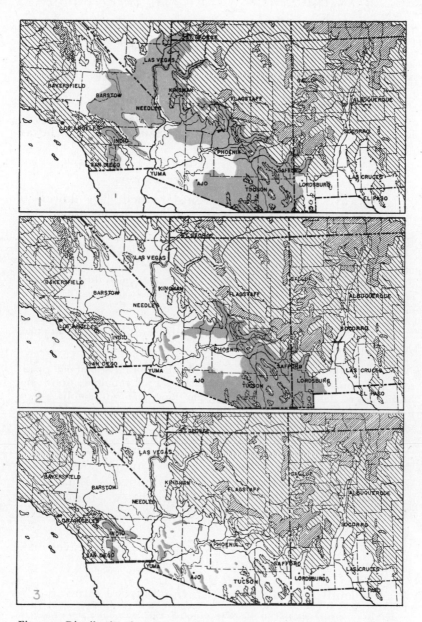

Fig. 73.—Distributional maps: *1*, western desert willow, *Chilopsis linearis* var. *arcuata; 2*, anisacanthus, chuparosa, or desert "honeysuckle," *Anisacanthus Thurberi; 3*, California beloperone, *Beloperone californica.*

1c. *Chilopsis linearis* (Cav.) Sweet var. *glutinosa* (Engelm.) Fosberg. STICKY DESERT WILLOW

Sterile branchlets and young leaves sticky; leaves mostly 5-8 mm. broad, not curved into arcs, tending to be erect instead of drooping.

Washes and bottom lands in the desert and the desert grassland at 3,000 to 5,000 feet elevation. New Mexico on the lower Rio Grande drainage south of Sierra County; western Texas; northeastern Mexico.

2. *TECOMA*. TRUMPET FLOWER

(1) Leaves pinnate, the margins toothed; (2) flowers of our species yellow; (3) pods flattened, 3-4½ inches long. (Fig. 71 *A*.)

Shrubs, trees, or woody vines. Leaves opposite. Flowers in racemes, alternate, opposite, or whorled; sepals 5, free from one another at the apices; petals forming a short tube at the base, a greatly expanded throat (the bulk of the corolla), and 5 somewhat irregular free lobes. Wing of the seed membranous.

1a. *Tecoma stans* (L.) Juss. var. *angustata* Rehder. YELLOW TRUMPET FLOWER (Fig. 71 *A*)

Shrub (within our range) 1-2 m. (3-6 feet) high; leaflets in about 4 pairs, with a terminal leaflet, lanceolate-attenuate, 4-7.5 cm. long, 10-18 mm. broad, green, glabrous; calyx about 5 mm. long, glabrous; corolla 4-6 cm. long, 14-17 mm. in diameter, the lobes nearly circular, about 10-14 mm. in diameter; pods 6-8 mm. long.

Rocky or gravelly slopes of the upper part of the desert, the desert grassland, and the lower oak woodland at 3,000 to 5,000 feet elevation. Arizona from the Pinal Mountains, Pinal County, to eastern Pima and Cochise counties; New Mexico in the Chihuahuan Desert (Doña Ana Mountains); western Texas; northern Mexico.

The attractive yellow flowers and bright green leaves make the plant desirable as an ornamental.

Family 40. *ACANTHACEAE*. THORN FAMILY

Herbs or shrubs similar to the Scrophulariaceae. Stamens 2 in our species. Corolla irregular and in our species red with some admixture of blue or in individuals of one species varying to orange or yellow. Seeds few, 2-10 in each of the 2 cells of the ovary. Fruit of our species stalked, flattened, with 2 seeds in each cell. (Pl. XXIX *left*; Fig. 72 *A-C*.)

KEY TO THE GENERA

1. Leaves lanceolate, very sparsely hairy; flowers red usually with some admixture of blue, varying to orange or yellow, the color not stable and not persisting as red in dried specimens; anthers symmetrical; bark exfoliating. (Fig. 72 *B*.)   1. ANISACANTHUS

1. Leaves ovate, densely short-hairy, at least at first; flowers red and remaining distinctly so when dry; anthers not symmetrical; the cells not placed at the same height on the filament; bark not exfoliating.

  2. Lower anther cell drawn out into a short, hard, white basal point (0.2-0.4 mm. long), the upper cell without a basal point; branchlets of our species clothed and completely obliterated by minute white hairs too small to be distinguished by the naked eye; branches about the inflorescence usually but not always leafless in our species. (Pl. XXIX *left;* Fig. 72 *A*.)   2. BELOPERONE

  2. Lower anther cell not drawn out into a hard, white basal point, scarcely differing from the upper cell of the same anther; branchlets more or less hairy but not obliterated, the hairs large enough to be distinguished with the naked eye; branches about the inflorescence leafy in our species. (Fig. 72 *C*.)   3. JACOBINIA

1. *ANISACANTHUS*. ANISACANTHUS

Shrubs. Bark exfoliating. Leaves lanceolate, very sparsely hairy. Petals red, usually with some admixture of blue, varying to orange or yellow, the color not stable in dried specimens; anthers symmetrical. Fruit flattened, with a long stalk. (Fig. 72 *B*.)

1. *Anisacanthus Thurberi* (Torr.) A. Gray. ANISACANTHUS; CHUPAROSA. (1) Branches tan, with exfoliating bark; (2) corolla red usually with some admixture of blue, varying to yellow or orange. (Fig. 72 *B*.)

Shrub 1-2 m. high; leaves 4-6 cm. long, 1-1.5 or sometimes 2 cm. broad; sepals very narrow, united only at the bases, about 1 cm. long; petals 2-3.5 cm. long, united half or three fifths of their length, narrow; fruit about 12-14 mm. long, the lower half forming a stalk; seeds flattened, 2 in each cell.

Rocky canyon bottoms and gravelly or sandy washes in the desert and the desert grassland at 2,000 to 5,000 feet elevation. Arizona in the Arizona Desert and the adjacent desert grassland; New Mexico in southern Grant County and in Hidalgo and Luna counties; Mexico. (Fig. 73 2.)

Anisacanthus is one of the better browse plants of the desert. Sometimes it is called desert honeysuckle.

2. *BELOPERONE.* Beloperone

Shrubs. Bark not exfoliating; branches in our species densely and finely hairy, the surface obliterated and the hairs too small to be seen with the naked eye. Leaves ovate, densely hairy. Petals red, the pigment stable during drying; anthers not symmetrical, the two cells placed at different levels on the apex of the filament, the lower one with a hard, white, basal point. Fruit stalked, with 2 seeds in each cell. (Pl. XXIX *left*; Fig. 72 *A*.)

1. *Beloperone californica* Benth. CALIFORNIA BELOPERONE. (1) Branches green, velvety-haired, flexible; (2) corolla red. (Pl. XXIX *left;* Fig. 72 *A*.)

Dense, bushy shrubs 1-2 m. (3-6 feet) high; leaves ovate, sometimes some of them ovate-lanceolate, mostly about 2 cm. long and 12-15 mm. broad, densely hairy, the hairs fine; flowers in bractless terminal racemes, the stem below the racemes leafless for some distance; sepals tapering their whole length (subulate), 4-5.5 mm. long; corolla 2-3.5 cm. long, the lower lip 12-14 mm. long; fruit about 2 cm. long, with a constriction in the apical swollen portion.

Gravelly or sandy soils along watercourses in the desert from sea level to 2,500 feet elevation. California in the Colorado Desert; Arizona in the Colorado Desert and the adjacent Arizona Desert as far eastward as the Superstition Mountains, Maricopa County, and the Baboquivari Mountains, Pima County; Baja California and Sonora, Mexico. (Fig. 73 *3*.)

A distinctive shrub with beautiful flowers. The brilliant red tubular corollas are attractive to hummingbirds. The tender young shoots are of limited forage value for livestock.

3. *JACOBINIA.* Jacobinia

Shrubs. Bark not exfoliating. Branches of our species hairy, but the hairs large enough to be distinguished with the naked eye, restricted to the last few internodes of new growth. Leaves ovate-attenuate, sometimes a few narrowly ovate, densely white-hairy at first, the hair falling away later or apparently so. Petals red, the pigment stable during drying; anthers not symmetrical, the two cells placed at different levels on the apex of the filament, the bases of the cells essentially alike, neither with a hard, white point. (Fig. 72 *C*.)

1a. **Jacobinia candicans** (Nees) Benth. & Hook. var. **subglabra** (S. Wats.) L. Benson, comb. nov. (Cf. p. 413.) JACOBINIA.

(1) Branches hairy at tips, smooth and tan on older growth; (2) corolla red; (3) restricted distribution. (Fig. 72 *C*.)

Shrub about 1 m. or more in height; leaves 2-4 cm. long, 1-2.5 cm. broad; flowers in the upper leaf axils; calyx 6-7 mm. long; corolla 2.5-3.5 cm. long; united about two thirds of its length.

Rocky foothills in the desert at approximately 2,000 feet elevation. Arizona in the Ajo Mountains, Pima County, and at Canyon Lake, near the Apache Trail in eastern Maricopa County; Mexico.

The variety occurs in at least Arizona, Baja California, and Sonora and it may include *Jacobinia ovata* A. Gray, which appears to be transitional to var. *candicans* (type from Oaxaca in southern Mexico). Branches and usually leaves subglabrous, smaller, narrow, attenuate; inflorescence very short (var. *candicans* having the opposed characters).

Family 41. *RUBIACEAE*. MADDER FAMILY

(1) Ovary inferior; (2) leaves simple and entire; (3) fruit dry, splitting into two 1-seeded parts.

Shrubs or herbs or sometimes trees. Leaves opposite or whorled. Sepals, petals, and stamens 4 or rarely 5, the sepals sometimes none; petals united; styles 1 or 2.

1. *CEPHALANTHUS*. BUTTONBUSH

Large shrubs or sometimes small trees. Flowers in dense, stalked, nearly spheroidal heads or "buttons." Corolla tubular, style greatly surpassing the corolla; stigma forming a knob. Fruit an inverted pyramid, hard.

1a. *Cephalanthus occidentalis* L. var. *californicus* Benth.
BUTTON WILLOW

Large shrub or reported to become a small tree, 2-8 m. (6-24 feet) high; leaves elliptic-acute to ovate or somewhat lanceolate or oblanceolate, 4-12 cm. long, 1-6 cm. broad, the tip somewhat attenuate or merely acute, short-petioled, rather thick and leathery; stipules minute or none; heads 1-2 cm. in diameter; sepals green; petals white; fruits slender, 4-5 mm. long, 1.5-2 mm. in diameter.

Wet soil along streams in the upper part of the desert, the desert grassland, the oak woodland, and the lower part of the yellow pine forest from near sea level to possibly 6,000 or 7,000 feet elevation, depending upon the vicinity. Here and there throughout our range; widely distributed in western North America.

The distinctive balls of flowers have given rise to application of a variety of vernacular names, including button willow, globe flower, honeyballs, and snowball. The species is desirable as an ornamental.

Family 42. *CAPRIFOLIACEAE*. HONEYSUCKLE FAMILY

(1) Ovary inferior; (2) leaves of our species pinnate, the leaflets with saw-toothed margins; (3) fruit a berry or berrylike, rarely a dry pod, never so in our species.

Shrubs, woody vines, or trees. Leaves opposite. Sepals, petals, and stamens usually 5, rarely 4, the sepals usually small or minute; petals united.

1. *SAMBUCUS*. ELDERBERRY

Large shrubs to fair-sized trees. Flowers in large, dense, flat-topped or pyramidal clusters. Corolla spreading like a saucer, the petals united only at the bases. Ovary 3-5-celled; style short, the stigmas 3-5. Fruit an edible berry.

1a. *Sambucus cerulea* Raf. var. *mexicana* (Presl.) L. Benson.
DESERT ELDERBERRY; MEXICAN ELDER

Usually a small or fair-sized tree, 6-12 m. (18-36 feet) high, the trunk 2-6 dm. in diameter; leaflets 3-5, mostly elliptical, ovate, or obovate but sometimes narrower, mostly 3-8 cm. long, 1-5 cm. broad, the tips short-attenuate, the surfaces hairy or glabrous, thick and leathery or relatively so; inflorescence flat-topped, 5-20 cm. in diameter, composed of many smaller clusters; petals yellowish white, the corolla 5-7 mm. in diameter; fruits 4-6 mm. in diameter, blue-black but lightened by the bluish white bloom (glaucous).

Watercourses and important drainages in the desert and desert grassland at mostly 2,000 to 4,000 feet elevation. California in the mountains from Santa Barbara and Kern counties to San Diego County; Arizona from Mohave County to Pima and Cochise counties; New Mexico on the Gila River drainage and the lower Rio Grande drainage; western Texas; Mexico.

The desert elderberry and the related blue elderberry (typical *Sambucus cerulea* known also as *Sambucus glauca,* a later and therefore unusable name) are the largest elders in the United States. Both may become trees 30 feet or more in height and with a trunk diameter of 1 or 2 feet. The dark blue fruits are utilized by man, being used particularly in pies, jellies, and wine, and they are relished by birds. The trees are planted as ornamentals.

Family 43. *COMPOSITAE.* Sᴜɴꜰʟᴏᴡᴇʀ Fᴀᴍɪʟʏ

(1) Flowers in dense heads each of which is surrounded by one or more series of scalelike bracts (an involucre), the heads composed of ray flowers (with corollas flattened out and resembling separate petals) or disc flowers (corollas tubular) or both, the entire head usually resembling a single flower, the ray flowers simulating petals and the disc flowers simulating the other parts; (2) sepals specialized as a pappus of scales or bristles which aid usually in dissemination of the fruits (e.g., dandelion), sometimes none; (3) petals 5, united; (4) stamens 5, united by the anthers but not by the filaments; (5) style 1, the stigmas or style branches 2, these usually hairy on the outside, the hairs serving as a brush which scrubs the pollen from the inside of the anther tube as the style elongates and pushes the stigmas upward. (Fig. 74 in particular and Figs. 75 to 84; Pls. XXX to XXXIV.)

KEY TO THE TRIBES

1. Stamens united to one another by the anthers, forming a tube around the style; flowers usually bisexual but sometimes all or some of them unisexual; heads not burlike.

2. Corolla 2-lipped, that is, with the petals in 2 strongly differentiated groups, with 2 petals in the upper lip and 3 in the lower, the lower lips of the marginal flowers often elongated; ray flowers none.

Tribe 1. ᴍᴜᴛɪꜱɪᴇᴀᴇ

2. Corolla not 2-lipped in all the flowers of the head, rarely so in the outer disc flowers when ray flowers are lacking.

3. Receptacle almost always naked; that is, with no elongated bristles and with no chaffy bracts subtending or surrounding the disc flowers.

4. Pappus not soft and fluffy (capillary in the extreme sense).

5. Involucral bracts not either lavender-tinged or scarious (thin, white or colorless, and translucent) or rarely so, sometimes the margins scarious; not large shrubs with wandlike branches and reddish purple disc flowers.

6. Plants with bisexual flowers or rarely some or all of them unisexual and the staminate and pistillate flowers on the same individual.

7. Style branches (or stigmas) shaped like clubs or baseball bats (sometimes greatly elongated but

THE SUNFLOWER FAMILY

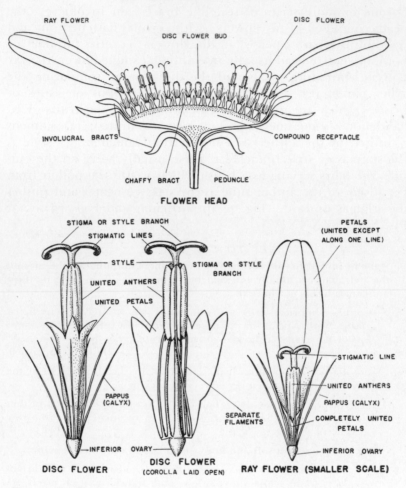

RAY FLOWER

DISC FLOWER BUD

DISC FLOWER

INVOLUCRAL BRACTS

COMPOUND RECEPTACLE

CHAFFY BRACT

PEDUNCLE

FLOWER HEAD

STIGMA OR STYLE BRANCH

STIGMATIC LINES

STYLE

UNITED ANTHERS

UNITED PETALS

PAPPUS
(CALYX)

INFERIOR OVARY

DISC FLOWER

STIGMA OR STYLE
BRANCH

SEPARATE
FILAMENTS

DISC FLOWER
(COROLLA LAID OPEN)

PETALS
(UNITED EXCEPT
ALONG ONE LINE)

STIGMATIC LINE

UNITED ANTHERS

PAPPUS (CALYX)

COMPLETELY UNITED
PETALS

INFERIOR OVARY

RAY FLOWER (SMALLER SCALE)

Fig. 74.—Sunflower family, Compositae: structure of the flower head and of ray and disc flowers.

gradually enlarged upward); involucral bracts of the semishrubby species commonly striate; ray flowers none; flowers white or greenish.

Tribe 2. EUPATORIEAE

7. Style branches not swollen above like clubs or base-ball bats, not greatly elongated, linear or broad at the middles, not enlarged markedly toward the ends; involucral bracts not striate; ray flowers commonly present; flowers of various colors or sometimes white, the disc flowers usually yellow.

8. Style branches with a stigmatic line along each margin of the lower half of each, the terminal portion of each branch not stigmatic, usually short-hairy, broad at the base and tapering to the acute apex (seen readily under low power of a compound microscope and fairly well under a dissecting microscope or high-powered hand lens); involucral bracts commonly in several series of graduated lengths. (Fig. 75; Pls. XXX; XXXI; XXXII.) Tribe 3. ASTEREAE

8. Style branches with the stigmatic lines running to the apices, linear, each branch commonly with an apical tuft of hairs, the apex chopped off abruptly, rarely with a short terminal bristle.

Tribe 4. HELENIEAE

6. Plants with unisexual flowers, the staminate and pistillate flowers on different plants, as shown by the longer ovaries and lack of stamens in some and the correspondingly shorter ovaries and large stamens in others at flowering time or by the elongated pappus in some plants and not in others at fruiting time. (Fig. 75 F; Pl. XXXII.) Tribe 3. ASTEREAE

5. Involucral bracts either lavender-tinged or scarious over most of the surface; pappus of bristles; ray flowers none; the shrub species with wandlike branches and reddish purple disc flowers and occurring along watercourses. (Fig. 81 A.) Tribe 5. INULEAE

4. Pappus of soft, fluffy, copious, usually white bristles, these capillary in the extreme sense. (Pl. XXXIII A; Fig. 81 D.) Tribe 6. SENECIONEAE

3. Receptacle with chafflike bracts (scales), 1 subtending each disc flower. (Pls. XXXIIIB; XXXIV; Fig. 80.) Tribe 7. HELIANTHEAE

1. Stamens separate from one another or practically so; flowers or some of them unisexual, the plants practically always with the staminate and

pistillate flowers on the same individual, the staminate heads in terminal racemes or spikes and the pistillate (usually burlike heads) produced lower on the same branch or an adjacent one. (Figs. 81 *B*, *C*; 83.)

Tribe 8. AMBROSIEAE

Tribe 1. *MUTISIEAE*. MUTISIA TRIBE

Herbs or shrubs, the juice not milky. Corolla 2-lipped: that is, with the petals in two strongly differentiated groups, with 2 petals in the upper lip and 3 in the lower, the lower lip often elongated; ray flowers none; flowers bisexual; anthers with long accessory tails at the bases (not to be confused with the filaments, which are free from one another).

The tribe is included for reference purposes, since in our area it embraces no true shrubs. *Trixis californica* Kell. is our only shrubby plant, and ordinarily it is scarcely a shrub but rather of a suffrutescent type. It is recognized by the yellow, obviously 2-lipped corollas present in all the flowers of the head. The stems are numerous from the base, and usually they are 1 or 2 feet high. The plant occurs in California in the Colorado Desert and in nearly all of the desert in Arizona.

Tribe 2. *EUPATORIEAE*. EUPATORY TRIBE

Herbs, suffrutescent plants, or small shrubs, the juice not milky. Bracts of the involucre in usually 2 or more series, sometimes all of about the same length, often of graduated lengths; those of most of our more shrubby species markedly striate; receptacle not with chaffy (scalelike) bracts among or around the disc flowers. Ray flowers none; disc flowers white or greenish; pappus of scales, or commonly of bristles, not fluffy and capillary in the extreme sense; disc corollas regular; anthers united, not with accessory tails; style branches shaped like clubs (swollen at the tips) or baseball bats (sometimes greatly elongated but gradually enlarged upward).

KEY TO THE GENERA

1. Achenes 5-nerved or -ridged; pappus bristles of our species dilated at the bases (not in 2 series as described in many books); leaf blades small, one fourth to one half as long as the slender petioles (in our species).

1. HOFMEISTERIA

1. Achenes 10-nerved; pappus of bristles, these sometimes plumose; leaf blades commonly distinctly longer than the petioles. 2. BRICKELLIA

1. *HOFMEISTERIA*

(1) Leaves small, more or less ovate or triangular, much shorter than the elongated slender petioles; (2) achenes 5-nerved.

Bushy shrubs. Leaves alternate or the lower ones opposite. Heads of our species rather small; involucral bracts markedly striate; disc flowers white or whitish; pappus bristles (or some of them) dilated and membranous at the bases; achenes markedly 5-nerved.

1. *Hofmeisteria pluriseta* A. Gray.

Shrub usually less than 1 m. high; herbage with rough and inconspicuous gland-tipped hairs, green; leaves ovate-attenuate to deltoid-ovate, entire to laciniately 3- 9- or 11-toothed, the larger ones mostly 1-1.5 cm. long, 5-12 mm. broad, the petioles 2-5 cm. long, slender; heads bell-shaped or broadly so, about 1 cm. in diameter; involucral bracts markedly striate with usually 3 nerves; pappus bristles mostly about 12-16.

Common on rocky slopes and canyon sides in the deserts from near sea level to 2,000 or occasionally 3,000 feet elevation. California in Inyo County and the Death Valley region and southward to the Mojave and Colorado Deserts; southern Nevada; southwestern Utah; Arizona in Mohave and Yuma counties and in the Organ Pipe Cactus National Monument in Pima County; northern Baja California and probably Sonora.

2. *BRICKELLIA*

Recognized by the proportionately shorter petioles of the leaves, the blades exceeding them in length, and by the 10-nerved achenes. The genus includes many plants on the borderline between herbs and shrubs, and the distinction is a difficult one to maintain. The species treated here may be classified definitely as desert shrubs or essentially shrubs. In addition the following species may barely qualify for inclusion in this work on either geographical grounds or the basis of woody habit: *Brickellia longifolia* S. Wats., *Brickellia multiflora* Kell., *Brickellia scabra* (A. Gray) A. Nels., *Brickellia Pringlei* A. Gray, *Brickellia californica* (Torr. & Gray) A. Gray.

Bushy to distinctly shrubby or herbaceous. Leaves alternate. Heads rather small; involucral bracts markedly striate; disc flowers whitish or tinged with green or purple; pappus of scabrous to plumose bristles, not dilated; achenes 10-nerved.

KEY TO THE SPECIES

1. Heads solitary, terminating the branches, 1-2.5 cm. long and 1-3.5 cm. in diameter at fruiting time; leaves sessile or nearly so, entire, the petioles none or not more than 1-2 mm. long.

2. Herbage densely and conspicuously matted with short, white, woolly hairs, the involucral bracts also woolly; heads about 2-2.5 cm. long and 2-3.5 cm. in diameter at fruiting time; achenes about 8 mm. long, the striations largely obscured by white wool; leaves subcordate and strictly sessile; large bushy shrubs about 1 m. high and 1 m. in diameter. 1. *Brickellia incana*

2. Herbage finely glandular-puberulent or with branched hairs, green and appearing more or less glabrous, the involucral bracts green; heads 1-1.5 cm. long and 1-1.3 cm. in diameter at fruiting time; achenes 4-5 mm. long, the striations not obscured by wool; leaves ovate, or when approaching subcordate, with petioles about 1-2 mm. long; low shrubs about 3-4 dm. tall.

   3. Leaves ovate-acute or somewhat attenuate, the larger ones 1.5-2.5 cm. long, 1-1.5 cm. broad; herbage finely glandular-puberulent, the hairs not elongated and soft (pilose) or kinky.
   2. *Brickellia atractyloides*

   3. Leaves oblanceolate, the larger ones 0.7-1 cm. long, 0.2-0.3 cm. broad; herbage with elongated and soft (pilose) kinky hairs.
   3. *Brickellia frutescens*

1. Heads in dense or loose clusters, 6-10 mm. long and 3-4 or sometimes 8 mm. in diameter at fruiting time; leaves distinctly petioled, the petioles at least 3 mm. long, the blades distinctly toothed.

   2. Heads sessile, in dense clusters of about 3-8 at the ends of leafy branches or sometimes in the axils of the upper leaves as well; pappus bristles about 15-25.

   3. Involucral bracts or nearly all of them each with a short apical cusp; leaves with short hairs covering the surface, not with spot-like glands. 4. *Brickellia californica*

   3. Involucral bracts obtuse or barely acute, not cuspidate; leaves glabrous, covered with dark, spotlike glands.

   4. Heads 14-20-flowered; leaves leathery and rather thick, conspicuously reticulate-veiny beneath. 5. *Brickellia baccharidea*

   4. Heads 8-11-flowered; leaves not leathery, thin, not reticulate-veiny beneath. 6. *Brickellia laciniata*

   2. Heads with peduncles 6-25 mm. long, in loose, leafless, terminal subcymose clusters of 3 to about 10; pappus bristles about 30-40.
   7. *Brickellia Coulteri*

   1. *Brickellia incana* A. Gray. (1) Heads solitary, terminating the branches, ½ to 1½ inches in diameter at fruiting time; (2) leaves without stalks, not toothed or lobed; (3) entire plant densely white-woolly.

Plate XXXII.—Desert broom, *Baccharis sarothroides: A,* pistillate shrub in flower; *B,* staminate heads; *C,* pistillate heads; *D,* plant in fruit; *E,* plant shedding fruits. (Photographs by Robert A. Darrow.)

Plate XXXIII.—Groundsel and zinnia: *A,* willow-leaf groundsel, *Senecio salignus* in flower; *B,* desert zinnia, *Zinnia pumila* in flower. The white ray flower corollas persist on the plant at fruiting time. (Photographs: *A* by Robert A. Darrow; *B* by Walter S. Phillips.)

Large white bush forming a sphere about 1 m. in diameter; branches white, shining, the larger ones with gray bark; leaves subcordate, entire, the larger ones 2-2.5 cm. long, about 1.5-2 cm. broad, becoming green only in age; heads solitary, terminating the branches, about 2 cm. long and 2-3.5 cm. in diameter at fruiting time; involucral bracts woolly, the striations apparent on only the inner sides; achenes about 8 mm. long, the striations partly or largely obscured by short, dense hairs; pappus bristles about 1 cm. long, with short, fine branch hairs.

Rocky slopes and desert flats at 1,200 to 4,100 feet elevation. California in the Death Valley region (Langford Wells) and southward through the eastern Mojave Desert to the northern edge of the Colorado Desert; southern Nevada; Arizona in western Mohave County.

2a. *Brickellia atractyloides* A. Gray. var. *atractyloides*. (1) Heads solitary, about ½ inch in diameter at fruiting time; (2) leaves ovate-acute, spiny-toothed, bright green, shining, not visibly hairy, with stalks not more than $^1/_{12}$ inch long.

Rather diffusely branched low shrub 3-4 dm. high; branches gray, some of them markedly woody and up to 1 cm. in diameter; herbage appearing glabrous, actually finely glandular-puberulent; leaves ovate-acute or somewhat attenuate, the larger ones 1.5-2.5 cm. long, 1-1.5 cm. broad, the petioles 1-2 mm. long; heads solitary, pedunculate, 13-15 mm. long, 10-13 mm. in diameter; involucral bracts green, the broader ones almost leaflike, tending to be ovate-acute or ovate-lanceolate, 3-4 or 5 mm. broad; achene, about 5 mm. long, very slender, finely but not densely hairy; pappus bristles white, 5-6 mm. long.

Rocky canyons in the desert at 2,500 to 3,500 feet elevation. Southern Nevada in Clark and Nye counties; southwestern Utah; Arizona from Mohave and Yuma counties to the Grand Canyon and to the mountains below the Mogollon Rim as far southeastward as Gila and eastern Pima counties.

2b. *Brickellia atractyloides* A. Gray var. *arguta* (Rob.) Jepson

Leaves, branchlets, and peduncles with longer gland-tipped hairs; larger involucral bracts narrowly lanceolate, 1-2 mm. broad.

Desert slopes and canyons at 3,000 to 4,000 rarely up to 7,000 feet elevation. California in Inyo County and southward through the desert mountains to the northern edge of Baja California, Mexico.

One form along the western edge of the Colorado Desert has the outer involucral bracts conspicuously dentately toothed. It has been called var. *odontolepis* (Rob.) Jepson.

3. *Brickellia frutescens* A. Gray. (1) Heads solitary, terminating the branches, about ½ inch in diameter at fruiting time; (2) leaves oblanceolate, not toothed or lobed, green, with soft, rather long, kinky hairs (these also on the stems and peduncles), the stalks not more than $1/_{12}$ inch long.

Low, rigid, intricately branched shrub 3-4 dm. high; branches becoming gray, distinctly woody; leaves 7-10 mm. long, 2-3 mm. broad; involucral bracts not markedly hairy, linear, 1-1.5 mm. broad; achenes about 4 mm. long, slightly hairy, tan; pappus bristles white, about 6 mm. long.

Rocky slopes in the desert at 2,000 to 3,000 feet elevation. California along the western edge of the Colorado Desert; southern Nevada; Arizona in the Kofa Mountains, Yuma County, and the Ajo Mountains, Pima County; Baja California, Mexico.

4a. *Brickellia californica* (Torr. & Gray) A. Gray var. *desortorum* (Cov.) Parish. (1) Heads not stalked, in dense clusters of about $3/_8$ at the ends of leafy branches; (2) leaves stalked, the stalks $1/_8$ to $1/_5$ inch long, the blades covered with short hairs; (3) each involucral bract with a short sharp point at the apex.

Intricately branched bushy shrub 0.5-1.5 m. high and up to 3 m. in diameter; branches and branchlets white, the older branches becoming gray below as bark is formed; herbage with short, rough hairs (scabrous), the leaves green; leaves deltoid-ovate, crenate-serrate, the larger ones 10-17 mm. long, 8-14 or 17 mm. broad, the petioles slender, 3-5 mm. long; heads about 7-10 mm. long, 3 mm. in diameter; involucral bracts glabrous, green, linear, less than 1 mm. board; achenes about 2.5 mm. long, somewhat hairy; pappus bristles about 15, about 5 mm. long.

Rocky slopes in the desert at 1,000 to 4,000 feet elevation. California from the Death Valley region to the western edge of the desert areas; southern Nevada; Arizona in Mohave and Yuma counties (Pierce's Ferry, Oatman, and the Kofa Mountains).

Brickellia californica var. *californica* is said to be occasional in occurrence on the Mojave Desert, but the writer is not certain whether it grows actually on the desert or just above the upper edge of it. It is distinguished from variety *desertorum* by the larger flowering head, approximately 14 mm. long and by the glabrous involucres. The typical variety is common in creek beds and washes and on dry slopes west of the main mountain axis in California, and it occurs eastward at elevations just above the deserts to Colorada and Texas and southward to northwestern Mexico.

5. *Brickellia baccharidea* A. Gray. (1) Heads not stalked, in dense clusters of about $^5/_8$ at the ends of leafy branches or in the upper leaf axils as well; (2) leaves stalked, the blades glabrous, covered with minute, dark, circular glands; (3) involucral bracts obtuse or barely acute, not with sharp apical points.

Shrubs about 1 m. tall; branches tannish but changing to gray as bark is formed; herbage green, glabrous; leaves ovate, laciniate-dentate toward the apices, 1-3 or 3.5 cm. long, 1-2 cm. broad, leathery, markedly reticulate-veined beneath; heads about 1 cm. long, 4 mm. in diameter, about 14-20-flowered; involucral bracts glabrous, green, narrowly lanceolate, about 1 mm. broad; achenes about 2-2.5 mm. long, finely hairy; pappus bristles about 15-25, about 7 mm. long.

Rocky slopes of mostly limestone hills in the desert and the desert grassland at about 3,500 to 5,500 feet elevation. Arizona in Yuma County and in southeastern Pima County and in Greenlee, Santa Cruz, and Cochise counties; New Mexico near Santa Rita; Texas near El Paso.

6. *Brickellia laciniata* A. Gray

Similar to *Brickellia baccharidea* and probably a variety of it; leaves somewhat smaller, thinner, not reticulate beneath; heads 8-11-flowered; achenes 2.8-3 mm. long; pappus bristles about 5 mm. long.

Slopes and plains in the desert at 3,000 to 4,000 feet elevation. New Mexico in the Organ Mountains; Texas west of the Pecos River; Chihuahua, Coahuila, and Nuevo Leon, Mexico.

7. *Brickellia Coulteri* A. Gray. (1) Heads in loose clusters, the stalks (peduncles) ¼ to 1 inch long; (2) leaves petioled (stalked), deltoid-cordate, attenuate.

Exceedingly brittle suffrutescent plant up to 1 m. high, the least shrubby of the seven species treated here; branches greenish, changing to gray, sometimes whitish at an intermediate stage; herbage with short, rough hairs (scabrous), these gland-tipped when occurring on the branches; leaves laciniately toothed near the bases, the larger ones 1.5-2.5 or 3.5 cm. long. 1-1.8 or 3 cm. broad, thin; heads subcymose, 3 to about 10 in a leafless cluster, about 8 mm. in diameter, about 15-flowered, the flowers and fruits not crowded in the head; involucral bracts few, glabrous, green, linear, about 1 mm. broad; achenes about 3 mm. long, dark gray, sparsely short-hairy; pappus bristles about 30-40, about 5 mm. long.

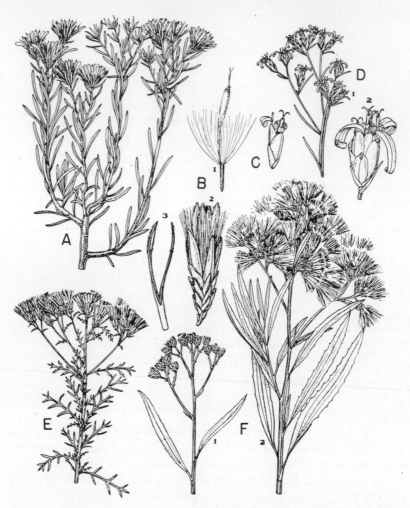

Fig. 75.—Aster tribe: *A*, turpentine bush, *Haplopappus laricifolius*, branch with leaves and heads of flowers; *B*, rabbit brush *Chrysothamnus nauseosus*, *1*, single disc flower, *2*, head of flowers, showing the vertical series of involucral bracts, *3*, apex of the style and the two style branches or stigmas, the terminal portion of each sterile and hairy, the base of each with a stigmatic line along each margin; *C*, snakeweed, *Gutierrezia lucida*, head of flowers, the longest involucral bract enclosing the solitary ray flower, the next the disc flower; *D*, snakeweed, *Gutierrezia Sarothrae*, *1*, branch with leaves and heads, *2*, head showing involucral bracts and ray and disc flowers; *E*, burroweed, *Haplopappus tenuisectus*, branch with pinnatifid leaves and with heads of fruits; *F*, seep willow or batamote, *Baccharis glutinosa*, *1*, branch with staminate heads, *2*, leafy branch with pistillate heads in fruit. (x $^2/_3$ except *B 1*, *2*, *C*, *D* 2 x $2^1/_3$; *B 3* x 23.)

Rocky hillsides in the desert at about 2,000 to 4,000 feet elevation. Arizona from southern Yavapai County to Yuma, Pima, and Graham counties; Baja California and southeastward in Mexico.

Brickellia Knappiana Drew occurs in the Panamint Mountains and near the Mojave River, California. It is reported to be a willowlike shrub 2-8 feet high, but the plant is not known to the writers.

Tribe 3. *ASTEREAE*. ASTER TRIBE

Herbs or shrubs, the juice not milky, the surface of the plant often (especially in the shrubs) resinous, usually not particularly odoriferous. Involucre usually but not always in several series of nonscarious bracts of various lengths, the bracts sometimes sharp but the head not burlike; receptacle not with chaffy bracts; that is, not with the bracts subtending or surrounding the disc flowers, not bristly. Heads with both ray and disc flowers or lacking ray flowers, the ray flowers of various colors but, except in a few genera, the disc flowers yellow; flowers bisexual or rarely unisexual; pappus of awns or bristles, these not fine and fluffy, not capillary in the extreme sense, rarely of scales or scales ending in bristles or none; disc corollas regular; anthers united, not with accessory tails; style branches (except in *Baccharis*) with a stigmatic line along each margin of the lower half of each, the terminal portion of each branch not stigmatic, usually short-hairy, broad at the base and tapering to the acute apex. (Fig. 75; Pls. XXX; XXXI; XXXII.)

KEY TO THE GENERA

1. Plants with bisexual flowers or some or all of them unisexual and the staminate and pistillate flowers on the same plant; style branches with a stigmatic line along each margin of the lower half of each, the terminal portion of each branch not stigmatic, usually short-hairy, broad at the base and tapering to the acute apex.

    2. Pappus of scales or of strongly and obviously flattened bristles.

        3. Involucral bracts not with broad membranous and fringed margins; pappus of scales or, when of flattened bristles, the tips not dilated.

            4. Leaves linear-lanceolate to linear, often narrowly so; pappus none or of separate scales; plant not spiny, barely shrubby, the branches wandlike, parallel; herbage resinous; disc flowers fertile or sterile.

                5. Pappus none or barely vestigial; ray flowers shorter than the disc flowers, the spreading part of the corolla much reduced, not rolled up in dried specimens.   1. SELLOA

5. Pappus present, formed from separate scales; ray flowers longer than the disc flowers, the spreading part of the corolla well developed, rolled up in dried specimens. (Fig. 75 *C, D*; Pl. XXX *A.*)   2. GUTIERREZIA

4. Leaves narrowly elliptic-acute to obovate; pappus of the ray flower of slender, elongated, tapering scales, the pappus of the disc flower of flattened, toothed bristles united into a basal saucerlike structure; plants with spines developed as pointed branches; shrubs intricately and divergently branched; herbage not resinous; disc flowers sterile.

3. AMPHIPAPPUS

3. Involucral bracts each with a broad scarious (thin, membranous, and translucent) margin, the extreme margin fringed somewhat like the sleeve of a buckskin shirt; pappus of flattened bristles, the tips dilated; achene very densely covered with long, stiff, appressed hairs.   4. ACAMPTOPAPPUS

2. Pappus of bristles, the bristles not markedly flattened.
3. Involucral bracts overlapping one another as shingles do, not arranged in obvious vertical rows. (Fig. 75 *A, E*; Pl. XXX *B.*)

5. HAPLOPAPPUS

3. Involucral bracts overlapping one another but arranged in obvious vertical rows. (Fig. 75 *B.*)   6. CHRYSOTHAMNUS

1. Plants with unisexual flowers, the pistillate and staminate flowers on different plants, as shown by the longer ovaries and absence of stamens in some plants and the correspondingly shorter ovaries and large stamens in others at flowering time or by the elongated pappus in some plants and not others at fruiting time; style branches linear. (Fig. 75 *F;* Pl. XXXII.)   7. BACCHARIS

1. *SELLOA.* GYMNOSPERMA

The single species within our range is suffrutescent rather than truly shrubby, and it is included here because of its close affinity and strong resemblance in appearance to *Gutierrezia,* a genus included for its importance as a range weed despite its scarcely shrubby character. (1) Pappus practically none, consisting of the slightest vestiges of scales; (2) leaves linear-lanceolate; (3) spines none; (4) herbage resinous; (5) ray flowers reduced, shorter than the disc flowers, Characters 1 and 5 are distinctions from *Gutierrezia;* 2-4 are distinctions from other genera, particularly *Amphipappus.*

1. *Selloa glutinosa* Spreng. Gymnosperma

Somewhat shrubby plants, the branches wandlike, woody at the bases, 0.5-1 m. high; leaves mostly linear- lanceolate, 5-9 cm. long, 3-6 or 10 mm. broad; heads 3-4 mm. long, 1.5-2 mm. in diameter, congested in more or less corymbose terminal clusters 2-5 cm. in diameter; involucral bracts greenish to straw colored.

Rocky slopes in the upper desert, the desert grassland, and the oak woodland at 2,000 to 6,000 feet elevation. Arizona in the Sierra Estrella, Maricopa County, and eastward and southward in the mountains south of the Gila River; southern New Mexico as far east as the White Mountains; western Texas; Mexico; Central America.

2. *GUTIERREZIA*. Snakeweed; Match Weed; Broom Weed

(1) Pappus of separate scales; (2) leaves linear or narrowly so; (3) spines none; (4) herbage resinous; (5) ray flowers longer than the disc flowers. (Fig. 75 *C, D*; Pls. XXX *A*; XXXI *B*.)

Herbs or suffrutescent bushes of low stature; branches wandlike, elongated from the perennial woody base of the plant. Leaves simple and entire, green on both surfaces, glabrous, markedly resinous-glandular. Flower heads small, in dense or loose terminal clusters with the appearance of cymes; involucral bracts tough and rather leathery, with warty tips, resinous, the outer ones shorter and with median ridges, the margins thin and membranous. Ray and disc flowers usually few; pappus of scales, usually shorter in the ray flowers; ray flowers fertile, pistillate; disc flowers bisexual or staminate; ovary hairy.

This genus is included despite its suffrutescent rather than shrubby character, since two or three of the half-shrubby species are among the plants most frequently sent to the University of Arizona for identification. All of them are significant as range weeds invading overgrazed areas.

KEY TO THE SPECIES
1. Disc flowers fertile, the ovaries well developed.
    2. Heads top-shaped, not approaching spheroidal; ray flowers 3-8; disc flowers commonly 3-8, rarely fewer; flowering from midsummer until autumn. (Fig. 75 *D*.) 1. *Gutierrezia Sarothrae*

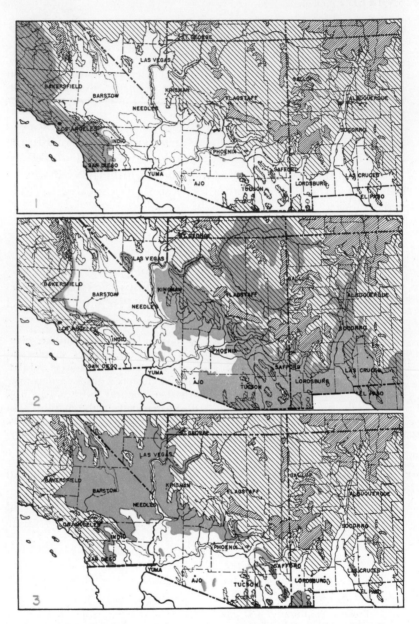

Fig. 76.—Distributional maps: *1*, California snakeweed, *Gutierrezia califor-nica;* *2*, snakeweed, *Gutierrezia lucida;* *3*, goldenhead, *Acamptopappus sphaero-cephalus;* *4*, big snakeweed, *Gutierrezia longifolia.*

2. Heads spheroidal or very broadly top-shaped; ray flowers 7 or 9-14; disc flowers 7-15 or 24; flowering from late spring (the latter part of April) until midsummer or sometimes August.

2. *Gutierrezia californica*

1. Disc flowers sterile, the ovaries very small.

2. Heads commonly with only 1 ray flower and 1 disc flower, rarely with 2 of either, with 2 principal involucral bracts, the longer enclosing the ray flower, the shorter enclosing the disc flower and with about 2-3 much shorter bracts, the head very small, less than 1 mm. in diameter, about 3 mm. long, cylindroidal, yellowish and straw-colored; largest leaves about 1-2 mm. broad. (Fig. 75 *C*; Pl. XXX *A*.)

3. *Gutierrezia lucida*

2. Heads with 2-3 ray flowers and 2-3 disc flowers, these subtended by several involucral bracts of graduated lengths, the head 1.5-2 mm. in diameter, 3-4 mm. long, between cylindroidal and top-shaped, partly green; largest leaves 3-4 mm. broad.

4. *Gutierrezia longifolia*

1a. *Gutierrezia Sarothrae* (Pursh) Britt. var. *Sarothrae*. SNAKEWEED. (1) Disc flowers commonly 3-8, with well-developed ovaries (fertile); (2) ray flowers 3-8; (3) heads top-shaped, never spheroidal, about 3 mm. in diameter; (4) flowering from midsummer until autumn. (Fig. 75 *D*; Pl. XXXI *B*.)

Plant with a woody base, the lower portions of the branches somewhat woody, but the branches essentially herbaceous; stems mostly 2-4 dm. high; leaves narrowly linear, mostly 1-4 cm. long, 1-2 mm. broad; heads congested mostly not stalked. Synonym: *Gutierrezia Euthamiae* (Nutt.) Torr. & Gray.

Plains and slopes in the upper creosote-bush desert, the desert grasssland, and the oak woodland at 3,000 to 7,000 feet elevation; occurring on a wide range of soils. Southern California from Los Angeles County to San Diego County and in the western Mojave Desert and southeastward to the New York Mountains; Great Basin and Rocky Mountain regions from Nevada and Montana southward; Arizona at 3,000 to 6,000 feet or more elevation; New Mexico; Baja California and southeastward in Mexico.

Snakeweed is aggressive, and in most of its distributional range it invades livestock ranges where the better forage grasses have been depleted or destroyed by overgrazing. On such ranges this and other species of snakeweed may constitute the principal vegetational cover. When better forage is lacking, snakeweed provides limited food for sheep and horses.

In one form the heads are solitary at the ends of the branches of the inflorescence. This form has been called *Gutierrezia divaricata* (Nutt.) Torr. & Gray. In a type occurring in southwestern New Mexico the branches, leaves, and outer involucral bracts are reported to be densely scaly (lepidote). This plant has been called *Gutierrezia furfuracea* Greene.

1b. *Gutierrezia Sarothrae* (Push) Britt. var. *microcephala* (DC.) L. Benson

Heads narrowly top-shaped, about 1.5 mm. in diameter; ray flowers about 4-5; disc flowers 1-3 or 4. Synonyms: *Gutierrezia microcephala* (DC.) A. Gray; *Gutierrezia Euthamiae* (Nutt.) Torr. & Gray var. *microcephala* (DC.) A. Gray.

Idaho to northern and southeastern Arizona, New Mexico, and western Texas; southward in Mexico as far as Coahuila.

2a. *Gutierrezia californica* (DC.) Torr. & Gray var. *californica*. CALIFORNIA SNAKEWEED. (1) Disc flowers 7-15 or 24, with well-developed ovaries (fertile) ; (2) ray flowers 7 or 9-14; (3) heads spheroidal or very broadly top-shaped; (4) flowering from the late April until midsummer, sometimes as late as August.

Plant with the base only slightly woody, the branches distinctly herbaceous, 2-5 dm. high; leaves narrowly linear, 1-4 cm. long, 1-2 mm. broad, heads stalked, 4-5 mm. in diameter and length, not congested at the ends of the branchlets of the inflorescence.

Alluvial plains and slopes in the desert, the chaparral, and the desert grassland from near sea level to 4,000 feet elevation. California from the South Coast ranges and the San Joaquin Valley to coastal Southern California and along the western borders of the Colorado Desert; Arizona in the Arizona Desert and on the upper Gila River drainage from Yavapai County to eastern Pima County and Cochise County; Baja California to Chihuahua, Mexico. (Fig. 76 *1*.)

2b. *Gutierrezia californica* (DC.) Torr. & Gray var. *bracteata* (Abrams) H. M. Hall

Branchlets strongly divergent, clothed with numerous bractlike leaves which are later deciduous; heads few, about 6 mm. long and of nearly the same diameter.

Hills and plains in the desert from near sea level to about 2,000 feet elevation. California in the Colorado Desert from San Gorgonio Pass to Palm Springs.

3. *Gutierrezia lucida* Greene. (1) Disc flower 1, very rarely 2, the ovary not developed, minute (sterile) ; (2) ray flower 1, very rarely 2; (3) principal bracts of the involucre 2, the others much shorter, the longest bract enclosing the ray flower, the next the disc flower; (4) leaves $^1/_{24}$ to $^1/_{12}$ inch broad. (Fig. 75 *C*; Pl. XXX *A*.)

Plant with the basal portion more woody than in the two preceding species, the bases of the branches commonly distinctly woody, the stems mostly 3-5 or 7 dm. high; leaves narrowly linear, mostly 1-4 cm. long, 1-2 mm. broad; heads congested in clusters, mostly not stalked. Synonym: *Gutierrezia glomerella* Greene.

Alluvial plains, slopes, and hillsides in the desert, the desert grassland, the oak woodland, and the pinyon-juniper woodland at mostly 2,000 to 6,000 feet elevation. California from the White Mountains, Inyo County, to the Little San Bernardino Mountains; southern Nevada; southern Colorado; Arizona; New Mexico; western Texas; Mexico. (Fig. 76 2.)

This species is the common snakeweed of the desert grassland ranges in southern Arizona and New Mexico.

4. *Gutierrezia longifolia* Greene, BIG SNAKEWEED. (1) Disc flowers 2-3, with undeveloped, minute ovaries (sterile) ; (2) ray flowers 2-3; (3) bracts of the involucre several, graduated in length; (4) larger leaves $^1/_8$ to $^1/_6$ inch broad.

Plant with the lower parts of the branches distinctly woody for some distance, the stems mostly 5-8 or 10 dm. high; leaves linear or very narrowly oblanceolate, 2-5 cm. long, the larger ones 3-4 mm. broad; some heads stalked, others not. Synonym: *Gutierrezia linoides* Greene.

Alluvial plains and slopes in the desert grassland, the oak woodland, and the yellow pine forest. Southern Colorado; southeastern Arizona in the Baboquivari, Graham, Mule, and Chiricahua mountains; New Mexico. (Pl. 76 *4*.)

3. *AMPHIPAPPUS*. CHAFF BUSH

(1) Pappus of narrow, elongated, tapering scales in the ray flowers and of elongated, flattened, finely toothed bristles joined basally into a saucer in the disc flowers; (2) leaves narrowly

elliptic-acute or obovate; (3) lower branches with some twigs specialized as nearly leafless spines; (4) herbage not resinous, glabrous.

Bushy shrubs with divergent, stiff branches. Leaves simple and entire, green on both surfaces, glabrous. Flower heads in dense, terminal, cymelike clusters; involucral bracts pale green, broad and blunt, thin, the narrow margins membranous. Ray and disc flowers few.

1. *Amphipappus Fremontii* Torr. & Gray. CHAFF BUSH

Plant usually 4-6 dm. high; new branches green, those of the previous season white, the old ones with gray bark; leaves 8-12 mm. long, 4-6 mm. broad; heads about 6-8 mm. long, 2-3 mm. in diameter, subcylindroidal; ray flowers 1-2; disc flowers about 3-6; bristles of the disc flower pappus somewhat contorted; ray achenes hairy; disc achenes with a few scattered hairs or glabrous.

Rocky slopes and gravelly washes in the upper desert. California in the northern and eastern Mojave Desert from the Coso and Argus mountains to the Providence Mountains; southern Nevada in Clark County; southwestern Utah; Arizona in the Mojave Desert to northern Maricopa County. (Fig. 77 *1*.)

4. *ACAMPTOPAPPUS*

The chief character is the fringes on the margins of the involucral bracts. The margins thin, membranous, and translucent, the extreme margin with a fringe resembling slightly the fringe on the sleeve of a buckskin shirt.

Shrubs small, rounded; branches slender, rigid; herbage practically glabrous. Leaves small, simple, entire, alternate, not petioled. Heads spheroidal; ray flowers present or absent, yellow when present. Pappus of flattened bristles dilated at the apices. Achenes very densely covered with long, stiff, appressed hairs.

KEY TO THE SPECIES

1. Ray flowers none; heads about 1 cm. in diameter, in clusters; leaves narrowly oblanceolate.   1. *Acamptopappus sphaerocephalus*
1. Ray flowers present; heads about 1.5 cm. in diameter, solitary; leaves oblanceolate-oblong.   2. *Acamptopappus Schockleyi*

1. *Acamptopappus sphaerocephalus* (Harv. & Gray) A. Gray. GOLDENHEAD

Low shrub 0.3-0.5 dm. high; stems definitely woody below; bark gray; leaves narrowly oblanceolate, 1-1.5 cm. long, 1-2 mm. broad; heads clustered, nearly spheroidal, about 1 cm. or slightly less in diameter; ray flowers none; achenes 3-4 mm. long, about 2 mm. broad, obpyramidal.

Gravelly or sandy mesas and slopes in the desert at mostly 1,500 to 4,000 feet elevation. California in the southern Mojave Desert and on the western side of the Colorado Desert; southwestern Utah; Arizona in the Mojave Desert, along the northern border of the Arizona Desert as far eastward as Graham County, and in the Ajo and Quiijotoa mountains, Pima County. (Fig. 76 3.)

2. *Acamptopappus Shockleyi* A. Gray

Similar to *Acamptopappus sphaerocephalus*; leaves oblanceolate-oblong, 2-3 mm. broad; heads solitary, about 1.5 cm. in diameter; ray flowers present, about 13-15 mm. long; achenes 4-5 mm. long.

Mesas and slopes in the desert mountains. California in the Mojave Desert from the Death Valley region southward to the vicinity of Baker; Nevada in southern Mineral, Clark, and Nye counties.

5. *HAPLOPAPPUS*[11]

(1) Ray flowers yellow; (2) pappus of bristles, these not flattened; (3) involucral bracts overlapping one another as do the shingles of a roof, not arranged in vertical rows, in most of our species of several lengths.

The genus is a large and exceedingly variable one, but the numerous apparently dissimilar types which make it up are connected by intermediate species. However, segregation of some of the included groups as separate genera might not be illogical. (Fig. 75 *A, E*; Pl. XXX *B*.)

Herbs, bushes, or well-developed shrubs; not spiny. Leaves alternate, simple, entire to pinnatifid, often dotted with resin glands. Flower heads of various sizes and shapes, solitary or arranged in panicles or clusters; involucral bracts tough and leathery, with or without warty greenish areas at the tips, these areas when present bearing dotlike resin glands. Ray flowers yellow or sometimes not present; pappus of bristles, these with minute, sharp projections (scabrous), not strongly flattened, of various lengths.

11. The name has been spelled *Aplopappus* by some botanists and *Haplopappus* by others. The problem has been settled by conservation of *Haplopappus*, cf. International Code of Botanical Nomenclature Adopted by the Seventh International Botanical Congress, Stockholm, July, 1950, prepared by J. Lanjouw, et al. 139. 1952. *Haplopappus* is a *nomen conservandum*; *Aplopappus* is rejected.

Although the first group (section *Isocoma*) of three species is barely shrubby, it is of special interest for the poisonous plants and the range weeds it includes. It is difficult of classification, and it is in need of further study as a unit. The species have a strong tendency to intergrade, and it is possible that some of them are better considered as varieties.

KEY TO THE SPECIES

1. Involucre from cylindroidal to top-shaped, 3-9 mm. in diameter, the bracts in several series, of a variety of lengths; ray flowers present or commonly wanting; pappus of coarse, off-white bristles.

    2. Tube of the corolla dilated abruptly; leaves either oblanceolate, linear-oblanceolate, or pinnatifid with narrow divisions. (Section 1. ISOCOMA.)

        3. Fully developed leaves pinnatifid (pinnately divided or deeply parted), the divisions elongated and narrow, the main blades 20-35 mm. long, about 1 mm. broad, the divisions 2-22 mm. long, about 1 mm. broad. (Fig. 75 *E*; Pls. XXX *B*; XXXI *A*.)
            1. *Haplopappus tenuisectus*

        3. Fully developed leaves entire to toothed or slashed into lobes or rarely deeply cleft, the lobes when present not or scarcely longer than the breadth of the main axis.

            4. Free portion of the petal 1 or commonly 1.2-1.5 mm. long, often somewhat attenuate; involucral bracts usually not each with a thickened, warty, green spot near the apex.
                2. *Haplopappus pluriflorus*

            4. Free portion of the petal 0.5-0.7 or occasionally 1 mm. long, merely acute; involucral bracts usually each with a thickened, warty, green (when fresh) spot near the apex, this dotted with resin glands.
                3. *Haplopappus acradenius*

    2. Tube of the corolla dilated gradually from base to apex; leaves either linear, filiform (threadlike, or, in this case, somewhat like pine needles), or rarely obovate or oblanceolate. (Section 2. ERICAMERIA.)

        3. Flower heads produced on distinctly leafy short branches, solitary or few.

            4. Flower-bearing branches arranged racemosely; ray flowers none.
                4. *Haplopappus propinquus*

            4. Flower-bearing branches arranged corymbosely; ray flowers usually 3-6, sometimes none. (Fig. 75 *A*.)
                5. *Haplopappus laricifolius*

3. Flower heads produced on essentially leafless short branches, these arranged in corymbs.

4. Leaves linear-oblanceolate, 1-2 mm. broad; involucral bracts spreading widely at fruiting time; ray flowers usually 1-2; disc flowers 5-8.   6. *Haplopappus Cooperi*

4. Leaves cuneate to obovate, 4 or commonly 7-12 mm. broad; involucral bracts not spreading widely at fruiting time; ray flowers in our variety none.   7. *Haplopappus cuneatus*

1. Involucre broadly hemispheroidal to nearly saucer-shaped, 14-18 mm. in diameter, the bracts mostly in about 2 relatively long series; ray flowers present and conspicuous; pappus of relatively soft white bristles. Section 3. STENOTOPSIS.)   8. *Haplopappus linearifolius*

1. *Haplopappus tenuisectus* (Greene) Blake. BURROWEED. Leaves dissected into narrow, elongated divisions, the leaves therefore pinnatifid. (Fig. 75 *E*; Pl. XXX *B*; XXXI *A*.)

Semishrub forming a hemispheroidal or nearly spheroidal bush, 0.5-1 m. in diameter and 0.5-0.7 or sometimes 1 m. high; branches woody below, the bark of the larger branches gray; leaves glandular, sometimes strongly so and rarely with stalked glands, the main axis of the blade in each of the larger leaves 20-35 mm. long, about 1 mm. broad, the divisions 2-22 mm. long, about 1 mm. broad; each involucral bract with a thickened, green, warty apical spot, this with minute resin glands; apical portion of the involucre at fruiting time 3-4 mm. in diameter, the head containing 8-12 or rarely 6 or in one specimen 15 flowers; pappus bristles 30-60; corolla lobes about 1 mm. long, acute.

Alluvial plains and slopes in the desert and the desert grassland at 2,000 to 4,500 feet elevation. Arizona in the Arizona Desert and the adjacent desert grassland south of the Gila River; extreme western New Mexico; Texas along the Rio Grande in the Big Bend region; Sonora to Chihuahua, Mexico. (Fig. 77 2.)

Burroweed is significant as an invader of depleted range lands, and often it constitutes the principal vegetational cover. Ordinarily the plants are not browsed upon when other forage is available, but, in periods of drought, excessive use of this species may cause serious livestock poisoning. Eradication and control of this weed in desert grassland is a serious and difficult problem.

2. *Haplopappus pluriflorus* (A. Gray) H. M. Hall. JIMMY-WEED. (1) Leaves linear-oblanceolate, entire or with a few short

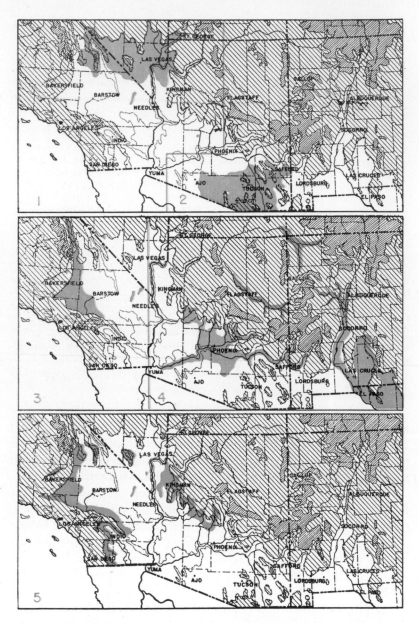

Fig. 77.—Distributional maps: *1*, chaff bush, *Amphipappus Fremontii*; *2*, burroweed, *Happlopappus tenuisectus*; *3*, *Haplopappus Cooperi*; *4*, jimmyweed, *Haplopappus pluriflorus*; *5*, stenotosis, *Haplopappus linearifolius* var. *interior*.

teeth; (2) involucral bract usually with no thickened, green, glandular area at the apex; (3) corolla lobes 1 or commonly 1.2-1.5 mm. long, commonly somewhat attenuate.

Similar to *Haplopappus tenuisectus*; bark and older growth grayish; leaves 2-6.5 cm. long, mostly 2-4 mm. broad. Synonym: *Haplopappus heterophyllus* (A. Gray) Blake.

Alluvial bottoms, plains, and gentle slopes in the desert and the desert grassland at 1,000 to 6,000 feet elevation. Southern Colorado; Arizona on the drainage of the Gila River proper and its northern tributaries from Yuma County and southern Yavapai County eastward; New Mexico on the Gila River, Rio Grande, and Pecos River drainages; western Texas; northern Mexico. (Fig. 77 *4*.)

Jimmyweed, like the closely related burroweed, is an aggressive invader of depleted grassland ranges. It is not grazed by livestock when other forage plants are available, but in drought periods cattle may eat sufficient quantities to cause "milk sickness" or "trembles." This malady is transmissible through milk to human beings.

This species intergrades in southern Pinal County, Arizona, with *Haplopappus tenuisectus,* the burroweed, and in the lower Gila River region it is not always distinguishable from *Haplopappus acradenius.*

3. *Haplopappus acradenius* (Greene) Blake. (1) Leaves oblong or oblanceolate, entire or toothed or lobed to shallowly parted; (2) involucral bract usually with an apical thickened, wartlike, green area bearing minute dotlike resin glands; (3) corolla lobes 0.5-0.7 or occasionally 1 mm. long, nearly acute.

Bark and older growth light tan to nearly white, shining; larger leaves 1-4.5 cm. long, mostly 4-9 mm. broad. Synonym: *Isocoma veneta* (H.B.K.) Greene var. *acradenia* (Greene) H. M. Hall.

Alkaline soils in the desert and the Pacific prairie from near sea level to about 2,000 feet elevation. California in the upper San Joaquin Valley in Tulare and Kern counties, along the western edge of the Mojave Desert in the vicinity of Antelope Valley, and in the Salton Sea Basin of the Colorado Desert; southern Nevada in Clark County; Arizona in the Grand Canyon region and the Mojave Desert and southward to southern Yuma County, Quitovaquito in western Pima County, and in Maricopa County; Baja California and at least northwestern Sonora, Mexico.

4. *Haplopappus propinquus* Blake.

Shrubs 1-2 m. high; leaves and twigs with resin glands; leaves narrowly linear, mostly 1.2-2 cm. long, the shorter ones often in fascicles; heads in a panicle of few-headed racemes; involucral bracts overlapping as shingles do; heads 5-8 mm. high; ray flowers none; disc flowers 8-12; achenes with dense, long hairs. Synonym: *Ericameria brachylepis* (A. Gray) H. M. Hall.

Alluvial plains and slopes in the upper desert and the lower part of the chaparral. Infrequent in California in the mountains of southeastern San Diego County along the edge of the Colorado Desert; Baja California, Mexico.

Haplopappus Palmeri A. Gray var. *pachylepis* (H. M. Hall) Munz. Similar to *Haplopappus propinquus*; readily distinguished by the presence of ray flowers. California from Santa Barbara County to Riverside County; reaching the edge of the desert through the passes.

5. *Haplopappus laricifolius* A. Gray. TURPENTINE BUSH (Fig. 75 *A*)

Flat-topped shrubs usually 5-8 dm. high, the terminal branches parallel and densely leafy; branches light colored, tannish; leaves green, glandular, linear to linear-oblanceolate, 1-2 cm. long, 1-2 mm. broad; heads terminating short, slender, leafy branches, these arranged corymbosely, 8-10 mm. high, 5-10 mm. in diameter; involucral bracts overlapping as shingles do, not spreading at fruiting time; ray flowers usually 3-6; disc flowers 9-13; linear, greatly elongated; achenes with long appressed hairs.

Rocky or gravelly slopes and plains in the upper desert, the desert grassland, and the lower oak woodland at 3,000 to 6,000 feet elevation. Arizona in the higher mountains of the Mojave and Arizona deserts and in the mountains below the Mogollon Rim; New Mexico in the mountains along the Gila River and eastward to the Organ Mountains; western Texas; Sonora to Chihuahua, Mexico. (Fig. 78 2.)

Turpentine bush is common on rocky mountain slopes just below or among the lowermost oaks, and it may constitute the chief vegetational cover. The plant is remarkably resinous, and the crushed foliage emits an odor similar to turpentine. The plants are of no value as forage for livestock. They contain a small amount of rubber.

6. *Haplopappus Cooperi* (A. Gray) H. M. Hall

Shrubs 0.5-1 m. high, appearing flat-topped because of the dense terminal foliage along each of many parallel branches; twigs light colored, the bark of the older stems gray; leaves green, glandular, linear-oblanceolate, 1-2 cm. long, 1-2 mm. broad; heads in corymblike clusters, 5-6 mm. high, 3-5 mm. in diameter; involucral bracts usually 8-12, overlapping as shingles do, spreading widely at fruiting time; ray flowers usually 1-2; disc flowers 5-8; stigmas narrowly lanceolate; achenes with dense long, straight, appressed hairs.

Alluvial slopes and plains in the desert and in areas along its borders. California from Big Pine, Inyo County, southward through Owens Valley and the Death Valley region to the Mojave Desert and the desert slopes of the San Bernardino Mountains; also in isolated colonies near Los Angeles and Riverside; southern Nevada in Esmeralda and Nye counties; doubtfully recorded from Baja California, Mexico. The plant is particularly common on the western edge of the Mojave Desert. (Fig. 77 3.)

7a. *Haplopappus cuneatus* A. Gray var. *spathulatus* (A. Gray) Blake

Low shrubs 3-6 dm. or rarely 1 m. high, often forming mats on rocks or growing in rock crevices; twigs either light colored or gray, the bark of the older branches gray or sometimes even black; leaves green, glandular, cuneate (wedge-shaped) or obovate, the larger ones 1-2 cm. long, 4- or commonly 7-12 mm. broad; heads in corymbose clusters, 7-9 mm. high, 5-6 mm. in diameter; involucral bracts overlapping as shingles do, not markedly spreading at fruiting time; ray flowers none; disc flowers commonly 15-20; achenes with straight appressed hairs.

Rocky ledges and crevices in the upper desert and in the pinyon-juniper and oak woodlands. California along Kern River and Caliente Creek, in the Slate and Panamint mountains, Inyo County, and along the western borders of the Mojave and Colorado deserts; southern Nevada; Arizona in the higher mountains bordering the desert from Mohave and Yavapai counties southeastward to Pima and Cochise counties; Baja California and probably Sonora, Mexico.

8a. *Haplopappus linearifolius* DC. var. *interior* (Cov.) M. E. Jones. STENOTOPSIS

Low, rounded to hemispheroidal shrubs 0.5-1 m. high; leaves green, glandular, linear to very narrowly linear-oblanceolate, mostly 1.5-2.5 cm. long, 1-3 mm. broad; heads solitary on short leafy branches, the upper portion of each branch forming a slender peduncle 2-3 cm. long, the heads 10-14 mm. high, 16-22 mm. in diameter; involucre 14-18 mm. in diameter, the bracts mostly in about two relatively long series; ray flowers mostly 14-18, conspicuous, 1.5-2 cm. long; disc flowers many; pappus with many soft, fine, white bristles; achene with appressed shining white hairs.

Mesas and slopes of the sagebrush and creosote-bush deserts and the adjacent woodlands at mostly 2,000 to 5,000 feet elevation. California in eastern Ventura County, the Tehachapi Mountains, and the Mojave and Colorado deserts; southern Utah; southwestern Colorado; Arizona in Mohave, Yavapai, and eastern Maricopa counties; Baja California, Mexico. (Fig. 77 5.)

The flower heads are large and conspicuous, and the species is a prominent part of the desert landscape in the spring.

6. *CHRYSOTHAMNUS*. RABBIT BRUSH

(1) Flowers bisexual; (2) pappus of bristles; (3) involucral bracts arranged in vertical rows. (Fig. 75 *B*.)

Suffrutescent plants or shrubs; not spiny. Leaves alternate, simple, entire, linear; either dotted with resin glands or not glandular. Flowers arranged in small clusters or large or small panicles; involucral bracts tough and leathery, with or without greenish thickened glandular areas at the apices. Ray flowers none; pappus of bristles, these with minute, rough projections (scabrous), not strongly flattened, of various lengths.

KEY TO THE SPECIES

1. Twigs and leaves strongly resinous, with depressed resin glands; leaves nearly circular in cross section.

    2. Heads solitary or in groups of 2 or 3, peduncled, arranged in panicles of racemes, numerous in the panicle as a whole; involucral bracts not with apical thickened glandular areas. 1. *Chrysothamnus paniculatus*

    2. Heads in compact clusters at the ends of branches, most of them not stalked, relatively few on each twig; involucral bracts each with an apical thickened glandular area.   2. *Chrysothamnus teretifolius*

1. Twigs and leaves not resinous, not with depressed glands; leaves obviously flattened.

2. Twigs and leaves glabrous or with short nonwoolly hairs.
3. *Chrysothamnus pulchellus*

2. Twigs and leaves woolly or partly so, the wool often feltlike, sometimes matted. (Fig. 75 *B*.)   4. *Chrysothamnus nauseosus*

1. *Chrysothamnus paniculatus* (A. Gray) H. M. Hall

Shrubs 0.5-2 m. high; twigs green, becoming tan; leaves green, linear, nearly circular in cross section, the larger ones 1-4 cm. long, 1 mm. or less broad, glabrous, strongly resinous, sticky, the resin glands sunken; heads solitary or few on short branches which are arranged in a panicle of racemes, numerous in the panicle as a whole, 6-7 mm. long, 3-4 mm. in diameter; involucre about 5 mm. long, the bracts not with apical glandular thickened areas; disc flowers 5-8; achenes appressed-hairy, elongated.

Gravelly or sandy washes and rocky canyon slopes in the desert. California in the Death Valley region and in the Mojave and Colorado deserts; southern Nevada in Clark County; southwestern Utah; Arizona in the Mojave Desert and at Rye Creek, Gila County; Sonora, Mexico.

2. *Chrysothamnus teretifolius* (Dur. & Hilg.) H. M. Hall

Shrubs 0.5-1 m. high; twigs tannish, the bark of the older branches gray to black; leaves green, linear, nearly circular in cross section, the larger ones 1.5-2 cm. long, 1 mm. or less broad, glabrous, strongly resinous, sticky, the resin glands sunken; heads in dense clusters at the ends of the branches, most of them not stalked, relatively few on each twig, 6-8 mm. long, 4-5 mm. in diameter; involucre about 5 mm. long at flowering time, increasing later to 6-8 mm.; each bract with an apical thickened glandular spot, disc flowers 5-6; achenes appressed-hairy, elongated.

Gravelly slopes and rocky canyons in the sagebrush and creosote-bush deserts at 3,000 to 6,000 feet elevation. California from the White and Inyo Mountains and the Death Valley region, Inyo County, to the Mojave Desert and at San Gorgonio Pass and in the Santa Rosa Mountains in the Colorado Desert; southern Nevada; southwestern Utah; Arizona in the Black Mountains, Mohave County. (Fig. 78 *3*.)

3. *Chrysothamnus pulchellus* (A. Gray) Greene

Shrub 0.3-0.5 m. high; twigs light colored, glabrous; bark of the old branches gray or brown; leaves green, markedly flattened in cross section, sometimes rolled backward (revolute), glabrous, not resinous; heads in small corymbose clusters at the ends of the branches; involucre 10-13 mm.

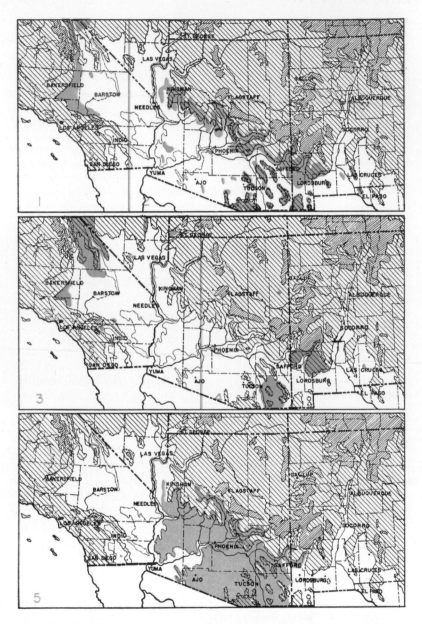

Fig. 78.—Distributional maps: *1*, rabbit brush. *Chrysothamnus nauseosus* var. *viridulus*; *2*, turpentine bush, *Haplopappus laricifolius*; *3*, rabbit brush, *Chrysothamnus teretifolius*; *4*, rabbit brush, *Chrysothamnus nauseosus* var. *latisquameus*; *5*, desert broom, *Baccharis sarothroides*.

high, the bracts greenish toward the apices; flowers about 5; achenes minutely hairy or glabrous.[12]

Mesas and slopes in the sagebrush desert, the upper part of the creosote-bush desert, and the desert grassland. Utah; southern Colorado; western Kansas; northern Arizona; New Mexico at Deming, Luna County, and at the White Sands, Otero County; western Texas; northern Mexico.

Chrysothamnus pulchellus (A. Gray) Greene subsp. *elatior* (Standl.) H. M. Hall differs in averaging about 1 m. tall and in having hairy leaves. Southern New Mexico, in the San Andreas Mountains, Doña Ana County. The plant is not known to the writers.

4. *Chrysothamnus nauseosus* (Pall.) Britt. RABBIT BRUSH (Fig. 75 *B*)

This wide-ranging and exceedingly variable species is represented in the Southwestern deserts and the desert grasslands by ten varieties, and these are segregated following the discussion of the species as a whole. The typical variety does not occur within our range. The varieties are those recognized by H. M. Hall and data for parts of the keys and descriptions are drawn from Hall's publications. Most of these varieties seem to be significant entries, but some are doubtfully of varietal rank. The problem is too complex to be taken up with the small amount of material available, and its solution would require years of field study applied to the special group of plants.

Rabbit brush is abundant throughout the Great Basin and adjacent areas, and it is particularly common on deteriorated range lands where it replaces the more valuable perennial grasses. The plant contains a small amount of rubber in the foliage and upper branches and a greater quantity in the lower woody portions.

KEY TO THE VARIETIES

1. Outermost short involucral bracts and sometimes the inner longer ones with woolly hairs on the backs or margins.

    2. Sterile terminal portion of the stigma (or style branch) shorter than the basal portion bearing the stigmatic lines; inner bracts usually at least slightly hairy.

12. Description adapted from H. M. Hall, Carnegie Inst. Wash. Publ. (326) : 193-4. 1923.

3. Wool of the twigs and leaves matted, the vegetative parts gray or yellowish green; corolla tube not with loose, woolly, elongated hairs in addition to shorter ones.   4a. Var. *gnaphalodes*

3. Wool of the twigs and leaves not matted, loose, the vegetative parts of the plant white; corolla tube usually with loose, woolly, elongated hairs in addition to shorter ones.   4b. Var. *hololeucus*

2. Sterile terminal portion of the stigma (or style branch) longer than the basal portion bearing the stigmatic lines; inner bracts glabrous.
4c. Var. *latisquameus*

1. Outermost short involucral bracts as well as the inner longer ones glabrous.

2. Achenes (fruits) glabrous. (The pappus bristles are not to be confused with hairs on the bodies of the fruits.)   4d. Var. *abbreviatus*

2. Achenes hairy.

3. Leaves 1-2 mm. broad, linear.   4e. Var. *graveolens*

3. Leaves not more than 1 mm. broad, very narrowly linear to threadlike (filiform).

4. Tip of the involucral bract not forming a sharp, narrow, clearly differentiated point (mucro), merely acute or obtuse.

5. Corolla lobes (free ends of the petals beyond the corolla tube) glabrous.

6. Involucral bracts not in sharply angular rows, few, the involucre 7-9 mm. long.

7. Twigs mostly 1-2 mm. in diameter; corolla lobes 1-2 mm. long.   4f. Var. *consimilis*

7. Twigs mostly 2-3 mm. in diameter; corolla lobes 1.7-2.5 mm. long.   4g. Var. *viridulus*

6. Involucral bracts in sharply angular rows, numerous, the involucre 9-10 mm. long.   4h. Var. *mohavensis*

5. Corolla lobes long-hairy before the flower opens; leaves few.   4i. Var. *junceus*

4. Tip of the involucral bract forming a sharp, narrow, clearly differentiated, recurved point (mucro). 4j. Var. *ceruminosus*

4a. *Chrysothamnus nauseosus* (Pall.) Britt. var. *gnaphalodes* (Greene) H. M. Hall

Shrubs usually 0.5-1.5 m. high; twigs grayish or yellow-green, the hairs matted or closely packed; leaves not more than 1 mm. broad; inflorescence small, rounded; involucre 6-7 mm. high, not strongly angled, all the bracts at least apically woolly; corolla 7-8 mm. long, the tube short-hairy, the lobes not more than 1 mm. long; sterile terminal portion of the stigma (or style branch) shorter than the basal portion bearing the stigmatic lines; achenes hairy.

Alluvial slopes and plains of the sagebrush and creosote-bush deserts and the pinyon-juniper woodland. California on the eastern slopes of the Sierra Nevada in Mono and Inyo counties, in the Mojave Desert, along the western border of the Colorado Desert near Banning, and on mesas near Colton, Riverside County; western Nevada; northern Arizona in Coconino and Apache counties.

4b. *Chrysothamnus nauseosus* (Pall.) Britt. var. *hololeucus* (A. Gray) H. M. Hall

Shrubs usually 0.5 1.5 dm. high; twigs densely white-woolly, the wool not matted, loose; leaves 1 mm. broad or sometimes broader, white-woolly like the twigs; inflorescence rounded, dense; involucre 6-7 mm. high, not strongly angled, all the bracts woolly; corolla 7-8 mm. long, the tube with loose, woolly, elongated hairs in addition to shorter ones, the lobes not more than 1 mm. long; sterile terminal portion of the stigma (or style branch) shorter than the basal portion bearing the stigmatic lines; achenes hairy.

Slopes and plains in the sagebrush and creosote-bush deserts. California along the eastern edge of the Sierra Nevada and the Tehachapi mountains from Mono County to Antelope Valley, Kern County; western Nevada from Washoe County to Esmeralda County.

4c. *Chrysothamnus nauseosus* (Pall.) Britt. var. *latisquameus* (A. Gray) H. M. Hall

Shrubs 1-2 m. high, the bases 2-4 cm. or more in diameter; twigs white with dense loose or somewhat matted wool; leaves 1 mm. or less broad, white-woolly like the twigs; inflorescence dense, a considerably branched panicle; involucre 7-8 mm. high, not strongly angled, only the outer short bracts woolly, the inner elongated ones glabrous; corolla about 8 mm. long, the tube often hairy, not woolly, the lobes not more than 1 mm. long; sterile apical portion of the stigma longer than the basal portion bearing the stigmatic lines; achenes hairy.

Gravelly or sandy soils along drainages in the upper part of the desert and the desert grassland. Arizona on the Little Colorado River drainage and in eastern Pima and Santa Cruz counties and Cochise County; New Mexico on the Gila River and Rio Grande drainages and in the Tularosa Basin; Sonora, Mexico. (Fig. 78 *4*.)

4d. *Chrysothamnus nauseosus* (Pall.) Britt. var. *abbreviatus* (M. E. Jones) Blake

Shrubs 0.5-1 m. high; twigs greenish to white, the wool closely packed; leaves very narrow, considerably less than 1 mm. broad, greenish or somewhat whitened; inflorescence very small and compact, rounded; involucre about 7 mm. high, not strongly angled, glabrous; corolla usually 6-7 mm. long, the tube usually somewhat hairy, the lobes much less than 1 mm. long; sterile terminal portion of the stigma longer than the basal portion bearing the stigmatic lines; achenes glabrous.

Alluvial plains and slopes in the desert. California in the Providence Mountains; southern Nevada in Mineral and Lincoln counties; southern Utah.

4e. *Chrysothamnus nauseosus* (Pall.) Britt. var. *graveolens* (Nutt.) Piper

Shrubs 0.5-1.5 m. high; twigs greenish to more or less whitened, the wool tending to be matted; leaves relatively broad, 1-2 mm. wide, green, only slightly woolly; inflorescence rounded, compact; involucre 6-8 mm. high, not strongly angled, the bracts glabrous; corolla about 8 mm. long, the tube hairy or glabrous, the lobes up to 1.5 mm. long; terminal sterile portion of the stigma longer than the basal portion bearing the stigmatic lines; achenes hairy.

Mesas and slopes in the sagebrush desert, the upper part of the creosote-bush desert, the desert grassland, and the pinyon-juniper woodland. Idaho and North Dakota to Utah and Colorado; Arizona from the Hualpai Mountains, Mohave County, eastward to the Little Colorado River drainage in Navajo and Apache counties; New Mexico on the San Juan River and Rio Grande drainages and southward to the White Mountains, Lincoln County. A widespread variety, particularly abundant in the Great Basin.

4f. *Chrysothamnus nauseosus* (Pall.) Britt. var. *consimilis* (Greene) H. M. Hall

Shrubs 0.5-1.5 m. high; twigs with matted wool, green; leaves less than 1 mm. broad, green, sometimes rather woolly; inflorescence elongated, rather narrow; involucre about 7-8 mm. high, not strongly angled, the bracts glabrous; corolla 7-8 mm. long, the tube usually glabrous, the lobes 1-2 mm. long; sterile apical portion of the stigma longer than the basal portion bearing the stigmatic lines; achenes hairy.

Alkaline soil of alluvial plains and gentle slopes in the sagebrush desert, the creosote-bush desert, and the grassland. Eastern

Oregon and Idaho to western Wyoming and Colorado; California in Siskiyou and Modoc counties and southward along the eastern slopes of the Sierra Nevada to Mono County, also in the Tantillas Mountains, San Diego County; Nevada, Arizona on the Colorado Plateau, at Kirkland, Yavapai County, and in the Santa Rita and Santa Catalina mountains, Pima County; northern New Mexico.

4g. *Chrysothamnus nauseosus* (Pall.) Britt. var. *viridulus* H. M. Hall

Shrub 1-2 m. high; twigs with feltlike hair, greenish; leaves 1 mm. broad, greenish, somewhat hairy; inflorescence compact, rounded; involucre about 7 mm. high, not strongly angled, the bracts glabrous; corolla 7-9 mm. long, the tube usually glabrous, the lobes about 2 mm. long; terminal sterile portion of the stigma longer than the basal part bearing the stigmatic lines; achenes hairy.

Alkaline flats in the sagebrush and creosote-bush deserts. California in Mono and Inyo counties and southward on the western edge of the Mojave Desert to Antelope Valley and the desert slopes of the San Bernardino Mountains; western Nevada in Esmeralda County. (Fig. 78 *1*.)

4h. *Chrysothamnus nauseosus* (Pall.) Britt. var. *mohavensis* (Greene) H. M. Hall

Shrubs 0.5-1.5 m. high; twigs whitened or greenish; leaves often few, 1 mm. or less broad, only slightly woolly; inflorescence short or elongated; involucre 9-10 mm. long, narrow, the bracts numerous, arranged in well-marked and elongated vertical ranks and the involucre as a whole therefore strongly angled, glabrous; corolla 8-10 mm. long, the tube finely hairy, the lobes 1.5-2.5 mm. long; terminal sterile portion of the stigma longer than the basal stigmatic portion; achenes hairy.

Plains and slopes in the desert, the chaparral, and the coastal grasslands. California in the inner South Coast ranges from Santa Clara County to Ventura County and eastward to the western and southern borders of the Mojave Desert south of Antelope Valley, Kern County.

4i. *Chrysothamnus nauseosus* (Pall.) Britt. var. *junceus* (Greene) H. M. Hall

Shrub apparently about 1 m. high; twigs greenish, the wool matted; leaves few, threadlike, much less than 1 mm. broad (in material available); inflorescence small, compact; involucre about 10 mm. high, narrow, the bracts numerous, arranged in well-marked and elongated vertical rows and the involucre as a whole therefore strongly angled, glabrous; corolla 9 mm. long, the tube glabrous, the lobes with long hairs at least before opening of the flower; terminal sterile portion of the stigma longer than the basal portion bearing the stigmatic lines; achenes hairy.

Rocky or gravelly slopes in the desert and bordering areas; often on limestone. Arizona in the Grand Canyon region, at Kingman, Mohave County, and along the Gila River in eastern Greenlee County.

4j. *Chrysothamnus nauseosus* (Pall.) Britt. var. *ceruminosus* (Dur. & Hilg.) H. M. Hall

Shrub 0.5-1 m. high; twigs greenish, the wool matted; leaves less than 1 mm. long; inflorescence compact, rounded; involucre 7-8 mm. high, not strongly angled, each bract tipped with a clearly differentiated, sharp, narrow, recurved point (mucro) about or nearly 1 mm. long, glabrous; terminal sterile portion of the stigma longer than the basal part bearing the stigmatic lines; achenes hairy.

Alluvial slopes in the desert. California in South Fork Valley, Kern County, and along the western side of the Mojave Desert from Tehachapi and Tejon passes to Hesperia, San Bernardino County.

7. *BACCHARIS*

The species of *Baccharis* are of rather diverse aspect, but they may be distinguished from other members of the aster tribe by the considerable difference in the staminate and pistillate plants. Since bisexual flowers are the rule in the rest of the sunflower family, with the exception of only a few groups, this character sets *Baccharis* apart from nearly all the common composites. When the plants reach the fruiting or seed stage, the difference in the staminate and pistillate individuals is most striking, since the pistillate plants produce great quantities of "fuzz" or "cotton" (the pappus of each of many fruits) and the staminate plants have only dried-up heads which fail to show the pappus.

Shrubs or sometimes herbs. Twigs angled or nerved. Leaves alternate, simple, commonly elongate, entire, toothed or sometimes lobed. Heads unisexual, staminate flowers with well-developed corollas and large stamens, the ovary undeveloped; pistillate flowers with slender, threadlike corollas, no stamens, and a larger ovary, the pappus of each pistillate flower of most species elongating rapidly at fruiting time, with numerous bristles; style branches or stigmas slender, the apical sterile portion not well differentiated. Achenes with 4 or commonly 5 or 10 longitudinal nerves. (Fig. 75 *F*; Pl. XXXII.)

KEY TO THE SPECIES

1. Leaves willowlike, lanceolate or narrowly so, the larger ones 7-11.5 cm. long, entire or toothed; achenes with 5 longitudinal nerves. (Fig. 75 *F*.)
    2. Heads in flat-topped clusters terminating each of the main branches, not in small clusters on the short lateral branches; leaves markedly toothed, the teeth from serrate to denticulate; leaves and twigs markedly sticky with resins. (Fig. 75 *F*.)   1. *Baccharis glutinosa*
    2. Heads in flat-topped clusters terminating each of the main branches and also present on each of the many short lateral branches near the apex of the stem; leaves not toothed or sometimes denticulate; leaves and twigs scarcely sticky.   2. *Baccharis viminea*
1. Leaves not willowlike, rarely a few of them lanceolate, rarely more than 5 cm. long, entire to lobed.
    2. Achenes with 5 longitudinal nerves; low bush about 3-6 dm. high, the branches not wandlike, spreading at various angles, somewhat woody below; leaves linear, entire, 10-15 mm. long, 1-2 mm. broad; twigs and leaves with gland-tipped hairs.   3. *Baccharis brachyphylla*
    2. Achenes with 10 longitudinal nerves; shrubs 1-3 m. high; twigs and leaves not with gland-tipped hairs, glabrous.
        3. Twigs tan; twigs and leaves dotted with sunken resin glands; heads on short leafy branchlets, these arranged racemosely.
        4. *Baccharis pteronoides*
        3. Twigs green; twigs and leaves not with resin glands; heads on leafless or practically leafless branchlets.
            4. Pistillate heads including the pappus 6-7 mm. long at fruiting time, the pappus off-white, not lustrous, the bristles few; larger leaves narrowly obovate to obovate-lanceolate, or sometimes oblanceolate, 18-25 or 35 mm. long, 4-6 mm. broad, entire, or sometimes with a few small teeth.   5. *Baccharis sergilloides*
            4. Pistillate heads including the pappus 12-27 mm. long at fruiting time, the pappus white, lustrous, soft, the bristles numerous; leaves rarely both narrowly obovate and without teeth or lobes.
                5. Leaves linear, 12-25 mm. long, 1-1.5 mm. broad, entire; heads solitary on elongated nearly leafless branchlets, the pistillate including the pappus 18-27 mm. long at fruiting time. (Pl. XXXII.)   6. *Baccharis sarothroides*
                5. Larger leaves obovate to lanceolate or oblanceolate or rarely ovate, 2.5-5 or 7.5 cm. long, 6-12 or 25 mm. broad,

coarsely toothed or lobed or entire; pistillate heads including the pappus 12-14 mm. long at fruiting time.

7. *Baccharis Emoryi*

1. *Baccharis glutinosa* Pers. SEEP WILLOW; WATER WALLY; BATAMOTE. (1) Leaves 1-4½ inches long, resembling those of a willow, lanceolate or narrowly so; (2) heads in flat-topped clusters at the ends of the main branches, not in small lateral clusters along the branches. (Fig. 75 *F*.)

Shrubs 1.5-3 or 4 m. high; branches green becoming tan, wandlike, strongly many-angled, numerous; leaves mostly 8-15 mm. broad, strongly serrate or sometimes only denticulate, markedly sticky and resinous, glabrous; heads 4-5 mm. long and about 5 mm. in diameter at flowering time; pistillate heads including the elongated pappus about 8-10 mm. long in fruit; pappus somewhat off-white; achenes with 5 longitudinal nerves.

Stream banks, ditches, and semipermanent watercourses in the desert and the desert grassland from near sea level to 5,000 feet elevation. California along Kern River and in the Mojave and Colorado deserts; southern Nevada; southwestern Utah; Colorado; Arizona along the Colorado River drainage and throughout the deserts and the adjacent desert grassland; New Mexico in the Chihuahuan Desert and the adjacent desert grassland; western Texas; Mexico.

The seep willow is of importance in the control of streambank erosion since it often forms dense thickets along watercourses or intermittent streams. Indians prepared an eyewash from resinous leaves. The plant has no forage value for livestock.

2. *Baccharis viminea* DC. MULE FAT. (1) Leaves 1-3½ inches long, resembling those of a willow, lanceolate or narrowly so; (2) heads in flat topped clusters terminating each of the main branches but also present on each of many short lateral branches near the apex of the stem.

Shrubs 2-4 m. high; branches green, becoming tan, wandlike, strongly many-angled, numerous; leaves mostly 8-12 mm. broad, not toothed or sometimes denticulate, only slightly sticky and resinous, glabrous; heads, flowers, and fruits similar to *Baccharis glutinosa*.

Streams and semipermanent drainages in the desert, the grassland, the chaparral, and the oak woodland, California in the

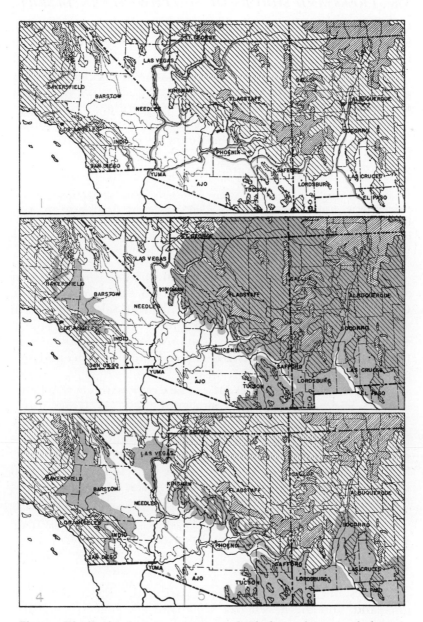

Fig. 79.—Distributional maps: *1*, arrow weed, *Pluchea sericea*; *2*, scale broom, *Lepidospartum squamatum*; *3*, thread-leaf groundsel, *Senecio Douglasii* var. *longilobus*; *4*, pigmy cedar, *Peucephyllum Schottii*; *5*, yerba de pasmo, *Baccharis pteronoides*.

Coast ranges from Lake County southward, in the Great Valley, in coastal southern California, and here and there eastward in the deserts; Arizona near the mouth of the Gila River and at Montezuma Castle National Monument. The species is closely related to the seep willow, *Bacchairs glutinosa*. It is exceedingly common in north-central and central California.

3. *Baccharis brachyphylla* A. Gray. (1) Bush 1-2 feet high, low, intricately branched, the branches not wandlike; (2) achenes (fruits) 5-ribbed; (3) leaves linear, not toothed, ½ inch long, $^1/_{16}$ inch broad, glandular-hairy.

Branches strongly 5-7 ridged, minutely hairy with gland-tipped hairs; twigs green; leaves rather densely glandular-hairy; heads few in short terminal racemes, 4-5 mm. long, 5-7 mm. in diameter at flowering time; pistillate heads including the pappus about 10-12 mm. long at fruiting time; achenes with 5 longitudinal nerves, rather sparsely short-hairy.

Alluvial plains and slopes in well-drained soils in the desert and the desert grassland at mostly 1,500 to 4,000 feet elevation. California in the mountains bordering the Salton Sea Basin (Morongo Pass and southern San Diego County); Arizona in the Tinajas Altas and Tule mountains, Yuma County, and in the southern Mojave and Arizona deserts and the adjacent desert grassland; Sonora, Mexico.

4. *Baccharis pteronoides* DC. YERBA DE PASMO. (1) Achenes (fruits) with 10 nerves running lengthwise; (2) larger leaves $^3/_8$ to ½ inch long, $^1/_6$ to somewhat less than $^1/_8$ inch broad, few-toothed at the apices; (3) pistillate heads including the pappus about ½ inch long at fruiting time, the pappus white, lustrous, abundant; (4) heads on short leafy branches arranged racemosely; (5) twigs tan (rather than green like nos. 3, 4, and 6-8.)

Shrubs 1-2 m. high; branches only moderately angled or nerved; twigs and leaves with small, sunken resin glands, glabrous; heads about 4 mm. long and 4 mm. in diameter at flowering time; achenes somewhat glandular between the nerves, sparsely hairy.

Slopes and plains in the upper part of the desert, the desert grassland, and the lowest oak woodland at 3,000 to 5,000 feet elevation. Arizona on the border of the Arizona Desert and in the mountains south of the Mogollon Rim; New Mexico in and

Plate XXXIV.—Brittle bush, *Encelia farinosa,* one of the most colorful plants in the desert; *above,* close-up view of the heads of flowers; *below,* several plants on a hillside. (Photographs by E. T. Nichols.)

adjacent to the Chihuahuan Desert from Socorro County southward; western Texas; Mexico. (Fig. 79 5.)

The vernacular name, yerba de pasmo, means "chill weed," and it alludes to use of leaf infusions as a remedy for chills. Livestock browse the plant. It is reported to be poisonous to sheep at certain seasons.

5. *Baccharis sergilloides* A. Gray. SQUAW WATERWEED. (1) Achenes (fruits) with 10 nerves running lengthwise; (2) larger leaves narrowly obovate to obovate-oblanceolate or sometimes oblanceolate, $3/4$ to 1 or rarely $1\frac{1}{2}$ inches long, $3/16$ to $5/16$ inch broad, entire or rarely with a few teeth; (3) pistillate heads including the pappus about $1/4$ inch long at fruiting time, the pappus off-white, not abundant or lustrous; (4) branches broomlike, not leafy.

Shrubs 1-2 m. high; branches strongly angled, with 3-4 principal ridges and an equal number of smaller intervening nerves; twigs green, sometimes finally forming weak spines; twigs and leaves not glandular, glabrous; heads on practically leafless short branches arranged in very loose racemes, 4-5 mm. long and about 5 mm. in diameter at flowering time; achenes glabrous.

Sandy washes and canyons in the desert and adjacent areas at about 2,000 to 5,000 feet elevation. California in the Panamint and Funeral ranges in the Death Valley region and along the western side of the Colorado Desert; southern Nevada; southwestern Utah; Arizona in the Mojave Desert and eastward to the Grand Canyon region and southward to Maricopa County; Sonora, Mexico.

6. *Baccharis sarothroides* A. Gray. DESERT BROOM. (1) Achenes (fruits) with 10 nerves running lengthwise; (2) larger leaves linear, $1/2$ to 1 inch long, about $1/16$ inch broad, not toothed; (3) pistillate heads including the pappus $3/4$ inch to 1 inch long at fruiting time, the pappus white, lustrous, copious; (4) heads solitary on elongated nearly leafless branches. (Pl. XXXII.)

Shrubs 1-3 m. high; branches green, strongly angled with about 5-7 nerves or ridges; vegetative parts not glandular, glabrous; pistillate heads cylindroidal, about 1 cm. long and 5 mm. in diameter at flowering time; staminate heads broadly obconical, about 5-7 mm. long and 5-7 mm. in diameter; achenes not glandular, glabrous.

Gravelly or sandy washes, watercourses, shallow drainages, flat, and low hills in the desert and the desert grassland at mostly 1,000 to 5,000 feet elevation. California near San Diego and in a few localities in the southern Mojave Desert and the Colorado Desert (Pinyon Wells, San Bernardino County; Gulliday Well, Chuckawalla Mountains; Salt Creek Wash, Imperial County); Arizona in the Mojave Desert south of Chloride, Mohave County, and in the Arizona Desert and the desert grassland; southwestern New Mexico in Grant County; Baja California and eastward in Mexico. (Fig. 78 5.)

The evergreen broomlike branches are attractive, and the shrub is used as an ornamental. During autumn the abundant masses of white, cottony "seeds" are contrasted sharply with the green branches. The resinous leaves and stems are not palatable for livestock.

7. *Baccharis Emoryi* A. Gray. EMORY BACCHARIS. (1) Achenes (fruits) with 10 nerves running lengthwise; (2) larger leaves narrowly obovate to lanceolate or oblanceolate or sometimes narrowly ovate, 1-2 or 3 inches long, ¼ to ½ or 1 inch broad, entire or coarsely few-toothed or lobed; (3) pistillate heads including the pappus about ½ or ⅝ inch long at fruiting time, the pappus white, lustrous, copious; (4) heads in small clusters at the ends of branches, not stalked.

Shrubs 1-3 m. high; branches green, strongly angled with about 5 ridges or nerves; vegetative parts not glandular, glabrous; pistillate heads cylindroidal, about 1 cm. long and 4 mm. in diameter at flowering time; staminate heads top-shaped, 5-7 mm. long, 4-5 mm. in diameter; achenes not glandular, glabrous.

Moist soil along streams and drainages in the desert and adjacent areas. California along Kern River near Bakersfield, in coastal Southern California, and in the Salton Sea Basin of the Colorado Desert; southern Nevada; southern Utah; southwestern Colorado; Arizona in the Mojave Desert, in scattered localities in the Colorado and Arizona deserts, and in the Huachuca Mountains; western Texas; northern Mexico.

Tribe 4. *HELENIEAE*. Sneezeweed Tribe

Herbs or suffrutescent plants, rarely truly woody, the juice not milky. Bracts of the involucre commonly in 1 or 2 series, commonly of about uniform length, little imbricated (i.e., not overlapping as shingles do), not striate; receptacle not with a chaffy (scalelike) bract subtending each disc flower. Ray flowers usually present, usually yellow; disc flowers commonly yellow, the corollas regular; anthers united, not with accessory tails; style branches linear, usually with an apical tuft of hairs, the stigmatic lines running to the truncate ("chopped-off") apices.

None of the plants in this tribe may be considered as a major shrub. However, one slightly woody plant, *Psilostrophe Cooperi,* the yellow paper daisy, is a conspicuous feature of the desert landscape in the springtime, and it is described briefly below. Some species of *Dyssodia* are slightly woody, and they are distinguished by the large glands of the stems, leaves, and involucral bracts. Another more or less shrubby plant, *Clappia suaedifolia,* extends into our range in south-central New Mexico.

Psilostrophe Cooperi A. Gray. YELLOW PAPER DAISY. Suffrutescent plants 2-5 dm. high; stems densely white-woolly; leaves linear to linear-oblanceolate, 2-5 cm. long, 1-5 mm. broad, green but with some white wool; heads showy; involucres bell-shaped, 6-8 mm. long, about 5 mm. broad, short-woolly; ray flowers 15-20 mm. long, 10-15 mm. broad, bright yellow, persistent and becoming papery at fruiting time; disc flowers few; pappus of 4-6 scales. Alluvial plains and slopes in the desert and the desert grassland. California in the Clark and Providence mountains in the southeastern Mojave Desert and in the Chuckawalla Mountains, Riverside County; southern Nevada; southwestern Utah; Arizona throughout the desert and the desert grassland; southwestern New Mexico in Grant County; Baja California and probably Sonora, Mexico.

Clappia suaedifolia A. Gray. Plants shrubby at the bases, the branches herbaceous, as much as 4.5 dm. tall; leaves alternate, markedly fleshy, the upper ones entire, the lower pinnately and laciniately divided, the divisions 3 or 5; heads solitary at the ends of the stems, markedly pedunculate, hemispheroidal, 1.5-2 cm. in diameter exclusive of the ray flowers, the involucral bracts elliptic, the larger ones 3-5 mm. long, 2.5-3 mm. broad, markedly striate, overlapping as shingles do, in about 3 series; ray flowers 12-15, the corollas narrowly oblanceolate, 1.5-2 cm. long; achenes dark, somewhat flattened, about 10-nerved, finely hairy on the nerves, about 2.5 mm. long, the pappus with 15-25 roughened, off-white bristles. Alkaline flats in the desert. New Mexico at the White Sands, Otero County, and near Roswell, Chaves County; western Texas; Mexico.

Tribe 5. *INULEAE.* EVERLASTING TRIBE

Mostly herbs, only one of our species a shrub. Herbage white-woolly or in our genus not so, the juice not milky. Leaves alternate or rarely opposite, entire or toothed. Bracts of the involucre of various types, sometimes highly specialized as sacs enclosing flowers, in most species scarious (thin, white or colorless, and translucent) over most of the surface. Ray flowers none; disc flowers white or yellowish or, in our genus, lavender to reddish purple, bisexual or unisexual; pappus of slender bristles; anthers caudate (with accessory tails) at the bases; style branches or stigmas with the stigmatic lines extending the entire length. (Fig. 81 *A*.)

1. *PLUCHEA*

Herbs or shrubs, erect and relatively large. Heads in flat-topped clusters. Involucre with overlapping, lavender-tinged bracts, not scarious. Disc flowers reddish purple or purplish. Outer flowers pistillate, the corollas very narrow; inner or central flowers potentially bisexual but sterile, with well-developed larger corollas. Pappus composed of bristles. (Fig. 81. *A*.)

1. *Pluchea sericea* (Nutt.) Cov. ARROW WEED (Fig. 81 *A*)

Shrubs 1-3 m. tall, the branches wandlike and suggestive of willows or of *Baccharis glutinosa* or *Baccharis viminea;* twigs obscurely nerved; densely matted with silvery appressed hairs; leaves numerous, thoroughly clothing the branches, lanceolate or commonly broadest at the middles, mostly 2-3 cm. long, 2-6 mm. broad, densely silky with appressed hairs on both faces; heads in small more or less corymbose clusters at the ends of the branches; involucral bracts firm and rather thick except on the scarious, fringed (fimbriate) margins, markedly tinged with lavender; disc flowers reddish purple to lavender.

Stream banks, watercourses, and ditches in the desert and adjacent areas. California from Cuyama Valley, San Luis Obispo County, to Bakersfield and to San Diego County and along the principal drainages in the Mojave and Colorado deserts; southern Nevada; southern Utah; southern Colorado; Arizona along the immediate Colorado River, Bill Williams River, and Gila River drainages and the large tributaries; New Mexico on the Rio Grande drainage from Socorro southward; western Texas; Baja California to Chihuahua, Mexico. (Fig. 79 *1*.)

Arrow weed is particularly abundant along the Colorado River and its permanent tributaries, and the Indians of this region have made extensive use of its long, straight, wandlike branches for manufacture of arrows and baskets.

Tribe 6. *SENECIONEAE*. GROUNDSEL TRIBE

Herbs or a few plants shrubby or slightly so, the juice not milky. Leaves alternate or rarely opposite, simple to pinnate. Involucral bracts in usually 1-2 or sometimes 3-4 series, usually not overlapping markedly, of nearly the same length, more or less greenish or white-woolly. Ray flowers usually present, nearly always yellow; disc flowers yellow or rarely otherwise; pappus with numerous soft, usually white bristles (capillary in the extreme); anthers not with accessory tails at the bases; stigmatic lines extending nearly the length of the stigma or style branch, hairs present at or near the apex of the stigma. (Pl. XXXIII A; Fig. 81 D.)

KEY TO THE GENERA

1. Involucral bracts 8 or more; leaves not spiny.

  2. Leaves not dotted with resin glands.

    3. Leaves large and well developed, at least some not linear in the shrubby species; ray flowers present in our species. (Pl. XXXIII A; Fig. 81 D.)   1. SENECIO

    3. Leaves either small and scalelike or linear; ray flowers none.

                                      2. LEPIDOSPARTUM

  2. Leaves dotted with resin glands.   3. PEUCEPHYLLUM

1. Involucral bracts 4-6; leaves spine-pointed or the first ones specialized as heavy spines.   4. TETRADYMIA

1. *SENECIO*. GROUNDSEL

Herbs or occasionally more or less shrubby plants. Leaves alternate, simple to pinnate, rarely palmately lobed. Heads in terminal flat-topped clusters. Ray flowers usually present, yellow; disc flowers yellow. (Pl. XXXIII A; Fig. 81 D.)

KEY TO THE SPECIES

1. Leaves pinnately divided (pinnatifid), the divisions linear; involucral bracts 15-25, attenuate, not yellow-margined. (Fig 81 D.)

                                1. *Senecio Douglasii*

1. Leaves entire, linear-lanceolate, firm, willowlike; involucral bracts about 8, rounded or obtuse, the margins yellow. (Pl. XXXIII A.)

                                2. *Senecio salignus*

1a. *Senecio Douglasii* DC. var. *Douglasii*. CREEK SENECIO. (1) Leaves pinnatifid, the divisions linear; (2) involucral bracts 15-20 long-pointed, not yellow-margined.

Bushy shrub commonly 0.7-2 m. high; branches leafy, rather densely white-woolly, the wool finally falling away; leaves 3-7 cm. long, pinnately divided, the divisions usually 5-9; heads rather broadly bell-shaped, 12-16 mm. long, averaging about 15 mm. in diameter; involucral bracts about 15-25, linear, attenuate; ray flowers conspicuous, about 2 cm. long, the corollas 2-3 mm. broad; bractlets at the apex of the flower stalk (peduncle) about $^2/_3$ as long as the involucre, slender.

Washes, dry stream beds, and alluvial plains in the desert, the chaparral, and the grasslands. California in the inner Coast ranges from eastern Lake County southward, on the western lower slopes of the Sierra Nevada, in coastal southern California, along the eastern base of the Sierra Nevada in Mono and Inyo counties, and on the western border of the Mojave; Baja California; reported from Sonora, Mexico.

1b. *Senecio Douglasii* DC. var. *monoensis* (Greene) Jepson

Smaller, usually 3-8 dm. high; herbaceous rather than woody; not woolly or only slightly so, glabrous or glabrate; bractlets of the upper part of the peduncle $^2/_5$ to $\frac{1}{2}$ as long as the involucral bracts.

Plains and slopes in the sagebrush and creosote-bush deserts, the desert grassland, and the oak woodland. California in Mono County and in the mountains of the northern and eastern Mojave Desert; southern Utah; nearly throughout Arizona; Mexico.

1c. *Senecio Douglasii* DC. var. *longilobus* (Benth.) L. Benson. THREAD-LEAF GROUNDSEL (Fig. 81 *D*)

Suffrutescent or somewhat shrubby, mostly 6-10 dm. high, densely woolly; bractlets of the upper portion of the peduncle inconspicuous, only $\frac{1}{4}$ to $^1/_3$ as long as the involucral bracts. Synonym: *Senecio filifolius* Nutt.

Plains, slopes, and washes in the upper creosote-bush desert, the sagebrush desert, the grasslands, and the oak woodland at 2,500 to 7,000 feet elevation. Arizona throughout the state at and above the desert border; southern Utah; Colorado; New Mexico; western Texas; northern Mexico. (Fig. 79 *3*.)

This variety is particularly abundant in the desert grassland in southern Arizona and New Mexico. Recent investigations have demonstrated that the plants are poisonous to cattle and horses, but livestock seldom eat them except in periods of prolonged drought or on badly overgrazed ranges.

2. *Senecio salignus* DC. JARILLA; WILLOW-LEAF GROUNDSEL. (1) Leaves entire, narrowly lanceolate, willowlike, firm; (2) involucral bracts about 8, rounded or obtuse at the apices, yellow-margined. (Pl. XXXIII *A*.)

Shrub about 0.5-1.5 m. high; stems several, erect; glabrous; leaves mostly 5-8 cm. long, the larger ones about 1 cm. broad; heads bell-shaped, about 1 cm. high, 8-10 mm. in diameter.

Deep, well-drained soils of flood plains and canyon bottoms in the desert grassland and the lower oak woodland at 4,000 to 5,500 feet elevation. Arizona in the mountains along the International Boundary in Santa Cruz and Cochise counties; Mexico; Guatemala.

The ill-scented flowers appear in early spring.

2. *LEPIDOSPARTUM*. Scale Broom

Small shrubs. Leaves alternate, simple, linear or scalelike, not glandular. Heads terminating long or short racemosely arranged branchlets. Involucral bracts (unlike most genera of the tribe) overlapping as shingles do, in 3-4 series. Ray flowers none. Disc flowers light yellow.

KEY TO THE SPECIES

1. Leaves of the mature branches scalelike, 1-2 or 3 mm. long; branchlets not markedly stirate; heads bell-shaped, 5-8 mm. high at flowering time; flowers about 10 or more; fruits glabrous; involucral bracts 1-2 mm. broad.   1. *Lepidospartum squamatum*

1. Leaves of the mature branches linear-filiform (threadlike), 1-5 cm. long; branchlets markedly angled; heads cylindroidal, 12-15 mm. long at flowering time; flowers about 4-6; fruits with dense, long, white, appressed hairs; involucral bracts about 3 mm. broad.
                                            2. *Lepidospartum latisquamum*

1. *Lepidospartum squamatum* A. Gray. SCALE BROOM. Scalelike leaflets of the mature branches about $^1/_{16}$ inch long.

Shrubs 1-2 m. high; branches not striate; leaves of the young, rapidly growing branchlets oblanceolate, 1 cm. or more in length, 1-3 mm. broad, densely woolly; heads terminating elongated scaly lateral branchlets or sometimes racemose or spicate along them, bell-shaped, 5-8 mm. long at flowering time; involucral bracts 1-2 mm. broad; disc flowers about 10-15; achenes glabrous.

Sandy washes and gravelly plains in the desert, the chaparral, and the grassland. California from Monterey to Kern County and to San Diego County and in the western parts of the Mojave and Colorado deserts; Baja California, Mexico. The species is especially abundant in the sand-dune area near San Gorgonia Pass. (Fig. 79 2.)

2. *Lepidospartum latisquamum* S. Wats. Elongated, threadlike leaflets about 1/2 inch to 2 inches long.

Shrubs 1-2 m. high; branches markedly angled; heads densely clustered in short racemes, cylindroidal, 12-15 mm. long at flowering time; involucral bracts about 3 mm. broad; disc flowers about 4-6; achenes densely hairy, the hairs white, appressed, long, obscuring the fruit.

Alluvial slopes and plains in the desert and the chaparral. California in the White and Inyo mountains and on the desert slopes of the San Gabriel Mountains; western Nevada in Esmeralda County and southern Nevada in the Charleston Mountains, Clark County.

3. *PEUCEPHYLLUM*

Shrubs; odoriferous; leaves alternate, simple, linear, bearing numerous dotlike glands. Heads solitary at the ends of leafy branches. Involucral bracts in 1-2 series, all of about the same length. Ray flowers none. Disc flowers pale yellow.

1. *Peucephyllum Schottii* A. Gray. PYGMY CEDAR

Shrubs 1-3 or 4 m. high; branchlets with a forked appearance, not angled, tannish, soon forming light gray bark; leaves abundant, crowded on the short terminal branchlets, linear, mostly 1.5-2 cm. long, less than 1 mm. broad; heads bell-shaped, some broadly so, about 10-13 mm. long, 10-12 mm. in diameter; involucral bracts linear, yellowish green, not membranous; flowers about 10-15; achenes densely clothed with rather short, white, appressed, shining hairs.

Rocky slopes and sandy or gravelly washes in the desert. California in the White and Inyo mountains and in the Mojave and Colorado deserts; southern Nevada in Clark County; western Arizona in the vicinity of the Colorado River from northern Mohave County to the Gila and Tule mountains in southern Yuma County; Baja California and Sonora, Mexico. (Fig. 79 *4*.)

The leaves are needlelike and they have a balsamic odor when they are crushed. The shrub is evergreen and it has some resemblance to a conifer.

4. *TETRADYMIA.* HORSE BRUSH

Low shrubs; usually woolly but the wool falling away early in some species; bark gray. Leaves alternate, linear, spinose-tipped. Heads in short, dense racemes at the ends of the branches or solitary or clustered in the axils; involucral bracts large, 4-6. Ray flowers none; disc flowers about 4-10, yellow.

KEY TO THE SPECIES

1. Leaves of the first season not specialized as rigid spines, merely with spinose tips, glabrous at maturity, 5-9 mm. long; flowers 4 in each head.
1. *Tetradymia glabrata*

1. Leaves of the first season rigid, forming spines, the body of the leaf sometimes flattened and more or less leaflike, however, and in this case densely woolly at maturity, mostly 2-5 cm. long; flowers 5-8 or more in each head.

    2. Leaves of the first season specialized as long spines but flat and leaflike, nearly linear, but gradually tapering, densely woolly; involucral bracts elliptic-oblong, flat, the margins not differentiated; achenes with long white hairs obscuring the pappus.
    2. *Tetradymia comosa*

    2. Leaves of the first season specialized as long spines, circular in cross section, tapering, not at all leaflike; involucral bracts flat or with the edges folded inward, narrowly oblong to nearly linear.

        3. Achenes with short, appressed hairs; heads in terminal cymose clusters; spines woolly at maturity; involucral bracts with the margins folded inward.
        3. *Tetradymia stenolepis*

        3. Achenes with long hairs surrounding and obscuring the pappus; heads solitary or in pairs on short branches in the leaf axils along the stem; spines bare at maturity; involucral bracts flat.
        4. *Tetradymia spinosa*

1. *Tetradymia glabrata* A. Gray. (1) Leaves of the first season very dense along the branches, not specialized as spines, merely with spinose tips, flattened, glabrous at maturity, ¼ to about ⅜ inch long (in the other species ¾ inch or more in length) ; (2) achenes with dense hair, the hairs overlapping the pappus and blending with it but not obscuring it.

Shrubs commonly less than 1 m. high; branchlets somewhat woolly at first but soon losing the wool except in the leaf axils; leaves linear, about 1 mm. broad, thick and slightly fleshy; heads in terminal clusters of small corymbs, top- to bell-shaped, about 12 mm. long, about 8 mm. in diameter; involucral bracts linear-oblong, about 7 mm. long, about 2 mm. broad, the margins thin; flowers 4.

Plains and slopes in the upper creosote-bush desert, the sagebrush desert, and the pinyon-juniper woodland. Eastern Oregon to Montana, Nevada, and Utah; California along the eastern slopes of the Sierra Nevada from Lassen County southward and along the western and southern edges of the Mojave Desert.

Ordinarily the plant is not palatable to livestock. In the spring months it may poison sheep provided they eat large quantities. The species is most abundant in the sagebrush desert of the Great Basin.

2. *Tetradymia comosa* A. Gray. (1) Leaves of the first season rigid and spine-tipped but flat and leaflike, linear, densely woolly; (2) achenes with long, conspicuous, white, ascending hairs; (3) heads in small terminal clusters.

Bushy shrubs usually less than 1 m. high; branches densely felted with short white wool; first leaves (spines) nearly linear, mostly 3-5 cm. long, 1.5-2.5 mm. broad, gradually tapering, soft when young; leaves of later seasons linear, short; heads corymbose, bell-shaped, 10-12 mm. long, about 10 mm. in diameter; involucral bracts elliptic-oblong, felted, 6-9 mm. long, 3-4 mm. broad, flat, the margins not differentiated; flowers about 6-8; hairs of the achene body long, white, obscuring the pappus.

Mesas and slopes in the chaparral and in the grassland and occasionally in the creosote-bush and sagebrush deserts. Southern California west of the mountain axis and in the western Mojave Desert from Owens Valley to the vicinity of Daggett and eastward to southern Nevada.

3. *Tetradymia stenolepis* Greene. MOJAVE HORSE BRUSH. (1) Leaves of the first season specialized as long spines, nearly circular in cross section, not at all leaflike, still woolly at maturity; (2) achenes with short appressed hairs.

Shrubs less than 1 m. high; bark gray; branches densely felted with short white wool; first leaves (spines) 2-3 cm. long, about 1 mm. in diameter, gradually tapering; heads in small terminal congested clusters, scarcely stalked, top-shaped, about 12 mm. long, mostly 7-8 mm. in diameter at the tops; involucral bracts narrow, the sides folded inward, 7-8 mm. long, about 2 mm. broad, only the extreme margins thin and translucent; flowers 5.

Mesas and slopes in the desert. California in the western Mojave Desert from Inyo County to the San Bernardino Mountains and in South Fork Valley, Kern County, and the Providence Mountains in the eastern Mojave Desert.

4. *Tetradymia spinosa* Hook. & Arn. COTTON THORN. (1) Leaves of the first season specialized as long, yellowish spines, nearly circular in cross section, not at all leaflike, glabrous at maturity; (2) achenes clothed with long hairs; (3) heads solitary or in pairs along the stem.

Shrubs mostly less than 1 m. high; branches densely felted with short white wool; first leaves (spines) 2-3 cm. long, about 1 mm. in diameter, gradually tapering, turning gray in later seasons; leaves of the second and later seasons lanceolate, 1.5-2 cm. long, 2-4 mm. broad; heads produced in the leaf axils along the stem, on somewhat leafy pedunculate branches 1-1.5 cm. long, bell-shaped, 1 cm. long, 1 cm. in diameter; involucral bracts narrowly oblong, about 6-8 mm. long, 2-3 mm. broad, densely woolly, flat, the narrow margins scarious (thin, translucent); flowers 5-7; achene with long white, conspicuous hairs from the body obscuring the pappus.

Plains and slopes in the sagebrush and creosote-bush deserts, the pinyon-juniper woodland, and the yellow pine forests. Eastern Oregon to Utah and Nevada; California on the eastern edge of the Sierra Nevada, in the western Mojave Desert, in South Fork Valley, Kern County, and in the Clark Mountains, San Bernardino County; Arizona southwest of Kingman, Mohave County. The long-spined form occurring in the Mojave Desert has been called var. *longispina* M. E. Jones.

Tribe 7. *HELIANTHEAE*. Sunflower Tribe

Herbs or a few plants shrubby or slightly so, juice not milky. Leaves alternate or opposite, commonly simple. Involucral bracts green or thickened, not thin and translucent, in 1 to several series. Ray flowers usually present, commonly yellow or white; disc flowers usually yellow, each one subtended by a chaffy bract (bract of the receptacle); pappus of scales or rigid awns or rarely cuplike; anthers not with accessory tails. (Pls. XXXIII B; XXXIV; Fig. 80.)

The outstanding diagnostic character of the group is the presence of a bract (specialized leaf) at the base of each disc flower. This may be detected usually but not always by pulling out the disc flowers, since the bracts are more securely fastened to the common receptacle and since they persist after removal of the flowers or after their natural disappearance at fruiting time. Nearly all the plants listed below are borderline cases in so far as woodiness is concerned, but the less woody ones are conspicuous in the desert flora for their showy flowers.

KEY TO THE GENERA

1. Ray flowers yellow or none; disc flowers producing fertile seeds.

   2. Pappus of rigid, awl-shaped (flat and tapering) awns or none, the awns when present not producing lateral hairs.

      3. Leaves alternate; achenes of the disc flowers strongly flattened.

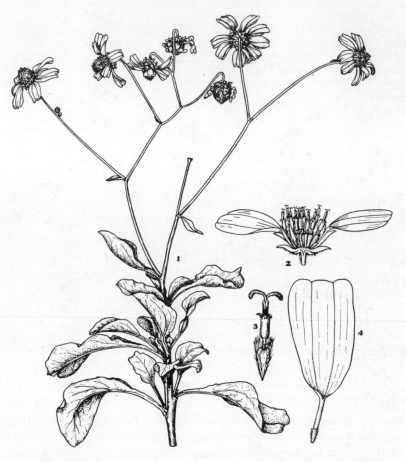

Fig. 80.—Brittle bush, *Encelia farinosa; 1,* branch with leaves and flowering and fruiting heads, *2,* longitudinal section of a head showing involucral bracts, ray flowers, and disc flowers, *3,* disc flower, *4,* ray flower. (*1* x $^1/_3$; *2* x $1^1/_3$; *3, 4* x $2^2/_3$.)

    4. Achenes with conspicuous hairs on the margins (ciliate); ray flowers present or absent. (Pl. XXXIV; Fig. 80.)   1. ENCELIA

    4. Achenes not with conspicuous hairs on the margins; ray flowers none.   2. FLUORENSIA

   3. Leaves (at least the lower ones) opposite; achenes of the disc flowers not strongly flattened, 4-angled, only slightly compressed at maturity (sometimes flattened in pressing of immature fruits).
                3. VIGUIERA

  2. Pappus of bristles bearing well-developed lateral hairs (plumose or featherlike).   4. BEBBIA

1. Ray flowers of our species white, sometimes tinged with lavender or purple; the corollas persistent on the achenes at fruiting time.

  2. Leaves opposite, in our species entire and linear; ray flowers conspicuous, the corollas large; disc flowers fertile, producing fertile achenes. (Pl. XXXIII *B*.)   5. ZINNIA

  2. Leaves alternate, in our species pinnately parted and ovate in outline; ray flowers inconspicuous, the corollas minute; disc flowers sterile, producing small, infertile achenes.   6. PARTHENIUM

1. *ENCELIA*

(1) Ray flowers yellow or sometimes none; (2) pappus of 2 rigid awns or none; (3) achenes or fruits strongly flattened, with conspicuous hairs along the margins; (4) leaves alternate. (Pl. XXXIV; Fig. 80.)

Herbs or shrubby or suffrutescent plants, the odor often pungent. Leaves simple and nearly entire. Ray flowers yellow or sometimes none, usually conspicuous when present, producing neither pollen nor fertile seeds; disc flowers yellow or purple.

KEY TO THE SPECIES

1. Heads produced in small, loose clusters on elongated leafless stalks, the individual peduncles glabrous.   1. *Encelia farinosa*

1. Heads solitary, the peduncles hairy.   2. *Encelia frutescens*

1. *Encelia farinosa* A. Gray. BRITTLE BUSH; INCIENSO. (1) Heads loosely clustered, on long naked branchlets; (2) leaves gray-green, densely hairy. (Pl. XXXIV; Fig. 80.)

Compact, scarcely woody, flat-topped bushes usually (exclusive of the projecting flowering stalks) 4-6 dm. high; leaves ovate-acute or broadly ovate-lanceolate, 2-5 cm. long, 1.5-2.5 cm. broad, whitened and densely covered with short, crooked hairs; stalks of the flower clusters leafless, arising in profusion from the compact leafy portion of the plant; heads hemispheroidal, about 1 cm. long, 2 cm. in diameter, the ray corollas large and conspicuous, 1-1.5 cm. long; disc flowers of some plants yellow, of others purple; pappus none.

Rocky or gravelly slopes and mesas in the desert and adjacent areas. California in the Mojave and Colorado deserts and in the interior valleys of coastal southern California (San Bernardino Valley, Lake Elsinore, western San Diego County); southern Nevada; southwestern Utah; Arizona throughout the deserts; Baja California and eastward in Mexico. (Fig. 82 *1*.)

Brittle bush is striking for its gray-green leaves and its bright yellow flower heads, and it is one of the most conspicuous shrubs on the desert mountains and hills. The brittle wood exudes a clear resin used by the Indians as glue, and in some parts of Mexico the resin is burned as incense in the churches. Hence the name "incienso."

2a. *Encelia frutescens* A. Gray var. *frutescens*. GREEN BRITTLE BUSH. (1) Heads solitary, on hairy peduncles; (2) leaves green, rough-hairy.

Low shrub or bush usually less than 1 m. tall; twigs white; leaves ovate or narrowly so, 1-3 cm. long, 8-15 mm. broad, roughened by stout, broad-based, stiff hairs, green, not flat (undulate), flower stalks numerous; heads hemispheroidal to broadly bell-shaped, 1-2 cm. in diameter at flowering time, enlarging sometimes to 2-3 cm. at fruiting, about 10-12 mm. long at flowering; ray flowers usually none, 12-15 mm. long when present; disc flowers yellow; pappus none.

Alluvial plains and slopes in the creosote-bush and sagebrush deserts. California on the west side of Walker Pass, Kern County, and in the Mojave and Colorado deserts; southern Nevada; southwestern Utah; Arizona throughout the deserts; probably northern Sonora, Mexico.

2b. *Encelia frutescens* A. Gray var. *actonii* (Elmer) Blake. ACTON BRITTLE BUSH

Leaves averaging larger, 2-3 cm. long, densely covered and whitened with short hairs, these with occasional appressed longer hairs among them, flat instead of wavy (i.e., not undulate); heads mostly 2-3 cm. in diameter, ray flowers present, usually 10-15, about 2 cm. long, conspicuous.

Mesas and slopes of the desert and adjacent regions. California west of the mountain axis of Southern California (Greenhorn Mountains, Kern County; Acton, Los Angeles County; San Jacinto; Palomar Mountains, San Diego County), in the Death Valley region, and in the western Mojave and Colorado deserts; western Nevada in Mineral, Esmeralda, and Nye counties. (Fig. 82 2.)

2. *FLOURENSIA*. Blackbrush; Tar Bush

(1) Ray flowers none; (2) pappus of 2 rigid awns, these unequal; (3) achenes compressed but rather thick, hairy but not more so along the margins than elsewhere; (4) leaves alternate.

Shrubs of low stature; resinous, the odor said to resemble that of hops. Leaves simple, entire. Disc flowers yellow.

1. *Flourensia cernua* DC. tar bush; black brush; hojase

Shrubs usually less than 1 m. high; leaves ovate or broadly ovate-lanceolate, 1.5-2.5 cm. long, 8-15 mm. broad, green, glabrous, scarcely petioled; heads on short leafy lateral branches and at the apex of each main branch, bell-shaped, 8-10 mm. long, 7-9 mm. in diameter; pappus awns nearly obscured by the long hairs of the body of the achene.

Mesas and slopes, often on limestone soils, in the desert and the desert grassland at 3,500 to 5,000 feet elevation. Arizona in the San Pedro, Sulphur Springs, and San Simon valleys in Cochise County; New Mexico in southern Grant County and Hidalgo County, in the Tularosa Basin, and on the Rio Grande and Pecos River drainages; western Texas; northern Mexico, particularly in Chihuahua. (Fig. 84 2.)

Tar bush is an indicator of the Chihuahuan Desert flora, and it occurs in isolated areas in southeastern Arizona. Here it is associated with a number of other species typical of the Chihuahuan Desert.

Leaves and flower heads are sold in the drug markets of northern Mexico as a remedy for indigestion.

3. *VIGUIERA*. Goldeneye

(1) Ray flowers yellow; (2) achenes of the disc flowers not flattened at maturity, 4-angled and only slightly compressed; (3) pappus of 2 awns and a few shorter scales or wanting; (4) leaves opposite or the upper ones alternate.

Herbs, suffrutescent plants, or small shrubs. Ray flowers of most species conspicuous, sterile, producing neither pollen nor fertile seeds; disc flowers yellow.

KEY TO THE SPECIES

1. Leaves pinnatifid with 3-7 narrowly linear divisions; pappus none; branches finely ridged and grooved. 1. *Viguiera stenoloba*

1. Leaves entire or toothed, triangular-ovate; pappus of bristles and smaller scales; branches not ridged and grooved. 2. *Viguiera deltoidea*

1. *Viguiera stenoloba* Blake. Leaves pinnatifid dissected into 3-7 narrow, elongated segments.

Shrub about 1 m. high; branches finely grooved and ridged, glabrous or clothed with rather dense short hairs; leaf divisions narrowly linear, mostly 2-6 cm. long, 1-4 mm. broad, green, with stiff appressed hairs particularly on the lower surface, these dense in the leaf axils; heads solitary on elongated peduncles; tending to be spheroidal, about 1 cm. in diameter; ray flowers about 10-12, 8-12 mm. long, not particularly conspicuous. Synonyms: *Heliomeris tenuifolia* A. Gray; *Gymnolomia tenuifolia* (A. Gray) Benth. & Hook.

Plains and slopes in the upper desert and the desert grassland. New Mexico in the mountains bordering the lower Rio Grande and the lower Pecos River drainages; western Texas; Mexico. (Fig. 82 5.)

2a. *Viguiera deltoidea* A. Gray var. *Parishii* (Greene) Vasey & Rose. Leaves entire or toothed, triangular-ovate.

Shrub or dense bush about 0.5 m. high, resembling *Encelia frutescens;* twigs and leaves with rigid, broad-based, rather short hairs; leaves 1-2 or 3 cm. long, 1-1.5 or 2 cm. broad, green, roughened and made harsh by the hairs; heads usually solitary but sometimes clustered on the elongated peduncles, about 1 cm. in diameter exclusive of the conspicuous ray flowers.

Rocky slopes and mesas in the desert at mostly 1,000 to 3,500 feet elevation. California in western San Diego County (San Luis Rey), in the Providence and Old Woman mountains in the eastern Mojave Desert, and the Colorado Desert; southern Nevada; Arizona in the southern Mojave, Colorado, and Arizona deserts as far eastward as Roosevelt Lake, Gila County; Baja California and Sonora, Mexico.

Virguiera reticulata S. Wats. is reported to be shrubby, but herbarium specimens do not indicate that it is. Plant with a striking resemblance to brittle bush, *Encelia farinosa,* 0.5-1 m. tall, probably shrubby only at the base if at all; branchlets and young leaves densely short-hairy (canescent) to satiny, the hairs white, the older branches and the lower sides of the leaves more or less glabrate; leaves ovate-attenuate or sometimes cordate, entire, the older ones strongly reticulate-veiny beneath, 2-5 or 6 cm. long, mostly 3-4 cm. broad, the petioles 1 cm. or less long; heads (exclusive of the ray flowers) 1-2 cm. in diameter; ray flowers about 6-9, with narrowly oblanceolate corollas, 1.5-2 cm. long; pappus of very short laciniate scales, practically wanting in the ray flowers. Rocky slopes and canyons in the desert. California in the Death Valley region and in northwestern San Bernardino County.

4. *BEBBIA.* Bebbia

(1) Stems elongated, scarcely woody, usually leafless; (2) ray flowers none; (3) pappus of bristles with well-developed branch hairs, therefore featherlike (plumose).

Bushy plants, the stems profusely branched. Leaves linear to linear-lanceolate. Heads solitary or few together. Involucral bracts in about 3 series. Disc flowers yellow.

1. *Bebbia juncea* (Benth.) Greene. BEBBIA

Bush up to about 1 m. high, often of greater diameter than height; stems not grooved, glabrous or with a few stout, usually appressed hairs; leaves few, linear or the larger ones linear-lanceolate, 1-4 cm. long, 1-3 or 4 mm. broad, glabrous or with stout, broad-based hairs; heads 1-2 cm. in diameter. Synonym: *Bebbia juncea* (Benth.) Greene var. *aspera* Greene.

Sandy washes and rocky slopes in the desert, the chaparral, and the grassland. California on the slopes and in the valleys of coastal southern California from San Bernardino southward and in the Mojave and Colorado deserts; southern Nevada in Clark County; Arizona in the Mojave Desert and eastward to the Grand Canyon region and in the Arizona and Colorado deserts; New Mexico in the Chihuahuan Desert (Organ Mountains); western Texas; Baja California and eastward in northern Mexico. Some authors have considered the desert form to be a separate variety *aspera.*

5. *ZINNIA.* Zinnia

(1) Ray flowers of our species white, conspicuous, large, persistent, becoming papery; (2) leaves opposite, in our species small, linear; (3) anthers not green. (Pl. XXXIII *B.*)

Herbs or sometimes suffrutescent plants or low bushes. Leaves simple and commonly entire. Heads solitary at the ends of branches; involucral bracts dry, of various lengths, overlapping as shingles do. Ray flowers (in the genus as a whole) yellow, white, red, or, in the magenta series, pistillate; achenes of the disc flowers compressed, fertile. Pappus of a few awns or scalelike teeth or none.

1. *Zinnia pumila* A. Gray. DESERT ZINNIA (Pl. XXXIII *B*)

Low bush 2-3 dm. high; stems woody at the bases; twigs and leaves with crooked or curled inconspicuous hairs; leaves linear, about 1 cm. long, 1 mm. broad; heads numerous and conspicuous, tending to be cylindroidal; ray flowers about 4-5, white, the corollas greatly expanded, nearly circular, 10-12 mm. long, about 10 mm. broad; disc flowers few.

Alluvial plains and slopes in the desert and the desert grassland at 2,000 to 5,000 feet elevation. Arizona from Yavapai County eastward in the Arizona Desert and the desert grassland; New Mexico in the desert grassland on the Gila River drainage and in the Chihuahuan Desert; western Texas; northern Mexico.

This attractive low shrub with persistent white flowers is abundant on caliche soils. It flowers profusely in the spring, and some flowers appear after the summer rains.

The yellow-flowered species *Zinnia grandiflora* Nutt. is equally conspicuous and attractive. The stems are scarcely if at all woody.

6. *PARTHENIUM*. GUAYULE

(1) Ray flowers white, the corollas very small and inconspicuous; (2) leaves alternate, parted, aromatic.

Shrubs or herbs; herbage gray with dense hair. Heads small, clustered, in our species the clusters flat-topped; ray flowers fertile; disc flowers sterile, not producing fertile achenes.

1. *Parthenium incanum* H. B. K. MARIOLA

Low, bushy shrubs usually about 4-6 dm. high; leaves ovate in outline, pinnately parted, the parts again lobed or toothed, 1-2 cm. long, about 1-1.5 cm. broad, gray; heads in small, dense clusters, the clusters in terminal flat-topped larger clusters.

Gravelly slopes and plains, usually on caliche soils, in the desert and the desert grassland at 2,500 to 5,000 feet elevation. Arizona in the Grand Canyon region, in the Hualpai Mountains, Mohave County, in the upper Verde River and Salt River drainages, and in eastern Pinal, eastern Pima, and Cochise counties; New Mexico in the Chihuahuan Desert and the adjacent desert grassland as far northward as Socorro County; western Texas; Mexico. (Fig. 82 *3*.)

Mariola is of interest as a relative of the Mexican rubber plant, guayule (*Parthenium argentatum* A. Gray). Mariola contains a small percentage of rubber, and this has been extracted commercially in Mexico. Guayule is native in the Big Bend region of western Texas and in the eastern half of the Mexican plateau, where it occurs on limestone soils. It does not occur in Arizona or New Mexico or in western Mexico. Some American enthusiasts have confused the brittle bush, *Encelia farinosa,* with guayule, and it is reported that natives of Sonora and Baja California use the name guayule for this plant, which contains only a trace of rubber, if any.

Tribe 8. *AMBROSIEAE*. Ragweed Tribe

(1) Staminate flowers in our genera, and most others, in ordinary heads with green, unspecialized involucral bracts, the flowers with corollas of the ordinary disc flower type, the pistillate heads below or distributed among the staminate, the involucral bracts highly specialized either as thin white wings below a single pistillate flower or as spines forming a bur (e.g., cocklebur) around 1 to several pistillate flowers, the pistillate flowers without other structures than the pistil or with the rudiment of a corolla; (2) stamens not united to one another by the anthers. (Figs. 81 *B, C*; 83.)

Herbs or shrubs. Leaves alternate or some of the lower ones opposite. Ray flowers none; disc flowers unisexual, the pistillate and staminate flowers on the same individual, in some genera in the same head but usually in different heads; staminate heads (or rarely heads of bisexual flowers) with a chaffy bract at the base of each flower; anthers not with tails; in our genera the pistillate involucre fused to the flowers.

The pollen of all of the genera is exceedingly light, and it is carried to the pistillate heads by the wind. The pollen is strongly toxic to individuals sensitized to it, and the ragweed tribe is one of the worst groups of hay-fever plants. The best-known ragweeds come into flower in accordance with the length of the day.

Consequently they bloom on a particular day every year in each given locality, and their victims' noses come into bloom at the same time. The true ragweeds of the genus *Ambrosia* are restricted to watercourses in the Southwestern deserts and for the most part they are at the higher elevations. Some of the shrubs of the genus *Franseria* are abundant on the mesas, bajadas, and hillsides, and many of them bloom in the springtime rather than in the summer as do the ragweeds. The shrubby franserias may be recognized by comparison with the figures in Fig. 83. There are a few herbaceous species in the desert as well.

KEY TO THE GENERA

1. Involucral bracts of the pistillate heads thin, silvery white, spreading below or enclosing the solitary pistillate flower; leaves threadlike or narrowly linear or pinnatifid with threadlike divisions. (Fig 81, *B, C.*)
1. HYMENOCLEA

1. Involucral bracts of the pistillate heads forming spines, the head becoming a bur in fruit, often resembling a cocklebur; the pistillate flowers 1-4; leaves of remarkably variable shape but never linear or threadlike or with threadlike divisions. (Fig. 83.)
2. FRANSERIA

1. *HYMENOCLEA.* Burro Brush

(1) Involucral bracts of the pistillate heads fused, the free portions thin, silvery white, spreading below or enclosing the single pistillate flower; (2) leaves very narrow and usually threadlike or with threadlike divisions. (Fig. 81 *B, C.*)

Shrubs, more or less bushy, the branches slender. Leaves alternate. Heads small, numerous, pistillate and staminate mingling in clusters along the branches or in terminal panicles, rarely tending to be restricted to different individuals. Staminate heads with several flowers, the involucral bracts united and forming a bowl; corolla not present.

KEY TO THE SPECIES

1. Terminal branchlets wandlike, elongated, produced from a wandlike main axis, leaves fewer, some of them (especially the lower ones) pinnatifid, the divisions threadlike; larger involucral bracts of the pistillate heads broadly fan-shaped to nearly circular or reniform, 2.5-8 mm. broad, in 1-4 series. (Fig. 81 *C.*)
1. *Hymenoclea Salsola*

1. Terminal branches short, the branching system more intricate, the divergence of the branchlets more pronounced; most of the leaves simple and threadlike, numerous, 2-5 cm, long, a few of the lower ones pinnatifid; involucral bracts of the pistillate heads narrowly wedge-

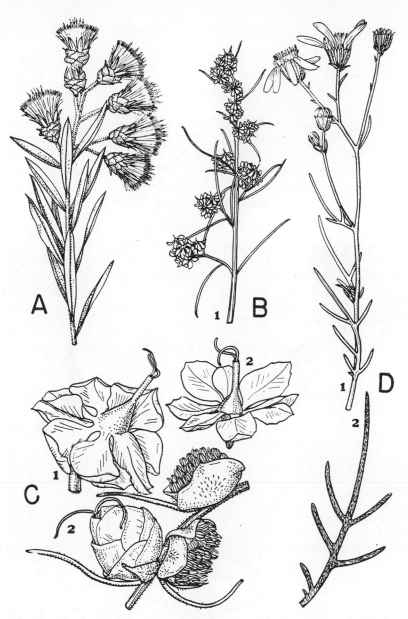

Fig. 81.—Arrow weed, burro brush, and groundsel: *A*, arrow weed, *Pluchea sericea*, flowering branch; *B*, burro brush, *Hymenoclea monogyra*, *1*, branch with pistillate heads, *2*, fruiting head; *C*, burro brush, *Hymenoclea Salsola*, *1*, fruiting head, *2*, staminate and pistillate heads in flower; *D*, thread-leaf groundsel, *Senecio Douglasii* var. *longilobus*, *1*, flowering branch, *2*, leaf. (*A*, *B* *1* x ²/₃; *B* *2* , *C* x 3¹/₃; *D* *1* x ¹/₃; *D* *2* x ²/₃.)

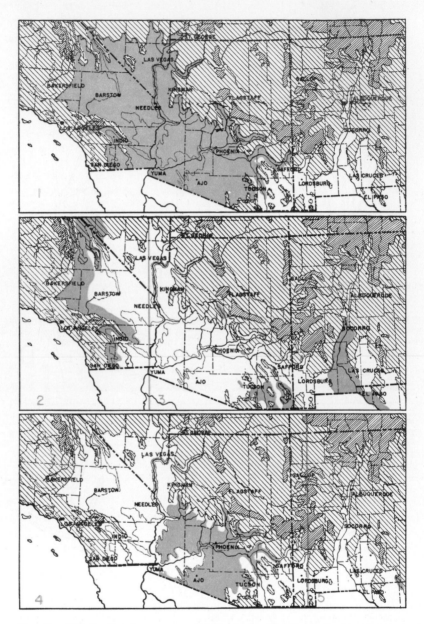

Fig. 82.—Distributional maps: *1*, brittle bush, *Encelia farinosa*; *2*, Acton brittle bush, *Encelia frutescens* var. *actonii*; *3*, mariola, *Parthenium incanum*; *4*, canyon ragweed, *Franseria ambrosioides*; *5*, *Viguiera stenoloba*.

shaped (cuneate) to obovate, 1-2 mm. broad, in a single series. (Fig. 81
B.)   2. *Hymenoclea monogyra*

1a. *Hymenoclea Salsola* Torr. & Gray var. *Salsola*. (1) Some
of the lower leaves pinnatifid; (2) involucral bracts of the pistillate heads broadly fan-shaped to nearly circular or reniform;
(3) flowering season in the spring. (Fig. 81 *C*.)

Shrubs commonly about 1 m. high; twigs light tan, the growing shoots
sparsely hairy; leaves few, mostly 1-4 cm. long, some pinnatifid and consisting of 3 or more threadlike divisions, the others entire and threadlike,
glabrous above, densely appressed-hairy beneath, the margins rolled downward and inward (revolute); heads in spikes or in small clusters along the
end of a branch, pistillate and staminate heads mingling or usually the
staminate tending to be above and the pistillate below; larger involucral
bracts of the pistillate heads about 12-18, in 3-4 series, overlapping as
shingles do, commonly 4-8 mm. broad.

Sandy washes, alluvial plains, and rocky slopes in the desert
and adjacent areas. California in scattered localities west of the
mountain axis (Cuyama Valley, San Luis Obispo County; Kern
County; near Banning, Riverside County), on the eastern side
of the Sierra Nevada in Inyo County, and in the Mojave and
Colorado deserts; western and southern Nevada from Mineral
County southward; southwestern Utah; Arizona in the Mojave
Desert and eastward to the Grand Canyon region and in the
Colorado and Arizona deserts in Mohave, Yuma, and western
Pima counties; Baja California and Sonora, Mexico.

Hymenoclea fasciculata A. Nels. is not well enough known
for thorough evaluation, but at best it seems to be merely a form
of *Hymenoclea Salsola*. It differs from the typical form as follows: involucral bracts of the pistillate heads remaining directed
upward as in the bud, not spreading out, the lower and larger
ones about 3-5 mm. broad. Both characters may be due to collection too early in the season.

1b. *Hymenoclea Salsola* Torr. & Gray var. *pentalepis* (Rydb.)
L. Benson

Involucral bracts of the pistillate heads 5-9, in 1 or 2 series, 2.5-4 mm.
broad.

Sandy or gravelly washes and plains in the desert. California
in the Colorado Desert (Chuckawalla Springs); Arizona in the

Colorado and Arizona deserts; Baja California and Sonora, Mexico. The variety *pentalepis* replaces the typical variety in most of the Arizona Desert.

This spring-flowering shrub is a hay-fever plant of considerable importance.

2. *Hymenoclea monogyra* Torr. & Gray. BURRO BRUSH. (1) Leaves all simple and threadlike, elongated; (2) involucral bracts $^1/_{25}$ to $^1/_{12}$ inch wide, in a single series; (3) flowering season in the autumn. (Fig. 81 *B*.)

Leaves 1-5 cm. long (averaging longer than in *Hymenoclea Salsola*), numerous; involucral bracts of the pistillate flowers in a single series, 7-12, 1-2 mm. broad, narrowly wedge-shaped (cuneate) to obovate.

Sandy washes in the desert and the desert grassland. California at Rialto, San Bernardino County, in Mission Valley, San Diego County, and along the immediate Colorado River drainage (Needles); Arizona in the Mojave Desert south of Kingman and in the Arizona Desert and the adjacent desert grassland; New Mexico on the Chihuahuan Desert and adjacent desert grassland northward as far as Socorro; western Texas; Baja California and northern Mexico. The plant is abundant on the principal drainages in the Arizona and Chihuahuan deserts. (Fig. 84 *3*.)

The species is of value in erosion control, but it is unpalatable to livestock.

2. *FRANSERIA*. BUR SAGE; WESTERN RAGWEED

(1) Involucral bracts of the staminate heads fused, spiny, the head becoming a bur in fruit, often resembling a cocklebur; (2) leaves of various shapes but never linear and threadlike or with threadlike divisions. (Fig. 83.)

Herbs or shrubs. Leaves all or mostly alternate. Heads in racemes or spikes, the staminate usually above and the pistillate below but in some species wholly or partly intermingling; staminate heads with the involucral bracts united, the involucre bowl- to top-shaped, the heads nodding; pistillate heads ellipsoid or ovoid, glandular, 1-4-flowered, the corollas none or vestigial, the stigmas protruding from involucral beaks enclosing them.

KEY TO THE SPECIES

1. Staminate heads in terminal spikes, the lower part of the panicle composed of short or sometimes elongated lateral spikes of pistillate heads,

Fig. 83.—Bur sages or western ragweeds, *Franseria: A,* canyon ragweed, *Fran-seria ambrosioides, 1,* leaf, *2,* branch with a terminal raceme of staminate heads and lateral racemes of pistillate cockleburlike heads, the lowest and longest apically staminate; *B,* bur sage or rabbit bush, *Franseria deltoidea, 1,* branch with an apical staminate raceme and two short lateral pistillate racemes; *2,* leaf; *C,* woolly bur sage, *Franseria eriocentra, 1,* terminal staminate heads and short lateral clusters of woolly pistillate heads, *2,* leaf; *D,* white bur sage, *Franseria dumosa, 1,* branch with intermingling staminate and pistillate heads, *2,* leaf; *E, Franseria cordifolia, 1,* branch with terminal staminate and lateral pistillate racemes, *2,* pistillate head in fruit; *F,* hollyleaf bur sage, *Franseria ilicifolia,* leafy branch with terminal staminate raceme and lateral pistillate racemes of cocklebur heads. *(A, F* x ¹⁄₈; *B-D, E 1* x ²⁄₃; *E 2* x 2.)

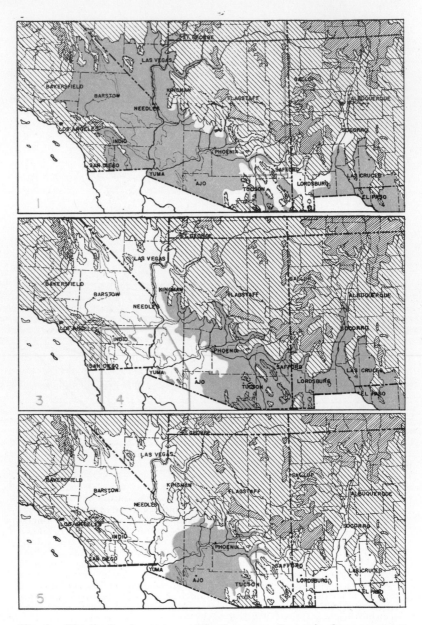

Fig. 84.—Distributional maps: *1*, white bur sage, *Franseria dumosa; 2*, tar bush, *Flourensia cernua; 3*, burro brush, *Hymenoclea monogyra; 4*, hollyleaf bur sage, *Franseria ilicifolia; 5*, bur sage, *Franseria deltoidea*.

these developing later than the terminal staminate spike, the longer ones sometimes terminated by a few staminate heads; leaves entire, toothed, lobed, or parted, these and the branches not completely obscured by short white hairs.

2. Pistillate heads 2-3-flowered, never obscured by dense long wool; thinly if at all hairy; leaves toothed, entire, or sometimes cordate and crenately lobed; spines of the fruiting heads hooked.

    3. Fruiting involucres resembling cockleburs, the spines slender, tapering, circular in cross section, the beaks enclosing the styles and stigmas separate, divergent, a pair of stigmas protruding from each of the 2, 3, or (?) rarely 4; free portions of the involucral bracts of the staminate heads sharp, acute.

        4. Leaves petioled, lanceolate or narrowly so, 5-12 cm. long, 1-3 cm. broad, saw-toothed (serrate), not spiny; pistillate flowers 3 in each head; staminate involucres about 7 mm. in diameter, the free portions of the bracts acute. (Fig. 83 *A*.)

                              1. *Franseria ambrosioides*

        4. Leaves not petioled, cordate-ovate, the bases clasping the stem, 3-9 cm. long, 2-6 cm. broad, strongly doubly dentate with spine-tipped teeth; pistillate flowers 2 in each head; staminate involucres about 10 mm. in diameter, the free portions of the bracts slender, spine-pointed. (Fig. 83 *F*.)

                              2. *Franseria ilicifolia*

    3. Fruiting involucres not strongly resembling cockleburs, the spines broad, flattened or thickened at the bases, the beaks enclosing the styles and stigmas fused, the 2 pairs of protruding stigmas side by side; free portions of the involucral bracts of the staminate heads low, broad, and rounded.

        4. Leaves narrowly triangular-ovate to lanceolate, finely toothed, the bases tapering into the petioles, the lower surfaces densely matted with short wool; bracts of the pistillate involucre strongly flattened in the normal plane of flattening of leaves, the beak of the involucre slender. (Fig. 83 *B*.)

                              3. *Franseria deltoidea*

        4. Leaves cordate or cordate-ovate, crenately lobed, the lobes few-toothed, the bases distinctly indented (cordate) in all but a few specimens, the lower surfaces with stiff, rather harsh hairs; bracts of the pistillate involucre strongly thickened at the bases, some of them flattened but in almost any plane, the beak of the involucre about as broad as long, at least not slender. (Fig. 83 *E*.)

                            4. *Franseria cordifolia*

2. Pistillate heads 1-flowered, partly obscured by dense long wool; leaves pinnately cleft or parted; spines of the fruiting heads not hooked. (Fig. 83 C.)   5. *Franseria eriocentra*

1. Staminate and pistillate heads intermingling in the terminal spike and in the short lateral spikes of the panicle; leaves pinnatifid and again lobed, these and the branchlets densely covered with short hairs, white, the green color completely obscured; spines of the fruiting heads not hooked. (Fig. 83 D.)   6. *Franseria dumosa*

1. *Franseria ambrosioides* Cav. CANYON RAGWEED. (1) Fruiting heads resembling cockleburs, with slender spines; (2) leaves elongated (lanceolate or narrowly so), mostly 2-5 inches long, mostly ½ to 1 inch broad, saw-toothed on the margins, not spiny, with stalks (petioles). (Fig. 83 A.)

Shrub about 1 m. high; branches reddish brown, with long, conspicuous but not dense, white hairs; leaves green above and below, with rather harsh hairs, the bases obtusely angled or truncate, veiny, the apices somewhat attenuate; staminate heads in a terminal spike or rarely a few terminating the longer lateral branches of the panicle, about 10 mm. in diameter, the involucres about 7 mm. in diameter, the free apical portions of bracts acute; fruiting heads in short lateral spikes of the panicle, ellipsoidal, about 10-13 mm. long, 3-flowered, the bracts slender, hooked, tapering, circular in cross section, each of the 3 styles and pairs of stigmas enclosed in a separate beak, the beaks divergent, the surface of the involucre with stalked glands, these not dense.

Sandy washes and rocky or gravelly canyon bottoms and slopes in the desert. California near San Diego; Arizona in southern Mohave County and in the Arizona Desert; Baja California and eastward in northern Mexico. Abundant in the desert mountains of central Arizona. (Fig. 82 4.)

Medicinal properties have been ascribed to the plant by the natives of Mexico. The shrub flowers during the spring, and it is an important hay-fever plant within the more or less restricted areas of its occurrence.

2. *Franseria ilicifolia* A. Gray. HOLLYLEAF BUR SAGE. (1) Fruiting heads resembling cockleburs, with slender spines; (2) leaves cordate-ovate, mostly 1½ to 3½ inches long, mostly 1-2 inches broad, with numerous spiny teeth, not stalked, the bases clasping the stem. (Fig. 83 F.)

Shrub 7-10 dm. high; branches thick, light tan or whitish, with rigid but inconspicuous hairs; leaves strongly doubly dentate with spine-tipped teeth, green on both surfaces, with short harsh hairs, strongly reticulate-veiny;

staminate heads in a terminal spike, about 12-13 mm. in diameter, the involucres about 10 mm. in diameter, the free apical portions of the bracts slender, spine-tipped; fruiting heads in short lateral spikes of the panicle, ellipsoidal, about 15 mm. long, the bracts slender, hooked, tapering, circular in cross section, each of the 2 styles and pairs of stigmas enclosed in a separate beak, the beaks divergent, the surface of the involucre rather covered with short gland-tipped hairs.

Sandy washes and canyon bottoms in the desert mountains from near sea level to about 1,200 feet elevation. California in the Colorado Desert (Signal Mountain and Maria and Chuckawalla mountains) ; Arizona in the mountains of southern Yuma County (Gila, Cabeza Prieta, Tule, Mohawk, and Castle Dome mountains) ; Baja California and probably northwestern Sonora, Mexico. A distinctive shrub of the arid ranges along the Colorado River. (Fig. 84 *4*.)

3. *Franseria deltoidea* Torr. BUR SAGE. (1) Fruiting heads somewhat resembling cockleburs but the spines all strongly flattened in the normal plane of leaves; (2) leaves narrowly triangular-ovate to lanceolate, finely toothed, the lower surfaces with densely matted short wool. (Fig. 83 *B*.)

Shrub about 3-6 dm. high, usually rounded or flat-topped; branches dark brown, ridged, strongly resinous, sticky, glabrous; leaves 2-3 cm. long 1-1.5 cm. broad, serrate or serrulate, dark green above, pale or white beneath, veiny, thick; staminate heads in terminal spikes, about 6-7 mm. in diameter, the free portions of the bracts short, rounded, much broader than long; fruiting heads in very short lateral spikes, crowded, about 5-7 mm. long and of equal diameter, the bracts very broad at the bases, tapering, hooked, the 2 styles and pairs of stigmas enclosed in the same (fused) beak, this slender, the surface of the involucre with minute stiped glands, these of only moderate density.

Alluvial plains and rocky or gravelly slopes in the desert; particularly abundant on bajadas. Arizona in the Arizona Desert and the adjacent Colorado Desert east of the Tule and Mohawk mountains, Yuma County; Sonora, Mexico. An abundant shrub in the palo verde-cactus vegetational type in the Arizona Desert, where it assumes the place of the white bur sage, *Franseria dumosa,* in the deserts of California. (Fig. 84 *5*.)

Bur sage or rabbit bush, as some call it, is one of the worst hay-fever plants of the early spring. It flowers in March and April.

4. *Franseria cordifolia* A. Gray. (1) Fruiting heads not strongly resembling cockleburs, the spines strongly thickened at the bases, some of them flattened but in almost any plane; (2) leaves cordate or cordate-ovate, crenately lobed, the lobes few-toothed. (Fig. 83 *E*.)

Semishrub up to about 1 m. high, some of the main branches more or less wandlike; twigs grayish or brownish, ridged, finely hairy at first; leaves mostly 2-4 cm. long, 1.5-3.5 cm, broad, green on both surfaces, the lower surface in particular with rather harsh hairs, veiny, of moderate thickness; staminate heads in a somewhat elongated terminal spike, appearing considerably before the pistillate heads, about 5 mm. in diameter, free portions of the involucral bracts low, rounded, much broader than long; fruiting heads in short lateral spikes, crowded, narrowly ellipsoidal in outline, 8-10 mm. long, the bracts relatively few, tapering upward from the thickened bases, hooked or curved at the apices, the surface of the involucre with minute stalked glands.

Rocky or gravelly slopes in the desert mountains at about 1,500 to 3,000 feet elevation. Arizona in the Mohawk, Ajo, Tucson, and Santa Catalina mountains, at Sycamore Canyon near Ruby, Santa Cruz County, and at Horse Mesa Dam, Maricopa County; northern Mexico.

5. *Franseria eriocentra* A. Gray. WOOLLY BUR SAGE. (1) Fruiting heads partly obscured by dense long woolly hairs; (2) leaves pinnately cleft or parted. (Fig. 83 *C*.)

Shrubs usually less than 1 m. high; twigs grayish or brownish, not ridged, with some very long and many, very short hairs; leaves mostly 2-3 cm. long, 8-13 mm. broad, green, white beneath, with some patches of short, crooked hairs above and a complete, dense cover beneath; staminate heads in short terminal spikes, appearing considerably before the pistillate heads, about 7-8 mm. in diameter, free portions of the involucral bracts a little longer than broad, acute, woolly; pistillate heads in short lateral spikes, congested, 8-9 mm. long, the bracts few, flattened in the normal plane of leaves, narrow, tapering, not curved or hooked at the apices, these and the body of the involucre with stalked glands and with conspicuous elongated woolly hairs.

Alluvial plains and slopes in the desert. California in the Providence and New York mountains in the Mojave Desert; southern Nevada in Clark and Lincoln counties; southwestern Utah; Arizona in the Mojave Desert and southeastward in the northern Arizona Desert to western Gila County.

6. *Franseria dumosa* A. Gray. WHITE BUR SAGE. (1) Staminate and pistillate heads intermingling both in the terminal spike and the lateral spikes of the panicle; (2) leaves bipinnatifid, these and the branchlets whitened by a dense cover of short hairs, the green color completely obscured. (Fig. 83 *D*.)

Low, bushy shrubs about 0.5 dm. high; leaves mostly 1.5-2 cm. long, 8-11 mm. broad, the divisions often narrow but not linear, of various shapes, staminate heads, 3-4 mm. in diameter, the free portions of the involucral bracts a little longer than broad, acute, woolly; fruiting heads 5-6 mm. long, rather resembling cockleburs but the spines broad and relatively thin at the bases, deeply grooved on the upper surfaces and ridged below, tapering, not hooked or curved at the apices, these and the involucre hairy or glabrous.

Mesas and alluvial slopes and plains in the desert at mostly 500 to 2,500 feet elevation. California in the Mohave and Colorado deserts; southern Nevada; southwestern Utah; Arizona in the Mojave, Colorado, and Arizona deserts as far eastward as Safford and Tucson; Baja California and eastward in Mexico. This is one of the most abundant shrubs in the deserts, and it is associated with the creosote bush over large areas. (Fig. 84 *1*.)

In California the plant is known sometimes as burroweed, as it provides forage for donkeys and cattle. As burroweed this species is not to be confused with *Haplopappus tenuisectus*.

APPENDIX

SCIENTIFIC SYNONYMS AND TYPE COLLECTIONS

ABUTILON (p. 266)

1. A. PRINGLEI Hochreutiner, Conserv. et Jard. Bot. Genève Ann. 6: 14. 1902. Tucson Mts., Ariz., *Pringle* in 1884.

ACACIA (p. 153)

1. A. GREGGII A. Gray, Pl. Wright. 1: 65. 1852. West of Patos, northern Mexico, *Gregg. A. Durandiana* Buckley, Proc. Acad. Phila. 1861: 453. 1861. Fort Belknap, Texas. *Senegalia Greggii* Britt. & Rose, N. Amer. Fl. 23: 110. 1928.

2. A. MILLEFOLIA S. Wats. Proc. Amer. Acad. 21: 427. 1886. Hacienda San Jose, southwestern Chihuahua, *Palmer 45* in 1885. *Senegalia millefolia* Britt. & Rose, N. Amer. Fl. 23: 111. 1928.

3a. A. ANGUSTISSIMA (Mill.) Kuntze var. HIRTA (Nutt.) Rob. Rhodora 10: 33. 1908. *A. hirta* Nutt. ex Torr. & Gray, Fl. N. Amer. 1: 404. 1840. Arkansas and Red rivers, *Nutall. A. suffrutescens* Rose, Contr. U.S. Nat. Herb. 12: 409. 1909. Santa Cruz Valley, Arizona, *Pringle* in 1881. *Acaciella hirta* Britt. & Rose, N. Amer. Fl. 23: 102. 1928. *Acaciella suffrutescens* Britt. & Rose, loc. cit. 103. *Acacia hirta* var. *suffrutescens* Kearney & Peebles, Jour. Wash. Acad. Sci. 29: 482. 1939. *Acacia angustissima* subsp. *suffrutescens* Wiggins, Contr. Dudley Herb. 3: 232. 1942.

3b. Var. CUSPIDATA (Schlecht.) L. Benson, Amer. Jour. Bot. 30: 238. 1943. *A. cuspidata* Schlecht. Linnaea 12: 573. 1838. Mexico, *Mühlenpfordt. A. texensis* Torr. & Gray, Fl. N. Amer. 1: 404. 1840. Texas, *Drummond.*

4a. A. CONSTRICTA Benth. ex A. Gray, Pl. Wright. 1: 66. 1852. Pass of the Limpia, Texas, *Wright 162* in 1851. *A. constricta* var. *paucispina* Woot. & Standl. Bull. Torrey Club. 36: 105. 1909. Animas Creek, Black Mountains, Sierra Co., N. Mex., *Metcalfe 1123. Acaciopsis constricta* Britt. & Rose, N. Amer. Fl. 23: 96. 1928. *Acaciopsis constricta* var. *paucispina* Moldenke, Rev. Sudam. Bot. 4: 15. 1937.

4b. Var. VERNICOSA (Standl.) L. Benson, Amer. Jour. Bot. 30: 238. 1943. *A. vernicosa* Standl. Contr. U.S. Nat. Herb. 20: 187. 1919. Santa Rosalía, Chihuahua, *Palmer 385* in 1908. *Acaciopsis vernicosa* Britt. & Rose, N. Amer. Fl. 23: 96. 1928.

5. A. FARNESIANA (L.) Humb. & Bonpl. ex Willd. in L. Sp. Pl. ed. 4. 4: 1083. 1806. *Mimosa Farnesiana* L. Sp. Pl. 521. 1753. San Domingo, *Farnes. A. acicularis* Willd. Enum. 1056. 1809. America meridionali. *Vachellia Farnesiana* Britt. & Rose, N. Amer. Fl. 23: 87. 1928.

391

ACALYPHA (p. 236)

1. A. PRINGLEI S. Wats. Proc. Amer. Acad. 20: 373. 1885. Ravines, shore of the Gulf of California, 150 miles south of the boundary, Sonora, *Pringle,* March 29, 1884.

ACAMPTOPAPPUS (p. 338)

1. A. SPHAEROCEPHALUS (Harv. & Gray) A. Gray, Proc. Amer. Acad. 8: 634. 1873. *Haplopappus Sphaerocephalus* Harv. & Gray in A. Gray, Mem. Amer. Acad. II. 4: 76. 1849. Calif., *Coulter.*

2. A. SHOCKLEYI A. Gray, Proc. Amer. Acad. 17: 208. 1882. Western Nevada, near Candelaria, Esmeralda Co., *Shockley.*

AGAVE (p. 76)

1. A. PARVIFLORA Torr. in Emory, Rept. U.S. & Mex. Bound. Surv. 214. 1859. Pimeria, Sonora, *Schott.*

2. A. TOUMEYANA Trel. in Bailey, Stand. Cyclop. Hort. 1: 238. 1914; in Standl. Contr. U.S. Nat. Herb. 23: 140. 1920. Pinal Mts., Arizona, *Toumey,* cf. Rept. Mo. Bot. Gard. 5: 164-5. *pl. 32.* 1894.

3a. A. SCHOTTII Engelm. Trans. St. Louis Acad. Sci. 3: 305. 1875. Sierra del Pajarito, west of Nogales, Arizona, *Schott. A. geminiflora* Gawl. var. *sonorae* Torr. in Emory, Rept. U.S. & Mex. Bound. Surv. 2: 214. 1859. Same type. *A. Schottii* var. *serrulata* Mulford, Rept. Mo. Bot. Gard. 7: 73. 1896. Rincon Mts., Pima Co., Arizona, *Toumey* in 1894. *A. Mulfordiana* Trel. in Standl. Contr. U.S. Nat. Herb. 23: 140. 1920. Nom. nov. for var. *serrulata.*

3b. Var. TRELEASEI (Toumey) Kearney & Peebles, Jour. Wash. Acad. Sci. 49: 474. 1939. *A. Treleasei* Toumey, Rept. Mo. Bot. Gard. 12: 75. 1901. Castle Rock, Santa Catalina Mts., Pima Co., Arizona, *Toumey* in 1896.

4. A. LECHEGUILLA Torr. in Emory, Bot. U.S. & Mex. Bound. Surv. 2: 213. 1859. Rio Grande at and below El Paso, Texas, *Wright 682* near Del Rio and along Devils River, in southern Val Verde County, Texas. *A. poselgeri* Salm-Dyck, Bonplandia 7: 92. 1859 (April). Probably near Saltillo or San Luis Potosi, Mexico, *Poselger.*

5. A. UTAHENSIS Engelm. in S. Wats. in King, Rept. U.S. Geol. Expl. 40th Par. 5: 497. 1871. St. George, Utah, *Palmer; J. E. Johnson. A. Newberryi* Engelm. Trans. St. Louis Acad. Sci. 3: 310. 1875. Peach Springs, Mohave Co., Arizona, *Newberry* in 1848. *A. utahensis* var. *nevadensis* Engelm. ex Greenm. & Roush, Ann. Mo. Bot. Gard. 16: 390. 1929. Ivanpah, Mojave Desert, Calif., *S. B. & W. F. Parish 418. A. scaphoidea* Greenm. & Roush, loc. cit. 391. St. George, Utah, *Palmer* in 1877. *A. utahensis* var. *scaphoidea* M. E. Jones, Contr. W. Bot. (17): 19. 1930. *A. utahensis* var. *discreta* M. E. Jones, loc. cit. Oatman, Mohave Co., Arizona, *M. E. Jones. A. eborospina* Hester, Cact. & Succ. Jour. 15: 131. 1943. Peek-a-boo Peak,

Sheep Range Mts., 35 miles northwest of Las Vegas, Nev., *Hester* in July, 1942, Dudley Herb. *285573*. *A. nevadensis* Hester, loc. cit. 133.

6a. A. PARRYI Engelm. Trans. St. Louis Acad. Sci. 3: 311. 1875. *Rothrock 274*. *A. americana* L. var. *latifolia* Torr. in Emory, Rept. U.S. & Mex. Bound. Surv. 2: 213. 1859. *A. applanata* Lemaire var. *Parryi* Mulford, Rept. Mo. Bot. Gard. 7: 83. *pls. 36-39*. 1896. *A. Couesii* Engelm. ex Trel. Rept. Mo. Bot. Gard. 22: 94. *pls. 94-97*. 1911. Fort Whipple, *Coues & Palmer 253*. *A. neomexicana* Woot. & Standl. Contr. U.S. Nat. Herb. 16: 115. *pl. 48*. 1913. Organ Mts., N. Mex., *Standley 541*. *A. Parryi* var. *Couesii* Kearney & Peebles, Jour. Wash. Acad. Sci. 29: 474. 1939.

6b. Var. HUACHUCENSIS (Baker) Little ex L. Benson, Amer. Jour. Bot. 30: 235. 1943. *A. huachucensis* Baker, Handb. Amaryll. 172. 1888. Huachuca Mts., Arizona, *Pringle*. *A. applanata* Lemaire var. *huachucensis* Mulford, Rept. Mo. Bot. Gard. 7: 85. 1896.

7. A. DESERTII Engelm. Trans. St. Louis Acad. Sci. 3: 310. 1875. Valcitron near San Felipe, Calif., *Emory* in 1846; Southern California, *G. N. Hitchcock, Palmer*. *A. consociata* Trel. Rept. Mo. Bot. Gard. 22: 53. 1911.

8. A. MURPHEYI F. Gibson, Contr. Boyce Thompson Inst. 7: 83. 1935. Superior, Arizona, *F. Gibson*.

9a. A. PALMERI Engelm. Trans. St. Louis Acad. Sci. 3: 319. 1875. Southern Arizona, *Schott* in 1855; *Palmer* in 1869; *Rothrock* in 1874.

9b. Var. CHRYSANTHA (Peebles) Little ex L. Benson, Amer. Jour. Bot. 30: 235. 1943. *A. chrysantha* Peebles, Proc. Biol. Soc. Wash. 48: 139. 1935. Queen Canyon, Pinal Mts., Arizona, *Peebles & Harrison 5543*.

ALLENROLFEA (p. 129)

1. A. OCCIDENTALIS (S. Wats.) Kuntze, Rev. Gen. et Sp. Pl. 2: 546. 1891. *Halostachys occidentalis* S. Wats. in King, Rept. U.S. Geol. Surv. 40th Par. 2: 293. 1871. Great Salt Lake, Carson and Humboldt rivers, *S. Watson*.

AMPHIPAPPUS (p. 337)

1. A. FREMONTII Torr. & Gray, Proc. Bost. Soc. Nat. Hist. 1: 211. 1845. Along the Mojave River, Calif., *Fremont. Amphiachyris Fremontii* A. Gray, Proc. Amer. Acad. 8: 633. 1873. *Amphiachyris Fremontii* var. *spinosa* A. Nels. Bot. Gaz. 47: 431. 1909. Moapa, Nev., *Goodding 2199*. *Amphipappus spinosa* A. Nels., Amer. Jour. Bot. 21: 579. 1934. Canyon of the Virgin River, Nev., *Goodding 707*. *Amphipappus Fremontii* var. *spinosa* C. L. Porter, Amer. Jour. Bot. 30: 483. 1943, based on var. *spinosa*.

ANISACANTHUS (p. 317)

1. A. THURBERI (Torr.) A. Gray, Syn. Fl. N. Amer. 2 (1): 328. 1878. *Drejera Thurberi* Torr. in Emory, Rept. U.S. & Mex. Bound. Surv. Bot. 2: 124. 1859. Las Animas, Sonora, *Thurber*.

APLOPAPPUS

See *Haplopappus*.

ARGYTHAMNIA (p. 233)

1a. **A. Brandegei** Millsp. var. **intonsa** Ingram, comb. nov. *D. Brandegei* (Millsp.) Rose & Standl. var. *intonsa* I. M. Johnston, Proc. Calif. Acad. Sci. IV. 12: 1062. 1924. Coronados Island, Gulf of California, *I. M. Johnston 3764*, May 18, 1921.

ASCLEPIAS (p. 283)

1. A. SUBULATA Dec. in DC. Prodr. 8: 571. 1844, not Larrañaga in 1923. Mexico, perhaps by Sessé and Mociño.

2. A. ALBICANS S. Wats. Proc. Amer. Acad. 24: 59. 1889. Los Angeles Bay, Baja Calif., *Palmer 588* in 1887.

ATAMISQUEA (p. 135)

1. A. EMARGINATA Miers, Trav. Chile 2: 529. 1826, nom. nud.; Miers ex Hook. & Arn. in Hook. Bot. Misc. 3: 143. 1833; Miers, Trans. Linn. Soc. 21: 1. *pl. 1*. 1855. Province of Mendoza, Chile, *Miers. Capparis Atamisquea* Kuntze, Rev. Gen. 3 (2): 6. 1898. Nom. nov. for *A. emarginata*.

ATRIPLEX (p. 118)

1a. A. CANESCENS (Pursh) Nutt. Gen. Pl. 1: 197. 1818. *Calligonum canescens* Pursh, Fl. Amer. Sept. 370. 1814. Big Bend, Missouri River, *Lewis*. *Obione canescens* Moq. Monogr. Chenop. 74. 1840. *O. occidentalis* (Torr.) Moq. var. *angustifolia* Torr. in Emory, Rept. U.S. & Mex. Bound. Surv. 2: 184. 1859. *A. canescens* var. *angustifolia* S. Wats. Proc. Amer. Acad. 9: 121. 1874. New Mexico, several collections. *A. angustior* Cockerell, Proc. Devenp. Acad. 9: 7. 1902. Based upon var. *angustifolia*.

A. canescens var. *laciniata* Parish in Jepson, Fl. Calif. 1: 442. 1914. Caleb, Calif., *Parish 8256*.

1b. Var. MACILENTA Jepson, Fl. Calif. 1: 442. 1914. Holtville, Calif., *Parish 8258*. *A. linearis* S. Wats. Proc. Amer. Acad. 24: 72. 1889. Guaymas, Sonora, *Palmer 120, 121, 235* in 1887. *A. canescens* subsp. *linearis* Hall in Hall & Clements, Carnegie Inst. Wash. Publ. (326): 344. 1923. *A. canescens* var. *linearis* Munz, Man. S. Calif. Bot. 141, 598. 1935.

1c. Var. GARRETTII (Rydb.) L. Benson, Amer. Jour. Bot. 30: 236. 1943. *A. Garrettii* Rydb. Bull. Torrey Club 39: 312. 1912. Moab, Utah, *Rydberg & Garrett 8465*. *A. canescens* subsp. *Garrettii* Hall in Hall & Clements, Carnegie Inst. Wash. Publ. (326): 344. 1923.

2a. A. LENTIFORMIS (Torr.) S. Wats. Proc. Amer. Acad. 9: 118. 1874. *Obione lentiformis* Torr. in Sitgreaves, Rept. Zuñi & Colo. 169. 1863. Colorado River in Calif.

2b. Var. GRIFFITHSII (Standl.) L. Benson, Amer. Jour. Bot. 30: 236. 1943. *A. Griffithsii* Standl. N. Amer. Fl. 21: 63. 1916. Willcox, Arizona, *Griffiths 1895. A. lentiformis* subsp. *Griffithsii* Hall in Hall & Clements, Carnegie Inst. Wash. Publ. (326): 336. 1923.

2c. Var. TORREYI (S. Wats.) McMinn, Ill. Man. Calif. Shrubs 113. 1939. *Obione Torreyi* S. Wats. in King, Rept. U.S. Geol. Surv. 40th Par. 5: 290. 1871. Truckee and Carson rivers, Nevada, *Torrey 463, 984, S. Watson. A. Torreyi* S. Wats. Proc. Amer. Acad. 9: 119. 1874. *A. lentiformis* subsp. *Torreyi* Hall in Hall & Clements, Carnegie Inst. Wash. Publ. (326): 336. 1923.

3. A. CONFERTIFOLIA (Torr. & Frem.) S. Wats. Proc. Amer. Acad. 9: 119. 1874. *Obione confertifolia* Torr. & Frem. in Frem. Rept. Ore. & Calif. 318. 1845. South of Ogden, Utah, *Fremont. A. collina* Woot. & Standl. Contr. U.S. Nat. Herb. 16: 119. 1913. Carrizo Mts., N. Mex. *Standley 7481.*

4. A. SPINIFERA Macbr. Contr. Gray Herb. (53): 11. 1918. Maricopa Hills, Kern Co., Calif. *Eastwood 3269. Obione spinifera* Ulbrich in Engler & Prantl, Natur. Pflanzenf. ed. 2. 16C: 508, 1934.

5. A. PARRYI S. Wats. Proc. Amer. Acad. 17: 378. 1882. Lancaster, Calif., *Parry. Obione Parryi* Ulbrich in Engler & Prantl, Natur. Pflanzenf. ed. 2. 16C: 508. 1934.

6. A. HYMENELYTRA (Torr.) S. Wats. Proc. Amer. Acad. 9: 119. 1874. *Obione hymenelytra* Torr. Pac. R. R. Rept. 4: 129. 1857. Bill Williams River, Arizona, *Whipple Exped.*

7. A. POLYCARPA (Torr.) S. Wats. Pro. Amer. Acad. 9: 117. 1874. *Obione polycarpa* Torr. Pac. R. R. Rept. 4: 130. 1857. Bill Williams River, Arizona, *Whipple Exped.*

BACCHARIS (p. 354)

1. B. GLUTINOSA Pers. Syn. Pl. 425. 1807. Chile.

2. B. VIMINEA DC. Prodr. 5: 400. 1836. Calif. *Douglas.*

3. B. BRACHYPHYLLA A. Gray. Pl. Wright. 2: 83. 1853. "Between Conde's Camp and the Chiricahui Mountains. . . . " *Wright 1199.* Chiricahua Mts., Cochise Co., Ariz.

4. B. PTERONOIDES DC. Prodr. 5: 410. 1836. "In Mexico inter Tampico et Real Del Monte . . . Berlandier. . . ." *Haplopappus ramulosus* DC. loc. cit. 350. "In Mexico ad Tlapujahua legit et Keerl. . . ." Placed in synonymy under *B. pteronoides* by A. Gray, Proc. Amer. Acad. 17: 212. 1882. *Linosyris ramulosa* A. Gray, Pl. Wright. 2: 80. 1853. *B. ramulosa* A. Gray, Mem. Amer. Acad. II. 5: 301. 1854.

5. B. SERGILLOIDES A. Gray in Torr. in Emory, Rept. U.S. & Mex. Bound. Surv. 2: 83. 1859. Along the Gila or Colorado, *Emory* in 1846; 50 miles west of the Colorado, *Bigelow;* Southern Calif., *LeConte.*

6. B. SAROTHROIDES A. Gray, Proc. Amer. Acad. 17: 211. 1882. "Near the old Mission station, the boundary monument, &c. . . .," San Diego Co., Calif., *Hayes, Palmer. B. arizonica* Eastw. Proc. Calif. Acad. IV. 20: 155. 1931. Packard, Gila Co., Ariz., *Eastwood 15832, 15833.*

7. B. EMORYI A. Gray in Torr. in Emory, Rept. U.S. & Mex. Bound. Surv. 2: 83. 1859. Gila River, Ariz., *Emory* in 1846; Ft. Yuma, Calif., *Thomas.*

BEBBIA (p. 375)

1. B. JUNCEA (Benth.) Greene, Bull. Calif. Acad. 1: 180. 1885. *Carphephorus junceus* Benth. Bot. Voy. Sulph. 21. 1844. Magdalena Bay, Baja Calif., *Hinds. B. juncea* var. *aspera* Greene, loc. cit. "Southeastern borders of California, and adjacent Arizona." *B. aspera* A. Nels. Bot. Gaz. 37: 273. 1904.

BELOPERONE (p. 318)

1. B. CALIFORNICA Benth. Bot. Voy. Sulph. 38. 1844. Cape Lucas, Baja Calif. *B. californica* var. *conferta* Brandegee, Proc. Calif. Acad. II. 2: 194. 1889. San Julio Canyon, Baja Calif.

BERBERIS (p. 131)

1. B. HARRISONIANA Kearney & Peebles, Jour. Wash. Acad. Sci. 29: 477. 1939. Kofa Mts., Arizona, *Peebles & Loomis 6768.*

2. B. TRIFOLIOLATA Moric. Pl. Amer. Rar. 113. *pl. 69.* 1841. Between Laredo and Bejar, Mexico. *B. trifoliata* Hartw. ex Lindl. Bot. Reg. 27: misc. 149. 1841; 31: *pl. 10.* 1845. Between Zacatecas and San Luis Potosi, Mexico, *Hartweg. Mahonia trifoliata* Lav. Arb. Segrez. 16. 1877. *M. trifoliolata* Fedde in Engler, Bot. Jahrb. 31: 96. 1901. *Odostemon trifoliolatus* Heller, Muhlenbergia 7: 139. 1912.

3a. B. NEVINII A. Gray var. HAEMATOCARPA (Woot.) L. Benson, Amer. Jour. Bot. 30: 236. 1943. *B. haematocarpa* Woot. Bull. Torrey Club. 25: 304. 1898. Mescalero Agency, N. Mex. *Mahonia haematocarpa* Fedde in Engler, Bot. Jahrb. 31: 100. 1901. *Odostemon haematocarpus* Heller, Muhlenbergia 7: 139. 1912.

B. FREMONTII Torr. in Emory, Rept. U.S. & Mex. Bound. Surv. 2: 30. 1859. Virgin River, Utah, *Fremont. Mahonia Fremontii* Fedde in Engl. Bot. Jahrb. 31: 89. 1901. *Odostemon Fremontii* Rydb. Bull. Torrey Club. 33: 141. 1906.

BERNARDIA (p. 234)

1. B. INCANA Morton, Jour. Wash. Acad. Sci. 29: 376. 1939. Sierra Tucson, Pima County, Arizona, *Pringle,* April 21, 1884.

BRICKELLIA (p. 325)

1. B. INCANA A. Gray, Proc. Amer. Acad. 7: 350. 1868. Providence Mountains, Mojave Desert, Calif., *Cooper* in 1861. *Coleosanthus incanus* Kuntze, Rev. Gen. 1: 328. 1891.

2a. B. ATRACTYLOIDES A. Gray, Proc. Amer. Acad. 8: 290. 1870. Utah near the Colorado River, *Palmer. Coleosanthus atractyloides* Kuntze, Rev. Gen. 1: 328. 1891. *C. venulosus* A. Nels. Bot. Gaz. 37: 262. 1904. "The Pockets," southern Nev., *Goodding 678.*

2b. Var. ARGUTA (Rob.) Jepson, Man. Fl. Pl. Calif. 1016. 1925. *B. arguta* Rob. Mem. Gray Herb. 1: 102. 1917. Calif., no type designated, several specimens cited. *B. arguta* var. *odontolepis* Rob., loc. cit. 103. Type not designated; based on Colorado Desert, Calif., *Orcutt* in 1889, Gray Herb., and *Brandegee,* N. Y. Bot. Gard. *B. atractyloides* var. *odontolepis* Jepson, loc. cit.

3. B. FRUTESCENS A. Gray, Proc. Amer. Acad. 17: 207. 1882. Cantillas Canyon, northern edge of Baja Calif., *Palmer* in 1875. *Coleosanthus frutescens* Kuntze, Rev. Gen. 1: 328. 1891.

4a. B. DESERTORIUM Cov. Proc. Biol. Soc. Wash. 7: 68. 1892. Between Banning and Seven Palms, Colorado Desert, Calif. *Orcutt. B. californica* var. *desertorum* Parish ex H. M. Hall, Univ. Calif. Publ. Bot. 3: 33. 1907.

5. B. BACCHARIDEA A. Gray, Pl. Wright. (Smiths. Contr. Knowl. vol. 3) 1: 87. 1852. Mountains near El Paso, Tex., *Wright. Coleosanthus baccharideus* Kuntze, Rev. Gen. 1: 328. 1891.

6. B. LACINIATA A. Gray, Pl. Wright. (Smiths. Contr. Knowl. vol. 3) 1: 87. 1852. Mountain valley 40 miles east of El Paso, Tex., *Wright.* Lectotype designated by Woot. & Standl., Contr. U.S. Nat. Herb. 19: 652. 1915. *Coleosanthus laciniatus* Kuntze, Rev. Gen. 1: 328. 1891.

7. B. COULTERI A. Gray, Pl. Wright. 1: 86. 1852. Calif., *Coulter* (Hooker's Herbarium). *Coleosanthus Coulteri* Kuntze, Rev. Gen. 1: 328. 1891.

B. KNAPPIANA Drew, Pittonia 1: 260. 1888. Mojave River, California, *Knapp.*

BUDDLEJA (p. 280)

1. B. SESSILIFLORA H. B. K. Nov. Gen. et Sp. Pl. 2: 345 (quarto), 278 (folio). *pl. 182.* 1817. City of Mexico. *B. verticillata* H. B. K. loc. cit. 346 (quarto), 278 (folio). *pl. 184.* Between Acaguisotla and Chilpancingo, Mexico. *B. pseudoverticillata* Mart. and Gal. Bull. Acad. Brux. 12 (2): 24. 1845. Mexico, *Galleotti. B. Pringlei* A. Gray, Proc. Amer. Acad. 19: 86. 1893. Tucson, Arizona, *Pringle* in 1883. *B. simplex* Kränzlein, Ann. Naturhist. Hofmus. Wien 26: 396. 1912. Saltillo, Mexico, *Berlandier 1372.*

2. B. UTAHENSIS Cov. Proc. Biol. Soc. Wash. 7: 69. 1892. St. George, Utah, *Palmer* in 1877.

BUMELIA (p. 271)

1a. B. LANUGINOSA (Michx.) Pers. var. RIGIDA A. Gray, Syn. Fl. N. Amer. 2 (1): 68. 1886. S. Texas, *Wright, Palmer* to S. Ariz., *Pringle, Lemmon. B. rigida* Small, Bull. N. Y. Bot. Gard. 1: 444. 1900.

BURSERA (p. 225)

1. B. MICROPHYLLA A. Gray, Proc. Amer. Acad. 5: 155. 1861. Sierras Tulè, Sonora, *Schott. Terebinthus microphylla* Rose, Contr. U.S. Nat. Herb. 10: 120. 1906. *Elaphrium microphyllum* Rose, N. Amer. Fl. 25: 250. 1911.

2. B. FAGAROIDES (H. B. K.) Engler in DC. Monogr. Phan. 4: 48. 1883. *Elaphrium fagaroides* H. B. K. Nov. Gen. et Sp. 7: 29. 1825. *B. odorata* Brandegee, Proc. Calif. Acad. II. 2: 138. 1889. San Gregorio, Baja Calif., *Brandegee. Terebinthus odorata* Rose, Contr. U.S. Nat. Herb. 10: 121. 1906. *Elephrium odoratum* Rose, N. Amer. Fl. 25: 250. 1889.

CAESALPINIA (p. 180)

1. C. GILLIESII (Hook.) Wallich ex Hook. Bot. Misc. 1: 129. 1829. *Poinciana Gilliesii* Hook. loc. cit. Rio Quarto, Rio Quinto, La Punta de San Luis, and Mendoza, Americae meridionalis, *Gillies. Erythrostemon Gilliesii* Link, Klotsch & Otto, Icon. Pl. 97. 1841.

CALLIANDRA (p. 162)

1. C. ERIOPHYLLA Benth. in Hook. Lond. Jour. Bot. 3: 105. 1844. Chila, Puebla, *Andrieux 405. C. Chamedrys* Engelm. ex A. Gray, Mem. Amer. Acad. II. 4: 39. 1849. Bachimba, *Wislizenius;* Ojito Cañon, *Gregg. C. conferta* Benth. ex A. Gray, Pl. Wright. 1: 63. 1852. Head of San Felipe River, Zacate Creek, and Rio Grande, Texas, *Wright. Feuilleea texana* Kuntze, Rev. Gen. 1: 187. 1891. Nom. nov. for *C. conferta. F. eriophylla* Kuntze, loc. cit. *Anneslia eriophylla* Britt. Trans. N. Y. Acad. Sci. 14: 23. 1894.

2. C. SCHOTTII Torr. ex S. Wats. Proc. Amer. Acad. 20: 364. 1885. "Arroyo de los Samotas, Sierra Verde, Sonora," *Schott. Anneslia Schottii* Britt. & Rose, N. Amer. Fl. 23: 67. 1928.

CANOTIA (p. 252)

1. C. HOLACANTHA Torr. Pac. R. R. Rept. 4: 68. 1856. Bill Williams River, Ariz., *Bigelow* in 1854.

CASSIA (p. 188)

1. C. WISLIZENII A. Gray, Pl. Wright. 1: 60. 1852. Carrizal and Ojo Caliente, Chihuahua, *Wislizenius. Palmerocassia Wislizenii* Britt. N. Amer. Fl. 23: 254. 1930.

2. C. ARMATA S. Wats. Proc. Amer. Acad. 11: 136. 1876. Fort Mojave to Cajon Pass, Calif., *Cooper;* western Arizona, *Wheeler, Xerocassia armata* Britt. & Rose. N. Amer. Fl. 23: 246. 1930.

CELTIS (p. 114)

1a. C. LAEVIGATA Willd. var. RETICULATA (Torr.) L. Benson, Amer. Jour. Bot. 30: 235. 1943. *C. reticulata* Torr. Ann. Lyc. N. Y. 2: 247. 1824. Base of the Rocky Mountains, *Long Exped. C. Douglasii* Planch. Ann. Sci.

Nat. III. 10: 293. 1848. Columbia River, *Douglas. C. brevipes* S. Wats. Proc. Amer. Acad. 14: 297. 1879. Camp Grant, Arizona, *Rothrock. C. mississipiensis* Bosc. var. *reticulata* Sarg. Silva N. Amer. 7: 72. *pl. 319.* 1895. *C. laevigata* Willd. var. *brevipes* Sarg. Bot. Gaz. 67: 226. 1919.

2a. C. TALA Gillies var. PALLIDA (Torr.) Planch. in DC. Prodr. 17: 191. 1873. *C. pallida* Torr. in Emory, Rept. U.S. & Mex. Bound. Surv. 2: 203. 1859. Rio Grande, Texas, to Magdalena, Sonora, *Wright 1858; Berlandier 3021. Momisia pallida* Torr. ex Planch. loc. cit., as syn., nom. nud.

CEPHALANTHUS (p. 319)

1a. C. OCCIDENTALIS L. var. CALIFORNICUS Benth. Pl. Hartw. 314. 1848. Sacramento Valley, Calif., *Hartweg 1765(414). C. Hansenii* Wernh. Jour. Bot. Brit. & For. 55: 176. 1917. Crow Point, Amador Co., Calif., *Hansen 1163;* San Diego Canyon, Sierra Madre, Chih., *M. E. Jones.*

CERCIDIUM (p. 183)

1. C. FLORIDUM Benth. ex A. Gray, Pl. Wright. 1: 58. 1852. Sonora Alta near Hermosillo, *Coulter* in 1830, cf. L. Benson, Amer. Jour. Bot. 27; 186-7. 1940. *Parkinsonia florida* S. Wats. Proc. Amer. Acad. 11: 135. 1876. *P. Torreyana* S. Wats. loc. cit. Colorado Desert, Calif., *Williamson;* Fort Yuma, *Thomas & Du Barry. C. Torreyanum* Sarg. Gard. & For. 2: 388. 1889.

2. C. MICROPHYLLUM (Torr.) Rose & Johnston in Johnston, Contr. Gray Herb. II. (70): 66. 1924. *Parkinsonia microphylla* Torr. Pac. R. R. Rept. 4: 82. 1857. Fort Yuma, Calif., *Schott. Cercidiopsis microphylla* Britt. & Rose, N. Amer. Fl. 23: 306. 1930.

CERCIS (p. 191)

C. OCCIDENTALIS Torr. ex A. Gray, Bost. Jour. Nat. Hist. 6: 177. 1850. Upper Guadalupe River, Texas, *Lindheimer. C. californica* Torr. ex Benth. Pl. Hartw. 361. 1857. ". . . in montibus Sacramento," Calif., *Hartweg. Siliquastrum occidentale* Greene, Man. Bay Reg. Bot. 84. 1894. *C. nephrophylla* Greene, in Fedde, Repert. Sp. Nov. 11: 111. 1912. San Diego Co., Calif., *Palmer, Vasey. C. orbiculata* Greene, loc. cit. Diamond Valley, southern Utah, *Goodding* in 1902. *C. latissima* Greene, loc. cit. Calif., G. B. Grant. *C. arizonica* Patraw, Dept. Interior, U.S. Park Service, Tech. Bull. 6: 23. 1932, nom. nud; Rose ex N. N. Dodge, Grand Canyon Nat. Hist. Assn. Nat. Hist. Bull. (3): 56. 2 *photographs.* 1936, nom. nud. (no Latin diagnosis). Grand Canyon. *C. occidentalis* var. *orbiculata* Tidestrom in Tidestrom & Kittell, Fl. Ariz. & N. Mex. 155. 1941.

CHILOPSIS (p. 311)

1a. C. LINEARIS (Cav.) Sweet, Hort. Brit. ed. 1. 283. 1827. *Bignonia linearis* Cav. Icon. Pl. 3: 35. *pl. 269.* 1794. Type not known. *C. saligna* D. Don. Edinb. Phil. Jour. 9: no. 18, 261, 1823. *C. linearis* var. *originaria* Fosberg, Madroño 3: 365. 1936.

1b. Var. ARCUATA Fosberg, Madroño 3: 366. 1936. Mission Creek, San Bernardino Mts., Calif., *Fosberg 8600.*

1c. Var. GLUTINOSA (Engelm.) Fosberg, Madroño 3: 365. 1936. *C. glutinosa* Engelm. in Wisliz. Mem. Tour N. Mex. 94. 1848. New Mexico and Chihuahua.

CHOISYA (p. 223)

1a. C. DUMOSA (Torr.) A. Gray, Proc. Amer. Acad. 23: 224. 1888. *Atsrophyllum dumosum* Torr. Pac. R. R. Rept. 2 (2): 161. 1854. Organ Mts., N. Mex. *Pope.*

1b. Var. ARIZONICA (Standl.) L. Benson, Amer. Jour. Bot. 30: 239. 1943. *C. arizonica* Standl. Proc. Biol. Soc. Wash. 27: 222. 1914. Santa Rita Mts., Ariz., *Pringle* in 1884.

Var. MOLLIS (Standl.) L. Benson, Amer. Jour. Bot. 30: 630. 1943. *C. mollis* Standl. Proc. Biol. Soc. Wash. 27: 223. 1914. Sierra del Pajarito, Sonora (west of Nogales).

CHRYSOTHAMNUS (p. 346)

1. C. PANICULATUS (A. Gray) H. M. Hall, Univ. Calif. Publ. Bot. 3: 58. 1907. *Linosyris viscidiflora* (Nutt.) Torr & Gray var. *paniculata* A. Gray in Torr. in Emory, Rept. U.S. & Mex. Bound. Surv. 2: 80. 1859. California, *Schott. Bigelovia paniculata* A. Gray, Proc. Amer. Acad. 8: 644. 1873. *Aster Asae* Kuntze, Rev. Gen. 1: 315. 1891. *Chrysoma paniculata* Greene, Erythea 3: 12. 1895. *Ericameria paniculata* Rydb. Fl. Rocky Mts., & Adj. Plains 853. 1917.

2. C. TERETIFOLIUS (Dur. & Hilg.) H. M. Hall, Univ. Calif. Publ. Bot. 3: 57. 1907. *Linosyris teretifolia* Dur. & Hilg. Jour. Acad. Nat. Sci. Phila. II. 3: 41. 1855; Pac. R. R. Rept. 5 (3): 9. *pl. 7.* 1856. "All over the mountains around Tejon valley; September." (Pac. R. R. Rept.) *Aster Durandii* Kuntze, Rev. Gen. 1: 316. 1891.

3. C. PULCHELLUS (A. Gray) Greene, Erythea 3: 107. 1895. *Linosyris pulchella* A. Gray; Pl. Wright. 1: 96. 1852. No type designated. *Wright. Bigelovia pulchella* A. Gray, Proc. Amer. Acad. 8: 643. 1873. Here, "New Mexico, near the Rio Grande, etc." *Aster formosus* Kuntze, Rev. Gen. 1: 316. 1891. *C. Baileyi* Woot. & Standl. Contr. U.S. Nat. Herb. 16: 181. 1913. Guadaloupe Mts., N. Mex., *V. Bailey 498.* Possibly of varietal status. *C. pulchellus* subsp. *typicus* H. M. Hall, Carnegie Inst. Wash. Publ. (389): 194. 1928. *C. pulchellus* subsp. *Baileyi* H. M. Hall, loc. cit. *C. pulchellus* var. *Baileyi* Blake, Jour. Wash. Acad. 30: 467. 1940.

Subsp. ELATIOR (Standl.) H. M. Hall, loc. cit. *C. elatior* Standl. Proc. Biol. Soc. Wash. 26: 118. 1913. Goldenbergs, San Andreas Mts., N. Mex., *Wooton* in 1912.

4a. C. NAUSEOSUS (Pall.) Britt. var. GNAPHALODES (Greene) H. M. Hall, Univ. Calif. Publ. Bot. 7: 167. 1919. *C. speciosus* Nutt. var. *gnaphalodes*

Greene, Erythea 3: 110. 1895. Pyramid Lake, Nev., *Curran. C. gnaphalodes* Greene, Pittonia 4: 42. 1899. *C. nauseosus* subsp. *gnaphalodes* H. M. Hall, Carnegie Inst. Wash. Publ. (326): 211, 221. 1923.

4b. Var. HOLOLEUCUS (A. Gray) H. M. Hall, Univ. Calif. Publ. Bot. 7: 166. 1919. *Bigelovia graveolens* (Nutt.) A. Gray var. *hololeuca* Λ. Gray, Proc. Amer. Acad. 8: 645. 1873. Owens Valley, Calif., *Horn 2852. C. nauseosus* subsp. *hololeucus* H. M. Hall, Carnegie Inst. Wash. Publ. (326): 211, 221. 1923.

4c. Var. LATISQUAMEUS (A. Gray) H. M. Hall, Univ. Calif. Publ. Bot. 7: 167. 1919. *Bigelovia graveolens* (Nutt.) A. Gray var. *latisquamea* A. Gray, Proc. Amer. Acad. 8: 645. 1873. "New Mexico, *Dr. Bigelow, Dr. Henry." C. speciosus* Nutt. var. *latisquameus* Greene, Erythea 3: 110. 1895. *C. speciosus* var. *arizonicus* Greene, loc. cit. Santa Rita Mts., Ariz., *Brandegee. B. graveolens* var. *appendiculata* Eastw. Proc. Calif. Acad. III. 1: 74. *pl.* 6. 1897. White Sands, N. Mex., *Cockerell. C. latisquameus* Greene, Pittonia 4: 42. 1899. *C. appendiculatus* Heller, Muhlenbergia 1: 6. 1900. *C. nauseosus* subsp. *latisquameus* H. M. Hall, Carnegie Inst. Wash. Publ. (326): 212, 221. 1923.

4d. Var. ABBREVIATUS (M. E. Jones) Blake, Jour. Wash. Acad. Sci. 27: 377. 1937. *Bigelovia leiosperma* A. Gray, Syn. Fl. N. Amer. 1 (2): 139. 1884. St. George, Utah, *Palmer* in 1875; Candelaria, southwestern Nevada, *Shockley. Aster leiospermus* Kuntze, Rev. Gen. 1: 318. 1891. *B. leiosperma* var. *abbreviata* M. E. Jones, Proc. Calif. Acad. II. 5: 693. 1895. *C. leiospermus* Greene, Erythea 3: 113. 1895. *C. nauseosus* var. *leiospermus* H. M. Hall. Univ. Calif. Publ. Bot. 7: 173. 1919. *C. nauseosus* subsp. *leiospermus* H. M. Hall, Carnegie Inst. Wash. Publ. (326): 217, 221. 1923.

4e. Var. GRAVEOLENS (Nutt.) Piper, Contr. U.S. Nat. Herb. 11: 559. 1906. *C. graveolens* Nutt. Gen. N. Amer. Pl. 2: 136. 1818. "Banks of the Missouri in denudated soils . . ." *Bigelovia graveolens* A. Gray, Proc. Amer. Acad. 8. 644. 1873. *B. graveolens* var. *glabrata* A. Gray, loc. cit. No type designated. *Linosyris graveolens* var. *glabrata* Engelm. ex A. Gray, loc. cit., as syn. *C. graveolens* Greene, Pittonia 3: 108. 1895. *C. virens* Greene, Pittonia 5: 61. 1902. Canyon City, Colo., *Greene* in 1896. *C. laetevirens* Greene, loc. cit. Grand Junction, Colo., *Greene* in 1896. *C. graveolens* var. *glabrata* A. Nels. in Coult. & Nels. New Man. Rocky Mt. Bot. 496. 1909. *C. nauseosus* subsp. *graveolens* H. M. Hall, Carnegie Inst. Wash. Publ. (326): 214, 221. 1923.

4f. Var. CONSIMILIS (Greene) H. M. Hall, Univ. Calif. Publ. Bot. 7: 176. 1919. *C. consimilis* Greene, Pittonia 5: 60. 1902. Deeth, lower Humboldt River, Nev., *Greene* in 1895. *C. angustus* Greene, Pittonia 5: 64. 1902. Alturas, Modoc Co., Calif.

4g. Var. VIRIDULUS H. M. Hall, Univ. Calif. Publ. Bot. 7: 177. 1919. Benton, Mono Co., Calif., *H. M. Hall 10642. C. nauseosus* subsp. *viridulus* H. M. Hall, Carnegie Inst. Wash. Publ. (326): 215, 221. 1923.

4h. Var. MOHAVENSIS (Greene) H. M. Hall, Univ. Calif. Publ. Bot. 7: 179. 1919. *Bigelovia mohavensis* Greene in A. Gray, Syn. Fl. N. Amer. 1 (2): 138. 1884. Mojave Desert, Calif., *Greene, Parry, Pringle. Aster mohavensis* Kuntze, Rev. Gen. 1: 318. 1891. *C. mohavensis* Greene, Erythea 3: 113. 1895. *C. nauseosus* subsp. *mohavensis* H. M. Hall, Carnegie Inst. Wash. Publ. (326): 216, 221. 1923.

4i. Var. JUNCEUS (Greene) H. M. Hall, Univ. Calif. Publ. Bot. 7: 180. 1919. *Bigelovia juncea* Greene, Bot. Gaz. 6: 184. 1881. Gila River, Ariz., near the N. Mex. boundary, *Greene* in 1880. *Aster Edwardii* Kuntze, Rev. Gen. 1: 316. 1891. *C. junceus* Greene, Erythea 3: 113. 1895. *C. nauseosus* subsp. *junceus* H. M. Hall, Carnegie Inst. Wash. Publ. (326): 216, 221. 1923.

4j. Var. CERUMINOSUS (Dur. & Hilg.) H. M. Hall, Univ. Calif. Publ. Bot. 7: 175. 1919. *Linosyris ceruminosa* Dur. & Hilg. Jour. Acad. Nat. Sci. Phila. II. 3: 40. 1885. Tejon Pass, Kern Co., Calif., *Heermann* in 1853. *Bigelovia ceruminosa* A. Gray, Proc. Amer. Acad. 8: 643. 1873. *C. ceruminosus* Greene, Erythea 3: 94. 1895. *C. nauseosus* subsp. *ceruminosus* H. M. Hall, Carnegie Inst. Wash. Publ. (326): 216, 221. 1923.

CLEOME (p. 134)

1. C. ISOMERIS Greene, Pittonia 1: 200. 1888, not Cleome arborea Weinm. in 1824. *Isomeris arborea* Nutt. in Torr. & Gray, Fl. N. Amer. 1: 124. 1838. San Diego, Calif., *Nuttall. I. arborea* var. *globosa* Cov. Proc. Biol. Soc. Wash. 7: 73. 1892. Caliente Creek, Kern Co., Calif., *Coville* in 1891. *I. globosa* Heller, Muhlenbergia 2: 50. 1905. *I. arborea* var. *angustata* Parish, Muhlenbergia 3: 128. 1907. Near Palm Springs, *Parish* in 1907.

COLEOGYNE (p. 146)

1. C. RAMOSISSIMA Torr. Pl. Fremont. 8. *pl. 4.* 1854. Mojave River, Calif., *Fremont.*

COLUBRINA (p. 263)

1a. C. TEXENSIS (Torr. & Gray) A. Gray var. CALIFORNICA (I. M. Johnston) L. Benson, Amer. Jour. Bot. 30: 630. 1943. *C. californica* Johnston, Proc. Calif. Acad. IV. 12: 1085. 1924. Los Animas Bay, Baja Calif., *Johnston 3496.*

CONDALIA (p. 258)

1a. C. LYCIOIDES (A. Gray) Weberb. in Engler & Prantl, Nat. Pflanzenfam. 3 (5): 404. 1895. *Zizyphus lycioides* A. Gray. Bost. Jour. Nat. Hist. 6: 168. 1850. Between Matamoras and Mapima, *Gregg.*

1b. Var. CANESCENS (A. Gray) Trel. in A. Gray, Syn. Fl. N. Amer. 1 (1): 403. 1897. *Zizyphus lycioides* var. *canescens* A. Gray in Rothr. in Wheeler, Rept. U.S. Surv. W. of 100th Merid. 82. 1878. Gila River Valley, Ariz., *Rothrock 331. C. divaricata* A. Nels. Bot. Gaz. 47: 427. 1909. Las Vegas, Nev., *Goodding 2300. Z. divaricata* A. Nels. ex Davidson & Moxley, Fl. S. Calif. 226. 1923.

2. C. Parryi (Torr.) Weberb. in Engl. & Prantl, Nat. Pflanzenfam. 3 (5): 404. 1895. *Zizyphus Parryi* Torr. in Emory, Bot. U.S. & Mex. Bound. Surv. 2: 46. 1859. San Felipe, Colorado Desert, Calif., *Parry.*

3. C. spathulata A. Gray, Pl. Wright. 1: 32. 1852. Rio Grande and Prairies of the San Felipe, Texas, *Wright.*

4. C. globosa Johnston, Proc. Calif. Acad. IV. 12: 1086. 1924. La Paz, Baja Calif., *Johnston 3028. C. globosa* var. *pubescens* Johnston, loc. cit. San Esteban Bay, Baja Calif., *Johnston 3201.*

5. C. mexicana Schlect. Linnaea 15: 471. 1841. Zimapan, Schiede; Barranca de Acholoya, *Ehrenberg.* Mexico.

COURSETIA (p. 203)

1. C. glandulosa A. Gray, Proc. Amer. Acad. 5: 156. 1862. Cape San Lucas, Baja Calif., *Xantus 25* in 1859 or 1860. *C. microphylla* A. Gray, Proc. Amer. Acad. 17: 207. 1882. Santa Catalina Mts., Pima Co., Arizona, *Pringle, Lemmon.*

COWANIA (p. 142)

1. C. subintegra Kearney, Madroño 7: 15. 1943. Two miles west of Burro Creek crossing on the road from Wikieup to Hillside, Mohave Co., Arizona, *Darrow & Benson 10891.*

2a. C. mexicana Don. var. Stansburiana (Torr.) Jepson, Man. Fl. Pl. Calif. 498. 1925. *C. Stansburiana* Torr. in Stansb. Expl. Gt. Salt Lake 386. *pl. 3.* 1853. Stansbury Island, Great Salt Lake, Utah, *Stansbury. C. Davidsonii* Rydb. N. Amer. Fl. 22: 416. 1913. Blue River, White Mts., Arizona, *Davidson 754.*

CROSSOSOMA (p. 137)

1. C. Bigelovii S. Wats. Proc. Amer. Acad. 11: 122. 1876. Mouth of Bill Williams River, Arizona, *Bigelow. C. parviflorum* Rob. & Fern. Proc. Amer. Acad. 30: 114. 1894. Grand Canyon, Arizona, *A. Gray;* La Tinaja, Sonora, *Hartman 245. C. glaucum* Rydb. N. Amer. Fl. 22: 232. 1908. Hassayampa River, Arizona, *Palmer 560. C. Bigelovii* var. *glaucum* Kearney & Peebles, Jour. Wash. Acad. Sci. 29: 480. 1939.

CROTON (p. 231)

1. C. sonorae Torr. in Emory, Rept. U.S. & Mex. Bound. Surv. 2 (1): 194. 1859. Sierra de Nariz, Sonora, *Schott.*

2. C. ciliato-glandulosus Ort. Hort. Matr. Dec. 51. 1797. "Habitat in Insula Cuba. Floret mense Septembri in Reg. Horto Matrit. è seminibus missis per D. Sessé." Apparently not from Cuba but grown at Madrid from seeds sent from Mexico by Sessé.

DALEA (p. 206)

1. D. spinosa A. Gray, Mem. Amer. Acad. II. 5: 315. 1855. Gila River, *Thurber. Asagraea spinosa* Baill. Adansonia 9: 233. 1870. *D. spinescens*

Hemsl. Biol. Centr. Amer. Bot. 1: 247. 1880. Based on *D. spinosa. Parosela spinosa* Heller, Cat. N. Amer. Pl. ed. 2. 7. 1900.

2. D. SCHOTTII Torr. in Emory, Rept. U.S. & Mex. Bound. Surv. 2: 53. 1859. Colorado River, *Schott, Parosela Schottii* Heller, Cat. N. Amer. Pl. ed. 2. 6. 1900. *P. Schottii* var. *puberula* Parish, Bot. Gaz. 55: 312. 1913. Borregos Spring, Colorado Desert, Calif., *Brandegee* in 1904, in 1905; Cajon de Santa Maria, Baja Calif., *Brandegee* in 1889. *D. Schottii* var. *puberula* Munz, Man. S. Calif. Bot. 263, 598. 1935.

3a. D. FREMONTII Torr. in A. Gray, Mem. Amer. Acad. II. 5: 316. 1855. Piute country, California, *Fremont. Parosela Fremontii* Vail, Bull. Torrey Club 24: 16. 1897. *P. Wheeleri* Vail, loc. cit. 17. Nevada, *Wheeler. Psorodendron Fremontii* Rydb. N. Amer. Fl. 24: 42. 1919. *Parosela Fremontii* var. *Wheeleri* Rob. in Macbr. Contr. Gray Herb. II. (65): 16. 1922. *D. arborescens* Torr. var. *Wheeleri* Tidestrom in Tidestrom & Kittell, Fl. Ariz. & N. Mex. 179. 1941.

3b. Var. SAUNDERSII (Parish) Munz, Man. S. Calif. Bot. 262. 599. 1935. D. Saundersii Parish, Bull. S. Calif. Acad. 2: 83. *pl. 2.* 1903. Victorville, Mojave Desert, Calif., *Saunders* in 1903. *Parosela Saundersii* Abrams, Bull. N. Y. Bot. Gard. 6: 396. 1910. *P. Johnsonii* (S. Wats.) Vail var. *Sandersii* Parish, Bot. Gaz. 55: 308. 1913. *Psorodendron Saundersii* Rydb. N. Amer. Fl. 24: 44. 1919. *Parosela Fremontii* var. *Saundersii* Macbr. Contr. Gray Herb. II. (65): 16. 1922.

3c. Var. MINUTIFOLIA (Parish) L. Benson in Benson and Darrow, Man. S. W. Dcs. Trees & Shrubs, ed. 1. 202, 374. 1945. *D. Johnsonii* S. Wats. in King, Rept. U.S. Geol. Expl. 40th Par. 5: 64. 1871. St. George, Utah, *J. E. Johnson, Palmer* in 1870. *Parosela Johnsonii* Vail, Bull. Torrey Club 24: 16. 1897. *P. Johnsonii* var. *minutifolia* Parish, Bot. Gaz. 55: 308. 1913. Calif.; Panamint Canyon, *Hall & Chandler 7002;* Providence Mts., *Brandegee* in 1905. *Psorodendron Johnsonii* Rydb. N. Amer. Fl. 24: 43. 1919. *Parosela Fremontii* var. *Johnsonii* Jepson, Man. Fl. Pl. Calif. 558. 1925. *Dalea Fremontii* var. *Johnsonii* Munz, Man. S. Calif. Bot. 262, 598. 1935.

3d. Var. PUBESCENS (Parish) L. Benson, Amer. Jour. Bot. 30: 239. 1943. *D. amoena* S. Wats. Amer. Nat. 7: 300. 1873. Northern Arizona, *Mrs. E. P. Thompson. Parosela amoena* Vail, Bull. Torrey Club 24: 17. 1897. *P. Johnsonii* (S. Wats.) Vail var. *pubescens* Parish, Bot. Gaz. 55: 308. 1913. Lee's Ferry, Arizona, *M. E. Jones 3076. Psorodendron amoenum* Rydb. N. Amer. Fl. 24: 44. 1919. *D. amoena* var. *pubescens* Peebles, Jour. Wash. Acad. Sci. 30: 413. 1940. *D. Fremontii* var. *amoena* Tidestrom in Tidestrom & Kittell, Fl. Ariz. & N. Mex. 180. 1941.

3e. Var. SIMPLIFOLIA (Parish) L. Benson, Amer. Jour. Bot. 30: 239. 1943. *D. californica* S. Wats. Proc. Amer. Acad. 11: 132. 1876. San Bernardino Mts., Calif., *Parry. Parosela californica* Vail, Bull. Torrey Club 24: 17. 1897. *P. californica* var. *simplifolia* Parish, Bot. Gaz. 55: 309. 1913. Western part of Colorado Desert, Calif., *Gilman 51. Psorodendron californi-*

cum Rydb. N. Amer. Fl. 24: 43. 1919. *Parosela Fremontii* var. *californica* Jepson, Fl. Calif. 2: 333. 1936. *D. Fremontii* var. *californica* McMinn, Ill. Man. Calif. Shrubs 224. 1939.

4. D. ARBORESCENS Torr. apud A. Gray, Mem. Amer. Acad. II. 5: 316. 1855. Mountains near San Fernando, Calif., *Fremont. Parosela arborescens* Heller, Cat. N. Amer. Pl. ed. 2. 5. 1900. *P. neglecta* Parish, Bot. Gaz. 55: 306. 1913, not Rose in 1905. Daggett, Mojave Desert, Calif., *Parish 644* (probably actually *654*). *Psorodendron arborescens* Rydb. N. Amer. Fl. 24: 42. 1919.

5. D. POLYADENIA Torr. ex S. Wats. in King, U.S. Geol. Expl. 40th Par. 5: 64. *pl. 9.* 1871. Truckee Desert, Nevada, *W. W. Bailey;* Carson Desert, *Torrey. D. polyadenia* var. *subnuda* S. Wats. Bot. Calif. 2: 441. 1880. Owen's Valley, *Dr. W. Matthews. Parosela polyadenia* Heller, Cat. N. Amer. Pl. ed. 2. 6. 1900. *Parosela polyadenia* var. *subnuda* Parish, Bot. Gaz. 55: 305. 1913. *Psorothamnus polyadenia* Rydb. N. Amer. Fl. 24: 46. 1919. *Psorothamnus subnudus* Rydb. loc. cit.

6. D. EMORYI A. Gray, Mem. Amer. Acad. II. 5: 315. 1854. Gila River, Arizona, *Emory* in 1852. *Parosela Emoryi* Heller, Cat. N. Amer. Pl. ed. 2. 6. 1900. *Psorothamnus Emoryi* Rydb. N. Amer. Fl. 24: 47. 1919.

7. D. SCOPARIA A. Gray, Mem. Amer. Acad. II. 4: 32. 1849. Jornada del Muerto, N. Mex., *Wislizenius. Parosela scoparia* Heller, Cat. N. Amer. Pl. ed. 2. 7. 1900. *Psorothamnus scoparius* Rydb. N. Amer. Fl. 24: 48. 1919.

8. D. FORMOSA Torr. Ann. Lyc. N. Y. 2: 177. 1827. Rocky Mts., Long Exped., *James* in 1820. *Parosela formosa* Vail, Trans. N. Y. Acad. Sci. 14: 34. 1894.

9a. D. WISLIZENII A. Gray var. SESSILIS A. Gray, Proc. Amer. Acad. 16: 105. 1880. New Mexico, *Greene* in 1877; Arizona, *Lemmon* in 1880. *Parosela Wislizenii* Vail var. *sessilis* Vail, Bull. Torrey Club 24: 15. 1897. *P. sanctae-crucis* Rydb. N. Amer. Fl. 24: 103. 1920. Santa Cruz, Sonora, *Wright 986. P. sessilis* Rydb. loc. cit. 104. *P. Wislizenii* var. *sanctae-crucis* Macbr. Contr. Gray Herb. II. (65): 19. 1922. *D. Wislizenii* var. *sanctae-crucis* Kearney & Peebles, Jour. Wash. Acad. Sci. 29: 484. 1939. *D. sessilis* Tidestrom in Tidestrom & Kittell, Fl. Ariz. & N. Mex. 184. 1941. *D. Wislizenii* subsp. *sessilis* Gentry, Madroño 10: 246. 1950.

10. D. PULCHRA Gentry, Madroño 10: 227. 1950. Soldiers Canyon, Santa Catalina Mountains, Arizona, *Gould & Robbins 3534.*

DASYLIRION (p. 74)

1. D. WHEELERI S. Wats. in Wheeler, Rept. U.S. Surv. W. of 100th Merid. 6: 272. 1879. Ash Creek, Southern Arizona, *Wheeler.*

2. D. LEIOPHYLLUM Engelm. ex Trel. Proc. Amer. Phil. Soc. 50: 433. 1911. Presidio, Texas, *Havard* in 1880.

DODONAEA (p. 257)

1a. D. viscosa Jacq. var. angustifolia (L. f.) Benth. Fl. Austr. 1: 472. 1863. *D. angustifolia* L. f. Suppl. 218. 1781. "India australi. . . ." *D. arizonica* A. Nels. Amer. Jour. Bot. 21: 576. 1934. Between Canyon Lake and Roosevelt Dam, Apache Trail, Ariz., *A. Nelson 11276.*

ENCELIA (p. 371)

1. E. farinosa A. Gray ex Torr. in Emory, Notes Mil. Reconn. 143. 1848. Locality not given; *Emory* in 1846. *E. farinosa* forma *phoenicodonta* Blake, Proc. Amer. Acad. 49: Contr. Gray Herb. (41): 362. 1913. Canyon near San Quentin, Baja Calif., *Orcutt 1341. E. farinosa* var. *phoenicodonta* I. M. Johnston, Proc. Calif. Acad. IV. 12: 1198. 1924.

2a. E. frutescens (A. Gray) A. Gray, Proc. Amer. Acad. 8: 657. 1873. *Simsia frutescens* A. Gray apud Torr. in Emory, Rept. U.S. & Mex. Bound. Surv. 2: 89. 1859. Agua Caliente near the Gila River, Maricopa Co., Ariz., *Emory* in 1846. *E. virginensis* A. Nels. Bot. Gaz. 37: 272. 1904. "The Pockets," Virgin River, southern Nev., *Goodding 606. E. frutescens* forma *radiata* H. M. Hall, Univ. Calif. Publ. Bot. 3: 135. 1907. Northern Ariz., *Wilson* in 1893; Grand Canyon, *Grant 396;* S. E. Utah, *Eastwood* in 1892. *E. frutescens* forma *ovata* H. M. Hall, loc. cit. Signal Mt., Colorado Desert, Calif., *Abrams 3156;* Tucson, Ariz., *Pringle* in 1884; "Palmetto Spring," *Stephens 53. E. frutescens* forma *virginensis* H. M. Hall, loc cit. *E. frutescens* var. *virginensis* Blake, Proc. Amer. Acad. 49: 363. 1913.

2b. Var. actonii (Elmer) Blake, Proc. Amer. Acad. 49: Contr. Gray Herb. (41): 365. 1913. *E. actoni* Elmer, Bot. Gaz. 39: 47. 1905. Acton, Los Angeles Co., Calif., *Elmer 3724. E. frutescens* forma *actoni* H. M. Hall, Univ. Calif. Publ. 3: 135. 1907.

EPHEDRA (p. 47)

1. E. trifurca Torr. in Emory, Notes. Mil. Reconn. 153. 1848. Between the Del Norte and the Gila rivers and westward to Calif. *E. trifaria* Parl. in DC. Prodr. 16 (2): 359. 1868. Misspelling.

2. E. Torreyana S. Wats. Proc. Amer. Acad. 14: 299. 1879. N. Mex. to S. Utah, several collections.

3a. E. californica S. Wats. Proc. Amer. Acad. 14: 300. 1879. Near San Diego, Calif., *Palmer 346, 365* in 1875.

3b. Var. funerea (Cov. & Mort.) L. Benson, Amer. Jour. Bot. 30: 231. 1943. *E. funerea* Cov. & Mort. Jour. Wash. Acad. Sci. 25: 307. 1935. Furnace Creek Canyon, Death Valley, *Coville & Gilman 447.*

4a. E. nevadensis S. Wats. Proc. Amer. Acad. 14: 298. 1879. Smoky Valley, Nevada, *S. Watson 1108. E. antisyphilitica* C. A. Mey. var. *pedunculata* S. Wats. in King, Rept. U.S. Geol. Surv. 40th Par. 5: 329. 1871. Nevada, *H. Engelmann;* S. Utah, *Palmer.*

4b. Var. ASPERA (Engelm.) L. Benson, Amer. Jour. Bot. 30: 232. 1943. *E. aspera* Engelm. ex S. Wats. Proc. Amer. Acad. 18: 157. 1883. South of Saltillo, Coahuila, *Palmer 1288. E. peninsularis* Johnston, Univ. Calif. Publ. Bot. 7: 437. 1922. Magdalena I., Baja Calif., *Brandegee* in 1889. *E. fasciculata* A. Nels. Amer. Jour. Bot. 21: 573. 1935. Phoenix, Arizona, *A. Nelson 10268. E. Reedii* Cory, Rhodora 40: 216. 1938. 55 miles south of Alpine, Texas, *Cory 18547. E. Clokeyi* Cutler, Ann. Mo. Bot. Gard. 26: 402. 1939. Cottonwood Springs, Riverside Co., Calif., *Clokey 6513.*

5a. E. VIRIDIS Cov. Contr. U.S. Nat. Herb. 4: 220. 1893. Coso Mts., Inyo Co., Calif., *Coville* in 1892. *E. nevadensis* S. Wats. var. *viridis* M. E. Jones, Proc. Calif. Acad. II. 5: 726. 1895.

5b. Var. VISCIDA (Cutler) L. Benson, Amer. Jour. Bot. 30. 233. 1943. *E. Coryi* Reed var. *viscida* Cutler, Ann. Mo. Bot. Gard. 26: 413. 1939. Rock Point, Apache Co., Arizona, *Cutler 2209. E. Cutleri* Peebles, Jour. Wash. Acad. Sci. 30: 473. 1940. Nom. nov. for var. *viscida.*

ERYTHRINA (p. 199)

1. E. FLABELLIFORMIS Kearney, Trans. N. Y. Acad. Sci. 14: 321. 1894. Southeastern Arizona, (probably) *Wilcox.*

EUPHORBIA (p. 246)

1. E. MISERA Benth. Bot. Voy. Sulph. 51. 1844. San Diego, San Diego County, California (probably) *Hinds,* Oct., 1839. *Trichosterigma miserum* (Benth.) Klotzsch & Garcke, Abh. Akad. Berlin 1859 (Phys.): 42. 1860.

EUROTIA (p. 126)

1. E. LANATA (Pursh) Moq. Monogr. Chenop. 81. 1840. *Diotis lanata* Pursh, Fl. Amer. Sept. 2: 602. 1814. Missouri River, *Lewis. E. subspinosa* Rydb. Bull. Torrey Club 39: 312. 1912. St. George, Utah, *Goodding 810. E. lanata* var. *subspinosa* Kearney & Peebles, Jour. Wash. Acad. Sci. 29: 475. 1939.

EYSENHARDTIA (p. 204)

1. E. POLYSTACHYA (Ortega) Sarg. Silva N. Amer. 3: 29. 1892. *Viborquia polystachya* Ortega, Hort. Matr. Dec. 66. 1797. Mexico. *E. amorphoides* H. B. K. Nov. Gen. et Sp. 6: 491 (quarto), 384 (folio). *pl. 592.* 1824. San Augustin de las Cuevas and Guanaxuate, Mexico. *Varennea polystachya* DC. Prodr. 2: 522. 1825. *E. amorphoides* var. *orthocarpa* A. Gray, Pl. Wright, 2: 37. 1853. Guadalupe Pass, Arizona-N. Mex. line near the Mexican Boundary, *Wright 980. E. orthocarpa* S. Wats. Proc. Amer. Acad. 17: 339. 1882. *Wiborgia amorphoides* Kuntze, Rev. Gen. et Sp. Pl. 1: 213. 1891. *Viborquia orthocarpa* Cockerell, Bull. Amer. Mus. Nat. Hist. 24: 97. 1908.

FALLUGIA (p. 144)

F. PARADOXA (Don) Endl. Gen. Pl. 1246. 1840. *Sieversia paradoxa* Don, Trans. Linn. Soc. Bot. 14: 576. 1825. Mexico. *F. paradoxa* var. *acuminata*

Woot. Bull. Torrey Club 25: 306. 1898. Las Cruces, N. Mex., *Wooton 65.* *F. micrantha* Cockerell, Entom. News 1901: 41. 1901. Mesilla Park, N. Mex. *F. acuminata* Cockerell, Proc. Acad. Phila. 1903: 590. 1903.

FLOURENSIA (p. 373)

1. F. CERNUA DC. Prodr. 5: 593. 1836. Monterrey. Nuevo Leon, *Berlandier 1401. Helianthus cernuus* Benth. & Hook. ex Hemsl. Biol. Centr. Amer. Bot. 2: 179. 1881.

FORESTIERA (p. 276)

1. F. PHILLYREOIDES (Benth.) Torr. in Emory, Bot. U.S. & Mex. Bound. Surv. 2: 167. 1859. *Piptolepis phillyreoides* Benth. Pl. Hartw. 29. 1840. Guanajuato, Mexico, *Hartweg* in 1837. *F. Shrevei* Standl. Field Mus. Nat. Hist. Bot. Ser. 17: 205. 1937. Alamo Ranch, Ajo Mts., Pima Co., Ariz., *Shreve 6201.*

2. F. NEO-MEXICANA A. Gray, Proc. Amer. Acad. 12: 63. 1876. Based upon the following: *F. acuminata* Poir. var. *parvifolia* A. Gray, Proc. Amer. Acad. 4: 364. 1860. Near Santa Fe, N. Mex., *Fendler 547. F. neo-mexicana* var. *arizonica* A. Gray, Syn. Fl. N. Amer. 2 (1): 76. 1886. Near Prescott, Ariz., *Palmer. F. arizonica* Rydb. Amer. Bot. 27: 62. 1921.

FOUQUIERIA (p. 270)

1. F. SPLENDENS Engelm. in Wisliz. Mem. Tour. N. Mex. 98. 1848. ". . . Jornada del Muerto, New Mexico, to Chihuahua, Saltillo, and Monterrey. . . ." *Wislizenius.*

FRANSERIA (p. 382)

1. F. AMBROSIOIDES Cav. Icon. Pl. 2: 79. *pl. 200.* 1793. Mexico. *Xanthidium ambrosioides* Delpino, Stud. Comp. Artemis. 63. 1871. *Gaertnera ambrosioides* Kuntze, Rev. Gen. 1: 339. 1891.

2. F. ILICIFOLIA A. Gray, Proc. Amer. Acad. 11: 77. 1876. "Great Cañon of the Tantillas Mountains, near the northern border of Lower California, Dr. E. Palmer." *Gaertnera ilicifolia* Kuntze, Rev. Gen. 1: 339. 1891.

3. F. DELTOIDEA Torr. Pl. Fremont. 15. 1853. Gila River, Ariz., *Fremont. Gaertnera deltoidea* Kuntze, Rev. Gen. 1: 339. 1891.

4. F. CORDIFOLIA A. Gray, Syn. Fl. 1 (2): 445. 1884. Mountains near Tucson, Ariz., *Pringle, Parish.*

5. F. ERIOCENTRA A. Gray, Proc. Amer. Acad. 7: 355. 1868. Providence Mts., Mojave Desert, Calif., *Cooper* in 1861. *Gaertnera eriocentra* Kuntze, Rev. Gen. 1: 339. 1891.

6. F. DUMOSA A. Gray in Torr. Fremont's 2nd. Rept. 316. 1845. Sandy uplands of the Mojave River, *Fremont. F. albicaulis* Torr. Pl. Fremont. 16. 1853. Gila River. *F. dumosa* var. *albicaulis* A. Gray in Torr. in Emory, Rept. U.S. & Mex. Bound. Surv. 2: 87. 1859. *Gaertnera dumosa* Kuntze, Rev. Gen. 1: 339. 1891.

FRAXINUS (p. 273)

1a. F. VELUTINA Torr. in Emory, Notes Mil. Reconn. 149. 1848. Between the Del Norte and the Gila and on the Mimbres, N. Mex., *Emory*. *F. pistaciaefolia* Torr. Pac. R. R. Rept. 4: 128. 1856. Bill Williams River, Ariz., *Bigelow* in 1854. *F. americana* L. subsp. *typicum* var. *pistaciaefolia* Wesmael. Bull. Soc. Bot. Belg. 31 (1): 108. 1892. *F. Toumeyi* Britt. in Britt. & Shafer, N. Amer. Trees 803. *f. 732.* 1908. Tucson, Ariz., *Toumey* in 1895. *F. attenuata* Jones, Contr. W. Bot. (12): 59. 1908. Valley of Palms, Baja Calif., *Jones 3741. Calycomelia pistaciaefolia* Nieuwl. Amer. Midl. Nat. 3: 187. 1914. *F. velutina* var. *Toumeyi* Rehder, Proc. Amer. Acad. 53: 204. 1917. *F. velutina* var. *glabra* Rehder, loc. cit. 207. Santa Rita Range Reserve, Santa Rita Mts., Ariz., *Wooton* in 1911. *F. glabra* Thornber ex Rehder, loc. cit. 207, as syn. "Thornber in U.S. Herb." *F. Standleyi* Rehder, loc. cit. 208. Van Patten's Camp, Organ Mts., N. Mex., *Standley* in 1906. *F. Standleyi* var. *lasia* Rehder, loc. cit. 210. Oak Creek Canyon, Coconino Co., Ariz., *Rehder 585.*

1b. Var. CORIACEA. *F. coriacea* S. Wats. Amer. Nat. 7: 302. 1873. Ash Meadows, Nev., *Wheeler*; Devil's Run Canyon, Ariz., *Bigelow* in 1853-54. *F. oregona* Nutt. var. *glabra* Lingelsh. in Engl. Bot. Jahrb. 40: 43 1907. California, *Parish 540, Wright. F. velutina* var. *coriacea* Lingelsh. loc. cit. *F. velutina* var. *coriacea* Jepson, Man. Fl. Pl. Calif. 230. 1923.

F. ANOMALA Torr. in S. Wats. in King, Rept. U.S. Geol. Expl. 40th Par. 5: 283. 1871. Labyrinth Canyon, Utah, *Newberry* in 1859; St. George, Utah, *Palmer.*

FRAXINUS GOODDINGII Little, Jour. Wash. Acad. Sci. 42: 373. 1952.

GARRYA (p. 268)

G. FLAVESCENS S. Wats. Amer. Nat. 7: 301. 1873. "Southern Nev. and Utah to Ariz. and N. Mex." *G. Veatchii* var. *flavescens* C. & E. Bot. Gaz. 15: 96. 1890. *G. mollis* Greene. Leafl. Bot. Obs. & Crit. 2: 86. 1910. San Francisco Mts., Ariz., *Pearson* in 1909.

GOSSYPIUM (p. 265)

1. G. THURBERI Tod. Prodr. Gossyp. 7. 1878. Based upon the following: *Thurberia thespesioides* A. Gray, Mem. Amer. Acad. II. 5: 308. 1854, not *G. thespesioides* F. Muell. in 1875. *Ingenhouzia triloba* of authors, not of DC., cf. Kearney, Amer. Jour. Bot. 24: 298-300. 1937.

GRAYIA (p. 126)

1. G. SPINOSA (Hook.) Moq. in DC. Prodr. 13 (2): 119. 1894. *Chenopodium spinosum* Hook. Fl. Bor. Amer. 2: 127. 1838. Columbia River, *Douglas.*

GUTIERREZIA (p. 333)

1a. G. SAROTHRAE (Pursh) Britt. & Rusby, Trans. N. Y. Acad. Sci. 7: 10. 1887. *Solidago Sarothrae* Pursh. Fl. Amer. Sept. 540. 1814. Plains of the

Missouri River, *Lewis. Brachyris Euthamiae* Nutt. Gen. N. Amer. Pl. 2: 163. 1818. "On the arid hills of the Missouri from the Arikarees to the mountains?" *Brachyachris Euthamiae* Spreng. Syst. 3: 374. 1825. *G. Euthamiae* Torr. & Gray, Fl. N. Amer. 2: 193. 1842. *G. divaricata* Torr. & Gray, loc. cit. 193. *G. tenuis* Greene, Pittonia 4: 55. 1899. Mountains back of Silver City, N. Mex., *Greene* in 1880. *G. juncea* Greene, loc. cit. 56. Gray, N. Mex., *Skehan 78* in 1898. *G. linearis* Rydb. Bull. Torrey Club 31: 647. 1905. Gray, N. Mex., *Earle 474. G. furfuracea* Greene in Fedde, Repert. Nov. Sp. 7: 195. 1909. *G. corymbosa* A. Nels. Amer. Jour. Bot. 23: 265. 1936. Ten miles east of Santa Fe, N. Mex., *A. Nelson 11759* (this species acc. Tidestrom).

1b. Var. MICROCEPHALA (DC.) L. Benson, Amer. Jour. Bot. 30: 631. 1943. *Brachyris microcephala* DC. Prodr. 5: 313. 1836. ". . . In Mexico prope locum dictum *Sallito* legit cl. Berlandier januar. . . ." *G. microcephala* A. Gray, Mem. Amer. Acad. II. 4: 74. 1849. *G. Euthamiae* (Nutt.) Torr. & Gray var. *microcephala* (DC.) A. Gray, Syn. Fl. N. Amer. 1 (2): 115. 1884. *G. filifolia* Greene, Pittonia 4: 55. 1899. Round Mountain, White Mts., N. Mex., *Wooton* in 1897. *G. globosa* A. Nels. Amer. Jour. Bot. 23: 265. 1936. San Ysidro to Bernalillo, N. Mex. *A. Nelson 11739* (this var. acc. Tidestrom).

2a. G. CALIFORNICA (DC.) Torr. & Gray, Fl. N. Amer. 2: 193. 1842. *Brachyris californica* DC. Prodr. 5: 313. 1836. California, *Douglas. G. serotina* Greene, Pittonia 4: 57. 1889. Tucson, Ariz., *Toumey* in 1892. *G. divergens* Greene, loc. cit. 58. San Bernardino mesas, Calif., *Parish;* Fall Brook, San Diego Co., Calif., *Parish 2241. G. polyantha* A. Nels, Amer. Jour. Bot. 25: 117. 1938. North of Tucson, Ariz., *A. & R. Nelson 1638* in 1935.

2b. Var. BRACTEATA (Abrams) H. M. Hall, Univ. Calif. Publ. Bot. 3: 36. 1907. *G. bracteata* Abrams, Bull. Torrey Club 34: 265. 1907. Between Banning and Seven Palms, *Orcutt* in 1889, Gray Herbarium.

3. G. LUCIDA (Greene) Greene, Fl. Fran. 361. 1897. *Xanthocephalum lucidum* Greene, Pittonia 2: 282. 1892. Mojave Desert region, California. Segregated from *G. microcephala* (DC.) Torr. & Gray. *G. glomerella* Greene, Pittonia 4: 54. 1899. Organ Mts., N. Mex., *Wooton 449.*

4. G. LONGIFOLIA Greene, Pittonia 4: 53. 1889. White Mts., N. Mex., *Wooton* in 1897. *G. linoides* Greene, Leafl. Bot. Obs. & Crit. 2: 22. 1909. Chiricahua Mts., Ariz., *Blumer* in 1907.

HAPLOPAPPUS (p. 339)

1. H. TENUISECTUS (Greene) Blake ex L. Benson, Amer. Jour. Bot. 27: 188. 1940. *Linosyris coronopifolia* A. Gray, Pl. Wright. 1: 96. 1852, not *Haplopappus coronopifolius* DC. in 1836. Rio Grande, Texas, *Wright 289. Bigelovia coronopifolia* A. Gray, Proc. Amer. Acad. 8: 683. 1873. *Aster coronopifolius* Kuntze, Rev. Gen. 3: 7. 1891. *Isocoma coronopifolia* Greene,

Erythea 2: 111. 1894. *I. tenuisecta* Greene, Leafl. Bot. Obs. & Crit. 1: 169. 1906. Tucson, Ariz., *Smart* in 1867. *I. fruticosa* Rose & Standl. Contr. U.S. Nat. Herb. 16: 18. *pl. 13.* 1912. MacDougal Pass, pinacate Mts., Sonora, *MacDougal* in 1907. *H. fruticosa* Blake, Contr. U.S. Nat. Herb. 23: 1493. 1926.

2. **H. PLURIFLORUS** (Torr. & Gray) H. M. Hall, Carnegie Inst. Wash. Publ. (389): 237. 1928. *Linosyris pluriflora* Torr. & Gray, Fl. N. Amer. 2: 233. 1842. "Upper Missouri or Platte?" *James*. Arkansas or Platte River in or near eastern Colorado. *L. heterophylla* A. Gray, Pl. Wright. 1: 95. 1852. Pecos River Valley, *Wright. L. Wrightii* A. Gray, loc. cit. Rio Grande 60 or 70 miles below El Paso, Texas, *Wright. L. hirtella* A. Gray, loc. cit. Valley of the Limpia, Texas, *Wright. Bigelovia Wrightii* A. Gray, Proc. Amer. Acad. 8: 639. 1873. *B. pluriflora* A. Gray, loc. cit. *B. Wrightii* var. *hirtella* A. Gray, Syn. Fl. N. Amer. 1 (2): 142 1884 *Aster heterophyllus* Kuntze, Rev. Gen. 1: 316. 1891. *Isocoma pluriflora* Greene, Erythea 2: 111. 1894. *I. heterophylla* Greene, loc. cit. *I. hirtella* Heller, Muhlenbergia 1: 6. 1900. *I. pedicellata* Greene, Leafl. Bot. Obs. & Crit. 1: 170. 1906. Southwestern Texas, *Palmer* in 1879 or 1880. *I. Wrightii* Rydb. Bull. Torrey Club 33: 152. 1906. *I. limitanea* Rose & Standl. Contr. U.S. Nat. Herb. 16: 18. *pl. 14.* 1912. Sonoyta, Sonora, *MacDougal 14* in 1907. *I. oxylepis* Woot. & Standl. Contr. U.S. Nat. Herb. 16: 180. 1913. White Water, Chihuahua, *Mearns 2288. H. heterophyllus* Blake, Contr. U.S. Nat. Herb. 25: 546. 1925.

3. **H. ACRADENIUS** (Greene) Blake, Contr. U.S. Nat. Herb. 25: 546. 1925. *Bigelovia acradenia* Greene, Bull. Torrey Club 10: 126. 1883. Mojave Desert, Calif., *Parry & Greene* in 1891. *Aster acradenius* Kuntze, Rev. Gen. 1: 317. 1891. *Isocoma acradenia* Greene, Erythea 2: 111. 1894. *I. bracteosa* Greene, Leafl. Bot. Obs. & Crit. 1: 170. 1906. Tulare Co., Calif., *Sheldon* in 1899. *I. eremophila* Greene, loc. cit. 171. "Southwestern part of the Colorado Desert, Calif. . . ." *Orcutt 2223,* U.S. Nat. Herb. *I. veneta* (H.B.K.) Greene var. *acradenia* H. M. Hall, Univ. Calif. Publ. Bot. 3: 64. 1907. *II. acradenius* subsp. *typicus* H. M. Hall, Carnegie Inst. Wash. Publ. (389): 233. 1928. *H. acradenius* subsp. *eremophilus* H. M. Hall, loc. cit. *H. acradenius* subsp. *bracteosus* H. M. Hall, loc. cit.

4. **H. PROPINQUUS** Blake, Contr. U.S. Nat. Herb. 23: 1490. 1926. Nom. nov. for the following: *Bigelovia brachylepis* A. Gray in Brew. & Wats. Bot. Calif. 1: 614. 1876. Larken's Station, 80 miles northeast of San Diego, Calif., *Palmer. Aster brachylepis* Kuntze, Rev. Gen. 1: 317. 1891. *Bigelovia brachylepis* Greene, Erythea 3: 12. 1895. *Ericameria brachylepis* H. M. Hall, Univ. Calif. Publ. Bot. 3: 56. 1907. *Haplopappus brachylepis* H. M. Hall, loc. cit. 7: 273. 1919, not Phil. in 1894.

H. PALMERI A. Gray var. **PACHYLEPIS** (H. M. Hall) Munz, Man. S. Calif. Bot. 521, 601. 1935. *H. Palmeri* subsp. *pachylepis* H. M. Hall, Carnegie Inst. Wash. Publ. (389): 267. 1928. Summit of Box Springs Grade near Riverside, Calif., *Keck 262.*

5. H. LARICIFOLIUS A. Gray, Pl. Wright. 2: 80. 1853. Guadaloupe Pass, N. Mex., *Wright 1188, Chrysoma laricifolia* Greene, Erythea 3: 11. 1895.

6. H. COOPERI (A. Gray) H. M. Hall, Carnegie Inst. Wash. Publ. (389): 275. 1928. *Bigelovia Cooperi* A. Gray, Proc. Amer. Acad. 8: 640. 1873. Providence Mts., Calif., *Cooper. H. monactis* A. Gray, Proc. Amer. Acad. 19: 1. 1883. Borders of the Mojave Desert, Calif., *Palmer* in 1876, *S. B. & W. F. Parish* in 1881, *Pringle* in 1882. *Aster Cooperi* Kuntze, Rev. Gen. 317. *A. monactis* Kuntze, loc. cit. *Ericameria monactis* McClatchie, Erythea 2: 124. 1894. *Chrysoma Cooperi* Greene, Erythea 3: 12. 1895. *Acamptopappus microcephalus* M. E. Jones. Contr. W. Bot. 7: 30. 1898. *Chrysothamnus corymbosus* Elmer, Bot. Gaz. 39: 50. 1905. Lancaster, Mojave Desert, Calif., *Elmer 3668. Tumionella monactis* Greene, Leafl. Bot. Obs. & Crit. 1: 173. 1906. *Ericameria Cooperi* H. M. Hall, Univ. Calif. Publ. Bot. 3: 56. 1907.

7a H. CUNEATUS A. Gray var. SPATHULATUS (A. Gray) Blake, Contr. U.S. Nat. Herb. 23: 1489. 1926. *Bigelovia spathulata* A. Gray, Proc. Amer. Acad. 11: 74. 1876. "Tantillas Canyon," Baja Calif., *Palmer. B. rupestris* Greene, Bot. Gaz. 6: 183. 1881. San Francisco Mts., Ariz., Greene. *Chrysoma cuneata* (A. Gray) Greene var. *spathulata* Greene, Erythea 3: 11. 1895. *C. Merriamii* Eastw. Bull. Torrey Club 32: 215. 1905. Caliente Creek, Kern Co., Calif. *Merriam* in 1902. *Ericameria cuneata* (A. Gray) McClatchie var. *spathulata* H. M. Hall, Univ. Calif. Publ. Bot. 3: 52. 1907.

8a. H. LINEARIFOLIUS DC. var. INTERIOR (Cov.) M. E. Jones, Proc. Calif. Acad. II. 5: 697. 1895. *H. interior* Cov. Proc. Biol. Soc. Wash. 7: 65. 1892. Four miles southeast of Mill Canyon Divide, Darwin Mesa, Inyo Co., Calif., *Coville* in 1891. *Stenotus interior* Greene, Erythea 2: 72. 1894. *Stenotopsis interior* Rydb. Bull. Torrey Club 27: 617. 1900. *Stenotus linearifolius* (DC.) Torr. & Gray var. *interior* H. M. Hall, Univ. Calif. Publ. Bot. 3: 48. 1907. *H. linearifolius* subsp. *interior* H. M. Hall, Carnegie Inst. Wash. Publ. (389): 158. 1928.

HAPLOPHYTON (p. 281)

1. H. CROOKSII L. Benson, Amer. Jour. Bot. 30: 630. 1943. *H. cimicidum* A. DC. var. *Crooksii* L. Benson, Torreya 42: 9. 1942. "Prison Road" or Soldier Trail Highway, Santa Catalina Mts., Pima Co., Ariz., *Crooks & Darrow* in 1939.

HOFFMANSEGGIA (p. 188)

1. H. MICROPHYLLA Torr. in Emory, Rept. U.S. &. Mex. Bound Surv. 2: 58. 1859. Colorado Desert, Calif., *Schott. Caesalpinia virgata* E. M. Fisher, Bot. Gaz. 18: 123. 1893. Nom. nov. for *H. microphylla. Larrea microphylla* Britt. N. Amer. Fl. 23: 310. 1930.

HOFMEISTERIA (p. 324)

1. H. PLURISETA A. Gray in Torr. Expl. & Surv. R. R. Miss. Pac. 4: 96. 1857. Bill Williams River, Arizona, *Whipple Exped.*

HOLACANTHA (p. 224)

1. H. Emoryi A. Gray, Mem. Amer. Acad. II. 5: 310. 1854. Between the Gila River and Tucson, Ariz., and on the Salinas River north of the Gila, *Emory.*

HYMENOCLEA (p. 378)

1a. H. Salsola Torr. & Gray in A. Gray, Mem. Amer. Acad. II. 4: 79. 1849. "Sandy, saline uplands near the Mojave River, in the interior part of California, *Fremont.*" *H. fasciculata* A. Nels. Bot. Gaz. 37: 270. 1904. Kernan, southern Nev., *Goodding 662.*

1b. Var. pentalepis (Rydb.) L. Benson, Amer. Jour. Bot. 30: 631. 1943. *H. pentalepis* Rydb. N. Amer. Fl. 33: 14. 1922. Pima Canyon, Santa Catalina Mts., Pima Co., Ariz., *Griffiths 2630.* *H. hemidioica* A. Nels. Amer. Jour. Bot. 25: 117. 1938. East of Mohawk, Yuma Co., Ariz., *A. & R. Nelson 1340, 1341* in 1935.

2. H. monogyra Torr. & Gray in A. Gray, Mem. Amer. Acad. II. 4: 79. 1849. "Ojito," N. Mex.?, *Gregg.*

HYPTIS (p. 298)

1. H. Emoryi Torr. in Ives, Rept. Colo. River Surv. Bot. 20. 1860. Based upon *Hyptis lanata* in Emory, Rept. U.S. & Mex. Bound. Surv. 2: 129. 1859. Lower Gila River, *Emory.*

ISOMERIS (see Cleome)

JACOBINIA (p. 318)

1. **J. candicans** (Nees) Benth. & Hook. var. **subglabra** L. Benson, comb. nov. *J. ovata* var. *subglabra* S. Wats. Proc. Amer. Acad. 24: 67. 1889. Guaymas, Sonora, *Palmer 264.*

JATROPHA (p. 238)

1. J. cardiophylla (Torr.) Muell. Arg. in DC. Prodr. 15 (2): 1079. 1866. *Mozinna cardiophylla* Torr. in Emory, Rept. U.S. & Mex. Bound. Surv. 2 (1): 198. 1859. "Near Tucson and Sierra Verde, Sonora. . . ." June, *Schott.* Tucson is now in Arizona, and the Sierra Verde may be the Pozo Verde Mountains, now known as the Baboquivari Mountains.

2. J. cinerea (Ort.) Muell. Arg. in DC. Prodr. 15 (2): 1078. 1866. *Mozinna cinerea* Ort. Hort. Matr. Dec. 108. 1799. Grown in Madrid, Spain, from seed obtained from Mexico. *Mozinna canescens* Benth. Bot. Voy. Sulph. 52. *pl. 25.* 1844. Bay of Magdalena, Lower Calif. (probably) *Hinds.* Nov. 2, 1839. *J. canescens* (Benth.) Muell. Arg. loc. cit. 1079.

3. J. cuneata Wiggins & Rollins, Contr. Dudley Herb. 3 (8): 272. *pl. 42. f. 1.* 1943. "Collected 1.5 miles north of the village of Kino Bay, near the

gulf coast almost straight west of Hermosillo, Sonora, *Ira L. Wiggins and Reed C. Rollins 162*, Aug. 29, 1941."

JUGLANS (p. 110)

1a. **J. microcarpa** Berlandier var. **major** (Torr.) L. Benson, comb. nov. *J. rupestris* Engelm. var. *major* Torr. in Sitgreaves, Rept. Zuñi & Colo. 171. *pl. 16.* 1854. *J. major* Heller, Muhlenbergia 1: 50. 1904. Western N. Mex., *Woodhouse;* Santa Rita, N. Mex., *Bigelow.* Dr. Ivan M. Johnston (Jour. Arn. Arb. 25: 436. 1944) has shown that *juglans microcarpa* Berlandier, 1850, antedates *J. rupestris* Engelm., 1853.

KOEBERLINIA (p. 253)

1. K. spinosa Zucc. Flora 15 (2): Beibl. 73. 1832. Mexico.

1a. Var. tenuispina Kearney & Peebles, Jour. Wash. Acad. Sci. 29: 486. 1939. Horse Tanks, Castle Dome Mts., Yuma Co., Ariz., *Kearney & Peebles 10969.*

KRAMERIA (p. 192)

1. K. grayi Rose & Painter, Contr. U.S. Nat. Herb. 10: 108. 1906. Nom. nov. for the following: *K. canescens* A. Gray, Pl. Wright. 1: 42. 1852, not Willd. in 1825. Prairies near the Pecos River, Texas, *Wright* in 1851.

2. K. parvifolia Benth. Bot. Voy. Sulph. 6. *pl. 1.* 1844. Bay of Magdalena, Baja Calif., *Hinds* in 1841. *K. glandulosa* Rose & Painter, Contr. U.S. Nat. Herb. 10: 108. 1906. El Paso, Texas, *Rose 4904. K. parvifolia* var. *glandulosa* Macbr. Contr. Gray Herb. II. (56): 52. 1918. *K. parvifolia* var. *imparata* Macbr. loc. cit. Mountain Springs, San Diego Co., Calif. *Mary F. Spencer 763. K. imparata* Britton, N. Amer. Fl. 23: 199. 1930.

LARREA (p. 218)

1. L. divaricata Cav. Anal. Hist. Nat. 2: 119. *pl. 18-19.* 1800. Buenos Aires, Argentina, Née. Locality probably actually Chile. *Zygophyllum tridentatum* Moc. & Sessé in DC. Prodr. 1: 706. 1824. Mexico. *L. mexicana* Moric. Pl. Nouv. Amer. 71. 1839. San Luis Potosí, *Berlandier 1362. Z. californicum* Torr. & Frem. in Frem. 2nd Rept. 257. 1845. Walker Pass, Mojave Desert Kern Co., Calif., *Fremont. L. glutinosa* Engelm. in Wisliz. Mem. Tour. N. Mex. 93. 1848. "Ola and Fray Cristobal, in New Mexico, to Chihuahua and Saltillo; also about Presidio (Dr. Gregg). . . ." *L. tridentata* Cov. Contr. U.S. Nat. Herb. 4: 75. 1893. *Covillea divaracata* Vail, Bull. Torrey Club 22: 229. 1895. *C. glutinosa* Rydb. N. Amer. Fl. 25: 108. 1910. *L. tridentata* var. *glutinosa* Jepson, Man. Fl. Pl. Calif. 604. *f. 596.* 1925. *Schroeterella glutinosa* Briq. Veroff. Geobot. Inst. Rubel 3: 664. 1925. *Neo-schroetera glutinosa* Briq. Candollea 2: 514. 1926.

LEPIDOSPARTUM (p. 365)

1. L. squamatum (A. Gray) A. Gray, Proc. Amer. Acad. 19: 50. 1883. *Linosyris squamata* A. Gray, loc. cit. 8: 290. 1870. Based upon vars. *Breweri*

and *Palmeri* A. Gray, loc. cit., the var. *Breweri* chosen by L. C. Wheeler, Rhodora 40: 321. 1938, as the basis for the species. Santa Monica Mts., Los Angeles Co., Calif., *Brewer 71*. The var. *Palmeri* a form restricted to the upper end of the Coachella Valley of the Colorado Desert and marked by an abundance of scaly leaves on the fertile stems, these grading into the bracts of the involucre. *Tetradymia squamata* A. Gray. loc. cit. 9: 207. 1874. *T. squamata* var. *Breweri* A. Gray in Brew. & Wats. Bot. Calif. 1: 408. 1876. *L. squamatum* var. *Palmeri* L. C. Wheeler, loc. cit. *L. squamatum* var. *obtectum* Jepson, Man. Fl. Pl. Calif. 1159. 1925. Whitewater Wash, *Schellenger.*

2. L. LATISQUAMUM S. Wats. Proc. Amer. Acad. 25: 133. 1890. Soda Canyon. Esmeralda Co., Nev., *Shockley* in 1888. *L. striatum* Cov. Proc. Biol. Soc. Wash. 7: 73. 1892. Based on a duplicate of the type of *L. latisquamum.*

LIPPIA (p. 286)

1. L. WRIGHTII A. Gray, Amer. Jour. Sci. II. 16: 98. 1853. *Wright 1506. Aloysia Wrightii* Heller, Muhlenbergia 1: 147. 1906.

LYCIUM (p. 301)

1. L. MACRODON A. Gray, Proc. Amer. Acad. 6: 45. 1862. Expedition to Calif., *Fremont* in 1849. Probably S. Ariz.

2. L. COOPERI A. Gray, Proc. Amer. Acad. 7: 388. 1868. Providence Mts., Mojave Desert, San Bernardino Co., Calif., *Cooper* in 1861. *L. Cooperi* var. *pubiflora* A. Gray, Syn. Fl. N. Amer. 2 (1): 238. 1886. Southern Calif., or Ariz., *Palmer* in 1876. *L. Shockleyi* A. Gray, Proc. Amer. Acad. 22: 311. 1887. Candelaria, Nev., *Shockley 219* in 1882.

3a. L. PALLIDUM Miers, Ann. & Mag. Nat. Hist. II. 14: 131. 1854. Santa Fe Creek Valley, N. Mex., *Fendler 670. L. Schaffneri* A. Gray in Hemsl. Biol. Cent. Amer. Bot. 2: 426. 1882. San Luis Potosí, *Schaffner 54* in 1877.

3b. Var. OLIGOSPERMUM C. L. Hitchc. Ann. Mo. Bot. Gard. 19: 304. 1932. Barstow, Mojave Desert, Calif., *Jepson 6606.*

4. L. TORREYI A. Gray, Proc. Amer. Acad. 6: 47. 1862. Fort Yuma, Calif., *Thomas* in 1855. *L. Torreyi* var. *filiforme* M. E. Jones, Proc. Calif. Acad. II. 5: 714. 1895. Beaverdam, Mohave Co., Ariz., *M. E. Jones 5015.*

5. L. BREVIPES Benth. Bot. Voy. Sulph. 40. 1844. Baja Calif., *Hinds & Barclay, Xantus. L. Richii* A. Gray, Proc. Amer. Acad. 6: 46. 1862. La Paz, Baja Calif., *Rich. L. Palmeri* A. Gray, loc. cit. 8: 292. 1873. Yaqui River, Sonora, *Palmer. L. cedrosense* Green, Pittonia 1: 268. 1889. Southwest side of Cedros I., Baja Calif., *Pond* in 1889.

6. L. PARISHII A. Gray, Proc. Amer. Acad. 20: 305. 1885. San Bernardino Valley, Calif., *S. B. & W. F. Parish 795. L. Pringlei* A. Gray, loc. cit. Sonora, *Pringle* in 1884.

7. L. EXSERTUM A. Gray, Proc. Amer. Acad. 20: 305. 1885. Altar, Sonora, *Pringle* in 1884. *L. Fremontii* A. Gray var. *Bigelovii* A. Gray, Proc. Amer. Acad. 6: 47. 1862. Bill Williams River, Ariz., *Bigelow* in 1854. *L. retusum* Rob. & Fern. Proc. Amer. Acad. 30: 120. 1894. Oputo, Sonora, *Hartman 212* in 1890.

8. L. FREMONTII A. Gray, Proc. Amer. Acad. 6: 46. 1862. Interior Calif. or eastward, *Fremont* in 1849. *L. gracilipes* A. Gray, loc. cit. 12: 81. 1877. Bill Williams River, Ariz., *Palmer 423* in 1876. *L. Fremontii* var. *gracilipes* A. Gray, Syn. Fl. N. Amer. 2 (1): 437. 1886.

9. L. CALIFORNICUM Nutt. ex A. Gray in Brew. & Wats. Bot. Calif. 1: 542. 1876. San Diego, Calif., *Nuttall*. *L. californicum* var. *arizonicum* A. Gray, Syn. Fl. N. Amer. 2 (1): 437. 1886. Maricopa, Ariz., *A. Gray* in 1885. *L. carinatum* S. Wats. Proc. Amer. Acad. 24: 65. 1889. Guaymas, Sonora, *Palmer 178* in 1887.

10. L. BERLANDIERI Dunal in DC. Prodr. 13 (1): 520. 1852. Mexico opposite Laredo, Texas, *Berlandier 1411* in 1828. *L. senticosum* Miers, Ann. & Mag. Nat. Hist. II. 14: 138. 1854. Carrizal, near Monterrey, Neuvo Leon, *Berlandier 1426-166*. *L. stolidum* Miers, loc. cit. 191. Western Texas to El Paso, *Wright 542* in 1849. *L. parviflorum* A. Gray, Proc. Amer. Acad. 6: 48. 1862. Sonora, *Thurber 962*. *L. Berlandieri* f. *parviflorum* C. L. Hitchc. Ann. Mo. Bot. Gard. 19: 246. 1932. *L. Berlandieri* var. *longistylum* C. L. Hitchc. loc. cit. 248. Santa Catalina Mountains, Pima Co., Ariz., *Pringle* in 1881. *L. Berlandieri* var. *brevilobum* C. L. Hitchc. loc. cit. 250. Conception del Oro, Mexico, *Palmer 285* in 1904.

11a. L. ANDERSONII A. Gray, Proc. Amer. Acad. 7: 388. 1868. South-eastern Nev., *C. L. Andersson 151* in 1866. *L. Andersonii* var. *pubescens* S. Wats. Proc. Amer. Acad. 24: 65. 1889. Los Angeles Bay, Gulf of Calif., Baja Calif., *Palmer 559* in 1887.

11b. Var. DESERTICOLA C. L. Hitchc. Ann. Mo. Bot. Gard. 19: 280. 1932. Palm Springs, Riverside Co., Calif., *Parish 4132*.

11c. Var. WRIGHTII A. Gray in Brew. & Wats. Bot. Calif. 1: 543. 1876. "Saar de Cienega towards Chiricahui, Ariz.," *Wright 1610*.

LYSILOMA (p. 162)

1. L. MICROPHYLLA Benth. Lond. Jour. Bot. 3: 83. 1844. Mexico, *Hartweg 72*. *L. Watsonii* Rose, Contr. U.S. Nat. Herb. 1: 99. 1891. Alamos, Sonora, *Palmer 664* in 1890. *L. Thornberi* Britt. & Rose, N. Amer. Fl. 23: 83. 1928. Rincon Mts., Arizona, *Thornber* in 1926.

MANIHOT (p. 242)

1. M. DAVISIAE Croizat, Jour. Arn. Arb. 23: 224. 1942. Santa Catalina Mts., Pima Co., Ariz., *Lemmon* in 1883, U.S. Nat. Herb.

2. M. ANGUSTILOBA (Torr.) Muell. Arg. in DC. Prodr. 15 (2): 1073. 1866. *Janipha Manihot* H. B. K. var. *angustiloba* Torr. in Emory, Rept. U.S. &

Mex. Bound. Surv. 2 (1): 199. 1859. "Sierras oeste de Sta. Cruz y Tubac," i. e., mountains east of Santa Cruz (Sonora if the town is meant rather than the river), and Tubac, Santa Cruz County, Arizona; June-July, *Schott*.

MENODORA (p. 278)

1a. M. scabra A. Gray, Amer. Jour. Sci. II. 14: 44. 1852. "New Mexico, *Wislizenius*. . . ." *Bolivaria scabra* Engelm. ex A. Gray, loc. cit., as syn. *M. laevis* Woot. & Standl. Contr. U.S. Nat. Herb. 16: 158. 1913. Organ Mts., N. Mex., *Vasey* in 1881. *B. scabra* Engelm. ex Steyermark, Ann. Mo. Bot. Gard. 19: 135. 1932, as syn. *M. scabra* var. *laevis* Steyermark, loc. cit. 137. *M. scabra* var. *ramosissima* Steyermark, loc. cit. 139. El Paso, Texas, *Palmer 31083*. *M. scabra* var. *longituba* Steyermark, loc. cit. 141. Mazatzal Mountains, Ariz., *Smart 213* in 1867.

1b. Var. glabrescens A. Gray in Rothr. in Wheeler, Rept. U.S. Surv. W. of 100th Merid. 15. 1874. Arizona, *Wheeler*. *M. scoparia* Engelm. ex A. Gray in Brew. & Wats. Bot. Calif. 1: 471. 1880. Saltillo, Mexico, *Gregg*.

2. M. spinescens A. Gray, Proc. Amer. Acad. 7: 388. 1868. Southeastern Nev., *C. L. Andersson*. *M. spinescens* var. *mohavensis* Steyermark, Ann. Mo. Bot. Gard. 19: 155. 1932. 14 miles northeast of Barstow, Mojave Desert, Calif., *Parish 9795*.

MIMOSA (p. 166)

1. M. biuncifera Benth. Pl. Hartw. 12. 1939. Mexico, *Hartweg*. *M. flexuosa* Benth. ex A. Gray, Pl. Wright. 1: 62. 1852. Mountain valleys beyond the Limpia, Texas. *Wright*. *M. biuncifera* var. *glabrascens* A. Gray, loc. cit. 2: 51. 1853. Hills on the Sonoita, Sonora, *Wright 1039*. *M. biuncifera* var. *flexuosa* Rob. Proc. Amer. Acad. 33: 327. 1898. *Mimosopsis biuncifera* Britt. & Rose, N. Amer. Fl. 23: 176. 1928. *Mimosopsis flexuosa* Britt. & Rose, loc. cit.

2. M. Grahamii A. Gray, Pl. Wright. 2: 52. 1853. Between San Pedro and the Sonoita, Sonora, *Wright 1042*. *M. Lemmonii* A. Gray, Proc. Amer. Acad. 19: 76. 1883. Huachuca Mts., Arizona, near Ft. Huachuca and Cave Canyon, *Lemmon*. *M. Endlichii* Harms in Fedde, Repert. Sp. Nov. 18: 93. 1922. West of San Juan River, Chihuahua, *Endlich 1256*. *Mimosopsis Lemmonii* Britt. & Rose, N. Amer. Fl. 23: 176. 1928. *Mimosopsis Grahamii* Britt. & Rose, loc. cit. 178. *Mimosa Grahamii* var. *Lemmonii* Kearney & Peebles, Jour. Wash. Acad. Sci. 29: 482. 1939.

3a. M. dysocarpa Benth. ex A. Gray, Pl. Wright. 1: 62. 1852. Pass of the Limpia, Texas, *Wright*.

3b. Var. Wrightii (A. Gray) Kearney & Peebles, Jour. Wash. Acad. Sci. 29: 482. 1939. *M. Wrightii* A. Gray, Pl. Wright. 2: 52. 1853. On the Sonoita, Sonora, *Wright 1041*.

4. M. laxiflora Benth. in Hook. Lond. Jour. Bot. 5: 93. 1846. Sonora Alta, Mexico, *Coulter*. Probably near Hermosillo.

MORTONIA (p. 250)

1a. M. SCABRELLA A. Gray, Pl. Wright. 2: 28. 1853. San Pedro, Sonora, and mountains near El Paso, Texas, *Wright.*

1b. Var. UTAHENSIS Cov. ex Trel. in A. Gray, Syn. Fl. N. Amer. 1 (1): 400. 1897. Utah and Nev., *Coville. M. utahensis* A. Nels. Bot. Gaz. 47: 427. 1909.

NICOTIANA (p. 299)

1. N. GLAUCA Graham, Edinb. Jour. 5: 175. 1828. Buenos Aires, Argentina, *Smith.* Described from plants grown at Edinburgh, Scotland.

NOLINA (p. 70)

1a. N. BIGELOVII (Torr.) S. Wats. Proc. Amer. Acad. 14: 247. 1879. *Dasylirion Bigelovii* Torr. Pac. R. R. Rept. 4: 151. 1857. Plaza Larga, N. Mex. *Bigelow. Beaucarnea Bigelovii* Baker, Jour. Bot. Brit. & For. 10: 326. 1872.

1b. Var. PARRYI (S. Wats.) L. Benson in Benson and Darrow, Man. S. W. Des. Trees & Shrubs ed. 1. 76, 384. 1945. *N. Parryi* S. Wats. Proc. Amer. Acad. 14: 247. 1879. Mojave Desert, Calif., *Parry* in 1876.

1c. Var. **Wolfii** (Munz.) L. Benson, comb. nov. *N. Parryi* S. Wats. subsp. *Wolfii* Munz, E. Aliso 2: 221. 1950. Beck Spring (as Crystal Spring on the label), Kingston Mts., Mojave Desert, *C. B. Wolf 7655* (cf. p. 72).

2. N. MICROCARPA S. Wats. Proc. Amer. Acad. 14: 247. 1879. Rock Canyon, S. Arizona, *Rothrock 248* (described as *278*). *N. affinis* Trel. Proc. Amer. Phil. Soc. 50: 417. 1911. Chihuahua, *Pringle 1 and 2* in 1885. *N. caudata* Trel. loc. cit. Mule Mts., Arizona, *Toumey* in 1894. *N. Greenei* S. Wats. ex Trel. loc. cit. North of Trinidad, Colo.,*Greene* in 1880.

OLNEYA (p. 201)

1. O. TESOTA A. Gray, Mem. Amer. Acad. II. 5: 328. 1855. Gila River, *Thurber, Mr. Gray;* Bill Williams River, *Bigelow.*

PARKINSONIA (p. 181)

1. P. ACULEATA L. Sp. Pl. 375. 1753. America calidiore. *P. Thornberi* M. E. Jones, Contr. W. Bot. (12): 12. 1908. Cult. at Univ. of Arizona, Tucson. Plants brought by Dean Forbes from Guaymas, Sonora.

PARTHENIUM (p. 376)

1. P. INCANUM H. B. K. Nov. Gen. et Sp. Pl. 4: 260. 1820. "Colitur in horto botanico Mexicano."

PENSTEMON (p. 309)

1a. P. ANTIRRHINOIDES Benth. var. MICROPHYLLUS (A. Gray) Munz & Johnston, Bull. Torrey Club 49: 43. 1922. *P. microphyllus* A. Gray in Torr. Pac. R. R. Rept. 4: 119. 1857. Bill Williams River, Ariz., *Bigelow* in 1854. *P. Plummerae* Abrams, Bull. Torrey Club 33: 445. 1906. Mineral Park, northern Ariz., *Mr. & Mrs. J. G. Lemmon* in 1884.

PEUCEPHYLLUM (p. 366)

1. P. SCHOTTII A. Gray in Torr. in Emory, Rept. U.S. & Mex. Bound. Surv. 2: 74. 1859. Colorado River in Sonora, *Schott.*

PLATANUS (p. 136)

1a. P. RACEMOSA Nutt. in Audubon, Birds Amer. 4: *pl. 362* (folio). 1827-38, nom. nud.; in Michx. N. Amer. Sylva Suppl. 1: 47. *pl. 15.* 1843. San Diego, Calif., *Nuttall. P. orientalis* L. var. *racemosa* Kuntze, Rev. Gen. 2: 236. 1891.

1b. Var. WRIGHTII (S. Wats) L. Benson, Amer. Jour. Bot. 30: 237. 1943. *P. Wrightii* S. Wats. Proc. Amer. Acad. 10: 349. 1875. San Pedro, Arizona, *Wright.*

PLUCHEA (p. 362)

1. P. SERICEA (Nutt.) Cov. Contr. U.S. Nat. Herb. 4: 128. 1893. *Polypappus sericeus* Nutt. Jour. Acad. Sci. Phila. II. 1: 178. 1848. "Rocky Mountains of Upper California." *Tessaria borealis* Torr. & Gray ex A. Gray, Mem. Amer. Acad. II. 4: 75. 1849. ". . . In Fremont's, Coulter's, and, more recently, in Emory's Californian collections. . . ." *P. borealis* A. Gray, Proc. Amer. Acad. 17: 212. 1882. *Bertholetia sericea* Rydb. Bull. Torrey Club 33: 154. 1906.

POLIOMINTHA (p. 298)

1. P. INCANA (Torr.) A. Gray, Proc. Amer. Acad. 8: 296. 1873. *Hedeoma incana* Torr. in Emory, Rept. U.S. & Mex. Bound. Surv. 2: 130. 1859. El Paso, Texas, *Parry, Wright, & Bigelow.*

POPULUS (p. 108)

1a. P. FREMONTII S. Wats. Proc. Amer. Acad. 10: 350. 1875. Deer Creek, near "Lassen's," Upper Sacramento Valley, Calif., *Fremont. P. canadensis* Moench var. *Fremontii* Kuntze, Rev. Gen. et Sp. Pl. 2: 643. 1891. *P. MacDougalii* Rose, Smiths. Coll. 61 (12): 1. *pl. 1.* 1913. Mecca, Calif., *Parish 8471. P. Fremontii* var. *macrodisca* Sarg. Jour. Arn. Arb. 1: 62. 1919. Silver City, N. Mex., *Eastwood 8429. P. arizonica* Sarg. Bot. Gaz. 67: 210. Mar., 1919. Tucson, Arizona. *P. arizonica* var. *Jonesii* Sarg. loc. cit. 211. Valley of Palms, Mexico, *Jones 373. P. Fremontii* var. *Thornberi* Sarg. loc. cit. 213. Tucson, Arizona, *Sargent* in 1916. *P. Fremontii* var. *pubescens* Sarg. loc. cit. 213. San Bernardino and San Diego cos., Calif. *P. Fremontii* var. *Toumeyi* Sarg. loc. cit. 214. Tucson, Arizona, *Toumey* in 1894. *P. Fremontii* var. *MacDougalii* Jepson, Man. Fl. Pl. Calif. 268. 1923. *P. Fremontii* var. *arizonica* Jepson, loc. cit.

1b. Var. WISLIZENII S. Wats. Amer. Jour. Sci. III. 15: 3. 1878. Rio Grande. *P. Wislizenii* Sarg. Silva N. Amer. 14: 71. *pl. 732.* 1902.

PROSOPIS (p. 171)

(Cf. L. Benson, Amer. Jour. Bot. 28: 748-754. 1941)

1a. P. JULIFLORA (Swartz) DC. Prodr. 2: 447. 1825. *Mimosa juliflora* Swartz, Prodr. Veg. Ind. Occ. 85. 1788. Jamaica. *Acacia juliflora* Willd. in L. Sp. Pl. ed. 4. 4: 1076. 1806. *Neltuma juliflora* Raf. Sylva Tell. 119. 1838. *Algarobia juliflora* Benth. ex Heynhold, Nom. 2: 18. 1840.

1b. Var. VELUTINA (Woot.) Sarg. Silva N. Amer. 13: 15. 1902. *P. velutina* Woot. Bull. Torrey Club 25: 456. 1898. Arizona, *Pringle* in 1881. *P. chilensis* (Mol.) Stuntz var. *velutina* Standl. Contr. U.S. Nat. Herb. 23: 1658. 1926. *Neltuma velutina* Britt. & Rose, N. Amer. Fl. 23: 186. 1928.

1c. Var. TORREYANA L. Benson, Amer. Jour. Bot. 28: 751. 1941. Needles, Calif., *L. Benson 11000.*

1d. Var. GLANDULOSA (Torr.) Cockerell, Bull. N. Mex. Agric. Exp. Sta. 15: 58.1895. *P. glandulosa* Torr. Ann. Lyc. N. Y. 2: 192. 1827. Long Exped. to Rocky Mts., *James* in 1820, probably on the Canadian River. *Algarobia glandulosa* Torr. & Gray, Fl. N. Amer. 1: 399. 1840. *P. juliflora* var. *constricta* Sarg. Trees & Shrubs 2: 249. 1913. Shreveport, La., *Cocks* in 1907, *Cocks & Sargent* in 1908, *Coty* in 1908. *P. chilensis* (Mol.) Stuntz var. *glandulosa* Standl. Contr. U.S. Nat. Herb. 23: 1658. 1926. *Neltuma glandulosa* Britt. & Rose, N. Amer. Fl. 23: 186. 1928. *Neltuma neomexicana* Britt. N. Amer. Fl. 23: 186. 1928. Dog Springs, Dog Mts., N. Mex., *Mearns 2325.* *Neltuma constricta* Britt. & Rose, loc. cit.

2. P. PUBESCENS Benth. in Hook. Lond. Jour. Bot. 5: 82. 1846. Between San Miguel and Monterey, Calif., *Coulter. P. odorata* Torr. in Frem. 2nd Rept. 313. *pl. 1.* 1845, nom. confus. Mojave and Virgin rivers, *Fremont.* Flowers and leaves of *P. juliflora* var. *Torreyana* with screw-bean fruits. *P. Emoryi* Torr. in Emory, Notes. Mil. Reconn. 139. 1847. Gila River, *Emory* in 1846. *Strombocarpa pubescens* A. Gray, Pl. *Wright.* 1: 60. 1852. *S. brevifolia* Nutt. ex A. Gray, loc. cit., as syn. *S. odorata* A. Gray, Bot. U.S. Expl. Exped. (Wilkes Exped.) 1: 475. 1854, nom. nud. *S. odorata* Britt. & Rose, N. Amer. Fl. 23: 183. 1928.

PRUNUS (p. 146)

1. P. FREMONTII S. Wats. Bot. Calif. 2: 442. 1880. Oriflamme Canyon, San Diego Co., Calif., *Cleveland. Amygdaulus Fremontii* Abrams, Bull. N.Y. Bot. Gard. 6. 385. 1910. *P. eriogyna* S. C. Mason, Jour. Agr. Research 1: 168. *f. 5.* 1913. Tahquitz Canyon, near Palm Springs, Calif. (?) *P. Fremontii* var. *piluata* Jepson, Man. Fl. Pl. Calif. 507. 1925. Wagon Wash near Sentenac Canyon, *Jepson 8769,* the plant unknown to us and probably a distinct variety. *Emplectocladus Fremontii* Dayton, U.S. Dept. Agric. Misc. Publ. (101): 70. 1931.

2. FASCICULATA (Torr.) A. Gray, Proc. Amer. Acad. 10: 70. 1875. *Emplectocladus fasciculatus* Torr. Pl. Frem. 10. *pl. 5.* 1854. Locality uncertain, *Fremont.*

P. Andersonii A. Gray, Proc. Amer. Acad. 7: 337. 1868. Near Carson City, Nevada. *C. L. Anderson (Andersson). Amygdalus Andersonii* Greene, Fl. Fran. 49. 1891. *Emplectocladus Andersonii* Nels. & Ken. Muhlenbergia 3: 139. 1908.

PSILOSTROPHE (p. 361)

P. Cooperi (A. Gray) Greene, Pittonia 2: 176. 1891. *Riddellia Cooperi* A. Gray in Proc. Amer. Acad. 7: 358. 1868. Fort Mohave, Arizona, *Dr. J. G. Cooper.*

RHUS (p. 248)

1. R. microphylla Engelm. in A. Gray, Pl. Wright. 1: 31. 1852. Between New Braunfels and San Antonio, Texas, *Wright. Toxicodendron microphyllum* Kuntze, Rev. Gen. et Sp. Pl. 1: 154. 1891. *Schmaltzia microphylla* Small, Fl. S. E. U. S. 728. 1334. 1904. *Rhoeidium microphyllum* Greene, Leafl. Bot. Obs. & Crit. 1: 143. 1905.

2. R. Kearneyi Barkley, Ann. Mo. Bot. Gard. 24: 363. 1937. Tinajas Altas, Yuma Co., Ariz., *Harrison & Kearney 6573. Schmaltzia Kearneyi* Barkley, Amer. Midl. Nat. 24: 651. 1941.

RICINUS (p. 237)

1. R. communis L. Sp. Pl. 1007. 1753. *"Habitat in India utraque Africa, Europa australi."*

SAGERETIA (p. 262)

1. S. Wrightii S. Wats. Proc. Amer. Acad. 20: 358. 1885. Santa Cruz, Sonora, *Wright 925* in 1851.

SALAZARIA (p. 289)

1. S. mexicana Torr. in Emory, Rept. U.S. & Mex. Bound. Surv. 2: 133. 1859. Near the Rio Grande, Presidio Del Norte, Chih., *Parry.*

SALIX (p. 103)

1a. S. nigra Marsh. var. vallicola Dudley ex Abrams, Fl. Los Angeles 100. 1904. Orange, Calif., *Abrams 3256. S. Gooddingii* Ball. Bot. Gaz. 40: 376. *pl. 12. f. 1-2.* 1905. Muddy Creek, Lincoln Co., Nevada, *Goodding 689. S. vallicola* Britt. N. Amer. Trees 184. *f. 141.* 1908.

2a. S. amygdaloides Anderss. var. Wrightii (Anderss.) Schn. Bot. Gaz. 65: 14. 1918. *S. Wrightii* Anderss. Öfvers. Svensk. Vet.-Akad. Forh. 16: 115. Mar., 1858; Proc. Amer. Acad. 4: 55. 1860. New Mexico, *Wright 1877. S. nigra* Marsh var. *Wrightii* Anderss. in DC. Prodr. 16 (2): 201. 1868.

3a. S. Bonplandiana H. B. K. var. Toumeyi (Britt.) Schn. Bot. Gaz. 65: 21. 1918. *S. Toumeyi* Britt. in Britt. & Shafer, N. Amer. Trees 187. *pl. 145.* 1908. Canyons in Southern Arizona.

S. laevigata Bebb, Amer. Nat. 8: 202. 1874. Santa Cruz, Calif. *C. L. Andersson;* Ukiah, *Kellogg & Harford 921.*

4. S. EXIGUA Nutt. in Michx. Sylva N. Amer. Suppl. 1: 75. 1843. Probably Snake River, Idaho (acc. Schneider), *Nuttall*. *S. longifolia* Muhl. var. *exigua* Bebb. in S. Wats. Bot. Calif. 2: 85. 1879. *S. fluviatilis* Nutt. var. *exigua* Sarg. Silva N. Amer. 9: 124. 1896. *E. exigua* var. *virens* Rowlee, Bull. Torrey Club 27: 255. 1900. Arizona, *Rothrock*. *S. exigua* var. *stenophylla* Schn. Bot. Gaz. 65: 25. 1918. La Veta, Cuchara River, Colorado, *Rydberg & Vreeland 6393*.

S. SESSILIFOLIA Nutt. var. LEUCODENDROIDES (Rowlee) Schn. Bot. Gaz. 65: 26. 1918. *S. macrostachya* Nutt. var. *leucodendroides* Rowlee, Bull. Torrey Club 27: 250. 1900. Southern California, *Parish 2040*. *S. integrifolia* var. *leucodendroides* Rowlee, loc. cit., nom. nud. *S. Hindsiana* Benth. var. *leucodendroides* Ball, Madroño 6: 232. 1942.

S. ARGOPHYLLA Nutt. N. Amer. Sylva 1. 71. *pl. 20*. 1843. "The river Boiseé, toward its junction with the Shoshone." Snake River, Idaho.

S. TAXIFOLIA H. B. K. Nov. Gen. & Sp. Pl. 2: 22 (quarto), 18 (folio). 1817. Mexico.

SALVIA (p. 290)

1. S. PINGUIFOLIA (Fern.) Woot. & Standl. Contr. U.S. Nat. Herb. 16: 169. 1913. *S. ballotaeflora* Benth. var. *pinguifolia* Fern. Proc. Amer. Acad. 35: 523. 1900. Near Clifton, Greenlee Co., Ariz., *Greene 300*.

2. S. PARRYI A. Gray, Proc. Amer. Acad. 8: 369. 1870. Apache Springs, Ariz., *Parry*. *S. confinis* Fern. Proc. Amer. Acad. 35: 523. 1900. Ft. Huachuca, *Lemmon*.

3. S. FUNEREA M. E. Jones, Contr. W. Bot. 12: 71. 1908. Funeral Mts., east side of Death Valley, Calif., *M. E. Jones*. *S. funerea* var. *fornacis* Jepson, Man. Fl. Pl. Calif. 868. 1925. Furnace Creek, Funeral Mts., *Parish 10032*.

4. S. GREATAE Brandegee, Zoe 5: 229. 1908. Canyon Springs Wash near Dos Palmas, Riverside Co., Calif., *H. M. Hall & L. A. Greata*, Hall's *no. 5848*.

5a. S. CARNOSA Dougl. ex Benth. subsp. TYPICA Epl. Ann. Mo. Bot. Gard. 25: 130. 1938. *Salvia carnosa* Dougl. ex Benth. Bot. Reg. 17: *pl. 1469*. 1831. "On clayey banks of the Columbia and plains from Walla Walla to Spokane and on the south to the Sources of the Missouri." *Douglas*. *Audibertia incana* Benth. loc. cit. Upper Columbia River, *Douglas*. *Audibertiella incana* Briq. Bull. Herb. Boiss. 2: 73. 1894. *Ramona incana* Briq. loc. cit. 440. *S. carnosa* var. *typica* Munz, Bull. S. Calif. Acad. Sci. 26: 21. 1927.

5b. Subsp. MEARNSII (Britt.) Epl. Ann. Mo. Bot. Gard. 25: 131. 1938. *Audibertia Mearnsii* Britt. Trans. N.Y. Acad. Sci. 8: 71. 1889; Bull. Torrey Club 16: 202. 1889. Fort Verde, Ariz., *Mearns*.

5c. Subsp. ARGENTEA (Rydb.) Epl. Ann. Mo. Bot. Gard. 25: 131. 1938. *Audibertiella argentea* Rydb. Bull. Torrey Club 36: 683. 1909. Mokiak Pass, Ariz., *Palmer 395*.

5d. Subsp. GILMANII Epl. Ann. Mo. Bot. Gard. 25: 132. 1938. Pinyon Mesa, Wild Rose Canyon, Panamint Mts., Inyo Co., Calif., *Epling & Gilman.*

5e. Subsp. PILOSA (A. Gray) Epl. Ann. Mo. Bot. Gard. 25: 133. 1938. *Audibertia Dorrii* Kell. Proc. Calif. Acad. 2: 190. *f. 57.* 1863. Probably Virginia City, Nev., *C. H. Dorr, Audibertia incana* Benth. var. *pilosa* A. Gray, Syn. Fl. N. Amer. 2 (1): 461. 1886. Northern base of the San Bernardino Mts., Calif., *S. B. & W. F. Parish. S. pilosa* Cov. ex Merriam, N. Amer. Fauna (7): 322. 1893. *Audibertiella Dorrii* Briq. Bull. Herb. Boiss. 2: 73. 1894. *Ramona Dorrii* Abrams, Bull. N.Y. Bot. Gard. 6: 443. 1910. *S. carnosa* var. *pilosa* Jepson, Man. Fl. Pl. Calif. 870. 1925.

6. S. VASEYI (Porter) Parish, Muhlenbergia 3: 126. 1907. *Audibertia Vaseyi* Porter, Bot. Gaz. 6: 207. 1881. Mountain Springs, San Diego Co., Calif., *Vasey. Audibertiella Vaseyi* Briq. Bull. Herb. Boiss. 2: 73. 1894. *Ramona Vaseyi* Briq. loc. cit. 440.

7. S. APIANA Jepson, Muhlenbergia 3: 144. 1908. Based upon the following: *Audibertia polystachya* Benth., Lab. Gen. et Sp. 314. 1833, not *S. polystachya* Ort. Calif., *Douglas. Audibertiella polystachya* Briq. Bull. Herb. Boiss. 2: 73. 1894. *Ramona polystachya* Greene, Pittonia 2: 235. 1895. *S. californica* Jepson, Fl. W. Mid. Calif. 460. 1901, not Brandegee in 1889. Based upon *A. polystachya* Benth. *S. apiana* var. *typica* Munz, Bull. S. Calif., Acad. Sci. 26: 25. 1927. *S. apiana* var. *compacta* Munz, loc. cit. Morongo Wash, Riverside Co., Calif., *Munz & Johnston 5170.*

8. S. MOHAVENSIS Greene, Pittonia 2: 235. 1892. Based upon the following: *Audibertia capitata* A. Gray, Proc. Amer. Acad. 7: 387. 1868, not *S. capitata* Schlect. in 1853-5. Providence Mts., San Bernardino Co., Calif., *Cooper. Audibertiella capitata* Briq. Bull. Herb. Boiss. 2: 73. 1894. *Ramona capitata* Briq. loc. cit. 440.

9. S. EREMOSTACHYA Jepson, Man. Fl. Pl. Calif. 870. 1925. Indian Canyon, Collins Valley, Riverside Co., *Jepson 8847.*

SAMBUCUS (p. 320)

1a. S. CERULEA Raf. var. MEXICANA (Presl.) L. Benson, Amer. Jour. Bot. 30: 240. 1943. *S. mexicana* Presl. in DC. Prodr. 4: 322. 1830. Mexico, *Sternberg. S. canadensis* L. var. *mexicana* Sarg. Silva N. Amer. 5: 88. *pl. 221.* 1893. *S. caerulea* var. *arizonica* Sarg. Man. Trees N. Amer. ed. 2. 885. 1922. No type given. Arizona, New Mexico, Southern California. *S. glauca* Nutt var. *arizonica* Sarg. ex Jepson, Man. Fl. Pl. Calif. 965. 1925.

SAPINDUS (p. 255)

1a. S. SAPONARIA L. var. DRUMMONDII (Hook. & Arn.) L. Benson, Amer. Jour. Bot. 30: 239, 630. 1943. *S. Drummondii* Hook. & Arn. Bot. Beech Voy. 281. 1836-9. Texas, *Drummond.*

SAPIUM (p. 245)

1. S. BILOCULARE (S. Wats.) Pax in Engler, Pflanzenr. IV. 147 (5): 153, 221. 1912. *Sebastiana (?) bilocularis* S. Wats. Proc. Amer. Acad. 20: 374. 1885. Hills between Rayon and Ures, northwestern Sonora, *Thurber* in 1853.

SARCOBATUS (p. 128)

1a. S. VERMICULATUS (Hook.) Torr. in Emory, Notes Mil. Reconn. 150. 1848. *Batis vermiculata* Hook. Fl. Bor. Amer. 2: 128. 1838. Columbia River, *Douglas. Fremontia vermicularis* Torr. in Frem. Rept. Ore. & Calif. 317. *pl. 3.* 1845.

1b. Var. BAILEYI (Cov.) Jepson, Fl. Calif. 1: 446. 1914. *S. Baileyi* Cov. Contr. U.S. Nat. Herb. 4: 184. *pl. 20.* 1893. Nye Co., Nevada, *Vernon Bailey.*

SELLOA (p. 332)

1. S. GLUTINOSA Spreng. Nov. Provent. Hort. Hal. 36. 1819. Brazil, actually from North America. *Gymnosperma glutinosum* Less., Syn. Gen. Compos. 194. 1832. Matamoros, Mexico. *G. corymbosum* DC. Prodr. 5: 312. 1836. Matamoros, Mexico, *Berlandier. G. multiflorum* DC. loc. cit. Mexico. *G. scoparium* DC. loc. cit. 312. San Luis Potosí, *Berlandier.*

SENECIO (p. 363)

1a. S. DOUGLASII DC. Prodr. 6: 429. 1837. Monterey, Calif., *Douglas.*

1b. S. DOUGLASII var. MONOENSIS (Greene) Jepson, Man. Fl. Pl. Calif. 1149. 1925. *S. monoensis* Greene, Leafl. Bot. Obs. & Crit. 1: 221. 1906. White Mts., Mono Co., Calif., near Southern Belle Mine, *Heller 8330. S. lathyroides* Greene, loc. cit. 2: 21. 1909. Pierce's Spring, Ariz., *M. E. Jones 5077,* U.S. Nat. Herb. *S. filicifolius* Greenm. Ann. Mo. Bot. Gard. 1: 274. 1914. Santa Cruz River Valley, *Pringle 316* in 1881. *S. pectinatus* A. Nels. Univ. Wyo. Publ. Bot. 1: 141. 1926. Baboquivari Mts., Pima Co., Ariz., *Hanson 1020.*

1c. S. DOUGLASII var. LONGILOBUS (Benth.) L. Benson, Amer. Jour. Bot. 30: 631. 1943. *S. longilobus* Benth. Pl. Hartw. 18: 1839. Aguas Calientes, Mexico, *Hartweg* in 1837. *S. filifolius* Nutt. Trans. Amer. Phil. Soc. II. 7: 414. 1841, not Berg. in 1767. "The banks of the Missouri, toward the Rocky Mountains." *S. orthophyllus* Greene, Leafl. Bot. Obs. & Crit. 1: 221. 1906. Willow Springs, Ariz., *Palmer 479* in 1890, U.S. Nat. Herb.

2. S. SALIGNUS DC. Prodr. 6: 430. 1837. Between Cerro Ventoso and Moran, Mexico.

SIMMONDSIA (p. 247)

1. S. CHINENSIS (Link.) Schn. Ill. Handb. Laubholtz. 2: 141. 1912. *Buxus chinensis* Link. Enum. Pl. 2: 386. 1822. "Hab. in China?" Actually from the Southwest. *S. californica* Nutt. in Hook. Lond. Jour. Bot. 3: 401.

pl. 16. 1844. San Diego, Calif., *Nuttall. S. pabulosa* Kell. Proc. Calif. Acad. 2: 21. 1859, acc. Jepson, Fl. Calif. 2:443. 1936, 1863 on the title page. Cedros I., Baja Calif., *Veatch, Galphimia pabulosa* Kell. Hesperian 4: *pl.* opp. p. 392. Nov., 1860, cf. Muell. in DC. Prodr. 16 (1): 23. 1869.

SOPHORA (p. 200)

1. S. ARIZONICA S. Wats. Proc. Amer. Acad. 11: 135. 1876. Cactus Pass and White Cliff Creek, northwestern Arizona, *Bigelow.*

2. S. FORMOSA Kearney & Peebles, Jour. Wash. Acad. Sci. 29: 482. 1939. Frye Mesa, Graham (Pinaleno) Mts., Arizona, *Maguire 10993.*

TAMARIX (p. 267)

1. T. GALLICA L. var. PYCNOSTACHYS Ledeb. Fl. Ross. 1: 135. 1844. *T. pentandra* Pall. Fl. Ross. 1 (2): 72. 1784-1788.

TECOMA (p. 316)

1a. T. STANS (L.) H. B. K. var. ANGUSTATA Rehder, Mitt. Deutsch. Dendr. Ges. 1915: 227. 1915. El Paso, Texas, *Jones 4187. Stenolobium incisum* Rose & Standl. in Woot. & Standl. Contr. U.S. Nat. Herb. 16: 174. 1913. Chihuahua, Chih., Mexico, *Pringle 960* in 1886. *T. incisa* I. M. Johnston, Jour. Arn. Arb. 21: 264. 1940, not Sweet in 1827, nom. subnud. *S. Tronadora* Loes in Fedde, Repertorium 16: 210. 1919. Several syntypes from northern Mexico. *T. Tronadora* I. M. Johnston, Jour. Arn. Arb. 29: 197. 1948.

TETRACOCCUS (p. 229)

1. T. HALLII T. S. Brandegee, Zoe 5: 229. 1906. Chuckawalla Bench, midway between Cañon Springs and Chuckwalla Spring, Colorado Desert, Riverside County, California, *Hall & Greata 5865,* April, 1906. *Bernardia (?) fasciculata* S. Wats. Proc. Amer. Acad. 18: 153. 1883, nomen provisorum. 24 miles northeast of Monclova, Coahuila, Mexico, *Palmer 1233,* Sept. 1880. *Securinega fasciculata* I. M. Johnston, Univ. Calif. Publ. Bot. 7: 442. 1922. *S. Hallii* I. M. Johnston, loc. cit. *Halliophytum Hallii* I. M. Johnston, Contr. Gray Herb. 68: 88. 1923. *H. fasciculatum* I. M. Johnston, loc. cit. *S. fasciculata* I. M. Johnston var. *Hallii* Jepson, Man. Fl. Pl. Calif. 595. 1925. *H. fasciculata* I. M. Johnston var. *Hallii* McMinn, Ill. Man. Calif. Shrubs 249. 1939.

2. T. ILICIFOLIUS Cov. & Gilman, Jour. Wash. Acad. Sci. 26: 531. 1936. Large canyon north of Titus Canyon on the west slope of the Grapevine Mountains, Death Valley, Inyo County, California, *Gilman 2180,* May, 1936.

TETRADYMIA (p. 366)

1. T. GLABRATA A. Gray, Pac. R. R. Rept. 2 (2): 122. *pl. 5.* 1854. Sierra Nevada, Calif., *Beckwith.*

2. T. COMOSA A. Gray, Proc. Amer. Acad. 12: 60. 1876. "W. Nevada, Lemmon. S. E. borders of California, E. Palmer. Potrero, San Diego Co., D. Cleveland."

3. T. STENOLEPIS Greene, Bull. Calif. Acad. 1: 92. 1885. Between Cameron and Mojave, *Curran.* "Mountains of Kern County," Calif.

4. T. SPINOSA Hook. & Arn. Bot. Beech. Voy. 360. 1840. "Snake Country," Idaho. *T. spinosa* var. *longispina* M. E Jones, Proc. Calif. Acad. II. 5: 698. 1895. St. George, southwestern Utah, *M. E Jones 5110.* This form has longer spines, and the spines are straight. Possibly it is worthy of varietal status. *T. axillaris* A. Nels. Bot. Gaz. 37: 277. 1904. Meadow Valley Wash, southern Nev., *Goodding* in 1902. *T. longispina* Rydb. Bull. Torrey Club 37: 471. 1910.

THAMNOSMA (p. 221)

1. T. MONTANA Torr. & Frem. in Frem. 2nd Rept. 313. 1845. Virgin River, Utah or Arizona, *Fremont.*

VAUQUELINIA (p. 141)

1. V. CALIFORNICA (Torr.) Sarg. Gard. & For. 2: 400. 1889. *Spiraea californica* Torr. in Emory, Notes. Mil. Reconn. 140. 1848. Gila River in New Mexico or Arizona, *Emory. V. Torreyi* S. Wats. Proc. Amer. Acad. 11: 147. 1876. Nom. nov. for *S. californica.*

VIGUIERA (p. 373)

1. V. STENOLOBA Blake, Contr. Gray Herb. (54): 97. 1918. Based upon the following: *Heliomeris tenuifolia* A. Gray, Mem. Amer. Acad. II. 4: 84. 1849. "Dry valleys, at Rinconada, Saltillo, Mapimi, and Andabazo, Mexico, *Dr. Gregg . . ."* Not *V. tenuifolia* Gardn. in 1848. *Gymnolomia tenuifolia* Benth. & Hook. ex Hemsl. Biol. Centr. Amer Bot. 2: 163. 1881.

2a. V. DELTOIDEA A. Gray var. PARISHII (Greene) Vasey & Rose, Proc. U.S. Nat. Mus. 13: 148. 1890. *V. Parishii* Greene, Bull. Torrey Club 9: 15. 1882. San Luis Rey, Calif., *S. B. & W. F. Parish 963.*

WASHINGTONIA (p. 57)

1. W. FILIFERA (Linden) Wendl. Bot. Zeit. 37: 68, 148. 1879; S. Wats. in Brew. & Wats. Bot. Calif. 2: 211. 1880. *Pritchardia filifera* Linden ex André, Ill. Hort. 21: 28. 1874, nom. nud.; Cat. Spring 1875, nom. nud.; Ill. Hort. 2: 32, 105. 1877. Southern California. *Brahea filamentosa* Wendl. in Haage & Schmidt, Cat. Autumn, 1875, nom. nud. *P. filamentosa* Wendl. ex Fenzi, Bull. Soc. Toscana Ort. 1: 116. Apr., 1876, nom. nud.; Williams, Gard. Chron. II. 6: 80. July, 1876. Drude, Bot. Zeit. 34: 806. 1876, nom. nud. *W. filamentosa* Kuntze, Rev. Gen. et Sp. Pl. 2: 737. 1891. *Neowashingtonia filamentosa* Sudw. U.S. Div. Forestry Bull. (14): 105. 1897. *N. robusta* Heller, Cat. N. Amer. Pl. ed. 1. 3. 1898. *W. filifera* var. *robusta* Parish, Bot. Gaz. 44: 420. *f. 3-5.* Dec., 1907. *W. filifera* var. *microsperma* Becc. Webbia 2: 191. Dec., 1907; Becc. ex Parish, Bot. Gaz. 44: 420. Dec., 1907. Cult. on the Italian Riviera. *W. arizonica* O. F. Cook, Morning Sun, Yuma, Ariz. Dec. 5, 1923. Kofa Mts., Arizona. *W. filifera* var. *typica* M. E. Jones, Contr. W. Bot. (15): 53. 1929.

Var. GRACILIS (Parish) L. Benson, Amer. Jour. Bot. 30: 233. 1943. *W. robusta* Wendl. Gart. Zeit. Berlin 2: 98. 1883. Southern California. *Washingtonia sonorae* S. Wats. Proc. Amer. Acad. 24: 79. 1889, 25: 136. 1890. *Neowashingtonia sonorae* Rose, Contr. U.S. Nat. Herb. 5: 255. 1899. *Washingtonia filifera* var. *sonorae* M. E. Jones, contr. W. Bot. 15: 48. 1929. *W. robusta* Wendl. var. *gracilis* Parish ex Becc. Webbia 2: 197. Dec., 1907. *W. gracilis* Parish, Bot. Gaz. 44: 420. *f. 8-10.* Dec., 1907. Cult. at Riverside, Calif., *Parish 5536;* originally from Baja California or Sonora.

YUCCA (p. 60)

1. Y. ELATA (Engelm.) Engelm. Bot. Gaz. 7: 17. 1882. *Y. angustifolia* Pursh var. *radiosa* Engelm. in King, Rept. U.S. Geol. Expl. 40th Par. 5: 496. 1871. Central Arizona. *Y. angustifolia* var. *elata* Engelm. Trans. St. Louis Acad. Sci. 3: 50. 1873. West Texas to Utah, Arizona, and Northern Mexico. *Y. radiosa* Trel. Rept. Mo. Bot. Gard. 3: 163. 1892.

2. Y. GLAUCA Nutt. in Fraser's Cat. no. 89. 1813. Missouri River, lat. 49, *Nuttall*. *Y. angustifolia* Pursh, Fl. Amer. Sept. 227. 1814. Missouri River, *Nuttall*.

3. Y. WHIPPLEI Torr. in Emory, Rept. U.S. & Mex. Bound. Surv. 2: 222. 1859. San Pasqual, Southern California, *Schott*. *Y. graminifolia* Wood, Proc. Acad. Phila. 1868: 167. 1868. Los Angeles, *Wood* in 1866. *Hesperoyucca Whipplei* Baker, Kew Bull. 1892: 8. 1892. *Y. Whipplei* var. *Parishii* M. E. Jones, Contr. W. Bot. (15): 59. 1929. Desert, S. Calif. *Y. Whipplei* var. *caespitosa* M. E. Jones, loc. cit. Cajon Pass, Calif. *Y. Whipplei* subsp. *percursa* Haines, Madroño 6: 43. 1941. Cachuma Mt., Santa Barbara Co., Calif., *Haines*. *Y. Whipplei* subsp. *caespitosa* Haines, loc. cit. *Y. Whipplei* subsp. *intermedia* Haines, loc. cit. Malibu Lake, Calif., *Haines*. *Y. Whipplei* subsp. *typica* Haines, loc. cit. *Y. Whipplei* subsp. *Parishii* Haines, loc. cit.

YUCCA NEWBERRI McKelvey, Yuccas S. W. U.S. (2): 49. 1927. New Water Point, Colorado River, Mohave County, Arizona, *McKelvey 4087*.

4. Y. BREVIFOLIA Engelm. in S. Wats. in King, Rept. U.S. Geol. Expl. 40th Par. 5: 496. 1871. Deserts of S. Utah through Arizona to Calif. *Y. draconis* L. var. *arborescens* Torr. Pac. R. R. Rept. 4: 147. 1857. Mojave River, *Bigelow*. *Y. arborescens* Trel. Rept. Mo. Bot. Gard. 3: 163. *pls. 5, 49.* 1892. *Clistoyucca arborescens* Trel. loc. cit. 13: 41. 1902. *C. brevifolia* Rydb. Fl. Rocky Mts. & Adj. Plains 170. 1917. *C. brevifolia* Macbr. Contr. Gray Herb. II. (53): 6. 1918. *Y. brevifolia* var. *Jaegeriana* McKelvey, Jour. Arn. Arb. 16: 269. *pl. 139.* 1935. Shadow Mts., San Bernardino Co., Calif., *McKelvey 2732*. *Y. brevifolia* var. *Wolfei* M. E. Jones, Contr. W. Bot. (18): 125. April, 1935. Yucca Grove and Mountain Pass on the Arrowhead Highway, Southern California.

5. Y. SCHOTTII Engelm. Trans. St. Louis Acad. Sci. 3: 46. 1873. Santa Cruz River, Arizona, *Schott*. *Y. macrocarpa* Engelm. Bot.. Gaz. 6: 224. 1881, not *Y. baccata* var. *macrocarpa* Torr. or its later combination in specific rank, Cov. in 1893. Santa Rita Mts., Arizona, *Engelmann* in 1880.

6a. Y. BACCATA Torr. in Emory, Rept. U.S. & Mex. Bound. Surv. 2: 221. 1859. Hurrah Creek, N. Mex., *Bigelow. Y. baccata* var. *vespertina* McKelvey, Yuccas S. W. U. S. (1): 45. *pls. 13-15.* 1938. Peach Springs, Arizona, *McKelvey 2167.*

6b. Var. BREVIFOLIA (Schott ex Trel.) Benson & Darrow, Amer. Jour. Bot. 30: 234. 1943. *Y. brevifolia* Schott ex Torr. in Emory, Rept. U.S. & Mex. Bound. Surv. 2: 221. 1859, as syn., nom. ambig. *Y. brevifolia* Schott ex Trel. Rept. Mo. Bot. Gard. 13: 100. *pls. 57-59.* 1902, not Engelm. in 1871. *Y. Treleasei* Macbr. Contr. Gray Herb. II. (56): 15. 1918, not Sprenger in 1906. Nom. nov. for *Y. brevifolia* Schott. *Y. Thornberi* McKelvey, Jour. Arn. Arb. 16: 268. *pl. 138.* 1935. Rincon Mts., Pima Co., Arizona, *McKelvey 1627. Y. arizonica* McKelvey, loc. cit. 270. Nom. nov. for *Y. brevifolia* Schott. *Y. confinis* McKelvey, Yuccas S. W. U. S. (1): 49: *pls. 16-18.* 1938. 14 miles northeast of Douglas, Arizona, *McKelvey 2099.*

7. YUCCA TORREYI Shafer in Britt. & Shafer, N. Amer. Trees 157. *f. 117.* 1908. *Yucca baccata* Torr. var. *macrocarpa* Torr. in Emory, Rept. U.S. & Mex. Bound. Surv. 2: 221-2. 1859. Texas near the Limpia and Presidio del Norte, *Bigelow. Y. crassifolia* Engelm. Trans. St. Louis Acad. Sci. 3: 44. 1873, as syn., nom. nud. *Y. macrocarpa* Cov. ex Merriam, N. Amer. Fauna (7): 358. May, 1893; Contr. U.S. Nat. Herb. 4: 202. Nov., 1893, not Engelm. in 1881. Nom. nov. for var. *macrocarpa. Y. Torreyi* forma *parviflora* McKelvey, Yuccas S. W. U. S. 112. *pls. 27, 28.* 1938. Between El Paso, Texas, and the City of Chihuahua, *Wislizenius 221.*

8. Y. SCHIDIGERA Roezl ex Ortgies, Gartenflora 20: 110. 1871. San Diego, Calif., *Roezl. Y. californica* Nutt. ex Baker, Jour. Linn. Soc. Bot. 18: 229. 1881, as syn., nom. nud. *Y. mohavensis* Sarg. Gard. & For. 9: 104. 1896. Mojave Desert, *Coville.*

ZINNIA (p. 375)

1. Z. PUMILA A. Gray, Mem. Amer. Acad. II. 4: 81. 1849. "High plain near San Juan de la Vequeria, and at Castaniola, in Northern Mexico, *Dr. Gregg.*" *Crassina pumila* Kuntze, Rev. Gen. 1: 331. 1891.

INDEX

Page numbers are to the main reference. **Bold face** type indicates description of a species or variety. References to figures, plates, and distribution maps are given in the body of the text and not incorporated in the Index. An Appendix (pp. 391–428) lists the genera alphabetically with the synonymy of the scientific names. No references to the Appendix are given in the Index.

429